BEST GAY LOVE STORIES 2005

BEST GAY LOVE STORIES 2005

edited by

NICK STREET

This trade paperback original is published by Alyson Publications,
P.O. Box 4371, Los Angeles, California 90078-4371.
Distribution in the United Kingdom by Turnaround Publisher Services Ltd.,
Unit 3, Olympia Trading Estate, Coburg Road, Wood Green,
London N22 6TZ England.

First edition: January 2005

05 06 07 08 09 a 10 9 8 7 6 5 4 3 2 1

ISBN 1-55583-881-2

Library of Congress Cataloging-in-Publication Data

Best gay love stories, 2005 / edited by Nick Street.—1st ed.
ISBN 1-55583-881-2 (trade pbk.)
1. Gay men—Fiction. 2. Love stories, American. I. Street, Nick.
PS648.H57B463 2005
813'.085089206642—dc22 2004059498

Credits

Cover photography by Rob Lang/Taxi Collection/Getty Images.
Cover design by Matt Sams.

Contents

Introduction

By sheer coincidence, this book came into my life at a point when I was spending a lot of time thinking about love. Not because I was *falling in love*—a phrase that, in my current state of mind, conjures images of mud puddles and banana peels and bright yellow signs that read CUIDADO! PISO MOJADO! No, what I've been up to feels more like *crawling out of love.* Let me explain.

Not long ago I left my partner of nine years. (Nine years! That's almost two decades in hetero years!) We weren't fighting, we were still fucking, and he's actually a gem of a guy. Cute too—if you live in L.A. and you're interested, let me know. I'll try to hook you up.

Anyway, the issue for me was—well, *me.* Who am I? What do I want? What's my life all about? Where am I going? All the questions that a reasonably self-actualized and individuated queer boy should be able to answer left me scratching my head. And, more important, I was very unhappy about that.

Which is the point, after all: to be happy. Simple enough—just turn that frown upside down, right? Wrong.

Most of us fags carry more baggage than the belly of a 747. Mommy and Daddy didn't get us, we faked our way through high school (and the prom), we fucked like mad when we got to college (thence to WeHo, the Castro, Chelsea, or wherever), and now we're supposed to know how to hold a job, pay the rent, and relate in a fairly sane and civilized way to our neighbors, boyfriends, coworkers, tricks, shrinks, posses, pets, and fellow recovering (fill in the blank) addicts.

My questions for the studio audience: At what point during this whirlwind tour through the land of psychosis did anyone tell us how to be happy? And, to return to the topic at hand, when were we supposed to have learned how to be happy *in love*?

The answer to those questions, my bent brethren, is that—for better or worse—we just have to figure this stuff out on our own.

That hard but somehow blessed fact was my guiding star as I worked my way through the submissions to the anthology you now hold in your hands. I wanted to see stories in which guys were *figuring their shit out* as they tried to learn how to navigate relationships with other guys. Some of the stories end in disaster; in others the protagonists experience personal revelations that left me (sap that I am) in tears. I have a few favorites—J.A. Deveaux's ghost story holds pride of place at the beginning of the roster—and several of the stories are literally transporting: J.D. Roman and Bob Condron, for example, will carry you across the Pacific and the Atlantic, respectively. You'll see new work by some writers whose literary voices are among the strongest I've heard recently (Jim Gladstone and Timothy Lambert spring immediately to mind). And a couple of writers—Lawrence Schimel and Schuyler Bishop—deftly re-spin familiar tales, with wickedly insightful results.

Each of the stories in this collection spoke to me (and to my delicate condition) in some particularly meaningful way. I hope each of them will be just as affecting for you. To tell the truth, I found putting this book together something of a tonic. It was just the right task at just the right time. My "spiritual" friends here in L.A. will surely tell me that's because there's no such thing as a coincidence.

—Nick Street

Passing

J.A. Deveaux

It's early autumn, and the sun hangs on the edge of a mountaintop above the Flatirons, beginning a descent that will plunge the valley below into shadow. The warm air carries no hint of the crisp chill that will fall as soon as the sun disappears below the horizon. Travis is warm enough and happy in his shorts and flannel shirt as he swings his arm back to hurl his plastic disc into the sky, aiming for the gray, weathered tombstone that rests beneath the overhanging limbs of a gnarled and lightning-twisted pine tree.

Andy and Ben left an hour ago to get dinner before the cafeteria closed, but Travis has stayed behind to practice a few more throws. The old Ninth Street cemetery is their favorite course for disc golf. Every gravestone is a unique hole, although some of them are naturally better than others—shaped and configured among the others in such a way as to challenge the skill of the disc golfers. Hollows and traps are in the thickets, low-hanging pine boughs intercept throws, and even a stream must be traversed at least twice in a typical 18-hole game.

Now he eyes the tombstone underneath a jealous pine, and his lips tighten. He's never broken par on this hole. It's a long straight shot and shouldn't be too hard, except for a stray branch from the pine that loops down to curve over the tombstone like a lover. Sometimes he thinks the tree purposely bats his disc away.

He throws the disc as the sun dips farther west. Shadows pour off the mountain flanks and spill into the valley with the suddenness of a flash flood. Then in the twilight, just as he completes his throw, Travis sees a man standing in front of the grave. The disc soars toward the man like an escaped flywheel.

"Heads up!" Travis shouts, and then, "Fore!"

The man doesn't move. He is staring at Travis, but at the last second, he reaches up and snatches the disc out of the air.

Travis jogs up to the stranger. "Hey, great catch, man. You throw disc?"

The man doesn't say anything. He wears a cream-colored button-down shirt with suspenders that hold up black wool trousers. A silver chain runs from his pocket to the button of his suspenders. He has wavy black hair that's not quite long enough to touch his shoulders and dark-blue eyes under bushy black eyebrows. He's a bit taller than Travis and looks young—about Travis's age of 21. He still stares at Travis and he does not smile.

Travis stops short a few feet from the man standing at the grave. The wind has picked up as the sun has set, and a cold finger of air lifts Travis's long blond hair from the back of his neck, giving him goose bumps.

"Is he a relative?" Travis asks.

The man looks confused. "Who?"

"This guy here." Travis points at the grave. "The one you're almost standing on."

The man turns and seems to look for someone, then his eyes focus on the gravestone. Travis steps forward, ducking under the pine bough, and kneels next to the headstone. He brushes one hand along the top of the stone and recites from the weathered engraving:

JONATHAN T. WALKER
1868–1892
MAY HE REST IN PEACE

"Jonathan T. Walker," Travis says again. "Is he a relative?"

"No!" says the man.

"Didn't think so. He died a hundred years ago."

The man flushes red and asks, "Don't you have any respect for the dead?"

Travis raises an eyebrow. "Sure, I respect the dead."

The man brandishes the disc at him. "Then what about this?"

"It's only a plastic disc. It can't hurt a tombstone, now can it?"

"What about letting the dead rest in peace? Throwing this thing around and whacking all the stones, stepping on graves?"

Travis chuckles. "I really doubt that would disturb the dead. Look, this is an old graveyard. They hardly ever bury anyone here anymore. It's not like I'm throwing the disc across a funeral in progress. And I doubt any ghosts hang out here. It would be pretty boring to hang out at a graveyard all the time."

"Then what are you doing here?"

Travis smiles. "OK. Maybe graveyards aren't that boring. This is the best disc-golf course in town."

"That's no reason to disturb the dead."

"Look, if you really think ghosts would spend their time hanging out in a graveyard, don't you think they'd enjoy seeing people have a little fun? Playing a game, or reciting poetry? It livens up the place and makes it happy. That's a nicer sentiment of respect for these people than standing around acting mournful and somber and boring all the time."

The man just frowns.

"Well. I have to go now," says Travis. "Can I have my disc back?"

"What?"

"My disc." He points to the disc in the man's right hand. "I'm going now."

The man looks at the disc then hands it to Travis without saying anything.

"Thanks. See you around sometime," Travis says as he walks toward the cemetery gates. "Why don't you think about it? If you decide that ghosts can have a sense of humor too, come play some disc golf with us sometime. We're here almost every day."

Two days later Travis stays late at the cemetery to practice his throws. The days are getting shorter and the sun drops lower in the sky each evening. The shadows of the trees stretch out long and make it harder to see some of the gravestones in the course. He's practicing a boomerang throw on a hole where he needs to hit the back side of the gravestone, and he can barely see the stone in the shadows now. It's a long throw paralleling the stream that runs through the graveyard, and he crosses his fingers so that the disc won't hit the stream.

He watches the disc until it disappears behind the gravestone, but he doesn't hear the soft thunk of plastic on stone telling him he's scored a hole in one. He starts to jog to the grave, when he sees the stranger from the other day watching him from the shadows of the trees on the far side of the stream.

Travis waves with the spare disc he's carrying as he comes up to the tombstone and looks for his disc. "Aw, man, it's six inches away. I don't think I hit it. Did you see? Did I hit the gravestone?"

"No. It didn't hit the gravestone."

Travis picks up the disc and gives the plaque on the grave a light tap. "Par 2, Miss Martha. I'll get you yet!"

"What's a par?" the stranger asks.

"You know, like in golf. 'Par for the course.' This hole's a par 3, but I got it in two. Above average."

The man nods, but he looks confused.

"Like in golf… I brought a spare." He grins and holds up the second disc. "Wanna learn? Here, catch!" He throws the disc across the stream to the man and then follows it, taking a running jump across the narrows next to the grave. Travis lands at the edge of the bank. The ground is soft and it crumbles. He topples back toward the stream, and the man grabs him by the arm with his free hand and lifts Travis up and onto the ground before he can fall in.

"Jeez! You're strong," says Travis.

"You should be more careful," the man replies.

Travis looks back down at the stream. "Well, it's only water. But I'm glad you caught me. Thanks! My name's Travis," he says and sticks his hand out.

The man takes Travis's hand and says, "Um, I'm…Johnny."

"Hi, Johnny." Travis smiles at Johnny and tightens his grip on Johnny's hand. Johnny responds by starting to increase the pressure slightly, but then he blushes and lets go of Travis's hand.

Travis says, "I think we can do a nine-hole course before it's too dark to see. Want to?"

Johnny nods and looks at the disc in his hand.

"That one will glow in the dark," Travis says, pointing to the pale-greenish disc, "but this one," he waves his own black disc, "has a tendency to disappear."

They walk down a lane until Travis puts a hand on Johnny's shoulder and points out a large monument several yards down the path. "See that big gray one? That's the first hole. You have to hit the thing that looks like an acorn on the top. It's a par 3, so you get three throws to make the hole. This tree," he points to a big cottonwood on the right and draws out an imaginary line across the path with a sweep of his arm, "is the tee line. You can throw from any place before the line, but you get penalized if you cross the line. Give it a try."

Johnny looks down the tree-lined row to the grave beyond the T in the lane and says, "No. You first. I want to see how you do it."

"OK."

Travis backs up, takes a couple of running steps, swings his arm, and lets the disc go. The disc sails in the air and catches an updraft that lifts it higher but also farther to the left before it lands, skidding in the dirt along the lane, about 20 feet to the left of the monument.

"Your turn," Travis says with a nod.

Johnny throws his disc in the same manner as Travis, and the disc flies through the air. It starts to glide left, then veers back to curve into the acorn-topped monument, striking it where the acorn attaches to the top of the monument.

"You *have* played this game before," Travis says with a little pique in his voice.

"No. I really have not."

It's late, and Travis walks up Ninth Street toward the graveyard. Snow drifts down from the sky and sparkles in the cones of light cast by the street lamps. It's one of those early-autumn snows. Yesterday it was 70 degrees and sunny. Today, snow. Tomorrow the sun will be out again, and the six or so inches of snow will melt in an hour. Travis has been inside all day studying for a midterm. It's driving him crazy. He shuffles and kicks the powdery snow and makes snowballs to throw at the stop signs. The graveyard's the best place for solitude at night. No one goes to a graveyard after dark.

When he gets to the gates, Johnny is standing just inside, wrapped in a black wool long coat. "Travis! Where have you been? I've been waiting for you." He's holding the disc that Travis gave to him a couple of weeks ago.

"Johnny? How long have you been here?"

"Since about dusk."

"Aren't you freezing?"

Johnny shrugs.

"Never mind," Travis shakes his head. "It's been snowing all day and I had a test to study for. Disc golf is a summer sport. We probably won't get to play much more until spring."

Travis walks on down the lane, deeper into the cemetery, and Johnny falls into step beside him. Travis reaches into his coat pocket and, pulling out a pouch and some paper, he rolls a cigarette. Striking a match, he lights it and inhales deeply.

"Smoke?" He offers it to Johnny.

Johnny takes the cigarette. Holding it awkwardly, he puts it to his lips. Travis watches him inhale and expects him to cough, but he doesn't. As they walk on, it looks as if Johnny is holding his breath.

"You can breathe out anytime now," Travis says.

Johnny breathes out a cloud of smoke and looks at Travis. Then he coughs.

"You've never smoked before, have you?"

Johnny shakes his head.

Travis takes the cigarette back. "Well, don't let me corrupt you. First, disc golf, and now this. Who knows where it will end?"

Travis finishes the cigarette as they walk along the lane, occasionally stopping to look at an interesting tombstone or to admire the way the light from the nearby street lamps reflects off a snow-covered branch. Johnny surprises Travis with stories about some of the people buried in the graves they stop at.

"How do you know all that?"

Johnny shrugs. "I talk to them," he says quietly.

Travis looks sideways at Johnny. "What, to their ghosts?"

Johnny nods.

"No shit." Travis stops still and turns against the soft breeze. Light flares briefly as he strikes another match. The snow has stopped. Through a rent in the clouds, light from a half-moon pours down and sets the snowy lane afire with the silver sparkle of crystal. The trees look like old grandfathers with frosty beards on their branches.

Travis turns back to Johnny with the cigarette hanging from the corner of his mouth and tucks the matchbook back into his coat pocket. "You're an odd one, Johnny. Quite a storyteller. So, you really talk to them?"

Johnny looks down and timidly kicks a pile of snow with his boot. Then he suddenly bends down and scoops up a handful of snow, packing it between his hands.

"What are you…oh, no," says Travis as Johnny throws the snowball at him and hits him in the chest, snow spraying into his face. The cigarette falls into the snow, sizzling. Johnny runs.

"Why, you!" Travis shouts laughingly. He scoops up some snow and chases Johnny, but Johnny dives behind a tombstone and comes up throwing another snowball from behind the barrier. They whoop and yell as they chase and throw snowballs at each other. Travis has the better aim, and soon Johnny's wool coat is covered with snow. Ducking his head, Johnny yells and runs into Travis's next throw, and keeps on going. Travis tries to scoop up another snowball, but Johnny is on him before he can manage it and they roll over in a tumble.

They wrestle in the snow until Johnny pins Travis underneath him, trapping both of his arms. They stare into each other's eyes, and Travis is breathing heavily. Then he grins and licks Johnny on the nose. Johnny jerks back, gasping, and Travis pulls one arm free.

"Wuff!" says Travis, and they both laugh.

Travis reaches up and touches Johnny's face. Johnny starts at the touch, blinking. Travis's breath billows between them, and Johnny holds so still that he doesn't seem to breathing at all. Travis pulls gently at the back of Johnny's head, then they are together, and their lips are touching. Johnny's kiss is tentative and naive and his eyes are wide open. Johnny releases Travis's other hand, touches his hair, and nuzzles along Travis's neck.

"You're so warm!" says Travis. "Have you got a furnace under that coat or what?"

"Mmm," Johnny replies as he licks at the soft bristles of Travis's starter goatee. Travis laughs lightly.

"My butt is getting soaked through in the snow. We have to stand up. C'mon, get up."

They stagger up together, still touching and kissing, and they walk toward the cemetery gates. When they get close to the gates Johnny looks up and around.

"You're going. I don't want you to go," he says.

"It's freezing out here. We can't stay in the graveyard all night," says Travis. "Come back to the dorm with me. I've got a single."

"I can't," says Johnny. His voice goes up a notch.

"Why not?"

"I just can't," he says.

"Why? If my dorm's not OK, can we go to your place tonight?"

"No," says Johnny. He looks away. "Will you…will you come back here tomorrow night?"

"To the cemetery? What about the Sink instead? It's close, on the Hill. We can get pizza and some beer."

"No. Please. Just come here, and we'll talk about it tomorrow. Please?" He looks at Travis and sounds almost desperate.

"What? Are you afraid to be seen in public with another guy?" Travis asks.

Johnny looks down and doesn't say anything. Travis thinks he sees tears in Johnny's eyes, but it could just be the snow. He takes Johnny's hand and tugs on it a little.

"Come with me, please."

But Johnny just shakes his head.

"OK," says Travis. "OK. I'm going before I catch pneumonia. I'll see you here tomorrow, but you better think about it. We can't just meet only in the graveyard and avoid other people. You're going to have to come out sometime."

The skies do not clear the next day. It gets colder and it snows more. Johnny is standing just inside the gate when Travis gets there.

"Hi," says Travis.

"Hi."

"Let's walk a little. It's too cold to stand still."

They walk side by side along the lane. After a minute or so Travis takes Johnny's hand but doesn't say anything. He doesn't know what he should say, and he wonders how long it will take Johnny to open up.

They're approaching the earthen bridge that spans the stream when Johnny jerks at Travis's hand and says, "No. Let's go this way." Travis lets Johnny lead him to the left, off the lane and farther from the streetlights that edge the perimeter of the graveyard, and deeper into the darkness of the center.

They come through a stand of trees where the snow has drifted almost waist-high and walk across a shallow clearing. The moon finds a break in the clouds and lights the area. Travis recognizes the gnarled old pine that protects the tombstone that always knocks him off par in disc golf.

"Our old friend Jonathan T. Walker," Travis says. "I wonder how he's doing tonight? Got any good stories about this one?"

"No." Johnny turns away and sticks his hands in his pockets. He sounds angry. Travis watches him for a moment, then turns his back to the grave and falls down flat on it, the snow billowing around him in a puff.

Johnny whirls around. "What are you doing?"

Travis smiles, lying in the snow on the grave. "Snow angel. I think this guy needs one."

Travis flaps his arms and legs, fanning the snow aside, and

then he carefully sits up and moves away from the grave to stand beside Johnny.

"Do you think he'd like it?"

"Yes." Johnny's voice is cracking. "I do like it. I do."

Travis nudges Johnny. "I didn't ask if you like it, silly. I asked if you think Jon Walker would've liked it."

Johnny looks at Travis, and only then does Travis realize that he's crying. "You don't understand."

"Hey," Travis puts his arms around Johnny and hugs him tight. "I guess I don't. Why are you crying? Why won't you tell me what the problem is?"

Johnny pulls out of the hug and looks hard at him. "Travis, I'm Jonathan Walker."

Travis frowns. "You have the same name as the guy on the tombstone? Why is that a problem?"

"No, Travis! I *am* Jonathan Walker. Why won't you listen to me? My body is buried there beneath that tombstone. I'm dead. I'm a ghost."

Travis shakes his head and pushes back some hair that has fallen into his face. "That's not possible. What are you talking about? You're not dead. You're real, solid. I can touch you." He grabs Johnny by both shoulders and shakes him just a little. "We were kissing last night."

"I'm only solid because I'm working really hard, and because you want to believe what you see. I can prove it."

"I don't understand why you're doing this," says Travis as he starts to touch Johnny's face. But when his hand reaches Johnny's cheek, it doesn't stop. Instead, his face suddenly feels like warm electric jelly, and Travis's hand sinks into Johnny's head.

"Gah!" Travis tries to pull back, but Johnny grabs him by the arms and starts pulling him closer. At every point of contact, Travis slides into Johnny, feeling gooey and charged as if he's being dragged across a static-filled carpet. He loses his vision as his head sinks into Johnny's, and everything becomes a metallic rainbow of light flickering in the base of his skull.

Travis tries to struggle and pull away, but he can't even feel his body. Everything feels electric, like heat lightning leaping through a cloud bank on a hot, dry summer night when the sky is purple and black and bubbling.

And then it is over. Travis is sitting on Johnny Walker's grave with his back against the tombstone. His body is hot and steaming, and every hair stands on end. He realizes that he is hard and his pants are wet and sticky.

Johnny is kneeling beside him, and his hands are on Travis's shoulders. He tentatively touches Travis's face.

"I'm sorry, I'm sorry, are you all right? Please say something!"

Travis tries to talk, but some connection in his brain has shorted out, and his mouth tastes like burned wiring. He wonders if he's had a stroke, and thinks this must be what a lightning strike feels like. Finally, he feels a small leap of electricity somewhere deep inside his brain, and a word comes out. "I…"

Johnny is crying, and when he hears Travis speak he holds his head and kisses him on the forehead. It's warm and moist, and Travis feels his lips, just like they are supposed to feel. Johnny pulls him into his arms and cradles him. The arms feel solid and strong and warm.

"I…like you better…solid," he says between shallow breaths.

Later, after Travis regains some strength, they walk slowly back to the gates of the cemetery. The snow is still falling and it has gotten deeper. It's hard for Travis to walk. Johnny holds Travis the entire way, as if he's trying to make his presence as solid and reliable as possible. When they get to the gate they stop and stand in silence.

Johnny pulls Travis into an embrace and whispers, "I don't want you to go. I don't want to be alone again."

Travis feels tears welling in his eyes and he says, "I can't stay here. I can't be in a cemetery all the time. Why don't you come out?"

"I can't. I can't even see anything beyond the gate. It's all gray."

"There has to be more to it than that," whispers Travis. "There's a whole world out there."

"I don't know. I'm afraid. None of the others who passed

through ever came back. I don't think there's anything but gray."

"I can't stay here." Travis pulls back and looks Johnny in the eyes.

"I know."

Travis touches Johnny's face, and his tears start to fall. He begins to say something, but Johnny puts his hand to Travis lips.

"No. Don't say any more. You have to go. You're freezing."

They look at each other for a minute, then they kiss gently. Travis pulls away, and Johnny lets him go. He walks up to the gate, still a little shaky on his legs. Just before Travis passes out of the gate, Johnny calls out to him.

"Travis, wait!" He steps forward and holds out his hand. "I don't want you to go without me."

Travis takes his hand and looks at him. He nods and says, "OK then, together." And they step through the gate.

On the other side, the street is lit by yellow lamplight and covered with snow. There are no tracks. The neighborhood is still and silent and Travis is alone. His arm is stretched out to one side, hand curled as if he's holding something. Then his hand relaxes, flexes again, and he starts to grope about.

"Johnny?"

Travis looks around and calls out again. "Johnny!"

He looks at the gates of the cemetery and then steps back through them. "Johnny!"

But there is no answer to his calls, and he stands alone at the corner of the cemetery, with the snow drifting down in unsettled piles around him.

Deep Trouble Undercover

Vincent Diamond

"How far is too far, Sarge?"

Benton brushed back his graying hair. "What are you really asking me, Steven?" His drawl was smoother than Jack Daniel's. Like so many cops on the Jacksonville PD, he was just a good ol' boy who'd done well. Lots of them didn't care much for the younger, college-educated cops who came onboard. Benton was always cool with me, though, and he gave me my first shot at high-level undercover work. Undercover was a young man's gig—the guys over 40 didn't have much of a chance.

I had to know: "When you worked undercover, did you ever...sleep with a suspect?"

Benton's head jerked around, revealing some surprise on his worn features. He snapped the manila folder containing the Stalton crew's operations file on the desk. "No, I never did. But I came close. You sleeping with his sister?"

If he only knew.

"No, it's just...things are getting kinda squirrely, tense, you know." Working the Stalton gang was taking its toll on me; I hadn't been sleeping or eating well the past month. Our target was Conrad Stalton, a bulked-up, shaved-bald ravemaster who DJ'd for illegal street dances and—we suspected—fronted a team of drug runners who operated from Miami to Raleigh. I'd spent the last few weeks out at clubs all night, making the raves, drinking with the crowd, trying to worm my way into Stalton's good graces.

Benton clapped a hand on my shoulder. "Do what you have to, Steven. The Feds are in the case now, we can't blow it."

So I got the advice I needed: Fuck whoever you have to in order to make the bust.

The bust went bad. Yeah, we had our SWAT guys, who are damn good, but when you're bogged down with DEA and FBI guys who only run a raid like this once a year, things go really wrong, really fast. Instead of waiting until dawn to move in, some bigwig Fed decided to go in *during a rave*. Civilians all over the place, the crew we were after tucked away in an upstairs back room, and sure enough, things got blown to shit. No civvies dead, but we took some hits, and two of Conrad's crew got popped permanently.

I slammed up the stairs and found Conrad bending over Jason, one of his crew who had hero-worshiped him the most. The knees of his pants were soaked with Jason's blood, there was a bloody palm print on his white T-shirt, and the look in his eyes when he saw me with a badge around my neck and a gun pointed at him...betrayal, grief, rage.

"You lying son of a bitch!" he bellowed. Conrad stood and wiped more blood onto his shirt.

"Conrad...I—" My voice cracked. Below us, the SWAT team banged at the bottom of the stairs. Conrad flinched.

I'll never forget that night.

Or the night before, when he laid me on a rickety table in that room and took me to heaven with his lips and his tongue and his hands.

Never forget.

I let him run, let him get down the fire escape, let him skip away into the night.

The Feds let us take the heat for the deaths, milked the media for all it was worth, charged the ravers with whatever they could, and left town. The case was "closed," and I got sent back down to street units.

It took me over three months afterward to track down Conrad. Once the Internal Affairs investigation was over, I knew my career in law enforcement was finished. Oh, they put me back on the street, but I got the midnight shift in a tony part of town that never saw any action. After three weeks in a row with nothing more serious than a burglary call to an outside storage shed, I turned in my badge and my gun.

I vowed I'd never shoot one again.

I ran the beaches for a while and picked up some cash working the surf shops. It was fun at first, like being back in high school again. Nothing more to think about than the waves and the girls and whether I should wear the orange shorts or the green that day.

Except that I couldn't really think about the girls.

I cruised the streets some nights to look for ravers. But the dance scene had virtually ended once Conrad left; there was no one with the power and charisma to generate the interest, so no one had stepped in to make money on raves. I did find one crew, but no one would talk to me about the Stalton team.

It was the Net that helped me out. I finally lucked out while I was checking a Florida music message board. Some kid bragged a little too much about being in the scene, said he knew somebody who knew somebody who knew Conrad and, with some nudging from me (DanceBoy69), he dropped the dime on Conrad.

Conrad was in Tampa.

I turned in my keys to the surf shop the next day and packed for my trip.

My old friend Sheila was still at the bank. She was happy to plug in his debit card number, and sure enough, his Visa record listed a cluster of purchases along Florida Avenue in the central part of the city. Gas one week at a Mobil, groceries here and there, the liquor store once. CDs—of course—at a hip-hop store on Columbus Drive. All in a six-block radius.

Once I got there, I felt the stares from the neighborhood folks. I was too white in a car that was too fancy. But Conrad would blend right in here with his caramel-toned skin and dark eyes. I wondered why he chose this part of town when the university neighborhoods would have a better music scene.

It didn't take long to spot his souped-up Mustang at one of the motels on the strip deep in the heart of Hispanic Tampa. That was one of the things that intrigued me about him: his interest in old muscle cars. The 'stang was painted a rich metallic-eggplant that looked black at night and glinted with purple sparkles in the daytime.

I parked across the street and watched the motel for an hour, telling myself I was just being cautious, casing the joint. In case he was working a crew in there. Told myself I was still thinking like a cop.

I was just scared shitless.

I waited until after dark, then made myself drive over. I parked next to his Mustang, picked a door, and knocked fast, before I could chicken out.

I was wishing I knew what to say to him.

He answered the door without looking, bare-chested, work pants drooping loose over his hips like he'd just tugged them on. He was a big guy, over six feet, a solid 210, and had shoulders about three feet wide. And that caramel skin and full sweet-as-honey mouth—all the same. Just seeing him made me feel like I'd been punched in the stomach.

I swallowed and locked my knees.

"Who's with you?" Conrad whispered.

My belly tightened and I felt my testicles crawl upward. Fear felt like this. "What?" I stammered.

"I said, who's with you, dumbfuck! The Feds? Jax PD?"

"No one!" I put my palms up. "I'm alone. Really."

"I bet." Conrad folded his arms over his chest. His deep voice rumbled, a growl like a lion's. "Then what the hell are you doing here?"

I balled up my fists and shoved them in my pockets. I kept my gaze on him.

Don't back away, don't cringe. Be a man and face him.

"I needed to see you."

"And I should care?" It probably felt good to strike back at me, if only with words.

"Conrad..." I managed to take a shaky breath. "Please."

"You still a cop?"

"No."

He just stood there, muscled arms over his smooth-skinned chest. A shoulder shrug.

I tried to speak calmly. "So, can I come in?"

"Suit yourself." Conrad turned back into the room.

The first thing I noticed was that the room smelled like—Conrad. Not that it was dirty and sweaty, just that he'd apparently lived there long enough to make it his own. Both beds were neatly made; the pillows were propped up on one, and the outline of Conrad's body was clearly visible on the mattress. Two pairs of work boots rested on the floor next to the TV, a few clothes dangled on the rack—shirts and pants together. Tidy.

I watched him move to the low dresser and tug out a tank top. As he stretched it over his torso, our eyes met in the mirror. Conrad's movement slowed, then he shifted his gaze away and pulled down the shirt. Then he buttoned his pants.

Conrad flicked the remote, and the TV blared back to life. He stretched out on the bed again, seemingly relaxed.

"Uh, can I use your bathroom?" I asked. It was all I could manage to say.

"Over there." A dismissive hand waved toward the back of the room.

I leaned against the bathroom door once I shut it. My legs were trembling the same way they had that night in his apartment. I remembered being pressed against another door, watching its hinges move as he thrust into me, feeling his fire and ice burn me.

I was glad that the fan worked. I flipped it on and just stood at the sink, looking at my face in the mirror.

What am I doing here? What can I possibly say to this man to make him forgive me?

I looked at Conrad's toiletries carefully arranged on the sink. A damp towel hung over the shower curtain, and I had to stop myself from reaching for it.

Screw this. You drove over 300 miles—you have to face him.

"...so after three weeks of that, I quit." I finished my story. Conrad's eyes flicked back and forth to the TV. It was disconcerting to see him stretched out on the other bed like that; my eyes kept skimming down his body. Conrad had grown a goatee, which gave him a devilish, dangerous look. That, combined with his usual shaved head, made him look a little too satanic.

"That's all very interesting, Steven, but it doesn't explain to me why."

"Conrad, I got in too deep, too fast. This was way more than the undercover jobs I'd done before. Shit, for two years I'd been busting college kids for selling dope in their dorm rooms, nothing like this. Benton saw it, he tried to pull me out, but by then the Feds were involved, and they didn't want to blow the whole operation. So I stayed in, and look what happened."

A car commercial roared onto the screen, and Conrad's eyes moved back to the television. We watched the 30-second spot in silence.

I wanted him to look at me.

"I owe you my thanks for letting me go. Thank you. But that's all I owe you, Steven. Nothing else. I don't know what you're doing here."

"I guess I just wanted to explain my side to you."

Conrad's eyes went flat and cold. His shoulders bunched up, and for a second I thought he might stand up and slap me across the face.

Instead he twisted his feet onto the floor and glared at me. His jaw clenched, and I saw that famous Stalton temper—the temper that got him sent to prison on attempted-murder charges—rising to the surface.

I'd be lucky to get away with just a slap.

Conrad clenched the remote and threw it over my head. It crashed into the wall behind me and fell apart in a rain of cheap plastic.

"You fuckin' lied to me! You lied, Steven! That first time in my apartment and again that night at the club. I tell ya, kid, you should go to acting school or something, 'cause you sure pulled that shit over good with me." Conrad's throaty baritone deepened into a growl of rage I'd heard directed at other people who'd pissed him off.

"I'm sorry."

Conrad shook his head. "You know what makes me even stupider? Not just fooling myself that you were just some kid on someone's payroll or fooling myself about you and Julia. No, I went one worse. I fooled myself into thinking that you fucking cared." That pointing finger again, accusing and cold. "You were lying all along."

"I wasn't lying when I told you that I cared." I raised my palms and wished they weren't trembling. "I let you go at the club that night, Conrad. I...had to."

"Doesn't matter. The team's torn to shit anyway. And it's my fault! Marcus is hurt, probably for the rest of his life; he may never drive a big rig again. Laurie and Taylor are gone, Jason is fucking dead, my sister won't even talk to me..." Conrad seemed to calm down a little. He lay back on the bed again. "I fucked things up for a lot of people, Steven, all because I couldn't see through you. Or didn't want to."

"I'm sorry, really." My voice broke. I remembered that pain and put one hand on my chest. My heart thumped. It felt loud to me; I wondered if Conrad could hear it. "It killed me to watch you walk away like that, Conrad. It actually hurt my heart."

"Well, it's over, kid. You did your bit, you said your piece, so how about you just move the fuck on?"

"Stop calling me 'kid.' I'm as much a man as you are. Man enough to face *you*."

Conrad's mouth snapped shut. I stood and walked over to the television. I slammed it off with a palm on the power button and stood facing him.

"You're right, you don't owe me anything, Conrad." The words came fast now; I couldn't stop them and was past caring about stopping them. My hands knotted in my T-shirt. "I don't know exactly what happened between us, I just know that it's changed me and I can't go back to where I was and I can't keep running and I can't be here. Maybe you felt like this your first time and maybe you didn't have anyone to turn to, either, but this is fucking me up all over." I felt my face flush and lowered my head.

I heard Conrad rise off the bed, felt his warm bulk step closer. Three steps away, two.

Please. Please, just hold me and tell me this will all get better.

Conrad didn't touch me, though. I raised my head and saw him look at me with sadness and pity and something else in his eyes. To my embarrassment, my stomach rumbled loudly in the quiet room.

The tension broke and Conrad grinned. "Geez, is that a thunderstorm in your belly? When was the last time you ate?"

I was able to grin back. "I had breakfast this morning in Jacksonville."

"Why don't you grab a shower and I'll snag you some dinner. OK?"

"That'd be great, thanks." I reached out, got close enough to feel his body heat, but Conrad moved away.

He tugged on a pair of boots. He smiled at me once more, that slightly goofy grin that belied his ultracool persona on the street. He had one crooked incisor where his stepfather had punched him as a child. "You better learn to like Mexican food, whitebread."

"I love it," I lied, but who cared?

"Back in 20."

I spoke once more as he got to the door. "Conrad? Thank you. Really."

He didn't turn back. A quick nod and he was out the door.

Two hours later, I'd downed three Coronas, four enchiladas, beans, rice, and corn, plus chips and guacamole. Conrad noshed along with me—"I had dinner earlier," he said—but I knew his dining with me was more to be polite than from any real hunger. He was thinner too. I saw a little more of the clavicle bones in his shoulders and noticed that his arms were slimmer. A touch of oil from the enchilada glistened in his new goatee; it looked delicious, intriguing.

"Oh, man, that was so great!" I flopped back on the second bed and groaned in mock distress. I raised my arms over my head, a badly needed stretch after my drive. I felt sleepy and satisfied—my feelings of unease with Conrad had dissipated as we ate and chatted. "My stomach's gonna bust."

Conrad picked up our dinner leavings and tucked them into the bag. "Want another beer?"

"No, better not. I probably shouldn't drive yet."

Conrad looked down at me. Our eyes met for a long time. A siren warbled in the distance—there were memories for both of us in that sound. I held his gaze and eased my legs apart, just a little.

Conrad swallowed and crunched the bag together with a loud rustle. He moved toward the door. "You can crash here. For tonight."

I elbowed up on the bed. "Conrad?"

"I'm gonna dump this trash and, uh, take a walk for a while. You can clean up and get some sleep."

Before I could speak, Conrad was gone.

Shit. I blew it.

I made for the door and realized that I was a little light-headed; the beers and the tension had zonked me. Once I grabbed my overnight bag from the car I felt more normal again, just on edge and anxious. What would I do when he got back?

Should I say something to him or just touch him?

The image of Conrad in that back room still chilled me. The utter sense of betrayal and anger on his face wilted any sense of excitement I could sustain now. I stripped off my clothes and shoes. I stood for a minute in my shorts, debating, then took them off as well. The sheets on the second bed smelled like bleach, and the linens were rough, scratchy. I rolled back and forth a few times pillow-punching, and then the beer and the food and the stress of the day caught up to me and I faded into sleep.

I woke at 7, my usual time. For a second I didn't recognize the room, then the smells reminded me—the odor of greasy food, beer, and Conrad. A narrow shaft of pale sunlight shone into the room and Conrad stirred, then turned away from me. His broad back was smooth-skinned, unblemished, and delectable.

Before this—before Conrad—looking at other men had meant something completely different from what I was feeling now. It meant sizing them up. Sweeping over a silhouette for a concealed weapon, gauging height and weight for a report later, analyzing someone's bulk to make sure I could take a suspect down without getting hurt myself. And sure, I checked out other guys like all men did: just that quick appraisal to reassure myself that I was bigger, stronger.

But looking at Conrad in the dawn light was looking at beauty. It felt strange to think that a man could be beautiful, but he was. His features were strong enough to carry off that bald head: sculpted brows over his deep-set brown eyes, a thick nose, and full lips balancing it all. And his skin! Caramel, mocha, creamed coffee—whatever you wanted to call it—it was literally mouth-watering.

I'm one of those unusual guys who don't have morning wood, but I sure did today. My cock was heavy and it bonged right up on my belly, hard and oozing precome. I rolled over to avoid looking at him and to keep myself from jacking off.

Next thing I knew, I heard the shower going.

Wait for him to come out or go to him?

Go to him.

The steam in the bathroom wafted a little as I carefully opened the door, just enough to peek in. I saw his silhouette through the flimsy shower curtain. One hand moved below his waist, steady and even. His exhalations made the steam swirl, and I saw his head fall back. I stepped inside the room, naked and hard and oh, so scared.

He stopped moving. "What the fuck do you want?" His words were hoarse and guttural.

I managed just a whisper in the steam, the words wet. "You. I want you."

I grasped the shower curtain with white fingers. Conrad still had one hand around his cock—it was wine-red and thick. He moaned as I grabbed his bull neck, pulled him toward me, and kissed him hard.

The shower curtain snapped off its rings as he wrenched me into the tub. I lost my balance on the wet surface, he bent to catch me, and we went down together, wet and lost. The water pelted us. I pressed him against the wall and pushed our cocks together. He groaned, his torso twisted against mine, and we frantically rubbed our bodies together, panting in the steam.

"Look at us, look," he gasped, his gaze downcast.

I saw my cock thrust up against his. Mine was longer, more pink-toned against my golden pubic hair. His was thicker, wine-dark with black curls surrounding him. The sight grabbed me—the pink and burgundy flesh moving together. He put his hands on us, tunneled our cocks together, and we both thrust upward, bucking like horses.

The tub hurt my knees, I was vaguely aware of the pain, knew I'd have bruises, but didn't care. I wrapped my arms around his shoulders and pushed harder. He gripped my butt, pulled me close, bit my neck, and groaned as he spurted upward. His thick white spunk washed away in the spray of the shower.

Now.

I gave three more hard thrusts and exploded. Semen spurted out of my cock, and Conrad bent low to catch some on his face. It looked beautiful against his dark skin, like frosting over mocha cake. He scooped some up with his fingers and fed it to both of us. My loud cry echoed against the tile, and I feared someone would come running to see what was the matter.

We knelt there, foreheads to shoulders, panting and breathless for a long time. When I looked at him again, his face was calm and set, the anger gone.

I woke with a start. The knock on the door was sharp, and so was the voice behind it.

"Cirada?" A woman's voice, raspy.

"*No, vuelto mañana, por favor. Gracias, señora.*" Conrad's deep voice buzzed in my ear. I pressed closer to feel the vibration in my skull. "*Justa toallas.*" Conrad's Spanish was quick and smooth. I recognized a couple of the words—a cop in Florida had to learn some just to get by—but I was surprised at how well he spoke it.

More secrets.

"*Sí, senor.*"

I saw a shadow pass in front of the curtains and heard the squeak of a wheeled cart. I glanced over at the bedside clock: 3:45.

Conrad stretched, and his broad torso rippled against mine.

He rubbed my feet with his own. "Man, you got cold feet. Jeezus!"

I snorted. "Yeah, I always have. Maybe bad circulation or something."

"Probably just those long legs of yours." Conrad accented his words with a caress down my belly to my cock. "Lo-o-onnng legs." A low growl from Conrad and I was hard again, just like that.

"Oh, no, not again!" I sighed with mock dismay. Then I laughed with delight. Conrad pulled me on top to straddle him. I watched his face flush, and I bent to kiss him.

"Just like that first night." Conrad breathed hard. "Ride me."

I rode.

Later we showered again. I found Conrad's body utterly beautiful and couldn't stop stroking and tasting and nuzzling him. His new goatee was scratchy—my face and neck were a little raw. Beard burn. It felt so strange.

But nice.

I liked feeling stretched and sore, kissed and bruised. I'd never made love with a woman with such intensity or adventure. Conrad was tough enough to take my fiercest sexual energy and gentle enough to kiss my fears away.

"Hey, Conrad, this is wonderful. Thanks." I curled my arms around Conrad's waist, and our eyes met in the bathroom mirror.

"Yeah, this is pretty wonderful." Soft smiles linked us. Conrad pulled me close and kissed my forehead. "I'm glad you found me, Steven."

In the next week we established a simple routine. Conrad drove off to his job at the garage, and I worked days washing dishes and busing tables at a local Spanish café. It was hard labor and paid next to no money, but I didn't mind. I had Conrad.

I usually got back to our motel room first and showered. The throaty roar of the Mustang announced Conrad's arrival from blocks away, and by the time Conrad got in the door, I was hard and ready. I didn't even let Conrad shower away the day's grime and sweat—I just met him at the door and we grappled with each other standing up. After Conrad got cleaned up we'd hit the bed again, then head out to one of the neighborhood restaurants for dinner. He pushed me to expand my tastes—he got "Mr. Meat and Potatoes" from the Midwest eating Thai and Greek and Mexican and even sushi. Once.

Since I've been a teenager I've usually had to get up during the night to pee. I tried to ease out of the bed and not wake him, but Conrad always welcomed me back with a quick nuzzle and a sleepy sigh of contentment. He twisted his toes around my chilled feet and rubbed them until they were warm again.

One Friday night I'd propped pillows under my torso to watch television sideways over Conrad's broad shoulders. We took turns stretching out, one holding the other, and switched off as the shows ended and we cruised through commercials. I let my fingers ease over Conrad's back and arms. "This feels great, doesn't it?"

"Yeah, absolutely." Conrad turned toward me, his face furrowed. "You're spoiling me, I'm not used to this."

"Come on, you've had this before."

"Not really." Conrad shrugged. "It's not like we lay around in Raiford all cuddly, ya know."

Raiford was the maximum-security men's prison in north Florida, a bad place by anyone's standards. He'd done two years of time and didn't like to talk about it. I pushed a little more.

"What was it like?" I felt Conrad's torso tense, and he swiped a palm over his smooth forehead.

"Raiford was just about…need. Release." Conrad's eyes went flat. "Not much more than that."

"Did you—after Raiford—were you ever with another man?"

"Coupla times. There's a beach south of Jax for cruising."

"Spa Beach, yeah, the cops know about it."

Conrad looked up at me sharply. "Do they? Guess I was lucky, could have gotten busted again for getting a knob shine. Great." He sat up and scooted back to lean against the headboard. I resettled next to him.

I couldn't help but be curious. "Why did you do it?" He'd had groupies of both sexes after him in the dance scene and seemed to prefer the women.

Those broad shoulders shrugged again. "I don't really know. But there were some nights when I just wanted a man's touch. Something different, something...rough. I guess that's what it comes down to."

"You had Donalita."

Conrad reached for his iced tea on the nightstand. He swallowed a good third of the bottle before speaking. "I never really had her. Donalita let me borrow her when it suited her purposes."

"Oh. I thought you two were pretty much an item."

"She liked the music and the money and being the top dog's woman. If Johnny Jay had taken over that scene, she would have been with him." Another long swallow. "I think."

"I'm sorry, I shouldn't have pried, this is none of my business." I saw the hurt in Conrad's features.

Conrad glanced over at me then looked away to the television. "It's OK, Steve. I don't mind talking to you about stuff." A few seconds silence. "And what about you, you been with another man since that night?"

"No, no way."

"Why not?"

"I don't really want another man. I just want..." I stared hard at the ceiling. I felt his brown eyes on me, felt our arms pressed against one another. "I just want you." It felt a little silly to say it but he didn't tease me.

I kissed him and settled on his broad chest. We wrapped our arms around each other, and the blue light from the television glazed our faces. When I woke around 3 in the morning we were still holding each other close.

At dinner a week later Conrad talked though a beery burp. "Walk on the beach?"

We both grinned. "Yeah, that'd be great. All sappy and romantic like." I was tickled that Conrad asked me this time—"romantic" he wasn't.

We headed west across the bridge to Pass-A-Grille Beach. We walked our usual route: around the jutting finger of the point, past the snack bar, then into the quiet bay where I liked to swim. The water here was calmer, and the sea smell permeated the air that night.

I spotted a lump on the sand ahead. Driftwood, maybe, or a clump of seaweed. The half-moon shone on the gray sand.

A few steps more and Conrad stiffened next to me. "Whoa."

I smelled it now: death. I moved closer and made out the dark shape on the sand, curved like a sickle. It wasn't seaweed.

I heard the flies first and covered my nose. From six steps away I could see it clearly—a dolphin, eyes blackened in death, mouth open in a rictus.

We moved upwind.

"Oh, man, this sucks. Should we call somebody maybe? The Game Commission?" I asked.

Conrad shook his head. "It's after-hours, man, nobody'll answer. Who gives a shit about a dead dolphin anyway?"

The words were cruel, and I looked at him for a few seconds, pissed. "An adult, wouldn't you say? I don't see any wounds." I squatted in the sand to see more closely.

Conrad didn't answer. He put his hands in his pockets and stared out to the gulf.

"Wow, that's so sad." I remembered dolphins from my surfing days back in high school. That first frisson of fear at seeing a fin in the water, then the sweet relief as the school arced past, close enough to make the waves swell around me. Smiling creatures, I remembered.

"Let's go," Conrad said quietly.

I looked up at him. Conrad's eyes were dark, and his jaw muscles clenched tight.

Halfway back to the car, Conrad took my hand in his.

We didn't talk on the way back, but Conrad's hand was tight around mine, and our fingers clutched together. He ran his thumb up and over mine in a sensual caress. I was hard before we even got back to the Mustang.

I grabbed him, kissed him, and looped one hand tightly around his neck. I tasted the tang of seawater on his skin. I was ready to climb in the backseat and do whatever he wanted, but he stopped and held my face. "Take me home," he said, his voice rough.

It was normally an hour drive; I made it back in 35 minutes.

Once we were inside the door I pushed him against it, impatient and horny. My shorts were damp from precome that had soaked through while I was driving. Conrad raised his arms overhead and leaned back, waiting. I trailed kisses over his bare scalp and down his neck and chest as I tugged at his pants. Conrad's cock sprang free and I kissed it, feeling it grow and bob against my lips.

It was pure sweetness.

"Get your clothes off and get the stuff." Conrad's order was husky and rough.

I loved Conrad's eyes on me as I undressed—I took my time, teasing him a little. When I ran a palm down my torso, I saw Conrad swallow. By the time I got back to the door with the lube and condom packet, Conrad was naked as well.

And now. Now Conrad would fill me up and ride me and pump me. I was so hard that it hurt—my cock actually ached. My balls were tight against me and tender. Precome oozed out of me. My fingers trembled.

Conrad grabbed me—almost too hard—and our kiss was frantic. Conrad gasped when we parted and fumbled for the lube.

Oh, yeah, give it to me. Right now.

Conrad filled my head—the smell of the beach still on him, a touch of pepper in his kisses, the sound of his eager breath, and his beautiful bulk. I ground against him, loving the feel of our bodies pressed together. I heard the rip of the condom packet and thought I would scream with frustration.

Conrad pushed me away and looked down. I kissed his scalp and nuzzled at his ears. "Oh, Conrad, please. You're teasing me."

Conrad's hand closed around me, and with a shock of slippery wetness, I realized that Conrad meant to put the condom *on me*. Conrad's callused palms were rough, but his touch felt so good. The latex was cool, Conrad's tongue was hot on my neck, and the room filled with our urgent moans.

I grabbed Conrad's face and forced our eyes to meet. "Are you sure about this?"

"Oh, yeah, I am absolutely sure I want you to fuck me." Conrad knelt down and used his tongue on me before rolling the rubber down. Then he stood and turned around.

Right up against the door, just like my first time had been.

I moved closer and eased my cock between Conrad's buttocks. I looked down and my head filled with an erotic buzz. Conrad's skin was warm against me, and I marveled to see my own pale cock pressed against another man. I cupped Conrad's muscled ass in my hands and felt the curve of him against me. I fumbled some lube onto my middle finger and plunged it inside him, a little unsure, not really knowing what I was doing.

He gasped and his head jerked back. He clamped down on my finger and whispered, "Fuck me, Steven. God, I want you to fuck me."

Oh, God, I want to do this!

I thought I could go slowly, but once I pushed inside him I was gripped with fever. Conrad moaned against the door, and his body went rigid. Our sweat was slippery between us, and I thrust into Conrad over and over. This was nothing like being with a woman—this was dangerous and hot-blooded and rabid-wild. I gripped Conrad's fingers tight, saw his knuckles whiten, saw the flakes of paint on the wall next to us. We moved together, and the cheap door rattled as we rocked away.

"Oh, God, Steven, please!" Conrad gasped. "Harder, Steven, please!"

I grasped his shoulders and slammed into him with everything I could muster. Conrad's whole body grew tight, and he pushed backward and let out a moaning wail so loud that I knew anyone nearby would hear it. Conrad thrashed in my arms—I could barely hold him. I moved one hand down to Conrad's cock, felt it wet and spurting. Then I came myself hard, gushing inside him, and my ears filled with the sound of our groans and the buzz of orgasm.

Coming made me stagger. We lost our balance, and I smacked into the wall next to the door. We stayed connected, panting and gasping. I put my hands on Conrad's back and felt him trembling.

Conrad pulled away and fell to his knees on the carpet. He hunched over, hands over his bare skull, gleaming with sweat.

After a few seconds my head cleared. My legs trembled so much that I had to push away from the wall with my hands.

Conrad stayed on the floor.

"Conrad, are you OK?" I bent down and realized that he was still shaking. "Hey, hey, Conrad, come on, man, tell me what's wrong."

No answer.

"Conrad! Look at me!"

Conrad raised his head finally, revealing red-rimmed eyes. His face was flushed and sweaty.

My heart lurched. "Oh, God, did I hurt you? Oh, Conrad, I'm sorry, I didn't mean to!"

Conrad clasped my face and kissed me. "No, you didn't hurt me, it's all right. Let's lie down."

We settled on the bed, and Conrad lay his head on my chest. I shivered as our sweat cooled. He tugged the sheets over us. I nuzzled his forehead, hoping he would talk. Our legs wrapped around each other, and he brushed his own warm feet against my cold toes.

I think he would have stayed silent all night if I'd let him, but I wasn't going to. "Conrad, you kinda scared me there, I have to admit."

He sighed and pulled himself closer. "I just needed that, Steven. It's been a real long time for me that way."

"Since Raiford?"

"Yeah."

"So why tonight?"

"I dunno." Conrad trailed one finger down my torso.

"I'm not buying that. Come on, tell me. I know something's bothering you."

"Shut up and kiss me." He elbowed up.

I stopped him with one hand against his neck. "You got quiet after the dolphin. Please talk to me."

Conrad sat up, pulled his legs to his chest, and swiped a palm over his scalp. "Jason loved dolphins. He used to go down to the marine science center in Sarasota to watch them. He was kinda embarrassed about it. When he went down there the first time we teased him for a while. Called him Flipper Boy." Conrad snorted and looked away.

"Until you stopped it."

"Yeah...I saw that it was a break for him, something away from us, away from the clubs. One little thing that was his own."

I stroked Conrad's arm. He looked at me with soft, glistening eyes.

"I couldn't go back to the house after the raid—I knew cops would be all over the place." Conrad's voice choked. "I never got to go his funeral, never got to see his family. I never said goodbye to him."

Conrad turned his face away and clenched his fingers tight over his arms.

I pulled Conrad to me. I let him grieve, let him shed his tears, and then loved him again as best I knew how.

I got up about 4 in the morning. After finishing in the bathroom, I stood for a few seconds, looking down at Conrad in the bed. Our bed. My heart thumped unsteadily in my chest and my stomach clenched.

I'm not sure what this is, but I sure like it.

I lay down gently and tried to settle in without waking him. Conrad pulled me close and spooned against me. He settled one hand around my waist, the other on my shoulder, and pressed his lips against my neck. I felt his toes caress mine, intertwining and rubbing, warming the tops of my feet with his soles, holding my feet between his. The touches were sensual and efficient all at once.

The gesture told me what I needed to know. This was something more than mere lust, something precious.

I rubbed his toes too, pressed back against his broad chest, and fell asleep, knowing he would be there when I woke.

How far is too far? This was far enough.

Pop Music

Jim Gladstone

New Orleans is not the best place to try to revive a relationship: all those vine-strangled concrete crypts lying on the surface of the earth, all that brass band funeral music lingering in the sweaty air. I couldn't stop hearing it.

But I was 20, Nicky was 18, and nobody had told us that in N'awlins, in July, the brutal humidity turns the atmosphere into an above-ground swamp and that you're instantly too tired to work out anything. We had trouble doing much more than avoiding each other's glances and staring at the shirtless bar backs whose sweat dripped off their pecs into the giant plastic cups emblazoned with the name of the bar, becoming the secret ingredient in each overblown Hurricane.

Maybe three days in the sticky heat would help us stick together. Or maybe we would just melt down.

Nicky jumped up from the damp, threadbare divan on our French Quarter balcony. "I'm going for a walk."

For more drinks and a bar back or two, I thought. But I said nothing—all those Hurricanes had taken the storm out of me.

"Go," I mumbled. "Get."

He grinned to himself, strapped his silver CD Walkman around his waist, and snapped in Rick Astley's "Together Forever." That was Nicky: all shiny gizmos and relentlessly upbeat dance tunes. As he stepped away, I admired the way the hazy sun pushed through the wrought-iron bars of the balcony, throwing tendrils of shade on his khakis. I stared at the shadow vines that clung to his legs.

This is the story of the hazy son: the desire for optimism and the music that hangs in the air.

The harmony of *eros* and *thanatos*.

We don't compose the music we're forced to dance to.

I'd met Nicky on the night my father told me he was dying.

Sort of.

I'd been avoiding my father. We were living in the same city, but I saw him as little as possible. This was our agreement. When I told my parents that I was returning to the city where they raised me, I also insisted that they leave me alone. I wanted to disengage from our family.

I had my rights—to privacy, to a life of my own.

My aloofness drove my father crazy, but he generally went along with my wishes. He suggested my disengagement was a phase. Most of what I did displeased my father; consequently, he believed most of what I did was "just a phase": Eventually I'd be 10 again, and we'd pick up our game of catch in the backyard.

Dad telephoned one afternoon. It was the day before Rosh Hashanah—Jewish New Year. One of my brothers was still at home, in high school. The other was coming down from college for the weekend. Mom was cooking. Scads of aunts, uncles, and cousins—all of those people you try not to give a damn about when you're 20 and you're trying so hard to be an independent, freshly minted faggot—were coming for dinner.

"So tomorrow..." my dad began.

As he spoke I heard his stereo in the background. Not his usual Linda Ronstadt or the Three Tenors. It was Chet Baker singing Hoagy Carmichael. "I Get Along Without You Very Well."

"Dinner is at 6, but I need you guys to be here at 4:30. Your brother's taking an early train."

It was September, and I was sure that, like most years, Dad wanted to use the holiday gathering as a chance to enlist my brothers and me to move his heavy wrought-iron patio furniture down to the basement until next summer.

"I'm really busy, Dad," I said flatly. "I'll be there by 6."

"Son," he said softly. His voice wavered, then cracked. "It's important."

Not the patio furniture after all. Some kind of dramatic proclamation—organized, controlled, with kinfolk gathered around.

First flash: My parents were getting divorced. *No*, I thought. *Impossible*.

"What's wrong, Dad?" I asked. I was scared.

"We're *not* getting divorced," he said. He laughed nervously. "Get that thought out of your head."

"What is it, then?" Now *my* voice cracked. "Is something wrong with Mom?"

That's it, I thought. *Breast cancer.*

"No, no. There's nothing wrong with your mother."

"Then what—"

"Tomorrow. Four thirty. OK?"

"*Dad?* Are *you* all right?"

"I can't talk about this now." His voice was all effort, no control. "Tomorrow. Four thirty. I love you."

"I have to sit around and pretend nothing's going on," I sputtered to my friend Jackie over dinner that night. "Tomorrow afternoon he's going to tell us he has cancer or something, but I have to play ignorant because he wants to be *fair* or something. Needs to tell all of his sons simultaneously, like some Shakespearean drama. But I *know* already, at least the gist of it, and now I have to pretend not to know. I'm not allowed to be upset until he waves the starting flag. Damn it!"

Jackie listened quietly, all empathy and patience.

"I'm sorry," I hairpinned. "Maybe I'm being an asshole. It's his life, not mine, right? Do you think I'm being selfish? I should think about what *he* needs, right?"

"I think," said Jackie. "That you should wait. Maybe it's not something so big."

"It's big," I replied. I was certain. "But, hey, I don't know anything for sure yet. Right? So fuck it, let's do this review."

I'd been writing restaurant critiques for the local weekly where I interned. Jackie and I were sampling the menu at the subject of my next column: the New South Café, a little bistro on South Street with a fey New Orleans accent. Phyllo triangles with ground andouille filling, rock shrimp grits, bananas Foster crème brulée—that sort of thing. The place was decorated in pretty floral prints, green carpet, and twinkling votives. There were trellises against the walls, and Enya was on the stereo. But the servers were old-school South Street: sullen attitudes, safety pin earrings, vintage granny glasses, combat boots, and pink streaks in their hair. The overall effect was Laura Ashley meets *Invaders From Mars*. That's how I eventually described the scene in my write-up.

I also wrote, only half joking, that I felt sorry for the one bright-eyed, clean-cut Oxford-shirted waiter I kept an eye on across the room. He didn't seem to belong. It was as if he'd just stepped from the lawn-mower page of the Sears catalog into an alternative universe.

Jackie and I actually managed to have a few laughs over dinner. The next morning I ran over to the newspaper office, typed up my piece, and filed it.

At 4:41 (I looked down to check my watch), Dad said the word "leukemia." Even today, I couldn't tell you what type of leukemia it was, which sort of corpuscle was doing the wrong thing. For 20 minutes he filled the void created by our shock with data on his disease and meticulously considered technical details of his treatment. I heard the phrase "six years at the outside" and watched my mother's skin go blotchy. My brothers sat curled on the couch, closing in on themselves as they tried to pay attention.

The hazy afternoon light slanted through the blinds of my father's den. A million illuminated dust motes floated unguided in the air.

When the family meeting broke up and everyone else wandered off to their bedrooms, I stayed in that den full of golden dust and thumbed through my father's cabinet of vinyl LPs. The entire front row was my parents' everyday aural diet of John Denver, Barbara Streisand, Neil Diamond, and Roberta Flack. In the second row were the albums, rarely freed of their dust jackets, that my father had collected much earlier. Before he was my father, Dr. Longhair, Ruth Brown, Fats Domino, and Etta James had been in heavy rotation.

In less than an hour the doorbell started to chime. It was holiday dinnertime. Perfectly distracting—all those cousins and briskets and blessings. It was a brilliant bit of choreography.

Every night for the next two weeks I danced at Kurt's, a Playskool-bright gay club in the basement of the Adelphia apartments on Chestnut Street. The talcum disco smoke that occasionally billowed onto the dance floor bothered me; it smelled like my childhood barbershop. Still, I managed to lose myself in the flashing lights and the stupid, thumping music. Taylor Dayne sang "Tell It to My Heart," Rick Astley crooned "Never Gonna Give You Up," and Whitney Houston proclaimed that she wanted to dance with somebody who loved her. That was fine for Whitney. But *I* wanted to dance with someone who would take me to bed and let me pound away.

By the second Sunday of my debauchery I was tired. Around midnight my friend Greg sauntered over with another guy as I nursed a vodka at the bar.

"You two just *have* to meet each other!" Greg waved a hand at the freckle-faced, ginger-haired boy in Gap jeans and a navy turtleneck.

"Hi," I said as I pivoted nonchalantly on my bar stool.

Greg giggled—he was stoned.

"Guess what his job is," Greg said.

"How should I know?"

"Here's a clue: He got off from work just now!" Greg said, about to burst with mostly beneficent manipulation.

Greg's friend glanced over and rolled his eyes at me conspiratorially: *Indulge him.*

"Greg, I don't know," I said, a little exasperated. "I give up, OK?"

"All righty then," Greg spun on his heels and pointed at the other guy. "Why don't *you* guess what Jay's job is!"

"Umm...an astronaut?" the guy said, cocking his head and giving me the once over. "He looks like an astronaut."

I laughed.

"Fine then!" Greg huffed. "If you boys aren't going to be any fun, I'll just tell you." He paused and let a pouty, displeased smile play at his lips.

"Nick is a waiter, and Jay is a writer." With that Greg began to walk away, then turned back for just a moment. "He writes restaurant reviews," he told Nick.

"You! You're you!" Nick exclaimed. He settled on a stool right beside me. "I'm kind of pissed at you." I noticed that he smiled even when he was kind of pissed. "Why did you say I was a lawnmower boy?"

I looked at him—handsome, wholesome—and it all suddenly made sense. My turn of phrase had come to life. Nicky had stepped out of my restaurant review and into an alternative universe.

I didn't want him to feel offended, so I offered him a drink. Surely I could win him over.

"I lo-o-ove this song," Nicky babbled an hour later, crazy drunk and pressing hard against me on the dance floor. He was sweating and he smelled like milk.

The DJ was spinning Dead Or Alive. Nicky sang in my ear: "You spin me 'round like a record, baby!"

Despite his questionable taste in music, I needed him to be my boyfriend.

This is a story of the hazy son and the human shield.

I brought him to dinner at my parents' house once a week. I felt proud, self-satisfied. Nicky did all the talking.

Shake your love, sang Debbie Gibson. *I just can't shake your love.*

"Did you ever listen to Dr. Demento?" I asked Nicky in bed one night six months later.

"Oh, yeah! My gosh, I forgot about that."

"Fish heads, fish heads, roly-poly fish heads," I sang.

"Fish heads, fish heads, eat 'em up, yum!" He bit my nipple as he finished the tune.

At 9 o'clock on Sunday nights Dr. Demento, a Los Angeles–based disc jockey, hosted a nationally syndicated radio show that featured idiosyncratic selections from his vast, decades-spanning record collection. Old novelty tunes were his specialty, from passing fads like "The Streak" to the enduring satirical concoctions of Stan Freberg and Tom Lehrer to funky, dirty New Orleans R&B. When we were kids my brother and I would listen to Dr. Demento in Dad's den as we read the Sunday papers and Dad paid the bills. Dad would offer little verbal annotations to the oldies: "Your grandmother met Stan Freberg once" or "I played 'Monkey Bar Blues' on the harmonica in eighth grade."

"I would listen to the whole show," Nicky reminisced as he snuggled against me. "I always hoped he'd play Alvin and the Chipmunks."

"You're kidding!" I exclaimed, sounding harsher than I meant to. "Why?"

"I like them," he said defensively. "They're cute."

My father had found them irritating. He made us change the station whenever the Chipmunks came on. *Come on, Daddy*, we'd beg. *They're cute.*

Nicky sang in my ear, rodent-style, as he reached over and tickled my belly. "My friend the witch doctor, he told me to say..."

"Cut it out!" I growled. I turned my back to him and pressed my hands over my ears.

"He told me, Ooh-e, ooh-ahh-ahh, ting-tang, walla-walla bing-bang..." sang Nicky the Chipmunk, Nicky the innocent, Nicky the kid.

"Fuck you!" I snapped. I leapt from the bed and slammed the door as I stormed out of the room.

From the very beginning, Nicky and I were a battleground.

We were going to break up on Memorial Day. There was a picnic with friends, and ants, and insults. I made fun of Nicky for not knowing who Lou Reed and Leonard Cohen were.

"I'm from Indiana!" he whined.

Then he started to cry.

"I'm sorry," I said, meaning it. "I'm a prick." I wanted to love him so much.

And I was so angry with my father.

He had been depressed and gloomy and needy since his announcement.

His leukemia had marooned me mid rebellion. The man I was supposed to reconcile with was gone. He'd stepped right out of the story I'd scripted, and I couldn't follow the new plot.

Nicky and I fought and fought. Then we decided we should take a little vacation.

New Orleans.

After Nicky headed out into the Quarter, I sat on the balcony, looking at the peeling paint on the shutters across the street, and flipping through *The Southern Voice*, a free newspaper I'd grabbed in a bar the night before. A listing in a music column caught my eye: Clarence "Frogman" Henry, Thursday, 9 P.M.

No way! Even in that soggy heat I shivered with excitement.

Clarence "Frogman" Henry sang the 1956 single "Ain't Got No Home," a doleful but rambunctious Dr. Demento standard that my father had been crazy about when he was 16. On Sunday nights Dad always stopped his work to sing along: "I ain't got no fadduh, ain't got no muddah...I'm a lonely boy-e-e-e, I ain't got no home."

Just as the Frogman did on the record, Dad changed his voice for each of the verses. One normal, one falsetto ("I'm a lonely girl...") and one in the ridiculous croak that made the song a novelty hit ("I'm a lonely frog..."). My brother and I laughed hard as our father sang on those Sundays—we were delighted to see the glint of freedom in his eyes. Sometimes as he kissed us good night he belched "Gribbit."

I was shocked to see that Clarence "Frogman" Henry was playing live; I'd assumed he was dead. The concert had taken place three nights ago, but as I played the choppy piano chords and laid-back rhythm in my head, I realized that the Frogman was from swamp country—a local boy. So I picked up the telephone in our sweaty bed-and-breakfast room and dialed information.

An hour later I was in a yellow cab rolling north of the city across flat, sere, brown emptiness dotted with prefab houses and trailers. I was glad to be from somewhere else.

"Who you meeting out here again?" asked the driver after he squirted a jet of tobacco-browned spittle out his open window. "Ain't never taken no tourist out thisaway before."

"Frogman Henry," I reminded him. "A singer from the '50s. I can't believe you've never heard of him. He's a local legend."

"Nope," the cabby said. "Don't ring no bell."

The Frogman himself had seemed a bit surprised at his legendary status in my mind when I'd telephoned.

"Hello," he rasped.

"Is this..." I began. Of course it was. That voice had been imprinted on my brain years ago.

"Can I come see you?" I asked. "Just stop by and pay my respects?"

"Lemme axe my wife." He set down the phone, and I waited for the verdict. "She says you can drop by, but don't pay no mind to the house, because she don't have no time to do no cleaning today."

"Thank you so much!" I said. "I just want to say hello, touch base."

I told him that, for me, this was going to Graceland. "You have no idea how much this means to me," I said.

At the time, I suppose I didn't either.

Clarence "Frogman" Henry lived in a sagging white ranch

house. There was a billboard-size painting of a piano-playing amphibian propped in the yard. Though he cherished his own memories, he wasn't used to young visitors for whom his single hit song had as much significance as the entire oeuvre of the Beatles—for whom, the Frogman reminisced wistfully, he opened on 11 dates in Canada during their 1964 tour.

I couldn't find much to say. But I was happy to get this close to something that seemed important.

Clarence showed me the bathroom off his narrow front hall. "My wife don't like these," he confided, "so I keep 'em in here."

The walls were lined with handmade six-inch-high shelves that were crowded with figurines, salt- and pepper shakers, and rubber toys—all frogs. Clarence picked up a heavy pewter bullfrog statuette. "Bobby Darin give me this one," he rasped, beaming. He pointed to a bright-green frog-shaped coffee mug. "Brenda Lee give me this one."

I asked if I could bring the taxi driver inside to take a picture of us together in the john.

I broke things off with Nicky on the plane the next morning. As always, he smiled hard and struggled to remain upbeat. As we began the descent into my hometown, I felt the black film canister like dead weight in my pocket. A sad song welled up in my head, composing itself as the pressure dropped. I began to doubt that my father would even remember the Frogman. It started to feel more like my song than his.

It's 15 years later now. There have been great medical advances; there are astonishing new drugs for leukemia.

My father is still alive.

And there is a roll of undeveloped film rattling like a backbeat at the bottom of my writing desk drawer.

Sing it, Frogman. Sing it.

Catching Up

Simon Sheppard

Some things never change. Like the smell of high school corridors.

Updike High, Jesse realized with an oddly Proustian jolt, smelled just the same as he remembered: a heady blend of dirty gym clothes, cheap cologne, battered textbooks, and yesterday's school lunch. Twenty years later, he felt—uneasily—right at home.

Why had he come back? When he was a teenager he couldn't wait to be free of the place. He'd assiduously avoided high school reunions for years—and why not? Anyone he might want to catch up with was hardly likely to attend.

Then he'd gotten that e-mail from Craig. Craig McCarty had become a legend of sorts. He was also the first boy Jesse had fallen for, and the first to break his heart. The heartbreak part was easy enough to explain. Craig had been good-looking, popular, smart—football team *and* the National Honor Society.

Jesse had been Craig's friend but also, very cautiously, his admirer. Which is to say, he'd had an unrequited crush on Craig. Not that he was the only one. Back then, Craig attracted unrequited crushes like Jesse's dog gathered ticks in August. And of course, Craig had his pick of all the cutest girls in school. Why would he want Jesse, whose devotion mostly took the form of furtive glances in the locker room and furious, desperate jacking off at home?

It said something about his graduating class that Craig turned out to be the most famous of the bunch. Not for being a rock star or a politician or a Nobel Prize–winning scientist, not even for being a football star. Craig McCarty had been a famous fugitive: on the FBI's Ten Most Wanted list, in fact. Jesse remembered (or at least thought he remembered) the exact moment he'd found out. His third year in college he saw an article about his friend in the newspaper. Craig—smart, sociable, well-hung Craig—had joined the Weather Underground. He was a leftist radical on the run.

Jesse was both appalled and intrigued. Like everyone he knew, he was opposed to the war in Vietnam. But planting bombs in draft board offices? Clearly that was beyond the pale. No matter how handsome Craig was—even in the pictures on his wanted poster he looked pretty good—there was no way Jesse could approve. And yet...and yet. There was a rebel romanticism, a Che Guevara aura to the story, The idea that Craig—*his* Craig—was in any way evil just seemed too farfetched to Jesse.

When the war ground to a halt, the Weather Underground became marginalized and irrelevant. The last Jesse had heard of Craig, he'd finally turned himself in. Because the federal government had overstepped its bounds in chasing down the Weathermen, the charges had been dismissed. Except for Craig's subsequent marriage to a fellow radical, that was all Jesse knew about his high school crush–turned–outlaw. Lately he'd hardly ever come to mind.

Then he'd gotten the totally unexpected e-mail, which let loose a startling flood of feelings. Craig wanted to know if Jesse was thinking of going to their high school reunion. He wanted to "catch up," he said.

So one fine spring day Jesse found himself walking the halls of Updike High once again.

He soon found himself corralled by Elaine Orlovski, a bohemian chick who'd proudly hung out with brains, nerds, and social misfits and who had been a friend of Jesse's way back when. In the ensuing quarter century, she told him at excruciating length, she'd married well, raised three daughters, become a widow, and found Jesus. Found Jesus with a vengeance, it seemed: Elaine Orlovski-Barton peppered her monologue with complaints about "homos, rap music, and secular humanism" and punctuated her rants with "Praise the Lord."

Jesse ached for an escape. He furtively glanced around the gym, which had been festooned with a crepe paper–and–cardboard tribute to the theme of their senior prom: "Holiday in Venice." *"Death in Venice" is more like it,* Jesse thought.

"Elaine, honey," he finally said when Elaine paused for air, and he managed to get a word in edgewise. "There's something you should know."

"Yes, Jesse?" Her eyes were still the same bright blue they'd always been, even behind bifocals.

"Elaine, I'm a fag."

Her dewlapped jaw dropped. Taking advantage of her stunned silence, Jesse beat a path to the punch bowl. He was just taking a bite of one of those cream-cheese-and-stuff-rolled-up-in-a-pita hors d'oeuvres when he saw him: Craig...Craig McCarty.

Jesse recognized, somewhere in the middle-aged man across the badly lit gym, the young man he'd once found so beautiful. But as he approached his old friend—half eagerly, half apprehensively—he saw how very many years had gone by. Craig was no longer the limber teenage athlete or the dashing young revolutionary outlaw. Craig McCarty was a balding, slightly chubby guy in a plaid shirt, rumpled sport coat, and ill-fitting chinos.

Still, improbably, Jesse thought he was simply beautiful.

Craig turned and recognized him. His face bloomed with a broad smile.

"Jesse? Oh, man..." He extended his hand. When Jesse shook it, Craig moved in and enfolded his old friend in one of those warm but cautiously noncommittal hugs straight men inflict on each other. The physical contact went straight to Jesse's crotch, which seemed remarkably inappropriate under the circumstances. Fearing Craig might feel his stirring erection, he pushed away, breaking the clinch.

"How you *been*, pal?" Craig asked, beaming bonhomie.

"OK, Craig. Great." How could anybody sum up three decades while standing in a high school gym? "And what have you been up to?" It was a question Jesse immediately regretted asking. When he was young Jesse had seen an arty film called *Zabriskie Point*. It was a self-indulgent mess about anomic young dropouts, and he'd mercifully forgotten most of it. The only thing that stuck with him was the final scene, when a house in the desert explodes and the screen fills with shot after shot of the charred detritus of American bourgeois life careening through the air. It was an image he'd recalled on 9/11, and it was an image he thought of now.

"Well, Jesse," Craig said, "I've had my ups and downs, you know. *You* know."

Jesse did.

They made the rounds of the gym, saying hi to the people they remembered, trying to recall the others—now complete strangers—who seemed to remember *them*. Bob Bradbury, the class clown, was now a state senator. Dana Krauss, the beautiful cheerleader, still looked great, though she probably wouldn't be able to get up from a split anymore. Nancy Parsons and Ken Snyder, two impressive brains who'd been the ones to beat at the science fair, had gotten married and grown fat. They were grandparents now, still no doubt geniuses, and no less socially inept than they used to be.

Jesse and Craig soon adjourned to the local "ye olde colonial tavern" down the street—one of those George-Washington-got-drunk-here joints that litter the Northeast.

Over fake-pewter tankards of beer, Jesse told Craig about Paul. Not everything, since some things were hard to explain—like how, as the years had gone by, he and Paul had become not two people but three, really. The third character in the mix was, somehow, their relationship itself, a love-infused being made up of the best of both of them. But that intimate detail wasn't the sort of thing you'd casually mention to someone you hadn't seen in decades—especially not to someone who was maybe a Marxist, who presumably had little time for the vagaries of the heart.

"And then Paul died," Jesse said, "of what you'd think he'd die of."

"Time is a thief," Craig said, unexpectedly poetic. Then, even more unexpectedly, he reached across the table and grabbed Jesse's hand.

"I loved him, Craig," Jesse said. This was not what you were supposed to say to someone you hadn't seen in 30 years—certainly not in a touristy tavern, not with unplanned tears running down your cheeks. Craig, probably knowing better than to say anything at all, just squeezed his old friend's hand tighter.

At last, when he'd regained his composure, Jesse used his free hand—the one Craig wasn't touching—to wipe his face. "I'm sorry," he said.

"Nothing to apologize for," Craig said. "Nothing at all."

Jesse smiled and looked into Craig's eyes. "God, that Elaine...isn't she unbearable? And she used to be so promising..."

They both laughed.

"Hey," Craig said, more briskly than necessary. "Want to finish up here and come back to my room?"

As Jesse wiped his eyes he realized that the pressure of Craig's hand on his had made his dick hard. This was, of course, an utterly inappropriate thing to happen while he was supposed to be mourning the loss of his boyfriend. But happen it did, despite all his complicated emotions, despite the fact that Craig looked nothing like the young football player Jesse had had a crush on. Despite that. Or maybe because of.

The room was in an upscale hotel on the edge of town. It was, like so much out in that direction—garden apartments, an office park, the mall you'd see anywhere in the country—unfamiliar to Jesse, built since he'd left home.

"We were careful not to harm people," Craig said in response to Jesse's gentle questions about his past. "Not after the townhouse blew up." Jesse had followed the exploits of the Weather Underground closely enough to catch the reference. Still, though, he wasn't quite sure whether he bought Craig's protestations of harmless goodwill. It was all safely in the past—*almost* safely in the past. A lot of things were. Jesse tried to recall the end of *Zabriskie Point*, but found himself wondering what Craig looked like naked.

The two of them sat in a pair of thick-armed lounge chairs in Craig's room and slowly worked their way through the six-pack they'd picked up on the way from the tavern.

"And you," Craig said, "what do you do now? I've been so busy talking about myself—"

"I'm with the FBI," Jesse said.

Craig looked startled and a bit alarmed.

"No, just kidding," Jesse said. "I'm an accountant."

"For real?"

"Which would you rather it be? Evil fed or boring book-keeper?"

"Y'know, I'm not quite sure." They both smiled, and there was a long moment of silence.

Then Jesse just blurted it out: "I was in love with you."

"I know," Craig said. "I knew it all along."

"Even back then?"

"Maybe not in so many words, not so I could say it right out to myself. But I knew. I was young, not stupid."

"You didn't mind?"

"I liked you. We were friends, right? And I was young and insecure and full of myself, ready to accommodate all wor-shippers."

"And I guess I still am," Jesse said.

"In love with me?"

Jesse looked around the room—at the open suitcase laid out on one of the beds, the wrapped drinking glasses, and the remote for the TV in the cabinet. This wasn't how and where he'd thought this would happen. Actually, he never thought it would happen at all. But here it was, happening.

"Yes," Jesse said.

"In love, or a crush?"

"Dunno. Love, I think."

"Despite everything?"

"At least *you* never became an accountant."

"So you want to do something about it?"

"You mean?" *Actually,* thought Jesse, *there aren't all that many things "doing something about it" could mean.* "But you're straight, aren't you..." For a while Craig and his wife had been one of America's Ten Most-wanted Couples, living under assumed identities, like a rock and roll Bonnie and Clyde.

"Yes, I am. Though my marriage, um, it isn't what you'd call on a firm footing anymore." He sighed heavily. "That's why she's not here. One reason." Craig shot Jesse a significant look.

"It's OK if we don't do anything," Jesse said. Oddly, he felt like he might cry again.

"Back in the day," Craig said, "we good lefties thought that monogamy was bourgeois and mandatory heterosexuality a ruling-class oppression. So we all experimented. In my case, the experiment with being bisexual wasn't all that successful. So yes, I'm straight."

"Well, then," Jesse said.

"But you can suck my dick."

"I think I'd rather not, thanks."

"Get it out of your system."

"When you put it that way, I'm sure. No offense, but no."

But Craig McCarty was already grabbing at his own crotch. As Jesse sat there on the edge of the bed, Craig stood up, unzipped his fly, and pulled out his dick, which was almost hard. It was smaller than Jesse remembered, but then he'd seen a lot of other dicks in the years between.

"Suck it," Craig said with some urgency. "You know you want to."

And Jesse *did* want to. If he'd had an iota of self-respect, a modicum of good judgment, a soupçon of sense, he wouldn't have. He never would have said what he said, which was: "OK."

And there it was, right in his face, between his lips, in his mouth. The dick of a man he'd spent the last 30 years, more or less, mooning over. It was just another dick. But in a sense, of course, it wasn't just a dick, just as sex is never "just sex" but always, whatever people think, a dense, contentious tangle of desire and fear and lust and love and contempt, all tied up in one sloppy package.

I love you, Craig, Jesse let himself think as the not-all-that-large cock speared into his throat. He let himself think that, he heard himself think that, and if it weren't altogether true, it was far from false. He saw Paul's face in his mind and took his mouth off Craig.

"Go on," said Craig.

"You want to fuck me?" Jesse asked, pushing away Paul's face.

"Up the ass?"

"Where else?"

Craig was already taking off his pants. "Got a condom?" he asked.

"Always."

Naked, Craig was a shadow of his teenage self, if a shadow could be twice as big as the original. Truth to tell, if Craig had been some stranger off the street, Jesse might still have had sex with him, though not with any particular enthusiasm. But that wasn't all this was about for Jesse—just sex in the here and now. It was about getting fucked by the Craig in the room, and the Craig in his memories, and maybe even by the secret, criminal Craig that came between. As he watched his high school buddy unroll a rubber over his surprisingly stiff middle-aged cock, Jesse realized it was about the weird persistence of love.

They say—Thomas Wolfe and whoever else "they" are—that you can't go home again. But Jesse did go home—boarded a plane on Sunday night after the final reunion goodbyes and headed back to the other coast. On the plane, he thought about how readily Craig had fucked his ass—not expertly, perhaps, but with a lack of reluctance that made him suspect Craig had perhaps understated his bisexual training.

The fuck hadn't been bad, not bad at all, and if it hadn't fully resolved his feelings for Craig, at least Jesse had come, noisily and messily, all over the motel's sheets. Craig had been cordial and even a little cuddly afterward; if anyone had acted awkward and standoffish, it had been Jesse. But neither of them spoke very much about it, and that was fine.

In retrospect, the sex seemed like something preordained, something they'd both had to go through to prove something or to release something or to reestablish their bond or to finalize its ending. But whatever it was or meant, it was done, it was over, and being honest with himself, Jesse had to admit that, yes, he still loved Craig, but in a different way, now that he'd had Craig's prick up his ass. Or maybe not in such a different way at all.

The plane landed, Jesse exited the jetway, and there was Paul.

"Hey, honey," Paul said, "how was the flight?"

"What you'd expect. No legroom and little bags of pretzels."

"And how did the reunion go?" He took Jesse's carry-on and hoisted it over his shoulder.

"I'll tell you later, Paulie. I'm beat."

Jesse had figured he'd confess the lie he'd told Craig as soon as he saw Paul, or maybe on the ride home, or at least on his first night back. But he didn't, not then and not ever.

It wasn't that they were monogamous. Paul had known about Jesse's crush on Craig and been understanding to a fault. That was one of the reasons—the very many reasons—that Jesse loved Paul more than anything in the world. On the car ride home Paul asked, "So did you get it out of your system with that guy?" Jesse confirmed that he had, and Paul was, mercifully, unconcerned about the details.

So why had he told Craig that Paul was dead, on the spur of the moment inventing a story so distressing that it had, in the telling, unexpectedly made him cry? Lying in bed that first night home, the possible reasons flipped through Jesse's brain.

Was it an attempt to grab Craig's sympathy, a ploy to appear vulnerable and ripe for the picking? Was it the equivalent of a married man taking off his wedding band on a business trip? Maybe it was a stab at drama, an attempt to invent a past that was, if not as interesting as Craig's, at least less boring than his humdrum life as a minor West Coast functionary for the FBI. (The accountant bit had been a lie too.)

Or maybe it was a warped attempt to punish Paul in absentia for letting him go through with the whole reunion thing. Paul had even declined to go along, lest his presence make things awkward between Jesse and Craig. Who knows, maybe it was just a clear case of demonic possession, or a kind of autobiographical Tourette's. *Oh, well,* he concluded, *if the Weather Underground can wear disguises, I can too.*

He rolled over, cuddled his sleeping lover, and considered that people often underestimate the sheer joy of sleeping spoons. But this time even a warm cuddle didn't bring on sleep for Jesse, not right away. He lay there thinking about that last scene in *Zabriskie Point*.

Explosion. Slow motion. All sorts of things flying madly across the screen, propelled by some irresistible force: Yearbooks. Football helmets. Love. Wanted posters. *Old* love.

At last, Jesse slipped into his dreams.

Tokens to Tomorrow

Gavin Austin

Waiting for a train on this barren platform will strip you of time if you let it.

I am sitting in the small glass-vaulted passengers' room at Sandgate Railway Station. A lot of loneliness nurses my heart. I feel as I usually do after visiting the cemetery: that Heaven is on the drift. Yet I know true love has too many tokens to be robbed of Faith.

It is one of those rare, glorious days that eastern Australia usually reserves for April. A soft-sun day where the sky is Wedgwood-blue and the clouds are so skimpy and listless you can imagine the world has stopped revolving. You can pretend you are sitting in the Louvre, looking up at some enormous Renaissance painting: those feathery, filamentous clouds like seraphim that dreaming eyes have brushed upon the pale sky.

The keen teeth of guilt gnash at me, and I fight back, resolved to make good on a promise. It will be a couple of months before I visit again—tomorrow I leave for Scotland to find the boy in the man I loved.

Why do I recall the cadence of his Scottish accent more easily than the other beautiful things about him? The mind keeps its own counsel.

How can I explain Angus? Although he lived most of his life

in Australia, he could muster his Scottish accent whenever it suited him to be especially charming (or nonchalant). My most treasured memory of him is that moment, all those years ago, when he first told me he truly loved me. That I meant more than those fleeting liaisons with the faceless, nameless men that had preceded me.

"My love is no automatic bobbin tha' reels off when'er someone pedals my machine, Raoul," he explained.

"Then I'd better pedal long and slow," I said as I sank into his translucent blue eyes and felt something kindle within me.

That was before he started calling me Roo. We were both a little drunk that night.

I miss his well-muscled body beaded with water droplets as he stepped from the shower. And the way his wet, curly, tobacco-colored hair excited the core of my sexuality. How his curved smile stopped me in my tracks. He could bring a smile to my face as he nodded his head quickly but gently three or four times as those planetary eyes accented some point he insisted I understand.

His friends called him Pixie because of his exquisite, lobeless ears, which melded into the rear of his jawbone. They said it was a sign of oversexuality, and so far as Angus was concerned, I am inclined to agree. I soon learned my big handsome Scot was a true softy, incapable of malice. The worst thing I ever heard him say was about the treacherous old queen, Kissy-Kissy, who did a drag act on Friday nights in the only gay bar in our industrial city of Newcastle. "Aw, he's no' so bad," Angus said, "though sometimes 'e can sink lower than shark shite."

The toughest job was vetting visitors on those days when Angus was barely in this world, let alone in our bed. Our neighbors, a lesbian couple, were very understanding and would knock to see if there was shopping to be done or if someone was needed to sit with Angus while I ran errands in town. Our gay cartel was harder to handle, perhaps because they adored him more. I heard later that a couple of friends had complained to the rest of the troop that I denied them access to Angus. My "jealousy," they called it. Good God! If Angus had been able to cope, I would have invited the world in to say Farewell, Pixie.

I changed the sheets twice a day; it seemed I was forever loading and unloading the washing machine. I was no longer able to paint. There was no time and, in any case, I'd lost all inspiration. We survived on welfare. Angus received a disability pension after he had to give up his job as a furniture restorer for an antiques dealer. I received a carer's pension and, despite the cost of tonics, creams and medication, we somehow managed to struggle through each fortnight.

The few times I found a couple of hours free in the afternoon, I laid out my brushes and stared at a blank canvas. Stared until my eyes filled with tears, for the "miracle drugs" were failing him. I knew it and so did he.

Angus had Dorothy, the community nurse, in tears when he had asked: "Do people like me ever build up and get better?" Her eyes held such sadness when she glanced at me. She didn't know what to say, so she plumped his pillows and changed the subject to the weather.

On those lost afternoons, I blinked back tears, packed away my brushes, stripped, and snuggled against him in bed. Tenderly I hugged his crucified body. If he had allowed me, I would have kissed the angry purple blooms—"irises" he called them—that grew on his legs and across his chest. He had forbidden me to touch him like I had in earlier times: those passion-filled days when we had first moved in together, and before he received his news. It was the only demand he ever made of me. He had also made it clear he did not want to die in hospital.

"I hate hospitals, Roo. I hate hearing people being sick, or coughing their guts up. Relatives cryin' as they pass the doorway. It's all too sad t' see."

I promised him I would go to the Isle of Mull someday.

"When you do, Roo, wherever you wander, you will be in my childhood...an' I'll be beside ye."

Our last summer together, as I watched him become a skeleton in cotton boxers, I learned some of the greatest lessons of life.

The end was not nearly as dramatic as I had imagined. We

were lying together on our left sides in the spoons-in-a-drawer position—his favorite sleeping pose—so we were not even facing each other, just breathing softly together.

"I'm tired, Roo," he said. "Can I go now?"

"Yes, my love." I tightened my hold on him.

His pianissimo effort in what became the final cavatina of our love was barely audible, but I was instrumentally aware of it. Soon I was the only one of us breathing. It was such a mild, uncomplicated movement. I tried to die alongside him.

It wasn't easy for me to know he had left my world without a whimper of protest—just a simple request for permission. True to the end.

Has he gone on to some greater life somewhere? I know I will find him where the stark mountains glide into cloud and the silver water laps the sleepy shore of the Isle of Mull.

It has taken me almost four years working in an insurance office to scrape together the money to go. I begin my extended holiday today. It still doesn't feel like I'm really living my life, but going to Scotland is fitting.

A woman comes down the station steps looking bereft, but she's not dressed in black, so I assume she's not been to a funeral but is visiting a grave. She clutches a Vuitton handbag in front of her as she walks. Her dark hair is worn in a fashionable bob that frames her elegant oval face. She smiles a sad Mona Lisa smile as she sits beside me on the banquette provided in the waiting room. Her perfume drifts to my nostrils. I haul myself from the morose pit of memory and smile back at her.

"We couldn't have a nicer day to visit," I say.

"Pardon?"

"I said it's a beautiful day."

She looks at the gum trees, glitter-tipped on the other side of the track, then up to the sky before she agrees.

"Yes, it is. I can't remember such a sky. It's..."

"Renaissant?" I offer.

"That's a perfect way of putting it."

We look at each other with an understanding that's deeper

than our minds are capable of articulating at that moment. She is younger than I had at first thought, so for some strange reason I warn myself to speak softly but not tritely.

"It isn't easy," I say.

"It takes time. Perhaps it does get better."

"Maybe that just means time finally claims you too—death heals you of everything life inflicts on you."

"Now, that's a bit too pessimistic," she replies.

The old two-carriage red-rattler grumbles from a kilometer away, making more noise than the massive coal trains that hurtle along this line.

"At least something's on time," I remark.

"I'm glad," she says. "I'll make my Sydney connection at Hamilton. Do you live in Newcastle?" She cocks her head slightly.

"Part of me does."

"Don't think like that. Grieving alone is bad."

"It's not that," I say. "It's like something...*debilitating* has happened to me. You're from Sydney?"

"Yes. My husband was born here. He wanted to be buried in the family plot. He died a year ago today...throat cancer."

"It's true," I say. "Women are stronger than men."

"Perhaps we're just more resilient."

The train bumps noisily to a halt.

"My name is Raoul. May I sit with you?"

"I'd like that. I'm Elaine Finlay-Jones."

We sit facing each other. As the train leaves the station and picks up speed, each of us pensively watches the interminable railway fence flashing by the window. Finally, she steels herself and turns her gaze on me.

"How long since your—"

"My partner, Angus," I say. "He died almost four years ago."

Not a mascara'd eyelash stirs.

"Had you been together long?"

"Seven and a half years. He died of..." I suddenly find myself weeping.

"Raoul, please. Don't upset yourself."

"I'm sorry. I..." I sniff and shuffle my feet.

"My brother is gay. He's lost several people very close to him over the years."

She conjures a small notebook and a tiny pen from the universe of her handbag and writes with a flourish of pen strokes. She tears out a page and hands it to me.

"My address and phone number. Ring next time you're in Sydney. I'll cook dinner and invite my brother Simon over. He lives in Bronte."

I fold the small sheet carefully, as if my future might be inscribed there. She flips her notebook open to the center and removes something. Coyly she passes me a photograph of herself alongside a dark-haired young man.

"It doesn't do you justice," I tell her. "You're much—"

"Not me! I wanted you to see Simon."

I look closely at the two distractingly wonderful faces, then stumble over my next words. "But surely you're twins?"

"Mmm-hmm. So now you know what to expect." She stifles a giggle.

His wide, earnest eyes made him look implausibly young.

"But he may not approve of..."

Her light laughter ascends like the flock of wild mallards that take flight as we pass the Warrabrook wetlands.

She leans across the space that separates us and whispers conspiratorially: "Simon knows I'm a horrid, meddling matchmaker."

As the train rumbles toward Hamilton, she laughs heartily at her confession. Before I can reply, she comforts me with eyes that glow approval.

"But why are you—" I begin.

"Doing this? Because I have this not so timid feeling that you two may be, if not meant for each other, at least good for each other."

The train sputters to a stop, and she frisks me with a searching look.

"You will ring?" she asks.

"As surely as I shall never lose this notebook page you've given me."

We walk across to the Sydney platform, and I take her arm to help her down the steep second flight of steps. Her heels are higher than my spirits.

"Are you curious, Raoul?"

"About?"

"Simon! He's not as outgoing as you or I."

"Which means he may be a more proper person."

"Hmm. Perhaps. I like hearing the truth. So in return I should be truthful."

"As people should be friendly to strangers they meet at desolate stations?"

Again her eyes probe mine, questioning my question. I almost drown in her attention.

"How true," she says. "Sadly, it's not always so. I have another confession: I recognized you back at Sandgate. I remembered your face from the cover of one of Simon's magazines. And the article inside on how, as a struggling, self-taught Newcastle artist, you'd won the People's Choice Award in the Archibald Prize. Then you suddenly quit painting."

"Oh," I mouthed almost silently. I felt my eyes grow wide.

"Are you angry?"

"Not at all, Elaine, more like surprised."

I begin to grin, and the fine lines around her eyes relax.

"You should smile like that more often," she says, beaming back at me.

"Angus always said that too." A sonorous horn wails in the distance. "That must be your Sydney train, right on time."

"Not good timing this time."

"I have so enjoyed meeting you," I tell her.

"I hoped you'd say that."

When the train arrives, I open the nearest carriage door for her, then peer along the windows until I see her select a seat. She senses me watching, turns her head, smiles (looking so like her twin), and waves a few fingers as the train pulls away.

I walk home hurriedly, like a tardy schoolboy, my hands pushed into my pockets. Lines from *Hamlet* come to mind unbidden: *There's a divinity that shapes our ends / Rough-hew them how we will.*

I can't control my thoughts, so I begin to take an inventory: guilt and memory, mostly. Then this simple act of gentleness toward myself gives rise to hope. Angus would want me to find happiness again, if it were true happiness, such as I'd shared with him.

As I fit the key into the lock of the front door, I notice the camellia bush in the terra-cotta urn on the porch is in bud. I close the door behind me, lock away the world, and pause to straighten the portrait that hangs in the hallway.

I slowly walk to the bedroom, where I often find Angus in the wardrobe mirror. He is there, waiting for me, and my heart tightens like a fist. He stands where he stood a few days before he died—he'd hauled himself out of bed, with the aid of his IV drip pole, to look at his devastated body. His boxers stuck to his gaunt thighs on that hellishly sticky afternoon. I don't know how I found the breath to speak; given his agony, I don't know that my effort could truly be called courage.

"Let me sponge you," I said, "and change your shorts."

It seemed he hadn't heard me, then he gradually turned and spoke with an eerie voice. "Mebbe I shoulda 'ad meself preshrunk at 21. Y'know...the way jeans are Sanforized so th'll na' shrink."

"You idiot," I said, cracking a smile for the first time in days.

He started to giggle, and I joined him. It was our last laugh together. I wanted to sweep him into my arms and hold him. Instead, as if he were a child, I shooed him back to bed. To the brief eternity of the little that remained of his life.

"Only if you'll get me a cold Foster's," he said.

Oh, what the hell? The room was a furnace, and he wasn't eating anything that couldn't be sucked through a straw.

"All right. You'll get your Foster's as soon as I've made you comfortable."

"You OK, Roo? Y' look worried."

"I'm fine."

"Hey remember when we wen' to the Mardi Gras Fair an' I heard the bagpipers? And I ran off an' pissed m' pants?"

"I remember...when I found you I tied my jacket around your waist to cover the stain."

"Well, I've done it again."

"It's OK. I'll get you fresh boxers."

"Aye. Y' always were good t' me, Roo." He seemed unaware of his rushing tears.

"Shhhhh...stop crying."

"I don't wan' t' say goodbye to you, Roo."

"Then don't..."

After that day he never returned to look in the mirror.

I look deep into the silvered glass and am astounded that, instead of grieving silently in disheveled depression, I am crying shamelessly with the hunger of wanting to be loved. Can I forget you? Or will my heart always remind me? You know I will never forget you, Angus. I may have just fallen for a face in a photograph, but...perhaps only because I need to feel needed. I no longer feel exiled from passion, and I know the love I knew with Angus has not deserted me.

The world spins on its axis again, but it isn't enough. Everything life and love bestowed on me—everything I thought I had lost forever—returns to recharge my emotions. I cling to hope like a frightened kitten.

Tomorrow morning I will finish the last-minute packing, but there is something I want to take down from the top of the wardrobe right now. With great care, I wrap my brushes in a towel and add them to the overflowing suitcase lying beside our bed. Perhaps I'll discover the need to paint again, by the silver shore of the Isle of Mull with Angus looking over my shoulder.

I picture a young man's face in Sydney whose portrait is waiting to be painted. I say the other name—Simon—out loud for the first time.

The Love of My Life

Dale Chase

I met the love of my life 20 minutes after I lost the love of my life. Reeling from an unforeseen breakup, I boarded a plane for Los Angeles. During the one-hour flight I was resurrected and set adrift into what would ultimately become my life. So crazy, that awful mix of pain and promise, and so confusing.

Apparently Raymond had been planning the breakup for some time. To avoid a scene and an open-ended discussion, he purposely chose to tell me his news when he knew I had to get on a plane. Two seats were booked and paid for; only one was to be used.

He was talkative on the way to the airport, as if letting me get a word in might derail him. I'd witnessed this kind of hyper monologue from him when he was drunk, so I just attributed it to excitement. I didn't have a clue.

We'd both packed carry-ons, so he was safe there—no luggage going off with the jilted party. After we got our seats in the boarding area, 10 minutes had gone by when he said, "I'm not going with you."

"When?"

"Now. To L.A."

It took several seconds for this to sink in because it made no sense. When I understood what he meant, it still made no sense. "What?" I said.

"You heard me. I'm staying here. And while you're gone I'm moving out."

"What?"

"Stop saying that."

I turned toward him, though he kept facing forward. I spoke to his brown brush cut, to his ear. To the neck I had kissed that morning. "This makes no sense," I said.

He sighed heavily, as if he were annoyed with my incomprehension. "I'm breaking up with you," he said. "There's someone else."

"And you chose to tell me now, when you know I have to get on a plane?"

"Yes."

The weight of his betrayal, coupled with his unabashed manipulation, began to press down onto me with a heaviness that started in my chest and ended in my stomach. My heart began to pound. He was leaving me by default, leaving by way of staying.

"So you're leaving me," I managed.

"Yes."

"Just like that."

"No, not just like that. I've given it lots of thought, agonized over it actually. It didn't come easy."

"And you couldn't tell me there was a problem? Couldn't give me a chance to speak up? You had to wait until..." I looked around at families, at couples with their vinyl bags and strollers and kids, their magazines and their lives.

"There's nothing to talk about," he said, his voice sinking a notch.

"Nothing?" Seemed to me we had everything to talk about.

At that moment the flight was opened for boarding, and people began to move toward the gate in a polite stampede. I didn't move. "What's your number?" Raymond asked.

I clutched the boarding pass in my right hand, which hung limp between my legs. I didn't resist when he pulled it up to look: "132. You'll be in the last group."

The heaviness spread over me—I felt there was no way any machine could get me airborne. I wanted to dive into the matter at hand, but all I could do was skate blindly along the surface. "Poor planning," I mumbled. "If we'd gotten here sooner, I'd have been given a lower boarding number and I'd now be on the plane, but you're stuck. Another 10 minutes, at least." I stopped to do some quick addition in my head. "Five years," I counted, "four months, and 10 minutes."

He sighed again, uncrossed his legs, and glanced at the herd of people.

"What happened to forever?" I asked.

"I was wrong," he said. "I don't think things are meant to go that long, I just didn't know it until now."

"Who is he?"

"You don't know him."

"Where'd you meet?"

"That doesn't matter."

"It does to me."

"Look, what we had was great—"

"What we had?" I cut in. My voice rose and I heard it as so much noise, disturbing the hubbub around us. Heads turned but I kept going. "What we had?"

"Calm down," Raymond said. "This isn't helping."

"Oh, I'm supposed to help? Help you dump me in an airport, for God's sake? An airport, of all places. You're such a shit!"

"Stop shouting!"

Rows 33 to 100 were now boarding. Raymond took note. I could see him calculating our remaining time together. His eyes flitted everywhere but to me. I wanted to scream, but I found myself suddenly empty. When I went quiet, it made him attentive, which, in turn, made me want to throw up. Maybe onto his shoes. When the gate attendant called the final rows, I rose and joined the throng of people. I passed the threshold, moved down the jetway, and didn't look back.

Inside the plane the aisle was predictably clogged, and I waited. There was no longer any purpose to my life. I moved when I was allowed, stowed my bag, and dropped into my aisle seat in the next-to-last row—near the tail. I pictured it falling off en route to L.A. Tears welled in my eyes.

The flight attendant had to remind me to fasten my seat belt. Then the plane was airborne, and I imagined Raymond driving away, free of me. I had never felt so alone.

When the drinks cart came by I declined, but the guy in the window seat ordered a Bloody Mary. When it arrived, he handed it to me.

"What's this?" I rasped, barely able to speak.

"You look like you could use it."

My hand flew to my cheek. "Oh, God," I said as I frantically wiped the stream of tears. The drink was still in the guy's outstretched hand—the middle seat was empty—and when I didn't take it he pulled down my tray and set it before me, along with the napkin. I used the napkin to mop my tears, took a long swallow of the drink, and felt the spicy liquid free-fall into my stomach. "Thanks," I said.

I looked at him then: blond and blue-eyed, Raymond's opposite. His smile was tentative, as if he didn't want to make light of an obviously difficult moment. I tried to return the smile and found I couldn't, so I turned away. I wanted to empty my mind, but I couldn't shake the image of Raymond staring straight ahead as he told me our life—my life—was over. I could see him breezing along the freeway, talking into his cell, sharing his story with his new love. Free at last.

Maybe they'd planned a celebratory fuck. The idea sent a wave of anguish through me. I grabbed the drink and swigged.

"Hey, take it easy," my seatmate cautioned.

"Impossible," I snapped when I'd drained the glass. "In fact, I'm going to have another."

He said nothing as I summoned the attendant and mixed a new drink. The first had begun to work—loosening everything except Raymond, who still clung to me even as he sped toward a future that didn't include me.

"Want to talk about it?" the guy asked.

I shook my head. "Talking won't help. Killing might."

He turned to the window, and I knew I'd gotten too dramatic. I wanted to tell him I wasn't serious, but I kept quiet. There was some truth to the comment.

As I finished the second drink I wondered what I'd do if Raymond and Mr. Whoever were in front of me. I spent several minutes crafting a bloody scenario, knowing all the while I'd never commit such mayhem. Against myself, maybe. I let out a heavy sigh, drained my glass, sucked in an ice cube, and let it melt on my tongue.

When I had a third drink in hand, I told my seatmate my lover of five years had broken up with me 10 minutes before I boarded the plane.

"That's terrible," he said.

"It's more than I can handle." Tears started rising again. I downed more of the drink and let them come. He offered me a handkerchief, which I accepted.

I had four drinks during the one-hour flight, and Tom—we finally exchanged names—helped me off the plane. He got my bag from the overhead and carried it and his own, since it took all my concentration to walk. In the boarding area I collapsed into a chair.

"I shouldn't have gotten you started," he said.

I laughed. "If you hadn't, I would have. Sometimes getting drunk is all you can do."

"Where are you staying?" he asked.

It took a few moments to retrieve the information from my vodka-soaked brain. "Manhattan Beach, the Quality Inn on Sepulveda. I need to get my rental car."

"You're in no condition to drive. Why don't you get the car tomorrow; let me drive you now."

He was bigger than me, and I found that comforting. He exuded warmth and a calm assurance as he guided me up from the chair and out of the terminal. I walked slowly, moving along in a fog. We took the shuttle to long-term parking to retrieve his car. I slumped against the passenger's seat, and when Tom had the engine running he asked me, "You going to be OK alone?"

"I don't know," I replied, starting to cry again. He put his hand on my shoulder and squeezed gently. "How about you come home with me. I've got plenty of room."

"I'll be terrible company," I sobbed.

"I'm not looking for entertainment. I just don't think you should be alone."

I didn't pay attention to where he was taking me. We were on a freeway, things whizzed by, and I fixed on the blur. I stared out the side window as life truly passed me by.

When we got to Tom's apartment he had to help me out of the car. I tried to explain that I usually held my liquor better, but he shushed me gently. "It's OK. Come on up."

The stairs were a challenge. Partway up I began to list to one side, and Tom, behind me, put his hands around my waist to guide me. I liked the feel of him—his hands were bigger than Raymond's. "Easy," he said when I stumbled on the top step.

Once he had me inside, he pulled off my jacket, helped me lie down on the couch, and put a pillow under my head. "Think you can nap?" he asked.

"I have no idea," I said. That was the last thing I remembered until I woke hours later. It was night: Lamps were on, the drapes were drawn, and Tom sat across the room, reading. "What time is it?" I asked.

"Ten thirty-five."

"P.M., right?"

"Right."

"I wish it was A.M., because then this day would be over."

"You're almost there."

I sat up, and my head began to spin. "Whoa," I said.

"Still drunk?"

"A little, yeah."

"You're welcome to stay the night."

I took a long look at him. "All I want is sleep."

"That's fine."

I followed him to the bedroom and stripped while he turned back the covers. Nothing had ever looked so inviting as that big bed. I climbed in, curled up, shut my eyes. I felt Tom get in with me, but he made no move. *Nice,* I thought, as I drifted back to sleep.

Sometime during the night I reached for him. Awakening in confusion, then panic, I clutched his arm. He murmured, then stirred, rolled toward me, and put an arm around me. Together we drifted back to sleep.

I awoke before Tom. Dawn, the gray light of reality, seeped from behind the curtains as he softly snored. I eased from under his arm and took a good look at the man who had rescued me. Big but well-proportioned and furry: the embodiment of the classic bear. His golden hair was thick and cut short, while his eyebrows were brown. The pelt across his chest was more of the blond. I found this an interesting mix and couldn't resist pulling back the covers to see the rest. His lower half had more of the brown hair at his crotch, lightening to blond on his thighs. The mix gave him an endearing quality—earthy, not purebred.

Nestled in the patch between his legs was a sizable prick, which was fully hard. My own cock stirred at the sight of his, but my arousal brought Raymond to mind. We always started our day with sex. I imagined him in a bed like this one, and I hated the duplicity: same scene, different players. For all the wrong reasons, I slid a hand around Tom's cock and began to stroke him gently. He let out a moan and opened his eyes. "I need you," I said.

His look was tentative—the last thing I expected. I could see he knew what I really wanted was another rescue. "Please," I added, and he took me into his arms.

He was ardent, expert, forceful yet caring, and he took me to where I wanted to go—which, of course, ultimately proved to be a mistake. Seconds after I came, I burst into tears. Tom allowed me a good cry and, mercifully, he didn't scold me for creating an even trickier situation than the one I was already in. Not that I had forced him to do anything; he had, after all, enjoyed himself. But I saw he was one of those people who are actually concerned with the bigger picture.

Still, I didn't want to talk about what we had done. "I need to shower," I said, almost adding, "Maybe I can wash Raymond off." Fortunately, I kept this to myself, but as I stood under the strong spray, it all came back. As the airport scene played through my mind, I experienced the abandonment all over again. I emerged from the shower clean but less than invigorated.

Tom had coffee brewing when I found him in the kitchen. "Hungry?" he asked.

"Maybe some toast."

"You won't mind if I have bacon and eggs? Maybe the smell will make you hungry."

I doubted this. I climbed onto a stool at the kitchen counter and watched him work. In seconds he had bacon going, cracked eggs into a bowl with one hand, and began stirring them with a whisk. It was only then that I really looked at him.

He wore a blue T-shirt and white cutoffs. The sun coming in through the window over the sink highlighted the golden hair on his arms. His big hands were nimble, and he moved about his kitchen with an easy grace. He obviously enjoyed cooking. "Are you a chef?" I asked.

He laughed. "Landscape architect, but I do like to fix a good meal."

"Where are we?" I asked, suddenly realizing I had no idea.

"Santa Monica."

"What time is it?"

"Nine forty-two," he said, looking at his watch.

"Oh, shit. I'm due at a wedding at 2."

"No problem, we can get you there in plenty of time. Where is it?"

"Palos Verdes."

"Who's getting married?" he asked, sliding eggs onto a plate.

"My sister. The whole world will be there."

"Ah yes, the family function. So that's why you flew down?"

He asked in passing, part of everyday conversation, and the question would have had little impact if it had come from anyone else. As it was, the previous day appeared before me as if I'd never gotten through it, as if I were caught in my own version of *Groundhog Day.* For the millionth time, I heard Raymond telling me it was over.

I fell silent, and Tom settled onto the stool beside me. "I'm sorry," he said. "I shouldn't have said that so breezily."

"No, it's all right, I mean, it was an airplane ride and a person has a perfect right to talk about an airplane ride."

He said nothing more and concentrated on his meal, which was now starting to look good to me. When he noticed my interest, he handed me a piece of bacon.

He didn't have a dishwasher, which I found hilarious. Interesting how distress skews things. I heard myself laughing. "It's an old building," Tom said when I told him what I found funny. "No garbage disposal either." I watched as he washed dishes, and when he handed me a towel, I began to dry. It was oddly comforting.

"I should get to my motel," I said. I was feeling better and figured I should try to face the day. "And I need to get the rental car."

Tom nodded and said he would take me to Hertz whenever I wanted. I stood at his front window and looked out onto a courtyard thick with well-kept shrubbery, a few trees, and lots of colorful flowers. "Did you design that?" I asked. "It's beautiful."

"Yeah, it's mine. I've been here quite a while."

It would have been the time to ask about his life, his relationships, if he'd ever been dumped like me, if he'd ever been so much in love that he wanted to die, but I couldn't do it.

Instead I asked him to take me to bed again.

"I don't think that's a good idea," he said.

"All right, forget it," I snapped.

He took me by the shoulders and looked into my eyes. "You want it for the wrong reasons."

"You think I don't know that?"

"It will only make it worse."

"Nothing can make it worse and you're...you're so good, so steady. I don't think I can get through the day without you."

He conceded, and I think that was the moment when I fell in love with him. He set aside reason and everything practical, everything we both knew was right, in the interest of consoling a man who had lost everything. He knew that intimacy, no matter the context, was a salve, if not the cure. He took me to bed, and I spent most of an hour with him inside me.

"You need to get moving," he said as I lay in his arms afterward.

"Do you want me to go?" I asked.

"Of course not, but isn't there a wedding at 2? It's now..." He looked over at the clock. "Eleven thirty. You need to get your car, go to your motel, shower, change, and drive to Palos Verdes. You're going to be pressed for time."

My hand lay on his chest, petting his fur. I had found a calm space and I didn't want to leave it, not even for my sister. I matched my breathing to the rise and fall of Tom's chest. "I can dress here," I said. "Do the car, the motel, all that stuff later on if you'll drive me to the wedding. Hey, you could come with me!"

"I don't think that's a good idea," he said.

When I fell silent, he explained. "We just met, you've got a situation, and then there's your family."

"But that's OK," I said. "I'd love to show up with you."

"I'd like to think this isn't about that."

Oh, God, I thought. *I've blown it.* Panic seized me. "Of course it's not." I raised myself on my elbows and looked down at him. "Oh, Tom, God, no, I'm so sorry I said that, please forgive me. I'm just a mess and you know why, but it truly isn't about that. Forget I said it."

"OK, OK, calm down, calm down."

"I'm so fucked up," I offered.

He didn't deny this, which gave me a pang, but his silent criticism was well-deserved after my outburst. "OK, you're right, I should do the wedding on my own, face up to things, to my life. Oh, God, my life." I rolled away from him.

"You go to the wedding," Tom said as he turned to me and pressed his body into my back. "You'll do fine, you'll see your sister on the happiest day of her life, and it will let you out of your own pain for a while."

"Then can I come back here?"

"I don't think so," he said.

I couldn't speak. I was losing all over again. Tom explained himself as he held me: "You're coming off of the worst pain in your life, and I'm very lucky to have met you, but if we're at the beginning of something, I don't want it built on that. Whatever we have should stand on its own."

I sat up. "Are we at the beginning of something?"

"Feels that way to me."

I laughed, and my laughter morphed into a teary mess. "Me too," I said, reaching over to stroke that gorgeous fur.

"Then it will withstand a little absence. You need to get your footing. You've undoubtedly got a life up in San Francisco, even without what's-his-name. You need to go back to it, take some time. I'll be here."

"How long?"

Now he laughed. "Eager little fucker, aren't you."

"How long?"

"Three months. No contact."

"Then what—you'll just call?"

"No, you'll call. If you still find yourself wanting to know me after you've gotten your perspective back, you get in touch. I'll be here."

"I hate this."

"Of course you do. You're blasted right now, a member of the walking wounded. You're going to hate everything."

"But last night, you were so...and the sex, it was fabulous, and just everything about this morning."

"Can't argue with any of that, but let's find out what it's like when you've healed. I'm thinking it will really be something."

We drove to Hertz in silence. It felt like Raymond all over again, but the best part—the very best part, and one of the multitude of reasons why to this day I love Tom so dearly—was that Tom understood this. "I'm not leaving you by staying," he said.

"Oh, God," I gasped, tears stinging my eyes.

He handed me a handkerchief as we turned into the lot. "Want to come inside with me?" I asked, sniffling, knowing he wouldn't.

"No, you're on your own now. You'll do fine. And in three months you'll be even better."

"And how about you? How do I know you won't find someone else in the meantime?"

He shook his head in a way that said far more than words. Then he kissed me. "Go get your car. And have a good wedding."

"This is so hard," I said, not wanting to get out.

"I know, but it will make you a better man."

"That's a lousy reason."

He laughed. "Go get your car."

I wanted to tell him I loved him—that he was my future—but because I did love him, I kept quiet, knowing the declaration would be out of place. Those words wouldn't be right for another three months. I slid out of the car, shut the door, and looked back. He didn't take his eyes off me until I passed through the doors to the rental office, and that meant the world.

Magi

Scott D. Pomfret

Not to be outdone by their Catholic counterparts, the Unitarian Universalist youth group set up a Christmas crèche outside their church on Newbury Street about a block from the Boston Public Gardens. It was the usual style: a cutaway view into the barn, which was mounted on cinder blocks on the small patch of frozen grass between stone buttress and sidewalk. There was one lonely bale of hay in front. What caused the stir was what was in the barn. There were plenty of sheep and donkeys, but no Mary, two Josephs, and a baby Jesus who (the placard said) had been adopted from Korea and whose birth name was Kim Yun Park.

Within three days, the papier-mâché figures were torn and scattered, and the words FAGS DIE had been painted on the side of the plywood barn.

Alan was chief architect of the movement to rebuild the crèche. With the help of several other do-gooders, he taped and pasted the pieces back together, reassembled the menagerie, and posted a sign-up sheet at the Starbucks in the South End to enlist equally well-intentioned gay men to stand vigil to protect the crèche from further harm.

After a feature in the *Globe* described crèche duty as the hottest way to scope out eligible gay men, the sign-up list was overflowing with names. And phone numbers. Indeed, shortly before Christmas, Alan showed up for an evening shift and was told that 12 men who had signed up for the supper shift had refused to surrender their places. They had set up a space heater and had obviously taken the added precaution of fueling themselves with a little hot buttered rum. They were blowing kisses to passersby and to the fundamentalist protesters across the street. Prompted by church bells, they broke into a decidedly un-silent version of "Silent Night" that dissolved into giggles when they got to the part about the "round yon virgin."

"Drama queens!" Alan scolded. "Get out of the way! Your turn is over."

The men curtsied and laughed and told Alan not to get his panties in a bunch, and the cops, parked in a nearby cruiser, insisted that Alan get his ass out of the street and back on the sidewalk where he belonged.

"Christ!" Alan complained to no one in particular. "This place is absolutely overrun with gay men!"

"No shit, huh?" quipped Scott, another of the volunteers. "Even the wisemen are probably wearing Armani and Prada under their robes and bitching about how the weather in Bethlehem can't compare to South Beach."

Scott smiled, and Alan looked at him twice. The air between them tingled.

Across the street, protesters held signs that said SHAME and REPENT and MATTHEW SHEPHERD IS IN HELL. At one point it looked like one fundamentalist's red-faced kids were dragging their dad across the street to try to get him to make nice with the gay men. This sudden gesture of apparent goodwill made the cops nervous. They yanked at their belts and girded their loins and stopped wondering what in God's name they were going to get their wives for Christmas.

But the kids had no interest in evangelizing and dashed straight to the pet shop window next to the church like a pair of balloons caught in a hard wind. The kids stood open-mouthed, their heads tilted up in a sweet kind of awe. Inside, the puppies wrestled and tumbled and thrust their noses into one another's asses.

"They don't know how lucky they are," Scott said.

"The kids?" Alan asked.

"The puppies. There isn't one of *that* crowd of hard-core fundies you'd want to take you home." Scott hoped the longing in his voice wouldn't betray that he hadn't gotten laid in six weeks.

"I used to have a dog," Alan said.

"Yeah?"

"She was a seven-pound white Maltese. She was adorable. I called her Miss Fidget."

Scott laughed, then realized that Alan was not kidding. He tried to disguise his laughter as a cough.

When Alan had squared away the next shift of volunteers, he and Scott slipped away from the scene as a dusting of snow began to fall. The awnings over the shops on Newbury Street hung like heavy eyelids after a big feast. In the Macy's display window, mechanical elves harnessed mechanical reindeer again and again. Santa threw back his head and laughed. His sleigh was loaded like a promise, and stuck to every surface was glitter that would never fade, but would always be clean and glam and new.

Scott and Alan rented skates at the frozen Frog Pond in Boston Common. Each of them feigned klutziness so he'd have an excuse to put his hands on the other. Finally they collapsed onto one another, their limbs splayed, cold bums on colder ice, and wool mittens sticking to frozen pond. They laughed uproariously like drunks as the other skaters indulgently made their way around them. Scott thought Alan's red cheeks looked like a pair of roses over his charcoal scarf. Alan felt every chilly breath brought new excitement, and the world itself seemed covered with a kind of dazzling glitter.

Three years later, the crèche no longer caused a stir. No rum-soaked chortling Kenneth Cole Christmas elves were needed to guard it, and the protesters and their puppy-loving rug rats had disappeared, never to return. Christmas shoppers hurried by and gave the display only passing glances. They were obviously more troubled by Scott's dour countenance and his long black overcoat than by any shenanigans in the barn.

It was Christmas Eve, and Scott was staring at the two Josephs and the wise men and the tired bale of hay and the menagerie of little animals and the little Korean Christ-child in the manger. He was feeling nostalgic for a time when he felt he had a purpose in life—when the crèche had needed defending and warm puppies did not yet know rejection and little Christian children weren't filled with hate and deficit spending was not all the rage and everything in the whole world had been beautiful and honorable and new.

Someone shouted, "Hey!"

It was the baker, who was standing in the open door of the bakery next door, which had displaced the pet shop. The bakery's windows were fogged and inviting. In the window's dew, someone had freshly drawn a smiling face in an elf hat with his finger.

"Come on in," the baker said. "I've got something for you."

"I really shouldn't," Scott replied. "I've got to get home. Christmas Eve and all..."

The baker gave him a look, and Scott shuffled through the open door into an heavy, seductive warmth, all yeast and dried cranberries. Somewhere in the back of the bakery was a cup of brewing tea.

"Attaboy!" the baker boomed as she clapped Scott on the back. She was a silver-haired dyke with an expressive, meaty face. Her eyebrows were dusted with flour—she had obviously been kneading dough. Her plump forearms looked like a pair of sausages ready to split open over a fire.

"Where's your friend?" she asked.

"Alan? He's at home."

Waiting, Scott thought, *to see if I come home.* They had been talking about seeing other people, which turned into talking about splitting up after the holidays. Scott had tried to get Alan to consider this idea objectively and dispassionately, as if they were discussing other people's lives. Alan had found that notion preposterous.

"Here!" the baker said. She forced a warm bagged loaf into Scott's arms. "It's his favorite."

With the loaf tucked into the crook of his arm, Scott trudged down Clarendon Street past the point where the shopwindows ended and toward their apartment in the South End. There were only townhouses in this neighborhood—bay windows and magnificent windowed double doors showcasing chandeliers that promised something antique and fabulous, a throwback to the way it used to be.

Scott made a game of looking in these windows as he passed them to see the scenes analytically, to try to figure out why people split up or why they kept making excuses for not moving out. He saw exposed brick, a Crate & Barrel Rothko, clusters of black-and-white prints so skillfully arrayed as to be haphazard. Or perhaps the arrangement was in fact haphazard. The difference between accident and intention seemed so fine that perhaps it was unimportant.

In one house, the walls had been painted with fresh heather tones from Ralph Lauren, and a collection of tchotchkes was arranged along a massive mantel. A man with an large head had managed to skillfully perch himself on the mantel among the tchotchkes. He lifted a cocktail to his lips as he spun a jowly tale to someone Scott could not see.

He also did not see people lying in bed next to sudden strangers. He did not see them staring out the window with a warm unfamiliar body next to them. There were other people trapped in that sadness that follows the first act of infidelity—the sadness that comes when you look at a world at once the same and different and realize you've made a liar of yourself and ruined something pure.

In the block before the apartment where he and Alan lived, Scott spotted a shirtless guy—maybe 26 or 27, too young for the real estate—standing in a window. The guy was lost in thought, one arm extended toward the window frame as if to prop up the wall, and the other drawing circles on his belly in a languid, bored way as if he were a longtime practitioner of the erotic arts. The neighborhood was full of such exhibitionists living uncurtained lives. It was easy for Scott to stop here—or on any block he chose—and imagine himself in the scene on the other side of the window, and fantasize about the ways in which it might be better than what he had.

He glanced back the way he had come, then toward where he was going. The loaf of bread under his arm suddenly seemed meager and insufficient. He set off in the direction of Chester Park, where—even in the dead of winter—a wooden fruit stand was set up, its front cover raised like a salute.

"Try one of these, my friend," the vendor advised, pulling a paper bag from beneath the shelf and exhaling little clouds of frosty breath. He was bundled like the Michelin man against the cold. "These apples are delicious. I saved them just for you."

Scott admired the apples, which obviously pleased the vendor, confirming perhaps that there were other people out there just like him on Christmas Eve.

"Merry Christmas," the vendor said.

Impulsively, Scott asked, "Have you ever...?"

He had wanted to say, "Have you ever broken up with someone?" Instead he asked, "Have you ever been in love?"

The vendor smiled sympathetically. Scott spilled a confession, and when he finished, the vendor called attention to the yellowness of the bananas and how they would soon be perfectly ripe.

"You will come to see me then?" the vendor asked. "You will let me know how it goes?"

Scott had somehow expected more from the vendor—an anecdote, maybe, or some advice. He asked for a quart of strawberries, but the vendor argued that strawberries were not what Scott really wanted or needed. Without condescension, he patiently explained why strawberries at this time of year were not a good choice and he sent Scott off with an apple, free of charge.

In the apartment, the sconces over the fireplace had been dimmed to starlight. There was incense burning, giving off the smell of hay and grass. A tray of cookies and port glasses was set out as if a visitor were expected.

Alan was in the kitchen. He had on a red apron that said THE BEST SNACKS ARE BENEATH; an arrow pointed to his groin. His hair had begun to silver, which made him look as if he too had been out in the snow.

Alan helped Scott remove his overcoat. These loving gestures still came naturally to them: a laugh shared over something funny in the paper, a crumb wiped from Scott's lips, a collar straightened, a hand to steady Alan's elbow when he skidded on the icy sidewalk. To Scott, these gestures had become small eulogies, delivered on the spur of the moment, for things they suddenly knew were not going to happen again. Sometimes, he reflected, you know instantly when love is over; sometimes the eulogies come years later, as if it took the living a while to get news of the dying.

Alan spilled out a couple of glasses of chardonnay. It was evident from the spillage that these were not the first two glasses he'd poured.

"I was afraid you weren't coming," he said. The words hung in the air a moment and soured, and Alan washed them back with wine.

Scott set the bread on the table. When Alan opened the bag, steam escaped and fogged his glasses. He flashed Scott a quick, grateful smile.

"It'll be perfect," Alan declared.

Alan would have said the same thing even if the bread had been less than perfect—even if it had been moldy, misshapen, and tasteless—because Alan was the most gracious host in the history of the planet. From the fairy-tale mother who had raised him, Alan had learned to love domesticity more than he had ever learned to love Scott, who suddenly felt weary—too old to still be playing house.

Alan fluttered around their kitchen, chattering and frantic, as he put the final touches on dinner. He griped about something inconsequential: Some colleagues at work had insisted on their right to take a half day at the busiest time of the year to attend their children's Christmas pageant. They had left Alan alone in the shop, as if being somewhat single gave him nothing to do on Christmas Eve.

"Why let it bother you?" Scott interjected. "Let it go. Let them be stupid."

The tirade abruptly ended, and Alan put his hand on his hip in a defiant pose. He leaned over as if he were going to kiss

Scott but placed his hand over Scott's mouth instead.

"I don't want you to argue with me," he said from a range of six inches. "I want you to indulge me and tell me I'm right and agree that they're assholes."

He nodded and indicated that Scott should nod with him. His manner was slow and indulgent, as if he were talking to someone of limited intelligence, or teaching a small child the essentials of hygiene.

"Do I have to explain *everything*?" he asked.

His voice cracked on the last word, and Scott saw into Alan as clearly as if Alan had pulled aside a shade and exposed himself. He glimpsed all the ugliness, weakness, desperation, fear; every slight and delight, all the hurt feelings and dreams and tenderness and the watch-you-while-you-sleep sentimental indulgence. Then the window shut, and the view was gone, as fleeting as a shooting star.

"How humiliating," Alan murmured without rancor or passion. "I feel humiliated."

After dinner, Alan sat by himself in the window box in the living room and listened to Billie Holiday. The built-in shelves on either side of the window box held antique photographs. On one side were erect, mustachioed Victorians and their corseted wives. On the other: big, lusty men, hairy and drunk, with their legs splayed over the edge of a big wooden tub—a cask of whiskey sawed in half. Each man brandished a foot-long scrub brush and a bar of caustic soap, beckoning to voluptuous, bawdy women, who were scantily draped in their falling-off dresses and drinking from jugs marked XXX.

"I need to talk to you, Alan," Scott said. He stood stiffly as he downed the last molten sip of brandy from a balloon glass.

Alan rose from the window box and began to dance. With a start, Scott saw Alan from a different angle, saw him as the baker might see him, or the fruit vendor, or anyone else who had half a brain. He was beautiful, unabashed, and earnest. His cheeks were ablaze from the wine.

Alan moved close and ran his hands over Scott's face, over his shoulders, and down to his hips. He shimmied his crotch over Scott's ass. He lifted Scott's free arm and draped it over himself extravagantly, as if his flesh were clay, and the night full of miracles, and Alan could blow breath into him to make him come alive.

"I need to talk to you," Scott repeated. He felt agitated and fragile and needed to explain everything.

"I don't like the sound of that," Alan said. He went to turn up the stereo to block out Scott's words. Once again he snaked his arm around Scott's hip, and his drunkenness gave him a certain instinctive command of the situation that compelled Scott to move in time.

Scott gave himself to the bluesy rhythm. He tried to speak but couldn't hear himself over the din. He hardly trusted his own words, in any case. If a passerby had bothered to look up at their window, he couldn't be blamed for concluding that the two men dancing close on Christmas Eve knew what it meant to be in love.

To Another City

David Masello

Lyle went looking for Timothy's street in Brooklyn. Although his afternoon there had started out as a simple retreat from Manhattan, the idea to see where Timothy lived occurred to him on the walk to the subway. Lyle had a tendency to become virtually inert on certain Saturdays. On those days he was unable to do much more than clean his apartment, amble the river walk in the United Nations park at the end of his street, or pace his roof, where all sounds of the city were masked by the roar of the building's air-conditioning unit.

It was "Turkish Day" in New York. Turkey's consulate was two buildings down the block, and when Lyle leaned out his living-room window he could see the country's red and white flag rippling in the wind, its crescent moon and star the same colors as the giant neon Pepsi-Cola bottle across the river. A part of 47th Street—the spot where all U.N. political rallies and demonstrations took place—had been transformed into a bazaar right out of Istanbul. Lyle loved the muezzin's chanting and the twirling performers. The strains of lilting Arabic were seductive enough to pull him from his lethargy to dance barefoot, dervishlike, on his sisal carpet in a cobra-inspired frenzy.

But Lyle knew the din of the festivities would go on all day, reaching him on the 18th floor and making him desperate for escape and quiet. So he convinced himself to go on an expedition to Brooklyn, a place he'd always considered foreign. His coworker Timothy lived there, which made the idea even more appealing. Even though he saw Timothy—or at least e-mailed him—every day at the office, he wanted to be with Timothy away from work and see what might happen.

The goal he had in mind was to learn how the three contiguous neighborhoods of Cobble Hill (where Timothy lived), Brooklyn Heights, and Carroll Gardens were laid out and how they fit together. He had been to these parts of town very seldom during the years he lived in New York. When a Brooklyn friend called with a party or brunch invitation, he'd carefully record the host's instructions, writing down the names of fruits or Dutch explorers that served as the names of streets, and tactfully try to learn if there were any danger spots along the way. After completing the trip, he'd tell himself to remember the train he took, the landmarks he encountered, and the duration of the journey so that he could return another time.

"Now that I know how easy it is to get out here," he'd say flatteringly to a host he knew he'd never be close to simply because of their geography, "I'd love to come to the neighborhood more often and have lunch some Saturday, go exploring."

But he never had the inclination to go back, and each time he was forced to cross the East River he'd have to relearn the route. With each subsequent trip, everything was newly unfamiliar.

As Lyle was about to swipe his subway card through the turnstile, he overheard a Japanese tourist ask the station clerk for a subway map. Lyle decided to do the same. The map featured only a few of Brooklyn's main streets: sinuous gray lines drawn on an amorphous white expanse. The markings were all he needed, though, to know which direction to head, and there were landmarks indicated on the map for him to be able to guess where the transition points were between the good neighborhoods and the fearsome ones. The east sides of cemeteries, boulevards named for fallen civil rights heroes, and streets paralleling canals made him wary.

The outing began with his petting a goat, which hopped

between the open hatch of a pickup truck and a manger-size pen set up in front of Borough Hall. The goat's two kids nestled on a bed of hay inside the truck and periodically cried for some attention from their mother. Their velvety ears shook each time she bleated her answer to their pleading. A tiny rust-colored pig snuffled the ground with the purposefulness of an anteater, and a small black calf stood chewing its cud like the dumb beast it was. Children dug into sacks of grain and hay and fed the animals, which lapped their hands clean and left them glistening.

Lyle discovered the remnants of several fading Italian neighborhoods on the southern ends of Court, Hicks, and Henry streets. Uncannily quiet streets lined with rows of brownstones would suddenly burst with life at certain intersections. An Italian men's club figured into each of these ragged commercial clusters—usually nothing more than a storefront with painted-over windows or drawn Venetian blinds and a lump of a cat pressed against the glass. The club's front door would be open and upon passing it, Lyle would be hit, as palpably as from a blast of air conditioning, by the room's inertia and insularity. Men sat in rows of folding chairs beneath bare fluorescent tubes. Black and white photos of sweat-beaded batters and prizefighters coiled into themselves at the end of a home run swing hung on wood paneling. Guttural dialect punched the air. The elder members wore suit coats and narrow-brimmed hats tagged with single feathers, while the younger men, chewing on plastic straws, were dressed in sneakers, designer jeans, and tight T-shirts.

Lyle walked into what was advertised on the outside as a candy store, but found no sweets inside. In the rear, through a doorway, men were huddled around a green felt table, cigarette smoke hovering over them like a cloud. The man behind the counter looked to Lyle and said, "Buddy, we don't sell nuttin here."

"I'm just looking for a candy bar," Lyle said.

"I'm telling you, there's nuttin in here for you."

He heard men snicker when he stepped outside. Once Lyle figured out how the numbered avenues, streets, and places ran, he began to look for Timothy's. Sometimes he was fooled into thinking that Timothy's street would figure in an alphabetical sequence, but a chronological span of presidents or bodies of water might just as easily suddenly give way to another Dutch settler or Indian tribe.

Completely unknown to him until this trip was an industrial zone that lay between Cobble Hill and Park Slope. He tried to walk the area spanning the neighborhoods but was defeated by the distances and the spooky emptiness. He became aware of the zone as he walked farther south on Court Street. One shopkeeper said to him from a folding chair on the sidewalk when he asked for directions, "Let me tell you young man, turn around right here. Don't go no farther that way. The neighborhood's a *disaster*. Used to be *paisan*—you know, Italian—but now you can't imagine what it's become."

Down some side streets—lined with houses clad in aluminum siding or peeling faux brick sheets; parts of parked cars bound by electrical tape—Lyle saw hazy clouds from disturbed gravel. Although he had never touched Timothy's dark blond hair, had only felt sharp corners of it brush his face that made him wince when they'd lean over the desk at work, the strands always seemed dulled; thick with scent, and Lyle wondered if it was because they had been coated daily with the fine silt of this place. The neighborhood he had been exploring gave out along those side streets. He had discovered a landscape that seemed bigger than any other part of the borough.

Was it possible, Lyle wondered, that Timothy lived in a house this close to this bleak tract of land? Did Timothy look into it from a block's remove as Lyle did now, as if it was a museum diorama of American Industry or an expanse of territory behind a fence forbidden to outsiders—a minefield in North Korea, a military testing ground in central Nevada? Lyle thought, *How could I have lived in New York for so many years and never have seen this terrain or read about it in the paper? Never passed through it in a cab taking an alternative route to the airport?*

From the roof of Lyle's 35-story apartment building, Brooklyn appeared as a solid, unbroken, low-rise mass—this empty land didn't emerge from that vista. Whenever he was up there pacing, he would study the density before him until, like a stereogram that suddenly reveals a 3-D image, cars would come into view coursing the Grand Central Parkway or a train tracing an elevated track.

The safest street around the industrial zone appeared to be Third Place. Next to the last house at the corner of Smith Street was a yellow brick wall marking the division between subway tunnel and outside track. The sidewalk trembled from a train below that was about to exit the tunnel. Lyle realized that many of the surrounding houses must feel those vibrations all the time, perhaps causing Timothy, if he lived close enough, to shift in his sleep during the night.

Once Lyle was across Smith Street, he watched a train climb a concrete trestle, which at its farthest point looked like a roller coaster. An elevated highway, paralleling the tracks, was frantic with traffic. In the foreground, on giant stilts, the letters spelling out the name of a flooring manufacturer loomed against the sky. From Third Place, Lyle looked into the industrial landscape, which was bisected by a canal. Blocks away, three boys leaned over their bicycle handlebars and gazed into the water as if they were waiting for something to happen. Most of the warehouses and factories appeared fallow, but there were rows of semitrailers parked nearby. Their gleaming hooks were poised to mate with a truck cab. Something was still made in these buildings and shipped away.

Lyle came to a bridge over an arm of the viscous canal, which followed a course of right angles into the industrial sprawl. In the distance was the skyline of downtown Brooklyn, punctured by the pin-thin art deco tower of the Williamsburg Savings Bank. Nothing in that view was different than it had been since the 1930s. Lyle decided this was as far as he would go. He began his walk back to the subway.

But within a block of the station, Lyle found Timothy's street—a short stretch of brownstones that ran between Smith and Court streets. He stood in front of Timothy's building—each of its four floors defined by a projecting bay—but worried that Timothy might suddenly come out and find him there.

To Another City

Lyle considered the age difference between himself and Timothy. He had met Timothy at a journalism seminar at New York University. Timothy was in his last undergraduate year, and Lyle was at the event as one of several representatives of the New York publishing world—a senior editor at a travel magazine. When Lyle returned to his office he called Timothy at his dorm room and assigned him a book review, something he would never have done for anyone else whose writing clips he hadn't seen.

"How many sources do you need for the story?" Timothy asked with enthusiasm. "Feel free to edit me however you want."

By graduation day Timothy had published three short pieces in Lyle's magazine—one about taxi fares in cities around the world, another detailing the lengths of subway systems, and the review of a series of travel guidebooks. With these clips, Timothy had an advantage over every entry-level candidate for an editorial assistant's job that had opened at the magazine.

But the week Timothy started on-staff, Lyle was transferred to another company magazine—a general-interest title aimed at obscenely wealthy readers—that was located elsewhere in the building. In Timothy's daily e-mails to Lyle in his office a floor below, he tried to be funny and spirited. The messages were usually nothing more substantive than a recounting of lunch break adventures, but when Lyle's computer beeped and the envelope icon flashed indicating mail, he immediately grabbed the mouse and clicked around the screen to call up the message.

In one note, Timothy spoke of seeing two Korean men sitting next to him at a midtown noodle shop: "They're slurpin' away (which is cool, because that's how one is supposed to eat noodles), and then one of them unleashes this ferocious burp. I mean, LOUD. And then he treats everyone in the shop to two repeat performances. I wish you'd been there with me, we would've laughed together." In another missive, he mentioned a sign he saw in the atrium of an office building: "It didn't say 'No Smoking,' or 'Caution, Floor Slippery When Wet,' but simply 'Please Be Careful.' Enigmatic? You make the call?"

But it was in Lyle's postcards to Timothy from trips he took that he felt more free with him. When Lyle came across the right card to send, some outdated shot showing finned cars on a busy downtown street with pedestrians in hats and white gloves or a recipe for a regional pie, he'd feel an ache of anticipation about writing him. From Chicago, he wrote about his explorations of the dark, fire escape–lined streets south of the Loop—streets he referred to in his card to Timothy as "thrillingly bleak," a phrase Timothy continued to cite. From Los Angeles, he told Timothy about his daily morning walk to a tiny cemetery in Westwood, situated behind a drive-in bank, to see Truman Capote's grave: "I almost got beheaded by the barrier that lets cars in and out of the bank lot. To think that I can now see Capote's old apartment from my bedroom window in New York and now here I am at his remains—though the story is that only *half* his ashes are interred here. More on that later."

"Your postcards are so...well...quaint," Timothy told Lyle once. "I can't believe you still send them. I mean, they're great and all, but it's just that I don't know *anyone* who still writes them. I thought people only sent e-mail postcards."

But the habit had caught on with Timothy too, so that when he went to Seattle on a vacation he sent Lyle a postcard of a glistening metallic salmon on a bed of white shaved ice at Pike Place Market. "This is the best sight I've seen all day," his message began. "I suppose this is the silver lining in the clouds that hover here all the time," he added, making an oblique reference to the gleam of the fish.

On his first day back at work from the Seattle trip, Timothy walked into Lyle's office and closed the door. He handed Lyle a package containing a vacuum-packed smoked salmon fillet. It was the first souvenir they had exchanged. "I really wanted to get you *something*," Timothy said.

The gift set a precedent. When Lyle took a trip a few months later to the Oregon coast, he spent hours one afternoon searching the beach for the perfect clamshell to bring Timothy—one whose hinge was still intact and amber finish flawless.

"Cool," Timothy said when Lyle handed him the smooth souvenir, the faint reek of the ocean emanating from the swirling pearly-white inner shell.

"I found that," Lyle said.

"Like this?"

"Exactly. Though it wasn't easy. All along the edge of the water I kept seeing broken ones. There would be no hinge, or else there would be holes made by gulls, or the amber color would be washed away. It turns out the best shells are way up from where I thought the tide line would be, just stuck, white side up, in the sand."

"You mean you found it this way? It's not from a shell shop?"

Timothy held the tapering oval halves in his open palm as if it were a butterfly whose wings were positioned with pushpins.

Lyle remembered these office moments as he stood on Timothy's street. He knew what he would want if he were to enter the apartment before him. And he knew also what he'd probably find—he hadn't forgotten the way he used to live when he was Timothy's age. Once inside, he would be hit with the dense, sun-warmed mustiness of Timothy's room—a scent of still-warm sheets and blankets, the dome of a baseball cap, a brimming laundry sack behind a closet door, an unzipped gym bag with shoes spilled beside.

He also knew that Timothy had a dog. The way Lyle envisioned it, he would knock on Timothy's apartment door with the buzz of the front door still whining in his ear. Then he'd hear the click of paws on the floor and the rush of air through the dog's nostrils as it waited to see if Timothy would come to welcome the visitor. The dog would stand at a diagonal in the threshold, blocking Timothy and Lyle from greeting each other. Lyle would coax the dog out of the way by patting its side, sounding the hollow canister of its body, his fingers filling the gaps between her ribs.

"Hey, what a great surprise," he imagined Timothy saying. "I'm honored that a Manhattanite would venture all the way out here."

"Well, you are, after all, the borough's main attraction," Lyle would say.

"Hardly."

But Lyle didn't ring Timothy's bell. He was not yet ready to give up the thrill of pursuit. It was better still to imagine what he wanted to happen. So Lyle returned to Manhattan without having found Timothy.

A week later, it was Timothy who came to Lyle's apartment. Timothy called late on a Saturday afternoon and said, "I have some important news to tell. And I want to tell you in person, tonight. Can I come over?"

The moment Timothy arrived, Lyle suggested they go to the roof and have a drink. "Let's talk about your news up there."

As if he knew the geography of the roof, Timothy walked quickly to the east-facing edge as soon as they emerged from the stairwell. He parted the branches of a small tree anchored in a concrete planter. Together they looked through the opening to a barge cutting the glassy river, its deck edged with points of blue and red lights. Timothy pushed his hair behind each ear with his index finger and jumped atop the planter.

"My neighborhood—or rather, my soon-to-be neighborhood—is in there somewhere," he said, motioning to the pink sodium-vapored sprawl of Brooklyn and Queens. When he leaned over the parapet he remarked, "All this and the Turkish flag too," which was unfurling in the wind many stories below. "I guess my neighborhood might just as well as be Istanbul to you, it's so far away from here. I always did want to show it to you, have you visit my apartment, see how I live. I used to think some nights, 'Hey, I wish Lyle were here to sit with me on the stoop.' "

Timothy turned to Lyle and said, "Listen, the reason I came into the city was to tell you that Sarah and I are getting married. It's going to happen in a few months, in D.C. We're going to live there. I didn't want to just tell you over the phone. I'm sorry. Of course, I'm also happy."

Timothy leaned fearlessly against the parapet. Planes approaching Kennedy and LaGuardia hung at opposite ends of the sky like glowing ellipses.

That Lyle was on his roof on a summer night looking at Brooklyn with Timothy was part of a scenario he had been concocting since he'd met him. This image of them together, up so high, in the wind, the lighted city surrounding them, was one he had regularly imagined while pacing up here in the evenings. Lyle felt as if he had found Timothy against the odds—amid the crazy spider web of lights, canal paths that snaked their ways inland, and dark warehouses that conspired to keep them apart. He had discovered Timothy, armed him with some quick professional credentials while he was still a student, brought him into his workplace, got him to write him notes, and here he was now at his home.

But Lyle knew that the fantasy he had rehearsed would not be played out. He knew that Timothy had been seeing a young woman named Sarah who was in her first year of law school in Washington. Lyle had met her briefly at an office party. He remembered her small, sharp breasts, positioned like weaponry to keep people like Lyle away from Timothy. She had been cool to Lyle when she met him, perhaps sensing a threat.

"Oh, yes, Timothy talks about you all the time," she said. "It seems you gave him his start in journalism." Then she took Timothy's hand and led him to the dance floor.

Timothy expressed no regrets or fears about leaving his neighborhood and his job. "Sarah wants me to consider going to law school—and I may do that. It's hard to live well as a journalist, even if *she's* going to be a lawyer someday."

Timothy told Lyle that his phone had already been disconnected days ago, even though he wasn't moving out until next week. "I figured, why not," Timothy said. "At night, no one else calls me but Sarah—and you." Despite his youth and appeal, Timothy had made few friends in his time in New York; he had never made the city his home.

Lyle had pursued Timothy, and Timothy had responded. There was a portion of that nebulous sprawl before them—Timothy's neighborhood—that Lyle now knew, but he wondered how long it would seem familiar and negotiable, for it was part of another city he might never visit again.

Lovers' Morning Hold

Waide Aaron Riddle

Ross and Kirby

Ross McGregor slowly awoke to the sensation of gentle kisses on his face. His boyfriend, Kirby Matthews, brushed Ross's cheeks with his lips. The sweet smell of Brut aftershave filled Ross's morning mind.

"Mmm, you smell good," Ross said as he opened his eyes.

"Good morning, handsome." Kirby kissed Ross's cheeks some more.

Ross stretched and kissed him back. "Do you have to go right now? It's so early."

"Yeah, I do," Kirby said.

"Three interviews today, uh?"

Kirby nodded with a half grin.

"Break a leg," Ross said.

"It's just handy work in warehouses."

"It's not *just* handy work in warehouses—it's a job."

A brief but heavy silence fell between the two men, then Ross ran his fingers through Kirby's hair. "I don't know what I would have done without you," Ross said. "I don't know what I'd do..."

"Now, don't start gettin' weird on me again." Kirby's grin

shifted into a half smile. "I don't plan on leavin' this world anytime soon."

Ross snuggled up to him. "Good—see to it that you don't!"

"Happy anniversary, handsome," Kirby said. "Ten years with the greatest barber in the world."

"I love the way you say that."

"Now I really gotta go." Kirby rose from the bed.

"I know...get out of here," Ross teasingly scolded. "But be back—"

Kirby interrupted: "Yes, I'll be back in plenty of time for the lighting. I won't forget." He made his way through the kitchen and into the entry hall, where he grabbed his Yankees cap and put it on just so. Then he threw a jean jacket over his thermo shirt. His faded Levi's were tattered at the cuffs and fit loosely over aging brown leather boots.

"Love ya, handsome," he yelled toward the bedroom.

"Love you too," Ross yelled back as Kirby closed the door behind him and locked it. Then he was gone.

New York City, November 28, 2001

It was 8 A.M. on a Wednesday morning, and the city of New York was in a suspended state of melancholy. The air was balmy-cool as Kirby made his way on foot down sidewalks, across streets and avenues, and through the rank alleys.

He furiously smoked one cigarette after another. Out of work since September 11, he'd only been able to nail two "handy" jobs, as an electrician in private homes. The uncertainty of employment and the reality of unemployment were suddenly beginning to get to him.

Then there was Ross. Ross was bringing home the bacon and paying the bills—and not once had he spoken a negative word to Kirby. Shame stabbed him.

Kirby was up to more than a pack a day now, his appetite was poor-to-nothing, and so was his sex drive. Sleep was a nightmare: dreams of freefalling into dark, smoky voids. He'd awake with a start, swearing he could smell smoke.

Kirby decided to skip the subway—the walk would do him

good. He bought a cup of joe from a street vendor and continued on his way into Manhattan. Storefronts were decorated in red, green, silver, and gold. Christmas trees in apartment windows and storefronts were draped with glittered ribbons, twinkling bulbs, and tassels.

He turned a street corner and took a sip of the black Joe. As he did he listened to the overlap of Christmas music coming from the businesses he walked past. He took another sip and headed through the obstacle course of people.

The Little Black Girl

Ross poured himself a mug of coffee and sat at the kitchen table with a bowl of cereal and a glass of juice. A digital clock radio on a kitchen shelf read 8:45 A.M. Then it read 8:46. The radio played a Christmas carol, but Ross's attention was elsewhere. He'd had constant muscle aches for the past few weeks—much like the body aches one gets from a flu—and the throbbing discomfort was beginning to move in waves up and down his back. The stress had triggered a fiery headache, and the Advil he took minutes before had knocked that out but left his muscles pounding.

At 9:25 A.M. Ross took the subway into Manhattan. He sat quietly, as did everyone else in the packed car. A little black girl no more than 6 or 7 sat next to him with her mother. She looked at him and smiled a toothy smile. Ross smiled back at her.

"Hi," she said.

"Hello there," he said back at her.

"What's your name, mister?"

"My name is Ross McGregor. What's yours?"

"My name is Jenna Sommers."

Ross extended his hand and Jenna shook it.

"It's a pleasure to meet you, Jenna."

"It's a pleasure to meet you too, Ross."

"You have a mighty lovely name and a strong handshake."

"Thank you, you do too. This is my momma," she said proudly.

"Hi, momma," Ross said in kind acknowledgment. "Your Jenna is quite the beauty."

"Thank you," Jenna's momma said softly. She smiled a proud smile that resembled her daughter's.

The conversation ended at that, and silence returned.

The Barbershop, 10 A.M.

It was a typical barbershop with four standard haircutting stations. Ross had worked there for nearly five years and hoped to one day own it.

The aromas of Clubman talc and other hairdressing oils and tonics greeted each customer as they entered the shop. As they sat and relaxed on one of the leather couches, they could watch the news or sports on TV and wait their turn for a barber.

Ross's cutting station was perfection: His combs, clamps, clippers, scissors, sprays, gels, and sanitary supplies were arranged orderly and properly. Each grooming utensil was spotless and, if necessary, lubricated with a drop of oil.

He worked quietly and took his time on Russell Lloyd, his first client. Russell had been a regular of Ross's for over two years and was set up in the appointment book for a haircut every three weeks. Russell was what Ross called a simple cleanup job—just very detailed around the ears and neck with a minimal amount of scissors-over-comb technique.

Russell read *The New York Times* as Ross combed and snipped. The barbershop's radio played back-to-back Christmas carols.

"Christmas music already," Russell remarked flatly behind his paper.

"Yep, seems like it breezes by faster every year," Ross said without looking up from his work.

"Yep." Russell lowered the paper. "And that reminds me—happy anniversary." He smiled at Ross's reflection in the mirror. Ross looked up in pleasant surprise.

"Thank you," Ross said.

"It is today, right?"

"Yeah, you remembered."

"Absolutely. And you said it's been 10 years now."

"Good memory." Ross looked down and continued to comb and clean.

"How is Kirby doing these days?"

"Quite honestly, Russell, not so good."

"It's been a really bad slam to him, I bet."

"Yeah. It's hard for him to be out of work. He's been without a job for so long. There's always been something just around the corner, no matter what." Ross paused as his frustration began to surface. "The phone just isn't ringing," he said. The thought irritated him, which began to aggravate the pain in his back. "He's gone from one or two cigarettes a day to a pack or more. His sex drive is dead and—"

Russell broke in: "Well, Ross, don't feel so bad. My wife's sex drive died the day after our honeymoon, and that was 20 years ago."

They shared a laugh. The pain in Ross's back was rolling in waves. After the laughter subsided Russell became serious. "The whole city is going through fucking hell right now."

"I know," Ross replied.

An uncomfortable pause followed. Russell segued, "The two of you have plans for tonight?"

"We're going to Rockefeller Center for the tree lighting. After that, we'll just have a quiet one-on-one evening." Ross breathed deeply as the pain subsided.

"That's where the two of you met, right?"

"Yes, it is. He saw me through the crowd, and I saw him looking at me, and I knew right then and there I was going to spend the rest of my life with him."

Ross twisted open a container of hair gel and applied it sparingly to the finished haircut.

"Linda loves romantic stories like that," Russell said with a chuckle.

"Please tell her I say hello," Ross said. Then he reached for the talcum brush, dusted around Russell's ears and neck, and removed the cutting cape.

"I will. And you give my best to Kirby."

Ross offered Russell a hand mirror so he could inspect the

back, but Russell refused it. "I know it's perfect—it always is."

Ross was flattered. "Thank you," he said.

After the bill was paid, both gentlemen shook hands and wished each other a good day.

Kirby, the Old Black Woman...and Ground Zero, 3 P.M.

Kirby walked the streets of Manhattan. He puffed at a cigarette while his mind strayed over the day's interviews. He was annoyed by the outcome of each of them. All three of the HR reps had used the same line on him: "Thank you, we'll be in touch if anything comes up."

Yeah, right—screw you! Kirby thought. Then he cursed out loud: "Damn!" He took a deep drag of smoke and suddenly found himself passing by the barricades. He went numb as a gust of turmoil hit him, and his gut tightened as he looked out upon Hell.

He stopped in his tracks and stood in a mind-set of chaos as he took a final draw off the cigarette, dropped it to the pavement, and crushed it out with his shoe. Ground Zero still smoldered with the rank stink of depression and death. Like a dam exploding under the pressure of too much water, Kirby's eyes welled up and the tears flowed. He wept, and his hands began to shake.

"Mister, you feelin' sick?"

The voice startled him. He looked up from his misery to find an elderly black woman standing beside him.

"I'm sorry, honey," she said. "I didn't mean to frighten you."

Kirby nodded but didn't say anything.

"You gonna be OK?"

"I don't think so," he said honestly.

The old woman gently put her hand on his shoulder and spoke softly to him.

"Did you lose somebody that day, honey?"

He nodded again as tears streamed down his cheeks. "Yeah, three buddies," he said.

There was what seemed to be a freeze, a pause in real time, a moment that felt like an eternity of dread. In pained guttural torment, she said, "I lost my grandbaby." Kirby was shaken to his very core. He opened his arms and embraced her, and she embraced him in return. They both wept together.

Still Life

Nighttime in Manhattan: Rockefeller Center held a sea of people who had come together for the lighting of the Christmas tree. The air was cool, and for the first time in many weeks, many of the people in the crowd felt hopeful, secure, and even cheerful.

Ross and Kirby stood in the hustle and bustle, holding hands. Both of them were dressed casually in denim jackets, flannel, and jeans. Kirby wore his signature Yankees baseball cap.

There was both live and televised entertainment, and at exactly 8:56 P.M. the First Lady and the mayor threw the oversize candy-cane switch. The night was bathed in red, white, and blue light, and the sea of people became a roaring ocean of applause and cheering.

"Happy anniversary, handsome," Kirby said with his half smile.

"Happy anniversary," Ross said, and Kirby kissed him passionately.

Their kiss was like a still-life posed for a photographer or painter: a lovers' embrace forever captured in an old-fashioned Christmas card at a five-and-dime.

They put their arms around each other and made their way through the crowd beneath the city lights.

Lay the Cards on the Table, 9:45 P.M.

Serendipity, a coffee shop in Manhattan, was packed with romantics. Ross and Kirby sat; Ross with a hot chocolate and a slice of chocolate cake and Kirby with a coffee and piece of pumpkin pie.

"How's yours?" Kirby asked as he sipped from his cup.

"Chock-full of sugar," Ross said as he took a bite of his cake. "It couldn't be better, and the whipped cream melted just right. How's your coffee?"

"Black. Tastes like tar," Kirby chuckled.

"Just how you like it. Sure you don't want some half-and half?"

"Don't even think about it." Kirby grinned playfully—a welcome sight for Ross.

"I don't believe I've seen you pick up a cigarette all evening. What's wrong? Got a fever or something?" Ross joked gently.

"Ha ha! Keep it up and I'll have to take you home and spank you."

Ross looked at him with a pleading face. "Promise?"

Kirby chuckled again, reached across the table, and took Ross's free hand. He kissed his fingertips and held him close.

"I need to talk to you," Ross said, swinging the mood for both of them.

"Sure...you look pretty serious."

"I am."

"OK. I'm all ears...what's wrong?" Kirby was genuinely concerned.

"I know you're not happy, and I know you've been very depressed."

Kirby looked down at the table in defeat.

Ross smiled at him. "I love you." He breathed deeply and chose his words carefully. "It's not your fault that a bunch of lunatics and assholes decided to smash into our city. You and your friends decided to play hooky from work and go goof around at the World Trade Center with some of your customer buddies. You volunteered to get their breakfasts and take it back to them. You decided to chitchat with the people in line getting coffee. It is not your fault that they were in there when it happened..."

Kirby looked up and searched Ross's eyes. "But I should have gone back to help—" His voice broke.

"Bullshit!" Ross said. "You helped by staying on the street and doing what you could for the people there. Call me selfish, but if you had gone back, you wouldn't be here right now. I thank God you went to get the coffee. That's what saved you." He paused briefly. "Believe me, I'm so sorry for Mike, for John, and for Joe. My heart goes out to their families. It makes me sick to my stomach every time I think of it." He searched his soul for the best words to describe his emotions. "You don't think that I've lost anyone? Many of my clients are missing. Their bodies will never be found...but you...you're alive, and that's all I care about. By the grace of God you're here with me, and I thank Him for that. And everyone you helped will remember what you did for them and they won't forget it. So stop blaming yourself and come back to me. Please..."

Kirby was at a hush. There was nothing left to be said.

Desert and coffee were over.

In Darkness There Is Arousal

Ross unlocked the apartment door and pushed it open. Kirby went in first, then Ross shut, bolted, and chained the door behind them.

Darkness.

Ross fumbled for the light switch, and as he did he felt Kirby press his body against his from behind; his arms encircled him and held him firmly. He could feel the bulge of Kirby's sex grow and stiffen.

"Hey, handsome man..." Kirby whispered into Ross's ear with a kiss. "I just want to touch you."

Darkness.

There was sudden laughter from the neighbors next door.

Hands roamed his body.

Slowly.

Fingers unbuttoned his jacket...pulling at his shirt...fingers sliding underneath...squeezing at his chest...his nipples.

Ross was getting hard.

Darkness.

Outside a dog was barking.

Kirby pushed his hips into him; the whisper of his breath was heavy, and with it was a distinct edge.

Hands pushing at his jeans...sliding them...just below his buttocks...hands caressing and squeezing.

He felt Kirby's naked flesh on his.

Darkness.

A car alarm.

Singing...the neighbor's children...Christmas carols...

Lovers' Morning Hold

Holding his hand, Kirby led Ross to their bedroom and undressed him.

Sunrise broke.

Pale-blue shadows froze their bedroom as they lay nude in a lovers' morning hold.

A chain-link tattoo snaked and spiraled from Kirby's elbow to his shoulder then disappeared behind his back. The tattooed arm rested around Ross.

Kirby opened his eyes briefly, long enough to kiss Ross's nape. "I love you," he said, and then he fell back into his slumber.

Meet the Wilkinses

Tom Mendicino

"You'll like them. I know it."

I've never been a big one for socializing. Alice had to drag me out of the house kicking and screaming. This time she was insistent.

She was right. Why wouldn't I like them? They were probably lovely people, great folks, exactly the type of neighbors we were hoping for when we bought this splashily designed, poorly constructed, wildly expensive townhouse in the most exclusive gated community in the Triad.

"Give them a chance," she said.

I rolled over on my stomach and grunted. She sighed and settled back into her pillows, resigned to relying on Eudora Welty for companionship yet another night. It was fucking torture, pretending to be unconscious when I was in the grip of insomnia.

I used to fall asleep at the drop of a hat. Alice would accuse me of narcolepsy and threaten to inject me with caffeine. That was another lifetime, before falling asleep meant having to wake up and crawl out of bed, shave, brush my teeth, put on my Game Face. That was before I had to try to convince my father-in-law, the King of Unpainted Furniture, I was obsessed with lumber prices and consumed with mortgage rates—higher rates equating a drop in residential home sales, meaning fewer empty rooms begging to be filled with the affordable products of Tarheel Heritage Inc.

It's all her fault, I thought, irritated by the dry, chapping sound of thumb against paper as she turned the pages of her novel. We should have parted ways when I started graduate school. She shouldn't have followed me to Durham and taken that job at the Montessori school, teaching music appreciation to the precocious offspring of Duke's junior faculty. The school paid even less than my measly stipend from the Department of Comparative Literature. At least once a day I would accuse her of resenting our shabby circumstances. She'd just laugh and say, "Not as much as you do."

"It's completely up to you," she said when I pondered her father's job offer. Always a pragmatist, he'd decided if Alice was going to be so goddamn stubborn, if she was going to insist he accept me, then he would try to co-opt me. I was floundering anyway, insecure among the pretensions of more impressively pedigreed academics and highly susceptible to the power of suggestion. He never missed an opportunity to question how a man could call teaching four hours a week "work."

Alice assumed I had a choice. The King knew better. All he had to do was impugn my masculinity and it was goodbye Duke and hello Sales. He made only one condition. No more living in sin. We slipped off to City Hall before he could initiate the tactical maneuvers that would climax with the Big Church Wedding.

The money wasn't bad. It certainly impressed my old man, who'd been exasperated by every decision I'd ever made up till then. He'd refused to contribute a single dime for me to lounge around at Duke and read paperback novels, but he insisted on fronting the down payment on the townhouse, not wanting to be outdone by that blowhard, the uncrowned King, J. Curtis McDermott.

It was all my fault. I'd made the bed we were lying in. And Alice? She seemed happy enough with a spouse who was National Director of Sales and her career introducing the young scholars of the Greensboro Friends School to the glories of Wolfgang Amadeus.

She hadn't changed much since college, and I knew she missed the obnoxious, smelly boy she'd married, with his torn flannel shirts and shaggy hair, his stupid record collection and dog-eared volumes of the literature of the South. And so I lay there that night, the sheets feeling like a hair shirt, feeling guilty for blaming my wife for this fate I alone had chosen. I rolled over on my side, told her I'd love to meet them, and, as penance for my cruel thoughts, started making love to her. Eudora Welty was tossed to the floor.

Alice wanted to cook dinner for them. No, I said, willing to give in only so far, we'll meet at a restaurant. She wanted to avoid the awkward moment when the check was presented. No problem, I said, I'll give my card in advance, and at the end of the evening I'll slip away from the table and discreetly sign. She finally conceded, knowing I really did not want to meet the Wilkinses.

I started to relax as the waiter uncorked the second bottle of wine. The evening was going well, better than expected. In fact, it was an unqualified success. The Wilkinses, unlike most of our recent acquaintances, gave every indication they had learned how to read. There was plenty to talk about; there was a lot of laughter. Driving home, Alice asked what I'd thought of Nora. The question took me by surprise. I was having a hard time remembering her face.

"She seemed kind of quiet," I said, assuming shyness was the explanation for her failure to make an impression on me.

"Andy," Alice laughed, "she talked a blue streak all night!" Funny, I hadn't noticed.

"What did you think of Brian?" she asked.

I wondered if that was a trick question. "Seems like a nice guy," I said cautiously.

"You two really seemed to hit it off."

Did we? I felt a strange sensation in my chest. Good God, I thought, it sounded like an old cliché, but did my heart just skip a beat?

"What did you talk about?" she asked.

"I dunno," I said, suddenly becoming inarticulate.

What did we talk about? Work, obviously. Our wives, certainly. It was easier to remember what we didn't talk about.

Golf.

ACC hoops.

Cars.

Power tools.

"Swimming," I finally said.

"He's a swimmer too?" she asked.

"Yes."

"You guys ought to swim together sometime."

"Yeah, he mentioned something like that," I said, sounding nonchalant and noncommittal. "He said he'd call to set something up."

Two days later she was slipping on her Levi's while I cradled my foot, engrossed in a virgin blister on my heel. She asked if something was wrong. It must be the new shoes, I said. No, I don't mean that, she said. I'd thought she was blissfully unaware of my barely concealed agitation, of the nervous twitch I'd developed whenever the phone rang, of my impatient interruptions to ask who was on the line, and of my disappointment when the call was not the one I was so anxiously awaiting.

Wednesday night Nora Wilkins called and invited us to dinner Saturday night. Alice expressed our regrets, telling Nora we were visiting my parents this weekend.

"Wait, wait one minute, Nora, Andy's trying to tell me something." I was waving my hands furiously to get her attention.

"Nora? Andy says they canceled, that they're going out of town this weekend. Thanks for telling me, mister," she said, laughing, then told Nora, "We'd love to."

I made a mental note to square this little white lie with my mother, pronto, before she called and told Alice they were looking forward to seeing us this weekend and she'd gotten tickets to the garden show for the two of them.

I got a fresh haircut Saturday afternoon and bought a new shirt that brought out the color in my eyes.

At the Wilkinses' house that night Brian apologized. "I've been meaning to call you all week, Andy, but the days just got away from me."

"Oh, I'd forgotten all about it, to tell you the truth," I lied.

"This week definitely."

"Not good for me. I've got a sales meeting with a distributor in Atlanta."

"Damn. Soon then."

"I'll be back Wednesday night," I blurted.

Alice and Nora finished the house tour. "Andy, you must see

it," Alice said. "The Wilkinses have the most beautiful things."

If I hadn't known better, I might have thought Alice had a bit of a crush herself. Nora was so self-assured, a take-charge blond, slightly butch in a female-golf-pro sort of way. I made it a point to be more conscious of her, notice her mannerisms, pay attention to her offhand remarks. She was bossy, but in a way that was more brisk and efficient than aggressive, as if she'd already considered and rejected all the alternatives to her way of doing things before you had an opportunity to propose them. She must have reminded Alice of her sisters; maybe that explained why she was so immediately comfortable with her.

"Brian, it's time to light the grill. Andy, go help him."

Aye, aye, sir...er, ma'am.

Central casting would never have selected Brian Wilkins as the catalyst for my downfall. Hollywood's idea of a seducer was everything short, fair, nearsighted Brian Wilkins was not. That's not to say Brian wasn't attractive. In fact, years earlier, he told me, he'd been voted Cutest Boy by his high school graduating class. Best-Looking would have been a classmate with a more classic profile, better bone structure, and features that would only improve with time, unlike Brian, whose chipmunk cheeks were thickening even before middle age.

A minor inferno erupted when Brian tossed a match on the charcoal. His hand flew up to my chest and he pushed me back from the flame, saying, "Someday I'll figure out how much lighter fluid is too much."

I drank a little too much that night. And the more I drank, the less I cared our wives might have been dining in another solar system for all the attention we gave them.

"I told you you'd like them," Alice said triumphantly as I rolled into bed. "I knew it."

Brian called the next morning. He was wondering when we might get together for that swim. *Too bad this week didn't look so good. Hey, how about today? This afternoon. It's clear for me. How about you? We can burn off some of that alcohol. Let's make it 2 o'clock. Give me the directions. I'll find it.*

That's how easy it was. Alice's Sunday was committed to yet

another shower—either bridal or, more often those days, baby. *Oh, God, please, not another baby shower,* I hoped. Officially, we still believed we had the luxury of time ahead of us; Alice was far too young to feel her biological clock ticking. But something was stirring, an instinct awakened by gift wrapping all those playsuits and teddy bears. All the signs were there. The casual remarks about the house seeming a little small. The occasional comment that Joshua might be a good name for a boy, Sarah for a girl. She couldn't have known when she kissed me goodbye, telling me to have fun, that those dreams were about to be derailed by the events of that perfectly ordinary Sunday afternoon.

I hadn't expected him to be so nervous. He dropped his lock twice, fumbling through the combination. He turned his back to me when he stepped out of his briefs and into his trunks. His shoulders were wide without being impressive and were covered with a thin layer of hair. He coughed and bent down to swipe the soles of his bare feet. He finally turned to face me, red in the face and stammering.

"Andy, I'm really sorry about this."

"Sorry about what?" I asked, truly confused.

"I'm a terrible swimmer. I should have told you up front."

"Why didn't you?"

"Because I wanted to come swimming with you."

His forwardness made me self-conscious. I knew then why I had impulsively chosen to bring a pair of baggy gym shorts instead of my usual racing trunks. I was conscious of my naked chest and limbs as we walked to the pool. I took long strides, moving quickly, forcing him to keep pace, anxious for the protective cover of the warm chlorinated water. I chose my lane, dove quickly, and swam away.

He wasn't a bad swimmer—not in my league, but, of course, I was a former state high school champion in the breaststroke, the rare high point in an adolescence distinguished mainly by my ability to achieve new standards of awkwardness. He'd taken the next lane, and I passed him many times, coming and going, always averting my eyes and immersing myself in my laps. Half an hour passed. When I pulled myself out of the pool, he was waiting on the deck, his arms wrapped around his knees and his toes inches from my nose. He had huge feet, and before I could censor my thoughts I wondered if the old wives' tale—big hands, big feet, big everything—was true.

"You've got a beautiful stroke. I could watch you all day."

Barely 30, Brian Wilkins was progressing on his March to the Sea. He'd started in the tiny market of Rochester, Minnesota, fresh out of school, as associate producer of the 10 o'clock news broadcast, making his way south with an unbroken string of triumphs at small stations in the heart of the Midwest. The network took notice when he drove the Greensboro affiliate's 11 o'clock newscast to first place in the ratings in nine short months by dumping the venerable local anchor for a former drum majorette with big tits and a blazing white smile of after-dinner-mint teeth. He knew it was his certain destiny to command network operations in the District of Columbia, finally capping his career in Manhattan as executive producer of a national broadcast.

But, he'd explained the night before, he was always self-effacing and humble, and he positioned himself so his rivals and enemies would underestimate him. His work ethic was legendary. His instincts for what sold in the broadcast journalism market were remarkable. The fortress of his personal life was unassailable. His Valkyrie wife excelled at fulfilling the responsibilities of corporate wife and was willing to overlook his lack of interest in conjugal intimacy in exchange for a seat on the rocket launch to the top. They'd already accomplished one daughter, and a little brother or sister was scheduled to be in development in the near future.

There was only one slight problem—one potential pitfall Brian Wilkins was determined to avoid. Brian had certain needs that none of his successes could satisfy. And so he chose me to follow my predecessors abandoned in Rochester and Springfield, Illinois, and Davenport, Iowa, all of us married men with too much at stake to risk indiscretion and potential exposure. Later, I asked him how he'd known to pursue me.

"It was easy," he said, his smile almost a sneer. "You're smart. You figure it out."

I'd kept my mind a blank slate when it came to homoerotic attraction and proclivities. I would immediately extinguish the occasional—no, frequent—disturbing thoughts before they had an opportunity to reveal their nature, before they could identify themselves as ATTRACTION or DESIRE. Brian Wilkins must have caught me in that split second before I put the fire out, my eye lingering a second too long before I blushed and looked away.

And so it began.

It was just a matter of waiting for the right opportunity, which was not, of course, going to be there and then on the wet pool deck, trunks around the ankles, writhing and moaning in the face of appalled exercise buffs. In the open shower it was my turn to keep my back turned, feeling like I was back in high school, not able to trust my defiant penis. We shook hands in the parking lot, and I ignored it when he scratched my palm with his middle finger, not yet knowing the secret signals between closeted homosexuals.

"We should get together soon for drinks," he said, making it obvious that he meant alone, not with our wives.

"Give me a call," I said, hoping he couldn't hear the nerves in my voice. He asked if we could get together Wednesday night. I told him I had a late-afternoon flight out of Atlanta after my lunch meeting with the distributor. Great, he said, telling me where to meet him.

That night I attacked Alice so enthusiastically the bed collapsed. Once wasn't enough. Twice didn't satisfy me. Long after midnight Alice pulled the twisted sheets between her legs and sipped a glass of wine.

"You ought to exercise more often," she said.

A week later she waited for a reprise. But that night I fell asleep during *60 Minutes,* not to awaken until 7 the next morning. Everything had changed in those seven days.

I'd called home from the airport Wednesday afternoon and left a message on the machine, complaining that I'd missed my flight, that it was ridiculous to get routed through Columbus, Ohio, and the next nonstop didn't arrive until after midnight. *Don't wait up. Love you. Miss you.*

I thought his choice of bar was a little odd. The Tara Lounge at a Holiday Inn on the outskirts of Winston-Salem? His briefcase was in plain view and he put a thick ratings book on the table, evidence of a purely business purpose in the highly unlikely event someone who knew him stumbled upon us in a dark corner in the empty lounge in that tacky backwater. We started with beer and moved quickly to bourbon straight up. It wasn't long before enough alcohol had flowed to excuse his shins touching mine under the table. I didn't pull my leg away, and he pressed lightly, just enough to confirm it was intentional. We kept talking. He went to the bar for another round, and when he returned he kept his legs tucked beneath the seat. I slid my foot across the floor until it nudged his shoe. He put his hands on the table and looked me in the eyes.

"What do you think?"

There was a key, Room 206, between us on the table. I panicked, admitting I'd lied to Alice, told her I'd missed my flight—she might call Nora and find out I was not far from home, meeting him for a beer. He laughed so hard the bartender looked away from the television.

"Are you fucking crazy? Nora thinks I'm in D.C. and won't be back until tomorrow night."

I learned a few things that night. First, big hands and big feet do not necessarily mean big everything. Just as well. Christ only knows how I would have reacted if he'd unzipped his pants and pulled out a Long Red Snake. As fate would have it, Brian Wilkins was the proud owner of a Short Brown Snail. Second, I learned how my body could respond to a touch I truly desired. For the first time, I felt the fissures in the fault line of the life I'd created and the potential of my dry heart to crack and split.

Eight, nearly nine years of hindsight have taught me it wasn't love I felt for Brian Wilkins. I didn't know better at the time. What else but love could cause me to despair when I didn't hear from him for days, constantly debating the pros and cons of calling to break the silence? What other reason to be elated when I would pick up the phone and hear his voice? Only love could have inflated Brian Wilkins like a Macy's Thanksgiving Day balloon hovering over my every waking moment, while shrinking Alice, like her namesake, to a two-dimensional shadow to be accommodated, gently, during the intervals between rendezvous.

Yes, hindsight brings wisdom. I know now it wasn't love. It was fear, an absolute, abject fear that without him, I'd be back in the box, snapped shut, sealed tight, labeled HUSBAND and returned special delivery to WIFE.

He tried hard to appear sad the night he told me he'd got the transfer to Pittsburgh. But the sex was bad, hurried, obviously one last chore before departing, like registering your change of address with the post office. We had a Last Supper together, the four of us, on their last night in North Carolina. I tried to make eye contact over the table, hoping to pass secret signals, looking for some sign of regret. But Brian was having none of it, never letting the conversation drift from market demographics, advertising revenue streams, and the necessity to adapt to survive against the threat of the cable news networks.

I waited a week to call him at his new station. His secretary put me on hold for 10 minutes after I gave her my name. *Great to hear your voice,* he said, sounding distracted and, worse, irritated. He told me he'd stay in touch. I never heard from him again.

The box couldn't hold me for long. One night, alone in a hotel room in Dallas, the King of Unpainted Furniture safely snoring in a suite on a different floor, I called a cab and gave the driver the address of a bathhouse, where many hands touched and stroked me before the sun came up.

There was no turning back now, not even when, many months later, Nora Wilkins called to tell us that Brian had passed away, suddenly, stricken by a pneumonia from which he never recovered. Nora had left Pittsburgh and was back home in Minnesota. She and Alice made a vague promise to see each other soon, a sentimental gesture appropriate to the moment. But time passed quickly and Nora Wilkins slipped into our shared history, the visit never undertaken. Years later I remembered they were trying to have another child, and I wondered if Nora had been one of the lucky ones or if their daughter was orphaned now, another statistic in the Great Plague of the late 20th century.

The Law of Love

Rhysenn S.

Practicing law in Boston, David decided, was highly overrated. He wished someone had told him this *before* he went to law school.

Of course, it was probably part of the conspiracy that TV shows like *The Practice* helped propagate: the beautiful myth that lawyers in Boston had an endless flow of interesting clients. And that however heinous and depraved these people were (the murderers, not the network executives), there never seemed to be a problem paying legal fees.

David's clientele was markedly different. They didn't bring him severed heads in medical bags. They'd probably never held a knife to anyone's throat. They also didn't show any sign of wanting to pay their fees.

His small law firm, West & Halder, sat cramped on the second floor of a nondescript building on the very fringe of central Boston. His partner—*business* partner—was James Halder, now sitting across him in their office.

James's table was pushed against one wall, David's against the other. There was only one other tiny room, which they used as a conference room, for meeting clients—though the decor was barely presentable.

James slid a folder belching with paper across the table toward David.

The Law of Love

"Think it's your turn to play secretary tonight," his partner said with a grin. "Good news is, I won't ask you to get in my lap and hump me."

David groaned as he picked up the folder. "You know, as much as I hate to admit it, that's looking like the better option."

"No kidding," James said carelessly. "You'd pay to ride *me,* I should think."

James. Straight as an arrow, and just as sharp. They met at law school in Massachusetts, when David had drunkenly hit on him and James had returned the gesture—with his fist. Later, when they were both more sober, James had come over to apologize—and to remind David that sticking his hand down James's pants was something he should never attempt again. They'd been friends ever since.

"Oh, fuck this, let's go home." James yawned loudly and stretched. "Paperwork will still be here tomorrow, and for the rest of our long, glamorous careers in this fucking practice."

Two years out of law school and the last vestiges of idealism had long ago vanished. Idealism didn't pay the bills.

Just as David reached for his coat, there was a knock on the door, so soft that David wasn't sure he'd actually heard it. He crossed the office and opened the door.

A young man stood outside. He was dressed in faded denim jeans and a crumpled white shirt. A small backpack was slung over his shoulder; he was worrying the loose end of its strap with his fingers.

"Can I help you?" David asked.

"Hi." The young man sounded tense. His blond hair fell across his left eye, which seemed circled with the shadow of a bruise. "I saw your ad in the phone directory."

James came up next to him and curiously poked his head out the door. "Who's this?"

The young man shifted his weight from one foot to the other, looking even more nervous. "I…I'm looking for a lawyer."

"This is a law firm, but I'm afraid we've closed for the day," David said, eyeing him suspiciously. He didn't trust people who showed up at such late hours. "You can come back tomorrow."

"Please," said the young man earnestly. "I really, really need your help. Please, sir, just hear me out."

As much as he liked being called "sir" by a boy begging for his attention, David shot James a mildly skeptical look. James shrugged.

"OK," David sighed, pushing the door farther open. "Come on in."

The young man nodded and quickly stepped into their small office. David watched him carefully, thinking he could be a street punk looking for a quick robbery—not that he'd have much luck here. But there was a certain vulnerable quality about him: the hunch of his shoulders, the dull shuffle of his feet on the floor.

They did not proceed into the conference room. James propped himself on a desk, not even bothering to pick up a legal pad. David closed the door and leaned back against it.

"So," he said. "What can we do for you?"

"I need a lawyer," the young man began, and then hesitated. "But, uh, I…I don't have any money right now."

"Few of our clients ever do," David said wearily. "What kind of legal services are you looking for?"

"I want to sue my ex-lover," the young man replied staunchly. "I want to make him pay for what he did to me."

David's ears perked up. *He?* From the corner of his eye he caught an amused twitch on James's mouth that said *This one's your call.*

"I'm David West," he said, and then, gesturing toward James, "This is James Halder. And you are?"

"Shane," the young man answered. "Shane Caulfield."

"Mr. Caulfield," David began. "This—"

"Please, call me Shane." The young man gave him an embarrassed smile.

David looked at him and relented. "All right, Shane," he continued. "This is the situation. If you want to retain us as legal counsel, we'll need to hear more about your case first. And then there's some paperwork to be done to appoint us as your lawyers. All of which will be better done in the light of day."

"But will you take my case?" Shane persisted.

"We'll definitely consider it," David replied. "We'll meet you to discuss the details of your case tomorrow as well as the terms of the legal contract."

"So you'll be my lawyers?" Shane sounded almost desperate for reassurance.

"Yes, yes, we will," James swiftly cut in, before David could open his mouth. James grinned at Shane and reached out and patted David on his shoulder. "You've come to the right place. David, my partner here, he's the best lawyer you can find in this entire building. He'll help you sue the pants off your ex-lover, that lousy bastard."

From the wide-eyed expression on Shane's face, David couldn't tell if he was comforted or alarmed.

"We open at half past 9 in the morning," David informed him. "But we can pencil you in at 9, before our regular appointments." This was a little trick he'd learned to give the illusion that they were busy lawyers with much profitable work to do: In actuality, they opened at 9 every morning and didn't even keep an appointment book.

Shane nodded, but he had the look of someone who wanted to say something but didn't know how. Finally, in the interest of eventually making his way home, David prompted, "Is there anything else?"

"Um, well," Shane dithered before blurting out, "I was wondering if I could stay here for the night. I don't mean inside your office," he added hastily, "I can camp just outside and wait for you guys to come in tomorrow morning. That is, if you don't mind."

"Why don't you go on home?" David asked. "The office isn't going anywhere."

There was an awkward pause.

"I don't...exactly have anywhere, uh, that I can go," Shane muttered to the floor, unable to meet their eyes. "It's a long story, and I really don't want to hold you guys back..."

David felt a headache creeping up from the base of his skull. He wanted a drink. A margarita would be nice.

"Sure," James said nonchalantly. "We don't pay rent on the corridor. Go ahead."

Shane gave him a grateful smile. "Thanks."

James shrugged. "No problem." One day, David mused tiredly, straight guys like James would learn a range of gestures more communicative than the shrug and more subtle than the finger.

They made their way out of the office and stood in the corridor while James locked up the office door. Shane lingered next to David, who couldn't help noticing the way Shane kept running his fingers through his hair, although he never really pushed it out of his eyes.

"Thanks again," Shane said when James had finished locking up. In a softer voice he said, "See you, David."

David nodded, and he and James headed toward the stairs. In the last glance he cast over his shoulder, he saw Shane taking off his backpack and settling down on the floor.

"Very funny, about me being the best lawyer in this building," David said as they started down the stairs; he gave James a reproachful look. "There's only one law firm in this building. Us."

"God's honest truth, then." James gave him a wicked grin. "And by the way, that was really sensitive of you, telling him to go home." He rolled his eyes. "Your EQ really is quite appalling sometimes. You sure you're gay?"

They exited the building and walked toward their cars, parked in a side alley a distance away. David looked distractedly down the empty street.

"I don't think he should sleep in the corridor," he finally said.

"Oh, stop being such an idiot," James snapped. "What, are you afraid he's going to break in and steal our computers?"

"It's not that," David answered. "I mean, it's cold tonight. And that carpet's awfully moldy, no one's cleaned it in ages. It's disgusting."

"Yep," James said affirmatively, thumping him on his back, "you're still gay."

As they reached James's Volkswagen, David thought of an idea. "He can sleep at your place," he said.

James turned to him with an incredulous look.

"Dave, if anyone should be bringing a gay boy home, it's you, OK?" James shook his head as he started digging in his trouser pocket for his keys. "Anyway, it's not like you have a boyfriend. Just pretend it's Friday night or something."

"I am not going to sleep with him!" David protested hotly.

"No one said anything about sleeping with him." James unlocked his car door and turned to him with a knowing wink. "Overcompensating, are we?"

"He can't come to my place," David said flatly.

"And he can't come to mine either." James shrugged and got into his car. "So we'll just let him stay the night on that disgusting, moldy carpet, and you can go home by yourself and rough it out with your conscience."

David knew that James was being a complete pain in the ass. He also knew that Shane wouldn't be sleeping in the corridor that night.

"This is all your fault," he said mutinously.

"Why is it my fault, exactly?"

"I wanted to tell him to come back tomorrow, but you wanted to let him in!"

"Listen," said James, "you're the one who can't bear to see him camp out there all night, so it stands to reason that you should be the one to let him sleep on your sofa. Or bed. Whatever."

David glared at him. "Fuck you, James."

James laughed, then started the engine. "See you tomorrow, Dave."

David scowled as he watched James drive off. Then he turned around and headed back to the office.

When he reached the second floor, he found Shane curled up just outside their office. His head was pillowed on his backpack, although he obviously wasn't asleep; he bolted upright the moment David appeared at the top of the stairs but relaxed when he recognized him.

"Forget something?" Shane asked, trying to sound light.

David walked toward him, not answering until he reached Shane. "Come on," he said resignedly. "You can crash on my sofa tonight."

Shane looked up at him, puzzled and somewhat wary. "That's quite all right. I really don't mind sleeping here."

"The corridor is freezing, and the carpet is filthy," David said, impatience creeping into his voice. "You'll be sick by the morning."

Shane eyed David, still looking unsure. Finally he got to his feet, dusted off bits of carpet that clung to his shirt, and picked up his backpack. The shadows hooded the expression in his eyes as he said simply, "Thanks."

David nodded, then led the way out of the building and to his car. Shane sat quietly as David drove.

Not turning from the road, David asked, "What happened to your eye?"

Shane flinched slightly; it was a while before he answered. "He hit me." A pause. "Just before I left."

There was another silence. Outside the car, it was starting to rain.

"How old are you?" David asked evenly as he made a left turn onto his street.

"Twenty-two," Shane answered, and gave a forced laugh. "I know, you must think I'm a little young to be needing a lawyer."

"Not really," David replied, and left it at that.

He parked outside his apartment, and Shane followed him inside. They rode the elevator in silence; as they reached his apartment on the seventh floor, David opened the door and flicked on the light.

His apartment was modest but cozy and relatively well-kept. A sofa sprawled in the middle of the small living room, in front of the TV set. In the kitchen, this morning's coffee cup was still waiting to be washed in the sink. The bathroom was adjacent to his bedroom, down the hall.

"You live here alone?" Shane asked quietly.

David glanced at him. "Yes."

Shane walked toward the sofa and dropped his backpack but didn't sit down. The way he moved reminded David of a wild cub lost in unfamiliar territory, cagey in its surroundings.

"Do you want some ice for your eye?" David entered the kitchen and rinsed his cup for his nightly cup of tea.

"No, thanks." There was a careful tone in Shane's voice. "I'm all right."

"Well, you can use the bathroom now if you want." David hunted for a tea bag, finally realizing they were all gone. "I'll shower in the morning."

He stepped back out into the living room and found Shane just where he'd been before. Shane watched him, a guarded yet somewhat questioning look in his eyes.

David paused. "Do you want anything else?"

"No." Shane's voice hardened as he added too quickly, "Do you?"

David was surprised at the sudden defensiveness in Shane's voice.

"What do you mean?" he asked.

Shane looked at him for a moment, as if making up his mind; then he boldly walked toward David, stopping only inches away from him. Shane's eyes were veiled, and they shimmered in the half darkness

David blinked, startled by Shane's sudden closeness. The next thing he knew, Shane was kissing him.

His lips were warm and soft, and his tongue was wet as it slid into David's mouth. David found himself nudged back against the living room wall, Shane pressed up against him. An irresistible heat twitched to life between his legs, and David found himself responding, pulling Shane hard against him, kissing him feverishly.

David yanked Shane's shirt up and slid his hands under the fabric. His fingers scraped against bare flesh, warm and smooth; David felt Shane shiver and arch, rubbing against him with delicious friction. Vaguely aware of Shane's mouth leaving his, David tilted his head back, and a moan escaped his lips as Shane's tongue licked a wet trail down his neck, over his chest...

Then Shane was kneeling in front of him, his hands scrambling at the zipper of David's pants—

And finally a shred of coherent thought pierced the haze of arousal in David's mind: *You shouldn't.*

Shane's hands pried open his fly, and the teasing touch of his fingers sent a wild sensation blazing through every nerve in David's body.

You can't.

Mustering every ounce of his willpower, David shoved Shane away from him with such force that he knocked Shane to the floor.

David staggered backward, away from him.

"What the hell," David said breathlessly, glaring down at Shane, "do you think you're doing?"

Shane looked confused; his shirt was open, revealing his lean torso, and if David didn't force himself to keep his eyes on Shane's face, he'd be confused too.

"I—I thought you wanted—" Shane swallowed, and the delicate movement of his throat muscles rippling almost made David think, *Screw ethics—I'll bet Ethics hasn't had a good fuck in forever.*

David closed his eyes and steeled himself; then he turned and strode toward his bedroom. "Good night, Shane."

"You wanted it," Shane said, just as David stepped into his bedroom, the defiance in his voice almost masking the hurt.

David looked back, directly at Shane.

"Yes, I did," he answered, and then closed the bedroom door.

David had half expected to wake up to find Shane gone the next morning, but when he stepped out into the living room, Shane was still asleep on the sofa.

Breakfast was an awkward affair. So was the drive to work, which passed in uneasy silence. David was glad to finally reach the office, where he directed Shane into the conference room and closed the door firmly behind him so he wouldn't be able to hear what was discussed outside in the office.

James was already at his desk, drinking his first cup of coffee for the day and eyeing David with sly interest.

"Morning," he said, arching an eyebrow. "Did we sleep well?"

David threw down his briefcase—the obligatory black briefcase all lawyers carry to feel important and, occasionally, to contain documents—and glowered at James.

"Shane offered to pay me last night," he said.

James looked surprised. "I thought he doesn't have any money."

"That's right," David said meaningfully. "He doesn't."

"Oh. *Oh!*" James realized what David meant and burst out laughing. "Don't suppose he wants a receipt for that?"

David shot him a withering look. "Fuck you, James."

James gave him an impish grin. "Well, you know, it's not me you really want to—" He broke off and yelped as David threw a legal pad at him. "All right, all right! But you're still going to represent him, aren't you?"

"I don't think I have a choice," David answered with a sigh.

"Looks like he opted for an installment plan," James said, smirking.

David looked chagrined. "I'm serious, James."

James sobered. "Don't tell me you really like him?"

"Well..." David considered this for a moment. "I guess I'm...attracted."

"And you see this as a problem," James surmised, nodding wisely.

"Of course it's a goddamn problem," David snapped. "How the hell am I supposed to work with him when I can't help being attracted to him?"

"Then tell him you can't be his lawyer and ask him to try somewhere else." James shrugged. "You can probably recommend him half our alumni."

David felt like thwacking James on the head with something heavier than a legal pad. Preferably an encyclopedia. Instead he just glared at him, turned, and stalked away.

"Where are you going?" James called after him.

"To do my job," David replied over his shoulder.

"Wonder if payment in kind counts as a tax-deductible benefit," James mused aloud.

Unfortunately for David, he actually planned to use the legal pad he was holding. So he settled for hurling a balled-up piece of paper at James before he went into the conference room.

Shane was there, pacing nervously; he stopped short when David came in, then inched toward one of the chairs. He never took his eyes off David, which made David feel exposed, watched, uncomfortable. And reminded him of what had happened last night. But David managed to keep his calm as they sat down across each other at the table.

He cleared his throat and put on his best professional voice. "Mr. Caulfield." David tried not to think about how good it had felt to run his hands up and down Shane's body. "I'm here to discuss the facts of the lawsuit you would like our firm to represent you in."

"I want to sue my ex-lover," Shane replied quietly. "His name is Kendall Hughes."

"Kendall Hughes." David's brow furrowed. "Hmm. That name sounds familiar."

"He's an older guy. Very rich," Shane informed him. "He has a share in quite a few big companies. I met him late last year, while I was working as a dealer in a casino, the Red Top. He liked to play at my table."

"Did he give you any money on a personal basis?" David asked.

Shane looked embarrassed. "Yes. He gave me a credit card, but he canceled it when I walked out. He also let me stay in his hotel suite, just upstairs from the casino. It was all very discreet, and it worked out pretty well for the past two or three months."

"Until?" David queried.

"Until he lost a bet with one of his friends," Shane said, "this guy called Phil. Also very rich, a big name in one of the law firms, I can't remember which."

There was a brief, startled pause. "You don't mean happen to mean Phillip Travers, senior partner in Wilkin, Fordson, & Brookes, do you?" David finally asked. "Broad-built, brown hair, weird mustache..."

Shane nodded vigorously. "That's him. You know him too?"

"I applied to join his law firm when I graduated," David muttered darkly. "He interviewed me. He was a real jerk—and that's putting it nicely."

"He's one of Kendall's good friends." Shane leaned forward with intensity in his eyes. "They love to gamble together. Huge amounts of money. But last week..." He paused and took a deep breath. "Last week Kendall didn't bet money. He bet...me."

David couldn't believe his ears. "What?"

"Yes. Kendall said that Phil liked me a lot. Enough to bet on, I guess." Shane gave a bitter, humorless laugh. "And Kendall lost, so..."

There was a moment of silence in the conference room.

"Did he"—a lump formed in David's throat, making his words sound thick—"did Phillip Travers collect on his debt?"

Shane looked down at his hands; David saw that they were clenched very tightly, his knuckles white-tipped.

"Yes," Shane answered, and his voice broke slightly.

That single word pierced David's heart. "I'll get him," he swore, his voice filled with fierce determination. "I'll get that son of a bitch for what he did to you."

An abrupt quiet followed the blaze of David's words.

"Thank you," Shane whispered, gazing into David's eyes. "And I'm so sorry about last night."

David looked at him; he suddenly felt no anger, no disgust, not even pity. Just sadness.

"You thought I only brought you back to my place because I wanted to have sex with you." There was a subdued tone of understanding in David's voice. "You thought I was just like all the other guys you've known."

"I didn't know how else I could..." Shane trailed off and bit on his lower lip. "I just wanted—"

"To pay me back?" David finished; from the fleeting look in Shane's eyes, though, he could tell that wasn't quite what Shane had been meaning to say.

But Shane just nodded and drew a deep breath.

"I don't have any money now," he said fervently, "but I'll pay you out of the money I get from the lawsuit."

"And what makes you so sure you'll get the money from the lawsuit?" David asked.

Shane held his gaze. "Because you're my lawyer."

David and James drew up the lawsuit and served the papers to Kendall Hughes and Phillip Travers. Of course, Hughes and

Travers weren't the least bit intimidated by the prospect of a lawsuit from a fledgling law firm staffed by a couple of fresh graduates—what worried them most was the storm of bad publicity sure to eclipse the case itself.

They came back with an offer for settlement: $50,000.

James did a victory dance in their office. To spare Shane from his partner's sheer exuberance, David ushered him into the conference room to tell him the good news.

Shane's response was far from what David had expected.

"Is that all you think I'm worth?" Shane asked, his eyes flashing. "Fifty grand?"

David chose his words carefully. "No, that's not what I think. You should never let anyone put a price tag on what you're worth, Shane." He paused, then heaved a sigh. "But as far as this case goes—yes, I think you should accept their offer."

"What will they think of me if I settle just because they offer me money?" Shane shot back. "They'll think I'm a…a whore!"

"We don't give a damn about their opinion, Shane!" David answered, frustrated. "Who *cares* what they think?"

"And what about *you*?" Shane's voice was frayed at the edges, and his eyes shone intensely as he gazed at David. "What do you think of me?"

David looked at Shane for a long moment.

"I haven't gone on a date with anyone since I met you," David said quietly. "And it's not just because you're sleeping on my sofa."

Shane stared at David, completely taken aback; his initial anger was gone, and now disbelief gave way to a new emotion that shone in his eyes.

"Accept their offer," Shane finally said softly.

The meeting with Phillip Travers, senior partner of the prestigious Wilkin, Fordson, and Brookes, would have unnerved any young lawyer. But David had enough hatred for Travers to face him without a hint of fear.

"My client has decided to accept your offer to settle," David calmly informed him.

"Of course, settlement doesn't in any way imply that we

acknowledge liability in this allegation," Travers said imperiously. "But in favor of discretion and expediency—"

"You mean, in favor of sweeping this *in*discretion under the carpet, so the wife and kids won't get to read all about it in the morning papers," David interrupted.

Travers fixed him with an icy glare. "Your representation of the boy interests me, Mr. West. It's perfectly obvious that he has no money," Travers remarked succinctly. "Which makes me wonder who really is the *client*."

"Mr. Caulfield would like a check for the full amount to be made out in his name and couriered directly to our law firm," David continued, unfazed. He gave the older lawyer a thin smile, then picked up his black briefcase. "It has been a real pleasure meeting you again, Mr. Travers."

On Saturday morning David and Shane sat together on the sofa, sharing breakfast and the morning paper. David had the front page in front of him, although he wasn't really reading it. His eyes strayed to Shane, who was avidly reading the comics section and chortling to himself. David smiled.

Shane looked up and saw that David was watching him. "What?" He grinned sheepishly and held up the paper. "This one's really funny."

The ringing of his cell phone interrupted them; David reached out and grabbed it. "Yes?"

"Check just arrived by courier!" came James's excited voice on the phone. "Fifty thousand bucks, baby!"

"Already? That's fantastic!" David sat up straight and almost knocked over his cup of coffee with his elbow. Shane leaned over and moved the cup out of danger's way.

"Yep," James continued. "I just thought I'd let you and Shane know."

David thanked him and hung up. "Guess what?" he said to Shane, who put down the comics and looked at him expectantly. "Your money arrived today. As of this moment, you're $50,000 richer—well, minus our fee, of course."

A troubled shadow flitted across Shane's face, and David

guessed it was memories of a past he just wanted to forget. Then it was gone, like a trick of light, and Shane smiled at David.

"That's great news," Shane said genuinely, and then added, "I'm just so glad it's all over."

"Wow." David sat back with a satisfied sigh. "I can't believe we did it."

"You did it," Shane corrected quietly. "It was all you, David."

"So," David grinned at him. "Have you decided what you're going to do with all your money?"

"Well, at least now we'll be square on the legal fees." Shane tilted his head pensively. "And I can pay you back for letting me stay here all this time. Then I won't owe you anything."

David gazed at Shane for a moment. Then he took Shane's hand, pulled him closer, and kissed him on the lips.

"You never did," David whispered.

Rearview Mirror

Schuyler Bishop

Traffic stopped when Matt Broscious made his debut, and though it was only on the sidewalks of Greenwich, Connecticut, as his mother strolled him along, Joanna Broscious soon learned to allow an extra half hour when she took Matt to town with her. Whatever it was that caused them to gape—Matt's golden skin, his high, rose-tinged cheeks, those silver eyes that seemed to glow from within—strangers and friends, adults and children alike wanted to touch Matt, talk to him, bask in his splendor. And Matt let them bask, and charmed them with his smile, and got what he wanted with his puerile pout. And in the soft swirling eddies the stroller left in its wake, all anyone could talk about was "that beautiful Broscious boy."

When Matt went off to nursery school, the other children clamored to sit next to him, to be his partner, to be on his side. Over the years the clamor quieted, but the desire to be next to Matt didn't. Girls plotted ways to kiss him and the boys asked their mothers if Matt could come over to play, if Matt could sleep over. Even Matt's teachers, whether they knew it or not, were smitten. For them, Matt's thoughts on every subject were original and insightful, worthy of everyone's attention. "And what do you think, Matt?"

There were, of course, jealous mothers and fathers who,

among themselves, said that Matt's beauty wouldn't last, but they were wrong. The older Matt got, the more his beauty stood him apart. His princely blond locks turned a lovelier, darker shade, his face filled out, and as the other boys grew out of their bodies and sprouted pimples, Matt kept his clear skin and soft firmness even as he stayed fourth tallest in his class at Greenwich Country Day.

Matt had his choice of prep schools, but he liked living at home, so he went to Greenwich High, where he was assigned to Folsom House. There he came to understand that the boys who most wanted to be around him also liked to see him naked. Since he was a natural athlete—a midfielder in fall soccer and a pitcher for the baseball team—they got their chance to glimpse him in the locker room before and after practice. Matt liked to have other boys watch him, and, he soon came to realize, desire him. Not just horny desire, like when Matt and a couple of friends would pull down their pants and wank themselves or each other, but real desire: The kind that disrupted young lives, the kind that—Matt knew—with just a glance or a kind word from him, could cause a boy to sputter, lose his balance or his attention. Or, at the very least, set the boy's cheeks ablaze with crimson.

After being convinced that a boy's desire was real, that the boy was losing sleep because of his desire for him, Matt would give himself to the boy, no matter who he was, what he looked like, or what others thought of the boy. These couplings were wildly passionate, but for Matt they were pretend passion, because Matt never felt for these boys what they felt for him.

Of course, each of these boys, thinking Matt's passion was real, was destroyed when Matt would have nothing more to do with him. For them, Matt became a snob, a conceited bastard. But Matt just wanted to love someone as those boys loved him, to desire someone so deeply that a mere glance would turn Matt to jelly.

At the end of ninth grade, a girl he didn't know actually threw herself at him during an assembly. She was so stung by his rebuff—"I'd rather die!" he said, though he immediately wished he hadn't—that she burst into tears, collapsed to the floor, and had to be taken to a hospital, where she remained for two years.

In 11th grade, a slip of a boy named Jamie Peterson attached himself to Matt. Jamie's family had moved to Greenwich hoping to put a stop to the adulterous affairs of his father, the CEO of a giant media company.

Matt felt bad for Jamie, but his attempt to befriend him made matters even worse: Jamie fell harder for Matt than anyone else ever had. Whenever he could, he found Matt and followed him—or tried to. He attended Matt's soccer practices, his eyes following only Matt, and lustily cheered whenever Matt got anywhere near the ball. Matt put up with it until one day, in the hallway between classes, Jamie dropped to his knees before Matt and began to recite one of Shakespeare's love sonnets. Matt asked him to stop, and then asked him again, and still Jamie went on. That's when Matt lost his temper. In a barely controlled whisper that silenced the students and teachers gathered in the hall, Matt said, "I'm not in love with you, Jamie. I'm sorry, but I'm not. Now would you please just leave me alone." After a horrified silence, Jamie, through his tears, said, "Someday I hope you fall in love with someone you can't have, just so you know how it feels."

Of course, Matt did fall in love. And when he fell, he fell hard.

"There's something in the mail for you, dear," Matt's mother called from the kitchen when she heard Matt come through the back door.

"No, is there really?" Matt said.

"I put it on the breakfast table."

Matt dropped his books on the kitchen counter and, stumbling over his golden retriever, Robby, leaped into the breakfast room just as his books went sprawling all over the floor. Ignoring his books, which he knew his mother would pick up, he grabbed the envelope and tore it open.

"Mom, I got it! I got it! I passed. I got my license!" He was jumping up and down as he came back into the kitchen. "Oh, can I take the Porsche, please, please, please."

Matt's mother had a hard time refusing him anything. Even though he was smiling that smile that always won her over, she remembered how firm her husband had been about this issue. She said, "Why don't you take the Expedition?"

"I don't want to take the Expedition. Oh, please, can't I drive the Porsche?" Matt hugged and squeezed his mother, rendering her helpless to turn down his request. "That's not fair," she said. Matt wriggled. "Please, please, please."

Weakening, his mother said, "You know what your father said about the Porsche."

"Yeah, but you know what Dad's like. And he won't be back till Saturday. Just this once, please can't I take the Porsche? Just a little drive? Please. I just got my license. He won't find out. And I promise, I'll never ask you again."

Matt's mother crossed her arms and shook her head no. Matt looked around the kitchen and focused on the vase of daffodils his mother had picked while he was at school. "Are those from the garden? They're beautiful."

"They're from the ones we planted on the hillside."

"You didn't think they'd grow there, but I told you they would."

"You did, didn't you." Joanna glanced at her beautiful son—at his pouting lips, which she hated to see—then turned her attention back to the daffodils and lazily moved a couple of the stems. "OK," she said, "but just this once."

"Oh, Mom!" Matt grabbed his mother and kissed her hard.

"Half hour's all you get."

Matt whooped gleefully as he leaped sideways across the kitchen. "Oh, thank you, thank you, thank you. Thank you so much, Mom," he said, then he grabbed the keys and was out the back door.

The leather seat was cold, but after he turned the key and the engine kicked in, Matt didn't notice. He smiled at the roar of power at his control. He backed out of the garage, drove around the circle once and honked to his mother, who stood at the back door, waving. He drove out the long driveway at a reasonably slow speed.

Knowing his mother could hear his acceleration, Matt began

his drive as if she were sitting beside him. But the Porsche was so responsive to the little hills and sweet curves of the roads of Greenwich and New Canaan that Matt, amazed at how well he could drive, sped up. He was just driving, happily going nowhere, thrilled at the way the Porsche responded to his touch, when he saw a sign for the entrance to the Connecticut Turnpike.

Since he'd gone with his father to buy the Porsche he'd always wanted to see how fast it could go. Turning left onto the entrance to the turnpike, he floored the accelerator. The response was instantaneous—a little too instantaneous: the Porsche fish-tailed on the sandy roadway. Matt corrected his trajectory, steering into the skid and letting up on the accelerator, the way his father had shown him. Giddy and terrified at the Porsche's power, he floored it again. The sudden surge of power pushed Matt back into his seat. The tachometer redlined, dropped, redlined again, as the speedometer swept past 50, 60, 70.

Matt was doing 95 when he first thought to check for state troopers. But because he'd neglected to adjust the rearview mirror, what he saw when he glanced into the small silver pool was his own face. A shiver went down his spine, because he'd never before seen such beautiful eyes. Or lashes or brows. He was entranced by the golden glow of his own cheeks and the astonishing smoothness of his skin. No one else had hair so lovely or lips so inviting. Never before had Matt seen such beauty. He was so captivated, so deeply lost in the blush of first love, that he didn't see the flashing lights of the patrol car speeding up behind him, and he didn't see the fat man waving wildly for him to avoid the green van stalled just ahead in the middle of his lane.

Fatal accidents always slow traffic. But this accident—whether because of the gruesome sight of the accordioned Porsche or the thousands of daffodils that had tumbled from the overturned delivery van—*stopped* traffic.

Derelict

Steve Berman

Bravey Boy stood where strawberries had once grown. He nudged the earth with the toe of his worn sneaker, disturbing some brown weeds and cigarette butts. October in Philadelphia could be fickle. Wearing a jacket, he left the tenement building he lived in , but as the sky darkened the air turned warmer, and he unzipped the jacket to let the sweat cool on a bare chest the color of dark coffee.

Some years back a community garden had filled the lot where he stood. Nothing grand—just a plot large enough to bring local folks together to plant a few greens and build a place for the kids to play safely. Then six months ago, the mayor chanted "Safe Streets" to every news camera, paper, and council meeting. The cops went out to the corners, forcing the dealers elsewhere; they had found the garden an earthly delight where they could lounge about during the daylight and sell at night. Parents boycotted the garden and kept their children away, and the lot quickly fell into despair. When some other crime crisis drew the politician's attention, the cops returned the corners back to their rightful owners.

Thus an entire city block had been abandoned by everyone. Now nothing grew there but some withered brush and a couple of sickly trees next to the rusty fence. Then came the men and boys, looking for sex—yet another commerce of addiction.

Bravey heard the usual sounds of the night: hip-hop music banging as a car floated by, someone somewhere yelling, a bloody fight between feral dogs. A breeze blew past, bringing with it a deep, musky odor—a touch of old sweat on an unwashed body. Bravey closed his eyes and shook his head even as he breathed in deeply. *Please*, he thought to himself. *Not him, not tonight.*

A muttered "Yo, my brotha" came from behind him. The scent intensified. He turned around to see Demonte shuffling up to him.

He hadn't seen Demonte in over a week. The boy didn't look so good. His left eye was swollen shut, blood encrusted one nostril, and a limp robbed the blatino's strut of its usual swagger. Yet he swung his arm around Bravey as if nothing were wrong.

"What's up?" Bravey kept his tone steady and cool, though in his head he urged Demonte to move on and get lost. If Lashon saw them standing there, he might get cold feet.

Demonte shrugged. "Same shit." His breath smelled sickly sweet, like cheap, flavored wine. He reached over to tug lightly at Bravey's jacket, revealing more of his smooth, toned chest. "Heh, what have we here?" Fingers scuttled over one nipple.

"Don't," Bravey growled as he slapped Demonte's hand away from him.

"Oh, am I not good enough a lay for you?" Demonte plucked at the grungy 76ers jersey he wore. "Didn't complain on your first fuck."

A few months ago Bravey Boy could not stop staring at Demonte whenever he saw him around the neighborhood. He admired every bit of muscle that the young man's shorts and wifebeater revealed, and he ached to see the muscles that they obscured.

One night he got up the nerve to follow Demonte on his nightly rounds. After a winding route through some rough areas, Demonte finally ended up at the derelict garden. An old man seated on a bench muttered a greeting, and when Bravey looked down at him he saw the man's hands busy below the belt. That almost sent him running. But he didn't want to lose track of Demonte, so he didn't break his stride.

It took him awhile to navigate the garden; in the dark it seemed to expand to the size of a football field. Here and there he glimpsed men standing or sitting about. He felt their eyes on him, which made him tremble.

He found Demonte leaning against the thin trunk of a sorry-looking willow. One of the brother's hands lifted up his shirt, obscuring half the marijuana leaf emblazoned on it, to scratch at his flat belly and offer a peek of the waistband of the boxer shorts he wore.

Demonte nodded at Bravey, who forced himself to walk over to the object of his obsession.

"Yo, didn't know they let little boys in here," Demonte said.

If the guy hadn't been grinning as he said it, Bravey might have been hurt instead of slightly stung. He unconsciously took a step back.

"Don't leave. Come closer." Demonte reached out and took hold of one of the younger boy's belt loops and pulled Bravey toward him. The boy's arms went up and his hands landed squarely on Demonte's chest. The heat from the solid muscle coursed over Bravey's fingers, making him sweat and yearn.

"So what do you want to do?" Demonte asked.

Bravey felt his face burn. "I-I don't know." His mouth was dry, and the words came out as a hoarse whisper.

Demonte laughed, took hold of one of Bravey's hands by the wrist, and led him to some bushes. The boy noticed how the guy's pants and boxers slid down to show just a glimpse of his ass crack. Bravey swallowed hard. He was surprised how turned-on he was by the strangeness of the situation and how quickly it was unfolding.

Behind the cover of vegetation Demonte roughly pulled Bravey to the ground. Bravey suddenly grew scared, worried that the guy had been playing him all the time and now planned to beat the shit out of him. A dead faggot—in this neighborhood, who would care?

But instead of pounding Bravey's face, Demonte deftly undid the zipper of his jeans.

A moment later Demonte's warm, wet mouth engulfed Bravey's dick. Bravey squirmed in the dirt and bit his lip. He didn't want to cry out and let everyone in the garden know what was happening to him.

Then it stopped. Bravey looked up to see Demonte tugging his own pants down. Amid a forest of black hair, a thick cock pushed out of its sheath to wag at him. It leaked a strand of goo that caught the moonlight and turned silver before breaking.

"Have to get it wet," Demonte said as he manipulated Bravey's dick toward his furry crack. He grunted a few times, eyes closed, as the tip went in, and then he sat down, forcing the boy deep inside him.

If Demonte's mouth had been intense, his ass was a thousand times hotter, tighter, more demanding. Demonte rode him hard and slapped his chest. Neither of them lasted long, and when the sex was over, they lay in a sweaty, sticky heap until their breathing returned to normal.

Demonte didn't date or even fuck the same guy regularly. That had been made clear in the awkward aftermath of their encounter.

Still, that knowledge didn't stop Bravey Boy from finding his way back to the garden in the hope that he might change the guy's mind. But he was dissed, ignored, and ended up just jerking off by himself in the dark while he listened to someone else get laid.

Bravey promised himself that he was done with the garden—told himself just forget about it—but two nights later he was lying on the old mattress in his room thinking about what happened with Demonte in the garden. He tried to close his eyes and fall asleep, but his ceaseless thoughts wouldn't let him. So he threw on some clothes and sneaked out past his snoring grandma's bedroom door. He cursed himself with every step he took toward the garden, but he knew he had to go back.

He didn't find Demonte there, but an older guy in his 30s with construction-worker muscles approached him. Bravey wanted to kiss the man—to see if the man's goatee would tickle his face—but the man made it clear he only wanted to suck Bravey off. Bravey let him.

So it went. Bravey's craving was always satisfied too quickly after a trip to the garden, leaving him with a lingering need for something more. Bravey couldn't put a name to the need until Lashon, the new stock boy, bumped into him while he was on a break from bagging groceries.

Bravey couldn't step outside 'cause it was raining. Instead he wandered down the chips aisle to find himself a snack. That's when he saw the boy with a linebacker's build humming to himself as he carefully arranged bags of salty pork rinds. As Bravey watched, wasting precious fractions of his 15 minutes of freedom from ringing up cold raw chicken and boxes of mac and cheese, the stock boy paused in mid hum to sing the words of his tune in a high, sweet voice. Not some rap song but an old R&B hit Bravey's grandmother listened to on the radio.

The stock boy saw Bravey staring at him and smiled and nodded hello. He kept on shelving salty snack foods and humming despite the wary looks the other people in the aisle gave him.

Every day after work for the next week, Bravey and Lashon hung out, sipping soda and chatting. Bravey had never been so excited to come to work. Being with Lashon made Bravey feel alive. He wanted to sing songs of his own and learn to move to the new rhythm going through his head.

But at night, before he could find sleep, the worries started. He endlessly replayed every moment he spent with Lashon, trying to figure out if this look or that gesture or some word the fine boy had said meant that Lashon liked him too. More than liked. Did he ache too? Not knowing the answer drove Bravey crazy.

That was why Bravey had a fight with his manager, who told him to go home early. Lashon saw Bravey leaving in a huff and followed him, risking his own job to find out what happened. Bravey could barely find words through the fog of his rage, and suddenly, magically, Lashon was giving him a hug—in the parking lot, for everyone to see. The hug wasn't one of those quick slaps on the back or squeeze-and-release jobs either. Lashon held Bravey tight and softly sang in his ear: "If I have to sleep on your doorstep, all night and day...just to keep you from walkin' away. Let your friends laugh, even this I can stand...'cause I wanna keep you any way I can."

On the walk home Bravey didn't see the dilapidated buildings or the trash on the street or notice the dealers and drunks lazily lounging to pass the day. All he knew was the sensation of Lashon holding him, the smell of the boy, and the sound of his gentle voice.

Nervous as all hell—maybe he had misread the boy's meaning—he called Lashon that night. He told Lashon how to get to the old garden.

Demonte didn't seem ready to leave. He stepped so close that Bravey could feel the heat rising off the brotha's body. Coupled with the smell, the experience was like standing in a dump in July. Demonte smirked. "I know you remember it." He reached down, grabbed hold of Bravey's crotch, and expertly rubbed with his thumb the tip of the shaft to make it grow bigger. "See, this remembers me too."

The touch made Bravey gasp. He felt unsteady and leaned toward Demonte. Their heads touched. The guy's forehead felt damp and feverish. Bravey lifted an arm and laid it on Demonte's bare shoulder.

"Please," he muttered.

"Please what?" Demonte said, aping Bravey's voice. He started to slide his other hand into Bravey's jacket.

Bravey wasn't sure what to say. He no longer wanted whatever quick fix Demonte offered. Yet the old cravings could not be denied. When he heard the familiar whistle and saw in the darkness a figure walking toward them, the desire that had overtaken him turned to nauseating fear and shame. He pushed Demonte away with both arms.

The approaching figure turned out not to be Lashon—just a man dressed in overalls that had seen much better days. He looked the boys over with goggle eyes. "Any you boys want to party?" He held up a paper bag with the tip of a dark amber bottle showing at the top.

Demonte turned back to Bravey. His voice was low and dangerous. "Come on, one more time. You can ride me good—hard as you like." He slid down his baggy pants a little, showing where the trail of wiry hair led. "Let you bust a nut in me."

The man piped in with a desperate bleat, "Let me watch that shit at least."

"Get the fuck outta here," Bravey said to both of them.

Demonte's face fell. For once he wasn't a cocky young man but a scared little boy. The drunken man wobbled unsteady. "There's me," he said, looking hungrily at Demonte. He took a long sip at whatever was in the bag.

"Yeah, yeah," Demonte said as he grabbed hold of the man's arm. "Too bad, papí," he said to Bravey.

Bravey watched them walk away. In the moonlight it looked like Demonte's feet never touched the ground as he led the man deep into the garden. Bravey let out a long sigh, not realizing how tense he had just been. He started pacing back and forth, worried that Lashon wouldn't show, but the figure that approached him was the stock boy.

Bravey didn't bother with the usual greeting. Instead he hugged Lashon tightly, then eased into him and relaxed in the other boy's arms.

"This is some strange place," Lashon said, shaking his head. "Two guys came up to me lookin' to hook up. Freaks."

Bravey saw the look of disgust on Lashon's face and knew he had been wrong to ask Lashon to come to the garden. What had he been thinking? What did he want from this boy? Just a fast grope or a blow or a fuck in the dirt? No, none of that, not with this boy. Just a smile from him would be enough of a thrill to let Bravey end the night feeling satisfied.

Lashon must think me a ho, Bravey thought. "Yeah, you don't belong here," he said. Bravey hated himself and wondered whether he should just send the boy away. How could he deserve someone as fine as Lashon?

But his friend suddenly chuckled. "Like you do? Shit, look at this." Lashon gestured at Bravey's clothes. "You acting all sexy for me?" He laughed. "Trying to make me think you like me or somethin'?"

"No," Bravey lied, looking away. He could no longer meet the other boy's gaze. He backed up a few feet and then found himself walking away. He cursed himself for even thinking something good could ever happen in this wretched garden.

"Wait up. Why you leavin'?" Lashon called as he started after Bravey.

Bravey shrugged and kept walking. He didn't know what to say anymore. The two boys passed an overturned barbecue grill that was slowly becoming a rusted hulk. Not far from it a man lay on the ground.

"Damn," Lashon said. He nudged the guy with his foot, but the man didn't move.

Bravey saw the familiar paper bag wrapped around the brown bottle that leaned against the barbeque. The guy's pants were undone but hadn't been pulled down yet. He stank like sour milk and rotten meat. Demonte was nowhere to be seen.

"He's just drunk," Bravey said out loud. In truth, he wasn't so sure.

"This is some park," Lashon muttered.

"I'm sorry I asked you to come here."

"I'm not." Lashon cupped Bravey's chin with his fingers.

"No?" Bravey didn't dare smile, afraid that maybe he had heard wrong.

"Unless that's all you want." He pointed at the man on the ground. "What everyone else 'round here wants. I'm not trash and I won't be treated like it."

Bravey shook his head. "It's cool. I mean, I want..."

Lashon smiled and chuckled again. "Wanna go get somethin' to eat with me?"

Bravey nodded. Buttoning up his jacket, he was suddenly embarrassed by how much skin he showed.

"Cool," Lashon said. Together they headed back to the edge of the garden, walking so close and slow that every now and then they lightly bumped against one another. Lashon pulled out car keys and flicked them playfully into the air. Bravey reached to catch them but only managed to knock them to the ground.

"S'all right," Lashon said as he bent down to pick them up. "Damn," he said. He plucked something small and red from a clump of green near his foot.

Bravey looked at the strawberry the boy held up. Lashon smiled and lifted it to Bravey's lips. He opened his mouth. The tiny thing tasted like Elsewhere—sweet and strong. It lifted him away.

"How does it taste?" Lashon asked.

Bravey Boy leaned in and showed Lashon.

Feast

Lou Dellaguzzo

Merle sits near the Jesuits, about five in all. He likes listening to their catty chatter, glad he doesn't know the people getting skewered. A jukebox nearby thumps out an old disco tune. Resonant and nasally, the Jesuits' voices glide over the music. Their dramatic gestures add even more delight to Merle's Saturday evening diversion.

He enjoys the irony of sitting in a Greenwich Village gay bar, listening to the holy men's ferocious gossip. Merle considers the scene a minor validation. *That could be me*, he thinks. *If I could've stood the hypocrisy.*

Two brothers in the group—once his professors at college more than a decade ago—don't recognize Merle. They even cruised him when they first sat down.

Always was a quiet student, he thinks. And he has changed physically. The tall, scrawny body has been replaced by a hard, muscular one. His long red hair is clipped short. Peach fuzz on his face long ago thickened to a rich chestnut shadow. Even his slight nose has grown a little.

Who was that college boy anyway? Merle wonders. He scans the room, sees a couple guys he isn't interested in but who Cole at the other end is talking to. Theater guys—like Cole, but without his kindness, his genuine friendliness. Merle waits out the conversation. He suspects Cole has seen him and will work his way over eventually. When Cole is ready.

After his two acquaintances take their leave to scope the bar, Cole stays put, nursing his drink. He ponders what to do about Merle. How might he reach the guy; get Merle past the hang-ups he won't discuss? Cole wants to keep trying. But he'd like to see some possibility, its promise even. He doesn't want to risk the friendship—still green in its first season—by maybe scaring Merle away, making him think he won't relent, won't let the relationship settle into easy knowing, nothing more.

He wants to take special care. Cole has lost too many friends recently. Some have moved far away. Other friends—their ambitions beyond achievement, their bodies aging ungracefully—have grown too bitter for Cole to stand or have simply disappeared. A few friends have died in ways too sad to remember. Not with a drink in his hand.

Take it slow, he thinks, looking up from the bar and gazing at Merle. Cole waits for acknowledgment—an encouraging light from Merle's green eyes.

"Did you catch how those guys looked at me when I suggested going to the Feast? As if I asked you to visit a garbage dump—hey, watch it." Like a school safety guard, Cole blocks Merle from risking the long walk across Houston Street against the light. Merle doesn't pay much attention to traffic. Cole wonders how his friend manages to stay alive walking alone. He doesn't know that Merle lets Cole lead when they're together—a discreet form of closeness.

"They're Jesuits," Merle answers. "Prissy ones at that—if I'm not being redundant. Two of them were my profs at college. You wouldn't recognize them in a classroom. Very reserved. And their voices—maybe an octave lower." Merle doesn't mention that, as a freshman, he once contemplated the priesthood. But only briefly. By the end of his sophomore year he had become an agnostic—although he continues to attend Mass to experience liturgical ritual, breathe the alchemical incense. The words and smells help him recall a childhood belief in magic and relive the comfort it once brought.

Merle regrets ever mentioning his passing vocation to his family. Years later his change of heart still roils his mother when she thinks of it: "Christ's great gift to the family—the family's great gift to Christ. Abandoned."

"Those smells," Merle says as they enter Little Italy proper, catching a strong whiff of foods drenched in cheap fat. "They make me hungry and nauseous all at once." He smiles up at Cole, half a foot taller. Merle himself reaches 5 foot 11.

Cole pulls a face. "Looks like a *pick your poison* situation," he says, studying the makeshift food stalls, the slatternly purveyors. "I'm game if you are." He brushes fine blond bangs from his forehead. His large hand wanders down a brown mustache, a beard neatly trimmed to follow the sharp jawline.

Now that Cole has abandoned his spotty acting career, he can indulge a preference not to shave. Directors don't care what an aspiring playwright looks like. *No more second-guessing*, Cole had thought, relieved not to have to worry about his appearance during every audition, hoping he had the ineffable "right look." With playwriting, only the layered meanings of words matter. Cole has three different ideas for a play. If he could just get past the outline stage.

Merle examines a glutinous cheesy dish. It bares no resemblance to the real Italian cooking he enjoyed during his summer in Rome after grad school—his summer of freedom, adventure. With two hands, the stall worker can barely scrape her spatula under the burned, unidentifiable glob before she places an oozing slice on a customer's plate. Merle's stomach gets queasy.

"We should just walk around. People-watch." He decides to suggest a late dinner in SoHo. Something Asian.

Cole will oblige, as he does any of Merle's suggestions. Then Merle will take the long subway ride back to Woodside, Queens. Alone. Back to his aging mother, more fretful than ever about her eternal soul, about how the neighborhood—once an Irish-American enclave—has become "an immigrants' Tower of Babel." Merle has never liked the place more. The bustling commercial areas, filled with international shops and restaurants, stay active late into the night. His new street neighbors—Koreans, Pakistanis, Uzbeks—make him feel like a curious newcomer to his own birthplace. Helps relieve the quiet, steady desperation of his home life.

"This is nothing like the state fairs I went to in Milwaukee," Cole says. "Mostly the hawkers sold standard junk food. You know, hot dogs, burgers. And cotton candy—which my mom never liked me to eat. Called it 'tooth rot on a stick.' "

"Bet you had some anyway," Merle says, regarding Cole's erect figure covered in a burgundy sweatshirt and white carpenter's pants flapping over worn sneakers.

"Sure did—along with some of Mom's homemade pickles she entered in a contest every year. Liked the sweet 'n' sour effect, I guess. So did my brother. Cotton candy and pickles." Cole shakes his head. "Mom wouldn't even look at us while we ate them."

"Did she ever win?" Merle asks. "A pickling contest."

"Don't think so." Cole's voice grows softer. "No." *Never won much of anything*, he thinks, recalling his mom's difficult life as a single parent—her disastrous choice for a second husband during Cole's last year in high school. His older brother—long settled in Vancouver—still keeps in touch with their mom and stepfather. Maybe twice a year he writes Cole about the couple's latest setback, which usually involves a major tumble off the wagon.

Sometimes Cole considers a family reconciliation—especially around the more sappy holidays. But he keeps his distance. He can barely manage for himself in New York. If he can't help back in Milwaukee, he'd rather steer clear. Otherwise, he'd just feel more useless. Then he'd start overindulging himself. Misery all around.

"All this small talk." Cole didn't mean to say this aloud.

"What?" Merle stops walking. He looks hurt.

"Sorry," Cole apologizes quickly. "Got to thinking about other things. Bad memories." He grabs Merle by his long, sinewy neck, draws him close. "I'm enjoying myself, Merle. With you. I always have." He sees Merle's discomfort. Cole hasn't touched his reserved companion this affectionately before. Not in public.

"Sorry," Cole says, this time apologizing for the physical intimacy. But in his own defense: "You confuse me, Merle. Sometimes. I don't know where this is going." *There, I said it*, Cole thinks.

Merle makes like he didn't hear.

The two of them wander westward to the outskirts of the Feast. Here they find more space: some relief from pungent odors and deafening noises that echo along the teeming, grungy streets turned gaudy with multicolored lights hanging above.

Maybe it's better to talk about our friendship like this, Cole muses. *In a crowd.*

Whenever he brings up the subject with Merle in a quiet place—an intimate restaurant, at Cole's doorstep—Merle withdraws. He puts on a sad smile, and his bright eyes go blank. The ensuing silence leaves Cole in limbo until he switches to a more neutral topic.

To hell with neutral, Cole thinks. "I'd like to shake you sometimes," he says without heat. "Not to hurt you. Just wake you up. Make you come out of hiding—from what I don't know."

Merle laughs and jostles his friend. "Come on. Don't get melodramatic on me. Remember—you're a serious writer now. Not an actor."

"Don't make fun." Cole slouches from his great height, defensive about his new vocation—the blank pages that await inspiration, some vision Cole imagines would come easier if he had gone to college. "I want to accomplish something creative. Something that lasts. It's not too late." And then he can't help himself: "Christ, if *I* had a graduate degree, you wouldn't see *me* wasting my life in some backroom office, messing around with invoices and bills. Oh, shit. I'm sorry."

Merle laughs. "That's your *third* apology," he says, untroubled by Cole's critique—his summary—of Merle's professional life; his *anti*-vocation, as Merle sees it. "Three strikes, buddy."

"I didn't mean it."

"Yeah, you did." Merle lightly jabs his friend's shoulder. "You have a good point. I do lead a thoroughly ridiculous life. But there it is, Cole. Mine to live, as I wish."

"Never said 'ridiculous,'" Cole murmurs, feeling worse—and

a little suspicious his friend has used the faux pas to avoid another discussion about their friendship. And Cole's desire to make it something more.

"It's not you; it's me," Merle had said when Cole first broached the subject. Cole had heard that unconvincing line before, more so as the years went by. But when he looked hard at Merle, Cole believed him—could divine an amorphous, spectral damage in those green eyes, the tight jaw that would grind large white teeth now and then. When certain subjects came up. Sex especially. Merle and sex in particular.

Strangely, his friend's existential hurt encourages Cole. The rejection wasn't personal after all. Once they got to know each other, became fast friends, Cole believed he would find a way past Merle's inhibition. Break down his defenses with trust. Trust is everything.

Cole sees it first: the bullying. A small, young guy with wavy brown hair—his features stretched to a vicious sneer—threatens another guy smaller still. Wide eyes shine with terror as the shorter, less muscular kid looks around for help. The crowd dynamic works against him. These people, headed for the Feast, have another street show in mind. They make like nothing's happening.

Poor kid, Cole thinks. All he did was bump against the punk accidentally—his apology unaccepted.

Cole had seen it all. Moments before the mishap he had noticed the beleaguered boy, his angelic features aglow in smooth olive skin. The kid, barely a teenager, had been smiling then, expectation animating his oval face and his intelligent eyes. A pleasure to watch. Until the youth's fun evening turned into a potential nightmare.

Not tonight, Cole thinks. He can't walk by as the punk grabs his quarry's shirt, knocking the frightened boy against a wall, threatening him with a beer bottle half empty. *It's always booze*, Cole thinks, recalling his stepfather's bullying outbursts—habitually directed at younger, weaker males.

Cole knows how to work the situation. He got lots of practice protecting his smaller, older brother from the family interloper.

Cole's muscular 6-foot-5 frame makes him a persuasive peacemaker. Only once did he have to get physical with his stepfather, decking the man with wrestling skills that routinely won Cole trophies in school. That night the embarrassed drunk—puking on the carpet from his exertions—never realized his luck. He almost got his nose crushed against his blotchy face.

"That's enough," Cole says, reaching from behind the young punk. Like a vise his hand grips the kid's wrist, squeezing the bone with wide fingers. The bottle crashes to the ground. Beer splatters on the punk's black jeans and his gray sneakers. One look at Cole—his height, his breadth—and the kid swallows his threatening words.

Instead he says, "Fuck, man. You got me all wet. I hate to get wet." His breath smells of beer and too many cigarettes.

Wordless, the young victim backs away. He makes for the crowd—some police he remembers seeing a few blocks ahead—afraid to stay behind and thank Cole, paranoid his huge rescuer might have bad intentions himself. After all, this is New York.

Taking flight, the boy rams Merle by accident. They gaze at each other briefly. Merle helps the kid steady himself before the lithe child's body recoils, then retreats behind a shifting curtain of revelers a block away. The encounter rattles Merle. He knows that boy. Has seen him every day. Mostly in the mornings, when Merle stares at his yellowing dresser mirror in a panic, composing himself to face another day, to find comfort—joy, even—in the steady sameness of a life unlived. A life he has chosen.

"You're not going anywhere yet," Cole says. He keeps a steady grip as the punk—seeing his victim escape—grows angrier, keen to avenge his humiliation but losing an exploitable target. Reflexively the youth makes a fist with his free hand. He draws it back. "That would be your worst mistake," Cole says, clenching his free hand, banging it hard against a heavy plastic garbage can, its handle chained to a rail. Like a thin cracker, the dense, black lid buckles in half, plunging into the pail.

"Let me go, man." The punk takes care not to sound threatening. He wants to spit in fury at the ground, but his mouth, dry from fear and booze, can't manage a drop.

Cole maintains his grip. Silent, the kid grasps he won't get hurt if he behaves and bides his time. *What a waste*, Cole thinks, gazing at the guy's brown eyes filigreed with gold, his delicate features, coarsened—made less human—by meanness. He muses briefly about the shadow's dark, probably banal, source. *Not my problem*, Cole concludes.

Yet the situation disorients him—standing at the periphery of a sleazy fete, holding a hostile stranger against his will. And the young boy he helped? Cole has trouble recollecting his face. Gone. Only a few minutes have passed since he interceded. They seem more like several hours—and in a gym. Cole's muscles ache. He looks around for Merle, worried that his companion, disapproving, might've left as well, melding with the indifferent crowd. *How could I have forgotten him?* Cole wonders. As he gazes at Merle's impassive, unreadable face, Cole concedes he doesn't know his friend at all.

Alert to change, the punk considers both men. His feral instincts apprehend a difference other than physical size. A contrast in sensibility. Merle's blank stare—no glint of emotion in his green eyes—infuriates the kid, makes him feel invisible, like when the other boy—smelling of the suburbs, of nurturing—bumped into him.

"You gonna let this thing go?" Cole asks the punk, eager to end the situation, continue his evening with Merle. "Admit you were wrong?" He knows it's a dumb question. The kid probably wants to rip out his heart. Still, Cole needs to hear capitulation, no matter how begrudging.

"Yeah, yeah." The kid sounds dismissive. He won't look Cole in the eye. "I'm over it, man."

Bullshit, Cole thinks, dropping the kid's wrist. "OK," he says. "OK then." He backs off, nods for Merle to follow. The kid's hand tingles with blood let free to flow. It's hard to flex his throbbing fingers, but he won't rub them to show Cole the effect of his powerful grip. He watches the two men head west, further away from the Feast—its crowded periphery. He waits. His anger, festering, demands release. Otherwise, he'll carry his fury home.

Cracked in two on the pavement, the amber bottle sparkles,

an empowering jewel. He can't refuse. The glass neck fits snugly in his square 18-year-old hand, rough from hoisting boxes in a Brooklyn warehouse. A discarded flier hawking the Feast makes an effective bottle sleeve. Its bright print obscures jagged glass.

After he scrubs it with soap and alcohol, Merle sets the plastic foot stool in the tub for Cole to sit on as he bathes. Merle has heard about tenement apartments with bathtubs in kitchens. This is the first one he's seen. Chips and rust stains decorate the tub's surface. Long ago someone, a prior tenant, had painted the thing lime-green—perhaps to match the checkered linoleum worn down to black near the sink and the stove.

"Gimme a hand," Cole says. He edges his beefy ass onto the makeshift bathing chair, lifting his muscular right leg over the high rim into the warm water, where his blond hairs darken and cling to his skin. Cole rests his left leg on a thick blue towel that drapes the tub's splotchy enameled lip. Three toes—their wounds cleaned and stitched and dressed by an emergency room doctor at St. Vincent's—must stay dry until fully healed.

"I have no patience for this kinda stuff," Cole grumbles, pointing to the turbaned foot wrapped in thick white bandages halfway up his arch. "Two weeks! I'm gonna go crazy."

He thinks again about the kid who came after Merle and him from behind with a broken bottle. Cole expects the little punk is still in the ER, getting his jaw wired—*talk about going crazy*—with a policeman standing guard, waiting to take him away and process him.

Cole flexes his right hand. It still hurts. He didn't mean to hit that hard, but the jagged glass had flashed too near Merle's face. Cole had subdued the crazed kid with one deft blow. But then he made the mistake of holding onto his assailant. When Cole let go, the youth—howling in pain, still holding his weapon—collapsed at Cole's feet, where he rammed the broken bottle through one thin sneaker.

"Hey. Pay attention," Merle warns, drawing Cole from his thoughts. "You almost splashed some water on the bandages already."

"See what I mean?" A thin, gray fleck—shaped like a man's face in profile—drops into the tub water. Both men regard the ceiling—its peeling paint hangs at varying lengths from the powdery plaster like miniature stalactites. To Merle, the jagged forms resemble tiny, inverted tombstones. They cast sad shadows against each other. Merle has to look away.

"Rent control," Cole says. He points a dripping finger to the ceiling. "I'm fighting the landlord. By law, he's supposed to paint. A matter of principle," he mumbles unconvincingly, thinking he should've taken that summer repertory job in Massachusetts. Could've fattened his meager bank account. But the company wanted him to serve as fight manager as well—for the more violent plays. Some Shakespeare. A Sam Shepard or two. He never liked that supplementary responsibility. Besides, he didn't want to leave New York, felt sure a television commercial he was set for would tide him over until fall. But he lost the spot, thanks to a last-minute recast.

Some fight manager, Cole thinks, glaring at his bandaged foot again and knowing he'll have to temp soon to pay the more important bills without depleting his savings. Unemployment checks aren't enough.

"Like your back washed?" Merle asks, wanting to rescue his friend's sinking mood. It's been a long night for both of them. No time for Cole to think about money matters.

A broad, crooked smile diffuses Cole's beard, gives subtle glimpses of pale skin beneath. "You bet," Cole answers. He lets the paint chip settle, looks at Merle, expectant—frustrated. He'd have liked this treatment under quite different conditions.

Merle soaps a thin washrag to a froth. Then he hesitates; studies his friend's broad, muscled back. Cole's watchful profile turns toward him, grinning. "I'm waiting, Jeeves," he says with a posh British accent.

Hanging the yellow rag on the tub, not wanting flimsy, rough material to interpose, Merle soaps his hands, rubs them lightly across Cole's smooth, freckled skin. The sensation—sliding, pressing, but not grasping—Merle feels to his spine. Bubbles foam between his long, bony fingers, then disappear.

"Hey, I won't break," Cole jokes, dropping the accent. "You gotta rub hard to draw the tension away," although the reverse occurs. Merle's touch becomes stronger, brisker, and charges Cole with its equivocal intimacy. Its potential. "Hmmm. Much better." Like a large dog getting his stomach rubbed, Cole makes deep, grateful noises.

He's just a big kid, Merle thinks. *In some ways.* Despite Cole's assured street moves, his surprising prowess, Merle has a new appreciation for his friend's vulnerability, his need of caring. The contrast charms him—he finds it irresistible. Evocative. "Thanks, by the way," he says, needing to escape his reverie.

"For what?"

"For keeping me from getting scarred for life. Would've thanked you sooner, but I was angry with you."

"Oh yeah?"

"For putting me in danger to begin with."

Cole turns to Merle. It's uncomfortable, awkward, to twist his body with one leg dangling over the tub. His eyebrows rise at sharp, parallel angles, knotting his smooth, high forehead. "Yeah. Guess you're right," he says hollow-voiced. Cole turns away quickly, and his elevated foot nearly slips into the tub. "Sorry," he apologizes, dazed by the way Merle made his spirits soar—then sink—all in a few seconds.

"To be frank," Merle says casually, "since the fight turned out OK—except for your foot—I'm kind of glad it happened. If it *had* to happen in the first place."

Cole would like to know why. He's reluctant to ask, afraid Merle will make him feel worse; perhaps use the evening—the thoughtful attentions—as a kiss-off. *Maybe that's not the best term*, Cole thinks bitterly, *since we've never kissed.* All his patience, his effort, wasted.

"Back at the Feast," Cole says, approaching his friend's disclosure obliquely. "During the first encounter with the kid. When I turned around to look for you and saw your face. I felt I didn't know you. Like you were a stranger. Well, practically. The way you stared at me. And the kid. As if we were a different species, you know? Objects of study." Cole picks at the paint chip that has settled at the bottom of his tub. Partially dissolved—no longer resembling a man's profile—the chip has adhered to coarsened enamel. "I couldn't read anything," Cole continues. "In your face.

"For a moment, I thought you would leave me. Just take off—like that kid I helped. Sounds crazy now. But at that same moment, I thought of Don Quixote. Played him one *long* summer in Jersey," Cole explains. "Could even feel the itchy gray beard and eyebrows glued to my face." He peers at Merle, who sees confusion—and accusation—in his hazel eyes, puffy with fatigue. "Your blank stare," Cole says. "It made me feel alone. Kind of crazy, delusional—like the Don. You didn't reassure me as I had expected."

Cole's neck is sore from craning it. Reaching over his shoulder, he grabs Merle's hand and draws his friend to the front of the tub so the two men can face each other. "Guess I owe you another apology," Cole says. "For telling you this."

Merle bends for the soap bar he left behind Cole. It slips from his hand, plunging into the gray water. He fishes it up and starts sudsing his hands vigorously. Soapy rivulets glide down his forearms. Merle wipes them off on his thick plaid shirt. "Glad you told me," he finally says, pantomiming with minimal gestures that he wants to wash Cole's chest and arms. All of him.

"I can do that," Cole says, reluctant to overburden, yet hoping the task might please them both.

"Yeah. But I *want* to." Merle's smile—indulgent, teasing—masks his emotional upheaval.

"Fine with me," Cole says. Then: "Thanks." Still unable to read Merle, his intentions—if he has any—Cole decides to follow his friend's lead. Wherever it takes them.

"Just relax. You don't have to talk," Merle says. The suggestion implies a request. Cole stays mum. He leans back, enjoys his friend's touch, feeling Merle's strong, large hands soap his body—taking time. Each thoughtful stroke evokes the significance of ritual. *But what kind?* Cole wonders.

And Merle's face—his gaze. It seems divided—here yet elsewhere. *Don't get picky,* Cole scolds himself. *This is really nice. Good enough.*

How different Cole's solid body feels to Merle. How distinct from Johnny's diminished frame, the slack parchment skin Merle had bathed nightly for nearly a year—then soothed with prescription lotions to avoid dermatitis. Johnny. Johnny Boy.

The battered red stool had sparked the initial reverie when Merle helped Cole sit down for his bath. As Cole gingerly rested his leg, dangling and vulnerable, on the tub's rim, Merle had envisioned Johnny's frail body superimposed over Cole's vital form. Two men—one spectral—shared a bath and a body. The image lasted only a few seconds. Merle had to let it go or leave the apartment, take one of his marathon walks to work off the pain.

As Merle bathes his living, injured friend, Johnny makes a second appearance—more a reassuring memory than a mournful apparition.

It's been three years. Three years since Merle has felt another body this intimately. After Johnny, he didn't want such closeness again. Closeness had left Merle stranded, exhausted, when Johnny's time had come. Half dead but healthy, the survivor lived guilt-ridden over his continuing existence. Johnny appreciated, valued life more, Merle had thought. The wrong man remained.

Yet despite his reserve, his apprehension, Merle finds himself feasting in silence on the long-dormant sensation—touching another man, caring for someone worth the risk of more sorrow, someone who makes life less burdensome. Even pleasurable.

With jittery hands, Merle tries to knead Johnny's ethereal presence into Cole's warm, living skin. Using slow, fervent strokes, he can imagine Johnny's essence melting into Cole's warm, wet body—as the Eucharist melts in a communicant's warm, wet mouth, uniting spirit with flesh. Merle wants to incorporate Johnny's memory, his goodness, as protection.

Can't quite escape the magic, can you? Merle chides himself, despite feeling overwhelmed. *Religious ritual without belief,* he thinks as he keeps on soaping Cole with purifying white froth, working his way down the large, yielding body he can't let go for a moment.

"You OK?" Cole hesitates to ask, watching Merle clean his dangling leg and foot, careful not to wet the dressing. He can't read Merle's nervous focus, the firm, rhythmic press of unsteady hands.

"I'm the one who's sorry," Merle answers, not looking up, not able to face Cole. "I'm the one who should apologize. For always pushing you away when you wanted to get close." Merle sits back on his haunches. His words—his confession—have sapped his energy. Leaning against the tub's rim, Merle places his forehead on Cole's bandaged wound, barely touching the cold whiteness, not wishing to move, afraid of the future—the very next moment even—but knowing he won't go back.

Märchen to a Different Beat

Lawrence Schimel

Hansel pulled a Tootsie Roll from his pocket and undid the wrapper as he watched his sister try to comb the knots from her long brown hair. He popped the dark chocolate into his mouth and threw the crumpled wrapper onto Gretel's vanity.

"I don't know how you manage to eat that stuff all day long and you're still thin as a rail," his sister said, watching him in the mirror as she struggled with her hair. "It's a miracle you have any teeth left."

Hansel was always ravenously eating candy, even if he wasn't hungry. It was his way of coping with the way their stepmother had tried to get rid of them during the famine. Gretel had been bulimic for nearly two years after the incident, as if she hoped she'd become so thin that no one would notice her again. Though they were twins, they had very distinct responses to the traumas they'd suffered together.

"Let me," Hansel said, taking the brush from her. "You're so nervous, your hands are shaking." He pulled the comb gently through her hair, untangling the long silken strands.

"I do wish you'd come to the prom," Gretel said, for what must have been the 40th time. "I'd certainly feel much calmer if you did." She smiled at him in the mirror, making sure he knew she was just teasing with this bit of emotional blackmail, but also hoping it would work anyway.

"You know I don't want to go. I'd feel so left out if I went. Everyone would be there in couples except me, the homo, standing alone in the corner, watching everyone have the time of their lives." Gretel winced as the comb caught in a tangle, and Hansel continued tugging too hard. "Sorry."

Gretel smiled genuinely at him in the mirror. "It's OK."

"Promise you'll tell me all about it when you get home? Especially about Scott. And I mean *every*thing. You know what traditionally happens on prom night. Oh, he's so dreamy—and I'm so jealous. If you weren't my twin sister, I'd probably strangle you!"

The twins shared a laugh, and Gretel promised to tell him everything—yes, even about the sex, if they had any. They shared everything with each other, all their secrets—but then, for so many years, each was all the other had. They were so close that sometimes they almost sensed what the other was thinking or feeling before it was vocalized. They were alike in so many different ways. They even had the same taste in men.

"Gretel!" Their father's voice drifted up the stairs to Gretel's bedroom, interrupting their thoughts and preparations. "He's here!"

"How do I look?" Gretel asked Hansel.

"Gorgeous," Hansel said. And it was true: She was stunning.

The doorbell rang.

"That's him," she said, looking frantically over the top of the vanity for something, anything, she might have forgotten.

"You've done everything already, don't worry," Hansel said. "Just go and have a great time. And don't do anything you're not comfortable with. And tell me all about everything as soon as you get home! Wake me up if you have to!"

They heard the murmur of voices in the front hall—their father's deep double bass and a higher tenor that belonged to Gretel's date.

"I'm so excited!" Gretel whispered, squeezing her brother's hand. "You can still change your mind about coming, you know?"

"You don't let up!" Hansel laughed. "Go and have fun with Mr. Handsome downstairs."

Gretel gave her brother a hug. "I'll miss you," she said. Then she hurried out of the room before he had a chance to reply.

Hansel stayed where he was, listening to her descend the stairs, the appreciative comments Scott paid her, the stern lecture from their father about responsible behavior. He so wanted to be in her shoes right now, to be out on a Big Date like this with a guy he was mad about. To have their conservative, undemonstrative father tell him and his boyfriend to have fun but not to stay out too late, and all the other standard worries and concerns about their general physical and moral well-being.

But then, Hansel had always been a sucker for stories about romance and chivalry and all that. And what better moment for it was there than tonight, prom night?

And what bigger torment for him than being gay? Even a girl who wasn't asked out tonight still had the hope, the dreams, and the stories of generations of girls and boys who'd gone before her. But who ever heard about guys inviting other guys to the Prom, as Hansel so longed would happen to him? It seemed every story he'd ever read was about waiting for Prince Charming to come sweep him off his feet. Or at least to sweep *her* off her feet. But that's who he sympathized with—the girl—waiting for Mr. Right to come along.

"Hansel!" Their father's voice drifted up the stairs again, interrupting his musing. "I'm going over to the Parkers' to watch the game. Want to come along?"

His father was being kind to invite him, even though he knew that Hansel hated watching sports of any sort. "No, thanks, Dad!" Hansel shouted down.

"If you change your mind, you know where to find us."

"Roger and out," Hansel shouted back, just to let his father know that he'd heard.

Alone now in Gretel's empty bedroom, Hansel sat at the vanity where his sister had been moments before. He picked up the silver hand mirror, one of the few objects that had belonged to their birth mother, who died when they were both young. His sister and he looked enough alike that he could pass for her, he thought, with the right hair and clothes and such. He couldn't help thinking that if they'd been born twin girls, he might be going to the prom tonight as well, instead of sitting at home, alone, feeling sorry for himself.

"Oh, I wish..." Hansel began, staring at his reflection in the small silver hand mirror until his tears blurred the image. The words caught in his throat.

Suddenly, from behind him there was a scurry of flashes of light, like a strobe hitting a disco ball. Hansel blinked his eyes and caught a glimpse of another figure reflected in the silver hand mirror. Standing behind him, somehow, was the tallest woman he'd ever seen. She wore a dress made of blue sequins that shimmered in the light from the vanity's row of tiny bulbs.

Hansel spun around on the vanity's chair. "Who—" he began, looking the stranger up and down. She was well over six feet tall, even without heels. "Who are you?"

"You might say I'm your fairy godmother. Or godfather. Or whatever." The stranger spoke with the deepest bass voice Hansel had ever heard. "I'm an old friend of your mother's. I gave her that mirror, in fact, many years back. Anyway, why don't you just call me Mary? I'm your Mary Fairy." Mary threw her hands onto her hips and her elaborately painted lips pursed into a pucker, and Hansel suddenly realized that he was staring at a man in drag. Or a fairy in drag. Or whatever, as the stranger had said.

"A fairy godbeing," Hansel said calmly. He'd faced the fantastic before, so it didn't faze him—not completely, anyway. "Why me?"

Mary sashayed over to the bed and sat down, crossing his legs firmly one over the other and smoothing the taffeta frills of his dress. "Oh, we've been keeping an eye on you two, ever since that episode with the witch and the house of candy. Speaking of candies, you wouldn't happen to have a breath mint on you?"

Hansel rummaged in his pockets and came up with a tin of Altoids.

"You *are* a darling," Mary said, taking two tablets from the tin. His fingernails were at least an inch and a half long, and they were painted an iridescent shade of blue, like the back of some tropical beetle.

Hansel closed the tin and held it in his lap, unsure of what to say or do next.

Mary took the initiative. After all, that's why he was there. "So you want to go to the prom?"

"Yes," Hansel said. "No. Oh, I don't know. I mean, I want to go, but I don't want to go by myself. I don't want to go there and feel so alone, that there's no one else there like me. I mean, I know there are other gay men in the world, but...I want to meet someone my age. Someone who'll love me because of who I am, not because I'm young and cute and then toss me aside when they find someone younger or cuter. Someone who'll understand what it's like."

Hansel was shy about having revealed so much to a complete stranger, but he'd been desperate to talk to someone, someone who cared—and who could maybe help. *Mary said he'd been watching over me anyway*, Hansel thought.

Just how much of his life had Mary watched, Hansel wondered—every moment since the candy house, or just occasionally? Did he watch even when Hansel went to the bathroom? When he was showering? When he masturbated?

Now his self-revelation was forgotten, with newer worries.

"I'll be your date," Mary said, and the matter was decided. He looked at his charge's still-concerned face and placed Hansel's hand in his lap. "I may not be your age, but trust me," Mary said, his voice dropping a register, "I'm definitely male."

It had not been something Hansel had really doubted before, but now he felt the proof in the pudding, as it were. For the first time. He was speechless.

"So, let's see what I have to work with. Stand up."

Hansel, slightly in shock, did as he was bidden.

"Turn around. Hmmm. It's a shame to hide your cute butt with such baggy pants."

Hansel blushed and wondered just how much Mary could see and what he could see through, such as the baggy jeans. He began to feel that embarrassment he felt when he was naked in the locker room, then he realized it didn't matter—there was nothing he could do about it if Mary was indeed able to see through his clothes, as seemed to be the case. That knowledge, while reassuring logically, didn't make him stop blushing, however, as Mary looked him over frankly.

"OK, now let's see the shoes. It's part of the script, you know. What have you got available?"

They both stared down at his sad-looking Reebok sneakers, which had seen better days—years ago.

"Not a moment too soon," Mary said, his judgment final. He stood up, strode elegantly to the door of Gretel's closet, and flung open the doors with a grand flourish. "Come over here," Mary said.

Hansel—still a bit awed by Mary's presence, and also a bit cautious after his last interaction with the supernatural—did as he was told.

"Now, stand in here for a moment," Mary said, fiddling with some of the many bracelets on his long forearms.

Hansel stood where he was and laughed. "I thought a gay fairy godmother would help me come out of the closet, not go into one."

"Very cute, darling. Now, do you want to go to the prom and meet the man of your dreams or not?" Hansel nodded. "Then trust me and do as I ask, thank you."

Hansel stepped into the closet. His heart leaped into his stomach when Mary shut the doors on him, throwing him into complete darkness. Why had he trusted this outlandish, unheralded stranger, who could be as evil as the witch who'd trapped him in a cage and planned to roast and eat him once he was fattened up?

Because he desperately wanted to believe in what this Mary Fairy stood for, that there was hope for a boy like him who loved—or at least wanted to love—other boys.

Suddenly, Hansel felt a hand on him. He screamed and tried to pull away. But there were hands everywhere: hundreds of them, it felt. He had no idea whose they were or how they could even belong to any bodies—there were too many of them atop his body. His panic subsided when he realized the hands weren't hurting him—and that there was nothing he could do to escape them, in any case. Furthermore, he realized that they felt rather pleasurable, rubbing themselves over every square inch of his flesh. He had a raging erection, he noticed, and felt embarrassed by it. He wondered what would happen if Mary chose that exact moment to open the doors.

Which, of course, is what Mary did.

"Very nice," he said, staring down at Hansel, "if I do say so myself."

Hansel glanced down at himself, ready to cross his legs and hide his hard-on with his hands. But it wasn't even visible beneath the dapper black tuxedo with a bright blue cummerbund that matched Mary's dress. He also wore a pair of shiny black dress shoes with a square clear crystal at each buckle—his glass slippers.

Speechless, Hansel crossed to his sister's vanity and stared at his new, ultra-chic image. At first he could hardly believe how sophisticated he looked, then a feeling of overwhelming insecurity gripped him. He reached into his pocket for a piece of candy, but his pockets were empty—not even lint!

"Nice, isn't it?" Mary said. "Now, let's go show you off. Miss Thing doesn't have all night, you know. The prom only runs till midnight, remember."

"What happens at midnight?" Hansel asked, opening drawers in his sister's vanity. He remembered hearing stories of how fairy magic ran out at midnight.

Mary smiled. "Why, then the after-hours bars open, and the fun really starts. Come along—it's time for you to make an entrance." Mary swept out of the room in a cloud of taffeta and sequins.

At last Hansel found what he was looking for: a Hershey bar he'd tucked away as emergency rations. He had similar hiding spots all around the house for just such moments when his own supply ran out. He regretted not having eaten the Gobstopper that had been in his jeans before his magical change of costume, but looking himself over in the mirror, he couldn't argue that he was looking fine in these new threads.

As Hansel followed after Mary, he couldn't help wondering if his twin would recognize him when they showed up—if *anyone* would recognize him, for that matter. Was he making a horrible mistake?

"Hansel," the principal said, standing up from his chair behind the table that blocked the gymnasium entrance. "We didn't expect to see you here."

Hansel looked away from the principal's bespectacled stare, forgetting that he had every right to be there, just like any graduating senior. He glanced down at the fancy clothes he wore and knew that he cut a striking figure, no matter how small he felt inside. He stuck his hands inside his pockets and felt the candy bar—suddenly he felt more reassured. He looked up again. "Well, here I am," he said plainly. He smiled.

Mary put his arm around Hansel and squeezed his shoulder tightly.

"Yes," the principal continued, "here you are. With your lovely, um, companion."

Mary pursed his lips and kissed the air with a resounding SMACK!

"Well, then—do you have your tickets?" the principal asked, knowing very well that they did not. Hansel felt his back break out in a sudden cold sweat.

"We're on the guest list," Mary said, and began to walk past the principal into the auditorium, tugging Hansel with him.

"But we don't have a guest list!" the principal protested.

"You do now," Mary said, and turned his back on the man.

And sure enough, on the table before him was a clipboard with a sheet of paper on it that said GUEST LIST. There were only two names on it:

Mr. Hansel B. Gottsfried
Ms. Right To Mary

Inside the auditorium, his arm still around Hansel's shoulder, Mary whispered in Hansel's ear, "If you think a fairy gets upset when she's not invited to a christening, Honey, look out if you don't invite her to the prom!"

Hansel smiled, giddy with relief that they had pulled off their confrontation with the principal. Already he was beginning to feel like this wouldn't turn out as bad as he had feared. People were noticing that he was there—Hansel imagined they might've been making bets earlier as to whether he would show and who he might bring with him. They'd wondered if he'd bring a guy as his date, and he wondered what would've happened if he had.

Then Hansel realized that he *had* brought a man as his date—a man in drag—who looked as glamorous as any of the biological girls at the prom. They were making a spectacle of themselves, perhaps, by their very presence, but he enjoyed being the focus of everyone's attention. He was making them stand up and notice him—notice that he wasn't afraid of them and that he wouldn't back down in the face of their fears or prejudices, or because of the names they'd called him behind his back for years.

"I'll go get us some punch," Mary said, making a beeline for the beverage table. People moved out of his way—and not simply because he was such an imposing, tall figure.

Hansel scanned the room for people he knew. Everyone looked so different in their formal wear, as if they were all royalty: princes and princesses, for tonight at least. He saw a handsome man, lingered on him for a moment, and began to conjure fantasies of love and lust before he realized he was gazing at Scott, his sister's date. Hansel was jealous for a moment, and then he laughed at himself. He and Gretel were so alike in so many ways, even when it came to their sexual attraction.

Gretel, seeing her brother, squealed with delight and dragged her partner off the dance floor.

"Hansel! I'm so glad you're here. What made you change your mind?"

Mary appeared suddenly and handed Hansel a drink of red liquid. "Here you are, sorry it took so long. They were serving Kool-Aid, can you believe? It took me a moment to stiffen it up. Hello there." Mary extended his arm to Gretel, as if he expected it to be kissed.

"Gretel, this is...Mary," Hansel said. "Mary, this is my sister Gretel, as you know, and her date, Scott."

"Sister, will you forgive me," Mary asked, handing Gretel his drink, "if I steal this handsome man from you for one dance?" She grabbed Scott before anyone had a chance to protest, or even speak, and led him back onto the dance floor. "I promise to be gentle," Mary called over his shoulder. Scott held Mary stiffly as they began to dance. He kept glancing down at Mary's crotch, as if he were trying to determine what lay beneath all those folds of taffeta and lace.

" 'As you know?' You have some explaining to do," Gretel said. She looked down at the cup she was holding and wondered where Mary's lips had been. Then she took a long drink from the cup anyway.

"Mary is my fairy godmother," Hansel explained. "Or godfather. Or whatever. He appeared out of nowhere, just after you left with Scott. Did the whole presto–change-o magic thing, and before I knew it, here we are. Isn't he something?"

"You're not in love with him, are you?"

"With Mary?" Hansel scoffed. "No. He's hardly my type. But you must admit, he is something else, eh?"

"That's for sure," Gretel remarked, somewhat sourly. But then she smiled. "But I'm so glad you changed your mind and decided to come anyway. We'll have so much fun together!"

"Yes," Hansel agreed.

"Let's dance." Gretel left their cups on a bleacher and pulled her brother onto the floor. They danced together for a while, enjoying the magic and glamour of the moment.

"Look over there," Hansel whispered to her. "It's Jack Charming."

"Yummm," Gretel agreed, getting a quick glimpse of the boy they were discussing as the pair spun through their steps.

Jack had transferred in during the past semester, so hardly anyone knew him very well, though he was generally well-liked. He was very good-looking, got straight-A marks, and he'd been a star athlete at his previous school, though he chose not to compete at Henley High, taking phys ed. classes instead. No one knew why he had switched schools so suddenly during his final senior semester.

"Why is he being a wallflower?" Hansel asked as he and Gretel spun around. "I can't believe someone like him doesn't have a date for the prom."

"Who knows?" Gretel said. Their movements brought them next to Mary and Scott. "May we cut in?" Gretel asked, returning to her date's arms.

"Your sister found herself a keeper," Mary said as he stepped into Hansel's arms. For a moment Hansel wasn't sure whether he should lead or follow—Mary was taller than he by at least half a foot—but after a moment's hesitation he stepped forward and took the lead.

"So are you enjoying yourself, Honey?" Mary asked.

"Yes," Hansel replied. And it was true. He *was* enjoying himself. He was jealous of his sister's boyfriend, he had to admit—to himself, though he said nothing aloud. But he didn't really need to. That's why his Fairy Mary was here, after all: to help him out in this special moment. As they danced together, Hansel wondered what it would be like to dance with a boy his own age who was equally in love with him, who would wrap him up in all the romance of this special night and not let go for years and years.

Suddenly, Hansel's reverie was interrupted by a deep voice that asked, "Can I cut in?"

Hansel felt his heart sink, wondering who wanted to dance with Mary. Couldn't they see that he was a man in drag? But then Hansel hadn't recognized this fact at first. What would he do? He would feel so abandoned if he were left alone—everyone would stare at him, know he was gay, and think he didn't belong. He tightened his grip around Mary's waist. *Please don't let go of me*, he prayed silently to Mary, *or I'll fall*.

But Mary did let go.

Before Hansel knew what was happening, Jack had taken his hand and pulled him close. For a moment they didn't know what to do. Who should follow and who should lead? They stood frozen like that for a moment, indecisive. Then Jack stepped forward, and Hansel stepped back. Though Hansel wasn't used to following, his feet seemed to know what to do. *Perhaps it's Mary's magic*, he thought. Then he thought only of Jack.

They danced together, and as the song ended, Hansel felt something hard press against his thigh. The two boys stood close to one another during the break between songs, and Hansel reached into his pocket. "Want to split a candy bar?" Hansel asked.

Immediately, he felt lame—he couldn't believe that *those* were his first words to the man of his dreams! He should've said something flattering about Jack's eyes, or remarked on how handsome he was, or any of a hundred thoughts that suddenly flooded Hansel's brain at once. Now that it was too late.

Jack smiled. "I love Hersheys," he said. Hansel's face lit up with a smile too as he stared into Jack's blue eyes.

Across the room, Gretel noticed her brother and Jack had stopped dancing and moved off the dance floor. "I'm tired," Gretel told Scott, "let's rest." The moment she and Scott stopped, Mary was standing beside them, as if he'd materialized out of thin air. "Have you got anything left in one of those cups?" Gretel asked. "I'm parched."

"Afraid not, Child," Mary said, turning both empty cups bottoms up.

"Scott," Gretel asked sweetly, "could you please get us something to drink?"

He glanced at Mary, as if he were nervous to leave his girlfriend alone with him. Then he smiled and went in search of drinks.

"So now that you've gotten us alone," Mary said.

"Is he going to be OK?"

"It looks like he's likely to have the night of his life."

"But it's not all some fairy glamour that's going to wear off at the stroke of midnight, is it?"

Mary looked wistfully at Hansel and Jack, who'd rejoined the twirl and surge of dancing bodies. "No, not this one. But I can't know what will come of this—no one can. There are many different ways of working magic, Child. Sometimes all it takes is giving someone a little self-confidence and letting them take care of all the rest."

Gretel looked at her brother and Jack, who'd started dancing again happily together. "I'm glad it wasn't magic."

"Me too." Mary sighed deeply. He blotted at his eyes with a handkerchief that had appeared out of nowhere. "My mascara is going to run." Mary blew his nose noisily into the handkerchief, then looked up again at Hansel and Jack. "Ah, young love."

"Yeah," Gretel agreed. "It's so nice to see Hansel finding a happy ending at last."

"Child, we haven't even gotten to a happy ending yet."

"Oh? What'll that be?" Scott asked as he came up, handing them each a cup of punch.

"You should see how big Jack's beanstalk can grow!" Mary purred.

The Best I Can Do Under the Circumstances

Gary McCann

In a black T-shirt, bone-colored pants, and flip-flops, Ian breezes through the bookstore's clean glass doors with the hazy Southern California sun shining on the parking lot at his back. Ian's a graduate student, five years younger than I am, with black Irish hair falling on his pale forehead and a wiry, medium-size body a little smaller than mine. From where I'm standing, at the calendar display rack, I watch Ian avoid my gaze as he passes the gift book tables and disappears into the stockroom.

I pat the blond wood calendar rack a few times, as though I'm a bongo drummer, and glance at my own brown eyes and sandy head reflected in an interior window that looks into my office. I finger my wedding band, turning it. Dave and I started wearing rings five years ago when we agreed we could only live together if we were monogamous.

Resuming what I was doing before I stopped to watch Ian—pulling 1985 calendars that haven't sold—I pick up a dog-eared display copy of a baseball calendar and leaf through a few slick pages until I find a picture I've looked at before. A handsome-enough batter is leaning over home plate.

My favorite picture of Dave was taken during his brief ball career, when he played first base for the Wisconsin Rapids Twins, a farm team for Minnesota. Dave wasn't in his ball uniform in the picture. He was standing by an unmade bed, in a straw cowboy hat, an unbuttoned denim shirt, and black briefs. A nurse he was seeing—a female nurse—took the picture.

The batter hunched over home plate on the calendar could be anyone, for my knowledge of baseball. All I know about him is that I'd like to experience his body at its peak. As many men as I've had, I crave more. No one expects less of a straight man, even a married straight man, in his taste for women, do they?

Walking toward my office with a box full of calendars on my shoulder, I stop on the customer's side of the main counter, facing Ian on his stool behind the cash register. He looks up from a book open on his lap.

"Do you have plans for Friday evening, Ian?"

"Do you want me to work late and close up?"

"I want you to come to dinner, with Dave and me."

Ian's eyes glance out across the store and return to mine.

"Sorry, I'm tied up Friday evening, come to think of it."

"Saturday evening?"

"This week's bad. The next few weeks are bad. Thanks, though."

"You like me, Ian, and I like you. I know you'll like Dave, and he'll like you. I don't see a problem."

"No problem. I'm just busy."

I lower my gaze to the smooth black T-shirt stretched over his chest.

"I love seeing the points of your tits in that shirt."

"Lenny, back off."

"Why?"

"Because I'm asking you to."

"I know you're fucking Dave, Ian."

He stares past me, toward the plate glass windows at the front of the store.

"I don't know what you're talking about."

"I saw you two having coffee in the Dunkin' Donuts by the college."

"So I ran into a guy at Dunkin' Donuts and had a cup of coffee with him."

"Bullshit, Ian. You're a lying bastard. I tried to introduce you to Dave at Robert's party, and I could never get the two of you in the same room. Now I know why."

"Here comes a customer, Lenny."

Ian hops off his stool.

While he rings up a stack of mysteries for a pregnant woman, I drop the box of calendars on my desk, grab my jacket off the hook behind my office door, and sling it over my shoulder. I wait near the cash register until the pregnant woman wobbles away.

"I'm giving myself a couple hours off, Ian. I deserve it, don't you think?"

"Sure, why not?"

He picks up the book he was reading and climbs back onto his stool. He sits erect, holding the book open on his lap and staring straight ahead. I keep my eyes on him until he glances at me and shrugs.

"I won't tell Jane you left early."

"You can tell Jane whatever you want, bastard."

Jane's the neurotic proprietress of Fullerton Books, absent more than she's here.

I stomp out of the store into the parking lot, climb into my beige Rabbit, and slam the door.

At home I open a bottle of beer. It's 75 degrees outside, and the late-afternoon sun is shining into the back of our small house, a green stucco rancher built during the '50s. I'm used to getting home in the dark. I strip off my shirt and shoes, and carry my beer out to the patio. With the sun on my shoulders, I hold a hose pouring water into our birds-of-paradise and agapanthus.

I'm in the kitchen opening cans of corned beef hash when Dave comes in the back door. He's half a head taller than I am and broader in the shoulders. Dave's wearing khakis and a maroon pullover sweater. His brown hair, combed to the side, juts over his forehead above pale-blue eyes heavy-lidded, and a long straight nose. His expressive mouth and square jaw look at home under a cowboy hat when he wears one. My cowboy is a herpetologist.

"You look tired, Dave."

"I've been grading exams."

We kiss, and he carries his briefcase through the living room to his den.

He comes back into the kitchen wearing a white T-shirt flecked with maroon fuzz from the sweater he took off. I have salads ready, and the hash is hot. At our secondhand dining table in the living room, we eat watching the news on a small black-and-white TV on a corner of the table, and then carry our dirty plates into the kitchen and load them into the dishwasher. Dave fills the teakettle.

"I need to finish grading. I promised my 101 class I'd give back their exams tomorrow. Do you want coffee?"

"No, thanks."

I lean against the sink counter and watch him reach for a jar of instant coffee on a top shelf. His lats stretch the armpits of his T-shirt, shrunk from too many trips through the dryer.

"I know you're fucking Ian, Dave."

He sets the jar of coffee on the counter and looks over his shoulder. I watch his mouth open and close without sound.

"I thought I should tell you I know. I don't want to talk about it."

He turns toward me, and his large body freezes in the middle of our kitchen, like a big buck caught in the headlights of an oncoming car. I brush past him and through the doorway. In the living room I start a Judy Collins cassette I was listening to earlier and, with headphones over my ears, settle on the dark wood floor, my legs folded. I stare into the fireplace as though the log on the grate is burning.

Dave comes into the room. He sits on the floor beside me and puts his arm around my shoulders. I consider knocking it off. He lifts the headphones away from my ears and holds them on his lap.

"I didn't know who he was, Len. You never mentioned hiring a guy named 'Ian.' He didn't know who I was. He thought I had a wife. We saw each other jogging every day."

"I said I don't want to talk about it."

"What do you want me to do? Can you give me a little time?"

"I can give you the rest of my life. Go grade your tests."

I take the headphones from him and put them over my ears. He kisses the back of my neck. I let him kiss me on the mouth—I figure then he'll go away and leave me alone, hopefully for the evening, and he does.

In bed, we're both surprised when I won't stop kissing him. I pull him on top of me and raise my legs. I think of Ian doing the same thing, and my cock throbs so hard it aches.

After we're both sated, Dave collapses on my chest. I stroke the back of his neck while he cries.

I hold him, quiet and still. He raises his head.

"I'd break it off right now if I could. Can you understand that, Len?"

"I understand. Understanding doesn't mean I like it."

"I'm the only man he's ever had sex with. We haven't done anything unsafe."

"I trust you."

"If you want me to move out of the house for a while, I will."

"*No*. I don't want you to move out. You're infatuated, Dave—it'll pass. I'm pissed off at the moment—that'll pass too."

"Can you handle this for a time?"

"Do I have a choice?"

He doesn't answer.

"I fucked around when we were first together, Dave. You're fucking around now. Our timing's bad, but we're good together."

He lifts off my chest, wipes his nose with his hand, and rolls onto his side. I snuggle against him, and we fall asleep.

At work Thursday and Friday, Ian and I pretend to ignore each other. At home, Dave and I pretend Ian doesn't exist.

Late Friday night I'm standing in a gay disco on Garden Grove Boulevard, tasting my first hard liquor in five years. I've had two beers, my normal limit. Dave comes out of the head. I've hardly spoken to him all evening. We've been dancing with our friend Robert, a small bald man, head of the comp lit department at Cal State and like a gay uncle to us. Dave and I have our shirts off. Dave glances at the rocks glass in my hand.

"What are you doing, Lenny?"

"Minding my own business, which is more than I can say for some people."

I down my bourbon and signal the bartender for another double. Someone tugs on my T-shirt, tucked through a side belt loop of my jeans.

"I *must* feel that sweaty torso," an effeminate voice lilts in my ear.

JT, the man speaking, reminds me of my first lover and best friend, Michael, who died of AIDS last year. Michael was small with long brown hair, soft as a baby's, over which he wore a bandanna hippie-style, the way JT does. Michael was less effeminate than JT but effeminate enough to give the alpha dog in me, 17 when we were lovers, a nonstop hard-on.

JT moves in front of me and presses the heels of his hands to my rib cage. His fingers fan out across my pecs, avoiding my nipples. I'd like to squeeze his small waist, under his purple silk shirt, and bury my face in his long hair. I see JT's shy lover, Billy, standing back from us and staring at the floor. Billy's a crew-cut albino, skinny in a baggy gray T-shirt and green fatigues, with the bass voice of a bullfrog and an uncut dick the size, limp, of a large cucumber. Billy felt my biceps when we were alone in the kitchen at Robert's New Year's Day party.

JT moves from me to Dave, and JT's fingers splay around Dave's large nipples. Dave likes the flattery but doesn't have my eclectic taste in men. I step up to Billy and give him a tight hug, swelling my pecs against Billy's bony frame under his gray T-shirt. We both start to get hard, and, smiling, let go of each other.

I turn to the bar and pay for my second drink. JT and Billy take turns shouting in Robert's ear. "I Will Survive" is playing. Dave moves beside me.

"Just don't drink too much, Lenny."

I ignore him. I'm watching a man I noticed while we were dancing. He's walking toward the men's room, his fingers brushing back wavy dark hair, his olive-skinned chest thrust out and sporting its own mane. His pock-marked face, 40-ish but youthful, is creased across the brow—he sees me watching him, and he's curious.

I down my bourbon, plunk my glass on the bar, and follow him toward the men's room and through its propped-open door. I step up next to him at the trough urinal and watch him pee while I'm waiting to start. He has a short thick dick with a head the size of a plum. He finishes peeing and tucks his plum through the fly of his jeans. I catch his eye and grin.

"You have a nice bulbous cock head."

I affect my native Texas accent. He laughs, and I wink.

"My name's Lenny."

"Mine's Cleve."

I'm holding my gracefully arched dick between thumb and index finger. We both watch the pee start streaming out of it.

"If I keep flirting with you, Cleve, I'll get a boner."

A couple of guys cackle, and one of them says in a motherish tone, "No boners at the urinal."

Smiling, I shake my dick dry and turn around from the trough. I don't have a huge uncut cucumber like Billy, but I'm big enough to enjoy showing off. I walk toward the sink, tucking myself away and eyeing Cleve in the mirror. He watches me zip up my faded blue jeans and waits while I rinse my hands under the cold tap water. I follow him out the open door.

"Let's dance," I shout.

"Aren't you with your boyfriend?"

"I want to dance with you."

I take his hand and lead him onto the floor.

He's restrained—he'd rather watch me dance, I think. I smile and ogle his chest, turn around, and wiggle my butt for him.

We boogie through "It's Raining Men" and "YMCA," and then move to the bar, where Cleve orders a Miller Lite and I order my third double bourbon. The music's too loud for us to talk. Cleve's standing on my left side. Dave appears on my right and shouts in my ear while he pulls on a green T-shirt with a coiled snake on its front, a shirt he bought at the Cincinnati Zoo when we visited his folks last summer.

"Robert's gone to JT and Billy's for coffee. I said we'd be along."

"Go ahead."

JT and Billy have a house in Westminster, a 10-minute drive away. I glance into my drink and swallow what's left.

"We don't have to go if you don't want to, Len."

"Go. I'm getting my own ride home."

"You're drinking too much."

"Fuck off, Dave."

I turn toward Cleve. He's leaning back against the bar, pretending to watch the dancers. Dave moves a couple of steps so he can keep shouting in my ear.

"Don't do anything crazy tonight. If you have to do something, make it safe."

I stare at the shirtless sweaty men on the dance floor. The bar area's smoky and reeks of tobacco, spilled liquor, and mold from the carpet. The air conditioner's humming and dripping condensation.

"Promise me, Len."

"*Christ!*"

"I love you—nothing's changed about that."

I lean close to Dave's ear.

"I won't do anything unsafe! I saw what Michael went through! Go home, Dave! I'll get there!"

"If you're sure you want me to leave without you, I will."

"I'm sure!"

"Should I get your jacket from the car?"

"*Go*, goddamn it!"

I face the bar, with my back to Dave. He moves to my side and kisses me on the cheek. His mouth hovers near mine.

I turn my head and kiss him—long and hard.

"Now go."

He backs away from me, does an about-face and walks toward the door, his tall body swaying in its unself-conscious gait.

I glance at Cleve. He's facing the bar, his eyes raised to a suspended television playing a Madonna video without sound.

"He's your lover?"

"I don't know what he is."

"You wear wedding bands."

"You're going to take me home and feed me cock anyhow, aren't you?"

"If that's what you want."

"That's what I want. Let's have a nightcap and get out of here."

I order my bourbon neat. Cleve orders a Coke.

We down our drinks and wander bare-chested out to the parking lot in the clear cold night. I pull my T-shirt out of my belt loop and slip it on. Cleve unlocks the passenger side of a big metallic-green two-door Electra and picks up a silver bomber jacket from the front seat. As I slide into the car, I watch his hairy arms and chest disappear into the jacket.

The Buick floats down the Costa Mesa Freeway with a fluid motion that reminds me of lying on a raft in a gently undulating pool. The new-car smell and the blowing heater make my stomach queasy.

"You have a big-ass new car."

"It's a late '84—the last of the V-8s. The company I work for leases cars for us. I'm a pharmaceutical salesman."

"A pharmaceutical salesman? I like drugs. I like grass, anyhow. I don't smoke much anymore."

I pick up a business card lying between us on the wide dark red seat and squint at the embossed printing. I'm nauseated, I realize. I lay the card down, and it slides into the crevice between the seat and the seat back.

"I don't need the heater on, if you're running it for me."

Cleve turns off the heater fan.

"How much further?"

"15 minutes."

"I know you told me where you live, but I forget."

"Balboa."

"Balboa's near Newport?"

"Balboa's the next beach south of Newport; it's in Newport Beach city limits. I share a house. You're new here?"

"Five years."

My stomach's too upset for me to elaborate. I want out of the car.

We reach the end of the Costa Mesa Freeway, continue along Newport Boulevard, and stop at a red light. I spot a Shell station a block ahead on the right.

"I hate to tell you, but I've changed my mind about tonight.

Would you mind letting me out at that Shell station?"

The red light turns green. We drive through the intersection, ahead for a block, and through the next intersection, passing the Shell station without slowing down. I point back with my thumb.

"They had a pay phone—I could call a cab."

"You've changed your mind?"

"I'm sorry."

"Come to my place. We don't have to do anything."

"Maybe some other time."

We pass another gas station. I point back with my thumb again.

"They had a pay phone too."

Cleve pulls into a left-turn lane, and we stop at a red light. I feel weak.

"Where are we going?"

"I don't know. Where do you want to go?"

"Home."

"You're sure I can't talk you out of it?"

"Positive."

"Where's home?"

"Fullerton."

The light changes, and Cleve makes a U-turn around a center island.

"You can drop me wherever there's a phone."

"Will you call your lover?"

"I'll call a cab."

"A cab to Fullerton would cost you $100—if you could get a cab this late. I'll take you home."

"You don't have to."

"I'm apparently not doing anything else tonight."

I see an Exxon station ahead.

"Could we stop at that Exxon station so I can use the john?"

Cleve glances at me. "Are you feeling OK?"

"Not entirely."

I force a smile. He moves two lanes to the right.

"I'll gas up—otherwise they won't give you the key to the men's room."

He pulls into the Exxon station and parks by a pump. I open the big coupe's wide door, lean out, and heave. My barf splatters the cement like I'm flinging it from a pail. I heave a second time and a third. Slime hangs from my mouth as I fumble into my jeans pocket for a handkerchief. I taste and smell bourbon, almost as pure as it went down, and partially digested chicken, fries, and cherry pie à la mode, from dinner at Coco's, where Dave and I started the evening. I wipe my mouth with my handkerchief and mop off the car door threshold.

I look over at Cleve and grin. He smiles.

"Feel better, handsome?"

"Like a new man."

"Do you still want to use the bathroom?"

"Maybe we should shove off. People don't like you throwing up on their property. I learned that in college."

Cleve starts the car, and I close my door. We pull onto Newport Boulevard and move into the middle lane.

"What do you want to do now?"

"Go home. You don't have to take me. I can call Dave. He'll come and get me."

"Did you guys have a fight?"

"Not exactly."

"I'll take you home. I feel like a drive."

We ride several blocks along Newport Boulevard, past motels and fast-food joints, most of them closed for the night; past a car repair shop, a tire outlet, a Realtor's office, and other darkened businesses and small office buildings set close to the curbless highway. As we accelerate onto the freeway, I glance at Cleve.

"Are you pissed at me?"

"No, I'm not pissed."

He leans toward the dashboard and turns on the radio. Tammy Wynette is singing.

We roll up the Costa Mesa Freeway and over the interchange to the Santa Ana. I scoot down in my seat, lay my head back, and close my eyes.

"Are you feeling sick again?" Cleve asks.

"A little. I'm OK. The country music's soothing."

"I like country music for driving."

"I was thinking about what a nice guy you are."

"Will you remember I'm a nice guy if things don't work out between you and your lover?"

"I'll remember."

I reach over and take Cleve's hand. I hold it for a while, squeezing his fingers, and then ease his hand into my lap, laying his palm over my crotch.

Cleve's massaging my hard cock through my jeans as we drive up four-laned Brookhurst, lightly trafficked this late at night. In the middle of our block I tell him to make a U-turn and park in front of our house. I don't see any lights in the windows. Dave's in bed, I figure.

"Do you want to come in, and I'll make coffee?"

"Are you sure it'll be all right?"

"Dave's easygoing."

Unlocking the front door, I wonder if Dave's home. I step inside and see a dim light shining from the hall on the other side of the living room.

Cleve follows me into the kitchen. The room smells of Raid that I sprayed for ants just before Dave and I left for the evening. I flip on the ceiling lamp, pull the coffeemaker and a can of Folgers out from the back of the countertop.

"Have a seat."

I motion toward the washing machine, the only place to sit in the kitchen. Everything in my vision is slowly revolving, left to right.

Cleve leans against the washer and unzips his jacket far enough to show a lot of curly black chest hair. I fill the coffeemaker, turn it on, and lean against the sink counter to wait.

Dave appears in the kitchen doorway, dark green bikini underwear separating his muscled long white torso from his muscled long white legs. He glances at me. "You're home." He stares at Cleve.

"This is my friend Cleve." I'm slurring my words, I realize. "I got sick on the way to his house, and he brought me all the way back from Newport Beach. Stay up and have coffee with us. Cleve, this is Dave."

From a cabinet I take three unmatched mugs and hold one after the other under the coffee machine as the liquid drips down. I slide a glass carafe under the machine to catch the rest of the coffee.

"Cream or sugar, Cleve?"

"Black."

The odor of coffee and ant spray is making me want to throw up again.

"Let's go sit in the other room."

We pick up our coffee mugs, and I follow Dave and Cleve into the living room. Dave switches on a floor lamp by a chair at the end of the couch, sets his coffee on the chair's arm, and goes into the bedroom. Cleve and I sit at opposite ends of the couch and angle ourselves toward each other. I sip my coffee and feel sicker.

Dave comes out of the bedroom wearing his jeans and pulling his Cincinnati Zoo T-shirt over his head. He sits in the chair and picks up his coffee mug.

Smiling as well as I can, I rise on shaky legs.

"You guys get to know each other. I need to go to bed."

I lean over, reach inside Cleve's jacket, and rub my fingers in his chest hair.

"You're a sexy man. I shouldn't have come on to you, though. I'm sorry."

"I'm not complaining."

I stagger through the hall into the bedroom, where the covers are pushed down on our double bed. With my clothes on I climb onto my side of the mattress and kiss the sheet on Dave's side, warm from his body.

I roll onto my back. I learned in college to lie with one foot on the floor to keep the room from spinning. Our bed is too high.

I bring a knee up to my chest and untie one of the old brown saddle oxfords I wear for dancing. I pull off the shoe, hold it out from the bedside, let go, and listen to it thump on the wood floor. I raise my other knee, pull off my other shoe, and let go.

Light is shining through the doorway from the hall and the living room. I hear Dave and Cleve talking; I don't listen to what they're saying, only to the sound of their voices. I'm glad to be home, in my own bed, with Dave no farther away than the next room. I don't want Dave to be farther away ever.

Coral Song

Jay Quinn

Nate sighed, stood, and stretched, extending from long legs up through his still-lean hips and narrow waist through his raised arms, his fists clenched like the boxer he used to be. His knuckles nearly brushed my new popcorned ceiling. "That was excellent."

I gathered up the fish-bone-strewn plates and greasy flatware. "Glad you liked it, want another beer?"

Nate gathered himself in from his long stretch and shook his head like a wet dog. "Just some water, please. With ice and some more of that lime, if you have it."

I nodded toward the living room and said, "Sure. Go sit down and make yourself at home."

Nate nodded and strode off into the living room. I put the dishes in the sink and braced myself against the counter. It was almost spooky the way he turned up in Alex's Souvenir Shop that afternoon. I hadn't seen Nate in years, but I visited Alex's Souvenir Shop on Federal Highway every Saturday.

I remembered places like Alex's from when I was little. I guess I was looking for some of the same excitement and happiness I had back then running around with Nate, dashing into the souvenir shop with my allowance. I was always looking for treasures amid the trinkets. All the tourist crap, shells, gifts, and more reminded me of being the kind of happy I had been as a kid. They also reminded me of Nate.

Of course, other things reminded me of Nate. Fighting. Fucking. We did go way back, but there wasn't any of it that was anywhere near wonderful. I spent long years hating the son of a bitch, all the while admitting to myself he was the love of my life. And, as bad as I wanted him to, he'd never admit I was the one constant thing in his life either.

Looking out the kitchen window into the late sunset, I tried to stop myself from wondering if this time would end like all the others had when Nate and I got together. We'd talk, we'd reminisce, we'd fight, and then we'd end up in bed. It took all of that to get us naked and finally at a place we both hoped to end up from the beginning. It was getting old, but neither of us knew a way to skip the bruising part to get to the healing.

I busied myself making the glasses of ice water with slices of lime, thinking how he came and went like a hard wind, leaving everything in pieces and scattered for years in between.

Still, I was distracted by the thought of his touch, his taste, his strong heart beating hard under his chest as broad and bare as a long run of beach. That was the only place I truly felt at home. Now, again, Nate himself waited in my living room, and I gathered myself in from my own mental stretch. With a deep breath I turned and went to him, like I'd dreamed of in the long stitches of time joining my life with and without him.

"You sure have some coral collection," he said from the sofa.

"Yeah, I'm pretty proud of it. I've been working on it a long time.

Coral wasn't cheap. The longest slender branches set me back anywhere from 45 to 100 dollars. The small rounded coral heads themselves ran anywhere from 20 to 50 bucks. Each week I picked up a single branch or small coral head with careful consideration of its worth and its price balanced by my love for it.

The coral heads lined glass shelves, three high, along all the windows of my living room. I often wandered my eyes along the shelves happily, searching a shelf length at a time. Bleached, white, and lovely, they inspired a sort of reverence in me. Once, they were living things, these tiny fingers of calcium, providing shelter and comfort to brightly darting fish. Dry and dusty on the shelves of the souvenir shop, they mutely sighed to me, whispers of waves, from their hundreds of tiny open mouths. I felt like I was rescuing them in bringing them home to shelter, comforting the brightly darting fish of my daydreams.

"You know they just bash these pieces off the living reef," Nate said.

"I know, I feel guilty enough already, don't make it worse."

"Pretty soon all the coral will die; then the small fish will leave, then the predators. Eventually there won't be a reef worth diving left in the world." He stood and walked over to the shelves in the front window. "Did you get all this at the place where I ran into you this afternoon?"

I sat the glasses of water and lime on the coffee table and walked over to join him. "A lot of it." I picked up a piece of staghorn coral and handed it to him. "You gave me this piece. Do you remember? When we were younger?"

"Back how far?"

"I was 6 and you were 9."

Nate smiles. "My dad was still in the Marines then."

"Yeah. And you were meaner than any other military brat I knew."

Nate's smile grew to a rueful grin. "Being mean comes from moving around so much. I can remember being angry all the time. I can't believe I was ever so nice as to give you anything."

I nodded. "Yeah, right. Being mean comes from having a full-grown marine kicking the shit out of you every time he got a chance."

Nate glanced at my cheek and quickly looked away. "You always knew it, didn't you?"

"When he'd beat you? Yeah, I knew."

"That was OK. No matter what, you made me feel like I could handle it." He placed the piece of coral securely on its shelf and placed his large hand on the side of my head, his thumb finding and gently stroking the scar on my cheekbone. "It's been a long time."

I still had to look up to catch his eyes and hold them. They were still as blue. That was the sum of it, all the stupid clichéd things you're reduced to remembering when you recall the few good things in a kind of love that has dogged you your whole life. *I am small, he is big. I am 6, he is 9. I am pretty, he is not. I am gay, he is not. I am happy, he is angry. I am in love with him, he is...his eyes are such a deep ocean-blue.*

Nate dropped his hand and smiled at me, squaring his broad shoulders as if to say "Well?"

"Your meanness never mattered, Nate. I've been in love with you since we were little boys on the beach 40 years ago."

Nate walked back and sat down on the edge of the sofa, placed his forearms on his knees, and hung his head briefly before he turned to look at me again. "I've loved you since then too."

All I could say was "Nate," and in saying his name, all of the tiny coral mouths on all the dry, bony coral heads drew a thirsty breath and sang.

Nate patted the sofa beside him and adjusted himself sideways so we could look at each other, as we nervously left that suddenly bared admission to talk back and forth about the news, politics, jobs, and finally, the personal things in years that have passed.

"So, how's the wife and kids?" I asked.

Nate stirred his second serving of ice water with a long thick finger, then took a deep swallow. I watched the muscles in his throat move.

"They're fine, the kids I mean. Kelly and Kerry. You know we had twins?"

"Boys, right?"

Nate nodded. "They're 19 this year."

I smiled. I could picture them, rawboned and rangy, like their daddy was at that age.

"Their mother is doing well. We communicate on the backs of my checks these days."

This was news. I hesitated to ask.

"Divorced three years ago."

"I'm sorry."

Nate looked at me and laughed. "No, you're not. How about you? Where's that prissy dickhead...what was his name? I take it you two split up too."

"Gary. His name was Gary. Anyway, we called it quits years ago."

"I wish I could say I told you so."

I studied Nate carefully. Something hateful jumped into my mind, provoked by all the other unspoken things, but I didn't say it. Instead I just said, "I wish you had. What are you doing in Fort Lauderdale?"

"Business."

"And how did you happen to find yourself at Alex's Souvenir Shop?

"I was looking for shells…gifts..."

"Yeah, and more!"

Nate sighed. "I wasn't looking for you," he recovered quickly. "But I want to tell you, I'm very happy I found you." He leaned forward and sat his glass on the coffee table. "I don't know if you even want to hear that."

I leaned forward to sit my own glass on the coffee table and collect my thoughts before I said anything. This was old territory for both of us, but I...we…both had grown older, and I wasn't used to silencing my desires anymore. I sat back and put my arm across the back of the sofa. Betrayed by this physical Freudian slip of reaching toward him, I answered his question with a flanking feint. "I can see why, there's been times you made my life fucking miserable."

"Aw goddamn, Frankie. You know why."

I turned away and searched the end table's drawer for a pack of cigarettes I kept squirreled away there. I found them and lit one to cover myself while I searched for my point.

"Give me one of those, will ya?"

I slid the pack and the lighter across the coffee table. Nate reached for them, his hand covering mine briefly before I pulled it away, stood, and walked into the kitchen for an ashtray. I heard the lighter's click and quiet burn of Nate getting his cigarette lit as I walked back into the living room. He still sat, half folded and too big on my sofa. There was gray in his hair, platinum flickers in the close-cropped bright blond gone ash.

Sitting down, being a mirror of his hunkered crouch, I put the ashtray between us. "These days they'd say you were self-identified as straight."

Nate toyed with his cigarette, making much of rolling the ash off the tray's edges, then flicking the butt end with his thumb. He took a long hit off the cigarette and ground it out, then leaned back into the sofa with a great rush of exhaled smoke. "Yeah. I still am self-identified as straight," he said without irony. "What do *they* say about you these days?"

I chuckled harshly. "*They'd* say I was a self-loathing homosexual incapable of developing a well-adjusted relationship with another gay man."

"I don't get it."

"I guess that's my point, Nate."

"What's your point, Frankie? I'm straight and you're gay with some great big-ass capital G? What does that have to do with how we feel about each other? Why does it have to be all one fucking thing or the other?" Nate stood up and strode angrily around the limits of the living room as if he were caged, stopping finally to stand in front of me. "What the fuck, Frankie?"

"Because it's my life, Nate."

"Your *life*? Every goddamn thing you do, everything you say or feel, revolves around you wanting dick? Is that it?"

I felt calm in the face of this sudden storm. Nate could go from benign to bastard in under six seconds. He hadn't changed at all in that regard. I put out my cigarette, leaned back into the sofa, and said, "Pretty much."

"So why did you beg me to scar you up to make a man out of you? You could have stayed a perfect pretty-boy faggot—you'd have been a lot better off. Maybe you wouldn't be so *self-loathing*."

My hand went reflexively over the scar on my cheekbone. "That didn't have anything to do with it, Nate."

"Didn't it? You were so fucking beautiful. Perfect! You always were, since you were 6 years old. Goddamn got *my* dick hard when I was 9 and kept it up for years. Then we were at State, you walking around so smart, so fucking smug, all wrapped up in your own self like no one else was even on earth."

"No fair, Nate. Shut up."

He laughed. "I hit your sore nerve this time, didn't I? At State you acted like you didn't even know me. Even after what we'd done together. What *you* got *me* to do with you."

I held up my hands as if to block out what he was saying: 6, 16, or 26, and so in love with him I'd have done anything to have him. I *did* do anything to have him, but he didn't put up much of a fight; behind the 7-Eleven, alone in his car, or out in the dunes at noon or dark midnight. "No. No way, Nate. That's not how it was."

Nate actually growled in frustration, his fists clenched hard as he tossed his head back to stare at the ceiling.

"Quit growling and just sit down."

He glared at me before he flung himself into the armchair across from the sofa. "I'm not going to hit you again, if that's what you want. I could have killed you then and I could kill you now, one fucking punch."

"I know, Nate."

Compass needles point north no matter which direction you turn, and there are poles of attraction that are stable in every relationship, despite the different ways you twist to fit the truth. We sat staring at each other as the anger cooled in the air-conditioned hum.

Nate rubbed his face with his hands and stood up. "This isn't how I wanted this to go, Frankie." He turned toward the door.

"Did you know I used to come to watch you box intramural?"

Nate stopped, but he didn't turn around.

"Yeah, I came to every match. I stayed out of the way because I thought it would embarrass you, you know, having me there."

Nate turned around and looked at me.

"That's why I ignored you when we were at State. You were this pissed-off, big, tough straight guy and people stepped out of your way when they saw you coming. You got off on it."

"I did not."

"Yes, hell, you did then and you do now. That's what your damn daddy taught you. You've been bigger than anybody else since we were kids and you use it to keep everybody away. Especially anybody who loved you."

"You sound just like my ex-wife."

"Maybe I sound like her because we both love you, Nate."

"Fuck you," Nate said and started for the door.

"Wait a minute, let me finish."

Nate stopped, but he didn't turn around.

"Do you know why I begged you to hit me? You didn't always want to admit you loved me, but you did want to punch me all the damn time. That's what I could give you because I loved you so goddamned much."

Nate turned around slowly and looked back at me. I saw his filthy dorm room in his eyes. I felt the pain explode in my eye, my cheekbone crack, the slide of blood down my face. I felt him fucking me as he sobbed in time with his thrusts and tasted my blood on his lips. His tears dripped down to mix with our come on my chest as I held him, stroking his hair and trying to shush the hurt little boy hiding in his heart.

I stood up slowly and walked over to him. I got as close as I could to him without touching him and looked up into his face, giving him a clear picture. "You don't wear that ring anymore, do you?"

"What ring?"

"You know what ring, the one you had with the raised initials, your initials."

"I don't know what you're talking about."

"Yeah you do. You can read them right here on my face. Your dad had that ring made in Thailand so it would leave a scar on whoever you punched to remind them who did it to them. I got a pachinko machine and puka shells. You got something to hurt somebody with."

Nate took a step back and reached up to rub his eyes.

"You asked me why I begged you to punch me."

Nate dropped his hand and looked down at me.

"Beating me was the only way you knew how to love me."

Nate shook his head and took a step back. Before he turned away he said, "I wish I could love you that much."

"You do, Nate. Look at what you've given me."

"What have I ever given you?"

I turned and walked away from him, my heart mammocked into rags.

I heard him turn around and walk toward me before I felt his hands on my shoulders. "I said, what have I ever given you?"

He'd never, in a million years, understand it if I told him he gave me his tears. Without turning around, I asked him, "Nate, where exactly did you hope tonight would end up?"

He turned me around gently and looked down into my eyes. I saw him swallow hard.

"I didn't come looking for you, I swear. I just saw you in the window of that shell shop."

"It's OK, Nate." I whispered it more than I said it.

"Why do we keep doing this to each other after all these years?" His voice was soft and unutterably sad.

I still wanted him as bad as I ever had. I wanted him like I wanted his initials carved into the flesh of my face over my right cheekbone. I wanted him as simply as the coral heads wanted to be back in the sweet rocking sea. I reached up and took his thick wrist and drew his knuckles to my mouth to kiss. "It's just in our natures, I guess."

Nate twisted his wrist free gently and stroked my scar with the back of his fingers. "You're the only...you're the only guy. You know that, right?"

"Yeah, I know it. Lucky me."

Nate lifted my chin to look at him. "I wanted us to end up in bed, but you knew that all along. Why do we always have to bring up all this old shit to hurt each other?"

"Because I can't make it easy for you, Nate. I have to know you understand how much you mean to me. If it was just me sucking you off every time we ran into each other, we could have finished this off in the parking lot at Alex's Souvenir Shop. But that's not what this is about and it never has been."

Nate slipped his arm around my shoulder and pulled me to him. "You always make me prove it, don't you?"

I nodded against his chest and slipped my hands into his back pockets.

Nate bent down his face to kiss the top of my head. "It might take me a little while to, you know...get really hard. I've been having some problems."

I looked up at him and smiled. "I've gotten fat."

"You're still the most beautiful thing I've ever seen, girl *or* guy."

"And you're still the stud I remember. What's poking me doesn't seem like it has any problems."

Nate laughed. "There's one big difference since the last time we got together."

I squeezed his ass through his back pockets. "Yeah, what?"

"I got some Viagra, it takes a little while to kick in all the way, but I think we can use the time wisely. It's a good thing we're spending a hell of a lot longer time talking our way around to it."

"That's your choice. You always did need to be begged."

"Right now, I want to spend a long time doing it, if it's going to have to last me." He put his hand under my ass, between my legs, and lifted me up onto the balls of my feet.

I sighed genuinely. I couldn't help it. I could have told him that was his choice too, but he knew that. I broke away from him and started toward my bedroom.

"Wait a minute, I have to tell you something, Frankie."

I stopped and turned around.

Nate held out his hands. "C'mere."

I took the two steps back to him and let him take my hands and steer us back to the sofa. He sat and urged me down next to him.

"You need to know a couple of things."

I tried to read his face. Nate didn't communicate truths or confessions with this kind of calm. He shouted. He hit. He fucked. Nate didn't converse when it came to the important things, he just struck out. "I'm listening," I said finally after noting the tiredness around his eyes and the high flush under the skin of his face.

"I lied. I did come looking for you. I don't live too far away."

"Where?"

Nate shook his head as if I was being deliberately worrisome. "That doesn't matter."

I realized he was nearly crushing my hands, he was gripping them so hard. "Ease up a little, big guy, you're cutting off my circulation."

Nate eased up on his grip, but he didn't let go. Instead, he pulled me a bit closer. "Look, Frankie...it's complicated, but I don't want it to be years between us getting together anymore. But I don't...I can't go gay. You understand? I'm not going to start marching in any parades and shit, but I don't want to be so far away from you anymore."

The struggle in his face was heartbreaking. "What makes you think I'd ask you to start marching in parades? I don't march in parades, I'm self-loathing, remember?"

Nate laughed and let go of my hands. He slumped back against the sofa and craned his neck to look at the ceiling. "You still push me. You push hard, Frankie."

I wanted to touch him some way. Instead, I just leaned back sideways with my elbow on the back of the sofa, my scar hidden in my palm as I rested my face in my hand to look at him. "OK, so what is it, Nate?"

"I'm fucked-up, man. It's my heart. I take this medicine to thin out my blood and I can't get hard anymore half the time. I've been cut open twice since the last time I saw you. The doctor says the walls of my heart are like paper. I'm on disability. He says I can't even lift a bag of sugar over my head."

I reached up to put my hand on his shoulder, but Nate knocked it away gently. He leaned forward again, put his elbows on his knees, and rested his big noble head in his large scarred hands. "I ain't got anybody else. I've run off my wife and my kids. I've treated you like shit. I never was any good at..."

I couldn't sit where I was, staring at his back and his humbled, bent head while he beggared his pride next to me. I slid off the sofa into the narrow space between the sofa and the coffee table by his knees.

"Frankie, all I could ever do is work and fight and fuck. Take that away and I honestly don't know who I am. I'm just about worthless."

"You're not to me," I offered.

Nate stood up slowly and walked, not to the door but to the front window.

"Let's just concentrate on getting you well."

"Let's? Why would you do that? Even if I could get well, which I won't. I'm going to die, Frankie. Sooner rather than later."

"No!" I almost shouted.

Nate turned from the window to look at me and laughed. "You're the stubbornest son of a bitch I've ever met in my life. You say I'm not going to die like you could do something about it. You say 'Let's get you well' just like you don't know, if I did, I would walk away from you for the first woman who gave me a second look."

"So what?"

"I don't deserve it, that's what! Look at you down there on your knees, like a dog. What did I ever do to deserve that kind of loyalty?"

I stood up and walked toward the bedroom once more. Halfway to the door, I stopped and turned around to answer his question. "What did I ever do to deserve you? You walk in and out of my life as easy as if I sat up on a shelf somewhere, in suspended animation, until you come around again. But you know what, Nate? So what. So fucking what. All that matters to me, all that has ever mattered to me is that I love you. God*damn* it, I'm stuck with you. Here or dead and gone. You are a bastard and you always have been, but I love you and I can't quit you, just like you can't quit me."

"I can't fight anymore, Frankie." Nate said suddenly and rubbed his eyes again. He'd been doing it all night. "I'm too tired."

"Then don't. Your bed is in that room and I'm getting in it. Everything you want, everything you need, is right here. Make up your mind, Nate. Come on, or lock the door on your way out."

"You don't get it, do you Frankie? I don't know what to do."

"You knew enough to hunt me down. You knew enough to take

a damn Viagra. You need to quit fighting with yourself, not me."

Nate looked at me. He looked at the door and then off over my head.

"Wait a minute...or did you think you had to fuck me? Is that it? You scared you couldn't lean on me unless you bought me off with your dick?"

Nate took two steps toward me and held out his hands. "No goddamn it, I wouldn't play you that way. Is that what you think?"

It was my turn to laugh. "Nate, I don't give you that much credit for thinking ahead."

He snickered himself, then, seeing I wasn't mad, he gave up and laughed genuinely as well. "We're getting too old for this shit."

"Yeah, right. We'll be going over the same old arguments when we're in our 80s."

Nate shook his head and looked me in the eye. "No. We won't. Seriously, Frankie. I may not make 50."

Nate wasn't joking and he wasn't exaggerating. I knew it, but everything in me didn't want to.

"Can you put up with my bullshit for whatever's left?" He wasn't begging. It wasn't rhetorical. It was an honest question.

"Can you forget about the straight-or-gay shit and just let me love you?" It wasn't a challenge, it was an honest question. He'd landed one in my gut this time. I wanted a yes or no.

"I don't know, Frankie. I promise to try."

The three yards of polished hardwood floor seemed like miles between us. I knew he'd come as far as he could go. The rest of the way was up to me, but I couldn't take another step in his direction. Thirty-nine years and it all came down to three feet. I was frozen to the spot I stood on.

We stared at each other, never noting all the tiny open mouths on the coral heads that sat all around the room. This time their song and cries weren't for me. Bashed and broken from their living reefs, brokenhearted and beautiful in their places on the mantel, the tables, and in the baskets, they sang for Nate alone.

In the small space between us, I saw him wet and laughing, running into the sea with the sun on his golden back. Nate was 9 years old and beaten but not afraid, his bruises the color of the water he arced into. His ocean eyes sought me out, broke over me. Those days were a million miles away from the lanky beaten boxer, on the ropes so far from beach. Those suns gathered like the glints in his hair, the sparks he squeezed from my sighs, so much time in the distance to cover just two short strides across a hardwood floor.

The coral cried and Nate reached across the great distance over shells, gifts, and more that I'd laid at his feet for years to guide him back again and again. I caught him by the belt loops at his hips and pulled him safe over the polished stretch of floor.

"Don't talk, Frankie," he whispered and slid down between my hands. On his knees, he wrapped his arms around my waist. I hugged his head to my chest and rocked him as currents swelled to fill the thousands of thirsty mouths of the coral heads and we all found ourselves back home in the sea. If just for a little while, one more time could see out a lifetime.

"Let me come home, Frankie. Jesus God, I'm so scared you won't let me come home."

"Hush. You ain't never been gone."

The End of the Show

Timothy Lambert

"You make it impossible for me to—"

David stopped yelling, snatched up my *Ellen DeGeneres Show* coffee mug from the kitchen counter, and threw it at the wall. I cringed, expecting it to shatter into a million pieces upon impact. Ellen's strong spirit must have been infused into the mug's glazing process along with her name, because the mug broke through the plaster and remained intact. The handle stayed visible, protruding from my kitchen wall.

I looked intently at the damage, wondering how David had intended to finish his sentence. Impossible for him to do what? Remain sane? Apparently. Calculate logarithms? I didn't even know what those were. Love me? That seemed more likely.

I considered calling my friend Tatiana so she could come over and remove the damaged wall for her next installation at the Michael Baydar Gallery in SoHo. The sheetrock was obviously too dilapidated to remove in one piece. Still, entire murals were moved all the time. Tatiana had to know how it was done. She could title it *David's Disgust,* or maybe *Breaking Barriers* would be better. Either way, it might sell for thousands of dollars. I could get a cut and use the money to fix up my apartment. Or maybe there'd be enough for me to move into another apartment altogether.

That thought brought me back to reality; the subject of moving was the reason David and I were arguing. We were both very opinionated people and had heated discussions all the time. They were almost always about our relationship.

We'd been dating for two years but still maintained separate apartments in Manhattan. I lived in a run-down railroad apartment in the east Village. David had purchased a condo in a prewar building in Chelsea that had just recently gone co-op. He'd meticulously renovated and updated the apartment, using up a large portion of his savings. Our respective apartments said a lot about us as individuals.

David was eight years older as well as a responsible and well-respected photographer for a fashion magazine. He always dressed impeccably, as if eternally ready for someone to turn the camera around on him. His apartment was dressed just as stylishly, with a tasteful blend of modern art and antique furniture, highlighted with the latest gizmos and computer gadgetry.

My apartment was as disheveled as I was. It was furnished in what I liked to call "deprivation chic," with the finest castaways and sidewalk finds. The hinges on one of my closet doors had come away from the frame. I'd tried to rehang it, but the wood was rotting, so I gave up, resolved to lifting it in and out of the door frame. The broiler door on my stove was missing. My bathroom was split in two: the tub and sink in one tiny room, the toilet in another. I had to walk through the kitchen just to wash my hands after peeing.

"Well, that settles it." Trying to remain calm, I gestured to the Ellen mug lodged in my kitchen wall and said, "I can't move now. There's no way I'll get my deposit back after this."

"That's brilliant, Andrew. Very funny. Very childish. Keep it up. You're pushing me farther and farther away." David shook his head in annoyance and left, slamming the door behind him.

I stood in the middle of my kitchen, unsure what to do next. It was as if I were in a parallel universe. David never threw things or yelled. That was my role. David never stormed out of my apartment. I always stormed out of his, expecting him to come running after me. Which never happened, of course. No matter how much I wanted it, nobody ever chased after me when I walked out.

The Ellen mug suddenly succumbed to gravity and fell out of the wall, shattering into little pieces on the greasy tile of my kitchen floor. So much for Tatiana's next showing. I frowned and finally ran after David.

I knew exactly where he'd go. He'd stopped by my place to try to get me to go to lunch with him, which was always a source of contention. As a stand-up comic and part-time bartender, my schedule was later than the rest of the world's. I worked at night. Therefore, my day didn't start until noon, sometimes later. I'd just had breakfast when David dropped by, and I wasn't hungry.

I'd tried to suggest meeting later for dinner, but David apparently was in the mood to fight and clung to the rejection instead. He argued that if we lived together, we'd see each other more often and our different schedules wouldn't matter. I countered by stating that he obviously hated what I did for a living and was trying to change me, which would be easier for him if I moved into his place and he had the home-court advantage. We went on in that vein for a while until the Ellen mug hit the wall. Since he'd never done anything that brash in the two years we'd been arguing, I figured he had low blood sugar and had gone to the diner on the corner.

Sure enough, he was just sitting down at one of the diner's sidewalk tables.

"I'll have a club sandwich, please. Mayo on the side, and a Diet Coke," I heard him say.

I slipped into the chair opposite him and added, "No lemon in his Coke. I'll have a coffee. Black."

David sighed audibly as the waiter left us. He looked tired and unwilling. I was smiling and feeling like Barbra Streisand's character in *What's Up, Doc?* who always turned up where she wasn't wanted.

"New Hampshire," I finally said.

"What is the only state to border Maine?" David, who was a *Jeopardy!* buff, asked. "What are you talking about?"

The End of the Show

"You're always bugging me about where I come from. Now I'm telling you," I said.

"You've told me that. You're from Chadwick, New Hampshire."

"Actually, to be accurate, I'm from Chadwick Corners. Population: 1,500. At least it was in 1987, when I was 16. I don't know how many people live there now. People with money lived in Chadwick. People striving to reach lower middle-class, like my family, lived in Chadwick Corners. The corners were actually two country roads. At their intersection was an ancient general store with two gas pumps, which was Chadwick Corners' main attraction."

David said, "I'll bet it's really a quaint place. Like a Norman Rockwell painting come to life."

"Hell no. Chadwick was the Norman Rockwell painting," I said dryly. "Main Street was lined with businesses housed in red brick buildings, and they all had hand-carved wooden signs with gold lettering hanging from their storefronts. There were elm trees everywhere, and red brick crosswalks overlapping the streets. The pedestrian crossing signs were a formality, because nearly everyone in Chadwick stopped politely for people crossing the streets.

"At the top of Main Street was a small green park with a gazebo where a band gave Pops concerts on warm summer nights. Vegetable farmers from Chadwick Corners sold their wares every Friday at the farmers market. Lobstermen sold their catch of the day from the backs of their trucks on the weekend. The center of the park could be flooded, creating a safe place for kids to ice-skate in winter."

"Sounds cute," David commented.

"There wasn't much for a kid to do in Chadwick, but it was a lot more interesting for me to spend time there than watching pine trees grow in Chadwick Corners. There was a pool hall, a bookstore, a couple of cafés, and a cineplex out on the edge of town. I went to Chadwick High and always hung out in town after school. I hated going home at the end of the day."

"Why?" David asked.

"Home was boring. I was always plotting my escape to New York City. I used to buy *The Village Voice* every week and circle the Roommates Wanted ads. You know, just in case I had to get out," I answered. "I couldn't relate to my family, and they couldn't relate to me. I don't think any of us really tried, now that I look back on it. My father was a mechanic and ran his own garage. My brother helped him after school. My mother cut hair, managed our home, and rarely did anything for herself. On the surface, I guess we were a typical rural family. We managed. We got by. But we never talked to each other."

"How is that possible?" David asked.

I knew that concept would be difficult for David to understand. He came from a large Roman Catholic family and had five brothers and sisters. They grew up in an affluent Boston suburb and remained involved in one another's lives. David's mother was a teacher in his private school. His father was a prominent attorney but still managed to find time to coach his boys' soccer team. David talked to them at least three times a week. I hadn't spoken to my family in months.

"I don't know. Maybe I breathed wrong or something when I was a kid. My brother and I weren't what you'd call scholarly. I knew my brain wasn't going to be my ticket out of Chadwick Corners." David frowned at me. He hated self-deprecation. But he ate his sandwich quietly and let me continue. "I was into anything artistic. Painting, singing, acting, even photography."

"I didn't know that," David said.

"I used to be really great in a darkroom," I declared.

"You still are," David said saucily, obviously remembering a moment we'd shared in his studio a month ago.

"Anyway, my family couldn't or wouldn't relate to my interests. I didn't care. My only goal was to remain as invisible as possible when I was at home. Even in school, to a point. I squeaked by in academics so I'd be eligible for extracurricular activities after school. But my real passion was theater."

I stared at Third Avenue, but I didn't see dingy storefronts and litter, or the sidewalks teeming with pedestrians and beggars. Instead, I saw the granite edifice of the theater in Chadwick, where I'd spent every summer of my adolescence.

Colton Theater Co. was well-known in New England, especially for their summer stock program. Interns from all over the country would come to study various aspects of the theater: performance, technical, or management. Each summer they'd mount five musical productions from June to August. And each summer I'd get a job as an usher, showing people to their seats then watching every show from the steps that led up to the balcony.

It was strictly volunteer work, so I definitely wasn't in it for the money. I loved watching the productions, learning every line and studying the differences in each actor's performance from one show to the next. I hoped for technical difficulties, loving it when the actors were forced to ad-lib. I imagined myself onstage and dreamed that one day I'd be in their place, performing and making people laugh or cry.

"Sounds like the perfect job for a gay boy to me," David said when I told him about it.

"Definitely. Although I wasn't gay then," I said. David looked dubious, so I continued, "Well, of course I was. But I hadn't experimented with what I was feeling about my sexuality at that time. I was only 16, and hard-pressed to find other gay guys in Chadwick. Plus, I didn't know if I *wanted* to explore that side of myself yet."

"But working in a theater, there must've been lots of gay men around," David pointed out.

"That's such a stereotypical thing to assume," I said. "Well, yeah, of course there were. But they were all older than me. Then again, most of the interns were only four or five years older. I suppose they just seemed a lot older at the time."

"When you're 16, everyone seems ancient," David said. He gestured at me and added, "Or even when you're 33."

"Want to join me onstage at the Hysteria House tomorrow night?" I asked sarcastically. "Besides, I've never said you're ancient. Decrepit, maybe, but definitely not ancient."

"You're so mean to me," David stated, but I could tell he didn't mean it.

"Anyway, that's what I loved about the theater, more than anything else. Age didn't seem to matter. Everyone treated me like an equal. We all had a job to do and shared the same passion. Nobody ever talked down to me. I finally felt like I belonged somewhere. It was great."

"I'll bet it was," David concurred. He paid the check, saying, "Now I understand where you come from. Was that so difficult?"

"Yes. I'm flawed. You're not supposed to know that."

"We all are," David said, sounding exasperated. "What bothers me is that I had to yell and act like an animal before you'd open up to me."

"You wouldn't do that unless you cared," I said. He rolled his eyes, put away his wallet, then looked at his watch. I knew I'd only scratched the surface of what I wanted to tell him, so I asked, "Do you have somewhere to be right now?"

"Some of us have real jobs," he said, reminding me that he was still angry.

"Some of us are big jerks. Is this where you walk out on me again?"

It took a moment for him to say anything, as if he had to count to 10 to calm down. "Before today, you were always the one walking out on our fights. Not me. Maybe we should shelve this until later. Right now I have to go photograph an annoying socialite and her pied-à-terre on the upper east side. Are you bartending tonight?"

"No," I answered. "I'm not working or performing. That's why I suggested dinner."

"Why don't you come to my place later? At 8?"

"Nine," I offered. I felt as if we should seal the deal with a handshake, but David kissed me on the cheek before walking away and hailing a cab.

I had another refill and watched people walk by, trying to figure out why I was finally telling David about my past. Everyone had a past, didn't they? It wasn't like I'd lived some sordid life of crime. Or been a prostitute. Or a Boy Scout. I'd always been selective about what I revealed to other people. I probably always would be.

The End of the Show

Even during that summer in 1987, when Brent Adams, Colton Theater's house manager, offered me a job as head usher, I lied and said I'd told my parents about my promotion. He'd innocently assumed they'd be proud, especially since I'd be paid $25 a week. My parents were prouder of my brother Jeff, who was becoming more like my father every day as they worked together in the garage. I didn't want anything to do with that. I was learning everything I could about the theater, hoping it would be my ticket out of Chadwick Corners.

Until my promotion, I was content to read ticket stubs and make sure our patrons got to their correct seats. As head usher I was in charge of making sure we'd have at least 10 ushers for each performance. Our ushers were local kids from Chadwick, most of whom I hardly knew because they were all younger than me.

It was also my duty to sort out seating mishaps. I'd work it out while cracking jokes. *You didn't want to sit there anyway. This seat over here has a much better view. Trust me. That seat's been in danger of collapsing since 1942, when Bertha Strongbottom was a season ticket holder. It's an old theater legend. Ask anybody. Late at night, when the theater's closed, you can still hear old Bertha stuffing herself full of popcorn.*

One day Brent Adams asked me if I'd mind helping the box office interns count the ticket stubs. I wanted to watch that afternoon's matinee, but Brent was too nice a guy to refuse. I resigned myself to the lobby, hearing the overture to *Anything Goes* fading behind me as I went downstairs, where I saw two interns counting tickets instead of the usual three. Obviously, someone had called out sick or something.

"Hi, my name is Andrew," I said. "Brent asked me to help you guys."

One of them looked up and said, "Great. Hi, my name is Brenda, and I am a box office intern."

I knew next to nothing about 12-step programs, so her joke was lost on me. Instead, I remained fixated on the crystal-blue eyes of the other intern. Thinking of other men as attractive was a relatively new concept for me. I thought Corey Hart rocked, but I also thought he was extremely cute. I would've plastered my bedroom walls with pictures of Johnny Depp if I thought my brother wouldn't catch on and beat me up. Both Corey and Johnny had a certain gentle sweetness to them that was mirrored in the intern's gaze. His long, light brown hair was tied back in a ponytail. He had flawlessly pale skin and rather large eyeteeth, which made him look almost catlike when he smiled at me.

"I think we've got this under control, but thanks anyway," he said. There was something in his eyes that let me know he wasn't trying to be standoffish.

I stood there for a moment, trying to come up with a reason to stay. I wanted to know more about him. I wanted him to like me. I felt silly and slightly embarrassed, so I went back upstairs to watch the show and invent ways to get him to notice me. Brent Adams was sitting on the stairs with the ushers, watching the show, so I sat down next to him and whispered, "They didn't need me."

"I find that hard to believe. Anyone who can't find some use for you ought to have his head examined. So to speak," Brent said mischievously. He grinned, then scampered downstairs like a hit-and-run comedian. I hoped he wasn't going to scold the box office staff for not letting me help them, which would be embarrassing. But later they joined us to watch the second act and never said anything about it.

I was at the top of the stairs, and the blue-eyed object of my affection sat a couple of steps below me next to Brenda. He was so close that I could have touched him if I dared. I wanted to run my fingers through his hair, freeing it from the elastic that held it in place. Instead I stretched my legs and let my foot lightly bump his arm. He turned around, and I pretended to be aghast while whispering "Sorry!"

He smiled and gently picked up my foot, carefully putting it down a safe distance from himself. He pointed at it as if it were a dog and whispered, "Stay!"

It made me like him all the more.

Four nights later the manager of the cineplex offered the entire theater company free admission to a midnight screening of the new Batman movie. His daughter was one of my ushers, and he was a season ticket holder. Box Office Boy would be there, so I was consumed with the idea of going, although I didn't know how I'd manage it. My parents wouldn't care, but I couldn't drive yet, and I knew they wouldn't drive me because it was too late.

Brent Adams came to my rescue. When I said I wasn't sure if I was going, he insisted on being my personal chauffeur. At first I was worried that Brent would hit on me, then I found out he'd offered three other people a ride. Plus, his boyfriend was going too. I was still naive and didn't know anything about threesomes or affairs, but the ride to the theater was relatively uneventful and my virtue remained unblemished.

The concession stand was closed, which was fine with me since I didn't have any money. I ducked into the men's room to lose Brent and the other people I'd ridden with. When I came out and went into the theater I saw them taking seats near the front. Everybody sat either as close to the screen as possible or at the very back, leaving a wide valley of open seats in the middle. I couldn't see Box Office Boy anywhere, so I figured he hadn't arrived yet. I thought about waiting for him but couldn't figure out how to remain standing without looking like a complete idiot. I finally decided to sit alone in the very middle of the theater.

Shortly after I took a seat, Brenda and Box Office Boy ran down the aisle wearing Batman logo T-shirts, capes, and masks. They were loudly singing the Batman theme and soon everyone in the theater joined in. I was thrilled when they finally sat down in front of me.

"Ready for some Bat thrills and chills, Andrew?" Brenda asked.

"Holy free movie, Brenda! You bet I am!" I exclaimed. I felt like a dork, but that faded when Box Office Boy laughed then pretended to punch me.

"Pow!" he yelled.

"Bap!" Brenda screamed, throwing a punch his way.

The lights dimmed and all fake fighting ceased. I found it extremely difficult to concentrate on the movie because of Box Office Boy. I couldn't believe that I still didn't know his name. I was more worried about Brenda. Were they dating? They'd slumped down in their seats, which effectively sealed me off from further interaction. Every now and then they'd whisper, and I'd feel a knot form in my stomach when their heads would almost touch.

After the movie everybody filed up the aisle to leave, some groaning at how late it was, others still talking excitedly about Michael Keaton and Jack Nicholson. I was painfully aware that Box Office Boy was walking behind me as I left the theater. In the lobby he grabbed my shirt and asked, "Ever drive with the devil in the pale moonlight?"

"What are you?" I said, mimicking a line from the movie.

"That's his way of asking if you need a ride home," Brenda explained.

"Yeah, that'd be great," I said, wishing Box Office Boy wouldn't let go of my shirt. I wanted him to tear it off me. Unfortunately, he let go. "But I live way out in the boonies. It's a 20-minute drive from here. You don't have to."

"No, that's fine," Box Office Boy replied.

"Can you drop me off first?" Brenda begged. "I'm exhausted."

After Brenda was gone, I directed Box Office Boy down the country roads toward my house. I wanted the drive to last longer and contemplated taking a few detours. Instead, I finally asked him his name.

"John Thedry Evans."

"I don't mean to be rude, but Thedry? What kind of name is that?"

"It's a family name," he explained.

"Thank you for driving me home. I don't know how I would've managed it otherwise," I said. I wanted to sound relaxed and older, but instead I felt like a character in an Edith Wharton novel. "So how long have you and Brenda been together?"

"Just a couple of weeks," he replied. "Oh. Wait, no. We're not dating or anything. We're roommates. We got an apartment a block away from the theater."

"It must be nice to have an apartment. I'd love to see it sometime," I said.

"Someone's feeling brazen tonight?" he said, glancing at me briefly with a smile.

"I'm feeling kind of bold," I admitted. Throwing all caution to the wind, I added, "If you were to pull over and park on the shoulder of the road, I'd probably even let you kiss me."

"And did he?" David asked me later in his apartment. I paused, remembering the anxiety I'd felt 15 years earlier; my first kiss with a man. I gave my best Mona Lisa smile, and David said, "Of course he did. I can't say that I blame him. I'll bet you were a cute kid."

David refilled my wine glass. I told him all about my first kiss with John, and how it was like all the others that came after it: gentle, sweet, and exploratory. John had always seemed content to let me initiate everything, perhaps letting me figure out my own boundaries and how far I wanted to take our relationship.

"How old was John?" David asked.

"Twenty-five," I answered, waiting for David to be shocked or disgusted. He merely raised his eyebrows briefly before taking a long sip of wine, so I said, "He interned at Colton right after graduating from college. He wanted to run his own theater company some day."

"Does he?"

I thought about answering him. But that wasn't the point of the story.

"His parents didn't want him to," I said. "They were upper-crust psychologists from Connecticut, wanted him to follow in their footsteps, go to one of those ivy-covered universities. He refused. They refused to fund his education if he didn't play by their rules."

David didn't say anything for a while. I couldn't blame him. I wasn't sure how well I'd take it if he prattled on about some old boyfriend. But it wasn't something I did often, and he was the one who was always saying that our pasts shape us into the people we become. I decided he should be happy that I was finally spilling my guts, and forged onward.

"After our first kiss, I was completely smitten. I did everything I could to see him as often as I could. I'd spend entire days in Chadwick, going home only to eat and sleep. John would take me out to eat, we'd drive to the beach, go to movies. It took me about a month to get into his apartment. But once I did, I wanted to spend all of my time there. I imagined us living together, eating, sleeping, spending every minute of our lives together and loving it."

I could see David's eyes narrow over the rim of his wine glass.

"I was rather ignorant then," I hastily added. "John took me to a Suzanne Vega concert that summer. She sang this one song 'Gypsy'; to this day it still makes me think of him. And another song 'Calypso' totally made me cry. They were both about men who come into your life, who you fall in love with, then they leave you. Looking back, I should've realized that's what was going to happen with John."

"Did it?" David asked.

"Of course," I said. "By the end of that summer I was convinced I was in love with him. Oddly enough, it never dawned on me until practically the last minute to ask him what his plans were after Colton's summer internship ended. On the night of the last performance, I made up some lie for my parents and arranged to spend the night with him. I was extremely nervous. I'd never slept with him, or anyone else, before that night."

"Wait," David interjected. "You never had sex with him?"

"Nope. We held each other all night, and it was wonderful. Very sweet. The next morning I woke up and he was packing his things. He explained to me that he'd gotten a job with a theater company in Boston, managing their box office or something. I couldn't believe he'd just go and leave me alone in that horrible little town with my family who didn't give a shit about me."

"How selfish of you," David said. I glared at him but couldn't say anything, because he was right. "I still can't believe you two never had sex. I was expecting this story to be adopted by the New Hampshire Man-Boy Love Association."

"Sorry to disappoint you," I said.

"So that was it?"

"I walked him to the bus stop, helped him carry his bags, waited a half hour with him for the bus to Boston. When he left, I hugged him and he kissed me on the cheek. That was it. There was so much I wanted to say to him and thank him for." I paused, remembering how I listened to nothing but Suzanne Vega songs for days afterward while crying and wishing I were with him again. "But I couldn't get the words out, and I let him go."

"Did you ever see him again?" David asked.

I laughed and said, "A year later, I was in Manchester with some friends and ran into him. It was so out of the blue. We did the small-talk thing. He asked if I was getting along better with my family, how school was, that sort of thing. Nothing had changed for me. I found out he loved Boston and was doing well. He was late meeting his sister for dinner, so I hugged him goodbye.

"But that time, I finally told him what I didn't say the year before. I told him I loved him and thanked him. He asked what I was thanking him for, and I said that he'd taught me that I was capable of being loved. That I was worthy of someone's love."

I realized I was staring at my plate, at the remains of a pork chop. I was embarrassed by my story and my admission that I could be that fragile.

David stood up and took my hand, leading me to his sofa. He pulled me down and I lay in his arms, feeling his warm breath on the back of my neck.

"Sometimes," he said softly, "you make it impossible for me to love you."

"This sounds familiar," I said.

"But most of the time, you make it impossible for me not to love you."

I rolled over and kissed him.

Thirty-three Years

Michael Huxley

Malibu, December 31, 1999

In the closeted, paranoid years before meeting James, I made the majority of my sexual contacts while working. James, though he proved exceptional, was no exception.

Many lusted for me in my day, but holding myself as a standard for physical attractiveness limited the number of men with whom I touched bases, as I insisted that all considerations be at least near, equal to, or surpassing my appeal. James Sutton, in my strict estimation, slipped tightly into the last category.

Easiest were anonymous tricks. Such encounters oftentimes proved among the most gratifying physically but seldom amounted to anything more than a single event. Not that a man's disinclination to emotional involvement always precluded a longer acquaintance, but I inevitably became bored with what are now called fuck buddies.

Even so, I was never impervious to love; quite the contrary. Whenever hope fertilized opportunity, I purposely incubated its zygote, fanned love's spark, only to observe it atrophy over time and then spontaneously abort. Until James Sutton: the brilliant young artist, the spoiled brat, the most outstanding specimen of manhood I'd ever made love to, I had every reason to suspect that hope springs not eternal but temporary, for what only *seems* an eternity. Once done, there was no erasing James from my obsession.

We fell instantly in love.

That James was sole heir to a Hollywood fortune was incidental, as I inherited my father's high-end construction business (and talent for wise investment) when he and my mother were killed in an automobile accident during my senior year at UCLA. It was never about money, James and I, but worth. James was a true individualist, vibrated intelligence, was pissed off—and with good reason: He was born, wasn't he? His arrogance obfuscated the lesson to be learned that big boys have never been allowed to cry, not really, so big boys objectify. We lust and hope to come of age in vain, settle for spurting hot tears in hiding places. Firing round after round of thick, white compensation, we feel beatified. For a time.

Arousal and unutterable loneliness coalesce, recalling the day James entered my life early in the Summer of Love.

I was naked and painfully aroused, awaiting his return that late-May afternoon in 1967. Noting my reflection, replete with its pounding erection, in the patio sliders of his mother's noteworthy home in Santa Monica, I was lying on a large sunning mat by the pool, struggling to not masturbate. Every nerve fiber in my cock, every synapse in my brain, was shrieking for me to lose the battle, but I didn't.

As the Ormsby-Sutton driveway project was progressing ahead of schedule, I'd sent my crew home earlier than usual that afternoon, hoping that James would return sooner than he eventually did. Remaining on-site, I found my way to poolside, where I stripped, ending my frantic erection's denim confinement, and collapsed onto the sunning mat—a safe but visible distance from the sliders. Sudden physical inactivity unleashed my mind: *Why didn't you let James fuck you, let him suck you off? That's what you wanted. Why didn't you at least jerk off after he came in your mouth, allow him to witness your momentous shooting?*

Because...I rationalized...*I considered him too significant for a quickie, and told him so.*

But my reflection knew that was only partially true, that my objective was to addict young James—absurd as that notion now seems—by offering him a mere sample of my passion, confident that he would crave more. Afterward, when I informed him, unsolicited, that I intended to spend the night with him there, he accepted that as a given.

Where the fuck is he? I wondered from the sunning mat. *It must be well after 4 by now…* Receiving no answer, I returned to free association and my cock: *I sense great potential for success with this James. He qualifies, exudes substance.*

Remember though, Alan, my reflection countered, cautiously caressing his volatile erection in the sliders. *Even those you successfully hooked, who then were able to see beyond your beauty, ultimately proved incapable of intriguing or challenging you further.*

Tuning that consideration out, I removed my hands from my genital area, brought them to my face, and inhaled deeply: *Perfect.* I lifted one elbow and sniffed my armpit: *Yeah…* I was filthy after my day spent on the backhoe and would remain so until James arrived. My scent was too compelling to remove by diving into the pool, which would have been my first inclination upon arriving home after a normal workday.

He's late, my reflection persisted. *Just how many fixes do you think it will take?*

"I've been wrong before, but I suspect that young James Sutton has already succumbed to me," I replied.

Be aware, Alan! Wishful romanticism is a worldview you profess to scorn in others. Your theory is based not on concrete evidence but a 30-minute seduction over your lunch break, shared with a beautiful college boy who's house-sitting for his mother, that culminated with your giving him a good blow job in her kitchen.

So it was that I lay, irrational and suffering on that sunning mat. Had I been at all prescient, I would have put tormented misgivings aside and not underestimated James.

When I heard his Jag pull in, I thanked a god whose existence or nonexistence is an ongoing debate that has never interested me in the least.

Young James called my name. Because I had moved my truck

up to the garage entrance, he knew I was near. I heard my name shouted again, from a closer distance. *Come to me, James,* I projected. *Find me, like this...* I heard him enter the house, again calling out. *If he suspects that I might be inside, then the house was left unlocked when he departed for the library. He trusts me.* When I spied him through my reflection, his presence did not intimidate me, though I was vulnerable. I felt no shame in strumming my cock; indeed, its hardness intensified. *Come to me, James.*

He pulled my reflection aside and stepped through the slider entrance, his eyes fixed upon me. Approaching me, he raised his shirt above his head and tossed it to the pool deck, unveiling distended pectorals. He stood over me, eclipsing the late-afternoon sunshine, and kicked off his sandals. Our eyes locked.

"My god, you're a vision. Didn't you hear me call?" he queried while unbuttoning his frayed bell-bottoms.

"Thank god you're back," I responded, near breathless with yearning. "Jim, please...get down here."

He dropped his jeans and kicked them away. Making warm contact with my thigh, he fell to his knees beside me. I raised myself a touch and we slid into one another's embrace. Though our love would never produce offspring, we were together as our natures intended.

"Are you all right?" he inquired, genuinely concerned, stroking my beard.

"I will be soon," I replied. Our mouths, his positive, drawn to my negative, pulled closer. Jerking stiff by fits and starts in my hand, James's magnetic opposite pole had grown rigid in seconds.

He sighed when our tongues met, but our kissing only increased the relentless blood flow that seemed to stretch my cock shaft cruelly beyond its maximum length and girth.

I could not continue, and so pulled away. "I can't kiss you now, Jim; it hurts too much. Please, just get me off; I've gotta come. Waiting for you was torture; I've been hard for the past four hours." It was no ploy; I sounded desperate because I was. "Suck me off," I implored. "I've been oozing all day thinking about us in the kitchen earlier. Taste my cock; it's all yours now."

"You can relax," he reassured me. "I'm here now. Just let me look at you first; let me touch you. I need to relish you." He ran his hands up my sides, down my chest to my belly. "It's about your *body*..." he whispered. He moistened my neck and throat with kisses, sucked both nipples fleetingly, then continued downward, his tongue leaving a trail in the sweat and grime. He paused to eat out my navel. "You are fucking delicious," he swooned.

"Then eat my cock, Babe. I wanna fill your mouth."

"You will," he assured me, lifting my genital agony with his fingers. "Who could resist *this*?"

"Don't ask me," I moaned. "Just *do* me."

He cupped my scrotum: "Look at these *balls*; Jesus Christ, you're gifted." He buried his face beneath them, inhaled my scent: "Your odor's like a fuckin' drug I can't get enough of."

"Suck me off, man," I insisted. "I'll fill your mouth with come. Do it now, Jim; suck me clean."

"Like I'm not going to?" he slurred. "Like I'm not already *there*?" He ran his tongue, slimy with spit, up my tender underside, between crusty mid shaft and oozing glans. My foreskin, stretched tautly smooth, was practically maroon with oversustained arousal.

"Take me *down*," I begged.

"Just try to stop me." His lips parted. I strained to enter his incomparable face. His mouth at last locked around my urgency, and James lowered his lip ring until it kissed my matted pubes. Nurtured by the warm, salivating depths that lay within his head-giving, pain was transformed at once into its opposite. By the time we'd established a rhythm, his youthful expertise could not be denied.

In no time I was bucking my hips/fucking those lips, free at last to thrust and gyrate, growl and rotate with the lewd, uninhibited abandon of a true hedonist.

What my cock demanded, his mouth provided a hundred times over. I felt no greater imperative than to cock-feed that virile young babe the milky proof of my maleness.

I love cock. I love men. I love this man. I love James...

My eyes were shut, but oh, did I see clearly: I saw James approaching, the first moment my eyes feasted upon him. "Hey, you the foreman?" he had said, what, four hours before?

Four-hours, be-fore, fore-man, fore-skin, fore-play: Come what may, for-ever will that image burn indelibly in my memory. Feast your mind's eye, Alan; it is he who is working you. Feel the semen coursing through your tubes; feel it gather and pressurize. Feast your cock, Alan; launch your big load; feel the goodness, yeah...

I was oblivious, approaching my threshold, but managed to speak: something about James needing to raise his lips high on my shaft and remain there unmoving so I could slam my overdosage unrestrained into his mouth. He must have understood, for I felt his partial retreat.

I heard my voice cry out: "Oh, yeah..." Felt my man-nerve begin to glow nascent, nirvana-bound: "Oh, *yeah...*" Heating rapidly brighter and brighter, from imbedded root system to bursting seed pod, my cock conspired to fuse my senses and short-circuit my sanity: "Oh, *Jim...yeah...*" I found myself gladly lost at a crossroads in a void, where I was given no alternative but to shoot my heavy load straight up the mainline, to once again experience what is perhaps a man's most compelling creed, his most defiant need, his greatest greed, his dirty deed: the majestic pumping of his seed. "*Fuck* yeah..."

How many halcyon lost moments drifted by after that, I had no idea, but all at once I flashed: *Oh, my god...James!* I opened my eyes. He was kneeling above me, supported by one arm, his fist still wrapped around his dripping dick, his piss slit clouded with come. "Jim..." was all that emerged from my mouth.

"Holy *shit*, man," he panted, crashing down upon my torso. I circled my arms around him and we rolled, hyperventilating, onto our sides, my crotch slippery with his semen. At a loss for words, we kissed again and again while our breathing slowly calmed to normal.

"What the fuck just happened?" he asked when the appropriate moment arrived.

"What can I say? Thank you for saving my life." But my attempt at melodrama failed.

"No, really. You were fucking out of it, Alan. I suspect I'm *good*, but—"

"Good?" I cut in. "You blew me *away*."

"Well, then...thanks for the compliment—and the warning, by the way; before your orgasm, I mean. My god, how long has it been since you came? I didn't just taste you; I *drank* you."

"Was it OK?" I asked cautiously. "I didn't want you to gag."

"Of course. I want more, but...right now I'm more concerned about something else."

"Concerned?"

James addressed me meekly. "You said you loved me, Alan."

"I did?" I pulled away from him, rather concerned myself.

"Not 'I love you' exactly. You really don't remember, do you?"

"I'm sorry; no, I don't."

"Like I said, you were blitzed. But shortly before you came—*we* came—you said: 'I love cock. I love men. I love this man. I love James.' It was bizarre; I heard you distinctly. Did you mean me? You don't call me 'James.' "

"I'm not sure why, but I do in my mind, Jim. Yes, I did mean you. But those words occurred to me as thoughts—or so I presume incorrectly."

"Would you call me 'James' from now on? I prefer it."

I laughed softly with relief. "Yes."

"I'm feeling that I very well may love you too, Alan," he stated objectively before suddenly blurting: "Hell, who am I kidding? I'm way gone on you. And for once I'm not afraid to let myself go."

My heart was bursting with gladness—such an event for me! I hugged him with all my considerable might.

"Easy, python," he laughed. "Leave me some breath."

"I don't want to smother you, James, or scare you away. It's just that...I'm very happy right now. 'Happy' isn't usually my operative word."

"Good!" he replied, slapping his thighs. "Look, I know this is abrupt, but...I want a cigarette, bad."

"God, so do I," I agreed. "I chain-smoked the last of mine two hours ago."

"I've got plenty in the house. I smoke filters, though. How you can deal with Camel straights is beyond me, but I suppose we *are* from slightly different generations!"

"I'm well aware of that, James. Are you even 20 yet?"

"I will be, in August."

"Oh, shit," I laughed.

"I know, sorry about that, but...what about you? I estimate you're 32 or 33, right?"

"I just turned 33 and was *born* in '33—an only child of the Great Depression."

"And Christ's age when he died," he added, hopping up. "Hang on, I'll run in and get the smokes." My triumphant young love sped off, as beautifully naked as the day we were all, I suppose, reluctantly born, calling over his shoulder: "You wanna beer? I'm gonna have one."

"The biggest glass of ice water you can manage would suit me better."

"You got it," he said, dashing into the house.

Shade had encroached on the sunning mat, so I'd moved to the chaise longues on the far side of the pool. James reemerged carrying a tray and repaired to our new location—much to my surprise, with a decidedly expensive-looking camera slung over his shoulder.

"What's with the camera," I said, instantly snagging a cigarette.

He followed suit by firing up a Viceroy before answering: "I wanna photograph you."

"What, right now?" I replied.

"The camera's loaded, I've got extra film, and there's plenty enough daylight left. Let's do it!"

"Looking like this?" I said doubtfully. "I'm naked, James, and filthy. I was hoping to take a quick swim."

"*Especially* naked and filthy!" he insisted. "Your beauty is intimidating, Alan—certainly, you're aware of that. I almost can't handle it. You're a fucking *hunk*. You see? I'm getting hard again just saying it."

"You wanna take a little break first, then?" I suggested.

"No way, man. You're not getting out of it that easily! But afterward...I might be open to suggestions."

"All right then," I said, disappointed but enormously flattered, considering the source.

"Far out," he exclaimed excitedly.

From the shutter's first blink, James metamorphosed into an exacting photographer, to put it mildly, and the experience proved anything but fun. "Damn it! This isn't working. Shit!" he'd curse. "Put that cigarette out! Here, I'll do it. Goddamn it, I *told* you not to fucking move!" The shoot dragged on and on. He insisted that my cock's being not semi-hard but semi-*soft* was essential. Maintaining a full erection throughout would certainly have been easier, I pointed out, attempting to inject some levity into the situation, but oh, no! That did not suit his purpose at all. He became utterly humorless yet remained tantalizingly naked: an unnerving contradiction.

Mechanically he would "fluff" me between shots, then retreat when the desired degree of "softness" was attained, each withdrawal of his luscious lips an agony for me. James's barking commands, prodding me to assume various uncomfortable poses, and repeatedly cajoling me not to "fucking move," were my reward. Never was a "please" or "thank you" even implied. He stopped frequently, annoyed that my cock had become too hard or had gotten too flaccid. If the latter, he would fluff me again, acting the arrogant *artiste* the entire time.

So it went: set up and frame, fluff me, maintain, focus, then aim. *Click.* I was held hostage by his despotic mien through I don't know how many rolls of black-and-white he loaded (or how many beers he guzzled)—the sun sinking, my cock alternately swelling and shrinking beneath his unblinking insistence upon artistic perfection. He was a real prick.

"That's a wrap," he finally exclaimed. "The fun's over."

"Thank *god*..." I practically imploded with relief.

"Take five, Alan; you've earned it. I'll be back in a few." He vanished into the house, allowing me a generous recovery, and returned after some minutes with what appeared to be a shaving kit. Having approached me from behind, he began to massage my stressed trapezius muscles.

"That feels terrific," I purred. "What's the shaving kit for?"

"You'll see," he answered cryptically, sliding his arms over my shoulders and hugging me. "Thank you for putting up with my insanity. I know I'm horrible, but the photos are going to be so beautiful. I'm incredibly excited."

That more than made up for it all. From feeling abused arose an awareness of being adored, and I was suddenly filled to capacity with blatant desire.

"Whoa, look at you," he said, reaching down and firmly squeezing my hard-on. Working his tongue in my ear, he whispered: "Ready for another rumble, Babe?"

"You have to ask?" I replied.

Once again positioned on the mat, we sat facing one other, both our cocks jutting straight up, demanding attention. Despite the fact that he was cut and I'm not, I noticed for the first time that our cocks were nearly identical in both size and formation when erect.

"Have you noticed how similar our dicks are?"

"They really are, aren't they?" he observed. "Lucky me, huh?"

"No," I disagreed, "lucky *us*..." We played at our leisure: fondling, kissing, humping, masturbating, sucking cock. You know, "big boy" games!

"OK James," I said huskily, indicating the kit he was reaching for. "What's in the mystery bag?"

"Use your head, man," he smirked. "It's my sex works. I want the god I saw through the camera's frame to fuck me good. How does that sound to you?"

"Jesus, what do you think?" I flushed.

"I thought you might be willing," he smiled, unzipping his "works." "You wanna wear a cock ring?"

"I don't need one, but...sure. Why not?" I was beside myself with excitement as he withdrew two leather cock rings, hiked up my balls, strapped one on me, and snapped it snugly into place.

"Too tight?" he asked.

"No, it feels great."

After snapping himself secure, James withdrew a tube of K-Y from the kit, placed it within my easy reach and, lying back, raised his legs.

"God*damn* you feel sweet up there," I slurred, having slipped him my slathered middle finger.

"Try a couple more fingers. Don't worry; I know how to relax...yeah, there y'go...*whew*, that's nice."

"Doing this is makin' me wanna fuck you something fierce," I growled.

"Then *do* it."

I believe I will, James, I thought as I oiled my hard-on with a generous dose of K-Y. Thanks in part to the cock ring, my dick was pulsing prime-time with each lusty heartbeat and felt absolutely killer. Kneeling between James's invitingly spread thighs—his ass held high, his shiny, wet pucker positioned just right—I moved in for the thrill of my life.

"Rock me, Alan," he urged. "I'm *so* ready. You don't have to be gentle."

Insane with anticipation, aching for immediate entry, I poised my glans firmly against his rosy threshold and drove my hips boldly forward. James matched my motion and opened himself to receive my first inflamed inches. Oh, the sumptuous temperature I registered with those inches! To be engulfed to my bristles by that heat wave had become mandatory.

"Go for it; I'm no virgin. *Fuck* me," he implored.

Sighing "Oh, *James*...you feel so fucking *good*," I eased my full length into him. But—*man oh man alive*—my saying that was serious understatement. Sliding my cock into that gorgeous piece of ass was bliss beyond comprehension. Considering my size, James showed no sign of anything but churning passion, especially if the redwood-hard prick oozing in his fist was any indication. I began a slow hip rotation, drilling his ass for pleasure, and finding it...finding it...*finding* it...with each thrilling movement, no matter how slight. Inside James, there was no escape from ecstasy.

All at once, I was hot with motion, thrusting hard, thrusting deep. Again and again I ground my prolific ball sac against his ass with each ravenous downstroke. I pulled back some and thrust shallow for a while, back and forth rapidly, like a dynamo. I pulled out of James completely, met his pleading gaze, embraced its implication, then buried my bone deeply back into his torrid *n*th degree: *Home again, Babe. Y'miss me?* Reading my thought, his eyes half shut, he moaned: "*Yeah*, man, just keep *fuckin'* me..."

As if preordained, so our quintessential fornication evolved.

As my motion became gradually more primal, increasingly beyond my ability to control, James played my cock like a counterrhythmic virtuoso. When we were kissing, pressed together, he fucked my belly, gliding smoothly in his own precome. When propped apart, he masturbated. I looked down and watched my cock gliding in and out of his body: What an incredible sight! I looked up and wallowed in the state of grace our lubricated friction created and sustained: What a sensational place! Back and forth, over and over, James and me: Fucking, *yeah*...

Our eyes fused, and we spoke raggedly:

"If you could see who's fucking me," he thrilled, "you'd die, he's such a stud."

I was pounding into James almost violently. "I am dying...you're slaying me..."

"Alan...we're *rutting*... It's fuckin' amazing."

I had slowed down a bit, was stirring our passion with circular motion. "We're *screwing*, Babe; we're makin' *love*."

"And I'm...*loving it*," he barely managed to say.

"*It* is *us*, James."

"Oh, god," he groaned, closing his eyes. "I never want this to end..."

"But it will, and soon..." I was pressed as deeply into James as possible, mini-thrusting involuntarily. I swallowed hard. "Let yourself go, Babe; let it happen."

James was fully ascendant, jerking off fiercely, his head rolling from side to side. "It *is*," he confirmed, steaming with sweat. "I can feel it; I'm gonna come; I can't *stop*..."

"Dig it, James," I whispered, thrusting wildly toward my own frenzied departure.

The muscle grip on my penis abruptly relaxed when he shouted "Oh, *god*...Alan..." But feeling his internal spasms, observing his frenzied spurting, and seeing his face—*my god, that face*—vaporized any remaining reality I might have cared to acknowledge.

Sentenced to electrocution by orgasm, I began to sustain

repeated surges of high-voltage pleasure from my deepest socket, each jolt more searing than the one preceding it. *Oh, out-of-sight annihilation!* My moment had arrived: incessant wave after come-spurting wave blasting savagely from beneath the cock-ringed pedestal of my monolithic joy, deeply into James.

The sun had set, but it was not yet dark. We lay together, James and I, silently in each other's arms for quite some time before disengaging to the occasion of words.

Life with the love of my life proved no fairy tale for either of us, of course. We somehow managed to survive the '70s intact, with that decade's attendant clichés of debaucheries exacerbated by James's gathering fame. At 33, following his mother's death from pancreatic cancer—a death that deprived Hollywood of one of its most bankable screen legends, and us one of our most ardent supporters—James finally confronted his alcoholism. In sobriety his redirected rage provided the impetus that rekindled his flagging career, which, from that point forward, burgeoned with seemingly a life of its own.

So began the happier years of our life together, but we paid a dear price for his celebrity, *our* celebrity as an alternative "out" couple—not that we were lacking monetarily. No between his inheritance, the outrageous sums his photographs commanded, and my obsessive knack for venture capitalism, we amassed a sizable fortune.

Funny thing about inheritances, though: When James was diagnosed with metastasized pancreatic cancer earlier this year, naturally, we sat down and discussed his options rationally, like the big boys we were. Certainly the most cataclysmic event of my life thus far was enduring our protracted and wrenching farewell before he drove off—alone, at his insistence—to the anonymous hotel room where he took his own life. James, perhaps at the height of his creative prowess, who had grown significantly more beautiful to me than the day we met, was 52. We'd lived together for 33 years.

Sitting alone this bereft New Millennium's Eve, sustained

by memory, I am holding the exquisite, posthumously released collection in hands I scarcely recognize as my own. Though I received the promo copy from the publisher days ago, I've yet to remove the shrink-wrap, the book's title—*James Sutton: A Dawning of Love and Genius—The First Nude Series of Alan Talmadge, 1967*—and cover photograph being plenty hard enough to take just yet.

Promises in Every Star

Greg Herren

There's nothing else quite like the smell of a cornfield after a heavy rain.

I'd forgotten that in the 25 years since I'd left Kansas and never looked back. Off in the east I could see the black clouds and the mist that hung from them to the ground, blurring everything beyond it. I'd forgotten that the sky in Kansas surrounds you and goes on forever so that you could see the weather coming and the weather that was just there. There were no clouds overhead now, just sky that was something between azure and robin's egg, reaching down into the wet corn. The pavement of the county road beneath the tires of my rented red Mustang convertible was wet and splashing every once in a while, the water being thrown up making a slight slapping sound against the rubber. Twenty-five years. What else had I forgotten?

As I turned off onto the Allen Road, I slid Fleetwood Mac's *Rumours* into the CD player and turned it up. This was the way I used to drive to school when Mom let me have the car or one of my friends picked me up and I didn't have to ride the bus. It was a CD now rather than a scratchy eight-track player, and the sound quality was much better, but it was still the same. I smiled to myself as I saw my old green Chevrolet Bel Air, with holes rusted in the sides, running up the Allen Road, the old muffler pipe hanging too low from the back end. All the windows would be open to catch the breeze and eliminate the smell of the cigarette dangling from my lip. Stevie would be wailing about the thunder and the rain washing you clean and you'll know. I would be singing along at the top of my lungs, thumping my hand on the steering wheel with the bass line.

No, it didn't look too different, I thought as the Mustang sped along. The same fields, the same houses, the same barns. Every once in a while there'd be a clearing in the corn and a brick house I didn't remember would appear, laundry flapping in the sweet after-rain air on a clothesline, a couple of cars in the unpaved drive. I crossed the Cottonwood River bridge and saw a house coming up on the right. *The Gosses used to live there,* I thought as I drove by. Mrs. Goss was the school secretary, and Sue her spoiled only child. I couldn't remember what Mr. Goss did for a living, but I remember Sue had her own custom Mustang when we were in school, and she always dressed nice. Sue was cute, in a little girlish kind of way, and a lot of the guys thought she was sexy. I thought she was funny. She made me laugh. She also didn't strike me as the type who'd marry any of the boys in our school. Sue would, I thought even then, marry money.

The mailbox still said GOSS. I guessed the Gosses would probably be in their 70s by now, and why wouldn't they still be there? Sue was undoubtedly long gone, came home a couple of times with her kids to see them a year; every once in a while they'd get into their Buick and go see her.

I was curious to see my old classmates again after so many years. I wondered who would show up. I hadn't gone to the 10-year or the 20-year, and still wasn't sure why I was coming to the 25th. But as I drew closer, each step, I began to experience some anticipation, and every once in a while I would find myself smiling. I was definitely going to be the best- and youngest-looking man there. I was relatively certain I was the only one who went to the gym three times a week. My head was shaved into a military-looking crew cut. Three years earlier I'd surrendered the battle to my receding hairline and gotten it shorn. I'd never looked back from that decision. Smartest thing I ever did.

I looked down. I was wearing a white Calvin Klein tank T-shirt. It was a medium, and was cut tight in the pecs and low on the shoulders. My jean shorts were about two sizes too big and rolled up at the knees. When I stood, they hung loosely off my hips. My contacts were in. I'd shaved that morning and trimmed my goatee. I was wearing brown suede work boots that reached just above my ankles. I smiled at myself in the rearview mirror. They would probably be completely oblivious to it, but I was dressed totally as a gay party-boy clone. It was a safe bet that I'd be the only one dressed this way.

Then again, I really had no idea what straight Kansans in their mid 40s wore these days. There was bound to be a Wal-Mart in Greenfield, the county seat. Did they drive SUVs? That would be weird, I thought, and then laughed at myself. Just because I remembered Kansas as a foreign planet didn't mean it was one. Of course there were Wal-Marts in Kansas; probably outlet malls as well. Car dealerships sold the same cars all over the country, so there would undoubtedly be some SUVs at the reunion. Hell, there might even be a Lexus.

Maybe, I thought in a slight bit of a panic, the rented Mustang convertible might be too much. Why didn't I just rent a compact car like I usually do whenever I travel?

Because you wanted to impress these people, these rustic backcountry Kansas hicks who always made you feel like an outsider, that's why.

The newsletter Jenna Bradley had sent out had everyone's current address, marital status, and how many kids. Of course, the letter Jenna had included in mine also covered divorces, jail sentences, and alcohol problems. Out of a class of 48, only six of us no longer lived in Kansas, and only 12 of us lived outside a 100-mile radius of dear old Northern Heights High. So, the outsider, the homo, the faggot wanted to show up at the reunion in a totally bitchin' car, with about 6% body fat, and rub their noses in his sophistication, his urban glamour: the successful photographer just back from a shoot in Milan. And what do you do?

Of course, the shoot in Milan that had run up all of my credit cards, and I was still waiting for the check.

No need for them to know that.

I crossed the railroad tracks and entered the teeming metropolis of Allen, Kansas. The rusted metal sign right after the tracks read ALLEN: POPULATED 84. After a couple of blocks I came to the turnoff to Tony's house. Well, where Tony used to live. I took a left, thinking *Why the hell not?* and there it was, the second house on the right, practically the same as it had been all those years ago. Only now the mailbox said MATHERS, a name I didn't recognize. According to Jenna's newsletter, Tony now worked as a trash collector in Council Grove.

Nice work if you can get it.

I hadn't asked Jenna if Tony was coming. She'd mentioned that he had come to the 10 and 20, so it was fairly safe to assume he might come to the 25th. No one knew I was coming. Jenna was the only one I stayed in touch with, and that was via e-mail, and very sporadically. Jenna and I had reconnected prior to the 20-year, and according to her gossipy report afterward, everyone was very curious about me.

I just bet they were.

I sat there, the car idling, looking at the dilapidated house. Surely that couldn't be the same battered screen door? Christine McVie launched into "You Make Loving Fun."

I could see Tony just as clearly as if I'd seen him just yesterday. The first time I had seen him in his underwear, after football practice. He pulled on a pair of blue briefs with red trim. I'd never seen colored underwear before, and it hugged his white ass, outlining the cleft between the cheeks. His tanned muscular legs covered with wiry black hair. Someone called his name from across the locker room, and he turned and I saw his chest, thickly muscled with nipples the size of half-dollars.

And I fell in love in that moment; madly, passionately in love. For me, Tony was everything I could ever possibly want in a boy. I fantasized about kissing him on his thick, sensual lips, tasting his tongue. I dreamed about him lying on top of me, my hands running down his broad back to where it narrowed, cupping his hard buttocks and squeezing. I wondered how his cock would taste in my mouth. There I was, the new kid, transferred in from

Chicago, staring at this boy from across the locker room, not even caring if anyone could follow my line of sight.

We had a couple of classes together, and there was, after all, football practice. I started making an attempt to befriend him, and it didn't take long. For some reason, Tony wasn't particularly well-liked either. I never wondered about it, I was just grateful that he was outside the "in crowd," if such a small school could be said to have one: those arrogant jocks in our class who thought they were better than everyone else. They grudgingly tolerated me but made it very clear I wasn't a part of their crowd. I wasn't invited to their parties or their get-togethers. Neither was Tony, so it was relatively easy for me to become his friend. We had a sense of humor that was similar. And whatever personality differences there may have been my desire to be close to him heavily outweighed. I hated his girlfriend, Allyson, because she took Tony's time and attention away from me. It was, of course, *her* fault that Tony and I weren't together in the way that I wanted. We used to sleep over at each other's houses from time to time. I only stayed at Tony's house once or twice, though. I think he was a little ashamed of his family. His stepfather worked at the meatpacking plant in the county seat; his mother worked as a housekeeper at the Best Western on the highway. Their house didn't have central heat or air; the wall that separated his bedroom from his parents' was just paneling thrown up. His clothes were inexpensive and worn. My house, in the town of Americus, must have seemed palatial. Wall-to-wall carpeting, central heat and air, I had my own phone, and my mother didn't work. He was always stunned by the meals my mother would come up with for dinner when he stayed over: beef burgundy, pepper steak and rice, chicken Kiev.

I used to sneak glances at him in the locker room and in the showers, taking photographs with my mental camera that I could revisit later while masturbating. And sometimes, when he stayed over, we would wrestle in our underwear; nothing sexual, nothing overt, but I would memorize the silkiness of his skin, the way his chest felt, the strength of his arms, the odor between his legs when he would wrap them around my head and squeeze.

I put the car back in gear and turned it around.

The reunion was in the town park, next to the old, abandoned Allen High School that had closed in 1955 when the new consolidated high school opened. I was surprised to see the crumbling building still stood. Wasn't it a health hazard or something? The school district had always been a poor one; there had never been the money to tear the old building down. All the old town high schools had still stood when I was in school: Allen, Bushong, Miller, and Dunlap. Apparently, they still were standing.

The parking area behind Allen High School was filled with cars. I glanced at my watch and saw that I was about half an hour late. There was a keg of beer resting in a tin washtub underneath an old cottonwood tree; there was another washtub filled with soft drinks. Unlike the previous reunions, which Jenna had told me about, there weren't any small kids running around, shrieking and screaming and playing. Of course not—this was the 25-year reunion, and my classmates' kids were too old by now to be dragged along. The cars, I noticed, were mostly pickup trucks and various other small cars that appeared to be inexpensive; the Mustang was a bit much. I maneuvered into a parking spot and shut off the engine. I lit a cigarette and watched the small groupings of people.

Would I even recognize anyone?

I got out of the car and ground the cigarette out under my shoe in the dirt. I hadn't seen any of these people in so many years. Did I even want to see any of them now? Why had I come?

I decided to get something to drink and walked over to the washtubs. A taller bald man, maybe about 20 pounds overweight, was filling a plastic cup with beer from the keg. He was wearing a pair of faded jeans and a blue polo shirt. I stuck my hand into the icy water of the other tub and pulled out a Pepsi. I popped the top, and he turned and looked at me. His face was deeply lined and tanned, and somewhat familiar.

"Dennis?" His eyes squinted at me.

My heart sank. Of all people to run into first! Steve Mallon. He'd been part of the in crowd of jocks, and he'd never liked me much. He'd never been mean to me, but he'd rarely spoken to me, and usually with a scowl on his face when he'd had to.

"Steve?" I asked.

He smiled. "It is you. Hear you've finally come out of the closet, huh?"

"Well, yeah."

He stuck out his hand. "Glad to hear it." I took his callused hand and we shook. "There's nothin' worse than tryin' to be something you're not, is there?" He shook his head. "I knew when we were in school that you were just pretendin'." He laughed. "Didn't know what you were pretendin', but I knew you weren't what you were pretendin' to be."

I laughed with him, loosening up a bit. "Yeah, well, I just tried to fit in."

"Couldn't have been easy." He took a swig out of his beer. "Glad to hear that's all over and done with." He shrugged. "I just thought you were a phony in school, ya know? Didn't like it. Hear you're doing well for yourself."

"Yeah."

Jenna Bradley made her way over to us with a big grin on her face. Jenna had been a big girl in school: almost six feet tall and weighing in at well over 200 pounds. She'd lost most of the weight but was still carrying some extra. Her brown hair was shot through with gray. There were lines on her face that didn't used to be there, dark circles under her eyes, and the skin on her neck was starting to sag just a little bit. She threw her arms around me. "You came!" she whispered into my ear. She stepped back a bit and winked at me. "You are looking good, Dennis!"

I grinned at her. "Thanks, Jenna. You look great too."

She ran a hand through her hair. "You really think so? Hell, I'm just an old broad now. Got a daughter starting college this fall, can you believe it?" She shook her head. "Where did all the time go?"

This didn't seem to need an answer, so I let her tuck her arm through mine and lead me into the groups of people. They were all at least polite to me, some of them friendly. I got hugs from women and handshakes from the men. I met husbands and wives I'd never heard of. My classmates had, of course, all aged, and I thought I'd prepared myself for it. Doug Jennings, who'd been whip-thin in school, still had skinny legs but a big beer gut hanging over the waistband of his jeans. His blond frizzy hair was long gone. Homecoming Queen Brenda Littrell had gained at least 40 pounds, wore too much makeup, and her black hair, shellacked and large, was obviously dyed. Craig Jackson, my second biggest crush after Tony, who'd been blond and blue-eyed and had no body fat, had gone gray, his hairline was receded, and he was fleshy. I looked at pictures of kids, made the necessary small talk, and laughed. But nobody asked me about my life; nobody asked about my other half back home, nobody asked about my career or my adventures. It was all casual small talk, the kind you share with people you might have once had something in common with but who had become strangers.

After about half an hour of this I headed back to the parking lot to just breathe. I lit a cigarette and leaned against the Mustang. The reminiscing was starting now, the talk about why we lost the football game against Olpe, what happened the night of the prom, what happened at the hayride, and on and on. I had my own memories of those events, memories that, despite my classmates' casual acceptance of me, I didn't want to share. I didn't want to share on prom night I spent the whole night watching Tony and wishing I could dance with him. I didn't want to share that on the hayride I had watched Craig Jackson moon a truck driving by and had stared at his perfectly shaped ass glowing in the moonlight. I was still on the outside with these people. I would always be on the outside with them. They had their memories and the similar paths their lives had taken since graduation: the marriages, the kids, the worries about buying a house and money.

I sat there, smoking and wishing I had a joint.

A car pulled in and I didn't turn to see who it was. I wouldn't recognize the person anyway. The shock of connecting familiar names with unfamiliar faces had worn off, and I was getting a little tired of it all. I wondered how long it would be before I could safely beg off and head back for the hotel in Greenfield.

"Dennis?"

I knew the voice. I would know that voice anywhere. I turned and there he was. Tony Martin. "Tony?" I replied, my voice croaking just a little bit.

The face that I had loved so desperately in high school was the same, with just some added wrinkles, and the dark circles he'd always had under his blue eyes were still there, only deeper and darker. His thick black hair was cropped short, close to his scalp. The big, muscular arms that I remembered were thicker and sticking out of a red T-shirt he'd cut the sleeves from. His jeans were tight and his waist a little thicker than I remembered, but he looked so much the same. For a brief second I wondered if his underwear was blue with red trim.

He held out his hand and we shook. He was smiling. "Wondered if you would make it this time."

I shrugged. "Yeah, well."

He leaned back against the car with me, the car dropping a bit under the added weight. "Jenna says you're doing well."

"Yeah."

He looked at the park, the small crowd of people. "Every time I come to one of these things I always wonder why I bother. They haven't changed since school."

There was a moment of silence. I didn't know what to say to him. What do you say to someone who was your first real love after 25 years of nothing but silence? I knew he was on his second marriage. I knew he had three kids. I knew he was a garbageman in Council Grove.

He pulled a joint out of his jeans pocket and lit it. He offered it to me, and I took a couple of drags. It wasn't the best pot I've ever had. It was strong and acrid, and I choked a bit, coughing. I took a quick swig of my Pepsi after handing it back to him. He grinned, the same devilish grin he had all those years ago, his eyes sparkling, the one that always made me weak, made me want to kiss him. "I can't ever handle these people without being stoned."

I laughed. I was feeling a little bit of the buzz. "I wish I would have brought some."

"Anybody call you a fag?"

"No." I shrugged. "They've all been nice, but phony nice, I guess. They don't know what to say to me, what to ask me, so they all just tell me what they've been up to." I looked at him. "You didn't bring your wife?"

"We're getting divorced." He handed the joint back to me. "Happily-ever-after doesn't seem to be in the cards for me."

"Sorry to hear that."

"Don't be."

We smoked in silence for a little while until the joint was just a small roach, which he pinched out and put into his wallet. "So, what do you think of the Class of 1978?"

"Things haven't changed much, I guess." I sighed. "I was an outsider then, I'm an outsider now. I'm not sure why I came, to tell the truth." I wasn't going to tell him the reason I'd come was to see him. I hadn't realized it until then, but it was true, it was why I had come. I'd wanted to see him, to put to rest all the fantasies I'd had for 25 years. Now that he was here and we were sitting with only a few scant inches between our bodies, I was reacting the way I always had: glancing at him sideways out of the corner of my eyes, drinking in his muscular arms, the big chest wrapped tightly inside the red T-shirt, the strong legs in the tight jeans.

I still wanted him.

He laughed. "Well, you're the one who's changed, Mr. Big-Shot Photographer. Out of the closet, living a high life, traveling the world, meeting famous people. I knew you were destined for something different than the rest of us." He looked at me. "You got out, but you weren't from here to begin with. You weren't tied to this fucking place." He shrugged. "I wanted out of here so bad, and yet here I am, 25 years later, still stuck in Kansas. I knew you'd get out." He laughed. "I wanted to go with you."

I stared at him. "You did?"

"Yeah." He looked down at his shoes. "Part of the reason I liked you so much was because I wanted out, and I knew you'd get out." He looked over at me. "Remember the night we camped out in your backyard?"

I'd forgotten about that night. We had a tent and sleeping bags that we'd put up. We sat up and looked at the night sky and talked until the sun started coming up in the distant east, turning the night sky beautiful combinations of navy-blue, pinks, and oranges.

"You told me that night that every star was a promise, remember?"

"I did?"

He laughed. "Funny you don't remember; I've never forgotten. You said that every star was a promise, and the promises in every star were the kind that could never be broken."

Kind of poetic for a 17-year-old, I thought. "I said that?"

He nodded. "And we promised on a star, remember? We promised that we would always be friends; we would always be a part of each other's lives."

I did remember now, the two of us holding hands solemnly as we picked out a star and made our promise. And after we made the promise we had hugged tightly, holding onto each other, our bare chests pressed hard against each other, and my dick had gotten hard. That had spoiled the moment for me, my teenage erection, and I had pulled back and away from him, afraid he'd see it, afraid of the contempt I would see in his face. "Yes, I remember that." My heart ached for the 17-year-old I'd been, so desperate for love, so desperate to belong somewhere, so desperately afraid of who I really was.

"When you left I wished I had said something, asked to go with." Tony smiled.

"But I went away for college," I replied. "You couldn't have come with me."

"Sure I could have." He shrugged. "I wouldn't have been able to go to college, but we could have gotten an apartment together off campus, and I could have gotten a job, and then when you graduated, we could have moved to the big city together."

"I don't think that would have been a good idea." I imagined it. It would have been torture for me, seeing him every day in his underwear around the house, trying to sneak glances at him while he showered. The torture would have become even more when he brought girls home to fuck in his room, me listening to them fucking through his bedroom door, always terrified of being caught.

"Why? Because you were in love with me?"

"You knew?" There was no point in denying it. Apparently my acting in high school was not Academy Award caliber as I had always believed. What was the harm in admitting to it at this point anyway?

"I always wondered what would have happened if you'd ever tried anything." He gave me a quick glance and just as quickly glanced away.

"You'd have kicked my ass and told everyone at school."

"That's what you thought? No wonder you never tried anything."

I lit a cigarette. "Believe me, I wanted to." I blew out a plume of smoke. "But you never gave me any indication, and I wasn't about to initiate it." I could remember the fears, which took years to get past. Even after I had come out, how long did it take before I had the courage to approach another man in a bar?

He grinned at me. "What about our wrestling?"

"What about it?"

"I always got hard." He shrugged. "I always kinda thought that it might lead somewhere. But it never did."

"I guess we were both afraid."

"Yeah." He playfully punched me in the arm. "I guess we were both a pair of pussies."

I laughed. No one had referred to me as a "pussy" since my days in the fraternity. "Yeah, I guess."

"What are you doing later on tonight?"

Was he asking me for a date, for chrissake? I stared at him. "My flight back isn't until tomorrow, so I'm staying at the Best Western in Greenfield tonight."

"After this is over I have to go see my mom." He shrugged. "I can grab a pizza and a six-pack and come by, if you want."

"Yeah," I said softly. "I want."

The rest of the afternoon passed by in a blur. I talked to some people, made some lame jokes, laughed. Some of my classmates got drunk off the keg beer. Mine kept getting warm since I wasn't drinking it fast enough and had to keep pouring it out into the grass. My Senior Prom date, Lisette Kidwell Armitage, clung to my arm for over half an hour, bitching about her husband and how sorry she was she never got out of Kansas. What could I say to that? I just smiled and nodded, looking for rescue from any quarter. She stank of beer and sweat, her fine blond bangs plastered to her forehead with perspiration. There was dirt beneath her bitten fingernails. I finally escaped, pawning her off on Clay Perkins, her Homecoming date. Clay had never liked me in school, had once called me a "fag" at football practice. *Tit for tat,* I thought, *here ya go, breeder, you deal with her.* I smiled and excused myself. The party was breaking up; before I could make my escape I had to pose for pictures with people I barely remembered and the obligatory photo of the class. Tony knelt beside me in the front in the grass.

"You getting out of here?" he whispered to me.

"Soon as the picture's taken."

"I'll see you in a few hours then," he said and winked at me.

I made my goodbyes, gave my address to a few people I'd never hear from again, gave Jenna a big hug and a kiss, and got in the Mustang. Fleetwood Mac roared from the stereo as I drove out of the lot with a sigh of relief.

I'd never see any of them ever again, I thought, as I made the turn onto the Allen Road, heading back to Greenfield.

My stomach was growling, so I made my way up Sixth Street and hit the drive-through at the McDonald's. It amazed me that it was still there, but so little in Greenfield had changed in 25 years. The sweet smell from the Dolly Madison plant when I'd crossed the highway into town. The stink of slaughtered beef and sour blood from the meatpacking plant on the other side of town when I'd made the turn onto Sixth Street. When I turned into the drive-through, I felt as though I'd driven back into time for the second time that day.

I'd worked at that McDonald's when I was a senior, flipping burgers and getting the stink of the grease into my hair and my pores. The girl working the drive-through window was maybe 17, with her blond hair pulled back under her cap and a sprinkle of pimples across her young cheeks. She smiled and took my money, handed me the sack with my Quarter Pounder with cheese, gave me my change, then thanked me for stopping at McDonald's and asked me to stop by again. I just smiled at her, looking beyond her at the other kids in the ugly brown polyester uniforms, moving about, grabbing burgers and bags of fries, pouring drinks. I saw myself, fresh-faced, young, with feathered brown bangs sweeping back from my face, smiling and joking with the other kids, squirting ketchup and mustard onto toasted buns, two pickles on each one, then a handful of onions followed by yellow cheese, sweat running down my cheeks. I ate the Quarter Pounder as I drove back up Prairie Street, where the Best Western was perched on a slow-rising hill overlooking the highway that led to Kansas City. I crumpled up the wrapper, placed it in the bag, and threw it into the backseat. I stopped at the Coke machine and got myself a can.

I showered, washing the sweat and memories off me. I put on a clean pair of white 2(x)ist underwear, a pair of white cotton shorts, and a red tank top. I flipped through the channels on the meager cable channels provided, finally settling in to watch a really bad Joan Crawford movie, *Berserk,* on what was supposedly a "classic" movie channel.

Apparently, I fell asleep after a few minutes, because when the knocking on my door started I sat up, disoriented. The digital clock on the nightstand read 6:07. I wiped my eyes and walked across the darkened room to the door. I flipped on the light switch next to the door before opening it.

Tony smiled at me. In one hand he held a Pizza Hut box, in the other a plastic grocery store bag with a six-pack of Coors Light tall boys perspiring in the late-afternoon heat. "Hope you still like pepperoni and sausage."

"Come on in." I stood aside and let him pass. He set the pizza and beer down on the little round table right next to the air-conditioning unit and flipped the box top open. The room filled with the smell of cooked meats and melted cheese. Steam rose up from it in lazy tendrils. He popped the top on one of the beers and took a swig.

I sat down and took a beer. We talked while we ate the pizza and drank the beers, small talk that revealed nothing about either one of us, just two strangers making conversation. We talked about the Kansas City Royals; about how Kansas State had finally managed to turn its long-suffering football team around into a championship contender year in, year out; about our classmates and how badly most of them had aged. He didn't ask me about my life and I didn't ask him about his, as though by mutual unspoken agreement the topic was off-limits. I wanted to ask about his two wives, about his kids. I wanted to ask about his curiosity about sex with another man, if it was something he'd always felt and just never acted on. Finally, all that was left of the pizza was assorted crusts in a greasy cardboard box.

He popped the lid on another beer. "You remember Rob Hinton?"

"Yeah." Rob Hinton had been a year behind us in school. He had a good body, I remembered, a nice round hard ass, with very pale skin, blue eyes, and light brown hair. Rob and I had been friends at first, but when I was a senior that changed. I never really knew why. "How's he doing?"

"He died in a car accident a few years ago. Driving drunk." Tony settled back into his chair and crossed his right leg over his left. "Left a wife and three kids."

"That's too bad." I shrugged.

"You know he used to—" he looked away from me. "When we were in school—"

"What?"

"Aw, hell, it doesn't matter anymore." He looked me square in the eye. "Rob and I used to mess around some."

"Really?"

"Yeah. I mean, we never fucked or anything like that, but we used to beat each other off sometimes."

I laughed. "What a pair of fags."

He put his hand on my knee. It was damp. "I always wondered what it would be like, you know? To be with another guy. Really be with another guy."

I stood up and pulled my tank top over my head. He did the same, and we stood there, facing each other, scant inches apart, shirtless, both of us breathing harder than we had been just the moment before, and then I leaned in toward him and put my mouth on his.

It wasn't the way I had always fantasized it would be all those years ago. Back then I imagined our mouths coming together in a frenzy, all tongues and lips weaving in and around each other, pulling each other closer in a mad explosion of passion and lust. This kiss was soft, and gentle, our lips touching, our bodies still apart, not touching each other anywhere except at the lips. He tasted of stale smoke, beer, and slightly of pizza and garlic. His lips were soft. I reached out with my right hand and placed it on his hard chest, touching his nipple that hardened under my fingers.

I pulled my head back. He opened his eyes, those brilliant blue eyes, and smiled at me. "That's nice."

I took his hand and led him to the bed. We stood there, looking at each other, my body starting to respond to his. His chest was still big and muscular, but his stomach wasn't flat any more, just a little bit of a paunch, with the wiry black hairs around his navel trailing down to the waist of his shorts. He reached and undid mine, and I let them fall, stepping out of them. He pushed me gently and I fell back onto the bed, and he took off his shorts, standing there in a pair of white BVDs that had been washed many, many times, more grayish than white now, and he lay down beside me. Our arms went around each other and we kissed again, this time deeper, more passionately, and I could feel his own erection through the frail cotton of his underwear.

It wasn't like I thought it would be all those times as I lay in my bed with my eyes closed and my underwear bunched around my ankles; it wasn't fire and music and fireworks going off. It was unsure, tender, maybe a little on the sweet side, as our mouths and hands explored each other uncertainly. And when I finally entered him and he was able to relax enough to take me inside of him, a single tear rolled out of his left eye. I watched the tear slide down his cheek. His eyes closed as I slowly made my way into him and wondered what the tear was for. Was it for sadness at releasing himself so completely to me; was it for time lost, so much time gone by and water sweeping under the bridge between us? There was just that single tear, alone and orphaned, but his eyes remained closed as I worked, as I worked to bring us both to the climax we had waited so many years to have together.

And then it was over, and I was handing him a towel to wipe himself down with. I lit a cigarette. "Was it what you were expecting?" I asked finally. Tomorrow I would be on a plane back to my life, to my world, to my partner. Tonight Tony would be driving back to Council Grove and his life as a sanitation worker, with his soon-to-be divorced second wife and his kids.

"It hurt a little bit, but it also felt good." He didn't look at me. He slipped his underwear back on, pulled his tank top over his head. "I, um, I really have to get going."

I smiled. How many times had I heard that before in my life? How many times had I said it to someone? I blew smoke at the ceiling. "Long drive back to Council Grove."

He buckled his shorts and tied his shoelaces. "Yeah." He walked over to the door.

I got off the bed and walked over to the door naked. "Goodbye, Tony."

He looked at me and smiled a sad sort of smile that didn't touch his eyes. "What might have been, huh?" He touched my cheek with his right hand, rubbing it gently. "It was good seeing you."

"Likewise."

The door shut behind him. I stood there, for a moment, and remembered two teenage boys, sitting out underneath the stars in their sleeping bags, their hands locked together in a fierce grip, their futures uncertain but with a wealth of possibilities. I saw us again sitting together on the bus coming back from an away football game, laughing and teasing with the other guys on the team. I remembered studying for a history test, asking him questions and then having to give him the answers. I pulled my shorts on and walked outside, to the little balcony off my room. I saw him down in the parking lot getting into his car. He looked up at me, and smiled, and gave me a little wave. I waved back, with the same smile.

The sun had gone down and the sky was cobalt, sprinkled

with tiny little pinpoints of light that winked and blinked.

I looked up at them for a moment, and then back down as his car drove out of the parking lot.

"There are still promises in every star, Tony," I said, flicking my cigarette ash over the balcony's edge. I brushed a tear out of my eye. "They're just made to other people now."

And I went back inside.

A Man's Man

Steve Attwood

Tristan Arthur Jones sat in the sun lounger and looked over the shimmering city of Nelson, New Zealand. He loved the sun. Matron scolded him for pulling his chair out of the shade of the wisteria-draped veranda. She said he'd give himself skin cancer. He said, Who cared, at his age; at 86 you have to die of something, might as well be from sitting in the sun.

His only concession to the midsummer rays was his white bowling hat, rice paper–thin, and a pair of dark glasses that, he liked to think, gave him a somewhat rakish appearance. The hat was to protect his bald pate; Tristan had not started losing his hair until he was well into his 70s, but now little remained of it except for a few white wisps along the sides. The sunglasses were also a necessity: once rich brown, now his eyes were almost colorless and so sensitive to light he had to wear tinted spectacles just to watch the telly.

Matron was scolding again.

"Mr. J." She called everyone by their initials. "Mr. J you've not had your lunch. Shall I bring it on a tray? You must eat something!"

Tristan shook his head and turned, defiantly, to the view.

He never ate lunch, rarely finished his dinner, but ate heartily at breakfast. Porridge, he had decided, was more than sufficient for a man whose digestive system was not as robust as it used to be. It kept him regular, and regularity was important to the aged.

It's funny, he thought, how life is reduced to basics when you're old, like being regular, and if your teeth fit, and will there be dessert with the dinner tonight, because if it were apple pie, he'd have some. He liked apple pie.

Tristan knew he was lucky to be in Harbour View. It had been one of Nelson's finest homes once and was still in pretty good nick. The grand old rooms had been subdivided into units barely big enough for a single bed, a dresser, and wardrobe, but the kitchen was still huge, as was the dining room. Had to be, with 15 residents. The place cost a fortune, but still, Tristan was lucky. And, when his money ran out, the government would pay. But he'd be dead by then. With any luck.

Still, with what you paid, you'd think Matron would do a little bit of "yes Mr. J, certainly Mr. J." But they took away your rights along with your money. Convenient, he supposed, to have docile residents, easily controlled and regulated into predictable routines. Fewer staff that way. Kept the costs down.

So Tristan rebelled in little ways. Like sitting in the sunshine at midday and not eating his lunch.

The veranda was the attraction of Harbour View. High on the Ridgeway, the residence looked over the Boulder Bank and The Gap, where ships slipped through into the shelter of the port—matchbox toys on a playmat sea, tufts of dirty cotton wool sprouting from their funnels.

In the foreground, the wisteria framed a fiery pohutukawa tree melodious with tui. On the lower terraces: figs, banana palms, hibiscus, and a haphazard orchard of citrus. Passion fruit vine rambled over everything.

Tristan heard the chairlift whir, felt its vibrations where its guide rail joined the veranda. He leaned forward to see. It was hardly used these days. None of the ladies seemed to like it. It didn't look secure, they said. Tristan used to ride it down to the lower street every morning and walk 50 meters to the dairy to buy a paper. It was his small escape. He could just as easily have ordered a paper for his room.

But, a few months ago, the dairy closed. Some developer bought the section and slapped a modern monstrosity on it. Matron said it was ARCHITECT DESIGNED. She had a habit of talking in capital letters when she wanted to impress someone. Tristan said the ARCHITECT should be SHOT.

A gentleman was riding the chair up to the house. Tristan could tell he was a gentleman because he sat straight, wore clothes that fit, and carried a walking cane, rather than a crook-headed walking stick. The cane was carved, tipped with brass, and shone like a medal. The gentleman had a thick head of closely cut white hair, an equally trim mustache and the sort of skin color one used to associate with explorers or soldiers of fortune.

The chair shuddered to a halt. Tristan rose to greet the visitor. It was his right as king of the veranda. The women residents never ventured out of the shade.

"Now, now, Mr. J, curiosity killed the cat." Matron pushed the sun lounger into the back of Tristan's knees so he collapsed back into the chair. "Can't have you putting Mr. L off before he's decided to stay. You'll meet him soon enough if he does."

Matron's voice trailed back to Tristan as she herded her prospect inside.

"Lovely view…modern facilities…one other gentleman, an author…NO PETS."

Colonel Robert Leadley moved in a week later, taking the room next to Tristan's. He was 79, a Kiwi but had served in the British Army. World War Two and Korea. After that, various other battles in miscellaneous African states, depending on who was paying.

He'd volunteered at the start of the war in Europe and found that he liked it. "Not the fighting, that was bloody awful. But the blokes, you know. Damn good men. Lifelong friends. Nearly all dead now."

Tristan decided he liked the Colonel, especially when, on the second day, he told Matron he'd bloody well sit in the sun if he liked. And, if he couldn't have bacon, eggs, toast, and porridge for breakfast, he'd take his money elsewhere.

The colonel also had a car. "Can't drive much, hip freezes up. But on a warm day..."

None of the other residents had a car, so there was plenty of room for it in the car park on the top terrace. It was an old Roller, and Matron gave the Colonel the car park nearest the street. Where the neighbors could see it.

"Bit of a cliché, I know," the Colonel said when he took Tristan up to see it. "But I sound like a Pom, and look like one, so why not have the best bloody car they ever made eh? Besides, it was a present from a grateful African president. We won that one. I got the Rolls and he got a year at the top before some other bastard shot him. I got the best end of the bargain wouldn't you say?"

Tristan didn't reply. He was too busy checking his pulse and wondering if he was going to get his breath back before he died of a heart attack. He hadn't tackled the steps to the car park for some time.

There was another chair, but the Colonel had told him to buck up and take the steps. Told him it would do him the world of good. Tristan wasn't so sure. He rode the chair down. So did the Colonel.

There was another dairy. Right down on the waterfront. A steep path, just opposite The Monstrosity, cut through the bush and came out behind the shop. The Colonel decided he and Tristan would make it a daily excursion. Tristan decided the Colonel was a bigger bully than Matron.

On the first expedition Tristan made it down all right but couldn't manage the steps back up to The Monstrosity and the bottom of the chairlift. The Colonel walked up on his own, caught both chairlifts—his hip was giving him gyp—and got out the Roller. Tristan enjoyed the ride. He used to have a Rover, but it didn't compare with the Rolls.

By the end of the third week Tristan made it back up the steps with only a few rest breaks. He still had to ride the chair to the veranda. So did the Colonel.

Tristan was also eating his lunch, and all of his dinner.

At the end of the fifth week, Tristan made it from the shop to the chairlift without a break. To celebrate, the Colonel ordered

Matron to pack a picnic for two and informed her that he and Tristan would be out for the day on Sunday, provided it was fine. Matron tried to insist she come along. After all, neither Mr. L nor Mr. J were as young as they used to be.

She also wanted to be seen in the Roller. But the Colonel told her he'd never had a woman in the Rolls and he bloody well wasn't going to start.

"It has a car phone. If either one of us take ill, we shall call for help on that. Believe me, I'll make sure you're the last to know."

Matron wasn't sure if she'd heard right.

Sunday dawned fine and Tristan managed the stairs to the car park.

They drove to the "Center of New Zealand" viewpoint and sat under a huge spreading gum tree vibrating with cicadas. Beneath them was spread the whole vista of Nelson and Tasman Bay. A summer haze blue-tinted the apple fields and vineyards. The Colonel declared it a bloody fine place and decided it was warm enough to take off his tie.

The Colonel broached the gin they'd bought from a bottle store, produced a pocket knife to slice a lemon, and clunked some ice into a couple of glasses from the Roller's picnic set. The ice had come from the bottle store too. So had the tonic. The gin gurgled until it measured two of the Colonel's thin brown fingers up the side of the glass.

The sharp taste of quinine buzzed through Tristan's brain. Made him feel incautious.

"What do you mean," he asked, waving a cucumber sandwich toward the Rolls, "no woman?"

"Never cared for them myself," the Colonel replied. "Oh, nice enough to dance with and all that but not my cup of tea otherwise. I'm a man's man. That's why I stayed on soldiering. I was always afraid if I got a woman into the Roller, I'd never get her out."

"A confirmed bachelor then?"

"You could say so."

The Colonel looked a bit crafty when he said that, but Tristan recognized the final tone in the remark and made no further inquiry.

Later, they drove down to Tahuna Beach. They had both taken off their jackets. The Colonel had undone his top button. Tristan didn't have one to undo. They dabbled lumpy old toes in the sea, trousers rolled up to their knees. Tristan scrubbed his feet in the sand to wear down his calluses. They wandered among mothers and children and fat sunburned men. The Colonel said the lot of them needed some military discipline. He said there was no excuse for a man letting himself go to seed. Tristan thanked God that genetics blessed him with slim lines and defined muscles.

They drove to a local winery for a tasting session, browsed the Sunday flea market and decided, without phoning Matron, to stay out for dinner.

"Place I know, on the waterfront," the Colonel said. "Bloody nice seafood. Couple of chaps run it. Friends of mine. Excellent wine list."

They talked about the Colonel's battles, and men he had known, good lads most of them, black and white.

They talked about Tristan's novel and how it had done well but that no one wanted to read good books any more. The Colonel said what he liked about Our Duty to Die was that Tristan hadn't cluttered the bloody thing up with women. He said it was a good man's read. Tristan said he thought that was probably why it had stopped selling. He told how, at one writers and readers festival, a woman of indeterminate gender had asked him how he felt about promoting the macho male stereotype and why he had failed to acknowledge the contribution of women to the Allied victory. The Colonel said the bloody woman should have been shot. Tristan said she was entitled to her opinion and, anyway, he'd made quite a nest egg out of the book by then.

It was after midnight when the Colonel's friends poured one last port into the two old men and got one of their waiters to drive them home in the Roller.

Matron was not amused.

"I nearly had the police out for you. And," she sniffed, "you've been drinking. Mr. J is not supposed to drink, not on top of his heart pills."

Tristan said, Might as well die of something he enjoyed doing. The Colonel told her she was an interfering old biddy and to bugger off.

Tristan was in his pajamas when the Colonel called through the wall to ask if he wanted a nightcap. The Colonel was wearing an oriental dressing gown. Silk or something. Tristan noticed he didn't appear to have pajamas on underneath. His own tartan wool gown, with striped flannel legs poking out from under, seemed a cliché of old age. Sensible. Not adventurous.

"Whiskey?"

"Please."

The Colonel stretched himself across the bed. Tristan took the chair. A comfortable silence lasted through the first whiskey.

"Colonel?"

"Hmm?"

"Thanks for a bloody good day."

A second whiskey was poured.

"Colonel?"

"Hmm?"

"Have you never had a woman?"

"Once. Didn't like it. Too soft. I'm a man's man."

"My Lucy died when we were expecting our first. Never married again. Didn't seem much point. I hadn't enjoyed it. You know, with Lucy, in bed I mean. Later, I met David. But now he's dead too."

The Colonel cast an appraising eye at Tristan. "They all die," he said. "All of the good ones. They all die. Still, that David was a lucky fellow."

A third whiskey.

"Colonel."

"Hmm?"

"Move over."

The small bed moaned a protest.

"Bloody hell," the Colonel said. "I think I've got an erection. I haven't had one for years."

"I haven't," Tristan said. "I don't think I could manage. Too much booze, or too bloody old, or both, but it doesn't matter does it?"

"No," said the Colonel, pulling his friend to him. "No, it doesn't matter at all."

Ruins

Curtis C. Comer

I sat up onto my elbows, jarred awake by the sound of rumbling trucks in the valley below. Five or six Soviet-era Fiat flatbeds, carrying bulldozers, bounced and jiggled along the highway, throwing swirling dust clouds into the humid air. Abrahm, my 18-year-old companion, sat up, shielding his eyes from the sun. His dark curly hair stuck to his sweaty brow.

"They are headed to Zeugma," he observed matter-of-factly, lying back down in the grass.

Zeugma, located in the southern part of Turkey, was Abrahm's home and had been my home for the past three months. Unfortunately, thanks to the Turkish government and the pervasive need for water, much of it would soon be lying beneath the surface of the Euphrates.

I lay back down in the grass and smiled, enjoying a private joke. Turkey was the last place I ever thought I would end up after fleeing New York and a stagnant relationship.

It wasn't that I blamed David for the breakup, though; the truth of the matter was that, after 15 years, we had simply stopped caring. I realized that I couldn't stay in New York either; there were too many things there, too many shared things that refused to let me move on. So I took all of my savings and decided to try Europe for a while. I ruled out France immediately, realizing that it would only make me miss my francophile ex-partner. Ireland too was ruled out; we had talked for years about visiting there and, now, such a trip alone sounded like some sort of rude consolation prize.

Somehow, after toying with the idea of numerous countries, I had ended up at the train station in Istanbul, trying my best not to look too American, visions of *Midnight Express* and heroin smugglers running through my head. Even the country's flag, a field of red with a vertical crescent moon and five-pointed star, struck me as somewhat menacing. I wandered the city's ancient streets, trying to remain anonymous, sipping thick coffee in smoky cafés.

But no matter how hard I had tried, I couldn't stop thinking how much David would have loved to be here. In Ankara, the capital, I tore up a postcard I had written to him, swearing to myself that I could finally let go, determined that I was going to enjoy the trip and learn as much as I could without using David as a crutch.

It was in Ankara that I met Abrahm, who had traveled there from Zeugma for the purpose of exempting himself from compulsory military service. He based his claim of exemption on the grounds that his aging father needed constant care, and his mother and an older brother, Kamil, had been killed in a devastating earthquake four years earlier. For the third year in a row his request was granted. It was later that evening that I caught him staring at me in the smoky Café Anatolia. I had been terrified and titillated all at once, fearing that I might be looking too American or, worse in a predominantly Muslim country, too gay. I quickly decided to finish my ouzo and leave, preferring the safety of my cramped hotel room to the possibility of attack or imprisonment. On the sidewalk, though, the young man grabbed my arm, stopping me in my tracks; I held my breath, awaiting the worst.

"Stop," he said in broken English, smiling. "You are American, yes?"

"Yes," I heard myself admitting to the beautiful stranger. "What do you want?"

He smiled again, releasing my arm.

"You have a hotel room?" he whispered, glancing toward the street.

"Yes, but I don't think—" I began.

"Take me there," he interrupted, smiling.

"I don't think that's a good idea," I replied, looking around to see if anyone else was listening, but the street was empty.

"I missed the last train to Gaziantep," he persisted, "and you need company."

My head was spinning from the ouzo, and I was silent. I looked into the kid's eyes. He was beautifully brown-skinned with a halo of black unruly curls and a mouthful of white perfect teeth. He raised his eyebrows, silently imploring me.

Still, I thought, *he could be a robber or a police informant.* Languishing in a Turkish prison was the last thing that I needed after New York.

"Listen," he said, as if reading my mind, "I am not a police, I promise on the grave of my mother." Then, lowering his voice, "It has been a month since I have been with a man."

He reached over and took my hand, stroking my palm softly. I felt a stirring in my cotton pants that I hadn't felt in years.

"All right," I relented, noticing the fat bulge in his loose-fitting linen pants. "But only for tonight."

Fortunately, back at my hotel we found the elderly desk clerk dozing behind his desk, a half-eaten plate of something in front of him, and Abrahm slipped past unseen.

We were barely inside the room when Abrahm was on his knees in front of me, tugging at my fly and gobbling on my stiffening cock. I leaned back against the door and moaned, running my fingers through the messy hair that was bobbing back and forth at my waist. Again, David invaded my thoughts, thoughts of when our sex had been this passionate, thoughts of the Time Before. But that time was in the past now, never to return. I became angry with myself for allowing David in, into this reality, and forced Abrahm's head farther down on my angry cock, causing him to gag. He looked up at me in the darkness and smiled, amused at my willingness to use him. He stood up and, with the tug of a drawstring, allowed his pants to drop to his ankles, revealing his own erect cock. I pushed him onto my bed and devoured his stiff dick as if I were starving—and, truthfully, I was.

Abrahm lifted his legs above my head, allowing me access to his asshole, which smelled of summer and boy. I gratefully accepted, rimming him while I stroked my cock, the boy groaning beneath me. I pulled myself up and kissed his moist lips, which tasted of oranges, and he began to pull my stiff dick toward his asshole. Unfortunately, it was my first sexual encounter in a very long time, and I came before I was able to be inside him, waves of hot load pumping onto his smooth ass. Abrahm laughed and pulled me to his side while he jacked himself off, a finger up his ass.

I awoke the next morning as he was pulling on his pants.

"You like ruins?" he asked suddenly.

"Ruins?" I asked, rising onto an elbow. "Like old buildings?"

"Yes," he replied, smiling.

"I guess," I said slowly, nodding.

"There are many in Zeugma," he said, sitting on the bed next to me. "You will come with me to Zeugma?"

I agreed, realizing that, since he was obviously neither an informer nor a thief, I had no reason to decline. Besides, I wanted another opportunity to fuck him.

The train route to Zeugma took us through Kayseri and Kahramanmaras, and just like Abrahm promised, the passing landscape was littered with ancient ruins, their weathered columns jutting from the dry earth here and there. They reminded me of the home David and I had made together: a roof that sheltered us from storms, walls that made it ours, symbolizing what we thought was a strong foundation. Now, like these ruins, it was a relic, relegated to the past.

At Gaziantep we got off the train and boarded a bus that would take us into Zeugma, some 20 kilometers away. The ride was crowded and hot, and the bus, which I was sure had no shocks, bounced and flailed on the dusty roads. We passed more ruins.

Abrahm informed me that Zeugma, once a Roman outpost, was just 50 kilometers north of the Syrian border, with Iran to the southeast, and I again wondered just exactly what it was that I thought I was doing here.

As I lay in the grass with Abrahm three months later, naked under the baking sun, the sound of more trucks on the road below, I find myself wondering the same thing again.

I glanced over at him.

"What?" he asked, squinting at me.

"Come to the United States with me," I suggested.

"What about my father?" he asked, quickly sitting up and pulling on his shorts, dry grass clinging to the back of his head. "I cannot leave him here alone."

Because of the construction of the Birecik dam, the government had ordered the evacuation of some 30,000 residents in Zeugma and neighboring villages, including Abrahm and his father. Fortunately, they had been given a reprieve due to the discovery of some frescoes found in the ruins of an ancient Greco-Roman villa. The Turkish government had granted a team of French archaeologists permission to remove the frescoes from the site in order to save them from the flooding caused by the rising waters. These were the trucks on the road below us now.

"Once the archaeologists are gone the floodgates will be open," I pleaded. "I want you to come with me."

Abrahm, who had managed to pull on his flimsy tank top, smiled, leaning over to kiss me.

"Please?" I asked, touching his leg.

His face was serious, but he didn't respond.

For weeks his neighbors had been dismantling and carting away their houses—windows, wooden beams, doors. Anything they could use to rebuild elsewhere was taken.

"Do you think," Abrahm said suddenly, "that they will move us to a better place?"

"Who knows," I replied, shrugging. "Perhaps Gaziantep, perhaps Sanli Urfa…they're the closest."

Abrahm stood up from our grassy hiding place, peering down at the sound of more trucks below.

"What is so important about those ruins?" he asked, looking at me.

"They're history," I replied stupidly.

Abrahm and I had gone to see the tile frescoes one afternoon. There were a total of 14 of them, each depicting some piece of Greco-Roman mythology, and the brilliant colors of the tile were a stark contrast to the barren land surrounding them. The archaeologists were planning to remove them, we were told, so that they could be restored at the museum in Gaziantep.

"Ruins are important," I continued, "because we can learn from ancient cultures…and because they were able to leave something, some monument to their culture, behind."

Abrahm smiled at me and sat back down.

"You are funny," he said.

"What do you mean?" I asked, tousling his messy hair.

"You think that these old ruins are more important than the people's homes that will be destroyed, too."

"That's not true," I replied, looking at his beautiful face. But I knew that there was a bit of truth in what he was saying. Would a team of French archaeologists have been so willing to rush in and halt completion of a dam without antiquities here? Of course not. Soon the ancient ruins below, along with the more modest modern ruins, would be abandoned to the encroaching Euphrates.

"I think," said Abrahm, getting up and offering me his hand, which I took and joined him in standing, "no matter where they send us, there is no place like your home."

I nodded and hugged him under the hot sun. Of course he was right, despite the poor English.

And, maybe, just maybe, I would finally send David that postcard.

Me Too

David Puterbaugh

They had been driving in silence for more than an hour. The car they had rented for the weekend redefined the word *compact*, and yet the distance between them felt more like miles than the few inches that separated the driver's and passenger's seats.

Jason sat slouched in his seat with his arms folded across his chest, staring blankly out of the passenger window. He had not moved since they left Boston. Every few moments out of the corner of his eye he could see his boyfriend looking over at him. But when he would refuse to look back, Brian would give up and go back to driving.

How could he not tell me? The voice inside Jason's head was screaming loudly. *Especially today? How could he not tell me today?*

"So do you ever plan on telling me why you're mad?" Brian asked as he looked over at Jason. "Or are we never going to speak to one another again?"

Why am I mad? Is he kidding?

"I'm not mad," Jason lied.

"Well, you're obviously mad about something, Jason. You haven't said two words to me since we left the house."

"Nope. Not mad," Jason answered, slouching farther down in his seat.

You're not getting off the hook that easy, pal!

"Fine. Don't tell me," Brian said, turning back to the road. "I can't believe that you're doing this today."

WHAT? Jason snapped his head at Brian and sat up straight. "I'm doing this? I'm the one who's doing this? Yeah, right!"

"What's that supposed to mean?" Brian asked.

"I know perfectly well what today is, Brian! I'm not the one who needs to be reminded!"

Brian looked completely confused. "Jason, what the hell are you talking about? Is this about the watch? Because I told you that you can take it back if you don't like it."

"THIS IS NOT ABOUT THE WATCH, BRIAN! THIS IS ABOUT ME HAVING A BOYFRIEND WHO NEVER TELLS ME THAT HE LOVES ME!"

Brian's mouth hung wide open. "Are you serious? That's what you're so mad about?"

"Isn't that enough?" Jason asked incredulously.

"I told you that I loved you this morning!"

"No, you didn't."

"Yes I did! Jesus Christ, we made love this morning! How can you not remember?"

"Because you didn't say it."

"Oh really? Than tell me what I said."

"*Me too.*"

"What? Me too?"

"Yes. 'Me too.' "

"I didn't say that!"

"Oh yes you did. After we made love *I* told you that I loved *you*. And then you said it. *Me too.*"

Brian looked at Jason, then back at the road, then back at Jason again. "I…are you…really?"

"Yes, really! It's what you always say! Every time I tell you that I love you that's your response! Me too! Me too! ME FUCKING TOO!"

Jason's face was red with anger as he raged on.

"When we first started going out I thought it was cute. It reminded me of that movie *Ghost*, where every time Demi Moore tells Patrick Swayze that she loves him, he says 'Ditto.' I found it endearing. But you know what? After a couple of years it finally hit me. This guy has never actually told me that he loves me!"

"That's not true—"

"Yes it is, Brian!" Jason screamed. "You've never once told me that you love me. I always have to say it first. And even then you don't say 'I love you' back, you say 'Me too.' And whatever you may think, that is not the same thing!"

For a moment Brian just sat staring straight ahead. "Why now?" he asked quietly. "If this has been bothering you so much, why are you just bringing it up now?"

Tears began to form in Jason's eyes. "Because I never would have thought that on our third anniversary I would have to ask you to tell me that you love me."

The only sound for the next mile was from Jason blowing his nose.

"Jason, you know how hard it is for me to talk about stuff like this," Brian finally said. "You knew that when you met me."

Jason turned his head away and looked back out the window.

"But you know how I feel about you. I know that you know that," Brian continued.

"Knowing it and hearing it are two different things."

The road sign that they were now passing was welcoming them to Provincetown.

"So what do you want to do now?" Brian asked.

"I don't care."

"Well, we're here already. And we won't get the deposit back if we cancel now."

"Fine," Jason said.

"Fine," Brian answered.

They drove the rest of the way in silence.

Although the mood inside their car couldn't have been darker, the world outside the vehicle could not have been brighter. The sun shone down happily on the seaside resort as they drove into town, and even though it was a weekend in late September, this particular day was as warm and pleasant as a summer afternoon.

Me Too

Brian turned the car onto a narrow street and came to a stop in the driveway of a charming Victorian house. They had both been on separate vacations when they met at the Dashwood Inn three years ago. Both of them had been traveling alone, and Brian had first spotted Jason one morning reading a book in the inn's flower-filled garden.

A conversation about their favorite books led to a discussion about their favorite movies, and each was happy to learn that the other also lived in Boston. Jason told Brian that he planned to go to the beach and asked him if he wanted to come along.

They ended up spending the day together. And later, the night as well.

They had returned several times to the Dashwood Inn since then, and always on their anniversary, staying in the same room that Brian had on that first trip.

Jason climbed out of the car as Brian turned off the engine and slammed the door behind him. Each took his own bag from the backseat and headed for the front of the house.

The owners of the inn were a couple in their mid 50s named Dan and Terry. Both men had been teachers in the New York City school system when they had met more than 30 years before. They themselves had been frequent visitors to Provincetown during their years together, and after they retired they realized their shared dream of becoming innkeepers by opening a B&B.

The Dashwood Inn was a fairly large house by Provincetown standards. In addition to the private garden, the inn boasted a spacious library with an impressive collection of books, as well as 15 guest rooms. As large as the house was, Dan and Terry always made it a point to greet each of their guests personally on the day of their arrival.

Which is why Brian and Jason were very surprised when a middle-aged woman opened the front door. "Oh, hello. You must be Jason and Brian? I'm Lois. Gorgeous day today, isn't it?" she said with a smile as she stepped aside and held the door open for them.

Lois was a typical-looking New Englander with a warm smile

and a firm handshake. As if anticipating their question, she answered it before either one of them could ask it. "Dan and Terry are away today, but they will be back later this evening. They asked me to please tell you both how sorry they are that they weren't able to be here to welcome you in person. And they made me promise that I would do everything possible to make you both feel right at home. I'm the new office manager, by the way. I've just finished my first summer here."

She waved them into a small room off the foyer that served as the office.

"How was your drive?" she asked while her back was toward both of them.

"OK," Brian mumbled as Jason frowned at him.

"I see you've been with us several times before?" she said, taking a seat behind a small desk and squinting at the computer screen in front of her.

"Yes," Brian said. "We met here, actually."

"At the inn? Oh, how nice," Lois said, smiling at both of them. "I've always said that Provincetown is one of the most romantic places in the world."

Jason smiled politely but wished that Brian hadn't brought it up.

"And I see that you'll be staying in the Great Gatsby room again. Very nice."

All of the rooms in the house were named after famous characters from American and English literature. Jason had been staying in the Holden Caulfield room the first time he and Brian had met.

"Personally, I think that's one of the nicest rooms in the house," Lois said. "The Dorian Gray room is lovely too, but I think the Gatsby has the better view."

"Yes, I really love that room," Brian said.

"*Me too,*" Jason said.

Lois missed the angry look that Brian shot Jason as she turned to retrieve two sets of keys off a pegboard behind the desk. "The names of the rooms are fun, aren't they? Did you know that Dan and Terry were both English teachers?"

They both nodded yes, then Lois laughed out loud. "Although when I first arrived I thought for sure that the literary references must get lost on some of the younger guys they get through here during the summer. Well, sure enough, I had this one kid insisting that he had locked himself out of the Mrs. Doubtfire room. I nearly wet myself when I realized that he was staying in the Mrs. Dalloway!"

Jason and Brian declined Lois's offer to help them with their bags and made their own way to the second floor. Whatever negative thoughts they were having about being cooped up together vanished the moment they entered their room.

The Great Gatsby room was exactly as they both remembered. The massive queen-size canopy bed was positioned in an alcove off the large sitting room, which contained an antique writing desk, a love seat, and several comfortable chairs. A huge fireplace dominated the wall directly across from the bed, and its mantel was adorned with a vase full of fresh flowers with a personal note from their hosts, which read, "HAPPY ANNIVERSARY FROM DAN AND TERRY."

The best thing about the room, however, was the private balcony and its commanding view over all of the smaller houses to the beach and ocean beyond.

"I could stare at this view all day," Brian had said to Jason the first time he brought him out there.

It was also the first place where Brian had kissed him.

Jason began to feel very guilty as he thought of this now, watching Brian push open the balcony doors and step outside.

Of course he loves you, stupid! the voice in his head now said. *In his own way he loves you! You're being such a fool!*

Jason sat down on the bed, the very same bed where they had first made love, and pulled his bag onto his lap. Unzipping the front pocket, he took out a card that he had been planning to give to Brian. He had found it in a small shop right here in Provincetown on the trip that they had taken last year. Liking it so much, he had bought it then and put it away to save for their next anniversary. The card had been hand-painted by a local artist, and the scene depicted on the front of it was of two men walking hand in hand along a beach at sunset.

Jason took the card out of its matching envelope and reread the words that he had written inside: *You're always on my mind. And forever in my heart.*

He quickly stuffed the card into its envelope as Brian came back into the room.

"Still a great view." Brian mumbled, looking down at the floor. "Jason, I'm sorry—"

"Here," Jason said before Brian could say anything else, holding out the card to him.

"What's this?" Brian asked, taking it from him.

"Open it."

Brian sat down next to him. His face turned pinkish and a smile crept across his face as he read the card. "Aw, baby…"

"Happy anniversary," Jason said.

"Happy anniversary," Brian said as he leaned over and gave Jason a kiss.

"And I'm sorry," Jason said.

"I'm sorry too," Brian said.

"And I love you," Jason said.

"Me—"

Brian's hand flew up to cover his mouth. Jason stared at him in disbelief. "I don't believe it."

"Jason, I'm sorry, I—"

"Forget it," he said, getting up from the bed and heading for the door.

"Jason, wait! Where are you going?"

Jason didn't turn around or answer him. He just walked out of the room and closed the door behind him.

It was just after dark when Jason finally returned. Brian had not left the room, and had sat most of the evening in a chair across from the door, waiting for Jason to come back. "Where have you been?" he asked, sounding more worried than angry.

"Walking. I took a walk along the beach," Jason said as he

took a seat closer to the door. "I want to go home," he said.

"I want to talk first," Brian said.

Jason shook his head. "There's nothing to talk about Brian. You're not going to change, and neither am I. I just want to go home."

"So, what? I don't get to say anything?" Brian said, standing up. "You walk out on me and you won't even listen to me when you finally do come back?"

"Brian, I don't want to argue…" But it was Brian's turn to be mad now.

"Well, we are going to argue goddamn it! Because this is ridiculous! You know how I feel about you, Jason! It is not my fault that you're so damn insecure!"

"Shut up!"

"No I won't, because it's true! You always need to be reassured. God! You are so damn needy sometimes! You think that I don't say that I love you enough? Well you say it too much! All the cards and the flowers and the presents! It's like you don't believe that you're loving someone unless you're completely suffocating them!"

Jason jumped out of his chair. "Oh, poor you!" he shouted back. "How awful it must be for you to have a boyfriend who actually cares enough to tell you that he loves you! I wish that I had your problems!"

"Exactly!" Brian yelled, now standing inches from Jason's face. "You want me to love you exactly the way that you love me! And I can't do that!"

"Or you won't," Jason said.

Brian stared at him. "Do you really believe that?"

Jason didn't answer.

"Fine," Brian said, looking down at the floor and shaking his head. "You know what? You win. You want to go home? Here." He tossed the car keys onto a table. "Go home. I'm going to get a drink."

A tear fell down Jason's cheek as Brian shut the door behind him.

After half an hour, Jason couldn't stand being alone in the

room any longer. Closing the door quietly behind himself, he headed downstairs. Another 30-something male couple was going into their room, the Lady Macbeth, and they smiled at him as they passed in the hall.

For a moment after Brian walked out Jason had seriously considered leaving. *Brian can easily take the ferry back to Boston*, he thought. But Jason hated driving alone in the dark, and even though he thought about it, he knew that he could never actually bring himself to leave Brian behind. Besides, the idea of getting a drink himself was sounding like a better idea every minute.

He took the back staircase that led to an exit through his favorite part of the house. Breakfast was always served at the Dashwood Inn in the formal dining room, but when the weather was nice Jason would often take his coffee and go sit outside on the patio, where several small iron tables and chairs were surrounded by the inn's lush and tranquil garden.

Jason heard voices as he opened the door and stepped outside, and was surprised when he found Brian sitting at a table with one of their hosts.

"There he is!" Dan shouted as he jumped up from his chair and came over to kiss Jason hello. "Are you feeling better?" he asked.

"Huh?"

"Brian said that you had a headache."

Jason looked over at Brian, who was staring down at the table. "Oh, right. I'm feeling much better. Thanks."

"Good! Well come have a glass of wine with us," Dan said, pulling another chair over to the table. He tilted a wine glass toward Brian. "I caught this one on his way out but I convinced him to have a drink with me first," he said, pouring Jason a glass of wine and handing it to him. "It's so good to see you both again! So how was your first day back in P-Town?"

Even though they were now seated next to one another, neither Jason nor Brian would look at each other. "OK," they both said.

Jason noticed that, although Dan was happy to see them, he seemed very tired. He had dark circles under his eyes, and he looked like he hadn't had a good rest in months. They must have had a very busy summer season, Jason thought. But surely things must have calmed down by now? And having a new office manager must have taken some of the burden off them having to do all the work themselves.

"I'm sorry that Terry and I couldn't be here to meet you when you arrived today," Dan said. "Terry had an appointment this morning to see a doctor in Boston. We took the ferry over right after breakfast."

"Oh, I hope it was nothing serious," Jason said politely. No sooner had Jason spoken then Terry himself stepped out onto the patio.

Brian and Jason could not hide the shocked looks on their faces. The vibrant host they both remembered so fondly was now nowhere to be found. The man standing in front of them looked old and weak. Terry's once ruddy skin was now sickly white, and he walked with some difficulty with the aid of a cane. His left arm hung loosely at his side, and the entire left side of his face seemed to droop toward the ground.

"Have you told them about my stroke yet?" he asked, as Dan jumped up again and pulled another chair over to the table. The words came slowly from Terry's mouth, and his speech was somewhat slurred.

"I was just about to tell them," Dan said. "But you beat me to it."

"You know me. I always liked a dramatic entrance," Terry said with as full a smile as possible.

"When did this happen?" Jason asked, as he glanced over at Brian, who had not taken his eyes off Terry.

"Six months ago," Dan said. "We were over in Boston for the evening. It was a friend's birthday and his partner was having a special dinner for him at the Four Seasons. Terry had been complaining of a headache all day, but these were old friends and he didn't want to disappoint them, so we decided to go anyway."

Dan reached over and put his hand on Terry's knee.

"They were just clearing away the dessert when Terry suddenly collapsed at the table."

"Oh my God," Brian whispered.

"Talk about dramatic," Terry said with a wink at him.

"It was very scary," Dan said, frowning at Terry. "I was never so terrified in all of my life."

Terry took his good hand off his cane and rested it on top of Dan's hand. "My hero," he said with a smile.

"I would be lost without him and he knows it," Dan said.

"You've got Lois now," Terry answered, waving toward the house.

"But you're the one that I love," Dan said as he leaned over and kissed Terry on the head.

Terry closed his eyes and smiled. "Me too," he said.

Jason felt Brian staring at him.

"It's true what they say," Dan said. "You never really know what you have until you think that you're about to lose it. I remember sitting there in the hospital next to Terry's bed, wishing that we could go back and make up for all the time that we spent arguing about stupid stuff."

"We argued a lot, didn't we?" Terry laughed.

"One time years ago I forgot Terry's birthday," Dan laughed. "Oh my God, he was so mad at me!"

"I wouldn't talk to him for a week!" Terry said.

"I was working two jobs then and going to school at night," Dan said. "I couldn't remember where I had to be half the time, let alone what day it was!"

"I didn't care. I was so mad!" Terry said.

"Even after he forgave me he still talked about it for years," Dan laughed.

"I was such an evil bitch," Terry said.

They all laughed, and then Dan got very quiet. "All of the stuff, the Christmas presents and Valentine's candy and the I Love You balloons, all of the stuff that we pretend means something—none of that stuff means a damn thing if you don't have someone who will stick with you through it all," he said.

The two couples sat silently for the next few moments, each of them lost in their own personal thoughts.

"Oh my God!" Dan suddenly exclaimed. "We completely forgot. Happy anniversary!"

"Oh, yes," Terry said.

"Thank you," Jason managed to say convincingly. He had never felt so awkward.

"Yeah, thanks," Brian added.

"Everyone wait right here! I'll be right back!" Dan said as he rushed from the table into the house. He was back in no time with a bottle of champagne and more glasses. "I meant to send this up to your room tonight. Oh how I hate getting old and losing my mind!"

"Dan, you really shouldn't have bothered," Brian said. "The flowers were more than enough."

"Don't be silly," Dan said as he popped the cork. "You met each other here, for goodness' sake. How could we not celebrate that?"

Dan poured champagne for Brian, Jason, and himself, and gave Terry a glass of iced tea that he had brought back from the house.

"Sorry, hon. No booze. Doctor's orders," he said to Terry, who stuck his tongue at him. Then Dan raised his glass and made a toast. "To Brian and Jason. May you have as many happy and wonderful years together as Terry and I have had."

After everyone had taken a sip of their drinks, Terry leaned in close to the table and waved his hand for Brian and Jason to come closer. "Hold hands," he said.

Brian and Jason looked at one another and then back at Terry. "Hold hands?" Jason asked.

Terry cleared his throat and continued. "When I was lying in the hospital, I couldn't feel anything. Couldn't feel my legs, couldn't feel my face, couldn't talk. But I could feel something in my hand. I didn't know what it was at first, but I knew that it was there. And when I could finally open my eyes, I looked down and saw that it was Dan sitting there holding my hand."

Dan took Terry's hand in his now and squeezed it.

"Don't ever stop holding each other's hands," Terry said. He lifted his and Dan's hands toward them. "Go on."

Jason looked at Brian, and Brian looked at Jason, and then Brian held out his hand. And Jason took it.

Later, when they went back to their room (neither of them mentioned again the idea of leaving early), Jason began to feel for the second time that day like a complete asshole. Leaving Brian in the bedroom, he went into the bathroom and looked at himself in the mirror. *You are such an idiot! You have a great guy here who you know deep down really and truly loves you. Why are you trying to screw this up? It doesn't matter what he says or doesn't say! Words don't mean anything anyway! It's what he does that matters. And he's here with you now. He puts up with all of your bullshit and he's still here. And do you know why? Because he loves you, stupid.*

Jason smiled at himself and then went back into the bedroom. There he found Brian sitting on the bed with his face in his hands. He was crying.

"Brian? Honey? What is it?" Jason asked as he sat down on the bed next to him.

Brian looked at him. Tears were streaming down his face. "Do you have any idea how much..." he choked. "If anything ever happened to you..."

"Oh, Brian..." Jason started to say, but Brian stopped him before he could finish. He took Jason's head in his hands and he kissed him.

Brian then looked into Jason's eyes, which were quickly filling up with tears of their own. "The very best thing about my life is that I get to share it with you," he said. Then he put his head on Jason's chest and closed his eyes. "I love you," Brian said softly.

Jason closed his eyes and sighed. "Me too," he said.

Vamp

J.D. Roman

I know you'll think this is all *ho'omalimali*, but I swear I'm not bullshitting you.

He pressed one hand into the back of my knee before I knew he was behind me. I was up on my tiptoes on the University of Hawai'i Library footstool, reaching for *Haunted Hawai'i* on the top shelf, looking for material to spice up my tour guide rap. His cold hand startled me, and I lost my balance. His other hand slid up the back of my cutoffs. He cupped my *okole*, the left cheek, and pushed me back upright. I'm sure he was expecting underwear, but once I strip off my bright flowered work uniform, *pau hana*, I wear as little as possible.

He didn't take his hands away. He owned me with his touch. He could crumple me down or hold me up, however he pleased.

I don't know who he was, where he came from, or how long he'd been watching me.

His hand slipped down from my *okole* and crept into the tight cranny between my thighs, searching for my balls, but they were squashed tight and sweaty up under the denim inseam. My big legs make for a tight fit, and he gave up trying to extricate my *ohana* jewels. He ran his hands up and down my legs. I stared at those disembodied hands exploring my body, his skin on mine like white coconut meat against its tough brown husk. Even his long fingers couldn't make it all the way around my mountain-biking calves. He touched me like he couldn't believe I was real. I didn't turn around to face him. I didn't want to snap out of a surreal dream. Maybe this was Maui the Trickster playing a godly joke on me.

He had his nose right at my tailbone. He pulled my sleeveless tank out of my waistband. He ran his hands under my shirt, across my back, and around to my abs. My nipples were on high beam, what with his icy touch and the air-conditioning cooling my sweat. It didn't take long for his Braille exploration to find them, plus I've got big tits. He reached up and pinched them hard. He touched both hands to my throat.

He dipped his fingertips down my belly and into my waistband. He paused as he encountered the tip of my *ule*—like a second glance, but instead of sight, touch—surprised by its half-mast reach. No bragging, I'm a big dude, and my cock's proportionate. He popped open my fly. My shorts dropped easily to my ankles once he got them over my ass mounds—they're the size of the outer islands.

I had those sweet thong tan lines that come spreading out from your ass crack like embracing wings that reach around to cup your precious jewels. I could've sunbathed nude on my apartment's *lanai*, but I think those tiny lines look really hot on muscular bodies like mine. They make big asses look penetrable. Front and back, those lines draw the eye right to the point. That's one part of me I don't care to sunburn, plus I'm *hapa*, mixed race, and I like to think I've stuffed my white side right up my ass.

He pressed his lips, cold and dry and thin, right to my crack. I must have been real *hauna*, but he seemed to like that musky smell. He breathed me in and licked my salty skin. Fresh from a hard bike ride through the Manoa Valley, I'd hit the library more for the cold air than the books. My apartment's air-conditioning was busted, but they kept the library A/C cranked because mildew is such a problem on the collections, what with the humid climate.

His white hands snaked through my pubic hair, the same coarse dark curls as the ones on my head. He cupped my package, feeling its heft. My *ule* protested his freezing hands. I mean, I was naked in the library, for crying out loud. I've had some kicks before, but never anything like that. He laughed when I wilted. But with what his cold fist did to my uncertain *ule*, I was stiff as a surfboard in seconds.

He worked me over *wiki wiki*. I thought he rushed because he was afraid of getting caught. Later I realized he wanted to show me good and fast that I had absolutely nothing to do with it. All I could do was give up and follow his paces. He revved me up before I could really go, like peeling tires when you take off too fast. He laid a patch with my body, and afterward I felt like one of those retreads you see at the side of the road. I didn't have time to think about any of it. I gave up to him, just like that, pawing a little at the stool with my toes. His moving hand was a blur, like a white dove flapping her wings.

He bit my *okole*, and I erupted all over the book spines in seconds. So much for mildew.

I lost all strength to my legs. Weak-kneed, I sagged back against him, and he lifted me down. Yeah, lifted, like in the *Gone With the Wind* poster, me looking up at him in a faintish, goofy sort of way. Nobody's hefted my sizable carcass since I was a little *keiki*. I'm big. And I don't act queeny or vamp it up, so I don't look *mahu*. How did he know he wasn't going to get a fist in his face instead of my sweet *okole*? His confidence and assumption were what really grabbed my attention—well, that and what he did to me in the stacks, only I guess he grabbed more than that.

His power and my unresisting surrender went straight to my groin, and I went stiff again. My thick *ule* has this way of looking purple and angry and demanding when it's awake. It's a mean cock. It surprises people if they know me. The head roars, like you'd better think twice about letting it down, and right now it was pointing straight at him in stubborn command. He liked the Second Coming. I could tell by his smile. Plus, it was his first good look, like he'd had his face full of my twin volcanoes up till now.

He set my naked butt on the stool. It had one of those ribbed, non-skid rubber coverings, and it dug graph-paper lines into my *okole*, smarting where he'd given me the ass hickey. Only now my cock pointed straight up at me, like to say, "You big dummy."

"Just let me go wash my hands," he smiled down at me. "I'll be right back."

I sat there 38 minutes, until the librarian kicked me out after the third closing announcement. I almost asked her if she wanted to play tic-tac-toe on my ass, but I'd hiked up my shorts by then. I left the books all *kapakahi* where I'd almost pulled them down on myself while he milked my *poi*-pounder.

That's how it started.

I should have considered it a one-night stand—like why else would he ditch me naked on a library stool? But I knew he had something else in mind. He had purchased me from the shelves with those hands. He had marked me. I had to sit with my right ass cheek cocked up off the seat for a week because of my bruised *okole*, had to sleep on my *opu* because sleeping on my back aggravated the sore spot. There had to be something in it for him. I mean, I hadn't even touched him.

I prowled the stacks every night after dumping off busloads of sunburned tourists at their Waikiki hotels. How else was he going to find me? I even tried to jerk off standing there, but the librarian cruised by, so I packed myself away real quick.

Eventually I gave up and rode my bike to the other side of the island and up the trail to Sacred Falls. It was late by the time I got there, and no one was around, so I stripped. I climbed the rock cliff and dove into the freezing pool. The water was his body and breath against me. His icy touch, and his gaze, gripped and penetrated me. I frog-kicked across the pool, and the water fucked my ass crack.

I paddled my outrigger furiously under the water, needing the friction to heat my *ule*. I'd been sticking my hand in the freezer before masturbating—which was constantly—remembering his cold strokes. My waves splashed the surface as much as the waterfall.

I swam under the pounding falls. The avalanche of water beat at my body and suffocated me. I latched onto the rock ledge and splayed my legs. The cascading water slammed into my ass, making violent, fluid love to me. It pushed me down into the depths of the pool, drowning me as it fucked me.

I floated back to the surface in still water downstream, my cock bobbing up first like a shark fin. I hummed the *Jaws* theme. The cold water lost its grip, and the warm air caressed me. The mist from the falls was all I'd need to come, I was that close. But I splashed upright, taking in a lungful of water. My bike and shorts were gone from the rock bank. Not only had someone stolen my stuff, but they'd witnessed my little water ballet. And now I had to find my way back in the dark without my bike light. Naked.

I ran. My hungry cock led the way for a while, until it got smacked a couple of times by stray branches. The dense mountain foliage scratched me, and I tumbled over exposed roots. My callused *luau* feet could take the rocks. It was the fear of *menehunes* that bothered me. The evil Hawaiian version of leprechauns, they lurked at night, ready to attack. These creatures had haunted me since my old Tutu, who had raised me, told me ghost stories when I was a *keiki*. I hadn't outgrown the superstition. I had no idea how I was going to get home halfway around the island once I escaped the forest. I just knew I had to *hele* on out of those deserted woods before something grabbed me.

I staggered, naked, dirty, bruised, and scratched, into the dark parking lot. My bike was strapped to the trunk of his Porsche convertible. He didn't speak or wave, just watched.

Pissed, I strode over to him. Anger brings out my local features in hard lines, and I knew I looked mean. Only, my tiki torch lit up…I was that charged by his reappearance, so I guess I wasn't all that threatening. He just smiled. I like his smile.

There was no sign of my shorts.

I climbed into the passenger seat and fastened my seat belt. He touched my thigh, and I got chicken skin. He fingered a welt on my shaft. He shifted my gears and the car's as he drove. Without headlights. *Pupule*, man. Crazy. He took me to Paradise Park. The exotic birds squawked in their tourist trap.

"Ever been inside?"

"Not since elementary school." I told him how I'd gone

home crying over the caged birds, had drawn up daring plans to free them.

I followed him to the entrance. He had my clothes. He jimmied the front gate.

The giant birdcage is two stories tall and you enter at the top. We stood at the beginning of the descending path that zigzags down one side of the open-barred cage. The tropical birds, multicolored and beautiful, flapped their wings and shrieked at the late-night disturbance. I started to walk down the path, but he grabbed my hand. I jumped with its chill.

I kept walking. Now that his hand wasn't on my cock, I was mad again.

I couldn't pull free. He stood still and quiet, just holding me. I whiplashed back.

I liked the shock of it. I had really checked him out this time, and he looked too thin to push me around. He's almost as tall as me, and older, with washed-out blue eyes and blond hair slicked back, like one of those proper dudes on a boring public television movie about a different century. He wore light-colored linen clothes that whispered around his body in the trade wind. His style is expensive but simple, except he wears a few big-ass rings, like even on his thumbs, thick and gold and hammered. One caught on my cock head in the stacks, and later he liked to scratch me with the diamond one.

He's *haole*, real white. Like, white in a way even *haoles* in Hawaii just aren't. Walking between your car and the grocery store will give you color. I mean, how could you stay that white with a convertible in the tropics?

He stuffed my clothes into the cage, shoes and all. They fell to the bottom, two stories down, landing in crusted bird shit.

He grabbed my cock and led me down the path to the cage door at the bottom. He held it open for me. I stepped in, and the barred door slammed behind me with a clang. I tested it. Locked from both sides. I'd worry about that later. Right now he beckoned to me through the bars. I came up close, and he petted me. I thought I'd shoot instantly. I'd never been put in a cage before. But he wasn't about to allow that. He'd just started to play.

Tonight wasn't about coming *wiki wiki*–like at the library—it was about stretching out my torment.

He rattled a pocket full of change. The birds squawked for a midnight snack, expecting us to feed them treats out of the vending machines. He bought a pile of seeds for them, stuffing his pockets, and scattered them at my feet. They swooped down, screeching. The beaks and claws on those birds made me real nervous.

I stood with my back to him, my *okole* pressed against the bars. He reached into the cage to fondle me, the other hand alongside my *ule,* with a hand full of seeds. I wanted my dick to shrink down out of the birds' way, but he made sure it stood up for them. They flapped around me, screeching and pecking. He balanced a seed right on my cock head, and a nasty white parrot swooped in and pecked it off. I yelped and slammed back against the bars. He laughed. I like his laugh.

I felt a nagging tickle up my ass. He'd fitted me with a plumed tail. It wagged whenever I clenched my cheeks.

He allowed me to turn around, cock thrust out of the cage and swollen balls hooked up over a crossbar. He walked a few more steps up the path and extended his enticing fingers into the cage. Up I climbed while he strummed my ukulele, my "jumping flea," until he stood at the top again. Two stories up, I clung to the cold bars, slippery with my sweat, my cock demanding a feeding through the cage. The height didn't bother me. I'd climbed a lot higher up mountainous rock that hadn't offered such easy hand- and footholds. But the parrots worried me. They screamed and beat with their wings, suspicious of this tailed beast in their sanctuary. He encouraged their raucous dance around me, sprinkling seeds on my hair and shoulders, on my ass hills, and wedged in my ass crack above my tail.

I wanted to climb down a few notches and have him feed me his shaft. Polly wanted some *kau kau*. I wanted him to pound down into me, his passion threatening to dislodge me, the danger of a high-rise blow job heightening my lust. But he just kept petting me, a slow, persistent stroke. He plucked one of my tail feathers and dusted my *ule* with it. That's how slow he went. He had me clinging to that cage, speckled in bird crap, squawking as loud as the parrots.

I trembled from the strain of holding my weight up for so long. I started to climb down. But he took such a hold of my dick it seemed he'd rip it out by the root if I moved, so I stayed planted, him working me over, my tail drooping.

He picked up the pace, and Polly sang.

He made me turn around, a dangerous execution, my back to the cage as I clung to it, arms above me, heels tucked into an opening. He reached around to my cock. I rocked in his motionless fist, the dance up to me. The bars rattled as my ass beat back against them, crushing my tail. He crouched and bit my ass again. I yelped, almost losing my hold, but instead shot an impressive arc that fell like warm tropical rain. I lost my tail.

I turned around. I should have guessed. He was gone. Only this time he'd left me in a trickier spot than bare-assed on a library stool.

Muscles quivering with exhaustion, I climbed down, slipping off my foothold a couple of times and dangling dangerously. I pulled on my cutoffs, swearing as the white parrot crapped on my head. I'm not sure what made me look up, but there he stood at the top, expressionless, next to an unlatched cage door. I had to climb back up to get out.

Flopping through the door awhile later, seal-like, I heard him screech out of the parking lot. He left me a present with my bike: the most brilliant multihued feather I'd ever set eyes on. I'd heard a hell of a shriek and suspected it was fresh plucked.

I could hardly make it home. With twin hickeys on my ass cheeks, one fading and one fresh, I coasted into the sunrise, standing up on the pedals.

After that I masturbated with the feather instead of ice cubes.

He stopped making me wait so long between visits. He showed up without warning, always at night. Whenever he appeared, I *hele*'d on over as fast as I could, no matter where I was. I'd ditch my friends. Like takeout from Zippy's Drive-In couldn't compare to his *pupu* platter. After a while my buddies gave up on me and quit calling.

He drove me all over, often to the same places I took jackass happy tourists during the day. While the pink herds milled around outside snapping photos, I jerked off on the tour bus, remembering what he'd done to me on this very spot, hours before. I was marking his territory—namely, me. I preferred his package tours to mine. Despite the daytime crowds, the places were deserted at night. One look from him, his narrow nose flaring, and any strays scampered. He wasn't physically threatening, like I could be. There was just something about him, a powerful *mana*. Like *auwe*, dude, if you crossed him wrong. I did my share of scampering.

Our dates consisted of one thing: me naked and him touching me, watching me. No small talk.

He'd tease and torture me all night. When I staggered into work the next morning, my boss thought I was stoned on *pakalolo*. I started calling in sick. I was afraid I'd wreck the tour bus, shouting "*Alo-o-o-HA!*" as I rid the island of myself and a gaggle of tourists. I went surfing. The ocean purified me, his scratches stinging in the saltwater.

By the time he took me up to the old *heiau* above Waimea Bay, I was cranky. I was getting tired of this routine. All he did was push me around and watch me squirm. I had yet to touch him. He hadn't removed a scrap of clothing. He hadn't even kissed me. He paid my dick lots of attention, but that's it. I reached for his crotch in the car. He smacked my hand away, and I sulked. I thought about dumping him, moving on and finding a real relationship.

I knew I couldn't. There were worse things than a guy paying too much attention to your dick. But the thought made me feel like I had a choice.

The *heiau*'s not much more now than a low, crumbling rectangular wall of fist-size rocks overgrown with weeds. Wandering around the sacred temple of the ancient Hawaiian *kahuna* witch doctors really creeped me out. Humans had been sacrificed to the gods here, but he prowled around like he owned it, no fear. At least at night we didn't have to worry about throwing our shadows across the *kapu* rocks. The taboo would have brought a death curse down upon us, or so the old people believed. I wrapped a *ti* leaf around one of the rocks and set it down amidst similar offerings left by others. Plenty enough still believed.

"For good luck," I explained sheepishly.

"Amazing the power the dead have over us, isn't it?" he asked. I felt pretty stupid.

He couldn't get me off, though on the way over my cock had been raging. I was too intimidated by my childhood superstitions, and he seemed to like that even better than my unfailing hard-ons. He smacked my soft meat around a little bit, and I asked again if we could go someplace else.

He pushed me facedown, naked of course, across the *kapu* rocks I'd always avoided even with my shadow. He finger-fucked me, his first penetration of my body. I bucked at the shock, mostly because I hadn't expected it after all this time, and his finger was dry and cold. I wanted up but couldn't push him off. I struggled a moment, then gave up to him. I couldn't refuse him. He explored my insides a long time, brutally, adding fingers. I tried to crawl away, but he was leashed to my insides. He pulled me back, scraping my torso and cock on the volcanic shrapnel. I knew he wouldn't stop until I broke down and accepted that my body must obey him. I tried to relax and open myself to the invasion I'd been craving.

He rolled me over. My body rotated around his fist like a *huli huli* chicken. He licked at my stinging scrapes. I was still limp, playing slack key. He spread my legs, made me hike my ass up. He pulled his hand out and shoved my *ti* leaf–wrapped sacred rock right up my shameless *okole*.

"Dance," he said.

I don't know how he knew about my *hula*. I never talked about it. It was sacred, pure, the best part of me. I had refused to earn better money at it by entertaining the tourists.

"Why do you do this?" I rarely asked questions. When I did, he rarely answered.

"Because I'm bored."

Beats television.

I knew he wouldn't ask twice. If I said no, I'd never see him again.

I rose up on my knees and chanted in the ancient language. I knew better than to drop the rock.

Real *hula* isn't smiling girls in grass skirts shaking their skinny *okoles* for the tourists. Nobody danced that crap till the *haoles* came. Ancient *hula* used to be a preparation for war, serious business, men only. The *kanes* stomp and chant *mele*, telling a story with their hands. It's real macho, but graceful and beautiful.

I danced in the dirt and weeds inside the decomposing wall, the soil rich with ancient blood. I danced and danced, but I couldn't get it up. I knew I couldn't stop dancing until I'd proven that he ruled my body. He'd fitted me with the proverbial red shoes, only they were up my ass, and I was dancing where the spirits could kill me.

So instead of the rain and sea and volcanoes and ancient gods, I made up a chant, a dance, about him. He possessed and penetrated me, even when he wasn't near. I beseeched him, paid homage to him, offered myself as sacrifice for his pleasure. He filled my mind and body, invading every crevice. He could kill me with his curse, or rule me with his mercy.

My cock obeyed, growing as hard as the rock inside me. I felt huge and primal, like the petroglyph stick figures the ancients carved in rock, their phalluses monstrous and out of proportion.

I danced faster, building a crescendo with the *kaholo*, the "vamp" step. My muscles quivered with the struggle of holding the rock inside me. My insides were violated. My guts cramped up and I collapsed to my knees, but I didn't lose it. I crawled over to him. He made me squat over the crumbling wall and lay my rock. I sank down, my head in my hands.

He'd broken me. He had tested me and discovered no limits. He was God over me, *akua* and *aumakua*, greater and lesser. His worship left room for no others.

He didn't touch me.

He took me up to Waimea Falls, and I dove off the high cliff into the deep pool of water. I felt cleansed and let him fondle me when I climbed out. I wanted to come, desperately, a release for my conflicted emotions. But he wouldn't take me there. It pissed me off. The turmoil had exhausted me, and I reached down to finish myself off. He grabbed my wrist, but I was so close and the struggle such a turn-on, I knew I would come without direct contact. He threw me into the cold water. My cock retracted like a frightened snake.

He wound me up again on the ride home, then dumped me out of the car in front of my crummy apartment, right on the brink.

He had never deprived me of satisfaction before. I guess I expected a tip for my performance.

That's when he told he I couldn't come anymore when he wasn't around.

Yeah, right.

He waited a long time before turning up again.

When I next saw his blinking headlights, I trotted over, deserting the *luau* dinner package tour. He saw I'd obeyed. My barometer wouldn't lie. I bulged right out of my pineapple-print *malo*, and the loincloth's wedgie wasn't helping matters any. I couldn't keep the front flap down, and the ladies were tipping well. He reached over the car door and ripped it off, leaving it in a heap on the pavement. Tourist jaws dropped wider than the *kalua* pig's. I climbed in. He backed over my outfit before peeling away.

His hands gripped the steering wheel. I wished they'd grip something else. I ached. I needed him now. I didn't care about reality tomorrow.

He took me to his place for the first time. He has this massive house right on the water, with automatic gates and everything.

"You live here alone?"

"I keep a few houseguests."

I laid back on a scarlet couch, the type where fainting ladies in corsets stretch out. The chandelier over us actually had candles.

He kissed me. That was a first. I drank it up like crazy. I tried to rub against him, but he pulled away.

"Live with me," he said. "Be mine."

"OK."

A hell of a deal. So what if he couldn't get it up? Since I'd seen no action behind the fly of his tailored slacks, I'd guessed that impotence forced him to get his kicks through other displays of power. I could live with that.

He flipped me over and poured a bottle of celebration champagne up my ass. The liquid bubbles made me squirm and laugh, and he fucked me with the bottle. It was a hell of a lot better than the rock. I erupted just like the uncorked bottle. He didn't worry about ruining the velvet settee.

My groom led me—by my hand—to my suite of rooms. Yeah, suite. He had totally decked out my bedroom for a real wedding night, everything in white, and candles and flowers all over—he knew I'd say yes. A filmy canopy floated over the bed. We'd never done it in a bed before.

He shoved me facedown on the mattress, just dug right into my neck with his shark's teeth. He'd always nibbled at me, licking at my scratches, but nothing could have prepared me for this rabid penetration of my flesh in his intense lust and hunger. I went rigid, like in a paroxysm.

His cock bulged against my backside as he grew hard on my blood. I pressed back, wanting it in an unbelievable way. He was warm against me. I had my mouth open in one long, nonstop moan. Despite my sudden anemia, I stayed pumped up and wanting it, his expert hand reaching around to fondle me.

I wasn't surprised once it happened.

And I wasn't afraid.

He wanted a lover, not a victim, *make*, a corpse. I guess quickies had lost their flavor for him decades ago, just like they do for most of us. He wanted me to want it, passion returned in his all-consuming embrace. I would hunger for it like he hungered for me. I was addicted, infected, incurably diseased.

I knew what I was going to be.

It's not so different from what his type's been doing to our people for centuries.

Maybe you think I'm *lolo*, crazy, but what kind of future was I giving up? The land has been stripped and paved. No sugarcane. Everything's endangered, even water. What's left? I'd been serving *haoles* my ass on a plate all along, only I preferred the way he fed off me.

He turned me over so I could watch him. He undressed. There was nothing wrong with his anatomy as far as I could see, his white pecker swollen with my own blood coursing through his ancient veins.

He fucked me, missionary-style, just like the first religious invaders to the islands taught us. I gave myself to him. I am his. My body is *kapu* to all others now, off-limits, sacred, property of my king and god, *ali'i* and *akua*. He rammed hard and deep and cold, ruthless, his dick inside me, and latched on again with his mouth to my neck. It was like his two body parts, his dick and lips, connected somewhere deep inside me, like I could feel his dick straight through my body from my asshole up to the top of my spine. I went limp, and it was like an orgasm all through my body, like jamming my finger into an electric socket.

I bucked and gasped, body spasming, brain and body screaming, him half full and me half empty, helpless to anything he desired. His hard cock coursed with my own blood.

He knew my pace, my rhythm, when he could push me and when I couldn't take any more torment. All this time he'd been testing, training, wooing, punishing, and rewarding me, simultaneously. Because he had to time it just right, leaving me enough to stay hard while taking enough to pump up his lust and fuck me. He liked to make it last, but he didn't want to kill me.

He couldn't climax. The pleasure he got was the sensation of the fucking, of being alive, of the body beneath him wanting it, of sex linked with live prey.

We are symbiotic, the perfect couple. He needs me, and he's my dream lover. Would you leave a man who fucks you all night long and doesn't care about his own orgasm?

So, you see, no *ho'omalimali*, I lived to tell the tale. And I'll go on living. I'm not what you think I am. I'm not like him, not one of his kind. My body replenishes what he needs. I eat lots of steak. Watching me eat turns him on. Sure, he snacks on the occasional tourist, but their sunscreen makes him sick. As I gain in strength, his hunger and lust for me grows. And when I've healed from his lovemaking, he saps my strength again with a passion no human lover can match. But first I dance for him, singing his tale in the oral tradition of the ancients. The traditional dog-tooth anklets clatter as I chant, only I know these are no poodle canines. These others were disposable, human sacrifices. But me, he keeps.

Adam & Steve

Bob Condron

"HAVEN"T YOU GOT YOURSELF A GIRLFRIEND YET?" It wasn't so much a question as a statement. Auntie Madeline was preening herself in front of the gilt-framed hall mirror.

Adam pecked her on the cheek as he closed the door to the street outside and passed by on his way toward the hall stairs.

"Not as you'd notice," he replied for the umpteenth time.

Aunt Madeline was the only one who still bothered to raise the subject. She *always* raised the subject.

Resting against the kitchen doorway, his mother folded her arms across her chest and rolled her eyes toward the ceiling, as was her habit when discussing her son.

"Spends all his time in his bedroom listening to punk rock records."

Adam laughed. "Don't exaggerate, Mam!"

"Well? What else do you do!"

"Go to work...and then there's the gym."

"Not often enough! I tell you, Madeline, if I hear that bleedin' 'Boredom' record one more time I'll go mental."

"It's 1978, Mammy. Get with it!" He grinned and winked at Auntie Mad's reflection in the mirror. "Anyway, isn't it a bit late in the day to worry about going mental, Mam?

"Eh?" His mother's eyes followed him as he ducked and

turned to make his escape upstairs. The penny dropped. She raised her voice a notch and spoke to his back. "Don't think I'll ever be rid of him!"

Aunt Madeline smeared lipstick over her bottom lip with the aid of her middle finger. "Jaysus, Adam, it's Saturday night! How old are you now?" She answered her own question. "Twenty-one, is it?" And continued. "A big handsome fella like you should be out having adventures."

"Don't waste yer breath, Madeline," her elder sister said, slipping into her topcoat. "He's a lost cause, that one. A bloody recluse!"

Aunt Madeline leaned over the bottom rail of the banister and called after him. "And don't wait up for us. Some of us girls know how to have a good time!"

He started the bath running and retired to his bedroom. Good on you, Aunt Madeline, he thought to himself. It was she who refused to let Mam mope around after Da died; it was she who got her out of the house after too many years chained to the kitchen sink. The glamorous younger sister acting as Svengali. Freed of her cocoon, his Mammy was finally starting to bloom. In fact, she looked less of a Mammy than she ever had. She had lost two stone and 10 years over the past six months. Reintroduced to the hairdresser and fashionable clothes, she looked surprisingly younger than her 39th year. Why, she had even taken to wearing makeup—though a damn sight more discreetly than Auntie Mad.

Whilst undressing, his eyes focused on an array of wall posters. Muscular role models surrounded him on all sides. He had read somewhere that visualizing was the key to muscle gain, and somehow it had seemed reasonable at the time. There above his bed stood his absolute favorite; the one he fell asleep looking at, the one he aspired to emulate.

An old black-and-white photograph, a classic from the '50s. Purchased from the Dandelion flea market in his 18th year. How his hands had trembled as he flicked through the pile of old *Physique Pictorials* before stumbling upon Keith...whatever his name was: 6'3" 221 lbs. Chest 51" Waist 32.5". Flabbergasted by this incredible hulk in a fulsome posing pouch—a dream made flesh. The guy behind the counter had sniggered—or was it leered—as he had slipped it in a brown paper bag before handing it over. For once Adam didn't care. He had to have it, had to own it.

Finally naked, he stood before the full-length mirror and gazed at his own musculature, still pumped up from the gym. In this instance, his faith seemed to have paid dividends.

Dark Irish, he could pass for a Spaniard. "You're fucking gorgeous, Adam Patrick!" he said aloud and—not without a fine sense of the ridiculous—he struck the same pose as his beloved Keith.

Chest taut, one leg stretched behind, fists clenched, he cut an impressive figure. He grinned. Then fists unfurled, he adjusted his *wedding tackle*. His meat-and-two-veg was equally impressive. Everything in proportion.

As far back as he could remember, Adam Patrick Duffy had only one burning ambition—to suck cock. It kept him awake nights; kept him on his knees. He was sure to be doomed to hell. His fervent prayers seemed to fall on deaf ears and, despite a childlike faith, he couldn't shake off the conviction that he was beyond redemption. A lost thing.

So many years of praying it straight and where had it got him? Home alone on a Saturday night. If you didn't laugh, Adam concluded, you'd go mad.

Taps turned off, bathroom door closed. Squatting down now, Adam tentatively submerged his solid backside in a sea of foam. Sure, his Mammy's bath crystals would only be left to gather dust if he didn't use them. Maybe he had been a tad overgenerous this time, though. The water had turned bottle-green—"Aquamarine" if you believed the label on the bottle—and the smell! Overwhelming him with the tang of salt and seaweed. He grew dizzy and lay back, crossing his feet at the ankles and resting them on the white ceramic rim, idly focusing on the soap bubbles as they fizzled on his toes.

Condensation covered the four walls. Absent-mindedly he

pressed the tip of his index finger against the white tiling and began to write. A name. The name was Steve. Closing his eyes, he lay back. Moisture rose and all but erased the name, like a silent prayer carried away on a cloud of steam.

The scalding water had turned his skin bright pink. A penance of sorts. An attempt to purge his lustful flesh; stinging his unrepentant erection. Ah, but the drip, drip, drip of lascivious thoughts continued to torture him. He tried to imagine what Steve would look like today at age 21. What would he look like stripped jack naked? Adam had not seen him since they were 19. A chance meeting in the central bus station. Steve all alone, abandoned, packed and ready to go to England for the long haul.

He had been sitting atop a battered brown suitcase, swigging copiously on a bottle of cider. Passersby made disapproving faces, but no one would pass remark. He was every inch the grown man, and not the sort you would want to get into an argument with. He came from a family of redheads ("No hair. Just red heads!" was the running gag.) But his cropped halo had mellowed into bronze, now complemented by the dense peppering of stubble on his chin and top lip. Hair shone golden on forearms exposed below the rolled-up sleeves of his crisp white shirt. Thick fingers pulled at the tight collar and tie. Hand-me-downs? Most likely. He had the body of a young bullock, and it threatened to split his clothes at the seams. But most remarkable had been the look he had given Adam as his eyes first struggled to focus on his boyhood pal. The tenderness and regret in those eyes.

From playing cops and robbers in Mountjoy Park to a lockup in Mountjoy Prison had taken not more than a few short years. Prison had knocked some of the stuffing out of Steve. Resident for six months—protesting his innocence all the way. A classic case. Product of a broken home, a brief career in petty crime before going down for, what he called, trumped-up charges: fencing stolen goods. Shame had kept Steve from keeping in touch, Adam was certain of this much. Stupid fucking pride. Adam hadn't cared. He had loved Steve. At that moment, right there in the bus station, Adam had wanted to finally tell him...but didn't have the guts. And as the shuttle bus to the ferry pulled in and they had said their goodbyes, Adam believed he saw beyond Steve's remarkably green eyes. Steve had grabbed him and hugged him, and Adam had been astonished to feel the rough brushing of lips against his cheek. Steve had loved him too?

Four women sat in the lounge of Ryan's Bar. A circle of friends seated around the cluttered table next to the fire. Madeline, Dolores, Mary Coote, and Mammy (Doreen to her friends). They were already on their third round of vodka and red.

"Sex? No, I don't miss it!" said Mammy, emptying her glass with one swift slug. "It's only for the men's pleasure."

Timid Mary echoed her wistfully. "Sure, there's no pleasure in it for women."

Busty Dolores pursed her lips and joined the consensus. "Just so much shoving and pushing if you ask me…and for what? The only satisfaction I get is when the fat lump climbs off me and I can breathe again. I only do it for a quiet life. My Mick's a right old bollocks if he doesn't get his bit."

"Well…" said Madeline, after a considered pause, during which she patted her bottle-blond hairdo. "I think a woman owes it to herself to get pleasure from her body. Even if she has to use Do-It-Yourself."

Doreen turned pale. Mary tittered. Dolores let rip with a full-throated laugh. "You're joking!"

"Not at all. Look at me and my fuckwit of a husband. My wedding night was a bleeding nightmare and it's never altered. If you believed them women's magazines, I should have been crying out for more." She paused and took a demure sip from her vodka glass. "Come to think of it, I was! 'Is it in? *Is it in?*' I kept shouting."

At this point Dolores lost her composure completely and choked on her drink, jettisoning red rivulets down her nostrils. Mary unclipped her handbag and held out a clean hankie, while Doreen clapped Dolores on the back.

"They say size isn't important? Bollocks! Fuckwit couldn't satisfy our cat!" She drew breath before continuing matter-of-factly. "Finally, bought myself one of them vibrators. Thought if I didn't tickle my fancy, it'd never get tickled."

Dolores convulsed as she dabbed her nose. "Eh, Madeline. Stop! Stop! You'll finish me off. You're a wild one!"

The water was turning cool, but still Adam continued to soak his aching muscles. Preoccupied. If wishing made it so, he thought, then Steve would stand there before me. And if visualizing his own body big and strong had worked, why hadn't this other wish come true? Supernatural forces were at work in the universe; he wanted so desperately to believe this. *Why shouldn't my thoughts have power to make things happen?* Still, he wasn't convinced. He had been waiting and hoping for too long already.

There were times, God forgive him, when he would almost trade his soul for one taste of Steve's stiff cock. The image it brought to mind was so vivid that he could not help but luxuriate in the fantasy. What if he had simply dropped to his knees one time? His mouth opened reflexively at the memory, as if readying itself to receive Steven's long, hard length. He had loved Steve, damn it! Loved him! Loved the body, loved the heart and mind. Why wasn't he allowed the privilege to touch, to taste...

His bladder ached. It came as a sudden revelation. Adam paused, then raising his hips, let flow a stream of bright yellow piss upward onto his belly. Reveling in it. Taking perverse pleasure from it. Maybe he deserved no better.

Dolores's eyes scanned the bar. "Not many beauts in tonight."

"Dolores! You're a married woman!" Mary exclaimed disapprovingly.

"So?" came the indignant retort. "And that means I can't look, does it! Don't be such a tight arse, Sister Mary. Lighten up." She turned away curtly to Madeline and Doreen. "Guess who I saw the other day strolling up Grafton Street, large as life?"

She was met with two blank expressions. Dolores was off on one again.

"Of course, I barely recognised him at first. But that could have been 'cause my eyes were fixed on his arse..." Her eyes glazed over. "What an arse..." She regained composure. "Anyway, he turns his head to look back over his shoulder and his face cracks into a big smile. For a moment I thought I'd been caught. Fortunately not. It was that old pal of your Adam's, Dor. Steve...Steve Doolan."

Doreen froze.

"Well, he recognized me straight off. And you know what? He was as nice and friendly as anything. Gave me a kiss on the cheek. Asked after everyone in the old neighborhood. You wouldn't know the lad. He's a fine thing—turned into a real charmer."

Doreen remained frozen solid.

Mary piped up. "And he had such a rotten start in life. What with that drunken old fella for a father. And his mother—" She lowered her voice till it was barely audible. "—on *the game*."

Doreen's expression could have curdled milk. "I don't know how he could be so brazen as to show his face back here again!"

Madeline broke free of an uncharacteristic silence. "Our Doreen never did approve of their friendship, did you Dor?"

"He was a bad influence!"

Madeline smiled pointedly. "At least he got the lad out of the house."

"Yes, running wild! I never knew where he was or what he was up to. I didn't want him mixing with knackers!"

Dolores tried to calm troubled waters. "You'd be surprised if you saw him now, Doreen. He's obviously come up in the world."

"Well, you know what they say: *what's bred in the bone*. It'd take more than fancy clothes to impress me. You forget, I lived near them."

"Oh, for goodness sake! Give the lad a break!" Madeline was suddenly strident enough for Doreen to be startled. "Carol did her best to bring those kids up under difficult circumstances, and if you hadn't been such a snob, you'd have warmed to her too."

Mary's face was etched with sadness. "She had no life, and that's a fact. And then to finally—" Again her voice dropped to a whisper. "—get the big C." She shuddered. "Doesn't bear thinking about."

Madeline changed tack abruptly. "So what brings him back, Dolores?"

"His youngest sister's after getting married—today I think—to a Garda, of all things!"

Doreen rolled her eyeballs. "Wonders will never cease!"

The clacking sound of the brass door knocker echoed along the darkened hallway and spiralled up the staircase. Having refilled the bath and just that moment climbed in, Adam was not amused. He stretched out an arm and lifted his watch from the pink candlewick cover on the lid of the lavatory seat. It was 10:15. "Who the fuck could it be at this time?" He decided to ignore it, but the rapping continued unabated. Finally, he leaped from the bath and, wrapping a coarse white towel around his waist, paddled downstairs.

"OK...OK!" he growled as he undid the latch and yanked the door open. Then came the sharp intake of breath.

Steve filled the doorway. Swaying slightly. Large as life and twice as cocky. A beery grin laced his ruddy face as he reached out and, grabbing a stunned Adam, wrapped him in a fierce, all-consuming embrace.

"You're wet!" Steve laughed but clung on and rocked him in his arms for what struck Adam as an eternity of seconds.

Finally, Steve pulled back, holding Adam at arm's length. Beefy hands clasped meaty shoulders. Just then, Adam's towel fell to the floor. He made to retrieve it, but Steve held him fast. Teary-eyed.

"Now, let me look at you."

Doreen was off spending a penny. Busty Dolores leaned her weight on the bar as she ordered another round. Timid Mary brushed a fleck of tobacco off her skirt and sucked purposefully on her filter-tipped Major, her eyes gazing off into the middle distance.

"Madeline?"

"Yes?"

"Where did you get that vibrator from?"

"Mail order. Want the address?"

Mary hesitated, tittered again. "If it's no trouble?"

"No trouble at all."

"Men are crap in bed aren't they?"

"They haven't a clue."

"I'd rather have a cuddle any day of the week, but Brendan's not very good at being *affectionate* if you know what I mean?"

" 'In. Out. In. Out. Shake it all about'? I know exactly what you mean. I tell you, Mary, what you really want is the love of a good woman."

Silence. The reply caught in Mary's throat briefly before escaping in a strangulated moan. "You could be right there."

"There's a lot of it about these days, *Lesbefriends*, you know?"

"Oh, I know. I know there is..."

"And I'm not surprised for one."

"Me neither..."

"Good luck to them, I say!"

Timid Mary sucked the life out of her tab end and winced as it burned her fingers. She stubbed it out with a vengeance. "Me too."

Adam had turned red as a beetroot while Steve's green eyes had given him the once-over. He wasn't ashamed of his body, quite the opposite, but what if the neighbors saw him, saw past his visitor's broad shoulders! Steve let his eyes linger on Adam's groin and enough became enough. Adam pulled him inside and closed the door.

Once the towel was again in place the atmosphere relaxed a little. Adam led Steve through to the kitchen. "Tea? Coffee?" he asked.

"Any fairy cakes to go with it?" Steve quipped as he slumped down thankfully on a kitchen chair.

Adam made no reply. Instead, he busied himself with the kettle while Steve explained the reason for his return: that he had left the reception early once the happy couple had departed on their honeymoon and he was left to face a roomful of Gardai on his own! But, nah...he had wanted all along to call by but had needed to work up to it. A full day of drinking a mixture of champagne, whiskey, and Guinness had done the trick.

"But why did you have to work up to it? Didn't you know I'd be glad to see you?"

"Glad? Is that all?" Steve's face dropped.

Adam was perplexed at this sudden mood swing. "What do you want me to say? What do you want?"

A long pause and then, "You." The word was drawn out with difficulty. It seemed to emerge from the very pit of Steve's stomach.

For all the world, Adam appeared cool, calm, and collected, but inside the blood surged through his veins as his heart pumped fit to burst. That's how he knew he was totally present in the moment. Still, he couldn't help but recognize that another part of him was detached, observing the scene from above. Observing his own unruffled facade in contrast to Steve's torment; observing and considering also that Steve had never been good with words, at least not when it came to his feelings. Here was the big galoot, straining and shaking with an inner turmoil that was palpable.

Finally, Steve found his voice. "Remember that one time you kissed me on the mouth?"

"Yeah." Adam cringed. "It was Christmas. I was drunk."

"Not *that* drunk."

"It's history. You made yourself perfectly clear at the time."

"Did I? I don't think so. I liked it, Adam. I liked it *a lot*." Steve ran a hand over his mouth as if to block or muffle what he had to say. "That's the scary part, don't you see? I *liked* it... But I couldn't handle it. I can handle it now..." Laughter bubbled up from his throat. "I'm a man of the world—well...I've been as far as Amsterdam for the weekend." So far the speech had been delivered to the ceiling. Head tipped back, eyes fixed on some point only Steve could see. Then his eyes fixed on Adam. "I don't want Amsterdam, Adam..." Steve's voice faded into a whisper as his head fell forward, "I want you.

"It's OK. It's OK, Steve."

"No, it's not OK!" Steve addressed the floor. "I left with unfinished business. I ran away to England. And for why and for what? Time and space have made no fuckin' difference whatsoever." He lifted his eyes as they began to mist over. "So many years... Too many. I dream about you. I long for you, here…" He cupped his belly. "In here. I don't want to run from you no more, I'm so tired of running I want to come to you. I want to come home."

Adam hesitated, but only briefly. Crossing the room, he laid a hand on Steve's shoulder. "I think you need to lie down. Come on, brother. Come on up to bed…"

But Steve couldn't wait the distance. He pulled Adam down toward him and, meeting with no resistance, had him on the kitchen floor; had him right then and there on the black-and-white tiled linoleum.

Having packed Mary and Dolores into a taxi, Doreen and Madeline tottered arm in arm up O'Connell Street toward home, all the time fighting against the stiff wind. Doreen had wanted to chat but now found she couldn't get a word in edgeways. Madeline was chattering loudly in an effort to be heard for fear her words of wit and wisdom would be carried over her shoulder and blown back in the direction of the pub. It was only as they turned the corner toward Mountjoy Square and into the relative shelter of a side street that she realized her sister had been silent throughout.

"So, anyways, I'm thinking of having it off with the Scrapman *and* his horse…"

"That's nice," replied Doreen.

Madeline arched her pencil-thin eyebrows. "Doreen Duffy, you haven't been listening to a word I've said!"

Doreen's eyes flickered into focus. "Sorry, Mad. I was just thinking." Her brow furrowed.

"Looks painful!" Madeline quipped, then relented. " 'bout what? What's on your mind, Sis?"

"Us coming out and my lad stopping home. Should be the other way around."

"He's big enough to sort himself out, Doreen. Why worry about him!"

"Because he's not happy." A long pause followed. "Mad, can you keep a secret?"

"You know me…" she replied, tapping the side of her nose.

"Exactly. That's why I'm asking."

Madeline's lips puckered in indignation.

Doreen laughed and poked her in the ribs. Then the laughter faded. "I'm worried about him, Mad. I think…I think he might be one of them homosexuals…" Her voice trailed away as Madeline's ears pricked up.

"Whyever would you think that?"

"Found some books under his mattress. *Bare* men!"

"Doesn't leave much room for discussion then!"

"What am I going to do, Mad?"

"Do? Nothing! It's his life. Good luck to him!"

"But he's homosexual!"

"I believe they call them 'gay' these days, Dor."

Doreen replied, wholly innocent to the fact that her words were merely a variation of a well-worn cliché, "Gay? *Gay*? He's bloody *miserable*!"

Adam Patrick Duffy wasn't happy. No, he was ecstatic. Impaled on Steve's thick, pulsing mickey with his buttocks rocking back, grinding down against flat hips and firm thighs. Steve lay back, fingers locked behind his head, grinning like a Ginger Tom as Adam did all the work.

Eyes closed tight, Adam felt otherworldly.

The two sisters had had to make a last minute dash toward their local chippers. Alfredo's Tasty Place was about to close as they rounded the last corner. Alfredo himself was about to turn the cardboard OPEN sign to CLOSED. Instead, he held the door wide and, with a sweeping arm gesture and a low bow, bid them enter, flicking the latch after them.

Fifteen minutes later both were sat in Madeline's kitchen. Newspaper wrappings spread out on the formica tabletop as they unceremoniously ate fish and chips with their fingers.

"I was bleeding starving," Madeline exclaimed, having eaten up in record time. She stood, screwing the newspaper into a ball, and dropped it into the flip-top bin. "My stomach thought my throat had been cut." Doreen's meal was only half eaten. She struggled to bite on the chip held before her greasy lips.

"What am I to do, Mad?"

"Hand them over. I'll have them if you don't want them!"

Doreen pushed them toward her sister. "I mean about our Adam?"

"Do? I told you! *Nothing!* Love him and let him get on with it. That's enough. Now, fancy a nightcap?"

Adam and Steve slept together like spoons. Folded into each other, one curled around the other. No embarrassment. It felt perfectly natural. Supernatural, even. Under the covers of Adam's single bed there was to be no avoiding each other.

Outside, the wind and the rain battered and rattled the sash window. Inside, they had each other to ward off the cold. As Steve had assured him years before when they had camped together in the backyard, they were adopting a tried-and-tested survival technique. Direct body contact would double the body heat.

Steve hadn't been wrong then. He wasn't wrong now. Direct body contact generated more heat than any hot water bottle. Warm as toast, they slept like twin babies in a cot.

Contributors

Steve Attwood is an HIV/AIDS educator living in Christchurch, New Zealand. "A Man's Man" was written after a bitter experience of ageism in the gay world. "I wanted to show older men are sexy and have passion too," he says. An earlier story, "Weekend in Christchurch," was published in the Alyson collection *Slow Grind*.

Gavin Austin was raised in Victoria, Australia, but now calls Sydney home. He writes short fiction, poetry and articles for several Australian journals and anthologies as well as in the online literary journals Red River Review and Blithe House Quarterly.

New Jersey resident **Steve Berman** has long been fascinated with the two elements of ghosts and sex, both of which appear in many of the 50 articles and short stories he has published. "Derelict" was nominated for a 2004 Gaylactic Spectrum Award.

Schuyler Bishop's articles have appeared in *Sports Illustrated* and *The New York Times*. He has also written plays that have been performed off-off Broadway and a chunk of an anthology called *A Passion for Golf*. He is at work on a musical about noted homo Henry Thoreau and lives in New York City with Bryan Byers, who is still the object of his desires.

Dale Chase has been writing gay for seven years and has over 100 stories published in various magazines and anthologies, including the *Harrington Gay Men's Fiction Quarterly*. His erotic novel *The Great Man* was recently published, and *The Company He Keeps*, a collection of Victorian erotica, is due later this year.

Curtis C. Comer was born in rural Kansas and moved to San Francisco at the age of 21. While living in the Bay Area he began writing in his spare time; this is his third short story to be included in an anthology. Curtis currently resides in St. Louis with his partner of 12 years.

Bob Condron is the author of the two homoerotic novels *Easy Money* and *Sweating It Out* as well as numerous short stories that have been featured in Alyson's *Bearotica* and *Bar Stories*, and in other anthologies. STARbooks Press will release his anthology *Daddy's Boyz* in Spring 2005.

Lou Dellaguzzo is a freelance writer living in Washington, D.C. His short stories have appeared in *Lodestar Quarterly, Harrington Gay Men's Fiction Quarterly, Velvet Mafia*, and *Blithe House Quarterly*. He's just completed a short-story collection titled *All of a Suddenly*.You can reach him at dellagu@attglobal.net.

J.A. Deveaux is fascinated by awkward and improbable romances. Fantasy, magic realism, and queer fiction are uniquely suited for these explorations. A circus enthusiast, J.A. is often found catching and flying on the trapeze, or walking a slack rope while juggling and maintaining an all too precarious balance.

Vincent Diamond is a central Florida writer currently marketing his first novel to publishers. He is hard at work on its sequel as well as many more short stories for anthologies. Diamond's work has also appeared in *Chance Encounters* (Torquere Press) and *Men of Mystery* (StarBooks Press). Time away from the keyboard is spent riding horses and gardening.

Jim Gladstone is the author of *The Big Book of Misunderstanding*—lauded by the *Paris Voice* as "a heartwarming story of people who love each other so much they almost destroy one another." He is also the creator of *Gladstone's Games to Go* and editor of the forthcoming *Skin and Ink*. His writing has been published in a wide range of publications, from *The New York Times* to *BUTT* magazine. His Web site is www.gogladstone.com.

Greg Herren is the author of *Murder in the Rue St. Ann* and *Jackson Square Jazz* and editor of *Shadows of the Night* and *Upon a Midnight Clear*. His writing has appeared in *Harrington Gay Men's Fiction Quarterly, Rebel Yell 2*, the *Friction* series, *Men, Unzipped, Gay and Lesbian Review, A&U, Instinct*, and *Genre*. He lives in New Orleans.

Michael Huxley is Editorial Director of STARbooks Press. He is a published poet, and his short fiction has appeared in the anthologies *Seduced 2, Wild and Willing, Fantasies Made Flesh*, and *Saints and Sinners*. Michael lives in Sarasota, Florida, with his long-time lover, Paul. Find out more at STARbookspress.com.

Timothy Lambert coauthored *The Deal* with Becky Cochrane. He is a Gemini and lives in Houston with his cat, Lazlo. Timothy dedicates "The End of the Show" to Jim, Tim, and Becky (with whom he's coauthored four novels under the pseudonym Timothy James Beck) because they add to his happiness.

David Masello is a New York–based writer and editor. His essays, features, and poems have appeared in numerous periodicals, including *The New York Times, The Boston Globe, Newsweek*, and *Massachusetts Review*. Other works have been anthologized in *The Man I Might Become: Gay Men Write About Their Fathers, Wonderlands: Good Gay Travel Writing*, and in a forthcoming anthology from New York University Press. He is also the author of books about architecture and public art.

Gary McCann, an emeritus librarian at American University, lives with his domestic partner of 19 years in Washington, D.C. His story, "A Double Bed," appeared in the *Harrington Gay Men's Fiction Quarterly* in 2001. He is presently at work on a novel.

Tom Mendicino is a lawyer who lives in Philadelphia. "Meet the Wilkinses" is an excerpt from his novel *Probation*. He'd like to thank Casey Fuetsch for her prodding and encouragement.

Scott D. Pomfret is coauthor of the Romentics-brand line of romance novels for gay men (www.romentics.com). He has also written short stories for *Post Road Magazine*, *New Delta Review*, *Genre*, *Freshmen: Best New Gay Voices*, and many other magazines and anthologies. Alyson Books' *Friction* series routinely includes Pomfret's erotic stories; one will also appear in *Best Gay Erotica 2005* by Cleis Press. Pomfret is shopping his collection of short fiction, *Until the Sugar Is Caramel*, and his newly completed novel, *Only Say the Word*. He lives in Boston.

A firm believer in the old saying "write what you know," **David Puterbaugh** has collected his most colorful stories from his years of working for a luxury cruise line and is cultivating them into his first novel about love on a gay cruise ship. He lives in New York City.

Jay Quinn is the author of *The Mentor, Metes and Bounds*, and the forthcoming *Back Where He Started* and the editor of *Rebel Yell* and *Rebel Yell* 2. He lives in Florida with his partner of 13 years.

Waide Aaron Riddle was born in Kingsville, Texas, and raised in Houston. He is the winner of the National Author's Registry Honorable Mention prize in 1996 and its 1997 President's Award . Additionally, his awards include the 1997 Certificate of Achievement for Excellence in Poetry from the Amherst Foundation and third place in the California State Poetry Society's 2002 competition. Waide is the author of two self-published books: *All American*

Texan and *The Chocolate Man: A Children's Horror Tale*. His Web site is www.waideriddle.com

J.D. Roman was born and raised in Hawai'i as a fourth-generation islander. His credits include: *Friction 7: Best Gay Erotic Fiction*; *Wet Nightmares, Wet Dreams*; Velvet Mafia.com, and Mind Caviar.com.

Rhysenn S. is a freelance journalist who writes articles exploring the gay culture in different parts of the world, especially southeastern Asia. He particularly enjoys the fact that doing something one loves means never having to really work at all.

Lawrence Schimel's has presided over 70 books, including writing a collection of short stories, *The Drag Queen of Elfland,* and edited the anthology *Kosher Meat*. His *PoMoSexuals: Challenging Assumptions About Gender and Sexuality* (with Carol Queen) won a Lambda Literary Award. He has been widely anthologized in everything from Alyson's *Ultimate Gay Erotica, 2005 to The Random House Treasury of Light Verse*. He lives in Madrid.

Simon Sheppard is the author of both *In Deep* and *Kinkorama: Dispatches From the Front Lines of Perversion*. His next book, *Sex Parties 101*, is due in early 2005. He's the coeditor of *Rough Stuff* and *Roughed Up*, and his work appears in over 100 anthologies, including *The Best American Erotica 2005* and *Best Gay Erotica 2005*. He's also the author of the columns "Sex Talk" and "Perv," and loiters lovingly at www.simonsheppard.com.

Nursing Care Plans These Care Plans are outcomes-focused. They present students with selected expected outcomes and possible corresponding nursing interventions, and provide evaluations, for the situation presented in the corresponding case study.

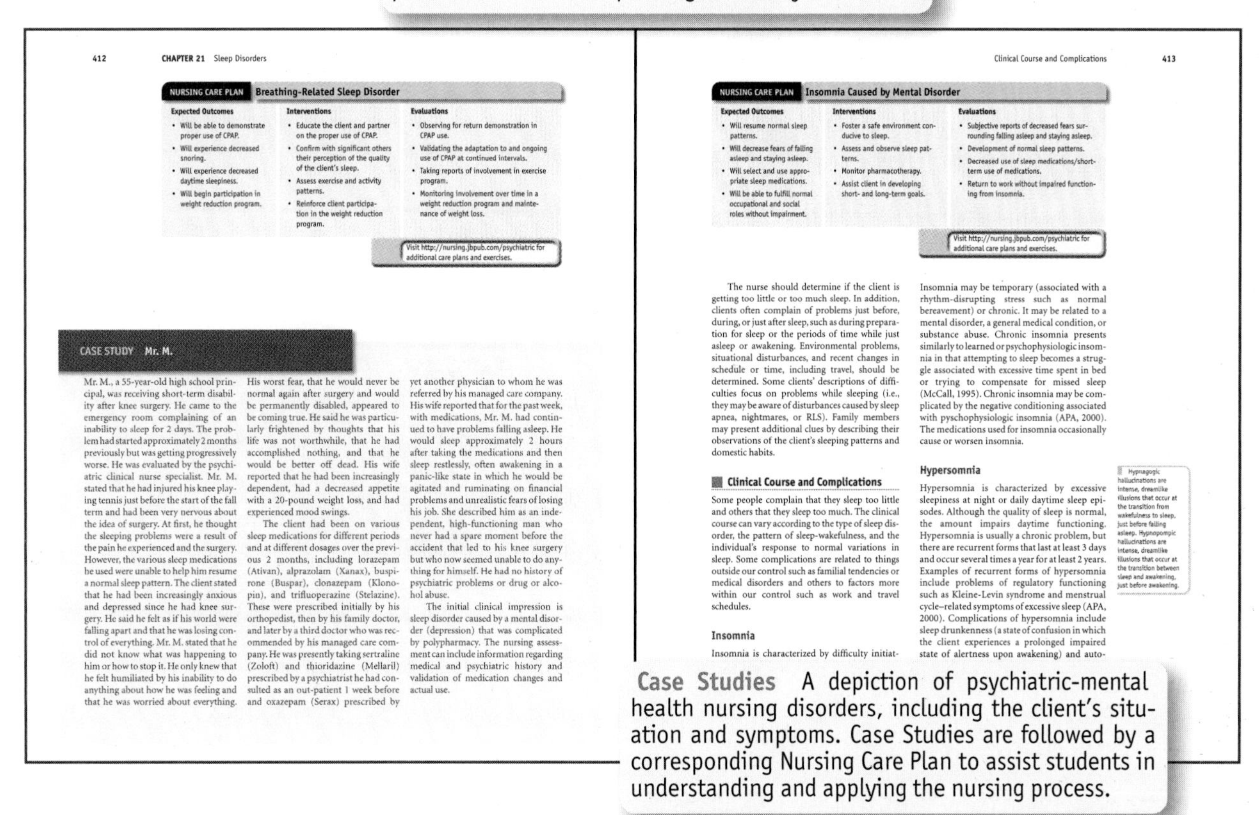

412 CHAPTER 21 Sleep Disorders

NURSING CARE PLAN Breathing-Related Sleep Disorder

Expected Outcomes	Interventions	Evaluations
• Will be able to demonstrate proper use of CPAP. • Will experience decreased snoring. • Will experience decreased daytime sleepiness. • Will begin participation in weight reduction program.	• Educate the client and partner on the proper use of CPAP. • Confirm with significant others their perception of the quality of the client's sleep. • Assess exercise and activity patterns. • Reinforce client participation in the weight reduction program.	• Observing for return demonstration in CPAP use. • Validating the adaptation to and ongoing use of CPAP at continued intervals. • Taking reports of involvement in exercise program. • Monitoring involvement over time in a weight reduction program and maintenance of weight loss.

Visit http://nursing.jbpub.com/psychiatric for additional care plans and exercises.

CASE STUDY Mr. M.

Mr. M., a 55-year-old high school principal, was receiving short-term disability after knee surgery. He came to the emergency room complaining of an inability to sleep for 2 days. The problem had started approximately 2 months previously but was getting progressively worse. He was evaluated by the psychiatric clinical nurse specialist. Mr. M. stated that he had injured his knee playing tennis just before the start of the fall term and had been very nervous about the idea of surgery. At first, he thought the sleeping problems were a result of the pain he experienced and the surgery. However, the various sleep medications he used were unable to help him resume a normal sleep pattern. The client stated that he had been increasingly anxious and depressed since he had knee surgery. He said he felt as if his world were falling apart and that he was losing control of everything. Mr. M. stated that he did not know what was happening to him or how to stop it. He only knew that he felt humiliated by his inability to do anything about how he was feeling and that he was worried about everything. His worst fear, that he would never be normal again after surgery and would be permanently disabled, appeared to be coming true. He said he was particularly frightened by thoughts that his life was not worthwhile, that he had accomplished nothing, and that he would be better off dead. His wife reported that he had been increasingly dependent, had a decreased appetite with a 20-pound weight loss, and had experienced mood swings.

The client had been on various sleep medications for different periods and at different dosages over the previous 2 months, including lorazepam (Ativan), alprazolam (Xanax), buspirone (Buspar), clonazepam (Klonopin), and trifluoperazine (Stelazine). These were prescribed initially by his orthopedist, then by his family doctor, and later by a third doctor who was recommended by his managed care company. He was presently taking sertraline (Zoloft) and thioridazine (Mellaril) prescribed by a psychiatrist he had consulted as an out-patient 1 week before and oxazepam (Serax) prescribed by yet another physician to whom he was referred by his managed care company. His wife reported that for the past week, with medications, Mr. M. had continued to have problems falling asleep. He would sleep approximately 2 hours after taking the medications and then sleep restlessly, often awakening in a panic-like state in which he would be agitated and ruminating on financial problems and unrealistic fears of losing his job. She described him as an independent, high-functioning man who never had a spare moment before the accident that led to his knee surgery but who now seemed unable to do anything for himself. He had no history of psychiatric problems or drug or alcohol abuse.

The initial clinical impression is sleep disorder caused by a mental disorder (depression) that was complicated by polypharmacy. The nursing assessment can include information regarding medical and psychiatric history and validation of medication changes and actual use.

Clinical Course and Complications 413

NURSING CARE PLAN Insomnia Caused by Mental Disorder

Expected Outcomes	Interventions	Evaluations
• Will resume normal sleep patterns. • Will decrease fears of falling asleep and staying asleep. • Will select and use appropriate sleep medications. • Will be able to fulfill normal occupational and social roles without impairment.	• Foster a safe environment conducive to sleep. • Assess and observe sleep patterns. • Monitor pharmacotherapy. • Assist client in developing short- and long-term goals.	• Subjective reports of decreased fears surrounding falling asleep and staying asleep. • Development of normal sleep patterns. • Decreased use of sleep medications/short-term use of medications. • Return to work without impaired functioning from insomnia.

Visit http://nursing.jbpub.com/psychiatric for additional care plans and exercises.

The nurse should determine if the client is getting too little or too much sleep. In addition, clients often complain of problems just before, during, or just after sleep, such as during preparation for sleep or the periods of time while just asleep or awakening. Environmental problems, situational disturbances, and recent changes in schedule or time, including travel, should be determined. Some clients' descriptions of difficulties focus on problems while sleeping (i.e., they may be aware of disturbances caused by sleep apnea, nightmares, or RLS). Family members may present additional clues by describing their observations of the client's sleeping patterns and domestic habits.

Clinical Course and Complications

Some people complain that they sleep too little and others that they sleep too much. The clinical course can vary according to the type of sleep disorder, the pattern of sleep-wakefulness, and the individual's response to normal variations in sleep. Some complications are related to things outside our control such as familial tendencies or medical disorders and others to factors more within our control such as work and travel schedules.

Insomnia

Insomnia is characterized by difficulty initiat-

Insomnia may be temporary (associated with a rhythm-disrupting stress such as normal bereavement) or chronic. It may be related to a mental disorder, a general medical condition, or substance abuse. Chronic insomnia presents similarly to learned or psychophysiologic insomnia in that attempting to sleep becomes a struggle associated with excessive time spent in bed or trying to compensate for missed sleep (McCall, 1995). Chronic insomnia may be complicated by the negative conditioning associated with pyschophysiologic insomnia (APA, 2000). The medications used for insomnia occasionally cause or worsen insomnia.

Hypersomnia

Hypersomnia is characterized by excessive sleepiness at night or daily daytime sleep episodes. Although the quality of sleep is normal, the amount impairs daytime functioning. Hypersomnia is usually a chronic problem, but there are recurrent forms that last at least 3 days and occur several times a year for at least 2 years. Examples of recurrent forms of hypersomnia include problems of regulatory functioning such as Kleine-Levin syndrome and menstrual cycle-related symptoms of excessive sleep (APA, 2000). Complications of hypersomnia include sleep drunkenness (a state of confusion in which the client experiences a prolonged impaired state of alertness upon awakening) and auto-

Hypnagogic hallucinations are intense, dreamlike illusions that occur at the transition from wakefulness to sleep, just before falling asleep. Hypnopompic hallucinations are intense, dreamlike illusions that occur at the transition between sleep and awakening, just before awakening.

Case Studies A depiction of psychiatric-mental health nursing disorders, including the client's situation and symptoms. Case Studies are followed by a corresponding Nursing Care Plan to assist students in understanding and applying the nursing process.

Implications for Evidence-Based Practice Nurses are expected to incorporate research into their professional practice. These sections highlight recent journal articles or research studies that provide research-based evidence for nursing interventions.

Impulse-Control Disorders 427

Implications for Evidence-Based Practice

A recent study (Grassi et al., 2006) focused on 100 individuals with medical illnesses who exhibited DSM-level psychosomatic symptoms associated with various adjustment disorders. Each of the subjects was interviewed using the Diagnostic Criteria for Psychosomatic Research (DCPR). A significant overlap was demonstrated between the symptoms associated with the adjustment disorders and the DCPR criteria related to abnormal behaviors associated with medical illness, most specifically health anxiety, tanatophobia (fear of death), nosophobia (fear of having a disease), illness denial, somatization, and demoralization. Because adjustment disorder is the most common psychiatric diagnosis found in the medically ill, it is important for nurses to understand the various manifestations of the stress of a medical illness on a client and to make appropriate interventions as the symptoms present, rather than having clients become further stressed and incapacitated by the psychiatric symptoms.

handling stressful events, especially identifying adaptive coping behaviors; teaching the client to use a problem-solving approach to deal with current and future problems; focusing on supportive resources and alternative solutions; educating the client and family about the precipitating stressor; and helping the client to identify appropriate family, social, work, and community resources (Krupnick & Wade, 1999). It is also helpful to assist the client in identifying other types of therapy that might relieve symptoms. These include relaxation techniques, guided imagery, meditation, exercise, biofeedback, occupational and physical therapy, vocational training, and specific education regarding the stressor, especially if it is a new medical condition or illness.

Considerations for Client and Family Education

Teaching clients experiencing an adjustment disorder should include helping both the client and the family identify, anticipate, and understand the situations and events that are stressors and causing the reaction. When possible, the client should be helped to identify and utilize adaptive coping behaviors. The client should be encouraged to utilize a combination of therapeutic modalities to cope with the stressors and to realize the importance of medication compliance if drugs are prescribed to assist with symptom management. If there is any concern that the client may harm him- or herself or others, the family or significant others should be counseled on how to contact emergency mental health services or to access appropriate resources. The client and family should be informed of community-based support services and the availability of educational materials.

Critical Thinking Question How can complementary therapies be used in conjunction with psychotherapy to positively assist a client in dealing with an adjustment disorder?

Medication is used on a limited basis. It is particularly helpful for short-term relief of particular symptoms. For example, a client with insomnia may have symptom relief after receiving a hypnotic such as flurazepam (Dalmane) for a short period, or a client with anxiety may be better able to address ways of coping after the acute anxiety has been relieved by a brief course of diazepam (Valium). A long-term need for medication could indicate that another, underlying mental disorder has not been identified.

Impulse-Control Disorders

There are five types of generally accepted impulse-control disorders: intermittent explosive disorder, kleptomania, ... logic gambling, and trichc... these conditions appear d... face, they all are character... or stimulus that is perceive... challenge, threat, or potent...

According to the Amer... ciation (2000, p. 609), inter... der (IED) is characterized b... failure to resist aggressive... serious assaults or destruc... are expressed as unwarram...; kleptomania is characterized by ... ure to resist impulses to steal objects not needed for personal or monetary value"; pyromania is

Five main impulse disorders: · Intermittent explosive disorder

Considerations for Client and Family Education A key element of psychiatric nursing, these recurring sections contain detailed instructions and insider tips for working with patients and their families.

Psychiatric Mental Health Nursing

An Introduction to Theory and Practice

Welcome to

It is our belief that, among all the textbooks in psychiatric-mental health nursing, this one presents the most balanced combination of practical application and theory-based content, in the most user-friendly format.

By reading the content, utilizing the key features shown here, and visiting the companion Web site (**http://nursing.jbpub.com/psychiatric**), students and instructors are ensured an up-to-date, straightforward introduction to the dynamic field of psychiatric nursing.

Key Features

Each chapter includes:

Chapter Opener:

Learning Objectives These objectives provide instructors and students with a snapshot of the key information they will encounter in each chapter. The objectives can serve as a checklist to help to guide and focus the learning process.

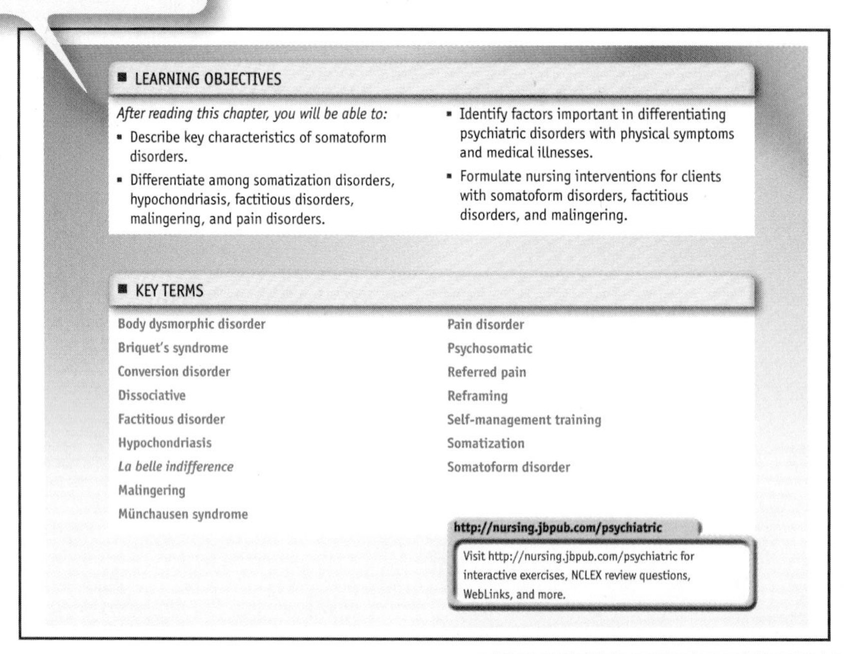

Key Terms These terms introduce essential vocabulary in psychiatric-mental health nursing, and are highlighted in colored text throughout the chapter. Visit http://nursing.jbpub.com/psychiatric to see these terms in an interactive glossary, and use flashcards and word puzzles to nail the definition!

Psychiatric Mental Health Nursing: An Introduction to Theory and Practice!

Throughout the Chapter:

Margin Notes These notes emphasize critical information contained in the text and assist the student in focusing on important content in the chapter. They will help foster critical thinking and a more comprehensive understanding of psychiatric-mental health nursing.

440 CHAPTER 23 Personality Disorders

A personality change that appears suddenly, in response to a life situation, is not diagnosed as a personality disorder. This holds true even though the change may be problematic, such as increased dependency after the death of a spouse. A personality disorder can coexist with an Axis I diagnosis, but the major features of some mental disorders, such as schizophrenia and anxiety disorders, are more properly associated with the primary diagnosis rather than a personality disorder.

Everyone at one time or another exhibits behaviors that characterize the various personality disorders. A person must have functional impairment as a result of the behaviors to actually be diagnosed with a personality disorder.

Nurses are likely to encounter clients with personality disorders in all healthcare settings and clinical specialties.

Types of Personality Disorders

The *DSM-IV-TR* identifies 10 specific personality disorders and 1 additional category for a personality disorder not otherwise specified. The personality disorders are organized into three clusters that define the predominant characteristics of the disorders. A pattern of behaviors is associated with each of the personality disorders (APA, 2000).

Cluster A

Cluster A includes odd or eccentric behavior. A person with paranoid personality disorder is distrustful and suspicious and tends to interpret others' motives as malevolent. Those with schizoid personality disorder are detached from social relationships and have a restricted range of emo-

with dependent p... sive, and their clingin... excessive need to be c... with obsessive-compuls... preoccupied with orde... control.

Not Otherwise Spe...

Personality disorder n... not meet the full crite... disorder. Rather, it has... one personality disor... impairment in functio...

Incidence and P...

The prevalence of per... cult to determine bec... sonality disorder var... because people may d... than one personality di... people who meet the d... sonality disorder enter... estimated that 10–20%... meets the criteria for o... orders (Andreasen & I... age is significantly h... populations, especially... Persons with obsessive...

ability of the client's report of pain but rather on increasing the client's repertoire of coping mechanisms to manage the pain. For example, massage, guided imagery, relaxation techniques, and behavior modification techniques are helpful when used alone or with other therapies. Acupuncture, cryoanalgesia, regional block analgesics or surgical blockades, trigger point injections, transcutaneous electrical nerve stimulation (TENS), and electromagnetic stimulation therapy (TheraStim) are considered useful adjuncts for some types of chronic pain. A client with chronic pain may be referred to a pain clinic for consultation. A multidisciplinary, individualized approach is particularly helpful (Turk, 1990). Referral is suggested if there is a history of self-medication, abnormal pain behaviors, complex problems, or history of inadequate treatment (Bouckoms & Hackett, 1997).

Clinicians can put clients in charge by encouraging them to keep a log of symptom relief using simple pain scales (intensity rating scales of 0–10, from no pain to the worst pain ever). The pain's location (site or area), descriptors (dull, pressing, throbbing, burning, sharp, stabbing), and duration (constant, intermittent, periodic, with diurnal variations) are important in assessment. The pain log alerts healthcare providers to changes in symptoms, the effectiveness of the current drug regimen, and concomitant stressors or environmental changes. The pain log also demonstrates acute changes or shows changes over time that may not be readily observed.

Critical Thinking Question What are some pharmacologic and nonpharmacologic methods of pain relief, and what are their potential side effects?

be changed before the client can accept alternative responses. If the environment cannot be changed, the clinician should attempt to alter the client's response to the environment. Reframing is a process of facilitating change by developing alternative options and interpretations.

Critical Thinking Question What are some possible staff reactions to a client's behavior when staff feel they have been manipulated or purposively deceived? Discuss some ways staff can minimize these reactions when they are aware of the underlying feelings.

Summary

The five main somatoform disorders are somatization disorder, hypochondriasis, conversion disorder, body dysmorphic disorder, and pain disorders. Somatoform disorders are often frustrating both for the client who feels that her or his complaints are not receiving the proper attention and for the caretakers who feel that the client does not recognize that medical or surgical care is not needed. While unexplained physical symptoms are a common phenomenon, the client with a somatoform disorder experiences multiple symptoms affecting multiple systems and often have a history of trauma or stress, psychological symptoms, and association of illness behaviors with primary and secondary gain.

It is important that the client feels supported. The healthcare provider should suggest ways to make the client more comfortable, involve him or her in treatment, and strengthen and maintain adequate coping mechanisms. Reassuring the client, recognizing changes and strengths, and reinforcing health choices allow the professional to engage the client in managing the symptoms rather than having the symptoms control the cli-

Critical Thinking Questions An integral part of the study process, critical thinking questions are presented by the authors based on their own clinical nursing experiences. How might you address such clinical situations as a nursing student or practicing nurse?

Additional Resources 107

- Explicit, consistent, written information is provided.
- Access to help is available when questions about the medication arise.
- Unpleasant symptoms return immediately after stopping a medication.

When the nurse makes the medication regimen simple and comfortable, patients are helped immeasurably in their quest for wellness. To accomplish this goal, the following guidelines are offered for increasing compliance:

- Teach the client and family members about the medications.
- Provide explicit, consistent, written information about the medications.
- Reinforce the importance of medication in relapse prevention.
- Explore specific ways that the medication is helpful.
- Provide for continuity of prescriber.
- Maintain a professional relationship.
- Express optimism about the medication's efficacy.
- Be available to answer questions about the medication or its side effects.
- Research the relationship between stopping medications and relapse in the past.
- Make the medication schedule as simple as possible.
- Arrange for as few doses per day as possible.
- Treat side effects aggressively.
- Teach the client about addiction potential.
- Encourage family and friends to support the use of medications.
- Equate taking medications with wellness and taking responsibility for oneself.

Summary

A broad range of psychotropic medications is available to manage the symptoms of mental disorders. The role of the nurse includes administration of the medication, evaluation of the client's response to the medication, and education of the client and family regarding all aspects of the medication.

This chapter reviews the usual dosage, actions, and side effects of drugs in each category of psychotropic agents. In addition, food and drug interactions that can alter medication absorption and produce untoward—and even life-threatening—effects are presented. Finally, factors that affect the client's compliance with prescribed medication regimens are discussed.

Annotated References

Goodwin, V., & Happel, B. (2006). In our own words: Consumers' views on the reality of consumer participation in mental health care. *Contemporary Nurse, 21*(1), 4–13.
This qualitative study provides insight into patients' views about ways to improve their participation in treatment.

Guy, W. (1976). *ECDEU assessment manual for psychopharmacology.* Washington, DC: U.S. Department of Health, Education and Welfare.
This is the original publication of the Abnormal Involuntary Movement Scale (AIMS).

National Institute of Mental Health. (2006). *Clinical antipsychotic trials of intervention effectiveness (CATIE): NIMH study to guide treatment choices for schizophrenia.* Retrieved April 1, 2006, from http://www.nimh.nih.gov/press/catie_phase2.cfm
The largest, longest, and most comprehensive independent trial ever done to examine existing therapies for schizophrenia.

Nierenberg, A. A., Fava, M., Trivedi, M. H., Wisniewski, S. R., Thase, M. E., et al. (2006). A comparison of lithium treatment and T3 augmentation following two failed medication treatments for depression. *American Journal of Psychiatry, 163*(9), 1519–1530.
This study identifies strategies that increase the effectiveness of antidepressant medications.

Additional Resources

Cooper, J. R., Bloom, F., & Roth, R. H. (2002). *The biochemical basis of neuropharmacology* (8th ed.). New York: Oxford University Press.
This classic text is a guide to neurotransmitters, their role in nervous system function, and their involvement in the mechanisms of psychiatric drug action.

Fuller, M., & Sajatovic, M. (2005). *Lexi-Comp's psychotropic drug information handbook for psychiatry* (6th ed.). Hudson, Ohio: Lexi-Comp.
A clinician's pocket guide to psychotropic drug information.

Kutcher, S. (Ed.). (2002). *Practical child and adolescent psychopharmacology.* New York: Cambridge University Press.
This text is a clinician's guide to psychotropic drug treatment of psychiatric disorders in children and adolescents.

Munetz, M. R., & Benjamin, S. (1988). How to examine patients using the Abnormal Involuntary Movement Scale. *Hospital and Community Psychiatry, 39*(11), 1172–1177.
This classic article provides detailed instructions for administering the Abnormal Involuntary Movement Scale.

Annotated References offer explanatory information on each reference.

Additional Resources, also annotated, for the student who wishes to pursue a subject in greater depth.

Parts II and III Include:

Clinical Examples These are concise vignettes that provide realistic illustrations of specific situations and disorders. Again, the authors' experience in the field benefits the reader!

How Groups Help 159

controversial issues that might divide their membership.

How Groups Help

A variety of dynamics common to self-help groups contribute to their vitality, popularity, and effectiveness.

Helper Therapy

The basic concept behind the helper-therapy principle (Riessman, 1965) is that those who help others gain special benefits themselves. In helping others, the helper experiences an increased sense of self-worth and self-esteem, often when it is most needed. The act of helping others also reinforces for the helper the principles, learning points, and/or program that the helper is following. Helpers develop a firmer understanding of their own recovery process and goals when helping others, as expressed in slogans sometimes heard in 12-step groups, such as, "If you help someone up the hill, you get closer to the top yourself." Even new members can experience the "helper's high" or increased sense of belonging when they listen to others and simply acknowledge with a nod to them that they truly understand what that person is saying. Through helper therapy, most groups turn what society considers a liability (i.e., one's experience as an addict, a widow, or a person with an illness) into an asset (that member's unique ability to provide help to others).

Helping others within the group has been reported as one of the more important benefits that members receive from their participation in the group (Bacon, Condon, & Fernsler, 2000; Fernsler & Manchester, 1997; Knight, 2006). In a study of members of self-help groups for co-occurring disorders, the experience of the helper-therapy process was associated with increases in abstinence from drug and/or alcohol abuse (Magura et al., 2003).

Positive Role Models

Experienced or veteran members demonstrate to new members that success, coping, and recovery are possible. They model competence and attest to how the problems that members face can be overcome. Their example and actions often provide needed encouragement and the installation of hope that otherwise is not available, because such role models are rarely found in agency settings or outside the group. The observance of role models by new members encourages them to assume more responsible action and pursue further learning.

Clinical Example

Some self-help groups have developed in response to the need for advocacy. For example, International Nurses Anonymous (www.intnursesanon.org) was started in 1988 in response to the special problems of nurses in recovery from chemical dependency. Nurses were regularly being denied licenses if they simply acknowledged that they were recovering alcoholics. INA developed as a fellowship of RNs, LPNs, and nursing students who were already in 12-step groups, but wanted to support and advocate for each other. Many other fellowships have developed for health professionals, such as Anesthetists in Recovery, a national support network for recovering nurse anesthetists; International Doctors in AA; and International Pharmacists Anonymous.

Clinical Example

Miguel is a 35-year-old married man who was admitted to the hospital with a blood alcohol level over 350. While hospitalized and treated for withdrawal symptoms, Miguel tells hospital staff that he feels lonely and isolated. Separated from his family, with no legal status in the United States, Miguel has been working long hours in order to send money to his family back home. He is frustrated because of the separation from his family and his inability to speak English. Staff have encouraged him to recognize the need to abstain from alcohol, and Miguel expresses a desire to stop drinking. The nurse is able to contact AA/Intergroup and find a meeting for Miguel in his own language and in his own neighborhood.

Accessibility

Because there are no fees, groups are financially accessible. Many groups are geographically accessible in the community and schedule meeting times that are more convenient than most professional services. They also are psychologically more accessible in several ways. In the many anonymous 12-step groups, last names are not given. Most groups require no registration. One can go to a group simply for education, which is much more affordable both emotionally and financially than having to assume the role of patienthood for mental health treatment. Yet these self-help groups often "grease the skids" for needed referrals of individuals to professional treatment services by both destigmatizing problems and explaining the true

Diagnostic Criteria Indicate where certain disorders fall under the *DSM-IV-TR*, found in text and tables throughout.

442 CHAPTER 23 Personality Disorders

them. The impulsive aggression associated with borderline personality disorder has been attributed to deficits in the neurotransmitter serotonin and to alterations in the functioning of the prefrontal cortex (Goodman, New, & Siever, 2004).

Researchers have discovered familial links between some of the personality disorders and the Axis I mental disorders that suggest a genetic basis. An increased incidence of schizotypal personality disorder is seen among the relatives of schizophrenics, and a familial link exists between paranoid personality disorder and paranoid schizophrenia. Persons with borderline personality disorder are at risk for developing major depression. Symptoms of personality disorder in elderly clients may be associated with disability and impaired social and interpersonal functioning after an acute depressive episode (Abrams, Spielman, Alexopoulos, & Klausner, 1998).

Impulsiveness, avoidance, and aggression have been associated with reduced monoamine oxidase (MAO) activity (Stalenheim, von Knorring, & Oreland, 1997). Electroencephalographic (EEG) abnormalities in persons with borderline and antisocial personality disorders suggest that a subtle brain injury or defect may cause the behavioral manifestations. A disturbance in fetal or childhood development of the brain and nervous system may be at least partially responsible for borderline personality disorder (Hampton, 1997). A recent review of the neurobiological models of personality concludes that current understanding is not sufficient to explain the structure of personality traits and disorders (Paris, 2005). However, the neurobiologic study of personality disorders is in its infancy and has the potential to influence both diagnosis and treatment.

Few people with personality disorders display the traits of only the one disorder with which they have been diagnosed. Typically, people exhibit traits belonging to several of the defined personality disorders.

Clinical Presentation

The APA (2000) offers broad criteria to identify personality disorders as well as criteria specific to the individual personality disorders.

Diagnostic Criteria

The general diagnostic criteria for personality disorder aid in distinguishing a personality disorder from personality traits, an Axis I mental disorder, or an organically based personality change (**Table 23-2**).

Paranoid personality disorder begins in early adulthood.

Table 23-2 Diagnostic Criteria for a Personality Disorder

1. A pattern of behavior that includes at least two of the following:
    - Thought disturbances, including how one perceives and interprets him- or herself, others, and events
    - Mood disturbances, including the range, intensity, lability, and appropriateness of one's emotions
    - Troublesome interpersonal relationships
    - Impulsive behavior
2. These behaviors
    - Have their onset in adolescence or early adulthood
    - Deviate from expected cultural behavior
    - Are enduring, inflexible, and extend across a range of personal, social, and occupational situations
    - Cause significant distress
    - Are not a manifestation of another mental disorder
    - Are not due to a medical condition, a medication, or other substance

Source: Adapted from American Psychiatric Association, 2000.

Additional Criteria

The *DSM-IV-TR* provides additional criteria that establish the diagnosis of each of the recognized personality disorders (APA, 2000). These criteria focus on behaviors that characterize the disorder and help inform the nurse's assessment. Behaviors associated with each personality disorder are identified in the following sections, as are the likely functional areas in which the client may be experiencing distress.

Paranoid Personality Disorder

These clients are often difficult to get along with because of their argumentative, sarcastic, and often hostile manner of relating to others. Not surprisingly, their behavior elicits a negative response in others that only serves to justify their actions to themselves. Clients with paranoid personality disorder have a fundamentally suspicious view of the world that makes them view the simple mistakes of others as deliberate intentions to cause personal harm. These people usually have problems establishing and maintaining close relationships and often are guarded during interviews, making it difficult for the nurse to obtain a personal history.

Schizoid Personality Disorder

Clients with schizoid personality disorder have a profound inability to form personal relationships, even with members of their immediate

Psychiatric Mental Health Nursing

An Introduction to Theory and Practice

Editors

Patricia G. O'Brien, PhD, RN, CS/NP, BC
Director of Nursing and Inpatient Services, Behavioral Health
St. Vincent's Catholic Medical Center Manhattan
New York, New York

Winifred Z. Kennedy, MSN, RN, CS, BC
Senior Nurse Clinician Consultation and Emergency Psychiatry Service
Maimonides Medical Center
Brooklyn, New York

Clinical Associate, Hunter-Bellevue School of Nursing
Adjunct Clinical Professor, New York University Graduate Division

Karen A. Ballard, MA, RN
Adjunct Professor
Lienhard School of Nursing, Pace University
Pleasantville, New York

Guest Lecturer and Advisory Council Member
Division of Nursing, Molloy College
Rockville Centre, New York

Nursing Consultant
Professional Nursing Issues and Health Policy
New York, New York

JONES AND BARTLETT PUBLISHERS
Sudbury, Massachusetts
BOSTON TORONTO LONDON SINGAPORE

World Headquarters
Jones and Bartlett Publishers
40 Tall Pine Drive
Sudbury, MA 01776
978-443-5000
info@jbpub.com
www.jbpub.com

Jones and Bartlett Publishers Canada
6339 Ormindale Way
Mississauga, Ontario L5V 1J2
Canada

Jones and Bartlett Publishers International
Barb House, Barb Mews
London W6 7PA
United Kingdom

Jones and Bartlett's books and products are available through most bookstores and online booksellers. To contact Jones and Bartlett Publishers directly, call 800-832-0034, fax 978-443-8000, or visit our website www.jbpub.com.

Substantial discounts on bulk quantities of Jones and Bartlett's publications are available to corporations, professional associations, and other qualified organizations. For details and specific discount information, contact the special sales department at Jones and Bartlett via the above contact information or send an email to specialsales@jbpub.com.

Production Credits

Chief Executive Officer: Clayton Jones
Chief Operating Officer: Don W. Jones, Jr.
President, Higher Education and Professional Publishing: Robert W. Holland, Jr.
V.P., Sales and Marketing: William J. Kane
V.P., Design and Production: Anne Spencer
V.P., Manufacturing and Inventory Control: Therese Connell
Executive Editor: Kevin Sullivan
Acquisitions Editor: Emily Ekle
Associate Editor: Amy Sibley
Editorial Assistant: Patricia Donnelly
Production Director: Amy Rose
Production Editor: Carolyn F. Rogers
Senior Marketing Manager: Katrina Gosek
Associate Marketing Manager: Rebecca Wasley
Photo Research Manager and Photographer: Kimberly Potvin
Manufacturing and Inventory Control Supervisor: Amy Bacus
Composition: Graphic World
Interior Design: Anne Spencer
Cover Design: Kristin E. Ohlin
Cover Image: © Handy Widiyanto/ShutterStock, Inc.
Printing and Binding: Courier Kendallville
Cover Printing: Courier Kendallville

Library of Congress Cataloging-in-Publication Data

Psychiatric mental health nursing : an introduction to theory and practice / editors, Patricia G. O'Brien, Winifred Z. Kennedy, Karen A. Ballard.
p. ; cm.
Includes bibliographical references and index.
ISBN-13: 978-0-7637-4434-2 (pbk. : alk. paper)
ISBN-10: 0-7637-4434-4 (pbk. : alk. paper)
1. Psychiatric nursing. I. O'Brien, Patricia G. II. Kennedy, Winifred Z. III. Ballard, Karen A.
[DNLM: 1. Mental Disorders—nursing. 2. Psychiatric Nursing—methods. 3. Nursing Theory. WY 160 P972045 2008]
RC440.P7372 2008
616.89'0231—dc22

2007038401

6048

Printed in the United States of America
11 10 09 08 07 10 9 8 7 6 5 4 3 2 1

Contents

Introduction

Psychiatric Mental Health Nursing: An Introduction to Theory and Practice is intended as a basic text for the undergraduate nursing student and as a reference for both the nurse in a nonpsychiatric setting who is caring for a client with a psychiatric diagnosis and the nurse who is making a transition from another specialty into psychiatric nursing. The content applies to nursing practice in the range of clinical settings, including the hospital, the client's home, or other community settings.

Nursing interventions are identified for each of the mental health disorders. These interventions are linked to client behaviors and are the foundation for outcome-focused nursing care plans. The content is presented in a concise manner and provides essential information related to the theory and practice of psychiatric-mental health nursing, without overwhelming the novice practitioner. This text offers a practical alternative to lengthier, comprehensive texts without sacrificing critical content. The authors and publisher carefully considered the learning features and the content in order to achieve this focused presentation.

Each chapter includes:

- **Learning Objectives** to guide and focus study as students move through each topic
- **Key Terms** that list and define the most essential words and phrases
- **Margin Notes** to enhance content and provide emphasis of critical points
- **Critical Thinking Questions** to help students process and expand upon the material they are reading and absorbing
- **Annotated References** offer explanatory information on each reference
- **Additional Resources**, also annotated, for the student who wishes to pursue a subject in greater length

The chapters in both Part II and Part III include the following student aides:

- **Clinical Examples**, concise vignettes that provide realistic illustrations of specific content
- **Case Studies** offer detailed depictions of psychiatric disorders including the client's situation and symptoms
- **Nursing Care Plans** that provide expected outcomes, interventions, and evaluation in relation to the situation presented in the corresponding case study
- **Diagnostic Criteria** for psychiatric-mental health disorders under the *DSM-IV-TR*
- **Considerations for Client and Family Education** sections contain detailed instructions for passing on to patients and their families
- **Implications for Evidence-Based Practice** highlights recent studies or journal articles that provide research-based evidence for specific nursing interventions.

Part I is an overview of psychiatric-mental health nursing. Chapter 1 traces the development of psychiatric nursing, including conceptual models of selected nurse theorists. The chapter discusses the major treatment modalities as well as the nurse-client relationship.

Chapter 2 covers issues and trends in psychiatric-mental health nursing, including the nursing process, issues related to documentation, outcomes and research, practice settings, cultural issues, generalist and advanced practice roles, nursing diagnostic and *DSM-IV-TR* classifications, and professional organizations.

The psychiatric nursing evaluation is described in Chapter 3 in a way that supports and delineates the nurse's role in client assessment. This chapter also assists students with biopsychosocial history-taking and conducting a mental status exam. It will help guide the patient interview process, providing ideas for what questions to ask, giving examples of therapeutic and nontherapeutic communication. In addition, it outlines nursing diagnoses, outcome identification, and planning of care.

Chapter 4 provides a clear, in-depth understanding of neurobiologic theories of mental disorders, with down-to-earth examples illustrating these processes.

Chapter 5 combines up-to-date information on psychopharmacologic agents with a discussion of the nurse's role in medication administration and client education. Easy-to-read tables help the student to organize and learn actions, dosages, and side effects of the medications.

Chapter 6 introduces the principles of crisis intervention and provides direction to guide the nurse's actions in response to psychiatric emergencies. The principles are applied to a variety of clinical situations, including acute trauma, agitation and aggression, and disasters. Discussion includes alternatives to restraints or seclusion, as well as considerations for patient and staff safety when these interventions are used.

Legal and ethical considerations are discussed in Chapter 7, including issues related to the use of seclusion and restraint, informed consent, and client confidentiality.

Chapter 8 acknowledges the active role of the client in the healing process and the growing impact of self-help groups as adjuvant to traditional therapeutic interventions.

The use of an experiential format in Chapter 9 allows the student to be actively involved in learning about the application of complementary therapies to meet the biopsychospiritual needs of clients in the context of holistic nursing practice.

Chapter 10 addresses violence in the family, including the issues of child and elder abuse.

Part II addresses specific mental health disorders in a way that is consistent with the *DSM-IV-TR* classification, the official nomenclature used by multidisciplinary teams treating psychiatric clients. As members of the treatment team, nurses must be familiar with the process used to diagnose and assess mental disorders as well as be conversant in the language and terminology used by the team. The format for each chapter includes a general description of the specific disorder; information on incidence, prevalence, and etiology; physiology; clinical presentation, course and complications; differential diagnoses; treatment and nursing approaches; and a summary.

Part III provides information on the nursing management of discrete populations. These populations were selected based on the unique challenges associated with providing care specific to their needs. Topics include age-related issues associated with the care of children, adolescents, and the aging. Individual chapters are devoted to the special needs of clients diagnosed with mental retardation and developmental disabilities, dual diagnosis, and chronic mental illness.

The appendices include:

- **Appendix I**—The most current American Nurses Association's scope and standards of practice for psychiatric-mental health nursing.
- **Appendix II**—Aligns the most common *DSM-IV-TR* disorders with their corresponding NANDA-I nursing diagnoses. Completely unique to this text, this appendix allows for quick comparisons between the two systems and assists nurses in successfully working within a multidisciplinary team with the correct and most current diagnoses.

Ancillary Package

A full companion Web site has been designed to accompany *Psychiatric Mental Health Nursing: An Introduction to Theory and Practice,* found at **http://nursing.jbpub.com/psychiatric**. The special features here are designed to complement and expand upon concepts learned from the main text and through the typical classroom instruction. Designed to be as simple, yet as useful as possible, the features on the Web site can be accessed either by chapter number or by type of feature (e.g., Flash Cards or WebLinks).

Students

The student features can be used to supplement individual study time by the reader or assigned by the instructor as homework. They include the following:

- **Interactive Glossary, Crossword Puzzles, and Flashcards** to test your knowledge of key terminology and concepts
- **Interactive Anatomy Review** for reviewing parts of the human anatomy pertinent to psychiatric nursing
- **Additional Case Studies and Care Plans** similar to those in the book ask students to complete client care plans based on clinical case scenarios
- **WebLinks** contain applicable psychiatric and mental health nursing Web resources for easy clicking and linking for further information on specific topics
- **Pre-Test** allows students to test their knowledge of key content before moving on to more extensive review questions
- **NCLEX-RN® Review Questions** provide overall review of psych-nursing content and helps prepare for the NCLEX-RN® examination

Instructors

Instructors will have access to the student resources on the Web site, and will also have access to the following secure resources that are designed to make instructor's job easier:

- **PowerPoint Slides** outlining each chapter's content for classroom presentation
- **Instructor's Manual** containing suggestions for classroom discussions, activities, and group work, homework assignments, and lecture suggestions
- **TestBank** of NCLEX®-style questions for your use in creating exams and quizzes
- **Answers** to the additional care plans and case studies

Preface

This book has been designed to support nursing faculty in their important role of introducing novice nurses to the basics of psychiatric-mental health nursing. The organization of the content recognizes the need to provide the nursing student with a clear understanding of what psychiatric-mental health nursing is and the context in which it is practiced. We are very aware of the special challenge that faculty face to introduce a large volume of new information within limited didactic and clinical semester hours. Therefore, as authors, we have made an effort to present essential content in a way that does not sacrifice substance, but does not overwhelm the novice.

In the late 1990s when we collaborated on an earlier textbook, we made a decision to present the nursing interventions in the framework of the American Psychiatric Association's (APA) *Diagnostic and Statistical Manual of Mental Disorders (DSM-IV*; 1994). Other psychiatric nursing books have since followed a similar format. We think this confirms our belief that nurses must learn the common language of the multidisciplinary team that is so integral to the delivery of mental health services. We have updated the information on mental disorders to be consistent with the revised *DSM-IV-TR* (2000).

The NANDA-I (2007) nursing diagnoses are identified for each of the DSM diagnostic categories. This is in keeping with our belief that psychiatric-mental health nursing must be grounded in nursing theory. Each author has extensive experience as an advanced practice registered nurse. Our collective backgrounds, including teaching and mentoring nursing students, has informed our approach to this textbook. We retained features of the original book that faculty found helpful and included new features to bring clinical situations to life, promote critical thinking, and structure the course content.

The content has been organized to promote incremental learning and to accommodate both discrete psychiatric nursing courses and integrated nursing curricula. The initial chapters introduce the nursing student to the general knowledge and specific skills that are applicable to learning the nursing care of clients with specific mental disorders. The student traces the development of psychiatric-mental health nursing, learns about the nursing theorists who have had the most influence on the specialty, compares the *DSM-IV* nomenclature with NANDA-I, and reviews neurobiology, psychopharmacology, and psychiatric emergencies. Ethical concerns, including client competence, are introduced. There is a brief overview of the types of therapies offered to clients with psychiatric illness, including group therapy, somatic therapies, and cognitive behavioral therapy.

The chapter on psychiatric nursing assessment builds on the nursing process that the nursing student is already familiar with and then guides the student through the steps of taking a biopsychosocial history and conducting a mental status examination. It gives practical advice to guide the client interview, such as what questions to ask, and examples of therapeutic communication. Finally, it covers the nursing diagnosis and development of an outcome focused nursing care plan.

We heard from faculty of the increased emphasis on teaching documentation relevant to psychiatric-mental health nursing. A comprehensive list of what should be included in nursing documentation provides a handy reference for the nursing student and can be easily copied and utilized in the clinical setting.

The various categories of psychotropic medications are presented in a table format with dosage, intended actions, interactions, and side effects. The tables are designed to organize a considerable amount of information in a manner that will promote learning.

All of the fundamental knowledge and skills that are presented in Part I of the book are applied in Part II to the specific mental disorders. A uniform format is followed with each disorder: description, incidence and prevalence, etiology, physiology, clinical presentation, course and complications, differential diagnoses, treatment, and nursing interventions. Each chapter has a special section on client and family education because this is one of the major nursing interventions. The content is enriched with clinical examples, case studies, and outcome-focused nursing care plans. Throughout each chapter there are margin notes to highlight important and interesting facts, as well as critical thinking questions that can trigger classroom or post-clinical discussions. Implications for evidence-based practice are highlighted through the presentation of recent research. Again, content is well organized, concise, and complete.

The third section of the book covers special populations and lends itself to community health or courses on the nursing care of specific age groups, such as child, adult, or geriatric clients. Chapters are devoted to the special needs of clients diagnosed with mental retardation and developmental disabilities, dual diagnosis, and chronic mental illness.

We hope our readers, both faculty and students, find this book readable, interesting, and a resource that you can utilize in the practice of any nursing specialty. Of course, we would be pleased if this introduction to psychiatric-mental health nursing inspires some students to pursue careers as psychiatric-mental health nurses. But, regardless of where you practice, there will be clients who are living with mental illness. We are confident that this book will provide a knowledge and skill base necessary for the student and novice nurse to meet the psychiatric-mental health nursing needs of clients and families in any setting.

Note from the Publisher

The editors bring to this project extensive experience in the practice of psychiatric-mental health nursing. The combined experiences, specialized knowledge, and interests of the editors were enriched by those of our contributors. The resulting efforts communicate the spirit of discovery and hope associated with current advances in understanding the etiologies and treatments of psychiatric illnesses. As remarkable as these scientific advances are, they do not lessen the significance of the interpersonal component of care. Communication skills, so much the essence of nursing, will continue to be valued. This text provides nursing students and nurses with the fundamental knowledge to contribute to the care of clients living with mental illness.

Acknowledgments

The authors wish to thank the psychiatric-mental health nurses who have been our mentors throughout our professional careers. You continue to inspire us and we are indebted to you for your wisdom, your patience, your friendship, and your belief in us. In writing this book, through our clinical practice, and through our teachings, we endeavor to carry on your commitment to our fellow nurses.

The authors extend our appreciation to our contributors who, by sharing their knowledge and insight into psychiatric-mental health nursing and the care of clients and their families, have made this book possible.

We are also grateful to our nurse colleagues, the nurses with whom we work everyday, who continue to define and expand the practice of psychiatric-mental health nursing. You do make a difference.

We extend love and appreciation to our families and friends who have supported and encouraged us throughout this process. Thank you for your enthusiasm, understanding, and love.

We wish to express our appreciation for the editorial, production, and marketing direction and support of Kevin Sullivan, Carolyn Rogers, Emily Ekle, Tricia Donnelly, Katrina Gosek, and their colleagues.

Author Biographies

Patricia G. O'Brien, PhD, RN, CS/NP, BC is Director of Behavioral Health Nursing and Inpatient Services at St. Vincent's Catholic Medical Center, New York City. She is a licensed psychiatric nurse practitioner with prescriptive privileges and is board certified by the American Nurses Credentialing Center as both a nurse practitioner and clinical specialist in adult psychiatric-mental health nursing.

Dr. O'Brien was formerly Associate Vice President for Regulatory and Professional Affairs at the Greater New York Hospital Association, specializing in mental health policy issues. She has held leadership positions in psychiatric nursing at New York Hospital's Payne Whitney Clinic, and has maintained clinical practices as a nurse practitioner in a metropolitan hospital outpatient department and as a clinical nurse specialist in private practice.

Dr. O'Brien is a member of the American Psychiatric Nurses Association (APNA), and serves as expert consultanat to APNA's task forces on seclusion and restraint and violence in the workplace. She was appointed to the NYS Department of Education Task Force on the Nursing Shortage, and has been an item reviewer for the National Council Licensure Examination for Registered Professional Nursing (NCLEX-RN®).

Dr. O'Brien has a master of arts degree in nursing from New York University and a PhD in nursing from Adelphi University. A graduate of St. Vincent's Hospital School of Nursing, she received her undergraduate degree in nursing from Hunter College, the City University of New York. Dr. O'Brien completed a postgraduate fellowship in cognitive-behavioral therapy at the Institute for Behavior Therapy in New York City, and studied behavior therapy under the supervision of Dr. Herbert Fensterheim at the Cornell University College of Medicine.

Winifred Z. Kennedy, MSN, RN, CS, BC is a certified clinical specialist in adult psychiatric-mental health nursing. Ms. Kennedy graduated from Fordham University (BS in Experimental Psychology), NY Hospital-Cornell University School of Nursing (BSN), and Hunter-Bellevue Schools of Health Professions (MSN Psychobehavioral Nursing). She holds a certificate in marriage and family therapy from the Family Therapy Institute at the Health Science Center of the State University of New York, Downstate Division.

Ms. Kennedy's expertise is in the area of psychiatric consultation liaison nursing. She is currently employed by Maimonides Medical Center, the nation's third largest independent teaching hospital. Ms. Kennedy is a member of the Consultation and Emergency Psychiatry Service, an interdisciplinary team that practices in the emergency department as well as in the general medical center. Her experience includes the supervision of students and licensed clinicians in the practice setting and is affiliated with several undergraduate and graduate nursing programs in the metropolitan area. Current clinical affiliations include Hunter-Bellevue School of Nursing and New York University Graduate Division. She holds numerous elected and appointed positions within state and national professional nursing organizations.

Karen A. Ballard, MA, RN is a nurse consultant in private practice specializing in professional practice issues and health policy. Ms. Ballard is a guest lecturer and advisory council member in the Division of Nursing at Molloy College in Rockville Centre, NY. She is also an adjunct professor at the Lienhard School of Nursing at Pace University in Pleasantville, NY. Ms. Ballard is a graduate of Niagara University (BS in Nursing) and New York University (MA in Child and Adolescent Psychiatric-Mental Health Nursing). She is currently the Chair of the Nurses Work Group for Health Care Without Harm, an international coalition of more than 400 organizations in 52 countries working to transform the healthcare industry so it is no longer a source of harm to people and the environment. She is a member of the Steering Committee of Rekindling Reform, a grassroots effort in New York State dedicated to achieving access to affordable, quality health care for all.

Ms. Ballard was formerly a pediatric-mental health clinical nurse specialist with extensive experience in the care of abused children and chronically and terminally ill children and their families. She has developed guidelines for assisting children and their families to adjust to hospitalizations and has contributed to the development of the American Nurses Association's scope and standards of nursing practice. Ms. Ballard has published on child abuse, the politics of the HIV epidemic, and nursing intensity weights and frequently presents on professional practice issues, nurses as environmental health activists, and the legally protected scope of nursing practice.

Previously for 20 years, Ms. Ballard held various staff positions as a nursing practice and regulatory specialist with the New York State Nurses Association including Director of Special Projects and Director of the Practice and Governmental Affairs Program where she interpreted nursing practice issues, served as a lobbyist and addressed such issues as bioterrorism, HIV/AIDS, reimbursement, nursing acuity, and staffing and the nursing shortage. Ms. Ballard was chair and a member of ANA's Nursing Standards and Guidelines Committee (1994–2001), serving as chairperson for the 2003 version of *Nursing: Scope and Standards of Nursing Practice* and as a consultant to *Psychiatric-Mental Health Nursing: Scope and Standards of Practice* (2007). Ms. Ballard is president-elect of the New York State Nurses Association (2007–2009).

Contributors

Jeanne Anselmo, BSN, RN, BCIAC-SF, HN-BC
Holistic Nursing Consultant
Sea Cliff, NY

Blaine R. Beemer, BSc(Hons), RN, MN, CPMHN(C)
Staff Nurse
Psychiatric Emergency Services
Calgary Health Region Sessional Instructor
Faculty of Nursing
University of Calgary
Calgary, Alberta, Canada

Donna R. Falvo, RN, PhD, CRC
Clinical Professor
Rehabilitation Counseling and Psychology
Department of Allied Health Services
School of Medicine
The University of North Carolina at Chapel Hill
School of Medicine
Chapel Hill, NC

Loraine Fleming, APRN, BC, MA, CS
Director, Behavioral Health Services
The Queen's Medical Center
Honolulu, HI
Lecturer and Adjunct Clinical Instructor
University of Hawai'i at Manoa
School of Nursing and Dental Hygiene
Honolulu, HI

Sherry Goertz, MSN, APRN-PMH, BC, CNE
Instructor of Nursing
Pennsylvania State University
Mont Alto, PA

Beth Harris, MA, APRN, BC
Health Education Coordinator
New York-Presbyterian Hospital
White Plains, NY

Beverley E. Holland, PhD, ARNP
Associate Professor
Lansing School of Nursing and Health Services
Bellarmine University
Louisville, KY

Karan S. Kverno, PhD, CRNP-PMH
Assistant Professor
Department of Farming and Community Health
University of Maryland School of Nursing
Baltimore, MD

Edward J. Madara, MS
Director
American & N.J. Self-Help Group Clearinghouses
St. Clare's Health System
Dover, NJ

Valerie N. Markley, MSN, APRN, BC
Assistant Professor
Indiana University School of Nursing
Bloomington, IN

Joan C. Masters, MA, MBA, PhD(c), RN
Assistant Professor
Lansing School of Nursing and Health Sciences
Bellarmine University
Louisville, KY

Claudia Mitzeliotis, MS, APRN-BC, CASAC
Psychiatric Clinical Nurse Specialist
Veterans Administration, New York Harbor Health-care System
Brooklyn, NY

Christine Carniaux Moran, LCSW, RN,C
Vice President for Behavioral Health Services
South Oaks Hospital
Amityville, New York

Bethany A. Murray, MSN, APRN, BC
Director of Nursing
Center for Behavioral Health
Bloomington, IN

Julia Balzer Riley, RN, MN, AHN-BC, CET
Expressive Arts Facilitator
TideWell Hospice and Palliative Care
Registered Expressive Arts Consultant and Educator
Constant Source Seminars
www.constantsource.com
Ellenton, FL

Cecelia M. Taylor, PhD, RN
Professor Emerita of Nursing
The College of St. Scholastica
Duluth, MN

Amy Wysoker, PhD, RN, APRN, BC
Professor of Nursing
Department of Nursing
Long Island University
Brookville, NY

Overview of Psychiatric-Mental Health Nursing

CHAPTER 1

Introduction to Psychiatric-Mental Health Nursing

Cecelia M. Taylor

LEARNING OBJECTIVES

After reading this chapter, you will be able to:

- Describe the evolution of psychiatric-mental health nursing care.
- List the members of the contemporary multidisciplinary treatment team and describe the distinctive abilities of each professional member.
- Explain two key concepts from each of the psychoanalytic, interpersonal, and behavioral conceptual models.
- Discuss the impact on psychiatric-mental health nursing of the works of Peplau, Orlando, King, Orem, and Riehl-Sisca.
- Describe the characteristics of individual therapy, family therapy, group therapy, milieu therapy, crisis intervention, and somatic therapies.

KEY TERMS

Anticipatory guidance
Anxiety
Apathy
Behavioral model
Classical conditioning
Cognitive model
Conceptual model
Coping mechanisms
Crisis
Developmental crises
Dynamisms
Ego defense mechanisms
Extinction
Family systems therapy
Genogram
Group therapy
Individual therapy
Levels of consciousness
Milieu therapy
Moral therapy
Multidisciplinary treatment team
Need for satisfaction
Need for security
Negative reinforcement
Neurobiologic model
Nurse-patient relationship
Operant conditioning
Personality, structure of
Positive reinforcement
Preoccupation
Psychoanalytic model
Psychodynamic nursing
Psychosexual theory of personality development
Punishment
Response cost
Security operations
Selective inattention
Self-care deficit nursing theory
Self-concept
Situational crises
Somatic therapies
Somnolent detachment
Structural family therapy
Therapeutic community

The use of the term *patient* in the first half of this chapter reflects historical usage.

http://nursing.jbpub.com/psychiatric

Visit http://nursing.jbpub.com/psychiatric for interactive exercises, NCLEX review questions, WebLinks, and more.

During the Middle Ages, mentally ill persons (the insane) were believed to be possessed by devils.

The inhumane treatment of insane persons reached its peak in the seventeenth century when almshouses, a combination of a jail and an asylum, confined both criminals and those who were mentally ill.

In 1792, Phillipe Pinel introduced moral therapy. Attendants were required to treat patients kindly and keep them busy with various activities.

Benjamin Rush (1745–1813) is considered the "father of American psychiatry." The first public psychiatric hospital in America was built in Williamsburg, Virginia, in 1773 and is still in operation today as the Eastern Psychiatric Hospital.

History

Society has always adopted measures designed to change the behavior of persons with mental illness. In prehistoric times, those measures were likely to have been tribal rites that, if unsuccessful, probably led to the abandonment of the ill person. During the Greek and Roman eras, the sick were treated in the temples, and treatment ranged from humane care to flogging, bleeding, and purging.

The plight of mentally-ill persons continued to be poor in the Middle Ages, when their care was determined by mistaken religious beliefs. The mentally ill were believed to be possessed by devils that could be exorcised by whippings and starvation. When the church stopped treating mentally ill persons during the sixteenth century, they were imprisoned in almshouses, which were a combination of a jail and an asylum. Those who were violent and delusional were placed in jails and dungeons. King Henry VIII officially dedicated Bethlehem Hospital in London as a lunatic asylum. Bethlehem Hospital soon became known as the notorious "Bedlam," whose hideous practices were immortalized by Hogarth, the famous cartoonist (**Figure 1-1**). The keepers at Bedlam were allowed to exhibit the most boisterous patients for 2 pence a look. The more harmless inmates were forced to seek charity on the streets of London; the "Bedlam beggars" of Shakespeare's King Lear were based on these prisoners (Taylor, 1994).

Figure 1-1 Bedlam, as depicted by William Hogarth. Note the well-dressed ladies, who made social visits to the prison to view the spectacle of the inmates as entertainment.

The inhumane treatment of mentally ill persons peaked in the seventeenth century when petty criminals and those who were mentally ill were confined together in almshouses. Treatment consisted of drastic purgings, bleedings, and whippings.

The Eighteenth and Nineteenth Centuries

In the eighteenth century, Europe, particularly France, underwent political and social reform. In 1792, Phillipe Pinel, the medical director of the Bicêtre asylum outside Paris, introduced a new treatment regimen termed **moral therapy**. Advocates of moral therapy believed that mental illness was related to immorality or faulty upbringing, and that a therapeutic environment could correct these weaknesses. Instead of harsh confinement, patients were kept busy with work, music, or other diversions. Moral therapy required that attendants treat patients with kindness and keep them involved in the treatment program (Wasserbauer & Brodie, 1992). The Quakers, under the Brothers Tuke, established the York Retreat and brought about the same dramatic reforms in England. The development of moral therapy and its reliance on attendants were the beginnings of current psychiatric nursing care.

The first place identified as a "poorhouse, workhouse, and house of correction" in the United States opened in New York City in 1736. In 1756, under the guidance of Benjamin Franklin, the Pennsylvania Hospital was completed. One of the first two patients admitted was described as a "lunatic." Although patients with a mental illness were relegated to the cellar, they were assured clean bedding and warm rooms. Benjamin Rush (1745–1813), a humanitarian and the "father of American psychiatry," began working at Pennsylvania Hospital in 1783.

The first public psychiatric hospital in America was built in Williamsburg, Virginia, in 1773 and is known today as Eastern Psychiatric Hospital. Most states, even as late as 1830, did not have facilities for treatment of the mentally ill, although a number of excellent private hospitals existed (most notably the Hartford Retreat, founded in 1818).

Dorothea Lynde Dix (1802–1887) was a schoolteacher who volunteered to tutor individuals confined to jails and poorhouses. She was horrified by the conditions in these facilities, and in 1841 began a campaign to convince state legislatures that suitable hospitals, not jails, were required for those with mental illnesses. Twenty states in the United States and the Canadian government responded directly to her appeals by authorizing the construction of large institutions for the mentally ill. This was the beginning of the state hospital system in the United States.

The original intent of the state hospital system was to treat those with mental illness and then discharge them to the community or the care of their families. Because so little was known about mental illness at that time, the goals of treatment and discharge were not able to be achieved. Consequently, state hospitals rapidly became overcrowded with chronically mentally ill patients. Paradoxically, the same state hospitals that were supposed to alleviate the suffering of violent persons who were previously imprisoned contributed to the ultimate demise of moral therapy, because this treatment could not be implemented in overcrowded settings.

In 1844, the Association of Medical Superintendents was formed as psychiatry began to develop as a profession and as physicians became increasingly responsible for the administration of asylums. This organization became the American Medico-Psychological Association in 1851, and was renamed the American Psychiatric Association (APA) in 1921. It was founded by medical superintendents from 13 asylums in the United States (Wasserbauer & Brodie, 1992).

By the 1870s, asylums were considered abysmal institutions with a terrible public image. Searching for ways to improve care, psychiatrists adopted the strategies already in use at general hospitals to improve patient services. These improvements included incorporating effective therapies that had a scientific basis and using graduate nurses instead of attendants. However, asylums were unable to attract enough nurses to improve patient care, so schools of nursing in asylums were established. The first school of this type was established at the McLean Asylum in Massachusetts in 1882 (Wasserbauer & Brodie, 1992).

The Twentieth Century

At the beginning of the twentieth century, treatment was still limited to restraints, isolation, water bath treatments, dietary regimens, and, eventually, early sedative drugs and shock treatments. Noticeable changes occurred in the state hospital system in 1908 when Clifford Beers, a psychiatric patient who was hospitalized several times, wrote a book about his experiences titled *A Mind That Found Itself*. The book's revelations led to the founding of the National Committee for Mental Hygiene. The committee, for the first time, espoused the prevention of mental illness and early intervention.

The most significant psychiatric revolution in the early twentieth century was a direct result of the work of Sigmund Freud (1856–1939). Freud made great contributions to the understanding of human behavior. Before his theories were introduced, human behavior, particularly the behavior of persons with mental illnesses, was shrouded in superstition, secrecy, and stigma. Freud brought the subject of human behavior to the public's attention. His theories served as a springboard for the scientific study of human behavior. Although much of Freudian theory is no longer embraced in scientific circles, some of his concepts have become so integrated into the mainstream that they have become part of everyday language (e.g., ego, conscience, unconscious).

The National Mental Health Act, passed in 1946, was one of the most progressive actions addressing mental illness the United States has ever taken. The legislation stemmed from the nation's concerns about the mental health of its citizens as a result of experiences during World War II. More men in the armed forces were disabled from mental disorders than from all other health problems related to military action. Immediately after the National Mental Health Act was passed, the National Institute of Mental Health (NIMH) was established in 1946. The NIMH provided funding to support research into the causes of mental illness and to provide tuition and stipends for education in the four core mental health disciplines: psychiatry, psychology, psychiatric nursing, and psychiatric social work. Major strides were made in increasing the number of mental health professionals as a result of this funding. For example, in the 1940s only five to seven graduate programs in psychiatric nursing existed; these numbers expanded greatly in the 1950s and 1960s as a result of NIMH funding.

Psychiatric nursing underwent a major change when *Interpersonal Relations in Nursing* by Hildegard Peplau was published in 1952. Reprinted in 1991 and now considered a classic, this book emphasized the significance of the relationship between the patient and nurse as a treatment modality. Dr. Peplau became the director of the graduate

> Dorothea Lynde Dix (1802–1887), an early advocate for the mentally ill, convinced state legislatures that suitable hospitals, not jails, were required for those with mental illnesses.

> A movement began in the 1870s to use graduate nurses instead of attendants in state hospitals. The first school of nursing at a state asylum was founded in 1882 at the McLean Asylum in Massachusetts.

> *A Mind That Found Itself*, by Clifford Beers, led to the founding of the National Committee for Mental Hygiene, which espoused the prevention of mental illness and early intervention.

> Sigmund Freud brought the subject of human behavior to the attention of the scientific community and public, although his theories are no longer universally acclaimed.

> One of the most progressive actions ever taken by the United States in response to mental illness was the passage of the National Mental Health Act in 1946 and the subsequent establishment of NIMH.

> A major turning point in psychiatric nursing was the publication of *Interpersonal Relations in Nursing* by Hildegard Peplau. This book emphasized the significance of the relationship between patient and nurse as a treatment modality.

program in psychiatric nursing at Rutgers, The State University of New Jersey, and is considered the "mother of modern psychiatric nursing."

The master's program in psychiatric nursing at Rutgers, along with many other programs, graduated hundreds of clinical nurse specialists (CNSs) in psychiatric nursing. These individuals quickly assumed leadership positions in organized nursing and lobbied for recognition as autonomous practitioners of mental health care, specifically psychotherapy. Currently, many states authorize certified psychiatric clinical nurse specialists and certified psychiatric nurse practitioners to prescribe psychopharmaceuticals, and Medicare and most insurance plans reimburse them for their services.

In 1953, the National League for Nursing required the inclusion of psychiatric nursing experience and coursework in the basic nursing curricula for all nursing students.

In 1953, the National League for Nursing, the accreditation agency for schools of nursing, required the inclusion of psychiatric nursing clinical experience and coursework in all basic curricula and required that these subjects be taught by nursing faculty. Thus, all nursing students had some exposure to the practice and theory of psychiatric nursing. However, it was not until the 1980s that the last school of nursing located in a psychiatric hospital closed.

The Mental Health Study Act of 1955 led to the establishment of the Joint Commission on Mental Illness; the commission's report, *Action for Mental Health*, provided a nationwide stimulus to develop more effective services for people in need of psychiatric care.

In 1955, the U.S. Congress passed the Mental Health Study Act. This act provided funds for a 5-year study of the problem of mental illness in the United States. As a result, the Joint Commission on Mental Illness was established. The commission's report, *Action for Mental Health*, provided the stimulus for developing more effective services for people in need of psychiatric care, and was the basis for additional legislation.

The care of persons with mental illness was revolutionized in the late 1950s when chlorpromazine (Thorazine) first became available for widespread use.

A revolution in care occurred in the late 1950s when the first effective antipsychotic medication, chlorpromazine (Thorazine), became widely available. Although many other, more effective, medications are currently available, none have had the impact of chlorpromazine when it was first introduced. This medication controlled many of the most distressing symptoms experienced by patients, resulting in their becoming more amenable to other forms of treatment and being able to function better both in and out of hospitals.

The 1963 Community Mental Health Centers Construction Act and its 1965 staffing amendments sought to revolutionize the provision of mental health care by emphasizing prevention and decentralized, local community treatment.

On February 5, 1963, President John F. Kennedy delivered a special message on mental illness and mental retardation to the Congress. He emphasized the goal of community care for persons with mental illnesses. In that same year, Congress authorized the Community Mental Health Centers Construction Act, which was followed in 1965 by amendments to provide for staffing in the centers (P.L. 89-105). These acts sought to revolutionize mental health care by emphasizing prevention and decentralized, local community treatment over institutional care, even for persons with the most severe psychiatric difficulties. The first federally funded centers opened in 1966, initiating the deinstitutionalization of persons with mental illness.

The first *Standards of Psychiatric and Mental Health Nursing Practice* was published in 1973 by the ANA.

In 1973, the executive committee of the division of psychiatric-mental health nursing practice of the American Nurses Association (ANA) published the first *Standards of Psychiatric and Mental Health Nursing Practice.* This document has been continually revised and reflects the current, accepted levels of practice that psychiatric nurses are expected to maintain. The most recent version is *Psychiatric-Mental Health Nursing: Scope and Standards of Practice* (2007).

In the late 1980s, NIMH shifted its focus and funding from education and service delivery to research. This legislative shift resulted, in part, from intense lobbying by the National Alliance for the Mentally Ill (NAMI), an advocacy group of families of mentally ill persons that demanded increased research into the cause and treatment of mental illness. Funding for the education of mental health practitioners was abolished, resulting in a dramatic decline in the number of nurses pursuing graduate degrees in psychiatric nursing.

Begun in the 1960s, deinstitutionalization was finally achieved in the late 1980s and early 1990s as a result of economic constraints and the availability of medications and services that enabled patients to function in the community. Currently, persons with mental illness who require hospitalization are likely to be admitted to a freestanding private hospital or a psychiatric unit in a general hospital. The nature of treatment has also changed. An individual admitted to the hospital no longer has to remain for months, with most staying for less than 2 weeks (Taylor, 1994).

Critical Thinking Question What are the advantages and disadvantages for clients, families, communities, and healthcare practitioners when short-term hospitalization is deemed necessary?

Finally, a major paradigm shift has occurred in understanding the causes of major mental illness, and this shift has altered the nature of psychiatric treatment. As a result of increasingly sophisticated technology, scientists have proposed that many of the most severe forms of mental illness have a neu-

Figure 1-2 An individual psychotherapy session.

robiologic basis. As a result, treatment relies heavily on the ever-expanding array of psychopharmaceuticals as well as the more traditional "talking" therapies (individual psychotherapy, group therapy, family therapy; see Figure 1-2). Furthermore, because of these findings, many graduate programs in psychiatric nursing have revised their curricula to emphasize neurobiology and psychopharmacology.

The Twenty-First Century

The understanding of the causes and treatment of mental illness has increased dramatically over the centuries. The availability of increasingly sophisticated technology ensures even more dramatic advances in knowledge. Because of the increasing scope and complexity of this burgeoning knowledge, it is necessary for the **multidisciplinary treatment team** to work closely together to achieve the goals of preventing mental illness and effectively treating those who are ill. Therefore, the psychiatric nurse in the twenty-first century works collaboratively in the community with other healthcare practitioners, clients, and their families, each an integral part of the multidisciplinary treatment team utilizing a variety of treatments. Recognition of the patient as an integral member of the treatment team is reflected in the contemporary use of the term *client* rather than *patient* when referring to the person in need of professional mental health services.

In addition to clients and their families, the multidisciplinary treatment team includes the psychiatrist, clinical psychologist, psychiatric mental health nurse, psychiatric social worker, and activities therapists such as life skills, art, and music. All mental health professionals share a common knowledge of and skill in interpersonal relationships and a deep appreciation of the inextricable relationship between mind and body. Each professional discipline has a distinctive knowledge base and skills that enrich the treatment team.

Psychiatrists are physicians with several years of supervised residency training in the medical specialty of psychiatry. The psychiatrist prescribes

Figure 1-3 A sample Rorschach "ink blot."

medications and administers other somatic therapies, such as electroconvulsive therapy. Psychiatrists are particularly skilled in identifying and treating persons whose problems have highly interrelated emotional physiological components.

Clinical psychologists have advanced education in the study of mental processes and the treatment of mental disorders. They have particular expertise in the use of inferential tools designed to assist in the diagnostic process and assessment of treatment effects. An example of such a tool is the Rorschach test, commonly known as the "ink blot" test (Figure 1-3).

Psychiatric-mental health nurse generalists and advanced practice psychiatric nurses work collaboratively in out-patient and in-patient treatment settings. According to the Society for Education and Research in Psychiatric-Mental Health Nursing (SERPN), psychiatric-mental health nurses are registered nurses who are educationally prepared in nursing, licensed to practice in their individual states, and qualified to practice in the psychiatric-mental health nursing specialty at one of two levels: basic or advanced. All nurses bring expertise in assessing the client's ability to engage in activities of daily living and to assist the client to cope as necessary. The nurse in an in-patient setting is responsible for establishing and maintaining an environment that is therapeutic for the client population as a whole. It is believed that the therapeutic nurse-client relationship is the hallmark of psychiatric nursing. For a more complete discussion of these roles, see Chapter 2.

Psychiatric social workers are prepared at the master's degree level and have particular skill in assessing familial, environmental, and social factors that contribute to the problems of clients and

Many of the most severe forms of mental illness most likely have a neurobiologic basis. As a result, treatment is based on the use of psychopharmaceuticals (i.e., drug therapy).

Figure 1-4 A client engaged in painting.

their families. They are also major contributors to discharge planning and the follow-up care of the client.

Activity therapists have at least a bachelor's degree, and increasingly a master's degree is required in their specialty field. The basis of activity therapy is the belief that persons can benefit from engaging in activities that focus outside of the self, such as exercise, crafts, writing, music, or painting (see **Figure 1-4**). These activities can be done either alone or in conjunction with other clients. Therefore, the activity therapist is skilled in the development, implementation, and evaluation of a highly individualized activity regimen designed to meet the needs of the person for whom it is designed.

A conceptual model is a framework of related concepts. Most mental health practitioners use a variety of approaches to assist clients in achieving mental health.

The founder of the psychoanalytic model is Sigmund Freud. Key Freudian concepts include levels of consciousness, structure of the personality, and psychosexual development.

The three levels of consciousness are the conscious, the preconscious, and the unconscious; the three aspects of the personality are the id, the ego, and the superego.

Conceptual Models

A **conceptual model** is a framework of related concepts. Conceptual models used by mental health practitioners address the bases for behavior in order to direct interventions. Although some mental health practitioners adhere strictly to one conceptual model, most practitioners in the United States use an eclectic approach in which they employ one or more approaches from several models. The most important conceptual models are the psychoanalytic, interpersonal, behavioral, cognitive, developmental, and neurobiologic models. We will discuss all the models in this chapter, but the last three models are discussed in more detail in other chapters of this book.

Critical Thinking Question Why would most mental health practitioners choose to use an eclectic approach to treatment? What are the advantages of this practice? Are there any disadvantages to this approach?

Psychoanalytic Model

Sigmund Freud is the founder of the **psychoanalytic model**. Freud was an Austrian physician who began his career as a neurologist. He developed an elaborate theory of human behavior based primarily on his work with persons suffering from disabling anxiety. The treatment approach derived from his theories is termed *psychoanalysis*. Key Freudian concepts include levels of consciousness, structure of the personality, and psychosexual development.

Three Levels of Consciousness

Freud believed in three **levels of consciousness**. The first level of consciousness is the conscious mind, that part of the mind that is aware of the present and functions only when the person is awake. It represents the smallest part of the mind and directs an individual's rational, thoughtful behavior.

The second level of consciousness is the preconscious. The preconscious (or subconscious) is the part of the mind in which thoughts, feelings, and sensations are stored. Although materials stored in the preconscious mind are outside of awareness, they can be brought to the conscious mind with the proper stimulus, such as a direct question.

The third level of consciousness is the unconscious. The unconscious represents the largest part of the mind and is the storehouse for all of the thoughts, feelings, and sensations experienced during the individual's lifetime. The individual is rarely aware of the unconscious mind, except when it demonstrates its presence through dreams, slips of the tongue, unexplained behavior, jokes, and lapses of memory (Taylor, 1994). These thoughts, feelings, and sensations cannot be recalled at will, but nevertheless exert a powerful influence on the person's behavior. Belief in the existence of the unconscious is the basis for the saying "All behavior has meaning."

Structure of the Personality

The second major concept developed by Freud is the **structure of the personality**. Freud believed that the personality consists of three aspects, the id, the ego, and the superego. The id is part of and derived from the unconscious. It is unlearned, primitive, and selfish. The id does not have a sense of right and wrong, and ruthlessly insists on immediate satisfaction of its impulses and desires, which are geared toward avoiding pain and experiencing pleasure. The personality of newborns consists solely of the id, a belief that is not difficult to accept when one observes the behavior of infants. They may, for example, cry lustily when hungry, regardless of the social appropriateness of such behavior. Even mature adults experience unceasing pressure from the id to satisfy its demands. The other parts of the personality are responsible for keeping the id under control.

The ego develops as a result of the infant's interaction with its environment. It establishes an acceptable compromise between the crude, pleasure-seeking strivings of the id and the inhibitions of the superego through reality testing. Reality testing is a process the ego employs to ascertain the likely consequences of behavior. The ego is the practical part of the personality. As an individual matures, the ego becomes the rational, reasonable, conscious part of the personality and strives to integrate the total personality into a smoothly functioning, coherent whole. In the mature adult, the ego represents the self to others and individualizes the person from other human beings (Taylor, 1994).

Chronologically, the superego develops last. The superego acts as the moral judge of the individual based on what the person has learned from significant others, such as parents and teachers. It operates mostly at the unconscious level and controls the id. The two aspects of the superego are the conscience, which punishes individuals through guilt and anxiety when their behavior deviates from the strict standards of the superego, and the ego ideal, which rewards individuals with feelings of well-being when their behavior achieves those standards believed desirable by the superego. Neither the punishing nor the rewarding functions of the superego are based on the reality of the situation. Rather, they are based on the individual's internalized standards of right and wrong and good and bad that were learned at an early age and are stored primarily in the unconscious (Taylor, 1994).

Freud believed that when id impulses unacceptable to the superego threaten to emerge, the individual experiences anxiety. **Anxiety** is a diffuse, vague sense of impending doom, and is always perceived as a negative emotion. Therefore, the person experiencing anxiety works to get rid of this feeling, often through the use of **ego defense mechanisms**, mental mechanisms derived from the ego that are designed to effect a compromise between the demands of the id and the superego to relieve anxiety. Ego defense mechanisms operate on the unconscious level, although an objective observer may be able to discern when others are using them. For example, a student who perceives herself as very intelligent but who fails a test may rationalize this otherwise anxiety-producing outcome by telling herself and others that the test was not important. Persons with whom she shares this belief may be very aware that she is using the ego defense mechanism of rationalization. **Table 1-1** details commonly used defense mechanisms.

In contrast to the unconscious nature of defense mechanisms, **coping mechanisms** are conscious mental strategies or behaviors the individual employs to lower anxiety. The various coping mechanisms cannot be listed because their number is as great as the creativity and resourcefulness of human beings. Coping mechanisms are categorized as short-term or long-term.

Short-term coping mechanisms are designed to address the immediate problem. For example, a person experiencing a great deal of work-related stress may drink alcohol as a means of coping. Although this action may relieve the immediate anxiety, it does not address the source of the stress or prevent the anxiety from reemerging. In contrast, long-term coping mechanisms address the cause of the anxiety and are likely to benefit the individual more than short-term coping mechanisms. Some examples are relaxation techniques, biofeedback, exercise, assertiveness training, setting goals, clarifying communications, visualization and guided imagery, meditation, yoga, seeking out peer support, and self-hypnosis.

Psychosexual Theory of Personality Development

Freud also defined the developmental stages of personality. His theory of personality development is termed the **psychosexual theory of personality development**. Prior to this theory, children were seen as miniature adults. Freud claimed that personality is a dynamic, evolving process that develops from birth through young adulthood. Freud's stages of psychosexual development are oral (birth to 18 months), anal (18 months to 3 years), phallic (3 to 6 years), and genital (13 years to adulthood).

Although specific portions of Freud's theory are now viewed as an outgrowth of the Victorian era in which he lived, his theories provided the foundation for the work of subsequent theorists. Erik Erikson expanded Freud's theory of personality development to include the entire life span, and emphasized the importance of culture as a

Anxiety is a diffuse, vague sense of impending doom and is perceived by the individual as a negative emotion.

One way in which people control their anxiety is through ego defense mechanisms, which operate on an unconscious level. Coping mechanisms (short-term or long-term) are conscious mental strategies or behaviors used to lower anxiety and adjust to demands in a purposeful manner.

Freud developed the psychosexual theory of personality development. He claimed that personality develops in stages (oral, anal, phallic, latency, genital) from birth through young adulthood.

Erik Erikson expanded Freud's theory of personality development to include the entire life span from a psychosocial framework. Erikson's theory is known as the Eight Ages of Man—trust versus mistrust, autonomy versus shame and doubt, initiative versus guilt, industry versus inferiority, identity versus role confusion, intimacy versus isolation, generativity versus stagnation, and ego integrity versus despair.

Table 1-1 Ego Defense Mechanisms

Defense Mechanism	Definition	Example
Compensation	Exaggerating one trait to make up for feelings of inadequacy or inferiority in another dimension.	A physically small man verbally bullies his employees.
Displacement	Attributing feelings to a person or object that are really directed at another person or object.	A young woman kicks her cat after a telephone argument with her boss.
Denial	Failing to perceive some threatening object or event in the external world.	A woman sets a place for dinner for her husband, who has just been killed.
Fixation	Remaining "stuck" in a developmental stage.	A husband depends totally on his wife for most of his activities of daily living.
Sublimation	Redirecting socially unacceptable urges into socially acceptable behavior.	An angry, hostile young man becomes a boxer.
Reaction formation	Substituting directly opposite wishes for one's true wishes.	An adult who grew up in a very messy home is compulsively neat in his or her own home.
Identification	Integrating desired attributes of an admired person to compensate for perceived inadequacy.	A shy adolescent girl styles her hair identically to that of a popular rock star.
Introjection	Incorporating another person to avoid the threat posed by the person or by one's own urges.	A psychotically depressed woman attempts suicide to kill her mother, who she states is in her stomach.
Undoing	Engaging in certain thoughts and actions so as to cancel out or atone for threatening thoughts or actions that have previously occurred.	A business executive studies to become a nursery school teacher after having an abortion.
Isolation	Severing the connection between the thoughts and feelings associated with an event so the event can remain conscious without undue anxiety.	A single parent talks unemotionally about her only child's recent diagnosis of a malignant brain tumor.
Rationalization	Substituting a fictitious, socially acceptable reason for the genuine, unacceptable reason for one's wishes or actions.	"I would have helped you if I could, but I had to take my dog to the vet."
Repression	Forcibly dismissing anxiety-producing thoughts, feelings, or events from consciousness.	A woman is unable to remember being raped by her brother when she was 10 years old.
Regression	Returning to patterns of behavior characteristic of a less anxiety-producing stage of development.	A 6-year-old girl begins to wet the bed at night after her mother's remarriage.
Projection	Attributing to others an objectionable trait or feeling that really emanates from oneself.	"My husband is cheating on me."
Symbolization and condensation	Using a neutral idea or object to represent an unacceptable idea or object.	A 40-year-old man has unconscious feelings of inadequacy as a male and spends all his money on guns and all his time polishing and cleaning them.
Conversion	Expressing unconscious emotional conflicts through a physical symptom with no demonstrable organic basis.	A young woman wakes up paralyzed from the waist down on the morning of her wedding day.

Source: Taylor, C. M. (1994). *Essentials of Psychiatric Nursing* (p. 211). St. Louis: Mosby Yearbook. Reprinted with permission.

major determinant of personality development. Erikson's theory of psychosocial development is called the Eight Ages of Man and encompasses trust versus mistrust (infancy, 0 to 1 year), autonomy versus shame and doubt (early childhood, 1 to 3 years), initiative versus guilt (preschool, 3 to 6 years), industry versus inferiority (school age, 6 to 12 years), identity versus role confusion (adolescence, 12 to 18 years), intimacy versus isolation (young adulthood, 18 to 25 years), generativity versus stagnation (adulthood, 25 to 45 years), and ego integrity versus despair (older adulthood, 45 years to death).

Interpersonal Model

The interpersonal model was first developed by an American-born psychiatrist, Harry Stack Sullivan (1892–1949). Sullivan believed the most critical factor in the development of the individual's personality, and thus his or her behavior, is the person's relationship with significant others.

Sullivan believed that all human behavior is goal-directed toward the fulfillment of two needs, the need for satisfaction and the need for security. The **need for satisfaction** derives from the person's biologic needs for air, food, sex, shelter, and so on. The **need for security** derives from the person's emotional needs for feeling states such as interpersonal intimacy, status, and self-esteem. When these needs are perceived, internal tension results and the individual employs a variety of methods to meet them and thereby reduce the tension. Sullivan termed these methods **dynamisms**. He emphasized that dynamisms are age-specific, which helps to explain the characteristics of each stage of personality development, from infancy (birth to 18 months), childhood (18 months to 6 years), juvenile (6 to 9 years), preadolescence (9 to 12 years), early adolescence (12 to 14 years), and late adolescence (14 to 21 years). During infancy, the oral cavity is used almost exclusively to meet the needs for satisfaction (by crying to be fed) and the needs for security (by crying to be held). Therefore, the stage of infancy is characterized by the oral dynamism, because it is the means through which the individual establishes interpersonal contact to meet needs and reduce tension (Taylor, 1994).

The concept of anxiety is central to Sullivan's theory. He postulated that anxiety is a response to feelings of disapproval from a significant adult. These feelings of disapproval may not be based on reality, and the adult whose disapproval is feared may be real or a symbolic representation. Sullivan believed that people defend against such anxiety by using **security operations**, including apathy, somnolent detachment, selective inattention, and preoccupation. Individuals use **apathy** by not allowing themselves to feel the emotion associated with an anxiety-producing event. Thus, an individual appears indifferent in a situation expected to elicit a great deal of anxiety in most persons. **Somnolent detachment** is a primitive defense in which the individual falls asleep when confronted by a highly threatening, anxiety-producing experience. More common is **selective inattention**, in which anxiety-producing aspects of a situation are not allowed into awareness, enabling the individual to maintain a sense of stability. Finally, the security operation of **preoccupation** manifests as a consuming interest in a person, thought, or event to the exclusion of the anxiety-producing reality.

Sullivan defined the **self-concept** as the result of reflected appraisals of significant others. He believed that the development of the self-concept begins in the stage of infancy and is closely related to the quality of the infant's feeding experiences. If infants frequently experience satisfaction and security from the mothering they receive during the feeding process, they begin to see themselves as worthwhile individuals; they start to develop what Sullivan refers to as "good me" self-concepts. However, if their needs for satisfaction and security often are not met, anxiety results and infants believe they are not worthwhile; this lays the foundation for the development of "bad me" self-concepts. In extreme cases where infants are severely deprived or when the majority of interpersonal relationships are fraught with great threats to their existence, infants defend themselves by dissociating the anxiety-generating experiences. As a result, because they cannot develop a sense of self from reflected appraisals, infants develop a "not me" self-concept, which may lead to severe emotional problems.

Once developed, the self-concept tends to self-perpetuate because people behave in a manner consistent with their self-concept and elicit interpersonal responses from others that reinforce their self-concept. Persons with good me self-concepts tend to relate to others in a positive way, eliciting positive responses that reinforce the self-concept. People with bad me self-concepts tend to relate to others in a manner that reflects their poor view of themselves and, predictably, elicits responses that reinforce this view. Anxiety occurs when others' responses are incongruent with the person's self-concept. People deal with this anxiety by utilizing security operations that enable them to ignore

> The interpersonal model is based on relationships. Harry Stack Sullivan believed that all human behavior is goal-directed toward the fulfillment of two needs, the need for satisfaction and the need for security. When these needs are perceived, internal tension results, and the individual uses dynamisms to relieve the tension.

> People defend against anxiety by using the security operations of apathy, somnolent detachment, selective inattention, and preoccupation.

> The self-concept is the result of reflected appraisals of significant others and may include "good me," "bad me," and "not me."

differing input. This theory helps to explain why some persons succeed against all odds and others fail despite all advantages.

Behavioral Model

Unlike the psychoanalytic and interpersonal models, **behavioral models** are concerned with the here and now, not with how or why people developed the behavior they currently exhibit. Ivan Pavlov (1849–1936) was the first behavioral researcher. His work on classical conditioning is well known to all students of psychology. **Classical conditioning** focuses on involuntary behaviors, such as blinking and salivation. In classical conditioning, a person has a reaction to a neutral event because the reaction and the event have become associated. For example, a person who exhibits the involuntary symptoms of anxiety (pounding heart, rapid respirations) when he or she sees a picture of a tall building somehow has learned to associate tall buildings or heights with danger.

Ivan Pavlov developed the theory of classical conditioning in which events and reactions become associated. B. F. Skinner developed the theory of operant conditioning, which addresses the relationship between voluntary behavior and the environment.

The theory of **operant conditioning** has been credited to B. F. Skinner (1904–1990) and his associates. Operant conditioning is concerned with the relationship between voluntary behavior and the environment. Skinner demonstrated that behaviors are influenced by their consequences; those behaviors that have a positive consequence increase in strength and are likely to be repeated, whereas behaviors that result in negative consequences are weakened and are less likely to be repeated (Stuart, Laraia, & Sundeen, 1998).

A desired behavior can be increased through positive and negative reinforcement. Behavior is decreased through punishment, response cost, and extinction.

Increasing a desired behavior is achieved through positive and negative reinforcement. **Positive reinforcement** rewards the desired behavior. For example, a person who receives a pay raise because he or she produced more widgets is likely to continue trying to produce even more widgets, assuming that he or she values an increase in pay. **Negative reinforcement** increases the frequency of a behavior by reinforcing the behavior's power to control a negative stimulus. For example, children quickly learn which behaviors are likely to prevent their parents from yelling at them.

Decreasing behavior is a more difficult task. It is achieved through punishment, response cost, and extinction. **Punishment** is an aversive stimulus that occurs after the behavior and serves to decrease its future occurrence. For example, a child whose parents make him take a "time out" by standing in the corner every time he uses a swear word is likely to decrease his use of swear words after several time outs. In **response cost**, a person experiences a loss or penalty as a consequence of engaging in a certain behavior. The teenager who is "grounded" 1 day for every 5 minutes she is late coming home from a date is likely to arrive home on time after several experiences of being grounded. **Extinction** is the process of eliminating a behavior by ignoring or not rewarding it. Repeatedly ignoring a child's temper tantrums is an example of extinction. Efforts to increase or decrease behavior require a plan of treatment that is consistently implemented and avoids unintended secondary gains, such as getting much-desired attention.

Cognitive Models

Jean Piaget was the first theorist to describe cognitive development (sensorimotor, preoperational, concrete operations, formal operations).

Cognitive models of development examine the perceptual and intellectual growth of the individual. Although individuals appear to follow a pattern in cognitive development, such timetables can be very individual. Children often appear to develop in one area while falling behind in others (e.g., learning to talk before or after walking, but not simultaneously).

An early cognitive theorist of the 1930s named Jean Piaget (1896–1980) focused on the process involved in a child's ability to know and understand. Like Freud, Piaget's theories are less accepted by today's therapists. However, he was the first theorist to postulate the different maturation cycles involved in how children gain an awareness of self through cognitive abilities. His stages of cognitive development include: sensorimotor (birth to 18 months), preoperational (2 to 7 years), concrete operations (6 to 12 years), and formal operations (12 years to adulthood). For more on this topic, see Chapter 24.

Developmental Models

There are a variety of developmental models offered by theorists that assist one in understanding how growth and development impact upon an individual's mental health. These include:

- An attachment model (John Bowlby, 1907–1990) based on the establishment of trust, bonding, and attachment as essential to the survival of the human species.
- A behavior modification model in which children are taught how to establish controls from within and that there are consequences (natural, logical, and unrelated) to one's behavior.

- A psychosocial model (Erik Erikson, 1902–1994) based on the importance of trust as a basic building block for normal psychological development, that includes eight stages of developmental growth (see Chapter 24).

Neurobiologic Model

In the last several decades, it has become apparent that an understanding of the brain and the nervous system is basic to understanding the symptoms, processes, and treatment of mental illnesses and disorders. Molecular biology is the foundation for molecular psychiatry.

Psychiatric-mental health nurses and other clinicians are increasingly challenged to understand neurons, neuronal transmitter brain receptors, ion channel variants, and intercellular neuronal molecules and their effect on neural circuits, and ultimately, the behavior of individuals. The **neurobiologic model** and its associated psychopharmcologic treatments will be driving forces in the next era of psychiatric interventions. For most clients, pharmacologic treatment controls the main symptoms of the mental illness or disorder and is used in conjunction with supportive therapies such as individual psychotherapy, group therapy, family therapy, and self-help groups (see Chapter 4).

Selected Nurse Theorists and Their Conceptual Models

Several nurse theorists stress the interpersonal dimension of nursing in their conceptual models and believe that some form of personal interaction with clients is the basis of the profession. A brief description of some of these theorists and their models follows.

Hildegard Peplau

Hildegard Peplau has had the greatest impact on the development and practice of psychiatric nursing. Although Peplau has held a number of significant positions, she is best known for initiating and developing the graduate program in psychiatric nursing at Rutgers, where she was the director from 1954 until her retirement in 1974. Her textbook, *Interpersonal Relations in Nursing*, first published in 1952, significantly changed psychiatric nursing from a medical model to an interpersonal model in which the nurse has a major role in therapeutic interventions. It was empowering to nurses and the nursing profession at a critical time when their contributions to the care of patients were not recognized. Furthermore, her theories were widely applicable to the practice of nursing in all settings and with all types of patients. The major concepts of Peplau's theories are **psychodynamic nursing**, the **nurse-patient relationship**, and nursing roles.

As described by Marriner-Tomey, "Psychodynamic nursing is being able to understand one's own behavior to help others identify felt difficulties, and to apply principles of human relations to the problems that arise at all levels of experience" (1998, p. 327). The therapeutic nurse-patient relationship is the concept for which Peplau is best known. She describes an interaction between the nurse and patient as having four distinct yet overlapping phases: orientation, identification, exploitation, and resolution. In the orientation phase there is a "felt need," and professional assistance is sought by the patient. Identification occurs after the patient has clarified the situation and begins to respond selectively to the various healthcare practitioners. In the exploitation phase, the patient has identified with a specific nurse and makes full use of all offered services. The resolution phase occurs as the patient gradually relinquishes identification with the caregivers (nurses and others) and is once again independent (Peplau, 1952).

Finally, Peplau describes six different nursing roles that emerge in the various phases of the nurse-patient relationship: stranger, resource person, teacher, leader, surrogate, and counselor. The roles change with the patients and the circumstances. Peplau emphasized that skill in these roles is developed only through practice and with ongoing, competent supervision.

Ida Jean Orlando (Pelletier)

Orlando's first book, *The Dynamic Nurse-Patient Relationship: Function, Process and Principles of Professional Nursing Practice*, was published in 1961. Of all Orlando's work, this book's theories, emphasizing the reciprocal relationship between patient and nurse, have had the greatest impact on psychiatric nursing.

Orlando was one of the first leaders of nursing to emphasize the elements of the nursing process and the critical importance of the patient's participation during the nursing process (Marriner-Tomey, 1998). As with Peplau's theories, Orlando's theories apply to all nurse-patient interactions.

> The neurobiologic model and its associated psychopharmacologic treatments are the driving forces in the next era of psychiatric-mental health care.

> Nurse theorists such as Peplau, Orlando, King, Orem, and Riehl-Sisca emphasize the interpersonal dimension of nursing in their respective conceptual models.

> No other nurse has had a greater impact on the development and practice of psychiatric nursing than Hildegard Peplau. The major concepts of Peplau's theories are psychodynamic nursing, the nurse-patient relationship, and nursing roles.

> *The Dynamic Nurse-Patient Relationship: Function, Process and Principles of Professional Nursing Practice*, written by Ida Jean Orlando and published in 1961, emphasizes the reciprocal relationship between patient and nurse.

The conceptual framework Imogene King formulated represents personal, interpersonal, and social systems as the domain of nursing.

The self-care deficit nursing theory was developed by Dorothea E. Orem and is based on an interactive process between the nurse and the patient.

Joan Riehl-Sisca applies the sociologic theory of symbolic interactionism to nursing.

Individual therapy focuses on the person. Almost all conceptual models are now implemented as types of individual therapy.

Family therapy is based on the belief that the person who is identified as ill exhibits symptoms that emanate from problems within the family system.

Family systems therapy is based on the belief that families are systems in which change in one aspect of the system affects the entire system.

Imogene King

Imogene King's first book, *Toward a Theory for Nursing: General Concepts of Human Behavior*, was published in 1971. King's theory of goal attainment is heavily based on systems theory. The conceptual framework she formulated represents personal, interpersonal, and social systems as the domain of nursing (Marriner-Tomey, 1998).

Dorothea E. Orem

Dorothea E. Orem's first book, *Nursing: Concepts of Practice*, was published initially in 1971. Orem's theory, termed **self-care deficit nursing theory**, describes how the actions of nurse and patient are determined by the patient's self-care agency, "the complex acquired ability to meet one's continuing requirements for care that regulates life processes, maintains or promotes integrity of human structure and functioning and human development, and promotes well being" (Marriner-Tomey, 1998, p. 190). Nursing is an interactive process based on the amount and kind of nursing agency needed.

Joan Riehl-Sisca

Joan Riehl-Sisca applies the sociologic theory of symbolic interactionism to nursing. Riehl-Sisca believes that

> . . . the nurse must view the actions of the individual as he perceives them. By role playing, explicitly or implicitly the nurse is able to understand why the patient does what he does and is thus better able to identify the source of difficulty, or nursing diagnosis. Then, having interpreted the patient's action and studied the process recordings, the nurse is able to intervene with a plan of care. The plan of care involves helping the patient and/or family assume roles they have used in the past, or are currently using, to cope with the present illness. The evaluation process is then used to determine the success of this "role taking." (Marriner-Tomey, 1998, p. 373)

Critical Thinking Question Which of the above nursing models do you think would be most useful in the practice of psychiatric-mental health nursing, and why?

Treatment Modalities

Based on the conceptual models used by the therapist and an assessment of the needs of the client, a treatment modality is selected, implemented, and evaluated. The following briefly describes the most commonly used treatments.

Individual Therapy

Individual therapy focuses on the person and includes other aspects of the person's life only as they relate to the individual. Psychoanalysis was the original form of individual therapy, although almost all conceptual models are now implemented as types of individual therapy. Individual therapy continues to be the most commonly used form of mental health therapy, although most therapists agree that treating individuals in the absence of their social support groups is the least desirable form of treatment.

Family Therapy

Although all nurses are concerned with the family's impact on the client, only those educated as advanced practice psychiatric nurses function as family therapists. Family therapy is based on the belief that the person identified as ill, the identified client, exhibits symptoms that emanate from problems within the family system. Therefore, treatment of the identified client in isolation from his or her family is doomed to failure. Two of the theoretical bases of family therapy are family systems therapy and **structural family therapy**.

Family systems therapy was developed by Murray Bowen in the 1950s, and is based on the belief that families are systems in which change in one aspect of the system affects the entire system. Therefore, when there is a change in the functioning of one family member, the entire family is affected. Family systems theory consists of seven interlocking concepts. Three concepts apply to overall characteristics of family systems: differentiation of self, triangles, and the nuclear family emotional system. The other four concepts are related to the central family characteristics: multigenerational transmission process, family projection process, sibling position, and emotional cutoff (Stuart et al., 1998).

Bowen believes that a member's movement toward either increased emotional closeness or distance is reflexive and predictable. The higher the level of differentiation, the higher the level of functioning. Differentiating the self from "weness" is the ultimate goal of treatment (Stuart et al., 1998). Family genograms are commonly used to depict the familial emotional system through generations (**Figure 1-5**). A **genogram** is a diagram or map of multiple generations of a family indicating family relationships, life events, family functioning, and significant developmental events. Men are represented by boxes, women by circles. Other symbols and lines represent births,

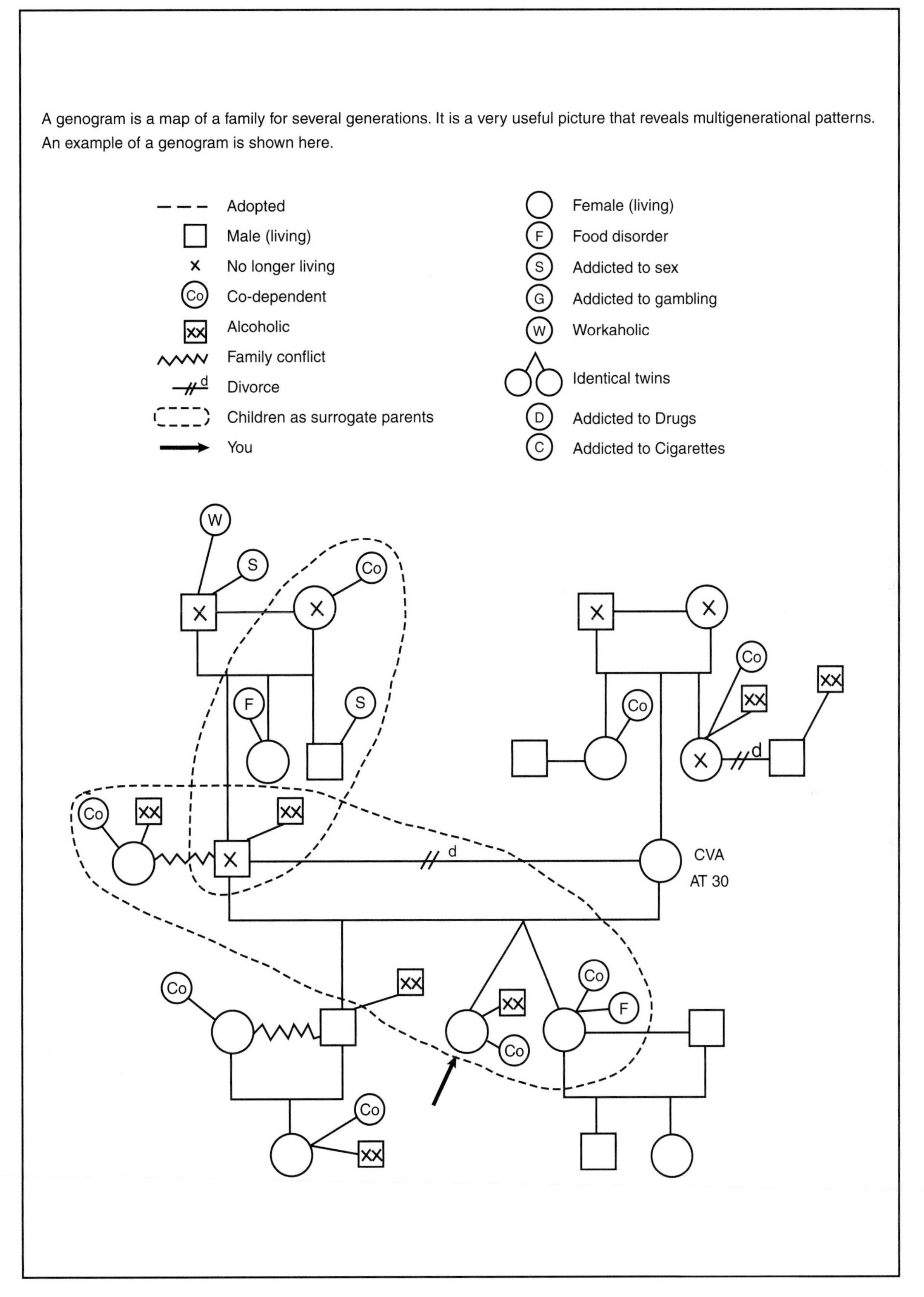

Figure 1-5 An example of a genogram.

deaths, marriages, cohabitation, children, pregnancies, adoptions, divorces and separations, ethnic and religious origin, health and illness, risk factors, and geographic locations.

Structural family therapy is based on understanding the individual within a social context.

Structural family therapy was developed by family therapist Salvatore Minuchin. It is based on understanding the individual within a social context. Minuchin postulated that behavior is a consequence of the family's organization and the interactional patterns between members. Changing the family organization and the feedback processes between members changes the context in which a person functions. Thus, the person's inner processes and behavior change (Stuart et al., 1998).

Group Therapy

Group therapy became a standard intervention for the treatment of persons diagnosed with a mental illness during and immediately after World War II. A group is an identifiable system composed of three or more individuals who engage in certain tasks to achieve a common goal. The therapeutic group differs from a social group because its goal is to assist individuals to alter their behavior patterns and to develop new and more effective ways of dealing with the stressors of daily living. This goal may be achieved through many forms of group therapy, including task groups, socialization groups, self-help groups, psychotherapy groups, teaching and learning groups, and supportive therapy groups.

The therapeutic group differs from a social group because its goal is to assist individuals to alter their behavior patterns and to develop new and more effective ways of dealing with the stressors of daily living.

Regardless of their type, all groups go through four developmental phases, and certain group behaviors characterize each phase. The first phase is the preaffiliation phase, during which members become acquainted with each other and develop trust in one another and in the group leader. Some groups are never able to move beyond this first phase. If the group is successful in achieving trust, it enters the second phase, termed the power and control phase. During this phase, intragroup conflict is experienced as members test each other and the group leader. If this phase is successfully negotiated, the group enters the third phase, termed the working phase. During this phase, the goal of the group is addressed directly. For example, in a task group the members are now able to address the task the group was formed to accomplish.

There are four developmental phases for all groups: the preaffiliation phase, the power and control phase, the working phase, and the termination phase.

The final phase is the termination phase. Group members integrate what they have learned about themselves and the behavioral changes they have made so that they can use these skills in the future. The success of the group is determined to some extent by the skill of the group leader or co-leaders whose interventions must be appropriate to the group's development. For example, the question "What is our purpose?" in the first phase is likely to be an attempt to set boundaries and orient group members. Therefore, a direct, factual answer is most appropriate. The same question asked during the next stage of group development is likely to represent a testing behavior and is best answered by reflecting the question back to the group as a whole.

Group theorist Irvin D. Yalom identified 11 operative factors that influence the therapeutic efficacy of groups.

Group theorist Irvin D. Yalom has identified 11 operative factors that appear to account for the therapeutic efficacy of groups: the imparting of information, the instillation of hope, universality, altruism, corrective recapitulation of the primary family group, development of socializing techniques, imitative behavior, interpersonal learning, existential factors, catharsis, and group cohesion (Yalom & Leszcz, 2005).

Milieu Therapy

Milieu therapy is the use of the environment as a therapeutic tool.

Milieu therapy is the use of the environment as a therapeutic tool. The basis of milieu therapy is the belief that all human beings are affected by their physical, social, and emotional climate. Therefore, the physical, social, and emotional climate may be structured to help those who have a mental illness. For example, research has documented that clients who are acutely ill respond best to a structured, consistent, and non-stimulating environment. In contrast, individuals with a mental illness who are well enough to live in the community often benefit from treatment environments they have actively helped to create and maintain (Taylor, 1994). Therapeutic treatment settings have the following characteristics:

- The client's physical needs are met.
- The client is respected as an individual with rights, needs, and opinions and is encouraged to express them.
- Decision-making authority is clearly defined and distributed appropriately among clients and staff.
- The client is protected from injury from self and others, but only those restrictions necessary to afford such protection are imposed.
- The client is afforded increasing opportunities for freedom of choice, commensurate with his or her ability to make decisions.
- The staff remains essentially constant.
- The environment provides a testing ground for the establishment of new patterns of behavior.

- Emphasis is placed on social interaction between and among clients and staff, and the environment's physical structure and appearance facilitate this interaction.
- Programming is structured but flexible.

The **therapeutic community** is a type of milieu therapy that strives to involve clients in their therapy, restore their self-confidence by providing many opportunities for decision making, increase their self-awareness, and focus their attention and concern away from the self and toward the needs of others. This treatment modality has been most successful with groups of clients who are in contact with reality (Taylor, 1994).

Crisis Intervention

A **crisis** is a "state of disequilibrium resulting from the interaction of an event with the individual's or family's coping mechanisms, which are inadequate to meet the demands of the situation, combined with the individual's or family's perception of the meaning of the event" (Taylor, 1994, p. 456). Thus, not every untoward event precipitates a crisis state in all individuals and families. Crisis intervention is of great interest to mental health professionals, because it provides a specific opportunity to prevent mental illness and to promote mental health. Research has documented that there are three potential outcomes to a crisis state: (1) the individual or family may re-integrate at a lower or less healthy level of functioning than the one before the crisis; (2) the individual or family may re-integrate at the same level of functioning as previously; or (3) the individual or family may re-integrate at a higher, healthier level of functioning than the level before the crisis experience. This last potential outcome promotes mental health and is most likely to be achieved with skilled intervention.

There are two types of crises, developmental and situational. The events that precipitate **developmental crises** are predictable and occur in conjunction with normal developmental transitions with which the individual and family are not prepared to cope. For example, the demands placed on a young couple by the birth of their first child may precipitate a crisis state if their idea of parenthood was fashioned by romantic notions of baby powder and teething biscuits. Developmental crises may be averted by **anticipatory guidance**, an educative process in which individuals and families are prepared for the normal life changes expected at each stage of development and are told about successful coping strategies. Self-help groups and books are common sources of anticipatory guidance.

In contrast, **situational crises** are precipitated by unpredictable events for which people cannot prepare, such as the sudden death of a child. Whereas the death of one's parent is a normal developmental event, the sudden death of one's child is an untoward event for which no one can be prepared. In such events, parents have no recourse other than general coping strategies, such as their religious faith and family cohesiveness. If these are adequate, a crisis state may be averted. If these or similar strategies do not exist or are insufficient, a crisis state occurs.

The goal of crisis intervention is to assist the individual and family to seek new and useful adaptive mechanisms within the context of the social support system. The steps of crisis intervention are deceptively simple: clients must achieve an accurate perception of the event that precipitated the crisis state, become aware of the human and material resources available to assist them, and learn how to manage their feelings. Even though these three steps seem simple, the crisis intervention counselor often spends hours helping clients tell and retell their experiences to identify the significance of the events and to identify and plan the use of resources. This process often must be repeated several times, but the reward of promoting the mental health of clients more than justifies the amount of time spent and the flexibility required.

Somatic Therapies

Somatic therapies are physiologically based interventions designed to produce behavioral change. Somatic therapies are based on the belief that an inextricable relationship exists between the mind and the body. In other words, the dichotomy between mind and body and between mental and physical illnesses is false. The most commonly used somatic therapies are electroconvulsive therapy (ECT) and pharmacologic therapy. These interventions are discussed in depth in Chapters 5 and 16.

The Therapeutic Relationship

Many consider the therapeutic relationship between nurse and client the hallmark of psychiatric nursing. In 1947, *Nurse-Patient Relationships in Psychiatry* by Helena Willis Render was published. Render was the first to introduce the

> The therapeutic community is a particular type of therapeutic environment that has been very successful for clients who are in contact with reality.

> A crisis results when the individual's or family's coping mechanisms are inadequate to deal with the demands of a particular event, causing a state of disequilibrium.

> There are three potential outcomes to a crisis state and two types of crises, developmental and situational.

> The goal of crisis intervention is to assist the individual and family to seek new and useful adaptive mechanisms within the context of the social support system.

> Somatic therapies are physiologically based interventions designed to produce behavioral change. The most commonly used somatic therapies are ECT and pharmacologic therapy.

> The therapeutic relationship between the nurse and client is a hallmark of psychiatric-mental health nursing.

idea that the relationship the nurse establishes with the client (patient) has a significant therapeutic potential. However, it was the 1952 publication of *Interpersonal Relations in Nursing* by Dr. Hildegard E. Peplau that essentially revolutionized the teaching and practice of psychiatric nursing in the United States. Peplau's text focused on the therapeutic potential of the one-to-one relationship at the same time that psychotropic drugs were starting to be used, enabling clients (patients) to benefit from interpersonally based treatment modalities (Taylor, 1994).

Critical Thinking Question What factors contribute to making the therapeutic relationship between the psychiatric nurse and the client the hallmark of psychiatric nursing?

To be truly helpful to clients, nurses need to understand the difference between professional and social relationships. Social relationships are interactions in which the needs of both persons are of equal importance. In contrast, professional relationships are those in which the needs of the client are paramount. To engage in professional relationships with clients, nurses must have a highly developed degree of self-awareness. Self-awareness means that nurses know those areas in which they are emotionally vulnerable, although they may not have an understanding of why these vulnerabilities exist.

Nurses need to understand the difference between professional and social relationships. A relationship exists between the client and nurse only when they become significant to each other.

All intentional interactions with clients that are helpful are considered therapeutic. However, not all nurse-client interactions constitute a relationship. A relationship exists between the client and the nurse only when they become significant to each other (i.e., the opinion of the other makes a difference in how one views oneself). When this occurs, the potential for corrective emotional experiences exists. If it is achieved, the relationship becomes therapeutic.

There are three phases of the nurse-client relationship: the orientation phase, the working phase, and the termination phase.

Nurses need to be aware that boundaries are critical in maintaining a professional therapeutic relationship. At the beginning of the relationship, an agreement or contract between the nurse and client should be established. This is an excellent opportunity to establish the rules and behaviors or boundaries that are expected between the nurse and client, such as the time and frequency of meetings; reimbursement for services; contact with family members, significant others, and other therapists; and prohibition against socialization.

Phases of the Nurse-Client Relationship

There are three phases of the nurse-client relationship. The initial phase is termed the *orientation phase* or *getting acquainted phase*. During this phase the nurse and client agree on a mutually acceptable contract that establishes the relationship's parameters. The goals of this phase are to develop trust and to establish the nurse as a significant other to the client. Although consistency and acceptance are desirable during all phases of the relationship, these behaviors are essential during the orientation phase. The client learns to trust the nurse only if the nurse is able to convey acceptance of the client (as a parent would of a child) and exhibit consistent behavior. Interestingly, once the client begins to trust the nurse, he or she may engage in behaviors designed to test the nurse's sincerity. During this stage, clients commonly arrive late for an appointment. Although the nurse should not condone all the client's behaviors, it is important to consistently convey acceptance of the client as a valued, worthwhile person.

Once trust has been achieved, the second phase of the relationship ensues. This phase is termed the *maintenance* or *working phase*. The goal of this phase is to identify and address the client's problems. Therefore, this phase is characterized by the highly individualized nature of the problems being addressed. During this phase the nurse assumes one or more of the roles identified by Peplau—socializing agent, counselor, or teacher—as the nurse and client tackle the issues facing the client.

The final phase of the relationship is the *concluding* or *termination phase*. The goal of this phase for both the client and nurse is to integrate helpful experiences so that what has been learned may be used in future relationships. Paradoxically, the more successful the relationship, the more emotionally painful is the termination. As a result, both the nurse and client are tempted to deny the inevitable and pretend that their parting is only temporary. They may use phrases such as "Keep in touch," "I'm sure we'll run into each other," and "See you later." These strategies are comforting in the short term but do not help either in the long run.

The therapeutic relationship remains the most useful tool available to nurses who work with a mentally ill client. However, the effectiveness of the relationship depends on the nurse's self-awareness.

Summary

Historically, mentally ill persons have been poorly treated by society, suffering abandonment, beatings, starvation, and imprisonment. More humane models of treatment were short-lived until the recent advent of therapeutic models of care and the availability of reliable psychopharmaceuticals. Because of the current scope and complexity of the burgeoning knowledge about the causes and treatment of mental illness, it is necessary for the multidisciplinary treatment team to work closely together to achieve the goals of preventing mental illness and effectively treating those who are ill.

The major conceptual models are the psychoanalytic, interpersonal, behavioral, cognitive, developmental, and neurobiologic models. These models of care are supplemented by the conceptual nursing models of Peplau, Orlando, King, Orem, and Riehl-Sisca. The treatment modalities commonly utilized include individual, family, group, milieu, and somatic therapies, with consideration of the need for crisis intervention. Establishing a professional therapeutic relationship is critical. The therapeutic nurse-client relationship is the hallmark of psychiatric nursing.

Annotated References

Marriner-Tomey, A. (1998). *Nursing theorists and their work.* St. Louis, MO: Mosby-Yearbook.

This text presents a discussion of the theories of all major nurse theorists. A lengthy reference list for each theorist is included.

Peplau, H. (1952). *Interpersonal relations in nursing.* New York: G. P. Putnam.

This classic psychiatric nursing textbook provides the basic concepts to guide professional nurses in establishing mature therapeutic relationships with clients (patients) with all types of conditions and in all settings.

Stuart, G. W., Laraia, M. T., & Sundeen, S. J. (1998). *Stuart & Sundeen's principles & practice of psychiatric nursing.* St. Louis, MO: Mosby-Yearbook.

This comprehensive textbook on psychiatric nursing is useful for the practicing nurse as well as for the beginning student.

Taylor, C. M. (1994). *Essentials of psychiatric nursing.* St. Louis: Mosby-Yearbook.

This classic text was designed for the beginning student. It includes many approaches to dealing with problem situations.

Wasserbauer, L. I., & Brodie, B. (1992). Early precursors of psychiatric nursing, 1838–1907. *Nursing Connections, 5,* 19–25.

This article provides an excellent description of the conditions and events contributing to the development of contemporary psychiatric nursing.

Yalom, I. D., & Leszcz, M. (2005). *The theory and practice of group psychotherapy.* New York: Basic Books.

This standard text about group psychotherapy covers all aspects of group psychotherapy with helpful hints for addressing difficult situations.

Additional Resources

Beers, C. (1923). *A mind that found itself.* New York: Doubleday.

This is Beers's autobiographical account of his mental illness, hospitalizations, treatment, and recovery.

Carter, E., Peplau, H. E., & Sills, G. M. (1997). The ins and outs of psychiatric-mental health nursing and the American Nurses Association. *Journal of the American Psychiatric Nurses Association, 3,* 10–16.

This article describes the profound influence of the American Nurses Association on the development of psychiatric-mental health nursing.

Joint Commission on Mental Illness. (1961). *Action for mental health.* New York: Basic Books.

This is the final report of the commission's recommendation for the development of more effective mental health services for the nation.

King, I. (1971). *Toward a theory for nursing: General concepts of human behavior.* New York: John Wiley.

In this book, King's first publication, she proposes a theory for nursing practice based on systems theory.

Olson, T. (1996). Fundamental and special: The dilemma of psychiatric-mental health nursing. *Archives of Psychiatric Nursing, 10,* 3–10.

This article explores the tension between defining psychiatric-mental health nursing as fundamental to the discipline yet also special. The formative works of Hildegard Peplau, Dorothy Mereness, and Claire Fagin are cited.

Orem, D. (2001). *Nursing: Concepts of practice.* St. Louis: Mosby-Yearbook.

First published in 1980, Orem's basic book explains her self-care deficit nursing theory.

Orlando, I. J. (1961). *The dynamic nurse-client relationship: Function, process, and principles of professional nursing practices.* New York: Putnam.

This book, Orlando's first publication, explores the nurse-client relationship.

Pickens, J. (1998). Formal and informal care of people with psychiatric disorders: Historical perspectives and current trends. *Journal of Psychosocial Nursing and Mental Health Services, 36*, 37–43.

This article describes the historical context and current trends in the care of people with psychiatric disorders.

Smoyak, S. (1993). American psychiatric nursing. *AAOHN Journal, 41*, 316–322.

This article provides a broad view of the work of psychiatric nurses in the United States during the past century.

Smoyak, S. A., & Rouslin, S. (1982). *A collection of classics in psychiatric nursing literature.* Thorofare, NJ: Charles B. Stock.

This book is a compilation of 36 articles written by leaders in psychiatric nursing prior to 1963. It provides a unique perspective on the "roots" of the specialty.

Internet Resources

http://nursing.jbpub.com/psychiatric

Visit http://nursing.jbpub.com/psychiatric for interactive exercises, NCLEX review questions, WebLinks, and more.

CHAPTER

2

Issues and Trends in Psychiatric-Mental Health Nursing

Karen A. Ballard

LEARNING OBJECTIVES

After reading this chapter, you will be able to:

- Discuss the applicability of standards of practice to psychiatric-mental health nursing.
- Explain the differences in primary, secondary, and tertiary prevention in the field of mental health.
- Describe the application of the nursing process to psychiatric-mental health nursing.
- Defend the need for mental health parity in health care.
- Contrast the differences and similarities in the practice of psychiatric-mental health registered nurses and psychiatric-mental health advanced practice registered nurses.

KEY TERMS

Advanced practice registered nurse (APRN)
Behavioral health
Case management
Diagnostic and Statistical Manual of Mental Disorders,* 4th ed., text revision *(DSM-IV-TR)
Evidence-based practice (EBP)
Managed care
Mental disorder or illness
Mental health
Mental health parity
Neurosis
Nurse practice acts
Nursing diagnosis
Nursing documentation
Nursing process
Outcomes of care
Primary mental health care
Primary, secondary, and tertiary prevention
Psychosis
Standards of practice
Standards of professional performance
Third-party reimbursement

http://nursing.jbpub.com/psychiatric

Visit http://nursing.jbpub.com/psychiatric for interactive exercises, NCLEX review questions, WebLinks, and more.

Overview

Psychiatric-mental health nursing is an integral part of the continuum of nursing practice. The American Nurses Association (ANA) describes psychiatric-mental health nursing as "a specialized area of nursing practice committed to promoting mental health through the assessment, diagnosis, and treatment of human responses to mental health problems and psychiatric disorders" (ANA, 2007, p. 1). As a core mental health profession, psychiatric-mental health nursing "employs a purposeful use of self as its art and a wide range of nursing, psychosocial, and neurobiological theories and research evidence as its science" (ANA, 2007, p. 1). The practice of psychiatric-mental health registered nurses includes the provision of "comprehensive, patient-centered mental health and psychiatric care and treatment and outcome evaluation in a variety of settings across the entire continuum of care" (ANA, 2007, p. 14).

What physically affects the body often has a mental component, and many mental disorders may manifest physically. It is important, always, to see the individual from a holistic perspective.

Mental Health Definitions

Karl Menninger described the state of **mental health** as "the adjustment of human beings to each other and to the world around them with a maximum of effectiveness and happiness" (1945, p. 1). Others see mental health as the individual's ability to be, to act, to grow, to master, and to become whatever the person wants to be. The ANA views mental health as "emotional and psychological wellness; the capacity to interact with others, deal with ordinary stress, and perceive one's surroundings realistically" (ANA, 2007, p. 67).

The ANA defines a **mental disorder or illness** as "a disturbance in thoughts or mood that causes maladaptive behavior, inability to cope with normal stresses, and/or impaired functioning. Etiology may include genetic, physical, chemical, biologic, psychological, or sociocultural factors" (ANA, 2007, p. 67). Mental illnesses have been traditionally categorized as neuroses or psychoses. A **neurosis** is a mental disorder usually characterized by anxiety and other uncomfortable and distressing symptoms for the individual while reality testing remains intact. A **psychosis** is a mental disorder in which the individual experiences gross impairment of reality testing, severe personality disintegration, and impairment in meeting the ordinary demands of everyday life.

A mental disorder or illness is a disturbance in thoughts or mood that causes maladaptive behavior, inability to cope with normal stresses, and impaired functioning.

Classification of mental disorders should not be seen as classification of people, but of the disorders that can affect people.

Concerned about the continued practice in health care of differentiating between mental and physical disorders, the American Psychiatric Association (APA) offers the following definition of a mental disorder:

> a clinically significant behavioral or psychological syndrome or pattern that occurs in an individual and that is associated with present distress (e.g., a painful symptom) or disability (i.e., impairment in one or more important areas of functioning) or with a significantly increased risk of suffering, death, pain, disability or an important loss of freedom. . . . It must currently be considered a manifestation of a behavioral, psychological, or biological dysfunction in the individual. (2000, p. xxxi)

The APA stresses that the classification of mental disorders should not be seen as a classification of people, but of the disorders that people manifest. Individuals should never be referred to as "the manic-depressive," "the alcoholic," or "the schizophrenic," but as "the client or individual with schizophrenia, manic-depressive episodes, or alcohol dependence." It is equally incorrect to view individuals as "the cardiac" or "the gallbladder." Such labeling reduces the person to a condition or disease and ignores his or her individuality and humanity.

In this era of managed care, the term **behavioral health** is increasingly being used instead of psychiatric or mental health care. Behavioral health is intended to encompass treatment for mental health disorders and substance abuse as well as issues addressed by employee assistance programs (EAPs). Some mental health practitioners are concerned that it may not be in the client's best interest nor facilitate obtaining appropriate mental health services to use such an imprecise term to describe the specialty. A client in commenting on the term "behavioral health" said that "To me, it implies if I would just change my behaviors, I wouldn't have a mental illness," and a nurse stated "Call it what it is. We have cardiac care units, not happy heart units" (Donohue, 2006).

Critical Thinking Question Describe how you think a person would feel and/or react to being labeled as "the schizophrenic," "the case with meningitis," "the manic nursing student," or the "alcoholic mother." How does such labeling potentially impact upon an individual's ability to function?

Nurse Practice Acts

Nurse practice acts provide a general description of what constitutes the legally protected scopes of practice of the RN, the LPN, and, in some states, different categories of APRN.

Psychiatric-mental health nurses are directed in both general and specialty practice by individual state **nurse practice acts** that establish the authority for professional nursing practice and the rules and regulations for each state. Most state nurse practice acts provide a general description of what constitutes the legally protected scope of practice in the state for registered professional nurses (RNs) and licensed practical nurses (LPNs). RNs are independent practitioners of nursing, whereas LPNs are dependent practitioners who deliver nursing care under the direction or supervision of a registered professional nurse, physician, or other legally authorized healthcare practitioner. Some states also describe the scope of practice of **advanced practice registered nurses (APRNs)** or advanced practice nurses (APNs) such as nurse practitioners (NPs), clinical nurse specialists (CNSs), certified nurse midwives (CNMs), and certified registered nurse anesthetists (CRNAs). The title APRN was suggested by the National Council of State Boards of Nursing as an umbrella classification (not a state title) to clarify the nomenclature in the regulation of advanced practice.

All nurses are responsible for knowing the statutes, rules, and regulations for nursing practice in the states in which they are licensed to practice. In specialties such as psychiatric-mental health nursing, nurses are responsible for acquiring and maintaining competency through appropriate education, knowledge, training, and experience.

Scope and Standards of Practice

Nurses receive direction for both general and specialty practice from such documents as the ANA's *Nursing's Social Policy Statement*, *Code of Ethics for Nurses*, *Nursing: Scope and Standards of Practice*, and various statements and standards related to psychiatric-mental health nursing, child and adolescent psychiatric nursing, psychiatric consultation liaison nursing, addictions nursing, and intellectual and developmental disabilities nursing. The phenomena of concern specific to psychiatric-mental health nursing (ANA, 2007, pp. 15–16) include actual or potential mental health problems pertaining to the following:

- The promotion of optimal health and well-being and the prevention of mental illness
- Impaired ability to function related to psychiatric, emotional, and physiological distress
- Alterations in thinking, perceiving, and communicating due to psychiatric disorders or mental health problems
- Behaviors and mental states that indicate potential danger to self or others
- Emotional stress related to illness, pain, disability, and loss
- Symptom management, side effects, and toxicities associated with self-administered drugs, psychopharmacological intervention, and other treatment modalities
- Barriers to treatment efficacy and recovery posed by alcohol and substance abuse and dependence
- Self-concept and body image changes, developmental issues, life process changes, and end of life issues
- Physical symptoms that occur along with altered physiological status
- Psychological symptoms that occur along with altered physiological status
- Interpersonal, organizational, sociocultural, spiritual, or environmental circumstances and events that affect the mental and emotional well-being of the individual, family, or community
- Elements of recovery including the ability to maintain housing, employment, and social support that help individuals re-engage in the seeking of meaningful lives

Critical Thinking Question How are the psychiatric-mental health phenomena of concern manifested by clients in an in-patient psychiatric unit?

The ANA also states that standards are authoritative statements describing the responsibilities for which nurses are accountable, reflect the values and priorities of the profession, provide direction for professional nursing practice, provide a framework for the evaluation of nursing practice, define the profession's accountability to the public, and identify the client outcomes for which nurses are responsible (ANA, 2003). ANA's *Psychiatric-Mental Health Nursing: Scope and Standards of Practice* (2007) was collaboratively written by representatives of the American Nurses Association, American Psychiatric Nurses Association (APNA), and the International Society of Psychiatric-Mental Health Nurses (ISPN) and can be found in Appendix I.

Based on the generic *Nursing: Scope and Standards of Practice*, the specialty-specific *Psychiatric-Mental Health Nursing: Scope and Standards of Practice* is divided into **standards of practice** and **standards of professional performance**. The standards

Advanced practice registered nurse (APRN) is an umbrella classification used to describe the four nurse specialist categories:
- Certified registered nurse anesthetist (CRNA)
- Certified nurse midwife (CNM)
- Nurse practitioner (NP)
- Clinical nurse specialist (CNS)

The phenomena of concern specific to psychiatric-mental health nursing include actual or potential health problems related to mental disorders and conditions.

Standards are authoritative statements reflecting the values and priorities of the profession. They provide direction and a framework for practice while addressing client outcomes and the nurse's accountability.

The *Psychiatric-Mental Health Nursing: Scope and Standards of Practice* includes standards of practice and standards of professional performance. Standards of practice address the care that the mental health client receives and are based on the nursing process. Standards of professional performance address the nurse's behavior in the professional role of a psychiatric-mental health nurse.

of practice address the care that the client receives from the psychiatric-mental health registered nurse and are based on the **nursing process**. These standards cover assessment, diagnosis, outcome identification, planning, implementation (coordination of care, health teaching and promotion, milieu therapy, and pharmacological, biological, and complementary interventions), and evaluation. Additional standards of practice for APRNs include prescriptive authority and treatment, psychotherapy, and consultation. The standards of professional performance address the psychiatric-mental health registered nurse's professional functioning. These standards include quality of practice, education, evaluation, collegiality, collaboration, ethics, research, resource utilization, and leadership (ANA, 2007, p. vi).

In addition to standards, the ANA provides measurement criteria for each of the standards, which should be reviewed by all nurses interested in the specialty. For example, under the Diagnosis Standard, the psychiatric-mental health registered nurse "derives the diagnoses or problems from the assessment data," and under the Quality of Practice Standard, the psychiatric-mental health registered nurse "incorporates new knowledge to initiate changes in nursing practice if desired outcomes are not achieved" (ANA, 2007, pp. 29, 45). These standards and accompanying measurement criteria apply to the practice of psychiatric-mental health registered nurses in all settings and with all clients—individuals, families, groups, communities, or populations.

Psychiatric-Mental Health Registered Nurses

According to the Society for Education and Research in Psychiatric-Mental Health Nursing (SERPN, 1996), a division of ISPN, psychiatric-mental health nurses are registered nurses who are educationally prepared in nursing, are licensed to practice in their individual states, and are qualified to practice in the psychiatric-mental health nursing specialty at one of two levels: basic or advanced. These levels of practice are differentiated by the nurse's level of educational preparation, the complexity of the nurse's practice, and the performance of certain specialty nursing functions.

The psychiatric-mental health registered nurse, whose practice skills are more generalized, provides interventions such as health promotion and health maintenance, intake screening and evaluation, case management, provision of milieu therapy, promotion of self-care activities, assisting with psychobiological interventions, health teaching, counseling, crisis care, and psychiatric rehabilitation. These nurses combine unique skills to address the mental health client's physical, mental, emotional, social, and spiritual needs and may work in many diverse settings such as hospitals, ambulatory clinics, walk-in clinics, residential settings, halfway houses, occupational health offices, EAPs, and schools (ANA, 2007). To achieve professional certification, in addition to meeting the educational requirements, the psychiatric-mental health registered nurse must have specific direct care experience, have spent a specified time in the practice of psychiatric-mental health nursing, have participated in clinical supervision, have participated in continuing education, and have successfully completed a national certifying examination administered by the American Nurses Credentialing Center (ANCC).

Psychiatric-Mental Health Advanced Practice Nurses

APRNs in this specialty hold either master's or doctoral degrees in a psychiatric-mental health nursing specialty. Early in the development of the specialty, some psychiatric nurses received advanced education in allied mental health disciplines. There are four generally accepted categories of advanced practice registered nurses in the nursing profession: CRNAs, CNMs, NPs, and CNSs. In the psychiatric-mental health nursing specialty, advanced practice registered nurses are either NPs or CNSs. Some states require APRNs or APNs to have a second license whereas others issue certificates authorizing such advanced practice, and other states do not even address advanced practice as a separate category. States may recognize the practice of all four advanced practice categories or selectively recognize particular ones. This lack of uniformity has confused both nurses and the public.

Each state's nurse practice act grants the legal authority for the full scope of nursing practice. There has been pressure for separate recognition of advanced practice both to clarify the authority for practice and to ensure third-party reimbursement for the nurse's practice. Nurse practice acts should cover the full spectrum of nursing practice. In reality, a hodgepodge of different authorizations (second licensure, certification, guidelines) exists. There are amendments to the basic nurse practice acts, separate language for specific categories of APRNs (CRNAs, CNMs, NPs, CNSs), and, in some cases, separate practice acts, most notably for CNMs, whose practice is conceptualized as separate from nursing. Almost all the states have laws, regulations, or guidelines for advanced practice.

In the past, the movement for separate recognition of the different categories of APRNs was driven by the fears and beliefs that advanced nursing practice without separate authorization was illegal, the desire for prescriptive privileges, and the need for nurses in private practice to qualify for direct third-party reimbursement from traditional indemnity insurance plans, federal and state reimbursement plans, and managed care plans. Even the titles of APRN and APN were created to uniformly recognize and refer to these nurses because in some states and insurance programs the various specialty titles were unclear and often were used to refer to more than one category of practitioner, especially NP and CNS.

Nurses have a long history of collaborating with physicians in assessing, planning, implementing, and evaluating care. The difficulty is that too often organized medicine attempts to legislate control by physicians over the nurse specialist's practice by requiring direct supervision. This can limit the nurse's independent practice. In fact, the federal Drug Enforcement Agency (DEA) does not issue separate DEA numbers for prescribing controlled substances unless the APRN has independent (unencumbered) authorization to practice.

APRNs in psychiatric-mental health nursing may become certified specialists through the ANCC. There are specific requirements for educational preparation for a master's degree, including a minimum number of client contact hours, a number of hours of supervision from a certified specialist in psychiatric-mental health nursing, and the successful completion of a certifying examination.

Psychiatric-mental health registered nurses work in many different settings, including hospital in-patient units, ambulatory settings, clinics, long-term care institutions, residential settings, nursing homes, home care agencies, volunteer agencies or programs usually associated with specific charities or church groups, shelters, respite care, day care programs, schools, workplaces and EAPs, correctional facilities, and for the APRN individual private or group practices with other nurse specialists or other mental health practitioners.

Depending upon the individual nurse's level of practice, education, and special training, psychiatric-mental health registered nurses can utilize counseling; group therapy; family therapy; marital and couples therapy; milieu therapy; art, music, dance, and other expressive therapies; and alternative and complementary therapies such as imagery, therapeutic touch, and journaling. Psychiatric-mental health APRNs practice psychotherapy and psychoanalysis; may prescribe psychotropic medications and supervise medication regimens; act as consultants, educators, and clinical liaisons; and provide direct clinical supervision for psychiatric nurses and other APRNs. The areas of subspecialization in psychiatric-mental health nursing include adult, child, and adolescent; geriatric; addictions; chronically mentally ill; consultation-liaison; forensic; marital and family; home care; and case management.

Critical Thinking Question What are some specific differences in the scopes of practice of a psychiatric-mental health registered nurse and a psychiatric-mental health advanced practice registered nurse?

Third-Party Reimbursement

Third-party reimbursement for the services of APRNs in psychiatric-mental health care has been a longstanding problem. Such services may be reimbursed through traditional indemnity insurance plans; self-insured plans constructed by employers and other groups; managed care plans and state and federal government plans such as Medicare, Medicaid, and the Civilian Health and Medical Program of the Uniformed Services (CHAMPUS); and the Federal Employees Health Benefits Program (FEHBP). CNMs, NPs, and CNSs have been directly reimbursed by CHAMPUS since 1982, CRNAs since 1987. FEHBP has reimbursed NPs and CNMs since 1990, when the Office of Technology Assessment analyzed the fiscal implications of the initiative and found it cost-effective and revenue neutral. Often, the problem with obtaining payment for such services was that both mental health care as a covered service and the practitioner had to be included in the plan. For many years, most plans resisted adding mental health services and nurses as providers of those services, so psychiatric-mental health APRNs in private practice often became frustrated and discouraged.

From the 1970s through the 1990s, the ANA on a federal level, the state nurses associations on a local level, and the psychiatric nursing specialty organizations advocated in the states and in Congress the inclusion of the services of psychiatric mental health APRNs in all appropriate plans where mental health services were covered. Examples of some of these federal initiatives include four demonstration projects establishing community nursing organizations providing community-based nursing and ambulatory care services under the direction of RNs (1992), CNMs directly receiving reimbursement at 65% of the physician's prevailing fee (1987), NPs in all geographic areas and CNSs in rural areas under a physician's supervision being reimbursed for certifying and recertifying residents for skilled nursing care (1991), the Rural Nursing Incentive Act providing direct reimbursement at 75–85% of the physician's fee to NPs and CNSs who serve rural areas (1990), and NPs and CNMs providing covered services in federally qualified health centers (1992).

A significant reimbursement victory involved the legislation of Medicare reimbursement for CNSs and NPs in all specialty areas, regardless of geographic setting, in the 1997 federal Balanced Budget Act. Prior to this law's passage, Medicare paid only for NPs and CNSs in rural areas and for specific, limited NPs' services in nursing homes. As of January 1, 1998, if a service is covered under Medicare Part B and can be provided within the legal scope of practice of an NP or CNS, that service is reimbursable directly to the nurse, or, if the nurse agrees, the facility, physician, or group that employs the NP or CNS can submit the claim. However, payment is not made to both a facility and a nurse. The payment amount is either 85% of the physician's payment or 80% of the actual charge, whichever is smaller. The law also contains a definition of CNS for the sole purpose of implementing the law. It states that a CNS is a registered nurse who is licensed to practice in the state in which the nursing services are performed; these nurses are required to have a master's degree and certification in a defined clinical area of nursing. For NPs and CNSs to receive reimbursement, they have to be approved by the local fiscal intermediary for the Centers for Medicare and Medicaid Services (CMS) and must be granted Medicare provider numbers for Medicare Part B services.

The nursing process is a systematic and interactive problem-solving approach that includes individualized client assessment, planning, implementation, intervention, and evaluation.

Over the past decade, there has been growing debate concerning whether advanced-level practitioners in psychiatric-mental health nursing should be a CNS or an NP. In an interesting article in 1995, Lego and Caverly held opposing views. Lego argued that primary care and specialization are two separate entities. The educational preparation of NPs is varied, although CNSs have always been prepared at the master's level. Traditionally, the CNS practice model has been that of an advanced-level autonomous practitioner with no requirements for collaborative practice or supervision from medicine, whereas NPs work with medical supervision or collaboration. National certification from the ANA has been the method of credentialing the CNS. Finally, Lego suggests that two tracks should exist in graduate nursing programs, one for the NP in psychiatry and one for the psychiatric-mental health CNS. Caverly argues that the APRN category represents a significant public policy contribution and could result in an unprecedented unity within the profession. In addition, she urges the profession to focus on securing reimbursement, revising regressive nurse practice acts, explaining to the public the roles of psychiatric-mental health nurses, and simplifying for the public the titles used to describe the APRN (Lego & Caverly, 1995).

The Nursing Process and Classification Systems

The nursing process encompasses "all significant actions taken by registered nurses and forms the foundation of the nurse's decision-making" (ANA, 2003, p. 4). When applied to psychiatric-mental health nursing, the nursing process involves the following five areas.

Assessment

During the assessment interview and in subsequent interactions, the psychiatric-mental health registered nurse collects both subjective and objective data, including observations made during the interview. These may include: main complaint or problem; general physical, mental, and emotional health status; personal and family history; support systems in the family, social group, or community; activities of daily living (ADLs); health habits and beliefs; substance use or abuse; use of prescription medications; interpersonal relationships; risk of injury to self and others; coping patterns; spiritual beliefs and values; client's interest in changing behaviors; and any other factors that may influence the client's ability to function and respond to treatment.

Diagnosis

The psychiatric-mental health registered nurse uses the assessment data to identify the actual or potential problems. Depending on the nurse's level of practice and skill, the data are organized into an acceptable framework using one or more of the common classification systems. These systems are the North American Nursing Diagnosis Association's (NANDA) *Nursing Diagnosis Classification*, which includes appropriate psychiatric nursing diagnoses and the fourth edition, text revision, of the ***Diagnostic and Statistical Manual of Mental Disorders (DSM-IV-TR)***; and any future editions of these classifications.

Planning

The psychiatric-mental health registered nurse develops an individualized plan of care, clearly identifying the interventions that should be used to meet the expected outcomes. Each diagnosis should have at least one corresponding goal. Goals should be measurable, realistic, understandable, and prioritized. A time frame should be established for both short- and long-term goals. This plan of care is developed in collaboration with the client, family, and other clinicians. It provides continuity of care, reflects current psychiatric nursing practice, and can include both short- and long-term goals.

Intervention

Nursing activities or actions are identified and implemented to help the client meet the planned goals. The implementation interventions may include counseling, milieu therapy, self-care activities, medications, health education, health promotion, psychotherapy, and case management.

Evaluation

The psychiatric-mental health registered nurse determines whether the goals and expected outcomes were met and whether the interventions were effective. If they were not, the nurse should reconsider all steps of the process and consider changes in the plan and interventions.

Utilization of NANDA and *DSM-IV-TR* Classification Systems

A nursing diagnosis states the actual or potential nursing problems based on the nurse's critical appraisal and analysis of the assessment data, including responses and stressors, as they apply to individuals, families, and groups.

A **nursing diagnosis** states the actual or potential nursing problems based on the nurse's critical appraisal and analysis of the assessment data, including responses and stressors, as they apply to individuals, families, and groups (Reighley, 1988). Formulating a correct nursing diagnosis is a critical step in the nursing process. In writing the nursing diagnosis, the psychiatric-mental health registered nurse utilizes the NANDA-I Taxonomy II, identifies the etiology, and describes the specific signs and symptoms particular to the client. Some nursing diagnoses are specific to mental health problems. The taxonomy itself uses a multiaxial structure (see Appendix II). Many resources are available to students and instructors regarding nursing diagnoses and their use in the delivery of nursing care. These should be reviewed and used when constructing nursing care plans for clients with particular psychiatric-mental health problems. It is not within the scope of this book to explore in detail all potential nursing diagnoses in psychiatric-mental health nursing practice.

A variety of practitioners provide mental health services to clients, so the most frequently used diagnostic nomenclature utilized by the multidisciplinary team is the *DSM-IV-TR*. This manual, compiled by the American Psychiatric Association (APA), has its critics. There is concern that the *DSM* is gradually converting many of life's expected stresses and bad habits into mental disorders such as caffeine-induced anxiety disorder, inhalant abuse, telephone scatology, and Internet addiction disorder, and thus using the *DSM* to differentiate between the normal and the truly disordered has become increasingly difficult (Leo, 1997). In addition to the *DSM-IV-TR*, some APRNs in psychiatric mental health nursing may use the ninth edition, clinical modification of the *International Classification of Diseases* (*ICD-9-CM*) to identify and record diagnoses.

There are three levels of preventive intervention: primary, secondary, and tertiary. In the United States, more emphasis is placed on secondary and tertiary prevention.

Primary mental health care is holistic and addresses the needs and strengths of the whole person.

Interventions, Outcomes, and Research

Primary, Secondary, and Tertiary Prevention

There are three levels of preventive intervention: **primary, secondary, and tertiary prevention**. Currently in the United States, more emphasis is placed on secondary and tertiary prevention than on primary prevention. Continued interest by the healthcare professions, consumers, insurance plans, and government in health promotion and disease prevention should provide more support for activities that emphasize primary prevention.

Primary prevention focuses on reducing the incidence of mental disorders or the rates at which new cases develop by identifying the causes of specific mental health disorders and offering early intervention programs. These programs include health promotion and education, growth and development classes, parenting classes, stress management, biofeedback, relaxation techniques, and community or political activities.

Secondary prevention focuses on reducing the prevalence of mental disorders by decreasing the number of existing cases through screening and evaluating clients, identifying health needs and health problems, and providing crisis and emergency intervention, medication treatment, case management, and early treatment when symptoms are identified.

Tertiary prevention focuses on reducing the severity of a mental disorder and its associated disabilities through such activities as rehabilitation programs, educational programs that increase understanding of how to manage the symptoms of the disorder and medications, case management, social skills training, aftercare, vocational counseling, and job training (Klainberg, Holzemer, Leonard, & Arnold, 1998; Krupnick & Wade, 1993; Worley, 1997).

Haber and Billings identify the concept of **primary mental health care** as

> [the] care that is provided to those at risk of or already in need of mental health services . . . involving all of the continuous and comprehensive services necessary for the promotion of optimal mental health, prevention of mental illness and health maintenance, and includes the management (treatment) of and/or referral for mental and general health problems. (1995, p. 155)

This care is holistic and addresses the needs and strengths of the whole person. According to the ANA, primary mental health care from a nursing viewpoint is "a mode of service delivery that is initiated at the first point of contact with the mental health care system." It involves the "continuous and comprehensive mental health services necessary for promotion of optimal mental health, prevention of mental illness, and intervention, health maintenance, and rehabilitation" (ANA, 2007, p. 15). Increasingly, individuals with mental health conditions have been treated with interdisciplinary care. Therapists from the various disciplines of psychiatry; psychology; nursing; social work; art, dance, and music therapy; and more recently philosophical counseling are administering care interchangeably. Ideally, interdisciplinary care should focus on a team approach, with the overlapping strengths and knowledge of the various healthcare professionals matched to the needs of the client, family, group, or community and, as a result of this planned synergy, the **outcomes of care** are enhanced and more comprehensive (ANA, 2007).

Outcomes of Care

The ANA standards clearly state that psychiatric-mental health registered nurses must identify expected outcomes, develop plans of care to attain expected outcomes, and evaluate the client's progress in attaining expected outcomes. This participation is an integral part of psychiatric-mental health nursing practice (ANA, 2007).

There is increasing pressure on the healthcare industry to measure the quality of outcomes of care, including psychiatric-mental health care, through quality assurance, total quality management, and continuous quality improvement. It is often difficult to isolate the particular nursing interventions that produce specific client outcomes. Indicators are qualitative measures used in evaluating and monitoring outcomes; outcomes are measurable changes.

Dramatic shifts in the nursing workforce and concerns among nursing professionals regarding quality of care and client safety resulted in the formation of the National Database of Nursing Quality Indicators (NDNQI) (formerly the Safety and Quality Initiative) in ANA's The National Center for Nursing Quality Indicators (http://nursingworld.org/quality/database.

htm). The initiative is a national program tracking the quality of nursing care. The study addresses three categories of indicators:

- *Structure of care indicators:* Focus on the organization and delivery of nursing care (supply of nursing staff, skill mix, educational levels)
- *Process of care indicators:* Focus on the nature and amount of care provided (assessment, intervention, RN work satisfaction)
- *Outcome indicators:* Focus on the effects of interactions between nursing staff and clients (occurrence of pressure ulcers, falls, IV infiltrations)

Although directed toward acute care, many of the indicators apply to all nursing specialties, including psychiatric nursing, and all clinical settings. Some of the indicators currently being studied include nosocomial infection rates, client injury rate, client satisfaction with nursing care, client satisfaction with pain management, client satisfaction with educational information, client satisfaction with care, maintenance of skin integrity, nurse-staff interactions, staff mix (RN, LPN, nursing assistants), total nursing care hours provided per client day, pediatric pain assessment, and psychiatric, physical, and sexual assaults. The federal government established the Agency for Healthcare Research and Quality (AHRQ) (formerly the Agency for Health Care Policy and Research) to study the effectiveness of health care and produce guidelines to support "best practices" (http://www.ahrq.gov). Some examples of this agency's early work include the management of depression in primary care, acute pain management, the recognition of early Alzheimer's disease and related dementia, and the management of cancer pain; more recently it has established Evidence-Based Practice Centers (EPCs) to produce evidence reports on clinical conditions (http://www.ahrq.gov/clinic/epc/).

Implications for Evidence-Based Practice

Evidence-based practice (EBP) has been defined as "the integration of the best possible research to evidence with clinical expertise and with patient needs" (Malloch & Porter-O'Grady, 2006, p. 1) and "the conscientious, explicit, and judicious use of the best evidence from systematic research to make decisions about the care of individual patients" (Sackett, Rosenberg, Gray, Haynes, & Richardson, 1996, p. 71). In order for evidence-based practice to truly work and to impact upon today's health care and mental health delivery systems, it must arise from the practice setting, include the actual practitioners involved in the delivery of care, and represent the aggregation and integration of applied clinical experiences (Breslin & Lucas, 2003; Malloch & Porter-O'Grady, 2006).

Interest in utilizing evidence-based practice in the delivery of medical, nursing, and health care has increased in the last decade, buoyed by the incredible changes in technology that are available to researchers. Health care as an industry has been slow in utilizing these technologies in the practice setting at the point of care. Also, nurses and other healthcare practitioners can be reluctant to try "something new," and are often distracted from participating in a new approach by the ongoing problems (organizational, staffing, lack of support from peers and/or management) encountered in the practice setting. Some practitioners complain that it is "too much work" or "just not practical" to incorporate evidence-based practice into the clinical setting.

Stuart (2000) has identified levels of evidence that can be incorporated into evidence-based nursing practice (EBNP). In ascending order of the importance and reliability of these levels, they include opinions of reviewers based on their experience and knowledge, opinions promulgated by well-known experts and respected authorities, and results of research studies. Within the research studies, nonrandomized controlled studies provide the weakest evidence, small randomized controlled trials provide stronger evidence, and evidence from large randomized controlled trials and meta-analysis of studies supply the strongest evidence upon which to base practice and interventions (Stuart, 2000; Zauszniewski & Suresky, 2004). However, any evidence only becomes meaningful when it is successfully integrated into nursing practice.

A recent study of three years of published research (2000–2002) in the five most commonly read U.S. psychiatric nursing journals was inconclusive. The authors found that the main research foci were global perspectives, psychiatric nurses as subjects, family caregivers as subjects, clients across the life span, and testing of nursing interventions. Of the studies, 63% involved testing the recipients of mental health care and only 11% actually tested psychiatric nursing interventions

There are three categories of indicators: structure, process, and outcome.

(Zauszniewski & Suresky, 2004). A similar study of 12 leading mental health journals involving 1,076 studies demonstrated that less than 25% evaluated clinical interventions (Shumway & Sentell, 2004). There was little evidence for changes in clinical practice in either analysis. However, evidence-based practice is critically needed in order to provide quality care for mental health clients. Therefore, throughout this book, the reader will see examples of evidence-based practice and how it can influence psychiatric nursing interventions and client care.

More research is required to successfully combine psychodynamic, psychosocial, and psychobiologic interventions with psychiatric-mental health nursing practice.

Research

Nurse researchers need to conduct ongoing research regarding the effectiveness of psychiatric nursing interventions and the various mental health treatment modalities, including conventional therapies and complementary and alternative therapies. Additionally, research is required to successfully combine psychodynamic, psychosocial, and psychobiological interventions with psychiatric-mental health nursing practice. Nurse researchers need to clearly identify and interpret for psychiatric-mental health nurses the research findings that are applicable to clinical practice and have been adequately studied. In addition, nurse researchers need to collaborate with nurse administrators so that there is an organizational culture that supports both doing and implementing nursing research, especially when such research involves nursing interventions.

Psychiatric-mental health nurses are required to document all information, plans, interventions, and outcomes in an understandable and retrievable manner that can be accessed as needed by all members of the healthcare team.

Documentation and Client and Family Education

Documentation

An accurate record of the client's care is required for legal reasons, regulatory agencies, accrediting organizations, institutional requirements, staffing requirements, and, most important, to provide an accurate and comprehensive care plan for the client. Psychiatric-mental health registered nurses are required by state laws and regulations, facility policies, and standards of practice to document all information, plans, interventions, and outcomes in an understandable and retrievable manner that can be accessed as needed by all members of the healthcare team. Health care continues to use multiple methods for documenting care, from traditional paper charts to concept mapping to electronic records.

In the process of recording client care, two types of plans are generally used in psychiatric-mental health settings—nursing plans and multidisciplinary treatment plans. The latter is a record reflecting the care delivered by members of the treatment team and are termed treatment action plans, case management plans, or interdisciplinary care plans depending on the treatment setting (Rowland & Rowland, 1997). Nursing plans of care (e.g., standardized care plans; computerized records; concept mapping; CareMaps; clinical pathways; charting by exception; clinical protocols; critical paths; flow sheets; nursing interventions list; practice guidelines; problem, intervention, and evaluation [PIE] notes) provide documentation of the delivery of nursing care by establishing a record of the nursing assessment, identified problems, nursing diagnoses, short- and long-term goals, suggested and implemented nursing interventions, expected client outcomes, and discharge planning. The increased utilization of concept mapping in clinical practice settings should result in less paperwork, enhance the nurse's critical thinking skills and clinical reasoning, and assist in identifying priorities and determining critical relationships in the clinical data (Schuster, 2000).

Typical charting or documentation rules that generally apply in many settings include writing neatly and legibly, using proper spelling and grammar, using blue or black ink, employing military time, utilizing only institutionally approved abbreviations, and transcribing orders carefully. The nurse should also document complete information about medication administration, document punctually but never chart nursing care or observations ahead of time, clearly identify care that was given by another member of the healthcare team, and never leave blank spaces on charts or forms. Additionally, the nurse must correctly identify late or supplemental entries, correct mistaken entries properly, and avoid sounding tentative. The nurse should never tamper with or modify a record, never criticize the actions of other healthcare team members in the chart, and eliminate personal biases from the written descriptions of the client. Finally, the nurse precisely documents information reported to the physician or other team members and carefully records any client actions that might negatively influence the outcome of care (Frank-Stromberg, Christensen, & Do, 2001; Iyer, 1991a, 1991b).

Examples of types of specific observations, behaviors, and outcomes of care that should be included in **nursing documentation** are (Eggland, 1997; Finkelman, 1997; Menenberg, 1995):

- Behaviors specific to the presenting problems
- New behaviors
- Nutrition and ADLs
- Interactions with other clients, staff, and family
- Family response to and involvement in the treatment plan
- Positive responses to medications
- Side effects (tardive dyskinesia, fluid retention, dystonia, oculogyric crisis)
- Client and family educational needs and responses to teaching
- Comments on mood, affect, anxiety levels, reality testing, orientation, suicidal thoughts, or periods of aggression
- Symptom relief
- Improved ability to function
- Specific expressions of feelings
- Substance abuse
- Failure to comply with treatment plan
- Restraints and seclusion
- Aggression and potential for violence
- Life events

As the electronic health record (EHR) becomes increasingly utilized in mental healthcare settings, nurses need to have the appropriate computer skills and expertise. Regardless of the format of the documentation, the professional nurse retains responsibility for the accurate recording of the client's nursing care. Like all nurses, psychiatric-mental health nurses are ethically and legally responsible for maintaining the confidentiality of the client's record and information. Under the Health Insurance Portability and Accountability Act of 1996 (HIPAA), the federal government established more stringent regulations regarding the security and privacy of health data and new national standards for electronic healthcare transactions. For more information on documentation, see Chapter 3.

Critical Thinking Question When reviewing a client's healthcare record, you discover what appear to be major discrepancies in the observations and information recorded by medicine, nursing, and social work. What would be appropriate actions for you to take in this situation?

Education for Clients and Families

Psychoeducation has proven to reduce relapse rates and support the recovery of persons with mental illnesses. It has been established that the components of an effective client/family psychoeducation program include education, supportive resources during crisis periods, assistance with problem-solving skills, and emotional support (Dixon et al., 2001).

Clients and their families and significant others require basic knowledge of the mental disorder, the treatment plan, medications, and any support services or advocacy groups (e.g., National Alliance on Mental Illness [NAMI]) that might be involved. Such education promotes understanding and adherence to the mental health plan. Positive treatment outcomes are directly related to the client's and family's willingness to be engaged in the treatment process. If the client does not understand the mental health condition, the treatment plan, any medication regimen, and expectations for changes in behavior, the result will be poor outcomes of care. Psychoeducation can benefit clients by establishing a clear understanding of the treatment plan, increasing client motivation, improving compliance with medical and behavioral recommendations, and increasing the client's and family's overall satisfaction with the healthcare experience (O'Donohue & Levensky, 2006).

Case Management, Managed Care, and Mental Health Parity

Case Management

Case management is a method of assigning the coordination of an individual's care, whereas managed care is a method for delivering prepaid healthcare services. *Case management* and *managed care* are not interchangeable terms. According to Bower (1992, p. 3), "The fundamental focus of case management is to integrate, coordinate, and advocate for individuals, families, and groups requiring extensive services. . . . The goal is to achieve planned care outcomes by brokering services across the health care continuum." Case management may be a role, a technology, a process, a service, and a system. Case management is unique in that "it is episode-focused, viewing health issues and responding to the care needs of clients along the illness and/or care continuum often across multiple

Case management is a method of assigning the coordination of a client's care; it may be a role, a technology, a process, a service, and a system. The goals of case management are to:

- Assist the client in gaining access to appropriate resources
- Assist the client in making choices
- Support the client in making personal healthcare choices

settings" (Bower, p. 4). Case management is especially effective when used with selected populations such as frail and chronically disabled clients; clients with long-term, medically complex problems; and clients who are severely compromised by an acute episode of illness or an exacerbation of a chronic condition. The goals of case management are to assist the client in gaining access to appropriate resources and to help the client make personal healthcare and other choices.

Registered nurses typically have the special knowledge and skills that are appropriate to the case management field. Nurses are able to recognize the signs and symptoms of physical illness and mental health disorders, are taught to be good communicators, and understand group and family dynamics and the use and abuse of psychotropic medications. The psychiatric-mental health registered nurse can provide case management to coordinate the client's comprehensive health services and ensure continuity of care. According to Cohen and Cesta,

> By emphasizing care that is patient-centered, the nursing case management approach embraces techniques of business in which the patient is seen as a valuable consumer who has the right to demand the best in health care. . . . Placing the patient at the core of nursing's power base authorizes the profession to reconfirm its commitment to society. (1997, p. 18)

Managed Care

Managed care is both a delivery system and a reimbursement system; it is a healthcare system that aims to combine cost-effectiveness with quality care.

Some managed care buzzwords are alternative delivery system, capitation, case mix, gatekeeper, paneled provider, integrated delivery system, and seamless care.

Mental health parity means that the annual and lifetime limits in health plans for mental health benefits are equal to the plan's medical and surgical benefits.

Managed care is both a delivery system and a reimbursement system; this dual role has created implementation problems. It is probably impossible to concentrate on managing a client's care and addressing health needs while focusing on controlling costs and payments. Ultimately, concerns arise about the type of care being delivered, who is receiving it, under what circumstances, and by which provider. The ANA has questioned whether managed care, with its focus on cost containment and financing arrangements, puts at risk the traditional values of nursing such as patient advocacy, holistic care, and addressing the individual's specific health needs (ANA, 1998).

Managed care has been described as "a health care system that combines cost-effectiveness with quality care" (Klainberg et al., 1998, p. 392). Some examples of managed care entities are health maintenance organizations (HMOs), preferred provider organizations (PPOs), and point of service (POS) plans. Some terms that nurses encounter in managed care include alternate delivery system (services outside of the hospital), capitation (a method of providing a set payment per month per covered member to a provider), case mix (the frequency and intensity of the health needs of a population), gatekeeper (a practitioner who controls access to health care), paneled provider (practitioners who can provide care in a payment system), integrated delivery system (networks of providers joined for purposes of mutual benefit), and seamless care (coordinated care as the client moves along the health services continuum). To be identified as a managed care plan, a plan must comprise certain components: restricted service networks, control of payment for services, benefits designed to maximize services, aggressive care and case management, an active quality improvement program, and data gathering and dissemination of information on the health of the population being served by the plan (Al-Assaf, 1998).

Mental Health Parity

Health insurance plans such as traditional indemnity plans, self-insured plans, government programs, or managed care plans have a history of bias against covering mental health treatment. Recently, with considerable reluctance, these various third-party reimbursement plans have begun to provide mental health coverage, often with considerable annual and lifetime restrictions on the number of visits and total expenditure both annually and for the lifetime of the plan (e.g., a typical plan may pay for just 10 or 20 visits to a mental health practitioner, while a client with diabetics can see a physician as often as necessary). Other restrictions include in-patient versus outpatient care, the type of practitioner covered (psychiatrist, psychologist, registered nurse, social worker, various counselors), the use of psychotropic medication, higher deductibles than for physical conditions, and requirements for detailed treatment plans that may compromise the confidentiality of the record and increase the potential for job discrimination. The requirement for a detailed treatment plan may be viewed by some as quite intrusive, including requests for information on the total plan of care, incidences of trauma, substance abuse, the status of marital and family relationships, sexual dysfunction, sleep patterns, finances, aggressive acts toward self or others, school performance, and potential for contracting human immunodeficiency virus (HIV) (Hymowitz, 1998).

As a result of the federal Mental Health Parity Act (MHPA) of 1996, as of January 1, 1998, employer-sponsored health plans were required to provide coverage for mental health benefits, ensuring that the annual and lifetime limits for the medical and surgical benefits and the mental health benefits are equivalent. Limits could be imposed only if the plan also restricted the medical and surgical benefits for physical conditions; both limits must be the same. If a plan has different limits for different medical and surgical benefits, then an average aggregate limit is calculated for mental health benefits. The law did not require that a plan offer mental health benefits; however, if mental health benefits were offered in a plan, **mental health parity** became mandatory. The parity requirement did not apply to treatment for substance abuse or chemical dependency. There were two technical exemptions to this law. First, the parity requirement applied only to plans covering more than 50 employees. Second, group health plans were exempt from the parity requirement if they could demonstrate that enforcing the parity provisions would result in a cost increase of at least 1%.

For decades, health insurance plans used expense as a rationale for not providing mental health coverage. Many analysts now indicate that parity adds little to total health costs and may even save money, especially if the mental health benefit is provided through a managed care plan. Certain groups that have studied the cost of parity estimate that providing equitable insurance coverage for mental illnesses for an entire year for one employee costs as little as one cup of coffee. Equalizing the annual limit of a typical insurance policy will increase costs approximately $1 per employee under managed care, and removing limits on inpatient stays and outpatient visits will increase costs by less than $7 per enrollee per year. There are few or no cost implications of parity in a managed care setting in states that have already legislated health insurance parity (internal document, Alliance for the Mentally Ill of New York, 1998). Many employers responded to the original legislation by moving the mental health benefit into such programs as Value Behavioral Health, U.S. Behavioral Health, and Empire Choice (Melek, 1997). Although the MHPA worked to end discrimination against individuals who suffer from mental disorders and seek coverage under employer-sponsored insurance plans, the act had a sunset provision, with its supporters having to depend upon yearly extensions as more all-inclusive legislation makes its way through Congress.

In 2001, Senators Domenici and Wellstone and Representative Roukema introduced broader parity legislation that quickly was passed by both the Senate and the House of Representatives as an amendment to a Departments of Labor and Health and Human Services appropriations bill. Unfortunately, it was dropped by the Joint Conference Committee and returned to the original committees. In 2003, after the death of mental health advocate, Senator Paul Wellstone, Senators Domenici and Kennedy and Representatives Kennedy and Ramstad introduced the Senator Paul Wellstone Mental Health Equitable Treatment Act. In 2006, even with strong bipartisan support and a promise from President Bush to support mental health parity, action on this bill languished (http://www.nmha.org/go/parity and http://www.wellstone.org/network/index.aspx). In February 2007, it was once again introduced as the Mental Health Parity Act of 2007.

Critical Thinking Question How does inadequate access to mental health services impact upon the health of the individual, family, and community?

Home Care and Community Practice Settings

In psychiatric home care, many individuals have persistent mental disorders, are elderly, have significant medical conditions, and are homebound.

Offering psychiatric-mental health services to clients in their homes is a cost-effective method of providing services to this population. Psychiatric clients receiving services through home care agencies or similar outreach programs often have complex physical health problems in addition to the presenting mental disorder (often depression, anxiety, or difficulty coping with life situations). Most psychiatric home care is short-term care. Clients may be receiving multiple home healthcare services, have family caregivers on site, or have no readily available support systems. More information is needed on the specific psychiatric-mental health nursing interventions that are helpful to these clients and their caregivers (Horton-Deutsch, Farran, Loukissa, & Fogg, 1997). Increasing numbers of elderly clients, individuals with persistent mental disorders, clients with significant medical illnesses in addition to the mental disorder, and clients who are essentially homebound are receiving psychiatric home care.

According to Peplau (1995), psychiatric-mental health nurses are uniquely able to provide the multiple appropriate services needed by clients in a home setting, are able to integrate assessment of both physical and psychiatric needs into a treatment plan, can provide health education, can coordinate care, can supervise home health aides, and can integrate the family and significant others into a support system for the client. Peplau emphasized that the mental illness of the individual is a family problem. The family may thus fear that the mental health practitioner blames them for the family member's illness. This fear then negatively impacts what should be a positive collaboration between the practitioner and family (Peplau).

In the 1970s, under the direction of the National Institute of Mental Health, the community support system concept evolved, encouraging the development of formal and informal supportive networks of caring and responsible people to meet the needs of the mentally ill. According to Pickens (1998), currently there is a critical need for psychiatric nurses to help establish and join in a true collaboration and partnership with clients, family, and community groups. Pickens identifies attributes, skills, and knowledge nurses need, including an awareness of one's preconceptions, a nonjudgmental attitude, an awareness of cross-cultural variations, respect for others, and the ability to promote negotiation and consensus building. In addition, the nurse needs to respond to the feelings of family members, facilitate problem management and solving, share knowledge and expertise with all involved, include families in treatment and discharge planning, make referrals to community resources, participate in family support groups as a learner, and participate in mental health advocacy.

Community-based psychiatric-mental health nurses must combine multiple nursing skills to meet the increasingly complex and interdependent physical and mental health needs of clients living in a variety of alternative living arrangements.

As psychiatric-mental health clients are more often placed in less restrictive, more normal settings, psychiatric-mental health nurses will be increasingly required to move throughout the community, offering mental health services wherever clients are, including their homes, congregate housing, partial hospitalizations, soup kitchens, homeless shelters, single-room-occupancy hotels, adult homes, and assisted living arrangements. Psychiatric-mental health nurses will have to combine multiple nursing skills to meet clients' increasingly complex and interdependent physical and mental health needs in a variety of living arrangements.

Cultural Issues and Mental Health

An estimated 6 to 8 million immigrants entered the United States in the last decade of the twentieth century. The United States is a diverse country with strong immigrant roots, and the nation's diversity will continue to expand, with significant increases in African, Hispanic, and Asian populations. Psychiatric-mental health nurses will encounter clients of many different racial, ethnic, and cultural backgrounds. It is important that there be positive interactions between the culture of the healthcare practitioner, the culture of the client, and the culture of the setting (Dienemann, 1997).

Psychiatric-mental health nurses need to be both culturally sensitive and culturally competent.

Psychiatric-mental health nurses need to be both culturally sensitive and culturally competent. Cultural sensitivity refers to the psychiatric-mental health nurse's "ability to be aware of and respect the client's values and lifestyles even when these differ from the nurse's own"; cultural competence refers to "a multidimensional concept involving various aspects of knowledge, attitude and skills" (Louie, 1996, p. 572). Clients from diverse backgrounds have different ideas about the causes of mental illness and their acceptance of the illness. Some cultures believe that disorders may be caused by evil spirits, events in previous lives, bad thoughts or curses from other people, racism, or divine retribution. The nurse should carefully evaluate unusual or unexpected behaviors for cultural influences and the client's acceptance of the behavior before assuming the behaviors are intrinsic to a mental disorder. Language differences must be accommodated by using competent and sensitive translators, preferably not family members.

Clients may seek to replace conventional therapies or use them in conjunction with cultural therapies and complementary or alternative treatments. Such therapies include the treatment of herbalists, folk healers, and family healers; invocations of the good spirits; imagery; religious ceremonies; the use of magical, life-giving objects; healing touch; and communing with the spirit world for guidance and assistance. The psychiatric-mental health nurse must understand and appreciate the influence of culture on the client, family, and community support system. The nurse should learn to incorporate these cultural therapies into the plan of care to achieve the best outcomes.

Professional Psychiatric Nursing Organizations

The two major professional psychiatric nursing organizations are the American Psychiatric Nurses Association (APNA) and the International Society of Psychiatric-Mental Health Nurses (ISPN), which has three divisions—the Association of Child and Adolescent Psychiatric Nurses (ACAPN), the International Society of Psychiatric-Consultation Liaison Nurses (ISPCLN), and the Society for Education and Research in Psychiatric-Mental Health Nursing (SERPN). Prior to the 1996 dissolution of the ANA's Council on Psychiatric and Mental Health Nursing and the other specialty practice councils, the ANA's council and the APNA, ACAPN, and SERPN successfully collaborated on practice, political, and legislative issues as the Coalition of Psychiatric Nursing Organizations (COPNO).

Founded in 1987, APNA provides national leadership on psychiatric-mental health nursing issues. An organizational affiliate of the ANA, APNA works closely with the ANA on legislation, practice standards, certification of psychiatric nurses as generalists and specialists, and provision of continuing nursing education in the specialty. In 1997, the ANA, APNA, and many other mental health advocacy groups signed a bill of rights for individuals seeking treatment for psychiatric and substance-abuse disorders. This bill of rights includes:

- The individual's right to know what mental health benefits are included in an insurance plan
- The right to receive full information concerning the professional expertise of the treating practitioner
- The right to know if there are contractual arrangements between the treating practitioners and a third-party payer
- The right to receive information concerning how to submit complaints or grievances about care
- The right to guaranteed confidentiality
- The right to choose any duly licensed or certified mental health professional for care
- The right to receive mental health care
- Other rights related to discrimination, including receiving mental health services, the structure of mental health benefits plans, treatment review, and accountability

ACAPN was founded in 1971 and has focused on meeting the professional needs of nurses specializing in the mental health care of children and adolescents. In 1998, the ACAPN, ISPCLN, and SERPN agreed to form the International Society of Psychiatric Mental Health Nurses (ISPN), which now also includes the Association of Geropsychiatric-Mental Health Nurses (AGPN). Each of the four organizations is an ISPN division, maintaining its specialized focus and identity. The purposes of the new alliance were to unite and strengthen the presence and impact of specialized psychiatric-mental health nurses, to work together on major issues affecting the nursing profession, to impact health policy, and to promote equitable and quality care for individuals and families with mental health problems.

Summary

Many issues and trends influence the practice of psychiatric-mental health nursing. The chapter began with a look at definitions of mental health, mental disorders, and psychiatric-mental health nursing practice. The independent and dependent legal authorizations for practice in states' nurse practice acts and the profession's scope and standards of practice and psychiatric-mental health nursing practice were discussed. The nursing process (assessment, diagnosis, planning, intervention, and evaluation) and its application to psychiatric-mental health nursing were described. Documentation specific to psychiatric-mental health nursing was identified: client behaviors, new behaviors, interactions, responses to medications, symptom relief, substance abuse, restraints and seclusion, and life events. The need for research on psychiatric nursing interventions and the types of client outcomes related to psychiatric nursing practice (client satisfaction, return to functional status, response to educational interventions) were discussed. The unique role of managed care in the delivery of mental health services, the utilization of case management, and the need for mental health parity were reviewed. The roles and contributions of registered nurses and advanced practice registered nurses to the care of the mental health client were discussed and the missions of the various professional psychiatric nursing organizations were presented.

The major professional psychiatric nursing organizations are the American Psychiatric Nurses Association, the Association of Child and Adolescent Psychiatric Nurses, the International Society of Psychiatric-Consultation Liaison Nurses, and the Society for Education and Research in Psychiatric-Mental Health Nursing.

Annotated References

Al-Assaf, A. F. (Ed.). (1998). *Managed care quality: A practical guide.* New York: CRC Press.

This book provides a historical review of managed care and numerous discussions of achieving quality in a managed care system.

American Nurses Association. (2007). *Psychiatric-mental health nursing: Scope and standards of practice.* Washington, DC: Author.

This is an authoritative statement on the clinical aspects of psychiatric-mental health nursing practice, including the scope and standards of practice in keeping with the contemporary and future needs of clients. This document was a collaborative effort of the ANA, APNA, and ISPN.

American Nurses Association. (2003). *Nursing: Scope and standards of practice.* Washington, DC: Author.

This is a foundational document that articulates the essentials of nursing, its activities, and its accountabilities: the who, what, where, and how of practice. It provides 17 standards with accompanying measurement criteria.

American Nurses Association. (2000). *Nursing's scope* and *standards of practice.* Washington, DC: Author.

This document establishes the basic clinical nursing standards of care and standards of professional performance.

American Nurses Association. (1998). Nursing's values challenged by managed care. *Nursing Trends and Issues, 3*(1), 1–8.

This article is a thoughtful discussion of nursing's traditional ethical values and principles in relation to a managed health care environment.

American Nurses Association. (1996). *Nursing quality indicators: Definition and implications.* Washington, DC: Author.

This is the second in a series of publications on the outcomes of nursing care. The text proposes a study to accumulate and compare national data on nursing quality in acute care settings.

American Psychiatric Association. (2000). *Diagnostic and statistical manual of mental disorders* (4th ed.). Text Revision. Washington, DC: Author.

This is the fourth edition with text revision of the American Psychiatric Association's official nomenclature of psychiatric conditions and disorders. It provides a systematic listing of the official codes and categories, a description of the multiaxial system for diagnosis, and diagnostic criteria for each of the disorders. This book is used by psychiatrists, physicians, psychologists, registered nurses, social workers, therapists, and other mental health workers in all clinical settings.

Bower, K. (1992). *Case management by nurses.* Washington, DC: American Nurses.

This publication provides a guide for the continued development and expansion of case management practice.

Breslin, E., & Lucas, V. (2003). *Women's health nursing: Towards evidence based practice.* Chicago, IL: W. B. Saunders.

This book utilizes evidence-based practice as it explores women's health problems across the life span, highlighting key phenomena. It discusses foundational concepts essential to the care of women, and it covers health history, screening and diagnostic tests, and physical examinations.

Cohen, E., & Cesta, T. (1997). *Nursing case management.* St. Louis, MO: C. V. Mosby.

This book examines nursing case management by explaining its historical roots and current and future challenges.

Dienemann, J. (1997). *Cultural diversity in nursing: Issues, strategies and outcomes.* Washington, DC: American Academy of Nursing.

This monograph promotes culturally competent teamwork. It explores types of cultures, the cultural competence of U.S. nurses, intercultural counseling, and training for cultural sensitivity.

Dixon, L., McFarlane, W. R., Lefley, H., Lucksted, A., Cohen, M., Falloon I., et al. (2001). Evidence-based practices for services to families of people with psychiatric disabilities. *Psychiatric Services, 52*(7), 903–910.

This article examines the evidence-based practice that supports family psychoeducation that has been shown to reduce relapse rates and facilitate recovery of persons with psychiatric disabilities.

Donahue, A. B. (2006). Pecking orders, social permits, and reverse discrimination. Interview by Shirley A. Smoyak. *Journal of Psychosocial Nursing and Mental Health Services, 44*(5), 4–5.

This brief article is a commentary on how unspoken beliefs and "word compartments" create incredible pain and cause unnecessary delay in providing care.

Eggland, E. (1997). Charting tips: Documenting psychiatric and behavioral outcomes. *Nursing 97, 27*(4), 25.

This article provides a brief listing of specific suggestions for documenting nursing outcomes in psychiatric care.

Finkelman, A. W. (1997). *Psychiatric home care.* Gaithersberg, MD: Aspen.

This book provides a complete review of the care of the psychiatric client in a home care setting. Topics discussed include psychiatric rehabilitation, the family and significant others, psychoeducation, psychopharmacology, case management, and specific clinical problems.

Frank-Stromberg, M., Christensen, A., & Do, D. E. (2001). Nurse documentation: Not done or worse, done the wrong way—part II. *Oncology Nursing Forum, 28*(5), 841–846.

Educating nurses about the principles of documentation and the importance of implementing risk-reduction practices will help guard against liability and ultimately improve patient care.

Haber, J., & Billings, C. (1995). Primary mental health care: A model for psychiatric-mental health nursing. *Journal of the American Psychiatric Nurses Association, 1*(5), 154–163.

This article introduces and defines the concept of primary mental health care as a model for the delivery of community-based, comprehensive psychiatric-mental health nursing care.

Horton-Deutsch, S., Farran, C., Loukissa, D., & Fogg, L. (1997). Who are these patients and what services do they receive? *Home Healthcare Nurse, 15*(12), 847–854.

This article presents an interesting description of the psychiatric client in home care.

Hymowitz, C. (1998, February 9). Price of privacy: Many psychotherapy patients pay own bills. *The Daily Gazette,* p. B2.

This article describes the choices clients face when payment for mental health services requires that the therapist be permitted to share specific details of the client's life and treatment with the insurance company. The author's viewpoint is that many clients choose to pay directly for treatment and do not seek reimbursement to avoid losing confidentiality.

Iyer, P. (1991a). Six more charting rules: To keep you legally safe. *Nursing 91, 21*(7), 35–39.

This article focuses on what should not be documented in a chart and how to record clients' actions that contribute to personal injury.

Iyer, P. (1991b). Thirteen charting rules: To keep you legally safe. *Nursing 91, 21*(6), 40–44.

This article discusses the recommended mechanics of charting and documentation.

Klainberg, M., Holzemer, S., Leonard, M., & Arnold, J. (1998). *Community health nursing: An alliance for health.* New York: McGraw-Hill.

This concise textbook provides a focused and thorough introduction to community health nursing.

Krupnick, S., & Wade, A. (1993). *Psychiatric care planning.* Springhouse, PA: Springhouse.

This excellent reference includes specific suggestions for planning the care of psychiatric clients including psychiatric diagnostic categories, nursing diagnoses, outcome criteria, and discharge planning.

Lego, S., & Caverly, S. (1995). Coming to terms: Psychiatric nurse practitioner versus clinical nurse specialist. *Journal of the American Psychiatric Nurses Association, 1*(2), 61–65.

In this article, a point-versus-counterpoint article, two leaders of psychiatric nursing debate different points of view regarding advanced-practice titles and roles in the specialty.

Leo, J. (1997, October 27). Doing the disorder rag. *U.S. News and World Report,* p. 20.

This opinion article questions the appropriateness of reducing many of an individual's most common behaviors to potential mental disorders.

Louie, K. (1996). Cultural issues in psychiatric-mental health nursing. In S. Lego (Ed.), *Psychiatric nursing: A comprehensive reference* (2nd ed., pp. 572–575). Philadelphia: J. B. Lippincott.

This chapter identifies the changing demographics of the U.S. population and discusses cultural sensitivity, assessment, and competence in psychiatric-mental health nursing practice.

Malloch, K., & Porter-O'Grady, T. (2006). *Introduction to evidence-based practice in nursing and health care.* Sudbury, MA: Jones and Bartlett.

This introduction to the use of evidence-based practice in nursing and health care provides an excellent orientation to the basic principles of evidence-based practice and explores barriers and strengths within organizations seeking to implement such a process.

Melek, S. (1997, December). Making sense of the Mental Health Parity Act. *Milliman and Robertson's Perspectives,* pp. 1–3.

This article identifies the major components of the law that created mental health parity in healthcare plans across the nation.

Menenberg, S. (1995). Standards of care in documentation of psychiatric nursing care. *Clinical Nurse Specialist, 9*(3), 140–148.

This article discusses the multiple factors that require careful documentation of psychiatric care and the need to coordinate all aspects of the interdisciplinary care record.

Menninger, K. A. (1945). *The human mind* (3rd ed.). New York: Alfred Knopf.

This classic, early psychiatric textbook describes mental conditions and related behaviors.

O'Donohue, W., & Levensky, E. R. (2006). *Promoting treatment adherence.* Thousand Oaks, CA: Sage.

This practical handbook for clinicians offers comprehensive information and strategies for understanding and promoting treatment compliance.

Peplau, H. (1995). Some unresolved issues in the era of biopsychosocial nursing. *Journal of the American Psychiatric Nurses Association, 1*(3), 92–96.

Four unresolved issues of importance to psychiatric-mental health nurses are explored in this article: biology versus environment, community and family nursing, primary care and advanced practice, and external versus internal regulation of nursing.

Pickens, J. (1998). Formal and informal care of people with psychiatric disorders: Historical perspectives and current trends. *Journal of Psychosocial Nursing, 36*(1), 37–43.

This article provides a review of the historical relationship between formal and informal caregivers and those with serious mental illness and discusses the attributes and actions needed by nurses to develop a truly collaborative relationship with clients, families, and community advocacy groups.

Reighley, J. (1988). *Nursing care planning guides for mental health.* Baltimore, MD: Williams & Wilkins.

This classic reference guides the planning of nursing care for clients with mental health conditions through the application of a nursing diagnosis framework.

Rowland, H., & Rowland, B. (1997). *Nursing administration handbook* (4th ed.). Gaithersberg, MD: Aspen.
This comprehensive overview of the field of nursing administration can be used as a hands-on tool by nurse managers. It explains leadership skills, problem solving and decision making, the overall working environment, finances and budgeting, technology and informatics, the operation of a nursing service, human resources, research, and the impact of today's healthcare environment on the nurse manager.

Sackett, D. L., Rosenberg, W. M. C., Gray, J. A. M., Haynes, R. B., & Richardson, W. S. (1996). Evidence-based medicine: What it is and what it isn't. *British Medical Journal, 312*(7023), 71–72.
This article explores the potential limitations associated with evidence-based medicine.

Schuster, P. M. (2000). Concept mapping: Reducing clinical care plan paperwork and increasing learning. *Nurse Educator, 25*(2), 76–81.
The authors discuss how concept mapping reduces paperwork and enhances nursing students' critical thinking skills and clinical reasoning.

Shumway, M., & Sentell, T. L. (2004). An examination of leading mental health journals for evidence to inform evidence-based practice. *Psychiatric Services, 55*(6), 649–653.
This study examined whether data needed to inform evidence-based practice could be found in leading mental health journals. The results were disappointing.

Society for Education and Research in Psychiatric-Mental Health Nursing. (1996). *The Society for Education and Research in Psychiatric-Mental Health Nursing (SERPN) Division.* Retrieved July 25, 2007, from http://www.ispn-psych.org/html/serpn.html
SERPN focuses on graduate education in psychiatric nursing and the evolving research base for psychiatric nursing practice. Its members include nurse educators, researchers, and advanced practice registered nurses—all dedicated to addressing the mental health needs of the consumers via the education and development of the advanced practice workforce, research, and innovative practice models.

Stuart, G. W. (2000). Evidence-based psychiatric nursing practice. In G. W. Stuart & M. T. Laraia (Eds.), *Principles and practices of psychiatric nursing* (7th ed., pp. 76–85). St. Louis: Mosby.
An excellent psychiatric-mental health nursing textbook from one of the specialty's most competent and compelling educators.

Worley, N. (1997). *Mental health nursing in the community.* St. Louis: C. V. Mosby.
This book presents psychiatric-mental health nursing concepts with a focus on practicing in the community.

Zauszniewski, J. A., & Suresky, J. (2004). Evidence for psychiatric nursing practice: An analysis of three years of published research. *Online Journal of Issues in Nursing, 9*(1). Retrieved September 6, 2006, from http://nursingworld.org/ojin/hirsh/topic4/tpc4_1.htm
This State of the Evidence review analyzed 227 data-based studies published in the five most commonly read U.S. psychiatric nursing journals from January 2000 through December 2002.

Additional Resources

Alperin, R. (1997). *The impact of managed care on the practice of women in psychotherapy: Innovation, implementation and controversy.* New York: Bruner/Mazel.
This textbook considers treatment approaches, the controversies in managed care, and technological advances.

American Nurses Association. (2003). *Nursing's social policy statement* (2nd ed.). Washington, DC: ANA.
This document describes nursing care and its knowledge base, the scope of practice, and methods by which the profession is regulated.

Burgess, A. (1997). *Advanced practice psychiatric nursing.* Stamford, CT: Appleton & Lange.
This is an excellent text that examines many of the issues facing advanced-practice nurses, including case management, prescriptive privilege, interdisciplinary collaboration, role merging, and ethical issues.

Cohen, E. (1996). *Nurse case management in the 21st century.* St. Louis: C. V. Mosby.
This book provides practical techniques and outcomes for integrating case management across the continuum of care.

Lego, S. (1996). Long live the CNS and the NP in psychiatric nursing: Do not blend the roles. *Online Journal of Issues in Nursing.* Retrieved April 23, 2007, from http://www.nursingworld.org/ojin/tpc1/tpc1_1.htm
This article presents three options for maintaining the clinical nurse specialist role in psychiatric-mental health nursing.

Internet Resources

http://nursing.jbpub.com/psychiatric

Visit http://nursing.jbpub.com/psychiatric for interactive exercises, NCLEX review questions, WebLinks, and more.

CHAPTER 3

The Psychiatric Nursing Assessment

Christine Carniaux Moran

LEARNING OBJECTIVES

After reading this chapter, you will be able to:

- Identify the components of a holistic assessment, including mental status examination.
- Correctly use psychiatric terminology to describe a client's symptoms.
- Choose the appropriate interviewing techniques to gather information for a holistic assessment.
- Demonstrate an understanding of the role of psychological testing, including rating scales, in assessment.
- Demonstrate understanding of each of the five axes in a *DSM-IV-TR* diagnosis.

KEY TERMS

Affect
Biopsychosocial history
Chief complaint
Closed-ended questions
Collateral history
Concrete thought process
Coping skills
Countertransference
Delusions
Differential diagnosis
Diagnostic and Statistical Manual of Mental Disorders,* 4th ed., text revision *(DSM-IV-TR)
Empathy
Global assessment of functioning scale
Hallucinations
History of present illness (HPI)
Holistic psychiatric assessment
Homicidal thoughts
Impulse control
Insight
Judgment
Mental status examination
Mood
Multiaxial *DSM-IV-TR* diagnosis
Open-ended questions
Physical assessment
Psychiatric nursing interview
Psychological tests
Resistance
Self-disclosure
Suicidal thoughts
Therapeutic contract
Transference

http://nursing.jbpub.com/psychiatric

Visit http://nursing.jbpub.com/psychiatric for interactive exercises, NCLEX review questions, WebLinks, and more.

Introduction

The evaluation of psychiatric clients is a multifaceted endeavor, most effectively performed by an interdisciplinary team of mental health professionals. A comprehensive, **holistic psychiatric assessment** examines the physical, psychological, intellectual, social, and spiritual aspects of the individual. The **physical assessment** may include a physical examination, a study of the client's biologic life stage and genetic predisposition, laboratory tests, and diagnostic tests such as magnetic resonance imaging (MRI) and electroencephalography (EEG). The psychological evaluation surveys childhood experiences, personality, and current objective and subjective symptoms of psychiatric illness. This information is gathered by interviewing the client and family, by performing a **mental status examination**, and by administering specific **psychological tests** and rating scales. Cognitive functioning is best assessed by utilizing a standard measure such as the Mini-Mental State Examination. The social assessment consists of an exploration of cultural, environmental, and familial influences on the expression and experience of illness, and the spiritual assessment is an exploration of the client's religious and spiritual dimensions (**Table 3-1**).

The psychiatric nursing evaluation covers the assessment, diagnosis, outcome identification, and planning stages of the nursing process. The evaluation is ongoing; as more of the client's history and new **insights** into his or her issues come to light, the diagnosis and treatment plan evolve accordingly.

Assessment

The ability to assess clients is one of the psychiatric nurse's most important skills. The assessment process defines the client's problem and allows

Table 3-1 Holistic Psychiatric Nursing Assessment

Assessment Tool	Component Parts	Dimension Addressed
Biopsychosocial history	Chief complaint	Psychological
	History of present illness	Psychological
	Psychiatric history	Psychological
	Alcohol and substance use history	Psychological
	Medical history	Physical
	Family history	Psychological, physical, social
	Developmental history	Psychological, physical, social
	Social history	Social
	Occupational/educational history	Social
	Culture	Social
	Spirituality	Spiritual
	Coping skills	Psychological
Mental status examination	Behavior and appearance	Psychological, physical, social
	Emotions: mood and affect	Psychological
	Speech	Psychological, physical, social, intellectual
	Thought process and content	Psychological, social, intellectual, spiritual
	Perceptual disturbances	Psychological, physical
	Impulse control	Psychological, physical
	Cognition and sensorium	Intellectual, physical
	Knowledge, insight, and judgment	Intellectual, psychological
Psychological tests	Multiple tools, including rating scales	Psychological, intellectual
Physical assessment	Physical examination	Physical
	Assessment of activities of daily living	Physical
	Laboratory tests	Physical
	CT scans/other diagnostic tests	Physical

the nurse and client to establish a relationship. A thorough nursing assessment is a prerequisite for formulating an appropriate nursing diagnosis and plan of care. Assessment data also provide a baseline level of functioning that is used to evaluate, change, and respond to the treatment plan.

Data used for assessment are gathered not only from the client, but also from other sources. The client's self-assessment usually differs from the perception of family, coworkers, other clients in the hospital, and members of the treatment team; those views also vary between groups. Additionally, anyone's perception of the client will change over time.

Assessment guidelines vary according to the specific dimensions of the client being evaluated; however, the need for a structured interview and a data collection tool is widely accepted. Tools and guidelines for performing comprehensive nursing assessments assist in evaluating clients, improve the nurse's professional image, and increase job satisfaction (Catherman, 1990). Lengthy assessment tools are often met with resistance by staff nurses who struggle with time constraints in the workplace (Schreiber, 1991). This resistance is partially justified by shorter stays in the hospital, increased client acuity, and financial pressure to decrease the nurse-to-client ratio throughout the healthcare system.

Nurses must narrow the range of their data collection to the information judged most relevant. It is the quality and not the quantity of the assessment data that matters (Regan-Kubinski, 1995). The following guidelines for a holistic psychiatric nursing assessment should be tailored to meet the specific needs of the nurse, client, and situation. These guidelines provide instructions for conducting a **psychiatric nursing interview** to obtain data for a **biopsychosocial history** and mental status examination.

Psychiatric Nursing Interview

An interview is a conversation with a deliberate purpose that ideally is mutually accepted by the participants. It differs from a social conversation in that one participant (the nurse) is responsible for the content and flow of the interaction, while the other participant (the client) is the focus of the discussion. The interview must take place within a specific time frame. The purpose of the psychiatric nursing interview is to gather the information necessary to understand and treat the client.

The content and process of the interview vary according to the state of the participants and the context in which the interview takes place. For example, an agitated client has just been admitted to an acute psychiatric unit of a teaching hospital. The client's severe impairment, the nurse's need to budget time, and the busy nature of the setting indicate that a series of brief, structured interviews is the most viable approach. The members of the interdisciplinary treatment team (psychiatrist, nurse, social worker, and other specialists) share the responsibility for data collection. With consent, family or significant others may be approached to elucidate the client's story. The content of the initial interview should focus on eliciting information to help the staff provide a safe environment for the client and others (i.e., the client's potential for suicidal and violent behavior is assessed).

The content of the psychiatric nursing interview focuses on the client's biopsychosocial history and current mental status.

Content of the Psychiatric Nursing Interview: Biopsychosocial History

Biopsychosocial history is a comprehensive assessment of the client's lifetime biologic, psychological, and social functioning.

> Assessment guidelines and data collection tools should be individualized for each client during the psychiatric evaluation.

Identifying Data

A written biopsychosocial history begins with a succinct summary of the client's demographics: name, age, gender, marital status, ethnicity, religion, occupation, education, and current living situation.

> The chief complaint and HPI provide valuable data for psychiatric and medical clients.

Chief Complaint

The client's **chief complaint** is the reason for current contact with the mental health system. The chief complaint should be obtained in the client's own words. Because of the nature of the illness, the client's statement may differ greatly from the family's or evaluator's assessment of the situation (e.g., an in-patient insists that she is in the hospital for a medical checkup following her abduction by aliens). The chief complaint provides valuable data concerning the client's illness.

History of Present Illness

The **history of present illness (HPI)** is a chronologic account of the events leading up to the current contact with the mental health professional.

The HPI includes a description of the evolution of the client's symptoms that covers the onset, duration, and change of symptoms over time. Exacerbating and ameliorating factors of the current psychological distress must be explored, and the nurse should delineate factors that may have precipitated the current episode. These stressful events may be negative (e.g., job loss) or positive (e.g., job promotion). Attendant changes in somatic functioning (sleep pattern, appetite, cognitive ability, sexual functioning) should also be noted. This information is similar to that obtained when clients are evaluated for nonpsychiatric medical illnesses (see **Table 3-2**).

Psychiatric History

Information concerning past psychiatric illness must be obtained to understand the current episode, to make an accurate diagnosis, and to make a prognosis. Psychiatric illness may be a single event, chronic, or intermittent, and the course of the illness may improve or deteriorate over time.

Alcohol and Substance Use History

Studies have shown high co-morbidity of mental illness and alcohol or substance abuse. Causality is difficult to discern, because alcohol and drug abuse may precipitate an episode of mental illness or may represent a client's attempt to cope with a preexisting mental disorder. Research has shown that drug and alcohol use in the mentally ill adversely affects the course of their illness (Sadock, Kaplan, & Sadock, 2003).

The nurse should obtain a history of the client's caffeine and nicotine use; both are prevalent in psychiatric clients. Caffeine may supply energy to depressed and schizophrenic clients; caffeine and caffeine withdrawal may cause agitation as well. Nicotine use may increase attention span and memory in clients with schizophrenia but may decrease the efficacy of neuroleptics. Nicotine withdrawal may lead to agitation or depression (American Psychiatric Association [APA], 2000; Rauter, de Nesnera, & Grandfield, 1997).

Medical History

The nurse should ascertain significant illnesses, injuries, and treatments received. The client must be assessed for allergies and past and present side effects from medication. An Abnormal Involuntary Movement Scale (AIMS; Guy, 1976) examination may be done to measure psychotropic medication–induced motor side effects. In performing an AIMS examination, the nurse observes for abnormal muscle movement while the client performs a series of simple motor tasks. Women should be questioned concerning

Table 3-2 Comparison of Assessment for Physical and Mental Disorders

	Chief Complaint	
	Angina	**Depression**
Quality	"Chest tightening, with pain radiating down my left arm."	"Emotional pain that feels like I am going to die."
Severity	"Severe—a 9 on a scale of 1 to 10."	"Severe—a 9 on a scale of 1 to 10."
Timing	"It lasts about 5 minutes."	"It is constant."
	History of Present Illness	
	Angina	**Depression**
Factors that aggravate	Exercise, emotional stress, and meals	Stress at work, arguments with family members, and morning hours
Factors that alleviate	Rest and nitroglycerine tabs	Social contact, activities, and antidepressant medication
Associated symptoms	Dyspnea, nausea, and sweating	Anhedonia (chronic inability to experience pleasure), diminished appetite, and insomnia
Chronology	Started with chest pain on exertion 1 year ago; getting increasingly more severe and frequent	Started with a sad mood and feeling overwhelmed after a job promotion 6 months ago; getting increasingly more incapacitating and unrelated to life events over time

their menstrual cycles, pregnancies, and menopause; hormonal changes may have a significant impact on the client's mental health. The nurse should evaluate the client's risk for falling and skin breakdown and take note of assistive devices the client requires (e.g., eyeglasses, hearing aides, dentures, canes, walkers).

Family History

Families are no longer blamed for causing mental illness; rather, they are taught about the condition and engaged in the treatment process. Obtaining a family history of mental illness is important, because many of these disorders are hereditary. Bipolar and unipolar mood disorders, schizophrenia, and attention deficit disorder (ADD) have significant genetic components. The client's response to specific interventions may be inherited as well, and should be included in the family history (Sadock et al., 2003).

Developmental History

The developmental history is an account of the client's infancy, childhood, and adolescence. It may provide clues to the origin of current behaviors and aid in the diagnosis. Erikson (1963) created a developmental timetable to identify the psychosocial adaptation required during each stage of life. All stages, beginning with birth and extending through senescence, are characterized by developmental tasks. The successful completion of these tasks, crucial to both happiness and success with subsequent tasks, represents optimal adaptation at a given stage. In contrast, failure at these tasks may lead to difficulty completing future tasks and may stifle psychosocial growth. Self-esteem, self-control, and independence emerge during toddlerhood, peak during the industry versus inferiority stage (6 years of age through puberty), and represent key issues in assessing an adult's ability to cope with the stress of illness, for example (see **Table 3-3**).

Childhood mental disorders, temperament, and style of interpersonal relationships may remain with the client into adulthood. Additionally, psychic trauma (e.g., neglect or abuse, loss of parent) experienced by a client during childhood may adversely affect brain development, leading to **impulse control** problems, personality disorder, posttraumatic stress disorder (PTSD), depression, or other psychiatric illness (Terr, 1991). It is estimated that 25% of children under age 16 will experience some kind of trauma (National Child Traumatic Stress Network, 2004). Data show that 34–53% of the mentally ill population report childhood sexual or physical abuse, with a 29–43% rate of PTSD among the seriously mentally ill (Kessler et al., 1995).

Clinical Example

Jerry is a 34-year-old male diagnosed with chronic paranoid schizophrenia, brought to the hospital by the police after threatening to harm passersby on the street. Jerry became enraged when he discovered that the hospital was a smoke-free environment; he had been smoking one to two packs of cigarettes per day for 15 years. Jerry was offered treatment with a nicotine patch or gum; however, he adamantly refused this treatment. Jerry required physical restraint on one occasion and medication on several other occasions, due to psychotic agitation that was exacerbated by nicotine withdrawal. Jerry was stabilized on psychotropic medications and was discharged within 2 weeks. Upon discharge, Jerry resumed smoking and had a relapse of psychotic symptoms. His psychiatrist attributed the outpatient decompensation to the diminished efficacy of the antipsychotic medication, because the medication dose had been titrated in the hospital while Jerry was nicotine-free. Jerry's condition was stabilized with an increase in dose.

A high level of *comorbidity* exists between mental illness and alcohol or substance abuse, and there is evidence that both may have a genetic or familial component.

Social History

A client's ability to make and sustain relationships indicates the ability to utilize the therapeutic relationship and aids in the diagnosis. Larger social networks are correlated with decreased severity of mental illness and a more thorough recovery. It is often difficult to ascertain whether a client's social problems have precipitated or resulted from the mental illness.

The psychiatric nurse should inquire about the client's family and household members. How have family and significant others responded to the client's illness? Often, a family member's mental illness is extremely disruptive to the family system (Terkelson, 1987). Seek the client's permission to involve family members and significant others in the assessment and treatment process, unless this involvement would be counterproductive. Ascertain a history of the client's friendships and sexual partners.

The nurse should have the client describe these relationships or lack thereof. Is the client satisfied with his or her social role at this point in life? For example, some persons become distressed when they fail to accomplish social milestones such as marriage by a certain age. Assess the client's wider social network, including religious organizations, community centers, and clubs. The client's living situation is also integral to the assessment, because many of the client's stressors

Table 3-3 Erikson's Stages of Psychosocial Growth and Development

Age Group	Developmental Stage Task	Characteristics
Infancy	Trust vs. mistrust	The goal is the development of a sense of trust. Consistent attention to physical needs within a reasonable time period builds trust.
Toddlerhood	Autonomy vs. shame and doubt	The goal is the achievement of autonomy. An environment in which the child is able to explore surroundings in a safe way engenders autonomy. Successful toilet-training plays a key role.
Preschool age	Initiative vs. guilt	The goal is the development of a sense that the child's actions produce outcomes through opportunity to try to do things on one's own.
School age	Industry vs. inferiority	The goal is a feeling of self-worth, gained by mastering schoolwork, sports, and other competitive activities.
Adolescence	Identity vs. role confusion	The goal is to establish a unique identity, first by rejecting adults and identifying with peer group and later by developing individuality.
Young adulthood	Intimacy vs. isolation	Establishment of close relationships with members of both sexes.
Middle adulthood	Generativity vs. stagnation	The goal is a feeling of giving back to the younger generation or society, through successfully adjusting to changing roles in marriage, parenting, and career.
Late adulthood	Integrity vs. despair	The goals are to attain a sense of continuity of past, present, and future, of meaning in one's life as it was, and of acceptance of death. This is achieved through life review and reminiscence.

are environmental in origin. Homelessness, for example, is a severe social stressor (see **Figure 3-1**).

Occupational and Educational History

It is essential to establish a client's past and present level of function in work and school. A sporadic or chaotic employment history may indicate personality disorder or frequent episodes of mental decompensation. Work- or school-related stress may have precipitated the illness. Assess the impact that hospitalization or treatment may have on the client's function at work or school. The client's level of education partially determines how the nurse can most effectively communicate with and educate the client. Low socioeconomic status has been correlated with a relatively high rate of symptoms of mental illness (Gresenz, Sturm, & Tang, 2001).

Figure 3-1 Homelessness is a severe social stressor.

Culture

Ethnicity, race, social class, degree of acculturation, and language should be included in the cultural assessment. Culture can significantly influence the development, expression, and reporting of mental disorders; thereby affecting diagnosis. A clinician who is unfamiliar with the nuances of an individual's culture may see psychopathology when a behavior or experience may actually be a normal variation of the client's culture, such as a Native American who hears a dead relative's voice while grieving. Some symptom clusters are uniquely associated with certain cultures, such as an "ataque de nervios" (nervous attack) in the Hispanic population (APA, 2000). In clients with depression, biological symptoms (e.g., sleep and appetite disturbances) may tend to be universal, whereas psychological symptoms have been shown to vary by culture. Members of certain groups may be more likely to present with somatic complaints. Culture-specific rating scales may therefore be helpful in assessing clients from diverse backgrounds (Kinzie & Manson, 1987).

Culturally competent assessment also requires sensitivity to the process of assessment. The client's comfort level in regard to disclosing private issues with unfamiliar people, having physical closeness with unfamiliar people, involving family in the assessment process, and being addressed by first name varies among age, socioeconomic, and ethnic groups. Because of a history of negative experiences that certain groups such as Native Americans have had with mainstream medicine, members of these groups may be reluctant to participate in the traditional Western assessment or treatment process (Vedantam, 2005). The presence of language barriers must be carefully assessed, because clients who may appear to speak English adequately may be more comfortable in their native tongue, especially when discussing emotional issues. Ideally, interpreters are familiar with medical terminology and are not members of the client's own family (to decrease communication problems and protect the client's privacy).

The efficacy of different treatment modalities and beliefs regarding the etiology and treatment of mental illness may also vary among cultures and must be considered when developing a treatment plan. Among some people in certain cultures, mental illness may be viewed as a punishment for past wrong-doing or as a result of a curse; convincing clients with these beliefs that Western medication will treat the illness can be challenging. Enlisting the help of community elders or traditional healers, instead of arguing against the beliefs, may be helpful in this regard (Vedantam, 2005). The role of the extended family and community in assisting with the treatment of the mentally ill also differs among groups, which will also need to be considered when delineating care. In some cultures, the mentally ill tend to be ostracized whereas in others the community takes pride in caring for these individuals. Even the efficacy, dosing, and side effects of psychotropic medication may differ significantly among ethnic groups (Vedantam, 2005).

Although it is important to have a working knowledge of general differences among cultures, it is essential that the nurse avoid stereotyping individual clients on the basis of ethnic, racial, or social group membership. Data supporting that African Americans and whites presenting with comparable symptoms are diagnosed with different mental illnesses (with the African Americans more likely diagnosed with pervasive illnesses such as schizophrenia) point to continued prejudices within our healthcare system (Blow, Zeber, McCarthy, Valenstein, Gillon, & Bingham, 2004; Neighbors, Trierweiler, Ford, & Muroff, 2003). The first step toward culturally sensitive practice is healthcare workers' examination of their prejudices regarding other cultures and the effect that their own culture has on their work.

The psychiatric nurse must consider the client's culture without stereotyping the client.

Spirituality and Values

Spirituality is an often neglected aspect of assessment, especially in the acute care setting. Nursing as a profession may have overlooked the spiritual aspects of assessment and care as it has struggled to assert itself as a research-based profession (Govier, 2000). However, a client's lack of or sense of spirituality may have a tremendous impact on illness and treatment. The belief in a divine plan and a benevolent God is comforting to many clients (Carson & Arnold, 1996). Some clients feel that spirituality decreases their sense of aloneness and despair. Spirituality and religiosity may deter suicide and violence. Conversely, some clients may become angry with God for having caused their suffering and may lose faith. Spiritual aspects of treatment, such as the concept of a higher power in the 12-step treatment program for alcohol and drug abuse, may engage spiritually minded clients but deter those who are not religious. A diagnostic category of religious or spiritual problems has been included in the ***Diagnostic and Statistical Manual of Mental Disorders,* 4th Edition, Text Revision *(DSM-IV-TR)*** (APA, 2000).

Religion is a way of expressing spirituality through an organized framework and through rituals. Clients should be asked about religion and whether or not they would like clergy involved in their treatment. Religiosity is correlated with relatively high levels of social support, decreased rates of depression, high levels of cooperation, and high levels of cognitive functioning (Koenig, 2007; Koenig, George, & Titus, 2004). In adolescents, religiosity is correlated with lower levels of drug abuse, violence, and behavioral problems (Barnes, Plotnikoff, Fox, & Pendelton, 2000).

Spirituality is a much broader concept than religion; it includes sources of motivation and strength, and finding meaning and connectedness to one's self, others, the environment, and a higher power.

We often equate religion with spirituality; however, spirituality is a much broader concept. Although atheists do not believe in God and agnostics are unsure of God's existence, it cannot be assumed that spirituality is absent in members of these groups. Govier (2000) did an extensive literature search and determined that an exploration of reason, reflection, relationships, and restoration were other important components of spirituality that should be assessed. Reason and reflection refer to the client's sources of motivation and strength, and the client's ability to take time to reflect on the meaning of his or her life or situation. Relationships refer to the client's sense of connectedness to others and to the environment. Restoration refers to the ability of the spiritual dimension to positively influence the physical aspect of care. On the other hand, spiritual distress (which can be the outcome of certain adverse life events) can precipitate or aggravate a course of illness.

Nurses who are not in touch with their own spirituality will tend to shy away from including an in-depth spiritual assessment of clients, so self-awareness is the first step toward performing a competent spiritual assessment. Observing for the presence of a bible, cross, or star of David may also give clues to the client's spirituality. Being present with the client, using active listening skills, being nonjudgmental, and taking care not to impose one's personal beliefs onto the client are essential skills in addressing a client's spiritual side.

Critical Thinking Questions What kinds of challenges would you expect when working with a client whose cultural or spiritual background differs from yours? What would you do to overcome potential difficulties?

A client's past coping style may help identify useful strategies to cope with the present illness.

The acronym BEST PICK is a helpful way to remember the composition of the mental status examination:
Behavior and general appearance
Emotions: mood and affect
Speech
Thought content and process
Perceptual disturbances
Impulse control
Cognition and sensorium
Knowledge, insight, and judgment

Coping Skills

Coping skills are mechanisms people use to manage internal and external stressors. Coping behaviors can enable an individual to alter a stressful situation by controlling, or at least minimizing, the stress resulting from the situation. Clients with chronic psychiatric or life-threatening medical illness may be unable to alter their condition, but can attempt to control the stress and minimize its effect on their lives. A client in this situation may reveal several behavioral signs. They may seek more information about their illness and treatment options. These clients may participate in self-care and reach out to others, including healthcare professionals, family members, and friends. They may also attend support groups and express their feelings about self-concept, body image, and physical function. They may practice deep breathing relaxation exercises.

Conversely, maladaptive coping mechanisms are behaviors that ultimately interfere with the client's ability to confront the stressor, may be harmful, and usually produce additional stress. Unfortunately, they are "tried and true" mechanisms; the client has successfully used them in the past to maintain emotional stability in the short-term. Consequently, clients tend to rely on these coping mechanisms to deal with future stressors. Such behaviors include alcohol and drug abuse, overeating, inappropriate anger, and social withdrawal.

Discerning the client's characteristic pattern of coping—whether it is adaptive or maladaptive—helps the nurse to predict how the client may react during a current stressor. It is often helpful to spend time uncovering and encouraging the use of the adaptive coping mechanisms that have been successfully used by the client in the past, because clients in current crisis are often feeling overwhelmed and may need prompting to remember the skills in their arsenal.

Content of the Psychiatric Nursing Interview: Mental Status Examination

Whereas the biopsychosocial history is a record of the client's entire lifetime, the mental status examination is an evaluation of the client's present state. Behavior and general appearance, **mood** and **affect**, speech, thought process and content, perceptual disturbances, impulse control, cognition, knowledge, **judgment**, and insight are assessed. Although it is termed an "examination," this assessment guideline requires little direct questioning beyond what is required for taking a biopsychosocial history; most pertinent information is gleaned from the interview process and content.

The acronym BEST PICK can assist in the recall of the main elements of the mental status examination: **B**ehavior and general appearance; **E**motions: mood and affect; **S**peech; **T**hought content and process; **P**erceptual disturbances; **I**mpulse control; **C**ognition and sensorium; and **K**nowledge, insight, and judgment.

Behavior and General Appearance

Note the client's body frame, posture, dress, grooming, and age-appropriateness of appearance. Some common adjectives used to describe the client's general appearance include *disheveled*, *well-groomed*, *heavily made-up*, *younger* or *older looking than biologic age*, *tensely postured*, *under-* or *overweight*, and *casually dressed*.

In terms of behavior, assess the client's gait, activity level, gestures, mannerisms, and psychomotor activity. Manic clients may be agitated and unable to sit still, whereas clients with schizophrenia may exhibit bizarre postures or psychomotor retardation. Observe for the rare symptoms of echopraxia (a mimicking of the interviewer's behavior), catatonia (statue-like immobility), and waxy flexibility (when limbs can be moved by the interviewer into positions that the client then maintains). Attempt to differentiate between movement disturbances secondary to mental illness and those resulting from medication side effects. Some antipsychotic medications may cause akathisia (motor restlessness), dystonia (stiffness), or dyskinesia (involuntary muscle movement).

The psychiatric nurse should always evaluate how the client relates to the interviewer and to the interviewing process. Is the client cooperative or uncooperative, bored, angry, or flirtatious?

Emotions: Mood and Affect

The client's mood is the pervasive subjective emotional state, and the visible expression of this state is termed the *affect*. Observe the depth, range, and fluctuation of emotional expression during the interview. Ask the client directly about his or her mood if the information is not offered spontaneously. Both mood and affect can be described as *euthymic* (normal), *labile* (rapidly changing from one mood state to another), *depressed, irritable, anxious, angry, euphoric* (excessively happy), *frightened*, or *empty*. Variability in the client's affect should be noted, ranging from *flat* (no variability) to *labile* (rapid fluctuation in affect). It is important to note congruity or incongruity of mood and affect. For example, some depressed clients look depressed, whereas others who are depressed appear euthymic.

Speech

The psychiatric nurse must observe the rate, amount, style, and tone of speech the client uses during the interview. Speech may range from pressured to hesitant, loud to inaudible, spontaneous to nonspontaneous, slurred to clear, and monotonous to dramatic. The client may be described as talkative or taciturn, depending upon the quantity of speech. Observe for evidence of dysarthria (physical difficulty in vocalizing), echolalia (the repetition of the interviewer's words), perseveration (the repetition of the same words or themes), aphasia (difficulties in understanding or producing speech), and other disorders or oddities of speech.

Thought Content

The psychiatric nurse should note any abnormalities in the client's thought content. *Obsessions* are intrusive thoughts or ideas that the client recognizes as "crazy" but acts in accordance with anyway (e.g., compulsive hand washing from an obsessive fear of germs). Hypochondriasis is an obsession with physical concerns that do not exist in reality.

Delusions are convictions that have no basis in reality. Delusions may be *paranoid, grandiose, somatic* (involving bodily concerns), *erotic, nihilistic* (involving death or destruction), *guilty, bizarre*, or *referential* (believing that benign environmental occurrences relate to or have special meaning for the client). The degree of congruence between the client's mood and the type of delusion experienced should be noted. Delusional content is occasionally revealed spontaneously during the psychiatric interview. For example, a client may ask the nurse to help him to hide from a Mafia hit man. Conversely, the nurse should be aware that a paranoid client may be guarded in his or her discussion of delusions secondary to pervasive lack of trust. In most cases, clients have little insight that their thoughts are delusional, and do not label them as such. The validity of delusions should not be questioned by the interviewer; such questioning is ineffective in changing the client's beliefs and often causes alienation and anger (Sadock et al., 2003).

Assessment of suicidal and homicidal thoughts is a priority in all evaluations of thought content. **Suicidal thoughts** are the client's desires to kill or harm him- or herself, and *homicidal thoughts* are the client's desires to kill or harm

A *euthymic mood* is a normal mood. A *labile mood* is one that changes rapidly from one state to another. A *euphoric mood* is an excessively happy one.

Dysarthria is a physical difficulty in vocalizing. *Echolalia* is the repetition of the interviewer's words. *Perseveration* is the repetition of the same words or themes. *Aphasia* includes problems in understanding or producing speech.

Referential delusions (ideas of reference) are false beliefs that things in the environment relate to the client or have special meaning for the client.

Clinical Example

Laura is a 26-year-old female hospitalized with an acute exacerbation of chronic paranoid schizophrenia. After the clients watched a televised news segment about Jerusalem, Laura was overheard discussing with the other clients her need to go on a pilgrimage to Jerusalem. Laura verbalized that one particular newscaster was speaking directly to her during the show, which is how she knew that she needed to go there. After Laura was accidentally bumped into by her hospital roommate later that day, Laura told her nurse that she then realized that the roommate was determined to join her in the pilgrimage. The nurse recognized these interchanges as referential delusions, active symptoms of Laura's schizophrenia.

A detailed account of the client's suicidal and homicidal thoughts must be obtained through direct questioning.

others. Contrary to popular belief, discussing these feelings with a client does not increase, and may lower, the likelihood of the client's acting on them. Direct questioning is essential. Questions regarding suicidal and **homicidal thoughts** should elicit information regarding the client's exact plan (including method, extent of lethality of method, availability of the means to carry out the plan), motivation or desire to carry out the plan, steps already taken to complete the plan, and factors preventing the client from following through, such as religiosity. The presence of active suicidal or homicidal thoughts constitutes a psychiatric emergency, and immediate action to ensure the safety of the client or the object of the client's anger is necessary.

Thought Process

The *thought process* is the way in which the client thinks. It is often evinced in the client's speech. Loose associations are marked by an illogical, difficult-to-follow shifting of ideas. Tangential thinking is exhibited when the client wanders from the subject at hand to a related one and is unable to come back to the original topic. Loose associations, tangential thought, word salad (completely nonsensical combination of words), and neologisms (nonsensical string of sounds that are formed into made-up words) often indicate schizophrenic disorders.

Circumstantial thought is demonstrated by clients who get lost in details but eventually return to the relevant topic. *Thought blocking* occurs when the thinking process stops altogether and the mind goes "blank." *Flight of ideas,* as seen in mania, involves pressured speech with rapid topic changes; the topics may be associated, but in a strange way. For example, "I can see! The sea is washing away the shells." *Confabulation,* often indicating dementia, is a fabrication of information to fill in for memory gaps. For example, a client may give an elaborate but untrue story about how he or she spent the day.

A client with a **concrete thought process** as opposed to an *abstract thought process* is only able to understand conversations literally. For example, a client who is asked what brought him or her to the hospital and responds, "an ambulance," is manifesting concrete thinking. A client's ability to think abstractly may be ascertained by assessing the client's interpretation of a proverb such as "people in glass houses should not throw stones" or the client's ability to describe similarities between objects such as a chair and table. Concrete thought is common in clients with schizophrenic disorders. A concrete thought process is not pathological when exhibited by children, however, who developmentally may not have the capacity for abstract thought until early adolescence (Sadock et al., 2003).

Perceptual Disturbances

Illusions, which are common in delirium, are misinterpretations of true stimuli. An example is when a curtain in a dark room is mistaken for a person. **Hallucinations** are defined as sensations experienced by the client without real external stimuli. A patient may not have intact reality testing, the ability to accept evidence that these perceptions are not real. Clients who appear to be talking to imaginary others or pointing at nonexistent objects during the assessment are probably experiencing hallucinations or illusions. Direct questioning regarding perceptual disturbances is usually required to elicit the specific symptoms. Hallucinations may be auditory, visual, gustatory, olfactory, or tactile; clients may hear, see, taste, smell, or feel things that in reality do not exist. Auditory hallucinations are the most common type; the more unusual visual, gustatory, olfactory, and tactile hallucinations may indicate medical illness or substance intoxication or withdrawal.

Hypnagogic and hypnopompic hallucinations are false sensory perceptions that occur while falling asleep and while awakening from sleep, respectively. Depersonalization is a perceptual difficulty in which the client feels unreal, dead, or mechanical; derealization is the sensation that the outside world is unreal. Hypnagogic and hypnopompic hallucinations, derealization, and depersonalization are considered within the normal range of experience and are not considered pathologic unless they cause undue distress or problems with daily functioning.

Impulse Control

Impulse control is the ability to delay, modulate, or inhibit the expression of behaviors and feelings. Clues to the client's ability to control his or her impulses are found in the content and process of the general interview. A client who describes a recent history of binge drinking and indiscriminate sexual contacts has poor impulse control. A person who storms out of an interview when difficult topics are broached also evinces poor impulse control. Assessing the client's ability to control impulses is an integral part of determining potential for acting on suicidal and violent thoughts.

Cognition and Sensorium

Level of consciousness, orientation, concentration, and memory are especially important to determine when assessing clients with coexisting medical problems or those who reveal symptoms of dementia during the interview. During the psychiatric interview, clients provide many clues to their sensorium. A client with an altered level of consciousness during the interview demonstrates a fluctuating ability to maintain awareness of the environment. Orientation is assessed by simply asking the client additional questions regarding full name, current location, date, and time.

A client's memory and concentration are determined by the ability to answer questions regarding psychiatric history. Concentration may also be assessed by asking the client to count backward from 100 by 7s (100, 93, 86 . . .), and memory is tested by asking the client to remember three objects immediately and to recall them after 5 minutes. Be aware that clients may have impairments in remote, recent past, recent, and immediate memory. The Mini-Mental State Examination (MMSE) efficiently and objectively measures cognition (Folstein, Folstein, & McHugh, 1975). The psychiatrist, psychologist, or advanced practice nurse typically performs this examination.

The client's intellectual functioning (below average, average, superior) may be estimated from the interview process as well.

Knowledge, Insight, and Judgment

Knowledge, insight, and judgment are related concepts usually ascertained while taking the client's history and while observing and discussing the client's actions in social situations and in dealing with mental illness. *Judgment* is the capacity to identify possible courses of action, anticipate their consequences, and choose the appropriate behavior. *Insight* refers to the extent of the client's awareness of illness and maladaptive behaviors. A client who tells the interviewer of reuniting with a physically abusive spouse because she feels that the spouse will change demonstrates poor judgment and little insight. A client who is admitted to the hospital for the third time because of noncompliance with antipsychotic medication, and who states that he stopped taking the medication because he is not really mentally ill, lacks knowledge of and insight into his illness and demonstrates poor judgment in regard to treatment. A client's judgment may be assessed by evaluating the answer to a hypothetical question such as: "What would you do if you found a stamped, addressed envelope in the street?"

Critical Thinking Questions What kind of information gathered in the mental status examination would prompt you to take immediate action? Specifically, what action would you take?

The Process of the Psychiatric Nursing Interview

The psychiatric nurse must pay attention to both the content of the client's words and the process of communication. How the client interacts with the nurse and the behaviors the client exhibits during the interview often provide important information concerning the client's symptomatology and ability to relate to others.

The interviewing process varies, ranging from casually talking with clients while, at the same time, assisting them with activities of daily living, to utilizing a standardized rating scale. Different methods may yield different information.

Empathy is the ability to put oneself in someone else's place. The nurse who can empathize with a client is able to understand how the client feels in a particular situation.

Phases of the Interview

An interview consists of a beginning, middle, and termination phase. In the initial moments of the interview, the nurse should begin to develop a rapport with the client and to engage the client in the meeting. Establishing a good rapport with a client is not simple; the nurse must put the client at ease, empathize with the client's suffering (i.e., understand how the client feels in a particular situation by mentally putting oneself in the client's place), listen compassionately, become the client's ally, and instill trust in the client of the nurse's expertise. The nurse must clarify the purpose of the meeting, which is to gain an understanding of the client's problems and to determine the best way to help. The client should be informed about the healthcare setting and the interviewer's credentials, and the rules of confidentiality should be discussed; these are requisite to making the client feel comfortable enough to share information.

During the middle phase of the interview, data are collected and processed. The nurse obtains information from and gives information to the client. For example, the nurse may assist the client in identifying ways to cope with symptoms.

The termination phase of the interview summarizes what has been accomplished during the meeting. A tentative diagnosis and an initial care plan are formulated and shared with the client. The termination phase is also used to help the client relax from the often emotional interaction (Kadushin, 1997).

Interviewing Techniques

One of the most important interviewing skills is the ability to be silent and attentive. Nonverbal communication, such as nodding in understanding and leaning slightly toward the client, demonstrates caring and attentiveness. Encouraging words, such as "I see" or "go on," enable the nurse to gather information without bombarding the client with questions. Allowing the client to discuss the chief complaint during the first few minutes of the interview is often an effective strategy to induce the client to "open up." Paraphrasing or summarizing the content and feelings related during the interview demonstrates that the nurse understands what the client has said and helps both the interviewer and the client to process an abundance of information. The nurse may need to ask questions for clarification to avoid jumping to conclusions about nebulous communications. Gentle transition statements such as, "What you are telling me about is important; however, there is one more important thing that we still need to discuss," keeps the interview on track without offending the client. Interviewing techniques must be individualized to the client's specific problems and personality (**Table 3-4**).

Self-Disclosure

Revealing personal information about oneself is a controversial technique that requires nursing experience, insight, and sophistication on the part of the interviewer. The nurse should share personal information with a client only if, after careful evaluation, the nurse believes that this sharing would benefit the client and improve treatment. The nurse should never disclose personal information for selfish reasons.

Self-disclosure is a controversial intervention that should only be used to benefit the client and the therapeutic process, never for selfish reasons.

Clinical Example

A client is going through a bad breakup of a relationship. The nurse may feel tempted to tell the client of a similar experience (e.g., "I know how you feel. My boyfriend and I just split up."). The nurse may feel good revealing this; however, a client in acute distress may feel that the nurse is not understanding his or her unique feelings and circumstances.

Additionally, **self-disclosure** reverses the interviewer-client dynamic and severs the client from the role of information-giver. One unique issue of self-disclosure involves the health professional who divulges a personal history of mental illness. In this situation, as in others, the nurse should discuss with an experienced nurse or supervisor and be guided by what best serves the client's interests.

One piece of information important to disclose to the client to protect the client's rights is the interviewer's name, title, and position. Many students and beginning practitioners are reluctant to divulge their novice status. Clients, however, may pick up on an interviewer's newness. Thus, denying that you are new in the field may cause a lack of trust. Clients who seem distressed by the nurse's lack of experience should be encouraged to discuss this with the nurse and may be referred to the nurse's supervisor for reassurance if necessary. Psychiatric clients who have had previous experience with new nurses and students often come to expect this as the norm; certain clients actually take pride in "training" new nurses.

Critical Thinking Questions What kind of personal information would be appropriate to share with a nonpsychotic client on the first interview? How and in what context would you disclose this information?

Choosing Appropriate Questions

The client's state and the subject being evaluated determine whether to ask open-ended or **closed-ended questions**. **Open-ended questions** are vague and may be answered in many different ways. The nurse may say, "Tell me about your problem." Open-ended questions are most helpful in obtaining a broad range of information from clients without thought disorders. *Closed-ended questions* elicit specific and concise information. Disorganized clients who are unable to tolerate a long interview usually need to be guided by closed-ended questions when giving information. Some topics of discussion, such as suicidal thoughts, lend themselves to direct questioning; clients who are given more freedom to answer may skirt the issue or provide incomplete information. Questions typically become more specific or closed-ended as the interview progresses (Sadock et al., 2003).

Certain types of questions should be avoided when evaluating the client, because they may taint the information elicited. Leading questions such as, "You do not abuse street drugs, do

Table 3-4 Therapeutic Versus Nontherapeutic Interviewing Techniques

Goal	Therapeutic Techniques and Examples	Nontherapeutic Techniques and Examples
To engage the client in treatment	Offering self: "I will stay here with you for a while." Suggested collaboration: "Let's work together to see if we can identify when your problems began."	Giving false reassurance: "Don't worry; everything will be fine." Using platitudes: "Keep your chin up; tomorrow is another day."
To get the client to open up and share information	Judiciously using silence. Actively listening by nodding and leaning toward the client. Using encouraging verbalizations such as "yes" and "I understand." Offering general leads such as "please continue" or "I am interested in hearing more about that."	Asking questions that yield only "yes" or "no" answers. Asking incessant closed-ended questions, so that the conversation seems like an interrogation.
To convey to the client that you understand	Summarizing the content. Restating content: *Client:* "I am so depressed that I cannot even eat." *Nurse:* "So your depression has caused you to lose your appetite." Reflecting on process: "You seem anxious." "It seems difficult for you to talk about this."	Using premature interpretations that deny the client's feelings: "You're not really angry with your mother; you're just looking for attention." Inappropriately using self-disclosure: "I know just how you feel, because my boyfriend just broke up with me, too."
To get the client more actively involved in treatment	Reflecting client's questions back to him or her: *Client:* "What should I tell people at work about my hospitalization?" *Nurse:* "What are you thinking about telling them?" Encouraging comparison: "What have you done in the past when faced with such a difficult situation?" Encouraging decision making: "What will you do the next time that you find yourself in a similar situation?"	Overtly agreeing or disagreeing with the client: "What you did was definitely the right (or wrong) thing to do." Giving advice: "I think that you should . . ."
To explore a topic in more detail	Exploring: "Could you tell me more about that issue?" Focusing: "Let's go back and discuss that topic further."	Bombarding the client with multiple closed-ended questions on a topic.
To diffuse a client's nonpsychotic anger	Agreeing with the grain of truth in the client's complaint: *Client:* "I hate this hospital. It's like a jail." *Nurse:* "I can see how you would feel that way, with all of the rules and the locked door. Let's talk about how you can be more comfortable here."	Denying the client's reality: *Client:* "I hate this hospital. It's like a jail." *Nurse:* "You know that this is not a jail."
To help the client control aggressive behavior	Limit-setting: "I will not be able to continue to talk with you if you continue to act in a threatening manner." Giving positive reinforcement for calm behavior. Decreasing stimuli: Placing the client in a quiet area until he or she is calmer.	Punishing the client: "You are going to have to stay in your room for 1 hour because you cursed at me" (choosing an arbitrary time period, unrelated to the client's behavior).
To clarify information	Asking for clarification: "Could you explain that to me again?" "Let's see if I have this straight." Placing events in sequence: "Did you start to drink alcohol before or after becoming depressed?"	Jumping to conclusions about the meaning of a client's statement, instead of seeking clarification.
To determine causes of problems or behaviors	Nonjudgmentally exploring: "What is it that gets in the way of your getting up to make it to work on time?"	Asking confrontational "why" questions: "Why are you unable to get to work on time?"

continues

Table 3-4 Therapeutic Versus Nontherapeutic Interviewing Techniques, continued

Goal	Therapeutic Techniques and Examples	Nontherapeutic Techniques and Examples
To effectively address delusional content	Focusing on the feeling content of delusions: *Client:* "People are trying to kill me!" *Nurse:* "You must be very frightened."	Directly challenging a client's belief system: *Client:* "Laser beams are irradiating me!" *Nurse:* "There is no way that laser beams are being sent through you—that's impossible."
To move to another topic of discussion	Transitioning gently: "What you are saying is very important, and I want to give it proper attention when we have more time. Right now, however, we need to move on."	Rejecting a client's topic or abruptly changing the subject: "It's not necessary to go into that right now. Let's talk about your hallucinations instead."

you?" steer the client to answer in a certain way. Questions beginning with *why* may make the client become defensive. For example, "Why did you not follow your physician's instructions and take your medication?" is more confrontational than "Tell me more about your decision to stop taking medication." Questions leading to yes or no answers such as, "Do you drink alcohol?" may yield incomplete data, as opposed to an open-ended question, such as, "Describe your alcohol use."

Client-Related Factors Influencing the Interview

A client may provide unreliable information during the interview for several reasons. Symptoms of mental illness such as delusions, disorganized thought, or disorganized speech may interfere with communication and alter the client's sense of reality. The client's lack of insight may also lead to an altered perception of reality. For example, an alcoholic may tell the nurse that he or she only drinks "socially." Some clients may purposely distort or provide false information (e.g., an undocumented alien who feigns citizenship or a client with antisocial personality disorder who denies a criminal history). A client who is poorly motivated for treatment (e.g., an involuntary client) often resists giving information.

Clinician-Related Factors Influencing the Interview

The nurse's interviewing skills are based on experience, intuition, critical-thinking ability, personality, and communication style.

The nurse's level of skill affects the flow of the interview and the information obtained. Interviewing skills are related to the nurse's degree of psychiatric experience, use of intuition or "gut feeling," critical thinking abilities, personality, and communication style. The nurse's ability to convey acceptance and **empathy** helps the client to feel comfortable in sharing information that is of a sensitive nature. The nurse's interest and enthusiasm may help the client to overlook small interviewing errors and inexperience (Sadock et al., 2003). The nurse's ability to be genuine is also important, because clients usually sense when others are acting unlike their true personalities. For example, the nurse should not attempt to bond with an inner-city adolescent by using unfamiliar slang.

The nurse's culture, race, age, religion, gender, socioeconomic status, and intellect necessarily affect the interview process. A nurse must not avoid issues that are important to the client but that are difficult for the nurse because of personal background. For example, a nurse for whom spirituality is unimportant must not ignore the client's spirituality.

Transference

Transference is traditionally defined as a client's unrealistic and often inappropriate feelings, thoughts, and behaviors toward the therapist. Transference in this traditional sense is an unconscious displacement of attitudes originally held toward other significant persons in the client's life, especially from early childhood, onto the healthcare professional (Goldstein, 1995). The concept of transference includes an appreciation for the role that the reality of the therapeutic relationship plays in determining the client's response to treatment and attitude toward the healthcare worker. For example, a minority client who has been the victim of prejudice may be appropriately apprehensive about disclosing information to a therapist with the same ethnic background as his or her oppressors.

Depending upon the client, the mental health professional, and the specific relationship between the two, the client's reactions toward the professional comprise degrees of reality and fantasy. Reality reactions are more likely to occur with healthier clients whereas unconscious transference from displacement of prior relationships predominantly occurs in psychotic clients. Nurses who actively participate in the interview process correlate with more reality-based transference, because clients see these nurses as real people rather than blank screens onto which fantasies may be projected (Goldstein, 1995).

Countertransference

The healthcare professional's feelings and reactions toward the client are known as **countertransference**. Countertransference can be viewed similarly on a reality-fantasy continuum. Woods and Hollis (2000) believe that workers displace feelings, attitudes, and fantasies onto some clients more than others, depending on the workers' particular life experiences.

Vannicelli (1992) has identified the following indicators of the presence of countertransference: inappropriate emotional responses toward the client, feelings of exhaustion, stereotyped or fixed responses regardless of what the client is saying, exaggerated emotional responses, impulses to treat the client in a special way, and extreme over- or underinvolvement. Education, supervision, and consultation with colleagues are essential for the nurse to use the countertransference productively. Appropriately analyzed, countertransference may offer important clues to a client's diagnosis or symptoms. For example, a nurse's feelings of extreme anger during an interview may identify the client's hidden rage.

Power Disparity

One important source of transference and countertransference is the power disparity between the interview participants. The interviewer (the nurse) assumes the responsibility for moving the interaction forward to achieve a goal, while the client passively answers questions. This situation often results in a transference, which for the client represents a repetition of feelings and reactions from past experiences with authority figures. Depending upon the client's history and current symptoms, the client may be overly compliant with the interviewer (e.g., tell the interviewer exactly what the interviewer wants to hear) or overly oppositional (e.g., assert that the professional has "no right" to ask such personal questions). For the nurse, the power disparity may cause feelings of omnipotence and fantasies of being able to "save" the client. The nurse may fail to involve the client in the treatment plan and may feel anger toward noncompliant clients as well.

Transference consists of realistic and unrealistic feelings that the client has toward the mental health professional. *Countertransference* are the feelings the worker has toward the client.

Resistance

Resistance refers to anything that impedes the progress of the interview or treatment. A client's resistance is often self-protective, and in many cases reticence increases when the client is confronted directly. During the initial interview, the client genuinely may be too paranoid, disorganized, despondent, or agitated to respond to all the questions. Confronting this resistance by asking the client why he or she is not being "up-front" with the interviewer may cause the client to retreat further. Temporarily changing the subject when a client becomes extremely angry or upset may enable the client to continue with the interview. Validating the client's feelings that underlie the resistance often effectively encourages the client to speak. For example, a reluctant client is more likely to self-disclose if the nurse agrees that it must be scary to trust a virtual stranger with personal information.

Interview Duration

The duration of the evaluation interview depends on the purpose of the evaluation, the client's state, and the nurse's availability. The

Clinical Example

Leo is a 15-year-old male admitted to a residential treatment center for the treatment of oppositional defiant disorder. Immediately upon his arrival to the unit, the admitting nurse sat down with Leo to complete a four-page nursing assessment form. When the rest of the residents lined up to go to the cafeteria for dinner, Leo promptly got up to join them. The nurse shouted at Leo to sit back down because the assessment was not yet complete and he had not asked for permission to join the group. Leo cursed at the nurse and stated that he was hungry. The nurse shouted back to Leo that she—and not Leo—was in charge of the unit, and that if he "kept it up" she would ban him from the cafeteria for the rest of the week. The supervisor arrived at the scene and quickly recognized that a power struggle had developed between the nurse and the new resident, who were demonstrating countertransference and transference (respectively). The supervisor asked another nurse to go over the rule book with Leo and to inform him that food would soon be brought to the unit for him, while the supervisor discussed the problematic transaction privately with the admitting nurse.

interview should be relatively brief (10 to 15 minutes) if the client is acutely ill and unable to tolerate much contact and exploration. The interview may be spread out over several short interactions, and the nurse may need to sit on the floor or even stand if the client's state requires it. Focused evaluations, such as those evaluating a client for entry into an incest survivor group, are usually shorter than a broad evaluation interview because of the limited content. If an interview is abbreviated as a result of the nurse's workload, the nurse must return at a later time or delegate further interviewing tasks to a colleague.

Environmental Issues

Uncomfortable furniture, air temperature, and interruptions such as a ringing phone or beeper may impair the flow of an interview. A peaceful and comfortable environment enhances the interviewing process. The interview environment should be private enough so that confidentiality is not compromised. At the same time, the environment in which the interview takes place should also ensure the nurse's safety; leaving the door ajar and positioning oneself near the door of the room will usually conserve privacy while allowing for safe egress should a client become aggressive. Many settings have safety measures such as emergency buzzers and overhead paging systems by which other workers can be called in to assist in a crisis situation.

Collateral History

If a client is deemed an unreliable historian, additional history should be obtained from family, friends, colleagues, and mental health professionals who have had previous contact with the client; this **collateral history** may be obtained only with the client's consent, unless it is an emergency. Those accompanying the client to the evaluation interview should be interviewed at that time, if possible. The client may feel more or less comfortable being interviewed simultaneously with a significant other, and the nurse should follow the client's lead. Clients should also be allowed time alone with the interviewer; this gives them privacy to disclose important information they may not be willing to discuss in the presence of others.

> With the client's consent, a *collateral history* may be obtained from family, friends, colleagues, or mental health professionals to ensure an accurate account of the client's history.

Psychological Testing

Psychological testing involves evaluation tools that objectively measure personality, intelligence, or symptomatology of specific mental illnesses. *Neuropsychological testing* is useful in detecting subtle cognitive defects in clients who are not obviously demented or brain-damaged. Psychological and neuropsychological tests are usually performed by experts in the field or specially trained nurses/mental health professionals. At minimum, nurses should be sufficiently familiar with the different tests to be able to glean meaningful information about a client from reading the testing reports. Nurses must know enough to be able to recommend that certain tests be performed.

> Standardized rating scales provide objective data to supplement information obtained through the nurse-client interview.

Increasingly, nurses utilize standardized rating scales such as those used during the assessment process. Rating scales that are administered by trained healthcare professionals provide objective baseline data of a client's symptoms that can be compared to later scores to evaluate the efficacy of treatment. This is important given the current emphasis on quality assessment, cost-effectiveness, and managed care. Despite the trend toward using standardized tools for data collection, this mode of assessment cannot substitute for the nurse-client interview.

Some rating scales were designed for clients, and not professionals, to complete. Certain self-rating scales such as the Beck Depression Inventory yield reliable and valid data that can assist professionals in the diagnosis of mental illness or to gauge treatment progress. Other self-rating systems are less precise but are useful for the client's self-monitoring of illness symptoms and coping skills. A nurse and his or her client can even design their own rating scale for the client based on the client's specific illness symptoms, for use in relapse prevention. See **Table 3-5** for commonly performed psychological tests, including rating scales.

Physical Assessment

The term *mental disorder* implies a distinction between mental and physical disorders. In actuality, there is much "physical" in "mental" and much "mental" in "physical" disorders (APA, 2000). Some clients who present primarily with psychiatric symptoms may be suffering from an underlying medical illness, such as hypothyroidism or acute intermittent porphyria. As the population ages, more cases of acquired immunodeficiency syndrome (AIDS) appear, and as the incidences of substance abuse and polypharmacy increase, mental disorders resulting from general medical conditions have become more prevalent. The

Table 3-5 Commonly Performed Psychological Tests and Rating Scales

Name of Test	Purpose of Test	Description of Test
Wechsler Adult Intelligence Scale (WAIS)	Intelligence test	This test includes six verbal and five performance subtests, yielding a verbal intelligence quotient (IQ), a performance IQ, and a full-scale IQ. It is the most widely used IQ test.
Minnesota Multiphasic Personality Inventory (MMPI)	Personality assessment	This is a self-report inventory of over 500 yes or no questions, the results of which are scores on 10 different scales (e.g., depression scale, paranoia scale). The pattern of scores is interpreted by the tester by comparing the scores and subscores against standardized data.
Rorschach Test	Projective personality assessment	Clients are shown inkblots and asked to describe what they see. Clients project their needs, fantasies, and thoughts into the inkblots because of their ambiguity. This test is very difficult to analyze.
Substance Abuse Subtle Screening Inventory (SASSI)	To identify people who have a high probability of substance use disorders, even when they are unlikely to admit to the problem outright. There is one version of the test for adults, and another for adolescents.	A 15-minute questionnaire, including face valid items as well as subtle items that do not address substance misuse in a direct or apparent manner.
Abnormal Involuntary Movement Scale (AIMS)	To test for psychomotor side effects of psychotropic medication	A 12-item inventory performed by trained evaluators who rate the client's involuntary muscular movements on a scale of 0 to 4.
Hamilton Depression Rating Scale (HAM-D)	To test for severity of depression in clients already diagnosed with an affective disorder	A 21- or 17-item inventory performed by trained evaluators who rate physical and psychological symptoms of depression on a scale of 0 to 4.
Beck Depression Inventory (BDI)	To measure attitude and symptoms that are characteristic of depression	A 21-item inventory performed either by a trained professional *or* by the client, who rates depressive symptoms and attitudes on a scale of 0 to 3.
Brief Psychiatric Rating Scale (BPRS)	To assess psychopathology in clients with, or suspected of having, schizophrenia or other psychotic illness	A 16-item inventory of a broad range of psychiatric symptoms, scored by a trained professional using a 7-point Likert scale.
Mini-Mental State Examination (MMSE)	To screen for cognitive impairment caused by dementia	A nine-item structured clinician-rated interview scale incorporating pencil-and-paper tasks.

term *organic* is used in clinical practice to refer to these illnesses.

A medical workup may be completed to rule out organic illness. The medical workup also ensures that the client is well enough to tolerate psychopharmacologic and other psychiatric treatments safely. The physical examination is an essential part of the workup that may be performed by the advanced practice nurse. Basic-level nurses assess the client's vital signs, teach the client about the examination, and reassure him or her throughout the examination. Important clinical laboratory tests include serum and urine

Clinical Example

Kay, a 52-year-old woman, was admitted to the psychiatric unit from the emergency room. She presented primarily with agitation. She seemed to be hallucinating, speaking to people who were not there. On closer examination, Kay was delirious with waxing and waning cognitive abilities. She was disoriented to place and time, tachycardic, and diaphoretic. Kay was able to provide a history of hypothyroidism, which had been treated sporadically with thyroid replacement hormone. Her family provided additional history concerning Kay's chronic alcoholism. Kay was transferred to a medical unit where she was placed on a librium alcohol detoxification protocol, and her thyroid level was stabilized. Most of her presenting symptoms resolved.

The *medical workup* consists of a physical examination, clinical laboratory tests, and specialized diagnostic procedures.

drug screens; thyroid, liver, and kidney function tests; complete blood counts; and sexually transmitted disease screening. Serum tests are also used to evaluate the levels of psychotropic medications in the client's blood. A low lithium level, for example, may precipitate a manic episode. A number of medical illnesses present with psychiatric symptoms, and specific diagnostic tests are used to detect them (**Table 3-6**).

Specialized diagnostic procedures performed on psychiatric clients include an EEG, which discerns if a seizure-like basis for an illness, such as an impulse control disorder, exists. In delirium, as a result of metabolic problems, the EEG generally shows high-voltage, slow-wave activity. Other tests including MRI, computed tomography (CT), and positron emission tomography (PET) identify space-occupying lesions and metabolic brain disorders. The tests may also identify biologic markers of mental illness; researchers have found evidence of increased brain ventricle size detected by MRI and CT and decreased frontal cortex activity detected by PET in clients with certain forms of schizophrenia (Sadock et al., 2003).

Organizing Data: Diagnosis

Formulating the client's diagnosis is an integral part of the psychiatric evaluation. During the assessment, the nurse must keep an open mind and avoid settling on a definitive diagnosis early in the interview. All aspects of the holistic assessment must be considered.

Nursing Diagnosis

All registered nurses are licensed to diagnose and treat human response to actual or potential health problems.

The American Nurses Association (ANA, 2007) states that nurses diagnose "human responses to actual or potential health problems." The practice of nurses diagnosing clients has met with long-standing resistance. Many nurses who graduated prior to the inclusion of the nursing diagnosis in the college curricula feel that making a diagnosis is beyond their scope. Nurses who were exposed to the theoretical aspects of the nursing diagnosis in school often have difficulty translating this knowledge into practice. Other professionals, notably physicians, may fear that boundaries are being crossed when nurses formulate diagnoses. Clients may be wary when nurses take a leadership role in their treatment.

Nursing diagnoses were originally categorized by the North American Nursing Diagnosis Association (NANDA) in 1986, and were last revised for 2007–2008 (www.nanda.org). Nursing diagnoses may relate to actual problems, risks for problems, or wellness issues. A nursing diagnosis is a concisely worded statement that includes the diagnostic label/definition, related factors, and defining characteristics.

One example of a nursing diagnosis is "post-trauma syndrome related to physical abuse, as evidenced by flashbacks, nightmares, and hypervigilence."

Formulating nursing diagnoses is difficult because of the array of possible human responses and the causes of these responses (Regan-Kubinski, 1995). Prioritizing these diagnoses is therefore essential. Without question, safety issues must be of primary concern (e.g., the risk for self-directed violence). Some diagnoses are addressed immediately, and others require long-term intervention. Remember that several diagnoses may be addressed simultaneously and that they will continue to be addressed in the outpatient setting (e.g., with home care, day program, psychotherapy, psychopharmacology). The client and family should actively participate in prioritizing the nursing diagnoses.

Diagnostic and Statistical Manual of Mental Disorders

The *Diagnostic and Statistical Manual of Mental Disorders* has been the primary resource used throughout the United States for classifying mental disorders since its original publication in 1952. More than 1,000 health professionals analyzed scientific data and performed field trials to test for validity and reliability of diagnostic categories, to prepare the *DSM-IV* (APA, 1994). In 2000, the American Psychiatric Association revised parts of the text portion of the *DSM-IV* to include new research information regarding associated features; culture, age, and gender features; prevalence; course; and familial pattern of many of the mental disorders listed. This new version, *DSM-IV-TR*, included very few changes to the diagnostic categories; the most notable changes in this regard were with the tic disorders and the paraphilias, which may now be diagnosed even if the associated behaviors do not cause the person distress or impaired functioning (APA, 2000).

Table 3-6 Physical Illnesses Presenting with Psychiatric Symptoms

Physical Illness	Physical Symptoms	Psychiatric Symptoms	Tests Used to Diagnose Physical Illness
Acquired immunodeficiency syndrome (AIDS)	Fever, weight loss, ataxia, incontinence, seizures, and opportunistic infections	Progressive dementia, personality changes, and depression	HIV antibody test, CT scan, MRI, lumbar puncture, and blood cultures
Acute intermittent porphyria	Abdominal pain, fever, nausea, vomiting, constipation, peripheral neuropathy, and paralysis	Depression, agitation, paranoia, and visual hallucinations	CBC, pulse, and Δ-aminolevulinic acid and porphobilinogen levels
Brain neoplasm	Headache, vomiting, papilledema, and local finding on neurological examination	Personality changes	Lumbar puncture, skull x-ray, CT scan, and EEG
Hepatic encephalopathy	Hyperreflexia, ecchymosis, liver enlargement, and ataxia	Euphoria, disinhibition, psychosis, depression	LFTs, serum albumin level, and EEG
Huntington's disease	Rigidity and choreoathetoid movements	Depression and euphoria	Genetic testing
Hyperglycemia	Polyuria, anorexia, nausea, vomiting, dehydration, abdominal complaints, acetone on breath, and seizures	Anxiety, agitation, and delirium	Fingerstick for blood glucose and urine dipstick for glucose and ketones
Hyperthyroidism	Sweating, diarrhea, weight loss, tachycardia, tremor, palpitations, vomiting, and heat intolerance	Nervousness, irritability, pressured speech, insomnia, and psychosis	TFTs and ECG
Hypoglycemia	Sweating, drowsiness, stupor, coma, tachycardia, tremor, restlessness, and seizures	Anxiety, confusion, and agitation	Pulse rate and fingerstick for blood glucose
Hyponatremia	Excessive thirst, polydipsia, stupor, and coma	Confusion, lethargy, and personality changes	Serum electrolytes
Hypothyroidism	Dry skin, cold intolerance, constipation, weight gain, and goiter	Lethargy, depression, personality changes, and psychosis	TFTs and ECG
Multiple sclerosis	Sudden transient motor and sensory disturbances	Anxiety, euphoria, mania, and personality changes	Lumbar puncture and head CT
Seizure disorder	Sensory distortions and aura	Confusion, psychosis, dissociative states, catatonia-like states, violence, and bizarre behavior	EEG
Systemic lupus erythematosus	Fever, photosensitivity, butterfly rash, headache, and joint pain	Depression, mood changes, and psychosis	ANA, lupus erythematosus test, CBC, chest x-ray
Tertiary syphilis	Skin lesions, arthritis, respiratory distress, and progressive cardiovascular disease	Personality changes, decreased performance of activities of daily living, irritability, confusion, and psychosis	VDRL and lumbar puncture
Thiamine deficiency	Neuropathy, cardiomyopathy, nystagmus, and headache	Confusion and confabulation	Thiamine level
Vitamin B_{12} deficiency	Pallor, dizziness, peripheral neuropathy, and ataxia	Irritability, inattentiveness, and psychosis	Vitamin B_{12} level, Schilling test, and CBC

Note: HIV = human immunodeficiency virus; CT = computed tomography; MRI = magnetic resonance imaging; CBC = complete blood count; EEG = electroencephalogram; LFTs = liver function tests; TFTs = thyroid function tests; ECG = electrocardiograph; ANA = antinuclear antibody test; VDRL = venereal disease research laboratory test

Psychiatric nurses must be well versed in the classification system and terminology used in the *DSM-IV-TR*, but only the advanced practice registered nurse (APRN) may use the guide to diagnose a mental disorder. To diagnose a client with the *DSM-IV-TR*, an individual must have appropriate training and experience with the system (APA, 2000).

When working with the *DSM-IV-TR*, the nurse must remember that normal reactions to stressful events, such as the death of a loved one, are not considered mental disorders. Additionally, some phenomena, which in the mainstream would indicate a mental disorder, are not symptomatic for a mental disorder if they are culturally appropriate. For example, in certain Hispanic cultures persons may talk to their dead mother's ghost. Socially unacceptable behavior, such as crime, does not necessarily indicate a mental illness. Lastly, the nurse must remember that the person's diagnosis is being classified, not the person him- or herself; the client is not just a "schizophrenic," but a multifaceted individual who happens to have schizophrenia (APA, 2000).

Multiaxial *DSM-IV* Diagnosis

Diagnosing mental disorders with the *DSM-IV-TR* is not foolproof; various mental disorders have overlapping symptoms, and individuals with the same disorder may differ significantly. The manual provides text and decision-tree diagrams that assist in establishing the **differential diagnosis**. The *DSM-IV-TR* also provides guidance to diagnose clients with insufficient information or information that does not fit neatly into one category. A diagnosis may be deferred, declared provisional, or delineated as atypical or not otherwise specified (NOS; APA, 2000). The diagnostic categories of the *DSM-IV-TR* often include several subtypes as well as descriptive statements that indicate the severity and course of the illness.

CASE STUDY Mr. C.

Psychosocial history: Mr. C., a 60-year-old man, was brought to the hospital by ambulance immediately following a suicide attempt by hanging. This hospitalization marked his first contact with the mental healthcare system. Mr. C. arrived combative and in four-point restraints and presented with the chief complaint, "I just wanted to die. . . . I feel hopeless and lost." According to the client, he had been feeling depressed for 2 months preceding the attempt and had experienced diminished appetite, insomnia, anhedonia, hopelessness, helplessness, and worthlessness during the 2 weeks prior to his suicide attempt.

The client identified that his troubles began 1 year prior, when his cardiologist advised Mr. C. to leave a job that he had held for over 30 years because of his compromised physical condition following a coronary bypass operation. Although Mr. C. had not planned an early retirement, he heeded the physician's advice and applied for disability payments. He soon fell into debt, resulting from the lengthy waiting period for disability payments, family weekend gambling excursions to Atlantic City, and accumulating medical bills. Mr. C., who had always been the head of household in his traditional family, felt that he had no choice but to return to work. He also became noncompliant with his heart medications, began to withdraw from social events, had frequent arguments with his wife, and experienced a reemergence of chest pain.

Mr. C. finally terminated his employment a few months later, upon receipt of disability checks. A month prior to the suicide attempt, Mr. C. received notification from the disability office that he was ineligible for the entitlement because he had worked for those few months after having applied and that he owed $4,000 in back pay. It was also around this time that his teenaged grandson was incarcerated for armed robbery.

Mr. C. had no previous psychiatric history. He did not use drugs or alcohol, but has smoked one pack per day for 40 years. His medical history was significant for heart disease. Mr. C. had a family history of hypertension and heart disease. He reported that his mother suffered from postpartum depression after the birth of her third child, which resolved without treatment. Mr. C. was the oldest of three children in a middle class family. Mr. C. met normal developmental milestones. Mr. C.'s father died when he was 14 years of age, after which Mr. C. was forced to drop out of school in order to work to help support his family. Although Mr. C. was close with his siblings in his youth, he fell out of touch with them after their mother passed away. He and his wife had been married for nearly 40 years at the time of the hospitalization. Their two grown children were living out of state. Mr. C. was normally in close contact with his children by tele-

The **multiaxial *DSM-IV-TR* diagnosis** is divided into five categories, or axes.

Axis I

Axis I comprises mostly clinical disorders such as major depression, chronic schizophrenia, and attention deficit disorder. Specific diagnostic criteria, consisting of the signs and symptoms of the illnesses, are provided for each of these disorders. Some of these criteria must be present before a diagnosis is made, and other symptoms may accompany them. The information obtained through the interview and testing is compared with the signs and symptoms found in the descriptions of the *DSM-IV-TR* for specific disorders.

Axis II

Axis II includes personality disorders and mental retardation, along with the related diagnostic signs and symptoms. Axis II diagnoses are deemed secondary to Axis I diagnoses, unless it is clearly stated that the client's primary diagnosis is on Axis II. Axis I and Axis II together contain the entire classification of mental disorders, numbering over 300 illnesses. This list of disorders is large but incomplete because the classification system constantly evolves through research.

Axis III

Axis III denotes the client's physical disorders or medical conditions. A medical illness may be the cause of the mental disorder (e.g., human immunodeficiency virus [HIV] infection on Axis III with dementia secondary to HIV infection on Axis I), the result of the mental disorder (e.g., cirrhosis on Axis III with alcohol dependence on Axis I), or unrelated to the mental disorder.

Axis IV

Axis IV recognizes psychosocial and environmental factors that may precipitate, result from, or affect the treatment of mental illness. Axis IV lists

phone. He had several close friendships through his job and from his church, but lately had not been socially involved with anyone besides immediate family.

Although Mr. C. had never earned his high school diploma, he had a successful career with the local utilities company until his recent health problems. Mr. C. verbalized a strong belief that the male in the household should be the primary provider for his family and that the woman should tend to the home. Mr. C. considered himself religious, regularly attended services, and took comfort in his belief in God. When asked about coping skills, Mr. C. reported that in the past he talked about his problems with friends and his priest. He reported that smoking gives him some relief from anxiety.

On the mental status examination, Mr. C. was a well-groomed Caucasian man who appeared older than his years. His posture was poor, and he exhibited psychomotor retardation. He was cooperative with the interview for 20 minutes, after which point he stated that he was too tired to continue. The client's mood was depressed, with a depressed affect that was constricted in range. His speech was slow, soft, and nonspontaneous. Mr. C. evinced no formal thought disorder. Mr. C. denied experiencing hallucinations, and there was no evidence of delusional thought. He expressed ambivalence about having survived his suicide attempt but stated that he had no plan to try again while in the hospital, because he wanted to see if we could help him with his problems. Mr. C. stated that perhaps his surviving the attempt was God's way of telling him that other people needed him here on earth. His impulse control, judgment, and insight were poor to fair, as shown by his gambling, going back to work against his doctor's advice, noncompliance with cardiac medications, impulsive suicide attempt, and ambivalence about his survival. Mr. C. was alert and oriented to person, place, and time. His memory for recent history was intact, and his concentration seemed mildly impaired. His level of intellect was deemed average, and he seemed to be a reliable historian.

Mr. C. rated his depression by using the Beck Depression Inventory, scoring in the range indicative of severe depression. The review of Mr. C.'s activities of daily living was significant for diminished appetite with a 20-pound weight loss as well as initial insomnia over the past year. His laboratory tests were all within normal limits. Mr. C.'s physical examination was significant for hypertension.

See **Table 3-7** for the diagnostic formulation for Mr. C., and Nursing Care Plan: Depression for the associated nursing care plan.

Table 3-7 Diagnostic Formulation of Mr. C.

DSM-IV-TR Diagnosis	NANDA-I Diagnosis
Axis I: 296.2 Major Depressive Disorder, Single Episode Axis II: 312.31 Provisional Diagnosis: Pathological Gambling 799.9 Diagnosis deferred on Axis II Axis III: Atherosclerotic Heart Disease, Hypertension Axis IV: Adjustment to forced early retirement, medical illness, financial difficulties, family discord Axis V: GAF = 20 (on admission to hospital)	Risk for suicide related to depression and stressful life events, manifested by serious suicide attempt Ineffective health maintenance related to financial difficulties and depression, manifested by noncompliance with cardiac medication Imbalanced nutrition: less than body requirements related to depression, manifested by decreased appetite and weight loss Sleep deprivation related to depression, manifested by insomnia Situational low self-esteem related to medical illness, forced early retirement, and depression; manifested by inability to maintain family finances and marital discord

Note: DSM-IV-TR = Diagnostic and Statistical Manual of Mental Disorders, 4th ed., Text Revision; NANDA-I = *Nursing Diagnoses: Definitions and Classifications, 2007–2008;* GAF = global assessment of functioning

NURSING CARE PLAN Depression

Expected Outcomes	Interventions	Evaluations
• Will not make suicidal gestures.	• Monitor client on a 1:1 observation.	• Evaluating for suicidal thoughts, plan, intent, lethality, and access to means each shift. • Assessing the client's reasons to continue living.
• Will sleep 6–7 hours a night.	• Teach relaxation techniques.	• Evaluating the client's demonstration of relaxation techniques, evaluating number of hours slept nightly.
• Will improve nutritional intake.	• Assess for likes and dislikes, encouraging small, frequent meals, referring to a nutritionist.	• Monitoring for weight gain on a weekly basis.
• Will learn alternative coping mechanisms.	• Assist the client in identifying coping mechanisms that have worked in the past in similar situations.	• Observing for increased use of adaptive coping mechanisms.
• Will be compliant with treatment.	• Teach the client about heart disease and treatment.	• Monitoring compliance with cardiac medication.
• Will have improved sense of self-worth.	• Identify and assist in correcting cognitive distortions.	• Administering Beck Depression Inventory at regular intervals.
• Will establish contact with community resources.	• Discuss possible community resources and support systems.	• Evaluating the client's participation in a heart disease support group.

Visit http://nursing.jbpub.com/psychiatric for additional care plans and exercises.

psychosocial and environmental events that would have a strong impact on the average person and that were experienced by the client in the year preceding the evaluation. Events occurring prior to that time should not be included unless they are catastrophic, in which case they may be directly involved in the etiology of the mental disorder (e.g., childhood abuse leading to PTSD). Stressors may include negative events, such as job loss, as well as events ordinarily deemed positive, such as the birth of a child. The *DSM-IV-TR* categorizes these stressors into clusters that the clinician should use as evaluation guidelines. The client's specific problems should be listed under Axis IV.

Axis V

Axis V indicates the client's overall ability to function. Using the **Global Assessment of Functioning (GAF) scale**, the interviewer rates the client's total psychological, social, and occupational or academic well-being on a scale of 1 to 100 (1 being virtually nonfunctional and 100 being asymptomatic with superior function in all realms). Both the severity of psychiatric symptoms and the degree of social, work, or school impairment are considered on the scale, which represents a continuum of mental health and mental illness. A person's GAF score changes over time, thus the clinician must rate the client for the most pertinent time period (e.g., upon admission, upon discharge, highest level in past year) and identify the time frame of the rating. The GAF score is useful when operationalizing a client's progress from admission to discharge. It is also helpful in formulating a prognosis; a high premorbid GAF score portends a good prognosis.

Outcome Identification and Planning of Nursing Care

The initial nursing care plan is based on the comprehensive assessment and attendant nursing diagnoses, with consideration of the medical diagnosis. Initial planning of care marks the final phase of the psychiatric client's evaluation. The care plan consists of the nursing diagnoses or problem list, outcome goals, interventions used to attain these outcomes, and evaluation of the interventions and their efficacy in achieving desired outcomes. Outcome identification is an important part of the nursing process; interventions cannot be delineated without first outlining the goals of the interventions (ANA, 2007).

The outcome measures should be client-centered, realistic, observable, measurable, specific, time-limited, and mutually agreed upon by client and nurse. Some diagnoses lend themselves to easily operationalized outcome measures, and others present some difficulty as a result of the subjective nature of the probe. For example, outcome measures for altered nutrition are more easily quantified than are measures for self-esteem disturbance.

In early care planning, the goal is to identify and explore urgent problems. Initial care planning should be done in collaboration with the client, family, and other members of the interdisciplinary treatment team. The **therapeutic contract** is the agreement between the nurse and client to work on these mutually identified problems. A contract may be in written form or may be a verbal agreement. Especially in the beginning of treatment, the amount and type of collaboration client and family offers may be limited; the nurse must then accept the balance of responsibility for treatment. Some clients actively resist collaboration. When this is the case, the nurse's first priority is to engage the client in treatment by setting firm limits, providing positive reinforcement for small steps, and persevering against resistance.

Interventions in the nursing care plan focus on improving the client's ability to function and quality of life. Some examples of interventions available to the psychiatric nurse include counseling, milieu therapy, self-care assistance, medication administration, education, case management, and health promotion. In addition, advanced practice nurses may implement psychotherapy, prescribe pharmacologic agents, and provide consultation.

In many settings, generic or standardized nursing care plans and contracts for specific nursing diagnoses, medical diagnostic groups, or client problems exist. These plans are good guidelines but should be tailored to the individual client's needs.

> The comprehensive multiaxial *DSM-IV-TR* diagnosis is congruent with nursing's biopsychosocial paradigm.

> The nurse-client relationship is collaborative; the nurse and client share responsibility for the client's care. The healthier the client is, the more responsibility he or she is given.

Summary

Holistic evaluation of the psychiatric client consists of assessing the client's biopsychosocial history and current mental status through the psychiatric nursing interview. The specific content and process of the interview depends upon the nurse, the client, and the context in which the interview takes place. In terms of content, the biopsychosocial history includes the client's chief complaint; HPI; psychiatric history; alcohol and substance use history; medical, family, developmental, social, occupational, or educational histories; culture; spirituality; and coping skills. The mental status examination comprises an evaluation of the client's current behavior and appearance; emotions: mood and affect; speech; thought content and process; perceptual disturbances; impulse control; cognition and sensorium; and knowledge, insight, and judgment. The nurse may remember these components with the acronym *BEST PICK*.

In terms of process, the psychiatric nursing interview consists of a beginning, middle, and termination phase. The primary task of the beginning phase is to develop a rapport with the client. The bulk of information sharing is done during the middle phase. The termination phase relaxes the client and summarizes the meeting. Interviewing techniques such as nodding one's head, reflecting feelings, and restating content facilitate the interaction; bombarding the client with questions and denying his or her feelings are detrimental to the interview. Transference and countertransference (the conscious or unconscious feelings, expectations, beliefs, and attitudes the client and clinician have for one another) may also influence the interview positively or negatively.

The *DSM-IV-TR* diagnosis is a multiaxial medical diagnosis that considers major mental illness as well as personality, intellectual functioning, medical illness, psychosocial stressors, and global functioning. The assessment data from the psychiatric nursing interview (with consideration of the *DSM-IV-TR* diagnosis, psychological testing results, and medical workup outcome) are used to formulate nursing diagnoses. These diagnoses are prioritized with input from the client, and safety is the primary concern. The nurse collaborates with the client in formulating the initial nursing care plan, which consists of the identified problems (nursing diagnoses), projected treatment outcomes and interventions, and evaluation of the process.

Annotated References

American Nurses Association. (2007). *Psychiatric-mental health nursing: Scope and standards of practice.* Washington, DC: American Nurses Publishing.

This text outlines the ANA's recommendations for psychiatric nursing practice. It guides the practice of all psychiatric nurses, especially those new to the field. Psychiatric nurses should keep up with current nursing trends by reading the latest version of the ANA's statement.

American Psychiatric Association. (1994). *Diagnostic and statistical manual of mental disorders* (4th ed.). Washington, DC: Author.

This is the fourth edition of the American Psychiatric Association's official nomenclature of psychiatric conditions and disorders.

American Psychiatric Association. (2000). *Diagnostic and statistical manual of mental disorders* (4th ed., text rev.). Washington, DC: Author.

This is the text revision of the fourth edition of the American Psychiatric Association's official nomenclature of psychiatric conditions and disorders. It provides a systematic listing of the official codes and categories, a description of the multiaxial system for diagnosis, and diagnostic criteria for each of the disorders. It is used by psychiatrists, physicians, psychologists, registered nurses, social workers, therapists, and other mental health workers in all clinical settings. The 2000 text revision includes new research information regarding associated features; culture, age, and gender features; prevalence; course; and familial pattern of many of the mental disorders listed.

Barnes, L., Plotnikoff, G., Fox, K., & Pendelton, S. (2000). Spirituality, religion, and pediatrics: Intersecting worlds of healing. *Pediatrics, 106*(4 suppl.), 1–19.

This article covers the clash between spirituality and biomedicine, and the effect of spirituality on children's health and on the provider of health services.

Blow, F. C., Zeber, J. E., McCarthy, J. F., Valenstein, M., Gillon, L., & Bingham, C. R. (2004). Etnicity and diagnostic patterns in veterans with psychoses. *Social Psychiatry and Psychiatric Epidemiology, 39*(10), 841–851.

This study used a national database for veterans diagnosed with serious mental illness and confirmed continued ethnic disparities in diagnosing mental illness, with race being the demographic variable most strongly associated with a diagnosis of schizophrenia.

Carson, V. B., & Arnold, E. N. (1996). *Mental health nursing: The nurse-patient journey.* Philadelphia: W. B. Saunders.

This psychiatric nursing text focuses on the often forgotten spiritual aspect of the nurse-client relationship.

Catherman, A. (1990). Biopsychosocial nursing assessment: A way to enhance care plans. *Journal of Psychosocial Nursing and Mental Health Services, 28*(6), 31–35.

This article advocates for the use of scientific data collection tools by nurses as a way of enhancing professionalism and patient care.

Erikson, E. (1963). *Childhood and society* (2nd ed.). New York: W. W. Norton & Company.

This pioneering work regarding the evolution of personality over one's lifetime is easy to understand and apply to practice. Development is put into historical and sociological perspective, and the role of the child in society is also explored.

Folstein, M. F., Folstein, S. E., & McHugh, P. R. (1975). "Mini-Mental State," a practical method for grading the cognitive state of patients for the clinician. *Journal of Psychiatric Research, 12,* 189–198.

This article introduced the mini-mental status examination and scoring method.

Goldstein, E. G. (1995). *Ego psychology and social work practice* (2nd ed.). New York: Free Press.

Although aimed at a social work audience, this text applies to nursing practice; both professions are attracted to ego psychology's engagement of the health and strengths of the client. Assessment is viewed from an ego psychologic vantage point, stressing both defense mechanisms and the rational and problem-solving capacities of the ego. Problems in functioning are viewed in relation to possible coping deficits and the fit between inner capacities and environmental resources. The text's easy-to-understand chapter on the assessment of defense mechanisms is an excellent resource.

Govier, I. (2000). Spiritual care in nursing: A systematic approach. *Nursing Standard, 14*(17), 32–36.

This article advocates for taking a systemic approach to assessing clients' spiritual needs. The need for nurses to evaluate personal spirituality before effectively assessing clients' spiritual needs is also discussed.

Gresenz, C. R., Sturm, R., & Tang, L. (2001). Income and mental health: Unraveling community and individual level relationships. *Journal of Mental Health Policy and Economics, 4*(4), 197–203.

A study by the Rand Organization that examined the relationship between mental disorder and socioeconomic status. The findings confirmed earlier studies that showed individual income to be highly correlated with mental health status.

Guy, W. (1976). *ECDEU Assessment Manual for Psychopharmacology.* Washington, DC: U.S. Department of Health, Education and Welfare.

This is the original publication of the Abnormal Involuntary Movement Scale (AIMS).

Kadushin, A. (1997). *The social work interview: A guide for human services professionals* (4th ed.). New York: Columbia University Press.

This book applies to the work of all mental health professionals. It contains detailed discussion of the beginning, middle, and termination phases of the interview and of the clinician-client relationship. A thoughtful chapter is included regarding the use of humor and self-disclosure in the therapeutic relationship. This edition includes extended information on listening, nonverbal communication, use of interpreters, and interviewing involuntary adults and sexually abused children.

Kessler, R. C., Sonnega, A., Bromet, E., Hughes, M., & Nelson, C. B. (1995). Posttraumatic stress disorder in the National Co-morbidity Survey. *Archives of General Psychiatry, 52*, 1048–1060.

Epidemiological data on all aspects of PTSD: causes, prevalence, co-morbidity, duration, and sociodemographic correlates.

Kinzie, J. D., & Manson, S. M. (1987). The use of self-rating scales in cross-cultural psychiatry. *Hospital & Community Psychiatry, 38*(2), 190–196.

The authors review the use of seven psychiatric self-rating scales and discuss their usefulness across cultures.

Koenig, H. G., George, L. K., & Titus, P. (2004). Religion, spirituality, and health in medically ill hospitalized older patients. *Journal of American Geriatrics Society, 52*(4), 554–562

This nursing research study, based on patient interviews conducted at Duke University, identified measures of religiosity and spirituality. Religiousness and spirituality predicted fewer depressive symptoms, and organized religious activities predicted better physical functioning and less severe illness.

Koenig, H. G. (2007). Religion and depression in older medical inpatients, *American Journal of Geriatric Psychiatry, 15*(4), 282–291.

This study examined the relationship between religious characteristics of older medically ill patients with depression and those of medically ill nondepressed patients. Depression was less severe in patients who identified a religious affiliation and formal religious practices.

National Child Traumatic Stress Network (2004). *Childhood traumatic grief educational materials.* Los Angeles, CA: National Center for Child Traumatic Stress. www.NCTSNet.org

This is an in-depth general information guide to childhood traumatic grief with information specific to healthcare providers, parents, and school personnel. It includes a useful reference and resource list.

Neighbors, H. W., Trierweiler, S. J., Ford, B. C., & Muroff, J. R. (2003). Racial differences in DSM diagnosis using a semi-structured instrument: The importance of clinical judgment in the diagnosis of African-Americans. *Journal of Health and Social Behavior, 44*(3), 237–256.

This article analyzed data on 665 African Americans and white psychiatric patients and found that, even when a semi-structured diagnostic instrument and DSM criteria were used, whites were more likely than African Americans to receive a diagnosis of bipolar disorder and less likely to be diagnosed with schizophrenia.

Rauter, U. K., de Nesnera, A., & Grandfield, S. (1997). Up in smoke? Linking patient assaults to a psychiatric hospital's smoking ban. *Journal of Psychosocial Nursing and Mental Health Services, 35*(6), 35–40.

This overview of the effects of smoking and smoking cessation in psychiatric clients is essential to understanding the pros and cons of the recent antismoking movement in healthcare settings.

Regan-Kubinski, M. J. (1995). Clinical judgment in psychiatric nursing. *Perspectives in Psychiatric Care, 31*(3), 20–24.

This article stresses the importance of the nurse's use of his or her experience and judgment in the contemporary healthcare environment.

Sadock, B. J., Kaplan H. I., & Sadock V. A. (2003). *Kaplan & Sadock's synopsis of psychiatry: Behavioral sciences, clinical psychiatry* (9th ed.). Baltimore: Williams & Wilkins.

This text targets psychiatrists in training; thus, the authors tend to stress the biologic aspect of assessment (i.e., genetics, brain anatomy and physiology, neurotransmitters). It is an excellent reference for psychiatric nurses.

Schreiber, R. (1991). Psychiatric nursing assessment: A la King. *Nursing Management, 22*(5), 90–94.

This article outlines an efficient psychiatric nursing assessment model based on King's nursing theory.

Terkelson, K. G. (1987). The meaning of mental illness to families. In A. Hatsfield & H. Lefley (eds.), *Families of the mentally ill* (pp. 128–166). New York: Guilford Press.

This chapter provides a conceptual framework for viewing the family's experience of a relative's mental illness. The chapter discusses several factors associated with the family and the mentally ill relative that impact upon the meaning of the illness to the family.

Terr, L. C. (1991). Childhood traumas: An outline and overview. *American Journal of Psychiatry, 148*(1), 10–20.

This article investigates those aspects of childhood trauma that follow the patient into adulthood. The author delineates the consequences of single versus multiple childhood traumas and provides helpful case examples.

Vannicelli, M. (1992). *Removing the roadblocks: Group psychotherapy with substance abusers and family members.* New York: Guilford Press.

Although this book's focus is the specialty area of group therapy for substance abusers, the excellent information concerning transference, countertransference, and resistance generalizes to group and individual treatment of all psychiatric clients.

Vedantam, S. (2005, June 26). Patients' diversity is often discounted. *The Washington Post,* pp. A01, A10.

This article contains a discussion of how the presentation of mental illness differs across cultures.

Woods, M. E., & Hollis, F. (2000). *Casework: A psychosocial therapy* (5th ed.). New York: McGraw-Hill.

Although this book is intended for caseworkers and not nurses, it contains useful information regarding the therapeutic relationship that applies to a wide range of mental health professionals.

Internet Resources

http://nursing.jbpub.com/psychiatric

Visit http://nursing.jbpub.com/psychiatric for interactive exercises, NCLEX review questions, WebLinks, and more.

CHAPTER 4

Neurobiologic Considerations in Psychiatric Care

Karan S. Kverno and Sherry Goertz

LEARNING OBJECTIVES

After reading this chapter, you will be able to:

- Describe the neuroanatomy and neurophysiology of the brain in relation to mental health and illness.
- Explain the basic processes of neurotransmission and the role of neurotransmitters in the major mental disorders.
- Explain current neurobiological implications of major mental disorders as a basis for helping clients understand psychopharmacologic recommendations.

KEY TERMS

Allostatic load
Amine neurotransmitters
Amygdala
Apraxia
Ataxia
Autonomic nervous system (ANS)
Axons
Basal ganglia
Brain stem
Broca's area
Central nervous system (CNS)
Cerebellum
Cerebrum
Dendrites
Depolarization
Extrapyramidal pathways
Frontal lobe
Functional imaging
Genes
General adaptation syndrome (GAS)
Glial cells
Hippocampus
Hypothalamic-pituitary-adrenal (HPA) axis
Hypothalamus
Kindling
Limbic system
Medulla
Membrane potential
Midbrain
Myelin
Neurogenesis
Neuroimaging
Neuron
Neuroplasticity
Neurotransmitters
Parasympathetic nervous system
Peripheral nervous system (PNS)
Pons
Reticular activating system (RAS)
Sensitization
Somatic motor system
Stress-diathesis model
Stressor
Structural imaging
Sympathetic nervous system
Synapses
Temporal lobe
Thalamus
Wernicke's aphasia

http://nursing.jbpub.com/psychiatric

Visit http://nursing.jbpub.com/psychiatric for interactive exercises, NCLEX review questions, WebLinks, and more.

The Surgeon General's 1999 report at the end of the Decade of the Brain called for more rapid translation of neurobiological research findings into evidence-based treatments for individuals with mental disorders.

The Human Genome Project mapped the entire sequence of human genes by 2003.

The central nervous system (CNS) is composed of the brain and spinal cord. The peripheral nervous system (PNS) delivers information to and from the CNS.

A mnemonic for the cranial nerves: "On Old Olympus's Towering Top A Finn And German Viewed Some Hops."

Introduction

Although the human brain weighs only about 3 pounds, it is composed of approximately 100 billion **neurons** that form intricate communication pathways allowing complex thought, movement, and emotions. It is perhaps not surprising that the neurons, the chemicals that pass between them, and the genes that guide them can at times fail to function properly. Transforming the mental healthcare system into one that is evidence-based requires healthcare practitioners to have an appreciation of the complex biological, psychological, and social (biopsychosocial) contributions to mental health and mental illness (Institute of Medicine, 2005). This chapter is intended to provide a basic knowledge of the brain's structures and functions, the **neurotransmitters** and their pathways, and the mechanisms for the development of mental illnesses and disorders and their treatment.

New discoveries related to brain physiology, genetic risk factors, and mental illnesses and disorders were reported throughout the twentieth century, but especially during the 1990s, a time referred to as the "Decade of the Brain" when the U.S. Congress provided significant support and funding for brain research. The Surgeon General's report on mental illness (U.S. Department of Health and Human Services, 1999) concluded the decade with a mandate for greater understanding and translation of the neurobiological underpinnings of mental illness. By 2003, the Human Genome Project had mapped the entire sequence of human genes (http://www.genome.gov/HGP/). With continued progress and more advanced neuroimaging methods, much more is now known about the combined genetic and environmental risks and effective treatments for mental disorders.

Structure and Function of the Nervous System

The brain and spinal cord make up the **central nervous system (CNS)**. Columns of myelinated **axons** run up and down the spinal cord, delivering information from the periphery to the brain (afferent pathways) and from the brain to the periphery (efferent pathways). The **peripheral nervous system (PNS)** in turn delivers information to and from the spinal cord. **Figure 4-1** shows the divisions of the CNS and PNS. The PNS includes 12 pairs of cranial nerves (with the exception of cranial nerve II, the optic nerve that is part of the CNS; see **Table 4-1** and **Figure 4-2**), 31 pairs of spinal nerves, and two major divisions—the somatic and autonomic nervous systems. The **somatic motor system** is responsible for voluntary control of skeletal muscle. The cell bodies of the neurons that make up the

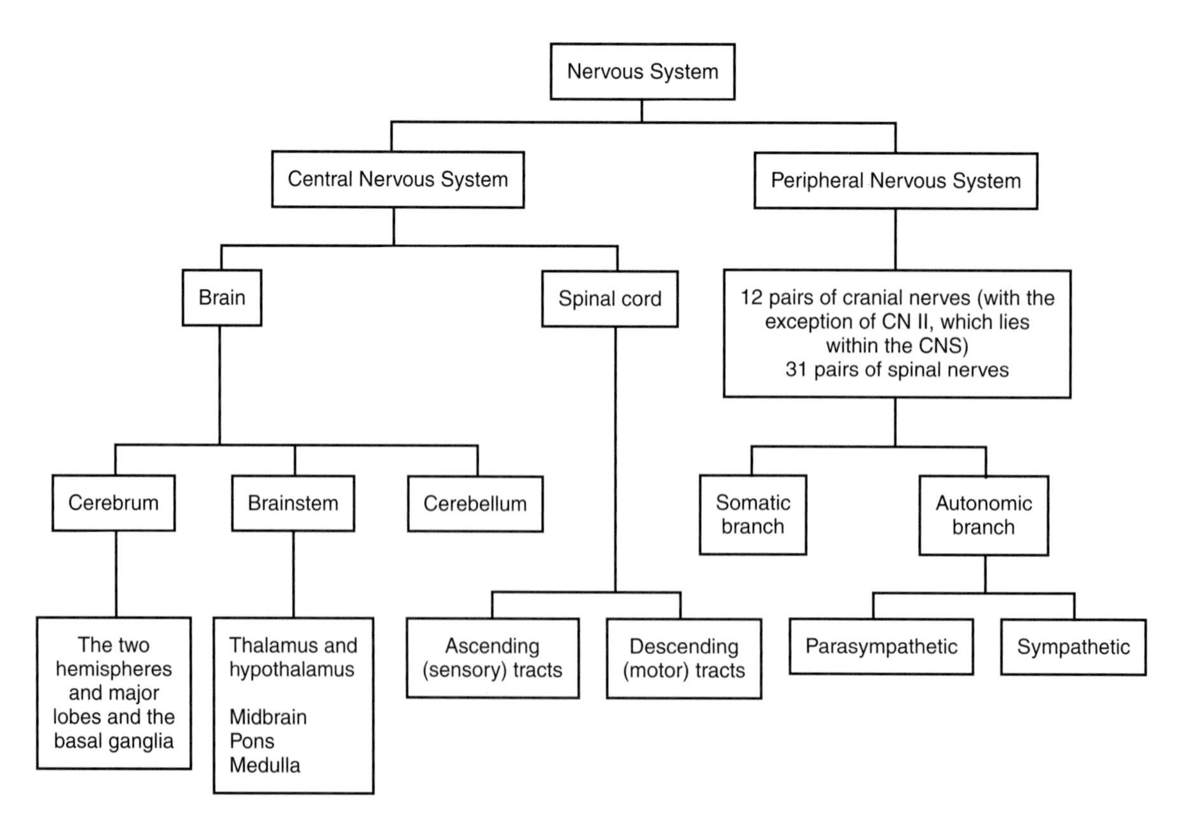

Figure 4-1 Organization of the nervous system.

Table 4-1 The Cranial Nerves

Cranial Nerve	Important Functions	Cranial Nerve	Important Functions
I. Olfactory	Sensation of smell	IX. Glossopharyngeal	Movements of muscles in the throat Parasympathetic control of the salivary glands Sensation of taste in posterior tongue Detection of blood pressure changes in the aorta
II. Optic	Sensation of vision		
III. Oculomotor	Movements of the eye and eyelid Parasympathetic control of pupil size		
IV. Trochlear	Movements of the eye		
V. Trigeminal	Sensation of touch to the face Movements of muscles of mastication	X. Vagus	Parasympathetic control of the heart, lungs, and abdominal organs Sensation of pain associated with viscera Movements of muscles in the throat
VI. Abducens	Movements of the eye		
VII. Facial	Movements of muscles of facial expression Sensation of taste in anterior tongue		
VIII. Auditory-vestibular	Sensation of hearing and balance	XI. Spinal accessory	Movements of muscles in the throat and neck
		XII. Hypoglossal	Movements of the tongue

somatic motor system lie within the CNS (in the brain stem or spinal cord) and their axons terminate at neuromuscular junctions. The release of acetylcholine (ACh) triggers contraction of the skeletal muscle. Somatic sensory information from the skin, muscles, and joints enters the spinal cord, and in return, the brain sends commands for voluntary movement.

Traditionally thought of as the involuntary nervous system, the **autonomic nervous system (ANS)** is responsible for the activities of the body that usually take place without conscious guidance—within the internal organs, glands, and vasculature. The two branches of the ANS allow the nervous system to maintain internal balance (homeostasis). Cell bodies for the ANS

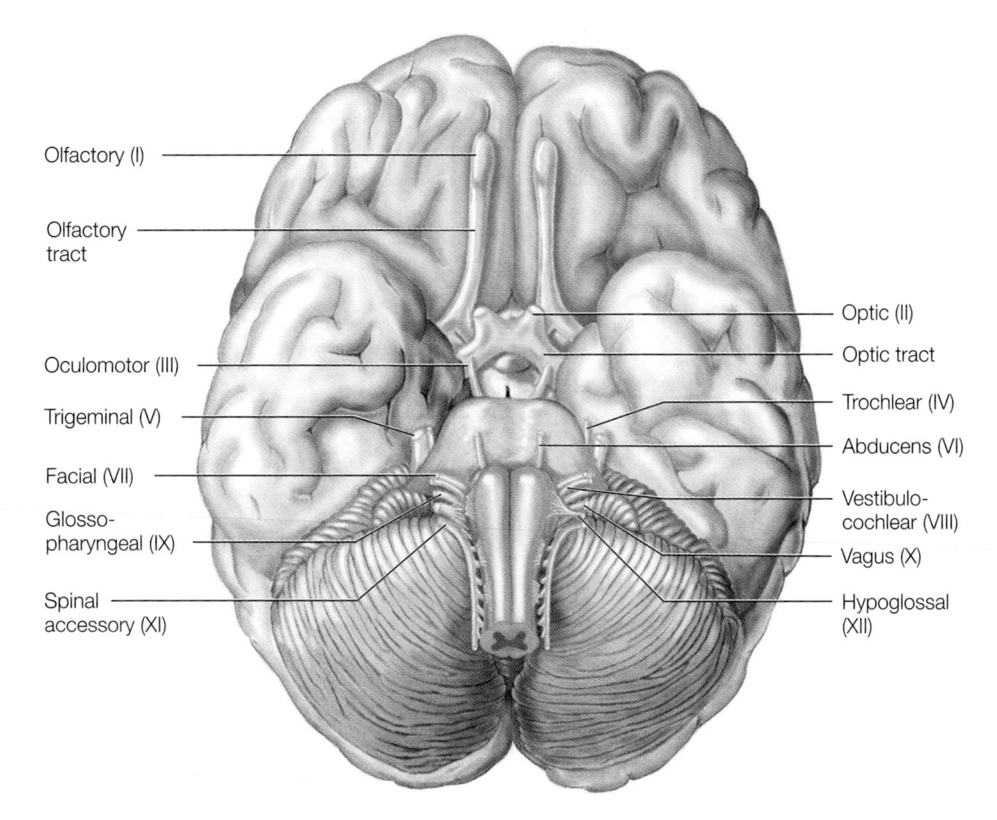

Figure 4-2 The cranial nerves.

The autonomic nervous system (ANS) is responsible for regulation of the organs, glands, and vasculature. The sympathetic and parasympathetic divisions maintain balance, allowing rapid responses to environmental demands, then return to homeostasis.

In hydrocephalus CSF builds up, causing the ventricles to enlarge and compress the brain. An increase in ventricular size due to atrophy is not called hydrocephalus.

lie outside of the CNS in clusters of cells called ganglia. The CNS activates them via preganglionic axons that utilize ACh as their neurotransmitter. Their postganglionic axons terminate on smooth muscle, cardiac muscle, and gland cells. By innervating the same organs, the two opposing systems respond effectively to environmental demands. The **parasympathetic nervous system** is responsible for resting functions such as digestion and bowel and bladder function. The vagus nerve (cranial nerve X) provides much of the parasympathetic innervation of the viscera. The remainder comes from the other cranial and sacral spinal nerves. Postganglionic axons in the parasympathetic nervous system also utilize ACh as their neurotransmitter. The **sympathetic nervous system** prepares one to fight or flee in an emergency by increasing heart rate and respiratory rate, dilating pupils and bronchi, and stimulating glucose mobilization. In an emergency, the sympathetic nervous system dominates. After the stressor subsides, the parasympathetic system increases in activity and balance is restored. Almost all postganglionic axons in the sympathetic nervous system utilize norepinephrine (NE) as their neurotransmitter.

The CNS is bathed in cerebrospinal fluid that flows through the ventricular system and protects the brain from injury. The ventricles of the brain can become enlarged when too much fluid is present (hydrocephalus) or when parts of the brain atrophy, leaving more space for CSF fluid. Figure 4-3 shows the location of the ventricles of the brain. The CNS can be divided into three major divisions: the cerebrum, the brainstem, and the cerebellum.

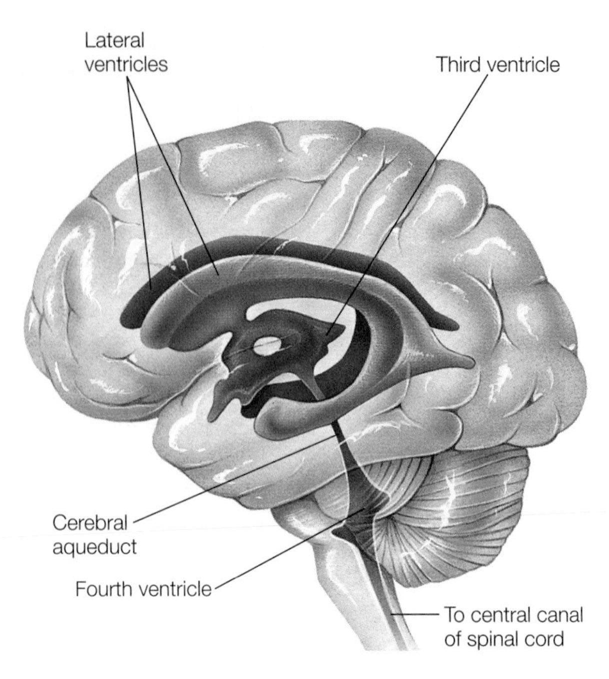

Figure 4-3 The ventricles are filled with cerebrospinal fluid.

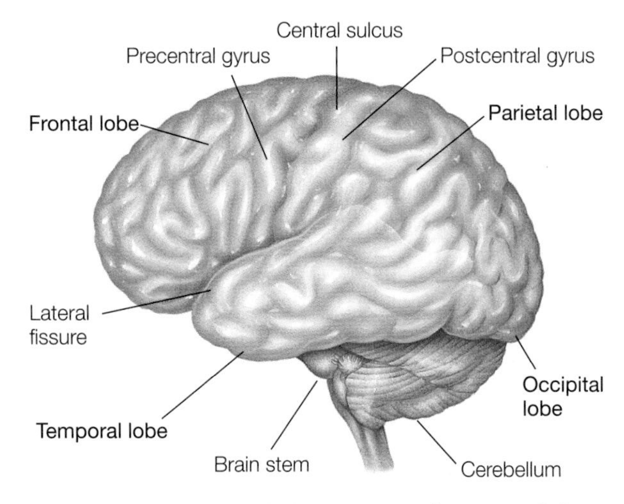

Figure 4-4 The lobes of the cerebrum. The cortex of the brain is identified by gyri (bumps) and sulci (grooves) or fissures (deep grooves).

Cerebrum

Cerebral Lobes

The **cerebrum** underlies the ability to reason, entertain abstract thoughts, and contemplate concepts like the "past" and the "future," as well as the ability to experience emotions. The cerebrum is the largest portion of the brain and is divided into a left and right hemisphere, each of which contains four major lobes: frontal, temporal, parietal, and occipital (Figure 4-4). A fifth area of cortex, called the insula, is less well known and understood and is not seen from the outer surface of the brain, though recent findings link it to the mental representation of bodily states and drug craving in nicotine addiction (Naqvi, Rudrauf, Damasio, & Bechara, 2007).

Sitting underneath the lobes are several structures referred to as the **basal ganglia**, which means deep nuclei. Together the cerebral hemispheres and basal ganglia are referred to as the telencephalon. A band of myelinated axons called the corpus callosum connects the two hemispheres, allowing information to pass between them in a unifying manner. The lobes of the brain serve different functions, and so it follows that injury or illness affecting these structures can result in specific alterations in functioning.

Frontal Lobes

The **frontal lobes** of the brain have evolved to be relatively larger in humans than in other species. In human beings, the frontal aspect of the brain, specifically the prefrontal cortex (anterior to the motor cortex), is responsible for executive functioning—planning, organizing, decision making, and working memory (short-term storage and processing of information). The frontal lobes also contain the primary motor, supplementary motor, and premotor cortex and are involved in the interpretation of incoming motor signals and planning and directing of motor responses. Injury to the frontal lobes can affect motor functioning on the opposite side of the body, executive functioning, and short-term working memory. For the majority of people, language functions are located primarily in the left hemisphere, and injury to **Broca's area** (**Figure 4-5**) can cause expressive aphasia, the inability to express oneself with language. The negative or deficit symptoms that we see with some of the psychiatric illnesses may be a reflection of underactivation or underutilization of the frontal executive functions.

The famous story of Phineas Gage helps us understand other functions of the frontal lobes. Gage was a foreman who worked for the railroad system back in the 1800s. One day an accidental explosion blew a tamping iron right through his skull, obliterating a portion of his frontal lobes. He recovered from the accident, but according to his physician, Dr. John Harlow, his personality changed drastically from one of being hardworking and easy-going to someone who was unmotivated, fitful, irreverent, and grossly profane.

Critical Thinking Question Can you think of any psychiatric or behavioral disorders associated with impulsivity? Do individuals with these disorders have additional problems with executive functioning?

Temporal Lobes

The **temporal lobes** are especially important in processing auditory information and consolidating long-term memories. Auditory hallucinations, receptive **Wernicke's aphasia** (the inability to understand spoken speech), and difficulty forming new long-term memories may reflect problems with the temporal lobes.

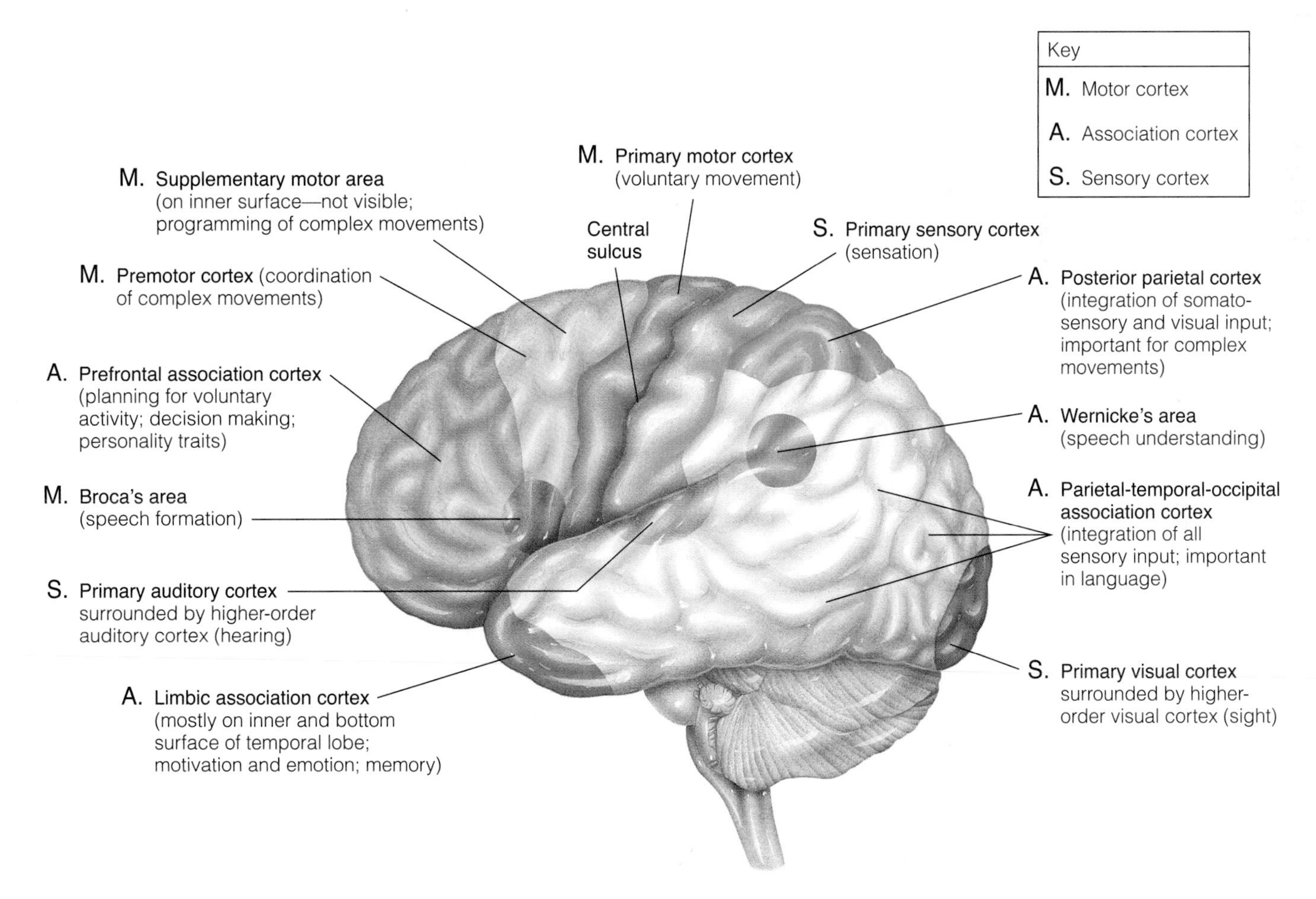

Figure 4-5 Functional regions of the cortex. Different functions can be localized to specific areas of the brain. The left hemisphere is dominant for language in the majority of people.

Two structures that reside within the temporal lobe are the **hippocampus** and the **amygdala**. The hippocampus, located within the medial temporal lobe, is important in the process of consolidating long-term memories. Without the hippocampus we would not be capable of storing new information about the facts and events in our lives.

A famous story about a man, referred to as HM, taught us much of what we know today about the functioning of the hippocampal structures. When he was young he had intractable seizures and probably would have died due to complications. In 1953, when he was 23, in an attempt to stop the seizures, surgeons removed both of the anterior portions of his temporal lobes, taking out both hippocampal structures. Following the surgery, HM recovered, and he could recall his life before surgery up to a certain point in time; then his ability to remember just stopped. This type of memory loss is called retrograde amnesia.

The worst problem, however, was that he never again stored or recalled any new facts or events (declarative memories). The inability to form new memories is called anterograde amnesia. Dr. Brenda Milner, a researcher at the Montreal Neurological Institute, has studied and worked with HM since the 1950s. She introduces herself each time she meets him because he has no recollection of ever meeting her. Some types of memory, such as the memory for riding a bike or other skills, are not dependent on the hippocampus. HM has improved his skill (procedural memory) at certain activities like table tennis despite not recalling that he has ever played (Milner, 2005).

The hippocampus is a vulnerable area of the brain. In dementing illnesses such as Alzheimer's disease, the hippocampus is one of the first areas to show cellular changes and shrinkage. The hippocampus is also vulnerable to chronically elevated levels of circulating cortisol, as might occur in chronic stress-related disorders and depression (Sapolsky, 2003a, b). Unfortunately we cannot avoid stress entirely. The good news is that the hippocampus retains its ability to regenerate neurons throughout life. This process is called **neurogenesis**, and it is facilitated by healthy behaviors such as exercise, good nutrition, and studying for exams.

The amygdala is a small almond-shaped structure that sits just anterior to the hippocampus in the temporal lobes. Like the hippocampus, the amygdala is important in memory consolidation; however, it specializes in emotional memories. The amygdala is also very important in relation to stress and appears to serve the function of detecting danger and activating fear and the stress response. The amygdala also appears to be an essential locus for the storage of fear-related memories (Schafe, Doyere, & LeDoux, 2005). Although extremely rare, individuals who do not have either amygdala cannot recognize negative emotion in others. The rare Kluver-Bucy syndrome demonstrates this phenomenon. When the anterior portions of the temporal lobes are removed through disease or injury, individuals display diminished fear and aggression, the tendency to identify objects by oral examination rather than visual inspection, and inappropriate sexual behavior.

For most of us, our amygdalas are present bilaterally, yet we all differ in sensitivity. Like a thermostat, some people seem to be able to take quite a lot of threat before triggering the stress or fear response system, whereas others appear to be extremely sensitive and hypervigilant. It is likely that a combination of genes and environmental experiences determines the level of sensitivity. Fortunately, both antidepressants and psychotherapy can reduce the sensitivity and reactivity of the amygdala.

Parietal Lobes

The parietal lobes contain the primary sensory cortex, which receives afferent sensory information about touch, pain, temperature, and proprioception (limb location), and the sensory association cortex where these signals are analyzed and interpreted. When the parietal lobes are injured or lesioned, such as can happen with a cerebrovascular accident, individuals may develop sensory and perceptual problems such as perceptual abnormalities of body image and spatial relationships—even the full neglect of one side of the body. Complex motor movements are coordinated between the frontal lobe (planning and motor) and the parietal lobe (sensory and limb position). A selective inability to perform complex motor acts is called **apraxia**. Problems with object recognition can also result from parietal lobe injuries or illness. These agnosias are defined by their functional deficits. For example, asterognosia refers to the inability to identify objects by touch (e.g., a key in one's pocket).

Occipital Lobes

The occipital lobes house the primary and association visual cortices, areas specialized in receiving visual signals and interpreting visual stimuli. Injuries or damage to the occipital cortex can result in vision changes and problems recognizing and interpreting visual information.

Basal Ganglia

The basal ganglia are a collection of neurons deep in the cerebrum. They consist of three major structures that cover the thalamus in each hemisphere: the caudate, putamen, and globus palidus. Together the caudate and putamen are sometimes referred to as the striatum. One of the most important functions of the basal ganglia is to facilitate the initiation of willed movements, such as walking or writing.

In psychiatric nursing and psychopharmacology, various terms are used in reference to the basal ganglia. **Extrapyramidal pathways** are pathways that are outside of the medullary pyramids (the descending corticospinal pathways). When you hear of the extrapyramidal symptoms (EPS) that include bradykinesia, tremor, and dystonia, what medical condition do you think of? If you thought of Parkinson's disease, you were right. One of the extrapyramidal pathways is a dopamine pathway that travels from the substantia nigra (dopamine-producing cells in the midbrain) to the striatum (of the basal ganglia). We refer to that pathway as the nigrostriatal pathway. "Nigro" tells you the origin of the pathway and "striatal" tells you the destination. In Parkinson's disease the dopamine-producing cells in the substantia nigra degenerate, decreasing the dopamine that is available in the basal ganglia for initiation of movement. EPS are common side effects in individuals who are taking the first generation antipsychotics that are potent dopamine antagonists. EPS side effects resemble a Parkinson's-like condition that is reversible once the dopamine antagonism is reduced in the nigrostriatal pathway.

Brain Stem

The **brain stem** consists of the central structures that sit below and support the cerebrum. The body's vital functions depend on neuron clusters within the brainstem. Also located within the brain stem is an area called the **reticular activating system**, whose function seems to be keeping us conscious and awake. Damage to this area of the brain stem can result in the sleep-like state of coma. The brain stem initiates a number of protective, automatic motor behaviors such as maintaining balance, blinking, and head movements.

Thalamus and Hypothalamus

At the superior aspect of the brain stem lie the thalamus and hypothalamus, together referred to as the diencephalon. Inside the **thalamus** are the major input and output relay nuclei that interact with every portion of the brain. Nerve impulses do not enter or exit the conscious brain without going through the thalamus. The thalamus sorts, amplifies, directs, and integrates sensory information.

The **hypothalamus** lies inferior to (beneath) the thalamus and superior to (above) the pituitary gland, where it helps maintain homeostasis by regulating vital functions, including body temperature, blood glucose level, salt and water balance, and our biologic clock. The hypothalamus is the major control center for the pituitary and is central in coordinating the physiological response to detected threats or stress via the **hypothalamic-pituitary-adrenal (HPA) axis**. Axons from the hypothalamic neurons release their neurotransmitters into the portal circulation of the anterior pituitary, influencing the release of pituitary hormones that act on the gonads, thyroid glands, adrenal glands, and mammary glands (**Figure 4-6**).

Midbrain

Clusters of cell bodies that produce monoamine neurotransmitters reside within the **midbrain**, also referred to as the mesencephalon. The midbrain is the origin of several of the diffuse regulatory pathways of the brain. The cluster of cell bodies that produces norepinephrine is collectively referred to as the locus coeruleus. The cluster that produces dopamine is referred to as the substantia nigra. As discussed earlier, the pathways are named by their origin and termination within the brain, so by knowing that "meso" refers to the mesencephalon, you would know that a mesolimbic pathway travels from the midbrain to the limbic structures of the brain.

Critical Thinking Question Name the origin and the destination of the following pathways of the brain: 1) corticospinal, 2) spinothalamic, and 3) Nebraska Avenue. Just kidding on number 3; however, sensible naming strategies for pathways make it easier to find your way around the brain than around most cities!

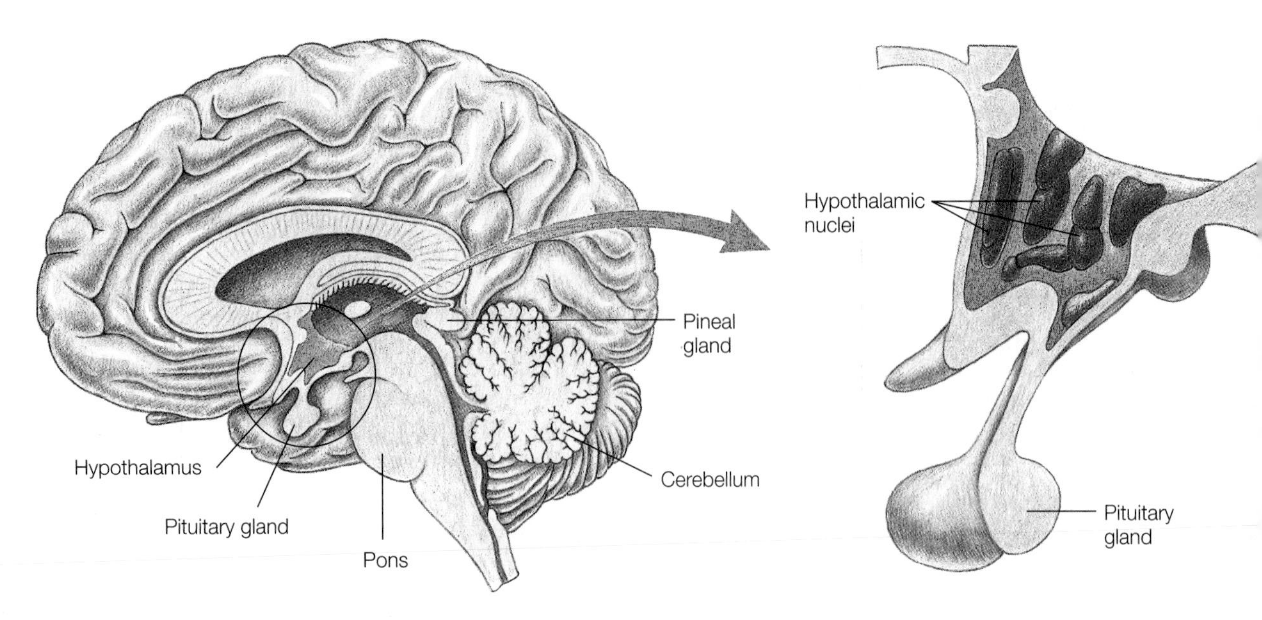

Figure 4-6 The hypothalamus is the master gland of the endocrine system.

Pons

Not only does the **pons** contain important neurotransmitter-producing cell bodies, but it also is a very important conduit for the ascending and descending pathways that pass between the cerebrum and cerebellum. Scattered groups of cell bodies referred to as the raphe nuclei produce serotonin in the midbrain, pons, and medulla.

Medulla

The descending corticospinal tracts cross (decussate) at the level of the **medulla**. This results in the right motor cortex controlling the muscles on the left side of the body and the left motor cortex controlling the muscles on the right side. The crossover accounts for how a cerebrovascular accident in one hemisphere of the brain creates functional difficulty for the other side of the body. The bundles of myelinated axons that course through the medulla are sometimes referred to as the "pyramids." As mentioned earlier, the pathways that lie outside of the pyramids are "extrapyramidal pathways."

Cerebellum

Bundles of axons travel between the pons and the **cerebellum**, providing a means for the cerebellum to communicate with the rest of the central and peripheral nervous systems. The cerebellum smoothes out and coordinates the sequence of muscle contractions that are necessary to control movements. Individuals with cerebellar damage will have difficulty touching finger to nose, or moving the arm to point from one location in space to another. An individual might also need to walk with a wide-based gait. The term **ataxia** refers to these uncoordinated and inaccurate movements. Substances such as alcohol can cause similar impairments to the cerebellar system.

Cellular Mechanisms of Communication

The Cells of the Brain

There are two main types of cells in the nervous system: the glia and neurons. The most abundant are the **glial cells**, which provide support and protection to the neurons. In early development, the glial cells also provide the structures upon which the neurons can migrate, with the help of neurotrophic (brain growth) factors, to appropriate sites in the brain. At least five types of glial cells have been identified. The astrocytes provide physical support to the neurons as well as regulating the extracellular environment to protect neurons from fluctuations in potassium and other chemicals. Two types of glial cells form the **myelin** sheaths that insulate axons: referred to as oligodendroglia in the CNS and Schwann cells in the PNS. The microglia act as phagocytes to remove cellular debris, and the ependymal cells form the lining of the fluid-filled ventricles of the brain.

Bear, Connors, and Paradiso (2007) use the analogy of a chocolate chip cookie to describe the relationship between neurons and glia. The chips (neurons) are surrounded and supported by the more plentiful dough (glia). Although we tend to think of neurons as being the most important cells in the brain, without glial cells they could not function. Indeed, Einstein's brain was found to have more glial cells relative to neurons in the posterior parietal cortex when compared to a control population (Diamond, Scheibel, Murphy, & Harvey, 1985).

The **neuron** is the basic functional unit of the brain for information processing. Neurons have three distinct parts—the cell body (soma), **dendrites**, and axon (see **Figure 4-7**). Central to the soma is the nucleus that contains the DNA. The DNA consists of sequences of amino acids, called **genes**, that determine the type, production, and distribution of proteins within the neuron and the functioning of the cell. Within the cytoplasm of the soma, outside of the nucleus, are several organelles that serve specific functions. Ribosomes are the sites of protein synthesis, golgi bodies cleave proteins into smaller functional units, and mitochondria produce the energy, adenosine triphosphate (ATP), needed for all cell activity. The proteins produced by neurons are transported to sites within the neuron where they serve as enzymes, receptors, ion channels, transport pumps, peptide neurotransmitters, and membrane and structural proteins.

Dendrites and axons distinguish the neuron from other cells in the body. The dendrites receive chemical signals from other neurons and the axons conduct electrical signals (action potentials) to their terminals that result in the release of chemical messengers (neurotransmitters), which activate the dendrites and cell bodies of other neurons. A gross inspection of the brain reveals both gray and white matter. The gray matter consists of the cell bodies and other nonmyelinated structures such as glia. The white matter is named for the white appearance of myelinated axons. Axons that are insulated with myelin sheaths are able to conduct the electrical signals more quickly and efficiently, with the axon potential jumping from one break in the myelin (also referred to as a "node of Ranvier") to the next (**Figure 4-8a**).

Critical Thinking Question Multiple sclerosis is a disease characterized by the destruction of myelin. Based on your knowledge of the function of myelin, what symptoms would you expect?

Neurotransmitters

Proteins are not the only substances produced by the neurons. Large peptide **neurotransmitters** (e.g., beta-endorphin) are produced in the soma and transported to the terminals for release. Smaller amine and amino acid neurotransmitters are produced in the axon terminals. There they are packaged into tiny synaptic vesicles and are released into the synapse upon the arrival of electrical signals (action potentials). **Figure 4-8b** depicts the arrival of an action potential at the terminal triggering the release of neurotransmitter from the vesicles. The neurotransmitter diffuses across the synapse and engages the receptors on the postsynaptic membrane. Notice the abundance of mitochondria in the terminal area indicating the great energy needs for the processes of neurotransmission, including re-establishing the membrane potential, transporting neurotransmitters back into the terminal, and repackaging them in vesicles.

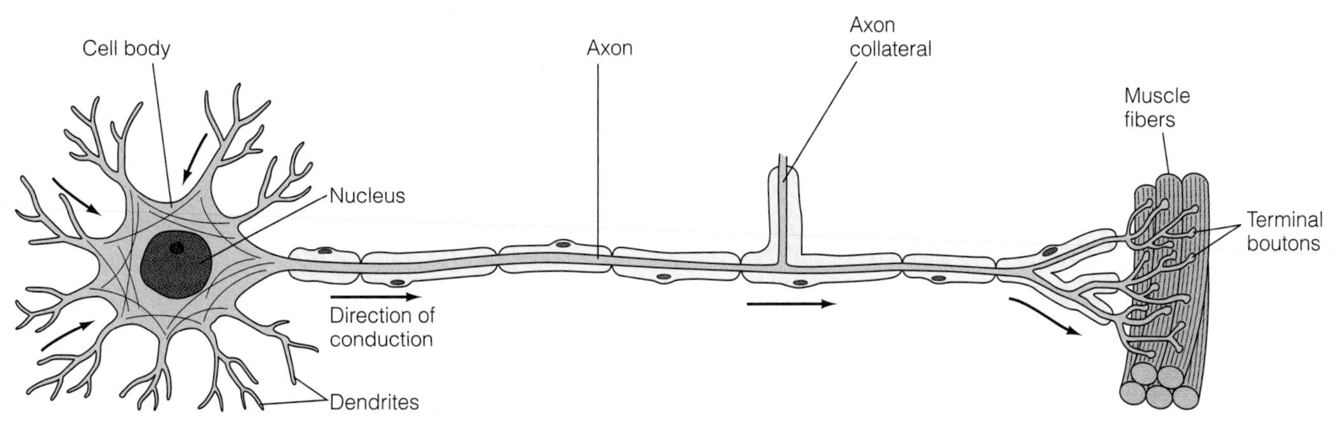

Figure 4-7 A prototypical neuron. Neurons are distinguished from other cells in the body by their dendrites and axons. Their terminals (sometimes called boutons) typically form synapses with the dendrites of other neurons, but may synapse on cell bodies or axons. This figure shows the axon terminating at the neuromuscular junction of skeletal muscle fibers.

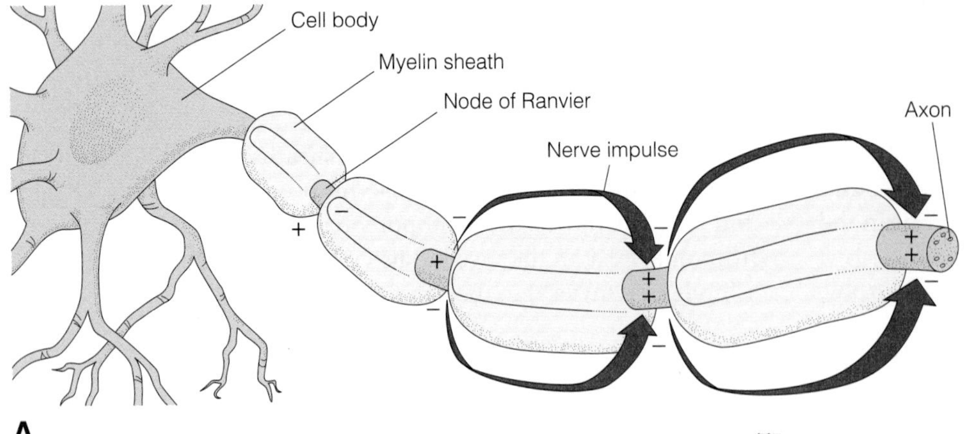

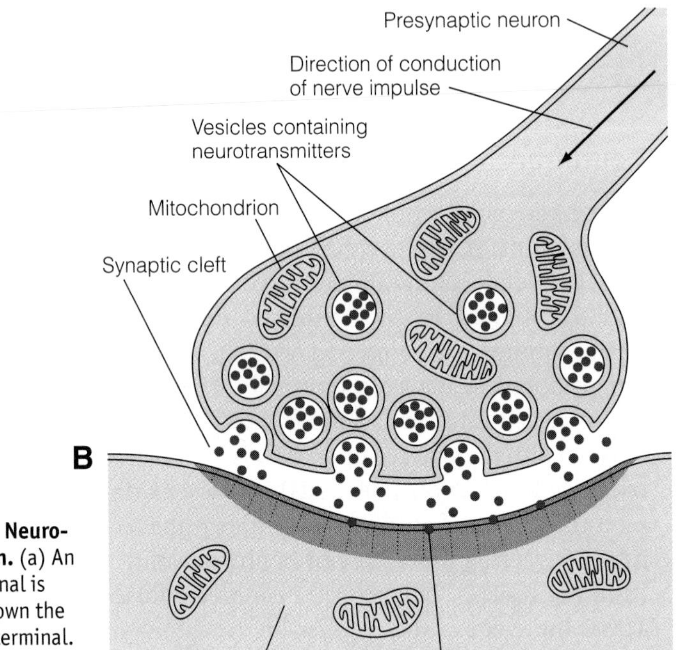

Figure 4-8 Neurotransmission. (a) An electrical signal is conducted down the axon to the terminal. (b) A chemical signal is released into the synapse.

Most notable to the etiology and treatment of mental illnesses are the **amine neurotransmitters**: acetylcholine (ACh), serotonin (5HT), dopamine (DA), and norepinephrine (NE). Epinephrine (E), commonly called adrenalin, is secreted by the adrenal medulla into the bloodstream in response to stress. The family of neurotransmitters called catecholamines refers to DA, NE, and E, all synthesized from a common amino acid precursor called tyrosine. See **Table 4-2** for a list of the common neurotransmitters and their functions. Clusters of cells that produce specific neurotransmitters are located in the midbrain and medulla, which send their axons into many areas of the cerebrum. The result is that the neurotransmitters are widely distributed throughout the brain and can have widespread regulatory effects on brain activity.

Neurotransmitters and their receptors mediate psychiatric disorders and are targets for psychopharmacologic interventions.

A synapse is the region of contact between neurons where information is transferred.

Neurotransmitters are chemical "messengers" that activate specific receptors.

Synapses

Although it might appear that neurons are part of one vast continuous network, they are actually separated from one another by small spaces called **synapses**. Upon the arrival of electrical signals (action potentials), chemical signals (neurotransmitters) diffuse across synapses from presynaptic terminals to postsynaptic receptors. The neurotransmitters do not actually pass into the postsynaptic cells. Instead, like keys, they activate receptors on postsynaptic membranes and then float back into the synapse where they await their fate. Some neurotransmitters float away, others are broken down by enzymes in the synapses, and the rest are pumped back into the terminal. Once in the terminal, the neurotransmitters may be broken down by enzymes (e.g., monoamine oxidase) or repackaged into vesicles for recycling. Note that several familiar psychotropic medications target the pumps (e.g., serotonin reuptake inhibitors) and the enzymes (e.g., monoamine oxidase inhibitors).

Critical Thinking Question Depression is thought to be related to diminished levels of serotonin and other monoamine neurotransmitters. How would you explain the mechanism of action of fluoxetine (Prozac) to a client?

Each neurotransmitter has several receptor types, and each given receptor type may have multiple subtypes with different actions. Thus, one neurotransmitter can cause multiple actions in different areas of the brain and spinal cord. Neurotransmitters are messengers that activate receptors. Some receptors are actually ion channels that open up in response to the neurotransmitter, allowing charged ion molecules to flow into or out of the postsynaptic cell. Others use a second messenger on the inside of the postsynaptic membrane to cause a cascade of chemical changes, eventually even influencing the expression of the genes that guide the cellular functions. The receptors that use a second messenger are called G-protein or metabotropic receptors. G-protein receptors have slower, longer-acting, modulating effects.

Let's look at glutamate as an example. Glutamate has four identified receptors (see Table 4-2). Three of the receptors are linked to ion channels and create rapid changes in the postsynaptic cell:

Table 4-2 Major Neurotransmitters in Mental Health and Illness

Chemical Classification	Neurotransmitter and Receptor Types	Major Pathways and Sites of Production	General Functions and Involvement in Symptoms of Mental Disorders and Medication Side Effects
Amines	Dopamine (DA) Five major receptor types with multiple subtypes: D1, D2, D3, D4, D5 The term *catecholamine* describes DA, NE, and E. NE is made from DA and E is made from NE.	Mesocortical: ventral tegmental area (VTA) to frontal cortex Mesolimbic: VTA to limbic areas of brain Nigrostriatal: Substantia nigra to basal ganglia Tuberoinfundibular: Hypothalamus to pituitary	Attention and executive functioning. Deficits (negative symptoms) in ADHD, schizophrenia, and depression. Emotion regulation, reward. Excesses (positive symptoms) in psychosis. All drugs of abuse increase DA in this pathway. Part of the extrapyramidal system that controls movement. Deficits in disorders such as Parkinson's disease, and EPS side effects of dopamine antagonist medications. Excess activity results in dyskinesias. Inhibits prolactin. Risk of lactation with dopamine antagonist (antipsychotic) therapy.
	Norepinephrine (NE) Two major receptor types with multiple subtypes: alpha and beta NE is converted to epinephrine (E) in the adrenal medulla. E is also known as adrenaline.	Locus coeruleus to frontal cortex Locus coeruleus to limbic system Locus coeruleus to cerebellum Postganglionic neurons of the sympathetic nervous system. Adrenal medulla releases E into the bloodstream in response to stress.	Concentration, working memory, speed of information processing. Deficits in cognitive disorders such as ADHD, depression, Alzheimer's. Mood: Deficits in depression, fatigue, and psychomotor retardation. Excesses in anxiety and psychomotor agitation. Regulation of motor movements. Excesses in tremor. Participates in the regulation of the autonomic nervous system. In response to stress, facilitates fight, flight, fright, and sex. E is involved in the coordination of the visceral response to stress.
	Serotonin (5HT) At least seven major receptor types with multiple subtypes: 5HT1–5HT7	Raphe nuclei to frontal cortex and limbic system. Raphe nuclei to basal ganglia Raphe nuclei to hypothalamus Raphe nuclei to brainstem regulatory centers. Raphe nuclei to spinal cord	Mood regulation. Deficits in depression and impulsivity. Dysregulated in anxiety and panic. Assists with control of movement. Deficits in obsessions and compulsions. Regulation of appetite and eating behavior. Dysregulated in eating disorders. Dysregulated in sleep disorders, vomiting. Other peripheral effects such as gastrointestinal motility.
	Acetylcholine (ACh) Two major receptor types with multiple subtypes: muscarinic and nicotinic	Nucleus of Meynert to hippocampus, amygdala, and throughout the cortex Other sites of cholinergic-producing neurons include the basal ganglia, lateral tegmental area, and all motor neurons in the spinal cord and brain stem.	Critical role in memory and higher cortical executive functions such as learning, problem solving, and judgment. Deficits resulting in learning and memory problems in cognitive decline, Alzheimer's dementia, and excessive medication-induced anticholinergic states. Causes contraction of skeletal muscle. Deficits result in muscle weakness (e.g., myasthenia gravis).

continues

Table 4-2 Major Neurotransmitters in Mental Health and Illness, continued

Chemical Classification	Neurotransmitter and Receptor Types	Major Pathways and Sites of Production	General Functions and Involvement in Symptoms of Mental Disorders and Medication Side Effects
Amines—cont'd		ACh is the preganglionic neurotransmitter of sympathetic and parasympathetic neurons, and the post-ganglionic neurotransmitter of parasympathetic neurons.	Effects on cardiac muscle: ACh slows heart rate. Parasympathetic ACh activity facilitates digestion, growth, immune responses, and energy storage. Activity of the parasympathetic nervous system is generally reciprocal to activity in the sympathetic system.
Amino acids	Glutamate Four major receptor types: NMDA, AMPA, kainate, and metabotropic	Synthesized from glucose and other precursors in all cells.	Serves as an excitatory neurotransmitter throughout the brain. The NMDA receptor is thought to mediate normal excitatory neurotransmission by opening ion channels to positively charged calcium. Too much excitability can result in too much calcium and death of cells. This so-called "excitotoxicity" is thought to be one of the mechanisms of cell death in neurodegenerative conditions such as Alzheimer's and Parkinson's disease. Other less toxic increases in glutamate may be related to other positive symptoms such as anxiety, panic, psychosis, and mania. Activation of the metabotrophic receptor by glutamate plays a key role in long-term potentiation of memory.
	Gamma-aminobutyric acid (GABA) Two major receptor types with several subtypes: GABA A and GABA B	Synthesized from glutamate in neurons that use it as a neurotransmitter. It is not one of the 20 amino acids used to make proteins.	Serves as an inhibitory neurotransmitter by allowing negatively charged chloride to enter, reducing the chances that a neuron will fire. Deficits in GABA inhibitory activity have been linked to anxiety disorders and insomnia. Excessive inhibitory activity can result in sedation, ataxia, and memory disturbance.

Source: Adapted from Bear, Connors, & Paradiso, 2007; Stahl, 2000.

NMDA, AMPA, and kainate. The NMDA receptor mediates normal excitatory neurotransmission. Too much glutamate action at NMDA receptors may eventually be excitotoxic to the cells, and may be part of the mechanism of neurodegeneration in illnesses such as Alzheimer's disease. The fourth glutamate receptor is a metabotropic receptor that uses a second messenger to create lasting changes in synapses, a process called long-term potentiation (LTP). LTP is thought to be a key neuroplastic change in the brain involved in forming long-term memories. Although the complexity of neurotransmitter-receptor actions is enormous, new receptor subtypes are continually being discovered, and as they are, newer drugs can be designed that have more specificity and fewer side effects. Memantine, a new NMDA glutamate receptor antagonist medication, holds promise for reducing the excitotoxic effects of excessive glutamate and is being used to decrease neurodegenerative processes in individuals with Alzheimer's disease and other dementias.

Neurotransmission

Due to a combination of diffusion and electrical factors, the inside of resting neurons is more negatively charged than the outside, polarized at about –65mV. The separation of charge between the outside and the inside of the neuron is referred to as the **membrane potential.** A great deal of cellular energy (ATP) is required to maintain the difference in potential. Because ATP is manufactured from oxygen and dietary sources of energy, when oxygen is lacking the pumps fail and the neurons can no longer function.

When an action potential arrives in the terminal it causes a brief **depolarization** of the membrane potential with the charge shifting towards 0 and above. The depolarization is what triggers the release of a neurotransmitter into the synaptic cleft. Following depolarization, the cell quickly repolarizes so that it can be ready to respond to the arrival of the next action potential.

So now imagine thousands of axon terminals releasing neurotransmitters into the synaptic clefts of the dendrites or the cell body of a single cell. The neurotransmitters may be excitatory (like glutamate) or inhibitory (like GABA). If the neurotransmitter is excitatory, it causes positively charged sodium or calcium to flow into the postsynaptic cell, depolarizing the neuron. If the neurotransmitter is inhibitory it causes negatively charged chloride to flow into the postsynaptic neuron or positively charged potassium to flow out, resulting in the cell becoming more negatively charged (returning the cell toward its resting potential), and less likely to fire off another action potential. Small currents build and move along the dendrites toward the cell body. Between the cell body and the axon is an area called the axon hillock, somewhat like a toll booth on a highway. If there is enough currency (depolarization) to pay the fare (shifting the charge from –65mV to a threshold level of about –40mV), then an all-or-none action potential is generated and it travels down the axon. If there is not enough depolarization at the axon hillock, the cell does not fire. The frequency and pattern of action potentials is like a Morse code of the brain, transmitting information to be processed and interpreted.

Neuroplasticity

The ability that we have to adapt to environmental changes, learn, and remember reflects the amazing **neuroplasticity** of the brain. It is difficult to imagine how complex thoughts, feelings, and behaviors emerge from small electrical and chemical signals in the brain. Neuroplasticity describes the dynamic nature of the brain and its functions. We now know that new cells are born (neurogenesis) across the lifetime. A peak number of synapses is present around age 6, followed by a period of extensive pruning and increased efficiency. Long-term potentiation or strengthening of synapses builds our memories. Long-term depression or weakening of synapses helps us forget. Receptors are up- or down-regulated depending on the availability and need for specific neurotransmitters. When a neurotransmitter is deficient, the receptors up-regulate in an attempt to compete for more of the neurotransmitter. Likewise, when a medication increases the levels of a neurotransmitter, the receptors down-regulate to decrease the overload. Feedback loops to the nucleus assure that cells are always responding to ever-changing environmental demands. Because the brain has so much plasticity in the early years, children have more capacity than adults to compensate for major brain injuries. Individuals who keep their brains active in later life have more of a buffer against neurodegenerative processes and dementia. So use it or lose it!

The membrane potential is the separation of charge between the outside and inside of the neuron.

Neuroplasticity describes the dynamic nature of the brain and its functions that permit humans to adapt to environmental changes, learn, and remember.

Neurogenesis is the birth of new neurons.

Regulation of Emotion

The Limbic System

The **limbic system** describes several structures that function as a system to regulate emotion, behavior, memory, and learning. **Figure 4-9** depicts the major structures together with their connections—the

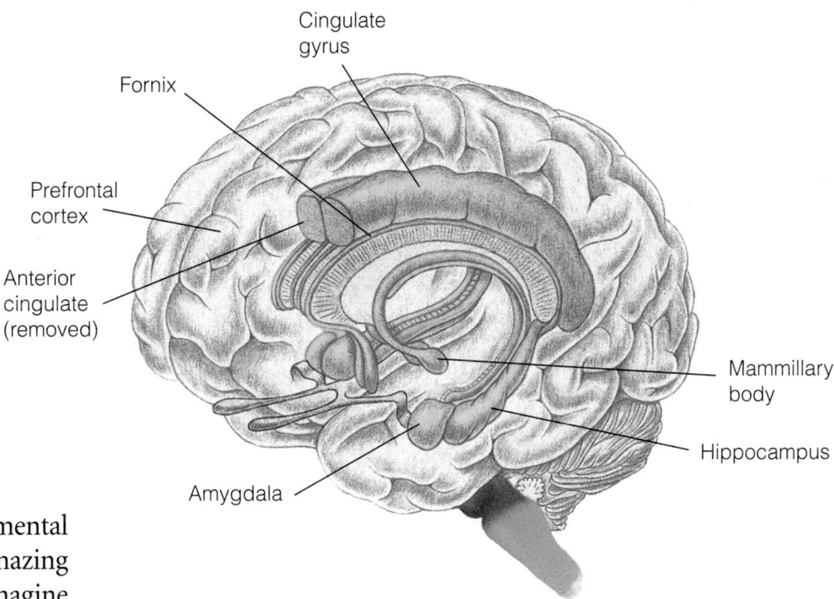

Figure 4-9 The limbic system. The limbic structures form a ring around the thalamus and hypothalamus (not shown). The structures and their connecting pathways (e.g., the fornix) are involved in the regulation of emotion and memory.

frontal cortex, thalamus, hypothalamus, cingulate gyrus, hippocampus, amygdala, and mammillary bodies. The limbic system is crucial to our motivation and important in producing behaviors that are critical to the survival of the species, such as behaviors that foster appropriate social interactions and success in producing offspring. Love and desire arise from this system, as well as fear and paranoia. Memory for the events of our lives and the emotional texture is what helps us make decisions and plan for the present and future. Mental disorders involve dysregulation of the limbic system.

The limbic system regulates emotion, learning, and memory.

The Stress Response

The modern-day concept of stress is influenced by the work of Hans Selye and the publication of his theory of **general adaptation syndrome (GAS)** in the 1930s (see Gabriel, n.d.). Selye identified three stages in the human response to stressors. In the first, the alarm stage, an individual becomes aware of the stress or stressor and the sympathetic nervous system springs into a "fight-or-flight" reaction. In the second stage, resistance, the body attempts to adapt to the stress response and in many instances adaptation occurs. If homeostasis is not restored, the third stage is that of exhaustion, where the body can no longer respond to the stress and over time may develop illnesses or die. Selye conceived of the response as nonspecific—in other words, the same response regardless of the type of stressor or the individual.

Selye's GAS model did not account for individual differences in stress reactivity. We now know that the stress response is triggered by challenge or threat when an individual perceives that the demands of a situation outweigh his or her capacity to adapt. What might be fun to some people (e.g., skydiving) is experienced as frightening and stressful to others. Some people seem more naturally resilient to stressors and demonstrate less reactivity than others. Genetic vulnerability as well as life experiences probably account for these differences.

Chronic stress, such as that experienced by individuals living in poverty or with illness, is characterized by elevated levels of cortisol and its physiological correlates.

Acute Stress

A **stressor** is anything that threatens homeostasis. Potential stressors may be acute physical challenges, such as hunger, cold, restraint, chemicals, shock, surgery, and bodily injuries, or psychological challenges, such as adversity, emotional illness, financial hardships, work issues, social hierarchy conflicts, and neglect. Our bodies are well adapted to dealing with acute stressors. The stress response is characterized by the activation of two major stress pathways: the **hypothalamic-pituitary-adrenal (HPA) axis**, yielding increases in the glucocorticoid called cortisol (**Figure 4-10**), and the sympathetic nervous system, yielding increases in the catecholamines NE and E. In response to stress, neurons in the hypothalamus release a peptide neurotransmitter called corticotropin-releasing hormone (CRH) into the blood of the pituitary circulation, triggering the release of adreno-corticotropic hormone (ACTH) into the general circulation. ACTH triggers the release of cortisol from the adrenal cortex. Amygdala activation stimulates the HPA axis, and hippocampal activation suppresses it. The associated autonomic physiological changes include the release of stored energy and increased cardiovascular tone. The pupils dilate, attention becomes sharper, and the individual prepares to fight or flee. If acute stress continues, short-term reversible impairments in memory may occur. Once the stressor is avoided or dealt with effectively, homeostasis is restored and digestion, growth, and other resting functions return.

A stressor (acute or chronic) is anything that threatens the body's homeostasis.

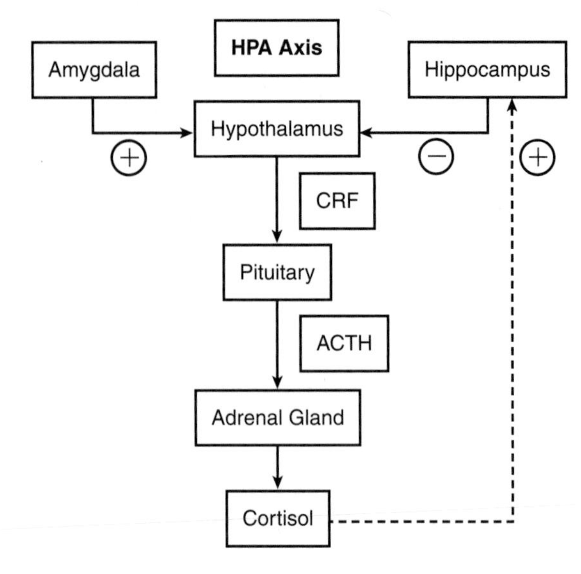

Figure 4-10 The HPA axis. In response to stress, neurons in the hypothalamus release a peptide neurotransmitter called corticotrophin-releasing hormone (CRH) into the blood of the pituitary circulation, triggering the release of adreno-corticotrophic hormone (ACTH) into the general circulation. ACTH triggers the release of cortisol from the adrenal cortex. Amygdala activation stimulates the HPA axis and hippocampal activation suppresses it.

Chronic Stress

Unfortunately, humans have many more things to worry about than being chased by predators and fighting or fleeing. Instead, we are bombarded by constant mild to major stressors. In addition, a large portion of our population suffers from the chronic stress of low socioeconomic status—poverty, hunger, manual labor, sleep deprivation, and low levels of personal control. Others are threatened by neglect or abuse, domestic or community violence, or even war. Persistent activation of the stress response appears to be a risk factor for the development of physical illness as well as depression and anxiety disorders. Although the fight-or-flight response may subside, the HPA axis remains overactive. Hippocampal neurons are especially vulnerable to the chronically elevated levels of cortisol resulting in hippocampal atrophy and associated memory changes (McEwen, 2000, 2001; Sapolsky, 2003a, 2003b, 2005). Other risks of chronic stress and elevated cortisol include deteriorated immune response, elevated blood pressure, increased abdominal fat, infertility, and mood disorders (Sapolsky, 2005).

McEwen (2001) refers to the process of maintaining stability or homeostasis through adaptation as allostasis. **Allostatic load** is the wear and tear produced by the repeated activation of allostatic (adaptive) mechanisms. He identifies four types of allostatic load: 1) repeated challenges/chronic stress, 2) failure to habituate with repeated challenges, 3) failure to shut off the response after the challenge is past, and 4) failure to mount an adequate response. Developmental or environmental determinants of differences in allostatic load can include early stressful life experiences resulting in increased reactivity of the HPA axis function and increased sensitization to later stress exposure (Charney, 2003), and stressful adult experiences that cause lasting changes in HPA functioning (Mason et al., 2001).

Stress is relevant to all of the psychiatric disorders, first because of its potential role in their etiology and maintenance, and second because of the chronic stress of living with mental disorders. Stress also contributes to the development, maintenance, and outcome of substance use disorders by increasing drug cravings, altering subjective responses to alcohol, and increasing alcohol consumption.

Mental Disorders

Are mental disorders inherited? The answer is yes, at least partially. Genetic factors provide the vulnerability or risk for mental illness but they do not explain the whole picture. Consider the case of two identical twins (monozygotic) who share the same genes but are discordant for an identified mental disorder. In monozygotic twins, concordance is thought to reflect genetic vulnerability, and discordance is thought to reflect the environmental contribution to mental disorders. All of the mental disorders have been found to show some degree of discordance. Reviews of twin studies indicate that the heritability is highest for schizophrenia (82–84%; Kendler, 2001) and bipolar disorder (85–89%; McGuffin et al., 2003), mid-level for alcoholism (52–58%; Kendler, 2001), and lowest for the anxiety disorders (37–43%; Kendler, 2001) and major depression (29–42%; Kendler, Gatz, Gardner, & Pedersen, 2006). The search is on to identify the various risks or "candidate" genes for each of the disorders.

Stahl (2000) describes a "two-hit" theory to explain the development of mental disorders. The first hit is the genetic contribution or risk factors; the second hit is the environmental contribution. A similar model is the **stress-diathesis model**. *Diathesis* refers to predisposition or vulnerability and *stress* describes the contribution of environmental factors. Environmental contributions to the development of mental illness may occur in utero, as in the case of one fetus getting more oxygen or more of a virus than the other. They may also stem from childhood experiences. Individuals who have experienced early childhood stress, such as the loss of a parent, neglect, or abuse, are much more vulnerable to depression and anxiety disorders later in life. Stress may also trigger the earlier onset of a mental disorder such as schizophrenia or bipolar disorder. In addition, extreme or chronic stress in adulthood is associated with vulnerability to anxiety and mood disorders. Finally, individual differences contribute to the environments that individuals choose to live in, so genes affect the environment and the environment affects the genes.

Mood Disorders

Unipolar Depression

Sadness and grief are normal responses. Prolonged periods of sadness or anhedonia (lack of pleasure) accompanied by other physiological symptoms such as appetite and weight changes, sleep disruption, fatigue, and psychomotor agitation or retardation are not normal. Persons with these symptoms are experiencing depression, a serious yet common illness. Findings from the most recent Global Burden of Disease Study (Ustun, Ayuso-Mateos, Chatterji, Mathers, & Murray, 2004) indicate that depression is the fourth leading cause of disability worldwide, creating an enormous burden for society.

The vulnerability to depression is heritable. Children of parents who have had depression have

Allostasis is the process of maintaining stability or homeostasis through adaptation.

The two-hit theory explains the development of psychiatric disorders. The first hit is the genetic vulnerability and the second hit is the environmental contribution.

Genetic factors provide the vulnerability or risk factors for an individual to develop a mental illness, but they do not explain the whole process.

The stress-diathesis theory explains the development of psychiatric disorders as a combination of diathesis (genetic predisposition) and environmental stress.

a higher risk for depression than their counterparts, yet early life stressors such as the loss of a parent, neglect, or abuse can predispose a person to the development of depression even without an obvious family history of depression (Gutman & Nemeroff, 2003). In addition, the illness is not the same for every person. Approximately half of individuals with depression have elevated levels of cortisol, suggesting a prolonged stress response (Lee, Ogle, & Sapolsky, 2002). These individuals may show a prolonged response to the dexamethosone suppression test, demonstrating a weakened ability to shut down cortisol activity in the body. Prolonged elevation of cortisol is toxic to the neurons of the hippocampus, the area of the brain involved in long-term memory consolidation.

Depression appears to be related to a depletion of monoamine neurotransmitters such as serotonin, norepinephrine, and dopamine.

Depression appears to be, to some extent, due to a depletion of monoamine neurotransmitters such as serotonin, norepinephrine, and dopamine. The exact mechanism for this is unclear; however, one possibility is that an enzyme that metabolizes monoamines is elevated, leading to lower than normal levels (Meyer et al., 2006). The monoamine reduction hypothesis is supported by the observation that antidepressants effectively reduce depression, and all antidepressants increase the availability of monoamine neurotransmitters. However, individuals differ in their responsiveness to antidepressants. Some individuals with depression respond best to antidepressants that specifically target the serotonin system (e.g., serotonin reuptake inhibitors [SSRIs]). Others do best with antidepressants that target the serotonin and norepinephrine systems (e.g., serotonin-norepinephrine reuptake inhibitors [SNRIs], tricyclics), and yet others do best with antidepressants that target the dopamine system (e.g., bupropion).

Serotonin reuptake inhibitors (SSRIs) inhibit the pumps that transport serotonin back into the presynaptic terminal, resulting in an increase in available serotonin in the synapse.

Monoamine oxidase inhibitors (MAOIs) block the enzyme MAO from destroying monoamine neurotransmitters, allowing them to accumulate in the presynaptic cell.

Critical Thinking Question Antidepressants increase the availability of monoamine neurotransmitters almost immediately. Why, then, does it take 3–6 weeks to achieve therapeutic reductions in depression? This is a very difficult question, and no one knows for sure; however, think through some of the neuroplastic changes or brain adjustments that take place over time. For example, consider the up-regulation of monoamine receptors that might occur in depression and the readjustment that might need to take place in recovery.

Bipolar Disorder

Bipolar disorders are characterized by the occurrence of manic (Bipolar I) or hypomanic (Bipolar II) episodes. Most individuals who have experienced manic episodes will also experience depressive episodes. Dr. Robert Post and his colleagues (Post et al., 2003) at the National Institute of Mental Health (NIMH) have spent years trying to identify the neurobiological underpinnings of bipolar illness and have come up with two descriptive concepts—sensitization and kindling. **Sensitization** describes the tendency for initial mood episodes to be linked to identified stressors, but later episodes require less of a stressor or none at all. People seem to become sensitized to the episodes themselves, such that the occurrence of mood episodes increases the risk for future episodes. **Kindling** is a term used to describe the lowered threshold for setting off neuronal activity in seizure disorders. Manic episodes are like seizures in that they result from too much neuronal activity, something like a limbic-lobe seizure. Support for this model is gained from the observation that anti-seizure drugs are effective in treating and preventing manic episodes. Lithium and the mood stabilizers appear to stabilize the neuronal membrane, making it less sensitive and increasing the threshold for activation. Bipolar depression may be treated with antidepressants; however, mood stabilizers are generally given concurrently to prevent swings from depression into mania.

Specific brain structural changes associated with bipolar disorder are reduced anterior cingulate volume (part of the limbic system that is important in directing attention), early-onset white matter (myelin) abnormalities, and, less consistently, reduced hippocampal volume and enlarged ventricular volume. Behavioral changes that might be accounted for by the structural changes are deficits in attention (anterior cingulate) and deficits in learning and memory (hippocampus). Prefrontal cortex abnormalities are suggested by abnormalities in the reward system of the brain, with a decreased responsiveness during periods of depression and an increased responsiveness during periods of mania. NIMH researchers Hasler, Drevets, Gould, Gottesman, and Manji (2006) suggest that these brain changes may be mediated by interactions among hypercortisolemia, glutamate neurotoxicity, and stress-induced reduction in neurotrophic (brain growth) factors.

Anxiety

Anxiety can be a symptom, a syndrome, or a disorder. As a symptom, anxiety and its stronger variant, fear, constitute the emotional component of a stress response. When the stress response is activated by a perceived threat, the sympathetic fight-or-flight response is accompanied by anxiety or fear. The main neurotransmitters involved in the sympathetic fight-or-flight response are NE and E. Aside from anxiety, other symptoms of noradrenergic (NE) and adrenergic (E) activation include tachycardia, tremor, and sweating.

Anxiety can also be part of a syndrome, associated with other disorders such as substance intoxication or withdrawal, or medical problems. The *DSM-IV-TR* (APA, 2000) lists anxiety as a part of a syndrome of intoxication for alcohol, amphetamine, caffeine, cannabis, cocaine, hallucinogens, inhalants, and phencyclidine, and of withdrawal for alcohol, cocaine, sedatives, hypnotics, and anxiolytics. In addition, anxiety is a common symptom associated with numerous over-the-counter and prescribed medications, including bronchodilators, corticosteroids, sympathomimetics, and thyroid preparations. All of these conditions and medications have the activation of the CNS in common.

The treatment of choice for anxiety as a symptom or as part of a syndrome is generally a sedative-hypnotic, like a benzodiazepine, which quiets down the CNS by enhancing the inhibitory activity of GABA. Other drugs are also used, depending on the target symptoms. Beta-blockers and other antihypertensives (e.g., clonidine) may be used to decrease the peripheral symptoms of tremor or behavioral activation, but are less powerful in blocking the subjective and emotional aspects of anxiety.

Finally, anxiety can be a mental disorder. The *DSM-IV-TR* anxiety disorders include panic disorder, simple phobia, social phobia, obsessive compulsive disorder (OCD), acute stress disorder, posttraumatic stress disorder (PTSD), and in children, separation anxiety disorder. The neurobiological mechanisms for the anxiety disorders are more complex, and treatment is not simply aimed at decreasing sympathetic activity or increasing inhibitory activity. In chronic anxiety, serotonergic dysregulation seems to be a factor, and the antidepressants, especially the SSRIs, are the treatment of choice.

Approximately 40% of individuals with OCD do not respond to the SSRIs alone (Stahl, 2000), implying that serotonin dysregulation cannot be the only explanation. OCD shares similarities with other disorders that involve the dopamine pathways of the basal ganglia: Tourette's disorder and pediatric autoimmune neuropsychiatric disorders associated with streptococci (PANDAS; Snider & Swedo, 2003). These disorders tend to be associated with movement irregularities or tics involving too much dopamine and OCD symptoms. Treatment with neuroleptics (dopamine antagonists) decreases both the tics of the body and the tics of the mind. Individuals with OCD who do not respond to SSRIs alone are often treated with the addition of a neuroleptic. Taken together these findings suggest that OCD may be a disorder involving dysregulation of serotonin and dopamine in the basal ganglia and its connections.

In summary, an individual's perception of threat and feelings of fear and anxiety are associated with the amygdala and its activation of the stress response pathways: 1) from the locus coeruleus to the sympathetic nervous system's release of norepinephrine, and 2) from the hypothalamus to the adrenal gland's (HPA axis) production of cortisol and epinephrine. Under normal conditions, once the stressor is gone, homeostasis is restored. Under chronic stress conditions, however, balance is not restored. Heightened peripheral sympathetic nervous system arousal may persist, especially in panic disorder and PTSD. The HPA axis may continue unabated, releasing CRH, ACTH, and cortisol, especially in PTSD. Eventually the elevations of cortisol can cause damage and eventual atrophy of the hippocampus, impairing hippocampal control over the HPA axis (**Figure 4-9**). Promising new research is evaluating CRH and glucocorticoids as possible targets for new drugs for anxiety disorders and depression.

Anxiety can be a symptom, a syndrome, or a mental disorder.

Critical Thinking Questions What stress management techniques do you use to reduce your own stress levels? Do you think that stress management should only be in the treatment plan of individuals with anxiety disorders? If not, why?

Schizophrenia

Schizophrenia, the most common psychotic disorder, generally gets diagnosed as a person reaches their late teens or early 20s, at a time when the prefrontal portions of the brain are completing their migration, connections, and pruning. The neurodevelopmental model is best for describing the pathology of schizophrenia. As the normal brain develops after birth, the maximum numbers of synapses are formed by around the age of 6, and after that a preprogrammed process of pruning takes place, ultimately making the brain more efficient. In schizophrenia, faulty migration and misalignment of neurons are suggested by early developmental delays in motor, cognitive, and social/emotional functioning. The brains of children and adolescents with schizophrenia also show enlarged ventricles and decreased gray matter maturation compared to their healthy age-matched peers (Rapoport, Addington, Frangou, & MRC Psych, 2005). This finding suggests that the cortical matter either has not developed as much compared to normal peers or was excessively pruned.

Schizophrenia involves both neurodevelopmental and neurodegenerative processes.

Neurodegenerative processes may also take place over time in the brains of individuals with schizophrenia. Structural scans of adults with schizophrenia show ventricular enlargement (indicating smaller brains), medial temporal lobe volume reductions (hippocampus), and frontal lobe volume reductions (Ross, Margolis, Reading, Pletnikov, & Coyle, 2006). Dysfunction of the prefrontal cortex is apparent on tasks of working memory and executive functioning.

Psychotic disorders such as schizophrenia are diagnosed by the presence of positive symptoms of hallucinations, delusions, disorganized speech, or disorganized behavior. The hypothesized mechanism for the positive symptoms involves excessive amounts of dopamine in the limbic system. Support for this hypothesis comes from the efficacy of dopamine antagonists in reducing positive symptoms.

Dopamine antagonists do not reduce the negative symptoms (e.g., affective flattening, alogia, and avolition) of schizophrenia. The conventional antipsychotics are especially strong antagonists of one of the dopamine receptors, called the D2 receptor. D2 antagonism in the dopamine pathways that terminate in the prefrontal cortex (involved in executive cognitive functioning) may even worsen negative symptoms. This is because dopamine is an important neurotransmitter in the prefrontal cortex and is important in mediating motivation and cognition. Fortunately the newer, atypical antipsychotics (serotonin-dopamine antagonists) spare dopaminergic functioning in the prefrontal cortex through the relation between serotonin and dopamine. The result is that with atypical antipsychotic treatment, individuals may experience decreases in both the positive and negative symptoms of schizophrenia.

Extrapyramidal Side Effects

EPS can occur as a result of treatment with conventional antipsychotics, and the nurse may be the first healthcare practitioner to identify and treat the symptoms. To understand the potential EPS, it is useful to know that there are four major dopaminergic pathways in the brain:

- The mesocortical pathway goes from the mesencephalon (another name for the midbrain) to the frontal cortex.
- The mesolimbic pathway travels from the midbrain to the limbic system.
- The nigrostriatal pathway travels from the substantia nigra in the midbrain to the striatum (the basal ganglia) and is involved in movement.
- The tuberoinfundibular pathway travels from the hypothalamus to the infundibulum (the stalk) of the anterior pituitary.

We have already discussed the hypothesis that, in schizophrenia, dopamine is elevated in the mesolimbic pathway and deficient in the mesocortical pathway. But what about the other two pathways?

The nigrostriatal dopinergic pathway is not usually affected by schizophrenia itself; however, when the pathway is blocked by a conventional antipsychotic, movement-related EPS can result. Bradykinesia, tremors, and dystonias are all possible antipsychotic-induced symptoms of Parkinsonism. Akathesia is severe restlessness. Another less common EPS side effect is lactation, which is caused by the antagonism of D2 receptors in the tuberoinfundibular pathway.

It is important for nurses to understand that the EPS are side effects and not changes in the psychotic disorder, and that they can be treated and reversed. The best practice today is to avoid the EPS by using an atypical antipsychotic as a first line agent. If the conventional agents are used, it may be necessary to add another medication such as an anticholinergic, antihistamine, benzodiazepine, beta blocker, or alpha adrenergic antagonist to reduce the side effects. Abnormal movements should be closely monitored for early intervention and evaluation of outcomes. The Abnormal Involuntary Movement Scale (AIMS; National Institute of Mental Health, 1975) is an excellent tool for that purpose. Treatment compliance is essential to recovery, and nurses are often the first healthcare practitioners to notice and report changes in functioning or condition.

Dementia

Dementia is the loss of memory and cognitive abilities. The most common cause of dementia is Alzheimer's disease (AD). Nearly 10% of individuals over the age of 65 and over 25–40% of individuals over the age of 85 have AD (Breitner et al.,

1999). Other forms of dementia are vascular, frontotemporal, Pick's disease, and Lewy body dementia. Dementia is also common in Parkinson's and Huntington's disease. A score of 24 or below on the Mini-Mental State Examination (MMSE; Folstein, Folstein, & McHugh, 1975) can alert the psychiatric nurse that a client needs further evaluation for possible dementia.

Alzheimer's Disease

Alzheimer's disease progresses slowly and is often mistaken for normal cognitive changes of aging until later in its course. Although the disease cannot be definitively diagnosed until the brain is biopsied at autopsy, the diagnosis may be given once a person manifests multiple cognitive deficits including memory impairment and cognitive disturbances (e.g., aphasia, apraxia, agnosia, executive deficits). Neuroimaging might reveal enlarged ventricles indicating brain atrophy. Microanatomical changes include accumulation of a protein called beta amyloid in the neurons, and neurofibrillary tangles created by clumps of structural components of the cell called microtubules. Needless to say, neurons that become stuffed with plaques of protein and tangles of microtubules are unable to perform their normal functions and eventually die.

Early on in the progression of the disease, acetylcholinesterase inhibitors can be prescribed to slow the metabolism of ACh, improving its availability for learning and memory. Later on, glutamate antagonists may slow the progressive neurodegenerative processes. But nothing has been found to halt disease progression entirely and, with or without treatment, it continues to destroy brain function. Fortunately, new research is addressing how we might someday be able to target the beta amyloid gene precursors to prevent amyloid plaques and other cellular changes.

Substance Disorders

The *DSM-IV-TR* (APA, 2000) lists substance-specific diagnostic criteria for 11 classes of substances. The *DSM-IV-TR* does not include the term addiction, referring to the loss of control over the use of a substance; rather, it defines substance abuse, dependence, intoxication, and withdrawal patterns. What seems remarkable is that although the substances can have strikingly different acute effects, they share the characteristic of being rewarding to the user, a quality that promotes repeated drug use, and in vulnerable individuals, the loss of control.

The brain mechanism of reward is thought to reside in the mesolimbic dopamine pathway. "Meso" refers to the mesencephalon, the Latin term for the midbrain. The dopamine-producing neurons have their cell bodies in the ventral portion of the midbrain, and their axons terminate in a location rich with cell bodies of other neurons, called the nucleus accumbens. All drugs of abuse increase dopaminergic transmission to the nucleus accumbens via this pathway (Nestler, 2005). The brain adapts to the chronic increase by decreasing baseline levels of dopamine, having the unfortunate result of decreasing sensitivity to normally rewarding activities like food or sex. Tolerance may develop as it takes more of the drug to have the same effect. Neural adaptations in other brain circuits occur as well. Chronic drug use appears to activate the amygdala and the HPA axis during withdrawal, resulting in fear, negative mood states, and stress. In addition, impairment in the executive functioning of the frontal cortex can lead individuals to become less able to inhibit sudden urges and actions related to drug seeking and taking.

Obviously not everyone who uses a drug becomes addicted or dependent. Risk factors for addiction include genetic vulnerability, sensitivity to environmental stressors and rewards, drug availability, adolescence, and mental illness. The first step towards treating substance disorders is to understand that the complex neuroplastic changes in the brain are long-lasting and that recovery takes time and patience. Treatment should include strategies that enhance the salience of natural rewards, strengthen inhibitory control and executive function, decrease drug cues and conditioned responses to them, and improve mood if disrupted (Volkow & Li, 2005).

Dementia is the loss of memory and cognitive abilities. The most common cause is Alzheimer's disease.

Neuroimaging

There are many ways to image the brain, but to date none of them provides definitive diagnoses for mental disorders. **Neuroimaging** has played an important role in expanding our knowledge base related to the structure, function, and neurochemistry of the CNS. Two categories of brain imaging may be used—structural imaging and functional imaging. **Structural imaging** with computed tomography (CT) and magnetic resonance imaging (MRI) gathers information regarding the physical constitution of the brain at any one point in time. These techniques are helpful in detecting structural changes that may result from injury or disease of the brain. The results are not dependent on

There are two types of brain neuroimaging—structural imaging (CT, MRI) and functional imaging (PET, fMRI). Though useful in understanding psychiatric disorders, they are not diagnostic.

thought, motor activity, or mood. **Functional imaging**, not surprisingly, tells us about the functioning of the brain. The two most common techniques for examining function are positron emission tomography (PET) and functional magnetic resonance imaging (fMRI). These methods detect changes in regional blood flow and metabolism during thought, motor activity, or mood changes.

Clinical indications for imaging in clients with psychiatric disorders are listed in Table 4-3. The newer American Psychiatric Association's practice guidelines suggest that neuroimaging may also be useful in formulating a diagnosis of dementia (Rabins, 2006). Although the neuroimaging of the brain provides important diagnostic clues, limitations exist (Fletcher, 2004) and the techniques are expensive to perform. These procedures are not routinely used with all clients who have psychiatric disorders. Many of the findings are nonspecific, showing only ventricular enlargements or generalized atrophy.

Structural Imaging

In CT, thin slices or tomographs of the brain are obtained by x-ray, reconstructed, and entered into a computer. With this technology, a variety of views of the brain can be produced, revealing the gross organization of the gray and white matter and the position of the ventricles. CT is superior to MRI for assessing calcification, acute hemorrhage, and bone injury. Though not diagnostic, CT studies in persons with schizophrenia have shown enlargement of ventricles and structural alterations in prefrontal and medial temporal areas, the corpus callosum, and cingulate (Fannon et al., 2000).

Table 4-3 Clinical Indications for Neuroimaging
• Psychiatric symptoms outside "clinical norms"
• Dementia or cognitive decline
• Traumatic brain injury
• New-onset mental illness after age 50
• Initial psychotic break
• Alcohol abuse
• Seizure disorders with psychiatric symptoms
• Movement disorders
• Autoimmune disorders
• Eating disorders
• Poison or toxin exposure
• Catatonia
• Focal neurological signs

Source: Adapted from Yudolfsky & Hales, 2004, p. 83.

MRI uses radio waves and magnets to obtain images. White and gray matter in the brain have different densities of hydrogen ions, so they respond differently to perturbations of a strong magnetic field. As a person rests quietly, the MRI scanner passes an electromagnetic wave (radio signal) through the head while it is positioned between the poles of a large magnet. When the magnetic fields are shifted, the movement of the hydrogen ions is detected and a detailed image of the whole brain, both gray and white matter, is obtained. MRI is superior to CT and generally is the preferred modality when assessing for subcortical lesions, demyelination, and lesions near bone. With MRIs, measurement of reduced hippocampal volumes has been reported in multiple studies of depression, bipolar disorder, PTSD, and dementia. MRIs taken of individuals with schizophrenia have shown enlarged ventricles, smaller total brain and hippocampal volumes, and less total gray matter in auditory and information processing centers (Sanz de la Torre, Barrios, & Junque, 2005). Figure 4-11 shows how follow-up MRIs have been used to detect schizophrenia-related brain changes over time.

The advantage of MRI over CT for structural imaging is that it does not require x-irradiation, the image is more detailed, and the computer can construct brain slices in any plane desired. The disadvantage is that it is difficult for individuals to lie still for the approximately 20 minutes that it takes to do an MRI, and some individuals feel frightened by the close proximity of the scanner and the loud noises that it emits. Fortunately, many sites now offer open MRIs that are not as confining.

Functional Imaging

Functional imaging gives us a sense of what is going on in the thinking, living brain. With functional imaging we are able to see which areas of the brain are active during certain types of mental tasks and how brain activation and metabolism changes as a result of brain lesions or mental illness. In psychia-

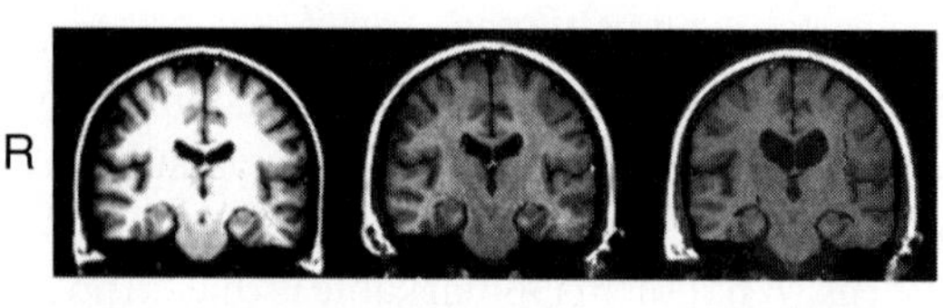

Figure 4-11 An MRI shows progressive atrophy and increased ventricular size in the same female with schizophrenia. She was 34 years old at the time of the 10-year follow-up.

try, the information is not diagnostic because of the considerable overlap in abnormalities of the limbic structures in mental disorders. Functional imaging has been used extensively in psychiatric research to help further our understanding of functional deficits and pharmacological therapies in clinically defined client groups. When the brain is active it utilizes more oxygen and glucose (recall that these are needed to make cellular ATP energy) and more blood is sent to the active regions. Both the fMRI and the PET scan can detect changes in regional blood flow and metabolism within the brain.

For a PET scan, an individual lies in the scanner and a radioactive solution is injected intravenously. As the individual performs a task, such as thinking of a series of numbers, blood flow and metabolism increase in the active areas of the brain. The PET detects the area of the brain that is most active during the task (see **Figure 4-12**). The disadvantages of PET are the radiation exposure and the relatively slow scanning time that limits the number of areas of the brain that can be studied in any one person at any one time.

The fMRI has the advantages of coupling structural scanning with images of brain activation, not requiring radiation exposure, and being completely noninvasive. Indirect measures of blood flow and metabolism are made by measuring the ratio of oxyhemoglobin (oxygenated form of hemoglobin) to deoxyhemoglobin (hemoglobin that has donated its oxygen). fMRI is the most widely used neuroimaging technique for studying cognitive dysfunction. An example of how fMRIs have helped us understand more about cognitive dysfunction comes from studies of individuals with schizophrenia. NIMH researchers (Weinberger et al., 2001) found that individuals with schizophrenia sometimes showed hypoactivation of the prefrontal cortex during working memory tasks, but at other times showed hyperactivation. The hypoactivation illuminated the difficulties that they had with staying on task, and the hyperactivation illuminated the reduced efficiency and automaticity of their prefrontal cortex. These types of findings would not have been possible using structural neuroimaging methods.

Other Neuroimaging Methods

Although less precise than PET, single photon emission computed tomography (SPECT) utilizes a radioisotope to show patterns of cerebral blood flow and metabolic activity. Areas of the brain that are more active absorb more of the radioisotope. SPECT can also be used to identify areas of hypoperfusion in the brain, such as might be seen in areas of neuronal degeneration in dementia.

Magnetic resonance spectroscopy (MRS) is used to detect and quantify brain tissue based chemicals, including brain levels of psychotropic medications. With MRS imaging, comparisons of the concentrations of substances can be made between healthy brains and brains with neuropsychiatric abnormalities. For example, investigators can detect a neuronal metabolite called N-acetyl-aspartate (NAA) that corresponds to neuronal health, a metabolite produced only in neurons. Reductions in NAA can indicate areas of neuronal degeneration.

Electroencephalography (EEG)

Electroencephalography (EEG) refers to the use of electrodes placed on the scalp to record the electrical activity of the brain. Large groups of neurons firing synchronously generate electrical potentials that can be monitored on the surface of the brain. With traditional EEG the pattern of brain activity at the surface of the brain is visible; however, the origin of activity from specific brain regions is not. Magnetoencephalography (MEG) is a technique that can detect neural activity deep

In electroencephalography (EEG) the pattern of the brain activity on the surface of the brain is visible, but the origin of the activity from within the brain's regions is not.

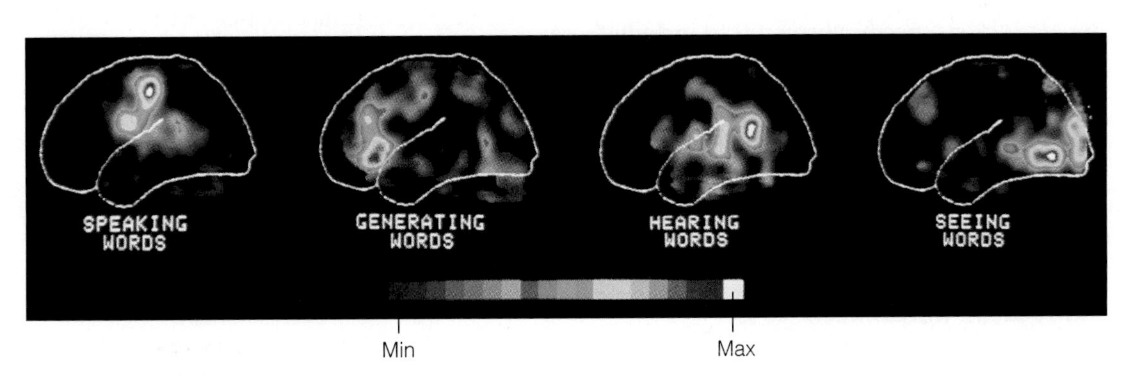

Figure 4-12 A PET scan shows areas of brain activation during cognitive tasks. The brighter the color, the more brain activation.

within the brain. It is noninvasive but is limited to use in research.

Critical Thinking Question What will you teach a client regarding the potential limitations from an MRI related to a diagnosis of mental illness?

Implications

Recent national reports and initiatives, such as the report from the President's Freedom Commission on Mental Health (2003), the Institute of Medicine's (2005) report on *Improving the Quality of Health Care for Mental and Substance-Use Conditions*, and the Department of Health and Human Services' Substance Abuse and Mental Health Services Administration's (SAMHSA, 2005) action steps for *Transforming Mental Health Care in America*, advocate transforming the mental health system to be more evidence-based and consumer driven. This will require nurses to keep up with the changes in our knowledge base regarding the causes and treatments of mental illness and to help translate these findings to clients and their families so that they can make informed decisions regarding their care. Helping clients, families, and the community at large understand the neurobiological considerations will help decrease the stigma and improve the care of individuals with mental illness.

Summary

This chapter has provided a basic knowledge of the brain's structures and their functions, the neurotransmitters and their pathways, and the mechanisms for the development of mental illnesses and disorders and their treatment. There was focused discussion of the structure and function of the nervous system, cellular mechanisms of communication, the role of neurotransmitters in mental illness, neurotransmission and neuroplasticity, the regulation of emotion and the limbic system, stress response (acute and chronic), and genetic factors. Conditions specifically discussed included mood disorders, anxiety, schizophrenia, and dementias. The role of various tests were presented: neuroimaging (CT, MRI), functional imaging (fMRI, PET), and electroencephalography (EEGs). The relationship between neurobiology and psychopharmacological treatment was highlighted.

Annotated References

American Psychiatric Association. (2000). *The diagnostic and statistical manual of mental disorders* (4th ed., text rev.). Washington, DC: Author.

DSM-IV-TR diagnostic categories describe clusters of symptoms that tend to co-occur, but are not based on neurophysiological etiologies.

Bear, M., Connors, B., and Paradiso, M. (2007). *Neuroscience: Exploring the brain* (3rd ed.). Baltimore, MD: Lippincott, Williams & Wilkins.

This text was developed for undergraduate students of neuroscience. It is highly readable and highly recommended.

Breitner, J., Wyse, B., Anthony, J., Welsh-Bohmer, K., Steffens, D., Norton, M., et al. (1999). APOE-epsilon4 count predicts age when prevalence of AD increases, then declines: The Cache County Study. *Neurology, 53*(2), 321–331.

Data from a study of 5,677 elderly residents of Cache County, Utah, were used to estimate the prevalence of Alzheimer's disease in the general population.

Charney, D. (2003). Neuroanatomical circuits modulating fear and anxiety disorders. *Acta Psychiatrica Scandinavica, 108*(Suppl. 417), 38–50.

Charney reviews the multiple neurotransmitter and structural abnormalities found in the various anxiety disorders and stresses the need to define the circuits related to the specific anxiety disorders as well as factors related to resilience to stress.

Diamond, M., Scheibel, A., Murphy, G., & Harvey, T. (1985). On the brain of a scientist: Albert Einstein. *Experimental Neurology, 88*(1), 198–204.

This article describes the analysis of Einstein's brain and the possible explanations given for his exemplary intellect.

Fannon, D. Chitnis, X., Doku, V., Tennakoon, L., O'Ceallaigh, S., Soni, W., et al. (2000). Features of structural brain abnormality detected in first episode psychosis. *The American Journal of Psychiatry, 157*(11), 1829–1835.

Structural deviations were found in those experiencing psychosis as significant cortical and temporal lobe gray matter reductions, reductions of total brain volumes, and enlargements of the lateral and third ventricles.

Fletcher, P. C. (2004). Functional neuroimaging of psychiatric disorders: Exploring hidden behaviors. *Psychological Medicine, 34*, 577–581.

The author of this editorial reports the progress in neuroimaging with PET and fMRI techniques over the past decade. Fletcher notes limitations and advances, and areas for continued research.

Folstein, M., Folstein, S., & McHugh, P. (1975). "Mini-mental state": A practical method for grading the cognitive state of patients for the clinician. *Journal of Psychiatric Research, 12*, 189.

The authors describe the MMSE and its scoring.

Gabriel, G. (n.d.). Hans Selye: The discovery of stress. Retrieved February 1, 2007, from http://www.brainconnection.com/topics/?main=fa/selye

The Brain Connection is a great online source for learning about the brain.

Gutman, D., & Nemeroff, C. (2003). Persistent central nervous system effects of an adverse early environment: Clinical and preclinical studies. *Physiology & Behavior, 79*, 471–478.

This article reviews animal and human studies showing persistent CRF, ACTH, and cortisol elevations in response to early childhood physical or sexual abuse.

Hasler, G., Drevets, W., Gould, T., Gottesman, I., & Manji, H. (2006). Toward constructing an endophenotype strategy for bipolar disorders. *Biological Psychiatry, 60*, 93–105.

These NIMH researchers identify genetically relevant aspects of the heterogeneous pathophysiology of the disease.

Institute of Medicine. Committee on Crossing the Quality Chasm: Adaptation to Mental Health and Addictive Disorders, Board on Health Care Services. (2005). *Improving the quality of health care for mental and substance-use conditions*. Washington, DC: National Academies Press.

This is a must-read for all healthcare professionals. The title is self-explanatory.

Kendler, K. (2001). Twin studies of psychiatric illness. *Archives of General Psychiatry, 58*, 1005–1014.

Kendler reviews heritability estimates for schizophrenia, alcoholism, and major depression from large twin studies.

Kendler, K., Gatz, M., Gardner, C., & Pedersen, N. (2006). A Swedish national twin study of lifetime major depression. *American Journal of Psychiatry, 163*(1), 109–114.

The lifetime prevalence of major depression was assessed in over 15,000 twin pairs.

Lee, A., Ogle, W., & Sapolsky, R. (2002). Stress and depression: Possible links to neuron death in the hippocampus. *Bipolar Disorders, 4*, 117–128.

This article presents a thorough review of the evidence for stress-related damage to the hippocampus.

Mason, J., Wang, S., Yehuda, R., Sherry, R., Charney, D., & Soputhwick, S. (2001). Psychogenic lowering of urinary cortisol levels linked to increased emotional numbing and a shame-depressive syndrome in combat-related posttraumatic stress disorder. *Psychosomatic Medicine, 63*(3), 387–401.

The purpose of the study was to search for the intrapsychic correlates of individual differences in cortisol levels in male Vietnam combat veterans with posttraumatic stress disorder.

McEwen, B. (2000). Effects of adverse experiences for brain structure and function. *Biological Psychiatry, 48*, 721–731.

McEwen reviews evidence for neuroplasticity in the hippocampus as a result of acute and chronic stress.

McEwen, B. (2001). Plasticity of the hippocampus: Adaptation to chronic stress and allostatic load. *Annals of the New York Academy of Sciences, 933*, 265–277.

McEwen reviews research that shows that repeated and long-term elevations in neurochemical, autonomic, and HPA reactivity, as seen in some individuals with recurrent depression or PTSD, might lead to hippocampal atrophy and even permanent damage.

McGuffin, P., Rijsdijk, F., Andrew, M., Sham, P., Katz, R., & Cardno, A. (2003). The heritability of bipolar affective disorder and the genetic relationship to unipolar depression. *Archives of General Psychiatry, 60*(5), 497–502.

The authors examined the lifetime risk of bipolar disorder among monozygotic and dizygotic twins.

Meyer, J., Ginovart, N., Boovariwala, A., Sagrati, S., Hussey, D., Garcia, A., et al. (2006). Elevated monoamine oxidase A levels in the brain: An explanation for the monoamine imbalance of major depression. *Archives of General Psychiatry, 63*(11), 1209–1216.

Presents recent evidence from a small comparison study that MAO-A levels may be elevated in individuals with depression.

Milner, B. (2005). The medial temporal-lobe amnesic syndrome. *Psychiatric Clinics of North America, 28*, 599–611.

This is a fascinating review of Dr. Brenda Milner's 40+ year observation of HM, a man who had bilateral medial temporal lobectomies.

Naqvi, N., Rudrauf, D., Damasio, H., & Bechara, A. (2007). Damage to the insula disrupts addiction to cigarette smoking. *Science, 315*, 531–534.

The researchers reported that damage to the insula area of the brain was associated with sudden cessation of smoking without cravings or relapse. It is as yet unclear whether the role of the insula in addiction to smoking might also apply to other drugs of abuse.

National Institute of Mental Health. (1975). *Development of a dyskinetic movement scale.* (Publ. No. 4). Rockville, MD: National Institute of Mental Health, Psychopharmacology Research Branch.

This scale became the Abnormal Involuntary Movement Scale and is useful for monitoring and documenting change in movements when patients are taking antipsychotics.

Nestler, E. (2005). Is there a common molecular pathway for addiction? *Nature Neuroscience, 8(11)*, 1445–1449.

Nestler describes how all drugs of abuse converge on the brain's reward pathways.

Post, R., Leverich, G., Altshuler, L., Frye, M., Suppes, T., Keck, P., et al. (2003). An overview of recent findings of the Stanley Foundation Bipolar Network (Part I). *Bipolar Disorders, 5*, 310–319.

The authors describe current understandings of bipolar symptoms and course of illness, including the effects of early environmental adversity on the brain.

President's Freedom Commission on Mental Health. (2003). *Achieving the promise: Transforming mental health in America. Final Report.* Rockville, MD: U.S. Department of Health and Human Services.

This well-known report challenged health professionals to understand the neurobiological causes of mental illness.

Rabins, P. (2006). *Guideline watch: Practice guideline for the treatment of patients with Alzheimer's disease and other dementias of late life.* Washington, DC: American Psychiatric Association. Available online at: http://www.psych.org/psych_pract/treatg/pg/prac_guide.cfm

This new addition to the practice guidelines suggests that neuroimaging may have a place in the diagnosis of Alzheimer's disease.

Rapoport, J., Addington, A., Frangou, S., & MRC Psych. (2005). The neurodevelopmental model of schizophrenia: Update 2005. *Molecular Psychiatry, 10*, 434–449.

These NIMH researchers present a clear update on neurodevelopmental changes in schizophrenia and the gene candidates that are under investigation.

Ross, C., Margolis, R., Reading, S., Pletnikov, M., & Coyle, J. (2006). Neurobiology of schizophrenia. *Neuron, 52*, 139–153.

These researchers review the brain development and neuroplasticity in schizophrenia and examine various susceptibility gene candidates.

Sanz de la Torre, J. C., Barrios, M., & Junque, C. (2005). Frontal lobe alterations in schizophrenia, neuroimaging and neuropsychological findings. *European Archives of Psychiatry and Clinical Neuroscience, 255*, 236–244.

This paper describes prefrontal and frontal brain differences in patients with schizophrenia compared to healthy controls.

Sapolsky, R. (2003a). Stress and plasticity in the limbic system. *Neurochemical Research, 28*(11), 1735–1742.

Sapolsky describes how stress affects the limbic system, in particular, the hippocampus.

Sapolsky, R. (2003b). Taming stress. *Scientific American, 289*(3), 88–95.

This is a very readable summary of the stress research and brain effects of stress.

Sapolsky, R. (2005). Sick of poverty. *Scientific American, 293*(6), 92–99.

This is a very readable summary of the effects of socioeconomic inequalities on physical and mental health.

Schafe, G., Doyere, V., & LeDoux, J. (2005). Tracking the fear engram: The lateral amygdala is an essential locus of fear memory storage. *The Journal of Neuroscience, 25*(43), 10010–10015.

LeDoux and his coworkers are world experts on the amygdala and its functions in mental health and illness. Memories of past threats are stored in the amygdala and influence its function.

Snider, L., & Swedo, S. (2003). Childhood-onset obsessive-compulsive disorder and tic disorders: Case report and literature review. *Journal of Child and Adolescent Psychopharmacology, 13*(Suppl. 1), S81–S88.

The authors review the literature showing a relationship between abrupt onset of tics and OCD and exposure to the streptococcus bacteria. The syndrome is called pediatric autoimmune neuropsychiatric disorder associated with streptococcus (PANDAS).

Stahl, S. (2000). *Essential psychopharmacology. Neuroscientific basis and practical applications* (2nd ed.). New York: Cambridge University Press.

Stahl assists the reader in understanding basic but potentially difficult concepts underlying the pharmacological treatment of psychiatric disorders. It is easy to read and filled with wonderful cartoon diagrams.

Substance Abuse and Mental Health Services Administration, U.S. Department of Health and Human Services. (2005). *Transforming mental health care in America. The federal action agenda: First steps.* DHHS Publication No. SMA-05-4060. Rockville, MD: DHHS.

This essential document outlines specific steps to take in improving mental health care.

U.S. Department of Health and Human Services. (1999). *Mental health: A report of the Surgeon General—executive summary*. Rockville, MD: Author.

This important report can be read online: http://mentalhealth.samhsa.gov/cmhs/surgeongeneral/surgeongeneralrpt.asp

Ustun, J., Ayuso-Mateos, S., Chatterji, S., Mathers, C., & Murray, C. (2004). Global burden of depressive disorders in the year 2000. *British Journal of Psychiatry, 184*, 386–392.

The authors selectively review evidence on the disability caused by depression in this large multi-national survey.

Volkow, N., & Li, T-K. (2005). The neuroscience of addiction. *Nature Neuroscience, 8*(11), 1429–1430.

Volkow and Li, the Directors of the National Institutes on Drug Abuse and on Alcohol Abuse and Alcoholism, write a concise summary of the neurobiological mechanisms of addiction.

Weinberger, D., Egan, M., Bertolino, A., Callicott, J., Mattay, V., Lipska, B., et al. (2001). Prefrontal neurons and the genetics of schizophrenia. *Biological Psychiatry, 50*, 825–844.

This is a wonderful summary by NIMH researchers of cognitive dysfunction in schizophrenia and its possible genetic risk factors.

Yudolfsky, S., & Hales, R. (2004). *Essentials of neuropsychiatry and clinical neurosciences.* Washington, DC: American Psychiatric Publishing.

This text is for the advanced practice psychiatric clinician. It reviews the psychiatric and neurologic evaluation and the use of neuroimaging in developing differential diagnoses.

Internet Resources

http://nursing.jbpub.com/psychiatric

Visit http://nursing.jbpub.com/psychiatric for interactive exercises, NCLEX review questions, WebLinks, and more.

CHAPTER 5

Psychopharmacology

Beth Harris

LEARNING OBJECTIVES

After reading this chapter, you will be able to:

- Name the five major families of psychotropic medications.
- List at least four indications for each family of psychotropic medications.
- Discuss at least three strategies for reducing side effects.
- Describe the management of at least three common side effects of each major family of psychotropic medications.
- Discuss at least three interventions that have been shown to increase client compliance.

KEY TERMS

Acetylcholine
Agonist
Akathisia
Akinesia
Antagonist
Antianxiety medication
Anticholinergic side effects
Antidepressants
Antidyskinetics
Antipsychotic medications
Atypical antipsychotic
Benzodiazepine
Compliance
Dopamine
Dystonia
Extrapyramidal
Hypnotic
Lag period
Minor tranquilizers
Monoamine oxidase inhibitor (MAOI)
Mood stabilizer
Negative psychotic symptoms
Neuroleptic malignant syndrome
Neurotransmitter
Norepinephrine
Positive symptoms
Psychopharmacologist
Psychopharmacology
Psychotropic medications
Sedative
Selective serotonin reuptake inhibitors (SSRIs)
Serotonin
Side effect
Stimulants
Tardive dyskinesia
Therapeutic effect

http://nursing.jbpub.com/psychiatric

Visit http://nursing.jbpub.com/psychiatric for interactive exercises, NCLEX review questions, WebLinks, and more.

Introduction

Psychopharmacology is the study of medications that affect the *psyche* (the Greek word that refers to a person's spirit or soul). In other words, psychopharmacology is the study of the medications used in psychiatry. These medications often are referred to as **psychotropic**, literally, medications that "move the spirit" or "move the soul."

Major families of psychotropic medications:
- Antipsychotics
- Antidepressants
- Mood stabilizers
- Antianxiety medications
- Stimulants
- Others

There are five major families of medications in psychiatry and an assortment of other smaller families. The five major families are closely related medications that are similar in chemical structure and similar in their physiologic effect on the body. Within each of the five families are a number of individual medications, each of which is approximately equally effective in a statistical sense (up to about 70% effective for most psychotropic medications). However, the effectiveness varies significantly among individuals who take them.

All the psychotropic medications alter some aspect of brain chemistry. Psychiatric symptoms and illnesses are caused by abnormalities in brain functioning, and the psychotropic medications restore the normal chemical balance of the brain, thus allowing the client to feel healthy and behave normally. For example, psychotic illnesses are thought to be related to overactivity of the chemical **neurotransmitters dopamine** and **serotonin**. Antipsychotic medications reduce the overactivity of one or both of these chemical neurotransmitters. Similarly, depression is thought to be related to an underactivity of the neurotransmitters **norepinephrine** and serotonin. Antidepressant medications specifically target these two neurotransmitters, increasing their activity and, by doing so, alleviating the depression. Similarly, each family of psychotropic medications works to restore a normal chemical balance in the brain.

Psychotropic medications do not cure mental illnesses any more than insulin cures diabetes. Like insulin for diabetes, the psychotropic medications treat the symptoms of the underlying illness, allowing the client to feel healthy and function normally.

Critical Thinking Question If psychotropic medications do not cure mental illness, what are the implications for length of treatment?

The nurse's role:
- Administer medications safely.
- Monitor desired (therapeutic) effects.
- Monitor for side effects.
- Teach client and family about medication management.

The Nurse's Role

Nurses play a pivotal role in psychopharmacology. Most psychiatric nurses administer and monitor psychotropic medications. In advanced practice, psychiatric nurse practitioners prescribe these medications.

The nurse's administration and monitoring role begins with the initial assessment of the client. Because one of the best ways of predicting a medication's effectiveness is to know if it previously worked well for the client or for a close family member (sister, brother, parent, child, grandparent, aunt, uncle, first cousin), the nurse asks about personal and family history of responsiveness to medications. The nurse also collects data about the client's potential reactions to **side effects**. For example, it would be inadvisable to give medication with hypotension as a common side effect to a client with a baseline blood pressure of 90/60 mmHg. Finally, the nurse asks about the person's feelings and attitudes about medication and seeks the client's opinion about what medication would be best.

As the client begins to take the medication, the nurse carefully administers each dose, gradually teaching the client about every aspect of the medication: the name of the medication; the exact dose, route, and schedule; and restrictions on certain foods and other medications. Whether the client takes 1 or 10 different psychotropic medications, the client should know the exact purpose of each. As the medication begins to enter the patient's bloodstream, the nurse monitors for the desired effects of the medication. The nurse identifies the target symptoms for the medication, and then regularly and consistently evaluates the presence and strength of each of those symptoms. With this information, the client and prescribing clinician are able to measure the medication's effectiveness in an objective way.

Critical Thinking Question When identifying target symptoms, why is it important to develop them in collaboration with the client?

The nurse's role in side-effect management is an important one. Psychotropic medications, like all medications, have side effects. For some people they are mild, and for others they are extremely uncomfortable and sometimes dangerous. The nurse teaches the client about the side effects that are most common with the medications being prescribed, so the client can share the task of monitoring for their presence. The client must be informed about side effects that are likely and that may be uncomfortable for the first few weeks or months. The client must be told that it is impossible to predict exactly what side effects will occur or how severe they will be. The nurse reassures the client that they will watch for side effects together and do whatever is necessary to minimize them.

It is extremely important that clients know that most side effects are temporary. Although the side effects begin right away, the desired or **therapeutic effect** may take weeks or months.

Clinical Example

A client with depression started taking an antidepressant. Because she was the mother of young children, she became anxious about her ability to care for her children because of the side effects she was experiencing: sleepiness, tremors, headache, stomach distress, and blurred vision. When taught that these side effects are temporary, usually subsiding within a few weeks, she expressed optimism about continuing to take the antidepressant.

Education for Clients and Families

Teaching clients about their medication is one of the most important functions of the psychiatric nurse. Medication teaching is begun as early as medications are discussed (usually at the initial assessment) and is continued throughout the course of treatment. Eventually, if capable, the client is taught to self-administer medication. If it is clear that the medication will be needed long term, even if there will be periodic attempts to reduce the dose, it is important to talk to the client about the course of treatment, because most people find it difficult to accept the long-term use of medications.

The nurse teaches the client and family the name and purpose of the medication, including target symptoms; the dose and exact schedule for taking each dose; the usual course and length of treatment; the importance of taking the medication as prescribed; alternative reminder devices to help remember each dose; the most common side effects and their management; long-term risks; addiction potential; food or medication restrictions; and the importance of informing the prescribing clinician of any problems with the medication.

If long-term risks are associated with taking the medication, clients should know about them so they can help monitor for their occurrence. Of all the psychotropic medications, the only ones that are potentially addictive are the antianxiety medications. Clients must be taught about the addictive potential of the **benzodiazepines** and about the absence of addictive potential for all the other psychotropic medications.

Most psychotropic medications take several weeks to begin working and must be taken consistently as prescribed, dose after dose and day after day, to be maximally effective. For example, many people feel little or no therapeutic effect from antidepressants for as long as 2 months. During this **lag period**, it is easy for clients to feel discouraged and demoralized. Most people expect medicines to work right away, similar to the way acetaminophen (Tylenol) helps a headache. They think that the medication either works within a half hour or so, or it does not work at all. The nurse needs to teach clients that taking psychotropic medications is not like taking acetaminophen (Tylenol) for a headache. Problems and discomforts that arise during the course of pharmacotherapy need to be discussed by the client and the prescribing clinician, so the medication can be adjusted until the target symptoms are controlled with a minimum of discomfort from side effects. For many people, this is a lengthy process during which a great deal of support is essential.

Because it is so integral to every aspect of our work, various aspects of client and family education are integrated throughout the chapter. A list of Internet resources to aid in client education is available on a Web site that is referenced at the end of this chapter.

Most psychotropic medications take several weeks to begin working and must be taken consistently as prescribed, dose after dose and day after day, to be maximally effective.

Critical Thinking Question Can you think of interventions to help a person accept the need for lifelong medications?

Psychotropic Medications

Most of the psychotropic medications fall into one of the following five categories: antipsychotic medications, antidepressant medications, mood stabilizers, antianxiety medications, and stimulants. Each of these five families will now be described in detail.

Clinical Example

A young man with bipolar disorder was stabilized on valproate (Depakote) following his first manic episode. When attending a medication group on the unit, he learned that bipolar disorder is lifelong and must be treated continuously with medication to prevent relapse into active symptoms. He expressed disbelief and anger that he would need to take medication for the rest of his life. Other members of the group who had a longer experience with bipolar disorder shared their own experiences of long periods of wellness stabilized on medication followed by relapse upon stopping their medication. After several such stories, the nurse encouraged the patient to think of his taking valproate as similar to a person with diabetes continuing to take insulin for a lifetime.

Common indications for antipsychotic medications:
- Schizophrenia
- Schizoaffective disorder
- Bipolar disorder
- Major depression with psychotic symptoms
- Tourette's disorder

Antipsychotic Medications

Antipsychotic medications (shown in **Table 5-1**) are used to treat psychotic symptoms. Target symptoms of antipsychotic medications are

- Agitation
- Apathy*
- Delusions
- Emotional withdrawal*
- Feelings of unreality
- Hallucinations
- Ideas of reference
- Lack of motivation*
- Lack of pleasure*
- Lack of spontaneity*
- Overreactive senses
- Paranoia
- Racing thoughts
- Rage
- Severe impulsiveness
- Social discomfort or isolation*
- Terror
- Unclear thoughts
- Uncontrollable hostility
- Uncontrollable negativism*

Table 5-1 Antipsychotics: Names and Usual Range of Daily Doses for Adults

Generic Name	Brand Name	mg/Day
Chlorpromazine	Thorazine	200–1,000
Thioridazine	Mellaril	25–600
Thiothixene	Navane	10–30
Trifluoperazine	Stelazine	6–40
Fluphenazine	Prolixin	5–40
Haloperidol	Haldol	2–40
Molindone	Moban	10–100
Loxapine	Loxitane	10–100
Perphenazine	Trilafon	8–32
Pimozide	Orap	4–10
Clozapine*	Clozaril*	200–900
Risperidone*	Risperdal*	4–8
Olanzapine*	Zyprexa*	5–20
Quetiapine*	Seroquel*	150–800
Ziprasidone*	Geodon*	80–160
Aripiprazole*	Abilify*	10–30
Paliperidone*	Invega	3–12

*Atypical antipsychotic

Whatever the cause of the psychosis, the symptoms themselves can be effectively treated with antipsychotics. The **negative psychotic symptoms** (marked above with an asterisk) are less responsive than the **positive symptoms**.

There are two groups of antipsychotics. The older group, first introduced in the mid-1950s, comprises the traditional antipsychotics. The newer group, the **atypical antipsychotics** (identified in **Table 5-1** by an asterisk), first became available in 1989 when clozapine (Clozaril) was approved by the Food and Drug Administration (FDA). The traditional antipsychotics work by creating a postsynaptic dopamine blockade in the brain in the subgroup of dopamine receptors called the D_2 receptors. The atypical antipsychotics have a lesser effect on the D_2 receptors and focus on blocking the serotonin postsynaptic receptors and other varieties of dopamine receptors (e.g., D_1 and D_5).

The atypical antipsychotics rarely cause one of the most problematic side effects of the traditional antipsychotics, **tardive dyskinesia**. For many years they were believed to induce fewer **extrapyramidal** (muscular) side effects, though this has been called into question in recent independent trials (see CATIE studies, below). The atypical antipsychotics are considerably more expensive than their older counterparts and, in the case of clozapine (Clozaril), they are more likely to be effective than the traditional antipsychotics. However, clozapine (Clozaril) causes agranulocytosis in slightly less than 1% of those who take it. As a result, safety requires that every person taking clozapine (Clozaril) have a white blood cell (WBC) count and careful clinical monitoring weekly for 6 months, every 2 weeks for an additional 6 months, and every month thereafter. Other problematic consequences of the atypical antipsychotics are the weight gain, metabolic changes, and diabetes mellitus that sometimes occur as side effects. When these occur they add greatly to the morbidity associated with the psychotic illness alone. **Table 5-2** lists side effects associated with antipsychotic medications.

Agranulocytosis rarely develops in persons who take clozapine (Clozaril), because of the mandatory WBC testing. When it does occur, agranulocytosis is detected before it becomes full-blown, thereby preventing danger, discomfort, and possible death. When agranulocytosis

Table 5-2 Antipsychotic Side Effects

Extrapyramidal or Muscular Side Effects	Other Side Effects
Dystonia (muscle cramp) Akinesia (lack of movement) Tremor Akathisia (motor restlessness) Tardive dyskinesia (abnormal, involuntary movements—more common with traditional antipsychotics) Finger rubbing or jerking Twitching or overactivity of the tongue Changes in posture Exaggerated blinking Puckering or chewing movements of the mouth Tic-like movements of the face **Sexual Side Effects** Delay in orgasm Reduced sex drive Amenorrhea **Anticholinergic Side Effects** Constipation Blurred vision Urinary retention or hesitancy Nasal congestion Dry mouth	Orthostatic hypotension Rash Reduced tolerance for alcohol Increased appetite with weight gain Sensitivity to sunburn Sedation Neuroleptic malignant syndrome High white blood cell count (WBC), high creatine phosphokinase (CPK) Muscular rigidity Increased or labile blood pressure, pulse, and respiration Fever Muteness Diaphoresis Drooling Dysphagia Agranulocytosis—1% risk with clozapine, very low risk with others Increased salivation Hypertension Fever (clozapine only) Nausea and vomiting (minimal risk except with clozapine) Seizures (minimal risk except with clozapine) Urinary incontinence (clozapine only)

does develop, the clozapine (Clozaril) must be stopped and cannot be used again due to the risk of agranulocytosis immediately recurring. In such cases, one of the newer atypical antipsychotics is usually substituted.

Neuroleptic malignant syndrome (NMS) is a rapidly developing syndrome of profound muscle stiffness, fever, and tremor. Within the space of a few hours, a person can become completely immobile, unable to swallow, to speak, or to move. NMS varies in its presentation, and may have a potentially fatal course or a relatively benign, self-limited course. The most important intervention for this side effect is to immediately stop administering the antipsychotic medication that is causing the problem. To do that, neuroleptic malignant syndrome must be recognized by its characteristic symptoms and laboratory findings (Table 5-2).

Once this syndrome is detected, the client is given supportive care (hydration, exercise, control of fever) for the few days it takes for the syndrome to resolve. Several **antidyskinetic** medications can be helpful in resolving the stiffness, including benzotropine (Cogentin), amantadine (Symmetrel), bromocriptine (Parlodel), and dantrolene (Dantrium) (**Table 5-3**).

Clinical Example

A young man with schizoaffective disorder says he stopped taking his medication after discharge because he does not "want to become a junkie." He and his nurse went online to the National Alliance on Mental Illness during their clinic appointment to find information that would reassure the client that his antipsychotic medication is not addictive.

Neuroleptic malignant syndrome is a rapidly developing syndrome of profound muscle stiffness, fever, and tremor. Medication should be stopped immediately.

A client with a lifelong psychiatric illness (e.g., schizophrenia, schizoaffective disorder,

Table 5-3 Antidyskinetic Medications: Names and Usual Range of Daily Doses for Adults

Generic Name	Brand Name	mg/Day
Benztropine	Cogentin	1–6
Biperiden	Akineton	2–8
Orphenadrine	Norflex	50–400
Diphenhydramine	Benadryl	25–300
Procyclidine	Kemadrin	7.5–20
Trihexyphenidyl	Artane	2–15
Amantadine	Symmetrel	100–400

Clinical Example

A retired lawyer whose bipolar disorder was stabilized with lithium for 30 years decided on retirement that the reduction of stress after giving up his law practice would eliminate the need for lithium. When he and his prescriber gradually decreased the dose, his symptoms that had been in control for many years began to reappear in the form of sleeplessness, pressured speech, and irritability. Rather than continue the dose reduction, the client decided to return indefinitely to the dose of lithium that had kept him well for so long.

Common indications for antidepressant medications:

- Attention-deficit hyperactivity disorder
- Bipolar disorder
- Bulimia or anorexia
- Dysthymic disorder
- Major depression
- Obsessive-compulsive disorder
- Panic disorder
- Schizoaffective disorder
- Social phobia

bipolar disorder) often needs to take antipsychotic medications indefinitely to maintain optimum symptom relief and functioning. The prescriber may make periodic attempts to reduce the dose, but for many people the course of treatment is lifelong.

Antidepressant Medications

Antidepressant medications (**Table 5-4**) are widely prescribed both in psychiatry and in other specialties where they are used to treat several pain syndromes, ulcers, and insomnia. Antidepressants fall into four major classifications, based on either their chemical structure or effect on the brain.

In psychiatry, they are the treatment of choice for the most common psychiatric disorder, major depression. In addition, they are an excellent treatment for several of the anxiety disorders. The target symptoms of the antidepressants when treating depression are

- Guilt
- Hopelessness and helplessness
- Increased or decreased appetite
- Insomnia or hypersomnia
- Loss of energy or sex drive or pleasure
- Preoccupation with death or suicide
- Psychomotor retardation or agitation
- Sad or anxious mood
- Trouble concentrating

Like the antipsychotics, antidepressants have a lag period during which the side effects appear (**Table 5-5**) but the therapeutic or desired

Implications for Evidence-Based Practice

The *Clinical Antipsychotic Trials of Intervention Effectiveness* (CATIE studies) (National Institute of Mental Health [NIMH], 2006), the largest, longest, and most comprehensive independent trial ever done to examine existing therapies for schizophrenia, had a number of important findings, including the following:

1. When four atypical antipsychotics (olanzapine, quetiapine, risperidone, and ziprasidone) and one traditional antipsychotic (perphenazine) were assigned randomly in a double-blind trial, all five medications were equally effective and *all* were associated with high rates of noncompliance due to intolerable side effects or poor symptom control.
2. Contrary to expectations, extrapyramidal side effects were *not* seen more frequently with the traditional antipsychotics than with the atypicals.
3. Olanzapine was better tolerated and produced greater symptom reduction than the others in this study, but this benefit was offset by the fact that persons taking olanzapine had considerably more weight gain and metabolic changes than those who were on the other four antipsychotics.
4. In phase 2 of the CATIE study, clozapine was found to be considerably more effective in reducing symptoms and considerably better tolerated than other antipsychotics, resulting in far better medication **compliance**.

The antipsychotics are not addictive. The major risks include agranulocytosis with clozapine (Clozaril); **neuroleptic malignant syndrome**, which occurs infrequently with both traditional and atypical antipsychotics but carries a mortality rate of 10%; and tardive dyskinesia (TD), potentially irreversible involuntary movements. Each of these risks can be minimized with early detection. Agranulocytosis is prevented by the required regular WBC counts, neuroleptic malignant syndrome can be detected by rapid clustering of its symptoms, and TD can be diagnosed at an early stage by regular screening using the Abnormal Involuntary Movement Scale (AIMS; **Figure 5-1**; Guy, 1976).

Table 5-4 Antidepressants: Names and Usual Range of Daily Doses for Adults

Generic Name	Brand Name	mg/Day
Imipramine	Tofranil	75–200
Amitriptyline	Elavil	75–200
Desipramine	Norpramin	75–200
Nortriptyline	Pamelor	25–100
Doxepin	Sinequan	75–200
Protriptyline	Vivactil	30–40
Trimipramine	Surmontil	75–200
Maprotiline	Ludiomil	150–200
Amoxapine	Asendin	100–400
Trazodone	Desyrel	200–400
Fluoxetine*	Prozac*	20–40
Bupropion	Wellbutrin	300–400
Clomipramine*	Anafranil*	75–250
Sertraline*	Zoloft*	50–200
Paroxetine*	Paxil*	20–50
Venlafaxine	Effexor	75–300
Nefazodone	Serzone	200–400
Fluvoxamine*	Luvox*	100–300
Mirtazapine	Remeron	15–30
Citalopram*	Celexa*	20–60
Escitalopram*	Lexapro*	10–20
Duloxetine	Cymbalta	40–60
Phenelzine†	Nardil†	15–90
Tranylcypromine†	Parnate†	30–40
Isocarboxazid†	Marplan†	10–60

*Selective serotonin reuptake inhibitor (SSRI)
†Monoamine oxidase inhibitor (MAOI)

Table 5-5 Most Common Antidepressant Side Effects

Orthostatic hypotension
Drowsiness or fatigue
Dry mouth
Constipation
Urinary hesitancy or retention
Palpitations or tachycardia
Blurred vision
Tremor
Diaphoresis
Sexual problems with desire or performance
Anxiety or agitation
Headache
Nausea or vomiting
Insomnia or nightmares
Hypertensive crisis *(MAOI only)*
- Stiff neck
- Headache
- Palpitations
- Chest pain
- Nausea
- Vomiting
- Flushing
- Chills
- Apprehension
- Pallor
- Sweating

Atropine psychosis *(anticholinergic delirium)*
- Purposeless overactivity
- Agitation
- Confusion
- Disorientation
- Dysarthria
- Dry, flushed skin
- Tachycardia
- Sluggish and dilated pupils

effect is not yet achieved. This can be a difficult and dangerous time for clients who are already depressed and have probably tried everything in their power to recover before resorting to antidepressant medications. After starting antidepressants, they often find themselves continuing to suffer from the symptoms of depression, and now also suffering from the antidepressant side effects.

Constant support and protection may be needed during this period to help clients survive until the beneficial effects of the medications begin.

A great deal of attention has been paid to a documented increase in suicidal ideation that occurs in children, adolescents, and adults taking antidepressant medications. Most studies show that although suicidal ideation is increased during the early weeks of treatment, there is no increase in the number of deaths from suicide. This increase in suicidal ideation in the early weeks of treatment, whether due to the lag period issues noted earlier or to a medication effect, must remain a focus of treatment until a full antidepressant response is seen.

Most of the time, the proper dose of antidepressant is determined by the client's clinical response. The prescriber starts with a low dose that is gradually raised until the client feels better, the side effects become too strong, or the dose has reached beyond the therapeutic range (see Table 5-4). For a few of the antidepressants, blood levels

Abnormal Involuntary Movement Scale (AIMS)

Patient's Name (Please print)__________ Patient's ID information __________

Examiner's Name__________

Current Medications and Total mg/day

Medication #1______ Total mg/day______ Medication #2 ______ Total mg/day______

Instructions: Complete the examination procedure before entering these ratings.

	None, normal	Minimal (may be extreme normal)	Mild	Moderate	Severe
Facial and Oral Movements					
1. Muscles of facial expression, e.g., movements of forehead, eyebrows, periorbital area, cheeks; include frowning, blinking, smiling, grimacing	☐ 0	☐ 1	☐ 2	☐ 3	☐ 4
2. Lips and perioral area, e.g., puckering, pouting, smacking	☐ 0	☐ 1	☐ 2	☐ 3	☐ 4
3. Jaw, e.g., biting, clenching, chewing, mouth opening, lateral movement	☐ 0	☐ 1	☐ 2	☐ 3	☐ 4
4. Tongue Rate only increases in movement both in and out of mouth, NOT inability to sustain movement	☐ 0	☐ 1	☐ 2	☐ 3	☐ 4
Extremity Movements					
5. Upper (arms, wrists, hands, fingers) Include choreic movements (i.e., rapid, objectively purposeless, irregular, spontaneous); athetoid movements (i.e., slow, irregular, complex, serpentine). DO NOT include tremor (i.e., repetitive, regular, rhythmic).	☐ 0	☐ 1	☐ 2	☐ 3	☐ 4
6. Lower (legs, knees, ankles, toes) e.g., lateral knee movement, foot tapping, heel dropping, foot squirming, inversion and eversion of foot	☐ 0	☐ 1	☐ 2	☐ 3	☐ 4
Trunk Movements					
7. Neck, shoulders, hips e.g., rocking, twisting, squirming, pelvic gyrations	☐ 0	☐ 1	☐ 2	☐ 3	☐ 4

SCORING:

- Score the highest amplitude or frequency in a movement on the 0–4 scale, not the average.
- Score activated movements the same way; do not lower those numbers as was proposed at one time.
- A POSITIVE AIMS EXAMINATION IS A SCORE OF 2 IN TWO OR MORE MOVEMENTS or a SCORE OF 3 OR 4 IN A SINGLE MOVEMENT.
- Do not sum the scores: e.g., a patient who has scores 1 in four movements DOES NOT have a positive AIMS score of 4.

Overall Severity					
8. Severity of abnormal movements	☐ 0	☐ 1	☐ 2	☐ 3	☐ 4
9. Incapacitation due to abnormal movements	☐ 0	☐ 1	☐ 2	☐ 3	☐ 4

	No awareness	Aware, no distress	Aware, mild distress	Aware, moderate distress	Aware, severe distress
10. Patient's awareness of abnormal movements (rate only patient's report)	☐ 0	☐ 1	☐ 2	☐ 3	☐ 4

Dental Status	Yes	No
11. Current problems with teeth and/or dentures?	☐	☐
12. Does patient usually wear dentures?	☐	☐

Comments:__________

Examiner's Signature__________ Next Exam Date __________

Figure 5-1 The Abnormal Involuntary Movement Scale (AIMS).

can be drawn that can be used to guide dosage if the clinical response is equivocal or disappointing. The antidepressant that is best guided by blood levels is nortriptyline (Pamelor), which works optimally only when blood levels are between 50 and 150 mg/ml.

The most widely used antidepressants are the **selective serotonin reuptake inhibitors (SSRIs)** (e.g., fluoxetine [Prozac] and paroxetine [Paxil]). Along with the "other" category of antidepressants (e.g., trazodone [Desyrel]), the SSRIs are considered an advance over the older tricyclic family (e.g., imipramine [Tofranil] and amytriptyline [Elavil]) because their side effects are considerably milder and more tolerable.

There is one subgroup, the **monoamine oxidase inhibitor (MAOI)** antidepressants (e.g., phenelzine [Nardil], tranylcypromine [Parnate], Isocarboxazid [Marplan], and selegiline [Emsam]), that requires some very important food and medication restrictions. This group is not widely used, but, in some instances, it may be the only effective alternative.

Table 5-6 lists the restrictions for people taking an MAOI; the restrictions are vitally important to follow, because eating the forbidden foods or taking the restricted medications can cause a life-threatening hypertensive crisis.

Someone with a strong family history of depression, who has had repeated episodes, or who has suffered a profoundly severe or damaging episode of depression may opt for lifetime maintenance with antidepressants. If not, the antidepressant is continued for a minimum of 6 to 12 months after recovery (which may, itself, take 6 to 12 months) and then slowly and gradually tapered until it is discontinued.

Some people have one episode of depression and do not become ill again. But about one half of people who have a first episode of major depression go on to have a series of depressions and a lifelong vulnerability to relapse in times of stress. This group of people, once they suffer a second episode, are said to have recurrent major depression. For them, there are strong arguments in favor of their continuing lifelong maintenance treatment with an antidepressant to prevent future relapses. Because antidepressants

Clinical Example

A woman, whose depression responded well to phenelzine (Nardil), took an over-the-counter cold medicine containing both an antihistamine and pseudoephedrine. She was aware that antihistamines were safe to take with her MAOI antidepressant, but did not think to check whether or not pseudoephedrine was contraindicated. Within a half-hour her blood pressure rose precipitously, causing a severe headache that brought her to her local emergency department where her hypertensive crisis was diagnosed and treated.

Table 5-6 Food and Medication Restrictions with Monoamine Oxidase Inhibitor (MAOI) Antidepressants

Foods that Must Be Avoided	Medications that Must Be Avoided
Aged cheese	Amphetamines
Liver	General anesthetics
Sausages	Local or spinal anesthetics containing epinephrine or levonordefrin
Bologna	Asthma or hay fever medications
Salami	Ritalin
Pepperoni	Over-the-counter cough, cold, and sinus medications
Tofu	Nasal decongestants
Pickled foods	Nonprescription sleeping pills
Smoked foods	Meperidine (Demerol)
Snow pea pods	Cocaine
Sauerkraut	Codeine
Fava beans	Morphine
Avocado	Hydrocodone
More than 1 oz chocolate	Stimulants
Red wine	Selective serotonin reuptake inhibitors
Beer	Percocet, Percodan
MSG	
Brewer's yeast	
Hydrolyzed protein extracts	

Table 5-7 Mood Stabilizers: Names and Usual Range of Daily Doses for Adults

Generic Name	Trade Name	mg/Day
Lithium carbonate	Eskalith	300–1,500
Carbamazepine	Tegretol	600–1,000
Valproate sodium	Depakote	750–5,000
Gabapentin	Neurontin	900–1,800
Lamotrigine	Lamictal	250–500
Topiramate	Topomax	100–400
Oxcarbazepine	Trileptal	600–2,400

are not addictive and because there are no long-term risks associated with their use, lifetime maintenance treatment is an excellent alternative for many people.

Common indications for mood stabilizers:
- Bipolar disorder
- Cyclothymic disorder
- Major depression

Mood Stabilizers

Mood stabilizers (**Table 5-7**) are used primarily to treat bipolar disorder (also called manic-depressive illness).

Contrary to intuition, the mood stabilizers both elevate depressed mood and suppress elated mood. It is unusual for a medication to have opposite effects on different people or opposite effects on the same person at different phases of illness, but that is, in fact, what mood stabilizers do. When a person with bipolar disorder is hypomanic or manic, the mood stabilizer brings the mood down to normal. During depression, the mood stabilizer elevates the mood. As a prophylactic medication, a mood stabilizer prevents both mania and depression, although the effect is often less robust in preventing depression. Bipolar disorder is almost always a lifelong condition, so people who take mood stabilizers ordinarily take them for a lifetime. Symptoms of mania targeted by the mood stabilizers are

- Increased social or work activity
- Increased talkativeness
- Rapid or racing thoughts
- Grandiosity
- Decreased need for sleep
- Distractibility
- Involvement in self-destructive activities such as overspending, reckless driving, bad business deals, or hypersexuality

Symptoms of depression targeted by mood stabilizers are

- Undereating or overeating
- Insomnia or oversleeping
- Agitation or general slowing down
- Loss of interest in usual activities
- Lack of energy or fatigue
- Feelings of worthlessness or guilt
- Inability to concentrate
- Recurrent thoughts of death or suicide

Mood stabilizers are a relatively recent addition to the psychopharmacologic arsenal. They were not available in the United States until 1970, when lithium was approved by the FDA. Lithium was the first mood stabilizer, and for a number of years it was the only one. Over the past three decades, other mood stabilizers have been gradually added. Lithium is used almost exclusively as a mood stabilizer, but all the other mood stabilizers were originally used for treating seizures and were only later discovered to be effective in stabilizing mood. All except lithium are still used for treating other conditions.

The mood stabilizers are unusual among psychotropic medications in that for some of them, their dosages are determined by the blood level of the drug. For clients who take lithium or carbamazepine (Tegretol), blood levels must be drawn every few months throughout the entire course of treatment.

None of the mood stabilizers are potentially addictive. Like the other medications discussed above, mood stabilizers have a lag period of a week or two before they become therapeutically effective. Side effects (**Table 5-8**) can be uncomfortable during the first few weeks while the dose is being adjusted and the body is getting accustomed to the medication.

Common indications for antianxiety medications:
- Agoraphobia
- Akathisia as a side effect of antipsychotics
- Clonazepam (Klonopin) in bipolar disorder
- Detoxification from alcohol or other sedative-hypnotics
- Generalized anxiety disorder
- LSD and PCP psychoses
- Panic disorder
- Sedation in mania or psychosis
- Situational or anticipatory anxiety
- Sleep disorders

Antianxiety Medications

Antianxiety medications, also called **minor tranquilizers** or **sedative/hypnotics**, are the oldest psychotropic medications (**Table 5-9**).

The earliest members of this family, the barbiturates (e.g., secobarbital, phenobarbital) and the nonbarbiturate, nonbenzodiazepine members (e.g., chloral hydrate, meprobamate), have fallen into relative disuse in psychiatry because of their high addiction potential and the danger of overdose from doses only slightly higher than therapeutic doses. The antianxiety medications in widest use today belong to the subgroup known as the benzodiazepines.

Table 5-8 Mood Stabilizer Side Effects

Generic Name	Brand Name	Common Side Effects
Lithium	Eskalith and others	Thirst Increased urination Loose stools Tremor Fatigue or weakness Nausea Swelling in hands or feet Weight gain Worsening of acne or psoriasis Thinning hair Decreased sexual interest and/or ability Memory problems Metallic taste in mouth Lithium toxicity (serum level too high), including tremor, nausea and vomiting, diarrhea, confusion, slurred speech, ataxia, poor coordination, hyperreflexia, tinnitus, nystagmus, seizures, coma, and death Hypothyroidism Diabetes insipidus
Carbamazepine	Tegretol and others	Nausea and vomiting Sedation Dizziness, lightheadedness Clumsiness Ataxia Rash (can be severe) Blurred vision Dry mouth Urinary retention Temporary double vision Confusion Slurred speech Paresthesias Sensitivity to sunlight Sore tongue Hair loss Problems with sexual desire or performance Elevated liver function tests (LFTs) Bone marrow suppression
Valproate	Depakote, Depakene	Nausea Mild stomach cramps Vomiting Sedation Weight gain Tremor Hair loss Menstrual irregularities Diarrhea Constipation Platelet problems Rash Dizziness Confusion Elevated LFTs

continues

Table 5-8 Mood Stabilizer Side Effects (continued)

Generic Name	Brand Name	Common Side Effects
Gabapentin	Neurontin	Sedation Dizziness Ataxia Fatigue or weakness Nystagmus Headache Nervousness Dry mouth
Lamotrigine	Lamictal	Rash (can be severe) Dizziness, ataxia Sleepiness Headache Double vision Blurred vision Nausea, vomiting
Topiramate	Topamax	Numbness Tingling Drowsiness Fatigue Psychomotor slowing Headaches Nausea Weight loss Dizziness Ataxia Memory problems
Oxcarbazepine	Trileptal	Dizziness Lightheadedness Drowsiness Ataxia Cough Fever Sneezing Sore throat Crying Dizziness Double vision Feelings of constant movement Abdominal pain Burning feeling in chest or stomach Nausea/vomiting Runny or stuffy nose

The benzodiazepines are used widely both inside and outside of psychiatry. When used to treat anxiety, the target symptoms for these drugs are

- Restlessness or feeling keyed up or on edge
- Difficulty concentrating or mind going blank
- Dizziness
- Insomnia
- Irritability
- Being easily fatigued
- Lump in the throat
- Muscle tension
- Nausea or upset stomach
- Palpitations
- Shortness of breath
- Sweating
- Tremors
- Weakness or tingling in the arms or legs

Table 5-9 Antianxiety Medications: Names and Usual Range of Daily Doses for Adults

Benzodiazepines		
Generic Name	**Brand Name**	**mg/Day**
Flurazepam	Dalmane	15–30
Chlordiazepoxide	Librium	5–100
Diazepam	Valium	2–40
Oxazepam	Serax	10–60
Lorazepam	Ativan	1–4
Temazepam	Restoril	15–30
Triazolam	Halcion	0.25–0.5
Alprazolam	Xanax	0.25–5
Clonazepam	Klonopin	0.5–5
Quazepam	Doral	7.5–15
Estazolam	ProSom	0.5–2
Clorazepate	Tranxene	7.5–60
Other Sedatives that Are Not Benzodiazepines		
Generic Name	**Brand Name**	**mg/Day**
Zolpidem	Ambien	5–20
Zaleplon	Sonata	5–10
Eszopiclone	Lunesta	2–3

There is a great deal of misunderstanding about the potential for addiction from the benzodiazepines. These medications clearly are capable of producing an addiction with the characteristics of craving, tolerance, and withdrawal. However, for most people who use them for the treatment of anxiety disorders, addiction is usually not a severe problem, even when benzodiazepines are taken for long-term prophylaxis. Although tolerance soon develops to the sedative properties of these medications, it is unusual to develop tolerance to the antianxiety properties. As a result, the client continues to get good anxiety relief with no loss of effectiveness at exactly the same dose for prolonged periods. If the decision is made to stop the medication, it must be slowly and gradually tapered to prevent severe withdrawal symptoms including grand mal seizures and death. Clearly, a physiological addiction occurs. However, as long as the client takes the benzodiazepine regularly, as prescribed, and undergoes a careful detoxification procedure when it is time to stop the medication, addiction may be a minor issue.

However, benzodiazepines can be abused or misused. One of the most common misuses is taking a benzodiazepine for a long time as a sleeping pill. As mentioned before, tolerance quickly develops for the sedative properties—usually within a month or two. When that occurs, the benzodiazepine no longer induces sleep unless its dosage is increased. This process repeats every few weeks, and higher and higher doses are required to induce sleep. If the dosage is not gradually raised to keep ahead of tolerance, the benzodiazepine becomes ineffective as a sleeping pill, even as it creates an addiction, necessitating eventual detoxification and causing the rebound insomnia that usually accompanies withdrawal from benzodiazepines. Benzodiazepines work well as short-term treatments for situational anxiety or insomnia. Most **psychopharmacologists** recommend continuing their use only for several days or weeks. For sporadic insomnia, occasional use (two or three nights a week) is recommended if other nonmedication interventions are unsuccessful.

For chronic conditions, such as panic disorder or agoraphobia, benzodiazepines can be used successfully for long periods (months or years) without risk or loss of effectiveness.

Unlike most of the medications used in psychiatry, there is no lag time before these medications become effective. The antianxiety effect can be felt within the first hour after the first dose. Side effects are usually mild and quite tolerable (**Table 5-10**).

One antianxiety medication, buspirone (BuSpar), is quite different from the benzodiazepines in that it has no addiction potential. Because a full response cannot be expected for 1–2 weeks of regular dosing, buspirone is ineffective as a prn (as needed) medication, and often is found to be unsatisfactory by those who previously had the

Clinical Example

A client with panic disorder unresponsive to antidepressants or beta blockers found that the only medication that reduced her anxiety enough for her to return to her job as a special education teacher was lorazepam (Ativan) 0.5 mg QID. Following a long discussion with her nurse practitioner about balancing the risk of addiction with the potential damage from being unable to work, she decided to continue the lorazepam for the remainder of the school year. At the end of that time, they would re-evaluate their plan.

Table 5-10 Side Effects of Antianxiety Medications

Daytime drowsiness or hangover
Decreased tolerance for alcohol and other sedating medications
Excitation
Impaired judgment
Impaired motor performance
Physical or emotional dependence
Restlessness
Trouble with learning or memory

experience of more immediate relief of anxiety with a benzodiazepine.

Indications for stimulants:
- Attention deficit disorder
- Attention deficit hyperactivity disorder
- Depression
- Narcolepsy

Stimulants

The **stimulants** (Table 5-11) are used primarily in the treatment of attention deficit disorder (ADD) and attention deficit hyperactivity disorder (ADHD).

These conditions initially occur in childhood but often continue into adulthood, although usually without the hyperactivity. For both children and adults, stimulants are the treatment of choice for ADD and ADHD. In people who do not have these conditions, stimulants cause stimulation, as their name suggests, but in ADD and ADHD they have an opposite, almost calming effect. Target symptoms of the stimulants when used for ADD and ADHD are

- Distractibility
- Impulsivity
- Irritability
- Overactivity
- Restlessness
- Short attention span

Table 5-11 Stimulants: Names and Usual Range of Daily Doses for Adults

Generic Name	Trade Name(s)	mg/Day
Pemoline	Cylert	37.5–112.5
Dextroamphetamine	Dexedrine	2.5–60
Methylphenidate	Ritalin, Concerta, Daytrana	10–60
Amphetamine mixture	Adderall	5–40
Modafinil	Provigil	5–100
Lisdexamfetamine	Vyvanse	30–70

Table 5-12 Side Effects of Stimulants

Abdominal pain or nausea
Agitation
Decreased appetite
Dizziness
Headache
Irritability
Palpitations
Psychosis
Sadness, listlessness, or lethargy
Temporary slowing of growth in children or adolescents
Tics
Tremor
Trouble falling asleep at night

The side effects of the stimulants (Table 5-12) are not usually problematic, but one of them is more noticeable than the others: when a child or adolescent is taking stimulants, growth in height and weight is temporarily slowed.

Often children and adolescents are directed to take their medication every school day, because the tight structure of a school day is particularly difficult for someone with untreated ADHD or ADD. During school breaks and vacations, including summer vacations, the medication is often stopped. The result for many of these young people is that they remain stable in height and weight during the school year but grow rapidly, catching up with their peers, during summer vacation and to a lesser extent during the longer midyear school breaks.

Other Medications Used in Psychiatry

Beta Blockers

The beta-adrenergic blockers (Table 5-13) have a variety of uses in psychiatry. One of the earliest uses was to treat performance anxiety or stage fright. A single dose taken 30 minutes before a performance

Table 5-13 Beta Blockers: Names and Usual Range of Daily Doses for Adults

Generic Name	Trade Name(s)	mg/Day
Atenolol	Tenormin	50–100
Metoprolol	Lopressor	100–200
Nadolol	Corgard	40–80
Pindolol	Visken	15–40
Propranolol	Inderal	40–80

reduces the physical manifestations of anxiety, such as tremors, sweating, and palpitations. Beta blockers perform a similar function for people with social phobia who are overwhelmingly anxious in specific, predictable circumstances.

Beta blockers also can be helpful to people who are overwhelmed by angry or violent feelings. They reduce the physiologic arousal associated with anger, thus allowing the person to regain and maintain control. Other uses of beta blockers include treatment of side effects of some of the psychotropic medications, including tremor from antidepressants or lithium, akathisia from antipsychotics, and palpitations or tachycardia from antidepressants or antipsychotics.

Alpha-adrenergic **antagonists**, including clonidine (Catapres) and guanfacine (Tenex), are used as adjuncts in detoxifying clients from alcohol or antianxiety medications. They are prescribed during the actual detoxification only (i.e., for a week or slightly less) to reduce discomfort from adrenaline-based symptoms of withdrawal: tremor, anxiety, agitation, tachycardia, or sweating.

Clonidine (Catapres) and guanfacine (Tenex) are sometimes effective in treating the adrenaline-based symptoms of posttraumatic stress disorder (PTSD), including palpitations, tremor, anxiety, sweating, flashbacks, and agitation. When they successfully treat the symptoms of PTSD, they are prescribed as a standing dose over a period of months or years. Both of these medicines are also sometimes used successfully in regular, consistent doses to treat the tics of Tourette's disorder or the hyperactivity of ADHD.

Cholinergic Agonists

There are four cholinergic **agonists**—donepezil (Aricept), tacrine (Cognex), rivastigmine (Exelon), and galantamine (Reminyl)—that improve cognitive functioning for some people, primarily in early-stage Alzheimer's disease. These medications prolong independent functioning by increasing the activity of the neurotransmitter **acetylcholine**. Another medication that is sometimes useful in later stages of Alzheimer's—memantine (Namenda)—has a different mechanism of action.

Addiction Medications

These medications are used for prevention and/or treatment of substance abuse and dependence. Disulfiram (Antabuse), acamprosate (Campral), and naltrexone (ReVia) are used as adjuncts in the treatment of alcoholism to help prevent relapse. Disulfiram acts as a deterrent to drinking because it induces extreme discomfort in a person who drinks even a small amount of alcohol, including symptoms of flushing, throbbing in the head and neck, headache, nausea, profuse vomiting, difficulty breathing, thirst, chest pain, palpitations, weakness, and blurred vision. Naltrexone works in a different way, blocking the desired effects of alcohol and opiates. Drugs, including alcohol, will not produce intoxication in a person taking naltrexone. Acamprosate lessens the sleeplessness and anxiety associated with alcohol withdrawal. Naltrexone is also useful in preventing a relapse into use of intravenous opioids, as are methadone (Dolophine) and buprenorphine (Subutex, Suboxone).

Naloxone (Narcan) is used in the emergency treatment of opiate overdose or intoxication. It is an opiate antagonist that, given intravenously, immediately cancels the effects of opiates.

Thyroid Medications

Sometimes thyroid medications (**Table 5-14**) are necessary as replacement therapy for people who have developed hypothyroidism as a side effect of lithium. Because thyroid function returns

Clinical Example

A young minister who has had attention deficit disorder since childhood is functioning well as a congregational minister, husband, and father stabilized on methylphenidate (Concerta). Prior to taking this medication, the minister found that the symptoms of his illness interfered with his ability to function in each of these roles.

Clinical Example

A concert violinist stabilized on lithium for her bipolar disorder finds her mild tremors tolerable except during performances. At these times, a small dose of atenolol (Tenormin) taken one hour before a performance prevents the tremors from interfering with her playing.

Table 5-14 Thyroid Medications: Names and Usual Range of Daily Doses for Adults

Generic Name	Trade Name	mcg/Day
L-triiodothyronine (T_3)	Cytomel	25–50
Levothyroxine (T_4)	Synthroid	75–125

Implications for Evidence-Based Practice

Thyroid medications are also used to augment antidepressant medications, even in cases where thyroid function is normal. The thyroid medications are prescribed for people who have only partially responded to an antidepressant and who wish to have a fuller response. A recently published study offers hope to clients who have failed to improve on two different antidepressants. This study found that the addition of thyroid medication brought about improvement in a significant number of previous nonresponders (Nierenberg et al., 2006).

to normal when lithium is withdrawn, thyroid hormone replacement therapy is only necessary as long as lithium is prescribed.

Drug-Drug and Food-Drug Interactions

Many clients take multiple medications, including both psychotropics and nonpsychotropics. Because many medications interact with one another, it's important to consider drug-drug interactions whenever a new medication is added to an existing regimen. Sometimes adding a new medication will raise the blood level of others and other times the opposite will happen. Food-drug and drug-drug interactions are complex. Of the large number of potential interactions, some are clinically significant, but many are not. **Tables 5-15** and **5-16** list the interactions that most often reach clinical significance.

The nurse must be alert to the variety of factors that influence the client's compliance with medication regimens.

Special Populations

Doses of the psychotropic medications are generally lower for children and the elderly. Side effect profiles may differ somewhat by age: Side effects are generally more pronounced in the elderly. For many psychotropic medications, there are special considerations in medicating pregnant or breastfeeding women. For these special populations, it is essential to check a reliable source such as your hospital formulary for any warnings or special considerations.

Compliance with Medication

Medications work only when they are being taken. Unfortunately, half the people who take medication for any condition—psychiatric or nonpsychiatric—take their medication incorrectly. Sometimes this is accidental or the result

Table 5-15 Drug-Drug and Other Interactions

Psychotropic Medication	Other Agent	Result
Antianxiety medications: benzodiazepines	Alcohol, other sedating medications	Respiratory suppression and increased sedation Increased sedation
	Some SSRI antidepressants, isoniazid, estrogens, disulfiram (Antabuse), and cimetidine (Tagamet)	Raised benzodiazepine levels
Antidepressants, general	Alcohol	Increased sedation and lowered antidepressant levels
	Other sedating medications	Increased sedation
	Guanethidine (Ismelin), clonidine (Catapres), and reserpine (Serpasil)	Antihypertensive effects are blocked with some antidepressants
	Anticonvulsants, barbiturates, glutethimide (Doriden), chloral hydrate, and oral contraceptives	Additive CNS depression
	Cimetidine (Tagamet), antipsychotics, and stimulants	Raised antidepressant levels

continues

Table 5-15 Drug-Drug and Other Interactions (continued)

Psychotropic Medication	Other Agent	Result
Antidepressants: tricyclic (e.g., amytriptyline [Elavil], imipramine [Tofranil])	MAOIs	Hypertension, tachycardia, convulsions
Antidepressants: SSRIs, (e.g., fluoxetine [Prozac], paroxetine [Paxil], fluvoxamine [Luvox])	Dextromethorphan, pseudoephedrine (Sudafed), MAOIs, triptans, and other serotonergic medications	Serotonin syndrome: hyperthermia, CNS irritability, hypertension, restlessness, myoclonus, hyper-reflexia, sweating, shivering, tremor, loss of consciousness, and seizures
Antidepressants: MAOIs, (e.g., phenelzine [Nardil], tranylcypromine [Parnate])	Amphetamines, methyldopa, levodopa, dopamine, epinephrine, norepinephrine, desipramine, guanethidine, reserpine	Hypertensive crisis
	Bupropion (Wellbutrin)	Delirium and grand mal seizure, hypertension
	Meperidine (Demerol), carbamazepine (Tegretol)	Hypertension or hypotension, coma, convulsions, death
Antipsychotics (e.g., chlorpromazine [Thorazine], haloperidol [Haldol], clozapine [Clozaril], risperidone [Risperdal])	Antidepressants, beta blockers, cimetidine (Tagamet), alprazolam (Xanax), chloramphenicol (Chloromycetin), disulfirum (Antabuse), MAOIs, acetaminophen (Tylenol), buspirone (Buspar), and fluoxetine (Prozac)	Raised blood levels of antipsychotic with increased risk of toxicity
	Clozapine (Clozaril) cannot be combined with other medications that suppress bone marrow	Increased bone marrow suppression
	Barbiturates, nicotine, phenytoin (Dilantin), cimetidine (Tagamet), carbamazepine (Tegretol), rifampin (Rifadin), and griseofulvin (Fulvicin)	Lowered antipsychotic levels with less therapeutic effect
	Antacids	Decreased absorption of oral antipsychotics
	Alcohol and other sedating medications	Increased sedation
	Antihypertensives	Increased antihypertensive effects
	Glutethimide (Doriden) and clonidine (Catapres)	Block antihypertensive effect of additional agents
Mood stabilizers: carbamazepine	Erythromycin, verapamil (Calcan), ketokonazole (Nizoral), diltiazem (Cardizem), dextropropoxyphene, propoxyphene (Darvon), isoniazid, and valproate (Depakene)	Raised carbamazepine levels
	Must not be combined with clozapine (Clozaril)	Increased risk of bone marrow suppression and agranulocytosis
	Antipsychotics, methadone, antiasthmatics, warfarin (Coumadin), valproate (Depakene), antidepressants, benzodiazepines, and hormonal contraceptives	Lowered levels of additional agents
Mood stabilizers: lithium	Theophylline	Increased excretion of lithium
	Nonsteroidal anti-inflammatory drugs (e.g., naproxen [Naprosyn], indomethacin [Indocin], phenylbutazone [Butazolidin], sulindac [Clinoril], diclofenac [Voltaren], thiazide diuretics, amiloride [Midamor])	Raised lithium levels
Mood stabilizers: valproate	Chlorpromazine (Thorazine), aspirin, fluoxetine (Prozac), and cimetidine (Tagamet)	Raised valproate levels
	Phenobarbital (Nembutal), benzodiazepines, phenytoin (Dilantin), and some antidepressants	Raised levels of phenobarbital, benzodiazepines, phenytoin, and some antidepressants with increased sedation
	Carbamazepine (Tegretol)	Lowered valproate level
	Warfarin (Coumadin)	Increased risk of bleeding

Table 5-16 Other Interactions

Psychotropic Medication	Substance	Result
Antidepressants, antipsychotics	Alcohol	Severe CNS depression
MAOIs	Food (see Table 5-6)	Hypertensive crisis
Liquid doxepin (Sinequan)	Grape juice	Precipitate forms
Liquid fluoxetine (Prozac)	Orange juice	Precipitate forms
Liquid fluphenazine (Prolixin) or perphenazine (Trilafon)	Caffeine-containing beverages, tea, apple juice	Precipitate forms
Antidepressants, antipsychotics	Cigarette smoking	Lowered blood levels of medications
Antianxiety medication (Ativan)	Grapefruit juice	Decreased blood levels
Calcium channel blockers	Grapefruit juice	Increased blood levels

of unintended error. Other times clients fail to take their medication correctly or at all because of one or more of the reasons listed below:

- Demand for changes in lifestyle or habits
- Complex recommendations
- Uncomfortable side effects
- Cost
- Fear of becoming addicted to the medication
- Very low level of anxiety
- Very high level of anxiety
- Lack of support from family or friends for taking medications
- Feeling well for a long time
- Hostility or aggression
- Lack of immediate return of symptoms when medication is stopped
- Desire for a return of symptoms such as grandiosity or elation
- Fear of the independence and responsibility that comes with recovery
- Equating taking medications with being ill
- Persistent delusion that the medications are harmful or poisonous

There are many things the nurse can do to improve compliance. Factors that increase compliance are listed below:

- Client believes that the illness is severe.
- Client feels personally at risk for relapse.
- Client is knowledgeable about the illness and its treatment.
- Client believes in the importance of the medication.
- Client has a moderate level of anxiety.
- Client has a stable family or home situation.
- Friends and family members support compliance.
- Client has a strong relationship with caregiver.
- Client has a long-standing relationship with caregiver.
- Client has a professional relationship with caregiver.
- Caregiver is optimistic about a medication's effectiveness.
- The medication's importance is stressed by the caregiver.

Implications for Evidence-Based Practice

The reader is referred to an excellent qualitative study that provides insight into clients' views about ways to improve their participation in treatment (Goodwin & Happel, 2006). Recipients of mental health services were interviewed in depth about what factors are important to them in establishing a working partnership with a nurse. The most important factor was whether the patient felt the nurse was respectful. Other factors important to clients were encouragement from the nurse, a spirit of working collaboratively with the nurse, and the nurse's ability and willingness to assist the client to overcoming barriers in the healthcare system. Nurses can learn from these findings how to strengthen their effectiveness as counselors and teachers. This can be most important in helping clients comply with medication treatments.

- Explicit, consistent, written information is provided.
- Access to help is available when questions about the medication arise.
- Unpleasant symptoms return immediately after stopping a medication.

When the nurse makes the medication regimen simple and comfortable, patients are helped immeasurably in their quest for wellness. To accomplish this goal, the following guidelines are offered for increasing compliance:

- Teach the client and family members about the medications.
- Provide explicit, consistent, written information about the medications.
- Reinforce the importance of medication in relapse prevention.
- Explore specific ways that the medication is helpful.
- Provide for continuity of prescriber.
- Maintain a professional relationship.
- Express optimism about the medication's efficacy.
- Be available to answer questions about the medication or its side effects.
- Research the relationship between stopping medications and relapse in the past.
- Make the medication schedule as simple as possible.
- Arrange for as few doses per day as possible.
- Treat side effects aggressively.
- Teach the client about addiction potential.
- Encourage family and friends to support the use of medications.
- Equate taking medications with wellness and taking responsibility for oneself.

Summary

A broad range of psychotropic medications is available to manage the symptoms of mental disorders. The role of the nurse includes administration of the medication, evaluation of the client's response to the medication, and education of the client and family regarding all aspects of the medication.

This chapter reviews the usual dosage, actions, and side effects of drugs in each category of psychotropic agents. In addition, food and drug interactions that can alter medication absorption and produce untoward—and even life-threatening—effects are presented. Finally, factors that affect the client's compliance with prescribed medication regimens are discussed.

Annotated References

Goodwin, V., & Happel, B. (2006). In our own words: Consumers' views on the reality of consumer participation in mental health care. *Contemporary Nurse, 21*(1), 4–13.

This qualitative study provides insight into patients' views about ways to improve their participation in treatment.

Guy, W. (1976). *ECDEU assessment manual for psychopharmacology.* Washington, DC: U.S. Department of Health, Education and Welfare.

This is the original publication of the Abnormal Involuntary Movement Scale (AIMS).

National Institute of Mental Health. (2006). *Clinical antipsychotic trials of intervention effectiveness (CATIE): NIMH study to guide treatment choices for schizophrenia.* Retrieved April 1, 2006, from http://www.nimh.nih.gov/press/catie_phase2.cfm

The largest, longest, and most comprehensive independent trial ever done to examine existing therapies for schizophrenia.

Nierenberg, A. A., Fave, M., Trivedi, M. H., Wisniewski, S. R., Thase, M. E., et al. (2006). A comparison of lithium treatment and T3 augmentation following two failed medication treatments for depression. *American Journal of Psychiatry, 163*(9), 1519–1530.

This study identifies strategies that increase the effectiveness of antidepressant medications.

Additional Resources

Cooper, J. R., Bloom, F., & Roth, R. H. (2002). *The biochemical basis of neuropharmacology* (8th ed.). New York: Oxford University Press.

This classic text is a guide to neurotransmitters, their role in nervous system function, and their involvement in the mechanisms of psychiatric drug action.

Fuller, M., & Sajatovic, M. (2005). *Lexi-Comp's psychotropic drug information handbook for psychiatry* (6th ed.). Hudson, Ohio: Lexi-Comp.

A clinician's pocket guide to psychotropic drug information.

Kutcher, S. (Ed.). (2002). *Practical child and adolescent psychopharmacology.* New York: Cambridge University Press.

This text is a clinician's guide to psychotropic drug treatment of psychiatric disorders in children and adolescents.

Munetz, M. R., & Benjamin, S. (1988). How to examine patients using the Abnormal Involuntary Movement Scale. *Hospital and Community Psychiatry, 39*(11), 1172–1177.

This classic article provides detailed instructions for administering the Abnormal Involuntary Movement Scale.

Nemeroff, C., & Kelsey, J. (2006). *Principles of psychopharmacology for mental health professionals.* Hoboken, NJ: Wiley-Liss.

This textbook was written specifically for the mental health professional who does not prescribe.

Rosenbaum J., Arana, G., Hyman, S., Labbate, L., & Fava, M. (2005). *Handbook of psychiatric drug therapy* (5th ed.). New York: Lippincott, Williams & Wilkins.

An excellent quick-reference handbook on the major classes of psychotropic medications.

Salzman, C. (2004). *Clinical geriatric psychopharmacology* (4th ed.). New York: Lippincott, Williams & Wilkins.

The authoritative clinical reference on psychopharmacology of the elderly client.

Schatzberg, A., Cole, J., & DeBattista, C. (2005). *Manual of clinical psychopharmacology.* Washington, DC: American Psychiatric Press.

The most recent edition of one of the classic texts on psychopharmacology.

Stein, D., Lerer, B., & Stahl, S. (Eds.). (2005). *Evidence-based psychopharmacology.* New York: Cambridge University Press.

This book is a collection of evidence-based practice findings for medication treatment of psychiatric disorders.

Trigoboff, E., Wilson, B. A., Shannon, M. T., & Stang, C. L. (2005). *Psychiatric drug guide.* Upper Saddle River, NJ: Pearson Educational.

One in a series of nurses drug guides that focuses on the psychotropic medications, including nursing implications.

Internet Resources

http://nursing.jbpub.com/psychiatric

Visit http://nursing.jbpub.com/psychiatric for interactive exercises, NCLEX review questions, WebLinks, and more.

CHAPTER 6

Crises, Psychiatric Emergencies, and Disasters

Winifred Z. Kennedy

LEARNING OBJECTIVES

After reading this chapter, you will be able to:

- Identify different variables that may contribute to a crisis or psychiatric emergency.
- Describe techniques of crisis intervention and how they can be used in the nursing process.
- Explain the effects crises, emergencies, and disasters may have upon victims and caregivers.
- Clarify the role of the nurse in dealing with crises, psychiatric emergencies, and disasters.

KEY TERMS

Acute stress disorder
Burnout
CODE-C
Compassion fatigue
Crisis
Crisis intervention
Critical incident stress management (CISM)
Debriefing
Defusing
Disaster
Dissociation
Maturational disturbance
Posttraumatic stress disorder (PTSD)
Psychiatric emergency
Situational disturbance
Suicide
Traumatic flashbacks
Triage
Vicarious traumatization

http://nursing.jbpub.com/psychiatric

Visit http://nursing.jbpub.com/psychiatric for interactive exercises, NCLEX review questions, WebLinks, and more.

Introduction

Psychiatric crises and emergencies are dynamic and unpredictable. The healthcare practitioner may treat a client with an urgent or emergent condition in an emergency room setting, or the client may be seen in his or her home, an ambulatory clinic, a mobile crisis unit, or a general hospital. The nurse may be responsible for **triage**, assessment, monitoring the client's condition or milieu, direct intervention or evaluation, education, mental health services, or referral for appropriate follow-up. Even those who do not consider themselves generalists or specialists in psychiatric care may be "on the front line" and called on to help.

An urgent condition requires prompt attention but is not immediately life threatening. An emergent condition requires immediate attention and is life threatening.

Urgent or emergent emotional, psychologic, or psychiatric problems are basically critical care problems; just as in a critical care situation, anticipation and preparation for the unexpected are necessary. Safety issues take precedence, regardless of the setting. Everyone is responsible for **suicide** prevention, assessing the potential for violence, and identifying suspected cases of abuse. All staff members are involved in considering the safety of the client, others in the area, and themselves. General assessment skills, people skills, basic knowledge about **crisis intervention** and normal and abnormal behavior, anticipation of and preparation for emergencies and disasters, and various intervention modalities are used to treat acute psychiatric problems. In any situation requiring immediate intervention and treatment, the goal is to stabilize the client as quickly as possible, address and normalize any variables that may be precipitating or sustaining the need for emergent care, and treat any life-threatening symptoms.

Overview

Psychiatric and behavioral health management skills are helpful in a variety of situations. When caring for individuals, families, or groups whose problems vary in urgency, the three main problem areas are times of crisis, emergency, and disaster. During these times, typical coping skills and normal functioning may be impaired, or the situation may be life threatening. Disturbances challenge previously held expectations or responses. Clients attempt to use normally held patterns, but internal and external resources are insufficient to meet these new demands on the system. The risk of regression, withdrawal, or failure exists, as well as the potential for new development or outreach.

When single or multiple stressors precipitate a crisis, the usual coping mechanisms or supports are inadequate or ineffective, anxiety and tension increase, and maladaptive responses or disorganized behavior result.

There are two types of disturbances. A **maturational disturbance** involves adaptation and transition of normal developmental phases. Some examples are the movement from childhood to adolescence, from high school pupil to college student, and from occupational employment to retirement. A **situational disturbance** involves accidental, planned, or imposed transitions, such as injury in a motor vehicle accident, a geographic relocation, or job insecurity related to layoff, termination, or employee displacement. Maturational and situational disturbances can occur alone or in combination, or several disturbances can occur periodically, sustaining the length of a crisis. For example, a person experiencing the developmental transition to middle age may be confronted with job termination and the diagnosis of a serious, life-threatening illness at the same time.

Crisis

A **crisis** is usually a self-limited transitional period in which the individual confronts an event or situation perceived to be threatening and potentially dangerous, which precipitates a period of psychologic disequilibrium and functional impairment. Traditionally, the potential for harm or change has been emphasized, as demonstrated by the root Chinese character for the word crisis, which combines the characters for danger and opportunity. A crisis may be developmental or maturational, situational or accidental, or psychosocial or physiologic in nature. The crisis may be related to one significant, potentially hazardous stressor or may be the cumulative result of a series or succession of stressors. Balancing factors include the presence or absence of the client's realistic perception of the event, adequate situational support, and previously learned or selected coping mechanisms. Crisis intervention, brief psychotherapy, cognitive therapy, and referrals to mutual self-help groups are useful interventions during crises. The goal of treatment is the client's return to the same or a higher level of functioning experienced prior to the crisis (Aguilera, 1998; Callahan, 2000).

Psychiatric Emergency

A **psychiatric emergency** is an unforeseen, acute, potentially serious and life-threatening event or situation in which the client is threatened or may represent a danger to him- or herself or others. The psychiatric emergency may be intrapsychic, interpersonal, biologic, or a combination of these factors. The emergency can manifest as a disturbance of affect, behavior, cognition, mood, perceptions, physiologic responses, relationships, or thoughts. Immediate intervention is necessary because of the potential for serious medical problems, self-harm, suicide, and violence toward others. Treatment options may involve stabilizing the client's medical and psychiatric conditions and referring the client for further intervention and out-patient or in-patient treatment on a voluntary, emergency, or involuntary basis (Callahan, 2000; Puskar & Obus, 1989).

Disaster

A **disaster** is an unpredicted, overpowering, traumatic event that disrupts usual life circumstances and assumptions. It devastates most individuals, overwhelms the usual coping responses and support systems, and impairs normal functioning. The threat to survival in a disaster can involve individual (e.g., hostage, fire victim) or collective trauma (e.g., communities of victims and survivors in the World Trade Center terrorist attacks, school shooting sprees, or hurricanes) (see **Figure 6-1**). Disasters may include natural and man-made catastrophic events, environmental hazards, armed conflict and civil unrest, and disease epidemics. Victims of disasters include those directly injured physically and emotionally, uninjured survivors, family members and friends of the victims and survivors, and the disaster workers.

Critical incident stress management (CISM) is a crisis intervention that allows all who are involved in the disaster experience to process what has occurred and begin the recovery process (Charney & Pearlman, 2000; Puskar & Obus, 1989; Raphael, 1986). CISM has been found to be helpful and supportive to those involved in a significant traumatic event and beneficial for preventing development of long-term problems that may interfere with functioning. Participation is voluntary, temporary, usually short term with some longitudinal follow-up or referral, and targeted to individuals or groups who have been involved in the same incident.

Steps in emergency trauma work utilize the format of consultation, outreach, debriefing and defusing, education, and crisis counseling (**CODE-C**; Myers & Wee, 2005). Interventions often involve crisis intervention, grief work and death and dying issues, and individual and group psychotherapy. Rescue workers and others who help in crisis intervention and disaster work often experience **vicarious traumatization** as a result of the urgency and camaraderie, physical and emotional demands of the disaster situation, intensity of countertransference issues, and close involvement with feelings of grief, hopelessness, and helplessness.

Figure 6-1 Arlington, Virginia (Sept. 11, 2001)—Medical personnel and volunteers work the first medical triage area set up outside the Pentagon after a hijacked commercial airliner crashed into the southwest corner of the building.

> Vicarious traumatization is a process in which traumatic damage is transferred to helpers or rescuers involved in crisis work by exposure to traumatic experience through their work or through their intense involvement in the experiences of others.

> Countertransference is the process in which positive or negative feelings from significant figures and conflicts in the clinician's past are transferred to the client.

> Critical incident stress management (CISM) is a method of individual and group intervention that allows those involved in crisis intervention to share thoughts and experiences, review events, give mutual support, normalize the experience, and provide meaning. This prevents dissociation and decreased functioning.

Stress-Related Disorders and *DSM-IV-TR*

The *Diagnostic and Statistical Manual of Mental Disorders*, 4th edition, text revision, lists many problems as conditions rather than as specific disorders, such as abuse or neglect (e.g., physical abuse of a child or adult), relational problems (e.g., parent-child or partner relational problems), and numerous conditions that may be the focus of clinical attention (e.g., bereavement and acculturation problems). They are coded as "v" codes on Axis I. Psychosocial stressors and environmental problems are also noted on Axis IV. Many of these conditions may appropriately describe the kinds of situational disturbances that crisis intervention targets. In addition, many clients who meet the requirements for specific disorders may present in crisis or as psychiatric emergencies. For example, a client with a history of dysthymic disorder may present after a suicide attempt, or a client with a panic attack may present with hyperventilation syndrome. Adjustment disorder also may be an appropriate diagnosis to describe responses to maturational or situational disturbances. Adjustment disorders may be specified as occurring with depression, anxiety, disturbances of conduct, or mixed (American Psychiatric Association [APA], 2000).

Acute stress disorder and **posttraumatic stress disorder (PTSD)** are two psychiatric disorders frequently associated with crises and emergencies. An acute stress disorder can occur 2 days to 4 weeks after a threatened or actual traumatic event. It involves combinations of affective, behavioral, cognitive, physiologic, and relational symptoms and dissociative symptoms that typically last from 2 days to 4 weeks. Symptoms are significant enough to impair functioning. PTSD can occur at any point following a threatened or actual traumatic event. It involves combinations of affective, behavioral, cognitive, physiologic, and relational symptoms that last at least 1 month and significantly interfere with normal functioning. The client may experience **traumatic flashbacks** or intensely reexperience the disturbance. The main differences between PTSD and acute stress disorder are the time to onset and duration of symptoms, and the presence or absence of dissociative symptoms and traumatic flashbacks (Aguilera, 1998; APA, 2000).

> Dissociation, an unconscious defense mechanism, involves distancing or numbing oneself to protect against painful emotions or thoughts associated with anxiety, conflict, or trauma. Symptoms may include detachment, depersonalization, derealization, decreased awareness of surroundings, and dissociative amnesia or fugue states.

Incidence and Prevalence

Some studies estimate that as many as 30% of all emergency room clients require psychiatric intervention (McCaig & Burt, 2004). Suicide attempts are life-threatening emergencies. In the United States, the incidence of suicide is 12.7 deaths per 100,000 people. The estimated prevalence ranges from 1% to 12%. The prevalence increases among those over 75 years of age—the elderly rate of suicide is two to three times higher than that of the rest of the population (Chiles & Strosahl, 1995).

> A traumatic flashback is a transient, intense, intrusive, repeated reexperience in the present of the thoughts, emotions, and physical sensations surrounding a past disturbance.

Research suggests that clients with chronic psychiatric conditions account for 7% to 18% of emergency service visits. The client may repeatedly visit the emergency room because of a gap in available services or providers (e.g., lack of a neighborhood continuing treatment or recovery program), a lack of insurance coverage for other services, no means of obtaining prescriptions, or to change a treatment plan established with another provider or agency (Fisher, 1989).

> Underlying problems such as medical conditions, cognitive disorders (dementia, delirium), drug and alcohol use, and history of psychiatric treatment should be identified.

Stress-related responses often include psychophysiologic reactions. An estimated 75% of victims of catastrophic or traumatic, life-threatening, stressful events experience somatic or physical body symptoms (Hardin, 1996). Clients may present in the emergency room with apparent psychiatric or functional symptoms that later are determined to be related to a medical illness or organic problem. Physical illness is responsible for psychiatric symptoms in approximately 50% of all emergency room visits (Dreyfus, 1987).

Etiology

The etiology of crises and emergencies varies. Internal and external stressors and resources change as people age and affect individual responses. For individuals in crisis, planned and unplanned developmental and situational issues may precipitate a crisis. Certain challenges and tasks are present at each maturational or developmental stage. The stages of infancy and childhood, latency and puberty, adolescence, adulthood (early, middle, late), retirement, and old age all require different responses from the individual for each task and life-changing event. Preparation, ability and capabilities, personality style, usual coping mechanisms, and social roles, norms, and relationships all influence the response. The physiologic integrity of the system, genetic predisposition, and biological levels of functioning influence the individual's ability to respond. The uncertainty and vulnerability associated with illness; perceptions of self-esteem and body image, as well as expectations of loss and decreased functioning; and the pain and suffering experienced in acute and chronic illness vary in different situations and periods of development. Some of the issues involving the responses to acute and chronic medical and mental illnesses are covered in Chapters 13 and 28.

Some of the underlying problems in psychiatric emergencies are outlined in **Table 6-1**. Many clients have medical problems that must be treated. Some clients with brain injury, dementia, or delirium may be at higher risk because of an altered level of consciousness and an inability to make their needs known or respond to internal and external stressors. Many behavioral or psychiatric symptoms are directly related to a physical or organic problem. These symptoms may be lessened or reversed by treating the medical problem. Many psychosocial problems or psychiatric disorders accompany or coexist with physical illness. Treatment of these underlying functional or psychiatric problems occasionally helps mitigate the client's physical symptoms or physiologic response to stress. Some of the medical problems associated with mental disorders are discussed in Chapter 13.

Puskar and Obus (1989) have categorized clients who present with psychiatric emergencies. Their problems include depression, anxiety, phobias, disorientation, suicidal threats or attempts, thought disorders, impulse control, alcohol or substance abuse, trauma or brutality, and those with social problems and homelessness. Alcoholic intoxication, acute schizophrenic reaction, psychotic depression, and acute situational disturbances appear to be the most common. Specific psychiatric disorders and special at-risk populations are discussed in other chapters.

Table 6-1 Underlying Problems

Condition	Symptoms or Issues
Delirium	Sepsis, endocrine disorders, electrolyte imbalance, encephalopathy, toxicity
Dementia	Cognitive impairment, regression, loss of social controls
Physical abuse (perpetrator)	History of violence, aggressive behavior
Physical abuse (victim)	History of unexplained injuries, fearful
Personality disorders	Antisocial, paranoid
Mood disorders	Depression, mania, suicidal ideation
Conduct and impulse disorders	Disorganized behavior, violence, legal problems, episodic loss of control or rage, fire setting, impulsive behavior (gambling, kleptomania, trichotillomania, eating disorders), blackouts, withdrawal, intoxication
Alcohol abuse	Intoxication, dependence, withdrawal, ethanol or methyl alcohol poisoning, toxicity, potentiation of other drugs or pharmaceuticals
Drug abuse	Hydrocarbons (glue, petroleum products, paint thinner), phencyclidine (PCP, angel dust), amphetamines (dextroamphetamine [Dexedrine] and methamphetamines), hallucinogens (LSD, mescaline), cocaine and crack cocaine, opioids, methadone, cannabinoids, "designer drugs" (Rohypnol, GHB [gamma-hydroxybutyric acid]), ecstasy, caffeine, tobacco, OTCs (over the counter), pain medications
Psychotic disorders	Delusions (paranoia, grandiosity, body dysmorphia or somatic delusions, jealousy, guilt, thought insertion or broadcasting, mind control or reading), hallucinations (auditory, visual, olfactory, or tactile), thought disorders, psychomotor disturbances (e.g., catatonia)
Disturbed perceptions	Illusions, hallucinations
Effects of prescription drugs	Polypharmacia, steroids, anticholinergic agents, cimetidine, sympathomimetic agents, overuse of pain medications, psychotropic medications (e.g., toxicity), neuroleptic malignant syndrome, serotonin overload, food-drug interactions with monoamine oxidase inhibitors, withdrawal especially with alchohol, benzodiazepines and barbiturates, extrapyramidal reactions, akathisia, acute dystonic reactions, tardive dyskinesia
Chronic pain	Loss of hope, polypharmacia, overdose
Disorders of thought or language	Illogical or overly detailed and circumstantial speech, problems in organizing thoughts, derailed or fragmented speech

Violence or the threat of violence can present as a psychiatric emergency in different ways. The staff may be treating the victim, perpetrator, or both at the same time. Some of the forms of potential and actual violence include:

- Self-inflicted violence (self-destructive behavior, self-mutilation, suicide threat or attempt)
- Intrafamily violence (child, partner or spouse, elder abuse)
- Interpersonal violence (aggressive and violent behaviors, assault, battery, muggings, attempted murder, murder, gang membership, criminal activity)
- Sexual harassment, coercion, assault, and rape
- Stalking
- Workplace violence

A family history of abuse is an important factor in the etiology of intergenerational exposure to violence and its repetition and recurrence in other situations. Physical, social, emotional, or economic isolation and dependence are factors in abuse and violence. At-risk clients often have a history of multiple unexplained or poorly explained injuries or use different healthcare practitioners to avoid detection.

Suicide

Suicide is a frequent psychiatric emergency. The threat or attempt may be associated with other physical or psychiatric disorders, alcohol or substance abuse, or acute situational disturbances. Clients may feel as if they would be better off dead because of pain, illness, changes in lifestyle or relationships, or a fear of being a burden to others. The client may have recurrent thoughts or fears of dying or may be preoccupied with death. These thoughts may be accompanied by a specific threat or plan. The client's fear of these thoughts, fear of loss of control, or fear of the responses of others with whom these thoughts have been shared can precipitate a crisis. Suicide threats and plans need to be evaluated to determine their potential lethality, how accessible the intended means for suicide is, and the likelihood of the act being carried out. The client's intent to act on the plan may have been demonstrated by a recent or past attempts, ongoing suicidal ideation and a specific plan, or the expression of intent to carry out the plan. Clients at greatest risk have impaired impulse control; concomitant psychiatric or medical illnesses; alcohol or substance abuse; feelings of hopelessness, helplessness, and guilt; no resolution of developmental, situational, or relational stressors; and a lack of situational supports.

Clients may be unaware of the potential lethality of over-the-counter medications (e.g., acetaminophen [Tylenol] overdose) and combinations of drugs (e.g., acetaminophen [Tylenol] and diphenhydramine [Benadryl], alcohol and a benzodiazepine [Valium]) or may misjudge the time frame in which they can be rescued.

Critical Thinking Question Identify client information that would be important to include as part of an assessment of suicide risk. What would be important factors to consider in determining immediate risk?

Substance Abuse Problems

Clients with drug and alcohol problems may present with problems associated with abuse such as intoxication, toxicity, dependence, or withdrawal. Clients may use these chemical substances to get "high" or intoxicated, to pass out, to anesthetize pain, or to avoid dealing with conflicts or relationships and intolerable emotions or thoughts. In addition, the client may have associated physical and mental disorders, may have made a suicide attempt, may have undergone trauma, or may have threatened aggressive behavior. Situational disturbances may alter typical patterns of abuse or have no relation to abuse and dependence. Abuse of sedatives, anxiolytics, and pain medications is often associated with alcohol abuse and dependence.

Medical and Mental Disorders

Clients often experience emergencies involving the onset of psychiatric disorders or acute exacerbations of known disorders. Sudden, unexpected, or debilitating symptoms of anxiety or panic may require emergency treatment. Acute and chronic grief reactions, sudden life losses or changes, and

Clinical Example

Linda, a 69-year-old homemaker, was brought to the emergency room by her family. They reported that she was not feeling well and appeared to be in pain. The physician who made the initial medical assessment did not find any significant problems and had ruled out a myocardial infarction. The family was distressed because the client seemed no better but was about to be discharged. The staff reported that the client was tearful and that the family stated she had a history of psychiatric problems. A psychiatric consultation was requested. The family told the psychiatric consultation liaison nurse specialist (PCLNS) that the client had been hospitalized for depression after the birth of her third child, 40 years ago, and again, approximately 20 years later, after the death of her spouse. They stated that she had been tearful "on and off" for a while and seemed withdrawn, but they were worried because she was "acting funny" (i.e., not remembering things, especially the recent death of her grandson). Several generations of the family had gathered together for the funeral of the young man, who had a history of lymphoma. They worried that Linda was depressed and unable to function, because she had not taken her usual role of matriarch at that family gathering. As part of the assessment, the nurse interviewed Linda and completed a mental status examination. The client was somewhat withdrawn and tearful during the interview, but her affect was labile and seemed to vary with no relation to the subject matter being discussed. The client reported having problems with her memory. When she was reminded of her grandson's death, she expressed concern and distress briefly. Based on the mental status examination, the nurse suggested that the client be evaluated for possible dementia. A computed tomography (CT) scan showed multiple lacunae infarcts as well as a right-sided infarct; an electroencephalogram (EEG) revealed marked bilateral dysfunction. In addition, the client's thyroid-stimulating hormone (TSH) level was elevated; she was treated for hypothyroidism.

Linda was facing a combination of maturational (aging and adjustment to decreased functioning) and situational (diagnosis of physical illness) changes. After the initial evaluation, the PCLNS assisted the client and family, helping them to adjust to this new loss and understand Linda's present capacity, at a time when they were dealing with another situational disturbance, a death in the family. The client, family, and staff also were told that the client's tearfulness was lability related to a dementia rather than a symptom of depression.

Clinical Example

Maria, a 42-year-old secretary with no previous medical history, was admitted to the hospital with acute abdominal pain. Exploratory laparotomy revealed metastatic ovarian cancer. A total hysterectomy and oophorectomy were performed. Postsurgery, the client had a myocardial infarction, coded, and was resuscitated three times. She was transferred to the surgical intensive care unit and was treated for septic shock.

A psychiatric consultation was requested for evaluation of anxiety. The client had no memory of her time in the intensive care unit, no problem sleeping in the hospital, and was eating. She had no history of depression or psychiatric follow-up. Maria was tearful and said she was upset about starting chemotherapy. She had been told that she would experience premature menopause, and she was frightened. She wanted to go home to her two young children before anything else went wrong. The spouse and children visited frequently. The client stated she wanted to do anything she could to help herself get better, but she did not want to ask too many questions or bother the staff. She felt they had saved her life and that she might seem ungrateful by worrying about menopause or talking about dying. At the same time, she did not want to add to the distress of her family by talking with them about her concerns.

The clinical impression was of adjustment disorder. In identifying issues and discussing different options with the psychiatric nurse, the client stated she felt better being able to talk about some of the things that were worrying her and learning about what to expect over time. She could ask questions, and the nurse anticipated some of her concerns and reassured her that she was responding in a normal manner. Maria did not know how to discuss the care of the children or her illness with her husband, because all he talked about was how much better she was. The nurse set up meetings with the client and spouse. An understanding of crisis intervention and grief counseling formed the basis of the interventions selected. The married couple's relationship and the stage of their marriage's development as parents of young children, the client's maturational stage and life tasks, and their children's development were important issues. Although Maria was unable to be home mothering the children and directing the household, she still took an active role in some of the tasks she missed. Then the children and both grandmothers, who had acted as caretakers during the client's hospitalization, were included in the discussions. After the client's immediate concerns were met and the psychiatric nurse had demonstrated her helpfulness, Maria became interested in anything that would help her with the chemotherapy and the discomfort she anticipated. Guided imagery was used as adjunctive therapy.

suicide threats and attempts all may be associated with depression. Deprivation and genetic predisposition may be involved in the development of depressive disorders. Researchers report that various biologic and genetic theories explain the development of psychotic symptoms. Psychosis also is associated with cognitive disorders and drug and alcohol abuse. Emergencies may be precipitated by taking psychiatric medications alone or in combination with other medications or substances of abuse.

Response of Caretakers

Intervention helps provide the support and feedback necessary for caretakers to continue their work. Caretakers with inadequate support risk **compassion fatigue** and **burnout**, which manifest as psychosomatic symptoms, fatigue and exhaustion, disturbed relationships, or "acting out" behaviors.

With compassion fatigue, the individual worker or volunteer is overwhelmed with the effects of chronic stress. The term *burnout* refers to an unproductive response to overwhelming and chronically stressful work situations. CISM is helpful for individual staff and groups.

The staff are like the members of a Greek chorus, standing witness to the suffering and tragedy around them. Past experiences of loss and childhood trauma can be reexperienced while facing loss, separation, and grief as adults, particularly if the experiences have not been successfully resolved. Research indicates that persons in the helping professions often have greater levels of perceived deprivation in childhood (Raphael, 1986). The shared concerns and experiences of the crisis or disaster, close involvement with loss and grief, and a sense of altruism and empathic involvement all place the individual at risk for emotional exhaustion (see **Figure 6-2**). To protect against painful feelings of loss, the individual may attempt to repress or deny these feelings. This can eventually lead to psychic numbing, detachment, and burnout. A sense of unbearable and overwhelming tragedy may be induced by certain normal or routine events in the helping professions,

Clarification of the immediate situation is helpful. The nurse should determine who brought the client to the emergency center or clinic (self-referral, involuntary, possible support systems); what circumstances or problems caused the client to seek help now, especially if the problem has existed for some time; when the problem started; and how similar situations were dealt with in the past (helpful and unhelpful methods, medications).

Figure 6-2 Emotional exhaustion or burnout can make it difficult to maintain a compassionate attitude.

such as the loss of a client who is well known to the staff or someone with whom the staff identify strongly. Conversely, an event may be outside the range of normal experience, such as a suicide on the unit, an accident or assault, or the unexpected death of another staff person. Concern for others demands openness and extending oneself to others. If the staff have lost the capacity to respond, the response may become blocked and mechanical. Treatment focuses on the event and the feelings experienced to break down the sense of isolation or craziness associated with symptoms of traumatic flashbacks or survivor guilt. This prevents the numbing that leads to the inability to feel or empathize with others (Raphael, 1983, 1986).

Burnout is a term used to describe an individual's maladaptive response to a chronically stressful work situation.

Defusing and Debriefing

Defusing and **debriefing** are interventions used to deal with staff responses to traumatic events. Defusing is a brief, immediate intervention used with small groups that focuses upon gathering facts (who, what, when, where, how), exploring thoughts, acknowledging feelings, and providing encouragement and anticipatory guidance. Debriefing focuses on larger-scale and time-limited structured groups to provide for screening, supporting, and education.

Staff should be offered voluntary opportunities for dealing with traumatic stress and grief that focuses on assessment, expression of feelings, opportunity for empathy and validation, encouragement of discovery and meaning, provision of didactic information, and time for recreational and self-management and self-care techniques (breathing and movement exercises, meditation and prayer, etc.).

Physiology

The initial response to stress, the fight-or-flight reaction, was identified by Walter Cannon in 1914. Previous studies attempted to show how the activation and arousal of physiologic systems that affected the ability of the individual to defend or to flee a perceived threat were adaptive and useful in the face of danger. The activation of biologic systems affects the system's response, including appropriate levels of alertness, decreased vegetative functions, changes in circulation and respiration, and focused attention to take aggressive action or to escape. In the 1930s, Hans Selye described the phases of alarm, resistance, and exhaustion of general adaptation or stress syndrome. The intensity and duration of the response, the resistance of the system, and the ability of the system to recover from the impact of the stress are all factors in the patterns of response that influence the system's ability to adapt. Activation of the autonomic nervous system is an immediate and normal response, but perseveration and continuation of the response, particularly when there is no immediate danger, leads to physical and psychological problems.

This model has been modified to show how the stress system response involves neurophysiologic and biochemical events associated with successful adaptation or dysregulation. Stress involves adrenergic, noradrenergic, and histaminic arousal responses. Facilitation of the fight-or-flight response is mediated by the behavioral inhibition system. The neurotransmitters epinephrine and norepinephrine are involved in the initial response. The stress system involves the effects of corticotropin-releasing hormone (CRH) and locus ceruleus-norepinephrine/autonomic release norepinephrine (LC-NE) systems and the hypothalamus-pituitary-renal axis. The LC activates noradrenergic arousal of the hypothalamus and limbic and central nervous systems. Low serotonin levels increase LC activity. The raphe nuclei in the brain stem affect serotonin modulations and pathways.

Researchers have hypothesized that the response is meant to be limited to actual threat and that excessive or chronic strain causes hypersecretion of CRH and influences the development of stress-related disorders (e.g., anxiety, anorexia, depression) and chronic disease (e.g., immunosuppressive response). Chrousos and

Gold (1992) hypothesized a V-shaped response in which hypo- or hyperfunctioning influences response and dysregulation. After initial arousal and preparation for fight or flight, catecholamine is released, norepinephrine levels increase, and cortisol levels decrease. The ratio of norepinephrine to cortisol, with increased norepinephrine from LC activation and decreased serotonin levels, is associated with the chronic stress of PTSD (Burgess & Hartman, 1996). The opioid-benzodiazepine system (LC, hypothalamus, amygdala) accounts for hormones that have an analgesic effect to control pain and activate the behavior-inhibiting cycle. Dysregulation may cause the symptoms of numbing or blunting associated with **dissociation** (Burgess & Hartman).

It is hypothesized that the amygdala is important in communicating anxiety and the hippocampus in encoding memories of trauma. Stimulation of the amygdala induces feelings of fear and anxiety and activates the sympathetic nervous system. The orbitofrontal cortex of the frontal lobe of the cortex is associated with the defensive experiences of fear and anxiety, and is the area of the cortex that influences information processing to the limbic system. Neurobiologic theories are discussed in depth in Chapter 4.

Clinical Presentation

The client may exhibit different signs of stress depending upon the situation and his or her personality and response repertoire. The client's appearance may vary. He or she may be well groomed or unkempt or show signs of possible abuse or trauma such as bruises, scars, or injury. The mood also may vary, and the client may be angry, anxious, or sad. The client's affect may be intense, labile, blunted, or inappropriate to the situation or topics being discussed. The client may be apathetic, detached, or in a daze. Conversely, she or he may be irritable, restless, or agitated and engaged in frantic overactivity. Visible signs of distress may appear, such as an unsteady voice, flushed face, tearfulness, tremulousness, distractibility, and hypersensitivity or hypervigilance to environmental stimuli. The client may experience some observable or measurable physiologic responses to stress, such as sweating or increased pulse, rapid respirations, elevated blood pressure, and elevated blood glucose levels. The client may describe subjective symptoms such as a feeling of internal restlessness, weakness or fatigue, or impending doom.

Triage

Triage for potential psychiatric emergencies requires the appropriate assessment of the client's needs, assurance of safety, and differentiation between organic and functional problems (Dreyfus, 1987; Rosenzweig, 1992). Immediate concerns include identification of medical and psychiatric problems and assessment of the risk for violence or elopement. Assurance of client and staff safety is established by assessing the client's potential for violence. The nurse should consider any threats of loss of control, aggression, self-harm, suicide, or homicide. Clients who are agitated, confused, intoxicated, manic, paranoid, or psychotic are at risk for losing control. A history of violence, brain injury, or substance abuse indicates the potential for violence. Clients receiving psychiatric treatment may have medical problems associated with their medications, such as a cholinergic response to neuroleptics or tricyclic antidepressants, neuroleptic malignant syndrome from neuroleptics, serotonin overload from serotonin reuptake inhibitors, toxicity from high doses of medications such as lithium or anticonvulsants, food-drug interactions such as hypertensive crisis with monoamine oxidase (MAO) inhibitors, and withdrawal, particularly from benzodiazepines and barbiturates (see Chapter 5).

Pusker and Obus (1989) divide psychiatric problems that present for triage into six groups:

- Emergent or life-threatening psychiatric emergencies that require immediate attention, including acutely agitated, violent, suicidal, or homicidal clients and clients brought in involuntarily by the police or protective services
- Urgent or serious psychiatric emergencies that are potentially life threatening, such as manic or psychotic clients; clients with a history of violence, self-harm, or drug abuse; or clients who appear restless, confused, or disoriented
- Potentially serious psychiatric problems or crisis situations, including most clients in crisis with a psychiatric problem who come in voluntarily and clients who require urgent medical attention or have a history

Sexual Assault

Outcomes	Interventions	Evaluations
• Participates in appropriate self-care	• Support client during assessment and physical evaluations.	• Demonstrates participation in self-care and tolerated examination and diagnostic procedures
• Experiences ability to express thoughts about the event	• Provide safe environment and time for client to recall and retell events.	• Subjective reports of appropriate grieving process and recovery
• Arranges follow-up care and appropriate support	• Assist client in identifying personal support sources (family, friends, etc.) and offer referral to therapists, support groups, and community resources.	• Identification of support sources and contact with appropriate referral sources
• Decrease in stress-related symptoms	• Teaching and anticipatory guidance appropriate to client's needs.	• Return demonstrations of self-management and self-care techniques

Visit http://nursing.jbpub.com/psychiatric for additional care plans and exercises.

CASE STUDY Ms. P.

Ms. P., an 18-year-old student, was brought to the emergency room by ambulance from her college campus. Her friends stated that she had complained of feeling dizzy and almost collapsed. When they had expressed their concern, the client protested that she was fine. However, her condition came to the attention of an instructor when she appeared dazed and unresponsive during class for a few minutes, and help was summoned. The client had missed 2 days of classes, which was unusual, but she had explained to her friends that she had a virus. Her friends said that she had looked tired and wan and attributed her withdrawn behavior to her recent illness. She admitted that she had not slept for 2 days before coming to the emergency center and had not eaten because she had a lump in her throat and "could not hold anything down." She complained that she felt alternately hot and then chilled. When the staff attempted to examine her, Ms. P. began to cry and would not allow the male physician to touch her. She eventually confided to the nurse that she had been raped 2 days earlier.

At first, Ms. P. stated that she did not remember any details of the attack. It seemed unreal to her, like a movie or something that had happened to someone else. Eventually, the story was pieced together. Ms. P. had stayed late in the computer resource room to finish a class project. She went to the restroom before leaving the building. No one appeared to be in the room, but a large man approached and quickly overpowered her, although she attempted to push past him. After the assault and rape, she felt degraded, humiliated, and helpless. She ran home and did not report the incident to anyone.

Ms. P. stated that she felt somewhat responsible for what had happened because she knew it was not safe to stay alone late at night. She said she had even felt uncomfortable about going to the restroom alone, but dismissed the feeling. She stated that she felt as if her skin was turned inside out and everything bothered her. For 2 days she had been afraid to leave her room, kept the door closed and the shades down, and had not answered the phone. She said she jumped at every sound and worried that the man would find her again. She was concerned that the man had given her a sexually transmitted disease, and she showered and cleaned herself repeatedly. She felt dirty. She could not concentrate on her school work. All she wanted to do was sleep and forget what had happened, but she was unable to rest and kept thinking about what had happened, what she felt she should have done, and what she would do if ever faced with a similar situation.

The medical protocol for rape involves a physical examination that includes inspection of the bruises or injuries incurred in the attack; inspection of the genitalia, anus, mouth, of medical illness associated with behavioral symptoms

- Crisis situations that present no immediate danger, including clients in nonacute and chronic situations with no situational support and clients with chronic psychiatric problems
- Situations where there is no immediate danger, threat, or change in situation or supports, such as a client with a history of psychiatric problems coming in for an unrelated physical complaint, reassurance, or renewal of psychiatric medications
- Problems resulting from a physical illness, including situations in which a medical problem is identified and no psychiatric problems are present or an underlying psychiatric problem is stable or does not require immediate attention

Clinical Course and Complications

The initial response to crisis is often denial, disorganization, and disruption of normal response patterns. The client may respond with feelings of anxiety and depression. Shock, confusion, lethargy, and heroics also have been noted in response to catastrophic stress (Hardin, 1996). Certain response strategies may be of particular value to an individual or may have been useful in other circumstances. The client may persevere in using the same response or regress to coping mechanisms that were useful in an earlier stage of development.

Many factors affect the clinical course. Some developmental stages, such as adolescence, may be more problematic in certain cultures. The client may not have successfully completed the normal, expected developmental tasks. This may lead to a

Triage is a classification process developed from battlefield techniques to rapidly assess acuity and attempt to balance needs and available resources. Derived from the French word *trier*, "to choose," triage is a way of making certain that the "right" client, place, time, and care provider are identified and treatment needs coordinated.

throat, or other areas violated in the assault; the collection of specimens of hair, semen, or other evidence of the assault; and the treatment of any injuries or sexually transmitted diseases. Many victims shower or douche or delay treatment immediately after an assault, complicating the examination and collection of evidence. Intervention is often needed to facilitate physical examination, the collection of specimens, and reports to legal authorities. Victims may need a supportive person to be with them through the examination and investigative procedures. Many police departments have special rape teams with women officers to help female victims feel comfortable in cooperating with the report and investigation procedures. Female victims may also have concerns about possible pregnancy and/or prevention of pregnancy. Male and female victims need assessment for the presence of alcohol or drugs that could have been used in commission of the assault and follow-up for the possible transmission of hepatitis, syphilis, and HIV.

Ms. P. was experiencing an acute, expressive reaction to the assault, but some victims respond by appearing calm, controlled, and untouched by the experience. The symptoms she experienced also are seen in acute stress disorders; many rape victims show signs of PTSD. Although Ms. P. did not feel she precipitated the attack and did not know her attacker, she felt, unrealistically, that she was partly to blame. Victims rarely precipitate or participate in sexual assault, but their beliefs and feelings about the assault can be complicated, particularly if they know the assailant. Ms. P.'s first impulse, to seclude herself and not tell anyone about the attack, isolated her and eliminated the possibility of getting help. It is difficult to establish information regarding the incidence and prevalence of sexual assault and rape because many victims do not report the crime because of fear, guilt, humiliation, or lack of faith in the criminal justice system.

Crisis intervention with Ms. P. focused on helping her safely explore what had had happened to her, cognitively and emotionally. She needed to recognize the symptoms she was experiencing and to know what she could expect to experience in the immediate future. The psychic numbing she was experiencing had some protective value but also limited her ability to cope with what had happened and to reach out to others for support. Intervention was needed to widen her available support base and to help her utilize the supports already in place. Long-range goals focused on minimizing the impact of rape-trauma syndrome—the emotional and behavioral consequences that affect adjustment and the ability to maintain relationships. Medical follow-up for possible sexually transmitted diseases and pregnancy should also be arranged.

NURSING CARE PLAN Survivor of Violence

Expected Outcomes	Interventions	Evaluations
• Will experience reduction in anxiety symptoms.	• Provide opportunity for nonjudgmental listening in safe environment.	• Demonstrates breathing techniques.
	• Teach breathing techniques.	• Able to relate feelings to anxiety.
• Will facilitate grieving process.	• Identify past and present effective coping mechanisms and reinforce use.	• Subjective reports of appropriate grieving process and recovery.
• Will identify appropriate support systems.	• Assist client in identifying supports that have been helpful to her.	• Decreased reluctance to utilize available supports appropriately.
• Will return to normal level of functioning.	• Involve client in identifying short- and long-term goals.	• Return to home and work activities without interference from psychological symptoms.

Visit http://nursing.jbpub.com/psychiatric for additional care plans and exercises.

CASE STUDY Ms. Q.

Ms. Q., a 45-year-old woman, was brought by ambulance from the train station to the emergency center. The client stated that she was on her way to work when she began to experience increased shortness of breath, palpitations, tearfulness, and feelings that she was going to die. Once on the train the client felt threatened with so many people around, and she started to breathe rapidly and "passed out." Ms. Q. had no history of anxiety disorder, panic attacks, or phobias. The staff requested a psychiatric evaluation.

Upon questioning by the psychiatric nurse, the client said she was not usually a nervous person but had been under stress recently. She was on her way to work for the first time in several weeks. She began to weep as she told of her 16-year-old son's murder approximately 2 months before. After her son died, she had been seen by a counselor from victim's services, who had been helpful. At first she had been overcome with guilt and plagued with repetitive, intrusive thoughts of her son's death. She could not sleep and kept imagining what he must have gone through and how she might have prevented it. After a while, she felt much better and decided to go back to work. She had not known it would be so difficult. She said that people were supportive after the murder, but most had returned to their own lives. Her married daughter, who had stayed with her for several weeks after the funeral, had returned home. The client did not want to burden her daughter. The counselor from victim's services was on vacation.

A few days before her scheduled return to work, Ms. Q. began to reexperience symptoms. She was awakened by thoughts about how her son looked when he left the house that evening and how she had felt when the police told her about his death. She felt partly responsible because he had bought a new jacket with money she had given him. Her son had been killed during an attempted robbery. Ms. Q. was a single mother—perhaps, she thought, if there had been a man in the household, he would have been better able to teach her son how to protect himself. She wondered if her son's murderers were still nearby. She wanted to look for them and see that they were caught. At the same time, she worried that she was a bad person and not true to her faith because she could not find it in her heart to forgive them.

The primary clinical intervention was to allow Ms. Q. to vent her feelings in a safe place and to help her tell her story and not to be overwhelmed by the intensity of her grief. The anxiety symptoms and traumatic flashbacks made Ms. Q. feel as if she were losing control. Ms. Q. was grieving appropriately and understood the extent of her loss. The only disturbance in her perception of the events were lingering feelings of guilt and the thought that she might have been able to change things.

Ms. Q. required assistance to strengthen and maintain her ability to cope during the temporary absence of the support person from victim's services. Often the network of social and community support is decreased by the crisis itself, loss of faith in the system, or the inability of former supports to bear the enormity of the tragedy. Victim's services becomes a valuable support that facilitates recovery and the client's ability to help the police and participate in court follow-up (Masters, 1998). The nurse taught Ms. Q. a self-management technique to help her control the symptoms of hyperventilation, if they recurred. The client was instructed to use deep-breathing techniques to relax and to slow her breathing further by placing her cupped hand or a paper bag over her mouth and nose. Arrangements were made for her to stay with her daughter. The client verbalized recognition of the need for follow-up and planned to return to victim's services for individual and group support.

limited repertoire of coping responses, less flexibility in coping responses, and less skill in learning new responses. Other mediating factors include family history, generational legacies of response patterns and learning skills, lack of supports, chronic physical illness, chronic psychiatric illness, poverty, guilt, hopelessness, helplessness, and alcohol and drug abuse. It is difficult to know why some situations or combinations of stresses are problematic for a particular individual or why two individuals at the same life stage respond very differently to similar sets of experiences, choices, and challenges.

In a psychiatric emergency, usually the client presents with symptoms of agitation or aggression, suicidal or homicidal ideation and behaviors, or with an acute problem such as drug intoxication or withdrawal or a sudden change in mental status. A client may present with a new psychiatric symptom such as psychosis or mania or with an acute exacerbation of a chronic problem such as schizophrenia. The client may present voluntarily, be brought in by family or police, or be an involuntary client that is sent for evaluation or who becomes agitated or threatening while receiving emergency care.

During a disaster, clients may have difficulty dealing with the immediate emotional impact. As in times of crisis, the initial response is most often denial and the second response is disbelief: "This could not happen here!" or "How could this happen to me?" Initial reactions may range from fear, guilt, anger, and sadness to heroic disregard for the client's own needs. Raphael (1986) describes the stages of response as victims face the sudden, unexpected warning or threat. Victims occasionally respond with disbelief and disregard, feelings of loss, or recognition of survival and response to being rescued by others or by their own heroic efforts. The sense of shared adventure, the closeness to others involved in the disaster and its aftermath, and learning to cope with a new experience initially may lead to a better level of functioning, followed by a return to previous or lesser levels of coping as the individual begins to deal with the long-term effects of extreme stress.

Persistence and stability may not function for a particular system during times of crisis. Occasionally, resistance must be overcome. The client may need to experiment with different coping methods before finding an adequate method and completing successful adaptation. Existing social support systems may not be used because they are fragile and tenuous, inadequate for the task at hand, involved in crisis themselves, psychologically or geographically distant, or lacking the durability to sustain the client during a particular crisis. The client may need encouragement to develop a new or different network that combines new and old support systems or to utilize the support system in different ways if external resources are inadequate. Formal and informal support systems are facilitated by involvement with professional support systems or mutual self-help groups. The process of reorganization reinforces what has been learned, defines the experience and response, and illustrates what can be anticipated and applied in the future. Many factors impact the individual's ability to participate in social learning.

Physical or Sexual Abuse

Situations involving physical or sexual abuse can complicate the clinical course. The client may be in a potentially dangerous situation. The risks or threats of remaining in the present situation should be investigated with the client. He or she may not cognitively or emotionally recognize the potential threat and may need help in identifying and avoiding it. Feelings of guilt, shame, anger, or fear may interfere with the client's ability to make choices that are self-protective and protective of others. The client may have difficulty initiating and maintaining healthy relationships. At-risk clients may need assistance in identifying the necessary legal and social support systems available. The client may avoid or delay treatment for injuries or may be unable to cooperate with treatment. The nurse may need to identify the steps in intervention (e.g., reporting abuse, getting an order of protection, arranging for a safe environment such as a shelter or safe house, leaving the relationship) and assist the client in following through with these steps. For long-term problems, the client still may be overwhelmed with feelings of anger, guilt, or fear that interfere with present coping and relationships and impair responses to other developmental and situational crises.

Risk of Suicide

The potential for suicide also complicates the clinical course. The nurse must identify the risk of suicide with direct questions. Thoughts about

Implications for Evidence-Based Practice

Cutcliffe, Stevenson, Jackson, & Smith (2006) utilized Glaserian grounded theory (identifying a basic psychosocial process and establishing a credible theory) to study the role of psychiatric nurses in the care of the suicidal person. The core variable centered on reconnecting the person with humanity by reflecting an image of humanity, guiding the individual back to humanity and learning to live. The authors identified the key processes to move the suicidal person from a "death-oriented" to a "life-oriented" focus. The nurse-patient relationship was described as "co-presencing." Further predictive research is indicated to identify specific suicidal behaviors and cognitive assumptions as well as specific nursing interventions involved.

suicide should be taken seriously, and if the client states that action may follow, these verbalizations also should be taken seriously. The questions should focus on attempting to evaluate the nature of the suicidal ideation and to clarify whether it is accompanied by threats or specific plans. If the client has a plan, the nurse should note whether it is vague or specific and whether the client has access to the means. The client also should be questioned about past attempts and whether treatment or hospitalization followed these attempts. Suicidal gestures (i.e., threats rarely carried out or threats made in the presence of others so intervention is readily available) are not intended to be lethal attempts. A client with a history of high lethality (serious overdose, gunshot wound, jumping from heights) or near lethality (attempt made without notifying others and discovered accidentally) is at high risk for suicide. The presence or absence of available supports is important in determining potential risk. Clients who live alone, have experienced multiple losses, have limited social skills and resources, and have unsatisfactory or no relationships are at high risk for suicide. Alcohol, a depressant that lowers impulse control, is an important risk factor, as are other substances of abuse. Impaired cognitive ability can interfere with the client's competency to make valid, informed decisions.

The nurse identifies the risk of suicide by the use of direct questions to determine the nature of the suicidal ideation, the existence of a plan, and the client's ability to carry out the plan.

Substance Abuse

Alcohol and substance abuse impede the client's ability to respond to crises, cloud the sensorium, and may precipitate a psychiatric emergency. Intoxication impairs insight and judgment, and complicates assessment procedures because an intoxicated client is unable to cooperate with examination or treatment. Diagnostic blood work may indicate anemia or elevated liver enzymes, and physical assessment may indicate other medical problems associated with chronic alcohol use, such as cardiac or liver disease. An increased tolerance is indicated by the client's relatively alert state accompanying intoxication, high blood alcohol levels, and need for differing amounts and duration of intake. The client may experience blackouts or a history of withdrawal syndrome with decreased use.

Alcohol and sub-stance abuse contribute to an increased risk of suicide.

Alcohol and drug abuse and dependence must be treated first. Other interventions and treatments may have to wait until treatment is completed. The client with chronic alcohol or substance abuse may have poor support systems or supports that are no longer available for contact. These clients may have lost their job, family, support systems, and housing and may have legal problems. Most clients with a dual diagnosis of mental disorder and substance abuse have multiple problems. Assessment of the potential risk of withdrawal is an important determinant in psychiatric emergencies, as is the possible interaction of alcohol with other substances of abuse and pharmaceuticals.

Medical Illness

Problems requiring medical treatment such as injuries from a recent suicide attempt, physical or sexual abuse, or trauma are added stressors that prompt their own psychophysiologic responses. Clients with acute or chronic medical illness are vulnerable to the effects of acute stress reactions, the long-term consequences of adaptation to illness, and the accompanying physical symptoms and distress. The diagnosis and treatment affect clients who also may be responding to the threat of illness or to maturational or situational disturbances unrelated to the physical disorder. In addition, the client may have difficulty adhering to diagnostic and treatment regimens as a result of the symptoms of chronic medical or mental illness. Prescription medications, singly or in combination and even at prescribed doses and therapeutic levels, may cause acute or chronic problems. The client with asthma, for example, may benefit from the use of pharmaceuticals while experiencing uncomfortable side effects. The use of steroids may prompt the symptoms of an affective or a delusional disorder. Clients may experience adverse long-term effects from medications that benefit them greatly. Clients who take antiseizure medications and those who take antipsychotics must balance the potential benefits with the potential burdens treatment places on them.

Violence

Threats or actual violence also can complicate the clinical course. Clients with a history of alcohol or other substance abuse may present with uncontrolled aggressive or self-destructive behaviors. Clients with a history of brain injury may experience an impulsive loss of control, changes in their typical personality because of the injury, or delusion syndromes. Many clients with behavioral symptoms of physical or psychiatric illness may experience periods of disorganized behavior or diminished capacity for making decisions and controlling volition. Disorganized behavior can present as withdrawal, illogical activity, negativism, excitation, or agitation. Irrational beliefs and magnified or wrongly perceived interactions with others and the environment can prompt abnormal responses. Issues involving intrafamily, interfamily, and workplace violence need to be reported and prevented whenever possible. Clients with a history of legal problems (e.g., recent arrest, past assaults, imprisonment) or gang membership are more likely to continue to be involved in violent acts. Acts of violence against healthcare workers are not unusual and are exacerbated by poor staffing, overcrowded physical environments, prolonged waiting time, and lack of health coverage.

This problem is not limited to the United States. In some places, legislation protects healthcare workers in the same manner as police and emergency workers.

Clinical Example

Ryan, a 27-year-old man, collapsed at a sheltered workshop during a period of record high summer temperatures and was brought to the emergency department when staff at the workshop noted the patient seemed to be confused before he collapsed. In the ED, Ryan had a temperature of 103.6 degrees, elevated blood pressure, rapid pulse, and was oriented to person only. He was dressed in multiple layers of clothing, some of which were the custom of a religious group and some of which seemed to be his own idiosyncratic style. He had been incontinent of urine. The patient had a history of serious persistent mental illness and was taking a combination of several antipsychotic medications and a seizure medication; he also had a history of hypertension, for which he took Vaseretic (enalapril maleate/hydrochlorothiazide). The patient was treated for neuroleptic malignant syndrome.

As the patient recovered, staff learned that he lived in a single room and did not have a fan or air conditioner. He was in the habit of making sure the window and door to the room were locked and he usually walked to the workshop rather than accept a ride on the bus. In addition, Ryan stated he did not like to use the water cooler at the workshop because others used it; and limited his use of fluids at home because he did not like to leave his room to use the bathroom in the residence.

Differential Diagnosis

Although the problem's initial description by the client or others suggests a psychiatric disorder, a careful assessment is necessary. Many organic and physical problems present as apparent functional psychiatric symptoms or behavioral manifestations related to psychiatric disorders. Cognitive, communication, and cultural problems may further complicate identification, assessment, and validation of the nurse's inferences. Past encounters with outside systems and agencies, belief systems concerning how to deal with emotions and medical or psychological problems, and experiences with illness or trauma all influence the client's communication with healthcare providers.

Critical Thinking Question In developing a comprehensive client assessment, what factors can facilitate or deter a client's ability to communicate with healthcare practitioners? What factors facilitate comprehensive service delivery?

It is important to speak with everyone involved to determine what happened and how the client usually responds to a crisis. The client's history (if available) and others with whom the client interacts can provide valuable information and assist the clinician in making sense of chaotic and

Clinical Example

Robert, a 23-year-old man, was brought to the emergency room following a suicide attempt. When interviewed by the psychiatric nurse, Robert was reflective and convincing in describing the suicide attempt as an impulsive, insignificant gesture that he now regretted. He stated that he was sorry that others had mistaken his actions and overreacted. Robert told the nurse that he would call his therapist for a crisis appointment and that he just wanted to take a shower, go home, and apologize to his family for causing problems.

The appearance of a calm client and a resolved situational disturbance is often deceiving. The emergency medical technicians who brought the client to the emergency room reported that the client was locked in his room and that after they forced entry, they found the client with a noose around his neck and a suicide note on the dresser. When contacted, the client's therapist stated that the client had not adhered to out-patient treatment plans, did not take medications as prescribed, and had a history of making nearly successful suicide attempts when he was depressed. The client's family stated that they were afraid to take the client home because he had made several threats in the past week and had been feeling increasingly hopeless because he had been unable to find a job whereas his younger brother had just successfully graduated from college. The parents stated that they were exhausted from taking turns sitting up all night to watch him. In the past, they had been able to support the client but were worried that they could no longer sustain the same level of involvement, because the client's father was scheduled for open-heart surgery the following week. Recognizing the importance of the collateral information and the stressors experienced by the patient and the family, the nurse clinician in the emergency room was able to evaluate the seriousness and potential lethality of the situation.

> Before presuming a psychiatric emergency, consider underlying medical problems; head injury or seizure; exposure to drugs, alcohol, or other toxins; and side effects from prescribed medications.

disorganized situations. Often, there is no traditional family system to rely on for information. However, neighbors, landlords, service providers such as bartenders or beauticians, clergy, primary healthcare providers, and community agencies may have had previous contacts with and knowledge of the client.

It is important to try to fit all the varied perceptions of the client's history, insight, present behavior, and support systems into a holistic assessment that considers possible stressors, support systems, standards of care, and reasonable expectations for the success or failure of different options. Decision making and treatment selection vary widely based on available information.

People usually respond in familiar, fairly predictable patterns. If a client's response is unusual for him or her, an effort should be made to evaluate the situation and determine what changed and if there are alternative explanations for the change. Do not assume that a client with a history of chronic psychiatric problems has come to the emergency room for treatment of a psychiatric problem. To assess clients with a history of psychiatric problems, information should be recorded about their usual symptoms, treatment, and response and how these match with the presenting problem. For example, a client with an identified psychiatric history may present with confused and disorganized behavior. If previous contacts during psychiatric crises have been confined to times when the client was depressed with mood-congruent psychotic features, alternative explanations for the change in mental status should be identified. Disorientation is more likely related to an underlying medical disorder. Before presuming a psychiatric emergency, consider underlying medical problems; head injury or seizure; exposure to drugs, alcohol, or other toxins; and side effects from prescribed medications.

In some situations, people remain biased against clients with known psychiatric problems. It is important to ensure that all clients receive the same standard of care. The physical complaints of clients with known psychiatric disorders should not be dismissed as somatic delusion or psychiatric symptoms. For example, clients with somatoform disorders (see Chapter 18) should have regular physical evaluations and evaluations of new symptoms so that new or concomitant physical problems are detected.

Clients with a history of medical or psychiatric problems may already take multiple medications, some of which have synergistic or competing effects. During a crisis or psychiatric emergency, clients may be unable to tell the interviewer all the medications they are taking or the reasons that they are taking a particular medication. The clinician should take nothing for granted and assume nothing. Clients may have their own supply of medication, may be taking another person's medication, or may be using additional substances. Clients may have been prescribed medications, but for a multitude of reasons are not taking them as directed. The client may be seeing multiple healthcare practitioners who are unaware that other prescriptions have been written. Another possibility is that the client may have been prescribed a medication for a purpose unknown to the interviewer or triage. This includes many herbal and nutritional supplements that may have side effects of their own or may interact with prescribed medications.

Management and Treatment

Management of psychiatric crises and emergencies begins with appropriate triage, assessment, and differentiation among functional or psychologic problems, organic or medical problems, and substance abuse problems. Determining the present disturbance includes evaluation of the potential for violence and appropriate intervention. The nurse should ask directly about issues of abuse, suicide, and violence and take the appropriate protective measures or protocols for reporting. Protection of the client, potential victim, and staff is important. The assessment of safety issues is as important with discharge arrangements as it is with the initial triage. Cognitive behavioral therapy is useful in dealing with stress and generalized anxiety. Crisis intervention techniques are useful in many situations. Hopkins (1994) emphasized the need for nurses to recognize the family's distress, particularly in trauma situations, and to provide them with comfort, information, visits with the client, time to adjust to the impact of change and role shifts, and the opportunity to meet with staff to discuss treatment and expected outcomes.

Occasionally, treatment options are limited by extrinsic factors such as legal constraints, insurance (or lack of insurance and eligibility for government-sponsored entitlements), and limits on disposition planning from lack of space or facilities, demands of managed care contracts, or other personnel and resource limitations. If the problems are not under the clinician's control, the choice of options, limits, and reasons that one option was chosen over another should be documented. Knowledge of internal and external systems and negotiation skills have become increasingly necessary both for survival and for advocacy.

The following principles guide the nurse's interaction with clients who present in crisis:

- Introduce yourself.
- Present a calm, nonthreatening demeanor.
- Speak in a low to normal tone.
- Attempt to make eye contact.
- Respect the client's personal space.
- Explain what you are going to do and what is going to happen next.
- Avoid competitive situations.

Nursing Interventions

Nursing interventions identify and address specific problematic symptoms and their commonly associated nursing diagnoses. Skilled interpersonal therapeutic intervention offers emotional support and empathy, an opportunity for catharsis, a model for interpersonal relationships, feedback regarding clients' thoughts and behaviors, and education to facilitate change. If the client is very disorganized or has regressed, the nurse may need to provide specific directives on how to meet basic daily needs. In most crisis and emergency situations, the nurse is concerned with

Considerations for Client and Family Education

- Focus on the present and the immediate problem.
- Provide specific directions on what needs to be done first and plan for the next step.
- Investigate options for possible support for the client and for the caretakers.
- Assist in developing perspective of the precipitating stressor and coping style.

Implications for Evidence-Based Practice

A study comparing hospital staff and relatives caring for clients with schizophrenia and depression showed that nearly one fourth of both groups showed a high degree of burnout. Subjects were interviewed using the Maslach Burnout Inventory, which measured emotional exhaustion, depersonalization, and personal accomplishment. A limitation of the groups was that the caregivers with the highest symptoms of burnout were more likely to have already withdrawn from caretaking responsibilities, and the use of untrained staff in the hospitals studied. The study suggested that mutual self-help groups, psycho-education groups, and support programs for partners of the mentally ill might be beneficial. For professional staff members, specific training was suggested (Angermeyer, Bull, Bernert, Dietrich, & Kopf, 2006). The study suggested that better-qualified staff would cope better with burnout. Further studies are needed regarding the common factors in professional and family caregivers' burnout in dealing with chronic mental illness, and how both groups can be supported.

immediate and short-term goals. The client may need physical or emotional attention, medication, and assistance in mobilizing resources, or direction and supervision. Assessment of the client's ability and reliability to follow the treatment plan is essential. The clinician needs to assess to what degree the initial reason for treatment was resolved. Total resolution may not be reasonably expected, but there should be some symptom relief or hope that further treatment will be reasonably successful. The availability and reliability of support systems help determine which treatment and follow-up plans are likely to succeed.

> When encouraging a client to verbalize feelings, it may be necessary to monitor and to titrate the client's catharsis (discharge of intense emotion) by pacing the interview and switching from specific to more general topics.

Stress Reduction

Comfort measures, distraction, touch (if tolerated by the client), and the nurse's quiet presence soothe clients who may be feeling vulnerable. Stress-reduction techniques are an important adjunct to other treatment interventions. During a crisis or psychiatric emergency, the client may be too anxious or preoccupied to participate fully in other treatment interventions. The nurse can be involved in offering support and may be a means for the client to become involved in self-management tasks. These stress-reduction techniques are easy to learn and to incorporate into treatment planning. The client may benefit from learning simple relaxation techniques.

> Stress-reduction techniques include:
> - Progressive relaxation
> - Deep-breathing exercises
> - Meditation
> - Guided imagery

> Desensitization uses relaxation induction to help the client cope with increasingly stressful images or situations.

The natural impulse in times of stress is to "stop breathing" or breathe rapidly. Teaching the client deep-breathing techniques involves them in self-care and takes the focus off distressing symptoms and feelings of helplessness. First, have the client take a deep breath and release it. Occasionally, it helps to have the client place his or her hand over the abdomen to feel the difference between shallow and deep breathing. Instruct the client to take a deep breath, hold it, and let it out slowly. This can be done over several minutes, gradually instructing the client to take deeper and longer breaths.

In progressive relaxation, the client is taught to tense and relax various muscle groups alternately for several seconds and then to increase gradually the length of time the muscles are tensed and relaxed. Clients are taught to tense and relax the toes, gradually move up and tense and relax the legs, trunk, upper limbs, and then the face.

Meditation is another relaxation technique. The client selects a word or phrase and slowly repeats the sounds while concentrating on slowing the breathing. In guided imagery, the client is presented with a vivid description of a pleasant or relaxing experience. The therapist uses a calm voice and images of as many sensory experiences as possible. Suggestions for successfully mastering an experience or facing troublesome symptoms can be incorporated.

In the technique of desensitization, the situation that causes stress is broken down into small, tolerable steps. This helps the client focus on manageable steps that can be successfully completed.

Working closely with people in crisis situations is demanding work. To prevent staff burnout, it is important to give the staff the opportunity to express their concerns and frustrations, access to support in dealing with the physical and emotional responses they experience, and ample clinical supervision. Nurses must know when they need help and when to ask for it. Too often, clinicians believe they can help others without taking care of themselves. This response leads to problems for the individual experiencing the stress. It also affects others in the environment in terms of lost productivity and may lead to lateral or horizontal workplace violence directed at co-workers.

Clinical Example

Everyone acknowledged that Barbara was a model nurse; she was just not the easiest person to work with. She was extremely competent and very career oriented. She volunteered regularly to take on the most difficult assignments and districts, never complained when asked to work overtime, and was inevitably the one who worked alone when the unit was short, letting the other nurses utilize the unlicensed assistive personnel. She occasionally took her breaks, rarely took lunch, and never called in sick. She often commented that it was easier to do things herself rather than ask for help because no one could do things as well as she could. She had little patience for others who did not meet her standard of perfection. She never seemed to have anything positive to say about her co-workers, the administration, or the hospital. Her co-workers were reluctant to ask her for help because she seemed so irritable and hypercritical. Her patients had no complaints, but said they did not want to ask for anything or bother her because she always seemed so busy and so tired. Over time Barbara had isolated herself from other staff and rarely participated in unit social activities or met with friends outside of work. Staff felt that some intervention was needed when Barbara was overheard telling the family of an orientee that she was not involved in precepting that the orientee was incompetent and should not be allowed near patients.

Critical Thinking Question Identify some strategies for recognizing signs of burnout in yourself or a colleague. What are some possible sources of support or organizational resources that can be used in dealing with this problem?

Crisis Intervention

Crisis intervention focuses on a particular identified disturbance and is meant to be brief and flexible. The first step in crisis intervention is the assessment of the client's perception of the present event, prior and present coping mechanisms, and available situational supports. Clients are encouraged to tell their stories of their crises and how they experienced them. A problematic crisis results when one or more balancing factors (realistic perception of event, adequate supports, viable coping mechanisms, ability to incorporate new methods of dealing with the situation) are absent or inadequate. Intervention primarily involves, but is not limited to, four goals:

- Assisting the client in developing intellectual understanding
- Gaining awareness of present feelings
- Examining alternate coping mechanisms
- Reopening the social system to incorporate new people and possibilities

The goal is to restore, replace, *or* revitalize the missing balancing factors to resolve the immediate crisis situation. Reinforcement of learning, successful adaptive coping mechanisms, and anticipatory guidance for future crises are important for resolution (Aguilera, 1998).

Psychiatric Emergencies

The management of psychiatric emergencies focuses on immediate treatment goals. To provide a safe environment, the nurse must ensure the client's safety as well as the safety of other clients and staff. If a client threatens self-harm or suicide, the client and the environment should be checked to limit access to potentially harmful objects or medications. The nurse may need to separate the client from the family if the client makes threats of elder, child, or spousal abuse. The nurse should take an active role in identifying possible cases of abuse, client assessment, and intervention. In abuse cases, the nurse should know the various reporting mechanisms and whether reporting of cases is mandatory. This may vary. For example, the reporting of child abuse and legal protocols for spousal assault may be mandatory, but the reporting of elder abuse may not be.

If the client threatens violence, isolating him or her in an area with minimal environmental stimuli may be necessary—a place with no access to potential weapons, victims, or hostages where the client can be closely observed and, if necessary, contained. If the client has threatened to harm another and violence is a risk, the clinician has the duty to warn the potential victim. This is based on the decision in *Tarasoff v. Regents of University of California* (1976), which stated that it is the legal duty of the therapist to warn a potential victim of danger. The nurse should be aware of the legal and professional guidelines regarding client restraint and seclusion.

Medication

During an emergency, medicating a client may have different implications, depending on whether the client accepts the medication on a voluntary or involuntary basis. This varies among agencies and legal jurisdictions. The nurse should be aware of the possible legal problems when administering medication on an involuntary basis. When administering any medication, the nurse should not assume that the client understands what is going on or that the client is incapable of understanding. Let the client know that a medication has been ordered, what it is, why it was ordered, anticipated action and side effects, and who will administer the medication. In most situations, medication is first offered in oral form (concentrate, tablets, capsules) before intramuscular (IM) form. In rapid tranquilization, the client is given neuroleptic or sedating medication or both on a regular, frequent basis until the intended effect of control or sedation is achieved. When rapid tranquilization is required, many medications can be administered intravenously. If the nurse believes that administering the medication may cause problems, it is a good idea to alert others and have them available in the area to assist if necessary.

Crisis intervention involves the use of cognitive and short-term psychotherapeutic techniques to help the client gain a realistic perception of events, become aware of feelings, develop active coping skills, and experience social support.

Once a medication is given, it is important to monitor the effects of pharmacotherapy and document the response and any untoward effects. A particular medication is selected based on its action, duration, effects, synergism or

Implications for Evidence-Based Practice

Murphy (2002) reviewed consensus guidelines for the treatment of potentially assaultive clients. Use of nonphysical interventions such as verbal intervention, voluntary medication, deescalation techniques, or show of force should be tried first. Research indicates that oral medication such as risperidone and a benzodiazepine or derivative or, less commonly, olanzapine or ziprasidone, can be used as an effective alternative to IM Haldol (haloperidol) and may limit side effects. Before restraints are used, the client should be evaluated by the appropriately authorized licensed independent healthcare practitioner (MD, PA, NP) and, if indicated, the family or healthcare proxy should be notified. Murphy suggests that an appropriate range of responses to potentially violent behavior may lead to a decrease in client and staff injury and patient side effects, an increase in long-term patient treatment compliance, and an improvement in staff-client relationships. Implications for further research include evaluation of guidelines across practice areas and evaluation of various medications in emergency situations.

interaction with other medications, and the client's past response to a particular medication regimen. Many psychiatric medications come in time-release or long-acting depot forms. The nurse must know what medications have been prescribed and what medications have actually been taken. For example, if a client is taking a depot medication, such as a long-acting form of haloperidol (Haldol) or fluphenazine (Prolixin), the nurse must know when the client received the last injection and when the next injection is scheduled. Taking a medication as prescribed requires the capacity to understand its purpose and benefits and a commitment to adhere to a treatment schedule. Involving the client in treatment planning, having flexible healthcare providers and clients, and providing anticipatory guidance and information regarding medication support groups improve adherence to medication schedules.

If a client's agitation continues to escalate and presents a significant danger to him- or herself or others, the nurse must set appropriate limits in a clear, calm, matter-of-fact manner and avoid competitive or conflicting confrontations with the client. Responses from all the staff involved should be consistent. Methods used to limit physical interventions include assessment, observation, verbal intervention, reduction of environmental stimuli, appropriate medication, awareness of territoriality, and physical space issues. Negotiation and conflict resolution skills are helpful but not always sufficient to deescalate potentially dangerous situations. If the client is about to lose control or has lost control, the staff may need to physically intervene and attempt to restrict the activity of or restrain the client. Preparation involves having an adequate number of experienced, properly trained staff and environmental controls in place. A course in self-protection and the management of violent clients with regular policy reviews and simulation of procedures may be included. The client may initiate a request for restraints or may have

Implications for Evidence-Based Practice

A review of the literature on deescalation (Cowin, 2003) showed that deescalation is an effective method when used by staff in dealing with potentially violent patients. Education in deescalation techniques is particularly effective with new or temporary staff. Implications for further nursing research include investigation of conflict and response of staff and patients as well as studies across different practice areas as to the effectiveness of the techniques for prevention and intervention.

given direction that restraints can be used in certain circumstances or appointed a proxy to make such decisions in an emergency. Restraints are discussed in more detail in the following section.

Restraints or Seclusion

Restraint or seclusion use is limited to emergencies where there is a risk that the client may harm him- or herself or others. To control extremely agitated or potentially violent psychiatric clients, as in a medical code management situation, the nurse should establish the person in charge of the team and identify each person's responsibility. An accepted routine should be in place as well as a method of calling upon ancillary support staff, including security guards, to ensure the presence of sufficient personnel to manage an emergency. If the opportunity is available, meet briefly when the team is assembled to plan for problems and review procedures. Initially, a show of force (i.e., having enough people present in the environment ready to intervene if necessary) may be all that is necessary to facilitate the client's cooperation. The nurse may still be able to "talk the client down," and verbal intervention should be employed to calm the client, communicate expectations, have the client consider alternatives, and offer acceptable choices and consequences (limit setting, medication, physical restraint, seclusion). The client may withdraw, accept medication, or even voluntarily agree to restraints. However, if a "take down" is necessary, having sufficient staff present ensures safety for both the client and staff. At least five people should be present, one person to protect the client's head and one for each limb. Safety restraining nets or other physical barriers such as mattresses can be used. Once the client is safe, he or she may need to be moved to another area, or the staff may utilize physical restraints or seclusion.

Legal restrictions and agency policies regarding ordering, assessment, observation, treatment, documentation, and time of use may vary, and the nurse should be aware of the legal and professional responsibilities inherent in the use of restraints and seclusion. Joint Commission on Accreditation of Healthcare Organizations (JCAHO) and Centers for Medicare and Medicaid Services (CMS) regulations specify who is able to start restraints (a licensed independent practitioner), and times of observation and reevaluation. In an emergency situation, the RN may initiate this intervention, but the client must be evaluated by the person responsible for ordering this procedure within a short period of time, usually one hour. The order is time limited, and times for a valid order differ for an adult and for a child. The client should be observed while in restraints. This may vary with the age of the client and the types of restraints used. In addition, the client needs to be released from restraints at regular intervals (e.g., with four-point restraints, one limb at a time can be released if necessary for client and staff safety). The client may have voluntarily requested to be placed in restraints or may have advanced care protocols or a healthcare proxy. As part of the nursing assessment, the client should be asked if they have ever been a victim of abuse or have been assaulted. If possible, the client should be asked what helps them calm down if they are upset or agitated and whether they have ever been placed in restraints or seclusion during previous hospitalizations.

Staff need to reassess the use of restraints and discontinue their use as soon as it is appropriate. The order for restraints needs to be renewed periodically, usually every 4 hours for adults, and the person ordering the restraints needs to reevaluate the client periodically, usually every 8 hours. When the client is released from restraints, the nurse can help the client reintegrate into the milieu. Once these interventions are used, their implications should be discussed with the client, allowing him or her to express thoughts, fears, and/or resentment and to explore alternative coping mechanisms.

Staff themselves also must have the time to review the event and have support to deal with the effects of any potentially traumatic event. Defusing is an effective method of dealing with these stressors within the regular work shift. If there are other more longstanding workplace issues or an acute overwhelming trauma, utilization of other CISM techniques such as debriefing may be helpful.

Disasters

Disasters may involve an individual, a group of individuals, a family, or larger communities. Many institutions and community agencies

When assessing a client's potential for violence, be aware of the client's affective, behavioral, and cognitive responses and your responses to the client. Learn to recognize cues of impending violence, such as increasing restlessness (inability to sit still, restlessness, pacing, agitation, kicking walls) and provocative verbal or physical behaviors (angry shouting, threats and cursing, raised fist, menacing posture, closure of territorial boundaries, picking up a weapon).

The Centers for Medicare and Medicaid Services (CMS) require training for staff in evaluating treatment approaches. This includes identification of possible staff and patient behaviors or environmental stimuli that might trigger use of restraints and seclusion, the safe application and monitoring of these procedures, alternate treatment techniques, and formal notification of clients and their families to ensure that client rights are protected and safety is ensured. See www.cms.hhs.gov.

Trust the feelings and intuitions you and your team members experience. If you feel threatened or frightened, ensure your own safety and the safety of the client and others.

Clinical Example

A state trooper had just completed his basic training when he was sent to New York City after 9/11. During a rest period, he was able to discuss his feelings regarding his assignment with a psychiatric nurse who had volunteered to work with rescue workers and survivors. The young trooper explained that this was his first time in New York City and that he had grown up in a rural upstate area. Not only was being in a large urban area a new experience for him, he had experienced a series of "worsts." First he thought that seeing the aftermath of the destruction was the worst thing he would ever experience. Then, it was helping survivors and family members search for missing friends and families that seemed to be the worst ever. It was even harder being the one who told people that the person they were searching for had not survived. Still there were more "worsts" to come—accompanying family members as they tried to identify remains and assignments to help bring remains to the city morgue for identification. The trooper was dealing with a series of situational and maturational crises. This was an opportunity for the nurse to help the trooper tell his story of the event, verbalize his emotional response to and distress regarding the trauma, and discuss normal adaptive reactions and stress management.

Clinical Example

Suzanne is a 32-year-old woman who relocated to another area after the loss of her home and job in New Orleans due to flooding. After recovering from the devastation, Suzanne felt she was managing well and that she was rebuilding her life. She married her fiancé, who had family in the area, and soon became pregnant. During the second trimester, the client found herself becoming more and more depressed, tearful for no reason, and unable to sleep or eat. The client sought help from her nurse midwife who referred her to a local mental health center. Suzanne told the staff she felt overwhelmed by everything that was happening to her, the changes in her life and in her body. She described how she missed her old friends and neighborhood. There she was surrounded by familiar people and things. She had lost all her family photographs and sentimental artifacts from her mother and grandmother in the flood. In speaking with the nurse at the mental health center, the client remembered that the anniversary of her mother's death a few years before and of the hurricane took place in the same month. Active listening was the key nursing intervention. The nurse was able to provide the patient with an opportunity to verbalize painful emotions, recognize how the response to stress was normal, deal with the normal stages of bereavement, and begin to plan for the future.

(hospitals; police, fire, and emergency medical departments; volunteer rescue teams; ambulance corps; federalized disaster teams; American Red Cross) incorporate planning and preparation for potential disasters into their general operating plans. Part of the planning process includes identifying resources, such as human resources, supplies, and communication networks; coordination of services with other public and private agencies; formation of crisis teams; and training and simulation exercises. The responsibilities of different team members, types of training, and available services may vary. The nurse may be a program administrator, triage nurse, team member or leader, consultant, community activist, or volunteer.

As pointed out by Nancy McKelvey, RN, MSN, chief nurse of the American Red Cross, "nurses bring a public trust; they bring an ability to translate technical knowledge into lay language; and they bring their whole health background to the table" (Palmer, 2002, p. 68). Preparedness is a key factor in disaster work, and nurses should be knowledgeable about their own role in the disaster plan at their place of employment as well as local, state, and national programs. Coordinating responses of workers and volunteers, maintaining services to the community, and planning for short- and long-term needs are important facets of disaster work. Training in crisis intervention techniques is necessary, as is the rapid mobilization of resources and response capabilities. In discussing the ethical questions of reporting for work in a disaster, Chaffee (2006) examined factors such as the potential for danger, the nurse's relationship to her or his clients and to her or his own family, degree of training, and duty schedules and other work or volunteer obligations.

Critical Thinking Question What factors would influence your decision to respond to a disaster situation? Do professionals have an obligation to prepare for disasters and to respond?

In disaster response, basic physical needs take precedence. Immediate treatment concerns include appropriate triage for medical and psychosocial intervention, provisions for safety and shelter, and establishing communication. The primary intervention may be directed at helping victims withstand the initial effects of shock and trauma. It is important to monitor responses to the acute stresses, projected recovery phases, and long-term consequences (Hardin, 1996). Intervention for victims and survivors usually includes referral for appropriate follow-up with clinics, community agencies, or support groups and mutual self-help groups, as well as voluntary referral for critical incident stress management for team members and volunteers.

Pharmacology

During times of acute stress or crisis, medications are sometimes used as an adjunct to other treatments in order to target specific symptoms such as anxiety or disturbances in sleep.

Selective serotonin reuptake inhibitors (SSRIs) such as escitalopram (Lexapro), citalopram (Celexa), paroxetine (Paxil), fluxetine (Prozac), and sertraline (Zoloft) are considered to be effective in the treatment of anxiety. Less typical medications such as the serotonin-norepinephrine reuptake inhibitor (SNRI) venlafaxine (Effexor) and the anxiolytic pregabalin (Lyrica), a gabapentinoid, are also effective, as is buspirone (BuSpar). Some tricyclic antidepressants (TCAs) and benzodiaziapines are used at times but are considered of limited use. TCAs are noted to have low tolerance due to side effects, and like buspirone (BuSpar) may take up to 2 weeks for effects to be noted; they should not be used along with a monoamine oxidase inhibitor (MAOI). Use of benzodiazepines has an association with the development of tolerance, a potential for abuse, and the danger of development of withdrawal symptoms with long-term use. Buspirone (BuSpar) should not be used in clients with seizure disorders (Baldwin & Polkinghorn, 2000). Sleep disturbances are covered in Chapter 21.

At times, medications are used in the prevention and treatment of PTSDs. SSRIs such as citalopram (Celexa), escitalopram (Lexapro), sertaline (Zoloft), fluoxetine (Prozac), and paroxetine (Paxil) are often the first-line medications used; recommendations for use are that they may be needed for up to 1 year after the significant event. Trials with benzodiazepines have not been considered to be effective. In clients who have been refractory to treatment, studies indicate that a combination of SSRIs and atypical antipsychotic medications such as olanzapine (Zyprexa), risperidone (Risperdal), and quetiapine (Seroquel) have been used. For treatment of refractory clients with mood symptoms, combinations of SSRIs and mood stabilizers such as lamotrigine (Lamictal), valproate (Depakene), and carbamazepine (Tegretol) have been effective (Portier, Bakker, van Balkom, & Stein, 2005).

Summary

Clients are extremely vulnerable during times of crisis, emergency, or disaster. Psychiatric emergencies or disaster situations bring rapid changes, and lives may be at risk. Triage and differentiation between urgent and emergent situations and between organic and functional problems are important. An acute response to stress and trauma is normal, just as bereavement is a normal grief response. Crisis intervention is used to treat maturational, developmental, and situational disturbances and involves an assessment of balancing factors such as the client's perception of the crisis, typical coping mechanisms, and the availability of support systems. As a result of the life-threatening potential of psychiatric emergencies, treatment usually focuses first on the immediate problem. Follow-up for crises and emergencies may include outpatient or in-patient treatment or referral to mutual self-help groups. Crisis intervention is intended to be short-term, flexible, and pragmatic. Treatment of victims of disasters involves immediate assessment; psychosocial support for individuals, groups, or communities; and referral for follow-up to stabilize functioning and minimize the risk of chronic stress reactions. Support should be made available to the staff to prevent burnout, compassion fatigue, or vicarious traumatization.

"A thorough crisis evaluation requires understanding of the client's premorbid personality, support systems, previous episodes of decompensation, past treatments, and the interaction of a precipitant with a particular personality structure" (Mindnich & Hart, 1995, p. 28).

Annotated References

Aguilera, D. C. (1998). *Crisis intervention: Theory and methodology* (8th ed.). St. Louis: Mosby-Year Book.

This classic text is an excellent guide for those interested in crisis intervention. Clear situational examples and guidelines are provided for applying crisis theory, problem solving, and short-term therapy techniques. Updated sections on legal implications of crisis work, professional Internet use and abuse, and violence are included.

American Psychiatric Association. (2000). *Diagnostic and statistical manual of mental disorders* (4th ed., text rev.). Washington, DC: Author.

This is the fourth edition, with text revision, of the American Psychiatric Association's official nomenclature of psychiatric conditions and disorders. It provides a systematic listing of the official codes and categories, a description of the multiaxial system for diagnosis, and diagnostic criteria for each of the disorders. It is used by psychiatrists, physicians, psychologists, registered nurses, social workers, therapists, and other mental health workers in all clinical settings.

Angermeyer, M. C., Bull, N., Bernert, S., Dietrich, S., & Kopf, A. (2006). Burnout of caregivers: A comparison of partners of psychiatric clients and nurses. *Archives of Psychiatric Nursing, 20*(4), 158–165.

This study compared German hospital staff and family caregivers, and showed that one quarter of each group scored high on burnout when dealing with clients with chronic mental illness.

Baldwin, D. S., & Polkinghorn, C. (2000). *Evidence-based pharmacotherapy of generalized anxiety disorders in evidence-based psychoparmacology.* Cambridge, UK: Cambridge University Press.

This is a review of treatment of generalized anxiety disorders.

Burgess, A. W., & Hartman, C. R. (1996). Rape trauma and posttraumatic stress disorder. In A. B. McBride & J. K. Austin (Eds.), *Psychiatric-mental health nursing: Integrating the behavioral and biological sciences* (pp. 53–81). Philadelphia: W.B. Saunders.

This chapter identifies the biologic and structural changes that occur when a client experiences a traumatic experience, and details the application of various therapeutic models and nursing interventions in case studies of rape and posttraumatic stress disorder.

Callahan, J. (2000). Crisis theory and crisis intervention in emergencies. In P. M. Kleespies (Ed.), *Emergencies in mental health practice: Evaluation and management* (pp. 22–40). New York: Guilford Press.

This chapter discusses the history and current theories of crisis work and applicable frameworks.

Chaffee, M. (2006). Making the decision to report to work in a disaster. *American Journal of Nursing, 106*(9), 54–67.

This article discusses the impact of disaster on the healthcare delivery system and the individual nurse's ethical decision making in terms of relationships to family, community, employer, clients, and companion animals.

Charney, A. E., & Pearlman, L. A. (2000). The ecstasy and the agony: The impact of disaster and trauma work on the self of the clinician. In P. M. Kleespies (Ed.), *Emergencies in mental health practice: Evaluation and management* (pp. 418–435). New York: Guilford Press.

This chapter discusses countertransference concerns and roles of the therapeutic helper in crisis work, and provides suggestions for protection from vicarious traumatization.

Chiles, J. A., & Strosahl, K. (1995). *The suicidal client: Principles of assessment, case management.* Washington, DC: American Psychiatric Press.

This guidebook discusses assessment, crisis management, and treatment of suicidal clients. It provides useful hints on how to manage clients with repeated suicidal behaviors and includes a description of the use of therapeutic contracts and crisis cards.

Chrousos, G. P., & Gold, P. W. (1992). The concepts of stress and stress system disorders: Overview of physical and behavioral homeostasis. *Journal of the American Medical Association, 267*(9), 1244–1252.

This article discusses the stress system response as a V-shaped curve of hypo- and hyperfunctioning. It suggests that chronic response can lead to disease, particularly stress-related disorders, and that this would impact diagnosis and treatment of stress-related disorders.

Cowin, L. (2003). De-escalating aggression and violence in the mental health setting. *International Journal of Mental Health Nursing, 12*(1), 64–73.

This article reviews the use of de-escalation techniques as an intervention to decrease potential for violence.

Cutcliffe, J. R., Stevenson, C., Jackson, S., & Smith, P. (2006). A modified grounded theory study of how psychiatric nurses work with suicidal people. *International Journal of Nursing Studies, 43*(7), 791–802.

This article is an investigation of the nurse-client relationship and identifies the concept of "co-presencing."

Dreyfus, J. K. (1987). Nursing assessment of the ED client with psychiatric symptoms: A quick reference. *Journal of Emergency Nursing, 13*(5), 278–282.

This article provides clear, step-by-step guidelines for performing a complete assessment of a client with psychiatric symptoms. The author covers the triage and post-triage phases of assessment, staff and client safety issues, and commonly seen diagnoses in the emergency room. It is very useful for anyone involved in triage or crisis work.

Fisher, H. L. (1989). Psychiatric crises: Making the most of an emergency room visit. *Journal of Psychosocial Nursing, 27*(11), 4–8.

This article discusses why clients go to the general or psychiatric emergency room. The author covers helpful strategies and the need for clear communication and consistency.

Hardin, S. B. (1996). Catastrophic stress. In A. B. McBride & J. K. Austin (Eds.), *Psychiatric-mental health nursing: Integrating the behavioral and biological sciences* (pp. 82–106). Philadelphia: W.B. Saunders.

This chapter provides a therapeutic model for viewing responses, reactions, and recovery from catastrophic stress.

Hopkins, A. G. (1994). The trauma nurse's role with families in crisis. *Critical Care Nurse, 14*(2), 35–43.

This article discusses trauma victims' and their families' responses to injury, potential nursing interventions, and expected outcomes.

Masters, R. (1998). Death on the doorstep: Helping the families of murder victims rejoin the community. *Family Therapy Networker, 22*(3), 38–44.

Intervention with victims and survivors is essential for their recovery. This article clearly shows the grief and trauma faced by these clients and their caregivers. Rosemary Masters, a lawyer and social worker who worked for Victim's Services in New York City, discusses some of the immediate and long-range forensic and psychosocial problems faced by this population and the wider community.

McCaig, L. F., & Burt, C. W. (2004). *National hospital ambulatory medical care survey: 2002 emergency department summary.* Advance data from Vital and Health Statistics no. 340. Hyattsville, MD: National Center for Health Statistics.

The National Hospital Ambulatory Medical Care Survey reviewed 53 million mental health related emergency department visits from 1992–2001 by using mental health related International Classification of Disease coded diagnoses. Review of data showed an increase in the number of emergency room visits for mental health conditions in most geographical areas in the United States except for the Midwest.

Mindnich, D. S., & Hart, B. (1995). Linking hospital and community. *Journal of Psychosocial Nursing, 33*(1), 25–28.

This article describes the role of the psychiatric consultation liaison nurse specialist (PCLNS) in an emergency room setting. The PCLNS functions as a bridge or link among the emergency room, psychiatric services, and the community.

Murphy, M. C. (2002). The agitated psychotic client: Guidelines to ensure staff and client safety. *Journal of the American Psychiatric Nurses Association, 8*(4), 2–8.

Reviews responses to client-perpetrated violence and use of restraints governed by guidelines of the Joint Commission on Accreditation of Healthcare Organizations and the Centers for Medicare and Medicaid Services as well as consensus guidelines for medicating agitated psychiatric clients.

Myers, D., & Wee, D. F. (2005). *Disaster mental health services: A primer for practitioners.* New York: Brunner-Routledge.

This book covers various topics dealing with crisis and psychiatric emergencies including CISM and CODE-C models, stress management, and responses to grief, trauma, disasters, terrorism, and weapons of mass destruction. The sections on the potential impact upon caregivers are particularly helpful.

Palmer, J. (2002). Building on the past, preparing for the future. In Sigma Theata Tau (Eds.), *Disaster, trauma and emergency nursing* (pp. 67–70). Indianapolis, IN: Sigma Theta Tau.

This article features a nurse in a nontraditional role as chief nurse of the American Red Cross since 1987. Nancy McKelvey, RN, discusses her role and the roles of nurses who may be in nontraditional roles in their communities as well as opportunities for volunteerism.

Portier, C. B., Bakker, A., van Balkom, A. J. L. M., & Stein, D. (2005). Evidence-based pharmacotherapy in post traumatic stress disorder. In D. Stein, B. Lerer, & S. Stahl (Eds.), *Evidence-based psychopharmacology* (pp. 121–136). Cambridge, UK: Cambridge University Press.

This chapter is an examination of treatment studies evaluating medication usage in PTSD.

Puskar, K., & Obus, N. (1989). Management of the psychiatric emergency. *Nurse Practitioner, 14*(7), 9–18, 23–26.

The treatment of psychiatric emergencies and crises is discussed in this article.

Raphael, B. (1983). *The anatomy of bereavement.* Northvale, NJ: Jason Aronson.

This book provides an excellent description of loss and bereavement issues across the life span, including normal bereavement and grief response, delayed bereavement, and chronic grief.

Raphael, B. (1986). *When disaster strikes: How individuals and communities cope with catastrophe.* New York: Basic Books.

This text describes the stresses experienced by those involved in disasters. Numerous case studies show the application of crisis theory with victims and survivors.

Rosenzweig, L. (1992). Psychiatric triage: A cost-effective approach to quality management in mental health. *Journal of Psychosocial Nursing, 30*(6), 5–8.

This article discusses some of the common dispositions of triaged clients, documentation, and placement problems identified by a task force studying problems in a Minnesota medical center. Useful examples of problem solving and quality improvement that led to the development of a psychiatric triage team are provided.

Tarasoff v. Regents of University of California. (1974). 529 P2d 553, 118 CalRptr129.

Tarasoff v. Regents of University of California. (1976). 17 Cal3d 425.551 P2d334, 131 CalRptr14.

These court cases set precedent regarding the therapist's duty to warn potential victims.

Additional Resources

Lindemann, E. (1979). *Beyond grief: Studies in crisis intervention.* New York: Jason Aronson.

This classic is based on the author's experiences helping victims of the Cocoanut Grove nightclub fire as well as clients at Massachusetts General Hospital, who were coping with illness and pain.

Saakvitne, K. W., & Pearlman, L. A. (1996). *Transforming the pain: A workbook on vicarious traumatization.* New York: W.W. Norton & Company.

This is a workbook on self-care issues for clinicians.

Sigma Theta Tau. (Ed.). (2006). *Disaster trauma and emergency nursing (NurseAdvance Collection).* Indianapolis, IN: Author.

This book contains a collection of evidence-based nursing articles on trauma and emergency nursing.

Stephan, S. (2006). *Emergency department treatment of the psychiatric patient: Policy issues and legal requirements.* New York: Oxford University Press.

Provides an overview of care of the mental health client's needs and problems seeking care.

Internet Resources

http://nursing.jbpub.com/psychiatric

Visit http://nursing.jbpub.com/psychiatric for interactive exercises, NCLEX review questions, WebLinks, and more.

CHAPTER 7

Legal and Ethical Considerations

Amy Wysoker

LEARNING OBJECTIVES

After reading this chapter, you will be able to:

- Identify legal and ethical issues that guide psychiatric-mental health nursing practice.
- Outline the elements for informed consent.
- Describe the issues related to confidentiality and the mentally ill client.
- Describe the legal issues related to psychopharmacology.
- List the responsibilities of nursing personnel when treating a suicidal client.
- Distinguish among mandatory hospitalization, involuntary out-patient treatment, and the right to refuse treatment.
- List the criteria to guide nursing practice with the use of seclusion and restraint.

KEY TERMS

Autonomy
Beneficence
Boundaries
Confidentiality
Duty to protect
Duty to warn
Electroconvulsive therapy (ECT)
Extrapyramidal symptoms (EPS)
Informed consent
Justice
Least restrictive environment
Mandatory out-patient treatment (MOT)
Privileged communication
Psychiatric advance directive (PAD)
Restraints
Right to refuse medication
Right to refuse treatment
Right to treatment
Seclusion
Sexual misconduct
Suicide
Tardive dyskinesia (TD)
Violence

http://nursing.jbpub.com/psychiatric

Visit http://nursing.jbpub.com/psychiatric for interactive exercises, NCLEX review questions, WebLinks, and more.

Introduction

Legal and ethical considerations pertaining to psychiatry are extremely pertinent to the psychiatric-mental health nurse and advanced practice psychiatric-mental health nurse (APRN). The goal of treatment is to provide safe, therapeutic care. Knowledge of the various legal and ethical issues can protect the nurse from professional confusion and litigation.

Nurse practice acts, established by individual states, are the legal basis for all nursing practice.

State Nurse Practice Acts

Licensure is the legal basis for the practice of nursing. State nurse practice acts are the legal documents that govern practice. These documents outline the nurse's legal mandates. The nurse practice acts primarily include a definition of nursing, requirements for licensure, exemptions from licensure, and what entails professional misconduct and unprofessional conduct. All nurses must know what is set forth in their state's nurse practice acts in order to be in legal compliance.

The three primary ethical principles that guide professional psychiatric-mental health nursing practice are autonomy or self-determination, beneficence, and justice.

Ethical Principles

Ethics in nursing refers to how nurses carry out their responsibilities and render care to clients. Three ethical principles guide the care that psychiatric nurses provide. **Autonomy** or self-determination is the underlying principle that allows clients to make their own decisions. Individuals have the right to make decisions that affect their lives, as long as the decision does not infringe on the rights of others. **Beneficence**, the second principle, means to act in the client's welfare by preventing harm and doing no harm. The third principle of **justice** states that people should be treated equally and fairly.

The Code of Ethics for Nurses of the American Nurses Association addresses such issues as respect for human dignity; the client's right to privacy; protection of information; protecting the health and safety of the client; acceptance of responsibility and accountability; personal responsibility for competence, consultation, and collaboration; the protection of the rights of human participants in research; responsibility to the public and the profession for standards; maintaining high-quality nursing care; protecting the public from misinformation and misrepresentation; and maintaining a professional relationship with other health-care disciplines.

Nurse practice acts encompass ethical concerns, and professional associations outline their specific codes of ethics in separate documents. The American Nurses Association (ANA; 2001) document entitled *Code of Ethics for Nurses with Interpretive Statements* specifies ethical responsibilities and emphasizes the nurse's role as client advocate. Nurses must be familiar with the components of the code of ethics.

In addition to being in compliance with the state's nurse practice act, professional nurses are required to follow standards of practice and standards of professional performance as established by the profession; accrediting organizations, institutions, and agencies; and the profession's code of ethics.

Standards of Practice and Professional Performance

Nurses also are judged according to standards of practice. In the profession of nursing, there are standards of practice and standards of professional performance for general nursing practice as well as for specialty areas. Psychiatric-mental health standards are available for both the general psychiatric nurse and the APRN (ANA, 2007). Additionally, standards of practice are outlined in numerous documents including institutional policy and procedure protocols, Joint Commission on Accreditation of Healthcare Organizations standards and those of other credentialing bodies, nursing textbooks, nursing journals, and governmental statutes and regulations. Professional standards of practice and performance and the code of ethics are the authoritative sources. While they are not legal documents, in a court of law the nurse is judged not only by the state's nurse practice act, but also by these authoritative sources.

Nurse practice acts, codes of ethics, and standards of practice guide the practice of psychiatric nursing. This chapter addresses the legal and ethical issues that apply to all psychiatric nurses. Topics such as informed consent, the right to receive and to refuse treatment, psychopharmacology, suicide, seclusion and restraints, electroconvulsive therapy (ECT), discharge planning, and sexual misconduct are all discussed.

Critical Thinking Question How does understanding the legal scope of practice as defined in state nurse practice acts and the profession's code of ethics impact upon the actual practice of a nurse in a clinical situation?

Informed Consent

All clients, including those receiving psychiatric care, have the right to determine their own treatment. This right is based on the principle of autonomy or self-determination. Information must be provided so that clients make informed decisions about the care they are to receive. Prior to obtaining **informed consent**, the nurse must determine that the client is competent to understand the necessary information. To be considered competent, the client must be able to comprehend the proposed treatment and the choices available and then be able to verbalize a choice.

It is not usually the nurse's responsibility to obtain informed consent. However, if a nurse is the authorized practitioner performing a procedure for which informed consent is required, the nurse can obtain that specific consent (see **Figure 7-1**). As client advocates, nurses should

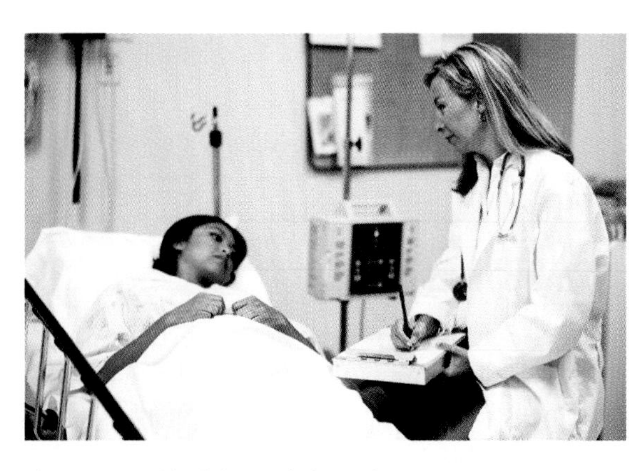

Figure 7-1 Obtaining an informed consent.

monitor the informed consent process. If questions arise concerning the client's ability to comprehend the process, the nurse must be able to discuss them in team conferences or with the physician or other mental health practitioner responsible for the client's care. Informed consent should include the following explanations (Appelbaum & Grisso, 1988; Grisso & Appelbaum, 1998):

- The proposed treatment in words the client understands
- The possible risks and side effects of treatment
- The possibility for a successful outcome
- The alternatives to proposed treatment
- The course of the illness if treatment is not instituted

The APRN can also be the primary therapist who is responsible for explaining and obtaining informed consent. Psychiatric personnel should not view informed consent as a single occurrence but rather as a continual process in which the client regularly receives current information. It is important to adhere to the informed consent process and document all discussions in the medical record. The MacArthur Competence Assessment Tool-Treatment (MacCAT-T) is utilized by therapists to determine a client's competency and ability to make informed treatment decisions (Grisso, Appelbaum, & Hill-Fotouhi, 1997).

Mental health practitioners functioning as psychotherapists must also stress self-disclosure in the therapeutic process (Galen, 1993). Nurse therapists must explain to clients the risks of withholding information and how sharing their thoughts and feelings can help them. It must be emphasized that not sharing all pertinent information can adversely affect treatment. The therapist must document that this was discussed. If clients injure themselves later in treatment, the nurse's liability is reduced because this information was discussed previously.

Nurses providing long-term psychotherapy must cover certain criteria during the informed consent process. They should explain the following (Wenning, 1993):

- The recommendation for treatment and the diagnostic model used
- The possible risks and benefits of the proposed treatment
- Other treatment options, including those that are less expensive and of shorter duration
- The reasons for psychotherapy
- Insurance coverage and possible restrictions by the insurance carrier
- The plans for continuous evaluation of the client's status

> Informed consent is the process of sharing information with the client regarding the proposed treatment. The client must be competent to understand the information provided, and the consent must be voluntary.

Research

In 1979, the National Commission for the Protection of Human Subjects of Biomedical and Behavioral Research issued the Belmont Report. This study discussed the relationship of three principles to the ethics of research. Respect for persons allows individuals to be treated as "autonomous agents" making informed decisions and affords additional protection for individuals with diminished autonomy who are incapable of making decisions. The concept of beneficence in research includes maximizing possible benefits and minimizing or preventing possible harm. The final concept, justice, states that everyone has the right to partake in research, and protects those who may be continuous targets of research (National Commission for the Protection of Human Subjects of Biomedical and Behavioral Research, 1979). In the course of their practice, psychiatric nurses facilitate the informed consent process, advocate for those who cannot make autonomous decisions, monitor the research process, remain alert for possible harm, and protect the rights of the mentally ill. Nurses involved in research with psychiatric clients should be cognizant of the requirements specified by the U.S. Department of Health and Human Services (DHHS; 1991) for informed consent when conducting research:

- A statement that the study involves research
- An explanation of the purpose of the research
- The duration of the subject's participation
- A description of the study procedures
- An explanation of any experimental aspect
- An explanation of foreseeable risks or discomforts that may result
- A description of benefits that may be expected
- A discussion of alternative procedures or treatments available
- A statement that confidentiality will be maintained
- Who can be contacted for information
- Who can be contacted if a research-related injury occurs
- A statement that participation is voluntary

- A statement that one can withdraw at any time without penalty or loss of benefits to which she or he would be entitled without consenting to the research

Nurses who participate in the research process and advocate for the client must ensure adherence to these criteria. This promotes ethical research. When embarking on research, nurses should check state laws for specific regulations in addition to federal requirements. All consent forms must be completed prior to initiating the research project, and a copy needs to be given to the client.

In 1972, the court in *Wyatt v. Stickney* ruled that all persons with mental illness or mental retardation must be treated in psychologically and physically humane facilities.

All individuals undergoing treatment for mental disorders have the right to the least restrictive environment.

Children in Research

The use of children in mental health studies and medication trials is often hotly debated by clinicians and society. Children are persons who have not attained the legal age for consent to treatments or procedures involved in research, under applicable law of the jurisdiction in which the research will be conducted. Generally the law considers any person under 18 years old to be a child, unless one has been determined to be an emancipated minor. The usual position is that children can be used as subjects in research as long as the dissent of children from and the assent of children to research are carefully safeguarded.

Currently, under the Department of Health and Human Services' Office for Human Research Protections (OHRP; 2000), when a proposed research study involves children and is supported or conducted by DHHS, the research institution's institutional review board (IRB) must take into consideration the mandated regulatory requirements that provide additional protection for the children involved in research. The IRB must consider the potential benefits, risks, and discomforts of the research to children and assess the justification for their inclusion in the research. In assessing the risks and potential benefits, the IRB should consider the circumstances of the children to be enrolled in the study (e.g., their health status, age, and ability to understand what is involved in the research) as well as the potential benefits to the subjects themselves, other children with the same disease or condition, or society as a whole.

For any protocol involving children, the IRB must determine which of the four categories of research apply to that study (DHHS, 2000). These categories are:

- Research not involving greater than minimal risk to the children
- Research involving greater than minimal risk but presenting the prospect of direct benefit to the individual children involved in the research
- Research involving greater than minimal risk and no prospect of direct benefit to the children involved in the research, but likely to yield generalized knowledge about the specific disorder or condition
- Research that the IRB believes does not meet the regulatory conditions, but that does present a reasonable opportunity to further the understanding, prevention, or alleviation of a serious problem affecting the health or welfare of children

In all circumstances, the research must be conducted in accordance with sound ethical principles and adequate provisions made for soliciting the assent of the children and the permission of their parents or legal guardians.

Critical Thinking Question How do the ethical principles of autonomy, beneficence, and justice relate to informed consent?

The Right to Treatment

In 1972, the court ruled in *Wyatt v. Stickney* that all clients with mental illness or mental retardation must be treated in psychologically and physically humane facilities that provide an adequate number of staff, individualized treatment plans, and an active therapeutic setting. The staffing must include therapists from multiple disciplines to provide a wide range of treatment. Individualized treatment plans that meet the client's needs are mandatory. These requirements adhere to nurses' ethical principle "to do good." If psychologically and physically humane treatment is not provided, the client's rights are being abused. These legal standards must be met for treatment to be provided.

Another ethical issue concerns the closure of psychiatric hospitals in recent years. What is the nurse's role in advocating for many different treatment modalities? Is the community the best place for treatment of all mentally ill clients? A large portion of the homeless population in the United States is mentally ill. The limited number of treatment facilities may have resulted in more homeless with mental illness. Is this population better cared for in psychiatric hospitals rather than community-based programs? Consumer groups have advocated for less hospitalization and more community services. However, it can be argued that the homeless client with mental illness may need in-patient hospitalization to receive adequate treatment.

The Right to the Least Restrictive Environment

There are many different types of treatment facilities. Clients have the right to the **least restrictive environment**, and this was acknowledged in *Dixon v. Weinberger* in 1975. When evaluating a facility, consider the type of setting, the institutional procedures for running the setting, client involvement, the consequences of breaking rules, the modes of treatment provided, the level of authority between employees and clients, and the clients' abilities to participate in their care related to their clinical needs (Garriston, 1983). The psychiatric team must evaluate all these areas when deciding which type of setting is appropriate for the client. Addressing these areas helps to define the least restrictive setting. This ensures that the ethical principle of beneficence is met.

The Right to Refuse Treatment, Including Hospitalization

All persons, including the mentally ill, have the right to refuse treatment. The right to refuse treatment includes the right to refuse hospitalization. This is based on clients' right to live as they choose and conduct themselves accordingly, as long as they do not interfere with the rights of others. Mentally ill individuals have the **right to refuse treatment** as long as they are not endangering themselves or others.

Nurses need to be aware of institutional policies regarding the hospitalization of a person against their will. The nurse is also guided by knowledge of specific state laws. In many states and hospitals, two physicians must certify that the client is a danger to oneself or others before the client can be hospitalized involuntarily. The staff needs to be careful to avoid violating the rights of clients; the hospital and treatment personnel are liable if violations occur. All psychiatric personnel must document in the medical records the behaviors and reasons leading to their decision to hospitalize the client involuntarily. This decreases liability in the event of litigation.

Clients have the legal right to submit a request for discharge if they disagree with their involuntary hospitalization. During this process, the hospital presents the reasons that involuntary hospitalization is necessary, and the client's legal representation submits reasons for opposing the hospitalization. The treatment staff, including nurses, may be asked to testify and describe the client's condition and needs. A judge then makes the final determination.

> All persons have the right to refuse treatment for a mental disorder or condition unless they represent a danger to themselves or others.

Involuntary Out-patient Treatment

> Laws that mandate involuntary outpatient mental health treatment are referred to as involuntary outpatient treatment, assisted outpatient treatment, or mandatory outpatient treatment.

Although clients have a right to refuse involuntary hospitalization, new laws been passed in 42 states that legislate involuntary out-patient treatment (Treatment Advocacy Center [TAC], 2000). These laws may be referred to as involuntary outpatient treatment, assisted out-patient treatment, or **mandatory out-patient treatment (MOT)**. Many of the laws have also been named after individuals who have lost their lives due to an act of a mentally ill person, such as Kendra's Law in New York State and Laura's Law in California. The American Psychiatric Nurses Association's (APNA) Position Paper on Mandatory Outpatient Treatment (2003) outlines the association's position on out-patient treatment. Recommendations include:

- Mandatory out-patient treatment should be a last resort that is used to protect the public and provide treatment to those in need of psychiatric treatment.
- Advance psychiatric directives should be incorporated into treatment.
- Services and a comprehensive treatment plan should be made available and independent panels should provide oversight.
- Therapeutic alliances should be established to promote medication adherence rather then mandatory medication; however, each case should be evaluated individually.
- Laws should not be named after individuals who have lost their lives because this continues to stigmatize the mentally ill.

The **psychiatric advance directive (PAD)** is an important document that psychiatric nurses should be educating clients on and advocating for its use. It provides a client the opportunity to share their wishes regarding treatment in writing. If and when the client relapses, their wishes can then be honored. A client's preferences for psychotropic medications, ECT, hospital, MOT, therapist, psychiatrist, and attorney, as well as any other preference, can be included in the advance directive. The client also has the right to change or revoke the advance directive when he or she is well and not experiencing acute symptoms (APNA, 2003; Geller, 2000; Mental Health Treatment Preference Declaration Act, 1990). The psychiatric advance directive can become an important document in assisting the psychiatric community and the courts if MOT needs to be implemented. State-by-state information on PADs is available online at the National Resource Center on Psychiatric Advance Directives (www.nrc-pad.org).

Although states differ in their wording, some of the criteria needed for involuntary commitment to occur include that the person must suffer from a mental illness, and based on clinical recommendations be unlikely to be safe in the community without oversight; have a history of nonadherence that has resulted in hospitalization or incarceration within a specified time frame; have had one or more acts, attempts, or threats of serious violent behaviors either toward self or others within a specified time frame; from past history is in need of out-patient treatment in order to prevent relapse; will not freely participate in treatment; and would benefit from treatment (TAC, 2000).

Involuntary out-patient treatment is a controversial issue. Balancing clients' rights and protection of the public is a legislative and nursing concern. The ANA *Code of Ethics* helps psychiatric nurses balance the mentally ill client's right to self-determination and the need to protect the public. The Code states:

> The nurse recognizes that there are situations in which the right to individual self-determination may be outweighed or limited by the rights, health and welfare of others, particularly in relation to pubic health considerations. Notwithstanding, the modification of individual rights must always be considered a serious deviation from the standard of care, justified only when there are no less restrictive means available to preserve the rights of others and the demands of justice. (ANA, 2001, p. 9)

All persons have the right to refuse medication except when, by refusing medication, they may represent a danger to themselves or others. Institutions and agencies should establish policies for the emergency administration of medication.

Advocating treatment for the mentally ill population and maintaining their rights is a priority of psychiatric nurses: "The need to safeguard patient rights and provide MOT is the challenge brought before the psychiatric community. Both can be done, but not one without the other" (Wysoker, Agrati, Collins, Marcus, & Thelander, 2004, p. 250).

Psychotropic medication effectively treats many mental illnesses and disorders. The benefits and risks of such treatment must be discussed with the individual before initiating treatment. Clients need to be carefully monitored for expected side effects and adverse reactions.

The Right to Refuse Medication

The **right to refuse medication** has been addressed in the courts. Nurses must be aware of the proper procedure when a client refuses to comply with treatment. The one exception to the right to refuse medication is in an emergency situation where the client is a danger to self or others. Only during such an occurrence can medication be administered against the wishes of the client. Hospital policy should inform the nurse of the protocol to follow for emergency administration. General guidelines include the following:

- Interventions have been attempted prior to the decision to medicate.
- The nurse has explained to the client that he or she is a danger to self or others.
- The procedures to inform the psychiatrist or other responsible treating mental health practitioner of the dangerous situation and the interventions to take have been followed.
- Documentation of these interventions is in the medical record.

The nurse gradually educates the client about the reasons for taking medication and how it can be beneficial. Thus, the client steadily gains an understanding of the medication's importance and is able to make an informed decision. If education is unsuccessful and the client continues to refuse medication, a court order needs to be obtained. Everything the nurse has taught the client must be documented in the medical record. The court then examines the client's response to educational intervention. Only court approval can override the client's decision. Nurses must verify in the medical record that court approval was granted, and the judge's order needs to be included with the documentation. It is imperative for the nurse to verify the document's presence prior to administering the medication. The court order should detail, among other specifications, the length of mandated medication therapy. Medication may be administered intramuscularly upon refusal, but only under court order.

Many ethical issues are raised when clients refuse medication. Nurses feel strongly that clients have the right to respect and self-determination. Conversely, the nurse may also strongly believe that the medication is necessary and may form the clinical judgment that administering the medication without a court order will "do good" or "prevent harm." Alternatively, the nurse may believe the client has the right to decide his or her own fate by refusing medication. The nurse may then experience conflict about giving the medication intramuscularly as detailed in the court order. The client may need to be held down to administer the medication, thus compromising the client's dignity and respect. Issues of "doing good" versus "doing harm" must be explored carefully, and the nurse may need assistance from nursing colleagues and other clinicians in deciding on a course of action.

Critical Thinking Question What are the ethical issues impacting on mandatory out-patient treatment, and how are they different or not different from the ethical issues surrounding mandatory medication administration?

Psychopharmacology

Psychotropic medication has dramatically improved the quality of life of clients with mental illness. However, the accompanying side effects of these medications have raised questions concerning the benefits of treatment versus the risks of incurring serious problems. The prescribing practitioner, psychiatrist or APRN, must weigh the risks and benefits when deciding the course of treatment. Prior to the initiation of therapy, clients must be informed of the benefits and risks and agree to the treatment plan. They must be part of the decision-making process. This is part of nurses' professional responsibilities as client advocates. Nurses need to be aware of medication side effects, such as **extrapyramidal symptoms (EPS)** and **tardive dyskinesia (TD)**. If side effects are observed, they must be reported to the prescribing practitioner, and treatment must be initiated. To decrease side effects, the dose may be changed, a different medication may be prescribed, or an anti-parkinsonian drug may be added to the regimen. The interventions taken and the rationale for this course of treatment must be documented in the client's record. Alternative options should also be addressed. The client's understanding of the chosen treatment regimen must be noted as well. Consent forms for the administration of medication are now being used in many institutions. However, many professionals still use the medical record, because consent is an ongoing process and indicates the client's continual involvement. Many states have laws requiring written consent. Nurses should be familiar with state laws and follow them accordingly.

The Abnormal Involuntary Movement Scale (AIMS) measures the presence of TD. It is recommended for all clients receiving antipsychotic medication. The American Psychiatric Association's Task Force on TD recommends regular examinations for the presence of TD at least every 3 to 6 months, and that informed consent should be documented in a progress note (APA, 1992).

Nurses must listen to the client and family to determine which treatments have been effective and ineffective in the past. The dosage should be monitored, and appropriate action should be taken if side effects occur. Communication among psychiatric personnel is crucial; it improves the health of clients and minimizes the negative consequences of medication.

Many nurses question the ethics of using medications when the side effects are commonplace. Nurses confronted with these concerns must weigh the benefits of ameliorating the symptoms versus the risks of side effects. Doing good and preventing harm frequently create an ethical dilemma when treating clients with medication.

Critical Thinking Question Knowing that psychotropic medication is a very important treatment modality for mental illness, but can also cause serious side effects, how can the nurse best provide medication education?

Electroconvulsive Therapy

Electroconvulsive therapy (ECT) is a mode of treatment that is used primarily to treat clinical depression. It is generally used for clients whose medical conditions contraindicate the use of antidepressants or antipsychotics, those who have not responded to their medication regimen, and those who are severely ill and need a rapid treatment response. The following rules for ECT guide the nurse and decrease the liability risk (APA, 1990, 2001):

- Informed consent must be obtained.
- A comprehensive medical examination must have been performed.
- Emergency management procedures must be in place and have been followed in the event of an emergency.
- Adequate client supervision must be provided during and after the treatment.

ECT has a long history of effective use, abuse, and misunderstanding. As a result, a stigma has been attached to the therapy by both the public and nurses. It is important for the nurse to understand both the benefits and the side effects of this treatment. There are many resources that describe when ECT should be an option for treatment, as well as the role of the nurse in the procedure and the treatment of accompanying side effects (Fitzsimons, 1995; Kelly & Zisselman, 2000). A greater understanding of this therapy helps nurses to make informed decisions and prevents them from feeling like they are providing ethically compromised care. When nurses adhere to ECT

Electroconvulsive therapy (ECT) is primarily used to treat clinical depression for clients who cannot receive psychotropic medications because of other medical conditions, those who have not responded to a trial of psychotropic medication, or those who are so severely depressed that immediate intervention is needed.

Suicide is a complex matter that requires an intensive multidisciplinary approach for prevention and protection.

guidelines, they will be ethically and legally meeting standards of care (Wysoker, 2003a).

Critical Thinking Question What should the nurse know about ECT treatment, and how best can nurses provide information to clients and families?

Suicide

Suicide is a major concern for psychiatric nurses, because they are entrusted with the client's care 24 hours a day. If a client successfully commits **suicide**, much blame and guilt are usually placed on nursing personnel. However, the treatment of a suicidal client is a complex matter, and the psychiatric staff needs to work collectively to prevent this occurrence. One of the most frequent reasons for hospital admission is due to risk of suicide. The goal of hospital admission is to provide a safe environment for the client (Billings, 2003). The therapist must address the issues that are making the client want to end his or her life. The nursing staff need to provide interventions to help clients balance their negative and positive views of life. The nurse's first priority is to protect the client from immediate harm. The responsibilities of nursing personnel include:

- Assessing the client's suicidal risk
- Informing other staff of suicidal risk
- Ensuring a protective environment
- Intervening to protect the client from harm
- Eliminating all dangerous objects that could be used for suicide
- Initiating appropriate observation by the staff, either one-to-one, 15-minute checks, or 30-minute checks
- Documenting actions taken in the medical record as dictated by hospital policy
- Documenting the client's status, including all behaviors observed and therapeutic interventions initiated

One-to-one observation requires that the client be observed by one member of the nursing or treatment staff at all times. The client must never be out of sight of the staff member for any reason.

Following these guidelines helps to decrease the risk of a successful suicide. At the same time, the nursing administration must carefully consider the institution's suicide watch policies and comply with written policies. A typical protocol involves assigning one staff member to a one-to-one observation for his or her entire shift, relieved only during lunch and break periods. One-to-one observation means that one staff member observes one client at all times. However, to implement this type of observation, sufficient staff must be available to carry out the entire unit's responsibilities. Frequently, a staff member is assigned to one-to-one observation but is given other unit responsibilities as well. This contradicts the definition of one-to-one observation and minimizes the seriousness of the client's condition. When this staffing pattern is condoned, the possibility of suicidal behavior resulting in death increases. Nurses must make the administration aware of these conflicting orders to avoid placing themselves and the treatment facility at greater risk for litigation should suicide occur. More important, these orders prevent clients from being kept safe and receiving the excellent nursing care they deserve (Wysoker, 1997, 2003c).

The common practice of assigning one staff member to watch one suicidal client for the entire shift raises other ethical concerns. It may not be in the best interests of the client or the institution. Realistically, one staff member cannot effectively watch a suicidal client for an entire shift. It is difficult, if not impossible, to watch someone every minute for seven or more hours. This practice actually provides clients with more opportunities to engage in a dangerous act. A client who is continually observed by the same person may also experience increased anxiety, which negates the benefits of therapy (Wysoker, 1997). Assigning different nursing personnel every 2 hours (at a minimum) increases client interaction with various staff members, allows for better distribution of staff assignments, and prevents administrators from breaking their institution's written policies. This is also a more realistic intervention. Nurses should not institute unethical policies that may do more harm than good.

APRNs in private practice need to be aware of their additional responsibilities when treating a potentially suicidal client. In some instances, managed care has hampered the care that practitioners provide. The ethical principle of justice raises the issue of fair distribution of resources in mental health care. Cost-containment efforts often conflict with clinical decisions. Negotiating hospitalization for a suicidal client may be difficult. It is therefore imperative that if the nurse therapist judges hospitalization necessary to protect the client from harm, treatment must be negotiated with the appropriate insurance company. If a managed care company denies hospitalization, the practitioner must appeal the decision. The courts have determined that practitioners are liable if the decision is not appealed (*Wilson v. Blue Cross of Southern California*, 1990). Clinical decisions must prevail, and the nurse should advocate on the client's behalf for the right to receive appropriate treatment. Ethically and legally, nurses who overlook these important issues are neglecting their professional responsibilities.

Seclusion and Restraints

The use of **seclusion** and **restraints** as therapy is fraught with controversy. General guidelines, however, exist for these interventions. Seclusion and restraints should be used only as a last resort after all other therapeutic interventions have failed. Furthermore, this therapy must only be employed to prevent clients from harming themselves or others.

In 1999 federal legislation was passed governing the use of seclusion and restraints (42 CFR Part 482 Section 482.13, Condition of Participation: Patients' Rights). The following statements provide guidance to agencies and nursing personnel:

- The patient (client) has the right to be free from any form of restraints that are not deemed medically necessary or are used as coercion, as a form of discipline, convenience, or retaliation by staff.
- The term *restraints* pertains to both physical restraints and drugs that are used as a means to restrain a person (client).
- Physical restraint is any type of manual method, physical or mechanical device, material, or any type of equipment that is attached to one's body and cannot be removed by that person and restrains movement.
- Drugs used as restraints are those that are used to control behavior or to limit movement and are not standard treatment for the person's condition.
- Seclusion is when a person is involuntarily confined in a room or area and is physically not permitted to leave.
- Seclusion or restraints can only be used in emergency situations if necessary to ensure safety, after less restrictive interventions have been ineffective.
- Only a licensed physician or practitioner legally authorized by state law to order restraints and seclusions may do so. The treating physician must be contacted if he or she is not the practitioner that ordered the restraint or seclusion.
- Orders can never be written as standing or prn (if necessary) orders.
- A licensed practitioner, as defined by state law, must see and evaluate the need for restraint or seclusion within 1 hour after the initiation of this intervention.
- Each written order for a physical restraint or seclusion is limited to 4 hours for adults, 2 hours for children and adolescents from 9 to 17 years, and 1 hour for children under 9 years.
- The restraint must be implemented in the least restrictive manner.
- Safe appropriate restraining techniques must be used and ended at the earliest time.
- Restraints and the use of seclusion cannot be used together unless a staff member is continually monitoring the patient (client) face to face or by staff using both video and audio equipment and in close location.
- Patient's (client's) condition must be continually assessed, monitored, and re-evaluated.
- Staff must have ongoing education and training in the proper use and safe application of seclusion and restraints and must learn alternative methods for handling behavioral symptoms.
- Hospitals need to report any death when the patient (client) is restrained or in seclusion or death is related to its use.

> Seclusion is the process of placing a client in a safe, contained environment separate from other clients. Restraints are mechanical or manual devices used to limit the client's physical mobility. These should never be used as forms of punishment.

As a result of a strengthened federal patients' rights rule, since early in 2007 the Centers for Medicare and Medicaid has been requiring stricter training and documentation requirements for nurses and physicians who place patients (clients) in restraints. The new training is aimed at ensuring that the treatment is appropriate and that the individual's rights are not violated. This federal rule is a condition of participation for Medicare and Medicaid healthcare facilities and applies to short-term, psychiatric, rehabilitation, long-term care, pediatric, and substance abuse facilities (Centers for Medicare and Medicaid Services, n.d.).

Nursing personnel must create an environment in which these treatment methods are required only in emergency situations. If they become necessary, the nurse must follow institutional policy regarding the application of restraints and placement in seclusion. These policies should follow state regulations and laws and must specify the following (Johnson, 1994):

- The types of restraints permissible under state law
- How to initiate and apply these treatments safely

- Who can apply the restraints
- The type of written orders needed and from which level of practitioner
- The length of time that clients may be kept restrained or in seclusion
- The interventions needed to monitor care
- The physical care interventions
- The necessary documentation

Nurses are frequently placed in an ethical dilemma when considering the use of restraints. Restraining a client is a treatment of last resort and should be instituted only when clients present a danger to themselves or others. If the decision is made to restrain a client, that individual's right to freedom is removed. Nursing personnel who are responsible for initiating this treatment modality must be prepared to explain the rationale for using this treatment. Nurses are both ethically and legally responsible when implementing this treatment modality.

The nurse needs to be particularly aware of the negative consequences of using restraints on clients with a history of sexual abuse. Clients who have been sexually abused have been placed in positions where they were unable to resist their abuser. Restraints limit free movement and can bring back terrible memories of the past when escape was impossible. Furthermore, the act of tying someone down and positioning their legs and arms far apart may intensify the memories of sexual abuse. Seclusion is indicated, rather than restraints, for clients with a history of sexual abuse. Sensitivity to individual histories can direct specific interventions accordingly. Clients may also be asked which calming methods are most helpful and least traumatic for them. A staff and client debriefing session should follow any use of restraints or seclusion to facilitate learning from the situation and to prevent further use.

Discharge planning and plans for aftercare treatment should be developed by the multidisciplinary treatment team in collaboration with the client, family, and significant others to ensure the client's agreement and compliance.

Critical Thinking Question What are the psychological issues related to the use of restraints? With this understanding, how can a nurse best provide treatment if and when it may be necessary to incorporate restraints into treatment?

Discharge Planning

Legal issues surface when clients are improperly prepared for discharge through inadequate discharge planning. Psychiatric nurses are instrumental in instructing clients about medication and follow-up appointments. Nurses need to include the client and family in the discharge plan to ensure agreement and compliance. The discharge plan, acceptance by the client and family, and the plan's rationale must be documented in the medical record. Discharge summaries should include all the pertinent information for the next treatment facility. If necessary information is omitted and legal action results, the facility and staff may be held liable for not providing adequate information, especially for suicidal clients.

Another ethical dilemma confronting nurses is that current hospital stays, as a result of managed care, are of shorter duration than in previous years. Discharged clients who are supposed to receive follow-up ambulatory care may find that adequate referral sources are limited. From an ethical standpoint, what should the nurse do when it is apparent that the referral source may not meet the client's needs? Should the nurse follow the discharge plan or advocate for more treatment time until an appropriate referral source can be located? This second course of action may restrict the client to unnecessary in-patient hospitalization no longer warranted by his or her condition.

Privileged communication is confidential information provided by a client that is shared with a person in a position of trust, such as a mental health practitioner, who has a legal duty not to disclose the shared information in a court of law.

Confidentiality

Confidentiality takes on an added dimension in psychiatry because of the stigma related to mental illness. Like all nurses, psychiatric nurses must keep the client's information confidential. It is an ethical and legal responsibility. A frequent breach of confidentiality occurs when nurses and other healthcare practitioners discuss clients in areas where other people may overhear the conversation. In addition, nurses often have the most access to medical records. Thus, it is imperative that they prevent anyone not directly related to the case from viewing the medical record.

Family members are frequently interviewed to obtain information to aid in the assessment. When interviewing family members, the psychiatric nurse must carefully refrain from inadvertently discussing information the client has shared. In this way, the nurse protects the client's confidentiality. In addition, clients have the right to refuse to allow the nurse to speak with others. This request must be honored, even if it prevents the nurse from learning important information. Nurses frequently have difficulty with this concept, because they believe it is in the client's best interest to gather all possible information. It is unethical to do so, and the nurse must address this ethical dilemma.

The Health Insurance Portability and Accountability Act (HIPAA) of 1996 was the first federal law mandating individuals' right to privacy of their personal health information. Under this law, enacted in 2003, healthcare providers do not need to obtain an individual's consent prior to disclosing protected health information for three purposes: to provide treatment to the client, to obtain payment for the treatment, and to carry out healthcare operations (45 C.F.R.164.506; Wysoker, 2003b). Although psychiatric nurses need to understand that HIPAA permits these uses, they still need to use their professional nursing judgment as to what information should be shared and for what specific reasons.

Confidentiality issues concerning discharge planning need to be addressed and must be documented accordingly. For nurses to disclose information to referring parties, the client must understand what, why, with whom, and when this information will be shared. The client must agree to disclosure. Many facilities have begun using consent forms to facilitate this process.

Another area taken into consideration in HIPAA pertained to incidental disclosures. HIPAA makes adjustments when a client's information may be inadvertently overheard as long as the facility has taken reasonable safeguards to protect this from occurring on a regular basis. Although psychiatric in-patient facilities have always been concerned about confidentiality, psychiatric nurses have not had areas designated where they can privately engage in therapeutic conversations. Psychiatric nurses do not have offices, and many interactions have occurred in treatment rooms and dayrooms where interruptions are a common occurrence. Psychiatric nurses, like other mental healthcare practitioners, should have a private area where they can engage in confidential conversations. Nurses should advocate for their clients' privacy. HIPAA may allow incidental disclosures; however, nurses should advocate for reasonable safeguards for their work with clients (Wysoker, 2003b).

Privileged Communication

Privileged communication is a legal term that refers to information shared between certain individuals as protected by law. Communication is privileged between physician and client, attorney and client, priest and parishioner, and husband and wife. These persons are not legally mandated to testify or share confidential information in certain legal proceedings if the other person wishes them not to do so. However, cases of suspected child abuse and clients who present a danger to others are exceptions to privileged communication, and this information needs to be reported to the appropriate authorities (Keglovits, 1992).

Although psychiatric nurses are not listed in the statutes of all states, a United States Supreme Court decision, *Jaffe v. Redmond* (1996), determined that psychotherapist-client confidentiality privileges exist. However, whether psychiatric nurse-client communication is privileged must be further defined by the courts in many states.

Duty to Protect and Duty to Warn

In *Tarasoff v. Regents of the University of California* (Monahan, 1993), the court ruled that mental health practitioners have a **duty to protect** those endangered by clients. Nurses working in ambulatory settings and APRNs conducting psychotherapy have a **duty to warn**; they must report information to the proper authorities if there is evidence that a client may inflict danger on a specific individual. It is the nurse's ethical responsibility both to provide care for the client and to protect others in the process. Despite the confidential nature of the therapeutic relationship, nurses must take legal action to protect others from harm.

Professional nurses have both an ethical responsibility and a legal obligation to provide nursing care and to protect clients and others from harm.

Felthous (1999) has developed an algorithm to help clinicians make decisions as to when to utilize the duty to disclose information to protect others. However, clinical judgment takes precedence. The algorithm is:

1. Is the client a danger to others?
2. Is the danger related to mental illness?
3. Is the danger imminent?
4. Is the danger aimed at a specific person?

Psychiatric nurses are also mandated by law to report suspected child abuse and, in some states, elder and spousal abuse. The nurse should be aware of state laws and follow them accordingly.

Critical Thinking Question You have established a trusting therapeutic relationship with a client. For some time the client has been discussing his relationship with his girlfriend of 8 years. One day he is very anxious and agitated and shared that his girlfriend broke up with him. He angrily shouts that he will never let her leave him. What ethical and legal issues need to be considered, and what interventions should the nurse consider?

Violence

Nursing staff are with clients 24 hours a day, and are therefore in the best position to assess for possible **violence**. Nurses are ethically responsible for protecting clients from being harmed by others as well as protecting themselves and other psychiatric personnel. In addition to the client's psychiatric condition, other factors must be considered to decrease the incidence of violence. Overcrowding, lack of privacy, an unappealing milieu, staff inexperience in dealing with potentially violent individuals, and poor staff attitudes toward clients all contribute to a potentially explosive environment (Davis, 1991). When nursing personnel address these issues, client care improves and violent episodes decrease. Collaboration among personnel and teamwork within the psychiatric unit is critical. Whenever violence erupts and injury results, liability issues place the nurse in a difficult position. Thus, prevention and early intervention are crucial.

Sexual Misconduct

Nursing personnel must constantly be aware of their interactions with clients. The nurse's primary responsibility is to provide appropriate and therapeutic care. The relationship needs to remain professional. **Sexual misconduct** includes the expression of any thoughts, feelings, or gestures that could be construed by the client as romantic or erotic. This inappropriate behavior is deemed unethical and has no place in psychiatric nursing.

Boundaries are limits that permit the client and mental health professional to have a therapeutic relationship based on the needs of the client.

The concept of **boundaries** is important, and nurses must be very careful not to cross the boundaries of acceptable professional behavior. The National Council of State Boards of Nursing (NCSBN) has published a guide for nurses on the importance of appropriate professional boundaries (NCSBN, n.d.). Four concepts are identified:

1. Professional boundaries are the spaces between the nurse's power and the client's vulnerability.
2. Boundary violations can result when there is confusion between the needs of the nurse and those of the client.
3. Boundary crossings are brief excursions across boundaries that may be inadvertent, thoughtless, or even purposeful if done to meet a special therapeutic need.
4. Professional sexual misconduct is an extreme form of a boundary violation and includes any behavior that is seductive, sexually demeaning, harassing, or reasonably interpreted as sexual by the client.

Although not every boundary crossing indicates sexual misconduct, the court does not look favorably on them. Violations of boundaries (Gutheil & Gabbard, 1993) include:

- Using first names
- Ongoing conversations concerning the nurse's personal life
- Body contact such as pats on the shoulder
- Accepting or giving gifts
- Wearing clothing inappropriate to the professional relationship
- Meeting at inappropriate times and places (e.g., late night meetings outside the office)
- Physical contact that can be misinterpreted (e.g., hugging the client when he or she is distressed)

Some of the actions listed above do not indicate sexual misconduct. In fact, frequently crossing one of these boundaries may be harmless as long as sound clinical judgment supplies an appropriate rationale. It is imperative for the nurse to document the rationale in the medical record. In addition, nurses need to be cognizant of the client's perceptions of interventions. What may seem to the nurse an innocent intervention (e.g., a pat on the arm or shoulder, see **Figure 7-2**) may be misinterpreted by the client. These misinterpretations should be explored with the client, and the behavior must be omitted to eliminate further confusion.

Figure 7-2 Although intended innocently, body contact can be misconstrued by clients.

Implications for Evidence-Based Practice

The legal and ethical considerations associated with psychiatric-mental health nursing are areas where more research studies are definitely needed. A 2002 study assessed and compared patients' and staff members' attitudes about what rights hospitalized psychiatric patients should have. The results indicated that the patients were less likely than staff to express the view that involuntary hospitalization, the use of force or physical restrictions, or the compromise of confidentiality is justified; there were no significant differences in the attitudes of the staff and patients toward patients' rights to obtain information about their illness and treatment and their right to refuse treatment (Roe, Weishut, Jaglom, & Rabinowitz, 2002).

In their study of the factors that influenced the decision-making process around seclusion, Wynaden, Chapman, McGowan, Holmes, Ash, and Boschman (2002) interviewed seven psychiatric-mental health nurses and one physician within 48 hours after the decision was made to seclude a patient. Findings indicated that seclusion was utilized only after all other interventions that were less restrictive were not successful. The American Psychiatric Nurses Association (2001) document, *Seclusion and Restraint: Position Statement & Standards of Practice*, is an important document that helps psychiatric nurses guide their practice in this treatment choice.

Nurses are often particularly concerned about how to meet the needs of clients who have attempted suicide and what is the appropriate follow-up treatment. In a study conducted by Brown and colleagues (2005), it was found that when cognitive therapy was given to patients who had recently attempted suicide they were 50% less likely to attempt to take their lives again within 18 months, compared to individuals who did not receive the therapy.

To prevent boundary violations of a sexual nature, Epstein and Simon (1990) formulated a tool (Exploitation Index) that provides therapists with guidance to help them monitor their behavior and act as a signal that boundary violations may be occurring. Psychiatric-mental health clinical nurse specialists and psychiatric nurse practitioners need to be continually evaluating their professional behaviors. Consultation with peers will assist this evaluation process. Continuing education needs to be available to help nurses stay current on boundary issues and the related ethical and legal concerns (Wysoker, 2000).

Critical Thinking Question What should a nurse be aware of when she or he begins to have personal feelings for a client? What ethical and legal principles apply, and how should the nurse proceed?

Summary

Psychiatric nurses are responsible for providing safe, quality care to clients with mental illness. Nursing's code of ethics requires professional behavior at all times. At the same time, nurses and other clinicians must provide care in a litigious society. As a result, much pressure is placed on the practitioner to provide quality care while protecting his or her professional license. An awareness of the legal and ethical issues accomplishes both goals without compromising either, and allows the nurse to provide excellent and appropriate psychiatric-mental health nursing care.

Annotated References

American Nurses Association. (2007). *Scope and standards of psychiatric-mental health nursing practice.* Silver Spring, MD: Author.

This book provides definitions and descriptions of basic and advanced psychiatric-mental health clinical nursing practice and the standards of practice and professional performance associated with that practice.

American Nurses Association. (2001). *Code of ethics for nurses with interpretative statements.* Washington, DC: Author.

This text discusses the code of ethics for professional nurses and is based on the belief of the independent, autonomous nature of individuals, nursing, health, and society.

American Psychiatric Association. (2001). *A task force report on the practice of electroconvulsive therapy: Recommendations for treatment, training and privileging* (2nd ed.). Washington, DC: Author.

This source establishes guidelines for using electroconvulsive therapy as a treatment modality in psychiatry.

American Psychiatric Association. (1992). *Tardive dyskinesia: A task force report.* Washington, DC: Author.

This report comprehensively reviews tardive dyskinesia, one of the main side effects associated with psychotropic drugs, and includes recommendations for the psychiatric clinician.

American Psychiatric Association. (1990). *The practice of electroconvulsive therapy: Recommendations for treatment, training and privileging.* Washington, DC: Author.

This source establishes guidelines for using electroconvulsive therapy as a treatment modality in psychiatry.

American Psychiatric Nurses Association. (2003). *Position statement on mandatory outpatient treatment.* Arlington, VA: Author.

Provides specific guidelines to be followed when utilizing mandatory out-patient treatment in the care of a psychiatric client.

American Psychiatric Nurses Association. (2001). *Seclusion and restraint: Position statement and standards of practice.* Arlington, VA: Author.

This text provides a position statement and standards of practice for psychiatric nurses regarding seclusion and restraints.

Appelbaum, P. S., & Grisso, T. (1988). Assessing patients' capacities to consent to treatment. *New England Journal of Medicine, 319*(25), 1635–1638.

This well-written article discusses specific criteria psychiatric clinicians can use to assess the client's ability to understand and provide informed consent to treatment.

Billings, C. (2003). Psychiatric in-patient suicide: Assessment strategies. *American Journal of Psychiatric Nursing, 9*(5), 176–178.

This article presents an overview of in-patient suicide and suggests various assessment strategies.

Brown, G. K., Have, T. T., Henriques, G. R., Xie, S. X., Hollander, J. E., & Beck, A. T. (2005). Cognitive therapy for the prevention of suicide attempts: A randomized controlled trial. *Journal of the American Medical Association, 295,* 563–570.

This article explores cognitive therapy as a means of decreasing future suicide attempts in patients who have attempted it.

Centers for Medicare and Medicaid Services. (n.d.). *Homepage.* Retrieved February 10, 2007, from http://www.cms.hhs.gov

The initial website portal for information on the variety of programs available through the Centers for Medicare and Medicaid services including Medicare, Medicaid, and low-cost health insurance for children (SCHIP).

Davis, S. (1991). Violence by psychiatric patients: A review. *Hospital and Community Psychiatry, 44*(6), 125–132.

This article comprehensively reviews the different violent behaviors exhibited by psychiatric clients, risk factors, and suggestions for intervention.

Department of Health and Human Services. (1991). *Regulations for protection of human subjects* (45 CFR Section 46.116). Washington, DC: Government Printing Office.

This federal document establishes national guidelines for the protection of human subjects in research.

Department of Health and Human Services, Office for Human Research Protections (OHRP). (2000). *Special protections for children as research subjects.* Retrieved November 10, 2006, from http://www.hhs.gov/ohrp/children/

The Department of Health and Human Services, Office for Human Research Protections website provides comprehensive information on conducting research on human subjects in the United States.

Epstein, R. S., & Simon, R. I. (1990). The exploitation index: An early warning indicatory of boundary violations in psychotherapy. *Bulletin of the Menninger Clinic, 54*(4), 450–465.

The authors provide a self-assessment questionnaire (Exploitation Index) for therapists that serves as an early warning indicator of boundary violations.

Fitzsimons, L. M., & Mayer, R. L. (1995). Soaring beyond the cuckoo's nest: Health care reform and ECT. *Journal of Psychosocial Nursing and Mental Health Services, 33*(12), 10–13.

A commentary on the need for healthcare reform in the management of ECT services.

Felthous, A. R. (1999). The clinician's duty to protect third parties. *Psychiatric Clinics of North America, 22*(1), 49–60.

A discussion on a clinician's duty to protect third parties, including an algorithm to aid mental health practitioners in making critical decisions regarding hospitalization and disclosures to protect others.

Galen, K. D. (1993). Assessing psychiatric patients' competency to agree to treatment plans. *Hospital & Community Psychiatry, 44*(4), 361–363.

This article provides simple and direct suggestions for psychiatric clinicians to assess appropriately a client's competency and ability to understand and agree to a treatment plan.

Garritson, S. H. (1983). Degrees of restrictiveness in psychosocial nursing. *Journal of Psychosocial Nursing, 21*(12), 9–16.

This article was written when psychiatric-mental health nursing first adopted the concept of least restrictiveness. It explores the premise that least restrictiveness is more than a set of techniques, and involves the adoption and incorporation of certain social and philosophical issues.

Geller, J. (2000). The use of advance directives by persons with serious mental illness for psychiatric treatment. *Psychiatric Quarterly, 71*(1), 1–13.

This article focuses on the use of psychiatric advance directives.

Grisso, T., Appelbaum, T. S., & Hill-Fotouhi, C. (November, 1997).The MacCAT-T: A clinical tool to assess patients' capacities to make treatment decisions. *Psychiatric Services, 48*(11), 1415–1419.

This study concluded that the MacCAT-T offers a flexible yet structured method with which caregivers can assess, rate, and report patients' abilities relevant for evaluating competence to consent to treatment.

Grisso, T., & Appelbaum, P. S. (1998). *Assessing competence to consent to treatment: A guide for physicians and other health professionals.* New York: Oxford University Press.

This is an excellent practical guide to assess patients' competency to consent to treatment.

Gutheil, T., & Gabbard, G. (1993). The concept of boundaries in clinical practice: Theoretical and risk management dimensions. *American Journal of Psychiatry, 150*(2), 188–196.

This article provides an excellent discussion about establishing boundaries in psychiatric practice and the various risk-management considerations.

Jaffe v. Redmond, 64 U.S.L. LW 4491 (1996).

This Supreme Court case established the existence of the psychotherapist-client confidentiality privilege.

Johnson, V. P. (1994). Psychiatry. In L. M. Harpsler & M. S. Veach (Eds.), *Risk management handbook for health care facilities* (pp. 165–176). Chicago: American Hospital Association.

This chapter addresses risk-management cases in psychiatry.

Keglovits, J. (1992). Legal issues and clients' rights. In K. S. Wilson & C. R. Kneisel (Eds.), *Psychiatric nursing* (pp. 930–952). Redwood City, CA: Addison-Wesley.

This chapter offers an extensive review of the various constitutional and legal issues and rights of clients.

Kelly, K. G., & Zisselman, M. (2000). Update on electroconvulsive therapy (ECT) in older adults. *Journal of the American Geriatrics Society, 48*(5), 560–566.

This article provides an update on the indications for ECT, how it is administered, common complications, its efficacy, and recommendations for management.

Mental Health Treatment Preference Declaration Act, Illinois Stat. Public Act 86-1190. (1990).

Illinois law establishing the parameters under which an adult can establish guidelines for what type of mental health treatment the adult would want and under what circumstances.

Monahan, J. (1993). Limiting therapist exposure to *Tarasoff* liability. *American Psychologist, 48*(3), 242–250.

This article discusses implications of the *Tarasoff* case for therapists.

National Commission for the Protection of Human Subjects of Biomedical and Behavioral Research. (1979). *The Belmont report: Ethical principles and guidelines for the protection of human subjects of research.* Washington, DC: Department of Health, Education, and Welfare (Publication Nos. OS-78-0013 and OS-78-0014).

This classic document established the current guidelines for using human subjects in clinical research projects.

National Council of State Boards of Nursing. (n.d.). *Professional boundaries.* Chicago, IL: Author. Retrieved March 10, 2007, from http://www.ncsbn.org/ProfessionalBoundaries.pdf

This is a guide for professional nurses on the importance of appropriate professional boundaries.

Roe, D., Weishut, D. J., Jaglom, M., & Rabinowitz, J. (2002). Patients' and staff members' attitudes about the rights of hospitalized psychiatric patients. *Psychiatric Services, 53*(1), 87–91.

This is a research study that interviewed both patients and staff members regarding the rights of hospitalized mentally ill patients.

Treatment Advocacy Center. (2000). *Model law for assisted treatment.* Retrieved August 14, 2007, from http://www.psychlaws.org/LegalResources/ModelLaw.htm

This organization works to eliminate barriers to timely treatment of severe mental illnesses.

Wenning, K. (1993). Long-term psychotherapy and informed consent. *Hospital and Community Psychiatry, 44*(4), 364–366.

This article discusses the problems in determining ongoing informed consent for treatment when the client is engaged in long-term therapy.

Wilson v. Blue Cross of Southern California, 271 Cal. Rptr. 876 (1990); 222 Cal. App. 3 dsp 660 (1990).

This case established a practitioner's responsibility to appeal the decision of a managed care company to deny care if the practitioner thinks that the patient will suffer because care was denied.

Wyatt v. Stickney, 344 Fed. Supp. 373 (1972).

This case established that all clients with mental illness or mental retardation must be treated in psychologically and physically humane facilities.

Wynaden, D., Chapman, R., McGowan, S., Holmes, C., Ash, P., & Boschman, A. (2002). Through the eye of the beholder: To seclude or not to seclude. *International Journal of Psychiatric Nursing, 11*(4), 260.

This article discusses the decision-making process involved in deciding to use seclusion with a patient.

Wysoker, A. (2003a). Legal and ethical considerations: Electroconvulsive therapy. *Journal of the American Psychiatric Nurses Association, 9,* 103–105.

This article responds to the stigma associated with ECT and how psychiatric nurses need to speak from an evidence-based background and educate the public.

Wysoker, A. (2003b). Legal and ethical considerations: HIPAA and psychiatric nurses. *Journal of the American Psychiatric Nurses Association, 9,* 173–175.

This article addresses HIPAA's implications for psychiatric nursing.

Wysoker, A. (2003c). Risk management in psychiatry. In F. Kavaler & A. Speigel (Eds.), *Health care risk management: A strategic approach* (pp. 225–294). Boston: Jones & Bartlett.

This 2nd edition chapter provides a more extensive and current discussion of risk-management issues in psychiatry.

Wysoker, A. (2000). Sexual misconduct. *Journal of the American Psychiatric Nurses Association, 6,* 131–132.

This article reviews sexual misconduct in psychiatric nursing.

Wysoker, A. (1997). Risk management in psychiatry. In F. Kavaler & A. Speigel (Eds.), *Health care risk management: A strategic approach* (pp. 225–294). Boston: Jones & Bartlett.

This chapter provides a more extensive discussion of risk-management issues in psychiatry.

Wysoker, A., Agrati, G., Collins, J., Marcus, P., & Thelander, B. (2004). Legal and ethical considerations: Mandatory out-patient treatment. *Journal of the American Psychiatric Nurses Association, 10,* 247–253.

This article explains the American Psychiatric Nurses Association position statement on mandatory out-patient treatment.

Internet Resources

http://nursing.jbpub.com/psychiatric

Visit http://nursing.jbpub.com/psychiatric for interactive exercises, NCLEX review questions, WebLinks, and more.

CHAPTER 8

Self-Help Groups: Options for Support, Education, and Advocacy

Edward J. Madara

LEARNING OBJECTIVES

After reading this chapter, you will be able to:

- Describe the types and characteristics of self-help groups available to clients, practitioners, families, and the community.
- Explain the primary functions of a self-help group and the distinctive benefits they, as community groups or online self-help networks, can provide.
- Describe different ways in which nurses can tap into, develop, and support self-help groups.

KEY TERMS

12 step
Advocacy
Mental health consumers
Psychoneuroimmunology
Self-help clearinghouses
Self-help groups
Self-help networks

http://nursing.jbpub.com/psychiatric

Visit http://nursing.jbpub.com/psychiatric for interactive exercises, NCLEX review questions, WebLinks, and more.

Introduction

Thousands of community self-help groups and an ever-increasing number of online **self-help networks** help individuals and families to better cope with a wide variety of illnesses, disabilities, addictions, caregiver concerns, bereavement situations, and other stressful life problems and transitions. However, **self-help groups** in general continue to be understudied and relatively untapped, primarily due to the lack of professional education on the benefits of social support and on self-help groups, and resulting attitudes among professionals who therefore fail to recognize the benefits of these member-run groups and the helpful roles nurses can play in helping clients benefit from such supports (Stewart, 1990b). Although an increasing number of health organizations and professionals do recognize value in groups, another reason for not investing staff time in nurturing linkages is the apparent inability of self-help groups to generate revenue as therapy groups do. Nurses who have worked with self-help groups have found that they are in a better position to understand and meet the needs of clients and the community (Adamsen & Rasmussen, 2003). Whether advising a stroke client and his or her family of the availability of a local stroke group, speaking on stress reduction techniques before an existing Well Spouse Association group, or assisting parents of children with cancer to organize a local chapter of Candlelighters, nurses can both tap into and develop these client care resources to expand the degree, reach, and long-term impact of their nursing care.

A self-help group is a nonprofit support group run by and for people who join together on the basis of common experience to help one another. It is not professionally run, although professionals are frequently found in supportive ancillary roles.

Many clients seek self-help groups for the basic emotional support, practical education, and sometimes the advocacy help that these groups provide. Kessler and colleagues found that 18.1% of the U.S. population has participated in a member-run self-help group at some time, and 7.1% did so in 1996 (Kessler, Frank, et al., 1997). These researchers also found that "those who reported having less supportive social networks were more likely to attend a self-help group than those with more supportive networks" (Kessler, Frank, et al., p. 35). In a separate national study on the epidemiology of psychiatric disorders, Kessler, Mickelson, and Zhao (1997) discovered that self-help groups were the most utilized single service sector in the mental and addictive disorders treatment system. Respondents who sought help for psychiatric problems indicated that 40% of all visits were to self-help groups, compared to 35% to the mental health specialty service sector, 8% to the general medical sector, and 16.5% to the human services sector.

A number of healthcare and social trends are contributing to the increased use and relevancy of the groups. The prevalence of chronic illness and disability continues to grow as the percentage of the aged population grows larger. At the same time, continuing medical advancements succeed in both saving lives and extending life expectancy. Yet traditional sources of social support and practical information, formerly found within extended families, neighborhoods, and community organizations, have become less available.

As the move to more efficient and patient-centered health care encourages patients to take more responsibility for their health care and participate in making more-informed health decisions, self-help groups in both their traditional community and new online forms remain a valuable but still relatively untapped volunteer-run resource. With attention to continuous quality improvement (CQI) practices in hospitals and healthcare agencies, self-help groups can provide informed customer feedback and serve as potential partners for health service planning, delivery, and evaluation. Finally, with increasing work pressures, self-help groups serve as welcome allies for those nurses who risk burnout because they are expected to be all things to their clients.

One of the only nationally known proponents of self-help groups was Dr. C. Everett Koop, who when in office, held a national Surgeon General's Workshop on Self-Help and Public Health (U.S. Department of Health and Human Services, 1988). He brought together researchers, policymakers, group leaders, and health professionals to develop recommendations for promoting the potential of self-help groups for the nation's public health. Of the more than 60 recommendations that were developed over the 2 days, the recommendation given the highest priority was the need to incorporate knowledge about self-help groups into the training and practice of professionals. Although no federal funding was provided to ensure such education, Dr. Koop worked to advocate for its introduction.

Although studies continue to indicate the value of self-help groups and reflect how professional interaction with self-help groups is desirable (Law, King, Stewart, & King, 2001), lack of education and information on groups has served as a barrier to such involvement (Stewart, 1990b), resulting in large part in an underutilization of self-help groups and the attendant benefits groups

Implications for Evidence-Based Practice

One of the earliest nursing articles that examined self-help groups (Bumbalo & Young, 1973) stressed how members of the health profession could learn a great deal from such groups, and cautioned against direct intervention by nurses because it might endanger self-help group autonomy and its associated benefits. Subsequent literature cites supportive but ancillary roles that nurses can play, but point out how nurses still have had scant knowledge and experience in using self-help groups (Hildingh, Fridlund, & Segesten, 1995; Stewart, 1990b). Further research is needed to evaluate nurses' level of knowledge about and use of self-help groups and the roles of nurses in self-help groups.

could provide to a broad spectrum of patients and families.

Several years after his national workshop, Dr. Koop wrote:

> My years as a medical practitioner, as well as my own firsthand experience, has taught me how important self-help groups are in assisting their members in dealing with problems, stress, hardship and pain. . . . Today, the benefits of mutual aid are experienced by millions of people who turn to others with a similar problem to attempt to deal with their isolation, powerlessness, alienation, and the awful feeling that nobody understands. . . . Health and human service providers are learning that they can indeed provide a superior service when they help their patients and clients find appropriate peer support. (1992, p. ix)

Critical Thinking Question In what particular ways might students better educate themselves in understanding the value, variety, and dynamics of self-help groups?

The Beginnings of Self-Help Groups

The number and variety of member-run self-help groups have continued to multiply since the very first group, Alcoholics Anonymous, was started in 1935. Approximately 100 different groups have now adapted the **12-step** approach developed by Alcoholics Anonymous to apply to a variety of other specific addictions and problems. See **Table 8-1**.

The second oldest group is Recovery, Inc., a group that was started in 1937 with the help of a psychiatrist, Dr. Abraham A. Low, whose book detailing Recovery techniques is still used by members worldwide. Recovery is run by those suffering from various emotional and mental conditions. The Recovery Method teaches people how to change the thoughts, reactions, and behaviors that cause their physical and emotional symptoms. The principles are similar to those found in cognitive-behavioral therapy. Recovery groups today continue to be especially open to working in partnership with professionals, as reflected in their willingness to provide demonstrational meetings for professionals and students (Snyder & Weyer, 2000).

If one examines the development of most health associations and movements in the United States, a small self-help support group of clients or families can usually be identified as the initial seed for that growth. For example, Sylvia Lawry, whose brother had multiple sclerosis, placed an ad in a Brooklyn newspaper to bring together others with the disease and their families to form what in 1946 became the Multiple Sclerosis Society. It was a small group of parents of children with developmental disabilities who organized the Association for Retarded Citizens (ARC) in the 1950s. Marjorie Guthrie, the wife of the folksinger Woody Guthrie, pulled families together to form what became the Huntington's Disease Society in 1967. She said her one regret was that no professional had encouraged her 10 years earlier to bring together families, when her husband was first diagnosed with Huntington's—for if that had happened, "We would be a decade further down the road in terms of research by now."

In some cases, self-help groups develop well before a particular health problem is recognized by professionals. Years before postpolio syndrome was officially recognized as a disorder by the medical community, groups of polio survivors were banding together in self-help groups to compare the pain and weakness that they were experiencing and to advocate for needed research. It was a self-help group of Vietnam veterans who, having lost a member to suicide, were instrumental in advocating for recognition of what eventually became known as PTSD (posttraumatic stress disorder) by the Veterans Administration (National Public Radio, 2003). Families of Vietnam veterans who were suffering from Agent Orange exposure, and subsequently families of Iraqi war veterans with Gulf War syndrome, both compared notes and advocated for research through their respective early mutual support networks.

Polly Murray, a housewife with no formal training, is credited with most of the epidemiologic groundwork that led to the discovery of Lyme disease in the United States and the development of the first support group in her hometown of Lyme, Connecticut. In 1995, ELASTIC (Education for Latex Allergy Support Team Information Coalition) was started by nurses and other medical professionals who were experiencing serious debilitating allergies associated with the protective gloves they wore. Their organization, which grew to have over 50 local self-help groups, advocated for hospital protocols to protect allergy-sensitive staff and clients, as well as for research and changes in the manufacturing of latex gloves.

Nurses who work with self-help groups can learn from the groups and expand the impact of their nursing interventions.

Table 8-1 A Small Sample of Self-Help Groups

For the addictions category only, the figures reflect international group estimates. The remaining categories reflect national group estimates for the United States.

Category	Group	Number
Addictions	Alcoholics Anonymous	106,202
	Narcotics Anonymous	33,500
	Cocaine Anonymous	2,500
	Gamblers Anonymous	1,300
	Al-Anon (families/friends of alcoholics)	26,000
	Nar-Anon (families/friends of drug addicts)	1,600
	Gam-Anon (families/friends of gamblers)	325
	Families Anonymous (families/friends of those with drug, alcohol, or behavioral	220
	problems)	950
	Sexaholics Anonymous	550
	Debtors Anonymous	
Bereavement	Compassionate Friends (death of a child)	600
	Parents of Murdered Children, Inc.	235
	Heartbeat (suicide of a loved one)	35
	Widowed or general bereavement (unaffiliated)	numerous
Disability	Amputee Coalition of America	240
	Brain Injury Association	275
	Spinal Cord Society	200
	Hearing Loss Association of America	240
Mental Health	Depressive & Bipolar Support Alliance	800
	National Alliance on Mental Illness (primarily families)	1,100
	Recovery, Inc.	500
	Emotions Anonymous	427
	Dual Recovery Anonymous (co-occurring disorders)	336
	Double Trouble in Recovery (co-occurring disorders)	250
	Schizophrenics Anonymous	156
	mental health consumer groups (most unaffiliated)	3,315
Other Parenting Groups	Adoptive Families of America	375
	Grandparents Raising Grandchildren	120
	Parents Anonymous (at risk of child abuse)	662
	National Parent Network on Disabilities	175
	Candlelighters (children with cancer)	300
	"Because I Love You" (out-of-control adolescents)	45
	Moms Clubs (mothers at home)	numerous
Sample of Other Groups	T.O.P.S. (for weight loss)	8,757
	Mended Hearts (any cardiac disorder)	285
	Us Too International (prostate cancer)	300
	CHADD (attention-deficit disorder)	200
	Stroke Clubs International	900
	American Chronic Pain Association	400
	Well Spouse Association (partners of those ill or with disability)	60
	Sisters Network (African American breast cancer survivors)	45
	Divorce and separation self-help groups (unaffiliated)	numerous

Self-help groups have developed to address a wide variety of illnesses, disabilities, and addictions, along with bereavement, parenting, and many other stressful life problems from arthritis to vestibular disorders, from groups for parents of premature babies to those for persons caring for an elderly frail relative. Some of the larger groups are not well known to professionals (see **Table 8-1**). This results, in part, from the fact that a significant number of the national and numerous local groups operate informally from "kitchen-table offices," without budgets for publicity.

The Variety of Self-Help Groups

Many individuals and families who face a disorder, illness, addiction, disability, loss, or other disruptive life event often seek out those who have been "in the same boat" to learn about the expectations, coping skills, available resources, options, and successes those persons had in facing that same challenge.

There are about 400 self-help groups for specific illnesses and disorders, and more are developing each year. They range from the Aarskog Syndrome Family Support Network to the Xeroderma Pigmentosum Society, from Arthritis Clubs across the country to the White Lung Association with local groups for asbestos victims and their families. There are many disability groups such as those for amputees or for people who are ventilator-dependent. There is the national Phoenix Society for burn victims and even a Lightning Strike and Electric Shock Survivors International organization, whose members work with medical professionals to assess effects on their long-term health. There are also survivor groups for victims of incest, sexual assault, and other crimes.

Because of the broad range of interests, there are very few human problems for which self-help groups cannot be used as a resource for referrals or as partners for patient education. Nurses, too, have formed self-help groups to deal with stress, such as one for nurses serving terminally ill and dying patients (Cullinan, 1992). Student-led support groups for nursing students have been developed for undergraduate students (Heinrich, Robinson, & Scales, 1998) and for graduate students (Hamrin, Weycer, Pachler, & Fournier, 2006), both of which have been evaluated as very helpful to students in coping better with the different stresses that they faced.

Mental Health

There are several national self-help groups for persons with depression or bipolar disorder and their families, most notably the national Depression and Bipolar Support Alliance (DBSA), which like most other national groups, provides interactive message boards and a wide variety of downloadable brochures, posters, and videos for patients, families, and professionals at their website, www.dbsalliance.org. As one example of their efforts to sensitize professionals to the experience of illness and treatment, with funding from SAMHSA, they produced a 19-minute video "Partners in Recovery: Creating Successful Practitioner-Consumer Alliances," viewable at www.stopstigma.samhsa.gov/partnersinrecovery.htm. Other groups that address depression and bipolar disorder include Recovery Inc., Depressed Anonymous, GROW, and Emotions Anonymous.

For those persons with a diagnosis of schizophrenia, the primary group available is Schizophrenics Anonymous, which provides a six-step program that members follow. There are also local self-help groups for persons with phobias, anxiety disorders, obsessive-compulsive disorders, or anorexia and bulimia.

NAMI, which has changed its name to the National Alliance on Mental Illness, has about 900 local self-help groups for families of those with a mental illness, but also now has 185 NAMI-CARE groups for **mental health consumers**. The national Federation of Families for Children's Mental Health has affiliated chapters with local support groups for parents of children and youth with emotional, behavioral, and mental health challenges. The local state parent organizations have also been developing mutual support groups for youth.

The National Institute of Mental Health, and later the Center for Mental Health Services, through the national Community Support Program first provided federal funding for annual national mental health consumer conferences in 1985. Subsequent funding has been provided for national technical assistance centers, research centers, and state programs that promote a wide variety of consumer-run centers and related services, of which local self-help and advocacy groups for mental health consumers are but one part of their accomplishments. For local self-help group information, visit the webpage of the National Mental Health Consumers' Self-Help Clearinghouse at www.cdsdirectory.org/programs.html#SupportGroup. For state contacts, which can also advise on local self-help groups, visit the webpage of the National Empowerment Center at www.power2u.org/consumer-run-statewide.html.

Similar to how the field of alcoholism treatment recognized the special value of employing those who were in recovery to serve as professional counselors, there has been increasing recognition of how "consumer/survivor providers" (Bluebird, 2004) can provide professional services as peer specialists based upon their firsthand knowledge of mental illness, recovery, and health-care system shortfalls.

A number of 12-step groups have been developed just for those persons with co-occurring disorders (such as recovering from alcohol/drug abuse and a mental illness). One study of members of 21 Double Trouble in Recovery groups in

The number of national self-help groups continues to increase as needs are identified.

Self-help groups help their members cope with a variety of illnesses, disabilities, and addictions, as well as bereavement, parenting, and many other stressful problems.

New York City found that drug/alcohol abstinence among surveyed members increased from 54% at baseline to 72% a year later (Magura et al., 2003). Other groups for co-occurring disorders that have local groups are Dual Recovery Anonymous, Dual Disorders Anonymous, and Dual Diagnosis Anonymous.

Parenting

There are hundreds of different groups for parents, including groups for single parents, adoptive parents, potentially abusive parents, and parents of children with special needs. The last group alone includes the Fetal Alcohol Network, for those caring for children with fetal alcohol syndrome; the Association of Birth Defect Children, for parents of children with defects due to environmental agents; and the National Father's Network, with local groups for fathers of special-needs children. Some groups address prevention, such as Sidelines, where mothers who had complicated pregnancies and premature births help high-risk expectant mothers.

A 12-step approach encourages members to follow a program based on learning and applying 12 steps, which are usually adapted from the 12 steps of Alcoholics Anonymous.

Bereavement

There are a wide variety of groups for adults who have lost a loved one, from young widowed persons (www.youngwidow.org) to adults who have lost a sibling (www.adultsiblinggrief.com). In many communities, there are unaffiliated, local groups open to any adult who has lost a loved one. Groups can be quite specific, such as COPS (Concerns of Police Survivors) for families of police killed in the line of duty, and the national Twinless Twin Support Group for those who have lost a twin. Compassionate Friends and Bereaved Parents of the USA are the two main national groups for parents who have lost a child. SHARE is one national group that helps parents who have experienced a miscarriage, stillborn, or early infant death. Self-help groups now exist just for parents who have lost children to sudden infant death syndrome, miscarriage, heart defects, drunk driving, murder, suicide, or a drug overdose. For those parents who have lost one or more children in multiple births, there are two international support networks; and there is one for parents who have lost an only child or all their children. A number of national groups have been started by parents who lost children to newborn disorders.

Addiction

In addition to those groups cited in Table 8-1, there are other groups like Crystal Meth Anonymous, Heroin Anonymous, Marijuana Anonymous, Nicotine Anonymous, Overeaters Anonymous (for compulsive overeating), Cleptomaniacs and Shoplifters Anonymous, and Workaholics Anonymous. There are also national addiction groups that have developed as alternatives to the 12-step approach, such as Secular Organizations for Sobriety and Women for Sobriety. For self-help groups for family and friends of addicts, there are national groups like Al-Anon, Alateen, Nar-Anon, Gam-Anon, Adult Children of Alcoholics, Families Anonymous, and S-Anon (sexual addiction).

"Hidden Clients"

A large number of groups exist for family members and friends, who are often "hidden clients" and whose own health can be adversely affected by the stress of an illness or stressful situation. We just reviewed groups dealing with addiction. For others, when family members are often the key caregivers and their well-being and support are crucial to the health outcome of the client, there are groups like the Well Spouse Association, adult children caring for elderly parents, and Siblings for Significant Change (siblings of those with a disability). There are also model groups, like Mothers Supporting Daughters with Breast Cancer in Maryland, that can be replicated in other parts of the country.

Rare Disorders

In addition to the groups for the vast majority of chronic illnesses, there are an ever-increasing number of rare disorder self-help groups. Their growth had been made possible primarily by the Internet and the ease with which one can start an online self-help network. Cardio-Facio-Cutaneous International was started in 1997 by the mother of a child with the very rare genetic disorder who developed an e-mail discussion group, and now has almost a hundred families worldwide. But a few rare disorder groups, once organized, seem to attract more members than original estimates had calculated; for example, the founder of the Ehlers-Danlos National Foundation noted how the incidence of E.D. syndrome had gone from 1 per 750,000, to 1 per 5,000 within 10 years. The groups feel their education of both professionals and the public regarding their disorders plays a key role in improved recognition of the disorder.

Disaster Recovery

Following both natural and man-made disasters, survivors have sometimes improvised their own self-help groups to help cope with the postdisaster turmoil and grief they face. In the case of natural disasters, the groups have usually taken the form of local community groups after a tornado, flood, or earthquake. With widespread destruction, some groups form in relocation areas, as with Hurricane Katrina in 2005, or in refugee camps. Man-made disasters include aviation and industrial accidents, fires, and war-related or terriorist incidents. Myers and Wee (2005) describe how self-help groups not only provide emotional support, practical information, and an enhanced sense of community, but also increase members' sense of control, political empowerment, and opportunities to help others. Myers and Wee go on to describe the importance and uniqueness of empathy provided by other survivors, noting how even with professionally run support groups,

> Trauma comes with its own unique constellation of suffering that can only really be grasped by others who are similarly affected. Regardless of the capacity for empathy of the facilitators, only other survivors know just how they feel. . . . The sense of being understood in this basic and profound way reduces isolation and is an essential ingredient of recovery. (pp. 216–217)

Some tragedies reflect a repeated cycle of surviors' willingness or need to reach out and help survivors of similar future disasters. For example, Betty Polec, who founded the Flight 255 Family Support Group after losing her daughter in the Detroit Airport crash in 1987, reached out to help Pan Am 103 families in late 1988. In turn, Pan Am 103 Families Group aided Heidi Snow, who lost her fiance in the 1996 TWA Flight 800 disaster, and went on to found the ongoing self-help group ACCESS (AirCraft Casualty Emotional Support Services) for those who lose a loved one in any type of air crash. As traumatologist Charles R. Figley noted,

> Trauma survivors . . . they become thrivers, and they become teachers. They can go back and remember various things, and answer all those questions we have. They have hope, and they have sense, and the ability to care about other people . . . to look into the eyes of others who have gone through the things that they have gone through, and to be at peace with that, and to show that they did it. (Gift from Within, 2001)

Other Stressful Life Situations

Self-help groups have developed to help people with a range of other potential difficulties such as for divorce, job layoffs, career changes, sexual orientation, being an incest survivor, or another type of crime victim. There are also general women's groups and men's groups that examine the concerns that members raise. There are also cultural variations; for example, for stay-at-home mothers of color, there is the national network of groups Mocha Moms, and for African American breast cancer survivors there is the national Sisters Network.

Characteristics of Self-Help Groups

Mutual Help

Self-help groups can be more appropriately described as mutual-help groups, because this is the primary way that members help one another within their self-help group or network. Mutual help is usually provided as members share their experiences, strengths, and hopes in small, face-to-face group meetings. Since the mid-1990s, an increasing number of new types of self-help networks have developed on the Internet. As many national and international self-help groups established an online presence, they started online self-help networks of their own.

Member-Run

Groups are run by their members, not professionals, although professional assistance is often provided. In one of the very first books on self-help groups, Katz (1961) used the term *self-organized groups* to describe what later became known as self-help groups. Because self-help groups are member-run, they provide a true sense of community and feeling of belonging. In being member-run, they are also more sensitive and responsive to their members' needs.

A self-help network provides mutual help to members through an interactive newsletter, correspondence, telephone, video, or online exchange.

Composed of Peers

Members share the same problem or experience. They know that others in the group understand because "they have been there." These groups aid in learning, because people can assimilate new knowledge better when it is presented by peers (Stewart, 1990b).

Self-help groups provide social support, education, and sometimes advocacy. Education consists of the practical information, successful coping techniques, and related "experiential knowledge" pooled from members' shared experiences.

Nonprofit

There are no fees and only minimal dues to sustain support costs, if any. The group is nonproprietary. Self-help group members were first referred to as being "prosumers" (Toffler, 1980) in that they develop services for themselves, rather than being only consumers of another's service.

Primary Functions

All self-help groups perform two major functions: support and education. Some groups take on an additional third function: advocacy.

Advocacy promotes a specific educational, political, or social cause or change in the community or society.

Social Support

In one of the increasing number of studies showing the health-related benefits of social support, Duke University researchers who examined the value of social support to the life expectancy of cardiac clients concluded that "a support group may be as effective as costly medical treatment. Simply put, having someone to talk to is very powerful medicine" (Brody, 1992, p. C12). Clients and their families report finding comfort and relief from isolation when they finally meet with peers in a group. Some describe it as an instant sense of community. They receive stress-buffering support from others who truly understand their problems and emotions. Support is often provided between meetings through buddy systems, phone calls, newsletters, e-mail contacts, social events, and sometimes through home and hospital visitation programs. As one group leader expressed it, "The heart of our message is 'You are not alone.' Our strength has come from sharing our experiences and giving hope to others."

Education

When group members share what has and has not worked for them, they actually develop a collective wisdom or "experiential knowledge" (Borkman, 1975) base, drawn from members' pooling their experiences around the common challenges they have faced. Members share the practical coping skills and resource information that they have found helpful in coping on a daily basis with a chronic illness, disability, or other stressful life problem. Quist (1989, p. 89) observes that, in groups of those caring for elderly relatives, "many caregivers are ingenious when it comes to devising solutions to their problems." Members' experiences, coping strategies, and successes provide other members with a range of options for problem solving and help new members realize that they are not helpless.

Members discuss and evaluate professional and social services (e.g., entitlements, housing, health care, legal information, and employment) and learn how to negotiate the systems. Groups are adept at collecting educational and journal articles and at tapping professional knowledge bases. Groups that are open to professional involvement at meetings frequently have professionals as guest speakers to share their insights, perspectives, and engage in discussion and joint learning. Some groups also discover their "strength in numbers" ability to tap professionals for their knowledge by having them as free guest speakers, or for training workshops, contributions to group newsletters and websites, and in service on advisory boards. Such interactions can foster additional collaboration in education, treatment, and research development efforts.

Critical Thinking Question Consider how "experiential knowledge" is often first articulated by clients and then used by practitioners to improve the quality of a business, health care, or other service delivery. Can you think of an example?

Advocacy

Many, but not all, groups engage in advocacy to address needs that cannot be met within the group, such as deficiencies that may exist in the healthcare system or the larger society. Advocates work to educate the public or professionals about the lack of awareness of a disorder, lack of treatment or rehabilitation services, or the presence of discrimination. Local groups often support national and international advocacy efforts. For example, self-help groups for persons with disabilities successfully advocated passage of the Americans with Disabilities Act, and Mothers Against Drunk Driving (MADD) have worked for tougher laws to reduce drunk driving. However, 12-step groups do not engage in advocacy efforts because of their tradition of not endorsing or lending their name to outside interests. It was strongly felt that such actions would divert them from their primary purpose, and introduce controversial issues that might divide their membership.

How Groups Help

A variety of dynamics common to self-help groups contribute to their vitality, popularity, and effectiveness.

Helper Therapy

The basic concept behind the helper-therapy principle (Riessman, 1965) is that those who help others gain special benefits themselves. In helping others, the helper experiences an increased sense of self-worth and self-esteem, often when it is most needed. The act of helping others also reinforces for the helper the principles, learning points, and/or program that the helper is following. Helpers develop a firmer understanding of their own recovery process and goals when helping others, as expressed in slogans sometimes heard in 12-step groups, such as, "If you help someone up the hill, you get closer to the top yourself." Even new members can experience the "helper's high" or increased sense of belonging when they listen to others and simply acknowledge with a nod to them that they truly understand what that person is saying. Through helper therapy, most groups turn what society considers a liability (i.e., one's experience as an addict, a widow, or a person with an illness) into an asset (that member's unique ability to provide help to others).

Helping others within the group has been reported as one of the more important benefits that members receive from their participation in the group (Bacon, Condon, & Fernsler, 2000; Fernsler & Manchester, 1997; Knight, 2006). In a study of members of self-help groups for co-occurring disorders, the experience of the helper-therapy process was associated with increases in abstinence from drug and/or alcohol abuse (Magura et al., 2003).

Clinical Example

Some self-help groups have developed in response to the need for advocacy. For example, International Nurses Anonymous (www.intnursesanon.org) was started in 1988 in response to the special problems of nurses in recovery from chemical dependency. Nurses were regularly being denied licenses if they simply acknowledged that they were recovering alcoholics. INA developed as a fellowship of RNs, LPNs, and nursing students who were already in 12-step groups, but wanted to support and advocate for each other. Many other fellowships have developed for health professionals, such as Anesthetists in Recovery, a national support network for recovering nurse anesthetists; International Doctors in AA; and International Pharmacists Anonymous.

Clinical Example

Miguel is a 35-year-old married man who was admitted to the hospital with a blood alcohol level over 350. While hospitalized and treated for withdrawal symptoms, Miguel tells hospital staff that he feels lonely and isolated. Separated from his family, with no legal status in the United States, Miguel has been working long hours in order to send money to his family back home. He is frustrated because of the separation from his family and his inability to speak English. Staff have encouraged him to recognize the need to abstain from alcohol, and Miguel expresses a desire to stop drinking. The nurse is able to contact AA/Intergroup and find a meeting for Miguel in his own language and in his own neighborhood.

Positive Role Models

Experienced or veteran members demonstrate to new members that success, coping, and recovery are possible. They model competence and attest to how the problems that members face can be overcome. Their example and actions often provide needed encouragement and the installation of hope that otherwise is not available, because such role models are rarely found in agency settings or outside the group. The observance of role models by new members encourages them to assume more responsible action and pursue further learning.

Accessibility

Because there are no fees, groups are financially accessible. Many groups are geographically accessible in the community and schedule meeting times that are more convenient than most professional services. They also are psychologically more accessible in several ways. In the many anonymous 12-step groups, last names are not given. Most groups require no registration. One can go to a group simply for education, which is much more affordable both emotionally and financially than having to assume the role of patienthood for mental health treatment. Yet these self-help groups often "grease the skids" for needed referrals of individuals to professional treatment services by both destigmatizing problems and explaining the true

Clinical Example

Lara is a 29-year-old married woman who speaks of feeling depressed over the last few weeks. She has had difficulty sleeping, and has experienced a loss of appetite. Except for the delivery of an abnormal stillborn baby a little over a year ago, her medical history was unremarkable. Lara tells the nurse in the clinic she feels as if she has been managing well, and she does not want to burden her family by telling them how she feels. She does not feel as if anyone understands the loss she has experienced. The nurse points out that sometimes people re-experience feelings of loss around the anniversary of the event. In reinforcing how her feelings are normal, the nurse discusses options for referral including referral to a self-help group composed of other women who have experienced a similar loss.

benefits and processes of professional treatment, as only those who have experienced it can.

Normalization

For many people, the experience of illness, disability, or trauma results in isolation and alienation. After new members meet with others who have similar experiences, they often report feeling "normal" again. People are comforted by knowing that their experiences and feelings are not unusual. They also can satisfy their human need for basic feedback as to how they are doing in comparison with others.

Alternatives

As members pool experiences, literature, and problem-solving skills, they are exposed to a range of different coping strategies and options for dealing with their individual situation. This can be especially helpful for new members who come to a meeting feeling helpless and hopeless.

Clinical Example

One example of the dedication of group members occurred in the wake of the September 11, 2001, terrorist attack on the World Trade Center. Members of the Oklahoma City bombing Family Support Group, the Victims of Pan Am 103 family group, and the Beirut Connection for families of the marines killed in the terrorist barracks bombing in Lebanon volunteered to travel at their own expense to comfort families who had lost loved ones in the 9/11 attack. In several meetings in the months after the tragedy, they consoled 9/11 families and assured them, as no one else could, that although the pain of their loss would never go away, it would ease and they would once again be able to experience joy in life.

Prevention Equation

To varying degrees, self-help groups serve a preventive function by enhancing social ties and connections that serve as a buffer to stress and by promoting the ability of people to cope with stress and adversity for many of life's transitions and crises. Silverman (1985) points out that although many stressful life transitions cannot be prevented, the mutual-help group may be one of the more powerful modalities for facilitating the acquisition of coping skills subsequent to stress. Albee's prevention equation (1982) theorizes how groups help prevent or lessen the incidence of psychopathology and stress-related illness by strengthening social support, coping skills, and competence:

$$\text{Incidence of dysfunction} = \frac{\text{stress} + \text{constitutional vulnerabilities}}{\text{social support} + \text{coping skills} + \text{competence}}$$

Although the literature on social support already reflects how such support improves health status and lowers mortality rates, additional research in the field of **psychoneuroimmunology** may be expected to contribute a clearer understanding of how the social support of an understanding and caring community strengthens immune system resistance and improves health (Stewart, 1990a).

Empowerment

Group members are empowered not only because they learn by doing, but also because they are changed by doing (Hedrick, Isenberg, & Martini, 1992). Seeing how others have taken responsibility for their health and recovery encourages members to take responsibility to educate themselves, become self-reliant, change their lifestyles, gain valuable self-advocacy skills, and support others. This, along with any group advocacy efforts, contributes to an increased sense of personal and collective efficacy.

Source of Altruism and Meaning

Some members remain in self-help groups long after they themselves have been helped, because they find the work in helping others personally satisfying and rewarding. In many groups, including those for persons with terminal illness, members report that the group has helped them to find new meaning, direction, or spirituality in their lives. Frankl (1959, p. 116) noted,

> We must never forget that we may also find meaning in life even when confronted with a hopeless situation, when facing a fate that cannot be changed. For what then matters is to bear witness to the uniquely human potential at its best, which is to transform a personal tragedy into a triumph, to turn one's predicament into a human achievement.

Growth of Online Self-Help Networks

The number of online self-help networks has increased dramatically over the last decade; for example, Yahoo! Groups recently indicated that 34,851 e-mail groups were available under the "Support" heading of their Health & Wellness category (http://groups.yahoo.com). Although the average American can choose from among several dozen different face-to-face self-help groups in his or her local area, Internet access allows that same person to participate in any one of thousands of different online self-help groups. At the same time, a Pew Internet study found that at least half of the American adult population has already turned to the Internet to seek health information, making it the third most popular online activity (Fox & Fallows, 2003).

Online computer systems are removing many of the barriers that previously prevented people from participating in a community self-help group, including the lack of any local group, an individual's lack of transportation to an existing group, the limitations of disabilities or chronic illnesses that prevent access to community groups, 24-hour-a-day caregiver or parenting responsibilities, and the rarity of an illness or condition that made it previously impossible to draw together enough people to have a local meeting (Bacon, Condon, & Fernsler, 2000). Expanding Internet access has prompted the development of new self-help groups not previously available in the community, such as support groups for men with breast cancer, for people facing hip replacement surgery, or for those with agoraphobia. It is not unusual to read a message posted that says, "I've never before talked to people with my disorder."

The three primary ways that people currently participate in online self-help groups are through website message boards or forums, e-mail discussion groups or electronic mailing lists, and live chat room meetings. The most prevalent form of online mutual help is the message threads found on various website message boards. These messages are often displayed as discussion threads, which are similar to self-help group discussions but evolve in slower motion. Unlike real-time group discussions, these responses are usually carefully and thoughtfully prepared offline before being posted. This asynchronous dialogue, available 24/7, is often richer than real-time meeting exchanges. One example is the Totally Hip website and discussion board (www.totallyhip.org), developed by a woman who went through two hip replacement surgeries. There are more than 800 registered members, including those anticipating the surgery who can learn from those who have been through it. Questions are answered by members—some of whom are physicians who have gone through the surgery—whose fears are addressed, and practical solutions to common problems are shared. Contacts between online members from the same area have even led to the development of several local community self-help groups.

> Online self-help networks are growing, eliminating many barriers that previously kept people from developing or participating in a community group. They primarily take the form of interactive websites, e-mail discussion groups, newsgroups, and commercial forums or conferences.

Second, there are e-mail discussion groups or listservs that allow subscribing members to send and receive messages using e-mail. Each message and every response is sent to all subscribers as individual e-mails, or as one daily digest that compiles all messages of the previous day into one e-mail message. One good example is the Association of Cancer Oncology Resources (www.ACOR.org), which has over 140 separate e-mail discussion groups dealing with specific cancers and some caregiver situations (such as partners of breast cancer patients, or those facing the death of a loved one). ACOR, which was started by the husband of a cancer patient after he found e-mail discussion groups to be very helpful to him and his wife but not easy to locate, generates over 1.5 million individual e-mail messages shared by members each week. Ferguson (2000) describes how one cancer patient, having been aided by an ACOR e-mail list, developed a very comprehensive website for lung cancer patients, where she works with leading physicians to help promote patient awareness of their work.

Third, there are online chat rooms where groups meet in real time mostly for group discussion or, in fewer cases, for a guest speaker or resource person. Meetings are often scheduled for evenings or weekends. One example is the National Ataxia Foundation (www.ataxia.org), which has been having three real-time group meetings scheduled at the same time each week for several years. The foundation also has a message board or bulletin for exchanges at other times.

Although online support networks lack some attributes of face-to-face self-help groups (nonverbal communication such as handshakes, hugs, and human presence), they do provide mutual support, information, a sense of belonging, and medical and resource referrals as needed. Lieberman, Golant, Winzelberg, McTavish, & Gustafson (2003–2004) studied differences among several different professionally run and "self-directed" or self-help online groups for breast cancer patients, and determined that groups conducted by professionals expressed significantly more negative emotions, anxiety, hostility, and depression, and fewer positive emotions than self-directed groups. The researchers noted that professionals had encouraged the greater expression of negative emotions in their groups because the open expression of such emotions has been shown to be beneficial, whereas the lay leaders more often responded with support and reassurance to members who expressed painful emotions.

A study of one online support network found that most respondents rated as most helpful the group's ability to help them "put cancer in perspective," obtain needed information, lessen their "sense of isolation," and permit them "to help others" (Fernsler & Manchester, 1997). In a study of one online group for parents of children with special needs, "the majority of participants not only obtained what they sought, but found more than expected in terms of insight and people to trust" (Baum, 2004, p. 29).

In assessing the validity of an online self-help network, one should check that the online community is nonproprietary, provides mutual help, is run primarily by peers, and is alive as a vibrant and caring community. This can be done primarily by reviewing the messages to see that postings are current, responded to, and of a caring and helpful nature. In the case of e-mail discussion lists, one can review the archive of messages. But ultimately, just as one should be routinely assessing client feedback on community groups, one should similarly be requesting feedback on whether particular online support networks are meeting clients' needs.

In addition to the online self-help networks, the vast majority of traditional national and international self-help groups now have websites with message boards and/or e-mail lists. As the availability and popularity of online services continues to grow, more patients will be seeking online peer support.

Clinical Example

Deanna is a 24-year-old single mother of three who is hospitalized with renal insufficiency. She is newly diagnosed with systemic lupus erythematosus (SLE). She mentions to the staff that because she has three young children it is difficult for her to find time under normal circumstances to leave home without the children and find a babysitter. One thing she enjoys doing is keeping in touch with her family and friends using the computer. Deanna is eager to learn about SLE. As part of patient teaching at discharge, the nurse discusses possible referral to an online support group in addition to other referrals for follow-up care.

Roles for Nurses

Identify and Refer to Groups

Identifying local groups is not always an easy task, but some areas of the country and the world are served by local **self-help clearinghouses** (such as http://www.mentalhelp.net/selfhelp/selfhelp.php?id=859), which provide local group contacts and sometimes online or hardcopy directories. If a local clearinghouse is not available, local help lines and mental health associations can sometimes provide group contacts and listings. The American Self-Help Clearinghouse provides a keyword-searchable database of over 1,100 national, international, model, and online self-help groups at its website (http://mentalhelp.net/selfhelp). There one enters a keyword, and then is provided any national group website, where access to information on the existing local groups is usually available. Group brochures, publications, newsletters, conference announcements and reports, and videos are increasingly available via download, and/or they may be ordered online.

Groups have different problem-solving approaches, not all of which are a good fit for all clients. Some groups have spiritual overtones, which may make some clients uncomfortable. Gray (1996) notes that some patients cope best with their illness by being alone, and that their need for solitude should be respected. When providing information to a client or family member, it is appropriate to mention the potential value of the group and how the group has been helpful to others, but note how only the individual client can determine if the group is right for him or her.

Self-help groups are not regulated or credentialed, which has made it possible for groups to be started by lay persons and operate with no fees. Groups both in the community and online are in various stages of development and decline. A group may have difficulty recruiting members or retaining adequate leadership. Therefore, it is appropriate to routinely request client feedback as to whether the local self-help group has proven helpful. If not found helpful, determine whether any problem was experienced that may be threatening the group's ability to help its members.

Liaison

If a nurse often works with clients with a certain disorder or problem, he or she can request or order literature from appropriate local groups, post meeting notices, and keep a supply or display of brochures on hand. They can also consider subscribing to the group's newsletter and establishing an ongoing liaison. When nurses provide referrals, local groups sometimes reciprocate by distributing agency materials and providing referrals to the professional health services.

Resource Person

Some local groups invite professionals to speak to their members. Nurses may offer to speak or help to identify speakers. They may help the group meet its needs for professional advisers, consultants, researchers, or special services. It is important to determine group needs that an agency might meet, such as providing meeting space, help with mailings, photocopying, or secretarial help.

Education

Group representatives can be invited to provide an overview of their work and issues at staff meetings or to speak at in-service training sessions, workshops, or conferences. Group members bring real experiences and personal insights to education. Linking groups with other community agencies might be considered. Some groups have a special interest in doing outreach focused on prevention of specific health problems, such as laryngectomy groups speaking on smoking cessation in schools or spinal cord injury groups speaking on pool or driver safety.

When planning new programs, nurses might consider delivering them within the framework of a support group. For example, Alexander (1983) brought together mothers with similar child care concerns as part of a community health education program. Group discussions were based on the needs and priorities of the mothers, which took precedence over planned instruction. The staff and mothers were partners rather than providers and receivers. As a result, there were fewer unnecessary emergency visits, and valuable knowledge and sensitivity to families' functioning were gained by the staff.

Nurses can make clients aware of groups, serve as resource persons to groups in multiple ways, tap groups for various educational efforts, and help develop needed new groups.

Development

Nurses are in a favorable position to identify, encourage, and link people who could join with others to start a local self-help group. Nurses are

Considerations for Client and Family Education

- Self-help groups can be a valuable resource for mutual support and education.
- Participation in a self-help group can provide an opportunity to develop alternate coping strategies.
- Roles within a self-help group vary and participants can find ways to help and advocate for themselves and others.
- When contact with others with similar problems or access to services is difficult, online self-help groups and support networks are a valuable source of support and information.

Implications for Evidence-Based Practice

One of the first published nursing journal articles on the self-help group phenomenon recognized that nurses could serve as helpful resource persons. However, it cautioned against benign cooptation: "We are convinced that direct nursing intervention in self-help groups should be avoided [since it] certainly would interfere with the operation of the helper-therapy principle" (Bumbalo & Young, 1973, p. 1591). Further research should also include a differentiation of roles for nurses working with self-help groups and include predictive studies as to the effect of nurse participation.

Implications for Evidence-Based Practice

Group representatives can be invited to speak to nursing students about their work and their experience of illness. In a survey of 26 university schools of nursing, Stewart (1990b) reported her conclusion that experiential learning opportunities for nurses could include more direct involvement or linkage with self-help groups and greater preparation of nurses as partners and consultants with groups. Another option to help students better understand the value, dynamics, and facilitation skills involved in a self-help group could be to help students co-facilitate their own student-run groups. Heinrich, Robinson, & Scales (1998) found that such experiences in developing caring communities not only enlightened students about group theory and dynamics, but also gave them "an appreciation for the power of nurses supporting nurses that they are applying in their clinical settings." Findings from these studies emphasized the benefits for the nurse in participating in self-help groups. Further research could focus on varied samples and longitudinal investigations. It is possible that nurses exposed to self-help groups as students will be more likely to refer clients to self-help groups or be involved in groups themselves.

Implications for Evidence-Based Practice

Trupin (1993) and other nurses noticed and substantiated the declining health status of grandparents who were raising their grandchildren full time because of the crack addiction of the children's parents. Because of the success of the first grandparents' support groups, which helped members cope and promoted needed legislation, training sessions in group facilitation were held for interested members to run additional groups. Further studies could investigate the development of needs assessment for other groups and the involvement of nurses in identifying the needs of various client groups.

often the first to recognize common unmet needs among clients.

In terms of productivity, a health professional can help start several self-help groups serving different patient and community health needs in less time than it takes for that same professional to plan and lead just one group by themselves for a year. Moreover, those ongoing self-help groups can provide a greater spectrum of empowering and supportive benefits, often to many more members, long after that professional is no longer available.

After a local need is identified, the nurse could determine if a national or model self-help group exists to meet that need. The group headquarters could then be contacted for how-to materials, suggestions, and possible referrals. If a local self-help group clearinghouse is available, it can be contacted for help in this process. Through personal contacts and other outreach, two or more people who are willing to start, not just join, the group should be identified. Recruitment efforts might piggyback with educational sessions, workshops, or conferences provided for that particular population. Once identified, the potential cofounders can share the responsibilities of planning, publicizing, and running the first meetings with the help of the nurse. To promote self-help group leadership, the nurse serves as a consultant in the development of the group, providing encouragement and suggestions, but defers decision making and leadership to the group. As Halper (1984) notes, once the group functions independently, the nurse may offer to continue as a resource person.

The key to group vitality is the members' sense of ownership. The more that the members feel the group is theirs, the more responsibility they assume, and the more time and effort they invest in their own group's success. If they perceive that the group belongs to a professional or an institution, they will be much more passive, expecting the staff person and agency to run the group.

Summary

Self-help groups continue to grow because they meet needs for support, education, and advocacy. Better understanding, use, and support of these community and online resources by nurses can help them to better meet their patients' and communities' health needs.

Annotated References

Adamsen, L., & Rasmussen, J. M. (2003). Exploring and encouraging through social interaction: A qualitative study of nurses' participation in self-help groups for cancer patients. *Cancer Nursing, 26*(1), 28–36.

This study explored the experiences oncology nurses had with cancer patients and self-help groups, reflecting how nurses function as social networkers encouraging relationships between patients and the formation of informal self-help groups for patients with cancer.

Albee, G. W. (1982). Preventing psychopathology and promoting human potential. *American Psychologist, 37*, 1043–1050.

Dr. Albee was a leading authority on prevention. Here he reviews various theories, reflecting on their value and potential implementation.

Alexander, J. S. (1983). Support group for mothers. *American Journal of Nursing, 83*, 1702.

This text describes how a support group helped nurses to learn more about the mothers' culture and problems, reduced unnecessary emergency room visits, and supplemented the nurses' role in patient education.

Bacon, E. S., Condon, E. H., & Fernsler, J. I. (2000). Young widows' experience with an Internet self-help group. *Journal of Psychosocial Nursing and Mental Health Services, 38*(7), 24–33.

The authors researched perceptions of members of one online group. They determined that the group was useful in reducing isolation and helping members to cope. The article suggests that nurses can guide their patients to Internet support groups for self-care when traditional groups are not available.

Baum, L. S. (2004). Internet parent support groups for primary caregivers of a child with special health care needs. *Pediatric Nursing, 30*(5), 381–388.

An exploratory study of 114 parents/caregivers who participated in online groups reflected that they had found more than they expected in terms of insight and people to trust. The strongest outcome factor was related to their satisfaction with an improved caregiver-child relationship.

Bluebird, G. (2004). Redefining consumer roles: Changing culture and practice in mental health care settings. *Journal of Psychosocial Nursing and Mental Health Services, 42*(9), 46–53.

This article explains how professionals who have personal experience in recovery from mental illness can uniquely serve as positive role models, instilling hope and empowering patients, while also responding to systemic deficiencies of which they may have firsthand knowledge.

Borkman, T. (1975). Experiential knowledge: A new concept for the analysis of self-help groups. *Social Service Review, 50*, 445–456.

This is an in-depth analysis of experiential knowledge, how self-help groups develop it, and how it differs from professional knowledge.

Brody, J. E. (1992, February 5). Personal health: Maintaining friendships for the sake of your health. *New York Times*, p. C12.

This is a review of research studies that have shown the value of social support to surviving health challenges.

Bumbalo, J. A., & Young, D. E. (1973). The self-help phenomenon. *American Journal of Nursing, 73*, 1588–1591.

This is an early nursing article that describes the dynamics and benefits of self-help groups, as well as what health professionals can learn from them.

Cullinan, A. L. (1992). The impact of a self-help group on nurses and their dying patients. In A. H. Katz, H. L. Hedrick, D. H. Isenberg, L. M. Thompson, T. Goodrich, & A. H. Kutscher (Eds.), *Self-help: Concepts and applications* (pp. 97–104). Philadelphia: Charles Press.

This chapter describes the development of a support group for nurses to help them cope with the stresses of working with terminal patients.

Ferguson, T. (2000). Online patient-helpers and physicians working together: A new partnership for high quality health care. *British Medical Journal, 321*, 1129–1132.

Dr. Ferguson describes the value of an online website for lung cancer, developed by a cancer survivor. The article speaks to the growing demand for online health information, and the benefits to physicians aiding patients in their efforts and working with online patient helpers.

Fernsler, J. I., & Manchester, L. J. (1997). Evaluation of a computer-based cancer support network. *Cancer Practice, 5*, 46–51.

This article compiles the results of a study conducted by two nurses, one of whom had cancer, and initiated the research of the Compuserve Cancer Forum.

Fox S., & Fallows, D. (2003). *Internet health resources: Health searches and email have become more commonplace, but there is room for improvement in searches and overall Internet access.* Washington, DC: Pew Internet & American Life Project. Retrieved August 14, 2007, from http://www.pewinternet.org/PPF/r/95/report_display.asp

This article reviews the impact of Internet searches and intervention on health care consumers' behavior and choices. The PEW Internet & American Life Project is one source of search engines that provides reports on the impact and trends of the Internet on daily life including use of peer-to-peer networks, resources to make health care decisions, and public opinion.

Frankl, V. E. (1959). *Man's search for meaning.* New York: Beacon Press.

This is an account of a psychiatrist's dehumanizing experiences in Nazi death camps that led to his development of logo therapy, a form of existential analysis.

Gift from Within. (2001). *Recovering from traumatic events: The healing process* (video). Camden, Maine: Gift from Within.

Narrated by members of International Society for Traumatic Stress Studies, who discuss practical approaches to recovery, with survivors recounting their experiences and recovery. It reflects how survivors can learn to be "thrivers," and then teachers of the healing process.

Gray, J. (1996). HIV report: Meeting psychosocial needs. *RN, 59*, 23–27.

This article describes the stresses of acquired immunodeficiency syndrome (AIDS) as a progressive illness and how group peer support is one resource.

Halper, J. (1984). Multiple sclerosis and self-help: New roles for nursing. *Journal of Community Health Nursing, 3*, 153–157.

This article, based upon nurses' experiences in starting several multiple sclerosis groups, outlines roles nurses can play in developing groups.

Hamrin, V., Weycer, A., Pachler, M., & Fournier, D. (2006). Evaluation of peer-led support groups for graduate nursing students. *Journal of Nursing Education, 45*(1), 39–43.

This article describes how peer support groups were developed and evaluated, based upon the students' group therapy training and Yalom's interpersonal group therapy model.

Hedrick, H. L., Isenberg, D. H., & Martini, C. J. (1992). Self-help groups: Empowerment through policy and partnerships. In A. H. Katz, H. L. Hedrick, D. H. Isenberg, L. M. Thompson, T. Goodrich, & A. H. Kutscher (Eds.), *Self-help: Concepts and applications* (pp. 3–55). Philadelphia: Charles Press.

This is a review of the value and dynamics of self-help groups and related national policy recommendations. It includes descriptions of self-help clearinghouses.

Heinrich, K. T., Robinson, C. M., & Scales, M. E. (1998). Support groups: An empowering, experiential strategy. *Nurse Educator, 23*(4), 8–10.

A description of RN-BSN student-run support groups that students reported as helpful to their understanding of group theory, a greater appreciation for the value of nurses helping nurses, and an increased willingness to utilize such groups in future work settings.

Hildingh, C., Fridlund B., & Segesten, K. (1995). Cardiac nurses' preparedness to use self-help groups as a support strategy. *Journal of Advanced Nursing, 22*(5), 921–928.

This study examined nurses' knowledge of social support and self-help groups. It concluded that lack of knowledge of social support and self-help groups affected the nurses' attitudes towards lay care and was probably the reason for not using self-help groups as a support strategy.

Katz, A. H. (1961). *Parents of the handicapped.* Springfield, IL: Charles C Thomas.

This is the first book to describe the earliest self-help groups that evolved into national organizations of parents who have children with specific disabilities.

Kessler, R. C, Frank, R. G., Edlund, M., Katz, S. J., Lin, E., & Leaf, P. (1997). Differences in the use of psychiatric outpatient services between the United States and Ontario. *New England Journal of Medicine, 336*(8), 551–557.

An international study that examined the types of outpatient services utilized for psychiatric problems in the United States and Ontario, which revealed a high percentage of visits to self-help groups by Americans when compared to other specialty professional services.

Kessler, R. C., Mickelson, K. D., & Zhao, S. (1997). Patterns and correlates of self-help group membership in the United States. *Social Policy, 27*, 27–46.

This article describes a major national study of self-help group membership.

Knight, E. L. (2006). Self-help and serious mental illness. *Medscape General Medicine, 8*(1), 68. Retrieved August 14, 2007, from http://www.medscape.com/viewarticle/519009

This article provides a review of various reports and studies that have examined the meaning and value of self-help groups, primarily for persons who have serious mental illnesses.

Koop, C. E. (1992). Foreword. In A. H. Katz, H. L. Hedrick, D. H. Isenberg, L. M. Thompson, T. Goodrich, & A. H. Kutscher (Eds.), *Self-help: Concepts and applications* (pp. xvii–xviii). Philadelphia: Charles Press.

Dr. Koop briefly points out the need for cooperation between self-help groups and organized medicine to achieve the best health care for the lowest cost.

Law, M., King, S., Stewart, D., & King, G. (2001). The perceived effects of parent-led support groups for parents of children with disabilities. *Physical & Occupational Therapy in Pediatrics, 21*(2/3), 29–48.

A qualitative study of members of nine groups indicated that the effects of belonging to a parent-led parent support group were substantial. Parents reported increased skills in dealing with day-to-day issues, an increased sense of power, support, and a sense of belonging.

Lieberman, M. A., Golant, M., Winzelberg, A., McTavish, F., & Gustafson, D. H. (2003–2004). Comparisons: Professionally-directed and self-directed Internet groups for women with breast cancer. *International Journal of Self Help and Self Care, 2*(3), 219–235.

Researchers compared support group messages from professionally run and self-directed online groups for women with breast cancer, and found professionally run groups expressed significantly more negative emotions and fewer positive emotions than self-directed ones.

Magura S., Laudet, A. B., Mahmood, D., Rosenblum, A., Vogel, H. S., & Knight, E. L. (2003). Role of self-help processes in achieving abstinence among dually diagnosed persons. *Addictive Behaviors, 28*(3), 399–413.

This study found that drug/alcohol abstinence among members of 21 Double Trouble in Recovery groups increased from 54% at baseline to 72% a year later. Helper-therapy and reciprocal-learning activities within the group were associated with better abstinence outcomes.

Myers, D., & Wee, D. F. (2005). *Disaster mental health services.* New York: Brunner-Routledge.

Chapter 6, "Support Groups in Disaster Mental Health Programs," discusses the use of self-help groups as one form of support group that provides opportunities for emotional support and information sharing, helping others, maintaining personal sense of control, and increasing political involvement.

National Public Radio. (2003, August 19). "All Things Considered": Post-traumatic stress disorder. Retrieved August 14, 2007, from http://www.npr.org/templates/story/story.php?storyId=1401789

NPR's Alix Spiegel traces the creation of the concept of posttraumatic stress disorder. He interviews Vietnam War veteran Jack Smith regarding his group's action in taking the head of the Veterans Administration hostage for a teach-in. Psychiatrists Robert Jay Lifton and Art Blank, who were invited to the group's meetings, are also interviewed.

Quist, J. C. (1989). RN at home: Helping a caregiver keep up the good work. *RN, 52*, 87–91.

This article explains how support groups can help nurses to lighten the load of caregivers.

Riessman, F. (1965). The helper therapy principle. *Social Work, 10*, 26–32.

This article examines the various benefits derived when people with a problem help others with the same problem, as originally reflected in student tutoring programs but especially found in self-help groups.

Silverman, P. (1985). Tertiary/secondary prevention-preventive intervention: The case for mutual help groups. In R. K. Conyne (Ed.), *The group workers' handbook* (pp. 237–258). Springfield, IL: Charles C Thomas.

This chapter presents ways in which self-help groups contribute to prevention and reduce the risk of relapse.

Snyder, M. D., & Weyer, M. E. (2000). Collaboration and partnership: Nursing education and self-help groups. *Nursing Connections, 13*(1), 5–12.

This article describes the development of a collaborative partnership between a psychiatric nursing course and Recovery, Inc., which afforded undergraduate students a better appreciation of the role of self-help groups and provided some students with personal insights into the universality of the human experience.

Stewart, M. (1990a). Expanding theoretical conceptualizations of self-help groups. *Social Science & Medicine, 31*(9), 1057–1066.

The author provides a review of the theoretical underpinnings related to self-help group benefits, with special attention to social support, social learning, and psychoneuroimmunology.

Stewart, M. (1990b). Professional interface with mutual-aid self-help groups: A review. *Social Science & Medicine, 31*(10), 1143–1158.

Dr. Stewart at the School of Nursing at Dalhousie University in Halifax examined empirical studies and concludes that the consultant role appears most supportive of self-help groups.

Toffler, A. (1980). *The third wave.* New York: William Morrow.

A futurist analyzes the different forces contributing to a third stage in the development of civilization, following the agricultural and industrial revolutions.

Trupin, S. (1993). Moral support for grandparents who care: A nursing success story. *American Journal of Nursing, 93*, 52–56.

This article reflects how nurses identified a need and provided training and facilitation assistance to develop groups that address advocacy needs.

U.S. Department of Health and Human Services. (1988). *Surgeon general's workshop on self-help and public health.* Washington, DC: Author.

This report contains plenary session presentations on self-help groups, proposed national recommendations, and Dr. Koop's response to them.

Additional Resources

Humphreys, K., & Moos, R. H. (2007). Encouraging posttreatment self-help group involvement to reduce demand for continuing care services: Two-year clinical and utilization outcomes. *Alcoholism Clinical and Experimental Research, 31*(1), 64–68.

This study of male substance-dependent patients showed that those referred for aftercare to 12-step-based self-help groups showed a higher rate of drug abstinence after two years and a cost savings for care related to less frequent use of out-patient and in-patient mental health services.

Katz, A. H., & Bender, E. I. (Eds.). (1998). *The strength in us.* New York: New Viewpoints.

This is a classic review of early history that focuses on the workings of several different groups worldwide.

Miller Resnick, W. (1988). *The manual for affective disorder support groups.* Baltimore: The Depression and Related Affective Disorders Association.

This is a how-to guide, written by a registered nurse, for starting one of the most requested types of support group.

White, B. J., & Madara, E. J. (Eds.). (2002). *Self-help group sourcebook* (7th ed.). Denville, NJ: Self Help Clearing House.

This guide contains information on better understanding self-help groups' dynamics and benefits, and provides descriptions of over a thousand national, international, and model groups. It includes chapters on starting community groups, and summaries of rigorous research outcome studies. The 42 research studies of self-help groups may be viewed online at http://www.chce.research.med.va.gov/chce/pdfs/Kyrouz%20Humphreys%20Loomis%202002.pdf

Internet Resources

http://nursing.jbpub.com/psychiatric

Visit http://nursing.jbpub.com/psychiatric for interactive exercises, NCLEX review questions, WebLinks, and more.

CHAPTER 9

Holistic Nursing and Complementary Modalities

Jeanne Anselmo and Julia Balzer Riley

LEARNING OBJECTIVES

After reading this chapter, you will be able to:

- Discuss the spiritual roots of nursing practice.
- Identify the beliefs and philosophy of holistic nursing.
- Describe the use of complementary therapies in psychiatric nursing practice.

KEY TERMS

Acupuncture
Autogenic training
Biofeedback training
Bodymindspirit
Breathing
Centering
Holistic nursing
Hypnosis
Imagery
Inner reflection
Intention
Journaling
Mindfulness meditation
Progressive muscle relaxation
Relaxation
Therapeutic touch (TT)

http://nursing.jbpub.com/psychiatric

Visit http://nursing.jbpub.com/psychiatric for interactive exercises, NCLEX review questions, WebLinks, and more.

Introduction

Contemplating the mysteries of life and death, finding meaning in suffering, cultivating hope, finding peace, exploring religion and our beliefs, and dealing with growth, change, loss, chaos, illness, and healing comprise the spiritual or psychospiritual dimensions of nursing. These life experiences touch us deeply and invite us to explore our personal beliefs, our understanding of our place in the universe, our reason for being here, the sacredness of living, and our relationship to a power greater than ourselves.

We touch dimensions of the sacred each day in nursing. Understanding how spirit and our sense of interconnectedness, meaning, and purpose impact our health and life continuously offers us new opportunities for growth, renewal, deepening, and learning. Whether we are new nurses or experienced practitioners, the journey continues to unfold.

> A nurse's own belief system about illness, spirituality, health, and self-healing could impact the client and the plan of care.

In this chapter you will explore psychospiritual and holistic nursing practice. You will focus on the roots of spirituality in nursing, nursing's role in psychospiritual health and healing, and your own personal experiences, beliefs, attitudes, expectations, and intentions that can impact professional practice. You develop insight into these issues by inner reflection and active exploration of information. This active learning will encourage you to be mindful of your beliefs, reflections, and attitudes rather than to be passive recipients of information. To introduce you to holistic nursing practices, we begin by exploring the art of **centering**, **inner reflection**, and **journaling**.

> Experiential healing practices expand our capacity for intuitive knowing, awareness of subtle cues, insight, and compassion. These practices also support our direct experience of how we can impact our own healing.

Take a moment to quiet your mind and relax your body. Turn off any extraneous noises, lower or turn off your phone ringer, and find a comfortable position on a bed or chair. You can read through this exercise and then try it yourself, invite someone to read it to you slowly, or tape this exercise so you can just relax and listen.

Uncross your arms and legs. Find a comfortable position on a bed or a chair (see **Figure 9-1**). If you are sitting, place your feet on the floor. Close your eyes or focus on a point, so your attention can turn inward rather than outward. Focus your attention on your **breathing**, taking a long, slow breath. Imagine as you exhale that you are allowing all the tension to be released from your "**bodymindspirit**." As you inhale, imagine you are breathing in quiet and calm. Allow this to happen at your own pace, continuing to focus on your breathing. As you exhale, breathe out any tension. Sometimes it helps to say the words as you breathe, "I am breathing in calm," and as you exhale, "I am blowing out any tension or negativity." Allow yourself to be in the moment. Gently focus your attention on your breath. Then, when you are ready:

- Reflect for a moment on what moved you to enter nursing. Maybe you remember some event or experience that helped you to know that this is what you wanted to do as your life's work. What qualities did you notice or experience in that moment? Pause. Reflect. Breathe.
- Try to remember your first experience of healing. How have you carried this experience into your life and work? How has it helped you in your life? Pause. Reflect. Breathe.

When you are ready, again focus on your breathing and gently scan how you feel in your bodymindspirit. Note any changes. There is no right or wrong way to do this. Whatever is happening is okay. Just note and observe it. Breathe and be present. Then gently bring your attention back. Write down any reflections, images, ideas, and remembrances in a journal or notebook, or on a piece of paper. Throughout the chapter you will be invited to reflect and record in your journal as part of this experiential learning journey (**Figure 9-2**).

> **Critical Thinking Question** Reflect on how you felt as you focused your attention on your breathing. What thoughts did you have as you focused on your path to nursing practice and your first experience of healing?

Breathing, centering, inner reflection, and journaling are complementary therapies used for

Figure 9-1 Start your centering exercise in a relaxed position.

Figure 9-2 Journaling can help reveal insights into your nursing practice.

self-care, self-healing, and self-awareness and offer insight into the **holistic nursing** process. These practices offer an opportunity to release the tensions of the day, concentrate your attention, and open yourself to new ideas and greater awareness for your own healing journey.

During the breathing and centering practice, you may experience a variety of responses from feeling calm, relaxed, quiet, and at ease, to feeling no change or to feeling aware of your stress. Each awareness practice gives you information about yourself that can help you on the path of personal and professional growth. The more we expand our awareness and deepen our appreciation for subtle and intuitive ways of knowing, the greater the potential for growth of our creativity, healing capacities, insight, and understanding. Holistic and complementary practices are learned first through experience and practice. This is a very different model of learning from our Western, scientific model of education, which focuses on learning about a subject or technique we may not have experienced personally. Practicing these holistic healing arts offers us the: (1) direct experience of the therapy; (2) opportunity to explore its personal impact; (3) understanding of our own personal path needed to learn this practice; (4) knowledge of how our beliefs, expectations, and attitudes are impacted by these practices; and (5) enhancement of our sense of well-being and empowerment.

Understanding more about ourselves helps us to understand others. By reflecting on personal and professional themes, we begin to understand some of the challenges our clients face that we might not otherwise explore until or unless illness or trauma affects us personally. Through inner reflection we contact our personal and professional beliefs that help us to be open as well as those beliefs that hold us back from being open with our clients.

Breathing, centering, reflecting, and journaling offer nurses who are exploring psychospiritual and holistic dimensions of nursing practical tools to develop compassion, insight, caring, understanding, and awareness necessary for quality care, professional practice, and personal growth. Give yourself permission to make your journal a visual journal, including doodles, scribbles, or drawings. Experiment with different colors and different media such as crayons, markers, or watercolor.

Taking advantages of these practices for self-care helps nurses to be able to recommend them to clients with confidence. Breathing, centering, inner reflection, and journaling help decrease reactivity to potentially stressful situations, a stress-buffering effect; promote relaxation, which can combat the stress response; and offer contemplative moments to pay attention and learn from the body's responses to the individual's life journey.

Clinical Example

A nursing student practiced what she had learned in a nursing elective on complementary and alternative modalities. Working, going to school, and being a mother could be stressful. One night when she had a headache and the demands of the children "were stressing me out," she remembered a centering exercise from class (**Table 9-1**). The student explained, "I changed some of the words so I could use them at home. It helped me to clear my head. I never realized that, with just slowing down for a moment, I could somehow relax, even for a short time. It made me think more clearly. It made me realize that my daughter was tired and then I became more patient" (personal communication, 2006).

Critical Thinking Questions Holistic self-care is the foundation of holistic nursing. How can exercising these self-care practices and reflecting on insights help you in your nursing practice? What benefit does this active learning and experiential practice offer you?

Table 9-1 Centering Technique for Healthcaring

1. Before you enter a client's room, take a moment to clear your mind of distractions so you can give your full attention to your client in this moment.
2. Take a deep breath.
3. Remind yourself that you are entering your client's personal space, a sacred act.
4. Set the intention that your work is for the "greater good of the client, with harm to none" (Dossey, Keegan, & Guzzetta, 2005, p. 176).
5. Center yourself by using a heart-centered modality such as that used by healing touch and therapeutic touch practitioners. They are taught to "stay in their hearts," which is how they define centering (Dossey, Keegan, & Guzzetta, 2005, p. 194).
6. Remember you are a co-participant with your client in the creation of a healing environment.
7. Create an affirmation that works for you, such as "I am an instrument of healing," or "I am peaceful and calm, offering my best self."
8. Release expectations of a specific outcome for the interaction.
9. Take another deep breath to still your mind.

Source: Adapted from Dossey, Keegan, & Guzzetta, 2005.

In the following sections, we explore how our nursing ancestors and nursing theorists reflected on these issues. Keep your journal on hand to write down your reflections.

Spiritual Roots of Nursing

Across time and throughout the various cultures of the world, nurturing, caring, compassion, healing, and nursing have held a special place in society. Nursing historians link the roots of the nursing profession to wise women, witches, ancient shamans, midwives, and healers. In ancient Greece, the roots of nursing are traced to Hygeia, the goddess of health and healing. Medicine traces its roots to Asclepios, the Greek god of medicine. Our impulse to help, heal, and offer care and compassion arises from a long lineage of spirited and compassionate women who nurtured and served in the ordinariness of everyday life as well as the catastrophes of war, plague, famine, and disaster. This lineage includes many saints and members of religious orders from all different cultures and traditions.

Critical Thinking Questions What does this lineage of spiritual roots mean for nursing today? How does this lineage impact your understanding of the psycho-spiritual dimensions of nursing?

Florence Nightingale, the "midwife" of modern nursing, was a visionary of great practicality, wisdom, and spirit. "Nature alone cures," and "what nursing has to do is to put the patient in the best condition for nature to act upon him" (Nightingale, 1992, p. 75). Nightingale acquired her nursing knowledge through observation and experience, and was of the belief that health was not an arbitrary gift from God, but, rather, was a state human beings must achieve for themselves. For Nightingale, service to God was service to humanity. "Mystical union with God is not an end in itself, but the source of strength and guidance for doing one's work in the world" (Calabria & Macrae, 1994, p. xviii). In Nightingale's writings, we can see how the spiritual lineage of nursing reflects a connection to something larger than the individual self, to the mystical, the numerous, the All, Spirit, and to God.

Suggestions for Thought by Florence Nightingale (Calabria & Macrae, 1994) is a demonstration of how nursing leaders lived, their questions and beliefs, and their exploration and development of new approaches and understandings. As we enter the twenty-first century, the spiritual issues facing nursing are much more complex than 100 years ago. Like Nightingale, we need to develop continuously our ability to look deeply into our experience, wisdom, heart, and spirit to be active participants in unfolding changes. Each of us influences the changes health care, healing, and nursing are going through, either for better or for worse. To face the challenges of a rapidly changing healthcare system, we need to be both leaders and learners. As we look back on nursing's roots, we see the spiritual dimensions of nursing practice carried forward in various forms to pass on to the next generation of nurses.

From Spiritual Roots to Modern Theorists

Modern nursing theorists continue this spirituality in nursing. Jean Watson, founder of the Center for Human Caring at the University of Colorado Health Sciences Center, proposed a philosophy and science of caring. Watson focuses on the quality of the caring relationship, to promote health and individual or family growth. She defines health as "unity and harmony within the mind, body, and soul" (Watson, 1988, p. 48.). Nurses using Watson's framework focus on health promotion through preventive health actions. They do this by providing situational support, teaching, and problem-solving techniques and by recognizing and developing coping skills and adaptation to loss. In Watson's theory, compassion, mind, body, and soul continue nursing's connection to spirit and caring.

Another nurse theorist, Margaret Newman, describes the life process as a progression toward higher levels of consciousness: "The expansion of consciousness is what life and therefore health [are] all about" (Newman, 1979, p. 66). An interesting dimension of Newman's theory is her views on disease as a meaningful manifestation of the pattern of the whole, based on the premise that life is an ongoing process of expanding consciousness. "Illness reflected the life patterns of the person and that what was needed was the recognition of that pattern and acceptance of it for what it meant to that person" (Newman, 1989, p. 3).

Critical Thinking Questions How would Watson's theory on caring influence your practice of nursing and the qualities you would want to bring to your work? How would Newman's theory on health and illness impact your view of your client's diagnoses and medical prognoses?

Can you imagine someone with a life-challenging illness telling you that this was the best thing that ever happened to him or her? How would that impact your life and work? *Breathe. Center. Close your eyes. Stop and journal.*

Can you imagine a time when you were going through a difficult challenge or illness? What helped you get through it? What impact or meaning did this event have in your life? What changes did you make as a result of that event? *Stop. Breathe. Center. Reflect. Journal.*

If you cannot remember an event or illness (e.g., loss of a loved one, divorce, a new job, moving to a new town, losing your job, facing a big challenge you did not think you could overcome), try to remember a friend, family member, or client you know who did go through a difficult challenge or illness, and try the same exercise. *Stop. Breathe. Center. Reflect. Journal.*

If you were the person going through the experience or could imagine yourself going through what a family, friend, or client experienced, what qualities would you want in the helping professionals involved in your care? What kind of relationship would you want with your helping professional? How much active participation would you want in planning out your care or course of action or treatment? What inner and outer resources would you draw on to help you through it? *Stop. Breathe. Center. Reflect. Journal.*

Reflecting on the last experience, you might have thought of resources that helped you, family members, friends, or clients through a difficult illness or challenge, most likely including family, friends, community, co-workers, and clergy as well as your own inner resources of faith, hope, belief in love, nature, and a relationship with a higher power. The qualities in the therapeutic relationship that you envisioned may have included caring, compassion, empathy, safety, trust, mutuality, connectedness, openness, understanding, insight, wisdom, skill, expertise, commitment, and hope. These are qualities that resonate with Watson's theory of nursing. The meaning and impact this event had on your life would have depended on a variety of factors, including how well you coped with past challenges, role models, ways role models directly or indirectly taught you to traverse adversity, and your self-esteem, confidence, resourcefulness, resilience, skill, hope for the future, and belief in finding meaning and purpose in the experience. The amount of active participation you would want in your care may also vary depending on the situation, personal preference, circumstances, sense of self-efficacy, belief in self-healing, empowerment, and the qualities, capabilities, and practice philosophy of your healthcare team.

Exploring these issues helps us to recognize the impact of beliefs, attitudes, expectations, and behaviors on people during crisis and to realize that our belief systems can impact clients emotionally,

CASE STUDY Effect of Belief System on Treatment Outcomes

A biofeedback researcher reported an experience in his biofeedback headache-relief clinic. The therapist in the research laboratory was able to teach 9 out of 10 clients to warm their hands, resulting in a reduction or elimination of migraine headaches in approximately 10 to 15 sessions. However, when the therapist went on vacation, another biofeedback therapist took over his sessions. During that time, the effectiveness of the therapy reversed, with 9 out of 10 clients unable to relieve migraines. The researcher compared the two clinicians and determined that each had comparable skills; but, the first practitioner believed clients could warm their hands and reduce their migraine headaches and the second practitioner did not.

How many times have we heard about clients being affected by a belief system of a helping professional? "I'm sorry Ms. X, there is nothing we can do. You have only a short time to live." This communicates hopelessness and despair. Sometimes the client just needs to hear the diagnosis for panic to set in. The diagnoses of cancer and acquired immunodeficiency syndrome (AIDS) send terror through most clients.

physically, psychically, and behaviorally. An example of how important the professional's own belief system is can be found in the true story discussed in the case study.

Critical Thinking Questions What if you, as a nurse, had a belief system similar to Newman's theory in which illness or disease is viewed as a meaningful manifestation of the patterns of life, and you recognized that what is needed is recognition of what the disease or illness means to the client (Newman, 1989)? How, then, might you interact with a client who has just been diagnosed with ovarian cancer?

Examine **Table 9-2**, A Nurse's Personal and Professional Self-Assessment. Ongoing self-development has always been essential professionally, but as we connect or reconnect to our roots of healing, caring, and spirituality in nursing, such development becomes even more important.

Table 9-2 A Nurse's Personal and Professional Self-Assessment

Reflect upon the following:

- Your intention in working with this client.
- Your reason for entering into this profession.
- Your belief about the contribution of nursing to spiritual and psychospiritual care of clients.
- Your philosophy of nursing practice.
- Your experiences that are similar to or different from your client.
- Your support network, resources, colleagues, pastoral care, community, and clergy.
- Your beliefs about spirituality, religion, a person's ability to heal, the meaning of illness, and forgiveness, and your comfort in dealing with death and dying issues.
- Your ability to introduce a complementary modality into your plan of care (i.e., breathing, relaxation, prayer, journaling). These are some of the practices most easily introduced by nurses and are usually most familiar to nurses and clients.

Questions to ask:

- What nursing collegial resources can you bring to this client (therapeutic touch practitioners, nurse healers, nurse psychotherapists, holistic nursing practitioners)?
- What theoretical framework best supports your practice perspective? Most nurses practice utilizing a synthesis of theories, although some nurses specialize in one nurse theorist's perspective of care.
- What caring dimensions of the nurse-client relationships are your strengths (building trust, developing safety, caring presence, receptive listening, empathy)?

Spiritual Roots in Other Cultures

Traditional healers in other cultures recognize the importance of cultivating spirituality, compassion, interconnectedness with all beings, empathy, forgiveness, knowledge of healing remedies, and their relationships with a higher power. In shamanism, there is the belief that persons who have been struck by illness have a great opportunity. If sick people are able to heal themselves, they return as wounded healers, bringing their healing abilities back to the tribe. Delores Krieger, a nurse researcher and developer of **therapeutic touch (TT)**, a noninvasive healing practice, writes about the wounded healer (or shaman) in her book *Living the Therapeutic Touch* (1987). There are two basic interpretations of the wounded healer:

> [In] one version . . . an individual who has been ill, wounded, or otherwise traumatized . . . experiences his or her own healing by healing others. . . . Ultimately, this leads the Wounded Healer to a realization of the profundity of the process of being healed, of being made whole. A sense of at-oneness may occur while he or she is engaged in the healing act. Here, there is conscious recognition that others are also fundamentally at one, whole, even though they may be ill, wounded, or weakened. With conscious recognition of this fundamental similarity, the Healer reaches out to heal.
>
> . . . [In] another version the Wounded Healer is an individual who has suffered, but who decided to help others so that they need not undergo the pain, weakness, discomfort, and dependency of similar suffering. The compassionate intent points toward the model for compassion that is known in Buddhism as the Bodhisattva vow. In this tradition, an individual who has completed the fullness of human evolution and attained spiritual enlightenment may leave this world of pain and sorrow for other higher realms of consciousness, achieving a state of perpetual bliss. The Bodhisattva, however, renounces this world until all other beings have reached a similar state. It is from the depths of this comate grace that transformation occurs. (p. 18)

Another example comes from Tibet, where healers believe in the connection of self-development, spirituality, healing, and quality of care. Tibetan Buddhist healers study, pray, and meditate to cultivate their compassion, wisdom, and connection with healing energies and deities. During the 1990s, many of these healing practices were incorporated into our Western healthcare system with the introduction of yoga, prayer, and meditation for both healing and self-development.

Critical Thinking Questions What similarities do you find in Krieger's description of the wounded healer and your own initial reflections on why you became a nurse and your first experience of healing? How is the wounded healer reflected in other cultures and religious traditions? How could learning about these stories and practices help you in dealing with clients in spiritual crisis?

Beliefs and Philosophy of Holistic Nursing

During the past few decades, some nurses have committed their nursing practice to cultivating self-care and self-healing practices for themselves and clients. Their focus has been on seeing human beings as whole and bringing spirituality into nursing practices. Many have chosen to call themselves holistic nurses. Understanding the framework of what we do and the theory and philosophy of why we do it is an important dimension of holistic nursing.

Nurses as Psychospiritual Counselors

Spirituality is a dimension of every human life, whether or not one recognizes or acknowledges it; not everyone practices a religion. Asking clients about experiences of wholeness or experiences in which they feel interconnected, allowing them to experience a sense of timelessness, peace, inner calm, or joy, helps clients to understand what spiritual experiences are. Most people, if given the opportunity, can speak of simple ways in which they nourish their spirit, even if they do not practice or believe in a religious tradition. You can ask, "Do you have a faith practice that helps you?" Nurses as psychospiritual counselors help clients make peace with life and death. Nurses can help clients recognize their ability to cope with the natural flow of life. Often clients are so fearful of death, loss, or illness that they cannot live their present life, even when they are not actively ill or dying. Helping clients to connect with what is healing in their lives, with what gives them hope, peace, or joy is a simple yet profound intervention. Weaving these kinds of topics, questions, and issues into interactions with clients helps bring out much more authentic responses than those elicited by just asking direct questions, such as "What religion are you?" Exploring for more authentic responses also helps to foster the nurse-client therapeutic relationship.

Nurses have access to clients in their most vulnerable and intimate moments—the birth of a child, the moment of death, and the traumas, pains, joys, and fears of life. Many times we are the spiritual support that holds the hand, witnesses the first breath or the last breath, and offers solace and understanding.

Helping clients recognize the difference between their religious beliefs and their spiritual beliefs and teaching clients to seek purpose, meaning, wholeness, and understanding of the mysteries of life are important contributions of nursing. Forgiveness, prayer, meditation, reconciliation, and connection to family and community are all vital elements of exploring spiritual and psychospiritual dimensions of nursing care.

Seeking out pastoral collaborators within institutions and the clergy of various religious establishments in the community is very important. Building a relationship with the clergy in the community before making a referral is essential. Working with the clergy, you can offer the client a broader base of healing possibilities. We recognize that there are wide variations in individual clergy's belief systems. Clergy specially trained in pastoral care can be quite flexible and versatile in dealing with a variety of beliefs; other clerics may not have that flexibility and skill. The client's support system includes the client's family, friends, and community and, when appropriate, clergy and religious centers. Nurses involved in psychospiritual counseling are resources and advocates to help the client navigate his or her life's challenge within their support system.

Critical Thinking Questions How do you see spirituality and religion? Are they the same? How are they different? How has psychospiritual support been helpful for you or for your clients?

Description of Holistic Nursing

Holistic nursing is directed at healing the whole person, and, as defined by the American Holistic Nurses Association (AHNA), is a specialty based on a body of knowledge, evidence-based research, sophisticated skill sets, defined standards of practice, and a philosophy of living and being that is grounded in caring, relationship, and interconnectedness (2006). Being a holistic nurse is *who* the nurse is rather than *what* the nurse does. It is the quality of your presence and being (i.e., a caring capacity) that in its essence describes holistic nursing. And at our best, all nursing is holistic. Calling yourself a holistic nurse could mean that complementary or holistic modalities are incorporated into your practice; it also could mean, for example, that if you work as a nurse in an intensive care unit (ICU) you can offer presence, touch, caring, compassion, counsel, skillfulness, healing, and wisdom, call yourself holistic, and truly be accurate.

Holistic nursing is officially recognized by the American Nurses Association as a nursing specialty with a defined scope and standards of practice (AHNA, 2006).

The holistic nurse is an instrument of healing and a facilitator in the healing process. Holistic nurses honor the individual's subjective experience about health, health beliefs, and values. To become therapeutic partners with individuals, families, and communities, holistic nursing practice draws on nursing knowledge, theories, expertise, intuition, and creativity.

Complementary Modalities in Holistic Nursing Practice

Holistic nursing is nursing practice that has care of the whole person as its goal.

Holistic self-care is the foundation of holistic nursing practice.

Once considered alternative, complementary healthcare practices are now integrated into the Western scientific system of practice.

Biofeedback relaxation, centering, breathing, and meditation are self-healing and self-regulating practices.

Over the past 35 to 50 years, our culture has begun to explore ancient healing practices and traditions from cultures around the world, especially the East, such as yoga, meditation, Zen, Buddhism, healing, Hinduism, shamanism, Native American healers, mysticism, Chinese medicine, acupuncture, herbs, Ayurveda, and chanting. People in our culture are just becoming aware of the benefits of these ancient healing practices, many of which have been practiced for over 5,000 years.

Critical Thinking Questions What cultural healing practices did your family (great-grandparents, grandparents, mother, father, uncles, or aunts) practice? How have you or your family integrated this healing information into your current healthcare beliefs or practices?

In this section you will explore an overview of some of the most frequently used complementary modalities, with suggestions for use in hospitals, home care, and community health. A list of resource materials and organizations are found at the end of this chapter, and practice exercises are included at the end of this section.

As you explore this section, review what we have discussed regarding learning from the inside out, experiential learning, active participation, empowerment and self-healing, caring in the therapeutic relationship, the meaning of illness and health, nursing theories, and holistic nursing. These nursing theories, perspectives, therapeutic alliances, and views on illness, self-healing, wholeness, health, and empowerment are reflected in these ancient and modern practices.

Self-Healing and Self-Regulation

Self-regulation practices are very different from those practices that rely on the intervention of a therapist. Self-regulation practices depend deeply on the person's own inner commitment and participation.

Doing the centering and breathing practices on your own are examples of self-regulation exercises that arise from the principle that people can heal themselves. Many cultures and traditions perform self-healing practices the way others perform morning hygiene for self-care and health.

These practices can be used as therapeutic interventions as you guide clients in self-regulation methods. This is done with the intention that clients learn to use the practices for self-healing and self-care. Biofeedback, relaxation, meditation, and breathing are a few of the self-healing and self-regulating practices.

Relaxation

Relaxation exercises have always been part of yoga, Chinese energy practices, and meditation. The ancient healing traditions underscore the importance of deep rest, that is, quieting the mind, body, emotions, and spirit and allowing a peaceful, deep, harmonious rest to arise. Deep rest supports and facilitates the natural ability of our bodymindspirit to heal. "Nature alone heals . . ." Nightingale reminds us (1992, p. 75). Relaxation exercises include the dimensions of breathing, awareness, and attending to the body.

Relaxation practices are effective interventions for pre- or postprocedure anxiety, sleep difficulty, anxiety, restlessness, stress, presurgical preparation, and pain relief.

Progressive Muscle Relaxation

Progressive muscle relaxation, developed by Edmund Jacobson, invites clients to attend to subtle as well as distinctive signals associated with sequentially tensing and relaxing each muscle group. Progressive muscle relaxation is performed with the intention to help clients (1) recognize the difference between tension and relaxation in the body (this is important, in that many people habituate to levels of tension in the body and consider that normal), and (2) learn how to relax at will. The original practice focused on only tensing and releasing muscle groups without the use of visualization. Since then, most clinicians have devised modified progressive muscle relaxation to include imagery and autogenic phrases that induce sensations of calm and relaxation.

A sample progressive muscle relaxation practice follows: Instruct the client to focus attention on a muscle group such as the hand, becoming aware of the area, noticing how it feels, then tensing or clenching the fist. Hold it. Count to 5. Then release and notice the difference in body awareness. Go through all the muscle groups from head to toe, sequentially using the same process, and close with an opportunity for the client to focus on the body's response to the experience.

Research has demonstrated that progressive relaxation is helpful with low back pain, postpartum depression, hypertension, tension headache, and asthma (Dossey, Keegan, & Guzzetta, 2005; Snyder & Lindquist, 2002). Caution should be used when performing progressive muscle relaxation with clients who are experiencing muscle spasms. It is important to be sure that they are able to relax after tensing their muscles during the exercise.

Autogenic Training

Autogenic training is a popular relaxation technique that focuses on using self-statements suggesting heaviness and warmth (e.g., "My arms are heavy and my hands are warm. Warmth is flowing down my arms and into my hands."). Research has compared the impact of autogenic training with progressive muscle relaxation. Both were found to be effective in treating anxiety and depression by reducing the intensity of symptoms (Dossey, Keegan, & Guzzetta, 2005).

The most important aspect is to learn any relaxation practice from the inside out. Practice on yourself, your family, and your colleagues first to understand the many possible reactions each practice can elicit. When working with clients, monitor signals of their relaxation response through visual cues. Even with their eyes closed, you may note rapid eye movement (REM), increased swallowing, change in skin coloring, vasodilatation of blood vessels in the hands, loosening or relaxing of jaw and shoulders, and deepening and slowing down of respirations. These are all signs of a decrease in sympathetic activity and an increase in parasympathetic activity. Track clients on insulin, hypertensive medications, anti-anxiety medications, and pain medications as they learn, practice, and improve their self-regulation abilities. You may notice clients reporting less need for medication, and it is helpful to work with prescribing professionals in order to titrate clients' medications appropriately.

You can incorporate breathing, progressive muscle relaxation (tense and then relax), and autogenic phrases ("I am calm; my hands are warm") in a relaxation exercise script or practice. This can be used as an intervention on its own, or in conjunction with biofeedback and imagery.

When introducing a client to the practice of relaxation it is important to create an unhurried environment, conducive to learning the new skill. Gauge how much time you have to spend with your client and leave time for the client to open his or her eyes, return to the moment, and share some experiences with you. Save approximately 3 to 6 minutes for this waking up and debriefing. You may choose to focus on only one or two areas of the body or to focus on places throughout the body from head to toe. Areas you could include are the scalp, eyes, jaw, neck, shoulders, arms, hands, fingers, chest, breathing, lungs, and heart. ("My stomach is calm. I am allowing vitality and nourishment to flow through my whole body.") The exercise can be ended in one of following three ways: The first encourages patient self-care,

Clinical Example

Breathing exercises are familiar to nurses who have taught abdominal breathing pre- and postoperatively as well as during natural childbirth. Breathing practices can be used to help a child with asthma who must learn to belly breathe without overusing the trapezius muscles. (People with asthma have a tendency to brace their shoulders and overuse their chest muscles involved in breathing.) Breathing also is a useful exercise to reduce anxiety. It is a simple bedside intervention that can be practiced in the hospital, clinic, or home.

> Learning from the inside out arises out of practices such as breathing, quieting, and calming. Experiential learning draws on our personal experience, intuition, and inner knowledge.

> Experiment with doing the relaxation exercises with friends and ask for feedback. Check how you feel as you practice.

Design the exercise based on the client's needs and available time. Pain clients benefit by focusing on positive, soothing statements and overall well-being.

the second supports the client in awareness and awakening, and the third allows the client to continue relaxing quietly and possibly to drift to sleep:

1. This is your time. Your whole body is relaxing at its own pace. The benefits of this practice can continue after this exercise. You have the option of continuing to focus on any of these statements as part of your own practice, whether before sleep or anytime you want to bring more comfort or calm to yourself.
2. In a few moments I will invite you to begin to bring your attention back. Continue to focus on your breathing, while scanning yourself, and see if you notice any difference in how you feel. (Pause.) When you are ready, gradually take a deep breath and open your eyes.
3. Continue to state quietly and calmly to yourself in your mind: "I am allowing myself to be calm, relaxed, quiet, peaceful, and restful." Continue to breathe easily and repeat any of these phrases on your own, allowing yourself to tune into any sensations of calm and comfort. You can continue on your own just by breathing, and I will remain silent. (Sit for a few moments with the client and then leave quietly.)

Try this with a partner and notice how it feels practicing with "your client." Get feedback on your tone of voice, timing, and presence. Critiquing can help with your comfort level, confidence, and presentation when you do this with a client.

Now reverse and allow yourself to experience the exercise. How did you feel? What benefits did you experience? Note if you felt any changes in respirations, hand and foot temperature, heart rate, muscle tension, and emotional well-being. What would you expect to see happen to blood pressure and oxygen saturation rate after introducing this exercise? Try taking your own blood pressure before and after the exercise, noting any differences.

Biofeedback Training

Biofeedback training uses technology, including electronic thermometers (to measure temperature and peripheral blood flow), electromyography (EMG; to measure muscle activity), electroencephalography (EEG; to measure brain wave activity), heart rate monitors, blood pressure monitors, and electrodermal response (to measure sympathetic nervous system outflow) to feed back information to clients who can learn to regulate or change an imbalance in their systems.

Specialized training and certification are available in biofeedback. Even without extensive study,

CASE STUDY Relaxation Exercises

When introducing relaxation practices to a client, start by quieting the environment. Turn off any extraneous noises, and turn down any bright lighting. You may want to play soft, soothing music in the background or just allow silence.

If using a relaxation script, read the phrases or script slowly, allowing time between each statement. A good practice is to do the relaxation technique along with the client. Slow your breathing and allow two or three breaths between each statement as a timing device and as a means to monitor your own level of participation. An autogenic relaxation script follows:

Start by taking a long, slow, deep breath and releasing it. Allow yourself to follow the rhythm of your breathing. Focus your attention on a specific point or close your eyes. When you are ready, pay attention to your forehead. Begin by telling yourself to breathe, and repeat the word "breathe" three times between each of the following phrases:

I am allowing my forehead to relax.
I am allowing my forehead to relax.
I am allowing my forehead to relax.

Allow time to observe the sensations in your forehead. Relax and quiet yourself at your own pace. Then focus attention on your jaw. Allow your jaw to loosen slightly by leaving a space between your upper and lower teeth. Then say gently in your mind, "Breathe," and repeat three times between each of the following phrases:

I am allowing my jaw to relax.
I am allowing my jaw to relax.
I am allowing my jaw to relax.

Then continue the exercise by focusing your attention on each part of the body, using similar phases and releasing or loosening each area, such as unclenching the fist, uncurling toes, and allowing the shoulders to release.

you can apply simple biofeedback principles in nursing practice in the home, hospital, critical care unit, and ambulatory care center by tracking clients' responses on monitors, if available, and feeding back the information (reading with interpretation) to inform, teach, and empower.

Some nurses have incorporated biofeedback for urinary and fecal incontinence as a part of their practice, which also includes TT, health counseling, and relaxation.

Neurofeedback, formerly known as EEG biofeedback, offers clients a vehicle with which to work with epilepsy, sleep disorders, attention deficit hyperactivity disorder (ADHD), and trauma. These areas require specialized education and practice. Many insurance carriers reimburse for biofeedback to treat incontinence as well as generalized feedback for stress-related disorders. Biofeedback clients need to be screened for non-stress-related causes of their symptoms by a nurse practitioner or physician prior to initiating the biofeedback process.

Imagery

Imagery can be used in conjunction with biofeedback monitoring or can be practiced on its own. Imagery is the practice of assisting clients to self-heal and self-regulate by bringing them into a state of relaxation (see script for relaxation) and then inviting them to visualize, using any or all of their senses. Images can be felt, sensed, heard, visualized, intuited, tasted, and smelled. Imagery has been helpful in improving immune function, in reducing pain and anxiety, and in working with insight (Dossey, Keegan, & Guzzetta, 2005; Snyder & Lindquist, 2002). A simple imagery practice is to imagine a healing place.

Try this for yourself. Allow yourself to focus on the special qualities of a healing place, the beauty of nature, the sense of peace and healing that it brings to you. Use all your senses to help bring out the healing qualities this place embodies for you. Use your journal as a place to record your images, dreams, and reflections to track your self-healing from the unconscious to the conscious mind.

Mindfulness Meditation

Mindfulness meditation is an ancient spiritual practice found in traditions around the world of learning to be in the present moment, practicing awareness, focusing on breathing, and focusing on moment-to-moment attention. An example of one breathing awareness practice is:

Clinical Example

A client may learn how to relax or reduce muscle tension and spasm in the shoulder or trapezium muscles based on feedback information from an EMG. A client also may learn how to regulate blood flow to relieve suffering from a migraine headache by relying on feedback from a thermometer that measures hand temperature.

Clinical Example

A client practicing a relaxation exercise while having blood pressure, heart rate, and oxygen saturation monitored can get feedback about the efficacy of the relaxation practice and compare this to the subjective reaction to the exercise. ("Your blood pressure went down 10 points while doing that breathing exercise. This is very good. If you practice this regularly, you may be able to keep your pressure down. How did it feel to you?")

Clinical Example

Annette was receiving hospice services due to severe chronic obstructive pulmonary disease (COPD). It would sometimes take her 5 minutes to catch her breath after just answering the door. She would sit on the seat on her walker, tethered by her oxygen tubing. Annette had begun to fulfill her dream to paint watercolor flowers, and although this was helping, she was becoming more anxious as it took her longer and longer to still her breathing. The nurse understood her love for color and flowers from earlier discussions, and asked if Annette had ever used imagery to relax. She had not. The nurse asked her to think of a place she could remember or dream of that was beautiful and peaceful for her. Annette said she loved Hawaii. With encouragement, she was able to describe a flower garden she loved there, and closed her eyes when the nurse asked her to imagine the sights, sounds, smells, and climate she experienced there. Annette smiled and agreed she would try this at night to help her relax and when she felt anxious. Over time, and with practice, Annette was able to use all of her senses to experience the flower garden, and within minutes, even seconds at times, a feeling of calmness would come over her and her breathing would ease.

> Breathing in, I am aware of breathing in.
> Breathing out, I am aware of breathing out.
> In. Out. (Thich Nhat Hanh, 1992, p. 8)

Follow your breathing as you use this practice. Observe your breathing and enjoy just being.

Mindful walking meditation is a movement practice of awareness of mind, breath, and being with each footstep (see **Figure 9-3**). These practices have great spiritual benefit, enhancing peace, joy, hope, calmness, and helping with depression, pain, hypertension, insomnia, and stress reduction (Snyder & Lindquist, 2002).

Figure 9-3 Walking a meditation path.

Hypnosis

Hypnosis is the practice of working with an altered state of consciousness or trance for therapeutic benefit. The therapeutic use of hypnosis has been effective in treating pain, addiction, anxiety, and posttraumatic stress and in inducing anesthesia, sleep, and memory (Dossey, Keegan, & Guzzetta, 2005). Nurses have developed specialized nursing practices that incorporate hypnosis as their main focus. Various schools of philosophy and practice are available. Eriksonian hypnosis based on the work of Milton Erickson is a nonauthoritarian approach (Haley, 1993). Practitioners of hypnosis can offer various methods of supporting clients to deepen their abilities to self-heal and self-regulate.

Therapeutic Touch

Therapeutic touch (TT), as mentioned earlier, is a form of energy healing, a frequently used intervention in holistic nursing practice. Derived from laying on of hands, TT invites nurses to focus on their **intention** to heal, center, assess, and then treat by directing life energy to the client using their hands. The client takes on and internalizes this energy to facilitate healing and restore balance.

TT has been shown to be of benefit for the relief of pain, anxiety, and discomfort, resulting in an improved sense of well-being, accelerated healing, reduction of blood pressure, reduction of fight-or-flight response, and improved oxygen saturation levels (Snyder & Lindquist, 2002). A patient satisfaction study of 605 clients who had received TT treatments in a general hospital reported that most clients reported a positive result, such as decreased pain and anxiety (Newshan & Schuller-Civitella, 2003).

TT consists of centering, assessment, unruffling, and transmitting energy. The centering that nurses practice is similar to the simple breathing practice at the beginning of this chapter. During this centering, your attention should be focused on helping, healing, and visualizing your client as whole. The next phase of practice focuses on assessing the client's energy field by scanning the field with the palms held above the body approximately 2 to 5 inches. Starting at the head, move the palms gradually to the feet making a mental note of any differences in sensation, temperature, density, activity, or lack of activity along the way. When possible, it is of value to assess both the front and back of the client.

Unruffling is the use of sweeping hand motions through areas of congestion in the energy field to enhance receptivity to energy. Transferring energy occurs when you intentionally and consciously act as a vehicle or channel for the universal life force to flow through you into the client. Imagining healing colors such as blue light for calming and white light for wholeness and healing is a vehicle for modulating the energy to support the energy needs of the client. Many nurses end each session by placing their hands on the insteps of the client's feet to ground and support the client. Information on the study of TT is available through the Nurse Healers Professional Association (see Internet Resources).

Massage

Massage is one area of expertise currently referred to as *bodywork*. It has a long history as a nursing intervention and in healing. The therapeutic use of hands and touch has been found significant in growth and development and has been used with newborns and in neonatal care. Stroking, holding, and massaging offer tactile nurturance, improve circulation, and enhance a feeling of safety, calm, and connection found in the relaxation response (**Figure 9-4**). This benefit has been demonstrated in people with cancer, hospice clients, institutionalized elders, and those suffering from dementia (Snyder & Lindquist, 2002). A literature review found that most of 22 studies on the effect of massage on relaxation, comfort, and sleep showed either physiologic relaxation or significant anxiety reduction (Richards, Gibson, & Overton-McCoy, 2000).

Massage is generally a practice of working with long strokes running down the muscles of the body, as in Swedish massage; however, there are numerous techniques and styles of practice. Different

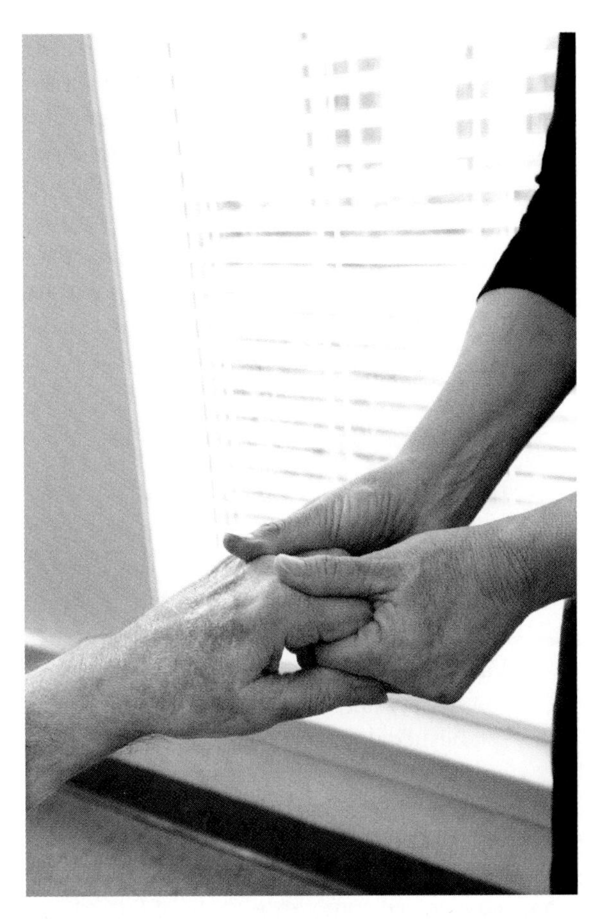

Figure 9-4 Massage can enhance a sense of peacefulness and relaxation.

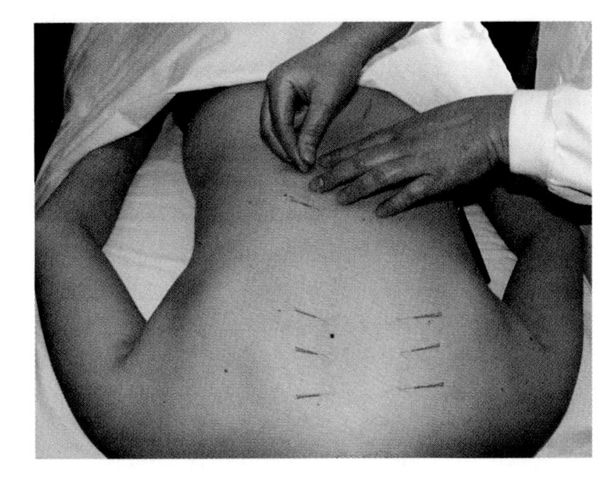

Figure 9-5 Acupuncture can help relieve many physical and mental problems.

states have different standards for who can practice "massage therapy" and the education required.

Back massage has been demonstrated to effect a relaxation response in some clients and sympathetic arousal in others. Overall, massage has been found to promote relaxation, facilitate sleep, lessen pain and fatigue, reduce edema, improve mobility, lessen anxiety and depression, and enhance well-being (Snyder & Lindquist, 2002). This ancient form of healing practice offers a connection between you and the client and may be helpful in pinpointing areas of soreness, tenderness, or discomfort.

Reflexology is the practice of massaging the hands and feet with an awareness that the whole body system is mapped onto the hands and feet. By massaging the arch of the foot, one can help the spine to relax. This practice offers easy access to help support, quiet, and calm the client while relieving pain, anxiety, and discomfort.

Acupuncture

Acupuncture is one of the ancient arts of traditional Chinese medicine (see **Figure 9-5**). Dating back 5,000 years, Chinese practitioners learned how to work with *chi* or universal life force or energy. They activate, balance, and harmonize this energy through the use of breathing, awareness, internal chi kung, tai chi, Chinese herbs, massage, energy transfer (external chi kung), and acupuncture. Acupuncture requires specialized study and is reimbursed by some insurance companies. It is used to relieve pain, stress-related illnesses, asthma, headaches, and muscle pain; to enhance immune system function; and to treat addictions (smoking, eating, drugs). A landmark study established acupuncture as an effective complement to conventional arthritis management. This rigorous study demonstrated that acupuncture reduces pain and functional impairment of osteoarthritis of the knee (Berman et al., 2004).

Shiatsu or *acupressure* is acupuncture without needles. Using the same map of the body as in acupuncture, the shiatsu practitioner activates meridian or energy points along the body. Through stretching and variations in pressure, this practice focuses on restoring energy, balance, relaxation, and relief from discomfort and anxiety.

Critical Thinking Question Think of a client for whom you have recently cared. How could you introduce one or more of these practices into his or her care?

Herbal Remedies

Herbal medicines are easily available and frequently used in the United States (Beaubrun & Gray, 2000). Be sure to include questions about a patient's use of natural remedies, herbal medicines, or over-the-counter medications when inquiring about medication use. Clients may be reluctant to reveal such information or forget to include it, not considering such preparations to be "medications." Your data obtained on the patient's use of herbals is an important nursing function. As part of patient education, it is important to convey that just because these medicines are "natural" does not mean they are safe. The research data are not conclusive and are often contradictory about the effectiveness and safety of herbals. In particular, the nurse practitioner with prescriptive privileges needs to be aware and make sure clients are aware of potential interactions between prescribed medications and herbal preparations that the client may be using, and nurses need to include this information as part of patient and family education.

Psychiatric clients may self-medicate with some of the following:

- St. John's wort (*Hypericum perforatum*) is used for self-treatment of depression and has been reported to have fewer side effects than antidepressants. Although it has been useful in people with mild to moderate depression, there is insufficient evidence of its effectiveness in severe depression (Ernst, 2001). Cautions include photosensitivity leading to a rash and possible blisters in fair-skinned people; also, people with a history of affective disorders, mania, or hypomania may find their condition triggered by this remedy (McGovern et al., 2003; Pilkington, Boshnakova, & Richardson, 2006). When used with serotonin reuptake inhibitors, serotonin syndrome may result, causing changes in mental status and motor and autonomic function (Ernst, 2001). Clients with HIV need to know that the herb can decrease the effectiveness of some protease inhibitors.
- Ginkgo (*Ginkgo biloba*) is used to treat age-related memory impairment, dementia, and senility. Some studies have shown ginkgo to be effective in "delaying clinical deterioration of patients or in bringing about symptomatic improvement" (Ernst, 2001, p. 105; Cass, 2004). Ginkgo potentiates the action of anticoagulants and increases the effects of monoamine oxidase inhibitors (MAOIs), a class of antidepressants (Cuellar, 2006; Ernst, 2001; Herbert-Ashton & Clarkson, 2005).
- Kava kava (*Piper methysticum*) is used for short-term treatment of anxiety or stress. As with other substances marketed as herbal supplements, kava has not had to undergo the quality requirements of the Food and Drug Administration (FDA). It was reported that one patient developed persistent Parkinsonism when being treated with extract of kava for anxiety (Meseguer et al., 2002). Kava kava potentiates drugs that act on the central nervous system, including alcohol, benzodiazepines, and barbiturates, and may decrease the effects of levodopa, used to treat Parkinson's disease (Cuellar, 2006; Ernst, 2001; Spencer & Jacobs, 2003). Kava kava can be toxic to the liver and is contraindicated for patients with liver disease (Herbert-Ashton & Clarkson, 2005).
- Valerian root (*Valeriana officinalis*) is used for anxiety and insomnia. Research has not established its effectiveness beyond a reasonable doubt, but early evidence indicates it might be useful by itself to promote sleep. In theory, it can potentiate the effects of sedatives or other CNS depressants at high dosages (Ernst, 2001). Clients should not drink alcohol, take other CNS depressants, or operate heavy machinery while taking valerian (Herbert-Ashton & Clarkson, 2005).

Holistic Nursing Practice

Nurses develop individualized models of holistic practice often based on their area of specialization and unique strengths. The principles of holistic assessment form the foundation for all models of holistic nursing practice.

Client Assessment

It is important to establish a therapeutic relationship with the client. A psychospiritual assessment can be performed through questions, interviews, and discussions with the client to explore the client's (1) sense of well-being and inner strengths (what brings joy, peace, a sense of wholeness into life), (2) support systems that are currently available (community, family, spiritual or religious support, work-related support), and (3) traditional or cultural rituals appropriate for the client's experience. Explore the client's purpose in life; feelings about suffering and illness; experience with self-healing; sense of hope and faith;

Implications for Evidence-Based Practice

Studies supporting the efficacy of complementary modalities have been referenced throughout the chapter and have implications for evidence-based practice. It is important for the psychiatric nurse to be aware of these complementary therapies and be ready to assist clients to integrate these therapies into their traditional treatments. In addition to knowing which therapies are effective in treating symptoms of mental illness, the nurse has a responsibility to educate clients as to their shortcomings. For example, for clients to make informed decisions, they need to know that, although studies have found St. John's wort to be more effective than placebos for the treatment of mild to moderate depression, data are not as conclusive when comparing it with standard medications for depression (Pilkington et al., 2006).

Future research is likely to help explain why complementary therapies are effective. A study of Buddhist practitioners of meditation, ranging from 15 to 40 years of age, has demonstrated EEG changes that "could reflect a change in the quality of their moment-to-moment awareness" (Matters of Note, 2005, p. 163). This study illustrates the concept of neuroplasticity, the idea that the adult human brain can continue to reorganize, forming new neural connections, with a natural reparative ability. Such findings can be expected to gain further acceptance of these modalities as adjuncts to traditional therapies.

capacity for forgiveness; comfort with death and dying; belief in religion, God, or a higher power; and comfort with spiritual practices such as prayer, meditation, healing and holistic practices, relaxation, and imagery. Include how the client connects to nature (gardening, walking in nature), cycles of the seasons, the environment, and the planet and learn which pets, plants, and other living things support the client's well-being each day.

In a wellness model that focuses on self-healing and empowerment, including the client in the planning of care is essential. Levels of participation by the client will vary, depending on the individual's capacity and comfort level. Even clients in crisis, coma, and trauma who are not verbal can be included by involving the client's family, friends, or proxy in this phase of care. Many nurses have also found centering, meditation, and reflecting, using inner dialogue or directly speaking to clients in a coma, reflects and honors this commitment to a client's needs and participation.

A Practice Model

Holistic nursing practice can occur in a variety of settings: on hospital in-patient or out-patient services, as part of a holistic health center, in the client's home, or in the nurse's private office. Holistic nursing utilizes the holistic practices described in this chapter, including biofeedback, relaxation, healthcare teaching and counseling, stress reduction, mindfulness meditation, and imagery, in nurses' work with a variety of clients.

Treatment may focus on relieving stress, anxiety, headaches, hypertension, or pain. It is always important that clients have a full evaluation by a nurse practitioner or physician to rule out non-stress-related physical conditions. Holistic nursing practices can be effective for clients with life-threatening illnesses; for example, guided imagery for cancer as well as biofeedback and relaxation for immune enhancement (Dossey, Keegan, & Guzzetta, 2005; Snyder & Lindquist, 2002).

The holistic nurse supports clients in developing a plan of care, exploring treatment options, developing self-healing practices, exploring the meaning of the crisis and their illness, developing family support, and dealing with bereavement, loss, and death. The nurse can help clients take a proactive, empowered stance with physicians and other healthcare professionals.

One of the authors worked in an urban health center with homeless women recovering from addiction and incorporated general healthcare teaching on wellness, holistic health, safe sex practices, hypertension, headaches, premenstrual syndrome, women's health issues, anxiety, and depression. The women shared their feelings and experiences by writing, drawing, or writing poetry after a meditation or imagery session. Many offered spontaneous poetry and have continued to write in their journals.

Embellishing Your Nursing Practice with Your Own Gifts: Creative Expression in Action

Holistic nurses embellish their nursing practice with their own gifts. Nurses who sing, sing to their comatose clients. Nurses who pray, say a prayer before they work or during the day. Nurses who write poetry, write poems to cope with their own stress or to honor clients. Nurses who are good at organization might take charge of social events to build team morale.

Holistic nurses embellish their nursing practice with their own gifts.

An author of this chapter followed an interest in expressive arts in healing. Expressive art is different than art therapy. Expressive art focuses on the artistic process for emotional expression and release and includes such arts as visual arts, music, dance and movement, and drama. This nurse became an expressive arts facilitator in hospices and nursing homes, incorporating visual arts such as collage and painting, along with music and expressive puppetry.

These approaches were effective with clients with dementia. Some clients benefited from aromatherapy—lavender oil for relaxation, lemon oil for energizing, or orange or grapefruit oil to dissipate strong smells in the room. Clients relax, lose a sense of time, become distracted from their pain, and find moments of joy and play.

Research tells us that during experiences with expressive arts, hormones shift the body to a healing mode, and blood flow shifts to bring nutrients and immune cells to fight cancer and infection (Samuels & Lane, 1998). Clients often report that they feel at peace and are able to access healing images.

Critical Thinking Question What special interests do you have that you might use to add your own creative touch to your practice?

See **Table 9-3**, Getting Started Right Now, to explore how you could incorporate these practices into your nursing practice.

Table 9-3 Getting Started Right Now

- Start each day with a centering practice of your choice. Use the one in this chapter or simply say a prayer to bring your best self to work and assist clients, families, and colleagues.
- Remember to focus on the sacred nature of our work. We are standing on holy ground in health care, privileged to journey with clients in their most intimate moments.
- Teach clients to relax by "breathing in peace and calm" and "blowing out tension." You try it, too!
- Help create a healing environment for others by paying attention to your own attitude. Be positive.
- Combat cynicism. When a colleague is negative, try: "That may be how you choose to see things, but I prefer to take a more positive view. Would you like to hear what I do to stay positive?" Refuse to listen to gossip and, instead, offer a compliment when possible or help other staff before they have to ask.
- Keep your sense of humor to keep perspective. Allow time to laugh and play.
- Experiment with modalities for yourself. Have a massage. Take a workshop on therapeutic touch or on another complementary modality.
- Read a book on meditation and practice it. Stay open.
- Role-play with a colleague on ways to introduce modalities to clients.
- Set the intention and follow through to practice self-care.

Summary

What we are able to implement varies according to our skill level, the client's receptivity, and the culture of our practice setting. Innovation, inclusion of complementary modalities, and multidisciplinary care are rapidly becoming a part of healthcare practice. Exploring possibilities of what is available in individual facilities and communities to offer clients the best possible care is an essential responsibility of nursing practice. There is a joy in nursing that is nourished by these self-care and complementary practices, for both you and the client. These practices afford us a great opportunity to offer empowered quality care to our clients and professional self-development to ourselves. We owe it to ourselves, our clients, our society, and to nursing. Enjoy the journey.

Annotated References

American Holistic Nurses Association. (2006, December 1). Holistic nursing achieves ANA specialty status. Press Release. Retrieved November 10, 2006, from http://www.ahna.org/new/specialty.html

This announcement by the official organization for holistic nurses defines holistic nursing and explains the implications of specialty recognition by the American Nurses Association for the future of holistic nursing.

Beaubrun, R., & Gray, G. (2000). Review of herbal medicines for psychiatric disorders. *Psychiatric Services, 51*(9), 1130–1133.

This is a useful article for psychiatric nursing regarding the herbal medicines clients may be using for self-medication.

Berman, B. M., Lao, L., Langenberg, P., Lee, W. L., Gilpin, A. M. K., & Hochberg, M. C. (2004). Effectiveness of acupuncture as adjunctive therapy in osteoarthritis of the knee: A randomized, controlled trial. *Annals of Internal Medicine, 141*, 901–910.

This article describes a randomized, controlled trial that demonstrates the effectiveness of acupuncture to improve function and pain relief as an adjunctive therapy when compared with credible sham acupuncture.

Calabria, M., & Macrae, J. (Eds.). (1994). *Suggestions for thought by Florence Nightingale.* Philadelphia: University of Pennsylvania Press.

This is an important work on the spiritual roots of nursing. Those interested in the spiritual philosophy of the founder of modern nursing will be drawn to this carefully edited edition, which offers insights about nursing, spirituality, and Nightingale herself.

Cass, H. (2004). Herbs for the nervous system: Ginkgo, kava, valerian, passionflower. *Seminars in Integrative Medicine, 2*(2), 82–88.

This article is a useful introduction to these herbals, featuring current research.

Cuellar, N. G. (2006). *Conversations in complementary and alternative medicine: Insights and perspectives from leading practitioners.* Sudbury, MA: Jones and Bartlett.

This book uses interviews to teach information about complementary modalities.

Dossey, B. M., Keegan, L., & Guzzetta, C. E. (2005). *Holistic nursing: A handbook for practice* (4th ed.). Sudbury, MA: Jones and Bartlett.

This text is a classic primer offering a detailed overview of holistic nursing and practice. It is a wonderful introduction to the areas of holistic nursing practice.

Ernst, E. (2001). *The desktop guide to complementary and alternative medicine: An evidence-based approach.* Edinburgh: Mosby.

This is an easy-to-use resource for research on CAMs.

Haley, J. (1993). *Uncommon therapy: The psychiatric techniques of Milton H. Erickson.* New York: W. W. Norton.

This author presents the theories of Erickson using interesting case studies.

Herbert-Ashton, M. J., & Clarkson, N. E. (2005). *Quick look nursing: Pharmacology.* Sudbury, MA: Jones and Bartlett.

This text is a quick reference book, useful for clinical practice.

Krieger, D. (1987). *Living the therapeutic touch: Healing as a lifestyle.* New York: Dodd, Mead.

This personal and scientific volume focuses on therapeutic touch and the autobiographic story of a personal transformation. This is an important volume for nurses interested in healing and holism.

Matters of Note. (2005). Can meditation change your brain? *Explore, 1*(3), 163.

This article highlights research on meditation and advanced brain functioning.

McGovern, K., Lockhart, A., Malay, P., et al (Eds.). (2003). *Nurse's handbook of alternative and complementary therapies.* Philadelphia: Lippincott Williams & Wilkins.

This easy-to-read text is a quick reference for an overview of alternative and complementary modalities.

Meseguer, E., Taboada, R., Sanchez, V., Mena, M. A., Campos, V., & De Yebenees, J. G. (2002). Life-threatening Parkinsonism induced by kava-kava. *Movement Disorders, 17*(1), 195–196.

This article raises the issue of the safety of kava-kava.

Newman, M. (1979). *Theory development in nursing.* Philadelphia: F. A. Davis.

This text focuses on a holistic approach of nursing, examining pattern recognition as reflective of the whole. Time, space, movements, and consciousness are examined at the macrocosmic, microcosmic, and humanistic levels.

Newman, M. (1989). The spirit of nursing. *Holistic Nursing Practice, 3*(3), 1–6.

This article in the journal of the American Holistic Nursing Association explores Newman's perspectives on nursing, health, disease, life as an ongoing process of expanding consciousness, and patterns that evolve and expand over time. A good introduction to her work.

Newshan, G., & Schuller-Civitella, D. (2003). Large clinical study shows value of therapeutic touch program. *Holistic Nursing Practice, 17*(4), 189–192.

This article reports findings of the largest published sample size of therapeutic touch outcomes using data from a continuous quality improvement clinical study and a patient satisfaction survey. Although this is not a research study, tools were developed to evaluate a TT program in a hospital.

Nightingale, F. (1992). *Notes on nursing: What it is and what it is not* (commemorative ed.). Philadelphia: J. P. Lippincott.

This classic text in nursing by Nightingale is a must for every nurse who wishes to connect with the clinical roots of nursing practice.

Pilkington, K., Boshnakova, A., & Richardson, J. (2006). St John's wort for depression: Time for a different perspective? *Complementary Therapies in Medicine.* Retrieved September 26, 2006, from www.sciencedirect.com

This article provides a literature review of meta-analyses, systematic reviews, and qualitative studies of St John's wort for the treatment of depression.

Richards, K. C., Gibson R., &, Overton-McCoy, A. L. (2000). Effects of massage in acute and critical care. *AACN Clinical Issues, 11*(1), 77–96.

This article discusses the results of a systematic review of 22 articles examining the effects of massage on relaxation, comfort, and sleep.

Samuels, M., & Lane, M. R. (1998). *Creative healing.* San Francisco: Harper.

This book offers useful information on the integration of creative expression and healing.

Snyder, M., & Lindquist, R. (2002). *Complementary/alternative therapies in nursing* (4th ed.). New York: Springer.

This book encourages nurses to explore the modalities that can be offered without physicians' orders, thereby developing autonomy in professional practice. These modalities include music, therapeutic touch, imagery, relaxation, movement, prayer, humor, advocacy, support groups, and biofeedback.

Spencer, J. W., & Jacobs, J. J. (2003). *Complementary and alternative medicine: An evidence-based approach.* St. Louis, MO: Mosby.

This text is a valuable reference book that emphasizes research, analyzes the effectiveness of each therapy, and provides practical information on how the therapies can be used to treat illness.

Thich Nhat Hanh. (1992). *Peace is every step: The path of mindfulness in everyday life.* New York: Bantam Books.

Vietnamese Zen Master's guidance on integrating the practice of mindfulness and being in the moment into everyday moments and actions of life. It includes a useful discussion of looking at strong emotions, such as anger and dealing with violence.

Watson, J. (1988). *Nursing: Human science and human care: A theory of nursing.* New York: National League for Nursing.

This is Jean Watson's second major work, which addresses philosophic issues and problems in order to "better our contribution to society." This text focuses on human care in nursing science.

Additional Resources

Childre, D. L., & Marint, H. (2000). *The HeartMath solution: The Institute of HeartMath's revolutionary program for engaging the power of the heart's intelligence.* San Francisco, CA: Harper.

This is an interesting text offering research on the value of centering.

Dossey, B. M., Keegan, L., & Guzzetta, C. E. (2005). *Pocket guide for holistic nursing.* Sudbury, MA: Jones and Bartlett.

This pocket guide is a quick reference for the most important concepts from holistic nursing.

Fontaine, K. L. (2005). *Complementary & alternative therapies for nursing practice.* Upper Saddle River, NJ: Pearson/Prentice Hall.

An excellent, readable introduction to holistic nursing practice.

Frisch, N., Dossey, B. M., Guzzetta, C., & Quinn, J. (2000). *AHNA standards of holistic nursing practice: Guidelines for caring and healing.* Sudbury, MA: Jones and Bartlett.

This book is the first to put holistic caring-healing interventions into action. Endorsed by the American Holistic Nurses Association, it offers explicit guidelines for over 50 standards of holistic nursing.

Ganim, B. (1999). *Art and healing: Using expressive art to heal your body, mind, and spirit.* New York: Three Rivers Press.

This is an in-depth exploration on the use of images in healing.

O'Brien, M. E. (2008). *Spirituality in nursing: Standing on holy ground* (3rd ed.). Sudbury, MA: Jones and Bartlett.

O'Brien discusses the relationship between spirituality and nursing from over 20 years of research and includes interventions and a spiritual needs assessment. This edition includes a chapter dedicated to September 11.

Thornton, L. (1998). RX. RN. Self-renewal and nurturing for holistic nurses. *Alternative and Complementary Therapies, 4*(5), 364–366.

This is a useful article that supports the belief that the foundation of holistic nursing is holistic self-care by the nurse.

Internet Resources

http://nursing.jbpub.com/psychiatric

Visit http://nursing.jbpub.com/psychiatric for interactive exercises, NCLEX review questions, WebLinks, and more.

CHAPTER 10

Family and Intimate Partner Violence

Claudia Mitzeliotis and Winifred Z. Kennedy

LEARNING OBJECTIVES

After reading this chapter, you will be able to:

- Identify what constitutes intimate partner abuse, child abuse, and elder abuse.
- Recognize the prevalence and clinical presentation of various types of family abuse and violence.
- Understand the cycle of abuse and victimization.
- Discuss the various types of family violence and appropriate nursing interventions.

KEY TERMS

Active neglect
Battered child syndrome
Battered partner syndrome
Batterer
Child abuse
Domestic violence
Empathy
Empowerment
Family violence
Incest
Intimate partner violence
Material exploitation
Neglect
Passive neglect
Victim

http://nursing.jbpub.com/psychiatric

Visit http://nursing.jbpub.com/psychiatric for interactive exercises, NCLEX review questions, WebLinks, and more.

Introduction

The potential for abuse or violence exists within the home, the community, the workplace, and other institutions. Abuse or violence can occur between individuals, intimate partners, family members, or adults and children within the community. Family violence has become a national issue, and one that cannot be taken lightly. Healthy People 2010, the framework for a national prevention agenda, has listed violence as one of its top 10 agenda items. Some of the other healthcare issues in the top 10 are tobacco use, overweight and obesity, mental health, and substance abuse. The Healthy People 2010 initiative is dedicated to designing national health objectives, identifying the most significant preventable threats to health, and establishing national goals to reduce these threats. Family violence, including child maltreatment and physical abuse and intimate partner assault, is a threat to the safety and well-being of all family

Family violence is the use or threat of physical, emotional, sexual, or economic abuse to control a family member.

A victim is any person of any age who is violated by acts of disorderly conduct, harassment, reckless endangerment, entrapment, or assault, including attempted assault.

In overt behavior, the person acts openly. The agenda is clearly defined. In covert behavior, the abuser conceals his or her agenda.

In domestic violence, the abuser acts violently toward the intimate partner. Intimate partner violence is not associated with a particular social or economic group.

members, not only the victim. This chapter will focus on three forms of **domestic violence**: intimate partner violence, child abuse, and elder abuse (U.S. Department of Health and Human Services, 2005).

The emphasis on safety highlighted by the Joint Commission for Accreditation of Healthcare Organizations (JCAHO) includes screening all adolescents and adults for intimate partner violence, or domestic abuse, child abuse, maltreatment, and exploitation.

General Description

Family is defined as any group of two or more people who live together and are emotionally involved with each other. Although families are usually considered a refuge from the turbulent outside world, some homes experience a great deal of domestic turmoil. The emotional involvement can be of a loving and caring nature or one of violence. The incidence of **family violence** has steadily increased, and many people do not feel safe in their own homes.

Family violence consists of one family member threatening or mistreating another family member or partner as a way to control that individual. Family violence manifests itself in various forms of spousal or intimate partner abuse, child abuse, or elder abuse. These forms of abuse are addressed separately in this chapter.

Family violence is not identified with a particular class or culture. The **victim** may be of either gender. Most victims of **intimate partner violence** are women. The nurse must remember that men also can be victims; however, abused men are usually reluctant to come forward, fearing humiliation. Violence is not limited to physical acts; the phrase encompasses a wide variety of behaviors. Victims may be subjected to economic abuse that limits their expenditures or earnings and results in monetary losses. Emotional, sexual, and psychologic abuse are considered forms of family violence. It is important for the nurse to identify the signs of family violence, because the victim's environment may be life-threatening. Physical abuse need not be present. Emotional abuse can have an equally life-threatening impact.

Intrafamily violence, intimate partner violence, and child and elder abuse are not classified on Axis I or II in the *Diagnostic and Statistical Manual of Mental Disorders,* Fourth Edition, Text Revision (*DSM-IV-TR*; American Psychiatric Association [APA], 2000). Rather, these problems are identified in the section concerning conditions that may be a focus of clinical attention. Included under relational problems are relational problem related to a mental disorder or general medical condition, parent-child relational problem, partner relational problem, and sibling relational problem. Specific coding for domestic violence distinguishes physical or sexual abuse of an adult versus a child, and also indicates whether the focus of clinical attention is the victim or perpetrator of the abuse. Included under problems related to abuse and **neglect** are physical abuse of a child, sexual abuse of a child, neglect of a child, physical abuse of an adult, and sexual abuse of an adult. The client may meet an Axis I category related to the abuse such as a mood or anxiety disorder, acute stress disorder, or posttraumatic stress disorder. In addition, the client may meet criteria for an Axis II disorder such as intermittent explosive disorder, impulse-control disorder, or a personality disorder.

There have been many myths and misconceptions associated with family violence. These myths have been ingrained into our society and have deterred interventions, leading to adverse outcomes for clients. There are five well-known myths on this subject, which are shown in **Table 10-1**.

If these myths are seen as truths, the victim is in danger of not getting the help he or she needs. The healthcare worker will perpetuate the abuse by not believing the victim.

Table 10-1 Myths of Family Violence

1. Myth: The victim caused the violence, "He or she asked for it."
   Fact: The batterer caused the violence. He or she is responsible for his or her actions.
2. Myth: The victim enjoys the abuse or else he or she would have left.
   Fact: No one enjoys being abused or victimized.
3. Myth: If the victim left the violence would stop.
   Fact: Victims have been found to be in more danger after they left.
4. Myth: Family violence only occurs in low socioeconomic groups.
   Fact: Family violence occurs in all socioeconomic groups.
5. Myth: The assault is an isolated incident and will not occur again.
   Fact: Battering is a complex pattern related to power and control.

Epidemiology of Family Violence

Violence may be associated with crime, gangs, mental health problems, substance abuse, and alcohol problems. Aggression may range from sneering or verbal harassment to bullying, school violence, sexual harassment and assault, and the use of hand guns or assault weapons. Exposure to violence comes in many forms from the media, movies, games, and even music or the reporting of the daily news. It can also be a learned behavior, often associated with lower economic class, poor education, and cultural expectations. It has been hypothesized that there is an intergenerational transmission between aggressors and victims, and the victims then go on to victimize others. Although certain risk factors have been identified, intrafamily violence has been found across varied racial, economic, and educational backgrounds. Some common triggers are seen in **Table 10-2.**

Many theories have been proposed to explain why a victim remains in an abusive relationship. It is important to remember that this is a phenomenon that is difficult to generalize and theorize. Each victim is an individual, and why he or she chose to stay in an abusive relationship is unclear and cannot be generalized.

Carnes (1997) theorized that a bonding described as "traumatic bonding" takes place in relationships that have domestic violence. Two primary characteristics of this theory are (1) that the victim feels dominated by the abuser, setting up an imbalance, and (2) that the abuse is not continuous but rather intermittent.

Table 10-2 Common Triggers of Family Violence

Critical Crisis	Economic Issues
Alcohol or substance abuse	Unemployment
Serious or long-term injury	Change in employment
A death in the family	Retirement
Pregnancy or birth of a child	Partner's employment status
Separation or divorce	Income level
Mental health problems	Caretaking burden
Chronic medical problems	Lack of medical insurance
Cognitive changes in family member	Credit card spending

Note: These are merely stimuli that can provoke an episode, not the actual cause. The causes of domestic violence are more serious underlying issues.

Clinical Example

A woman living in a shelter decided to return to her partner. She found that he had not changed. She stated that the emotional abuse does not leave physical scars, but scars were left on her heart. She named emotional abuse, financial abuse, and destruction of property and pets as leaving her scarred. Her return is characteristic of psychological entrapment. She continues to give power to the abuser and her self-esteem is low.

Other theories that have been associated with family violence include learned helplessness, psychological entrapment, and the Stockholm syndrome. These theories focused on the victim and why they remained in the relationship. For example, in the description of Stockholm syndrome, victims are compared to hostages in that if the aggressors showed the hostages any degree of kindness, the hostages would have some **empathy** for their captors because they had shared a common experience and survived. This is similar to the victim having empathy for the **batterer** once kindness and remorse are shown.

In a situation of learned helplessness, the victim gives up. In an animal experiment, subjects who were shocked repeatedly eventually gave up trying to escape the shock. In a similar manner, victims of repeated abuse become demoralized and begin to lose motivation to try to escape the abuse. Victims may feel pressured by cultural or community expectations, or may be fearful of being involved in the legal system or of being unprotected by the court system.

Patterns of Abuse

The patterns of abuse escalate slowly, making identification difficult. The abuser appears loving, and the overprotectiveness is seen as caring. The abuser's goal is to completely control the victim. There are three distinct phases of abuse:

- In the escalation phase, the batterer begins to control and isolate the victim. This subtle stage often masks the abuser's true motives. The batterer often prevents the victim from working full time. This initially isolates the victim and establishes financial control.
- In the acute phase, the batterer uses threats and force to instill fear and to reinforce control. Physical violence is common.
- The de-escalation phase follows immediately after the acute phase. The batterer

Patterns of Abuse

Escalation phase: Tensions build until the abuser loses control. In this phase, a victim might provoke the batterer to strike "to get it over with."

Acute phase: Battering and abuse occur, whether physical or verbal. The victim does not fight back; emotional detachment decreases confrontation.

De-escalation phase: The victim seeks a reward for submission. The batterer is loving and promises to care for the victim.

becomes apologetic and promises never to harm the victim again, giving the victim false hope for improvement. The apologies tend to work if this is the first offense. Over time, as the pattern continues, the victim lives in constant fear of further attacks.

Clinical Presentation

The following symptoms and psychological complaints may indicate an ongoing abusive situation. The common types of injuries associated with family violence include contusions, lacerations, abrasions, stab wounds, human bites, burns, gunshot wounds, sprains, and fractures. These injuries are usually seen on the head, neck, chest, breasts, abdomen, and genital area. It is important to question the cause of injuries, even minor ones.

The nurse must investigate all medical complaints and findings. A history of repeated falls or chronic injuries should be questioned. The nurse should also look for injuries in different stages of healing. Clients may complain of unexplained medical symptoms of chronic pain, psychogenic pain, or pain-related trauma without visible signs of injuries.

Other common complaints voiced by clients who have been abused include decreased concentration, chronic headache, and sexual dysfunction as well as abdominal, gynecologic, and gastrointestinal complaints. Some clients experience frequent vaginal or urinary tract infections. The clinician should be aware of frequent visits to medical personnel with vague complaints but no physical findings.

Psychiatric symptoms are most prevalent when abuse is present. Clients commonly are isolated. The clinician may note evidence of overt or covert signs of suicide attempts or gestures. Psychiatric symptoms range from anxiety attacks to panic attacks. It is also common for clients to exhibit depression. The nurse should observe for posttraumatic stress disorder. Clients may exhibit sleep and appetite disturbances and may also abuse drugs or alcohol. Statistics show that clients often return to their batterers, making intervention very difficult. Taking photographs will help in monitoring the abuse and can be used later in the judicial system. However, the patient must sign a consent form to be photographed, and a witness must also sign. The consent form becomes part of the patient's records along with the pictures taken.

Intimate Partner Violence

As mentioned earlier, domestic violence is not associated with any particular socioeconomic status, gender, race, ethnic group, age, or employment status. In intimate partner violence, the threat of abuse or intimidation is found between heterosexual or homosexual couples and current or former spouses. Women account for the majority of victims of intimate partner violence, approximately 85% of cases. In most cases the abuse or assaults are never reported. The National Crime Victimization Survey estimates that there are approximately 1 million cases of intimate partner violence each year. This accounts for 6% of all rape and sexual assault cases, 11% of all murders, and 30% of all female murders. The highest rates of intimate partner violence are for women between 20 and 24 years old (U.S. Department of Justice, 2006).

Critical Thinking Questions Susan has come to the emergency room four times this past month with repeated injuries she refers to as falls/accidents. How will you gain her confidence and try to assess whether she is a victim of domestic violence? In examining Susan you feel it is important to document with photos the markings on her body. It is important to consider Susan's feelings on this, as well as the legal ramifications. What steps are needed before you can take photos of the victim's body demonstrating the degree of abuse?

Critical Thinking Question Tom is living with his wife, who calls him names and humiliates him in front of the children. She tells him to leave and that she hates him and will kill him in his sleep. He is emotionally paralyzed and stays. He tells the nurse he wants a family. He is hoping she will change because at times she is nice. He also feels it is his fault. He continues to stay in his marriage being emotionally and verbally abused. What interventions would you use to help Tom?

Special Considerations: Teen Dating/Relationship Abuse

Dating is a time when one begins to once again explore the concept of trust. In early childhood development one learns to trust the caregiver; in dating this concept is once again touched upon. One does not want to believe that the person they chose to date would abuse them. However, intimate partner violence and sexual assault are common forms of violence among adolescents and young adults. This can have long-term damaging

NURSING CARE PLAN Intimate Partner Violence

Expected Outcomes	Interventions	Evaluations
• Will decrease risk of injury by self or others. • Will evaluate possible history of or presence of intrafamily violence. • Will decrease fear and anxiety. • Will assist client in developing a safety plan.	• Assessment of risk for self-harm, assault, suicide, and homicide. • Provision of appropriate assessment and evaluation. • Development of nurse-patient relationship. • Discuss options for referral and follow-up.	• Client is able to contract for safety and recognizes choices. • Documentation of physical status, appropriate photographs, and collection of evidence. • Empowerment to participate in assessment and counseling. • Client verbalizes willingness to take the next step to protect self from abuse and violence.

Visit http://nursing.jbpub.com/psychiatric for additional care plans and exercises.

effects on self-concept, self-esteem, and choosing a partner in the future. As in domestic violence, relationship abuse can be any one of the four methods: sexual abuse, emotional abuse, physical abuse, or psychological abuse. It is difficult to identify relationship abuse because most young people would not discuss this with anyone, and these crimes are often unreported. It is important if you are a school nurse to be aware that this is occurring within the community. Studies indicate that 1 in 10 female high school students report being physically and/or sexually abused while dating (Centers for Disease Control and Prevention, 2006). Surveys of female college students indicate that 1 in 4 had experienced some form of intimate partner violence (U. S. Department of Justice, 2006).

It is the role of the nurse working in high schools, junior high schools, and universities to teach students the characteristics of an abusive relationship. Included in most programs is also information regarding "date rape" and behaviors that may place individuals at risk for this and other problems. It is important to implement support groups. The risk of abuse and violence is higher for young women, but both young men and women need to know that they have a right to be treated with dignity and respect. Abuse and violence awareness programs can be designed by nurses to educate young people on the signs of an abuser and safe dating. It is important in these programs to include common characteristics of abusers and warning signs. These programs should be made available to both genders because, as with domestic violence, dating violence is not limited to heterosexual relationships. Emergency room nurses and psychiatric nurses need to include questions regarding relationship status and potential assault in their assessments of young people.

CASE STUDY Ms. C.

Ms. C. was taken to the emergency department after ingestion of approximately 30 tabs of acetaminophen for a headache. She told the staff that she had impulsively taken the medication after a fight with her spouse and had not intended to kill herself. She minimized the event, telling everyone how stupid she was. The pain was so bad she just hadn't realized how many pills she had taken. However, when the nurse asked her if she felt safe at home, Ms. C. began to cry and shake. Although there was no reason for his jealousy and rage, her partner often became violent and had beaten her. He had returned to the house drunk and was verbally accusatory. She could never do anything right. No wonder he had to drink. She couldn't keep the house clean, the dog quiet, and the bills from piling up. He was provocative, throwing things around the house and breaking furniture. The last time this had happened he had tried to choke her and she passed out. Ms. C. told the nurse that the only reason she thought she hadn't died that time was that he was too drunk to finish her off. She felt that the only way to get away from the house and from him was to take the medication. She didn't really care if she died; she was desparate to find a way out. She felt so ashamed; she would rather be dead than return home.

Clinical Example

An 18-year-old female comes to the emergency room with bruises on her arms and legs and a black eye. She says she injured herself falling off her bicycle. You accept this and treat her injuries. She returns 2 weeks later with similar bruises. She tells you that she had a fight with her roommate. She doesn't want to report it because she has to share the room with her and doesn't want to make waves. You decide at this point you will have to report this and have her room changed. She stops you and begins to sob, confiding that it is actually her boyfriend on campus who has assaulted her. She insists he does not mean to hurt her; but admits that when he drinks, he loses control. She states that she feels responsible because she did not want to have sex with him. She feels lucky that he is dating her because he usually does not date girls who will not have sex with him.

The Centers for Disease Control and Prevention (CDC) have developed a special program, the National Youth Violence Prevention Resource Center and website (www.safeyouth.org) to help teens and the people who care about them to understand relationship abuse. This website is helpful and has creative programs that can be implemented to assist in educating young people on relationship abuse.

Studies indicate that drug use is a common factor in most cases of sexual assault. In addition, date rape drugs are used in approximately 5% of the cases involving women (Preidt, 2006). Common date rape drugs such as Rohypnol (flunitrazepam) and GHB (gamma hyroxybutyrate) are tasteless and odorless, making prevention difficult. One group of nursing students utilized the College of Registered Nurses of British Columbia standards for nursing practice highlighting client education and advocacy to work with the police to develop Student Nurses for Clean Drugs, an education project spotlighting the dangers to young people (Priest, 2005).

Batterers or abusive individuals share several characteristics. They deny responsibility for their actions, and they are unable to trust people; this is projected in all relationships. Batterers expect immediate gratification from their partners. They are extremely jealous and unwilling to negotiate.

Clinical Course and Complications

Emotional abuse ranges from name calling to yelling, constantly criticizing, or undermining behavior directed toward the spouse or partner. The victim becomes isolated, especially if the abuser is jealous. The jealous abuser makes it difficult for the victim to see family or friends. Occasional incidents of public humiliation reinforce that isolation. See **Table 10-3**.

Economic abuse is also considered a type of domestic violence. Perpetrators may deny the victim access to bank accounts and credit cards. They may insist that the victim account for every expenditure. This category also includes preventing a person from getting a job or returning to school. Economic control may place restraints on receiving adequate health and dental care and filling prescriptions.

Threats are as damaging as any of the other behaviors. They can leave a victim feeling paralyzed and helpless. Threats vary in degrees ranging from inflicting harm on the person to kidnapping the victim's child. Weapons are often displayed as an additional means of threatening the individual. The victim lives in a state of fear, trying to remain neutral in order to avoid the threats. The abuser uses anger to manipulate the individual.

Physical violence associated with domestic violence includes grabbing, pushing, hitting, kicking, choking, biting, punching, and slapping. The nurse must remember that pregnancy does not protect a woman from physical violence. Pregnant women have been thrown down the stairs or punched in the stomach, resulting in miscarriages. In the clinical setting, clients may present with gynecological disorders, sexually transmitted diseases, pregnancy difficulties, or orthopedic problems. Also, the potential for violence continues even after the relationship with the abuser has ended.

Differential Diagnosis

To obtain a comprehensive history, it is vital that the nurse maintain a supportive and nonjudgmental atmosphere. Victims need safety

Implications for Evidence-Based Practice

Biroscat et al. (2006) investigated the Michigan Intimate Partner Violence Against Woman (IPVAW) interventions in 23 emergency departments across the state over a 2-year period. Chart review confirmed 2,926 incidents of physical and/or sexual assault, and more than one third of these cases were attributable to intimate partner violence. A considerable proportion of the victims were young women abused by an ex-boyfriend. Further research and a wider sample are needed to determine the extent of relationship abuse.

Table 10-3 Abusive Behavior

Behavior	Description
Breaking promises	Not following through, not taking responsibility, refusing to help with childcare or household duties.
Emotional withholding	Not expressing how they feel, not being supportive, not giving compliments; disregards the rights or opinions of others.
Minimizing, denying, and blaming	Making light of the behavior; not taking the concerns or feelings of the victim seriously. Denying the abuse happened; shifting the responsibility. Blames the victim for upsetting them.
Economic control	Interfering with the victim's work or not allowing the person to work. Refusing to give money.
Self-destructive behavior	Abusing substances, threatening to kill themselves.
Isolation	Preventing victim from seeing or making it difficult to see friends or relatives. Monitoring phone calls, telling the victim where to go.
Harassment	Making uninvited visits or calls, following the victim, checking up on them, refusing to leave, and embarrassing them in public.
Pressure tactic	Using guilt trips to force the victim into making decisions. Manipulating the children, telling them what to do.
Destructive criticism/verbal abuse	This can range from name calling and yelling to swearing and mocking.
Abusing authority	Always claiming to be right, telling the person what to do.
Disrespect	Interrupting, changing topics, not listening or responding, twisting the person's words or statements, putting the person down in public.

and a chance to speak openly. Questioning the victim in the presence of the abuser may lead to more violence because the victim may be unable to communicate openly in this situation. Therefore, it is necessary to interview the victim separately.

Initially, the victim may not have enough trust in the nurse to discuss these issues. It is helpful to use action verbs such as hit, kick, or yell when asking questions. This helps victims verbalize the form of abuse. The nurse should rephrase questions when necessary if the client gives evasive answers. When questioning victims about violence during follow-up visits, the nurse must reassure the victim that his or her safety is a primary concern. Clinicians must also be aware of their own beliefs when interviewing a potential victim. It is important to be nonjudgmental and to remember that domestic violence is not associated with a certain class or group.

It is helpful to show the patient the Domestic Abuse Intervention Project Power and Control Wheel and have them point out which sections on the wheel diagram they identify with. The Power and Control Wheel diagram was developed from the experiences of abused women and has been used to help during the assessment stage of treatment (The Duluth Project, 1987). It includes descriptions of types of physical abuse ranging from pushing and shoving to using a weapon. Forms of power and control range from isolation and intimidation to economic and sexual abuse. It helps the victim to feel not alone and to identify specific incidents of abuse.

> Empowerment: Survivors of abuse gain self-esteem and self-confidence to control their environment.

There is also a "wheel" diagram that was designed during a domestic violence project to demonstrate how the healthcare system can perpetuate the abuse. Categories described in this wheel include:

- *Violating confidentiality:* Interviewing in front of family, telling colleagues topics discussed in confidence without the patient's permission, calling the police without the patient's consent
- *Trivializing and minimizing the abuse:* Ignoring the complaints and not taking them seriously
- *Blaming the victim:* Asking the victim why she or he did not leave or what they did to upset him or her.
- *Not respecting the victim's autonomy:* Giving suggestions on what the victim should do (e.g., go to a shelter, go to the police)
- *Ignoring her or his need for safety:* Not acknowledging the danger the victim is in

Battered partner syndrome is a term used to describe a victim who is exposed to multiple traumas, is passive and socially isolated, and often finds it difficult to leave the batterer.

- *Normalizing victimization:* Seeing her or his abuse as normal in the relationship, failure to respond to her or his disclosure of the abuse

Management and Treatment of Intimate Partner Violence

Nurses have many roles that they use when delivering quality care to clients. The key component is self-reflection. The nurse must first identify his or her own feelings about the subject and concepts of domestic violence. Empathy is one of the key elements needed to assist the victim. An important role the nurse will utilize is the role of advocate. See **Table 10-4** for sample interview questions to determine whether the client is being abused or feels unsafe at home. The following categories are seen as key components of the advocate role:

- *Respect confidentiality:* Interviews should take place in a private area away from family members. This simple tactic will enhance the therapeutic relationship and build a trusting relationship.
- *Respect the victim's autonomy:* Respect their right to make decisions in their life in their own time frame.
- *Believe and validate the client's experiences:* Listen to her or him and believe her or him. Reassure the victim that he or she is not alone.
- *Acknowledge the injustice:* The violence is not his or her fault. No one deserves to be abused.
- *Help plan for future safety:* Explore what measures were taken in the past and if they were helpful. Is the victim aware of agencies and shelters that can help?
- *Promote access to community services:* Have a list of shelters available to give the client. Provide a hotline number the client can use at any time.

Table 10-4 Sample Interview Questions

"I have noticed you have a number of marks and bruises on your body. Could you tell me how this happened? Has anyone hurt you?"
"I have heard from patients I treated that a person close to them has hurt them. Has this happened to you?"
"You shared that sometimes your partner loses his temper. Could you describe what happens when he loses his temper? Has he ever hurt you?"
"Do your verbal fights sometimes get physical?"
"Does your partner sometimes try to control your actions?"

Table 10-5 Education for Clients and Families for Intimate Partner Violence

- Recognize that some individuals do not see themselves as being abused.
- Provide a supportive setting.
- Help the person identify alternatives rather than returning to the batterer.
- Provide information on obtaining legal assistance and a court order for protection.
- Identify and treat extreme mental and physical fatigue.
- Reassure the victim that she or he is not alone.
- Identify feelings of guilt and self-blame.
- Recognize that counseling alone has limited effectiveness while the violence continues; counseling works only when the victim is safe and the abuser is in treatment as well.
- Inform the battered partner that she or he may leave and return several times before making a final decision, and that plans for safety should be continued.
- Provide a 24-hour hotline and shelter information.

Some clinicians may want to keep a checklist of interventions they can refer to when working with the battered partner. See **Table 10-5** for some interventions for battered partners.

Include intervention goals such as developing independence and promoting love of self and feelings of self-worth to promote assertiveness that can be used to demonstrate components of a "healthy relationship." Respect, responsiblity, honesty and accountability, economic and social partnership, negotiation, and fairness are key hallmarks of a healthy relationship.

The client should help decide the composition of the treatment plan. This is the first step to empowering the client. Knowledge of the components of a healthy relationship is useful in helping to show the client what is acceptable in a mature relationship and allowing the client to make choices. It is important to allow the client the autonomy to make these decisions. If the nurse makes the decisions she or he is only reinforcing the abuse by reinforcing the client's place in a helpless situation.

It is frightening to leave home when one is financially dependent upon someone else. The client can benefit from joining a domestic violence support group or self-help group. These groups provide resource information and empower the victim. **Empowerment** is the key to successful treatment. The forced isolation experienced by victims may have been responsible for restricting access to family, friends, or community resources with their employers and healthcare practitioners. Reestablishing these links to social networks helps decrease the perceived isolation and increase support.

Implications for Evidence-Based Practice

In a randomized controlled study of two prenatal clinics in the Northwest and Midwest, 1,000 woman between 13 and 23 weeks gestation were offered either an abuse video or access to a nurse case manger; participants identified as at risk for abusive relationships received nursing case management throughout their pregnancy. Curry, Durham, Bullock, Bloom, & Davis (2006) concluded that nurses needed to focus on client-identified needs, which may not be the abusive relationship. This study has implications for patient teaching and interventions.

Clients should have access to emergency shelters and hotlines to assist them in times of crisis. Many times the client is afraid to even accept information, fearing that their partner may find evidence that they have spoken with someone outside of the household about the abuse. For this reason, the referral information is often printed on wallet-sized cards or even matchbooks so they may be confidentially and safely carried by the client. The nurse must work with the client to explore the benefits and drawbacks of remaining at home. The client should be assisted to develop a step-wise safety plan. Part of the nursing intervention is helping the client recognize the importance of having a plan and planning to use it. The client can be asked when she or he will feel ready to take the next step. It is important to remember that many times the victim leaves and returns to the batterer. The nurse must always remain objective and supportive.

It is also valuable to consider that once the client makes a decision, a shelter may well be the last and only safe alternative. Many times women in particular escape in the middle of the night with their children and only the clothes on their back. Shelters often are not set up to accept male clients alone or with children, and other resources must be found. These clients are running for their lives and their sanity to a shelter. For these clients, anonymity and refuge are essential. Once at the shelter they will be examined by the nurse and interviewed by caseworkers. Children are placed in the local school and try to carry on as if all is well. The children tend to be upset and some cry, talking mom into returning to the batterer. Remember, the batterer may not have abused the children, and even when there is **child abuse** also, the child may want to return. The children are frightened and want to return to a familiar setting. Some woman do not stay in the shelter system, and return to their home. It is important to remain nonjudgemental. The main thing in caring for these clients is self-reflection. It is important to assess your own feelings and be able to treat these clients objectively.

A diagnosis of **battered partner syndrome** is associated with a battered person who is unable to leave the batterer. In this case an individual develops a set of personality traits initiated by the abuse, making survival in the relationship possible. The victim has become tuned in to the cycle of domestic violence. She or he anticipates the next explosion and may passively comply with the assault in order to go on to the next phase where the batterer will express remorse and vow never to be abusive again. The victim is not fighting back, has become withdrawn, and has given up. The battered partner sees escape as impossible, and depression compounds this

Implications for Evidence-Based Practice

In a randomized study of two groups, one who received a referral card and another who received a case management protocol, McFarlane, Groff, O'Brien, & Watson (2006) found that women in both groups experienced a significant increase in safety behaviors and a decrease in utilization of costly in-patient and out-patient services. The process of abuse assessment and subsequent disclosure of abuse has the potential to interrupt the cycle of abuse and increase safety. Inclusion of abuse assessment was shown to be an important nursing intervention.

entrapment. Assessment and treatment of this syndrome are vital if the victim is to survive. Recidivism is a barrier to treatment.

In conjunction with these patterns, the survivor of intimate partner violence is also faced with the conflicting concepts of love, hope, and fear: The idea of love for your partner, and the thought that any relationship has its good points and is not all bad. The hope that things will change; it was not like this at the beginning, and the batterer will change. The very real fear that the threats to kill you or your family are real.

Child Abuse

Child abuse has existed for centuries and across national boundaries. Nurses are considered mandated reporters for suspected cases of child abuse and neglect. (Additional discussion of child abuse can be found in Chapter 24.)

Child abuse consists of physical injury, emotional abuse, or sexual abuse that occurs when the child is neglected, isolated, or shamed and demeaned.

Incidence and Prevalence

The World Health Organization (WHO; 2006) report on preventing child maltreatment notes that the prevalence of child abuse is higher in societies where there is a tolerance for violence, gender and social inequality, poor living standards, and child pornography, prostitution, and child labor. The 2002 incidence of deaths related to child abuse was 31,000 deaths per 100,000 cases of reported violence and neglect by parents or close family members. Depending upon the country, from one fourth to one half of all children report experiencing some form of child abuse in their lifetime. Nearly 20% of women and 10% of men report a history of early sexual abuse. It is estimated that in the United States, the cost of child abuse is $94 billion a year, or nearly 1% of the gross national product. Hospital costs related to child abuse are $13 billion a year, mental health costs $425 million, child welfare costs $14.4 billion, and costs related to criminal activity approximately $55.4 billion a year (WHO, 2006).

Epidemiology

Incest involves sexual intercourse or intimate sexual behavior with members of the same family. In the treatment of incest, it is important to remember to collect evidence, because criminal charges may be filed.

Child abuse may be related to a parental history of abuse or sexual assault, a parental history of engaging in substance abuse or criminal activity, medical or mental health problems, or difficulty bonding or physical problems at birth. Isolation, poverty, and lack of self-control and impulse control have also been identified as factors (WHO, 2006).

Child abuse, maltreatment, or neglect, as in other categories of family violence, should not be associated with a particular social class or ethnic group. However, it is possible that incidents of neglect and physical abuse may correlate to higher levels of financial stress.

A child living in a home where domestic violence occurs is considered a victim of abuse. A child in this environment lives in fear and anticipation of losing a parent to violence. Living with domestic violence can also have long-term effects. For example, the child may eventually be diagnosed with an Axis I disorder, be involved in an abusive situation as a victim or batterer, have chronic health problems, or have long-term problems forming relationships.

Child abuse occurs when a temporary or primary caregiver intentionally harms or threatens a child. It is also defined as maltreatment either by physical abuse, sexual abuse, emotional abuse, or neglect. Emotional abuse varies from an emotionally distant parent to one who is overbearing or demeaning. Forms of emotional abuse include name calling and humiliating a child in public. Pressuring children to meet unrealistic expectations can damage them emotionally. Interfering with the child's social and psychological development in any way is also considered emotional abuse. Neglect can be life-threatening. In these instances, the caregiver fails to provide the basic requirements of food, shelter, medical care, and supervision. Children have died from this form of abuse.

Physical abuse can also be life-threatening. This type of abuse consists of inflicting bodily harm. Forcing children to exercise excessively or to participate in activities against their will is also considered physical abuse.

Sexual abuse ranges from exposing the child inappropriately to sexual acts or materials to using the child for sexual stimulation. It is important to remember that in addition to other types of abuses, sexual abuse of children occurs in all socioeconomic classes.

Incest is a serious form of sexual abuse that is not easily detected. Children often do not report these occurrences. They are filled with fear and confusion, especially if the violator is a parent. Incest is defined as intimate sexual contact between members of the same family; in this case, the family members are closely enough related to be legally prohibited from marrying one another.

Critical Thinking Question Ms. Smith brings her daughter, age 5, in for her annual physical. Alice used to be a smiling and joking child. She now is quiet and withdrawn. You comment on the change you noticed. Her mom dismisses it and says she is growing up and maturing. You notice that Alice is uncomfortable with taking off her clothes and being examined. You ask her if anything hurts and she says it hurts when she urinates. You ask how long she has been having pain. She says since daddy has been sleeping in her bed at night. Her mother chuckles and dismisses this as her imagination. You are uncomfortable with pursuing your thoughts. You dismiss the child's statements and go on with your nursing tasks. This case scenario took place 40 years ago. Alice, today in therapy at the age of 45, shared the abuse she endured. Her father repeatedly sexually abused her. He penetrated her at age 5, and this went on for almost 5 years until her parents were divorced. Her mother continues to deny that any abuse took place. Alice felt used by both parents—the abuser and her mother who never rescued her or allowed her to be rescued. Today, how would this situation be handled?

Clinical Example

Rick was the youngest of three children. The household was chaotic and his father was physically abusive towards his mother. His father was later imprisoned, and his parents separated. When Rick was 3 years old, his mother, who was using drugs, was charged with neglect. He and his older siblings were placed in care with his grandmother. A few years later, Rick was returned to live with his mother. This plan failed when Rick was physically abused by his stepfather; teachers in school noted physical bruising and frequent absences. Rick was placed in foster care. He had some behavioral problems and was moved through several foster homes and group homes. Things seemed to be looking up for Rick when he was 13 years old and he returned to live with his mother and several of his siblings. However, when he was 15 years old, his mother told him that it was her turn for a good life. She told him that she was going to remarry and that he would have to leave the apartment. For several months Rick carried on going to school. Sometimes he stayed with relatives and sometimes he slept over at friends' apartments. Then the nights that he had no place to stay became more frequent. He dropped out of school and began to live on the street.

Clinical Presentation

To assess whether maltreatment has occurred, the nurse must be understanding and empathetic. This will encourage the child to disclose events. A concise interview, including a thorough psychosocial and medical history, aids in detecting signs of abuse. Repetitive bruising is an indication of abuse and must be explored, although the child may deny any abusive incidents. If children exhibit overly aggressive behaviors, this also may be a sign of physical abuse. This trait is seen most often in boys, but it can be observed in girls as well.

As mentioned previously, child abuse may be present where domestic violence occurs. If a husband physically abuses his wife, he most likely will also physically abuse the child. Even when the wife leaves the batterer, the perpetrator will use the child or children as a means of control.

Children are afraid to report abuse in the home. It is important to remember that the child is loyal to the family and may initially fear the repercussions of disclosure. As in all cases where abuse is suspected, separate interviews with the victim and suspected perpetrator are advised. Simple interviewing techniques to remember include establishing eye contact and adopting an open body position that shows interest. An interviewer might say, "Do people in your family hit each other when they get mad?" It is important to coordinate interviews by clinicians and state agencies, because multiple interviews can be upsetting and not in the child's best interest.

Multiple lesions or bruises at different stages of healing are considered suspicious and warrant further investigation. **Battered child syndrome** refers to children who exhibit multiple traumas and who appear to have been beaten repeatedly. Battered child syndrome is associated with children 3 years of age and younger. These children are shaken, beaten, or otherwise traumatized brutally, causing severe injuries and even death. Multiple fractures and bruises are associated with this syndrome. Repetitive bruising is an indication to explore these incidents further. You may suspect child abuse, but the child may deny it.

The child's development and growth pattern should be assessed. A weight of less than the fifth percentile for the age group may indicate signs of neglect. Complaints of genital or abdominal pain without cause are other indicators of possible abuse. The symptom of a child who has been exposed to an act of incest is similar to that of a child who has been sexually abused: expressions of fear, aggressive behaviors, and sexual behaviors. These symptoms can appear together or as isolated occurrences.

The nurse demonstrates empathy when viewing the client's world from his or her internal frame of reference. This involves the nurse's sensitivity to the client's current feelings and the ability to communicate this to the client in a language that can be understood. This technique is most useful in establishing trust and expresses understanding and concern.

Table 10-6 Education for Clients and Families for Abused Children

- Identify the child's fears caused by a violent home environment.
- Teach the abused child to express feelings rather than act them out.
- Allow the child to express feelings of guilt, particularly if the child is angry with the abuser.
- Aid and encourage the parent and child to discuss their fears openly.
- Teach children acceptable ways of expressing their emotions. Denial is used as a protective device. Through play therapy, young children are able to express their feelings openly.
- Focus on helping older children work through emotions of guilt, shame, responsibility, anger, and depression.

Table 10-7 Education for Abusive Parents

- Encourage the abusive parent to express feelings freely.
- Remain nonjudgmental.
- Empathize with the parents' frustrations.
- Provide information on parenting support groups.
- Explore alternative childcare services.
- Help parents identify triggers to abusive behavior.
- Discuss alternate coping mechanisms.
- Identify sources of community and family support.
- Refer for appropriate treatment if indicated.
- Assist the parent during the referral and reporting process.

The child should be observed for nightmares or withdrawn behavior. Child victims may exhibit fear when they see perpetrators. Another symptom caused by fear is regression. Symptoms of aggressive behavior are hitting, biting, breaking toys, head banging, and tantrums. These symptoms appear as a result of the intense anger the child is experiencing. The child is angry at the person who has abused him or her and at the parent who was trusted to protect the child. The child who is a victim of incest feels emotionally abandoned by the nonabusive parent if the abuse goes undetected.

Reporting child abuse is mandated by legislation in the United States. Statutory requirements override the client-patient confidentiality rule. Failure to report can result in penalties. Professional immunity may be granted when reporting suspicions. Nurses should be familiar with the requirements for reporting child abuse in the states where they practice.

Battered child syndrome takes place when a child has multiple traumas and has been beaten repeatedly. Shaken baby syndrome refers to rough handling and shaking of infants that results in brain injury and possible death.

Management and Treatment of Child Abuse

It is difficult to single-handedly treat a case of child abuse. The clinician should coordinate treatment with social workers, attorneys, and medical personnel. No consensus has been reached concerning the most effective form of treatment. Foster care offers some respite, but may also be abusive, causing further trauma when the child is separated from the family. Children who have been sexually abused or who are victims of incest should not be returned to the abuser.

Maintaining the continuity of the family during treatment, however, is also a consideration. The nurse must attempt to involve the family and assess their social, physical, economic, and emotional needs if the child is to remain in the home during treatment. Community resources can provide a sense of security for the family and increase the members' self-esteem and sense of control. See **Table 10-6** for potential interventions for abused children.

It is important to incorporate the abusive parent/parents in your treatment plan. There are a number of interventions that can be used; see **Table 10-7**.

Elder Abuse

The media and healthcare profession have only recently begun to address elder abuse. In the 1990s, the U.S. Department of Health and Human Services created a task force to define and identify preventive measures that would be beneficial to the treatment of abused elders. In some states, elder abuse is covered under domestic violence laws or laws applying to nursing homes and home healthcare agencies, whereas in others there are specific laws covering manadatory reporting.

The characteristics of elder abuse are similar to other types of abuse and may be intentional and direct or unintentional and indirect; it is often unrecognized and underreported. Because the victim may be frail and in poor health, it is often difficult to dertmine the source of bruising, fractures, or poor nutritional status. In addition, there may be sensory, language, or cognitive problems contributing to poor communication. The elderly person depends on his or her caregiver for the basic necessities, and may be reluctant to contribute potentially damaging information. There are four types of elder abuse: physical abuse including sexual abuse, emotional abuse, material exploitation or misappropriation of funds, and neglect (Paris, Meier, Goldstein, Weiss, & Fein, 1995).

Elders are at particular risk for the effects of physical abuse due to the effects of aging and concurrent physical disorders or the side effects of medication. Physical abuse is when an act is carried out with the intent of causing physical pain or bodily harm. Violent actions range from slapping and hitting to occasionally using objects to strike others. One slap may not be considered to be a pattern of abuse, but can cause injury in a vulnerable and frail adult. Such mistreatment can result in lacerations, bruises, burns, abrasions, and occasionally skeletal fractures. When the client has a history of falls at home, is demented and may accidentally leave the stove on, or is on blood thinning agents which can cause bruising after minor injuries, it is difficult to assess whether the injuries are due to intentional maltreatment by others. The elder may not be able to communicate or remember what happened. Victims of abuse may be able to file for an order of protection against the abuser.

Psychological or emotional abuse is any threat that causes emotional pain. Threats to abandon or institutionalize the victim increase the elder's sense of insecurity and heighten the emotions of fear and despair. Insulting the elder and humiliating him or her are characteristics of psychological and emotional abuse.

Material exploitation and/or misappropriation of funds are another form of elder abuse. The caregiver may cash the elder's social security or pension check and keep the money. Force is often used to coerce the victim into signing over the checks. Caregivers may convince their victims to sign over all their assets and change their wills to benefit the caregiver. At times the address is changed and statements are sent to another home, or there may be a change in the volume of usual banking activity with suspicious signatures or unusually large withdrawals.

Neglect is difficult to define clearly, because it depends on the caregiver's abilities and the elder's needs and capacity. One caregiver may have a knowledge deficit and be unable to deliver the care needed or provide access to proper medical care (**passive neglect**) whereas another caregiver may deliberately choose not to provide adequate food for the elder (**active neglect**). Therefore, it is important to distinguish between passive and active neglect. Neglect is identified in a person who should be but is not thriving in the community. All aspects of the elder's health and dietary needs, social needs, and safety should be examined when looking for signs of neglect.

An extreme form of neglect would be abandonment. Abandonment is when the person who as assumed care of the elder or is responsible for care deserts the elder or does not provide care. In cases of abandonment, there is refusal to fulfill obligations to an elder by the family or caregiver.

Elder abuse describes acts of commission or omission resulting in harm or threatened harm to the health or welfare of an older adult. Elder abuse may include physical, emotional, or economic abuse as well as neglect.

Incidence and Prevalence

It is difficult to estimate the prevalence of the elder abuse problem due to differences in definition, reporting mechanisms, and data collection. Mandatory reporting of elder abuse is not required in all states. It is estimated that 1 in 14 incidents of elder abuse are reported and only 1 in 25 cases of material exploitatation. The frequency of elder abuse is estimated to range from 2% to 10% depending on the sampling, survey methods, and case definitions of the studies done (National Center on Elder Abuse [NCEA], 2005).

The 1998 National Elder Abuse Incidence Study estimated that approximately 551,000 community-dwelling elders, those living in their

Material exploitation is an example of economic abuse using resources inappropriate for one's own needs.

Implications for Evidence-Based Practice

Baker and Heitkemper (2005) reported that elders who live independently are at lowest risk for elder abuse, as are those with social support. Those with dementia, particularly those with aggressive or disruptive behaviors, are at highest risk. Caregivers with a history of mental illness, aggressive personality style, dependence on the victim for support, and substance and alcohol abuse are more likely to be abusive. In institutional settings, risk factors for abusers include poor staffing, mandatory overtime, and lack of training and clinical supervision. Roles for nurses in preventing elder abuse include being educators, researchers, and case managers, and providing expert consultation on public policy and community service project teams.

own home or with a family member, were abused or neglected. A state-by-state survey in 2000 estimated the number of reports to be 473,813. Under the Long Term Care Ombudsman program, there were 20,673 cases of suspected abuse investigated in nursing home residents (NCEA, 2005). Additional cases of self-neglect have not been estimated.

Neglect is a condition in which a caregiver fails to provide physical and/or emotional care to a child or elderly person.

The incidence of abuse increases with age. It is estimated that the rate of abuse is two to three times higher for those 80 years old and above. The incidence also is higher among elders not physically able to care for themselves (International Council of Nursing, 2006). Accurate estimates are not available for elders living in institutional settings, but these elders are considered to be at highest risk for all types of elder abuse.

Clinical Example

Alice was released from the hospital after she broke her ankle and wrist after a fall. The hospital arranged for some part-time assistance at home. Alice was comfortable with home care arrangements and looking forward to going home and regaining her independence. However, over the next few weeks, her friends became more and more concerned. It became increasingly difficult for them to contact Alice directly, and they were told that she was not receiving visitors. When one friend went directly to the home, she was denied access. The friend became anxious and contacted the police. The police found Alice in the company of a woman who identified herself first as Alice's relative and later as a tenant. Alice's residence was unkempt, drug paraphernalia was in view, and there were several adults and children living in the home. When the police insisted on speaking with Alice, they found her dehydrated, confused and disoriented, and laying on a soiled mattress covered in feces. Alice was brought to the hospital. The tenant who had befriended Alice had apparently moved in, stopped the home care follow-up, taken possession of Alice's checkbook, and denied Alice access to contact with her friends and neighbors. Isolated and neglected, denied access to her ususal medications and medical care, Alice had become ill and increasingly dependent upon her abuser.

Epidemiology

A rapidly growing elder population and a society ill-prepared for caretaking responsibilities increase the risk for possible abuse. Underlying abuse in a domestic situation may be a long-standing history of domestic abuse, impaired parent-child relations, criminal or substance abuse problems, and chronic physical and mental health problems. Intergenerational relations, financial and caregiver stress, and the increased dependency of a frail elderly spouse or parent can upset a previously stable but fragile balance. Elders may be isolated in the community and dependent upon strangers or transient caretakers. Institutionalized abuse may be complicated by financial problems, lack of health care, or overcrowded conditions.

Clinical Presentation

Assessing elder abuse can be challenging. Frequent accidents and unexplained bruises should be evaluated thoroughly. The clinician must establish an atmosphere to encourage full disclosure. The victim may not report incidents, fearing institutionalization or separation from the family member. As mentioned earlier, however, reporting elder abuse is mandatory in some but not all states.

The nurse must utilize several resources. Interviewing a number of family members is helpful. As in all types of family violence, all parties involved should be interviewed separately. The nurse may ask the elder how meals are pre-

CASE STUDY Mr. S.

Mr. S. is an elderly man who recently lost his wife. He has a daughter, Susan, who lives in another state; a son, David, who is busy working and has an active family life; and another son, James, who never married and who lives upstairs. James has a history of intermittent substance abuse and unemployment. David speaks to his father every morning and visits him twice a week. He has noticed in his telephone conversations that his father is getting more distressed and complaining of missing money. At first David thinks his dad may have misplaced his money. He notices, however, that this has been occurring more often, and begins to investigate. He believes his brother may be taking advantage of his father.

You are interviewing Mr. S. for his annual physical and noticed he is losing weight and forgetful. David shares that his father is misplacing his money, which reinforces your observation of cognitive changes. Mr. S. also begins to complain about his other son and shares with you that he feels he is taking his money. He becomes angry, however, and attacks you when you mention reporting his son James for elder abuse. It is critical that this case be handled with care and respect for Mr. S.

NURSING CARE PLAN Elder Abuse

Expected Outcomes	Interventions	Evaluations
• Will establish trust with the client and family. • Will identify if the patient is a victim of elder abuse or neglect. • Will explore alternative coping mechanisms and ways of managing his finances. • Will establish contact with community resources for follow-up care.	• Orient client and family. • Question client and family separately. • Maintain confidentiality. • Identify necessary resources. • Assess the client's mental status; perform a mini-mental exam. • Assess the client for changes in thought process and mood. • Assess the client's ADL. • Assess the client's nutritional intake. • Assist the client in identifying coping mechanisms that have worked in the past in similar situations. • Discuss possible community resources and support systems with the client and appropriate family members.	• Validate inferences. • Make appropriate referrals to other healthcare providers, social service, and behavioral health. • Score mini-mental and evaluate the patient's perception of the test. • Observe the quality of speech and content for paranoid statements. • Observe client's appearance and interview him focusing on his grooming habits and daily activities. • Review with the client his dietary intake. Does he eat alone? Who prepares his meals? • Review with the client how he monitors his finances. • Determine if referral for further evaluation of exploitation is needed. • Evaluate the client's participation with follow-up care.

Visit http://nursing.jbpub.com/psychiatric for additional care plans and exercises.

pared or ask the person to describe a typical day to establish communication. It is also appropriate to ask if violence has occurred in the home or if the victim fears abandonment.

Psychological or emotional abuse is difficult to assess. At times the elder may be isolated from usual contacts and become increasingly dependent upon the abuser. The elderly person must be evaluated for signs of depression. Clients may exhibit signs of withdrawal, express anxiety, have vague health complaints, or express a desire to die. These covert signs indicate that the individual may be living in an abusive environment. If these symptoms worsen, early intervention can prevent further deterioration.

Education facilitates the diagnosis of elder abuse. Discussing and teaching the client the appropriate quality of life and health expectations prompt more accurate answers to future questions. A checklist is helpful when querying the victim. The following sample questions can help elicit information: Has anyone ever taken something of yours without permission? Are you home alone for long periods? Has anyone ever hit you? Have you ever felt fear of abandonment? Describe a typical day at home. This last entry allows the nurse to assess the patterns of daily living including mealtimes, general hygiene, medical needs, and administration of medications.

Management and Treatment of Elder Abuse

The victim's wishes should be considered when developing the treatment plan. The victim's input often helps to remedy the situation. Caregivers are often overburdened and unaware of available resources. The situation resolves once caregivers receive aid. Conversely, the elder may be in serious danger and require different living arrangements. See **Table 10-8** for interventions with abused elderly clients.

Prevention is a key part of treatment of the elderly. Neighbors, friends, or relatives should visit often. Encourage elderly clients to participate in community activities and have them make arrangements to have their social security checks or pensions placed by direct deposit into a bank account. Meet with family members to decide who will be available to help if the elderly person becomes incapacitated. The clinician should assist the elder to evaluate a family member's ability to

Passive neglect is an unintentional failure to deliver caregiving obligations, or inflicting distress without willful intent. Active neglect is intentional failure to fulfill the caregiving obligations, or inflicting physical or emotional distress.

Table 10-8 Education for Clients and Families for Abused Elders

- Provide a supportive, empathetic, and nonjudgmental atmosphere.
- Interview both parties separately.
- Emphasize the importance of remaining socially active with family and friends.
- Remind the elder that one does not have to live with a violent person.
- Assess whether abuse is intentional or related to a knowledge deficit, and act accordingly.
- Know the state laws regarding reporting.
- Include the elderly person in the treatment plan.
- Contact significant others or a protective service if the elderly person is unable to make decisions.

provide home care. Discuss resources available to the elder such as Meals on Wheels, supportive services, assisted living options, or nursing homes if the elder can no longer live at home. If necessary, the client may be referred to Protective Services for Adults or other abuse prevention programs for further evaluation and intervention. Alternate housing for the abuser or for the elder may be suggested.

Summary

Family violence has become more prevalent. Domestic and intimate partner violence, child abuse, and elder abuse share similar characteristics. The abuser in all incidents attempts to control and isolate the victim. The false sense of power and security fuels further acts of violence. Typically a honeymoon phase follows the abusive act. The abuser apologizes and promises the abuse will never happen again. The victim wants very much to believe this, and therefore stays in the relationship. Elderly and younger people tend to fear abandonment or placement outside the home.

The nurse must remain objective and empathetic, and demonstrate concerned interest during the interview. Low self-esteem may prevent the victim from trusting anyone. Thus, the healthcare provider must establish an atmosphere of trust. The parties should be interviewed separately for accuracy of information, confidentiality, and safety. Additionally, it is important to know the laws of the state regarding mandatory reporting.

Documentation must be accurate and concise, quoting the victim clearly without interjecting the nurse's opinion. A diagram should document the location of physical injuries, and, if possible, color pictures of the injuries are taken. These become part of the victim's permanent health record.

Flexible treatment plans that focus on safety should improve the client's living conditions. Ultimately, clinicians seek to improve the victim's quality of life. The nurse should urge the batterer to seek help by referral to appropriate agencies. Healthcare professionals' responsibilities involve assessing the client's global quality of life, including the home environment.

In all cases, prevention is the best intervention. Parenting classes and support groups can provide much-needed outlets for the frustrations experienced during the parenting years. Teaching the batterer and victim responsibility and mutual respect may be the first step toward resolution. Providing assistance to caregivers decreases stress.

The literature also demonstrates that there are characteristics of the abuser the nurse can be made aware of, and that it is often difficult for the victim to leave the situation or to report the abuse. It is always important not to generalize, and to treat the individual as unique. Evidence-based research can help the nurse understand the phenomenon and explore treatment modalities that have proven to be beneficial.

Annotated References

American Psychiatric Association. (2000). *Diagnostic and statistical manual of mental disorders* (4th ed.). Washington, DC: Author.

This is the fourth edition of the American Psychiatric Association's official nomenclature of psychiatric conditions and disorders. It provides a systematic listing of the official codes and categories, a description of the multiaxial system for diagnosis, and diagnostic criteria for each of the disorders. It is used by psychiatrists, physicians, psychologists, registered nurses, social workers, therapists, and other mental health workers in all clinical settings.

Baker, M. W., & Heitkemper, M. M. (2005). The roles of nurses on interprofessional teams to combat elder mistreatment. *Nursing Outlook, 53*(3), 253–259.

Discusses the role of nurses on Elder Abuse Project teams in the Seattle, Washington, area to help recognize and manage abuse, including assessment and screening, mandatory reporting, direct care, and investigation of complaints.

Biroscat, B., Smith, P., Roznowski, H., Tucker, J., & Carlson, G. (2006). Intimate partner violence against women: Findings from one state's E.D.

surveillance system. *Journal of Emergency Nursing, 32*(1), 12–16.

This study is a 2-year review of 2,926 cases of intimate partner violence cases seen in Wisconsin emergency departments. It found most violence to be directed toward younger women.

Carnes, P. (1997). *The betrayal bond: Breaking free of exploitative relationships.* Deerfield Part, FL: Health Communications, Inc.

Traumatic bonding and intimate partner violence is explained.

Centers for Disease Control and Prevention. (2006). Physical dating violence among high school students—U.S., 2003. *Morbidity and Mortality Weekly Report (MMRW) 55*(19), 532–535.

This study reviewed data from a 2003 national survey of students in grades 9–12 who self-reported incidents of physical dating violence in the preceding 12 months.

Curry, M. A., Durham, L., Bullock, L., Bloom, T., & Davis, J. (2006). Nurse case management for pregnant women experiencing or at risk for abuse. *Journal of Obstetrics, Gynecological, and Neonatal Nursing, 35*(2), 181–192.

A multisite study of two groups of pregnant women receiving safety information concluded that the women experienced a significant reduction in stress.

The Duluth Project. (1987). Power and control equality wheels. Duluth, MN: Domestic Abuse Intervention Project, Minnesota Program Development, Inc. Retrieved June 15, 2007, from http://www.duluth-model.org

Information regarding the use of "wheel" diagrams for Power and Control, Equality, Child Abuse, Nurturing, and the Creator. The diagrams can be copied for educational purposes as long as they are credited to the Domestic Abuse Intervention Project.

International Council of Nursing. (2006). *Fact sheet on elder abuse.* Retrieved August 22, 2007, from http://www.icn.ch/matters_elder.htm

Information and policy statement on elder abuse and other topics are available from the International Council of Nursing.

McFarlane, J. M., Groff, J. Y., O'Brien, J. A., & Watson, K. (2006). Secondary prevention of intimate partner violence: A randomized control study. *Nursing Research, 55*(1), 52–61.

Women attending urban primary care clinics were offered a referral card or a 20-minute case management protocol. Both groups showed an increase in safety behaviors and a decrease in utilization of community resources.

National Center on Elder Abuse. (2005). *Elder abuse prevalence and incidence. National Center on Elder Abuse fact sheet.* Washington, DC: Author.

Information on elder abuse.

Paris, C. E. B., Meier, E. D., Goldstein, T., Weiss, M., & Fein, E. D. (1995). Elder abuse and neglect: How to recognize warning signs and intervene. *Geriatrics, 50*(4), 47–52.

This article presents a case study to assist the reader in learning how to recognize and treat cases of elder abuse. The client is first seen in the emergency room. As the clinician assesses the victim, the reader learns how to detect elderly abuse and neglect.

Preidt, R. (2006, May 11). Sexual assaults. *Health Day.* News release. University of Illinois at Chicago.

Identified risk factors in sexual assault cases.

Priest, A. (2005, April). Student nurses for clean drinks. *Nursing BC, 37*(2), 7–11.

Describes nursing students who organized a group for client education and advocacy concerning date rape drugs.

Ressnison, C. (2005). *Intimate partner violence 1993–2001.* Washington, D.C.: Bureau of Justice Statistics, U.S. Department of Justice, Publication No. NCJ197838.

This study reviewed data from the National Crime Victimization Survey for the incidence of intimate partner violence.

U.S. Department of Health and Human Services. (2005). *Healthy people 2010: The cornerstone of prevention.* Retrieved August 22, 2007, from http://www.healthypeople.gov/Publications/Cornerstone.pdf

Guidelines for Healthy People 2010.

U.S. Department of Justice, Bureau of Justice Statistics. (2006). *National crime victimization survey.* Retrieved August 22, 2007, from http://www.ojp.usdoj.gov/bjs/abstract/cvusst.htm

Data regarding crimes and characteristics of victimization.

World Health Organization. (2006). *Preventing child maltreatment: A guide to taking action and generating evidence.* Geneva, Switzerland: Author.

An extensive report on violence against children.

Additional Resources

Bremner, J. D., & Narayan, M. (1998). The effects of stress on memory and the hippocampus throughout the life cycle: Implications for childhood development and aging. *Developmental Psychopathology, 10*, 871–886.

Research on the long-term effects of trauma upon delayed memory recall and traumatic amnesia.

Bremner, J. D., Randall, P. R., Scott, T. M., Bronen, R. A., Delaney, R. C., et al. (1995). MRI-based measurement of hippocampal volume in patients with combat-related posttraumatic stress disorder. *American Journal of Psychiatry, 152*, 973–981.

Research on the mechanisms of physiologic reactivity generated by long-term effects of traumatic experience.

Carpenito, J. L. (1996). Domestic violence: Why do they stay? *Nursing Forum, 31*(2), 3–5.

The author defines domestic violence, what a victim is, and the emotions felt by these victims. This article also provides guidelines for reducing domestic violence.

Helfrich, C., & Simpson, E. (2006). Improving services for lesbian clients: What do domestic violence agencies need to do? *Health Care for Women International, 27*(4), 344–361.

This article deals with the needs of lesbian clients faced with domestic violence.

Jordan, C. E., Nietzel, M. T., Walker, R., & Logan, T. K. (2005). Intimate partner violence: A clinical training guide for mental health professionals. New York: Springer.

A guide to the assessment of violence and victimization, and interventions with victims and offenders.

LaViolette, A. D., & Barnett, O. W. (2002). *It could happen to anyone: Why battered women stay.* Thousand Oaks, CA: Sage.

This text discusses theories applicable to the subject. The authors use case histories to explain family violence and the cycle of abuse.

Martin, D. (1981). *Battered wives.* Volcano, CA: Volcano Press.

This is one of the earliest pieces of literature that focuses on the subject of domestic violence. It is considered to be a classic among practitioners who work with battered women. One section focuses on legal issues and survival tactics.

Peterman, L., & Dixon, C. (2003). Domestic violence between same-sex partners: Implications for counseling. *Journal of Counseling & Developmental Psychology, 81*(1), 40–48.

Information on intimate partner abuse in same-sex relationships.

Podnieks, E., Kosberg, J. I., & Lowenstein, A. (Eds.). (2005). Elder abuse: Selected papers from the World Congress on Family Violence. San Diego, CA: Haworth Maltreatment and Trauma Press.

Information regarding elder abuse and evidence-based research.

Reece, M. R. (1994). *Child abuse: Medical diagnosis and management.* Philadelphia: Lea & Febiger.

This book helps medical practitioners identify, evaluate, and treat the medical conditions related to child abuse. One section describes symptoms that can be mistaken as child abuse and sexual abuse. There is also a chapter devoted to documentation, reporting, and testifying in abuse cases.

Schofield, R. B. (2006). Office of Justice programs focusing on studying and preventing elder abuse. *Journal of Forensic Nursing, 2*(3), 150–153.

Information on research on elder abuse, neglect, and exploitation.

Shea, C. A., & Mahoney, M. (1997). Breaking through the barriers to domestic violence intervention. *American Journal of Nursing, 97*(6), 26–34.

This article discusses screening tools, advocacy issues, and educational programs needed to help sensitize staff and to facilitate identification of domestic violence victims.

Wang, J., Lin, J., & Lee, F. (2005). Psychological abusive behavior by those caring for the elderly in a domestic context. *Geriatric Nursing, 27*(5), 284–291.

A study to identify possible risk factors for abusive behavior by caretakers.

Weiss, E. (2003). Family and friend's guide to domestic violence: How to listen, talk, and take action when someone you care about is being abused. Volcano, CA: Volcano Press.

Provides useful interventions for patient and family teaching.

Internet Resources

http://nursing.jbpub.com/psychiatric

Visit http://nursing.jbpub.com/psychiatric for interactive exercises, NCLEX review questions, WebLinks, and more.

Mental Health Disorders and Conditions

CHAPTER 11

Disorders Diagnosed in Infancy, Childhood, or Adolescence

Bethany A. Murray

LEARNING OBJECTIVES

After reading this chapter, you will be able to:

- Discuss how childhood communication disorders relate to childhood onset of psychiatric or behavioral disorders.
- Describe common child and adolescent behavioral disorders.
- Differentiate the symptoms of mood and affective disorders in children from those disorders in adults.
- Discuss the impact of early childhood trauma on a child's mental health.
- Identify nursing interventions for a child or adolescent with a psychiatric or behavioral disorder.
- Develop teaching plans for children with psychiatric or behavioral disorders and their families.

KEY TERMS

Attention deficit hyperactivity disorder (ADHD)
Bipolar disorder
Communication disorder
Conduct disorder
Encopresis
Enuresis
Expressive language disorder
Generalized anxiety disorder (GAD)
Individualized Education Program/Plan (IEP)
Learning disorders
Major depressive disorder
Obsessive-compulsive disorder (OCD)
Oppositional defiant disorder (ODD)
Pediatric autoimmune neuropsychiatric disorder associated with group A streptococcus (PANDAS)
Pervasive developmental disorder
Reactive attachment disorder (RAD)
Selective mutism
Separation anxiety
Stuttering
Tourette's disorder (TD)

http://nursing.jbpub.com/psychiatric

Visit http://nursing.jbpub.com/psychiatric for interactive exercises, NCLEX review questions, WebLinks, and more.

Introduction

The Surgeon General of the United States of America has reported that as many as 20% of U.S. children suffer from a diagnosable mental health or behavior disorder sometime between the ages of 9 and 17 years (U. S. Department of Health and Human Services, 1999). The *Diagnostic and Statistical Manual of Psychiatric Disorders,* Fourth Edition, Text Revision (*DSM-IV-TR*; American Psychiatric Association [APA], 2002) has identified a number of disorders that are first seen in childhood. However, children may also have emotional or psychiatric problems that are more frequently diagnosed in adults. Childhood psychiatric illnesses may look similar to adult-onset disorders, or the child may present with significant differences in symptoms based on the child's level of cognitive, emotional, mental, and physical development. Similarly, although it might seem logical to assume that disorders arising first in infancy, childhood, or adolescence will persist into adulthood, there is very little evidence to support this. Problems in development such as mental retardation or autism will almost certainly continue into adulthood, whereas other problems such as childhood anxiety may be self-limiting and disappear by adolescence. However, many adults with psychiatric illnesses will report that they have had problems since childhood. Severe disorders such as schizophrenia are commonly recognized as having an average onset in mid to late adolescence (for further discussion refer to Chapter 15), although symptoms may begin in the school-age child as well. Yung and McGorry (2004) identified three "at risk" behaviors or mental states in early childhood that may be associated with adult onset schizophrenia. These included abnormal social behaviors, cognitive problems, and delayed walking. These risk factors were even more robust when the child had a first-degree relative with a psychotic disorder.

Infancy is the period from birth to approximately 12 months; childhood refers to the period from 1 year of age to approximately 13 years; and adolescence is the transitional period from puberty to adulthood, usually ending with high school graduation.

Classification of Disorders

Current *DSM-IV-TR* classification of disorders usually first diagnosed in infancy, childhood, or adolescence include mental retardation, learning disorders, motor skills disorders, communication disorders, pervasive developmental disorders, attention deficit and disruptive behavior disorders, feeding and eating disorders, tic disorders, elimination disorders, and other occurring disorders. Generally, childhood disorders are coded on Axis I except for mental retardation, which is coded on Axis II (discussed in Chapter 26). Childhood disorders in this chapter are conceptually grouped into the following categories:

- Disorders related to development (expressive language disorder, phonological disorder, stuttering, Tourette's disorder, enuresis, encopresis)
- Disorders related to behavior (attention deficit hyperactivity disorder, oppositional defiant disorder, conduct disorder)
- Disorders related to anxiety (separation anxiety, selective mutism, generalized anxiety disorder, obsessive-compulsive disorder)
- Disorders related to trauma or abuse (reactive attachment disorder)
- Disorders related to mood (major depressive disorder, bipolar disorder)

Disorders Related to Development

Mental retardation, pervasive developmental disorder, autism, and Asperger's syndrome are frequently seen in the child mental healthcare setting, and may occur along with psychiatric illnesses such as obsessive-compulsive disorder, anxiety disorders, attention deficit disorder, major depressive disorder, and bipolar disorder. The *DSM-IV-TR* provides criteria for differentiating these neurobiological disorders. Consult Chapter 26 of this text for a more thorough discussion of the prevalence, recognition, management, and nursing care of the child with a pervasive developmental disorder.

Learning Disorders

Learning disorders (learning disabilities) that involve reading, writing, or mathematical concepts are frequently encountered in the academic setting and are rarely thought of as a psychiatric problem. However, learning disabilities often present in mental health care as secondary or complicating variables to treatment. A learning disorder is diagnosed when an individual's achievement on a standardized test is substantially below that expected for age, schooling, and level of intelligence. Again, Chapter 26 of this text can be consulted for an in-depth discussion of the numbers and types of learning disorders identified in the *DSM-IV-TR*.

Communication and Language Disorders

Communication disorders that will be discussed here consist of expressive language disorder, phonological disorder, and stuttering. An **expressive language disorder** requires that the child scores lower than expected on standardized tests that measure language development. A phonological disorder is a failure to use developmentally expected speech sounds. **Stuttering** differs from phonological problems in that the pronunciation of the letters and words is not impaired, but there is a disturbance in the fluency and time patterning of the speech. Stuttering may be absent when reading aloud, singing, or talking to pets or toys. Environmental factors and regional dialects should be considered when assessing a child's speech (APA, 2002).

Incidence and Prevalence

Language delays, in particular expressive language disorders, are common in children under the age of 3 years (10–15%); however, by school age the prevalence drops to around 3% to 7% of the population. Phonological development problems are more prominent in males than in females and occur in about 2% of the population. About three-quarters of children affected by phonological disorders spontaneously decrease by age 6. Stuttering is three times more common in males than in females and occurs in 1% of children prior to puberty (0.8% postpubescent; APA, 2002).

Etiology

Communication and language disabilities may be associated with other developmental delays (mental retardation, fragile X syndrome) or there may be no identifiable precipitants. Toxic insults such as prenatal drug or alcohol exposure may affect learning. Disorders may also be associated with brain injury (hypoxia, trauma) or poisonings (lead). Phonological and speech problems are commonly seen in children with hearing loss and deafness (APA, 2002).

Physiology

Communication and language delays cannot be identified or diagnosed on computerized axial tomography (CAT) scans, magnetic resonance imaging (MRI), positive emission tomography (PET), or x-rays. Laboratory tests are used to rule out other physical disorders.

Clinical Presentation

The child with an expressive language disorder will have difficulty answering questions and may seem to provide information that differs from that requested. In responding, the child may hesitate before speaking, and then select words that are not quite accurate or may seem unusual. For example, when asked "Where does your father work?" the response may be "When you go to town, and there's a place there and people park there." Frequently, the child will demonstrate word-finding or vocabulary errors, a limited range of word choices, a limited amount of speech, difficulty acquiring new words, simplified or shortened sentences, use of unusual words or word order, omissions of parts of sentences, and a slow rate of language development that is inconsistent with intellectual capabilities. Phonological disorders are exhibited as errors of pronunciation. Common errors are mispronunciations of letters, or substitutions of one sound for another (*t* for *k*). Lisping (*th* for *s*) is also relatively common.

> When evaluating a child's speech pattern it is important to consider environmental factors, regional dialects, and hearing.

In stuttering there may be frequent repetitions or prolongations of sounds, syllables, or words. Blocking (silences between words), broken words (pauses within a word), word substitutions, or other disturbances may be seen. The extent and intensity of the disturbance varies between situations and is often more severe when the individual is feeling under pressure or anxious. Motor movements such as eye blinking or head jerking may accompany stuttering (APA, 2002).

Differential Diagnosis

Expressive language disorders may exist alone, or in combination with receptive language problems. An in-depth speech and language evaluation, often offered by universities or available through the public school system, will help to make this differentiation. Mental retardation and other **pervasive developmental disorders** may be present and should be assessed. Severe environmental neglect may produce language delays as well.

Clinical Course and Complications

> Expressive language disorders may exist alone, or in combination with receptive language problems.

An expressive language disorder is usually recognized by age 3 years. An acquired disorder may occur suddenly following a traumatic injury to the brain. The majority of children improve significantly by adulthood; however, some may have symptoms as adults and subtle language difficulties will persist. Children are occasionally perceived as being oppositional, defiant, or inattentive by parents and may present for psychiatric evaluations for these symptoms. Approximately three-fourths of children with mild to moderate phonological problems show normalization of the disorder by age 6. Stuttering may develop from around age 2 to 5 years over many months; it tends to be more insidious and has some waxing and waning of symptoms. Most children

(20–80%) recover spontaneously from stuttering before the age of 16 years (APA, 2002).

Communication and language disorders are associated with lowered self-esteem, negative self-image, peer problems (teasing, bullying), academic delays (which may lead to parental conflict), and social withdrawal. These disorders are also correlated with higher rates of attention problems and ADHD, mood disorders, and anxiety (APA, 2002).

Management and Treatment

Treatment of communication and language disabilities consists of a speech and language evaluation, academic (achievement) testing, individualized instruction or tutoring, and an **Individualized Education Program (IEP)**, sometimes referred to as a Plan. Medication management is not helpful or appropriate. Speech therapy through the school system may be indicated for phonological disorders and stuttering. Relaxation counseling can help individuals (children and adults) to live with stuttering.

Tourette's Disorder

Tourette's disorder (TD) is a severe neurobiological disorder consisting of a pattern of chronic motor and vocal tics.

Tourette's disorder (TD) is a severe neurobiological disorder whose hallmarks are chronic, unpredictable, and unremitting vocal and motor tics (involuntary skeletal muscle spasms). Chronic tic symptoms can be extremely embarrassing to the individual and lead to fears of rejection or humiliation in social situations. Tourette's disorder is often accompanied by other psychiatric, developmental, or behavioral problems, which may include Asperger's syndrome or other social skills deficits, obsessive-compulsive disorder or traits, attention deficit hyperactivity disorder, learning disabilities, or mood disorders.

Incidence and Prevalence

Tourette's disorder occurs in approximately 4 per every 10,000 children in the United States. The onset is before 18 years. More transient tic disorders occur in 15–20% of school-age children. Tourette's disorder occurs 3–4 times more often in boys as compared to girls, and the onset is usually around age 6 or 7 years (Coffey et al., 2000).

Coprolalia, a complex vocal tic occurring in less than 10% of individuals with Tourette's disorder, involves the spontaneous uttering of obscenities.

Etiology

The causes of TD are unclear. The disturbance is not due to the direct physiological effects of a general medical or substance condition. An inherited susceptibility is suspected. Dopamine receptor hypersensitivity has been the primary hypothesis for tic disorder and TD (Coffey, 2002).

Physiology

Tourette's disorder is thought to involve several neurotransmitters and neuromodulators, including dopamine, serotonin, and endogenous opioids. Dopamine receptors have been implicated due to the responsiveness of the motor and vocal tics to dopamine antagonists (haloperidol, risperidone, ziprasidone) and agonists (aripiprazole; Coffey, 2002). Tourette's disorder is undetectable on typical CAT, PET, or MRI scans. There are no laboratory tests to aid in making the diagnosis. The most promising research is in genetic studies (APA, 2002).

Clinical Presentation

Common simple motor symptoms associated with Tourette's disorder include eye blinking, facial scrunching or grimacing, neck jerking, head turning, tongue protrusion, and licking (**Figure 11-1**). Complex tics may involve stooping, walking, twirling, or other multi-step activities. Vocal tics may be expressed as grunts, squeaks, squeals, sniffs, snorts, coughs, barks, throat clearing, or whole words or phrases. Coprolalia, a complex vocal tic occurring in less than 10% of individuals with Tourette's disorder, involves the spontaneous uttering of obscenities.

Differential Diagnosis

Tourette's disorder cannot be diagnosed when substances such as stimulant medications have been used, or when a medical condition such as Huntington's chorea or viral encephalitis is

Figure 11-1 Facial tics are commonly associated with Tourette's disorder.

present. Tourette's disorder symptoms must begin prior to the age of 18 years.

Clinical Course and Complications

Tourette's disorder may be lifelong, or it may spontaneously remit. The severity, frequency, disruptiveness, and variability of the tics can wax and wane over time, and the characteristics of the tics can change without warning. Anxiety or "nervousness" tends to exacerbate tics, making school performance demands difficult for the child.

Tourette's disorder has been associated with a number of other psychiatric problems, in particular anxiety disorders (25–40% incidence), attention deficit hyperactivity disorder (50–70% incidence), obsessive-compulsive disorder (40% have the disorder, up to 90% have traits), mood disorders such as major depressive disorder (up to 50% incidence), bipolar disorder (16% incidence), and other developmental disorders (20% incidence; Coffey, 2002).

Management and Treatment

Children with TD often present a complicated clinical picture. Therapy is not indicated for the specific treatment of tic disorders or TD. Counseling is extremely useful for the co-morbid conditions, especially when self-esteem problems and depression occur. Motor and vocal tics are not harmful and can be left untreated if they are mild and not bothersome to the child. More severe tics or tics that result in social ostracization should be managed with medications.

Medications are very beneficial in reducing the frequency and intensity of tics. Primary medication treatment should be with the alpha-adrenergic agonist medications clonidine (Catapres) and guanfacine (Tenex), which have norepinephrine activity. Second line choices include the new-generation "atypical" antipsychotics, which alter dopamine transmission in the brain. These include risperidone (Risperdal), aripiprazole (Abilify), olanzapine (Zyprexa), quietiapine (Seroquel), and ziprasidone (Geodon). Despite their established effectiveness, none of the alpha-adrenergic medications or new-generation antipsychotics has Food and Drug Administration (FDA) approval for TD. Older medications including pimozide (Orap) and haloperidol (Haldol) are FDA-approved and are useful; however, side effects occur often with these drugs. Stimulants (methylphenidate, amphetamine) tend to exacerbate or worsen motor and vocal tics (Coffey, 2002).

Enuresis and Encopresis

Two types of elimination disorders are identified in the *DSM-IV-TR*, encopresis and enuresis. **Encopresis** is the involuntary (or voluntary) passage of feces at inappropriate times or in inappropriate places. In *primary encopresis*, the child has never obtained bowel control. Primary encopresis may be associated with other developmental delays (mental retardation) or with inadequate toilet training and/or parental neglect. *Secondary encopresis* occurs when a previously bowel-trained child develops fecal incontinence, usually between the ages of 5 and 8 years. Secondary encopresis is more often related to psychosocial stress such as a parental divorce or birth of a sibling, physical or sexual abuse, or other distressing

> Normal children soil their underwear; this is not necessarily a pathologic or psychiatric symptom. Daytime control is usually attained before nighttime control, and bowel control is usually attained before full bladder control.

Implications for Evidence-Based Practice

Coffey looked at 156 individuals ages 5–20 years diagnosed with Tourette's disorder for correlations between co-morbid conditions and psychiatric hospitalizations. They found hospitalization rates of 12% in the study group. Illness morbidity was strongly associated with mood disorder co-morbidity (major depressive disorder, bipolar disorder), more so than with the frequency or severity of the motor and vocal tics. The researchers concluded that major depressive disorder and bipolar disorder, in the presence of Tourette's disorder, were robust predictors of psychiatric hospitalization (Coffey et al., 2000). This information is important to the healthcare practitioner when assessing a client with Tourette's disorder. A thorough history should be obtained, paying particular attention to the possibility of depression, suicidal thoughts or other self-harm behaviors, aggression, severe moodiness, explosive outbursts, or other symptoms of a mood disorder. More intensive services may be needed when this combination of symptoms is present.

events. To be diagnosed as a psychiatric or behavioral disturbance, medical causes must first be ruled out. A nursing history should include consideration of issues such as history of toilet training, discipline, family conflict, abuse, or molestation. Encopresis can be socially devastating to a child resulting in embarrassment and teasing by other children (APA, 2002).

Enuresis is the involuntary (or voluntary) passage of urine at inappropriate times or in inappropriate places. Enuresis is subdivided into "nocturnal only," "diurnal only," and "both nocturnal and diurnal" subtypes. Enuretic episodes must occur at least twice a week for 3 months or more in a child who is age 5 or older. The amount of impairment associated with enuresis depends on the age of the child, type of wetting, and how the wetting impacts peer and family relationships.

The essential feature of encopresis is the passing of feces either voluntarily or involuntarily into inappropriate places (clothing, closets, floor, or toy box). Children with enuresis have voiding accidents either involuntary or intentionally during the day (diurnal type), at night (nocturnal type), or both.

Incidence and Prevalence

Approximately 1% of 5-year-old boys have encopresis, with the disorder being more prevalent in males than in females. Prevalence rates for enuresis are relatively high: 5–10% of children age 5 years, 3%–5% of children ages 5–10 years, and around 1% of children ages 15 years or older. Seventy-five percent of all children with primary enuresis have a first-degree biological relative who has had the disorder (APA, 2002).

Etiology

Encopresis is often the result of constipation or impaction, which may be due to psychological stress (anxiety, fear, defiance) or illnesses such as dehydration. Painful stool passage will predispose the child to avoidance behavior, which will in turn increase the withholding and constipation (APA, 2002). While there appears to be a strong genetic component, for most children with enuresis a specific etiological factor cannot be determined. It is important to assess for urological, developmental, psychosocial, and sleep related causes (American Academy of Child and Adolescent Psychiatry [AACAP], 2004).

Physiology

Primary encopresis may be associated with gastrointestinal disorders, or it may lead to severe stool retention and impaction. Children will complain of nausea and stomach pain when this occurs. Enuresis can be the result of a urological malformation (shortened urethra) or a urinary tract infection.

Clinical Presentation

The essential feature of encopresis is the passing of feces (either voluntarily or involuntarily) into inappropriate places (clothing, closets, floor, or toy box). The behavior must occur at least once a month for 3 months or longer in a child over the age of 4. Children with enuresis will have voiding accidents (either involuntary or intentional) during the day (diurnal type), at night (nocturnal type), or both several times a week for 3 months or longer. The child must be over the age of 5 to make this diagnosis.

Differential Diagnosis

Medical causes must always be ruled out for both encopresis and enuresis before psychological treatment is initiated. Encopresis cannot be diagnosed in the presence of other medical disorders that are associated with constipation, and the disorder cannot be diagnosed when due to the direct effects of a substance such as a laxative. Enuresis can be diagnosed when medical disorders are present (e.g., bladder infections, neurogenic bladder) but only if the child was previously continent of urine, and developed a secondary incontinence.

Clinical Course and Complications

Encopresis can persist with intermittent exacerbations for years. It can be improved with psychological counseling (secondary types), parent education, and bowel retraining programs. Enuresis occurs more often in children with attention deficit hyperactivity disorder, developmental delays, or sleep disorders (sleepwalking, sleep terrors). Enuresis is less related to psychological distress than is encopresis, and often spontaneously remits. Spontaneous remission rates are around 5–10% by adolescence (APA, 2002). Both enuresis and encopresis can severely limit a child's social development, can cause negative self-esteem in the child, and can result in parental disapproval, anger, resentment, and rejection.

Management and Treatment

It is imperative to address both the self-esteem of the child and the parents' embarrassment in any management program. Treatment for encopresis involves bowel-retraining programs. The child is usually put on a daily laxative such as mineral oil and may also be given a fiber supplement. Parents should be educated about high fiber diets that include fruit juices, whole fruits, vegetables, and whole grain cereals. The parents should toilet the child on a regular basis, usually right after breakfast, asking the child to sit without straining for several minutes (not more than 5 minutes at a time). A set of clean clothes should be kept at school for the child. Alerting the school nurse, classroom teacher, and school aide of the problem may help to diminish some of the social and personal embarrassment associated with encopresis. Prior to beginning the program, parents should be counseled to never ridicule the child for lack of control, threaten to tell peers, or deprive the child of peer, school, social, or family activities because of wetting or soiling.

Psychological counseling for the child and family, including an assessment for physical or sexual abuse, is helpful in determining what psychosocial stressors may be present and to help the family to manage the emotions aroused by the toileting accidents. Once medical causes are ruled out, the treatment of enuresis is usually a combination of medications and behavior modification. Medications used include DDAVP (desmopressin), a synthetic antidiuretic hormone; Detrol or Ditropan, used to treat adult incontinence; and imipramine (Tofranil), a tricyclic antidepressant. DDAVP is available orally or in a nasal spray (one spray in each nostril). Detrol and Ditropan are also oral and may be given during the day or at bedtime. Imipramine is only available orally and is usually given at bedtime in low doses. Imipramine at doses higher than 20 mg places the child at risk for slowed cardiac conduction, thus an EKG tracing is advised during follow-up visits.

Two types of behavior management are useful for treating enuresis. Parents may purchase a pad that sets off an alarm when it becomes wet, which is designed to wake the child, prompting use of the toilet. Parents can set an alarm clock and check on the child at increasingly earlier hours nightly until they find the point at which the bed becomes wet. They then wake the child prior to that "wetting time" and escort the child to the bathroom. Additionally, it is prudent to restrict fluids within an hour of bedtime, and to ask the child to urinate before retiring. Pull-up diapers at night may be acceptable in young children, but they can be emotionally traumatic for the older child. Diurnal, or daytime, wetting is best treated by toileting routines of sending the child to the bathroom every 2–3 hours (AACAP, 2004).

Clinical Example: Disorders of Development

Billy is an 8-year-old boy referred by his pediatrician for the evaluation and management of multiple motor and vocal tics, aggressive behaviors, school failure, poor social skills, and intermittent nocturnal bedwetting. During the assessment, the nurse notes that he gets overly concerned with the "rules" at school, and he doesn't seem to be able to differentiate between friendly joking by peers and "being made fun of." His mother reports that he has attacked peers on the playground several times, and spends more time in the office than in the classroom. Academically, Billy is unable to read words that are longer than three or four letters, but he has already memorized his multiplication tables. He passed the math portion of the fall ISTEP (standardized test) but has failed the language portion. His full scale IQ was tested at 85, but the tester noted a vast discrepancy between language and performance scores. At home, Billy tells his parents that he is "stupid" and "no one likes me." He demonstrates a variety of motor tics including eye blinking, head jerking to the right, and sticking out his tongue. He also makes chirping noises and grunts. Billy is diagnosed with Tourette's disorder, reading disorder, enuresis (nocturnal), and a rule-out for childhood depression. He is started on risperidone (Risperdal) 0.25 mg TID to treat both the tics and aggression, and he is given DDAVP 0.1 mg tablets to take at bedtime for the enuresis. Additionally, his family is referred to a Tourette's disorder support group in the community and scheduled with a child and family therapist and advised to advocate for an IEP (Individualized Education Program) at school, which should include a smaller, more self-contained classroom setting to minimize peer conflicts; an individualized reading tutorial; and more predictable routines and structure.

Critical Thinking Questions What are some normal or typical childhood activities that might be more difficult for a child who has a developmental disorder? What modifications might be made so that the child with a developmental disorder can have a more rewarding social experience?

Disorders Related to Behavior

Perhaps the most commonly seen presenting complaint of parents or teachers is "behavior problems." Children, more than adults, are likely to act out in a variety of ways when under stress, which may include challenges in the academic setting. A behavior problem can be minor such as repeatedly bothering other kids, talking out in class, or running in the hallways, or it can be quite significant such as throwing furniture, kicking or hitting others, screaming for long periods, threatening self-harm, or running away. The clinician is charged with examining the behavior and its implications for the child in the home, school, and social settings. A behavior in and of itself does not provide much information as to the cause or diagnosis of the child until it is taken in context with developmental age, family circumstances, and other environmental or medical factors. The most commonly observed behavior disorders in the child/adolescent mental health setting include attention deficit hyperactivity disorder, oppositional defiant disorder, and conduct disorder.

Children with ADHD are often described as "constant engines." These children have trouble sitting quietly. They are always running and often are impulsive, hurtful towards others, quick-tempered, disorganized, prone to accidents, unpopular, loners, and poor students.

Attention Deficit Hyperactivity Disorder

Attention deficit hyperactivity disorder (ADHD) is the most frequently encountered psychiatric diagnosis in children. ADHD has been described in the literature since the 1930s, although terminology has changed over time. Early diagnoses included minimal brain disease or dysfunction, because it was felt that ADHD symptoms were similar to behaviors seen in individuals with central nervous system injuries. Since that time, ADHD has been called hyperactive child syndrome (1950s), hyperkinetic reaction of childhood (1968), then attention deficit disorder (ADD) or attention deficit hyperactivity disorder (ADHD). In 1984, the *DSM-IV* further defined the diagnosis, stating that there is only one ADHD, but subtypes include "with hyperactivity," "without hyperactivity," or "combined presentation" (APA, 2002).

Many ADHD symptoms are developmentally normal at certain ages, which contribute to much of the difficulty in making the diagnosis. For example, very young children are talkative, impulsive, and very active. Tired children are inattentive and have poor concentration. Excited children are distractible. A diagnosis of ADHD can only be made when the symptoms are determined to be at a level that is greater than expected for the average child of the same age and in similar circumstances.

Incidence and Prevalence

Prevalence rates for ADHD are around 4% (3–7%), with a ratio of boys to girls of 4:1 (APA, 2002). In 2003, the National Health Interview Survey of children's health looked at 4.4 million U.S. children (ages 4–17 years) diagnosed with ADHD and found that 56% (2.5 million) were receiving medications for their disorder. Additionally, 60–85% of the children still met the criteria for ADHD by late adolescence (Centers for Disease Control and Prevention, 2004).

Etiology

The cause of ADHD is not known. It has been found to be more common among first-degree biological relatives, and clinicians note that many ADHD children have at least one ADHD parent. In some children, there may be a history of child abuse or neglect, lead or other toxin exposures, brain infections, prenatal drug or alcohol exposure, or mental retardation. Prematurity, low birth weight, and maternal nicotine dependence have been associated with ADHD, though there is no clear research evidence to support these correlations (APA, 2002).

Physiology

There are no laboratory tests or radiological exams that are used in making the diagnosis of ADHD. PET scans have been used to demonstrate some changes in brain activity in children with ADHD, though no clear information yet exists. ADHD is more likely to occur in children and adolescents who have other brain injuries or psychiatric/behavioral disorders.

Clinical Presentation

The inattentive features of ADHD consist of persistent difficulties in maintaining attention or focus, high distractibility, difficulty in getting organized, forgetfulness, losing things, poor listening skills, and reluctance to engage in any activities that require mental effort, such as homework (**Figure 11-2**). The impulse/hyperactive subtype is characterized by higher than usual levels of impulsivity, hyperactivity, poor judgment, a lack of patience (taking turns), interrupting or intruding on others, talking excessively, restlessness, and running about or climbing excessively (APA, 2002).

Figure 11-2 The inattentive features of ADHD can make it difficult to pay attention during school.

Features that are not direct symptoms of ADHD but are associated with the disorder may include low frustration tolerance, temper outbursts, emotional lability or moodiness, stubbornness, bossiness, demands that needs be met immediately, and significant academic impairment in the absence of any other learning disorders. Lost recess time, in-school suspensions, frequent visits to the principal's office, and suspensions and expulsions may be seen, which serve to further interrupt the learning process. Individuals with the predominantly inattentive type have fewer behavior problems, but they tend to be withdrawn, socially passive, poor school performers, and neglected by peers (APA, 2002).

Differential Diagnosis

Physical examinations should be done to rule out other causes of hyperactivity (e.g., thyroid disease) or mood lability (e.g., Type 1 diabetes mellitus). A parent's history is the best source of diagnostic information because most parents first observe ADHD symptoms when the child is a toddler, although most treatment options begin at age 6. Other psychiatric disorders such as depression or social anxiety may mimic the inattentive components of ADHD.

Clinical Course and Complications

Most parents report increased motor activity when the child is a toddler. The diagnosis is usually made once the child enters the school system around age 4 or 5 years. Children with ADHD, predominantly inattentive subtype, may not be identified until later, when teachers note that the child's intelligence and abilities are not consistent with academic performance. The hyperactive and impulsive symptoms of ADHD often change or attenuate through adolescence and young adulthood, although the inattentiveness and poor concentration symptoms tend to remain more constant (APA, 2002). As late as the early 1970s, ADHD was thought to occur only in childhood, but we now know that adult ADHD prevalence rates are around 4.4% of the population (Kessler, Adler, & Barkley, 2005).

Approximately half of the children diagnosed with ADHD will also have oppositional or defiant behaviors, or conduct disorders, and almost one third will have another psychiatric/behavioral disorder. The most common co-morbid conditions seen are oppositional defiant disorder, conduct disorder, anxiety disorders, mood disorders (both major depressive disorder and bipolar disorder), learning disorders, tic disorders including Tourette's disorder, and communication disorders (APA, 2002).

Management and Treatment

> Children with ADHD and their families need ongoing support to cope with the multiple disorganizing symptoms of the disorder, the medication therapy, and the changing family dynamics.

The treatment of ADHD consists of parent education, teaching the child internal controls and more acceptable behaviors, behavior management and coaching, reinforcing structure (routines) in the child's environment, strengthening peer and family relationships, environmental modifications, academic testing, evaluations for other psychiatric or learning disorders, individualized educational programs or plans (IEPs), and medications.

Medication interventions can significantly reduce ADHD symptoms and lead to a dramatic improvement in functioning. Stimulants are highly effective and are considered the first-line treatment. These drugs work by delaying the release of dopamine from the neurotransmitters in the brain, thus slowing or regulating chemical conduction at the neuron level. Some children tolerate one type of stimulant better than another. Stimulant medications work within 15–30 minutes, and are completely metabolized and eliminated by the body in the same day. They provide a lot of flexibility in dosing; some parents choose to utilize them on school days only. Side effects to stimulant medications (even at therapeutic doses) include jitteriness, stomach upset, decreased appetite, and insomnia. Rarely do seizures occur. Weight and height, blood pressure, and heart rate should be checked at each follow-up appointment. Indications that the medication level is too high include mental dulling, flat emotions, agitation, or moodiness. Overdosage can result in hallucinations, psychosis, tachycardia, and cardiac arrhythmias. Occasionally children may develop motor or vocal tics, which may require dose adjustments or additional medications. Laboratory testing is not necessary when utilizing stimulant medications because dosages are determined based on clinical response and side effects. Stimulant medications fall into two groups: methylphenidate based and amphetamine based. **Table 11-1** provides more information on the number and types of stimulant preparations currently available (Spencer, Biederman, & Wilens, 2000).

Table 11-1 Stimulant Medications for Attention Deficit Hyperactivity Disorder

Methylphenidate-Based	Dosage	Delivery	Duration	Special Comments
Ritalin (generic)	5–60 mg daily	oral tablets	3–4 hours	Given TID-QID
Ritalin SR, Ritalin LA	5–60 mg daily	oral capsules	6–8 hours	Extended release Qam-BID
Metadate ER, Metadate CD	5–60 mg daily	oral capsules	6–8 hours	Extended release Qam-BID
Concerta	18, 27, 36, 54 mg tablets	oral tablets	12 hours	Qam, occasionally repeated at noon
Daytrana	10, 15, 20, 30 mg	Transdermal skin patch	9 hours	Applied in a.m. Taken off in 9 hours.
Methylin solution	5–60 mg daily	oral liquid syrup	3–4 hours	Given TID-QID
Focalin	2.5–30 mg daily	oral tablets	3–4 hours	Isoenzyme of Ritalin. TID
Focalin XR	2.5–30 mg daily	oral capsules	6–8 hours	Extended release Qam-BID
Amphetamine-Based	**Dosage**	**Delivery**	**Duration**	**Special Comments**
Adderall (generic)	5–60 mg daily	oral tablets	4–6 hours	Three amphetamine isomers. BID
Adderall XR	5–60 mg daily	oral capsules	12 hours	Three amphetamine isomers. Extended release Qam
Dexedrine (generic)	5–60 mg daily	oral capsules	4 hours	Single amphetamine isomer. Dose TID
Dexedrine spansules	Up to 60 mg daily	oral capsules	8 hours	Single amphetamine. Extended release Qam-BID

Source: Information taken from Spencer, T., Biederman, J., & Wilens, T. (2000). Pharmacotherapy of attention deficit hyperactivity disorder. *Psychopharmacology, 9*(1), 77–97.

Atomoxetine (Strattera) treats ADHD in a different way. Strattera is a norepinephrine-reuptake inhibitor; it slows down the transmission of norepinephrine through the neuronal pathways of the brain. Strattera is highly effective in reducing hyperactive-impulsive symptoms, and moderately effective in improving the inattention symptoms. It may also be useful for modulating the moodiness and irritability experienced by some children. Strattera is not immediately effective; it requires a titration over 4–5 days, and then it takes 2–4 weeks to achieve a steady state. Dosing is based on the weight of the child. Common side effects reported include stomach upset and insomnia. Rare side effects associated with Strattera include suicidal thoughts (Food and Drug Administration "black box" warning) and liver problems. The norepinephrine activity may precipitate mania in an undiagnosed bipolar client, but is helpful in an ADHD child with co-morbid anxiety. Strattera is not associated with the development of motor or vocal tics (Spencer et al., 2000).

Many other medications are also used off-label to treat the symptoms of ADHD. These include the alpha-adrenergic medications, clonidine (Catapres) and guanfacine (Tenex), which act by reducing norepinephrine in the frontal part of the brain; older tricyclic antidepressants, which are potent norepinephrine-reuptake inhibitors; and newer generation antipsychotics, which have dopamine blocking activities. Finally, the prohistamine modafinil (Provigil) is under FDA study for ADHD due to its ability to improve wakefulness, attention, and concentration in adults, and its low side effect profile in adults and in early child studies. Clonidine, guanfacine, and modafinil will not induce or contribute to the development of motor or vocal tics, and they are not asso-

Implications for Evidence-Based Practice

The National Institutes of Health (NIH) and National Institute of Mental Health (NIMH) supported the *Multimodal Treatment Study of Children with ADHD*, published in 1999, which examined 579 children between the ages of 7 and 9.9 years over a 14-month period, all of whom had a diagnosis of attention deficit hyperactivity disorder. The study compared and examined four treatment modalities: medication alone (stimulant medications were used), medication plus behavioral therapy, behavioral therapy alone, and community-based (nonpsychiatric) care. The study found that 56% of the children who received medication alone improved significantly, as compared to 60% of the children with medication plus behavioral therapy, 45% of the children with behavioral therapy but no medications, and 36% of the children cared for by primary care providers or in support group programs (community-based care; NIMH, 1999).

The Multimodal Study of ADHD treatment provides good guidelines for evidence-based practice. Well over half of ADHD children improved with medications and only 4% of children on medications did better when behavioral therapy was in place. This seems to suggest that utilizing medications is an integral part of the treatment of ADHD and should not be minimized or ignored by the clinician.

Pressman and colleagues (2006) examined family environmental factors and their relationship to ADHD in a study of 220 families with an ADHD child. They reported strong links between increased functional impairment in children with ADHD and high family conflict, low family overall achievement, and low family organization.

Research such as Pressman's could lead the nurse to hypothesize that chaotic, highly conflicted, and disorganized families may contribute to more dysfunction in ADHD children. Additionally, because there is a high degree of familial ADHD, functioning in families with ADHD parents might be lower than in families without an ADHD parent, a potential area for future research.

ciated with weight loss or insomnia (Spencer et al., 2000).

Oppositional Defiant Disorder

Oppositional defiant disorder (ODD) is characterized by a recurrent pattern of negative, defiant, and/or hostile behavior toward authority figures and sometimes peers to a degree that is not developmentally appropriate. Parents of children with ODD describe them as having a "bad attitude," as being stubborn or unwilling to compromise, or as being very disagreeable and difficult to live with.

Incidence and Prevalence

Rates of oppositional defiant disorder have been reported as low as 2% and as high as 16%, depending on the population sampled and the methodology used. The behavior is more common in males than females before puberty; after puberty, it occurs equally (APA, 2002).

Etiology

Oppositional defiant disorder has no clear cause. When it occurs in males, it has been shown to be more prevalent in those who had problematic temperaments or high motor activity in the preschool years. ODD appears to be more common in families in which at least one parent has a history of mood disorder, oppositional defiant disorder, conduct disorder, ADHD, antisocial personality, or a substance-related disorder. ODD is also more common in families with a high degree of marital discord (APA, 2002).

Physiology

There are no specific physiological findings described in the child with an oppositional defiant disorder.

Clinical Presentation

Children with ODD often lose their temper, argue frequently with adults, defy rules or refuse to comply with requests of adults, deliberately annoy

Parents of children with oppositional defiant disorder (ODD) describe them as having a "bad attitude," as being stubborn or unwilling to compromise, or as being very disagreeable and difficult to live with.

others or blame others for their own mistakes, tend to be resentful and angry, and can be spiteful or vindictive. They may even be unhappy about the high degree of conflict in their lives, but seem to be unable control their behaviors (APA, 2002).

Differential Diagnosis

Oppositionality and defiance may be a result of an atypical episode of major depressive disorder, particularly in adolescents. Commonly ODD symptoms can be confused with conduct disorder or bipolar disorder of childhood as well. ODD occurs more often in the presence of ADHD; a careful documentation of the child's symptoms will aid in making an accurate diagnosis.

Children with conduct disorders appear not to care about anything, have no remorse or feelings of guilt, and generally have very poor self-esteem. Setting fires is a particularly dangerous symptom observed in these children.

Clinical Course and Complications

ODD usually becomes evident in early childhood before the age of 8 years. Onset is typically gradual over months or years. Children with ODD may or may not progress to developing a conduct disorder. Some of the ODD symptoms such as irritability and anger may also be characteristics of childhood depression, and a thorough assessment for depression should be done. ODD is highly present in children with ADHD, with as many as 50% of these children being both inattentive/hyperactive and oppositional-defiant (APA, 2002).

Management and Treatment

Treatment for ODD consists of individual and family therapy, and behavior modification (rewards/consequences). Medications are not particularly helpful, although an underlying depressive disorder should be carefully considered and, if found, antidepressants may be found to be helpful. If antidepressants are started, a selective serotonin inhibitor (SSRI) is usually prescribed.

Conduct Disorder

The main features of a **conduct disorder** are repetitive and persistent patterns of behavior in which the rights of others or social rules are consistently violated (APA, 2002).

CASE STUDY Joey

Joey is a 10-year-old boy who is being treated by his pediatrician for attention deficit hyperactivity disorder. He is in the fifth grade of elementary school, but is reading at the third-grade level due to his problems with staying focused and paying attention to what he is reading. He has been taking Adderall XR 30 mg every morning for about 3 years.

Joey is admitted to the child behavioral unit of the local hospital after he became agitated and aggressive toward his teacher and other children in the school. He had started to scream and curse, threw his books across the room, and overturned the desks.

The nurse doing the admission assessment interviews both Joey and his parents, and obtains the following information: Joey has been arguing and defiant at home for several months. His temper ignites quickly, and once angered he loses all sense of reason and will damage property or attempt to hurt his parents and siblings. It seems to take him hours to calm down. His parents are "fed up" with his behavior and have been seeing a counselor for marital therapy because they are fighting with one another over how to handle him. There are three younger children at home and Joey's mother fears for their safety as well. Joey is failing in school because he is in the principal's office nearly every day for acting out. The school is considering expelling him; the parents would have to provide home schooling if this occurs.

The admitting nurse notes that Joey is in the 10th percentile of weight for his age group, and is in the 85th percentile for height. His mother notes that Joey is too angry to eat breakfast, and his medication causes him to have a loss of appetite at lunchtime. He eats some dinner with the family, but he prefers "junk" food and high sugar content foods. He throws fits if they do not provide what he wants.

The nurse identifies the following problem list:

- Aggressive to others and destructive of property
- Unpredictable and prolonged outbursts
- Poor control of impulses
- Poor attention span, focus, and concentration
- Failing in school
- Problems getting along with parents/siblings/peers
- Not gaining weight as expected due to medication side effects

Some nursing diagnoses that can be utilized in planning for the care of a child with attention deficit hyperactivity disorder include impaired nutrition related to medication side effects and poor eating habits, as evidenced by body weight in the 10th percentile for age/height; interrupted family processes related to the child's out-of-control behaviors, as evidenced by the parents' report of marital conflict; and risk for other-directed violence related to poor impulse control, as evidenced by unpredictable and prolonged outbursts.

NURSING CARE PLAN Attention Deficit Hyperactivity Disorder

Expected Outcomes	Interventions	Evaluation
• Child will not harm others.	• Assess for triggers that typically induce outbursts in client. Most outbursts are associated with specific triggers, and identifying them may help to prevent problems. • Identify nonverbal behaviors that precede aggression. Increasing anxiety can be seen as pacing, restlessness, fleeting eye contact, or loud voice tone.	• Child does not harm others or destroy property. • Outbursts are reduced to less than once per week.
• Child will talk about how he is feeling to others, and will express his anger appropriately.	• Teach child other ways to express feelings (drawing, writing, talking). Children may lack the innate ability to verbalize their feelings, and can benefit from being given tools to do so.	• Child is writing or drawing pictures in his daily journal.
	• Teach child physical means to help displace anger (exercise) as increased stress hormones (e.g., fight-or-flight response) may be alleviated through vigorous physical activity. • Maintain a calm, non-confrontational approach as responding to anger with more anger or agitation will worsen the behavior.	• Child asks to shoot baskets in the gymnasium when he is feeling upset, and identifies riding his bicycle at home as an activity that he can do.
• Parents will identify ways to cope effectively with child's behaviors including community support networks.	• Assess family functioning and the presence of any pathology in family members as parental depression may significantly impact the ability to manage family dynamics. • Educate parents as to child's diagnosis and "typical" behaviors that they may see as understanding that the child has a brain-based disorder that he cannot control may help to reduce some blaming by the parents. Learning about the disorder will help parents be better able to advocate for their child.	• Parents are both fully involved in learning about the child's diagnosis and treatment. • Parents can identify behaviors that will not be tolerated and agree on consequences for these behaviors. • Family maintains a balanced structure of work time, play time, and so on, and schedules meals, bedtime routines, etc.
• Parents will implement behavior management techniques for ADHD children.	• Teach parents how to structure the home environment more predictably as providing external routines and structure reduces anxiety for a child who lacks internal self-control.	• Parents utilize "star charts" and identify behaviors that will be rewarded
	• Teach parents how to use reward and consequence-based behavior management techniques as behavior management techniques will act to promote positive, adaptive behaviors and extinguish maladaptive patterns.	• Parents attend at least one ADHD support group.
	• Provide the parents with referral information (e.g., ADHD support group) as families benefit from getting advice and suggestions, or making friends with other families having similar problems. • Refer parents and children for family therapy as family therapy can help to restructure the power and control of the family system, and empower the parents to feel that they have taken back management of their family life.	• Parents make and keep an appointment with a family therapist.

continues

NURSING CARE PLAN **Attention Deficit Hyperactivity Disorder (continued)**

Expected Outcomes	Interventions	Evaluation
• Child will gain weight to at least the 50th percentile for height and age.	• Teach parents to ensure that child is provided a full breakfast and adequate time to eat it in the morning (may involve waking up earlier), pack a nutritious lunch and afternoon snack, and provide the child with a high-calorie, high-nutrition bedtime snack (e.g., peanut butter sandwich with whole milk).	• Child is eating a wider range of foods. • Child gets a bedtime snack incorporated into his routine every night.
	• Provide Boost, Pediasure, or other nutritional supplements daily, or mix Carnation Instant Breakfast with whole milk for client daily as supplements will add 240–360 additional calories daily.	• Parents are providing more nutritious meals, snacks, and supplements.
	• Put child on a daily multivitamin as a vitamin supplement will help the child to get necessary nutrients that he is missing in his diet.	
• Parents report child is making better food choices.	• Teach parents to role-model good eating habits (e.g., family dinners, a variety of fresh fruits and vegetables, and minimal sugary snacks or colas) as the child will feel like a part of the family and will eat more nutritiously if the entire family is eating healthier. • Consult with the prescribing practitioner to determine if medication can be tailored or adjusted to reduce anorexia side effects as other, equally efficacious, ADHD medications may be used that have less appetite suppression as a side effect. • Check weight once a week on the same day of the week to monitor progress as children should gain a pound of body weight or more every month.	• Child returns to at least 50th percentile for body weight.

Source: Adapted from Ackley, B. J., & Ladwig, G. B. (2005).

Visit http://nursing.jbpub.com/psychiatric for additional care plans and exercises.

Incidence and Prevalence

Prevalence reports vary from 1% to 10% of the child/adolescent population. Rates appear to have increased over the last few decades, and urban setting rates are higher than are those in more rural environments. Males are more likely than females to have a conduct disorder, but this is changing over time as more and more girls are committing violent acts (APA, 2002).

Etiology

Conduct disorder is influenced by both genetic and environmental factors. The risk for conduct disorder is increased in families where one parent has an antisocial personality disorder or a sibling has conduct disorder. It may also be higher in families where one parent has a substance-related disorder, alcohol dependence, mood disorders, or schizophrenia (APA, 2002).

Physiology

There are no medical correlates to conduct disorder. Some studies have suggested lower heart rate and lower skin conductance (both measures used in polygraph or "lie detector" tests) in individuals with conduct disorder.

Clinical Presentation

Children or adolescents with this disorder often act aggressively toward others and they display little empathy or concern for the feelings of others. They may feel justified in their behaviors, and feelings of guilt or remorse are often absent. Poor frustration tolerance, recklessness, irritability, and temper outbursts are associated features. Truancy, promiscuity, gang activity, setting fires, drug use, and other criminal actions may exist, and children with conduct disorder are frequently involved with the legal system (APA, 2002).

Differential Diagnosis

Children with a conduct disorder should be evaluated for ADHD, learning or communication disorders, anxiety disorders, mood disorders, and substance-abuse problems. Many children have periods of antisocial behavior that are bothersome and require intervention. This transient behavior does not necessarily constitute a conduct disorder.

Clinical Course and Complications

The first significant symptoms of conduct disorder usually emerge in middle childhood to early adolescence. Onset is rare after age 16 years. In a majority of individuals, the disorder will abate by adulthood. However, a high proportion of these children will go on to demonstrate adult antisocial personality disorder. The earlier the onset, the worse is the prospect for lifelong legal and substance-abuse problems associated with the disorder.

Management and Treatment

Treatment for conduct disorder consists of individual and family therapy. Such intervention teaches the adults living with the child how to control the unacceptable behavior in an age-appropriate manner for the child and to control their own aggressive and angry responses to the child's behavior. The child needs to be helped to understand internal conflicts and moods. These children often have no understanding of how their feelings relate to their actions. Often the parents are themselves products of a violently disturbed family and may need to learn new, acceptable behaviors through role modeling. Occasionally, the child may require residential treatment that provides a safe environment, defuses an angry family situation, and permits the child and family members to learn new behaviors. Frequently, the child or adolescent is involved with the legal system in the form of probation, deferred prosecution, or even juvenile detention. Medications have not been found to be of benefit for this disorder.

Clinical Example: Disorders of Behavior

Sean is a 10-year-old boy presenting for an evaluation due to academic and behavior problems without an apparent learning disability or developmental disorder. His parents report that he has always been "all boy." He likes to climb trees, he rode a bike without training wheels by age 4, and he is always "on the go." He has trouble staying in his seat throughout a meal, and runs off from his parents when out in public. He is in the fourth grade for the second time (did not meet academic requirements the previous school term) and he is making D's and F's in most of his subjects. He tends to rush through his worksheets, and he often says he doesn't have any homework, when he does. Many times he will lose his homework before turning it in. In fact, he loses shoes, toys, jackets, and other things frequently. The teacher says he talks out of turn and "pesters" the other children. When corrected, he argues or refuses to comply with requests. He has trouble completing tasks that require more than two steps, and he is easily distracted by activity in other parts of the room. His parents complain that he "back-talks" and that he has a "bad attitude." Sean is physically healthy and well developed. He sleeps well, but has trouble winding down to sleep at night. Testing has revealed his IQ to be 76 with equal verbal and performance scores. Sean is diagnosed with attention deficit hyperactivity disorder (combined type) and oppositional defiant disorder. His parents are referred to a support group for ADHD and family therapy to work on behavioral management techniques. Sean is started on Concerta 18 mg, one tablet every morning. A release of information is signed to the school to coordinate services.

Critical Thinking Questions Other than medications, what are some ways a parent or a teacher can manage a child with a behavior disorder? How can a child be taught to understand how one's feelings relate to actions and behaviors?

Disorders Related to Anxiety

Anxiety disorders in children and adolescents are not uncommon and can be frightening to both the child and the family. Disorders such as separation anxiety and selective mutism are specifically classified by the *DSM-IV-TR* as childhood-onset disorders, whereas generalized anxiety disorder, obsessive-compulsive disorder, and other anxiety problems may begin at any point in life. For a complete discussion of anxiety and dissociative disorders see Chapter 17.

Anxiety Disorders

Often parents think that the panic demonstrated by a child when faced with an anxiety-provoking situation is defiance or rebellion, and family stress levels may be quite high as a result. Children and adolescents with anxiety disorders suffer in their schoolwork and their peer relationships as well. Many times frequent and unnecessary visits to the healthcare practitioner's office due to vague physical complaints (headaches, stomachaches, lethargy) may result, leading to high absenteeism or truancy.

Incidence and Prevalence

The prevalence of **generalized anxiety disorder (GAD)** in children and adolescents is estimated to be around 3%, with females more likely to be overanxious than males (approximately 3:1) (APA, 2002). **Obsessive-compulsive disorder (OCD)** occurs in approximately 1–2.3% of persons, including children, with rates significantly higher when the child has Tourette's disorder (35–50%). OCD is more common in boys than in girls during childhood, which reverses in adults when the disorder becomes more common in women (APA, 2002).

Separation anxiety disorder should not be confused with the developmentally normal separation anxiety that occurs in children between 1 and 3 years of age. Nor should it be confused with the tolerance some cultures have for supporting interdependence among children and other family members.

Separation anxiety occurs in approximately 4% of the population of children and young adolescents and is not considered an uncommon disorder. It occurs more frequently in children who have parents with anxiety disorders. In most clinical samples, males are approximately equal to females; however, epidemiological studies suggest that the disorder is more common in females (APA, 2002). **Selective mutism** is highly correlated with other anxiety disorders, but with a prevalence rate of 1% it is rarely seen alone (APA, 2002).

Etiology

The causes for anxiety disorders in children, as with all mental health or behavioral disorders, are basically unknown. There are no specific physical findings or laboratory tests that aid in making the diagnosis of an anxiety disorder. Individuals with generalized anxiety disorder frequently report symptoms starting very early in life. Obsessive-compulsive disorders have been noted to be strongly associated with disruptions in the brain's neurotransmitters.

One particular type of OCD, **pediatric autoimmune neuropsychiatric disorder associated with group A streptococcus (PANDAS)**, can arise abruptly following an infection with a streptococcus bacterium. PANDAS are associated with both OCD and the rapid onset of tic disorders. In a study of 12 children with PANDAS, the mean age at onset was found to be 7 years with a 4:1 ratio of males to females. All of these children developed a rapid onset of OCD or tic disorder following a streptococcus throat infection; parents could identify the exact day the symptoms began. Prior to this date, there was no evidence of any neuropsychiatric disorders in any of the children. Seventy-five percent of the compulsions were bacteria related, and more than half also had urinary urgency and frequency without infection. The children were treated with broad-spectrum antibiotics for 10 days, and the OCD symptoms resolved in 14 days. Six of the children relapsed and again had positive throat cultures for group A streptococcus. Recommendations of the study were to consider PANDAS in a child with a sudden onset of strange behaviors following a recent sore throat or fever. The child should be placed on a course of antibiotics in addition to any psychiatric interventions. Currently it is not known if PANDAS is predictive of a later onset OCD or tic disorder (Hughes, 2002).

Separation anxiety tends to be more often found in families that are very close to one another. Cultural variations exist in the amount of interdependence sanctioned by families. The disorder may arise following a major life stressor such as the death of a parent or grandparent; it may be characterized by periods of exacerbations and remissions (APA, 2002). Selective mutism is intricately linked with other anxiety disorders including posttraumatic stress disorder, and is not related to any known specific causal factor (APA, 2002).

Physiology

When children or adolescents are confronted with an anxiety-provoking event or situation, they may demonstrate symptoms of a panic attack. A panic attack is a discrete period of intense fear in the absence of any real danger. Panic attacks have numerous cognitive and physical symptoms including an increase in heart rate and blood pressure (followed by a rapid drop in blood pressure when a vasovagal response occurs), shortness of breath, chest palpitations, sweating, tremors, choking sensations, nausea, dizziness, numbness, extreme fearfulness, a fear of dying, or an overwhelming sense of doom. Children having panic attacks often cannot describe what they are feeling, and may be perceived by adults as having tantrums. Adolescents with panic attacks more closely resemble adults, and they are better able to describe what they are experiencing. Panic attacks are accompanied by a desire to escape or flee. They may last for minutes to an hour or more, and can be quite disabling to the child or adolescent (APA, 2002).

Clinical Presentation

An understanding of normal growth and development is essential in the identification and treatment of an anxiety disorder in a child (e.g., a fear of strangers is normative in a 2-year-old but should become less intense as the child ages).

Children with generalized anxiety disorder can have such problems as trembling, feeling shaky inside, muscle aches or soreness, sweating, nausea and diarrhea, and exaggerated startle responses. Children with GAD seek out constant reassurance from others. They may complain of vague stomachaches or headaches or have other physical complaints or they may worry about a variety of "adult" issues such as paying bills, buying groceries, or keeping appointments. School functioning can be significantly impacted due to the child's preoccupation with home life worries.

Children with obsessive-compulsive disorder have recurrent obsessions (intrusive thoughts) or compulsions (ritualistic behaviors) that cause marked distress to the child, are usually unwanted, and are severe enough to be time consuming. The intrusive thoughts associated with obsessions may seem to arise without reason. Children with OCD may not recognize that their thoughts or actions are excessive or unreasonable. Common obsessions include fears of germ or disease contamination, repeated worry or doubt, or a need to have things in order. Children with obsessions initially attempt to ignore or suppress the thoughts, later often finding behaviors that provide some temporary relief from the anxiety. The compulsive behaviors may have some logical association with the obsession (e.g., washing hands with a germ phobia) or they may not. The most common compulsive behaviors include counting, checking, cleaning or washing, rank ordering, demanding assurances, or repeating actions. Panic attacks are associated with OCD when the child feels unable to carry out the compulsive behavior. Compulsive behaviors can take hours to perform and can be quite disabling for the child and disruptive to family life.

Separation anxiety may be hard to recognize in an older child because the behaviors exhibited may be more indirectly related to the anxiety. Fears of monsters, concerns over the death of loved ones, aggression with authority figures, or an eagerness to please all can be symptoms of the disorder. Separation anxiety is characterized by excessive fear and apprehension when separated from home or from close attachment figures such as parents or the main caregiver. The anxiety experienced must be developmentally excessive and last for at least 4 weeks. Symptoms leading to the diagnosis must be present prior to the age of 18, and cause significant impairment in social, academic, or other areas of functioning. Children with separation anxiety often demonstrate extreme homesickness when away from attachment figures and they may ask repeatedly about them or want to telephone them frequently. They fantasize that their loved ones are ill or injured, or that they themselves will be lost. The preoccupation with returning home can overwhelm the child and make it impossible to attend to any other activities. Children with separation anxiety also frequently complain of physical symptoms (upset stomach, headaches, and dizziness) and they may be unable to sleep alone without having nightmares or panic symptoms.

Children with selective mutism persistently refuse to speak in social situations, interfering with peer relations, education, and other important areas of functioning. Children with selective mutism may communicate with gestures, monosyllabic words, or even by using an altered voice (AACAP, 2006; APA, 2002).

> Children having panic attacks often cannot describe what they are feeling and may be perceived as having tantrums; adolescents having panic attacks more closely resemble adult experiences and are better able to describe what they are experiencing.

Differential Diagnosis

Anxiety disorders are differentiated from one another based on the ability to identify the stressor, or anxiety-provoking event. It is critical that medical conditions or their treatments that could be causing the behaviors be ruled out (e.g., hyperthyroidism, asthma). Selective mutism cannot be diagnosed if the refusal is related to embarrassment over a phonological or communication disorder, or when the language is not native to the child.

Clinical Course and Complications

For the most part, anxiety disorders all begin at some point in childhood and may worsen, remit entirely by adolescence, or continue to exacerbate and remit throughout adulthood. Anxiety disorders are highly co-morbid with other psychiatric disorders of childhood, and an assessment for anxiety should be done when any mental health problem is suspected in a child or adolescent. Most of the time, separation anxiety and selective mutism symptoms are gone by adulthood. Selective mutism is intricately linked with other anxiety disorders including posttraumatic stress disorder, and is not related to any known specific causal factor (APA, 2002).

Management and Treatment

Treatment for generalized anxiety disorder and obsessive-compulsive disorder should include individual therapy with the child. Cognitive-behavioral therapy and exposure therapy are generally the most helpful. Cognitive-behavioral techniques help the child to rehearse the association among thoughts, feelings, and behavioral responses. Exposure therapy gradually exposes the child to the feared object or situation. Children respond very well to relaxation training and guided imagery, which can significantly help in preventing the anxiety from advancing to a panic state (Chard & Gilman, 2005). The treatment of separation anxiety and selective mutism consists of individual and family therapy and incorporating rewards for increasing levels of autonomy. Medications are of limited usefulness in separation anxiety.

However, medications are very effective in treating generalized anxiety disorder and obsessive-compulsive disorder in children. The most effective medications are selective serotonin reuptake inhibitors (SSRIs) such as sertraline (Zoloft), which is the only FDA-approved SSRI medication for use in childhood. It is approved specifically for OCD down to age 6 years. Other effective medications used include citalopram (Celexa), escitalopram (Lexapro), mirtazapine (Remeron), and fluoxetine (Prozac). Luvox (fluvoxamine) is specifically indicated for OCD and has FDA approval for older children and adolescents, but it is sedating and has several drug interactions. Anafranil (clomipramine), a tricyclic antidepressant, was FDA-approved in the 1980s for use in children down to age 10 years; however, it has a significant number of side effects such as weight gain, sedation, cardiac conduction problems, and an increased seizure risk. Other tricyclic antidepressants (imipramine, desipramine, nortriptyline, and amitriptyline) are all also effective for treating anxiety and OCD, but they also have problematic side effects including a risk for cardiac conduction problems that may lead to dangerous cardiac arrhythmias (AACAP, 2006).

Reactive attachment disorder (RAD; inhibited or disinhibited) is a failure to develop appropriate social relatedness associated with grossly pathological caretaking.

Disorders Related to Trauma and Abuse

Posttraumatic Stress Disorder and Acute Stress Disorder

Stressful or traumatic events in early childhood may have long-lasting effects on brain development, affecting neural and endocrine systems that mediate the response to stress and exhibit persistent alterations after the trauma (Gillespie & Nemeroff, 2005). Posttraumatic stress disorder (PTSD) and acute stress disorder (ASD) occur in response to a personal experience of an event where there is actual or threatened death or serious injury, in response to witnessing an event that involves death or serious injury, in response to learning about unexpected or violent death, or in response to childhood abuse or neglect, serious harm, or threat of death or injury to a family member or close friend. The individual responds with feelings of intense fear, helplessness, or horror. Children may express agitated or disorganized behaviors (APA, 2002). For a more detailed discussion of both PTSD and ASD, please refer to Chapter 24; for information on family violence and child abuse, see Chapters 10 and 14.

Reactive Attachment Disorder

Reactive attachment disorder (RAD) is a failure to develop appropriate social relatedness associated with grossly pathological caretaking. There are two subtypes: inhibited and disinhibited. The pathological care history may include a persistent disregard for the child's basic physical or emotional needs, or repeated changes in caregivers that prevent formulation of stable attachments. This disorder is frequently seen in children with a long history of foster home placement, particularly when they have been moved often, or in children raised primarily in orphanages (APA, 2002).

There are conflicting data on the prevalence of RAD. The *DSM-IV-TR* reports that it appears to be uncommon. However, the practice parameters for RAD published by the American Academy of Child and Adolescent Psychiatry (AACAP) report a likely rate of 1% of the U.S. population of children. Other studies have indicated rates as high as 38–44% in children in orphanages or foster care (AACAP, 2005). The cause of RAD appears to be grossly pathological care; in fact, severe neglect is required in order to make the diagnosis. Physical examinations of the child with RAD may reveal other evidence of neglect and/or abuse including failure to thrive, growth delays, malnutrition, vitamin deficiencies, bruising, or old fractures on x-rays (APA, 2002). Developmental delays in the absence of neglect cannot be considered a cause for RAD.

In the inhibited type of RAD, the child demonstrates a pattern of hypervigilant, ambivalent, or highly inhibited behaviors toward caregivers. The child may be resistant to comfort measures, or appear to be watchful or suspicious of others. In the disinhibited type, the child will show diffuse and nondiscriminatory attachments toward others, with behaviors such as hugging or climbing into the lap of relative strangers. Safety of the child may be a particular concern for the caregivers.

The onset of RAD is usually prior to the age of 5 years, although the diagnosis may not be made until later. The severity and duration varies according to the intensity of the environmental deprivation and/or abuse, and the consistency of interventions. Indiscriminate sociability (disinhibited type of RAD) may persist for years. The child or adolescent should be assessed for other signs of trauma including flashbacks, nightmares, hypervigilance, and dissociation, all symptoms of acute or chronic posttraumatic stress disorder. Major depressive disorder should also be considered. There are very few long-term studies of these children and their outcomes (APA, 2002).

Reactive attachment disorder treatment consists of a combination of family therapy, which may involve foster or adoptive parents, and a stable, nurturing, permanent home and caregivers. Medications are useful only if there is a comorbid anxiety or other disorders responsive to medication. Some therapists have used so called "rebirthing techniques" or "compression holding therapy" as treatments. These interventions, which include physically restraining a child to improve attachment, are controversial and can be very dangerous. Withholding or forcing food and water may also be used. At least six documented child fatalities have occurred related to the use of these unproven methods (AACAP, 2005).

Critical Thinking Questions What effect do you think the extensive television coverage of events such as the 9/11 attacks, the wars in Afghanistan and Iraq, and Hurricane Katrina has on children who have been previously traumatized? What factors might serve as "protective" for a traumatized child?

Other Disorders in Childhood Related to Mood and Affect

In addition to discussing conditions most often present first in childhood, *The Diagnostic and Statistical Manual of Mental Disorders* discusses variations in disorders based upon developmental stages and includes children in the other *DSM-IV* diagnostic categories when their symptoms meet the criteria for the disorder (e.g., major depressive disorder, bipolar disorder, adjustment disorders, and anxiety disorders; problems related to abuse or neglect). Regardless of the diagnostic category, nurses must recognize symptoms indicating that a child is having problems and intervene appropriately. The following discussion highlights major depressive disorder and bipolar disorder.

Two controversial interventions, "rebirthing techniques" and "compression holding therapy," include physically restraining a child to improve attachment, and can be very dangerous, having resulted in death.

Clinical Example: Disorders of Trauma and Abuse

Missy is a 15-year-old girl who is seen in the office with her group home houseparent. Missy has been in three unsuccessful foster homes since the death of her mother 2 years previously. When younger, Missy was molested by her father, and her mother was found "unable to protect" her. She was placed with her maternal grandmother from the age of 2 to 13. After her grandmother died, Missy was moved to her mother's home. At 13 she found her mother dead of a drug overdose and she was moved to foster care. While in foster care, Missy became depressed and started self-mutilating. She reported seeing her dead mother's face in her room at night and said she felt "numb all over." After a brief hospitalization, she was moved to another foster home. While there she ran away with an 18-year-old boy she had known for 2 weeks. She was then moved to a third foster home, where she was caught fondling an 8-year-old girl in the home. At this point, she was placed in a group home setting where she remains. Missy is diagnosed with PTSD and a reactive attachment disorder. Individual therapy is recommended along with Zoloft 50 mg every morning.

Disorders Related to Mood and Affect

Mood disorders and anxiety disorders are present in a high proportion of children presenting for treatment in a mental health setting. Although disorders of behavior are often identified and referred for care, disorders of mood and affect are subtler in children and can be easily overlooked, leading to potentially dire consequences including chronic self-esteem and socialization problems, impaired learning, more family conflict, and even self-harm behaviors.

Major Depressive Disorder

Major depressive disorder is characterized by a period of at least 2 weeks during which there is either a loss of interest or pleasure in nearly all activities or a significantly depressed or irritable mood. Children and adolescents tend to present with grouchiness or irritability in addition to, or instead of, overt sadness (APA, 2002). For a complete discussion of this disorder consult Chapter 16.

An understanding of normal growth and development rates for children and adolescents and the corresponding behaviors is essential in order to assess for and diagnose depression. Three percent of children and up to 8% of adolescents become depressed (Wagner et al., 2003). This number is higher for children with one or more family members with major depressive disorder and for children who have experienced a major loss or trauma, including abuse (APA, 2002). Many medical disorders present an increased risk for major depressive disorder in children, including hypothyroidism and Type 1 diabetes mellitus. Laboratory findings and changes in brain imaging found in depressed adults (elevated glucocorticoid secretion, blunted growth hormone, and thyroid-stimulating hormone and prolactin responses to test agents) are not usually seen in children or young adolescents.

Children and adolescents with major depressive disorder often think that it would be better if they had never been born, and exhibit behaviors such as sleep changes, appetite problems, listlessness, apathy, disinterest in social or play activities, trouble concentrating on schoolwork, or preoccupations with themes of death or violence.

Children and adolescents with major depressive disorder may exhibit sleep changes, appetite problems, listlessness, apathy, disinterest in social or play activities, trouble concentrating on schoolwork, or preoccupations with themes of death or violence. They may say that they never really feel happy or that they think the family would be better off if they had never been born. Depressed children and adolescents stop caring about hobbies or activities, including spending time with friends or family, or at school. Common sleep disturbances in a child with depression consist of normal to slightly delayed onset of sleep followed by middle of the night wakening. Sleep is described as "not restful," and children may report nightmares or be found wandering about the house. Fatigue and low energy are pronounced during the day. Adolescents who are depressed become self-isolating and disinterested in activities with friends or family. Grades may drop at school and they may exhibit more tardiness, truancy, or other behavior problems including substance experimentation (Wagner et al., 2003).

Concentration problems and behavior problems may lead children to be misdiagnosed as having ADHD or an oppositional defiant disorder. Somatic (physical) complaints are fairly common in depressed children. Anxiety symptoms may present in combination with depression. Depressive symptoms usually develop over several weeks. An untreated episode of major depressive disorder may last 4 months or longer, in children as well as in adults (APA, 2002).

The most critical complication of major depressive disorder for children as well as adults is the very real possibility of suicide. Suicide is the sixth leading cause of death for 5–14-year-olds, and the third leading cause of death (after accidents and homicide) for 15–24-year-olds. Children and adolescents who are contemplating suicide may provide "hints" such as giving away prized possessions, writing about it in diaries or journals, or making verbal comments such as "you won't have to worry about me anymore." The presence of any hallucinations or delusions is also a risk factor for suicide (Wagner et al., 2003).

Treatment for major depressive disorder in a child or adolescent generally includes a combination of individual and family therapy. Children may respond to antidepressant medications; selective serotonin reuptake inhibitors (SSRIs) or the dopaminergic medication buproprion (Wellbutrin) are often used. Fluoxetine (Prozac) is approved for use in children down to age 12. Caution should always be taken when giving children and adolescents SSRIs and other antidepressant medications because in 2005, the U.S. Food and Drug Administration placed a "black box warning" on antidepressant use in children due to an increase in suicidal thoughts and behaviors in children on antidepressants (3.6%) as compared to depressed children not taking medications (1%). Theories as to why this occurs include the following: antidepressants may cause the child to act on previously only contemplated thoughts (discussed in the adult literature fairly extensively); antidepressants may precipitate bipolar, manic states in children and adolescents; or the research methodology used did not account for extraneous other variables. Nevertheless, when antidepressants are used, treatment staff must follow the child closely (weekly appointments are recommended) and parents should be well educated on signs of suicidal thoughts or behaviors (Wagner et al., 2003).

Major depressive disorder in the child or adolescent clearly has serious implications that should not be ignored by the healthcare practitioner. Family discord and parental depression may be associated with the development of major depressive disorder and anxiety disorders later in life; substance-related disorders are higher in depressed children and adolescents; and suicide attempts are a real risk. Nurses should obtain thorough family histories when assessing children and adolescents, and they should keep the child's safety in mind as a top priority when developing care plans.

Bipolar Disorder of Childhood

Childhood **bipolar disorder** is a controversial diagnosis that has only recently (since the mid-1990s) been recognized as occurring in children and adolescents. These children typically are unpredictably explosive, moody, and aggressive toward themselves and others. Traditionally these children have carried a variety of diagnoses (intermittent explosive, impulse control, mood, and conduct disorders) and have been treated with a combination of medications including lithium, antiepileptics, sedatives, and antipsychotics. Institutionalization may have been recommended by healthcare practitioners in the past to protect the family and the community from the child's unpredictable behaviors. Society has since moved away from large, regional, residential placements and toward an emphasis on deinstitutionalization of the mentally ill, adults as well as children, with the result being that more children are living at home, attending public school, and being treated in an out-patient setting. These children can be very difficult to manage and often require a multidisciplinary team approach to their care. Polypharmacy is common due to the high co-morbidity with other psychiatric illnesses. Healthcare practitioners have little data on the safety of many medications used for bipolar disorder in children and adolescents, due in large part to the lack of agreement on diagnostic criteria. Clark (2004) discusses this diagnostic controversy as arising from two basic questions:

- Does diagnosing bipolar disorder in children require discrete episodes of mania, as in adults, or can it be chronic and unremitting?
- Must elation of mood and/or grandiosity be present, or can irritability and mood lability suffice?

The classic mania/hypomania episodes seen in adults are rarely seen in a child or younger adolescents (Clark, 2004).

Massat and Victor (2005) found that problems with diagnosing children with bipolar disorder arise from skepticism that the disorder could exist, misdiagnosis due to inconsistent diagnostic criteria, and overlapping symptoms with other psychiatric disorders of children including ADHD. They describe the atypical picture in children as characterized by persistent irritability, violent behaviors, affective "storms," and prolonged or aggressive temper outbursts. Symptoms of grandiosity or hypersexuality commonly seen in adults with manic episodes are uncommon or difficult to diagnose in a prepubescent child or young adolescent. Overlapping symptoms with other disorders include overactivity, irritability, distractibility, emotional lability, impulsivity, and racing speech or talkativeness (Massat & Victor, 2005).

There are no laboratory or imaging studies that help to make the diagnosis of bipolar disorder. Meyer and Carlson (2003) discuss the relationship between parents with a known bipolar disorder and their children, noting that children with one or more bipolar disorder–diagnosed parents exhibited more motor restlessness, motor agitation, anxiety, mood lability, inattentiveness, stubbornness, and excitability than did children without bipolar disorder–diagnosed parents. The *DSM-IV-TR* reports that 4–24% of individuals with bipolar disorders have first-degree relatives with either bipolar I disorder or major depressive disorder (APA, 2002).

> Children with bipolar disorder have atypical symptoms including persistent irritability, violent behaviors, affective "storms," and prolonged or aggressive temper outbursts, contributing to the difficulty with diagnosing the disorder.

Children with bipolar disorders almost always have a mixed presentation. Cycling of moods is less clearly differentiated than in adult clients. Mania is frequently characterized less by euphoria and more by agitation, with explosive anger outbursts and violent episodes. These outbursts can be triggered with very little provocation; both the intensity and the abruptness of the outburst may be very frightening for those around the child. "Normal" temper tantrums in children are usually self-limiting and respond to firm directives. Outbursts seen in a child with a bipolar disorder are much more intense and may involve hitting or kicking adults, biting, destroying property, attacking pets or younger children, or using weapons. The duration of these episodes can last from a few minutes to several hours and they usually do not end until the child is exhausted.

Children with bipolar disorder may exhibit symptoms as early as age 3, with parents often reporting that the child always "had a bad temper" or was difficult to calm. Early childhood disorders tend to be episodic and chronic. By the late teens, the adolescent may have fewer rage outbursts and the disorder may disappear completely, or the mood swings may become more cyclical in nature, more closely approaching the criteria for a bipolar I disorder (APA, 2002). Bipolar disorder

Implications for Evidence-Based Practice

Geller and Luby (1997) did a 10-year literature review of child and adolescent bipolar disorder using literature online with Medline, previous research in the field, their own research and clinical experiences, and data from the National Institute of Mental Health. They looked at epidemiology, course of the disorder, co-morbidity, and treatment. They concluded that childhood bipolar disorder is a nonepisodic, chronic, rapid cycling, and mixed manic state that may be either co-morbid with ADHD and conduct disorder or preceded by ADHD and conduct disorder. For nurses assessing and caring for children with this condition, it is important to know that these researchers found that four *DSM-IV-TR* criteria have the least overlap between bipolar disorder (BPD) of children and other psychiatric illnesses, thus they are the most useful in making a differential diagnosis. These are as follows (Geller & Luby):

1. *Elated mood:* 89.3% in BPD and 13.6% in ADHD
2. *Grandiosity:* 86% in BPD and 4.9% in ADHD
3. *Decreased need for sleep:* 39.8% in BPD and 6.2% in ADHD
4. *Flight of ideas/racing thoughts:* 71% in BPD and 9.9% in ADHD

Clinical Example: Disorders Related to Mood and Affect

Sara is a 13-year-old girl who is brought in for an assessment by her parents because of concerns they have over her moodiness and self-harm thoughts. Sara is physically healthy and experienced menarche 4 months before the appointment. In the past 4 months she has been crying frequently with very little provocation. She feels that none of the girls at school like her, and she has been isolating herself in her room. Her grades have dropped from an honor roll level to a C average. She recently has refused to eat with the family, and her mother believes she may have lost 10 pounds; she is 5′2″ and weighs 95 pounds. She is having trouble staying asleep at night. The evening prior to the assessment, her mother found her making some superficial cuts on her left wrist. When asked, Sara said she wanted to be in heaven with her grandmother and she didn't think anyone would miss her. She was started on fluoxetine 20 mg daily. Six days later, her parents called the emergency services to report that Sara was agitated, screaming at them, stomping through the house, not sleeping, and was tearing apart her room. She was admitted to the hospital's adolescent psychiatric unit and diagnosed with bipolar I disorder. She was taken off of the fluoxetine and started on a titration of lamotrigine (Lamictal) up to 100 mg BID along with individual and group therapy. Her parents were also entered into family therapy, and referred to a community support group for family members of individuals with bipolar disorder.

co-morbidity with other psychiatric conditions is very high. Wilens and colleagues (2004) reported that in a study of 57 adolescents meeting the criteria for bipolar disorder, 74% had ADHD, 63% had conduct disorder, 93% met the criteria for ODD, 91% had met the criteria for major depressive disorder at some point, psychosis occurred in 28%, multiple anxiety disorders were found in 79%, and 32% had substance abuse disorders, while 21% smoked cigarettes.

The treatment of bipolar disorder nearly always includes mood-stabilizing medications. Lithium is the only FDA-approved medication specifically for bipolar disorder in children (12 years and older). The response rate to lithium is only about 50%, however, and it is associated with side effects including tremors and a narrow therapeutic-to-toxic range. Risperdal (risperidone) was recently approved for irritability, aggression, and mood swings associated with autistic disorder in children ages 5–16 years. All of the medications used in adults are also utilized in children "off label," or without FDA approval. Many mood stabilizers are also antiepileptics and have FDA approval for the treatment of seizure disorders in children, but they are not approved for bipolar disorder. Mood-stabilizing medications have a variety of side effects. Sedation, appetite increases, and weight gain are common. Newer generation antipsychotics are generally thought to be safer, but still carry risks for extrapyramidal side effects (EPS) and tardive dyskinesia (Clark, 2004).

Critical Thinking Questions What are the benefits and risks to utilizing antidepressant medications in children and adolescents with major depressive disorder, anxiety disorder, or bipolar disorder? What are some ethical concerns in using non-FDA approved "off-label" medications in children and adolescents?

Implications for Evidence-Based Practice

Pilowsky and colleagues (2006) looked at the effects of parental depression and family discord on offspring psychopathology. This longitudinal study interviewed 182 subjects in 83 families at age 17 years and again 20 years later. Results indicated that parental depression and family discord are consistent risk factors for the development of major depressive disorder and various anxiety disorders later in adulthood. Wagner and colleagues (2003) reported a literature review of 376 children and adolescents with major depressive disorder. They found frequent hospitalizations, with almost 50% of the subjects attempting suicide at some point. Additionally, up to 25% had experienced some form of substance abuse.

Education for Clients and Families

Historically, mental health treatment has been provided with the individual client in mind; however, children and adolescents rarely live in a vacuum. The impact of a healthy and well-functioning family unit cannot be overemphasized. Nursing has long recognized that the individual exists in a holistic environment where physical, mental, social, emotional, and spiritual needs cannot be separated from the individual. A nurse who would exclude the impact of the family or environment on the child would not be very effective.

Assessment for mental health problems in parents and other family members is an integral

CASE STUDY Sandra

Sandra is a 15-year-old girl whose parents divorced two years ago. She chose to live with her mother and finish school, and her father moved to a neighboring state, but she continued to see him over holidays and in the summer. She is an only child. Sandra's father was killed in a motor vehicle accident while driving drunk 6 months ago. It occurred during a weekend that she normally would have visited him, but she wanted to go to a cheerleading camp instead. Since his death, Sandra has been increasingly isolating herself at home. Her mother says she has stopped going to practices, she won't talk to her friends on the phone anymore, and she cries in her room at night. Sandra's grades are worsening and she is more listless and apathetic in her schoolwork. Sandra's mother found a letter in which Sandra says her family would be "better off" if she were dead, and it's her fault her father died. In the letter, Sandra outlines different ways she could kill herself and which ones would be more likely to be effective. Her letter also alludes to "visits" from her deceased father at night, and hearing his voice calling her name as if he is beckoning her to join him.

Sandra is admitted to the in-patient adolescent behavioral healthcare unit for major depressive disorder, single episode, with psychotic features and started on antidepressant medications. During her admitting assessment, the nurse notes that she has lost about 10 pounds in the past 6 weeks, but she is still within normal height and weight range for her age. Sandra says she can't sleep at night—she is tossing and turning, has dreams about her dad, and wakes frequently. Consequently, she feels fatigued and exhausted during the day. She can't concentrate at school, and she "just wants this to be over with."

The nurse identifies the following problem list:

- Bereavement
- Depressed and guilty mood
- Lack of interest or motivation in activities
- Impaired social interactions (not seeing her friends)
- School performance failure
- Thoughts of suicide
- Vague reports of auditory and visual hallucinations
- Insomnia

In establishing a plan of care, the nurse identifies the following nursing diagnoses:

1. Dysfunctional grieving related to the death of her father, as evidenced by persistent depressed moods, insomnia, dreams of her father, thoughts of suicide, and feeling that he is visiting her at night or speaking to her
2. Sleep deprivation related to depressive disorder, as evidenced by fitful and restless sleep, decreased total sleep hours, and lack of feeling refreshed the next day
3. Social isolation, self-imposed isolation related to depressive disorder, as evidenced by her refusal to see or call friends or go places with them

NURSING CARE PLAN Major Depressive Disorder

Expected Outcomes	Interventions	Evaluation
• Child will be able to freely express her feelings over her father's death without becoming completely overwhelmed or suicidal.	• Assess child's stage of grieving as having an understanding of where the child is in the grief process will help to guide interventions. • Encourage child to talk openly about her father and to express her feelings associated with how he died (including feelings of guilt) as child may have felt that she could not talk about her father without upsetting her mother, or that she needed to be "strong." • Encourage child to cry as crying helps to release pent-up feelings and reduce some of the distress associated with them.	• Child talks about her father's death and her own feelings in individual and group sessions.
	• Encourage child to keep a journal and write in it her thoughts and feelings about her father.	• Child writes about the experience in her personal journal.
	• Assist child in starting a scrapbook, or "memory book" of memories of her father. Ask her mother to assist her in finding photos, etc., to put in the memory book as reviewing memories will aid in the grief process.	• Child begins a scrapbook or "memory book" about her father.
	• Refer child to community-based grief support group programs, especially those designed specifically for children/adolescents as adolescents respond well to peer interaction based on their normal developmental tasks, and the child may find a great deal of relief in meeting other children with similar losses.	• Child attends at least one bereavement support group.
	• Refer child for individual counseling after she leaves the hospital as a trained therapist can help her to continue to gently challenge false beliefs (i.e., responsibility over her father's death) and let go of her guilt. • Educate child's mother that the child will need to feel okay about having good memories of her father (and she may seem to "forget" conflicts between her parents prior to the divorce) as loved ones may be idealized for a period of time after their death by those left behind, which is a normal process.	• Child agrees to meet privately with a therapist for ongoing counseling and support.
• Child will be sleeping no less than 6 uninterrupted hours per night, or 8 hours total. • Child will report feeling better rested and more energetic the next day.	• Assess things that may be preventing adequate rest (e.g., caffeine, leaving the television on at night). • Encourage child to do quiet, restful activities at bedtime such as taking a warm bath or reading a book as this will allow the child to become gradually drowsy and eventually fall asleep. • Keep the environment around child quiet at night (turn down telephone ringers, keep staff voices low) as a noisy environment can be disruptive to sleep.	• Child is reading books before bedtime, and is avoiding caffeine or television right before sleep.
	• Obtain orders for a PRN sleep medication that's safe for use in adolescents.	• Child asks for her PRN sleep medication 30 minutes prior to bedtime.

NURSING CARE PLAN **Major Depressive Disorder (continued)**

Expected Outcomes	Interventions	Evaluation
• Child will be able to identify activities that she normally enjoys. • Child will participate in her usual pre-illness activities again.	• Use active listening skills to establish a therapeutic relationship with child as presenting self as actively interested in child will promote self-esteem and verbalization. • Encourage child to list things she enjoys doing with her friends as this will help the child to review and remember things that she enjoys in life. • Encourage letters to friends and visitations from friends while in the hospital as doing so will keep the child connected with those who care about her.	• Child is observed talking more about things she wants to do with friends once she leaves the hospital. • Child has a more positive outlook and be future-oriented.

Source: Adapted from Ackley, B. J., & Ladwig, G. B. (2005).

Visit http://nursing.jbpub.com/psychiatric for additional care plans and exercises.

part of treating children and adolescents. Many of the disorders discussed in this chapter have familial associations and heritability factors; it is common to find more than one person in a family with a diagnosable psychiatric illness. Gartstein and Sheeber (2004) examined 69 mothers of 3–6-year-old children who had been diagnosed with major depressive disorder, looking at issues of parenting competence, attachment to the child, the child's impact on the family unit, and the child's behavior problems. Findings were that child behavior problems were associated with maternal depression, with a positive relationship among high maternal depression, high family dysfunction, and low maternal self-perception of parenting competence.

A basic understanding of normal developmental tasks of childhood is essential in managing the child with a mental health disorder. Often families are not well versed in normal developmental stages (e.g., they may perceive normal defiance associated with a 2-year-old and a 14-year-old as pathological when it is not). Parents should be helped to learn normal and expected developmental behaviors of their child.

Education of the family is essential for the child psychiatric-mental health nurse. Education regarding the specific psychiatric-mental health disorders once they are diagnosed is necessary to help parents understand that the behavior exhibited is not intentional or malicious, nor is the child always in control. Parents can be directed to a number of resources (library, Internet) that will aid in this process. Many support groups exist (e.g., Children and Adults with Attention Deficit Disorder [CHADD], Tourette's support, autism support programs) where parents have the opportunity to network with other families with children having similar problems.

Medication treatment can be overwhelming and confusing to parents because there is a proliferation of medications being used, and often many medications used in child psychiatry are "off label." Parents should be taught the specific reason the child is receiving a particular medication, its dosage schedule, any dietary limitations, side effects and adverse effects (especially any requiring an FDA "black box" warning), and what to do if they are concerned that the child is having a reaction to the medication.

Education regarding the specific psychiatric-mental health disorders once they are diagnosed is necessary to help parents understand that the behavior exhibited is not intentional or malicious, nor is the child always in control.

The nurse should not assume that parents have a good grasp of basic parenting or behavior management techniques. Families vary widely in their parenting knowledge, tolerance for routines and structure, or use of rewards and consequences. Some parents enforce strict bedtimes and expect their children to do chores, while other parents are more laissez-faire and tolerate more casual, or even chaotic, home environments. Parenting classes are excellent means of providing some basic parenting instruction and may be more acceptable to some families that perceive family therapy as an implication of personal deficiencies.

All children in the United States are guaranteed an education. Many times, children with psychiatric or behavioral disorders are a challenge in the classroom. Parents of children who are struggling to learn should be advised that they can request intelligence (IQ) and academic testing, speech and language evaluations, hearing tests, and other necessary evaluations from the school system. The school system is required to make appropriate accommodations for a child who has "special" learning, developmental, emotional, or mental health needs. Parents should be meeting frequently with their child's teacher and other representatives of the school system to ensure that an Individualized Education Program (IEP) is in place when needed.

Summary

Disorders of infancy, childhood, and adolescence have profound effects on the child and family and often have a lifelong impact on the individual's ability to function in a family and in society. This chapter has presented information on disorders in childhood related to development, behavior, anxiety, trauma or abuse, and mood.

A basic understanding of normal developmental tasks of childhood is essential in managing the child with a mental health disorder. A childhood disorder that is not treated adequately will cause problems in adulthood. Education regarding the specific psychiatric-mental health disorders is necessary to help parents understand that the child's behavior is not intentional or malicious, nor is the child always in control, and to provide the parents and caregivers with necessary information and skills.

Annotated References

Ackley, B. J., & Ladwig, G. B. (2005). *North American Nursing Diagnosis Association, Taxonomy II. Nursing diagnosis handbook: A guide to planning care* (7th ed.). Retrieved September 30, 2006, from http://www.evolve.elsevier.com

This handbook helps the nursing student or practicing nurse make diagnoses and plan care utilizing the diagnoses approved by the North American Nursing Diagnosis Association (NANDA). Additionally, nursing outcomes classifications (NOC) and nursing interventions classifications (NIC) are provided.

American Academy of Child and Adolescent Psychiatry. (2004). Practice parameter for the assessment and treatment of children and adolescents with enuresis. *Journal of the American Academy of Child and Adolescent Psychiatry, 43*(12), 1540–1550.

The AACAP has developed standardized criteria expanding on the *DSM-IV-TR* manual looking at the specific etiology, diagnosis, and treatment of child psychiatric disorders. This article presents the practice parameters for enuresis including etiology, assessment, and treatment of the disorder.

American Academy of Child and Adolescent Psychiatry. (2005). Practice parameter for the assessment and treatment of children and adolescents with reactive attachment disorder of infancy and early childhood. *Journal of the American Academy of Child and Adolescent Psychiatry, 44*(11), 1206–1219.

The AACAP has developed standardized criteria expanding on the *DSM-IV-TR* manual looking at the specific etiology, diagnosis, and treatment of child psychiatric disorders. This article presents the practice parameters for reactive attachment disorder including etiology, assessment, and treatment of the disorder.

American Academy of Child and Adolescent Psychiatry. (2006). Practice parameter for the assessment and treatment of children and adolescents with anxiety disorders. Retrieved December 5, 2006, from http://www.aacap.org/galleries/PracticeParameters/JAACAP_Anxiety_2007.pdf

The AACAP has developed standardized criteria expanding on the *DSM-IV-TR* manual looking at the specific etiology, diagnosis, and treatment of child psychiatric disorders. The practice parameter for anxiety disorders was approved June 17, 2006, and published in February 2007. This parameter presents data based on extensive literature reviews of the etiology, assessment, and treatment (both pharmacologic and nonpharmacologic) of anxiety disorders in children and adolescents.

American Psychiatric Association. (2002). *Diagnostic and statistical manual of mental disorders* (4th ed., text rev.) Washington, DC: Author.

The *DSM-IV-TR* applies a standard nomenclature based on relatively stringent diagnostic criteria to provide the psychiatric clinician with a standardized text for recognizing, differentiating, and diagnosing psychiatric, behavioral, and substance use disorders.

Chard, K. M., & Gilman, R. (2005). Counseling trauma victims: 4 brief therapies meet the test. *Current Psychiatry, 4*(8), 50–64.

The authors discuss adapting cognitive-behavioral therapy techniques to posttraumatic stress disorder clients, with a discussion of modifications specific for children and adolescents.

Clark, A. (2004). Particular aspects of diagnosis, management, and treatment of bipolar disorders in children and adolescents. *Clinical Approaches in Bipolar Disorders, 3*(2), 49–54.

The author reviews issues related to diagnostic confusion in childhood bipolar disorder including methods of assessment, criteria used, and differential diagnoses and co-morbidity. Additionally, the author offers expert opinion on appropriate management and pharmacologic treatment of the disorder.

Coffey, B. (2002, March 16). *Tics and Tourette's disorder.* Paper presented at the Conference on Child and Adolescent Psychopharmacology, Boston, MA.

Lecture notes from the 2002 Psychopharmacology of Childhood Conference in Boston, Massachusetts, as presented by Dr. Barbara Coffey on the subject of Tourette's disorder.

Coffey, B., Biederman, J., Geller, D., Spencer, T., Kim, G., et al. (2000). Distinguishing illness severity from tic severity in children and adolescents with Tourette's disorder. *Journal of the American Academy of Child and Adolescent Psychiatry, 39*(5), 556–561.

This article examines a study of 156 youth ages 5–20 years who were diagnosed with Tourette's disorder and discusses the co-morbidity of other psychiatric disorders found in these children and adolescents.

Gartstein, M., & Sheeber, L. (2004). Child behavior problems and maternal symptoms of depression: A mediational model. *Journal of Child and Adolescent Psychiatric Nursing, 17*(4), 141–150.

The article suggests an association between maternal depression and child behavior problems in a study of 69 mothers of 3–6-year-old children, and examines three variables that may be mediating for the severity of dysfunction in the mother.

Geller, B., & Luby, J. (1997). Child and adolescent bipolar disorder: A review of the past 10 years. *Journal of the American Academy of Child and Adolescent Psychiatry, 36*(9), 1168–1176.

The authors conducted a 10-year literature review of child and adolescent bipolar disorder looking at epidemiology, course of the disorder, co-morbidity, and treatment.

Gillespie, C. F., & Nemeroff, C. B. (2005). Early life stress and depression. *Current Psychiatry, 4*(10), 15–30.

This article examines the impact of early life stress as a risk factor for the development of mood and anxiety disorders.

Hughes, D. (2002). Sudden onset of obsessive-compulsive disorder may point to PANDAS. *Neurology Reviews.com, 10*(4). Retrieved September 22, 2006, from http://www.neurologyreviews.com/apr02/pandas.html

The website Neurology Reviews covers emerging news in neurology and neuroscience and is updated monthly, with a focus on practical approaches to treating neurologic disorders. This report discusses one of the first systematic studies that looked at PANDAS and their relationship to obsessive-compulsive disorder.

Kessler, R. C., Adler, L. A., & Barkley, R. (2005). Patterns and predictors of attention-deficit/hyperactivity disorder persistence into adulthood: Results from the National Comorbidity survey replications. *Biological Psychiatry, 57,* 1442–1451.

The authors replicated the National Comorbidity survey by screening 3,199 individuals ages 19–44 years, finding the prevalence rate of attention deficit hyperactivity disorder to be 4.4% in the sample.

Massat, I., & Victor, L. (2005). Early bipolar disorder and ADHD: Differences and similarities in pre-pubertal and early adolescence. *Clinical Approaches in Bipolar Disorder, 4*(1), 20–28.

The article discusses a number of studies including clinical, cognition, neuroimaging, genetic, and pharmacologic that highlight the differences and similarities between childhood bipolar disorder and attention deficit hyperactivity disorder.

Meyer, S. E., & Carlson, G. A. (2003). Bipolar disorder in youth: An update. *Current Psychosis and Therapeutic Reports, 1*(2), 79–84.

The authors highlight findings in childhood bipolar disorder literature regarding definition of the disorder, epidemiology, co-morbidity, developmental aspects, family studies, medication responsiveness, and treatment.

National Institute of Mental Health. (1999). NIMH research on treatment for attention deficit hyperactivity disorder (ADHD): The Multimodal Treatment Study—questions and answers. Retrieved September 22, 2006, from http://www.nimh.nih.gov/childhp/mtaqa.cfm

The Multimodal Treatment Study of Children with ADHD brought together 18 nationally recognized authorities in ADHD at 6 different university medical centers and hospitals to evaluate the leading treatments for ADHD, including various forms of behavior therapy and medications. It included nearly 600 elementary school children. The NIMH website reports the results of that study.

Pilowsky, D., Wickramaratne, P., Nomura, Y., & Weissman, M. (2006). Family discord, parental depression, and psychopathology in offspring: 20-year follow-up. *Journal of the Academy of Child and Adolescent Psychiatry, 45*(4), 452–460.

The authors look at the independent effects of parental depression and family discord on children at high and low risk of depression over a 20-year span.

Pressman, L., Loo, S., Carpenter, E., Asarnow, J., Lynn, D., et al. (2006). Relationship of family environment and parental psychiatric diagnosis to impairment in ADHD. *Journal of the American Academy of Child and Adolescent Psychiatry, 45*(3), 346–354.

The authors examine the links among family environment, parental psychiatric diagnosis, and child impairment in 220 families that had at least two children with the diagnosis of attention deficit hyperactivity disorder.

Spencer, T., Biederman, J., & Wilens, T. (2000). Pharmacotherapy of attention deficit hyperactivity disorder. *Psychopharmacology, 9*(1), 77–97.

This article discusses the current pharmacotherapy models for the treatment of attention deficit hyperactivity disorder utilizing recommendations of the American Academy of Child and Adolescent Psychiatry practice parameters.

U.S. Department of Health and Human Services. (1999). *Mental Health: A report of the surgeon general.* Retrieved October 2, 2007, from http://www.surgeongeneral.gov/library/mentalhealth/home.html

Wagner, K., Ambrosini, P., Rynn, M., Wohlberg, C., Yang, R., et al. (2003). Efficacy of sertraline in the treatment of children and adolescents with major depressive disorder. *Journal of the American Medical Association, 290*(8), 1033–1041.

Two randomized controlled trials discuss major depressive disorder in children and adolescents, and examine the safety and tolerability of selective serotonin reuptake inhibitors in 376 youths ages 6 to 17 years.

Wilens, T., Biederman, J., Kwon, A., Ditterline, J., Forkner, P., et al. (2004). Risk of substance use disorders in adolescents with bipolar disorder. *Journal of the American Academy of Child and Adolescent Psychiatry, 43*(11), 1380–1386.

The authors examine the risk of substance use disorder in children with a diagnosis of bipolar disorder (n = 57) and without a diagnosis of bipolar disorder (n = 46).

Yung, A., & McGorry, P. (2004). Precursors of schizophrenia. *Current Psychosis and Therapeutics Reports, 2*(2), 67–72.

The authors attempt to detect a precursor stage for emerging psychosis associated with the onset of schizophrenia by reviewing precursor research and assimilating their findings.

Internet Resources

http://nursing.jbpub.com/psychiatric

Visit http://nursing.jbpub.com/psychiatric for interactive exercises, NCLEX review questions, WebLinks, and more.

CHAPTER 12

Dementia, Delirium, Amnesia, and Other Cognitive Disorders

Winifred Z. Kennedy

LEARNING OBJECTIVES

After reading this chapter, you will be able to:

- Differentiate among delirium, dementia, amnesia, and other cognitive disorders.
- Discuss common etiologic factors associated with dementia and delirium.
- Describe symptoms of common types of dementia and delirium.
- Identify effective nursing interventions for the confused client.

KEY TERMS

Agnosia
Alzheimer's disease
Amnesia
Anterograde amnesia
Aphasia
Apoptosis
Apraxia
Asterixis
Creutzfeldt-Jakob disease
Delirium
Dementia
Huntington's disease
Korsakoff's syndrome
Lewy body disease
Parkinson's disease
Pick's disease
Prion
Retrograde amnesia
Sundowning
Vascular dementia

http://nursing.jbpub.com/psychiatric

Visit http://nursing.jbpub.com/psychiatric for interactive exercises, NCLEX review questions, WebLinks, and more.

Introduction

Christopher Reeve (1996) spoke of the great need for research into brain and spinal cord problems, which affect one in every five U.S. families during their lifetime. He said, "If we can conquer outer space, we should be able to conquer inner space, too. . . . that's the frontier of the brain, the central nervous system, and all the [other] afflictions of the body that destroy so many lives and rob our country of so much potential." Cognitive disorders are dysfunctions or deteriorations of brain functioning. The *Diagnostic and Statistical Manual of Mental Disorders,* Fourth Edition, Text Revision (*DSM-IV-TR*) classifies the various cognitive disorders in terms of delirium, dementia, amnesia, and other general categories to describe acute, chronic, and progressive impairments of brain functioning (American Psychiatric Association [APA], 2000). These impairments are evidenced by changes that may occur in a person's affect, language skills, cognition, behavior, or personality because of anoxic, chemical or endocrinologic, structural, thermal, toxic, traumatic, or vascular conditions that have altered the function of the brain. Dementia, delirium, and amnesia are cognitive disorders symptomatic of mental or psychologic problems believed to be caused by physiologic problems such as structural or metabolic changes in brain functioning or drug abuse.

General Descriptions of the Disorders

Cognitive disorders are types of brain disorders affecting higher order brain functions such as cognition, perception, memory, reasoning, learning, creativity, judgment, and decision making. The *DSM-IV-TR* identifies these disorders as delirium, dementia, substance-induced delirium, and amnesia.

The *DSM-IV-TR* divides the classification of **delirium** between delirium as a result of a general medical condition (see Chapter 13) and substance-induced delirium (see Chapter 14). When significant cognitive impairment related to substance abuse persists beyond the period of intoxication and withdrawal, a diagnosis of *substance*-induced persisting dementia can be made, substituting the name of the specific substance or substances (APA, 2000). The diagnosis differs because the causative agent differs. In delirium associated with a general medical condition, the etiology or etiologies, if known, are specified on Axis I. The history and diagnostic testing that confirm drug use indicate a substance-induced delirium or withdrawal (APA, 2000).

> Delirium is a sudden deterioration in a client's condition, and is often linked to an identifiable cause that can be treated and potentially reversed. It is a common problem complicating hospital admissions. Clients with an underlying dementia may be more prone to developing delirium.

Amnesia is a separate diagnostic category related to memory impairment and can be transient or chronic. Amnestic disorders can be classified as due to a general medical condition, substance-induced persisting amnestic disorder, or, if not meeting criteria for other disorders, amnestic disorder not otherwise specified (NOS).

> As the world's population ages, the incidence of all types of dementia increases, particularly in the more developed countries. Many forms of dementia are chronic and cause a progressive decline in functioning.

Diagnostic criteria for **dementia** are based on the presumed or identified etiology and are specific for dementia of the **Alzheimer's** type, **vascular dementia** (multi-infarct dementia), and dementias related to **Lewy body disease**, **Parkinson's disease**, **Pick's disease**, **Huntington's disease**, **Creutzfeldt-Jakob disease**, normal pressure hydrocephalus, and human immunodeficiency virus (HIV). In all these types of dementia, the presence of delirium, delusions, or depressed mood also can be specified. Dementia is usually noted on Axis I. Dementia can be specified as being with early onset (age 65 years or younger) or with late onset (after age 65 years), and further specified as to being with or without behavioral disturbance. Other disorders such as significant mood disorder or psychosis should also be coded on Axis I.

Cognitive disorders that do not meet complete criteria for delirium, dementia, or amnesiac disorder can be classified as a cognitive disorder not otherwise specified (NOS).

Incidence and Prevalence

World health studies predict that both the incidence and prevalence of degenerative and hereditary central nervous system (CNS) disorders and cerebral vascular accidents (CVAs) will increase globally by the year 2020. This is partly because of declining mortality rates as a result of better prenatal and infectious disease care and the gradual aging of society; the prevalence of these disorders increases greatly in the elderly. The 2006 World Health Report predicted that the number of persons over 65 years of age in developing countries will increase by 200–400% over the next 25 years (Lopez, Mathers, Ezzati, Janison, & Murray, 2006).

Delirium affects an estimated 10–20% of hospitalized clients, making it a disorder frequently seen in the emergency room, particularly in the very young and very old. Delirium is most prevalent in hospitalized clients older than 65 years of age and in clients with an underlying baseline dementia. It is often associated with sepsis, anoxia, polypharmacy, arrhythmia, intoxication, or substance abuse. A sudden deterioration in the client's condition is often linked to an identifiable cause that can be treated and potentially reversed.

Although not a sign of the normal aging process, dementia is more common among individuals 60 years of age and older, and the incidence rises rapidly for clients 80 years of age and older. For example, although less than 2% of the population younger than 60 years of age is diagnosed with Alzheimer's disease, it is estimated that approximately 50% of persons older than 80 years of age have this diagnosis. The 2006 World Health Organization (WHO) report estimated that approximately 22 million individuals worldwide are affected by Alzheimer's disease and vascular dementias and predicted that approximately 80 million people will be affected by the year 2020 (Ferri et al., 2006; Lopez et al., 2006).

Dementia occurs more commonly in developing and developed countries. Alzheimer's disease has been determined to be the fourth leading cause of death in the United States. Cardiovascular disease, the third leading cause of death in the United States, increases the risk for developing arrhythmias, transient ischemic attacks (TIAs), or CVAs that can lead to vascular or multi-infarct dementia. Smoking, alcohol abuse, diabetes, vasculitis, and coagulopathies also increase the risk for vascular dementia. In the United States, the National Stroke Association (NSA) estimates that the risk of stroke is greater for women and for those over 55 years of age; two-thirds of all stroke clients are older than 65 years of age. WHO estimates that the incidence of Parkinson's disease is approximately 500 per 100,000 with a prevalence of 0.07%. Huntington's disease is estimated to have a frequency of 4–7%. Creutzfeldt-Jakob disease, a rare disorder in which clients show progressive signs of deterioration similar to clients with Alzheimer's disease, occurs with an incidence of one case per 1 million people each year (Lopez et al., 2006). Some researchers posit an association between Creutzfeldt-Jakob disease and "mad cow disease" or bovine spongiform encephalopathy (BSE). Although the incidence of both of these diseases is low, Creutzfeldt-Jakob disease has an increased prevalence along with BSE (also known as new-variant Creutzfeldt-Jakob disease) due to improvement of the sensitivity and specificity of diagnostic testing, identification of wider genetic susceptibility, and a possible carrier status, as well as the potential uncertainty regarding the incubation period (Seitz et al., 2007).

Etiology

Cognitive disorders may occur from temporary or permanent changes in the function of the brain as a result of genetic predisposition, infections, toxins, metabolic disorders, or injury. Delirium may be caused by general medical conditions, substance abuse, multiple causes, or it may have an unknown etiology. Dementia may be caused by Alzheimer's disease, a vascular or medical condition, or a substance abuse–induced pathology.

Deliriums are usually considered to be temporary and potentially reversible states. Some physiologic causes of delirium include infections, particularly those affecting the CNS; encephalopathies; toxic metabolic events; acute or chronic exposure to heavy metals or industrial toxins; intoxicants; inhalants and volatile solvents; cannabinoids or hallucinogens; and overdoses of prescription or over-the-counter (OTC) medications. Many prescription medications can, by themselves or in combination with other medications, contribute to the development of delirium. These medications include anesthetics and pain medications, antihistamines, commonly used gastrointestinal medications and hypnotics, steroids, and psychotropic medications. Delirium can be caused by drug intoxication or withdrawal. Malabsorption problems and dietary problems also cause cognitive changes that may be reversible. These include chronic alcohol abuse that can result in a vitamin B_{12} deficiency, pellagra resulting from a niacin deficiency, or an amnesiac syndrome such as **Korsakoff's syndrome** resulting from a thiamine deficiency. In clients with seizure disorders, the frequency and duration of seizures, the prolonged use of medication or overmedication, and the underlying disease or injury can contribute to the development of cognitive disorders. The physiologic changes experienced by a client with grand mal, petit mal, temporal lobe, or psychomotor seizures may present in an acute confusional state as a result of continuous or breakthrough seizure activity, as well as a postictal state.

Isolation, sleep deprivation, and immobilization also can contribute to the development of delirium. The most common example of this phenomenon is that of demented clients who experience worsening of confusion and restlessness at night. This is known as **sundowning**. The routine practice of giving hypnotics or antianxiety medications to demented clients who have been isolated in the strange new environment of a hospital room to quiet them down exacerbates this problem. The commonly used term *intensive*

Deliriums are usually temporary and reversible. Dementias are typically chronic and progressive.

Clinical Example

Betty is a 67-year-old woman who called the police for assistance and was found screaming in her apartment that her family was trying to poison her and wanted her dead. Her family reported that Betty had no past history of psychiatric problems and no medical problems except for hypertension, which seemed to be controlled with medication. They reported no changes in her health or regular medication. They mentioned that the patient was a little nervous anticipating traveling to visit her daughter in another state. Because she was having some trouble sleeping, the patient had been taking an over-the-counter medication containing diphenhydramine (Benadryl). Using a new prescribed medication or over-the-counter medication can lead to new symptoms usually associated with a psychiatric disorder.

Implications for Evidence-Based Practice

Foreman, Mion, Trygstad, & Fletcher (2003) identified strategies for nursing assessment and supportive nursing care for patients with delirium. Basic to assessment is obtaining baseline information, evaluating alertness, attention, and current medical status. Supportive nursing care includes comfort measures, preventing the hazards of immobility, clear communication, and family education. Further research is needed on the standardization of assessment tools and validation of nursing actions.

care unit (ICU) psychosis usually inaccurately describes the disoriented, disorganized behavior of a client who is delirious. The delirium may be caused by an underlying medical problem or an iatrogenic problem as a result of the use of restraints or medical or surgical interventions.

Dementias are usually considered chronic and progressive. Alzheimer's disease is probably the most frequently encountered dementia. As mentioned earlier, a distinction is made between clients who have early-onset dementia and those who have late-onset dementia. Dementia may be accompanied by symptoms of delirium, delusions, depressed mood, hallucinations or other perceptual problems, behavior disorders, or communication problems. Some of the disorders most commonly associated with dementia are as follows:

- *Degenerative dementias:* These include Alzheimer's disease, Lewy body disease, amyotrophic lateral sclerosis (ALS), Pick's disease, Creutzfeldt-Jakob disease, Parkinson's disease, Parkinson's plus (Parkinson-like syndromes with multiple system degeneration), Huntington's disease, and BSE/new-variant Creutzfeldt-Jakob disease.
- *Ventricular disorders:* Ventricular disorders include normal pressure hydrocephalus (NPH) and obstructive and nonobstructive hydrocephalus.
- *Infectious disorders:* These include human immunodeficiency virus type 1 (HIV-1), encephalopathies, and neurosyphilis.
- *Vascular disorders:* The vascular disorders are Binswanger's (subcortical arteriosclerotic encephalopathy), subarachnoid and subdural hematomas, vasculitis, small vessel disorders, and CVAs.
- *Immunologic disorders:* These include multiple sclerosis (MS), systemic lupus erythematosus (SLE), and HIV-1.
- *Convulsive disorders:* These may result from injury, epilepsy, stroke, or metabolic disorders.
- *Systemic disorders:* Systemic disorders include brain cancer and metastatic disease, uremia or renal failure, and other metabolic, endocrinologic, or electrolytic imbalances.
- *Traumatic injury:* Examples of trauma include head injury and postanoxic states.
- *Toxicity:* Toxicity results from exposure to toxins, heavy metals, or alcohol or other drug abuse.

Amnesic disorders include short- and long-term memory problems that can be caused by trauma, brain lesions, strokes, encephalitis, or chronic alcohol abuse. Transient global amnesia, a period of less than 24 hours of memory loss and confusion, is thought to be primarily vascular in origin. Other medical conditions or surgical interventions also may be associated with amnesic disorders (APA, 2000).

Physiology

Dementias

Dementias are usually considered chronic, progressive disorders. Some of the most common degenerative disorders are Alzheimer's disease, Lewy body disorders, frontal and frontal-temporal lobe dementias, and Down syndrome.

Alzheimer's disease involves the development of neurofibrils, neurofibrillary tangles, and beta-plated amyloid plaques, first in the cortex and hippocampus and later in the frontal, parietal, and temporal lobes. Additional changes include cortical atrophy, increased ventricular dilation, and decreased levels of acetylcholine, norepinephrine, and other neurotransmitters. Many of the changes are in the basal forebrain, which is the cortex's source of acetycholine. This process differs from the normal developmental process of **apoptosis**, the naturally occurring cell death that is part of aging, which may involve the development of amyloid plaques. Acetylcholine is believed to play an important role in memory. Researchers have posited that a genetic link may predispose some individuals to Alzheimer's disease. In addition, there is some indication that long-term exposure to pollutants or intoxicants may contribute to the development of the disease in those individuals with a predisposition to Alzheimer's.

Some studies have indicated that persons with relatives who have Parkinson's disease also have cortical symptoms. In clients with frontal lobe dementias such as Pick's disease, ALS, and progressive supranuclear palsy, there can be frontal temporal lobe hypometabolism and a progressive, degenerative course similar to Alzheimer's. Lewy body dementias also have the plaques and tangles associated with Alzheimer's disease as well as Lewy bodies in the substantia nigra and the cortex, as in Parkinson's disease. In clients with Lewy body disease, visual hallucinations and delusions are usually more prominent than would be suspected by the degree of cognitive impairment, and the client may have extrapyramidal symptoms as do clients with Parkinson's disease.

Parkinson's disease and Huntington's disease are primarily subcortical dementias. The predominant features of these diseases tend to be the symptoms of movement disorders, mood disorders such as depression, and changes in personality (regressive behavior). Clients with Parkinson's disease have degeneration of the substantia nigra. Parkinson's disease is caused primarily by a dopamine deficiency in the substantia nigra, caudate, and putamen that results in basal ganglia dysfunction. Lewy bodies are also found mainly in the autonomic nervous system and brain. Extrapyramidal symptoms such as rigid posture, tremors, and bradykinesia (slowed movements) are common. The observation of family clusters of Huntington's disease has led to genetic mapping studies that have identified Huntington's as an autosomal-dominant disease in which the hypermetabolism of glucose and tissue atrophy cause choreic movements (jerking, ticlike involuntary movements) and progressive dementia.

In most multi-infarct dementias, encephalopathies, infectious diseases, systemic illnesses, endocrinopathies, and exposure to drugs and toxins, both cortical and subcortical damage occur. Disorders that are transmitted, such as Creutzfeldt-Jakob disease and BSE/new-variant Creutzfeldt-Jakob disease, are thought to be caused by **prions** (proteinaceous infectious particles containing deoxyribonucleic acid [DNA]). Prions are almost indestructible particles that self-replicate by connecting to other proteins and accumulate, form plaques, and cause spongiform vacuoles, or spongelike holes that damage neurons.

> Prions are almost indestructible particles that accumulate, form plaques, and damage neurons.

Immunologic and infectious disorders such as multiple sclerosis (MS), neurosyphilis, and human immunodeficiency virus-1 (HIV-1) also cause symptoms of a cognitive disorder as a result of changes to the CNS. In HIV-1, as the disease progresses, white matter and subcortical structures are often destroyed. However, the damage can be complicated by reduced resistance to other infections including meningitis, toxoplasmosis, cytomegalovirus (CMV), and neoplasms such as lymphoma and Kaposi's sarcoma. MS is an autoimmune disease in which extensive periventricular demyelination causes symptoms of dementia with no correlation to the duration of the illness or to other symptoms of disease progression (Mendez & Cummings, 2003).

Cardiac, vascular, and pulmonary problems may cause disturbances in the regulation of cerebral blood flow. This can cause oxidative damage and hypoperfusion in the subcortical white matter of the brain. This damage is shown by changes in microglial cell activation, beta-amyloid processing, and long-term potentiation on glutamate-mediated neurotransmitters. In vascular dementias, ischemic events or emboli as well as vascular changes may affect certain areas in the brain and after a time are seen as ischemic changes to the white matter. Following a TIA, damage may be only temporary or not apparent at all. However, over time the client may develop lacunae infarcts in which the surface of the brain is pitted from small infarcts. Damage to vital areas may also occur. Damage to certain areas may cause speech and language problems.

An **aphasia** is a speech or language disorder. Left-sided temporal lobe lesions often cause Wernicke's aphasia, a receptive disorder in which there are problems comprehending sensory stimuli. Left-sided temporal lobe lesions cause Broca's aphasia, an expressive disorder in which there are problems with speech or speaking. Clients with right-hemisphere lesions often present with an abnormal posture, apathy, an altered perception of body image that causes inattention to or denial of disability, and problems with constructional ability (inability to reproduce figures correctly), recognition (difficulty in identifying objects or faces), and spatial orientation (Pinel, 2006).

A client with grand mal, petit mal, temporal lobe, or psychomotor seizures undergoes physiologic changes that may result in either an acute confusional state from continuous or breakthrough seizure activity or a postictal state in which periods of amnesia are experienced. Trauma to the head, such as the repetitive injury and abuse boxers or football players suffer, can cause physiologic and structural changes that produce symptoms of dementia or amnesia. Neurofibrillary tangles and amyloid plaques, which are associated with memory and cognitive functioning, can develop.

Taking a complete client history may help to identify the various causes of head injuries. Elderly clients may hurt themselves by falling, epileptics from seizures, and alcoholics from abuse. Sports injuries and motor vehicle or bicycle accidents also are frequent causes of brain injury.

Amnesias

The memory disturbances of amnesia are thought to be caused by interruptions to cerebral blood flow, blows to the head, effects of medication, or drug abuse. Damage to the hippocampus in the medial temporal lobe or to the cortex can cause amnesia. Korsakoff's syndrome is associated with chronic alcohol use. Memory loss may be attributable to thiamine deficiency and possibly to lesions in the brain and damage to the mediodorsal nuclei of the mediodorsal thalamus. Wernicke's encephalopathy is caused by acute thiamine deficiency. It is seen in chronically malnourished alcoholics who may have a genetic predisposition that prevents thiamine bonding. Wernicke's encephalopathy is an acute confusional state that usually resolves with treatment. Clients with a persistent or profound memory loss, particularly for recent events, usually have brain lesions and chronic impairment and exhibit the symptoms of dementia or Korsakoff's syndrome (Mendez & Cummings, 2003; Pinel, 2006).

Clinical Presentation

The signs and symptoms of changes in mental status are often the first clues to the presence of cognitive impairment. Other signs include changes in the individual's ability in one or more areas of comprehension, object naming, organizational skills, insight and judgment, spatial and visual abilities, and the ability to perform complex sequences of tasks. The mental status of a client is assessed by examination of appearance, alertness, affect and mood, speech and language, general cognitive functioning, and psychologic state.

The mental status examination often begins by observing the level of consciousness, which is usually defined as part of a continuum of interaction with or sensitivity to environmental stimuli. It includes the level of consciousness and ability to attend and recognize stimuli. The client may exhibit anything from hypervigilance to alertness, lethargy, stupor, obtundation, and coma. An alert client is fully awake and responsive and readily interacts with the examiner. A lethargic client may appear to be sleeping, may respond readily to verbal stimuli but is unable to attend to the interviewer and soon falls back to sleep if not continuously stimulated. In contrast, a stuporous

Implications for Evidence-Based Practice

Mezey and Maslow (2007) reviewed best practices in assessment and recognition of dementia in hospitalized older adults. By using targeted questions regarding memory problems, diagnosis of Alzheimer's disease or dementia, family questionnaire of daily activities and memory, and patient behavior triggers to record symptoms of possible dementia, nurses could increase recognition of dementia. Merzey and Maslow suggest incorporating questions and behavior profiles in the nursing assessment and hospital forms. Basic questions focused on forgetfulness, repetition, problems following directions, and problems managing the household and making decisions and staff recorded behavioral symptoms usually associated with dementia. A history of dementia is often not listed in the hospital record or used in determination of acuity. Further research is needed regarding whether early identification of dementia and delirium would be beneficial in identifying high risk patients in the hospital, as well as in reducing problems such as falls, agitated and aggressive behaviors, and functional decline.

client may appear to be sleeping soundly. An obtunded client may be only minimally responsive to painful stimuli, and a comatose client may not respond at all. Unless the client is fully alert, it is difficult to involve him or her in an assessment. The client would be unable to focus and to shift attention at will.

Family members and other caretakers can be questioned to determine if the level of consciousness or alertness of the client varies or fluctuates throughout the day, worsens at night, or occurs in response to a specific event or stressor. If a CVA is suspected, it is important to note when the changes occurred and whether the changes were witnessed (e.g., the client was observed having problems speaking) or unwitnessed (e.g., the client was found unresponsive on the floor) that lasted for a particular length of time. Family members or caretakers also can describe the client's usual living arrangements and whether the client functions independently, requires some assistance with household responsibilities, or needs supervision of personal activities of daily living (ADLs). These changes may have occurred so slowly that the client or family may not be aware of the accommodations that have been made for progressive disability. Conversely, abrupt changes in the client's usual level of functioning may also occur.

Observation of the client's appearance, ability to communicate, and behavior is also important. The nurse must check to see if the client is groomed properly and if the clothing is appropriate for the situation and season. The nurse should note if there are bruises or signs of injury. The nurse must also note if the client's features are symmetrical and if posture, gait, mouth, or tongue are impaired. Clients with dementia may exhibit the loss of the ability to perform skilled motor acts, a condition referred to as **apraxia**. The client's speech and language skills can be observed as they interact with others in identifying and recalling objects, responding to questions, and making their needs known.

Also of importance is the client's ability to recall personal identity, to orient to his or her present location, and to give the date and time. The nurse should see if the client can describe his or her living situation and give details such as the names of the primary healthcare provider, family members or caretaker, and usual medications. The nurse can perform a quick assessment of the client's reading and comprehension skills. If the responses are spontaneous and fluent, a formal cognitive test may not be needed unless a specific problem is suspected or the client's history suggests a problem such as noncompliance with medical treatment (possibly attributable to comprehension or memory problems). The nurse must observe whether the client has trouble concentrating or performing the task at hand. The nurse should look for signs of problems with immediate memory (recalling new ongoing events), recent memory (recalling contemporary events), or remote memory (recalling past events). Often a client will mention having problems with memory or concentration. At this point, a more formal measure of cognition such as the Mini-Mental State Examination or another brief cognitive rating scale can be introduced as a natural extension of the interviewer's assessment.

Clinical Example

Roberto is an employed 63-year-old man who was brought to the emergency department after he was observed by his family to have a period of slurred speech and inability to move his right arm when awakening from a nap at home. The patient had been watching a ballgame on television and had fallen asleep. The family is concerned because Roberto didn't seem to recognize them at first and didn't seem able to communicate with them. Roberto appeared to recover in a few minutes. Now despite some weakness in his right arm, he insists he is fine and wants to go home. His wife recalls that he had a similar episode several weeks before but the symptoms disappeared so quickly the patient said his arm must have fallen asleep.

The mental status examination is an important part of client assessment. Many of the same symptoms can be found in clients with cognitive disorders and functional psychiatric disorders. The mental status examination initially helps the clinician build a foundation for the differential diagnosis.

Agnosia, or the inability to recognize objects that cannot be explained by a reduced level of alertness, may suggest a dementia. Any unusual preoccupations such as paranoid beliefs, delusional thinking, or unusual experiences such as hallucinations are important to note, as are assessments for suicidal or homicidal thoughts and the potential for aggressive or violent behavior. The presence of visual hallucinations usually indicates a delirium rather than psychotic features of a functional psychiatric disorder. Visual hallucinations can be prominent in Lewy body dementias and are often not distressing or frightening to the client.

Differential Diagnosis

The differential diagnosis of a cognitive disorder as a reflection of abnormal brain functioning is often determined by the onset, progression, and types of symptoms that occur. The onset of delirium is

NURSING CARE PLAN Dementia

Expected Outcomes	Interventions	Evaluations
• Will decrease potential for injury.	• To provide anticipatory guidance to the family regarding the patient's disabilities.	• The client has begun to wear a Medical Alert bracelet.
• Will be able to interact with others to maximum of cognitive ability.	• To discuss options for possible referral to an adult day care program.	• The client participates in an adult care program with activities for demented clients.
• Will experience improved interaction and support with family.	• To refer the family to an Alzheimer's Association family support group.	• Family members verbalize feelings of loss.
• Will be able to accomplish activities of daily living by self or with support of others.	• To educate the client and the client's family regarding the need for memory cues such as clocks, calendars, and lists of routines.	• The family has set up stable household routines.

Visit http://nursing.jbpub.com/psychiatric for additional care plans and exercises.

usually sudden and progresses rapidly, but symptoms may appear to fluctuate during the day and worsen at night, or they may fluctuate from day to day. The client's level of consciousness and orientation may be impaired or seem to fluctuate at times. The client may perceive common environmental stimuli incorrectly or have visual as well as other types of hallucinations. Memory problems are common and may affect recall and short- and long-term memory.

Asterixis, known as "liver flap," is a condition of motor tremors where the client is unable to maintain a posture or position without moving. For example, the client is unable to hold his or her

CASE STUDY Ms. S.

Ms. S. is a 60-year-old woman with no psychiatric or drug abuse history whose son brought her to the psychiatric center. The client was evaluated by the advanced practice nurse. The client's son stated that he had become alarmed during a visit when his father told him that his mother had been acting "very strangely" and "crazy." The client's son and husband attributed these changes to her early retirement 3 years ago. The family stated that the client had been a home attendant and had worked regularly up until then, although the agency for which she worked had been hiring her less and less for about a year before her retirement and had eventually stopped calling her. In addition, they said that she formerly had done everything in the house, was very strong and healthy, and took no medications. However, she had been forgetting to pay bills lately, leaving the stove on, burning dinners, and neglecting the housework and her appearance. She had stopped doing many of her usual activities such as going to church, and she previously had been very active in church work. Her husband said that he noticed that she never read the Bible any more, which had been very important to her.

The previous night she had left the house without saying anything to her husband and was gone for hours. He assumed that she was acting strangely again and had gone to her sister's house. However, when she did not return the following morning, and her sister said that she had not visited, her husband went looking for her. He found her walking up and down the block several streets from their home. Her only explanation at the time was that "the house was wrong." During the interview, the client seemed very embarrassed and apologized to everyone. She was unable to recall objects, do simple arithmetic problems, recite the months of the year backward, or draw a simple figure of an open cross. The initial clinical impression was dementia of the Alzheimer's type with early onset (before age 65) (see **Table 12-1**), and she was referred for a dementia workup, which may include neurologic examination; diagnostic tests for possible sepsis, anemia, electrolyte imbalances, vitamin B_{12} deficiency, folate deficiency, syphilis (VDRL), and thyroid functioning; computed tomography (CT) scan of the head; electroencephalogram (EEG); toxicology screen; ammonia levels; and liver function tests.

Table 12-1 Assessment for Dementia

1. History of cognitive decline (e.g., progressive decline in Alzheimer's type dementia or more sudden or step-wise decline in vascular type dementia)
2. Evidence of cognitive impairment (e.g., Mini Mental State Score of less than 26/30, aphasia, apraxia, agnosia, history of impairment in higher cortical functioning such as inability to do abstractions or problem solving)
3. Examples of decline from pre-morbid functioning (e.g., inability to maintain household, inability to drive car)
4. Elimination of possible reversible causes of impairment (e.g., decreased vitamin B_{12}, folate, or niacin, and abnormal thyroid or liver functioning; positive VDRL; sepsis)
5. Elimination of possible medical disorders that better explain functional problems (e.g., Huntington disease, Parkinson disorder central nervous, normal pressure hydrocephalus)
6. Elimination of possible mental disorders that better explain functional problems (e.g., depression, psychosis, developmental disorder)
7. Identification of presence or absence of behavioral problems (e.g., severe agitation, wandering) associated with the decline in cognitive functioning

Table 12-2 Assessment for Delirium

1. Identification of sudden change in mental status (e.g., changes within a few hours or days) or history of pre-existing dementia that may make the person more prone to development of delirium (e.g., previous history of post-op delirium in client with known dementia, confusion in client with known history of stroke who showed behavior changes in past when diagnosed with urinary tract infection)
2. Observation of levels of consciousness that show sudden and fluctuating changes (e.g., periods of clarity alternating with lethargy, presence of visual hallucinations or illusions)
3. Development of cognitive changes that may also be sudden and fluctuating (e.g., periods of disorientation, communication problems, memory problems) not better explained by pre-existing disorder such as dementia or central nervous system disorders
4. Identification of specific medical disorder or reversible cause for symptoms (e.g., sepsis, exposure to toxins or substances of abuse, electrolyte imbalance)

CASE STUDY Ms. T.

Ms. T. is a 72-year-old woman who was brought to the emergency room by police after her neighbors called to report that she had been found wandering in the hallway of the apartment building. Neighbors stated that she was screaming about snakes in her room that were coming out of the floor and ceiling. The neighbors stated that Ms. T. was normally a very quiet woman who was very active in the senior center but had not been performing her usual activities for several days. When the client's family was called, they were very upset to see Ms. T. Her daughter stated that she had seen her mother 2 days earlier to help her with shopping and that everything had seemed fine. The client had called her daughter the day before and said that she did not feel well and thought she had a slight cold, so she was going to stay home. Her daughter stated that she would not have recognized her mother, who now appeared unkempt and tremulous. This was an abrupt change from the client's usual well-groomed and confident appearance. The client was described as a very strong and forceful woman who required only minimal assistance with household management. The daughter added that the client was proud that she had never been sick a day in her life, was on no prescription medications, and rarely took any OTC medications other than aspirin. There was no psychiatric history. Now the client appeared frightened and asked her daughter to stay near her because she did not understand why she had been arrested and brought to the police station. The client became more distressed when the curtain was drawn around her bed in the emergency room. She complained that there were worms moving on the striped curtain. The client had a slight cough and elevated temperature, and the staff reported that the initial chest x-ray indicated pneumonia.

The initial clinical impression was of delirium (**Table 12-2**), and diagnostic testing was done to determine if the client was septic. It would be expected that the delirium would resolve as the infection was treated. Because an underlying dementia can sometimes cause a client to be more prone to developing delirium, the client should be evaluated for possible dementia after the delirium resolves. If the delirium is superimposed upon a preexisting dementia, the diagnosis would be dementia with delirium (APA, 2000). Delirium is a symptom of a medical emergency, and the client should be evaluated to determine the cause of the delirium.

NURSING CARE PLAN Delirium

Expected Outcomes	Interventions	Evaluations
• Will be oriented to environment and assisted to maintain orientation when needed.	• To provide reorientation for the client (e.g., introducing self, explaining procedures, having a clock and calendar in the room).	• Observation of increased levels of functioning and orientation with appropriate cueing.
• Will experience decreased anxiety.	• To observe and identify ways in which the client expresses anxiety related to confusion.	• Observation of decreased anxiety.
• Will decrease potential for injury to self or others.	• To review fall precautions and other safety policies with unlicensed assistive personnel involved in care of the client.	• Supervision of fall precautions on the unit.
• Will receive assistance in identifying and coping with symptoms of hallucinations.	• To assess the client's cognitive status and presence of visual hallucinations.	• Involvement of the staff in client assessment and appropriate interventions.

Visit http://nursing.jbpub.com/psychiatric for additional care plans and exercises.

hands in a flexed position without "flapping" them. To test for asterixis, clients are asked to extend their arms outward and raise the fingers so that the palms of their hands face outward. The nurse should also be aware of the presence of sepsis, a systemic disorder, substance abuse, exposure to toxins, or structural damage as a result of an accident or stroke, because these are all possible causes of delirium. Asterixis can be found in patients with metabolic encephalopathies, electrolyte imbalance, and drug use.

The differential diagnoses of dementia or delirium should include consideration of any underlying psychiatric disorders and drug and alcohol abuse.

Taking a complete history of any trauma, medication use, operative and postoperative complications, cardiac disease, and hypertension is important to understand the etiology of the disorder as well as contributing factors that, if treated, could resolve the delirium. Behavioral changes are not always a clear indication of delirium because the client may either be agitated and hyperactive or withdrawn and sedated. Overmedication, drug interactions, and substance abuse may be related to the development of delirium. If related to substance abuse withdrawal, treatment for withdrawal symptoms may be indicated or the client may need to be tapered slowly from the offending agent to avoid seizures or autonomic instability. Although delirium is considered a temporary and potentially reversible problem, recovery time may be prolonged in the elderly or those who are medically compromised.

An important differential is to determine whether the symptoms represent pseudodementia or dementia-like symptoms of poor memory and functioning that are actually caused by a mood disorder, usually depression. Whereas clients with dementia usually attempt to cooperate with cognitive testing or to minimize and hide deficits, clients with pseudodementia have inconsistent responses that make them appear to be worse than they actually are. For example, they may have better immediate and short-term memory than long-term memory and improve in the hospital rather than worsen in the new environment or at night. Treatment of the depression improves the cognitive impairment of a client with pseudodementia. Observations and meth-

Implications for Evidence-Based Practice

Gaudreau and colleagues (2005) studied use of a brief five-item observational scale noting disorientation, inappropriate behavior, disorganized communication, illusions/hallucinations, and psychomotor retardation to identify clients with manifestations of delirium. Inter-rater reliability was determined between nurses and physicians and between the scale used and the CAM, a more widely used scale. Use of the Nursing Delirium Screening Scale (Nu-DESC) was validated and beneficial in helping recognized unidentified cases.

ods used to differentiate among delirium, dementia, vascular dementia, and pseudodementia are given in **Table 12-3**.

Dementia may be the initial presenting problem or an underlying problem predisposing the development of delirium. Dementia should be distinguished from the normal aging process. Identifying the cause of dementia assists in treatment and management. Other medical conditions should be eliminated as contributing factors. There may be multiple etiologic factors identified with the dementia. In a vascular dementia there are usually associated focal neurologic signs. It is common to find combinations of Alzheimer's and vascular dementia.

Clinical Example

Dennis a 65-year-old man, has been having increasing problems concentrating since he retired. He worries about problems with his memory and loses track of bills and appointments. He has lost interest in his usual activities, and doesn't shower or shave regularly saying, "What's the difference; I'm not going anywhere." He appears to have lost weight since his last clinic visit. He identifies his biggest problem as fatigue and states he has had trouble falling asleep and staying asleep. During questioning, Dennis answers "I don't know. I just don't know" to simple questions while appearing to easily answer more difficult questions. Clients with depression may be indifferent to testing or highlight their inability to answer questions, and some may frequently "give up" and not answer. This is in contrast to clients with dementia who may struggle with the test, ask for frequent feedback on responses, or answer with a "near miss."

Clinical Course and Complications

The clinical course in cognitive disorders varies from acute to chronic conditions and may be accompanied by other physical and psychiatric disorders. An outline of the clinical course of delirium, Alzheimer's disease, and other forms of dementia appears in **Table 12-4**.

Delirium is usually associated with an acute medical condition and is potentially reversible.

Many clients present with a mixed picture of symptoms that may be attributable to several different disorders. For example, a demented client may become delirious, a client with Alzheimer's disease may also have a vascular dementia, or a client with a substance-abuse disorder may have normal pressure hydrocephalus.

Table 12-3 Comparison of Delirium, Dementia, Vascular Dementia, and Pseudodementia

	Delirium	Dementia	Vascular Dementia	Pseudodementia/ Depression
Onset	Acute	Chronic	Acute or chronic	Chronic
Clinical course	Sudden	Slowly progressive	Sudden, gradual, or stepwise	Acute or chronic
Impairment	Fluctuating	Progressive	Discrete or global problems	Inconsistent
Disorientation	Usually	Progressive	Sometimes	Intact
Cognitive impairment	Rarely	Progressive	Usually	Patchy
Language	Sometimes	Naming objects	+/- Speech problems	None
Perceptual	+/− visual hallucinations; +/− tactile hallucinations	Sometimes	Sometimes	Rarely, +/− auditory hallucinations
Aphasia	Occasionally	Sometimes	+/− speech and language problems	Rarely
Apraxia	Rarely	Progressive	Sometimes	Rarely
Agnosia	Rarely	Progressive	Sometimes	Rarely
Asterixis	+/− asterixis	Rarely	Rarely	Rarely
CT scan	Normal	Atrophy	Abnormal	Normal
EEG	Abnormal	Normal or slowed; slowing increases when advanced	+/− abnormalities	Normal
MRI	+/− changes	Normal or hippocampal atrophy	White matter disease; ischemic changes	Normal

Note: CT = computed tomography; EEG = electroencephalogram; MRI = magnetic resonance imaging.

Table 12-4 Clinical Course of Delirium, Dementia, and Amnesia

	Onset	Clinical Course	Signs and Symptoms
Delirium	Sudden	Acute, reversible	Confusion and disorientation
Dementia	Varies with disease	Generally irreversible	Varies with disease
Alzheimer's disease	Gradual < age 65	Progressive	Cognitive decline, disorientation, incontinence, wandering, and behavior changes
Vascular dementia	Acute	Stepwise	Cognitive changes, speech problems, and paresis
Parkinson's disease	> age 40	Progressive	Bradykinesia, tremor, and gait and posture problems
Pick's disease	Sudden	Rapid and progressive	Personality changes and cognitive decline
Huntington's disease	Age 35–40	Progressive	Movement disorder, emotional instability, and personality changes
Creutzfeldt-Jakob (CJD)	Age 40–60	Progressive	Cognitive disorder and personality changes
BSE (new variant CJD)	Age varies	Progressive	Similar to CJD
Normal pressure hydrocephalus	Gradual; > age 50	Chronic and possibly reversible	Apathy/depression, gait problems, and incontinence
HIV	Varies	Varies	Increased by presence of other disorders and acute/chronic infection
Substance-induced	Drug abuse history	Acute or chronic; +/– withdrawal	Memory problems, cognitive problems, and behavior changes
Amnesia	Sudden; not part of delirium	Depends on cause	Memory problems: anterograde, retrograde, and transient global

Clients with preexisting dementia may be more prone to developing the symptoms of a delirium when they experience the physiologic changes associated with an electrolyte imbalance, pharmacotherapy, or medical illness (see Chapter 13). It is important to identify and treat the underlying cause of the delirium as well as to avoid anything that may cause or contribute to the delirium. Untreated pain or overmedication with pain medications can contribute to delirium. Screening should include a history of medications, herbals, and supplements the client may be taking as well as a determination of substance use and abuse. The symptoms of delirium may vary during the course of the illness in terms of the level of alertness and orientation and as to the presence or absence of symptoms of agitation, delusions, or hallucinations.

Clients with Alzheimer's disease may experience a gradual progression of symptoms for several years. This may include periods when symptoms occasionally level off or stabilize. The problem typically noted first is delayed recall. As the disease progresses, problems include difficulties in recognizing and naming objects, problems in recognizing people, and socially inappropriate and disinhibited behaviors. At this point, the client requires total care and supervision of ADLs. The onset of vascular dementia may be more noticeable and rapid for both client and family. The disease may progress for many years, but symptoms may not be seen until a critical area of the brain is affected or the additive effects to many different areas of the brain are apparent.

Critical Thinking Question At times changes in cognition may be so slow and gradual that the client and family accommodate to these changes, making it difficult for them to recognize and acknowledge problems. Problems may not be recognized until the client is in a new environment such as the hospital. How can client and family teaching be used to assist the client and family in recognizing when further assessment or assistance might be needed? Give an example of how these topics could be introduced to the client and family.

In amnesic disorders, the onset may be rapid and is usually associated with trauma or disease. In many cases, memory gradually returns over time. Past events are usually remembered first. However, there may be no memory of the traumatic event itself or the events immediately preceding or following it. With **anterograde amnesia**, the client has problems learning new material. With **retrograde amnesia**, the client has problems recalling past events or learned material.

Management and Treatment

Nursing Interventions

Management of cognitive disorders includes reorientation. The nurse should restructure the environment and activities of the client to maximize his or her abilities and minimize distractions and hazards. This restores the individual to an optimum level of functioning.

Remotivatating involves the client as much as possible in self-care activities and appropriate social activities and reinforces appropriate coping mechanisms, adaptive skills, and social supports. In addition, clients are encouraged to reminisce and review their lifetime memories as well as developmental stages and tasks. Dysfunctional symptoms are regulated by treating coexisting illnesses and administering the appropriate medications as required.

Disorientation is often a problem; therefore, frequent reorientation may be necessary. Based on an assessment of the client's deficits, the staff frequently will need to incorporate information to help the client reestablish a correct orientation to person, place, and time. Environmental cues such as easily read calendars and wall clocks, appropriate signs and area decorations, color coding of different areas, and access to information and news sources are important. Staff members should be aware of any sensory deficits and memory and language problems when they provide explanations or interact with a disoriented client in any way.

Critical Thinking Question Identify environmental factors that can contribute to confusion and some strategies and suggestions for dealing with these problems. How can these suggestions be adapted to the home environment?

The client's attention span and ability to concentrate may be impaired, or there may be varying levels of consciousness. There also may be physical disabilities as a result of illness or a movement disorder. Because of these factors, the environment must be physically safe, accessible for those with disabilities, and structured to minimize dangers. At times having a family member present helps reorient the client. If the client is agitated or wanders, a companion or sitter at the bedside may help. It may be necessary to evaluate whether the use of partial side rails or safety restraints and full side rails on beds is needed. The staff needs to be aware of the problems that

Predominant features complicating the clinical course of a dementia may include the presence of delirium delusions, depressed mood, or behavioral disturbances.

Considerations for Client and Family Education

- Develop awareness of changes in levels of confusion and symptoms that may indicate the need for treatment of medical or psychiatric illnesses.
- Assist the client and family to anticipate and prepare for some changes in roles and caretaking responsibilities.
- Recognize the importance of developing support systems for both the client and caretakers.
- Provide guidance in recognizing and dealing with symptoms of stress and fatigue.

Implications for Evidence-Based Practice

Futrell and Melillo (2002) identified assessment criteria for wandering including identification of the consequences of wandering, travel patterns, wandering behaviors, and risk factor of premorbid lifestyle characteristics. Appropriate environmental modifications such as providing a secure place to wander, providing cueing, and making exits less accessible in addition to providing appropriate therapeutic interventions such as regular structured activities including exercise, music, and social interaction are effective in decreasing wandering. Further studies of effective assessment tools and interventions would be helpful.

may actually be caused by restraint use. Proper lighting during the day and night lights in the evening are helpful. Ensuring that clients have appropriate supervision, assistance with ADLs, and access to their eyeglasses, hearing aids, dentures, and other adaptive aids is important. Clients with memory problems or wandering (a problem occurring in the later stages of some dementias) may need to wear a Medical Alert bracelet or some other form of identification, and their physical environment may need to be changed to ensure safety.

Restoring the client to an optimum level of functioning may be difficult as a result of communication or other cognitive problems, isolation, poor nutrition, or inadequate access to health care. The client may not understand instructions or take prescribed medications. It is important to ensure that the client is getting proper nutrition. The nurse must assess whether problems exist with feeding, dentition, and gum disease, as well as if there are mechanical problems with chewing or swallowing. Fatigue, limited mobility or movement disorders, incontinence, and alterations in sleep patterns may require changes in a client's routine and physical environment. In addition to the assessment and treatment of their medical problems, clients should be evaluated for the necessity of speech, physical, and occupational therapies.

Critical Thinking Questions With progressive symptoms of dementia, the client may eventually be unable to take food orally. How can dysphagia be evaluated? What quality of life and ethical factors might the client or family consider in deciding on the option for tube or PEG feedings?

Clients may have low self-esteem and an altered body image. Feelings of hopelessness, helplessness, and isolation may require the staff to become involved in remotivating the client. Social interaction, group support, and activities should be geared to the client's abilities. Art, music, and movement therapies are useful adjuncts, as is appropriate involvement in exercise groups. The staff should provide access to familiar religious and cultural activities as well as to the person's usual religious or spiritual advisor. Hospital chaplain services also should be provided. The staff should assess if the client is able to make decisions. Once that determination is made, the staff should encourage the client's participation in choosing care, planning activities, and problem solving.

The nurse must identify the strengths of clients, instruct them thoroughly, and modify their behavior and environment. This will reinforce appropriate coping and adaptive skills. Family members may require respite services or advice regarding guardianship laws. The client or family may require referral to legal or social services as well as to community and self-help organizations.

Clients should reminisce and review their lives; this is an important developmental task. It helps them reflect upon their life experiences and relationships and maximizes the use of remote memory, which is usually the last to deteriorate. Reminiscing increases feelings of mastery and self-esteem. Family photographs, oral or video recordings, and familiar objects or artifacts from home can be used to stimulate memories and social interaction and to encourage clients to relate their personal histories and to express their feelings regarding the purpose and worth of their lives and relationships.

Regulating the problematic symptoms of coexisting psychiatric disorders, such as anxiety, depression, and behavioral problems, allows the client to remain involved and active. Relaxation therapies to treat anxiety and supportive-

Implications for Evidence-Based Practice

Hendry and Douglas (2003) focused on identification of a multidimensional approach to meet the needs of clients diagnosed with dementia using stage-specific communication and recreational interventions as well as adjunctive therapies and the therapeutic interactive process. They concluded that this interaction best meets the cognitive, functional, and developmental needs of the client and improves quality of life. Further research is indicated as to the specific staging and interventions used.

Implications for Evidence-Based Practice

Gerder (2001) investigated the use of individualized music selections in the management of agitation in confused elderly. Structured monitoring of the use of individualized patient-preferred music to reduce agitation and combativeness, medication use, and physical restraints showed that this can be an effective intervention. Further research across settings, the involvement of family members in selecting music, and the correlation of the music selected and the degree of significance to the individual would be useful.

Implications for Evidence-Based Practice

Kolanowski, Fink, Waller, & Ahern (2006) reviewed administrative data from an insurance company and found that approximately 27% of the sample of clients with dementia who lived in the community were prescribed antipsychotic medications compared to a previous study that found 18.2% of nursing home residents with dementia were receiving these medications (perhaps because of regulatory requirements in long term settings). The risk of polypharmacy, side effects, and adverse events were significant. The risk of hip fractures was higher among clients prescribed both typical and atypical antipsychotic. Patient and family teaching regarding non-pharmacologic interventions for behavioral and psychological symptoms related to dementia can have significant benefits. Further research as to the use of antipsychotic medications in varied samples is needed. Research as to the efficacy of various nonpharmacolgic and pharmacologic interventions would be helpful.

expressive and cognitive therapies to treat depression have been helpful. Physical and movement therapies as well as ambulation can help reduce restlessness or agitation. Paranoia or delusional thinking, hallucinations, and depressive disorders all may be present in clients with dementia or delirium and require treatment. Behavioral problems such as restlessness, agitation, aggressiveness, or socially inappropriate behavior should be monitored and exposure to possible stimuli limited.

Pharmacology

The causes of acute delirious states can usually be identified and treated. The treatment of Alzheimer's disease, particularly in the early stages, focuses on attempts to slow memory loss and cognitive decline. In early stages of mild or moderate dementia, a 3-month trial with a cholinesterase inhibitor (ChEI) is suggested because this may mitigate some of the effects of the disease process. By blocking cholinesterase enzymes, it is expected that the levels and action of acetylcholine will increase in the synapses, facilitating cholinergic neurotransmission. The most common medications used are donepezil (Aricept), galantamine (Reminyl), and rivastigmine (Exelon), and there are some differences in their dosage schedules and reported side effects. Tacrine (Cognex), one of the first ChEIs, is only rarely used because it may cause nausea and liver damage. Titration of beginning doses and gradual increases in the doses of donepezil, galantamine, and rivastigmine are recommended. Adverse effects are common and should be monitored. When it is suspected that a drug may no longer be helpful, a drug holiday or trial discontinuation for a short period is recommended. There is evidence that memantine (Namenda), a low-affinity NMDA (*N*-methyl-D-aspartate), may be effective in clients with Alzheimer's vascular and mixed dementias (Evans, Wilcock, & Birks, 2005). Exelon (rivastigmine transdermal) is thought to minimize side effects in its patch form and may benefit clients who have problems swallowing.

Remember the six Rs:
*R*eorient the client.
*R*estructure the environment.
*R*estore normal functioning and health.
*R*emotivate the client and involve him or her in
*R*eminiscence.
*R*egulate dysfunctional psychiatric symptoms.

Many clients find the use of vitamin E supplements, Gingko biloba, statins, folate, and estrogen supplements to be helpful. Research is continuing to determine the usefulness of these products to treat the symptoms of dementia. Selegiline, an MAO-B inhibitor that does not require tyramine dietary modifications, has been used elsewhere as an adjunct to treatment for Parkinson's disease and to slow neuronal damage in Alzheimer's disease; however, research continues to determine its clinical effectiveness and long-term value (Evans et al., 2005).

The treatment of vascular dementia may include aspirin or other anticoagulants, ticlopidine (Ticlid), a clot dissolving agent such as streptokinase (Streptase), exercise, and antioxidants coupled with medications for accompanying conditions such as hypertension, hyperlipidemia, diabetes, smoking, and vasculitis. Limited studies have been completed regarding the effectiveness of medications to increase blood flow such as pentoxifylline (Trental) and ergoloid mesylates (Hydergin). Further study is indicated regarding neural protective medications such as nimodipine (Nimotop), propentofylline, and posatirelin.

Behavioral and Psychological Symptoms

Due to the possibility of side effects, polypharmacy, risk of adverse effects, and studies showing limited efficacy of using antipsychotic medications with patients with dementia, non-pharmacological interventions should be utilized first. The Food and Drug Administration has issued warnings regarding use of typical and atypical antipsychotic medications in dementia. However, if a client who displays agitation or aggressive behavior needs to be evaluated for medication, a sedating serotonergic agent such as trazodone (Desyrel) or mirtazapine (Remeron) may be used if psychotic symptoms are not present. Antipsychotic medications are used with caution in the elderly due to the risk of extrapyramidal symptoms. Many sedating agents have been associated with lowered blood pressure and raised heart rate. Orthostatic hypotension is a particular problem with the risk of falls. Atypical antipsychotic medications such as olanzapine (Zyprexa), risperidone (Risperdal), and quetiapine (Seroquel) have been used in low doses; however, there is some evidence to suggest that these medications may not be effective with clients with dementia. Onor and colleagues (2006) found that low doses of risperidone (Risperdal) appear to be well tolerated by clients with Alzheimer's disease and appeared effective in reducing behavioral and psychotic symptoms. At times, low doses of haloperidol (Haldol), sometimes given in combination with low doses of lorazepam (Ativan), are used to control symptoms of severe agitation, hallucinations, or delusions. Benzodiazepines are used cautiously due to the risk of over sedation, confusion, and falls. In a double-blind study, Holmes and colleagues (2004) studied the efficacy of donepezil (Aricept) for treatment of behavioral and psychological symptoms in dementia. Significant reduction in behavioral symptoms was found over a 12-week period, as well as a reduction in distress experienced by caretakers for these patients. The possible cognitive benefits of donepezil (Aricept) were found to be reduced by concomitant use of antipsychotic medications. Elderly persons or those with additional medical problems must be kept under observation as any of the medications have cumulative effects and potential side effects which can be more of a burden than the possible benefit of the medications.

Depression

Clients who exhibit symptoms of depression are usually treated with nonsedating selective serotonin reuptake inhibitors (SSRIs) such as escitalopram (Lexapro), citalopram (Celexa), fluoxetine (Prozac), paroxetine (Paxil), sertraline (Zoloft), and venlafaxine (Effexor). Clients with depressive disorders with agitation and other severe symptoms may benefit from an evaluation to determine if a small dose of a tricyclic antidepressant such as desipramine (Norpramin), nortriptyline (Aventyl), doxepin (Sinequan), and amitriptyline (Elavil) should be used. In medically ill clients plagued by fatigue and depression as well as dementia, psychostimulants such as methylphenidate (Ritalin) or pemoline (Cylert) are occasionally used.

Buspirone (Buspar) or short-acting antianxiety medications such as alprazolam (Xanax), lorazepam (Ativan), or oxazepam (Serax) treat the symptoms of anxiety as well as panic disorders. As with other medications, the elderly client may require a reduction of the normal dose.

Summary

Cognitive disorders encompass a number of problems that produce changes in the function of the brain. Deliriums and dementias are differentiated in that deliriums are felt to be temporary and potentially reversible and dementias are chronic and irreversible. It is important to identify and treat any underlying or concomitant disorders for both syndromes. Treatment consists of avoiding infections, trauma, or agents that may cause brain dysfunction and minimize any problematic symptoms. Treating the causes of the delirium will hopefully return the client to baseline functioning without sequelae. The treatment of dementia focuses on stabilizing the client's abilities and delaying disease progression for as long as possible. When treating clients with amnesia, the symptoms must be explained well, and reassurance should be given. Reorientation and rehabilitation are priorities. Restraints, whether chemical or mechanical, should be used cautiously and only for client safety, not for staff convenience, because restraints and restrictions can exacerbate confusion and agitation. Treatment of coexisting behavioral disorders or psychiatric symptoms involves a combination of environmental and behavioral modifications and pharmacologic intervention that minimize sedative, anticholinergic, and extrapyramidal side effects. For the pseudodementia of depression, treatment of the underlying depressive disorder with antidepressants is indicated. Any coexisting medical illnesses also are treated, and considerable effort is made to minimize the anticholinergic side effects of the medications.

Annotated References

American Psychiatric Association. (2000). *Diagnostic and statistical manual of mental disorders* (4th ed., text rev.). Washington, DC: Author.

This is the fourth edition, text revision, of the American Psychiatric Association's official nomenclature of psychiatric conditions and disorders. It provides a systematic listing of the official codes and categories, a description of the multiaxial system for diagnosis, and diagnostic criteria for each of the disorders. It is used by psychiatrists, physicians, psychologists, registered nurses, social workers, therapists, and other mental health workers in all clinical settings.

Evans, J. G., Wilcock, G., & Birks, J. (2005). Evidence-based pharmacotherapy of Alzheimer's disease. In D. Stein, B. Lerer, & S. Stahl (Eds.), *Evidence-based psychopharmacotherapy* (pp. 290–319). Cambridge, UK: Cambridge University Press.

A review of medications used to treat Alzheimer's disease.

Foreman, M. D., Mion, L., Trygstad, L., & Fletcher, K. (2003). Delirium: Strategies for assessing and treatment. In M. Mezey, T. Fulmer, I. Abraham, & D. A. Zwicker (Eds.), *Geriatric nursing protocols for best practice* (pp. 116–140). New York: Springer.

Guidelines for rapid assessment and nursing interventions for clients with delirium.

Futrell, M., & Melillo, K. D. (2002). *Evidence-based protocol: Wandering.* Iowa City, IA: University of Iowa Gerontological Nursing Interventions Research Center.

Guidelines for the identification of type of wandering, consequences, and behaviors and development of environmental modifications and interventions.

Gaudreau, J. D., Gagnon, P., Harel, F., Tremblay, A., & Roy, M. A. (2005). Fast, systematic, and continuous delirium assessment in hospitalized clients: The nursing delirium screening scale. *Journal of Pain and Symptom Management, 29*(4), 368–375.

Discusses the use of a five-item scale, the Nursing Delirium Screening Scale (Nu-DESC) to standardize observation for signs of delirium in hospitalized clients.

Gerder, L. (2001). *Evidence-based protocol: Individualized music.* Iowa City, Iowa: University of Iowa Gerontological Nursing Interventions Research Center.

The author studied using music that has some meaning to the client in order to reduce restlessness and agitation in confused clients.

Hendry, K. C., & Douglas, D. H. (2003). Promoting quality of life for clients diagnosed with dementia. *Journal of the American Psychiatric Association, 9*(3), 96–102.

This article focuses on the need for a multidimensional approach focusing on client strengths, developmental needs, and stage of dementia to improve quality of life rather than focusing on behavioral disturbances.

Holmes, C., Wilkinson, D., Dean, C., Vethanayagam, S., Olivieri, S., Langley, A., et al. (2004). The efficacy of donepezil in the treatment of neuropsychiatric symptoms in Alzheimer disease. *Neurology, 63*(2), 214–219.

Randomized study of patients with dementia and neuropsychiatric symptoms who received donepezil showed that donepezil had significant efficacy in the treatment of patients with mild to moderate Alzheimer's disease.

Kolanowski, A., Fink, D., Waller, J. L., & Ahern, F. (2006). Outcomes of antipsychotic drug use in community-dwelling elders with dementia. *Archives of psychiatric nursing, 20*(5), 217–225.

Reviewed administrative data of 959 cases over a 3-year period to determine use of antipsychotic medication with community-dwelling elders with dementia. There was a high risk of polypharmacy, side effects, and adverse events in use of these medications particularly among patients receiving both typical and atypical antipsychotic medications.

Lopez, A. D., Mathers, C. D., Ezzati, M., Janison, D. T., & Murray, C. J. L. (Eds.). (2006). *Global burden of disease and risk factors.* New York: World Bank Publications.

This is a good source of public health data and information regarding the global impact of disease and disability.

Mendez, M., & Cummings, J. L. (2003). *Dementia: A clinical approach.* Boston: Butterworth-Heinemann.

This is a serious text for the industrious student who wants an in-depth discussion of dementia and delirium or for the researcher who needs information on a specific topic or disorder. This book contains everything you need to know about dementia-related topics from AIDS to Wernicke-Korsakoff syndrome.

Mezey, M., & Maslow, K. (2007). Recognition of dementia in hospitalized older adults. *Try This: Best Practices in Nursing Care for Hospitalized Older Adults, 1*(D5). New York: The Hartford Institute for Geriatric Nursing, Division of Nursing, New York University.

A study of best practices in identifying at-risk hospitalized older adults.

Onor, M. L., Saina, M., Trevisiol, M., Cristante, T., & Auglia, E. (2006). Clinical experience with risperidone in the treatment of behavioral and psychological symptoms of dementia. *Progress in Neuro-psychopharmacology and Biological Psychiatry, 31*(1), 205–209.

Studied efficacy and tolerability of use of risperidone to treat behavioral and psychological symptoms in clients with dementia.

Pinel, J. P. J. (2006). *Biopsychology.* 6th ed. London: Allyn & Bacon.

This is a user-friendly text and CD for those interested in a biologic and psychologic approach to learn more about the anatomic, physiologic, psychologic, and behavioral characteristics and learned and inherited features of cognition, memory, and amnesia. The text describes different problems that can affect cognitive functioning, including organic brain syndromes and disorders.

Reeve, C. (1996). Democratic National Convention Floor Speech. Retrieved July 4, 2007, from http://www.pbs.org/newshour/convention96/floor_speeches/reeve

Transcript of speech from 1996 Democratic National Convention in Chicago, IL. Also available on video from American Rhetoric, Product ID 101704, on www.learnoutloud.com.

Seitz, R., von Auer, F., Blumel, J., Burger, R., Buschmann, A., Dietz, K., et al. (2007). Impact of vCJD on blood supply. *Biologicals, 35*(2), 79–97.

Review of possible transmission and risk assesment for BSE and vCJD as well as screening methods and precautionary measures.

Additional Resources

Ferri, C. P., Prince, M., Brayne, C., Brodaty, H., Fratiglioni, L., et al. (2005–2006). Global prevalence of dementia: A Delphi consensus study. *The Lancet, 366*(9503), 2112–2117.

Due to changes in underdeveloped countries, an aging worldwide population, and changes in mortality, estimates in the prevalence of dementia are important in forecasting future needs and costs in health care.

LoboPrabhu, S. M., Molinari, V. A., & Lomax, J. W. (Eds.). (2006). *Supporting the caregiver in dementia: A guide for health care professionals.* Baltimore, MD: The Johns Hopkins University Press.

Provides helpful evidence-based information on the relationship and experiences of caregiver and dementia clients as well as suggestions for caregiving.

Mace, N. L., & Rabins, P. V. (2001). *The 36-hour day: A family guide to caring for persons with Alzheimer's disease, related dementing illnesses, and memory loss in later life.* New York: Warner Books.

This text describes the often unending demands on families and caretakers in meeting the overwhelming needs of clients with dementia. The tremendous toll upon family life, the concerns and ambivalence of caretakers, and descriptions of the stages of disability are discussed.

Strauss, C. J. (2002). *Talking to Alzheimer's: Simple ways to connect when you visit with a family member or friend.* Oakland, CA: New Harbinger.

A simple guide for professionals or consumers who want to facilitate communication and contact with clients with cognitive disorders.

Waszyniski, C. M. (2001). Confusion Assessment Method (CAM). *Try this: Best practices in nursing care to older adults.* New York: The Hartford Institute for Geriatric Nursing, Division of Nursing, New York University.

An evidence based evaluation of the use of the Confusion Assessment Method (CAM) for assessment of the presence or absence of delirium.

Wexler, A. (1996). *Mapping fate: A memoir of family, risk, and genetic research.* Berkeley, CA: University of California Press.

This is a first-hand account dealing with family members who are confronted with Huntington's disease. As research continues to find possible genetic links for many forms of dementia, the concerns facing the individual who may or may not want to know the risks involved or those who must face these challenges may become more common. Many ethical questions involving research, healthcare planning, public accessibility to information, and individual rights to privacy are discussed.

Internet Resources

http://nursing.jbpub.com/psychiatric

Visit http://nursing.jbpub.com/psychiatric for interactive exercises, NCLEX review questions, WebLinks, and more.

CHAPTER 13

Mental Disorders Due to General Medical Conditions

Joan C. Masters

LEARNING OBJECTIVES

After reading this chapter, you will be able to:

- Identify indications a mental disorder may be due to a medical condition.
- Describe the most common medical disorders that may cause psychiatric symptoms.
- Discuss the nurse's responsibility in assessing clients for mental disorders due to a general medical condition.

KEY TERMS

Mental disorder

Personality disorder

http://nursing.jbpub.com/psychiatric

Visit http://nursing.jbpub.com/psychiatric for interactive exercises, NCLEX review questions, WebLinks, and more.

Introduction

This chapter discusses **mental disorders** caused by the direct physiologic effects of a medical condition. It is important to note, however, that mental disorders and medical conditions can be related to each other through several mechanisms. The cause and effect of the condition are not always readily discernible, thus, it is often difficult to determine which appeared first. The clinician must remember that a mental disorder is not an expected or normal response to a particular event such as the death of a loved one. Independent of the original cause, the disorder must be considered a manifestation of a behavioral, psychologic, or biologic dysfunction (American Psychiatric Association [APA], 2000).

Medical conditions can affect mental health and well-being whether the observed behavior results from physiologic or nonphysiologic processes. This is termed a *secondary mental disorder*. Conversely, a medical condition may exacerbate a *primary mental disorder*. A primary mental disorder is caused by a medical condition and is not substance induced from the effect of drugs such as alcohol, side effects from prescribed medications, or toxins.

Regardless of the clinical setting, nurses have traditionally used a combined psychologic, biologic, cultural, and spiritual approach to assess clients. Florence Nightingale expressed concern about the body's effect on the mind: "The sick suffer to excess from mental as well as bodily pain" (Nightingale, 1946, p. 34). The *Diagnostic and Statistical Manual of Mental Disorders,* Fourth Edition, Text Revision (*DSM-IV-TR*) distinguishes mental disorders due to medical conditions, but this does not mean that fundamental differences exist between mental disorders and medical conditions. Nor does it mean that mental disorders are unrelated to physiologic or biologic factors or that medical conditions are unrelated to behavioral or psychosocial factors or processes. Mental disorders and medical conditions are distinguished to encourage

> The psychiatric disorder may be a direct physiologic consequence of the medical condition. Client history, including history of present illness, physical examination, and laboratory tests and other diagnostic findings, support this relationship.

> Signs and symptoms of psychoactive drug withdrawal or toxic exposure are not considered disorders due to a general medical condition but are substance-induced disorders.

thorough evaluations and to enhance communication among healthcare providers (APA, 2000). A comprehensive assessment of the client helps the entire healthcare team to be aware of alternative or differential diagnoses.

General Description

Medical conditions that can cause mental disorders were originally categorized as organic mental syndromes and disorders by the *Diagnostic and Statistical Manual of Mental Disorders*, Third Edition, Revised (*DSM-III-R*). Delirium, dementia, and psychoactive substance-induced mental disorders were included in this category (see Chapter 12). The authors of the *DSM-IV-TR* used the term *general medical condition* to categorize medical conditions not listed under mental and behavioral disorders in the International Classification of Diseases (ICD). "General" represents several medical conditions in which the physiologic effects manifest as mental disorders (**Table 13-1**).

Excluding substance-induced mental disorders, a mental disorder that is a direct physiologic consequence of a medical condition is diagnosed as a mental disorder due to a general medical condition (**Table 13-2**). Medical and mental conditions are coded using the *DSM-IV-TR's* Multiaxial Assessment (see Chapter 3). The mental disorder is noted on Axis I along with the associated medical condition. The medical condition, along with its ICD-9-CM code, is noted on Axis III. For example, a mood disorder resulting from hypothyroidism with depressive features is coded on Axis I, whereas hypothyroidism is coded on Axis III.

Table 13-1 General Medical Conditions

- Infectious and parasitic diseases
- Neoplasms
- Endocrine, nutritional, and metabolic diseases and immunity disorders
- Diseases of the blood and blood-forming organs
- Diseases of the nervous system and sense organs
- Diseases of the circulatory system
- Diseases of the respiratory system
- Diseases of the digestive system
- Diseases of the genitourinary system
- Complications of pregnancy, childbirth, and puerperium
- Diseases of the skin and subcutaneous tissue
- Congenital anomalies
- Certain conditions originating in the perinatal period
- Symptoms, signs, and ill-defined conditions

Table 13-2 Major Mental Disorders Due to a General Medical Condition

- Delirium
- Dementia
- Amnestic disorder
- Psychotic disorders
- Mood disorders
- Anxiety disorders
- Sleep disorders
- Sexual dysfunction
- Acute brain syndrome that develops rapidly (within hours or days) and is characterized by cognitive impairment not induced by a preexisting or evolving dementia. Signs and symptoms fluctuate daily and include clouding of consciousness, disorientation, memory impairment, and decreased ability to focus, shift, or sustain attention.
- Diffuse brain dysfunction characterized by a gradual, progressive, and chronic deterioration of intellectual function. Judgment, memory, affect, cognition, and attention span are affected.
- Memory disturbance resulting in impaired ability to learn new information or recall previously learned information or past events.
- Mental disorder characterized by impaired thought, communication, and interpretation of reality.
- Disorder of mood characterized by depression, mania, and hypomania.
- Disorder characterized by excessive worry, uncertainty, and uneasiness about events or activities. The anxiety must occur more often than not for at least 6 months to be classed as a disorder.
- Disorder characterized by abnormalities in sleep-wake generating or timing mechanisms.
- Disturbance in sexual desire and the psychologic and physiologic changes that characterize the sexual response cycles.

Physical illnesses are common among psychiatric clients, and in some cases these physical illnesses worsen or even cause psychiatric problems. The *DSM-IV-TR* classifies disorders that present with psychiatric signs and symptoms but that are medical in origin as "mental disorders due to a general medical condition." This group of disorders is grouped with delirium, dementias, and amnestic disorders, but is distinguished from them in an important way. Delirium, dementias, and amnestic disorders are characterized primarily by cognitive impairment, that is, deficiencies in attention, language, and memory. People who have a mental disorder due to a general medical condition may have some cognitive impairment, but cognitive impairment is not the predominant problem; instead they present with other psychiatric symptoms such as psychosis, mood disorder, or personality and behavioral changes. It is important with all clients to consider whether a medical illness may be contributing to what initially appears to be a psychiatric issue (Sadock & Sadock, 2003).

Nurses may see these clients in psychiatric settings either because the medical basis for their apparent psychiatric problems are not recognized or because their behavior is so disruptive they cannot be cared for on a medical unit. These clients are frequently seen in the emergency department (ED); approximately one-third of clients with a psychosis seen in the ED have an underlying medical condition causing the psychotic symptoms (Koran et al., 2002; Larkin, Classen, Edmond, Pelletier, & Camargo, 2005; Saliou, Fichele, McLaughlin, Thauin, & Lejeux, 2005).

It is important nurses understand that psychiatric symptoms can originate from medical conditions, so clients can be correctly treated. Misdiagnoses can lead to delayed treatment or no treatment, resulting in a client suffering, potentially even dying, and at the very least increased healthcare costs. It can be difficult to accurately diagnose clients with changes in behavior and/or thinking whose problems suggest a primary psychiatric illness but whose illness is medical in origin.

Incidence and Prevalence

The extent of the problem of mental disorders due to a general medical condition is not clear because by their nature these disorders are thought to be frequently misdiagnosed or overlooked. However, there are indications from some research studies that physical health problems are common among psychiatric clients, and that these problems may cause or worsen a client's psychiatric illness.

Signs and symptoms of a mental disorder occurring during a delirium are considered associated features of the delirium. Signs and symptoms occurring other than during a delirium suggest a primary mental disorder.

Etiology

General medical conditions may be linked to mental disorders in several ways (**Table 13-3**). The clinician must distinguish whether the medical condition is causing or exacerbating the mental symptoms.

Mental disorders unrelated to a medical condition are coded separately on the multiaxial

Implications for Evidence-Based Practice

A group of researchers interested in the extent and severity of medical illnesses in psychiatric patients assessed 289 patients who were admitted to an in-patient psychiatric unit over a 6-month period. The patients were given a routine physical exam and laboratory tests (complete blood count, blood chemistry, thyroid function, vitamin B_{12}, folate levels, and urine analysis). The patients also completed a 10-item medical symptom questionnaire. The patients were referred for a medical consultation if the physical exam, laboratory tests, or questionnaire indicated an active or serious medical disorder. The majority of patients were diagnosed with schizophrenia (62%) and mood disorder (24%). The remainder were diagnosed with adjustment disorders (9%), or dementia and other disorders (4%). Of the 289 patients in the study, 29% (84) had active and serious medical disorders. Of the 119 disorders detected (some patients had more than one disorder), 20% (24) were undiagnosed before the study.

In only one case was a disorder, hypothyroidism, detected that was considered to have caused psychiatric symptoms. In two other patients with schizophrenia, their worsening psychosis was attributed to hypothyroidism. For 14 other patients, physical problems caused or worsened psychiatric symptoms. These included drug withdrawal, epileptic psychosis, postconcussion syndrome, hyperthyroidism with hypoparathyroidism, myocardial infarction, quadriplegia with anemia, dementia co-morbid with schizophrenia, and cerebral degeneration co-morbid with major depression.

A number of medical disorders were diagnosed in the study, which while not an immediate threat to the patients' mental health had the potential to cause psychiatric symptoms if not treated. These included syphilis (two patients), anemia (six patients), diabetes, alcoholic cirrhosis (three patients), thalassemia, vitamin B_{12} deficiency, hepatitis, chronic obstructive pulmonary disease, urinary tract infections, cellulitis, and proteinuria (Koran et al., 2002).

Table 13-3 Etiology of Mental Disorders Due to Medical Condition

Mental Disorder	Medical Condition
Delirium	Hypoxia, hypercarbia, hypoglycemia, fluid or electrolyte imbalances, hepatic or renal disease, thiamine deficiency, postanesthesia states, emergence delirium, hypertensive encephalopathy, focal lesions of right parietal lobe, and inferomedial surface of the occipital lobe
Dementia	Pick's disease; normal pressure hydrocephalus; Parkinson's disease; Huntington's disease; traumatic brain injury; anoxia; human immunodeficiency virus (HIV); syphilis; hypothyroidism; hypercalcemia; hypoglycemia; thiamine, niacin, and B_{12} deficiency; systemic lupus erythematosus (SLE); hepatic conditions; metabolic disorders; multiple sclerosis
Amnestic disorder	Cerebrovascular disease; metabolic conditions; seizures; closed head trauma; damage to medial, diencephalic, and temporal lobe brain structures (penetrating wounds, surgical intervention, hypoxia); infarction of posterior cerebral artery; herpes simplex encephalitis
Psychotic disorder	Neoplasms, cerebralvascualar disease, Huntington's disease, epilepsy, auditory nerve damage, hypo/hyperglycemia, hypo/hyperthyroidism, fluid or electrolyte imbalances, hepatic or renal disease, autoimmune disease (e.g., SLE)
Mood disorder	Parkinson's disease, Huntington's disease, cerebrovascular disease (stroke), B_{12} deficiency, hypo/hyperthyroidism, hypoadrenocorticism, autoimmune disease (e.g., SLE), hepatitis, mononucleosis, HIV, cancer of pancreas
Anxiety disorder	Vitamin B_{12} deficiency, porphyria, hypo/hyperthyroidism, hypoglycemia, pheochromocytoma, congestive heart failure, pulmonary embolism, arrhythmia, chronic obstructive pulmonary disease, pneumonia, hyperventilation, neuroneoplasms, vestibular dysfunction, encephalitis
Sleep disorder	Parkinson's disease, Huntington's disease, cerebrovascular disease (upper brainstem vascular lesions), hypo/hyperthyroidism, viral encephalitis producing insomnia, insomnia caused by pain or cough from pulmonary disease
Sexual dysfunction	MS, spinal cord lesion, neuropathy, temporal lobe lesion, diabetes mellitus, hypo/hyperadrenocorticism, pituitary dysfunction, vascular conditions, genitourinary conditions

assessment. Mental disorders that are reactions to a medical condition are termed *adjustment disorders.* These disorders occur within 6 months of the event and are coded as follows: A client who develops an adjustment disorder with depressed mood, reacting to a diagnosis of breast cancer, is coded on Axis I. Breast cancer is coded on Axis III.

Additionally, certain medical conditions, not directly related to the mental disorder, have important prognostic and treatment implications. One example is the choice of an antidepressant for the client who takes cardiac medications such as antiarrythmics. Another example is insulin monitoring for the diabetic client who is also schizophrenic.

Physiology

Along with the client's history, physical examination, and laboratory results, the chronologic relationship between the physiologic and mental disorder should be determined.

Medical Conditions

The clinician must determine when onset, exacerbation, and remission of both the medical condition and the mental disorder occurred. Did the mental disorder resolve after initiating specific medical treatment? For example, following surgical excision of parathyroid tissue, which restores normal calcium levels, the client's anxiety resolves.

The symptoms of a mental disorder may be seen before the underlying pathology of systemic or cerebral disease is detected. The depression that precedes choreiform movements in Huntington's disease exemplifies this. Conversely, treating the general medical condition may not resolve the mental disorder, such as failing to improve depressed mood despite administering thyroid hormone replacement for hypothyroidism. Treating the mental disorder and medical condition concurrently often symptomatically relieves both conditions. Treatment that targets the medical condition, however, provides stronger etiologic evidence.

Atypical features of a primary mental disorder include:

- The onset of schizophrenic-like symptoms of delusions, hallucinations, disorganized speech, and grossly disorganized behavior at 75 years of age, when the typical age of onset is late teens to early 30s
- Significant weight loss with only mild depressive symptoms
- Disproportionate cognitive deficits
- Detection and location of a brain lesion or known pathophysiologic mechanism likely to affect brain function

Catatonia

A central nervous system (CNS) motor disturbance characterizes catatonia due to a general medical condition (**Table 13-4**). This motor disturbance is a direct physiologic effect of the medical condition. Client history, physical examination, and laboratory findings exclude the following neurologic conditions and metabolic disorders: malignant brain neoplasm and other neoplasms, head trauma, cerebrovascular accident, encephalitis, hypercalcemia, hepatic encephalopathy, homocystinuria, and diabetic ketoacidosis.

Table 13-4 Signs and Symptoms of Catatonia

Signs and Symptoms	Features
Motor immobilization	Fully conscious but unresponsive and mute
Motor excitability	Uncontrolled, aimless motor activity
Negativism	Refusal to cooperate with simple requests for no apparent reason
Sterotype	Repeated but non-goal-oriented movements (e.g., rocking)
Peculiarities of voluntary movement	Bizarre or uncomfortable postures (e.g., squatting) for long periods
Ecopraxia	Mimicking the gestures of another person
Echolalia	Parrot-like repetitions of another person's words or phrases

Personality Changes

Personality changes from a general medical condition's direct physiologic effects involve a pathologic disturbance in functioning brain systems. These systems mediate language, perception, memory, attention, and other cognitive systems. Normal behavior is assessed as a by-product of these functional systems. Thus, compromised function alters behavior. Knowledge of particular brain system functions is vital in recognizing corresponding behavioral changes. A fundamental review of these systems and their functions is presented in **Table 13-5**.

Diagnostic tests are valuable therapeutic tools for evaluating direct physiologic effects.

Clients with cognitive changes generally ignore or minimize perceived behavioral changes; therefore, it is necessary to interview family members because they are often the first to notice these changes and can provide vital information.

Personality changes can result from many neurologic and medical conditions. The most common causes include closed head injury (symptoms occurring years after the injury), traumatic lesions of the frontal and temporal lobe, and tumors and strokes affecting the frontal lobe. Other causes include Huntington's disease, Wilson's disease, epilepsy, infectious diseases with CNS involvement, endocrine conditions, and systemic lupus erythematosus.

As the personality changes progress, behavior becomes grossly inappropriate. The client is at risk of injuring him- or herself or others and may require hospitalization.

Personality changes resulting from a general medical condition may present as a predominant symptom associated with the affected brain system. Common manifestations include affective instability, poor impulse control, outbursts of aggression or rage disproportionate to the precipitating stressor, apathy, suspiciousness, and

Table 13-5 How Systems of the Brain Affect Human Behavior

System	Functions
Prefrontal	Social judgment
	Volition
	Integration of new information
	Ability to plan and make decisions
	Ability to generate new thoughts and ideas
	Mediation of attention and perceptions, affect, and emotions
Limbic system and hypothalamus	Emotional stability
	Adherence to social and sexual mores and norms
Basal ganglia	Regulation of emotion and cognition

Table 13-6 Personality Changes Due to a General Medical Condition (Categorized by the Predominant Symptom)

Type	Predominant Symptom
Labile	Affective lability
Disinhibited	Poor impulse control, sexual indiscretion
Aggressive	Violent and aggressive behavior
Apathetic	Marked indifference and apathy
Paranoid	Suspiciousness, hypervigliance, paranoid ideation
Other	May be associated with a seizure disorder
Combined	One or more predominant features
Unspecified	Absence of a predominant feature

paranoid ideation. The *DSM-IV-TR* categorizes particular personality changes by the predominant symptom (**Table 13-6**).

Clinical Presentation

There are certain characteristics of medical disorders that present with psychiatric symptoms. These include:

- *An atypical presentation:* The psychiatric symptoms seen in disorders with a medical origin are not classic psychiatric symptoms (Chuang & Forman, 2006).
- *An early or late onset (before age 12 or after age 40) of psychiatric symptoms:* Except for the dementias, psychiatric disorders tend to develop early in life. Psychiatric disorders occurring later in life suggest a possibly physical origin (Reeves, Pendarvis, & Kimble, 2000).
- *A rapid onset of symptoms:* New symptoms, particularly vague somatic complaints or symptoms of confusion and disorganization, may be preclinical or prediagnostic manifestations of underlying medical disorders (Chuang & Forman, 2006).
- *A lack of response or an atypical response to treatment for psychiatric symptoms:* If a client is treated for what is assumed to be a psychiatric condition but which is actually a medical condition, they may react in an unexpected way; for example, they may not improve or may get worse instead of better (Chuang & Forman, 2006).
- *Visual or tactile hallucinations:* Auditory hallucinations are characteristic of psychiatric, not medical, disorders (Reeves et al., 2000).
- *Altered level of consciousness or disorientation:* Clients with psychiatric disorders may demonstrate odd behavior and speech but they are usually awake and alert and not disoriented (Reeves et al., 2000).
- *Unusual physical signs:* Unusual findings will be present on the physical exam (Reeves et al., 2000).
- *Suggestions of toxin ingestion or exposure:* The client or a collateral informant may report that the client has taken an overdose of medication or some other substance, a urine and serum blood screen is positive for illicit substances, or the client may have evidence of product on them, for example, traces of paint on their face and hair (Reeves et al., 2000).
- *A history of a medical illness:* If a person has a new onset of psychiatric symptoms and is known to have a medical illness, the medical illness should be investigated at the beginning of the assessment as the source of the person's problems. Clients should also be asked about their use of prescribed and over-the-counter medications (Chuang & Forman, 2006).
- *Abnormal vital signs:* Psychiatric disorders do not usually alter vital signs (Chuang & Forman, 2006; Reeves et al., 2000).
- *No history of psychiatric illnesses in the client or family:* The index of suspicion of a possible medical illness is higher if there is no preexisting history of similar psychiatric symptoms in the client or no family history of psychiatric illness (Chuang & Forman, 2006).

Differential Diagnosis

One makes a differential diagnosis to determine whether the mental disorder is caused by a direct physiologic mechanism, which distinguishes the disorder from a primary mental disorder. The following questions also aid the clinician:

- *Does the medical condition precipitate or exacerbate a mental disorder without a known physiologic link?* For example, there is no known physiologic link between osteoarthritis and depression. People with arthritis may experience an adjustment disorder with depressive features, but this is not physiologically based.

- *Is there evidence of recent substance abuse?* This includes prescribed medications with psychoactive effects as well as herbals, nutritional supplements, and over-the-counter medications and substances commonly abused.
- *Is there evidence of withdrawal from a substance? Has the client been exposed to a toxin?* Urine and blood toxicology screens as well as other laboratory data help establish this diagnosis.
- *Does the clinical presentation represent the combined effects of a general medical condition and substance abuse, including medications?* These presentations may include delirium, dementia, psychotic disorder, anxiety disorder, sleep disorder, and sexual dysfunction (see Table 13-2 earlier in the chapter). Both mental disorders due to a general medical condition and substance-induced mental disorders apply in these cases.
- *Does the disturbance occur only during periods of delirium?* For example, psychosis, mood disorder, and anxiety occurring only during periods of delirium are considered associated features of delirium and do not require a separate diagnosis. Should these signs and symptoms occur other than during a delirium, mental disorder due to a general medical condition may be diagnosed, such as depression from hypothyroidism.
- *Does a mix of different symptoms complicate assigning the condition to one category?* If yes, a subcategory is used based on the predominant clinical features. Finally, if it is impossible to determine whether the mental symptoms are primary, substance-induced, or resulting from a general medical condition, use the not otherwise specified (NOS) category (see Tables 13-1, 13-2, and 13-3 earlier in the chapter).

Clinical Course and Complications

In a review of the medical records of 64 clients who had been admitted to the hospital with changes in mental status, a group of researchers found a variety of unrecognized medical conditions (Reeves et al., 2000). Clients had been inappropriately referred from the emergency department to the psychiatric service with such serious and potentially life-threatening conditions as severe alcohol or drug intoxication (34.4%), alcohol or drug withdrawal (12.5%), and overdose of a prescription medication (12.5%). A variety of other diagnoses were also overlooked including hypoglycemia, diabetic ketoacidosis, lithium toxicity, anticonvulsant toxicity, neuroleptic malignant syndrome, pneumonia, urinary tract infection, sepsis, cerebrovascular accident, heart failure, neurosyphilis, subdural hematoma, hyperthyroidism, hepatic encephalopathy, and uremic encephalopathy. Instead of being diagnosed with a medical illness, the clients were incorrectly admitted with diagnoses of schizophrenia (46.9%), psychotic disorder not otherwise specified (26.6%), depression (14.1%), and bipolar disorder (12.5%). In reviewing the client records the researchers found that in 80% of the clients, the only part of the mental status exam done was assessment of orientation. Not one of the 64 clients had received a comprehensive mental status exam, and physical exams were omitted or incomplete in 44% of the clients. Indicated laboratory tests and radiological exams were overlooked in 34% of the cases. Other errors included failure to obtain an available history (34%), ignoring abnormal vital signs (8%), and failure to obtain indicated neuroimaging (3%); some errors occurred more than once in some clients.

The researchers concluded that ED staff were too quick to diagnose that altered mental status and behavioral problems were due to a psychiatric condition, and therefore did not carry out a detailed workup. Even a brief mental status exam would have picked up most problems of the 64 clients. A majority of the clients (43; 67.1%) had a previous psychiatric diagnosis, and this may have biased the examiners toward a psychiatric diagnosis. However, a psychiatric history does not preclude having a medical illness (Reeves et al., 2000). According to the *DSM-IV-TR*, mental conditions due to a general medical disorder can only be diagnosed when there is a direct physiological link between signs and symptoms and the medical disorder. (This is in contrast to primary psychiatric disorders, in which the link is more tenuous.)

Mental conditions due to a general medical disorder are organized by symptoms in the *DSM-IV-TR*. For example, disorders characterized by problems in mood would be found with the mood disorders, but also with mood disorders due to a general medical condition in the mental disorders due to a general medical condition section. The major categories of mental disorders due to a general medical condition are as follows:

- Mood Disorder Due to a General Medical Condition
- Psychotic Disorders Due to a General Medical Condition
- Anxiety Disorders Due to a General Medical Condition
- Sleep Disorders Due to a General Medical Condition
- Sexual Dysfunction Disorders Due to a General Medical Condition
- Mental Disorders Due to a General Medical Condition Not Elsewhere Classified. This category includes three types of disorders, Catatonia Due to a General Medical Condition, Personality Change Due to a General Medical Condition, and Mental Disorder Not Otherwise Specified Due to a General Medical Condition (Sadock & Sadock, 2003).

Mood Disorders Due to a General Medical Condition

People with mood disorders due to a general medical condition (also known as secondary mood disorders) experience depression or mania (an elevated or expansive mood) directly related to a physical condition. These disorders have not been widely studied and the number of people affected is not known. However, mild and major depression are frequently seen in people experiencing neurological disorders such as Parkinson's disease, Huntington's disease, stroke, multiple sclerosis (MS), and infections such as HIV and syphilis. Mania is less common than depression as a secondary mood disorder. The goal in treatment is to address the underlying medical disorder. Clients may also benefit from treatment with antidepressants or electroconvulsive therapy (ECT; Sadock & Sadock, 2003).

Other medical conditions are also known to present with depressive symptoms. For example, pancreatic cancer is notorious for presenting as depression. Pancreatic cancer should always be suspected in middle-aged adults who have a new onset of depression; depression may precede physical symptoms of cancer by as much as 6 months. Other medical causes of depression include hypothyroidism, Addison's disease, Cushing's syndrome, lupus, hypoparathyroidism, hyperparathyroidism, hepatic encephalopathy, acute intermittent porphyria, Wilson's disease (an autosomal recessive disorder of copper metabolism), and AIDS. Like MS, Huntington's disease may also cause depression or euphoria (Sadock & Sadock, 2003).

Multiple Sclerosis

Multiple sclerosis (MS) is a disorder in which mood is frequently affected. People with MS can have both cognitive and psychiatric symptoms. Although depression is common, about 25% of people with MS develop euphoria that is unrelated to anything going on in their lives. Clients may spontaneously cry or laugh but do not understand this emotional lability and can become very distressed.

About 350,000 people in the United States have MS; it is the most common chronic neurological disease in young adults. Depression is the most common psychiatric diagnosis in people with MS, with a lifetime risk of 40% to 60%. The etiology of depression in MS is complex but is thought to be related to focal demyelination in areas of the brain involved in regulating mood, immune dysfunction, adverse effects of treatment with interferon B, the psychosocial stress of disability, decreased social support, and unemployment (Wallin, Wilken, Turner, Williams, & Kane, 2006). Depressed clients also have been shown to have an increased immune response, and MS is a chronic inflammatory disease with immune dysfunction.

People with MS should be routinely screened for depression. It is important to keep in mind that many "vegetative" symptoms of depression, such as disturbed sleep and fatigue, are common in people with MS who are not depressed, so a careful distinction needs to be made so as not to overinterpret physical symptoms.

There is an increased risk of suicide in people with MS. In a study of people with MS in Denmark the risk of suicide was almost double that of the rest of the population; in a Canadian study, for 15% of the clients with MS who died, suicide was the cause of death (Feinstein, 1997; Wallin et al., 2006).

NURSING CARE PLAN Multiple Sclerosis

Expected Outcomes	Interventions	Evaluations
• Client and family will be involved in learning about illness and treatment. • Client and family will understand that personality and mood symptoms are related to medical problem. • Client will recognize possible symptoms related to stress, physical fatigue, or medications. • Client will experience hopeful sense of future.	• To involve client and family in assessment, education, and treatment planning. • To discuss options for treatment and follow-up with client and family. • To refer client and family to client education groups and MS Center. • To involve client and family in discussions and problem solving. • To discuss mechanisms for coping with stress. • To assist client in evaluating personal goals and sense of future with regard to adaptation and serviceable sense of denial.	• Client and family discuss potential problems and needs. • Client verbalizes recognition of need for continued medical follow-up. • Client's involvement in group activities helps maintain sense of control and mastery. • Client is able to identify activities that are pleasurable and increase positive perception of self-esteem and sense of personal well-being. • Client is able to adapt interests to present abilities and choose activities to help maintain a healthy lifestyle. • Client is able to avoid situations and activities that increase stress and fatigue.

Visit http://nursing.jbpub.com/psychiatric for additional care plans and exercises.

CASE STUDY Ms. S.

Ms. S. is a 33-year-old teacher admitted to the hospital with complaints of weakness, blurred vision, and ataxia. While on the unit, her family tell the staff they are worried that she is depressed and needs a psychiatric evaluation. They report she is tearful at times, "crying for no reason." In the months prior to admission, she seems to have become a different person (i.e., irritable at times, suspicious of others, and easily distracted). During the preceding summer, she had become less active, giving up her usual interests in jogging and tennis, and had become more isolated. Her memory was poor. She had not been sleeping regularly, although she frequently complained of being fatigued. Since she has been hospitalized, they are worried that she may not be able to cope with a possible medical diagnosis.

When the psychiatric consultation liaison nurse specialist speaks with Ms. S., Ms. S. says she can understand why her family was worried about her. She denies being depressed, but has been very worried that she was going crazy. Ms. S. states that she does not know whether she should be upset because she is undergoing diagnostic testing for multiple sclerosis or relieved that she will finally find out what has been going on. Ms. S. reports that she felt as if she were losing her mind. During the summer, she had felt as if she were out of control (i.e., one day feeling like herself and another day feeling as if she couldn't do anything or remember anything). One day she would have muscle cramps and blurred vision, then those symptoms would go away. Another day she would feel giddy as if she were going to faint. She thought the symptoms she was having were not real and all in her mind. She had always been healthy and felt as if she were becoming a hypochondriac.

Once the school year restarted, she was concerned that she could not fulfill her job responsibilities. She was afraid to tell anyone and tried to pretend that there was nothing wrong. Now she feels that if the doctors know what is wrong with her, she will be able to get some help. Ms. S. tells the nurse that she thinks she recalls that Shirley Temple had multiple sclerosis, and that Shirley Temple had been able to do a great many things in her life. She hopes that she will still be able to do many things in her life.

Ms. S. tells the nurse that she is interested in learning everything she can about multiple sclerosis. She is worried about being a burden for her family and is reluctant to talk to them about her concerns. She doesn't want to worry them, although they have always been very supportive to her. Ms. S. states she dreads the idea that she might not be able to continue to teach, and doesn't know how she would cope if the doctors told her she could not go back to work.

Psychotic Disorders Due to a General Medical Condition

The extent of secondary psychotic disorders is unknown, but these disorders may be seen in any condition that affects brain function. Clients should first be evaluated for dementia; it is unusual but possible for people who have a degenerative brain disorder such as Alzheimer's disease or Huntington's disease to first present with psychotic symptoms such as hallucinations and delusions before showing the more common cognitive impairments (disorientation, memory loss) associated with these disorders. People experiencing a delirium may also experience psychotic symptoms, but they will have a fluctuating level of consciousness. In comparison, the person who has a psychosis due to a psychiatric condition such as schizophrenia will be awake and alert. As with all mental disorders due to a general medical condition, the prognosis depends on the effectiveness of treatment for the underlying disorder. Medical conditions that may cause a psychosis include seizure disorders, lupus, hepatic encephalopathy, vitamin B_{12} deficiency, Cushing's syndrome, Addison's disease, hyperthyroidism, AIDS, and neurosyphilis (Sadock & Sadock, 2003).

Neurosyphilis

Syphilis is a sexually transmitted disease caused by the bacterium *Treponema pallidum*. Before the widespread availability of penicillin in the 1940s, one in five admissions to psychiatric hospitals were due to neurosyphilis (tertiary syphilis). Today about 1% of psychiatric admissions are due to neurosyphilis (Ritchie & Perdigao, 1999). In 1941 there were 100,000 cases of syphilis reported in the United States; this number declined to 10,000 in 1951 but increased to 32,000 in 2002 (Centers for Disease Control [CDC], 2004). However, syphilis may be underdiagnosed. Even though effective treatment is available for syphilis, the incidence of neurosyphilis is increasing because of the increase in HIV, overall increase in syphilis, and undertreatment of syphilis. Infection does not convey immunity, and people may become repeatedly re-infected. People also may be asymptomatic or have symptoms but not realize what is wrong with them and not seek treatment (Ritchie & Perdigao).

Syphilis has been called "the great imitator" because the signs and symptoms mimic many other diseases (CDC, 2004). Psychiatric symptoms can develop ant any stage of the illness, but are more common later in the illness. Psychiatric symptoms are variable but include psychosis, mania, depression, irritability, paranoia, violent or other aberrant behavior, personality changes, memory loss, slowed thinking, and the inability to learn new material. Grandiose delusions undistinguishable from those seen in delirious mania are common. Neurologic symptoms include tremors, handwriting difficulties, stroke, and slowed speech. As the disease progresses the dementia is very much like dementias from other disorders (Ritchie & Perdigao, 1999). Neurosyphilis can also worsen a concurrent psychiatric illness, for example, precipitating relapse and making medications less effective in remission. About one-third of people with untreated late latent syphilis will develop tertiary syphilis. It used to take as long as 20 years for neurosyphilis to develop, but HIV-associated immunosuppression has shortened that time for many people (Ritchie & Perdigao).

The usual screening test for syphilis is the RPR (rapid plasma reagin), but neurosyphilis is difficult to diagnosis on the basis of one test, and a negative RPR does not mean a client does not have neurosyphilis. There should be a high suspicion of neurosyphilis in people who have new psychiatric or neurological symptoms. This is particularly true for those who are at high risk of a sexually transmitted disease, especially if they have another STD, or HIV or AIDS. Psychiatric clients with schizophrenia, bipolar disorder, and substance abuse are especially vulnerable to these disorders because of impaired judgment and insight, and impulsivity.

Anxiety Disorders Due to a General Medical Condition

Medical disorders where anxiety may be the most important presenting symptom include hyperthyroidism, hypoglycemia, hyperglycemia, hypoparathyroidism, MS, and pheochromocytosis. In all of these conditions the client would have behavioral problems and abnormal laboratory and physical examination findings.

Other Disorders Due to General Medical Condition

In rare circumstances, medical conditions may cause sleep disorders, sexual disorders, catatonia, personality changes, and mental disorders not otherwise specified (Sadock & Sadock, 2003).

Pellagra

Pellagra presents with the "Four Ds" of dermatitis, dementia, diarrhea, and death. Pellagra is a potentially fatal disease brought on by a deficiency of the vitamin niacin (nicotinic acid). It was once a common cause of dementia in the American South and was associated with an acorn-based diet. Adding vitamin supplements to the food supply has made pellagra almost entirely disappear from the United States, but its rarity may also mean that it is overlooked as the etiology for neuropsychiatric symptoms (Kertesz, 2001). The three systems involved in pellagra are the skin (rash, hyperpigmentation), gastrointestinal (nausea, vomiting, diarrhea, discomfort after meals, and glossitis), and neuropsychiatric (memory loss and other cognitive dysfunction, anxiety, depression, psychosis, seizures, and ataxia). The first signs are reddened skin, like sunburn, on areas of the body exposed to the sun.

Catatonia Due to a General Medical Condition

A central nervous system (CNS) motor disturbance characterizes catatonia due to a general medical condition (see Table 13-4 earlier in the chapter). This motor disturbance is a direct physiologic effect of the medical condition. Client history, physical examination, and laboratory findings exclude the following neurologic conditions and metabolic disorders: malignant brain neoplasm and other neoplasms, head trauma, cerebrovascular accident, encephalitis, hypercalcemia, hepatic encephalopathy, homocystinuria, and diabetic ketoacidosis.

The *DSM-IV-TR* helps to interpret information gathered from the client's mental and physical assessment and presents other criteria that aid in making a differential diagnosis of catatonia. For example, the *DSM-IV-TR* states that the disturbance is not better accounted for by another mental disorder such as a manic episode, or that the disturbance does not occur exclusively during the course of the delirium (APA, 2000).

Other conditions to rule out include medication-induced movement disorders. Abnormal positioning may result from neuroleptic-induced acute dystonia. Catatonic-type schizophrenia also must be ruled out. This is distinguished both by the absence of a general medical condition related etiologically to the catatonia and by the presence of characteristic signs of schizophrenia such as delusions, hallucinations, and disorganized speech.

Clinical Example

Gerald, an 81-year-old man who lived by himself, was brought to the hospital via ambulance after his neighbors called stating that he was becoming increasingly anxious at home and unable to manage. The neighbors reported that he had been having more trouble caring for himself and appeared to be losing weight. Gerald appeared visibly shaken and told staff that he felt panicky all the time and "just knew" that something terrible was going to happen. He could not explain why he was frightened or what was making him nervous. Gerald told staff he had food at home and was eating normally but was losing weight. Gerald had no past psychiatric history. Staff in the emergency department noted that he appeared jaundiced and his liver function tests were elevated. He was admitted to the hospital and was found to have a diagnosis of pancreatic cancer.

Clinical Example

A 58-year-old homeless man was admitted to the hospital with complaints of chest pain, fever, cough, 10-pound weight loss, night sweats, nausea, vomiting, watery diarrhea, a burning sensation on discolored skin, and a labile mood. The patient had been diagnosed with bipolar disorder in the past but although currently labile was neither manic nor depressed. The patient received an extensive physical examination and laboratory tests, all of which were negative, including those for tuberculosis and HIV, or were only mildly abnormal. The patient's nutritional history was then assessed. The patient reported that he did not eat at shelters and had lived mostly on alcoholic beverages and corn chips for 4 months. The patient was started on 100 milligrams of niacin twice a day and began to eat meals at a shelter. Within two weeks all of his symptoms, including his irritable mood, subsided (Kertesz, 2001).

The third condition to exclude is mood disorder with catatonic features. This is also distinguished by the absence of a general medical condition and the presence of symptoms that meet the criteria for a major manic or major depressive episode.

Personality Changes Due to a General Medical Condition

Clients sometimes experience personality changes due to a general medical condition because of brain lesions due to trauma, tumors, strokes, seizures, hyperthyroidism, and hypocorticolism, although any medical condition may cause a personality change (Sadock & Sadock, 2003). The type of symptoms a person experiences is related to the location of damage. People with a traumatic brain injury are more likely to have persistent problems with personality.

> Behavioral disturbances represent changes from the client's previous personality patterns.

> Personality changes that are associated features of a general medical condition are not coded as personality change due to a general medical condition.

Personality changes due to general medical conditions must be differentiated from personality disorder, the primary mental disorder that involves certain stable behaviors and patterns. Personality changes resulting from a general medical condition can only be diagnosed if a direct physiologic mechanism is established that has caused or maintained changes. The presence of chronic medical conditions associated with personality changes also facilitates the differential diagnosis. Conditions that cause pain and disability are often responsible for personality changes and thus should be excluded. In addition, if the criteria for dementia are met, a separate diagnosis of **personality disorder** caused by a general medical condition is not warranted. Similarly, personality changes occurring only during the delirium are not caused by a medical condition; they are considered associated features of the delirium. Personality changes may be caused by another mental disorder due to a general medical condition. Examples include mood disorder due to a brain tumor with depressive features, personality changes due to substance abuse, and personality changes due to other mental disorders. The absence of both a specific general medical condition and evidence of its direct physiologic effect strongly suggests a primary mental disorder. (See Table 13-6 earlier in the chapter.)

Although the term *personality* is commonly linked to both changes and disorders, personality changes due to a general medical condition are coded on Axis I, whereas personality disorders are coded on Axis II.

Management and Treatment

Management and treatment focus on the careful assessment and identification of the primary medical disorder. Proper treatment of the primary medical disorder can mitigate or reverse the psychiatric symptoms at times. However, other symptoms, such as personality changes or affective symptoms related to steroids, can develop or increase even if the client's medical problems are being adequately managed and the client has had no problems in the past with the same regime. If the psychiatric symptoms are disturbing to the client or interfere with functioning, the client should be evaluated to determine whether the symptoms can be managed with medication, changes in environment or medication, or psychotherapeutic intervention.

Considerations for Client and Family Education

- Clients or family members should be aware that when new or atypical psychiatric symptoms are present, even in a client with a previously identified mental disorder, careful assessment and evaluation are needed to determine if the symptoms are due to a medical disorder.
- It is possible that some psychiatric symptoms related to a medical disorder can be treated or reversed when the general medical disorder is treated.

Summary

Clients who present with psychiatric symptoms may be medically ill. It is essential for nurses to be intellectually curious and question psychiatric diagnoses in clients whose signs and symptoms are atypical and who do not respond well to psychiatric treatment. Nurses then need to be client advocates and work with other caregivers to be sure clients receive comprehensive assessments including physical exams, family and client history, laboratory and neuroimaging studies, and mental status evaluations. Mental disorders due to a general medical condition can have serious and even catastrophic consequences for people, and they deserve competent nursing care.

To diagnose a mental disorder due to a general medical condition, the etiology of the psychiatric disorder must be the result of the physiologic condition. Delirium, dementia, amnesia, psychosis, sexual dysfunction, and mood, anxiety, or sleep disorders may all be directly caused by medical conditions. To manage mental disorders due to a general medical condition, the underlying pathophysiology or etiology must be identified. Some general medical conditions are frequently associated with mental disorders. These are typical considerations in differential diagnoses. Examples of this type of commonly encountered association would be that between hypothyroidism and mood disorders or between hypoxemia and delirium. Once established, treatment targets the medical condition. Occasionally it is necessary to treat both conditions concurrently or to continue treating the mental disorder after the medical condition stabilizes. It is essential for medical and psychiatric practitioners to collaborate.

Annotated References

American Psychiatric Association. (2000). *Diagnostic and statistical manual of mental disorders* (4th ed., text rev.). Washington, DC: Author.

This is the fourth edition, with text revision, of the American Psychiatric Association's official nomenclature of psychiatric conditions and descriptions. It provides a systematic listing of the official codes and categories, a description of the multiaxial system for diagnosis, and diagnostic criteria for each of the disorders. It is used by psychiatrists, physicians, psychologists, registered nurses, social workers, therapists, and other mental health workers in all clinical settings.

Centers for Disease Control. (2004). Sexually transmitted diseases. Syphilis—CDC Fact Sheet. Retrieved October 29, 2006, from http://www.cdc.gov/std/Syphilis/STDFact-Syphilis.htm

Statistical data on syphilis.

Chuang, L., & Forman, N. (2006). Mental disorders secondary to general medical conditions. *Emedicine.* Retrieved April 24, 2006, from www.emedicing.com/med/topic3447.htm

Lists criteria for distinguishing medical and psychiatric origins of psychiatric symptoms.

Feinstein, A. (1997). Multiple sclerosis, depression, and suicide. *British Medical Journal, 315,* 691–692.

An editorial reviewing studies reporting high rates of depression in people with MS and increased risk of suicide.

Kertesz, S. G. (2001). Pellagra in 2 homeless men. *Mayo Clinic Proceedings, 76,* 315–318.

A discussion of case reports for clients with pellagra.

Koran, L. M., Sheline, Y., Imai, K., Kelsey, T. G., Freedland, K. E., Matthews, J., et al. (2002). Medical disorders among clients admitted to a public sector psychiatric inpatient unit. *Psychiatric Services, 53*(12), 1623–1625.

A research study on the extent of medical problems in psychiatric clients found that a large proportion of patients had newly diagnosed medical problems, and some had physical disorders, that may have increased symptoms of a mental disorder.

Larkin, G. L., Classen, C. A., Edmond, J. A., Pelletier, A. J. & Camargo, C. A. (2005). Trends in U.S. emergency department visits for mental health conditions, 1992–2001. *Psychiatric Services* 56 (6) 671–677.

This report studied trends in mental health related visits to emergency departments.

Nightingale, F. (1946). *Notes on nursing. What it is and what it is not.* Philadelphia: J.P. Lippincott.

Florence Nightingale's oberservations on nursing, first published in 1859.

Reeves, R. R., Pendarvis, E. J., & Kimble, R. (2000). Unrecognized medical emergencies admitted to psychiatric units. *American Journal of Emergency Medicine, 18,* 390–393.

The case records of 64 clients with unrecognized medical conditions who were inappropriately admitted to psychiatric units were reviewed. The most common missed diagnoses were alcohol or drug intoxication, alcohol or drug withdrawal or delirium tremens, or prescription medication overdose. The most common incorrect diagnoses was schizophrenia followed by psychosis NOS, depression, and bipolar disorder. Except for assessing orientation, mental status exams had not been done and few clients had a physical exam or indicated lab and diagnostic studies or x-rays. Discusses the problem of unrecognized medical problems in psychiatric clients.

Ritchie, M. A., & Perdigao, J. A. (1999). Neurosyphilis: Considerations for a psychiatrist. Retrieved October 5, 2006, from http://www.priory.com/psych/neurosyphilis.htm

Discusses neuropsychiatric complications of syphilis.

Sadock, B. J., & Sadock V. A. (2003). *Kaplan and Sadock's synopsis of psychiatry* (9th ed.). Philadelphia: Lippincott Williams & Wilkins.

A comprehensive textbook of psychiatry.

Saliou, V., Fichele, A., McLoughlin, M., Thauin, T., & Lejeux, M. L. (2005). Psychiatric disorders among patients admitted to a French emergency service. *General Hospital Psychiatry, 27*(4), 263–268.

This study of admissions to a French emergency service found that 29% of the patients had medical problems.

Wallin, M. T., Wilkin, J. A., Turner, A. P., Williams, R. M. & Kane, R. (2006). Depression and multiple sclerosis: Review of a lethal combination. *Journal of Rehabilitation Research & Development, 43*(1), 45–62.

This article reviews the association of depression with multiple sclerosis due to the psychosocial effects of disability, effects of lesions and interferon on brain structures, and immune dysfunctions. The need for assessment, screening, and treatment is discussed along with the risk factors for suicide.

Additional Resources

Bogousslavsky, J., & Cummings, J. F. (Eds.). (2000). *Behavior and mood in focal brain lesions.* New York: Cambridge University Press.

Describes the effects of various neurologic conditions on behavior and mood.

Foster, R., Olajide, D., & Everall, L. P. (2003). Antiretroviral therapy-induced psychosis: Case report and brief report of the literature. *HIV Medicine, 4,* 139–144.

One month after starting combination antiretroviral therapy a client developed persecutory delusions, mutism, and catatonia. After discontinuing the abacavir (ABC) and starting a low dose of an antipsychotic, the client's psychosis resolved.

Govoni, M., Castellino, G., Padovan, M., & Trotta, F. (2004). Recent advances and future perspective in neuroimaging in neuropsychiatric systemic lupus erythematosus. *Lupus, 13,* 149–158.

Neuropsychiatric symptoms occur in 14% to 75% of clients with SLE, but remained difficult to diagnosis.

Lubkin, I. M. (2006). *Chronic illness: Impact and intervention* (6th ed.). Sudbury, MA: Jones and Bartlett.

This text describes the impact of chronic illness upon the client and family members.

Mohr, D. C., Hart, S. L., Fonareva, I., & Tasch, E. S. (2006). Treatment of depression for clients with multiple sclerosis in neurology clinics. *Multiple Sclerosis, 12,* 204–208.

A discussion of treatment issues of depression in people with MS.

Morgante, L. (2000). Hope in multiple sclerosis: A nursing perspective. *International Journal of MS Care, 2*(2), 1–8.

Discusses hope as a nursing concept and psychosocial issues in caring for medically ill clients.

Wells, S. M. (2000). *A delicate balance: Living successfully with chronic illness.* Cambridge, MA: Perseus.

A helpful book for clients and families dealing with adjustment to chronic illness, including information on typical behavior patterns.

Internet Resources

http://nursing.jbpub.com/psychiatric

Visit http://nursing.jbpub.com/psychiatric for interactive exercises, NCLEX review questions, WebLinks, and more.

CHAPTER 14

Substance-Related Disorders

Patricia G. O'Brien

■ LEARNING OBJECTIVES

After reading this chapter, you will be able to:

- Define substance abuse, substance dependence, tolerance, intoxication, and withdrawal.
- Assess clients for signs and symptoms of substance-related disorders.
- Identify the issues relevant to the management and treatment of substance-related disorders, and use these to develop individualized nursing care plans.
- List at least five areas for client and family education related to substance use.

■ KEY TERMS

Blackouts
Codependence
Denial
Detoxification
Intoxication
Substance abuse
Substance dependence
Substance-induced disorders
Tolerance
12-step program
Wernicke-Korsakoff syndrome
Withdrawal
Withdrawal delirium

http://nursing.jbpub.com/psychiatric

Visit http://nursing.jbpub.com/psychiatric for interactive exercises, NCLEX review questions, WebLinks, and more.

Introduction

The *Diagnostic and Statistical Manual of Mental Disorders*, Fourth Edition, Text Revision (*DSM-IV-TR*) distinguishes between substance-induced disorders and substance-use disorders (American Psychiatric Association [APA], 2000). **Substance-induced disorders** refer to intoxication and withdrawal as well as to other disorders induced by substances, including delirium, dementia, amnesia, paranoia, depression, anxiety, sexual dysfunction, and sleep disorders. *Substance-use disorders* refer to **substance dependence** and **substance abuse**. The most commonly abused substances are categorized as central nervous system (CNS) depressants, CNS stimulants, opiates, hallucinogens, cannabinoids, phencyclidine (PCP), inhalants, and nicotine. This chapter discusses intoxication, withdrawal, substance abuse, and substance dependence, and presents the principles of diagnosis, treatment, and prevention.

Substance-Induced Disorders

Substance **intoxication** is a substance-specific syndrome that results from recent ingestion or exposure to a substance (APA, 2000). The cognitive and behavioral changes that occur are related to the effects the substance has on the CNS and vary depending on the person and the substance. Common responses include belligerence, labile mood, impaired judgment, and loss of motor coordination. The first substance disorder a person is most likely to experience is intoxication.

Substance **withdrawal** is a substance-specific response as well. It occurs when a person stops or decreases use after heavy, prolonged consumption. Signs and symptoms vary depending on the substance, dose, duration of use, and health of the person. The "morning-after hangover" with the accompanying symptoms of headache, dry mouth, and fine hand tremors is indicative of mild alcohol withdrawal.

Figure 14-1 Repeatedly driving under the influence is a sign of substance abuse.

Substance-Use Disorders

The *DSM-IV-TR* distinguishes between the two substance-use disorders: substance abuse and substance dependence.

The essential feature of **substance abuse** is a maladaptive pattern of substance use manifested by recurrent and significant adverse consequences related to the substance use (APA, 2000). According to *DSM-IV-TR* criteria, substance abuse can be diagnosed if one of the following criteria is met within a 12-month period, *and if the criteria for substance dependence are not met:*

- The substance abuse interferes with the person's major responsibilities at work, home, or school.
- Repeated use occurs in hazardous situations, such as driving when impaired (see Figure 14-1).
- The person is experiencing recurrent substance-related legal problems.
- The person has recurring social or interpersonal problems related to substance use.

Examples of behaviors that should be considered in making this diagnosis include frequent absences from work, arrests for driving while intoxicated (DWI), involvement in physical or verbal altercations, and missing significant family events. Substance abuse can include excessive use of substances over brief periods of time or it may occur as a chronic problem. However, there is an absence of physical or psychological dependence.

Clinical Example

Tom is 28-year-old single stockbroker who has developed a pattern of weekend drug abuse. Every Friday he joins co-workers after work for a few drinks. The other guys generally have a couple of beers before heading home, but Tom drinks faster than the others and averages four or five beers before the group breaks up. Tom drives home and usually stops to pick up a sandwich or a burger and a couple of six-packs of beer. He has a couple of beers with the sandwich before showering and dressing for the club scene. At the club, he mixes shots of vodka with beer, and "mellows out" with marijuana. It is not unusual for Tom and his friends to get into verbal and even physical altercations during these nights out. After sleeping late on Saturday, the partying continues with alcohol, marijuana, and sometimes the stimulant Ecstasy, which Tom uses to enhance his casual sexual encounters. Over the past couple of years, Tom has fallen into the same pattern every weekend. He stops all drinking and drug use early Sunday, noting that he has to "sober up" so he can be alert for work on Monday morning. However, twice this past month Tom did continue partying into Sunday, and was unable to work on Monday. Tom had a girlfriend for 3 months but she broke up with him because of her concern over his drug use.

Critical Thinking Question Which criteria can you find in the clinical example about Tom to support the diagnosis of substance abuse?

A diagnosis of **substance dependence** is made based on evidence of tolerance, withdrawal, or a pattern of compulsive behavior related to the substance. According to *DSM-IV-TR* criteria (APA, 2000), substance dependence requires the presence of three or more of the following at any time during a 12-month period:

- Tolerance
- Withdrawal
- Greater use of the substance than intended
- Inability to stop or control the substance use
- Preoccupation with obtaining, using, or recovering from the substance

- Giving up important activities in order to use the substance
- Continued use of the substance even when confronted with the risks

Tolerance refers to the person's need for increasing amounts of the substance to achieve the desired effects. Tolerance develops as a result of the body adapting to the presence of the substance. A decrease in the amount or effectiveness of the substance leads to withdrawal.

Withdrawal represents a physiologic dependence on the substance, and occurs when the person stops using the substance after a period of prolonged use. Withdrawal symptoms are not observed with all substances, and not all persons dependent on substances develop a physiologic dependence.

The additional diagnostic criteria for substance dependence are behaviors aimed at protecting and maintaining the substance use. The person uses greater amounts of the substance for longer periods than intended. He or she repeatedly plans to curtail or regulate substance use. The person spends a great deal of time using, obtaining, and recovering from the substance. Important social, work-related, or recreational activities are given up or reduced. Finally, the person continues to use the substance despite the knowledge that it is causing a psychological or physical problem.

Critical Thinking Question Which criteria can you find in the clinical example about Marcie to support the diagnosis of substance dependence?

Clinical Example

Marcie is a 40-year-old recently divorced, currently unemployed mother with a 10-year-old daughter, Tanya. Marcie was let go from her job as a bank teller due to frequent absences, which she attributed to chronic back pain. Doctors did not find a specific cause for the back pain, but Marcie had prescriptions for benzodiazepine medications, Valium, and Klonopin to help her cope with the pain. Marcie also uses these medications when she has difficulty sleeping. In the past month, Marcie has noted that she needs to take double the dose of these medications in order to fall asleep. She has been experiencing increasing difficulty managing her responsibilities with her daughter, and her ex-husband is threatening to seek custody. Just last month, she failed to pick Tanya up after school and the principal, unable to reach Marcie, had called Tanya's father who found Marcie at home, passed out on the couch with an empty bottle of wine on the table. Fearing losing custody of her daughter, Marcie promised to stop drinking at that time, but instead has managed to restrict her drinking to after Tanya goes to bed at night. She starts each night planning to have one glass of wine, but always has more, and usually loses count. This past week, Marcie has begun taking a Valium in the morning to steady her hands.

Incidence and Prevalence

In the United States alone, more than 100,000 people per year receive in-patient treatment for alcohol and other mind-altering drugs. Substance abuse occurs across all racial, socioeconomic, and ethnic lines. The incidence of alcoholism is higher in cultures that proscribe childhood use but encourage and accept heavy use in adulthood. In recent years, the medical community has become increasingly aware of substance abuse among women and the elderly. Persons between 18 and 24 years of age use the greatest amount of all substances, but there is concern about adolescent use as well. It is estimated that more than half of U.S. youths experiment with an illicit drug before finishing high school (Perkinson, 2001).

The popularity of certain drugs varies over time and depends to some extent on their availability and how easy they are to use. Marijuana and cocaine are the most commonly used illicit drugs. Among young people in particular, certain drugs have come to be known as "club drugs," referring to the dance clubs, bars, and parties (such as "raves") where they are commonly available and used. These drugs include Ecstasy and methamphetamine.

Chemical dependency comes first. Physical, social, and psychologic consequences are caused by the dependency.

Prescription drugs, primarily benzodiazepines, can lead to dependence and abuse that is often difficult to detect, because the withdrawal symptoms are similar to the anxiety or insomnia the drugs were originally prescribed to treat. Oxycodone is another prescribed medication that is frequently abused. Primarily because of their availability, over-the-counter (OTC) medications can also be drugs of abuse. In high doses, OTC cough and cold preparations can produce effects similar to PCP. The common decongestants, pseudoephedrine and ephedrine, have been used illegally to manufacture methamphetamine. Most states now restrict the sale of OTC medications with these ingredients.

Alcohol is still the most widely used and abused psychoactive substance in the United States and has been associated with 100,000 to 200,000 deaths each year. Some alcohol-related deaths include accidental or intentional overdoses, drug interactions, traffic or other accidents, injuries sustained in falls, and medically related illnesses.

Alcohol-related accidents and disorders account for 30% of all emergency room visits and 40% of all general hospital admissions.

Etiology

Substance abuse does not have just one cause. Rather, the etiology is a combination of neurobiologic, genetic, social, and psychologic factors (Allen, 1996). Classic studies conducted with children of alcoholics have established a genetic predisposition, but because the rate of alcoholism never reaches 100% for identical twins, other variables must be involved. Children of parents with substance-abuse disorders are considered at increased risk for developing these disorders. Parents' attitudes and the examples they set may contribute to this risk. Although there is no recognized addictive personality disorder, depression, low self-esteem, loneliness, stress, and behaviors such as pain avoidance and pleasure seeking all may contribute to a reliance on psychoactive substances. However, this situation is not simply one of cause and effect, because depression, low self-esteem, and loneliness may very well be consequences of the addiction. More research is required to discern the etiology of this complex disorder.

The onset of withdrawal is more rapid, and symptoms do not last as long with drugs that affect the body quickly and only for a short time, such as alcohol. The onset of withdrawal is delayed, and withdrawal symptoms last longer with drugs such as diazepam (Valium) that affect the body for a longer period of time.

Physiology

All abused psychoactive drugs directly affect the brain and CNS, altering the neurotransmitters essential for intercellular communication. This action results in changes in feelings, thoughts, and behaviors. Specific alterations depend on the substance, the route of administration, the amount of the dose, the presence of other drugs, and the general health of the individual. Drugs are commonly classified by the type of effect they exert on the CNS. The psychopharmacologic properties of the major classes of drugs that produce physical dependency are shown in **Table 14-1** (Allen, 1996; Deglin & Vallerand, 2006; Galanter & Kleber, 2004; Perkinson, 2001).

Substances of Abuse

CNS Depressants

Examples of CNS depressants include alcohol, benzodiazepines, minor tranquilizers, barbiturates, chloral hydrate, meprobamate, and methaqualone. Depressants affect the brainstem and respiratory centers. Mechanisms vary but are most likely related to altered concentrations of one or a combination of neurotransmitters. The effects of CNS depressants include the relaxation of muscles, sedation, and decreased anxiety. *Intoxication* from CNS depressants is characterized by slurred speech, ataxia, impaired judgment, agitation, and depression. Severe intoxication can result in paranoia, seizures, stupor, coma, apnea, and even death. Alcohol abuse has been associated with **blackouts** or periods of amnesia during which the person appears to function normally but later does not recall the events that transpired. Following a night of heavy drinking, a person may have no recollection of getting home. In more extreme examples, people report waking up in strange cities with no idea how they got there. An alcohol tolerance usually leads to cross-tolerance with barbiturates and other sedative hypnotics. Combining these drugs with alcohol potentiates the effects of intoxication, particularly respiratory depression.

The delirium experienced during withdrawal can be a life-threatening symptom.

Withdrawal Symptoms

The onset of withdrawal from CNS depressants occurs within hours or days after stopping or reducing drug use. Withdrawal may occur during prolonged use if the person's high tolerance has decreased the drug's effect. Because alcohol affects the body for only a short time, withdrawal symptoms are usually observed within 4 to 6 hours after drinking ceases. Conversely, diazepam (Valium) withdrawal may not be evident for 7 to 10 days. The time to onset of barbiturate withdrawal ranges from 12 hours to 3 days, depending on the half-life of the drug abused.

Symptoms of withdrawal include diaphoresis, elevated pulse and blood pressure, tremulousness (noted in the hand and extended tongue), nausea, vomiting, auditory and visual hallucinations, ataxia, agitation, and a subjective state of restlessness or anxiety. The risk of seizures is greatest in persons with a history of withdrawal seizures. The risk is highest 24 to 72 hours after the substance was last used. **Withdrawal delirium**, or delirium tremens (DTs), is a life-threatening complication of alcohol withdrawal and has a mortality rate of 15%. It is characterized by agitation, delusions, disorientation, visual hallucinations, elevated temperature, and cardiac arrhythmias.

Detoxification

Alcohol withdrawal is usually treated with progressively decreasing doses of chlordiazepoxide (Librium) at 4-hour intervals for a period of 5 days. Additional doses may be needed based

Table 14-1 Drug Categories that Produce Physical Dependency

Drug Category	Time to Onset of Withdrawal	Symptoms of Withdrawal	Detoxification
CNS depressants (alcohol, barbiturates, benzodiazepines)	From last use: 4–6 hours, peaking at 24 hours for alcohol; 12 hours to 3 days for barbiturates, depending on half-life; 7–10 days for diazepam (Valium)	Diaphoresis, elevated pulse and blood pressure, tremors, nausea, vomiting, agitation, auditory and visual hallucinations, and seizures	Doses of CNS depressants are tapered. Sample alcohol detoxification: chlordiazepoxide (Librium) 25 mg orally every 4 hours for 24 hours, then 20 mg every 4 hours for 24 hours, so that on the fifth and final day, the dose is 5 mg every 4 hours. Phenobarbital (Luminal Sodium), diazepam (Valium), and lorazepam (Ativan) are also used for detoxification. Detoxification can be extended up to 2 weeks when the drug of addiction is long acting.
CNS stimulants (cocaine, amphetamines, caffeine)	Wide variations in onset from a few hours to several days	Depression, agitation, suicidal ideation, fatigue, insomnia, vivid dreams, extended sleep, hunger, and drug craving	Stabilize vital signs; control behavior. Chlordiazepoxide (Librium), haloperidol (Haldol), and antihypertensives are usually effective.
Opiates (heroin, morphine, codeine, meperidine, methadone)	Onset within hours to days after use; symptoms last 7–10 days	Chills, sweating, dilated pupils, increased pulse and blood pressure, muscle aches, abdominal cramps, drug craving, rhinorrhea, yawning, drowsiness, and coma	Methadone is administered orally in decreasing doses over a period of about 10 days; clonidine (Catapres) 0.3–1.2 mg/day, decreased by 50%/day for 3 days then discontinued.
Cannabinoids (marijuana, hashish)	Mild physical dependence associated with chronic use of high doses	Restlessness, irritability, insomnia, nausea, vomiting, and sweating	No treatment required.
Nicotine (cigarettes, cigars, pipe and chewing tobacco)	Symptoms develop within 24 hours of tapering or not using drug	Irritability, nicotine craving, decreased heart rate, tremors, headache, difficulty concentrating, and insomnia	Nicotine is substituted in the form of gum or a patch, which is tapered and eventually discontinued.

on the presence of withdrawal symptoms, and are given as needed. Elderly clients may require lower doses of medication during withdrawal. Withdrawal from CNS depressants is usually accomplished with benzodiazepines or barbiturates. Long-acting drugs such as diazepam (Valium) and chlordiazepoxide provide a smoother **detoxification**, but some practitioners prefer short-acting drugs to prevent a cumulative effect. Short-acting drugs are indicated for clients whose physical or mental status is unclear, such as when laboratory tests are pending or a head injury is suspected. Short-acting drugs such as lorazepam (Ativan) are used to treat withdrawal in the presence of impaired liver function. Intravenous diazepam (Valium) is usually administered to treat withdrawal delirium. Anticonvulsants are occasionally prescribed prophylactically for clients with a history of withdrawal seizures.

CNS Stimulants

Examples of CNS stimulants are caffeine, cocaine, amphetamines, and methylphenidate (Ritalin). Crack, a less expensive and more readily available form of cocaine, is highly addictive and is characterized by a quick high and a sudden crash, accompanied by profound depression. Methamphetamine, another popular drug of abuse, is also less expensive than cocaine, produces a longer high, and, like crack, results in an intense crash.

Chlordiazepoxide (Librium) is contraindicated in the presence of impaired liver functioning. The liver's inability to metabolize chlordiazepoxide leads to accumulation of the drug and causes increased lethargy and coma.

Methamphetamine and amphetamines can be consumed by smoking, inhalation, or injection. Smoked methamphetamine is often referred to as "ice" or "crystal meth." Ecstasy, also known as MDMA (methylenedioxymethamphetamine), is a synthetic drug with amphetamine-like effects.

These drugs stimulate the CNS by enhancing the actions of the neurotransmitters dopamine and norepinephrine. CNS stimulants have the following effects: alertness, euphoria, decreased appetite, and an enhanced sexual response. *Intoxication* from CNS stimulants is characterized by anxiety, confusion, paranoia, irritability, grandiosity, rhinitis, insomnia, tactile hallucinations, elevated vital signs, chest pain, cardiac arrhythmias, dilated pupils, and respiratory distress. Seizures can result from cocaine intoxication. Alcohol can counter the undesirable effects of stimulants such as anxiety. The combination of stimulants and alcohol, however, is unpredictable.

CNS stimulants dilate the pupils.

Nearly 40 states have passed laws that limit the sale of cold medicines containing the decongestants pseudoephedrine and ephedrine, which illegal labs use to make methamphetamine.

Opiates constrict the pupils.

Opioid dependency is associated with a death rate as high as 1.5–2% a year. Deaths are related to overdose, accidents, injuries, AIDS, and general medical complications.

Withdrawal Symptoms

Depression, agitation, suicidal ideation, fatigue, insomnia, vivid dreams, extended sleep, hunger, and drug craving are all symptoms of withdrawal from CNS stimulants. Symptoms vary from person to person, and the onset can occur anywhere from a few hours to several days after ceasing or reducing drug use.

Detoxification

Detoxification includes stabilizing the client's vital signs and managing his or her behavior. This requires a combination of supportive therapy and medication with chlordiazepoxide (Librium) or haloperidol (Haldol). Intravenous antihypertensives may be necessary, and diazepam (Valium) may be used to control seizures. Clients who use an intravenous combination of cocaine and heroin, commonly referred to as "speed-ball," are detoxified with methadone.

Opiates

Examples of opiates include heroin, morphine, codeine, opium, meperidine (Demerol), and methadone. These drugs stimulate opiate receptors in the brain, mimicking the action of natural endorphins. Opiates produce an intense pleasure referred to as a "rush." Other effects of opiates include analgesia and decreased gastrointestinal motility. *Intoxication* from opiates is characterized by respiratory depression, slurred speech, constricted pupils, orthostatic hypotension, nausea, and vomiting. Clients taking phenothiazines or antidepressants are at greater risk for respiratory depression. An overdose of opiates is indicated by severe respiratory depression, pinpoint pupils, and coma. Intravenous naloxone (Narcan) is administered during acute intoxication to reverse opioid-induced respiratory depression. The effects of opiates are potentiated by all CNS depressants, including alcohol.

Withdrawal Symptoms

Symptoms of opiate withdrawal include chills, sweating, increased pulse and blood pressure, muscle aches, abdominal cramps, drug craving, rhinorrhea, yawning, drowsiness, and coma. These symptoms begin within hours to days after drug use ceases and usually subside in 7 to 14 days. The duration of withdrawal is shorter for heroin, a short-acting drug, and longer for methadone, a longer-acting drug. Methadone detoxification may be extended over several months.

Detoxification

Methadone is administered orally in decreasing doses to detoxify clients. Methadone administered as a maintenance treatment is another option. Women who are pregnant will be maintained on methadone until after delivery because of the risks that withdrawal poses for the fetus. It is safer to withdraw the baby after delivery. If the client is also withdrawing from a CNS depressant, phenobarbital is administered until opiate detoxification is complete. Once detoxification is finished, the phenobarbital is tapered and finally discontinued. Clonidine (Catapres), an alternative drug, manages the symptoms of opiate withdrawal, and, when combined with naltrexone, an opioid antagonist, can significantly shorten the length of time for complete withdrawal. Vital signs must be monitored before each dose of clonidine because of the associated side effects of sedation and hypotension. Nonsteroidal anti-inflammatory medications and anti-nausea agents are used to manage muscle aches and nausea during withdrawal.

Hallucinogens

Examples of hallucinogens include lysergic acid diethylamide (LSD), mescaline, psilocybin, ketamine, and the synthetic amphetamin-like "designer drug" Ecstasy. Hallucinogens have a sympathomimetic effect, but the exact mechanism of action has not been determined. These drugs alter the client's sensory perception: taste, smell, and touch are highly intensified; the sense of time and space is distorted; and the client experiences visual illusions and emotional lability. Intoxication with hallucinogens is characterized by tachycardia, hypertension, and dilated pupils. It has not been determined whether hallucinogens interact with alcohol.

Withdrawal Symptoms

No physical dependence develops with hallucinogen use; therefore, there are no withdrawal symptoms. However, adverse reactions can include a panic response or "bad trip," delirium manifested by hallucinations, paranoia, and agitation. These symptoms usually end within 24 hours, but psychotic symptoms occasionally persist and require treatment with psychotropic medications.

Detoxification

There is no need for detoxification. The effects of hallucinogens usually subside within 8 to 12 hours.

Cannabinoids

Two examples of cannabinoids are marijuana and hashish. These drugs depress the higher organizational centers in the brain. Cannabinoids produce the effects of euphoria and altered perceptions, and intoxication is characterized by anxiety, suspiciousness, impaired judgment, hallucinations, tachycardia, and red, irritated conjunctiva (bloodshot eyes). Cannabinoids potentiate the effects of CNS depressants, including alcohol.

Withdrawal Symptoms

Symptoms of withdrawal include restlessness, irritability, insomnia, sweating, nausea, and vomiting. Persons may also experience "bad trips," delirium, or flashbacks, but these are not as common with cannabinoids as with hallucinogens.

Detoxification

No treatment is indicated for detoxification from cannabinoids.

Phencyclidine (PCP)

PCP (angel dust) produces peripheral sympathetic and anticholinergic effects as well as central psychotomimetic, anticholinergic, and adrenergic effects. The drug is stored in the brain and adipose tissue, so the serum half-life can be extended for up to 3 days. Depending on the dose, PCP can act as an analgesic, depressant, or stimulant. Intoxication results in impaired judgment, nystagmus, elevated heart rate and blood pressure, muscle rigidity, ataxia, seizures, and delirium. Persons with PCP intoxication may become paranoid and exhibit unpredictable, violent behavior. It is not known whether PCP interacts with alcohol.

Withdrawal Symptoms

No withdrawal syndrome is associated with PCP, but clients may experience lethargy, depression, and drug craving.

Detoxification

No detoxification is required.

Inhalants

Inhalants cause diffuse impairment of brain function. Types of inhalants include glue, paint, paint solvents, aerosol sprays, cleaning fluids, gasoline, typewriter correction fluids, nitrous oxide, and amyl nitrite (**Figure 14-2**). These substances produce euphoria, or what is termed a "high," along with altered perceptions. Intoxication, which occurs during or shortly after use, is characterized by slurred speech, ataxia, impaired judgment, dizziness, tremors, and attacks on others. An interaction with alcohol has not been established.

Figure 14-2 Many common household products are used as inhalants.

> Persons who use hallucinogens can experience flashbacks, or recurrent drug experiences, for months after the last drug use.

> Over-the-counter drugs such as cough syrups that contain dextromethorphan, a synthetic derivative of morphine, can produce effects similar to those of PCP.

> On physical examination, persons who abuse inhalants may have a rash around the nose and mouth.

Inhalant use can result in sudden death, most likely due to acute arrhythmia, hypoxia, or electrolyte abnormalities.

Withdrawal Symptoms

Psychologic dependence forms from the use of inhalants, but physical withdrawal symptoms have not been documented.

Detoxification

Detoxification is not indicated for inhalants.

Nicotine

Nicotine exerts an agonist effect on nicotine receptors in the central and peripheral nervous systems to initiate drug actions. Cigarettes, cigars, and pipe and chewing tobacco all contain varying amounts of nicotine. Nicotine produces the dual effects of relaxation and stimulation, but it has no recognized intoxication. Nicotine combined with alcohol increases irritation to the oral mucosa, throat, and esophagus.

Nicotine dependence has a similar familial pattern as alcohol dependence. Twin and adoption studies indicate genetic factors contribute to the onset and continuation of smoking.

Withdrawal Symptoms

Symptoms develop within 24 hours of tapering or stopping nicotine use. These include irritability, nicotine craving, decreased heart rate, tremors, headache, difficulty concentrating, and insomnia.

An intoxicated client may not be a reliable informant.

Clients with substance abuse are at increased risk for suicide.

Detoxification

Nicotine patches or chewing gum are effective in relieving withdrawal symptoms, and their use is gradually tapered and discontinued.

Clinical Example

Jack W. was admitted to a medical detoxification unit of a large urban hospital. He had been found passed out on the street, obviously intoxicated, with alcohol on his breath. Jack, 70 years old, regained consciousness in the emergency room and admitted to being homeless and to drinking a fifth of whiskey a day. His last drink was reportedly that morning, approximately 5 hours before admission. Jack was already noted to have hand tremors, mild diaphoresis, and an elevated BP and pulse. He was started on 50 mg chlordiazepoxide by mouth every 4 hours with orders for decreasing doses over the next 5 days. On the second day of detoxification the nurse went to check Jack's vital signs and found him difficult to arouse. When he did wake up, he appeared confused. This change in sensorium alerted the nurse to check Jack's pupils. The left pupil was sluggish. Additional tests confirmed that Jack had a subdural hematoma, a collection of blood in the subdural space of the brain as a result of a ruptured blood vessel. It may have been easy to attribute the confusion and drowsiness to withdrawal, but the nurse knew that patients with substance abuse are often poor historians and may suffer injuries that they either dismiss or do not recall. The nurse's good judgment and knowledge may well have saved Jack's life.

Assessment of Clients with Substance-Abuse Disorders

If the client is intoxicated at the time of the assessment, it may be difficult to obtain accurate information. When possible, the nurse should obtain a complete history from both the client and another person who knows the client and his or her circumstances prior to the assessment. The information that is obtained should consist of medical, psychiatric, alcohol, and drug histories. The American Nurses Association has established a *Scope and Standards of Addictions Nursing Practice* (2004).

Physical Assessment

The nurse needs to consider all possible physiologic causes of the sensory changes associated with substance abuse and intoxication. For example, even in the presence of acute withdrawal, a client can experience acute hypoglycemia or, as the result of a fall, a subdural hematoma. Performing a neurologic examination, including pupil-check and level of consciousness, and vital signs are therefore of great importance.

Alcohol abuse can lead to a variety of medical problems, including pancreatitis, esophagitis, esophageal varices, gastritis, hepatitis, cardiomyopathy, dementia, and peripheral neuropathy. **Wernicke-Korsakoff syndrome**, also known as alcohol-induced persisting amnestic disorder, and characterized by severe memory impairment, is a serious neurotoxic effect of alcohol abuse. Hepatitis, endocarditis, and the human immunodeficiency virus (HIV) are complications of intravenous drug use. Pulmonary edema can result from opiate toxicity, and pulmonary, renal, and liver complications, cerebral atrophy, cerebellar degeneration, and an increased risk for acute myelocytic leukemia are associated with abuse of inhalants. Physical examination and relevant laboratory tests including blood chemistries, complete blood count with differential, liver function tests, and prothrombin time can aid in diagnosing potentially life-threatening illnesses. Screening for tuberculosis by skin testing or chest x-ray may also be indicated.

Psychiatric Assessment

Assessment should include a history of psychiatric symptoms, treatment, and hospitalizations. The hallucinations, paranoia, depression, and agitation that are frequently associated with substance abuse and intoxication may be induced by the substances or may be symptoms of an underlying psychiatric illness such as schizophrenia or a mood disorder. The clinician may find it easier to evaluate and diagnose clients after withdrawal and a period of sobriety. However, even after sobriety is achieved the diagnosis may not be straightforward. Clients will often report using substances to control psychotic or behavioral symptoms. It may be difficult to determine which came first, the substance abuse or the psychiatric disorder. Currently, the importance of a dual diagnosis is recognized, and integrated treatment is recommended. (See also Chapter 27.)

Alcohol and Drug History

Information that is obtained should include the type of substance or substances used, the length of time the substance was used, the amount of substance used, the method of administration, the history and frequency of use, and patterns of past intoxications and withdrawals, including seizures and delirium. Toxicology screenings of urine and blood are informative, because most psychoactive substances are detectable for up to 48 hours (and even longer) after use.

Given the high incidence of substance abuse among hospitalized clients, it is reasonable to include an alcohol and drug history as part of every assessment. It is not uncommon to have a patient go into withdrawal while recovering from orthopedic or other surgery. Hospitalization for any reason may be the first time that a client passes a few days without using alcohol or other drugs, and he or she may develop agitation, anxiety, tremors, and other withdrawal symptoms.

A matter-of-fact, nonjudgmental approach maximizes the likelihood of obtaining accurate information from the client. Understanding the progressive nature of dependence and the subtle process of **denial** that may bias the client's responses is helpful. For example, the client may have started drinking in a socially appropriate way but, because of a high tolerance, gradually increased the amount and frequency of drinking to achieve the desired effect. Progression may include sneaking drinks, hiding alcohol to keep it available, missing social functions, resolving to reduce consumption, experiencing blackouts, and bingeing. Binge drinking is a pattern of drinking that results in a blood alcohol concentration (BAC) of 0.08 grams percent or above. This typically happens when men consume more than four drinks and women consume more than three drinks in two hours (National Institute of Alcohol Abuse and Alcoholism, 2004). In most states, the legal BAC limit for drivers is 0.10%. However, many states are considering lowering that to 0.08%.

Clinical Example

At family gatherings Carl always volunteers to be the bartender. He prepares the drinks in the kitchen, and this allows him to sneak extra shots out of the sight of his wife and guests.

A group of co-workers agree to buy season tickets for the local baseball team. When Sam learns that the seats are in a no-drinking area, he declines.

Most psychoactive substances can be detected in the blood and urine for up to 48 hours after use.

Denial is a psychologic defense that is prominent among alcoholics and leads them to underestimate the amount of alcohol used.

Alcoholics may state that they have only two drinks per day. However, when questioned, they may acknowledge that the liquor is not measured in a shot glass but freely poured into a glass the size of a tumbler. Clients who abuse alcohol often understate their use, while clients who abuse benzodiazepines and heroin tend to exaggerate their use. Clients may report using five bags a day of heroin, or 15 bags, or more. It is good to ask how many bags the client needs to "get straight," or to ease the symptoms of withdrawal. This may be as little as two bags. This information will guide the nurse practitioner or other prescribing clinician to evaluate the initial dose of methadone to use for detoxification.

Frequently, clients' patterns of substance use reflect a loss of control over the amount and frequency of use and preoccupations with planning for the use or attainment of a substance. These behaviors, when pointed out to the client, can help break down denial and help the client to recognize the extent of the substance-abuse problem.

A widely used tool to assess for substance abuse is the CAGE test (Mayfield, McCleod, & Hall, 1974), which asks four questions that were originally directed at assessing alcohol abuse but can be adapted for use with other substances, as indicated:

- Have you ever felt you ought to Cut down on your drinking or drug use?
- Have people Annoyed you by criticizing your drinking or drug use?
- Have you ever felt bad or Guilty about your drinking or drug use?

- Have you ever had a drink or used drugs first thing in the morning to steady your nerves or get rid of a hangover (Eye-opener)?

Two or more positive answers are considered clinically significant, but even one positive response deserves follow-up.

A more thorough assessment will yield information that can be utilized to motivate the client to pursue treatment. This includes which substances, including prescription and over-the-counter medications, the client uses. It is helpful to know the frequency of use as well as the circumstances under which the substances are used. Adverse effects of the substance use, including withdrawal, seizures, and medical, social, or legal consequences, can be important in helping the client confront the extent of the substance abuse or dependence. Knowing if the person has had any past periods of sobriety can identify interventions that the client found helpful.

Management and Treatment

Detoxification

If the client is experiencing symptoms of physiological withdrawal, initial interventions are directed at safely detoxifying the client and observing for and treating complications (**Table 14-2**). Out-patient management is appropriate for patients with mild to moderate withdrawal symptoms, if they have no important coexisting conditions and have a support person willing to monitor their progress. However, patients with severe withdrawal symptoms, a history of complications, or co-existing medical or psychiatric disorders will require supervised in-patient treatment (Kosten & O'Connor, 2003).

During this stage, the client's mental status and vital signs, including temperature and pupils, should be checked frequently. Vital signs and other objective symptoms of withdrawal such as tremors are used to determine whether the client needs additional medication to control symptoms and maintain comfort. The client should be awakened, if necessary, to check for withdrawal symptoms. The nurse must remember that adequate medication can prevent life-threatening complications and that the detoxification process involves tapering and eventually discontinuing the drugs. This knowledge helps the nurse to avoid a power struggle with clients that can lead to withholding medication.

Table 14-2 Nursing Care During the Detoxification Stage of Treatment

- Check mental status and vital signs frequently
- Observe for withdrawal symptoms
- Administer adequate medication
- Maintain adequate nutrition and hydration
- Encourage behavioral interventions for insomnia
- Provide for the safety of clients with impaired judgment, ataxia, confusion, or suicidal ideation
- Anticipate memory deficits and keep instructions simple and repeat important information
- Develop a supportive relationship

During detoxification, nutrition, especially hydration, often requires supervision. The client's intake and output should be monitored closely during the initial days of the detoxification phase of treatment. Clients may benefit from nutritional supplements. The administration of thiamine prevents alcohol-related dementia. The twitching of muscles may indicate a need for magnesium, which is thought to exert a protective effect on the heart. During withdrawal and often for months afterward, clients may experience difficulty sleeping. Because benzodiazepines, and even nonbenzodiazepine hypnotics, can be addictive, behavioral interventions and other pharmacologic agents should be considered first. Behavioral interventions include maintaining a regular schedule for sleeping and waking, a relaxing bedtime routine before retiring, avoiding heavy meals, alcohol, nicotine or caffeine close to bedtime, and exercising regularly but not too close to bedtime. If these do not help, sedating antidepressants such as trazodone may be prescribed.

Nurses must provide for the safety of clients with impaired judgment, ataxia, confusion, or suicidal ideation. Memory deficits indicate the need for repetitive instructions and simple directions. Clients in this condition cannot be expected to remember scheduled times for meetings, meals, or medications. Failures to comply with requests must be understood as the result of the client's mental state and not a volitional act of defiance or control.

Nurse-Client Relationship

Developing a supportive relationship may be the only intervention available to treat some of the symptoms of intoxication and withdrawal. A positive relationship that has been established during the period of acute discomfort may be

Table 14-3 Enhancing Self-esteem Within the Nurse-Client Relationship

- Identify the client's strengths and accomplishments
- Validate the client's feelings and experiences
- Give positive feedback when indicated
- Set realistic goals and acknowledge progress
- Create opportunities for the client to contribute in groups or on the unit
- Maintain respectful communication style

instrumental in motivating the client to pursue long-term treatment and sobriety. Guilt-ridden, embarrassed, and experiencing low self-esteem, the client may be sensitive to even the slightest indication of rejection. Directing angry outbursts at the staff is one way clients attempt to extricate themselves from both the treatment setting and the uncertainty associated with giving up the substance to which they have become dependent.

The nurse must take any opportunity to improve the client's self-esteem (see **Table 14-3**). Learn the client's strengths and accomplishments, validate the discomfort the client is experiencing, give positive feedback when indicated, and create opportunities for the client to contribute to the unit or to assist another client. Most important, the nurse must have respect for the client as a person. This requires that the nurse examine his or her use of substances and also have a self-awareness of any personal prejudices regarding drug users and alcoholics.

Critical Thinking Question What personal experiences might influence your ability to work effectively with a substance-dependent client?

Treatment Plan

Within the context of the therapeutic relationship, the nurse learns about the client's personal history of alcohol and/or drug abuse. The circumstances surrounding his or her drug use and the effect of the addiction on the client's life are revealed. Past efforts at attaining sobriety are explored for information that can be helpful in the present. Therapy may include individual, group, and family work. Responsibility rests on the client not for the illness, but for participating in recovery. The nurse should reinforce the client's pursuit of treatment.

Clinical Example

Carrie, a 30-year-old nurse nearing completion of an in-patient detoxification from Valium and alcohol, had been working closely with one of the nurses to understand her substance dependence. One evening she became uncharacteristically hostile and argumentative with this nurse. Rather than respond defensively, or focus on the negative behavior, the nurse considered what feelings might be behind this behavior. The nurse knew that the client was struggling with a decision to transfer to an in-patient rehabilitation treatment center. Recognizing Carrie's anxiety regarding this huge step, the nurse praised her for the honesty and hard work she had exhibited up to this point in treatment. The compliment surprised Carrie, who became tearful. The nurse was thus able to change the interaction and help Carrie talk about her fear of failing in her efforts to become sober.

Motivational interviewing (Miller & Rollnick, 2002) offers specific strategies that have proven successful in helping persons with addictions recognize and accept the need for change. Also referred to as motivational enhancement therapy, this approach delivers interventions in a neutral and empathetic way, actively eliciting the client to identify the pros and cons of sobriety. This less defensive, more proactive approach is an alternative to the confrontational style of therapy traditionally used to shake the substance abuser's denial. Motivational therapy has six components summarized in the mnemonic FRAMES:

The nurse can be instrumental in motivating the client to accept treatment.

1. Feedback on personal impairment
2. Emphasis on personal Responsibility
3. Clear Advice to change
4. Menu of alternative options or choices
5. Empathy as a counseling style
6. Self-efficacy or removal of barriers to achieving goals

This intervention approach has been effective in reducing substance use among both older adults (Finfgeld-Connett, 2004) and adolescents (Simkin, 2002).

Cognitive-behavioral approaches have been used for clients who are interested in controlling but continuing their substance use. This non-abstinence approach remains controversial because it is not clear which clients actually benefit from it.

The usual treatment approach is total abstinence from all mind-altering drugs and the support of a **12-step program**, such as Alcoholics Anonymous (AA) or Narcotics Anonymous (NA). Related support groups are available to help family members deal with their feelings and correct the dysfunctional family interactions that have supported the addiction. These 12-step programs

AA has "open" meetings that non-alcoholics can attend. Anonymity should be respected at all times.

are supplemented with individual or group psychotherapy led by a professional acquainted with the dynamics of addiction and recovery.

Pharmacologic agents are also used to aid clients in attaining sobriety. The drug disulfiram (Antabuse) exerts an adverse effect when combined with alcohol. This deters the recovering alcoholic from drinking. The client must be careful not to use any product containing alcohol, such as cough syrup or colognes, while taking disulfiram (Antabuse). During a disulfiram (Antabuse) reaction, flushing, sweating, headache, chest pain, nausea, and vomiting occur. It should be used with caution in clients with a cardiac history. Naltrexone, a medication that blocks the effect of opiates and reduces the desire to drink, is a more recent addition to the treatment of alcoholism and opiate addictions. Methadone maintenance therapy in the form of daily doses is a long-standing treatment of opioid dependence. Buprenorphine has some similarities to both methadone and naltrexone, and is the newest medication for maintaining abstinence from opioids. Like methadone, buprenorphine is taken on a daily basis. The antidepressant bupropion (Wellbutrin, Zyban) has been shown to be effective in smoking cessation.

It is important that both the client and the nurse accept the fact that addiction is a chronic illness, and, therefore, the patient may experience a relapse. This should not be regarded as a failure. Rather, the nurse should help the client learn from the experience, make necessary changes in the treatment plan, and make a renewed commitment to recovery. Medication adherence and response rates have been found to be similar for drug dependence, type 2 diabetes mellitus, hypertension, and asthma (McLellan, Lewis, O'Brien, & Kleber, 2000). This finding supports the argument that substance abuse and substance depen-

CASE STUDY Mr. T.

Mr. T. is a 38-year-old divorced male, employed as a sergeant with the local sheriff's office. He is currently on disability for back and neck injuries sustained in an on-the-job auto accident 15 months earlier. He has been attending physical therapy twice a week. Mr. T. is brought to the hospital emergency room at 10 p.m. by a male friend, who is also a police officer, who went to Mr. T.'s home, at the request of his girlfriend, and found Mr. T. in a stuporous state, with slurred speech. He had told his girlfriend, in a phone conversation earlier in the day, that he had no reason to live. His girlfriend and his co-worker were concerned, given that Mr. T. had access to a gun.

In the emergency room, Mr. T. was cooperative. He was described as average height, overweight, appearing older than his age. A mental status exam noted he was alert but lethargic, with slurred, slowed speech. He was oriented to person and place, but unable to give the date, although he did know the month. He had difficulty with the cognitive task of serial subtraction, but had good memory, insight, and judgment, and was assessed to be of average intelligence. He described his mood as depressed and admitted passive suicidal ideation, but denied any plan. He denied homicidal ideation, and denied hallucinations or delusions. He admitted to frequent paranoia where he would think that groups of people on the street were talking about him.

On physical exam, Mr. T. was noted to have fine tremors of the hands and tongue, and slurred speech. His temperature was 98.8, blood pressure was 160/100, pulse 120, respirations 24. He reported using prescribed pain medication and benzodiazepines in daily doses that well exceeded the prescribed doses. This use had been a pattern for close to 1 year. What was new this day of admission was that the patient consumed nearly a quart of alcohol precipitated by the news from his physician that he was not cleared to return to work. Prior to that, he described his drinking as "occasional" until the past 3 months. At that time, he began drinking two to four drinks a day. This was in the context of keeping his girlfriend company at the bar where she had recently taken a job as bartender.

Mr. T. was divorced 4 years ago after 6 years of marriage. He shares custody of two sons, ages 9 and 7, with his ex-wife. Mr. T. takes the boys every other weekend, 2 weeks during the summer, and some major holidays. He lives alone and has been in a relationship with his girlfriend for 2 years. They met through a mutual friend. Three months ago, his girlfriend lost her job as a buyer at a major department store and took a job tending bar to supplement unemployment income. As noted, Mr. T. was injured a year ago in an auto accident while on duty with the sheriff's office and is on long-term disability. This leaves Mr. T. with much free time. He has two close friends from work and three male friends he has known since childhood who live in the area.

Mr. T.'s parents are both deceased. His mother died from complications of open-heart surgery when Mr. T. was 15 years old. His father, a retired fireman, died from cirrhosis of the liver at age 70.

dence ought to be covered by medical insurance, and diagnosed and treated the same as other chronic diseases. As with all chronic illnesses, relapses should be expected in clients with substance abuse disorders and is not a reflection of moral failure or character weakness.

Critical Thinking Question Does it affect your ability to care for a patient if you perceive the patient's illness to be the result of a lifestyle choice, such as drinking, intravenous drug use, unsafe sexual practices, smoking, or obesity?

Education for Clients and Family

Education is a large component of treatment. It is through education that the client can begin to understand the nature of addictions. Information must be kept simple, and the major points should be repeated to maximize learning in the presence of cognitive deficits.

Addiction is a chronic illness, and the causes are complex and not fully understood. The client is not responsible for the substance abuse or dependence, but is responsible for accepting treatment.

Clients and families need to learn about the specific actions and effects of the substances involved. They need to understand the concept of cross-tolerance for drugs in the same category. A person with a tolerance for alcohol will have a tolerance for all sedative-hypnotic drugs. Clients are advised to avoid all mood-altering drugs.

The best success has been with an abstinence model. Recovery often requires changes in the recovering person's lifestyle, including new friends and activities. Self-help groups, such as AA and NA, are excellent sources of support in this process and have a proven record of success in maintaining sobriety.

His father had a history of alcoholism and, at the time of his death, had been sober with the help of AA for 5 years. Mr. T. is the youngest of four children. His three older sisters are married and employed, with no known history of alcohol or drug abuse. His siblings and their families all live out of state, the closest being 2 hours away. They do not see each other often.

Mr. T.'s medical history is positive for gastroesophageal reflux disease (GERD), for which he takes Prevacid. He has no history of psychiatric treatment. Mr. T. first used alcohol and marijuana at age 16 with friends. He reports getting drunk the first time he drank alcohol and every time after, until he stopped drinking at age 21. He began inhaling cocaine at age 17 and continued, using 2–3 times a week, also until age 21. He stopped all alcohol and drug use at that time because he did not want to jeopardize his application for a job in law enforcement. About 10 years ago, he reports resuming alcohol on an occasional basis, mostly beer or whiskey, with dinner or with friends on the weekend, but "rarely" got drunk. As noted above, his drinking increased to 2–4 drinks a day over the past 3 months. He reports that this past year he started taking painkillers and sleeping medications after suffering back and neck injuries, and gradually began increasing the doses. At the time of admission, he was taking eight Vicodin tablets a day, rather than the three prescribed, and two 20-mg Valium tablets most nights to sleep. Mr. T. purposely saw two physicians, a physiatrist and an internist, so he would be able to get additional prescriptions. He was careful to fill the prescriptions at different pharmacies.

When in the emergency room, Mr. T. told the nurse practitioner that he had taken two Vicodin tablets that morning before going to his doctor's appointment, which was at 10 a.m. From 11 a.m. to 4 p.m. he consumed the fifth of whiskey, and talked to his girlfriend sometime in the afternoon. He then passed out on the couch and woke when his friend came by a little before 10 p.m.

Mr. T. denied any negative consequences related to his escalated drug and alcohol use, but his friend reported that Mr. T. was stopped once last month for driving while impaired, but the officer had let him off without a ticket and drove him home. Mr. T. admits being concerned about his drug and alcohol use, but denied making any efforts to stop or reduce use of these substances. He had two positive responses on the CAGE assessment inventory: he admitted becoming annoyed when his girlfriend and one of his friends in the sheriff's office spoke to him about his use of pills and alcohol.

Based on history and physical assessment, a diagnosis of alcohol and sedative-hypnotic dependence with physiological withdrawal was made and Mr. T. was admitted to the hospital for detoxification. An initial nursing care plan was developed at that time.

A week later, when Mr. T. moved to an out-patient substance abuse program, another nursing care plan was developed to reflect revised goals and outcomes.

NURSING CARE PLAN Substance Withdrawal

Expected Outcomes	Interventions	Evaluations
• Will not exhibit withdrawal complications and will have minimal discomfort. • Will be safe. • Will accept ongoing treatment for substance dependence.	• Frequent assessment by observation and evaluation of vital signs and temperature; administer medication as prescribed and PRN; ensure adequate fluids and nutrition; reassure that discomfort is temporary. • Observation; on-going mood evaluation for suicidal ideation and plans; encourage verbalization of feelings; remove sharp and dangerous objects. • Motivational therapy to increase responsibility and active involvement in recognizing and accepting treatment options; education on cross-tolerance of benzodiazepines, pain medications, and alcohol	• Able to taper and discontinue medications over several days; no further signs of withdrawal. • Absence of suicidal ideation. • Client makes appointment for out-patient substance abuse treatment and agrees to attend AA meetings.

Visit http://nursing.jbpub.com/psychiatric for additional care plans and exercises.

NURSING CARE PLAN Substance Dependence

Expected Outcomes	Interventions	Evaluations
• Will achieve abstinence. • Will learn new coping skills. • Will experience improved mood and self-esteem.	• Supportive individual and group therapy; identify antecedents to alcohol/drug use; AA; avoids bars; pharmacologic support with Antabuse. • Meditation and relaxation training for stress and back pain; encourage swimming for exercise and pain management; learn skills related to antecedents to alcohol/drug use (anger management, boredom, insomnia). • Help client to find meaningful activity as a substitute for work (explore creative outlets, volunteer work); on-going mental status evaluations; antidepressant medications if indicated.	• Attends out-patient sessions; gets a sponsor in AA; expresses satisfaction with life. • No longer takes pain or sleep medications; uses natural approaches to reduce insomnia. • Absence of depressive symptoms; engages in pleasurable activities.

Visit http://nursing.jbpub.com/psychiatric for additional care plans and exercises.

New coping skills, such as social skills, assertive communication, and relaxation techniques, can be taught to assist the recovering person to deal with stress and anger, ask for help, set limits, and express feelings appropriately. Often the client will have relied on drugs or alcohol to cope with these feelings or situations.

Clients need to learn to take care of themselves by getting adequate nutrition, sleep, and recreation. The importance of a balanced lifestyle as a defense against relapse needs to be understood.

Positive self-esteem is critical to staying sober, and clients should be advised to avoid people and situations that leave them feeling bad about themselves. Family members and significant others need to relate to the recovering person in a way that reinforces strengths and self-esteem. It is important that goals be realistic in order to maximize successful experiences.

Relationships and roles change when someone becomes sober. Frequently family members and significant others may not have been aware of how their behaviors actually supported or enabled the drinking or drug use, creating a **codependence**. The client, family members, and significant others need to be prepared to learn new roles and ways of relating. This can be a very difficult process for all involved, and families and

Implications for Evidence-Based Practice

Recent research points to changes in how substance abuse is viewed by the medical community and the legal system. Some recent studies are referenced here with a brief explanation of how the findings can be expected to have positive implications for the treatment of persons with substance abuse disorders.

Although there is evidence that drug dependence produces significant and lasting changes in brain chemistry and function, there continues to be resistance to viewing addictions as a chronic medical illness. An example of this is the different application of health insurance benefits for drug dependence compared to other medical illnesses. A literature review comparing drug dependence to type 2 diabetes, hypertension, and asthma showed similarities in the etiology, medication adherence, and relapse rates among these chronic disorders (McLellan et al., 2000). These findings support the argument that drug dependence should be insured, treated, and evaluated like other chronic illnesses.

Drug courts and diversion programs are beginning to treat first-time offenders and their families rather than taking a punitive approach (Simkin, 2002). Motivational interviewing provides an effective method for assessment and intervention that can be used by primary care physicians and nurse practitioners caring for persons with suspected substance abuse. The empathic approach is comfortable for most clinicians and allows the client to be less defensive and more proactive. The assessment of drug dependence in the primary-care setting will become increasingly important as the "baby boomer" generation ages. Research strongly supports positive outcomes of case finding, referral, and treatment of older adults who are abusing alcohol (Finfgeld-Connett, 2004; Stevenson, 2005).

The major changes in the treatment of substance-related disorders will come from advances in neuroscience and pharmacology. Addiction vaccines are in the development and testing stages. These vaccines would produce antibodies to specific drugs, preventing them from entering the bloodstream, making it nearly impossible for the drugs to produce a high. Pharmacological treatments are being targeted to the subtype of addiction, with most of the research focused on the use of different serotonin-modulating drugs in the treatment of clients with early and late-onset alcoholism (Johnson, 2003; Johnson et al., 2000). Acamprosate (Campral), a synthetic compound that stabilizes the glutamate system and reduces the pleasurable effects of alcohol as well as the craving, has become standard treatment for alcohol relapse prevention in many countries and is currently under consideration by the Food and Drug Administration.

A best practices approach for addictions has been developed for the Asian American community (Naegle, Ng, Barron, & Lai, 2002). Given our culturally diverse society, it is likely that specialized treatment approaches will be identified for other ethnic populations.

significant others can benefit from existing support groups, such as Al-Anon and Alateen.

In cases where the substance dependence or abuse is ongoing, the family and significant others need education on how to assist the client. Providing a nonjudgmental, factual description of the behavior is most effective (e.g., "You didn't come by to take the children to the baseball game last night."). Family members and significant others need to be cautioned against making excuses that cover up for the substance-abusing or dependent person. This behavior protects the abuser from facing the consequences of the illness.

Health teaching is an important component of nursing care for clients with addictions. In particular, the nurse can educate the client about hepatitis, sexually transmitted diseases, and HIV, with a focus on prevention. Because of impaired judgment, clients with substance abuse disorders may place themselves at risk for these illnesses.

Summary

Substance-use disorders include dependence and substance abuse. A person who is abusing a substance continues to use it despite serious problems that are clearly related to that use.

Withdrawal symptoms indicate a physical dependence on the substance. Substances that can be abused fall into many drug classifications, and symptoms of intoxication and withdrawal vary by classification. Withdrawal from alcohol can be life-threatening. Treatment includes managing the concomitant physical and psychiatric disorders, detoxifying the client if indicated, and establishing a therapeutic relationship to support the client in the decision to seek help for his or her addiction. With the assistance of a 12-step program, sobriety is the ultimate goal. The nurse can play a critical role in motivating the client to pursue treatment.

Annotated References

Allen, K. M. (1996). *Nursing care of the addicted client.* Philadelphia: J. B. Lippincott.

This is a comprehensive textbook and clinical resource for healthcare professionals at all levels of expertise in the area of addiction. It provides in-depth examination of addiction recognition and treatment in the clinical specialties of maternal-child health and psychiatry. It has chapters devoted to attrition, cultural competence, intimate behavior, legal issues, ethical issues, and research.

American Nurses Association. (2004). *Scope and standards of addictions nursing practice.* Washington, DC: Author.

This document establishes a scope of practice and standards of professional performance for the nurse specializing in addiction nursing.

American Psychiatric Association. (2000). *Diagnostic and statistical manual of mental disorders* (4th ed., text rev.). Washington, DC: Author.

This is the American Psychiatric Association's official nomenclature of psychiatric conditions and disorders. It provides a systematic listing of the official codes and categories, a description of the multiaxial system for diagnosis, and diagnostic criteria for each of the disorders. It is used by psychiatrists, physicians, psychologists, registered nurses, social workers, therapists, and other mental health workers in all clinical settings.

Deglin, J. H., & Vallerand, A. H. (2006). *Davis's drug guide for nurses* (10th ed.). Philadelphia: F. A. Davis.

Coauthored by a nurse and a pharmacist, this book is an excellent resource for medication information such as use, interactions, side effects, and client education needs.

Finfgeld-Connett, D. L. (2004). Treatment of substance misuse in older women: Using a brief intervention model. *Journal of Gerontological Nursing, 30*(8), 30–37.

Discusses the barriers to diagnosing and treating alcohol and benzodiazepine misuse among older women, and recommends brief interventions for use with this population.

Galanter, M., & Kleber, H. D. (2004). *Textbook of substance abuse treatment* (3rd ed.). Washington, DC: American Psychiatric Press.

This comprehensive text identifies treatment issues specific to each classification of drugs. It addresses individual, group, and family therapy and special programs including in-patient and adolescent programs, employee assistance programs, community-based treatment, and therapeutic communities.

Johnson, B. A. (2003). The role of serotonergic agents as treatments for alcoholism. *Drugs Today, 39*(9), 665–672.

This review summarizes studies on the use of selective serotonin reuptake inhibitors and serotonin antagonists in the treatment of subtypes of alcoholism.

Johnson, B.A., Roache, J. D., Javors, M. A., DiClemente, C. C., Clononger, C. R., Prihoda, T. J., et al. (2000). Ondansetron for reduction of drinking among biologically predisposed alcoholic patients: A randomized controlled trial. *Journal of the American Medical Association, 284*(8), 1016–1017.

In a randomized controlled study, ondansetron, a selective serotonin antagonist, was found to be an effective treatment for patients with early-onset alcoholism.

Kosten, T. R., & O'Connor, P. G. (2003). Management of drug and alcohol withdrawal. *The New England Journal of Medicine, 348*(18), 1786–1795.

A review article presenting current concepts for the treatment of withdrawal from alcohol, benzodiazepines, opioids, and stimulants.

Mayfield, D. G., McCleod, G., & Hall, D. (1974). The C.A.G.E. questionnaire. *American Journal of Psychiatry, 131,* 1121–1123.

This article introduces a brief tool to assess alcohol abuse.

McLellan, A. T., Lewis, D. C., O'Brien, C. P., & Kleber, H. D. (2000). Drug dependence, a chronic medical illness: Implications for treatment, insurance, and outcomes evaluation. *Journal of the American Medical Association, 284*(13), 1689–1695.

A literature review comparing the diagnoses, etiology, pathophysiology, and response to treatments of drug dependence vs type 2 diabetes mellitus, hypertension, and asthma.

Miller, W. R., & Rollnick, S. (2002). *Motivational interviewing, preparing people for change* (2nd ed.). New York: Guilford Press.

This work reviews the conceptual and research background supporting motivational interviewing, outlines specific strategies for building motivation and overcoming ambivalence to change, and provides clinical examples.

Naegle, M. A., Ng, A., Barron, C., & Lai, T. M. (2002). Best practice, topics in review, alcohol and substance abuse. *Western Journal of Medicine, 176*, 259–263.

Presents a culturally appropriate model for the treatment of alcohol and substance abuse in the Asian population.

National Institute of Alcohol Abuse and Alcoholism (2004). NIAA council approves definition of binge drinking. *NIAAA Newsletter, 3*, 3.

This article describes the NIAAA National Advisory Council's approved statement on the definition of binge drinking.

Perkinson, R. R. (2001). *Chemical dependency counseling: A practical guide* (2nd ed.). Thousand Oaks, CA: Sage.

This must-have book presents the dynamics of addiction and the essential clinical processes in assessing and treating the illness. It emphasizes the establishment of a therapeutic alliance and contains sections on adolescent and family issues. The appendix includes assessment tools and worksheets for relapse prevention and anger management. Chapter 8 presents a patient education series on such topics as the disease, defense mechanisms, addiction and recovery, and feelings.

Simkin, D. R. (2002). Adolescent substance use disorders and comorbidity. *Pediatric Clinics of North America, 49*(2), 463–477.

Discusses the importance of identifying risk factors associated with specific developmental stages, so that interventions can be made to reduce risk for future substance use disorders. Stresses the importance of primary care physicians using instruments to assess for mental disorders in children and adolescents.

Stevenson, J. S. (2005). Alcohol use, misuse, abuse, and dependence in later adulthood. *Annual Review of Nursing Research, 23*, 245–280.

This article provides a review of the considerable research on alcohol problems in older adults.

Additional Resources

AA World Services. (1975). *Living sober.* New York: Author.

This book provides strategies to help maintain sobriety. It is prepared by Alcoholics Anonymous, but is applicable to other substance addictions. The text addresses practical concerns such as dealing with drinking friends and situations, managing loneliness and insomnia, and keeping liquor in the house.

AA World Services. (1978). *Twelve steps and twelve traditions.* New York: Author.

This text explains the 12-step program of Alcoholics Anonymous.

Botelko, R. J., & Skinner, H. (1995). Motivating change in health behavior: Implications for health promotion and disease prevention. *Primary Care, 22*(4), 565–589.

The authors present a generic approach for helping practitioners motivate patients to change, introduce the principles of motivational interviewing as a way to help people recognize and do something about their problems, and make a distinction between traditional advice-giving and patient-centered advice-giving. A practical and thought-provoking guide to working with client resistance.

Elder, P. R. (1996). *Conducting group therapy with addicts: A handbook for professionals* (2nd ed.). New York: Sulzburger & Graham.

This book addresses students and mental health professionals. It discusses the nature of addiction and the benefits of group therapy in addressing the addict's denial and in achieving recovery. The book offers practical strategies to address common problems encountered in groups.

Estes, N. J., & Heinemann, M. E. (1986). *Alcoholism: Development, consequences, and interventions.* (3rd ed.). St. Louis: Mosby.

Contributors to this book represent a variety of disciplines. They address a broad spectrum of topics, including in-depth discussions of complex issues related to the treatment of alcoholism.

Moyers, W. (1998, March 29–31). *Moyers on addiction: Close to home* [Television series]. Public Broadcasting Service.

This three-part, 5 1/2-hour video is an interesting, informative, and moving overview of addiction: personal experiences, treatment issues, neurobiology, and policy concerns. It makes a case for replacing the military metaphor "war on drugs" with one compatible with the medical model for addiction.

Internet Resources

http://nursing.jbpub.com/psychiatric

Visit http://nursing.jbpub.com/psychiatric for interactive exercises, NCLEX review questions, WebLinks, and more.

CHAPTER 15

Schizophrenia and Other Psychotic Disorders

Winifred Z. Kennedy and Claudia Mitzeliotis

LEARNING OBJECTIVES

After reading this chapter, you will be able to:

- Differentiate among schizophrenia, schizophreniform disorder, schizoaffective disorder, delusional disorder, brief psychotic and shared psychotic disorders, psychotic disorder due to a general medical condition, and substance-induced psychotic disorder.
- Identify positive and negative symptoms of schizophrenia.
- Discuss the clinical course and complications of schizophrenia.
- Develop a nursing care plan for management of a client with hallucinations, delusions, and communication problems.

KEY TERMS

Affective flattening
Alogia
Anhedonia
Avolition
Catalepsy
Catatonia
Delusion
Echolalia
Epraxia
Hallucination
Negative symptoms
Neuroleptic malignant syndrome
Oculogyric crisis
Opisthotonus
Polydipsia
Positive symptoms
Psychosis
Tardive dyskinesia
Thought disorder

http://nursing.jbpub.com/psychiatric

Visit http://nursing.jbpub.com/psychiatric for interactive exercises, NCLEX review questions, WebLinks, and more.

Introduction

Schizophrenia is a psychiatric disorder characterized by significant disorganization of thinking manifested by problems with communication and cognition; impaired perceptions of reality manifested by hallucinations and delusions; and sometimes in significant decreases in functioning. Symptoms are usually first seen in adolescence or young adulthood and are often chronic and persistent.

In describing her experiences with a psychotic disorder, a young woman wrote,

> Schizophrenia is not just an illness, it is a way of life, and it is a life constantly disrupted by symptoms. I have dealt with a totally delusional world in which I was God—The Creator and The Sufferer—and the trees held magical power, while a great wall and glass dome cut me off from the rest of humanity. More recently, I have gone through excruciating periods of thought-interference and feelings that I did not exist, experiencing my body as a machine that I could see and feel

> but which I could not perceive as being in the world. The most frightening part for me is how quickly I can be taken by force and projected into another "state" in which all my perceptions are altered, and the world becomes a bizarre place. Sometimes there is confusion about which is the true reality—the objective world or the psychotic world. (Anonymous, 1986, C3)

General Description

Descriptions of schizophrenia and other psychotic disorders have been recorded throughout human history and across cultures. Bark (1988) noted descriptions of persecutory delusions and auditory hallucinations in the second millennium B.C., Mesopotamian–Old Babylonian period, and Indian Ayurvedic writings from 600 B.C. that describe "endogenous insanity," impaired intellect, incoherent speech, "noises in the ears," and "feeling of voidness in the head" that are remarkably similar to contemporary writings. Kin (1996) notes that descriptions and occurrences of bizarre behaviors are similar across Western and non-Western cultures.

In the late-nineteenth and early twentieth centuries, Kraepelin used the term *dementia praecox* to emphasize that symptoms began at an early age and were chronic and debilitating. Eugene Bleuler used the term *schizophrenia* to describe the "split mindedness" or the separations between affect, cognition, and emotions. At one time, clinicians utilized Bleuler's "4 A's"—associative looseness (difficulties in understanding client's verbiage), apathy (avolition), autistic thinking (self-inferential rather than objective), and ambivalence (inability to make decisions)—as the fundamental symptoms of schizophrenia. **Delusions** and **hallucinations** were considered accessory symptoms. Schneider later theorized first-rank symptoms (control of behavior through auditory hallucinations, thoughts spoken aloud, thought control, thought broadcasting, experiences of influence and control) and second-rank symptoms (other hallucinations, affectual blunting, mood disorders, perplexity; Black & Andreasen, 1999). Contemporary descriptions of the disorder consider clusters of positive, negative, cognitive, and mood symptoms. The **negative symptoms** of **affective flattening**, **anhedonia** (loss of feeling pleasure), **avolition**, and attentional impairment and the **positive symptoms** of hallucinations, delusions, and **thought disorder** are similar to classic descriptions of schizophrenia.

> Psychotic disorders are characterized by distortions of reality, speech, thought, behavior, and affect.

> The main diagnostic features of *schizophrenia* are the length of illness presentation—greater than 6 months—and the presence of psychotic symptoms and impaired functioning.

Psychosis describes significant impairment in functioning, ego boundaries, and reality testing. Impairments in affect, behavior, communication, cognition, perception, and social functioning may be present. Insight, judgment, and impulse control may be impaired. Psychotic symptoms can be present in many different psychiatric disorders including cognitive and mood disorders and schizophrenia.

The Diagnostic and Statistical Manual of Mental Disorders, Fourth Edition, Text Revision (*DSM-IV-TR*) identifies schizophrenia, schizophreniform disorder, schizoaffective disorder, delusional disorder, brief psychotic disorder, shared psychotic disorder, psychotic disorder due to a general medical condition, and substance-induced psychotic disorders as psychiatric disorders that manifest psychotic features of delusions, hallucinations, and disorganized speech and behavior singly or in combination (American Psychiatric Association [APA], 2000). Hallucinations are false sensory perceptions that exist without objective sensory stimuli. Thought disorders describe cognitive symptoms that may be demonstrated by problems in forming or organizing thoughts or communicating with others. Disorganized behaviors may be demonstrated by isolated, withdrawn, regressed, uncontrolled, or inappropriate, bizarre activity.

The *DSM-IV-TR* identifies delusional disorder, shared delusional disorder, brief psychotic disorder, psychotic disorder due to a general medical condition, and substance-induced psychotic disorder as disorders in which the client exhibits some prominent psychotic features but does not meet the criteria for schizophrenia, schizophreniform, or schizoaffective disorders because of the types of symptoms present or the duration of the symptoms. Delusional disorder and brief psychotic disorder do not generally result from a medical condition or substance abuse (APA, 2000).

Schizophrenia

The main criterion for schizophrenia is that the client has characteristic psychotic symptoms, more or less continuously, for at least 6 months, not related to medical condition or substance use, and serious enough to impair social and occupational functioning. The main subtypes of schizophrenia are paranoid, disorganized, catatonic, undifferentiated, and residual. Schizophrenia may be further specified as single episode, episodic, continuous, in full or partial remission, with prominent negative symptoms, or with another or unspecified pattern of symptoms or course.

Schizophreniform Disorder

The main criterion for schizophreniform disorder is that the symptoms of the psychotic disorder have been present for at least 1 month but less than 6 months. This differs from the diagnostic criteria for schizophrenia in that significant impairment in functioning is not required for diagnosis. Within the 6-month period when symptoms first appear, the diagnosis is considered provisional; if symptoms persist beyond the 6-month period, schizophrenia would be diagnosed. Generally, positive prognostic features for schizophreniform disorder are the presence of good premorbid functioning and the absence of impaired affect.

Schizoaffective Disorder

In schizoaffective disorder, there is the continuous diagnostic criteria for schizophrenia with at least 1 concurrent period when the client meets the diagnostic criteria for a major depressive or manic disorder. Psychotic features of delusions and hallucinations are present for at least 2 weeks when mood symptoms are not prominent. The main subtypes of schizoaffective disorder are bipolar type (major depressive, manic, or mixed episode symptoms are present) or depressive type (only symptoms of major depressive episodes are present).

Delusional Disorder

In a delusional disorder, the client focuses on the presence of a delusion (delusions are false beliefs that exist without objective evidence), and the criteria for schizophrenia are not met. Hallucinations, mood symptoms, or behavior problems, if present, can be explained by the delusion; other areas of functioning are not impaired. Delusional disorders can be further specified, based on the predominant theme of the delusion, as erotomanic, grandiose, jealous, persecutory, somatic, mixed, or unspecified.

Brief Psychotic and Shared Psychotic Disorders

A brief psychotic disorder is one in which the psychotic symptoms (delusions, hallucinations, disorganized speech or behaviors) are present for at least 1 day but less than 1 month. The disturbance may be related to specific stressors that would be disturbing to anyone with a similar cultural background. Symptoms are not related to a mood disorder, medical illness, or substance abuse and do not meet the criteria for schizophrenia or schizoaffective disorder. The diagnosis may be specified with or without marked stressors or with onset within 4 weeks postpartum. In shared psychotic disorder, the client has a close relationship, usually dependent, with someone who has a delusional disorder.

In *schizophreniform disorder*, symptoms are present less than 6 months.

Psychotic Disorder Due to a General Medical Condition

This disorder is associated with a medical illness in which hallucinations or delusions are present at times other than when the client is delirious. The disorder is further specified as to whether the predominant symptoms are delusions or hallucinations. The associated general medical condition is indicated on Axis I (e.g., psychotic disorder due to Huntington's disease), and the medical condition, Huntington's disease, along with the American Medical Association's (AMA) *International Classification of Diseases* (*ICD-9-CM*) code, is noted on Axis III (AMA, 2006).

The main diagnostic feature of *schizoaffective disorder* is symptoms of schizophrenia and an affective or mood disorder.

Shared psychotic disorder is relatively rare. The diagnostic criteria are broader than for historical descriptions of *folie à deux*, a shared delusional disorder.

Substance-Induced Psychotic Disorder

In a substance-induced psychotic disorder, delusions or hallucinations are the direct result of substance abuse, medications, or toxins and are present only when the client is delirious. Symptoms exceed what might normally be expected during periods of intoxication or withdrawal. The drug of abuse and the predominant symptom, delusions or hallucinations, are specified. Drugs of abuse commonly associated with psychotic disorders are alcohol, amphetamines, anxiolytics, cannabis, hallucinogens, hypnotics, inhalants, opioids, phencyclidine, and sedatives.

Incidence and Prevalence

The World Health Organization (WHO) estimates incidence rates for schizophrenia of 13.37 per 100,000 men and 12.94 per 100,000 women. The highest rate occurs in the group 20 to 64 years of age. The overall prevalence rate for men and women is 0.4% (Ustun & Sartorius, 2001). The estimated lifetime prevalence rate is 0.05% to 1% (APA, 2000). Schizophrenia is the most common disorder with psychotic symptoms and ranks in the top 10 for disease burden. The average life span of a patient with schizophrenia is reduced by 10 years (Lopez, Mathers, Ezzati, & Murray, 2006).

Progressive decline in functioning, particularly in economic potential ("downward drift"), occurs in most clients diagnosed with schizophrenia (APA, 2000). Clients with schizophrenia account for approximately 40% of in-patient admissions (Fox & Kane, 1996). It is estimated that approximately 25–50% of clients with schizophrenia may attempt suicide and from 4–13% will die from a suicide attempt (Meltzer, 2001).

Etiology

The complex syndrome of symptoms in schizophrenia has prompted a broad range of theories regarding its etiology. More than one area of the brain, one neurotransmitter, one gene, and one environmental factor appear to be involved. In addition, some structural abnormalities, endocrine and viral disorders, as well as hallucinogenic drugs or exposure to toxins have been known to simulate psychotic features similar to schizophrenia. Longitudinal phases of premorbid evolution (from conception to symptom development), psychotic decompensation, and long-term evolution (chronicity, residuals, remissions) were suggested by Ciompi as a biopsychosocial model emphasizing the interaction of genetic and environmental variables (Fox & Kane, 1996).

Most studies indicate a genetic link and familial pattern. The closer the degree of kinship to someone with schizophrenia, the greater the genetic risk for schizophrenia. The risk is greatest for monozygotic twins and decreases steadily for dizygotic twins, siblings, those with two affected parents, one parent, and cousins. Certain ethnic groups such as the Irish in Ireland, southwestern Croatians, Scandinavians in the United States, and West Indians in England show consistently higher rates (Kin, 1996), which is consistent with studies that indicate immigrants and migrating populations have a greater risk of schizophrenia than native populations. Other cross-cultural and environmental variables such as obstetrical complications, number of winter births, possible exposure to viruses, and neurodevelopmental disorders have to be considered as possibly responsible for increased rates in certain groups (Eagles, 1991). Research suggests that genes, brain development (particularly areas involved in language processing and cognitive functioning), timing of development, and environmental stressors are involved (Fox & Kane, 1996).

> No single etiologic factor has been found for schizophrenia. A genetic variant has been hypothesized, but no specific genotype has been identified. A "two-hit" hypothesis, a combination of genetic and environmental problems leading to neurologic problems, has been suggested (Fox & Kane, 1996).

The *neurodevelopment hypothesis* in the development of schizophrenia is based upon the observation of schizophrenia in infants exposed to viral infections in the second trimester as well as neurologic soft signs found in evaluating patients with schizophrenia. Developmental, neurostructural, biochemical, and environmental factors influence an individual's ability to process information. Problems in focusing attention, assessing stimuli, and assigning affectual meaning to experiences impair cognition and the ability to interact successfully with the environment. Neurostructural and biochemical factors influence how the individual experiences and perceives the world. As the individual develops and interactions become increasingly complex, the problems in processing information increase because development has been inadequate to meet demands or develop a repertoire necessary to meet new challenges. Impairments in information processing continue as the inability to modulate biologic and psychosocial stressors. Deficiencies in automaticity, the ability to re-create and retrieve past experiences to deal with a present situation, further impair the client's ability to deal with new situations (Fox & Kane, 1996).

Reduced frontal lobe activity in schizophrenics is thought to be associated with reductions in glutamatergic activity and with negative symptoms and cognitive deficits. Increased mesolimbic dopamine activity is hypothesized to be related to schizophrenia. The *dopamine hypothesis* for the development of schizophrenia is associated with the dopamine-blocking properties of antipsychotic medications and their effects on various neurotransmitter systems.

Research into the family's role in schizophrenia involves differentiation in families using a construct of *expressed emotion (EE)*. High EE families are seen as being critical and overinvolved. Schizophrenic clients living in households with high EE have a higher rate of relapse. Further research suggests that there are higher levels of arousal in schizophrenic clients living in high EE households. Social skills training and education for both the family and the client help reduce the levels of arousal and rate of relapse (Fox & Kane, 1996; Leff, 1994).

Psychologic theories hypothesize that a deficit in ego development and functioning leads to a failure of the ego to interpret reality correctly or to modulate id drives. Impaired functioning leads to ego decompensation and a return to more primitive functioning. Problems functioning and relating to others create anxiety. Ineffective coping causes further anxiety and impairment in functioning. Regression helps defend against anxiety but impairs the ego's ability to determine reality. The development of psychotic symptoms signals the individual's inability to differentiate between thoughts and reality; that is, subjective experience is misinterpreted as objective experience. Hallucinations and delusions are the ego's attempt to deal with the anxiety, and the symptoms hold symbolic meaning for the individual.

Critical Thinking Question What are some concerns a family might have regarding a relative's new diagnosis of schizophrenia? Discuss some strategies that could be used to help the family deal with this diagnosis.

Physiology

Neurobiologic theories of schizophrenia are discussed in Chapter 4. Schizophrenia has been defined as a neurodevelopmental disorder in which parts of the brain have not developed properly or function inadequately. The severity of the symptoms depends upon the extent of structural abnormalities and biochemical functioning. The vast diversity of symptoms indicates that more than one area of the brain is involved. Some clients show "soft" signs of neurologic problems; that is, the presence of primitive reflexes; grimacing; grunting; snuffling; mirroring; mild choreiform and tic-like movements; impaired motor skills, tone, or both; and coordination problems. Neurologic deficits may include impairments in attention, problem solving, memory, and comprehension. Some clients experience problems in concept formation and overall intellectual functioning. Research suggests that clients with schizophrenia are likely to have structural neuropathy. Computerized axial tomography (CAT scan), magnetic resonance imaging (MRI), and phototron emission studies have identified variations in structures that may influence functioning. Structural problems in the frontal cortex may influence negative symptoms, and structural problems in the limbic system may influence positive symptoms. Decreased brain volume and thalamic size, increased ventricular size, and prominent cortical sulci have been identified with schizophrenia. Enlarged ventricles suggest problems in development or loss of brain tissue. Reduced tissue mass has been found in the amygdala, hippocampus, parahippocampus, substantia nigra, internal globus pallidus, and frontal areas of the brain in clients with schizophrenia. Studies of the epidemiology of schizophrenia emphasize the interaction between infectious agents and genetic predisposition. Some of the diseases that have been implicated are influenza, rubella, polio, herpes simplex, cytomegalovirus, and toxoplasmosis (Yolken & Torrey, 2006).

Excess dopamine and defects in metabolism of serotonin may also be involved in schizophrenia. Problems in dopamine and other neurotransmitter pathways, or dysregulation, may cause abnormal transmission in the brain and influence the behaviors seen in schizophrenia. Based upon the actions of typical neuroleptics on D_2 dopamine receptor sites, hyperactivity of dopamine (a neurotransmitter associated with limbic and motor nuclei functioning) may be responsible for symptoms in schizophrenia. Studies of other neurotransmitters and receptor sites indicate that norepinephrine is increased or released in schizophrenia and gamma-aminobutyric acid (GABA) activity increases dopaminergic activity. Atypical neuroleptics affect D_3 and D_4 blockers of dopamine, and D_2 activity to a lesser degree, as well as affecting serotonin receptors. Hyperactivity of 5HT2, a serotonin receptor, may influence dopamine receptors and decrease monoamine oxidase (MAO). Serotonin is a neurotransmitter associated with calmness, pleasure, and the reduction of pain. Dysfunction of 5HT2 and hypersensitivity of postsynaptic receptors are associated with negative symptoms of schizophrenia.

Clinical Presentation

Clients with schizophrenia and related disorders may present with a mixture of signs and symptoms. Symptom presentation may have been chronic and progressive. Symptoms usually begin to appear when the client is young, usually in adolescence, and rarely after middle age. MRI studies of adolescents and young adults diagnosed with schizophrenia have shown the presence of gray matter brain changes at the time of

problematic symptoms and helping the client and the client's family deal with the illness, symptoms, and treatments. The various diagnoses may overlap, so treatment focuses on problematic symptoms. Chronic problems can be managed in partial hospitalization programs, continuing day treatment, rehabilitation programs, and ambulatory settings. Research indicates that a therapeutic relationship can influence improvement in the client's overall functioning (Frank & Gunderson, 1990; Hogarty, Greenwald, et al., 1997). Clients with serious, persistent mental illness may benefit from ongoing psychiatric case management and community support services.

Clients, family members, and others in the client's environment can be taught to identify symptoms and to recognize when intervention is needed. In addition, family support is often needed to assist or supervise the client in order to maintain involvement in self-care activities such as hygiene and health maintenance, social activities with the family or in the community, and adherence with medication regimes. Clients with schizophrenia, as with other chronic syndromes, are often susceptible to relapse if their medications are discontinued abruptly or without supervision. Stressful life events can be particularly difficult to navigate with a limited social network without family support. Family members can help facilitate the client's communication with members of the treatment team or act as healthcare proxy when the client is unable to communicate. Family involvement and willingness to participate in psychoeducation programs, opportunities for development of problem solving and communication techniques, and the need for support for family members should be included in assessment and treatment planning (Dixon, Adams, & Luksted, 2000).

Hospitalization may be necessary during an acute phase or when the client presents a danger to self or others. At the time of initial admission or during an acute phase, the client needs a complete medical and psychiatric workup. This helps diagnosis and treatment, particularly if the psychotic symptoms are related to a medical problem or to substance abuse. It is important that the nurse obtain a careful history, document any subjective complaints or objective findings, and assess the client's potential for self-harm and aggressive behaviors, particularly during the acute phase. Assessing and documenting the effects of pharmacotherapy assist the prescribing healthcare provider in deciding to change, increase, or decrease medications and facilitate client compliance with a more successful treatment regime. Family and friends can help validate the client's experiences or identify stressors or problems. They can often provide vital information on how the client usually deals with stress or conflicts and what is helpful for the client to maintain control.

In an in-patient unit, the nurse is responsible for maintaining a therapeutic milieu and identifying when the environment or social interactions

Considerations for Client and Family Education

- Assist client and family in identifying possible stressors and signs of decompensation.
- Identify client strengths and appropriate strategies for managing symptoms.
- Provide information regarding medications and possible side effects.
- Reinforce the need for ongoing support in dealing with a chronic illness.

Implications for Evidence-Based Practice

VanMeijel, van der Gaag, Kahn, & Grypdonck (2003) described a randomized trial of an interventional protocol based on review of the literature and consensus guidelines that utilized nurses and the clients' social network to prevent rehospitalization. Clients with chronic schizophrenia and delusional disorders were monitored on a regular basis for signs of decompensation. An action plan was instituted that provided 24-hour availability of professional assistance, medication, and stress reduction techniques. It was felt that the program was successful in providing psychoeducation for the client and the social network and in preventing rehospitalization. Further research is needed to monitor the interventional trajectory and determine the application within nursing practice.

Implications for Evidence-Based Practice

Dearing (2004) identified aspects of the nurse-patient relationship that influence compliance including establishing rapport, exploring skill development, setting and achieving goals, planning strategies and instilling hope, and approving and reinforcing changes. By providing validation for the nursing process and nurse-patient relationship, this study shows it is an important factor in improving treatment compliance. Further study is needed regarding the effects of the nursing assessment and therapeutic relationship and their impact on healthcare delivery and outcomes.

become over-stimulating or over-demanding. Limit setting may be necessary if the client's behaviors become disruptive, provocative, or threatening to others. Eventually the clients are helped to identify potential stressors and to modify their reactions to stressful situations.

Managing the Client with Hallucinations

The nurse must observe for signs that the client may be responding to the internal stimuli of hallucinations. Is the client talking to him- or herself or laughing? Does the client appear preoccupied during social interactions and unable to attend to the demands of the external environment? The nurse should investigate the underlying experience of the hallucination and help the client verbalize his or her anxiety. Early intervention is important to prevent aggressive outbursts or harm to self or others that may be the response to command hallucinations. The clinician should avoid touching the client and allow sufficient personal space and distance so that the client does not misinterpret the clinician's approach; the client may be paranoid and extremely sensitive to perceived threats and environmental stimuli.

The nurse must express acceptance and remain nonjudgmental. This allows the client to establish trust and to share the experience of the hallucination. As the client begins to talk about what is internally experienced, the nurse can assess the possibility of danger and injury to self and others. It is important not to reinforce the hallucination, and the nurse should refer to the hallucination as "voices" rather than as "he," "she," or "they." For example, the nurse may say, "The voices seem real to you, but I do not hear the same voices" rather than "They told you to kill the president, but they are wrong." The nurse should reassure the client that, although the voices are frightening, they are not real. The client may begin to realize that the voices are not real and begin to identify the experience of the hallucination and distinguish it from reality. The nurse should try to distract the client from the hallucination by involving him or her in interpersonal activities and by using clear directives and explanations.

Many clients experience hallucinations when they are anxious. Decreasing environmental stimuli and helping the client associate how and when hallucinations are experienced and controlled allows the client to develop mastery over the symptoms. The nurse should help clients identify those situations in which the experience of hallucinations is triggered (e.g., when they are under stress or withdrawn) and teach techniques that reduce the likelihood of experiencing a hallucination, such as getting involved in activities or social interactions.

Managing Clients with Communication Problems

Communication problems can affect the client's ability to engage in social activities or maintain occupational functioning. The nurse can help the client with some of these problems. Validation is one technique often used. Using this technique, the nurse can ask the client for feedback to determine if his or her inferences are correct. For example, "When you say (this), do you mean (that)?" The client may use language in an idiosyncratic or in a symbolic or metaphorical manner. The nurse can give feedback on the communication process. For example, the nurse may say "I do not understand what that means." This helps the client understand how he or she is being perceived and makes it clear that he or she is not understood. This technique helps the client to feel in control and encourages the client to help the nurse better understand what is being communicated.

Often, a client's disorganized or disruptive behavior is frightening. It is helpful to approach the client in a nonthreatening manner and explain how the behavior is perceived. The client may be unaware that the behavior is alienating others. It is important that the nurse convey empathy when helping the client manage problematic behaviors. Statements such as "That must be frightening," "That must have been confusing," or "Could there be another explanation?" demonstrate concern and encourage interaction and explanation.

Managing Clients with Delusions

When treating clients with delusions, the nurse must remember that the content of the delusion relates to an underlying anxiety or fear. Many clients experience the world as unsafe and distrust their own experiences and others. The nurse needs to reassure clients that they are in a safe place. Overwhelmed by anxiety, the client may develop a false belief to explain what is experienced or to cope with what he or she is feeling. These beliefs function as a defense mechanism to protect the client from painful unconscious or subconscious feelings. The outward expression is usually the opposite of the internal experience. For example, a client frightened by paranoid thoughts may be seen as angry and aggressive by others. If the delusion is the result of an organic problem, the client can be reassured that the cognitive problems are related to a medical condition, medication, or substance abuse and that the problems in the thinking process are temporary and caused by biochemical changes.

The content of a delusion relates to an underlying anxiety or fear.

The client's interactions with others or with the environment may be impaired because of the false beliefs. For example, if the client believes the food is poisoned, the nurse may have to arrange for food to be provided in individual, closed containers so that the client can maintain adequate nutrition. Careful observation may be necessary to determine if routines need to be changed or if the client is able to make valid, informed decisions regarding self-care activities.

It is not uncommon for the client to ask if the nurse believes what the client is saying. The nurse may respond by saying "I believe these beliefs seem real to you and explain how you see things." Arguing about the belief provokes anger or defensiveness, and putting forth logical or rational explanations is not helpful. Avoid competitive situations. If the dynamic of the delusion is understood, the nurse can attempt to validate the client's experience and provide reality-based explanations while focusing on the emotions identified with these thoughts. If the underlying feelings are identified and the level of anxiety surrounding the situation is reduced, the client may begin to focus less on the content of the delusion. Some clients find stress reduction and relaxation techniques helpful. Behavioral and cognitive interventions help the client refocus thoughts or practice thought-stopping or thought-switching techniques. Distraction can also help the client refocus on another experience and thoughts.

Psychoeducation and Psychotherapy

Psychoeducation and cognitive therapy have been helpful in assisting clients to gain mastery over problematic behaviors. Cognitive skills development begins in the in-patient unit and is continued during the various phases of out-patient rehabilitation, as tolerated by the client. Integrated psychologic therapy and social skills training (e.g., the Social and Independent Living Skills Series by the UCLA Clinical Research Center for Schizophrenia and Psychiatric Rehabilitation) have been identified as effective methods of helping clients deal with communication and social problems (Fox & Kane, 1996). In these structured programs, various exercises in social skills, role playing, problem solving, and task assignments are used to develop the practical skills clients need to facilitate independent functioning. Long-term follow-up indicates that skills in conversation and listening, medication, symptom management, and recreation can be generalized to other areas of psychosocial functioning. Social skills training includes opportunities for repetition, replication, and reinforcement of skills. Attention to information-processing deficits allows for learning to be facilitated (Liberman, Wallace, et al., 1998).

Research indicates that clients who participate in either psychoeducation or social skills training groups function better and that their relapse rates are greatly reduced (Hogarty, Anderson, et al., 1991).

Pharmacology

Pharmacotherapy plays a major role in treating and managing the symptoms of psychotic disorders. Medications have made a dramatic difference in the treatment of schizophrenia; they are particularly important in the acute phase. Because long-term use of some medications caused significant problems in the past, the client or the client's family may resist using medication to treat the disorder; however, the benefits of medications can outweigh any problems the client may experience in adhering to a medication regimen. The National Institute of Mental Health (NIMH)–funded longitudinal study CATIE (Clinical Antipsychotic Trials of Interventional Effectiveness) has provided information regarding drug efficacy, effectiveness, side effects, and discontinuation rates. Increased knowledge about drug dosage and side effects as well as new medications with decreased side effects have changed the ways in which medications are prescribed. Studies have also provided information regarding the high number of clients with symptoms of metabolic syndrome at baseline, indicating the need to emphasize the importance of monitoring clients for side effects. The high number of clients who discontinue medication (74%) highlights the importance of interventions to increase adherence to medication schedules (Lieberman et al., 2005).

Studies conducted as part of CUtLASS (Commentary on Cost Utility of the Latest Antipsychotic Drugs in Schizophrenia Study) suggest that the more recently developed atypical antipsychotic medications may be no more effective than the traditional antipsychotics in treatment of schizophrenia (Lieberman, 2006). Treatment needs to be individualized to recognize differences among clients who may be treatment resistant, susceptible to side effects, or have problems adhering to a particular medication regime, particularly with long-term use.

Client education and medication groups can reinforce adherence. Medication groups are task-oriented groups that provide peer support, educate clients regarding medication use and side effects, and identify benefits and possible problems with adherence to treatment plans. Medication management is a module of the Social and Independent Living Skills Series (Bellack, Mueser, Gingerich, & Agresta 2004; Liberman, Derisi, & Mueser 2001).

Medications

Two main groups of medications are used to treat these disorders, typical and atypical. Typical agents are the high-potency neuroleptics such as fluphenazine (Prolixin), haloperidol (Haldol), thiothixene (Navane), and trifluoperazine (Stelazine); moderate-potency neuroleptics such as molindone (Moban) and loxapine (Loxitane); and low-potency neuroleptics such as chlorpromazine (Thorazine) and thioridazine (Mellaril). These agents effectively block the dopamine reaction at the receptor site. The typical agents have been considered important in managing positive symptoms.

Atypical agents are the serotonergic-dopamine antagonists (SDAs). These agents, including risperidone (Risperdal), olanzapine (Zyprexa), quetiapine (Seroquel), and ziprasidone (Geodon), block specific serotonin and dopamine receptor sites. Because they are metabolized in the liver and excreted from the kidneys, careful monitoring of

> Pharmacotherapy is the foundation for treatment of problematic symptoms in schizophrenia. Oral antipsychotic medications or neuroleptics, depot medications, and atypical antipsychotic medications are used to control symptoms of psychosis. Mood stabilizers and antidepressants may be used for specific affective symptoms.

Implications for Evidence-Based Practice

Mahone (2004) studied medication decision making in clients with serious mental illness. Utilizing the Interaction Model of Client Health Behavior (IMCHB) that emphasizes nurse-client interaction, Mahone identified motivational enhancement, behavioral tailoring, and social skills training as nursing interventions that facilitate medication decision making and management. This study has implications for practice, client teaching, and nursing education. Suggested areas for further research include investigation of medication adherence themes, client empowerment, and interventions to address co-morbidities at different developmental levels.

liver and renal functioning is important. Clozapine (Clozaril) and quetiapine showed the lowest reports of extrapyramidal symptoms (EPS). Olanzapine (Zyprexa) is available in oral and injectable form, but treated patients showed more weight gain and glucose intolerance. Of all the atypical antipsychotics, clozapine is the most effective in treatment-resistant patients, but also is the most associated with side effects. Atypical agents are used to treat both positive and negative symptoms. Some research has indicated that olanzapine may help manage mood symptoms associated with psychotic disorders. Aripiprazole (Abilify) is an atypical antipsychotic medication, available as an injectable and as an oral medication, that is a dual dopamine autoreceptor agonist and postsynaptic D_2 receptor antagonist used to control agitation and psychotic symptoms in schizophrenia. Paliperidone (Invega), an atypical antipsychotic that delivers an active agent in risperidone, is available as an extended release tablet. Patients taking this medication, which passes slowly through the digestive tract, should be informed that they may see the capsules in their feces. An advantage to the extended release tablet is that it need only be taken once a day and may minimize side effects.

Clozapine is not considered a first-line treatment. It may lower seizure threshold and, because it may cause agranulocytosis, requires regular blood test monitoring. Dosage monitoring is required, particularly if treatment is stopped and restarted. Research indicates it can be effective for refractory treatment-resistant schizophrenia and is well tolerated in the sense that there is minimal association with EPS and akathisia. Risperidone, olanzapine, quetiapine, and haloperidol have also been used in treatment-resistant schizophrenia. Quetiapine has the advantage of not being associated with EPS or increases in prolactin secretion. Hyperprolactinemia is associated with menstrual disturbances and galactorrhea in women and sexual dysfunction and hypergonadism in men.

Review of current research indicates that atypical antipsychotic medications may be beneficial as first-line treatment because they are effective in the treatment of positive symptoms as well as negative symptoms and affective symptoms. Side effects are a large problem, particularly in long-term treatment and adherence to treatment regimes, and atypical antipsychotic medications are less associated with side effects. Atypical antipsychotic medication such as risperidone is available in a long-acting injection, making it a viable treatment alternative for patients requiring a depot medication. Aripiprazole has been found effective with positive and negative symptoms and mood disorders (Emsley & Oosthuizen, 2005).

Anticonvulsant medications such as carbamazepine (Tegretol), clonazepam (Klonopin), and valproic acid (Depakote, Depakene) sometimes are used to stabilize behavior and mood symptoms. Drug levels and possible drug interactions should be monitored.

Selection of a medication is based on its type, action, duration, potential side effects, and the client's past experiences and preferences. For example, typical high-potency neuroleptics such as haloperidol (Haldol) may be selected for agitated clients because intramuscular injections begin to work within 30 to 60 minutes, and small doses can be given at frequent intervals to allow for dosage monitoring and titration; low-potency medications may require 3 to 4 hours to take effect. Studies of injectable atypical antipsychotic medications show they are somewhat as effective as typical neuroleptics and that patients reported fewer side effects, particularly EPS. Ziprasidone (Geodon) is available in injection form and has been effective when used in situations when rapid tranquilization is required and EPS and prolactin levels are a concern. Some of these medications are available in depot (haloperidol, fluphenazine, risperadone [Risperdal]) or sustained action form, allowing the client to receive an injection every few weeks rather than daily parenteral doses. Extended release tablets such as paliperidone (Invega) allow for once a day dosing and are helpful in maintaining a steady state distribution of medication and minimizing side effects. These types are particularly useful with clients who have problems adhering to medication schedules.

Pharmacokinetics can be influenced by a client's gender, age, medical illness, use of tobacco, and drug interactions. Changes in drug clearance vary according to tobacco use; tobacco causes increased clearance rates and faster elimination rates. Levels of thiothixene (Navane), fluphenazine (Prolixin), haloperidol (Haldol), and olanzapine (Zyprexa) are influenced by tobacco use. Also, metabolism rates vary in the elderly, in different ethnic groups, and in clients who abuse alcohol (Ereshefsky, 1996). Studies indicate smoking and caffeine use are much higher among schizophrenics than the general population, and there is strong interdependence for chronic use of both by chronic schizophrenics. Smoking and caffeine can affect CYP1A2 metabolism of psychotropic medications such as clozapine and olanzapine, and blood levels of the drugs may be reduced (Strassnig, Brar, & Ganguli, 2006).

Side Effects

Common side effects associated with neuroleptic medications are anticholinergic effects; autonomic instability including orthostatic hypotension and temperature dysregulation; blood dyscrasias; drug-induced Parkinson's; extrapyramidal effects; movement disorders such as acute dystonias, akathisia, and **tardive dyskinesia**; **neuroleptic malignant syndrome**; photosensitivity; sedative effects; and interactions with other medications. Some side effects that are more common with typical antipsychotics include hyperprolactinemia, neuroleptic malignant syndrome, photosensitivity, QTc interval prolongation, temperature dysregulation, and weight gain. Other side effects such as abnormal glucose metabolism are more common with atypical antipsychotic medications. Agranulocystosis, myocarditis, seizures, and weight gain have been seen with clozapine.

Abnormal Glucose Metabolism

Abnormal glucose metabolism is a risk factor associated most commonly with atypical antipsychotic medications. Patients should be assessed for risk factors associated with diabetes such as family history, age, weight, hypertension, and hypertriglyceridemia. In addition, patients should be monitored for fasting blood glucose and lipid profile levels on a regular basis. Some medications such as olanzapine and clozapine are more associated with risk for metabolic problems than others.

Anticholinergic Side Effects

Anticholinergic side effects include dry mouth, constipation, and blurred vision. Clozapine has been associated with anticholinergic side effects. High-potency drugs such as haloperidol and fluphenazine have fewer anticholinergic side effects. Risperdone is not associated with anticholinergic side effects. Water, sugar-free candy, and alcohol-free and hydrating mouthwashes are sometimes helpful in dealing with dry mouth. Increased fluids and fiber help relieve constipation.

Blood Dyscrasias

Blood dyscrasias such as agranulocytosis, granulocytopenia, and leukopenia have been found in some clients taking antipsychotic medications. Clients taking clozapine in particular must have baseline and periodic blood and granulocyte counts.

Extrapyramidal Effects

Extrapyramidal effects have been associated more with antipsychotic and anti-Parkinsonian drugs. These include dystonias (**oculogyric crisis**, torticollis, **opisthotonus**), in which the client experiences muscle spasms, pseudo-Parkinsonism (shuffling gait, masklike faces, drooling, tremor, rigidity), akathesia (motor restlessness), and akinesia (weakness, fatigue, lack of movement). An *acute dystonic reaction* can be seen within hours of medication administration. Akathesia, an intense sensation of motor restlessness that can appear to be anxiety or agitation, is most associated with typical antipsychotics and can be seen within days of starting medication. It can be treated with anticholinergic agents, benzodiazepines, or sometimes beta-blockers such as propranolol (Inderal).

Parkinsonian Symptoms

Drug-induced Parkinsonian symptoms associated with typical antipsychotic medications, often seen weeks or months after starting medication, are characterized by muscle spasms and cramping of the neck, face, tongue, or back. Benztropine (Cogentin) or diphenhydramine (Benadryl) are used to reverse acute symptoms. To minimize risk of symptoms, benztropine is sometimes given prophylactically or continued on a regular basis if an acute episode has occurred. High-potency drugs such as haloperidol and fluphenazine are associated with extrapyramidal symptoms. Risperidone may be more associated with EPS than other atypical antipsychotic medications. However, low doses can often be well tolerated, and even atypical antipsychotic medications such as risperdone can be associated with dose-dependent EPS. Clozapine and quetiapine are considered to be less likely to cause EPS. Anti-Parkinson drugs such as trihexyphenidyl HCL (Artane) and benztropine mesylate (Cogentin) are commonly used to relieve EPS by blocking the action of acetylcholine. Antihistamines such as diphenhydramine are also used for EPS to suppress cholinergic activity. Tardive dyskinesia

Oculogyric crisis, a dystonia involving the eyes, results in an involuntary upward, lateral gaze.

(involuntary tic-like movements, particularly of the tongue, lips, and jaw; dystonia; jerky movements of limbs) often begins after long-term use of typical neuroleptics and is considered irreversible.

Most movement disorders in schizophrenia are drug induced. Those that start with new medication or dosage changes are often related to the dose or type of medication and are treatable. However, tardive dyskinesia, associated with chronic use of neuroleptics, is irreversible.

Neuroleptic malignant syndrome is a life-threatening emergency.

Neuropleptic Malignant Syndrome

Neuroleptic malignant syndrome (NMS) is a life-threatening emergency. Symptoms include elevated creatine phosphokinase levels, fever, diaphoresis, muscle rigidity (often called "lead pipe rigidity"), and autonomic instability. Management focuses on stopping the neuroleptic medication and treating symptoms through cooling, hydration, and prevention of emboli. Treatment with dantrolene (Dantrium) and bromocriptine (Parlodel) has been helpful. Benzodiazepines also have been used to treat symptoms. Some clients may tolerate treatment with clozapine or risperidone; however, NMS has also been found with the use of these drugs and can manifest without the symptom of muscle rigidity (Hasan & Buckley, 1998).

Orthostatic Hypotension

Orthostatic hypotension is a common side effect of some neuroleptics that block alpha-adrenergic receptors. Monitor blood pressure when the client is seated and after the client changes to a standing position (Figure 15-2). If symptoms are mild, the client can be instructed to change positions slowly and fall precautions may be instituted. If the symptoms are severe, the client may need intravenous fluids for hypovolemia or treatment with an alpha-adrenergic agonist such as norepinephrine (Levophed) or metaraminol (Aramine).

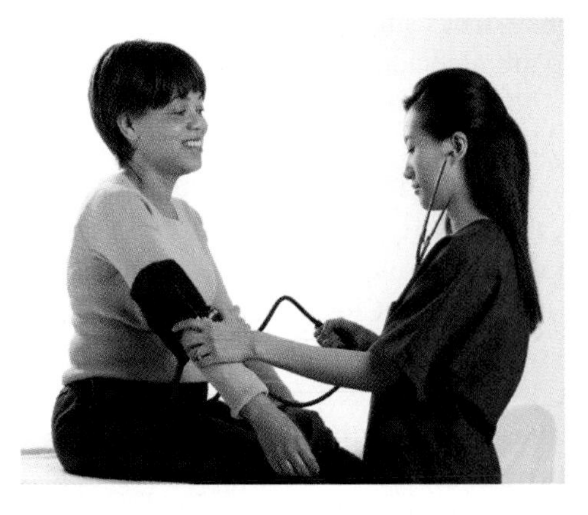

Figure 15-2 Differential blood pressure readings can help diagnose orthostatic hypotension.

Photosensitivity

Photosensitivity is a relatively common side effect of typical antipsychotics. Sunblock should be available, and clients should be taught to avoid prolonged exposure to strong sunlight.

Prolactin Elevations

Prolactin elevations are associated with typical antipsychotic medications and are more common with risperidone than with other atypical antipsychotic medications.

QT Prolongation

QTc interval prolongation has been a concern usually associated with other known cardiac risk factors and is sometimes dose dependant. This risk is associated with the typical antipsychotic thioridazine (Mellaril). Some research indicates that ziprasidone may be more associated with this side effect than other neuroleptics, and it is contraindicated in patients with known QTc prolongation (Emsley & Oosthuizen, 2005). Paliperidone (Invega) should not be used by clients with congenital long QT syndrome or those taking other drugs known to prolong QTc.

Thermal Regulation

Thermal regulation is another problem of autonomic system instability. Clients may experience decreased sweating, fever, and collapse. Environmental conditions should be monitored. This is especially important in hospital units where windows cannot be opened or individual controls of heating and cooling are not available in the rooms. Fluids should be made available and clients warned of the symptoms of heat stroke. Active, restless, and agitated clients may not be aware of the need to cool down.

Weight Gain

Weight gain is associated with typical antipsychotics as well as atypical antipsychotic medications such as clozapine, olanzapine, quetiapine, and risperidone.

Summary

Schizophrenia, schizophreniform disorder, schizoaffective disorder, delusional disorder, brief psychotic episodes, and shared psychotic episodes are all syndromes with psychotic symptoms. Psychotic symptoms also may result from medical disorders such as neurologic, viral, and autoimmune diseases or exposures to toxins or may be directly related to substance abuse (e.g., the visual and tactile hallucinations associated with alcohol withdrawal). Psychotic symptoms include hallucinations, disorganized speech and behaviors, delusions, and social and occupational impairment. Positive symptoms include disorganized or bizarre behavior, delusions, hallucinations, and thought and language problems. Negative symptoms include blunted or flattened affect, alogia, avolition, anhedonia, and attention problems that decrease intellectual functioning and the ability to filter out stimuli.

Management of the psychotic client has progressed from isolation and imprisonment, insulin shock, and ice baths to rehabilitation and case management. Treatment of schizophrenia and other psychotic disorders focuses on management of problematic symptoms such as hallucinations, delusions, disorganized thinking, disruptive behaviors, depression, or anxiety. Clients with these disorders are at great risk for self-harm and suicide; clients who experience command-type hallucinations telling them to harm themselves or others are at greatest risk. Psychotherapy, psychoeducation, cognitive and behavioral therapies, social skills training, and rehabilitation have helped clients deal with these symptoms.

Pharmacotherapy is often an essential part of treatment. In the past, negative symptoms often left the client unable to socialize or participate in activities. New medications that effectively treat negative symptoms have changed the outlook and lives of many clients. Some of the more common symptoms of schizophrenia such as catatonia are rarely seen now because of good pharmacologic management, but side effects of medication are still one of the main reasons for noncompliance.

The chronic course of many psychotic disorders with recurring symptoms, exacerbations of existing symptoms, and progressive decline in functioning is discouraging for the client and the client's family. Often, the client, family, and staff are very anxious when confronted with the symptoms experienced by the client. Clients and their families can learn to identify the prodromal symptoms of anxiety and depression and the psychotic symptoms that indicate decompensation or relapse. Early intervention and problem solving are helpful in dealing with chronic disorders. Due to the chronicity of schizophrenia, family support is essential for better treatment outcomes. Assistance and, when indicated, supervision by family members assists with the client's ability to adhere to treatment and medication regimes. As those closest to the client, family members are vital members of the treatment team.

Working with this population is well worth the challenge. One psychiatric nurse case manager working in the community with clients who had chronic schizophrenia stated that she admired her clients and was moved by their struggles as they sought "in very noble ways" to deal with difficult and debilitating disorders. Nurses must keep up with the rapid changes in theory and practice to ensure that quality care is being given.

Annotated References

American Medical Association. (2006). *International classification of diseases* (9th rev. ed.; Vols. 1, 2). Dover, DE: Author.

This is the code book for specifying diagnoses.

American Psychiatric Association. (2000). *Diagnostic and statistical manual of mental disorders* (4th ed., text rev.). Washington, DC: Author.

This is the fourth edition, text revision, of the American Psychiatric Association's official nomenclature of psychiatric conditions and disorders. It provides a systematic listing of the official codes and categories, a description of the multiaxial system for diagnosis, and diagnostic criteria for each of the disorders. It is used by psychiatrists, physicians, psychologists, registered nurses, social workers, therapists, and other mental health workers in all clinical settings.

Anonymous. (1986, March 18). "I feel I am trapped inside my head, banging against its walls, trying desperately to escape." *The New York Times,* p. C3.

A young woman with schizophrenia eloquently describes her personal experiences with schizophrenia in this article.

Bark, N. M. (1988). On the history of schizophrenia: Evidence of its existence before 1800. *New York State Journal of Medicine, 88*(7), 374–383.

This article discusses historical writings on mental illness that describe schizophrenia and related disorders.

Bellack, A. S., Mueser, K. T., Gingerich, S., & Agresta, J. (2004). *Social skills training for schizophrenia: A step-by-step guidebook* (2nd ed.). New York: Guilford Press.

Provides guidelines for social skills training.

Black, D. W., & Andreasen, N. C. (1999). Schizophrenia, schizophreniform disorder, and delusional (paranoid) disorder. In R. E. Hales, S. C. Yudofsky, & J. E. Talbot (Eds.), *The American Psychiatric*

Press Textbook of Psychiatry (3rd ed., pp. 411–463). Washington, DC: American Psychiatric Press.
This chapter discusses schizophrenia and other psychotic disorders.

Boyd, M. A., & Lapierre, E. D. (1996). Fluid imbalance and water intoxication. In A. B. McBride & J. K. Austin (Eds.), *Psychiatric-mental health nursing: Integrating the behavioral and biological sciences* (pp. 396–424). Philadelphia: W. B. Saunders.
This chapter provides an extensive review of polydipsia and hyponatremia.

Dearing, K. S. (2004). Getting it, together: How the nurse patient relationship influences compliance for patients with schizophrenia. *Archives of Psychiatric Nursing, 5*(8), 155–163.
In the days of doing more with less, this article reviews the basics of the therapeutic nurse-patient relationship and its relationship with patient compliance with treatment plans.

Dixon, L., Adams, C., & Lucksted, A. (2000). Update on family psychoeducation for schizophrenia. *Schizophrenia Bulletin, 26*(1), 5–20.
Review of family intervention studies to determine evidence-based practice guidelines for family and client education.

Eagles, J. M. (1991). The relationship between schizophrenia and immigration: Are there alternatives to psychosocial hypothesis? *The British Journal of Psychiatry, 159*(12), 783–789.
This article discusses the possible reasons for increased rates of schizophrenia in certain groups.

Emsley, R., & Oosthuizen, P. (2005). Evidence-based pharmacotherapy of schizophrenia. In D. Stein, B. Lerer, & S. Stahl (Eds.), *Evidence-based psychopharmacology* (pp. 56–87). Cambridge, UK: Cambridge University Press.
Reviews studies of pharmacotherapy in the treatment of schizophrenia.

Ereshefsky, L. (1996). Pharmacokinetics and drug interactions: Update for new antipsychotics. *Journal of Clinical Psychiatry, 57*(Suppl. 11), 12–25.
This article compares traditional antipsychotic medications with newer atypical antipsychotic medications.

Fox, J. C., & Kane, C. F. (1996). Information processing deficits in schizophrenia. In A. B. McBride & J. K. Austin (Eds.), *Psychiatric-mental health nursing: Integrating the behavioral and biological sciences* (pp. 321–347). Philadelphia: W. B. Saunders.
This excellent chapter discusses various theories regarding the etiology and treatment of schizophrenia.

Frank, A. R., & Gunderson, J. G. (1990). The role of the therapeutic alliance in the treatment of schizophrenia: Relationship to course and outcome. *Archives of General Psychiatry, 47*(3), 228–236.
This study indicates that a good therapeutic alliance increases adherence to treatment and provides better outcomes.

Hasan, S., & Buckley, P. (1998). Novel antipsychotics and neuroleptic malignant syndrome: A review and critique. *The American Journal of Psychiatry, 155*(8), 1113–1116.
This study reviewed reports of clozapine- and risperidone-induced neuroleptic malignant syndrome and possible drug interactions and concomitant medical and psychiatric problems.

Hogarty, G. E., Anderson, C. M., Reiss, D. J., Kornblith, S. J., Greenwald, D. P., et al. (1991). Family psychoeducation, social skills training, and maintenance chemotherapy in the aftercare treatment of schizophrenia. II. Two-year effects of a controlled study on relapse and adjustment. Environmental-Personal Indicators in the Course of Schizophrenia (EPICS) Research Group. *Archives of General Psychiatry, 48*(4), 340–347.
This study demonstrated that psychoeducation groups and social skills training reduce relapse rates by half. Clients who received a combination of these treatments had no relapses.

Hogarty, G. E., Greenwald, D., Ulrich, R. E, Kornblith, S. J., DiBarry, A. L., et al. (1997). Three-year trials of personal therapy among schizophrenic patients living with or independent of family. I: Descriptions of study and effects on relapse rates; three-year trials of personal therapy among schizophrenic patients living with or independent of family. II: Effects on adjustments of patients. *The American Journal of Psychiatry, 14*(11), 1504–1524.
These two articles discuss the results of a 3-year study on the effects of therapy on the personal and social adjustment of clients with schizophrenia. Therapy was found to help clients living with family and promoted continuity of care.

Kin, K-M. (1996). Cultural influences on the diagnosis of psychotic and organic disorders. In J. E. Mezzich, A. Kleinman, H. Fabrega, & D. L. Parron (Eds.), *Cultural and psychiatric diagnosis: A DSM-IV perspective* (pp. 49–62). Washington, DC: American Psychiatric Press.
This chapter discusses some of the cultural and cross-cultural issues that are encountered when identifying and treating psychotic symptoms.

Leff, J. (1994). Working with families of schizophrenic patients. *The British Journal of Psychiatry, 164*(suppl. 23), 71–76.
Research based on expressed emotion (EE) in families with schizophrenics. Family sessions in the home and relative support groups were used to provide education and expand social support.

Liberman, R. P., Derisi, W., & Mueser, K. T. (2001). *Social and independent living skills: Social skills training for psychiatric patients (psychology practice guidelines)*. Boston: Allyn & Bacon.
This is a manual for social skills training geared for client education.

Liberman, R. P., Wallace, C. J., Blackwell, G., Kopelowica, A., Vaccaro, J. V., et al. (1998). Skills training versus psychosocial occupational therapy for persons with persistent schizophrenia. *The American Journal of Psychiatry, 155*(8), 1087–1091.

This study compared groups of schizophrenic clients participating in social and independent living skills training and occupational therapy groups. Generalization of skills was found to be better with repetitive training, practice, and application of skills in the community.

Lieberman, J. A. (2006). Comparative effectiveness of antipsychotic drugs: A commentary on cost utility of the latest antipsychotic drugs in schizophrenia study (CUtLASS 1) and clinical antipsychotic trials of intervention effectiveness (CATIE). *Archives of General Psychiatry, 63*(10), 1069–1072.

Discusses the cost and effectiveness of antipsychotic medications.

Lieberman, J. L., Stroup, T. S., McEvoy, J. P., Swartz, M. S., Rosenheck, R. A., et al. (2005). Effectiveness of antipsychotic drugs in patients with chronic schizophrenia. *New England Journal of Medicine, 353,* 1209–1223.

Discusses the effectiveness of various neuroleptics and atypical antipsychotic medications in phase I of the CATIE.

Lopez, A. D., Mathers, C. D., Ezzati, D. T., & Murray, C. J. L. (2006). *Global burden of disease and risk factors.* New York: Oxford University Press.

Provides an assessment of trends and risks for disability and mortality by demographics for many diseases.

Mahone, I. H. (2004). Medication decision-making by persons with serious mental illness. *Archives of Psychiatric Nursing, 18*(4), 126–143.

Examination of client motivation as it relates to participation in the nurse-patient interaction and its relation to medication adherence and patient satisfaction.

Meltzer, H. Y. (2001). Treatment of suicidality in schizophrenia. *Annals of the New York Academy of Science, 932*(1), 44–60.

This article reviews some of the risk factors for suicidality in schizophrenia such as a history of past suicide attempts, depression and hopelessness, substance abuse and male gender as well as the effects of insight and the degree of cognitive impairment.

Reynolds, S. A., Schmid, M. W., & Broome, M. E. (2004). Polydipsia screening tool. *Archives of Psychiatric Nursing, 18*(2), 49–59.

The authors developed a 17-item screening tool for polydipsia and attempted to verify internal consistency, validity, and predictive value of the instrument.

Strassnig, M., Brar, J. S., & Ganguli, R. (2006). Increased caffeine and nicotine consumption in community-dwelling patients with schizophrenia. *Schizophrenia Research, 86*(1–3), 269–275.

The authors sampled out-patients to assess dietary habits, food choices, and use of caffeine and nicotine in schizophrenics in order to determine the need for patient education regarding lifestyle choices.

Ustun, T. B., & Sartorius, N. (2001). *Mental illness in general health care.* London: John Wiley.

Written in collaboration with the World Health Organization, these authors studied the impact of major mental illness on the public health and the economy and projected their impact across the globe. The information is useful for studies of statistical prevalence and the impact of mental disability.

VanMeijel, B., van der Gaag, M., Kahn, R. S., & Grypdonck, M. H. F. (2003). Relapse prevention in patients with schizophrenia: The application of an intervention protocol in nursing practice. *Archives of Psychiatric Nursing, 4*(8), 165–172.

The authors studied psychiatric nurses using an interventional protocol aimed at preventing rehospitalization of chronic psychiatric patients.

Whitford, T. J., Grieve, S. M., Farrow, F. D., Gomes, L., Brennan, J., et al. (2006). Progressive grey mater atrophy over the first 2–3 years of illness in first-episode schizophrenia: A tensor-based morphometry study. *NeuroImage, 32*(2), 511–519.

This study found progressive grey matter abnormalities present at time of diagnosis of the first psychotic symptoms and over the first few years of illness when comparing young schizophrenics and a control group. There are indications of the predictive value of MRI studies in identifying clients at risk for developing schizophrenia.

Yolken, R. H., & Torrey, E. F. (2006). Infectious agents and gene-environmental interactions in the etiopathogenesis of schizophrenia. *Clinical Neuroscience Research, 6*(1–2), 97–109.

These authors attempted to show the role of infections and other environmental factors as well as genetic predisposition and the importance of susceptibility for development of schizophrenia.

Additional Resources

De Leon, J., Diaz, F. J., Afuilar, M. C., Jurado, D., & Gurpegui, M. (2006). Does smoking reduce akathisia? Testing a narrow version of the self-medication hypothesis. *Schizophrenia Research, 86*(1–3), 256–268.

This study attempted to find a relationship between "self-medication" with smoking and schizophrenia because many patients describe smoking as relaxing and calming. Further study is needed to establish a linkage.

DeLisi, L. E. (2006). *100 questions & answers about schizophrenia: Painful minds.* Sudbury, MA: Jones & Bartlett.

Provides information for providers, families, and patients about schizophrenia and its treatment.

Kingdon, D. G., & Turkington, D. (2004). *Cognitive therapy of schizophrenia: Guides to individualized evidence-based treatment.* New York: The Guilford Press.

Describes treatment techniques suitable for schizophrenia and other psychotic disorders.

Levinson, D. F., Mahtani, M., Nancarrow, D. J., Brown, D. M., Kruglyak, L., et al. (1998). Genome scan of schizophrenia. *The American Journal of Psychiatry, 155*(6), 741–750.

This article discusses the possible genetic etiology for schizophrenia. A genome-wide map of different markers found five significant regions but no single gene responsible for schizophrenia.

Littrell, S. H., & Littrell, K. (1997). Recent advances in the understanding of negative symptoms in schizophrenia. *Journal of the American Psychiatric Nurses Association, 3*(4), 111–116.

This article focuses on negative symptoms and guides nurses in the delivery of care needed by these clients. It uses an extensive literature review and discusses etiologic factors and medications used to treat negative symptoms.

Torrey, E. F. (2001). *Surviving schizophrenia: A manual for families, consumers and providers.* New York: Collins.

Provides a description of schizophrenia and its impact, and information on coping with its effects.

Williams, C. L., & Davis, C. M. (2005). *Therapeutic interactions in nursing.* Sudbury, MA: Jones & Bartlett.

Describes the therapeutic use of self and nurse-patient relationship, giving examples of communication techniques.

Internet Resources

http://nursing.jbpub.com/psychiatric

Visit http://nursing.jbpub.com/psychiatric for interactive exercises, NCLEX review questions, WebLinks, and more.

CHAPTER 16

Mood Disorders

Valerie N. Markley

LEARNING OBJECTIVES

After reading this chapter, you will be able to:

- Describe the diagnostic criteria for mood disorders (unipolar and bipolar).
- Discuss the influence of mood disorders on a client's daily functioning.
- Identify nursing interventions to assist clients experiencing mood disorders.
- Review the major psychopharmacological agents available to treat clients with mood disorders.
- Identify measures for suicide prevention and assessment of risk.
- Discuss the teaching issues for clients and their families and the available peer support services and referral resources.

KEY TERMS

Affect
Anhedonia
Bipolar
Cognitive behavioral therapy
Cyclothymic disorder
Dysthymic disorder
Euphoria
Euthymia
Flight of ideas
Hypersomnia
Hypomania
Insomnia
Melancholia
Mood
Postpartum depression
Rapid cycling
Unipolar

http://nursing.jbpub.com/psychiatric

Visit http://nursing.jbpub.com/psychiatric for interactive exercises, NCLEX review questions, WebLinks, and more.

Introduction

This chapter focuses on both major depressive (**unipolar**) and **bipolar** disorders; discusses the diagnosis, treatment, and appropriate nursing interventions for each; and presents the assessment of risk and measures for the prevention of suicide associated with these disorders. Mood disorders include disorders ranging from major depression to bipolar disorder (see **Table 16-1**). These are separate and differ from the depression, sadness, and euphoria that are normal reactions to losses, disappointments, and joys experienced regularly in one's life. A term used to describe a normal **mood** experience is **euthymia**.

Even in ancient times there are recordings of people suffering from depression. The Old Testament speaks of King Saul's struggles with depression. He had David play the harp to soothe his troubled soul.

Table 16-1 *DSM-IV-TR* Categorization of Mood Disorders

Depressive disorders:
Major depressive disorder
Dysthymic disorder
Depressive disorder not otherwise specified (NOS)
Bipolar disorders:
Bipolar I disorder
Bipolar II disorder
Cyclothymic disorder
Bipolar disorder NOS
Mood disorder due to:
General medical condition
Substance-induced mood disorder
Mood disorder NOS
Specifiers:
Describing the severity:
Mild
Moderate
Severe
With psychotic features
In remission
Describing features:
Chronic
Catatonic
Melancholic
Atypical
Postpartum onset
Describing course:
Seasonal pattern
Rapid cycling

Source: Adapted from the American Psychiatric Association. (2000). *Diagnostic and statistical manual of mental disorders* (4th ed., text rev.). Washington, DC: Author.

Figure 16-1 Well-known historical figures have had to deal with depression.

Well-known figures from the worlds of politics, entertainment, the arts, and sports have acknowledged dealing with depression (e.g., Abraham Lincoln, Mike Wallace, Virginia Woolf, F. Scott Fitzgerald, Patty Duke, Margot Kidder, Vincent Van Gogh, Cole Porter, Buzz Aldrin, and Terry Bradshaw; see **Figure 16-1**).

> The severity of symptoms and length of time separate normal "blues" from diagnosable depression.

Mood disorders are categorized and coded on Axis I by the *Diagnostic and Statistical Manual of Mental Disorders,* Fourth Edition, Text Revision (*DSM-IV-TR*), as conditions in which the major feature is a disturbance in mood (American Psychiatric Association [APA], 2000). Mood disorders are separated into the depressive disorders (often termed *unipolar depression*), the bipolar disorders, and two disorders based on etiology—mood disorder due to a general medical condition and substance-induced mood disorder (APA, 2000). In addition, there are specifiers that denote the severity of the disorders (mild, moderate, severe, with psychotic features, in remission), describe features that add more specificity (chronic, catatonic, melancholic, atypical, postpartum onset), and connote the course of the disorder (seasonal pattern, rapid cycling; see **Table 16-1**).

Healthy, well-adjusted individuals in positive life circumstances can experience sad, difficult situations and losses of varying significance and are usually able to get through such situations. The severity of mood variations and the length of time they are experienced mark the major differences between what is generally considered normal sadness ("blues") or depression and an actual mood disorder.

Grieving is an issue that can fall into either category. Certainly with a significant loss individuals may have symptoms similar to those that occur with major depressive disorder, but they should not have a marked impairment to their social or occupational functioning that continues beyond the fairly immediate time of the loss or experience active suicidal ideation. The *DSM-IV-TR* notes a period of 2 months for normal bereavement (APA, 2000). Many authorities refer to longer time periods, and some cultures mark the entire first year after a family member's or close significant other's death as an official time of mourning. Elisabeth Kübler-Ross (1997), one of the most noted authorities on the subject of death and dying, delineated five stages that the dying person and those close to him or her can experience: (1) denial and isolation, (2) anger, (3) bargaining, (4) depression, and (5) acceptance. She emphasized that the time period spent in any stage varies with the individual, and that family members are likely to go through them at different times and in varying ways, often moving back and forth among the stages until the grieving is resolved.

People who have endured a significant loss need to be encouraged to talk about what has happened. They may repeat details over and over again. This is therapeutic and helps them to work through the normal process of grieving. Empathetic listening is one of the most therapeutic measures a nurse can utilize. It is beneficial to assist the person to go through this normal process, but no one can force an individual to move faster or to transition from one stage to another. Most individuals can get through this time without the need for psychiatric assistance or antidepressants. Individuals who experience grieving that extends beyond this description may benefit from mental health services. Some individuals have a delayed grieving time, which is usually more difficult. Some get stuck in the depression stage and seem unable to progress further. When symptoms are severe, the period of grieving continues unabated, or social and occupational functioning are seriously affected, intervention is strongly indicated.

Major Depressive Disorder

Depression has a significant impact on our national prosperity and well-being (Depression and Bipolar Support Alliance [DBSA], 2006). The estimated cost of depression in America is more than $80 billion a year (Greenberg et al., 2003). Major depressive disorder is the main cause of disability in the United States and leads to more days of disability and lost days of work than many other medical illnesses (Druss, Rosenheck, & Sledge, 2000). "Unipolar major depression is the No.1 cause of disability in the Americas, and is projected to be the single leading cause of disability worldwide by 2020, according to WHO's Global Burden of Disease (GBD) report" (National Alliance for Research on Schizophrenia and Depression [NARSAD], 2002, p. 25). "Stigma surrounding mental illness is one of the major barriers to access of mental health services" (DBSA, p. 4). This problem is also compounded by the fact that many clients do not receive sustained relief following initial treatment and need encouragement to continue treatment for lasting success.

The nursing assessment should begin with a physical examination and thorough history. The client should be questioned about current mood, feelings, thoughts, and level of functioning. Changes in eating and sleep patterns must be noted. A weight gain or loss may be significant. Psychomotor retardation or agitation should be observed, not based solely on the subjective report. The nurse considers the length of the current depressive state and reports of similar episodes in the past. The presence of suicidal thoughts must be assessed and dealt with seriously. Observed behavior should be recorded as well. Family members and significant others may provide additional information that should be documented carefully.

> WHO's Global Burden of Disease Report projects major depressive disorder will be the #1 cause of disability worldwide by 2020.

> Stigma associated with mental illness is one of the major barriers to access of mental health services.

Incidence and Prevalence

Major depressive disorder may occur at any time during the life cycle, but the average age of onset is in the mid-20s. The disorder is "1.5–2 times more common among first-degree biological relatives of persons with this disorder than among the general population" (APA, 2000, p. 373). The occurrence of *unipolar disorder*, a term used to describe depressive episodes with no occurrence of mania, is higher in women than in men. The lifetime risk for major depressive disorder as noted in the *DSM-IV-TR* varies from 10% to 25% for women and from 5% to 12% for men (APA). This gender differential becomes significant around the time of puberty.

> Major depressive disorder is the main cause of disability in the United States and leads to more days of disability than many other medical illnesses. It is a major public health problem and is costly to the client, families, communities, and employers.

> The estimated cost of depression in the United States is more than $80 billion a year.

Critical Thinking Question What are some possible reasons why the incidence of depression is equal in genders before puberty, but higher in females after puberty?

Mood disorders tend to be cyclical and naturally remitting. The *DSM-IV-TR* (APA, 2000) identifies individuals with a major depressive disorder as having a 60% chance of experiencing a second episode. After a second episode the risk for a third episode increases to 70%. Those who have had three episodes carry a 90% risk of having a fourth episode. This is strong impetus to support continuing with treatment. The severity of the initial episode appears to indicate the disorder's persistence. The presence of chronic medical illnesses also tends to be a risk factor for more persistent episodes (APA). The suicide rate is dangerously high for individuals with mood disorders. According to the *DSM-IV-TR*, the suicide rate for those with major depressive disorder is up to 15%.

Culture can affect one's expression of the symptoms associated with mood disorders and one's receptivity to intervention and treatment.

Culture can affect the experience of depression and the way in which the symptoms are communicated or the seriousness of the symptoms is judged (APA, 2000). Some examples of cultural differences are:

- Latinos often rely less on mental health services and frequently present with physical symptoms.
- African Americans depend more heavily on family and social support systems, church, and folk remedies for help.
- Asians may delay seeking psychiatric help until symptoms are more severe due to concern about stigmatization (Snyder & Matsuno, 2001).

Age and gender may also affect the ways in which depressive symptoms present. Children more often show somatic complaints, irritability, and social withdrawal, yet they are less likely to have delusions, excessive sleeping, and psychomotor retardation than are adolescents and adults. Before puberty and during adolescence, depressive symptoms are more likely to occur along with other mental disorders, including disruptive behavior disorders, attention deficit disorders (ADD), and anxiety disorders. Adolescents may also experience depressive symptoms along with substance-related disorders and eating disorders. In older adults, cognitive features such as memory loss, disorientation, and distractibility may be particularly apparent and the death rates are four times higher for individuals over 55 who have major depressive disorder (APA, 2000). Women are significantly more likely than men to experience depression sometime in their lives.

Genetic, biological, and environmental factors play a significant role in the cause of depression.

Morbidity is higher for clients with severe mental illness than for those in the general population. Individuals with diabetes, myocardial infarction, cancer, and stroke have a 20–25% risk for developing major depression (APA, 2000; Forrester et al., 1992). Nurses can be instrumental with these clients in working to help them in their struggles with conditions such as obesity and hypertension and to "address lifestyle issues of poor nutrition, lack of exercise, and smoking" (Kennedy, Salsberry, Nickel, Hunt, & Chipps, 2005, p. 50). Integrated health care could greatly improve both the mental and physical health of these clients.

Etiology

The causes of major depression have not been clearly determined. Research demonstrates that both biological and psychosocial factors play a significant role, with a combination of factors (multiple causality) being likely. The vulnerability to depression seems to be inherited; both research and clinicians confirm significant family histories of depression. Causation may also be linked to elevated cortisol levels or to a depletion of monoamine neurotransmitters such as serotonin, norepinephrine, and dopamine. (See Chapter 4.)

Every October in the United States in order to identify individuals, who are dealing with undiagnosed depression, a National Screening Day is held to educate and assess for depression. A screening tool is supplied by Mental Health America (formerly known as the National Mental Health Association) and has been expanded to include screening for manic depression or bipolar disorder. This is only a screening tool; it is not diagnostic. If a person scores over the number 8 for depression, for example, he or she should be referred to a mental health practitioner for further evaluation (www.depression-screening.org).

Biological Theories

Even with the evolution of the Human Genome Project (Garlow & Nemeroff, 2005), scientists have not been able to identify specific genes or chromosomes that are responsible for vulnerability to the range of mood disorders. Two areas of focus have been the effects of neurotransmitters and their action in the nerve synapse, and neurogenesis, the development of new neuronal tissue. Garlow and Nemeroff have stated "despite 40 years of concerted research, the primary neurochemical pathology of major depression has not been identified" (p. 454). More information is steadily emerging on the interrelationship of the physical and emotional components of depression. According to Goldstein and Potter "the neuroendocrine effects of stress and the neurotransmitter effects of depression are now recognized to interact in a tightly linked system that offers a homeostatic mechanism for responding to stress" (2004, pp. 21–22).

Adverse life events, significant loss, or other major stressors often can be found to have occurred in the year prior to the onset of depression (van Praag, de Kloet, & van Os, 2004). This relationship seems to be more apparent in the first episode of depression and decreases to some extent with following relapses. It is sometimes hard to tell whether the event or the depression came first. Chronic stress is often sited as a risk factor for major depression. These events may not be sufficient to cause the depression but add to other risk factors, such as biological ones. Some risk factors for depression include family history, a serious medical condition, a chronic disability, the lack of a support system, a history of abuse, trauma and/or stressful life events, early loss of a significant other, poverty, loss of employment or significant change in status, and medications or chemicals. In fact, it has been noted that "family, twin, and to a lesser extent adoption studies all point towards a genetic influence on depressive disorder" (van Praag, de Kloet, & van Os, p. 72). In addition to genes, chronic stress may be able to disturb monoaminergic functioning in the brain, producing a similar appearance to the way the brain looks in depression. There seems to be a strong interplay between genes and the environment in the causation of depression.

Psychosocial Theories

This approach attempts to explain how an individual's internal mental life, relationships with others, and life events contribute to depression. Interpersonal theory considers the ways in which a depressed person experiences and perceives loss. Psychodynamic theory addresses how individuals deal with developmental tasks and cope with stress. Important losses, such as the loss of a parent at a very young age, have been noted to increase one's risk for depression. Inadequate nurturing, extreme poverty, any significant change in health or life status, and other adverse conditions can also play a role and increase the risk for depression or another mood disorder.

Critical Thinking Questions What is the impact of life circumstances on the onset of mood disorders? What are the implications of those circumstances for someone living with a mood disorder?

Physiology

Neurotransmitters play an important role in depression. However, it is important to guard against a one-dimensional interpretation of the part they play. (See Chapter 4.) No laboratory findings have been identified to be diagnostic for major depression (APA, 2000). Sleep electroencephalogram (EEG) abnormalities may occur in as high as 90% of clients hospitalized with major depression (APA). According to the APA,

> the pathophysiology of a major depressive episode may involve a dysregulation of a number of neurotransmitter systems, including the serotonin, norepinephrine, dopamine, acetylcholine, and gamma-aminobutyric acid systems. There is also evidence of alterations of several neuropeptides, including corticotrophin-releasing hormone. Functional brain imaging studies document alterations in cerebral blood flow and metabolism in some individuals, including increased blood flow in limbic and paralimbic regions and decreased blood flow in the lateral prefrontal cortex. (p. 353)

Clients with depression regularly experience disruptions in their circadian rhythms, including "a reduction in the circadian rhythm of serotonin, norepinephrine, thyroid-stimulating hormone (TSH), and melatonin" (Glod, 1998, p. 351).

> Neurotransmission and neurogenesis both have an impact on the pathophysiology of mood disorders.

> The pathophysiology of a major depressive episode involves a dysregulation of a number of neurotransmitter systems, including the serotonin, norepinephrine, dopamine, acetylcholine, and gamma-aminobutyric acid systems.

Clinical Presentation

The essential characteristic of a major depressive episode is a period of at least 2 weeks of depressed mood or loss of interest in almost everything with no history of manic episodes. In children and adolescents the mood may present as irritable instead of sad. The symptoms must be accompanied by clinically significant impairment in social and occupational functioning (APA, 2000).

Some individuals may report aches and pains and other somatic complaints, show increased irritability and persistent feelings or expression of anger, or experience an almost total loss of interest or pleasure in everything. Most individuals have a greatly reduced appetite with a weight loss of more than 5% in a month, although some may instead gain weight. In

> Significant loss and major stress play a supporting role in the first episode of depression. Individuals with a major depressive disorder run a 60% chance of experiencing a second episode; after three episodes the risk increases to 90%.

Figure 16-2 Insomnia is a common symptom of depression.

depressed clients, the most common sleep disturbance is **insomnia** (**Figure 16-2**). Less common is the occurrence of **hypersomnia** or excessive sleeping, usually without any deep, restful sleep. There may be psychomotor agitation or retardation, a noticeable speeding up or slowing down of activity; a greatly reduced energy level with complaints of tiredness and fatigue without the output of physical efforts; or an overwhelming sense of worthlessness or guilt and negative views of self often accompanied by ruminations over past failures. There is often a sense of self-blame for being sick or depressed and failing to fulfill one's responsibilities. A pervasive inability to experience pleasure, called **anhedonia**, takes over the person.

Impairment may occur in the ability to think, concentrate, and process decisions with complaints of memory problems. Children may show a drop in school performance due to poor concentration. Adults may be unable to perform their jobs or home tasks. In older adults the primary complaint may be memory problems, which are often mistaken for the beginning signs of dementia. Of course, it is also true that a major depressive episode can occur at the onset of dementia when the individuals often realize they are having cognitive difficulty.

The depressed person may feel that others would be better off if he or she were gone. There are frequently thoughts or wishes for death and suicidal ideation or attempts of suicide. Certainly depressed persons represent a very high-risk group, yet "many studies have shown that it is not possible to predict accurately whether or when a particular individual with depression will attempt suicide" (APA, 2000, p. 351).

Chronic, catatonic, melancholic, atypical, and *postpartum onset* are terms used to further describe mood disorders.

Five features (chronic, catatonic, melancholic, atypical, postpartum onset) are used as further descriptors of mood disorders. It is "chronic" when the disorder has continued for at least 2 years. "Catatonic feature" is used when there is marked psychomotor disturbance involving motor immobility, extreme motor activity, excessive negativism, mutism, or other peculiarities of movement or speech. "Melancholic features" occur more commonly in middle aged or older depressed persons and are more likely to occur in a severe rather than mild form. With **melancholia**, there is a loss of interest in almost everything and no sense of pleasure. The individual does not even feel better if something good happens. Along with this is the distinct element of depression that is routinely worse in the morning and often with early morning awakening. Other characteristics are psychomotor retardation, significant weight loss or anorexia, and excessive guilt (APA, 2000). "Atypical features" is added when mood reactivity is present, meaning that the individual's mood improves when something positive happens. The client may gain weight or have an increased appetite and may sleep too much. There may be a feeling of heaviness in the arms and legs. In addition there is often a long history of feeling interpersonal rejection with significant resulting impairment in social or occupational functioning (APA).

Symptoms that are observed in "postpartum onset" are mood fluctuations and preoccupation with the well-being of the infant. According to the *DSM-IV-TR* (APA, 2000) the onset occurs within 4 weeks of delivery. However, many practitioners say the problem can occur anytime within the baby's first year. **Postpartum depression** can occur with or without psychotic features. The risk of danger to the infant is generally much greater with postpartum psychotic episodes. For a woman who has had a postpartum psychotic episode, there is a 30–50% chance of recurrence with every future delivery. With postpartum depression, the mother may experience a lack of interest, be afraid to be alone with the baby, or be overly zealous to the point of interfering with the infant's rest. It is very important to separate postpartum depression from "baby blues," which occur in as many as 70% of women during the first 10 days after delivery. These feelings are different in that they are transient and do not interfere with the mother's level of functioning (APA).

Critical Thinking Question What are some somatic behaviors that might be experienced by a college student who is experiencing the onset of a mood disorder?

Differential Diagnosis

Dysthymic disorder and major depressive disorder differ in terms of severity and chronicity. With dysthymic disorder the symptoms are less severe than in major depressive disorder, but the symptoms are on-going for at least a 2-year period for adults and for a 1-year period in children and adolescents (APA, 2000). In adults, dysthymic disorder occurs two to three times more often in women than in men. Personality issues or a diagnosable personality disorder are often present. Dysthymic disorder in children occurs equally in boys and girls until puberty, when the incidence increases for females. Reduced school performance and poor social interaction often result. Low self-esteem, poor social skills, and a pessimistic outlook tend to accompany this chronic disorder even in children (APA).

Mood disorder due to general medical condition is diagnosed when the alteration in mood is assessed to be a direct physiological result of the individual's general medical condition (APA, 2000). The medical condition could be any illness that a person can have. Certain medical conditions that are chronic, incurable, or involve great pain or disability place the individual at a high risk for suicide "(e.g. malignancy, spinal cord injury, peptic ulcer disease, Huntington's disease, . . . AIDS, end stage renal disease, head injury)" (APA, p. 402).

A substance-induced mood disorder is differentiated from major depressive disorder in that a substance (i.e., a medication, drug of abuse, or toxin), is judged to be the cause of the symptoms (APA, 2000). With individuals so affected, hopefully the symptoms will clear once the effects of the substance are no longer present. Of course, there is also a very strong co-morbidity between mood disorders and substance abuse, with many individuals stating they use substances to self-medicate against the depression.

Management and Treatment

Clients with a mood disorder should be screened for the possibility of other medical problems that could be producing symptoms of mood problems or compounding them. This review should include a complete history and physical, screening for substance abuse and a thorough mental status exam, an ECG (electrocardiogram), and a complete blood count with differentials, serum electrolytes, cholesterol test, and liver, thyroid, and renal function tests (Lehne, 2007). It is important to establish a baseline prior to starting a medication regimen because it provides vital information for tracking changes.

Dysthymic disorder is less severe than a major depressive disorder, but symptoms extend over 2 years for an adult and 1 year for children and adolescents.

The cooperative efforts of the interdisciplinary team are vital in the treatment of clients with mood disorders. Having the expertise of a group of professionals and support staff is of great benefit to clients and family members. It is to everyone's advantage for the team members to work together in a spirit of respect and collaboration with the client's best interest always as the central goal. In acute care settings and in all levels of community-based programs, healthcare practitioners from many disciplines are needed. It is vital to keep the focus of treatment on complete recovery and a meaningful role in one's community, not just symptom relief (DBSA, 2006).

Psychotherapeutic care including counseling, pharmacotherapy, and psychoeducation, and psychosocial care including environmental manipulation, as well as peer support, are important to consider in the treatment of those with mood disorders. With mild depression, psychotherapy alone is often an effective treatment. With more severe depression, better results are usually gained with a combination of treatment with antidepressants and psychotherapy.

All antidepressants have an equal opportunity to be effective, with results being more on an individual response basis with each client. If an individual or a close relative has responded positively to a certain medication in the past, the same medication is more likely to help the client (Glod, 1998). "About 40% of those given antidepressants achieve full remission; another 20% to 30% achieve at least 50% reduction in symptom severity" (Lehne, 2007, p. 330).

A substance-induced mood disorder is differentiated from major depressive disorder in that a substance such as a medication, drug of abuse, or toxin is judged to be the cause of the symptoms.

The four major groups of antidepressants are selective serotonin reuptake inhibitors (SSRIs), atypical or novel antidepressants, tricyclic antidepressants (TCAs), and monoamine oxidase inhibitors (MAOIs; see **Table 16-2**). Initial therapeutic response with all antidepressants has a lag time of 1–3 weeks, and maximum effectiveness

Table 16-2 Common Antidepressant Medications

Subgroup Categories	Daily Adult Dosage Range (mg)
Selective Serotonin Reuptake Inhibitors (SSRIs)	
Prozac (fluoxetine)	10–80
Prozac (fluoxetine) weekly	90 mg per week
Zoloft (sertraline)	25–200
Paxil (paroxetine)	10–60
Paxil (paroxetine) CR	12.5–75
Celexa (citalopram)	10–60
Lexapro (escitalopram)	10–20
Luvox (fluvoxamine)	50–300
Atypical (Novel) Antidepressants	
Wellbutrin (bupropion)	200–450
Wellbutrin (bupropion) SR/XL	150–300
Nefazodone (formerly available as Serzone)	150–600
Remeron (mirtazapine)	15–45
Asendin (amoxapine)	50–300
Desyrel (trazodone)	150–600
Atypicals, also called Serotonin Norepinephrine Reuptake Inhibitors (SNRIs)	
Effexor (venlafaxine)	75–225
Effexor (venlafaxine) XR	75–225
Cymbalta (duloxetine)	40–60
Tricyclic Antidepressants (TCAs)	
Tofranil (imipramine)	75–300
Elavil (amitriptyline)	50–300
Norpramin (desipramine)	75–300
Pamelor, Aventyl (nortriptyline)	50–150
Anafranil (clomipramine)	75–250
Monoamine Oxidase Inhibitors (MAOIs)	
Marplan (isocarboxazid)	20–60
Nardil (phenelzine)	15–90
Parnate (tranylcypromine)	30–60
Emsam (selegiline) transdermal patch	6, 9, or 12 mg/24 hr

Note: CR = controlled release; SR = sustained release; XL = extended release.

Source: Adapted from Crutchfield, D. B. (2006). *Review of psychotropic drugs.* Wilmington, DE: Astra Zeneca Pharmaceuticals; Keltner, N. L. & Folks, D. G. (2005). *Psychotropic drugs.* St. Louis, MO: Mosby; and Townsend, M. C. (2006). *Psychiatric mental health nursing* (5th ed.). Philadelphia: F. A. Davis Co.

The four major groups of antidepressants are selective serotonin reuptake inhibitors (SSRIs), atypical or novel antidepressants, tricyclic antidepressants (TCAs), and monoamine oxidase inhibitors (MAOIs).

takes 1–2 months to occur. All too frequently clients stop taking their antidepressants once they start feeling better. They need to be carefully informed about the negative impact of stopping the medication because it is very likely that it is the antidepressant that is making them feel better, and quitting it will likely result in a return of symptoms. It is recommended for antidepressant therapy to continue for 6 months to 1 year after symptoms have improved. If repeated episodes of depression occur, longer term therapy is strongly indicated. When treatment is first initiated, clients may feel the activating or increased energy that accompanies many of the agents before the mood benefits occur. This may give them the energy to act on any suicidal thoughts. Therefore, clients and their family members or caregivers need to be carefully instructed about this possibility, and clients must be closely monitored. Another serious precaution in the use of antidepressants is the possibility of precipitating mania in individuals with a predisposition for bipolar disorder.

The selective serotonin reuptake inhibitors (SSRIs), including Prozac (fluoxetine), Zoloft (sertraline), Paxil (paroxetine), Celexa (citalopram), and Lexapro (escitalopram), along with the atypical antidepressants, are the first line of medication treatment for depression. The SSRIs selectively block the reuptake of serotonin back into the nerve endings making more serotonin available in the neuronal synapse. Lehne (2007, p. 349) has observed "over time, this induces adaptive cellular responses that are ultimately responsible for relieving depression." The SSRIs present two major advantages over TCAs and MAOIs in that they have fewer side effects and are less lethal if used by a client in an intentional overdose. In a study of over 400 older subjects, the research results indicated decreased effectiveness of SSRIs with age for those diagnosed with the melancholic subtype of depression, whereas the effectiveness of TCAs did not appear to be influenced by age or depressive subtype (Parker, 2002). Two of the most common side effects of SSRIs are gastrointestinal upset and sexual dysfunction.

Atypical or novel antidepressants include a group of antidepressants that do not all have a similar pattern of neurotransmitter action. Wellbutrin (bupropion) has a chemical structure that is similar to amphetamine (Lehne, 2007). Remeron (mirtazapine) appears to work by increasing the release of serotonin and norepinephrine; it also blocks histamine receptors. Effexor (venlafaxine) and Cymbalta (duloxetine), also called serotonin norepinephrine reuptake inhibitors, seem to combine the best benefits of the TCAs and the SSRIs. Effexor tends to have fewer drug interactions than other antidepressants, and it does not increase the effects of alcohol (Keltner, 2007a). Cymbalta helps to reduce depressive symptoms and may reduce some of the physical pain that often accompanies depression.

The tricyclics, including Tofranil (imipramine), Elavil (amitriptyline), and Norpramin (desipramine) were the first class of antidepressants available for the treatment of depression. They work by blocking the reuptake of norepinephrine and serotonin at the nerve synapse. The most frequent adverse reactions are sedation, orthostatic hypotension, and anticholinergic effects, including dry mouth and constipation. Cardiotoxicity is the side effect of greatest concern because it can be lethal (Lehne, 2007). To reduce this risk of suicide, severely depressed clients should be given no more than a week's supply at one time. The combination of TCAs and MAOIs is contraindicated because the two together can precipitate a hypertensive crisis.

The monoamine oxidase inhibitors (MAOIs) are able to increase the amounts of norepinephrine, serotonin, and dopamine in the neuronal synapse by blocking monoamine oxidase, which is a main enzyme needed for the breakdown of these neurotransmitters. Although the MAOIs are as effective as other antidepressants, they are seldom used due to their serious side effects and the life-threatening increase in blood pressure that can occur when MAOIs are used in combination with certain foods and drugs (**Table 16-3**).

In 2006 the Food and Drug Administration (FDA) approved Emsam (selegiline), which is the first transdermal skin patch on the market for the treatment of depression. The drug is delivered via a once per day patch that supplies the selegiline, a monoamine oxidase inhibitor, through the skin directly into the bloodstream. According to the FDA, "at its lowest strength, Emsam can be used without the dietary restrictions that are needed for all oral MAOI inhibitors that are approved for treating major depression" (U.S. FDA, 2006, p. 1). Clients using patches with higher dosages are instructed to follow the dietary and drug restrictions that are necessary for those taking oral MAOIs.

Antidepressant medications must be taken for several weeks before they become effective. Side effects associated with antidepressant medications are divided into the following categories:

The side effects that are most likely to cause noncompliance with antidepressant medication regimens are weight gain, impotence, and decreased libido.

Table 16-3 Foods, Products, and Medications to Be Avoided By Clients Taking MAOIs

Foods	Products	Medications
Aged cheeses, most cheeses	Yeast extracts	All sympathomimetic agents
Sour cream	Ginseng	Methylphenidate (Ritalin)
Yogurt	Meat tenderizer	Amphetamines
Fermented meats (smoked/aged/spoiled)	Soy sauce	Cocaine
Salami, pepperoni, bologna		Cold remedies
Aged fish (cured/dried/smoked/pickled)		Nasal decongestants
Caviar		Asthma medications
Figs, bananas, avocados, especially if overripe		Meperidine (Demerol)
Fava beans		Tricyclic antidepressants
Sauerkraut		SSRI antidepressants
Soybean paste, fermented bean curd		Anti-Parkinsonian agents
Imported beers and wines, especially Chianti and other red wines		
Caffeinated coffee, soft drinks, tea (in large amounts)		
Chocolate		
Licorice		

central nervous system (CNS), anticholinergic, hypotensive, and cardiovascular effects.

Drowsiness is the most common CNS effect. CNS stimulation occurs occasionally and may include tremors, insomnia, psychomotor excitement, and agitation. Rapid eye movement (REM) sleep may be disturbed. The most common anticholinergic effects include dry mouth, blurred vision, tachycardia, constipation, urinary retention, and palpitations. The degree of distress varies. Dizziness and orthostatic hypotension are serious hypotensive effects that may require dosage or medication changes.

Numerous cardiovascular effects are caused by antidepressants. Tachycardia, bradycardia, ventricular extrasystoles, congestive heart failure, myocardial infarction, atrioventricular block, and bundle branch block have been seen in clients taking tricyclic antidepressants. An electrocardiogram (ECG) should be performed before medications are administered so that clients with cardiovascular problems do not receive them.

Antidepressant medications should be chosen based on the symptoms and distress associated with the depression and the severity of the side effects. For example, a client who is sensitive to the sedative effects of certain medications should be prescribed a nonsedating drug, whereas a client in an agitated depression may benefit from a sedative. Side effects such as weight gain, impotence, and decreased libido frequently cause clients to discontinue their medication. The client is often reluctant to discuss these side effects.

St. John's wort is one of the top-selling herbal preparations in the United States. It is widely touted as beneficial in the treatment of mild to moderate depression. It may decrease the uptake of serotonin, norepinephrine, and dopamine. Various studies have compared St. John's wort to TCAs and now to the SSRIs. There is some evidence that the herb is beneficial for individuals with mild to moderate depression. The main side effects reported are dry mouth, dizziness, insomnia, confusion, constipation, GI irritation, and photosensitivity. The herb has the potential risk for serotonin syndrome, especially if combined with other antidepressants. Practitioners, especially prescribers, need to ask clients if they are using herbs and teach them about the possible risks involved in "double dosing." This herb also has the potential for inducing mania. A major concern with the use of St. John's wort is that the ingredients in the product may vary with different vendors and dosage equivalency cannot be guaranteed.

Critical Thinking Question What are the indications and reasons for someone with a mood disorder to stay on medication during long periods of stability?

Electroconvulsive Therapy (ECT)

This can be a highly effective treatment, especially for severe, unrelenting depression. It is mainly used when antidepressant medications have failed to bring relief or when quick response is needed due to the significant risk of suicide. ECT is effective for about 50% of the clients who do not respond to medications. ECT can also be useful for severe depression with psychotic features and sometimes for severe mania. With ECT a low-energy electrical current is passed through the brain to cause a brain seizure lasting about one minute; it is thought to alter the flow of neurotransmitters in the brain. The treatments are usually given two to three times per week in a series of 6 to 12 treatments. ECT is given after careful medical screening and in a very controlled environment with an anesthesiologist or healthcare practitioner with anesthesia training present.

The main risks are those associated with brief anesthesia. Short-term memory loss, especially for the time period surrounding the treatment, may occur. More significant memory loss is rare with the modern application of this treatment. ECT is considered safer than medication for some older adults and for pregnant women after the first trimester, during which time anesthesia is considered an undesirable risk (Glod, 1998; Keltner, 2007b). ECT may have to be repeated, and sometimes maintenance treatments about once a month are indicated. About 100,000 clients per year receive ECT for the treatment of depression (DBSA, 2006).

Alternative Treatments

Some somatic or alternative therapies being used to treat depression include light therapy (phototherapy), vagus nerve stimulation (VNS), and transcranial magnetic stimulation (TMS). In phototherapy, broad-spectrum light exposure provides artificial lighting, brighter than usual indoor lighting, to the environment of an individual with seasonal affective disorder (SAD). Light therapy is based on biological rhythms. VNS involves the implanting of a pacemaker-like device to stimulate the vagus nerve, which is critical in relaying information to and from the central nervous system. In TMS therapy, "a special electromagnet delivers short bursts of energy to stimulate nerve cells in the brain" for the relief of severe depression that has not been relieved by traditional therapy (DBSA, 2006, p. 52). Even if they do not use any of these somatic or non-pharmacological treatments, clients suffering from unrelenting depression appreciate knowing that there are still other forms of treatment that might offer them some degree of relief.

Critical Thinking Question When obtaining a medication history, why is it important to obtain information on medications for mood disorders, other medical conditions, and over-the-counter medications that a client may be taking?

Nursing Interventions

Two primary concerns for clients with mood disorders are safety (suicidal potential) and self-esteem. Short-term goals include meeting the client's physical needs, resulting from the symptoms he or she is experiencing. After baseline data are collected and a physical assessment is completed, the nurse develops a care plan to address the client's physical and mental health needs. Clients who are very depressed may neglect both their health and safety. Nurses may need to provide basic care for clients who lack the energy or interest for self-care. Basic activities of daily living (ADLs) such as bathing, grooming, choosing clothes, and dressing may require assistance. Nurses must promote adequate nutrition and fluid intake for clients who have not been eating or drinking. Nutrition and fluid intake must be monitored and documented carefully. Restoring sleep patterns will provide adequate rest at night and wakefulness during the day, benefiting the client both physically and mentally. Because of the anticholinergic side effects of drug therapy, nurses must encourage good dental hygiene. Sipping water during the day and chewing sugarless gum can help to relieve dry mouth.

Women with mood disorders need special attention during pregnancy and the postpartum period. The nurse needs to talk with the mother and ask for her description of her mood and behavior. Mood changes during this time are too often overlooked. When these changes are discovered, they are treated very much like depression or mania in the general population except for the concern about medication. Although it is generally the best policy to avoid medications and unnecessary chemical intake during pregnancy or breastfeeding, nontreatment may put the mother and child at greater risk. Reaching out to these women can have enormous benefits for them, their children, and others close to them. They need a strong support system, adequate rest, and some time for themselves away from caretaking responsibilities.

Physical activity is very important and should be encouraged even if the client resists. If achievable, the nurse must encourage the client to take part in activities that were enjoyed previously. The client can begin with solitary activities before mixing with others. Physical activity both releases pent-up energy and increases feelings of well-being, accomplishment, and control. Bowel, bladder, and menstrual functions should be monitored, and the nurse should intervene as indicated for constipation, urinary retention, or lack of self-care.

Some helpful statements the nurse can say to someone who is depressed include:

- I know you have a real illness and that's what causes you to feel depressed.
- I can't understand exactly how you feel, but I want to understand and help you.
- Tell me what I can do right now to help you.
- You may not believe it, but the way you are feeling now will change.
- Talk to me; I am listening. (DBSA, 2005)

Nurses can provide positive reinforcement by acknowledging the client's accomplishments and validating progress. The nurse can promote the client's existing strengths and resources as well as help the client identify activities or plans that are reminders of past pleasures or future anticipations. In interactions with a client who is depressed the nurse needs to be mindful of her or his own **affect**. A pleasant but neutral affect is usually best. Too much cheerfulness can be almost painful for the client and may cause

ECT is a highly effective treatment, especially for severe, unrelenting depression. It is mainly used when antidepressant medications have failed to bring improvement or when there is a purposeful threat of suicide.

Nonpharmacological complementary therapies in conjunction with antidepressants can help clients with depression.

A primary nursing goal is to keep clients safe and prevent self-injury.

the client to withdraw and be unable to connect with the nurse. The client's low self-esteem and hopelessness often require the nurse to direct the client's actions. A conscious effort should be made to provide continuous and much needed encouragement, support, and reinforcement.

Some nursing diagnoses that can be utilized in care planning for clients with a mood disorder such as a major depressive disorder include:

- Risk for violence directed towards self or others
- Impaired social interactions
- Chronic low self-esteem
- Hopelessness
- Powerlessness
- Self-care deficit
- Altered thought processes
- Interrupted family processes
- Altered nutrition
- Disturbed sleep pattern
- Anxiety
- Risk for suicide (North American Nursing Diagnosis Association [NANDA], 2004)

See Appendix II for additional NANDA diagnoses.

Education for Clients and Families

Client education is very important. Nurses must provide information about the specific mood disorder, its typical symptoms and problems, the clinical course, treatment issues, and the medications used. It is essential to build a therapeutic nurse-client relationship based on trust. Family members and significant others should be involved in the educational process from the beginning of treatment. This creates a support system for the client that can be useful throughout the course of therapy for episodes of depression and to assist in recognizing signs of impending problems. Clients should be taught to identify the early signs of depression and to seek help when needed to avoid or limit recurrences. Clients should be counseled to continue taking medications even when they start to feel better. They also need to understand the synergistic relationship between some antide-

CASE STUDY Ms. S.

Ms. S., a 29-year-old married female with an attractive appearance, though somewhat unkempt and profoundly sad, is accompanied by her husband upon admission. She is a homemaker and has two sons, ages 4 years and 13 months. Ms. S. was admitted to the hospital because she was unable to function at home and care for her children, was having great difficulty sleeping, and began expressing some suicidal ideation. She has been crying almost continuously for the last month, has lost 15 pounds, seems withdrawn, and says she has no energy or interest to do anything. She had experienced some "postpartum blues" after the birth of her first child, but did not seek help. Ms. S. reports that she had more difficulty after the birth of her second child and was treated for postpartum depression by her family doctor. She had been prescribed Lexapro 20 mg daily. She reports that the medication helped her, but she did not want to be a "druggie" and quit taking the medication about 2 months ago when she started to feel better. She has been troubled by recurrent "yearnings for death" and feelings that her family would be better off without her. Ms. S. talks about feeling anxious and not wanting to be a "poor mother" to her children like her own mother who had several hospitalizations for psychotic depression during Ms. S.'s childhood. Ms. S.'s husband is with her on admission and seems supportive and concerned. He is caring but expresses difficulty understanding "what went wrong."

Ms. S. is diagnosed with a *DSM-IV-TR*, Axis I diagnosis of major depressive disorder, with postpartum onset. Some nursing diagnoses that could apply to a client with major depression include:

- Risk for self-directed violence related to depressed mood, as evidenced by her appearance, self-report, and "yearning for death"
- Self-care deficit related to lack of energy and interest in caring for herself or her family, as evidenced by her unkempt appearance, lack of attention to herself, and loss of weight
- Low self-esteem related to perceived role inadequacy, as evidenced by her stated guilt regarding her inability to care for her children, her home, or herself

NURSING CARE PLAN Major Depressive Disorder

Expected Outcomes	Nursing Interventions	Evaluations
Short-term:		
• Will take medication as prescribed.	• Administer prescribed medications such as Lexapro 20 mg, one every morning, or Trazadone 50 mg, one hour after bedtime if unable to sleep. • Regularly review medication regimen and repeat medication education from the beginning of hospital stay.	• Is able to correctly repeat information about and take her medication
• Will remain free of self–harm.	• Demonstrate an empathetic, caring relationship with client, letting her know your concern for her safety and gentle optimism for her future progression. • Regularly assess client for suicidal ideation/intent.	• States she no longer wishes to be dead. "I want to be the mother for my boys." • She also states that her spiritual beliefs strongly encourage her to value her life as a special gift.
• Will follow unit schedule and attend therapies. • Will bathe and groom daily.	• Monitor client's activities and remind her of the unit schedule.	• Follows the unit scheduled routines and activities • Bathes, grooms, and dresses neatly on her own.
• Will eat food, selected by her, that is served.	• Have dietician meet with client to discuss her preferences.	• Eats meals with other clients in the dining room.
• Will make specific daily goals that she can reasonably accomplish.	• Assist client in making daily specific goals that she can meet and thereby gradually boosting her self-esteem. • Offer client the opportunity to talk about caring for her children and other concerns that she wants to discuss.	• Asks for one-to-one time with her nurse to discuss goals and concerns.
	• In a matter-of-fact manner acknowledge accomplishments. ("You washed your hair today.")	• Acknowledges encouragement from others.
	• Encourage client to interact with other clients, both sharing and listening. • Teach client relaxation techniques and practice individually and in a group.	• Uses deep-breathing relaxation exercises in the evening in her room.
	• Encourage client to attend the family night group meeting with her husband.	• Attends family group meetings with her husband.
	• Review her discharge plan as it is developed. • Involve client's husband in a review of her discharge plan.	• Asks her husband to join her for the review of her discharge plan.
Long-term:		
• Will commit to plans for follow-up care at the psychiatric and counseling center. • Will participate in family psychoeducation classes with her husband.	• Engage client in discussion about the impact of follow-up care on maintaining emotional balance after hospitalization. • Involve client's husband in planning post-discharge activities.	• Schedule appointment for her initial, postdischarge appointment with the psychiatric and counseling center.
• Will attend the Depression and Bipolar Support Alliance (DBSA) bi-weekly groups for mothers of young children. • Will reconnect with her church group and utilize "Mom's Morning Out" program.	• Discuss with her and give her a brochure with information about the Depression and Bipolar Support Alliance (DBSA) group meetings with location, meeting times, and contact phone number.	• With client's permission, give her name and number to the local Depression and Bipolar Support Alliance (DBSA) contact person to put her on the list for a reminder of the meetings. Also, give client information and a phone contact for DBSA.

Visit http://nursing.jbpub.com/psychiatric for additional care plans and exercises.

pressants (e.g., MAOIs and TCAs) and certain foods and other drugs and that they are at greater risk for tooth and periodontal disease and should be attentive to their dental regimen and follow-up (McDermott, 2005).

Bipolar Disorder

Like with unipolar disorders, bipolar disorders occur in a range of severity levels. Bipolar I disorder, formerly known as manic-depressive disorder, is the most classic of these disorders and can be the most severe. Persons with bipolar I disorder experience one or more manic episodes or mixed episodes. Frequently individuals may have had one or more major depressive episodes prior to experiencing mania (APA, 2000). Bipolar II disorder is characterized by at least one hypomanic episode and one or more major depressive episodes. With this disorder the hypomanic episodes may not result in significant harm. However, the major depressive episodes tend to bring about considerable distress in relationships and occupational functioning. With bipolar disorder the person's mood vacillates in cycles from high to low over time. The *DSM-IV-TR* refers to this happening as "a shift in polarity" (APA, p. 382).

A "shift in polarity" describes the client's experience with mood cycles changing from highs to lows over a period of time.

With bipolar disorders there are four different types of mood episodes: manic, hypomanic, major depressive, and mixed.

With bipolar disorders, four different types of mood episodes can occur: manic episode, hypomanic episode, major depressive episode, and mixed episode. The most expansive type is the manic episode or mania, which often begins with an elevated sense of heightened energy, creativity, and a pleasurable social engagement. These feelings rapidly escalate to a high state of **euphoria** or severe irritability. Individuals with mania or in a manic episode typically lack insight into their situation. They remain in denial that anything is wrong and resist efforts for help. They tend to be very accusatory toward anyone who suggests they are ill. To be labeled as a manic episode the symptoms must be present for at least 1 week or be severe enough to result in hospitalization. In addition to the extreme euphoric or irritable mood the individual must meet three to four of the following criteria: having an inflated self-esteem or feeling of power and greatness; requiring little sleep yet having a high degree of energy; talking so fast that others cannot keep up; racing thoughts or flight of ideas; being easily distracted; increasing goal-directed activity at work, socially, or sexually; and engaging excessively in pleasurable activities without concern for potential negative consequences such as extreme spending, indiscrete sexual behavior, or foolish business endeavors. With a manic episode there is severe impairment in social or occupational functioning. The person may have to be hospitalized to prevent harm to self or others, and in extreme cases psychotic symptoms may occur (APA, 2000).

The hypomanic episode or **hypomania** is a less severe degree of mania with a distinct period of elevation or mania that must last at least 4 days. The symptoms are similar to mania but less severe and do not cause marked impairment in social and occupational functioning or have psychotic features. Many individuals like the experience of these episodes. They feel better and can be more productive. As a result, clients with bipolar disorder often quit taking their medication in an effort to extend this period of hypomania. These periods rarely last indefinitely, and it has been identified that "5–15% of individuals with hypomania will ultimately develop a Manic Episode" (APA, 2000, p. 367).

Depression is the downside of bipolar disorder. The symptoms that occur with this phase are the same as those already discussed under major depressive disorder. As with unipolar depression, psychotic features can be present in the depressed period of bipolar disorder. With a mixed episode, symptoms of both mania and depression occur at the same time or alternating, frequently nearly every day for at least a week. Individuals feel elevated or irritable like in the manic state, but are also depressed or agitated. Both the depressed and the mixed episodes cause marked impairment in social or occupational functioning (APA, 2000). Mixed episodes are difficult to endure and to treat. As a result of the high energy and the depression in combination, there is an especially high risk of suicide in these clients.

Incidence and Prevalence

Bipolar I disorder is characterized by periods of both manic episodes and major depressive episodes, and occurs equally in both sexes. There is no evidence of variation in the incidence of bipolar disorder in different racial and ethnic groups, but some practitioners are concerned that the disorder is under-diagnosed in certain groups. The typical individual with bipolar disorder will experience four episodes during the first 10 years after diagnosis (Kahn, Ross, Printz, & Sachs,

2000). A number of years can pass between the first two or three manic or depressive episodes, but without treatment most individuals tend to experience an increase in episodes. For some, moods occur in a seasonal pattern with an onset and remission at certain times of the year, especially the fall and the spring.

> The presence of winter-type seasonal pattern appears to vary with latitude, age, and sex. Prevalence increases with higher latitudes. Age is also a strong predictor of seasonality, with younger persons at a higher risk for winter depressive episodes and with women comprising 60%–90% of persons with seasonal pattern." (APA, 2000, p. 426)

Men are more likely to begin with a manic episode and women with a major depressive episode. With men the episodes of mania usually equal or exceed the number of depressions, but with women the depressive episodes are predominant. The specifier of **rapid cycling** is also more common in women. Rapid cycling is the occurrence of four or more mood episodes in a 1-year period. About 10–20% of those with bipolar disorder experience rapid cycling. Those with a rapid cycling course tend to have a more guarded long-term prognosis (APA, 2000, p. 428).

According to the *DSM-IV-TR*, a person's first manic episode typically occurs in their early 20s, but it can begin in adolescence or even after age 50 (APA, 2000). There are also some cases that happen in early childhood. There is a 10–20% risk for the development of bipolar I disorder in adolescents with repeated major depressive episodes. When the first manic episode occurs after age 50 with no previous history of such symptoms, the practitioner should be alert to the possibility of an undiagnosed neurological or other general medical condition or the effects of using alcohol, drugs, or prescribed medication.

Women with bipolar I disorder have a greater risk for having an episode during their postpartum period. In addition, women with major depressive, manic, mixed, or hypomanic episodes may experience more difficult symptoms during their premenstrual period (APA, 2000). Bipolar II occurs more often in women than in men, and the time period between episodes tends to get shorter with age. Nevertheless, about 85% of clients with this disorder experience quite functional times between episodes. Major changes in their sleep cycle or loss of sleep may trigger an episode (APA, 2000).

Clinical Example

Fifty-eight-year-old Pearl has been living with bipolar I disorder since her mid-teens. Every few months she experiences significant mood fluctuations—periods of euphoria, increased energy, and greatly reduced sleep. She has been known to bake hundreds of cookies for local workers such as the police, firefighters, and postal workers, showing up at odd times of the day or night to distribute her baked goods. On her last admission to the crisis unit, Pearl took off all of her clothes and marched down the hallway singing "Let Me Love You" while approaching other clients and staff in an overtly sexual manner.

Critical Thinking Question What are some of the concerns for treating women with bipolar disorder during their childbearing years, and what type of counseling is required if a woman is considering becoming pregnant?

In bipolar disorder "rapid cycling" is the occurrence of four or more mood episodes in a 1-year period. It is more common in women.

Etiology

Bipolar disorder appears to run in families. Many research studies have identified a number of different genes and specific brain structural changes that may be linked to the illness. Different studies indicate different results. The mode of inheritance in bipolar disorder is very complex. Only a fraction of those with the genetic risk actually get the disorder as "first degree biological relatives of individuals with Bipolar I Disorder have elevated rates of Bipolar I Disorder (4%–24%), Bipolar II Disorder (1%–5%), and Major Depressive Disorder (4%–24%)" (APA, 2000, p. 386). It also has been noted that clients with mood disorders in their first-degree biological relatives are more likely to have an earlier age at onset; extensive twin and adoption studies indicate strong evidence of a genetic influence for bipolar I disorder (APA, p. 386).

In older adults (age 50+) with no previous history or risk factors, baseline screening is especially vital to rule out other causes such as an undiagnosed neurological or other general medical condition or the effects of using alcohol, drugs, or prescribed medication.

Bipolar disorder appears to run in families, occurs equally in both sexes, and is often under-diagnosed in some racial and ethnic groups.

Physiology

No laboratory findings have yet been determined to be diagnostic for bipolar I or bipolar II disorder. The diagnosis is based on history, observation, interview, and client report. When compared with clients with major depressive disorder or individuals without any mood disorders, imaging studies "tend to show increased rates of right-hemispheric lesions, or bilateral subcortical or peri-ventricular lesions in those with Bipolar I Disorder" (APA, 2000, p. 385). Hypothyroidism may be associated with rapid cycling. On the other end, "hyperthyroidism may precipitate or worsen manic symptoms in individuals with a preexisting Mood Disorder" (APA, p. 385). Regardless of the exact biochemical nature of bipolar disorder, it is apparent that individuals with the disorder have an increased vulnerability to emotional and physical stressors. (See Chapter 4.)

The *DSM-IV-TR* notes that the lifetime risk for bipolar disorder varies from 0.4% to 1.6% (APA, 2000). Some sources quote data indicating higher rates for bipolar disorder. At the Sixth International Conference on Bipolar Disorder (2005), new figures were presented indicating that the incidence of bipolar disorder is considerably more prevalent than previously noted.

Clinical Presentation

Clients experiencing a manic episode have symptoms that can be observed by the nurse as changes in behavior, cognition, and emotions. Some of the signs that can be recognized in these three categories are discussed below.

Behavioral Signs

Clients in a manic episode wake up full of energy after little sleep, do not tire easily, do not need much sleep, and may have insomnia. They show extreme motor activity and an increased or a decreased appetite and pay no attention to hygiene, grooming, or health. The individual may exhibit uncharacteristic sexual activity or sexual behavior. These clients often dress flamboyantly, have exaggerated mannerisms, wear too much makeup, behave impulsively, and are often intrusive, demanding, domineering, and physically threatening. Family and friends may describe wild shopping sprees, excessive work hours, or elaborate schemes to acquire wealth or fame. Clients experiencing a manic episode are angered at any attempts to set limits; thus, personal interactions are strained. The client may disappear without explanation.

The three primary categories of medications used to treat bipolar disorder are mood stabilizers, antipsychotics, and antidepressants. When antidepressants are used they should be combined with a mood stabilizer to avoid pushing the client with bipolar disorder towards mania.

Cognitive Signs

Clients may report that their thoughts are racing, or they have shown poor judgment. They may be hypervigilant, easily distracted, or have impractical ideas. Their speech is pressured, rapid, loud, and even incoherent, with **flight of ideas**, which is pressured speech with rapid topic changes. Clients may have delusions of persecution, grandiosity, or religiosity or may experience hallucinations. They lack insight into their condition.

Emotional Signs

The client may have a labile mood that changes rapidly from elation or euphoria to irritability, anger, or rage. Affect may shift from happy to depressed, negative, or hostile. They typically appear excited and overconfident, feeling like they can accomplish anything. Clients may report feeling "on top of the world."

Differential Diagnosis

It can be difficult to distinguish between bipolar disorder and various other conditions, including anxiety disorders, schizophrenia, schizoaffective disorder, and sometimes substance disorders. Anxiety and psychotic symptoms and acting out behavior can occur in all of these disorders. It is also true that many clients with bipolar disorder have a co-occurring alcohol or other substance abuse disorder, especially those with an earlier onset of the bipolar disorder. In addition, other co-morbid mental conditions include anorexia, bulimia, ADHD, panic disorder, and social phobia (APA, 2000, p. 384). The *DSM-IV-TR* also states that: "Child abuse, spouse abuse, or other violent behavior may occur during severe Manic Episodes or during those with psychotic features. Other associated problems include school truancy, school failure, occupational failure, divorce, or episodic antisocial behavior" (APA, p. 384). In adolescents who experience recurrent major depressive episodes, about 10–15% will later develop bipolar I disorder.

Management and Treatment

A combination of psychotherapy and medication is usually the most effective approach in treating bipolar disorders. A careful baseline health assessment is also imperative. It is essential that this include evaluation of cardiac status with EKG, blood pressure, and heart rate; complete blood counts with differential; serum electrolytes; renal function; and complete thyroid function studies (Lehne, 2007).

Psychopharmacology

The three primary categories of medications used to treat bipolar disorder are mood stabilizers, antipsychotics, and antidepressants. Benzodiazepines may also be prescribed to help alleviate insomnia, anxiety, or restlessness, especially in the lag time before any of the three main groups of drugs begin to work. The most often prescribed mood stabilizers are lithium and antiepileptic drugs. The antipsychotics are used to help control agitation, anxiety, and insomnia during severe manic episodes even if no psychotic symptoms are present. The atypical antipsychotics have been found to have mood stabilizing properties and are now preferred over the traditional antipsychotics. Clients may also need antidepressant therapy. However, antidepressants must always be combined with a mood stabilizer when treating clients with bipolar disorder to avoid pushing them toward mania. Wellbutrin (bupropion), Effexor (venlafaxine), and the SSRIs are usually the preferred choices of antidepressants. The tricyclics have more serious side effects and may have a greater tendency to cause a manic episode (Kahn et al., 2000; Lehne, 2007).

Lithium

The usefulness of lithium was first reported in Australia in 1949, but lithium was not approved for use in the United States until 1970 (Lehne, 2007). Lithium appears to be more effective for clients with bipolar I who have the more euphoric mania and experience less depression with the elevated state. However, lithium can also be useful for depression and is often added with other medications. Lithium tends to be less effective in treating mixed manic states and rapid-cycling bipolar disorder (Kahn et al., 2000).

The exact mechanism of action by which lithium (lithium carbonate, Lithobid) stabilizes the mood is not known. However, the evidence suggests that lithium works by altering the distribution of calcium, sodium, and magnesium ions, which are vital to nerve function. It also affects the synthesis and release of norepinephrine, serotonin, and dopamine. Although the leveling of manic effects begins 5–7 days after treatment begins, maximum benefits may take 2–3 weeks.

The adverse effects of lithium (**Table 16-4**) are closely associated with serum levels. The side effects increase as the level of lithium in the blood increases toward the toxic level. Some of these adverse effects occur at therapeutic lithium levels, below 1.5 mEq/L. These milder effects include fine hand tremor, mild stomach irritation, abdominal bloating, mild thirst, polyuria, muscle weakness, tiredness, headache, and weight gain. Many of these mild effects subside, or at least decrease, with time. Clients should continue their lithium as ordered. As beginning toxic levels (1.5–2.0 mEq/L) are reached, the adverse effects increase dramatically. Severe and persistent gastrointestinal symptoms, coarse hand tremors, uncoordination, sedation, and EKG changes occur. Lithium should be withheld and lithium blood levels should be drawn. When severe levels of toxicity are reached (2.0–2.5 mEq/L), clients experience tinnitus, high output of dilute urine, serious EKG changes, severe hypotension, stupor, and seizures. As the level of lithium in the blood rises above 2.5 mEq/L, urine output ceases and cardiac arrhythmia occurs along with peripheral circulatory collapse. Coma and even death can occur (Lehne, 2007). The most frequent cause of severe toxicity is intentional overdose.

The most important way to minimize adverse effects is to sustain a steady state of lithium level and fluid and electrolyte balance. Clients need to maintain a normal salt or sodium intake and replace water lost due to perspiration, diarrhea,

Lithium is used for clients with bipolar I who have the more euphoric mania and experience less depression with the elevated state. It also can be useful for depression and is often added with other medications; it is less effective in treating mixed manic states and rapid-cycling bipolar disorder.

The adverse effects of lithium are closely associated with serum levels. Some of these adverse effects occur at therapeutic lithium levels, below 1.5 mEq/L. The toxic level occurs at 1.5–2.0 mEq/L, and monitoring blood lithium levels is critical.

Table 16-4 Recognizing Levels of Lithium Toxicity by Side Effects

Blood Level of 1.5 mEq/L	Blood Level of 1.5–2.5 mEq/L	Blood Level of 2.5 mEq/L or Greater
Vomiting	Ataxia	Unconsciousness
Weakness	Diarrhea	Hypotension
Drowsiness	Persistent nausea and vomiting	Increased temperature
Lethargy	Loss of coordination	Dysrhythmias
Muscle twitching	Blurred vision	Grand mal seizures
Mild ataxia	Stupor	Renal failure
Slight tremor	Clonic limb movements	Hallucinations
Dizziness	Syncope	Deep tendon hyperreflexia
Slurred speech	Delirium	Coma or death
Vomiting	EKG and/or EEG changes	
Abdominal pain	Nystagmus	

Note: EEG = electroencephalogram; EKG = electrocardiogram.

or heavy exercise by routinely drinking 8–12 glasses of liquids every day. They should avoid diuretics and nonsteroidal anti-inflammatory drugs (NSAIDs) such as ibuprofen and naproxen. NSAIDs, but not aspirin, can increase renal absorption of lithium and thus cause lithium levels to rise. Lithium should always be taken with food or milk to avoid stomach upset. Lithium can cause birth defects and should not be taken during pregnancy, especially during the first trimester or during breastfeeding (Lehne, 2007).

Monitoring of lithium levels in the blood is essential. There is a small margin between therapeutic and toxic serum levels. Maintaining an adequate fluid level in the body significantly affects the lithium level in the blood. At the onset of treatment, frequent blood samples, every 2–3 days, are required until therapeutic concentration is attained. After stabilization, blood levels should be taken every 1–3 months regularly. For proper evaluation, the blood should be drawn in the morning, 12 hours after the evening dose (Lehne, 2007).

Antiepileptic Drugs (AEDs)

Many of the medications used for the treatment of epilepsy are also used to treat bipolar disorder. These drugs are used to suppress mania and stabilize the mood of clients with the disorder (**Table 16-5**).

Atypical Antipsychotics

All of the atypical antipsychotics, except Clozaril (clozapine), are used to treat acute mania in bipolar disorder because of their mood stabilizing effects (**Table 16-6**). The traditional or typical antipsychotics are still used in the treatment of bipolar disorder. However, due to their higher rate of extrapyramidal side effects, including tardive dyskinesia, they are now prescribed less often than the atypical antipsychotics. All of the atypical antipsychotics except Clozaril have FDA approval for the treatment of acute mania. Zyprexa (olanzapine) is also approved for long-term use to prevent the recurrence of more mood episodes. Risperdal (risperidone) and Seroquel (quetiapine) are associated with a more moderate level of weight gain than Zyprexa. Seroquel is indicated for the treatment of depressive episodes in bipolar disorder in addition to acute mania. Geodon (ziprasidone) and Abilify (aripiprazole) are the two newest atypical antipsychotics on the market, and both have been shown to cause little or no weight gain. They are often referred to as weight neutral. All of the atypical antipsychotics can be used as monotherapy or in combination with lithium or one of the AEDs for the treatment of bipolar disorder (Keltner, 2007a; Lehne, 2007).

Mood stabilizers may take a few weeks to establish a favorable response, so other medica-

Table 16-5 Antiepileptic Drugs (AEDs) Used for Mood Stabilization

Trade Name	Generic	Advantages	Some Disadvantages
Depakote	divalproex sodium	Antimanic, particularly effective for treating acute mania; faster and safer than lithium (greater range between therapeutic and toxic levels); also useful for rapid cycling and mixed manic bipolar episodes	Weight gain, sedation, nausea, weak anti-depressant properties, rare cases of liver and pancreas toxicity and thrombocytopenia; possible fertility issues for females; hair loss
Lamictal	lamotrigine	Reduces cycle frequency; strong antidepressant effect; no significant weight gain	Stevens-Johnson rash, nausea, headache, blurred vision, dizziness
Tegretol	carbamazepine	Antimanic	Agranulocytosis; liver toxicity; reduced effectiveness for birth control pills; nausea
Neurontin	gabapentin	Adjunctive versus monotherapy; reduces anxiety	Fatigue, muscle aches, blurred vision
Trileptal	oxcarbazepine	Antimanic properties; fewer side effects than Tegretol	GI upsets; sedation; can reduce effectiveness of birth control pills
Topomax	topiramate	May prompt modest weight loss	Cognitive dulling; may reduce effectiveness of birth control pills; possible glaucoma; kidney stones

Table 16-6 Atypical Antipsychotics as Mood Stabilizers

Trade Name	Generic	Advantages	Some Disadvantages
Risperdal	risperidone	Antimanic; antipsychotic; may reduce cycling	Weight gain; increased prolactin levels
Zyprexa	olanzapine	Antimanic; antipsychotic; may reduce cycling	Weight gain (significant)
Seroquel	quetiapine	Antimanic; antipsychotic; may reduce cycling	Sedation; some weight gain; cognitive dulling
Geodon	ziprasidone	Antimanic; antipsychotic; may reduce cycling; weight neutral	Sedation; potential heart rhythm changes
Abilify	aripiprazole	Antimanic; antipsychotic; may reduce cycling; weight neutral	Insomnia or sedation; restlessness

tions may be used initially to provide more immediate relief from the agitation, nervousness, and insomnia that often accompany a manic episode. The antipsychotics mentioned above may have some calming effect before they help with mood stabilizing. They are also beneficial when psychotic symptoms are present. The benzodiazepines, such as Ativan (lorazepam) or Klonopin (clonazepam), are sometimes used, preferably only on a short-term basis (Kahn et al., 2000). These anxiolytics are schedule IV controlled substances and may lead to physical dependency with long-term dosing. Their use requires careful supervision, and extended use should be avoided for clients with a history of alcohol or drug abuse.

Critical Thinking Question Does taking antidepressants cause bipolar disorder? Support your answer with examples.

Nursing Interventions

Nurses should provide a quiet, stimulus-free environment for clients who are experiencing acute mania. Staff members must discourage clients from acting out in an attempt to entertain the staff with their behavior. A quiet room or "time out" should be used as needed. Seclusion or restraints are a last resort for clients with safety issues. Medications should be administered as needed.

Although a therapeutic relationship is difficult to establish initially, the client must be emotionally supported and encouraged to inform staff members when feelings of hostility or anger increase. The nurse should not confront clients or argue with them; it is best to maintain a quiet, calm approach and to have brief but frequent contact. The nurse-client therapeutic relationship involves teaching the client and family about the disorder and the need to monitor signs and symptoms carefully to recognize and handle impending recurrences at an early stage.

During an acute manic phase, the nurse must help the client maintain adequate nutrition, sleep, and cleanliness (personal hygiene). Because the client has increased motor activity, the nurse may need to provide finger foods and beverages in small containers that can be consumed "on the run." Documentation of intake and output is important. The client often needs assistance with hygiene, grooming, and dress. Medication may be administered to help the client get necessary and adequate rest.

The nurse should not confront clients or argue with them. The nurse should maintain a quiet, calm approach; have brief but frequent contact; and provide a quiet, stimulus-free environment when clients are experiencing acute mania.

Education for Clients and Families

The nurse must fully explain to the client and family members or significant others why the manic and depressive episodes recur. The nurse can increase the family's understanding and support by explaining that the disorder is an illness that can be treated effectively. Clients also must learn the effectiveness of each treatment and how to minimize side effects. The client should be able to recognize the early signs of mania, accept that treatment is necessary, and seek help as needed.

Clients with bipolar disorder must be warned that the antidepressants they take for depressive episodes may induce manic episodes. This knowledge allows the client and others to differentiate between lifting depression and impending mania. Clients who are receiving lithium should be advised to take food or milk to reduce gastric

NURSING CARE PLAN Bipolar I Disorder, Manic Episode

Expected Outcomes	Nursing Interventions	Evaluations
Short term:		
• Will contract not to harm self or others during hospital stay.	• Develop caring rapport with client. • Regularly assess client for safety.	• Client remains free of injury during inpatient hospital stay.
• Will follow unit rules.	• Review unit rules with client and give him any necessary reminders to help him display acceptable behavior.	• Client follows the unit's rules with minimal difficulty.
• Will experience a decrease in or cessation of psychotic ideation.	• Observe client for changes in psychotic ideation.	• He displays a calming energy level and his thoughts gradually return to a reality base within 72 hours. • Interacts coherently with staff and peers.
• Will not engage in substance abuse/misuse.	• Assess client for substance abuse/misuse.	• Client has no signs of substance abuse, with a normal blood alcohol level and drug screen.
• Will sleep at least 6 hours per night.	• Monitor sleep and promote positive sleep hygiene.	• Client is sleeping for at least 6 continuous hours during the night.
• Will achieve adequate food and fluid intake. • Will bathe and groom daily. • Will participate in unit activity schedule.	• Monitor food and fluid intake for adequacy.	• Client has appropriate food and fluid intake and is appropriately engaging in self-care and is groomed.
• Will make appointment for follow-up care with psychiatric and counseling center before discharge.	• Discuss the importance of on-going follow-up care in the prevention of relapse. • Discuss plans for future career options.	• Client is beginning to talk about his job situation and is expressing appropriate feelings of sadness and anger related to his loss and alteration in status. • Client is demonstrating appropriate behavior with staff and peers on the unit and is beginning to discuss his need for follow-up care for his bipolar disorder and excessive substance use.

CASE STUDY Mr. M.

Mr. M. is a 31-year-old professor of Italian at a major university. He is single, lives alone, and his family lives out of state. He had become depressed during the past year while he was applying for tenure. The psychiatrist he saw treated him with Zoloft. The medication was very effective in relieving his depression, but after about 8 months, he became hypomanic with increasing disturbances in his behavior. Prior to this he had not experienced any signs of mental illness. He had received an award as an outstanding professor with an impressive list of publications to his credit.

Mr. M. was brought to the ER by his girlfriend and admitted to the crisis unit. His girlfriend noted that his behavior had been escalating for several weeks. She reported the following behaviors:

- He had slept only a few hours in the past week, experiencing high energy levels with no desire to rest.
- His behavior had become uncontrolled and potentially dangerous, including drinking much more than usual and driving recklessly.
- He had recently been reported for being too friendly with several female students and assistant instructors, with two women filing sexual harassment charges against him.
- He stood up in class today and declared that he was receiving an important message from God and that he had "a plan for bringing peace to the world."
- He had also been spending money furiously, buying venture stocks with some inheritance money, and using his credit cards to buy Italian wines by the case to stock his wine cellar.
- He was calling old friends and colleagues on the phone at all hours of the night.

Tonight at the restaurant with his girlfriend he was loud and intrusive to other patrons and demanded to be

NURSING CARE PLAN **Bipolar I Disorder, Manic Episode (continued)**

Expected Outcomes	Nursing Interventions	Evaluations
	Psychopharmacological Intervention:	
• Will adhere to medication schedule. • Will attend medication group and will review his prescribed medications with his primary nurse.	• Administer prescribed medications such as lithium carbonate, 600 mg three times per day, and Seroquel, 100 mg daily on day one (with daily increase of Seroquel until therapeutic level is reached, usually 500–600 mg). • Monitor medication administration closely for adherence. • Teach client about his medications and review information to promote understanding.	• Demonstrates adherence with medication schedule and regularly attends medication group
Long-term:		**Referral:**
• Will actively engage in classes to learn about bipolar disorder. • Will continue in follow-up care after his hospitalization. • Will attend a DBSA support group soon after discharge. • Will keep a daily mood journal and also a list of essential topics to discuss in follow-up care with therapist.	• Review with client, family, and significant others post-discharge plans. • Discuss with client, family, and significant others the need to commit to follow-up care and to keep scheduled appointments. • Demonstrate to client how to keep a journal and explain its use in post-discharge plan of care.	• Schedule client's initial, postdischarge appointment with the psychiatric and counseling center. • With client's permission, give his name and number to the DBSA contact person to put his name on the list for a reminder of group meetings.

Visit http://nursing.jbpub.com/psychiatric for additional care plans and exercises.

given the "special attention deserved by someone of my notoriety." After only two drinks he started singing loudly and swinging around a decorative column. Four staff members struggled to get him out the front door. It was all his girlfriend could do to get him to the car. Against his wishes, she drove him straight to the hospital, yet upon arrival he did agree to sign for a voluntary admission.

The girlfriend tells the staff before leaving that she is concerned for Mr. M., especially since he just learned this week that his tenure has been denied, but she is really getting weary of struggling with this relationship. Mr. M. appears unshaven, with very wrinkled clothes, yet bursting with energy and unable to sit down for his intake interview.

Mr. M. has a *DSM-IV-TR*, Axis I diagnosis of bipolar I, most recent episode manic. His nursing diagnoses include:

- Injury, risk for, related to spiraling mania and delusional thinking, as evidenced by receiving a message from God, intrusive behavior in public, and high energy level.
- Sleep pattern disturbed related to the symptoms of mania, as evidenced by sleeping only a few hours in the past week without feeling tired.
- Self-esteem, risk for situational low, related to change in expected job progression, as evidenced by denial of tenure in his academic position and potential loss of current girlfriend.
- Ineffective coping related to manic state, as evidenced by drinking more than usual, driving recklessly, making unwelcome sexual advances, spending money excessively, and calling old friends at all hours, disruptive behavior, and deteriorating self-care.

irritation, expect fine hand tremors and an increase in urination and thirst as well as weight gain, maintain appropriate salt intake, avoid excess perspiration, drink 10 to 12 glasses of water a day, suck on hard candies, elevate feet for any edema, avoid pregnancy while on the drug, comply with having regular blood tests, and check with their prescribing practitioner before self-medicating for any condition.

Nurses must emphasize repeatedly the importance of taking medication as ordered, that effects will not be felt immediately, and that medication must not be discontinued just because the client feels better. Clients must be taught about nutrition because diet and fluid intake can greatly affect the action of the medication. Clients and family members should know when and how to seek help from crisis intervention services and their ongoing support system. The psychiatric nurse is often the practitioner that brings together the client and the needed community resources.

The possibility of suicide must always be considered when caring for clients with mood disorder; they should be asked whether they currently have or have had suicidal thoughts or plans. A "no suicide" contract can be a valuable treatment tool.

Critical Thinking Questions Should a client tell an employer that she or he has a bipolar disorder? How can such a decision impact upon the client's work situation?

Suicide and Mood Disorders

Suicide takes the lives of over 30,000 Americans a year, and worldwide suicide is the leading cause of violent death, outnumbering homicide and war-related deaths. It is the eleventh leading cause of death of all Americans; the eighth leading cause of death for all U.S. men, and the third leading cause of death among young people 15 to 24 years of age. More than four times as many men as women die by suicide, although women attempt suicide three times as often as men. The highest rates for suicide occur in white men age 85 and older (10.6% per 100,000), with suicide by firearms being the most common method (DBSA, 2006; National Institute of Mental Health [NIMH], 2003).

There is a suicide completion rate of 10–15% for individuals with bipolar I disorder. Both suicidal ideation and attempts happen more often during the time the person is in a depressed or mixed state (APA, 2000). This problem is compounded by the fact that

> on average, people with bipolar disorder see 3 to 4 doctors and spend over 8 years seeking treatment before they receive a correct diagnosis. Earlier diagnosis, proper treatment, and finding the right medications can help people avoid . . . suicide . . . alcohol/substance abuse . . . marital and work problems . . . treatment

Implications for Evidence-Based Practice

Recent studies indicate that clients with serious mental illness as well as physical health problems bear a greater burden of disease as they attempt to cope with their various conditions (Kennedy et al., 2005). Hagerty and Williams (1999) have demonstrated that higher levels of depression are associated with a lower sense of belonging. Studies using randomized clinical trials with 932 subjects produced evidence that psychotherapy in combination with antidepressant therapy is associated with significantly higher improvement rates than drug treatment alone. In studies that lasted longer than 12 weeks, the addition of psychotherapy was shown to have an even greater efficacy over drug treatment alone (Pampallona, Bollini, Tibaldi, Kupelnick, & Munizza, 2004). Another study (Simon, Ludman, Tutty, Operskalski, & Von Korff, 2004) consisted of 600 primary care clients with depression (mean age 46 years, 74% female) who began treatment with antidepressants. Results indicated a significant improvement in satisfaction with treatment and in clinical outcomes for those clients involved in a telephone program that integrated the management of their care and a structured form of psychotherapy using **cognitive behavioral therapy**.

These various studies support the importance and value when treating depressed clients of establishing a therapeutic nurse–client relationship to assist the clients in understanding their multiple problems, to improve their sense of self, and to participate in both psychotherapy and antidepressant therapy.

difficulties . . . incorrect, inappropriate, or partial treatment. (Kahn et al., 2000)

The risk of suicide tends to peak in the earlier years of the illness. The suicide rate is dangerously high with mood disorders. According to the *DSM-IV-TR* (APA, 2000) the suicide rate for individuals with major depressive disorder is up to 15% and for individuals with bipolar disorder is 10–15%.

A safety maxim when working with any individual is: *Every depressed client is potentially suicidal.* Risk factors and indicators are important to know, but these factors are based on statistics and a practitioner must not dismiss the potential risk of a client who does not fit the typical profile. Consider the fact that women of all ages and racial groups can kill themselves.

In addition to the presence of an existing mental illness, some significant indicators of suicide risk include: previous suicide attempt(s); having a plan in mind; significant change in expected patterns of behavior; age; gender; race; alcohol or substance abuse; serious medical problems; recent severe loss, unresolved grief, or threatened loss; financial loss or unemployment; hopelessness; disciplinary problems; work or school problems; imprisonment; and a poor social support system. In addition to maintaining safety and preventing self-injury, nurses must plan for the depressive or manic episodes that clients with mood disorders experience. The nurse may implement a formal agreement (no-suicide contract) specifying that clients will refrain from harming themselves and will notify the nurse or other staff of strong suicidal thoughts or urges. Clients with mood disorders must be regularly assessed for suicidality. Ask: "Are you thinking of hurting yourself?" If the answer is yes, it is imperative to ask: "Do you have a plan in mind?" If this answer is also yes, established suicide precautions must be taken.

Critical Thinking Question Is it ever appropriate to not be concerned if a client reports having ideas about wanting to be dead?

Summary

All individuals experience ups and downs of emotions in daily life, and these can be more marked in times of great loss or grieving. The mood disorders are separated into the depressive or unipolar disorders (major depressive disorder and dysthymic disorder) and bipolar disorders (bipolar I, bipolar II, and **cyclothymic disorder**). Additionally, mood disorders can be related to general medical conditions or can be substance-induced disorders, and they can occur seasonally or after delivery of an infant.

Clinical Example

Michael, who is in his mid-40s, was admitted to the psychiatric unit accompanied by his wife, who reported that in the last 3 weeks he was constantly crying, had stopped going to work, was rarely sleeping, and had lost over 20 pounds. During the night of admission, Michael went into the bathroom and while the door was briefly shut, separating him from observation, he stuffed a sock securely down his throat, lost consciousness, and collapsed to the floor where his body blocked the door. After several attempts, staff pulled him from the stall, removed the sock from his trachea and attempted resuscitation. It was unsuccessful and Michael died.

All of the mood disorders have a neurological basis, and genetics play a role because the disorders occur in families with psychosocial factors impacting upon the development and presentation of the disorders. Mood disorders are highly recurrent, with every episode increasing the likelihood of additional episodes. Women are twice as likely as men to experience depression and have a higher incidence rate of bipolar II disorder; bipolar I disorder with classic mania occurs about equally in both sexes.

Research indicates a higher improvement rate in the treatment of depression with a combination of psychotherapy and antidepressants. Supportive psychotherapy, cognitive behavioral therapy, and interpersonal therapy are various modalities. The selective serotonin reuptake inhibitors, atypical antidepressants, tricyclic antidepressants, and monoamine oxidase inhibitors can all be equally effective in treating the depressive disorders. Lithium remains an effective treatment for clients with bipolar I disorder with classic mania. The antiepileptic drugs also are effective in treating bipolar disorders. Antidepressants should never be given to a client with bipolar disorder without a concurrent mood stabilizer due to the concern of precipitating a manic episode. The goal of medication treatment is to fit the medication to the symptoms of the individual client with consideration for the particular drug actions, advantages, and side effects.

Recent studies indicate that clients with serious mental illness as well as physical health problems bear a greater burden of disease as they attempt to cope with their various conditions.

Clients with mood disorders should be regularly monitored for suicidal ideation because the suicide rate for this client population is 10–15%. Teaching clients and family members about their disorders, medications, and other available treatments is important. Nurses should refer clients and their families to peer support networks and other self-help resources.

Annotated References

American Psychiatric Association. (2000). *Diagnostic and statistical manual of mental disorders* (4th ed., text rev.). Washington, DC: Author.

This is the official nomenclature used by psychiatrists, other physicians, psychologists, registered professional nurses, social workers, occupational and recreational therapists, counselors, and other health and mental health professionals across all settings—in-patient, out-patient, partial hospital, consultation-liaison, clinic, private practice, and primary care, and with community populations.

Crutchfield, D. B. (2006). *Review of psychotropic drugs.* Wilmington, DE: Astra Zeneca Pharmaceuticals.

This book includes a review of current psychotropic drugs including their actions, side effects, adverse effects, and dosages.

Depression and Bipolar Support Alliance. (2005). *What helps and what hurts.* Chicago: Author.

This brochure from a national advocacy group provides suggestions to help family members communicate with clients who are dealing with symptoms of depression or bipolar disorder.

Depression and Bipolar Support Alliance. (2006). *The state of depression in America report.* Chicago: Author.

This report examines the economic, social, and individual burdens of this illness and explores opportunities to improve the availability and quality of care while working toward recovery and better lives for all Americans.

Druss, B. G., Rosenheck, R. A., & Sledge, W. H. (2000). Health and disability costs of depressive illness in a major U.S. corporation. *American Journal of Psychiatry, 157*(8), 1274–1278.

This article explores the cost of depression to a major employer. It concludes that the cost in lost workdays is as great as or greater than the cost of many other common medical illnesses, and the combination of depressive and other common illnesses is particularly costly. The strong association between depressive illness and sick days in younger workers suggests that the impact of depression may increase as these workers age.

Forrester, A. W., Lipsey, J. R., Teitelbaum, M. L., DePaulo, J. R., Andrzejewski, P. L., & Robinson, R. G. (1992). Depression following myocardial infarction. *International Journal of Psychiatry and Medicine, 22,* 33–46.

This study concluded that major depression is common in the acute post-myocardial infarction period and identified that major depressive syndromes were present in 19% (n 5 25) of the patients and were associated with prior history of mood disorder, large infarctions, and functional physical impairment.

Garlow, S. J., & Nemeroff, C. B. (2005). The neurochemistry of depressive disorders: Clinical studies. In D. S. Charney & E. J. Nestler (Eds.), *Neurobiology of mental illness* (pp. 440–460). New York: Oxford University Press.

Describes the state of knowledge of neurochemical mechanisms underlying psychiatric disorders and the implications for diagnosis and treatment.

Glod, C. A. (1998). *Contemporary psychiatric-mental health nursing: The brain-behavior connection.* Philadelphia: F. A. Davis.

A textbook for nursing students discussing the theories that are the foundation for linking brain and behavior; also explores healthy psychological development.

Goldstein, D. J., & Potter, W. Z. (2004). Biological theories of depression and implications for current and new treatments. In D. A. Ciraulo & R. I. Shader (Eds.), *Pharmacotherapy of depression* (pp. 1–32). Totowa, NJ: Humana Press.

Provides an orientation to the biological causes of depression as a basis for the safe and effective use of antidepressants.

Greenberg, P. E., Kessler, R. C., Birnbaum, H. G., Leong, S. A., Lowe, S. W., Bergland, P. A., et al. (2003). The economic burden of depression in the United States: How did it change between 1990 and 2000? *Journal of Clinical Psychiatry, 64*(12), 1465–1476.

Using a human capital approach, the authors developed prevalence-based estimates of three major cost categories: (1) direct costs, (2) mortality costs arising from depression-related suicides, and (3) costs associated with depression in the workplace. The results revealed that the economic burden of depression remained relatively stable between 1990 and 2000, despite a dramatic increase in the proportion of individuals who received treatment.

Hagerty, B. M., & Williams, R. A. (1999). The effects of sense of belonging, social support, conflict, and loneliness on depression. *Nursing Research, 48*(4), 215–219.

The study findings emphasize the importance of relationship-oriented experiences as part of assessment and intervention strategies for individuals with depression.

Kahn, D. A., Ross, R., Printz, D. J., & Sachs, G. S. (2000, April). Treatment of bipolar disorder: A guide for patients and families. In G. S. Sachs, D. J. Printz, D. A. Kahn, D. Carpenter, & J. P. Docherty (Eds.), The expert consensus guideline series: Medication treatment of bipolar disorder 2000. *Postgraduate Medicine Special Report,* pp. 97–104.

This guide is part of a consensus report on medication treatment of bipolar disorder. It is intended to answer some of the most commonly asked questions about bipolar disorder.

Keltner, N. L. (2007a). Antidepressant drugs. In N. L. Keltner, L. H. Schwecke, & C. E. Bostrom (Eds.), *Psychiatric nursing* (5th ed., pp. 232–251). St. Louis: Mosby.

This is the chapter on antidepressant medications in a textbook that takes a practical, clinical approach to nursing by integrating clinical realities with the theory taught in nursing schools, emphasizing those actions for which nurses are primarily responsible.

Keltner, N. L. (2007b). Somatic therapies. In N. L. Keltner, L. H. Schwecke, & C. E. Bostrom (Eds.), *Psychiatric nursing* (5th ed., pp. 232–251). St. Louis: Mosby.

This is the chapter on somatic therapies in a textbook that takes a practical, clinical approach to nursing by integrating clinical realities with the theory taught in nursing schools, emphasizing those actions for which nurses are primarily responsible.

Keltner, N. L., & Folks, D. G. (2005). *Psychotropic drugs.* St. Louis, MO: Mosby.

This book is a comprehensive discussion of the biologic basis of psychotropic drugs used for specific disorders; it includes disorder-specific narrative chapters and drug profiles.

Kennedy, C., Salsberry, P., Nickel, J., Hunt, C., & Chipps, E. (2005). The burden of disease in those with serious mental and physical illnesses. *Journal of the American Psychiatric Nurses Association, 11*(1), 45–51.

A review of the effects of both mental and physical conditions and illnesses on patients and the need for skilled nursing care.

Kübler-Ross, E. (1997). *On death and dying.* New York: Touchstone.

This is one of the most important books of the 20th century on death and dying. It introduced clinicians, patients, and their families to the grieving process and how one transitions from life.

Lehne, R. A. (2007). *Pharmacology for nursing care* (6th ed.) St. Louis, MO: Saunders.

In a student-friendly manner and with clinical precision and a clear focus on understanding drug prototypes, this book presents pharmacology in the context of nursing care.

McDermott, W. (Ed.). (2005, Winter). Antidepressants can lead to tooth, gum disease. *Schizophrenia Digest, 3*(1), 25.

The author discusses how antidepressants can cause tooth and gum disease and the need for good dental regimens and routine dental care for those taking these medications.

National Alliance for Research on Schizophrenia and Depression. (2002). Brain disorders top list of major cases of disability worldwide. *National Alliance for Research on Schizophrenia and Depression Research Newsletter, 14*(2), 25.

The World Health Organization in 2002 reported that brain disorders were the leading cause of disability from non-communicable diseases, and their impact was on the rise.

National Institute of Mental Health. (2003). *In harm's way: Suicide in America.* Retrieved September 20, 2006, from www.nimh.nih.gov/publicat/harmsway.cfm

Suicide is a major, preventable public health problem. This NIMH report presents a discussion of the statistics, the complexity of the behavior, and some of the risk factors (age, gender, or ethnic group) that may occur in combination or change over time.

North American Nursing Diagnosis Association (NANDA-I). (2004). *Nursing diagnoses: Definitions and classifications—2005–2006.* Philadelphia: Author.

The official compilation of nursing diagnoses from the North American Nursing Diagnosis Association.

Pampallona, S., Bollini, P., Tibaldi, G., Kupelnick, B., & Munizza, C. (2004). Combined pharmacotherapy and psychological treatment for depression: A systematic review. *Archives of General Psychiatry, 61*(7), 714–719.

The authors concluded that psychological treatment combined with antidepressant therapy is associated with a higher improvement rate than drug treatment alone and, in longer therapies, the addition of psychotherapy helps to keep patients in treatment.

Parker, G. (2002). Differential effectiveness of newer and older antidepressants appears mediated by an age effect on the phenotypic expression of depression. *Acta Psychiatrica Scandinavica, 106*(3), 168–170.

The author discusses why the broader-based tricyclic antidepressants may be more effective than SSRIs in implicating age and depressive subtype influences.

Simon, G. F., Ludman, E. J., Tutty, S., Operskalski, B., & Von Korff, M. (2004). Telephone psychotherapy and telephone care management for primary care patients starting antidepressant therapy. *Journal of the American Medical Association, 292*(8), 935–942.

The authors discovered that for primary care patients beginning antidepressant treatment, a telephone program integrating care management and structured cognitive-behavioral psychotherapy significantly improved satisfaction and clinical outcomes, suggesting a new public health model of psychotherapy for depression.

Snyder, A., & Matsuno, J. (2001). *Psychopharmacology handbook for nurses.* Provo, UT: Utah State Hospital.

An extensive review of drug therapies utilized in the treatment of mental illness.

Townsend, M. C. (2006). *Psychiatric mental health nursing* (5th ed.). Philadelphia: F. A. Davis Co.

A textbook of essential information for nursing students about psychiatric nursing. It includes highlighted patient education boxes.

U.S. Food and Drug Administration. (2006, February 28). *FDA approves Emsam (selegiline) as first drug patch for depression.* Retrieved November 12,

2006, from http://www.fda.gov/bbs/topics/News/2006/New01326.html
This is a link to the FDA's press release announcing its approval of Emsam (selegiline) as the first drug patch for depression, including its ability to be used at its lowest dose without the restrictions required of MAOI-class depression drugs.

van Praag, H. M., de Kloet, E. R., & van Os, J. (2004). *Stress, the brain, and depression.* Cambridge, UK: Cambridge University Press.
The authors examine the potential for traumatic life events causing depression. They examine three major themes: the pathophysiological role of stress in depression, whether or not a subtype of depression exists that is particularly stress-inducible, and finally, how best to diagnose and treat depression in relation to its biological basis.

Additional References

Earley, P. (2006). *Crazy—A father's search through America's mental health madness.* New York: G. P. Putnam.
In this book Earley, a noted journalist, applies the term *crazy* to the "broken system" the mentally ill face when trying to seek mental health care. He writes about his son's traumatic experiences when he became ill with bipolar disorder. He describes the mental health system, the hospital, out-patient care, the legal system, and the jails, which now house more mentally ill people than the hospitals. Earley also makes suggestions for ways to correct the system and emphasizes the necessity for legal reform and a properly trained crisis intervention team.

Jackson, J. (2004). *The handbook for survivors of suicide.* Washington, DC: American Association of Suicidology.
This book is written as a quick-reference guide for survivors of suicide by a survivor who lost his young wife to suicide. Jackson describes his own journey to recovery and also gives information on how to find support groups in one's area.

Jamison, K. R. (1995). *An unquiet mind.* New York: Vintage.
Dr. Jamison is a noted psychologist and a professor of psychiatry at Johns Hopkins University School of Medicine. This is an autobiography in which Jamison describes her own long-time struggles with the extreme highs and lows of bipolar disorder, including suicidal ideation and even suicidal behavior.

Sherman, M. D., & Sherman, D. M. (2006). *I'm not alone: A teen's guide to living with a parent who has a mental illness.* Minneapolis, MN: Seeds of Hope Books.
This book was written by a clinical psychologist and her mother for teenagers who are living with a parent with serious mental illness. The authors attempt to normalize the teen's wide range of emotions. They also give suggestions for positive coping strategies.

Internet Resources

http://nursing.jbpub.com/psychiatric

Visit http://nursing.jbpub.com/psychiatric for interactive exercises, NCLEX review questions, WebLinks, and more.

CHAPTER 17

Anxiety and Dissociative Disorders

Loraine Fleming and Patricia G. O'Brien

LEARNING OBJECTIVES

After reading this chapter, you will be able to:

- Identify the signs and symptoms of the anxiety disorders.
- Recognize the difference between normal and pathological anxiety.
- Identify modalities used in the treatment of anxiety disorders.
- Develop a nursing care plan for the client with an anxiety disorder.
- Define educational objectives for clients with anxiety disorders and their families.
- Identify signs and symptoms of dissociative disorders.
- Identify principles of nursing interventions for clients with dissociative disorders.

KEY TERMS

Agoraphobia
Anxiety
Behavior therapy
Cognitive therapy
Compulsion
Depersonalization
Derealization
Dissociation
Exposure
Flooding
Obsession
Panic attack
Phobia
Ritualistic behavior
Serotonin
Systematic desensitization

http://nursing.jbpub.com/psychiatric

Visit http://nursing.jbpub.com/psychiatric for interactive exercises, NCLEX review questions, WebLinks, and more.

Introduction

This chapter presents both anxiety and dissociative disorders. Alhough they are two distinct disorders, some anxiety disorders are characterized by dissociative behaviors, and the dissociative disorders, like the anxiety disorders, are rooted in a prior traumatic or stressful event.

It is not unusual for clients to seek treatment in an emergency room for the symptoms of a first panic attack, which is often attributed to "nervousness."

Panic attacks usually start after an illness, an accident, the break-up of a relationship, or the birth of a child.

Agoraphobia is a disabling complication of panic disorder, characterized by phobic avoidance.

Anxiety Disorders

Anxiety is a universally experienced feeling. It is a response to stress that generally has an adaptive function that alerts us to real danger and motivates us to prepare for and succeed in various situations. However, when feelings of anxiety are excessive and interfere significantly with a person's functioning, they are considered pathologic and are diagnosed as an anxiety disorder (American Psychiatric Association [APA], 2000).

The *Diagnostic and Statistical Manual of Mental Disorders*, Fourth Edition, Text Revision (*DSM-IV-TR*) codes anxiety disorders on Axis I. According to the APA, panic attacks and agoraphobia are not codable disorders; rather, they are considered components of the recognized disorders.

A **panic attack** is defined as the sudden onset of intense fear, in which the client experiences at least four of the following symptoms: sweating, palpitations, trembling, shortness of breath, choking sensation, chest pain, nausea or abdominal discomfort, lightheadedness or dizziness, derealization (feeling of unreality) or depersonalization (feeling as though one is outside one's body, observing), fear of losing control (sometimes described as "going crazy"), fear of dying, paresthesia (numbness or tingling sensation), and chills or hot flashes (see **Table 17-1**). The attack may be in response to a specific situation, such as being chased by a dog, or occur out of the blue. The attack generally lasts 5 to 30 minutes. Panic attacks can be a component of panic disorder, social phobia, specific phobic disorder, or major depressive disorder, or a panic attack may occur as an isolated episode (National Institute of Mental Health [NIMH], 2006).

Table 17-1 Symptoms of a Panic Attack

- Sweating
- Palpitations
- Trembling
- Shortness of breath
- Choking sensation
- Chest pain
- Nausea or abdominal discomfort
- Lightheadedness or dizziness
- Derealization (feeling of unreality) or depersonalization (feeling as though one is outside one's body, observing)
- Fear of losing control (sometimes described as "going crazy")
- Fear of dying
- Paresthesia (numbness or tingling sensation)
- Chills or hot flashes

The essential feature of **agoraphobia** is anxiety about being in places or situations from which escape may be difficult or in which help may not be available should a panic attack occur. This leads to the avoidance of situations such as leaving home, being in a crowd, or flying in an airplane. In agoraphobia the fear is not of the specific situation; the fear is of having a panic attack, losing control, and being helpless. Agoraphobia can interfere with the performance of routine activities such as grocery shopping, traveling to work, and enjoying social functions.

Essential Features of Anxiety Disorders

Although anxiety disorders may be manifested in a number of ways, there are essential features that distinguish the various disorders. Each of the anxiety disorders centers around an experience of irrational and disproportionate fear or dread. Whether the symptoms are physiological (e.g., palpitations, excessive sweating) or psychological (e.g., the experience of intrusive, disturbing thoughts), the underlying precipitant is fear.

Panic Disorder

Panic disorder is characterized by recurrent, unexpected panic attacks followed by at least 1 month of persistent concern about having another panic attack. The panic attack is not due to a general medical condition or the effects of an ingested substance. Attacks can occur with moderate frequency, perhaps once a week, for months at a time, or be more concentrated, such as daily for a shorter period of perhaps 1 week. It is not unusual for weeks or even months to go by with no attacks only for them to resume again. Agoraphobia may or may not be associated with panic disorder. There is a high incidence of major depressive disorder as well as other anxiety disorders associated with panic disorder.

Agoraphobia without History of Panic Disorder

In this disorder the client has never experienced unexpected recurrent panic attacks yet fears the occurrence of incapacitating or extremely embarrassing panic-like symptoms or limited-symptom attacks rather than full panic attacks (APA, 2000). In a limited-symptom panic attack, the client experiences fewer than 4 of the 13 symptoms of a panic attack (**Table 17-1**). For example, the client may feel short of breath and lightheaded, and have a fear of losing control.

Specific Phobia

The essential feature of a specific **phobia** is a marked and persistent fear of a particular object, place, or situation referred to as a *phobic stimulus.* Exposure to the phobic stimulus provokes an immediate anxiety response. As with all anxiety disorders, the diagnosis is appropriate only if avoidance or fear of the stimulus interferes significantly with the client's daily routine, occupational functioning, or social life or causes marked personal distress and is disproportionate to any real danger (APA, 2000). If recurrent panic attacks are always related to a specific stimulus, the diagnosis is specific phobia rather than panic disorder. A client with a specific fear of dogs may be able to go about his or her activities and only occasionally encounter a dog. In this example, the person's specific phobia is not considered a psychiatric disorder.

Clinical Example

Nancy has lived with a fear of elevators ever since a childhood experience when she was trapped in one for several hours. Nancy had successfully coordinated her life to avoid the need to use elevators. Now 37 years old, Nancy has been employed at the same publishing company for 15 years. The company just recently announced that it would be relocating from a second floor office suite to the 32nd floor of a new high-rise building.

Shortly after receiving this news, Nancy experienced heart palpitations, shortness of breath, ringing in her ears, nausea, and a feeling she described as "being far away." She told her supervisor she was feeling sick and went home. The symptoms subsided but returned the next day after she arrived at work. Nancy called her doctor who advised her to go to the nearest ER. By the time Nancy arrived at the ER, her symptoms had subsided. She was evaluated and no physiological cause was found for her symptoms. Nancy did not return to work that day, but the next day at work she again experienced the symptoms. Nancy went to see her primary physician, and upon further evaluation, her symptoms were recognized to be a panic attack. A psychiatrist subsequently diagnosed Nancy's condition as a specific phobic disorder.

Critical Thinking Questions In the clinical example, how do Nancy's symptoms satisfy the criteria for specific phobia? In this example, is the phobic stimulus the elevator or the office?

Social Phobia

Social phobia refers to a fear of social or performance situations in which embarrassment may occur and which, when experienced, produces an immediate anxiety response. Symptoms may include palpitations, tremors, confusion, blushing, muscle tension, sweating, and gastrointestinal distress. It is not unusual to experience some of these symptoms when asked to perform or speak in front of a large audience; therefore, diagnosis of the disorder depends on the degree of discomfort and resulting incapacitation that result from the anxiety. Social phobias are self-reinforcing; that is, the fear of performing leads to anxiety, which interferes with performance, causes embarrassment, and increases or reinforces the fear of performing. Persons with social phobias frequently lack social skills and experience severe social and work impairment.

Social phobias include fears of eating, drinking, speaking, and writing in front of others and avoidance of public restrooms, restaurants, public transportation, banks, stores, and other public places.

Social phobia is potentially debilitating. The impairment caused by the disorder may be extensive, affecting educational attainment, career advancement, and family and social relationships.

CASE STUDY Ms. M.

Ms. M. has a history of being shy and reclusive, and recalls being uncomfortable at social events all her life. She was even aware of this at childhood birthday parties, and the feelings of anxiety associated with social events led her to avoid socializing in high school and college. Ms. M. could be comfortable at an activity, such as a school football game, but, once the structured event was over, Ms. M. would become uncomfortable and would usually retreat to her room or the library.

Ms. M. did well academically and attained an excellent position in the computer field after college graduation. Her co-workers are also young and there is an expected office culture of socialization after work. The times that Ms. M. has accompanied her colleagues, she describes feeling like an outsider. She felt very tense, and experienced noticeable hand tremors, extreme nervousness, profuse sweating, and was unable to engage in any conversation. Ms. M. is concerned that her inability to socialize will have an impact on her ability to succeed at work. She also genuinely likes her co-workers and would welcome friends in her life.

NURSING CARE PLAN Social Phobia

Expected Outcome	Intervention	Evaluation
• Ms. M. will be more comfortable in social situations.	• Cognitive restructuring: Help Ms. M. identify the thoughts that inhibit social interaction (e.g., people will not like me; I won't know what to say; I will make a fool of myself). • Help Ms. M. challenge the reality of these thoughts and the consequences.	• Ms. M. is able to counter her negative thoughts with positive statements (e.g., is there any evidence that people do not like you? Is that "all people"? If people have different tastes, isn't it okay that some people may not like you? Even if this is true, are there some behaviors you can do despite this? If a friend had this same thought what would you suggest?).
	• Social skills training: Review basic social skills, including conversation starters, and listening skills. • Role-play social interactions. • Refer Ms. M. to self-help books.	• Ms. M. appears more confident during role-playing. • Ms. M. identifies strategies she will use in real-life encounters to increase her comfort level.
	• Develop a hierarchy of social activities: Ms. M. may initiate telephone calls to a colleague at work, have an in-office lunch with a colleague, attend an after office get-together for a specific short period of time, invite a colleague to a structured social event (e.g., a movie or a baseball game). Gradually increase activities and duration as comfort and skills increase.	• Ms. M. recognizes positive responses from persons she interacts with. • She reports decreased symptoms of anxiety before and during social events. • Ms. M. begins to attend more social functions. • Ms. M. reports increased ease at social events and has made friends.

Visit http://nursing.jbpub.com/psychiatric for additional care plans and exercises.

Obsessive-Compulsive Disorder

Obsessive-compulsive disorder (OCD) is characterized by **obsessions** (repetitive, intrusive thoughts that make little sense) and by **compulsions** (repetitive, **ritualistic behaviors** that strive to neutralize the anxiety associated with the obsessions). The obsession may take the form of a persistent worry or an unreasonable belief, such as an exaggerated fear of contracting an illness from the germs acquired by touching a doorknob. Obsessions may include a need to be perfect, can be violent in nature, and may involve a fear of hurting someone. The thoughts cause anxiety, which is partly relieved by compulsive, ritualistic behavior.

Obsessions are unwanted, recurrent ideas or impulses. Compulsions are repetitive behaviors done in response to obsessions. For example, fear of illness from germs is an obsession; frequent hand washing is a related compulsion.

For example, frequent hand washing may reduce the anxiety associated with the fear of illness resulting from touching the doorknob (**Figure 17-1**). Other compulsive behaviors are counting rituals, checking and rechecking, and precise arranging of objects in a particular order. The rituals must take more than 10 minutes a day (often much more time consuming than that) and must distress the client. Healthy people may also engage in rituals, such as checking several times to assure that they have unplugged the coffee maker before leaving for work. If the checking does not interfere with the person's daily life or cause undue stress, this activity would not be considered pathological.

OCD is a pervasive and potentially disabling anxiety disorder.

Figure 17-1 Overly frequent hand washing can be a compulsive behavior.

Posttraumatic Stress Disorder

A traumatic event that involved an actual or threatened death or physical injury that was personally directed at the client, witnessed by the client, or experienced by someone else and learned about by the client may be followed by posttraumatic stress disorder (PTSD). The presenting symptoms of PTSD vary and may include those associated with depression, anxiety, sleep disorder, sexual disorder, or even psychosis. Intense reexperiencing through traumatic memories is most common, and can involve flashbacks or hallucinations.

Examples of traumatic events are:

- *Personally experienced events:* Military combat, assault (rape, mugging), kidnapping, being a prisoner of war, internment in a concentration camp, natural disasters (tornado, flood), severe auto accident, or being diagnosed with a life-threatening illness
- *Witnessed events:* Injury or unnatural death of another person from a violent assault, war, accident, or disaster; unexpectedly witnessing a dead body or body parts
- *Learning about events experienced by others:* Assault, serious injury, or accident experienced by a family member or close friend; learning that one's child has a life-threatening disease

The response to the traumatic event involves a fear of helplessness and a sense of horror that is re-experienced in recurring thoughts or dreams. An event that resembles the original trauma can produce the same intense emotional and physiological response, including palpitations, shortness of breath, and other symptoms of anxiety. Persons may go to great lengths to avoid anything that reminds them of the trauma. The disorder is considered acute if symptoms last less than 3 months, and chronic if they last more than 3 months (APA, 2000).

Clinical Example

Isobel is intelligent but she is failing her first-period class in biology because she is always late to class or absent. She gets up at 5 a.m. to get to school on time. She spends the next 3 hours taking a long shower and then changing her clothes repeatedly until it "feels right." She finally packs and repacks her books until they are just the way she feels they should be, opens the front door, and prepares to walk down the front steps. She goes through a ritual of pausing on each step for the count of 10. Isobel is certain that if these behaviors are not done, something dreadful will happen to her. Even though she recognizes that her thoughts and behaviors are senseless, she feels compelled to complete her rituals. Once she has completed these rituals, she makes a mad dash for school and arrives when the first period is almost over (NIMH, 1994).

Prior psychiatric history and poor social support increase a person's vulnerability to PTSD.

The presenting symptoms of PTSD vary and may include those associated with depression, anxiety, sleep disorder, sexual disorder, or even psychosis.

CASE STUDY Mr. T.

Mr. T., 28 years old at the time, was a security guard at the World Trade Center in New York City on September 11, 2001, when two airplanes slammed into the twin towers. After the first plane hit one of the towers, Mr. T. redirected the many people rushing out of the other tower building back into the lobby to avoid being struck by the falling debris. Soon after, the second tower was also struck and, within an hour, both buildings collapsed, leaving 3,000 people dead and many wounded. Mr. T. suffered a broken arm and a deep facial cut that required 15 stitches. When Mr. T.'s wife met him at the hospital emergency department (ED), he was unable to recall how he came to be in the hospital, had trouble remembering details related to his actions that morning, and kept repeating, "This doesn't seem real." Mr. T. was discharged from the ED and returned to his home in a suburb of the city.

Within days of the attack, Mr. T.'s memory began to return, but he was having difficulty sleeping. When he was able to fall asleep, he would have terrible nightmares. Even when awake, Mr. T. would find himself reliving the experiences through vivid images of that day. A voracious reader, Mr. T. was unable to concentrate enough to enjoy a book or even the newspaper. He told his wife that he felt responsible for sending people back into the building and "causing their deaths." Mr. T. would not talk about the trauma, and when confronted with video coverage he experienced palpitations and tightness in his chest. He became increasingly withdrawn and irritable, becoming short-tempered with his wife and refusing to see friends and relatives who came by to visit. Mr. T.'s employer had contracts with several buildings throughout the city, and offered to accommodate Mr. T. with a desk job that he could manage until his arm healed. He asked Mr. T. to think about it and call him back when he was ready to return to work. After 3 weeks, Mr. T. had not returned the call and told his wife he did not think he could travel into the city again.

Because the symptoms occurred within 4 weeks of the trauma, the diagnosis is acute stress disorder. If untreated and the symptoms extended beyond 4 weeks, or if the symptoms subsided, only to reappear at a future time, perhaps triggered by another traumatic event, the diagnosis would then be posttraumatic stress disorder.

NURSING CARE PLAN Acute Stress Disorder

Expected Outcome	Intervention	Evaluation
• Mr. T. and his family will have an understanding of normal responses to stress and will be hopeful that improvement is possible.	• Provide information on neurobiological and cognitive theories of anxiety so they can understand the cause and treatment; inform client that symptoms usually subside in time.	• Mr. T. and his family will understand the need to diminish avoidance and will demonstrate a willingness to engage in treatment.
• Mr. T. will identify antecedents of acute symptoms of anxiety.	• Teach client to self-monitor symptoms and thoughts, events, circumstances, and dream content that appear to trigger anxiety.	• Mr. T. will be able to identify precipitants of his symptoms (e.g., thoughts of returning to work; nightmares of the traumatic events; video images of the events). • Mr. T. will be able to cope with stressors and experience a decrease in symptoms.
Mr. T. will learn symptom management to: • Reduce guilt • Improve sleep • Decrease irritability • Mr. T. will return to normal functioning.	• Identify and reinforce current coping skills that are effective. • Use cognitive restructuring to challenge personal responsibility for the deaths of the victims. • Educate on sleep hygiene (see Chapter 21). Refer for sleep medication if insomnia persists. • Teach relaxation techniques to assist with sleep. • Facilitate socialization and interpersonal activities; beginning with scheduling time for communication between Mr. T. and his wife; gradually introduce other activities and people.	• Mr. T. will be more communicative with wife and allow visits from friends. • Mr. T. will engage in activities outside the home (shopping, library, walks). • Mr. T. will return calls to his employer and will be able to consider returning to work.

Visit http://nursing.jbpub.com/psychiatric for additional care plans and exercises.

Complications of PTSD may include violent and aggressive behavior, alcohol and substance abuse, and poor impulse control.

Acute Stress Disorder

This disorder occurs with the development of anxiety, dissociative, and other symptoms within 1 month after exposure to an extremely traumatic stressor of the kind that can precipitate PTSD. In acute stress disorder, the response involves dissociation, which is defined as a disruption in the usually integrated functions of consciousness, memory, identity, or perception of the environment (APA, 2000). Dissociative symptoms include emotional numbing or detachment, derealization, amnesia, and depersonalization. Acute stress disorder, by definition, lasts at least 2 days, but no more than 1 month.

Dissociative symptoms are accompanied by symptoms of anxiety. The client typically expends much energy to avoid situations or people that might trigger recollection of the trauma. As with PTSD, the event and the emotional response are persistently re-experienced and lead to hypervigilant behavior directed at avoiding further trauma. The client may have an exaggerated startle response, difficulty sleeping, and a decreased ability to experience pleasure. The disturbance results in significant impairment in social and occupational functioning.

The primary difference between generalized anxiety disorder and the other anxiety disorders is the frequent absence of a focal symptom or trigger.

Critical Thinking Question In reviewing the case study, what are the signs and symptoms that would suggest that Mr. T. needs professional counseling to help him cope with this crisis?

Generalized Anxiety Disorder

The essential feature of generalized anxiety disorder (GAD) is excessive anxiety and worry for most days over a period of at least 6 months in response to several events or activities. The person is unable to control the worry and experiences at least three of the following symptoms: restlessness, fatigue, difficulty concentrating, irritability, difficulty sleeping, and muscle tension.

Substance-Induced Anxiety Disorder

A diagnosis of substance-induced anxiety disorder is made when prominent anxiety symptoms result from the direct, physiologic effects of a substance, which could be a drug of abuse, a prescribed or over-the-counter medication, or a toxin. Substance-induced anxiety disorder arises only in association with intoxication or withdrawal states. The predominant symptoms may be those of GAD, panic attacks, OCD, or phobic disorder.

Incidence and Prevalence

Anxiety disorders are the most common psychiatric disorders and frequently occur along with other physical or psychiatric illnesses (NIMH, 2006).

The majority of people with one anxiety disorder will also have another anxiety disorder, and people with anxiety disorders will also frequently experience depressive disorders or substance abuse. It is estimated that approximately 40 million American adults, ages 18 and older, or 18% of the population, experience an anxiety disorder in a given year, with the prevalence of each disorder estimated to be 2.7% (6 million) for panic disorder, 1% (2.2 million) for OCD, 3.5% (7.7 million) for PTSD, 3.1% (6.8 million) for GAD, 6.8% (15 million) for social phobia, and 8.7% (19.2 million) for specific phobia (Kessler, Chiu, Demler, & Walters, 2005).

The age of onset varies according to the type of anxiety disorder experienced. Specific phobia frequently begins in childhood, while social phobia may begin in early adolescence. Other anxiety disorders generally begin in early adulthood.

Genetics and gender also seem to be factors in the development of anxiety disorders, with women and first-degree relatives of clients with anxiety disorders being at higher risk for experiencing an anxiety disorder (APA, 2005). Panic disorders are known to affect women twice as often as they affect men (APA, 2000).

Etiology

The development of anxiety disorders can be attributed to a combination of neurobiologic and environmental factors. Influences on the development of anxiety disorders may vary depending on the specific disorder.

Neurobiologic Model

Complex interactions of various neurotransmitters and alterations in brain structures appear to contribute to the development of anxiety disorders. One theory is that the amygdala, the portion of the brain that regulates fear, is overactive and the cerebral cortex, the part of the brain that controls fear, is underactive.

Panic disorders and PTSD have been linked to cortisol disregulation, a physiological response to life stressors. Cortisol, a major stress hormone, is secreted as an adaptive response to an environmental stressor. Under acutely stressful situations cortisol release is beneficial, but chronic secretion of stress hormones such as cortisol may lead to cell destruction in the brain's hippocampus, which regulates mood, heart rate, and memory. Trauma and, possibly, abuse may affect brain structure and functioning, leading to neurobiologic dysfunction and resulting in dissociation, mood instability, and profound memory lapses (Glod & McEnany, 1995).

There are two main theories regarding the development of OCD. One suggests that there is an abnormality in the **serotonin** system; the other suggests that an abnormally high level of brain activity, measured by blood flow and glucose metabolism, occurs in the frontal lobe and basal ganglia, associated respectively with thoughts and movements (Glod & Cawley, 1997).

The elderly are prone to developing anxiety symptoms because of medical illness and polypharmacy.

GAD has been attributed to excessive noradrenergic activity in the locus coeruleus, a small area of the brainstem. Receptors for gamma-aminobutyric acid (GABA) are concentrated in the limbic area of the brain and are linked to anticipatory anxiety. Scientists postulate that excessive anticipatory anxiety may trigger a panic attack. Benzodiazepines are known to facilitate or enhance the inhibitory action of GABA.

OCD and specific phobia are anxiety disorders that may have a childhood onset.

The increased incidence of anxiety disorders among first-degree relatives supports the neurobiologic theory. Panic disorder is eight times more likely to occur in first-degree biological relatives of people who have the disorder (APA, 2000). A neurobiologic basis for anxiety is further supported by the efficacy of certain pharmacologic agents in the treatment of anxiety disorders. Neurobiologic theories hold promise for the development of effective medications to target specific anxiety symptoms.

Cognitive-Behavioral Model

Whereas the initial panic attack may be the result of genetic or biologic vulnerabilities or increased stress, the cognitive-behavioral model proposes that recurrent attacks and anticipatory fear are the result of a learned response. Initial panic attacks are interpreted as catastrophic, causing the person to become sensitized and focused on the body's arousal signals. This causes the person to misinterpret or overreact to normal sensations in a way that makes them seem dangerous. For example, heart palpitations, thought to signal an impending heart attack, further increase the anxiety, which intensifies the sensations and the desire to escape. Agoraphobia is the result of this avoidance conditioning. The individual learns to avoid situations that may lead to the feared sensations.

In OCD, the ritualistic behaviors reduce or neutralize the anxiety associated with obsessive thoughts, thereby reinforcing the compulsive rituals. This, in turn, reinforces the belief that the original obsessive thoughts were dangerous. The client thus learns that other experiences of anxiety may be reduced by compulsive rituals, and the compulsive behavior becomes more extensive.

According to the cognitive model, anxiety is the result of the client's interpretation of an event.

Clinical Course and Com plications

Anxiety disorders can cause major impairment in the level of functioning with a negative effect on the quality of life. They can be accompanied by substance abuse, depression, and suicide attempts. Although most clients with anxiety disorders improve with treatment, relapse is frequent, and maintenance pharmacotherapy is often required.

Nursing Assessment

Guidelines for the nursing assessment of clients with anxiety disorders are summarized in **Table 17-2**. When conducting a client interview, the nurse should observe for signs of anxiety. Clients may have trouble sitting still, tap their fingers, swing their leg, and pace. The mental status examination may reveal difficulty concentrating, poor memory, and distortions in thinking or hearing. The nurse may need to repeat questions to determine if an inappropriate response is the result of inattention or an altered perception of reality. The interview should be conducted without interruption in a private, quiet area. By limiting the amount of stimuli, the nurse can help contain the client's anxiety.

Table 17-2 Guidelines for Nursing Assessment of Clients with Anxiety Disorders

Guideline	Rationale
The interview should be conducted without interruption in a private, quiet area.	This is intended to limit stimulation and decrease anxiety.
The nurse may need to repeat questions.	This will help determine if an inappropriate response is the result of inattention or an altered perception of reality.
Mental status examination is part of the assessment.	The examination may reveal difficulty concentrating, poor memory, and distortions in thinking or hearing. Observe for signs of anxiety (trouble sitting still, tapping fingers, swinging foot, pacing).
Ask the client to state the problem.	This helps define the client as an active participant in the treatment process, which increases his or her sense of personal control, contributes to self-esteem, and does not foster dependency.
Is there a particular event that triggered the symptoms? How long has the client experienced anxiety? Has the client had this experience before, or is it something new? Is there a history of anxiety disorders in the client or family?	These questions help to reveal the nature and history of the client's anxiety symptoms.
How has the anxiety interfered with the client's life? Why is the client seeking help at this particular time?	This information will enlighten the nurse as to the client's level of distress and motivation to engage in treatment.
What is the client's underlying fear? Is there a fear of having a panic attack, or is there a fear of being embarrassed, helpless, or losing control?	The nature of the underlying fear experienced by the client is helpful in determining appropriate interventions.
What coping strategies has the client used to reduce anxiety?	This can help the client recognize strengths, contribute to self-esteem, and begin to engage in a problem-solving approach.
What is the client's understanding of the illness?	This will help identify educational needs.
Ask for permission to meet with family members.	An understanding of the client's disorder may help the family to relate more effectively with the client.
Take a psychiatric and medical history and a history of medication and substance use.	Another primary disorder, medications, or substance use may precipitate or worsen symptoms of anxiety.

It is important to determine why the client is seeking help at this particular time. This information will enlighten the nurse as to the client's level of distress and motivation to engage in treatment. Asking the client to state the problem helps define the client as an active participant in the treatment process, which increases his or her sense of personal control, contributes to self-esteem, and does not foster dependency.

Some questions the nurse may ask to learn the nature and history of the client's anxiety symptoms are: Is there a particular event that triggered the symptoms? How long has the client experienced anxiety? Has the client had this experience before, or is it something new? Is there a history of anxiety disorders in the client or family?

It is important to identify the nature of the underlying fear experienced by the client. Is there a fear of having a panic attack, or is there a fear of being embarrassed, helpless, or losing control? The client may not have thought about the anxiety objectively, and the nurse can provide a supportive relationship in which the client feels safe to consider the meaning of the anxiety.

The client should be helped to be as specific as possible about how the anxiety has interfered with his or her life. It is not unusual for clients to have developed intricate ways of avoiding fears that provoke anxiety, including limiting family, work, and social relationships to control these fears. The nurse must determine the coping strategies employed by the client to reduce anxiety and help the client recognize strengths and resources that will support treatment. This can be caring family or friends, community supports, personal accomplishments, or crises or difficulties that have been successfully handled. When clients are depressed over their current situation, they need help seeing these strengths. Through this discussion, the nurse helps counter the client's negative personal view and sense of hopelessness and contributes to the client's self-esteem.

The client's understanding of the illness will help identify educational needs. Typically, clients with anxiety disorders recognize that their behaviors or fears are exaggerated and irrational, but sometimes clients with OCD, out of shame and guilt, try to hide their behaviors or make them appear rational.

The nurse should ask for permission to meet with family members. They usually benefit from learning the nature of the client's illness and can then relate more effectively with the client.

Differential Diagnosis

The assessment is not complete without a medical history and a history of medication and substance use. Clients with anxiety symptoms should be assessed for depression, given the high comorbidity. Some medical conditions that can cause symptoms of anxiety include endocrine disorders, both hyperthyroidism and hypothyroidism; hypoglycemia; cardiovascular disease; respiratory problems, including hyperventilation; and neurologic conditions, including neoplasms and encephalitis. Substance intoxication and withdrawal also are associated with anxiety. A physical examination and laboratory and clinical tests should be conducted based on the client's presentation.

Treatment

Psychotherapy, primarily cognitive-behavioral therapy (CBT), and pharmacotherapy are the most frequently used modalities in the treatment of anxiety disorders. It is important to realize that each client is unique, and treatments must be individualized and modified according to a client's response.

Cognitive-Behavioral Therapy (CBT)

Psychotherapeutic treatment of anxiety disorders combines elements of **cognitive therapy**, **behavior therapy**, and support. The application of these approaches is specific for the type of disorder. CBT focuses on the interplay of maladaptive behavioral, emotional, and cognitive responses that characterize and perpetuate mental disorders (Matthews, Rayburn, & Otto, 2004).

An important initial step in therapy is educating the client on the role that the client's thoughts and beliefs play in activating anxiety. According to the cognitive model, anxiety is the result of distorted thinking. This can take the form of thinking the worst or "catastrophizing," focusing on negative outcomes, perceiving threats where none exist, and generalization, to name a few symptoms. Anxiety disorders are based on fear: fear of looking foolish (social phobia), fear of having a panic attack (simple phobia or panic disorder), or fear of some dire outcome if compulsions are not acted on (OCD). In addition, there is an assumption by the client that he or she lacks the resources to manage these perceived dangers or threats, and this further fuels the client's anxiety.

Clients with OCD are often successful in concealing their obsessive-compulsive symptoms from friends and co-workers before they become severe and time consuming.

Family members may show their anger and resentment, which often results in increased anxiety in the client.

Client education in treatment of panic disorder includes an overview of the fear cycle so that the client understands the rationale for treatment.

The cognitive model of panic disorder views the client's greatest fear as the fear of having a panic attack. Anticipatory anxiety and avoidance associated with panic attacks can be reduced if the client recognizes what causes and exacerbates the panic, as well as ways to reduce it. For clients who are medically cleared, purposeful hyperventilation will produce the panic symptoms and running in place or breathing into cupped hands will restore the carbon dioxide balance and eliminate the panic symptoms. This exercise educates the client about the nature of panic symptoms, demystifies the panic response, and gives the client increased control over the symptoms.

Cognitive restructuring helps the client to examine and challenge the thoughts that contribute to the experience of anxiety by examining the ABCs: antecedents, behavior, and the consequences of one's thoughts (**Table 17-3**). The goal of therapy is to interrupt this process by challenging the antecedent thoughts.

Cognitive restructuring involves asking the client questions to help him or her evaluate negative automatic thoughts and substitute more realistic thoughts.

These may include catastrophic thoughts such as "I will die" or "I am having a heart attack," personalizing thoughts such as "I am responsible for whatever happens," or assumptions regarding approval and perfectionism. Agoraphobic and social phobic clients believe that others can see their anxiety and will reject them because of it. Challenges to the person's automatic thoughts may include the following questions:

- What are the advantages and disadvantages of this thought?
- What is the evidence for and against this thought?
- Is the evidence convincing?
- What if the thought is true? Why would that bother you?
- If someone else had this problem, what advice would you give him?
- If someone else had this problem, would you judge him negatively, as you judge yourself? Why or why not?
- If the thought is true, are there some things you can do to improve the situation? (Leahy, 1996)

Critical Thinking Question How would you apply the challenges listed above to the example shown in Table 17-3?

Cognitive therapy and behavioral therapy are modalities aimed at helping people understand their thinking and the behavioral responses to their thoughts. Once clients have an understanding of their patterns of response they can learn to overcome irrational and erroneous fears and change their behavior. The client can be assisted to identify rational responses to frequently occurring anxious thoughts.

Exposure is a CBT technique that introduces repeated experience or contact with the stress-provoking situation with the goal of extinguishing the emotional response. Assigning time to worry, for example 30 minutes a day, exposes the client to the fears but with some control—a specific time, place, and by choice. This practice helps the client learn to accept and tolerate some level of anxiety.

Systematic desensitization refers to the gradual exposure to an increasing hierarchy of stress-provoking stimuli for the purpose of extinguishing the negative emotional response. This technique can be applied using both imagined and real-life (in vivo) situations. A client with a simple phobia of public speaking may be helped by creating a hierarchy of situations that would provoke anxiety, from the least stressful to the most stressful. The low end of the hierarchy may be standing in front of an empty auditorium; the high end may be presenting a marketing plan to the board of directors for a company. The client identifies a level of fear and negative thoughts (e.g., I will faint; I will blush; everyone will know I am nervous; I will forget what to say) prior to carrying out the activity, and then rates the feelings and validity of the negative thoughts during the real or imagined exposure. Each step in the hierarchy is repeated until the anxiety is reduced, and then the process is repeated for the next step.

Flooding is a more extreme form of exposure, where the client is confronted with the stress-

Table 17-3 Relationship of Thoughts to Anxiety: Social Phobia

Antecedent Thought	Behavior	Consequences
If I approach someone to speak with them, they will reject me and I will feel foolish.	I feel anxious and nervous and do not initiate social contact.	My anxiety lessens but I do not achieve my goal and I remain alone.

provoking stimulus for an extended period of time, again for the purpose of extinguishing the negative emotional response. A person with a specific phobia, say to elevators, would agree to enter an elevator with the therapist and ride to the top floor of a building and back to the ground floor.

The cognitive therapy approach to OCD also utilizes exposure without a neutralizing response. The client is asked to tolerate the obsessive thought without engaging in the usual ritualistic behaviors that neutralize or reduce the anxiety. In the clinical example of the student with OCD, described earlier in the chapter, Isobel was late for class due to extensive rituals that she felt compelled to follow. In cognitive therapy, the student might be asked to not stop and count on each step when leaving home. A compulsive hand washer would resist washing in spite of an obsession about germs. Tolerance can be introduced in time increments, such as not washing hands for 5 minutes, and gradually increasing exposure to the obsessive thoughts. This process requires that the client understand the rationale and is willing to tolerate the resulting anxiety.

The anxiety lessens with each exposure, *as long as it is not interrupted*. For this reason, during the exposure phase, the client should not use relaxation exercises or try to stop the thoughts as a way of reducing anxiety associated with obsessive thoughts. If the goal is to extinguish the obsessive-compulsive behavior, the client must experience and tolerate the thoughts without taking action to reduce the anxiety, neither carrying out the compulsive behavior nor inducing a state of relaxation. Neutralizing the anxiety would reinforce or strengthen the belief that the thought is indeed dangerous and has to be neutralized (Harvey & Rapee, 1995; Leahy, 1996).

CBT is a very specialized area of therapy, and the techniques should only be applied by clinicians who have received education and supervision in the field. However, it is important for the nurse to understand these concepts when caring for clients who are engaged in cognitive therapy for the treatment of an anxiety disorder. For example, a client hospitalized for OCD may be carrying out this exposure exercise in an in-patient setting. The nurse would need to be supportive without undermining the goal of increasing the client's tolerance for the anxiety.

Skills training is also employed in CBT and is tailored to the client's needs. Relaxation training can be helpful for the client with GAD, whereas social skills training may be indicated for the client with a social phobia. Problem-solving is a skill that is of benefit to most clients and can increase the client's sense of control over the anxiety and can transfer to other situations.

These CBT techniques can also be effective in treating clients with PTSD. Exposure is used to disrupt the connection between the cues that trigger memories of the traumatic event and the resulting emotional and physiological response and avoidance. Prolonged exposure to the traumatic memories has been most effective and has shown a 65% reduction in symptoms (Foa, Keane, & Friedman, 2000).

Although the short-term, symptom-focused cognitive therapy model has been demonstrated to be effective in the treatment of anxiety disorders, it requires that the client be ready and willing to actively participate in his or her treatment.

For some clients, this form of treatment is not comfortable, and traditional psychotherapy may be better suited to their needs. The focus of the therapy may include reducing vulnerability to stress, bolstering self-confidence, and improving interpersonal relationships. Psychodynamic psychotherapies are thought to have more utility in social anxiety than in the other phobic disorders because of the apparent roles of shame and humiliation (Reid, 1997).

Pharmacotherapy

Medication can be used alone or in combination with psychotherapy. As already described, some cognitive therapy approaches require that the client experience anxiety, so the use of medications in conjunction with cognitive therapy is controversial. Some clients may benefit from time-limited medication to reduce anxiety enough to engage in treatment and initiate some of the behavior exercises.

Knowledge about the neurobiology of anxiety disorders has developed based on the effectiveness of various pharmacologic agents in treating the related symptoms. The selective serotonin reuptake inhibitors (SSRIs), a class of antidepressants that includes fluoxetine (Prozac) and sertraline (Zoloft), are used in the treatment of OCD. In OCD, symptom relief depends on taking the medication; when the medication is stopped the symptoms return.

Clomipramine (Anafranil), a tricyclic antidepressant (TCA) that is also an SSRI, is the most consistently effective tricyclic in treating OCD, as

> Distraction, including thought stopping and relaxation, may maintain anxiety-provoking thoughts and situations and may reinforce the client's view that certain thoughts and images are to be avoided.

> Traditional psychotherapy may enhance the client's response to cognitive behavioral therapy and psychopharmacology.

> Knowledge that thoughts or behaviors are irrational or exaggerated is not sufficient to accomplish change. The client must experience anxiety as part of the treatment. There is a tension between having enough anxiety to motivate treatment and having so much anxiety that one runs from therapeutic situations that temporarily increase discomfort.

well as panic and phobic disorders. Not all clients react the same to a medication, and in the absence of a therapeutic response, it is reasonable that the client be given a trial with another antidepressant. In general, it takes 2 to 6 weeks for antidepressants to reduce panic and anxiety symptoms effectively.

Propranolol (Inderal) and other beta-adrenergic blockers may be used to alleviate anxiety and improve functioning in persons with phobic disorders, and are prescribed most often for performance phobia. Benzodiazepines act quickly and have fewer side effects than the TCAs or the monoamine oxidase inhibitors (MAOIs) and are frequently used to treat the symptoms of anxiety. Regular use of benzodiazepines, however, carries a risk of dependence and abuse. They can be helpful for persons with severe phobias who need time-limited, immediate relief, such as a person with a specific fear of airplane travel who has to fly for a family emergency or a business trip. Buspirone (BuSpar), a nonbenzodiazepine anxiolytic, can be effective for long-term treatment of anxiety, as in general anxiety disorder. It has few side effects, making it a good choice for the elderly. It takes 2 to 4 weeks to reach maximum therapeutic response.

Benzodiazepines can sedate, induce memory impairment, and increase the intoxicating potency of alcohol and may lead to abuse and dependence after long-term use. Treatment with benzodiazepines should be time-limited to prevent the complications of tolerance and dependence.

Anxiolytics, including the benzodiazepines, and beta blockers are also effective in treating acute symptoms of PTSD. Propranolol (Inderal) and clonidine (Catapres) have limited side effects and are the usual drugs of choice. Chronic symptoms are better treated with the SSRIs (fluoxetine [Prozac] and sertraline [Zoloft]) or with serotonin-norepinephrine reuptake inhibitors (SNRI), ven-lafaxine (Effexor) or duloxetine (Cymbalta). Trazodone or doxepin may be used to treat the insomnia frequently associated with PTSD.

As with all pharmacotherapy, the nurse must educate the client regarding the expected action and possible side effects of the medication. Some side effects decrease over time. The support of the nurse can be essential to client compliance. This is especially important when clients are on medication that requires several weeks to reach a therapeutic level necessary for the relief of symptoms.

Nursing Interventions

Working with clients who have anxiety disorders requires great patience on the part of the nurse. The initial contact with the client is a time for the nurse to communicate understanding and concern. This can be done by allowing the client to talk about stressful and traumatic experiences. The nurse can help the client identify thoughts and fears and how they relate to the anxiety.

It is important that the nurse not appear impatient with the client's behavior. This can be especially difficult with clients who have OCD. In the beginning of treatment, it is important to allow time for the client's rituals. It may be necessary to conduct the nursing assessment in segments to accommodate the client's behavior.

Efforts should be made to reduce environmental stimuli. Choose a quiet place to meet with the client and avoid interruptions. Anxiety may interfere with the client's ability to hear things correctly. The client may distort or misinterpret what the nurse says, so it is essential that the nurse asks questions to validate the client's responses. Simple sentences reduce the chance of misunderstanding.

The mental status examination may have reflected memory impairment, another frequent manifestation of anxiety. The anxious client may need reminders and should not be expected to recall appointment times or medication times. The client may find it helpful to write things down. This is an example of how the nurse can help the client identify ways to cope with the anxiety and its effect on functioning.

Critical Thinking Question In what ways might the nurse decrease or limit stimulation for a hospitalized patient with an anxiety disorder?

The nurse should involve the client in setting goals for care. Safety is a primary concern, and the client needs to know how and from whom to request help. Special attention should be paid to the client's nutritional status. Snacks and frequent small meals may work better for these clients than regularly scheduled meals. The nurse should convey acceptance and support but must be aware that clients experiencing anxiety may perceive any form of touch as a personal threat.

Client and Family Education

Initially, the focus of client and family education is on explaining the nature of the disorder. The clinician should discuss the symptoms the client may be experiencing and help both the client and family identify signs of exacerbation of the illness. The clinician should validate both the client

Implications for Evidence-Based Practice

Currently, research supports the use of SSRIs/SNRIs as first-line pharmacological interventions in the treatment of anxiety disorders (Silverstone, 2004). The literature also suggests that the use of atypical antipsychotic medications and antiseizure medications may augment the effects of the SSRIs/SNRIs in clients who do not respond to the first-line treatment (Kniele & Brawman-Mintzer, 2006). Additionally, work currently is being conducted to study the effects of DBS (deep brain stimulation) in the treatment of severe and refractory OCD (Greenberg et al., 2006). The initial results of the studies have been encouraging, although they are preliminary and will require more research.

The psychological intervention of choice in the treatment of anxiety disorders is cognitive-behavioral therapy (Culpepper et al., 2006). The techniques used may vary depending on the anxiety disorder experienced (Beck, 2005). Recent research has supported the idea that prolonged exposure therapy may actually reduce the symptom severity in clients with PTSD (Schnurr et al., 2007).

The Crisis Debriefing Model also has been used for many years in the treatment of PTSD. However, controversy has arisen about its efficacy, and there is even concern that it may exacerbate symptoms (Regehr, 2001).

Due to the extensive prevalence and potentially debilitating effects of anxiety disorders, early recognition and intervention are essential. Therefore, emergency services and primary care providers are encouraged to screen for anxiety disorders and address treatment issues with clients. Successful treatment and prevention of relapse depend on careful intervention and follow-up care (Culpepper et al., 2006).

and the family's understanding through their ability to describe the disorder in their own words. Once there is a basic understanding of the condition, the clinician can begin to educate the client and family regarding treatment options and the participation that is necessary for success.

Client education includes an understanding of the relationship among thoughts, fears, and anxiety. The nurse can use some of the questioning techniques from the cognitive therapy model to help the client achieve this understanding and to learn new coping behaviors.

The teaching of new skills is a major focus of helping the client handle and control the symptoms of anxiety and is an important nursing intervention. Skills training may include relaxation techniques, social skills, and problem-solving. It is important that the nurse recognizes the client's efforts and progress by verbal acknowledgment, a smile, or some other means, because this reinforcement helps the client sustain positive changes. A person with a social phobia, for example, should be praised for initiating a social contact or for participating in a group session. Family members can be taught to also utilize positive reinforcement to support the client's treatment.

If medications are part of the treatment protocol, the nurse assesses the client's response to medication and ensures that clients and families are given information and are able to articulate an understanding of side effects, drug or food interactions (including alcohol), proper administration, management of missed doses, and possible adverse reactions. The nurse needs to be aware of prescribed or over-the-counter medications that the client may be taking for other medical conditions, in order to assess for potentially harmful drug combinations.

It is important that the nurse educates the client regarding the potential risk of alcohol and drug abuse in persons with anxiety. This requires an open discussion, including an assessment of current use as well as information to increase the client's awareness of signs of escalated use or abuse.

It is a good idea to make clients and families aware of the costs of medication to be sure that they are able to afford the prescribed drug regimen. Based on financial need, some pharmaceutical companies offer medications at reduced rates. If this is not possible, and if other sources of financial aid are not available, the nurse practitioner or other prescribing clinician may need to consider alternative medications.

As noted above, the client's safety is a primary concern. Education should include the signs of depression as well as clear information for the client and family about ways to access help and resources in emergency situations.

Dissociative Disorders

Dissociation is a disruption of the usually integrated functions of consciousness, memory, identity, or perception of the environment. The *DSM-IV-TR* identifies five dissociative disorders, discussed in the following sections, and there is considerable overlap in both presentation and symptoms among the disorders. Dissociative disorders are conceptualized as posttraumatic stress syndromes. The dissociative symptoms of emotional numbing (detachment), **derealization**, amnesia, and **depersonalization** are often accompanied by symptoms of anxiety (APA, 2000).

Essential Features

The *DSM-IV-TR* identifies five dissociative disorders. As with the anxiety disorders, the dissociative disorders share common elements but are manifested in different ways.

Dissociative Amnesia

Dissociative amnesia is characterized by selective or generalized recall of repressed memories. This manifests as an inability to recall important personal information, usually of a traumatic or stressful nature, that is too extensive to be regarded as ordinary forgetfulness.

Dissociative Fugue

In dissociative fugue, clients experience sudden, unexpected travel away from either home or place of work accompanied by an inability to recall the past, or even their own names. This can result in the assumption of a new identity.

Dissociative Identity Disorder

Formerly referred to as multiple personality disorder, dissociative identity disorder refers to the presence of two or more distinct identities or personality states that reappear and take control of the individual's behavior. This disorder also includes amnesia for personal information that extends beyond ordinary forgetfulness.

Depersonalization Disorder

Depersonalization disorder involves a persistent or recurrent feeling of being detached from one's mental processes or body. Persons with this disorder may describe feeling as though they are in a dream state or that they are outside observers of their lives. Depersonalization is also a symptom of some anxiety disorders and schizophrenia. The experience is actually fairly common and must cause considerable distress to warrant a diagnosis. In depersonalization disorder, the client knows that this is a feeling, not reality.

Dissociative Disorder Not Otherwise Specified

The predominant feature in this disorder is a dissociative symptom—a disturbance in the usually integrated functions of memory, identity, consciousness, and perception of the environment that does not meet the criteria for a specific dissociative disorder. This could include trance-like states or a coma not explained by a medical condition.

Critical Thinking Question What is the underlying precipitant common to all dissociative disorders?

Incidence and Prevalence

There is little data on the prevalence of the dissociative disorders, although the rate is thought to be 1% or less of the population. Although dissociative disorders appear in both men and women, there are gender differences. Women are more likely to experience dissociative identity disorder and men more likely to experience dissociative fugue. Dissociative identity disorder is generally diagnosed when the client is in his or her 30s or 40s, and it is known to be more common in first-degree relatives of people with the disorder.

Etiology

The dissociative disorders are viewed as a response to a trauma, often one that occurred in childhood. The traumatic event may have involved physical or sexual abuse. The disorder is more common among family members than in the general population. It is hypothesized that at extreme stress levels associated with traumatic events, the hippocampus-based system basically shuts down while the amygdala-based system is enhanced. This change can lead to an abnormal encoding of the space-time context of memories (Gleaves & Williams, 2005).

Clinical Course and Complications

People with dissociative amnesia generally respond well to treatment and make a full recovery. This is true also for persons with fugue states that are of a short duration. Dissociative identity disorder usually requires long-term psychotherapy. Depersonalization disorder does not respond well to treatment and is often complicated by depression and anxiety.

Nursing Assessment

Nursing assessment includes a mental status examination, psychiatric and medical history, and information on medication and substance use. The nurse may request permission to question a relative, depending on the client's state of memory. Memory is a major focus of assessment, as well as any history of trauma. The nurse should determine how much understanding the client has about the disorder, as well as the way the disorder has affected the client's day-to-day functioning. It is always useful to learn what coping mechanisms the client has utilized and whether they have been effective in dealing with stress.

Differential Diagnosis

An organic basis, such as a brain tumor or seizure disorder, for dissociative symptoms must be ruled out. Other mental disorders, including factitious disorders and malingering, must also be considered, as well as depression, psychosis, and substance abuse.

Treatment

The primary approaches to treating the dissociative disorders are psychotherapy and medication.

Psychotherapy

The focus of psychotherapy is on the client's response to the traumatic event. If years have passed since the traumatic event occurred, it may be difficult for the client to achieve recall. The accuracy of the memory cannot be certain when the client remembers a long-ago traumatic event. Treatment is directed at obtaining relief for the client through the recovery of lost memories. A "recovered" memory, even under hypnosis or with the assistance of amobarbital (Amytal)-induced sedation, is likely to be altered to fit the needs and expectations of the client (Reid, 1997). Clinicians should remain open and nonjudgmental in their approach, neither confirming nor denying the accuracy of reported memories (Gleaves & Williams, 2005).

In dissociative identity disorder, the goal of treatment is the integration of the parts of the client's personality, referred to as *alters*. Integration of an *alter personality state* implies that it no longer exists by itself.

Pharmacotherapy

The symptoms of dissociative disorders respond to treatment with antidepressants; SSRIs are the medication of choice. Pharmacotherapy is most effective in these clients when it is combined with psychotherapy.

Nursing Interventions

The nurse's role with clients who have dissociative disorders is largely supportive. The client may be very concerned regarding the loss of memory. The nurse can facilitate the client's exploration of the past and expression of feelings. Safety of the client is a primary concern, especially if the client is depressed or suicidal. The nurse can assist the client to identify and practice healthy coping skills to respond to anxiety and stress.

Summary

Anxiety is a universal phenomenon, which allows the nurse to identify with the client's experience and discomfort. However, clients who present for the treatment of anxiety or dissociative disorders have often developed extreme, ineffective patterns of coping with stress. As a result, they usually suffer great personal discomfort combined with psychosocial problems. The client may be experiencing severe impairments in interpersonal functioning that affect his or her ability to enjoy life.

> The process of integrating alter personality states can be very frightening for the client.

Treatment requires the client to discover and learn new ways to cope more effectively with the symptoms of anxiety. Peplau referred to this process as "real learning."

> Real learning, . . . trains us to deal with anxiety. In the learning process, we are forced to endure uncertainty while we observe, describe, analyze and formulate the meaning of experience. In the learning process, we gain not only the knowledge needed to deal with new situations, but also we are conditioned to withstand anxiety. (Peplau, 1964, p. 43)

The nurse's role is to help the client with the process of real learning. This task can be both daunting and rewarding for the client. The nurse is privileged to be part of this process.

Annotated References

American Psychiatric Association. (2000). *Diagnostic and statistical manual of mental disorders* (4th ed., text rev.). Washington, DC: Author.

This is the revised fourth edition of the American Psychiatric Association's official nomenclature of psychiatric conditions and disorders. It provides a systematic listing of the official codes and categories, a description of the multiaxial system for diagnosis, and diagnostic criteria for each of the disorders. It is used by psychiatrists, physicians, psychologists, registered nurses, social workers, therapists, and other mental health workers in all clinical settings.

American Psychiatric Association. (2005). *Let's talk facts about anxiety disorders.* Washington, DC: Author.

This brochure contains concise information regarding anxiety disorders, including definitions, symptoms, and available treatments.

Beck, A. (2005). The current state of cognitive therapy. *Archives of General Psychiatry, 62,* 953–959.

The article presents a 40-year retrospective review of the development of the cognitive therapy model.

Culpepper, L., Judd, C. R., Moller, M. D., Nemeroff, C. B., Rapaport, M. H., et al. (2006, July). Clinicians on the front line: Active management of depression and anxiety. *Clinical Advisor: Supplement,* 4–21.

This supplement is a continuing medical education presentation that provides a thorough review of the factors influencing the diagnosis and treatment of depression and anxiety disorders.

Foa, E. B., Keane, T. C., & Friedman, M. (Eds.). (2000). *Effective treatments for PTSD: Practice guidelines from the International Society for Traumatic Stress Studies.* New York: Guilford Press.

A definitive guide for evidence-based treatment of PTSD.

Gleaves, D., & Williams, T. (2005). Critical questions: Trauma, memory, and dissociation. *Psychiatric Annals, 35*(8), 649–654.

A clear and concise review of dissociative disorders and their relation to trauma.

Glod, C. A., & Cawley, D. (1997). The neurobiology of obsessive-compulsive disorder. *Journal of the American Psychiatric Association, 3,* 120–122.

This article discusses theories of serotonin disregulation and increased brain activity as they relate to obsessive-compulsive disorder. The authors cite recent research findings and discuss nursing implications.

Glod, C. A., & McEnany, G. (1995). The neurobiology of posttraumatic stress disorder. *Journal of the American Psychiatric Association, 1*(6), 196–199.

This article thoroughly discusses the neurobiologic and neurodevelopmental effects of trauma and identifies the implications for nursing practice, education, and research.

Greenberg, B. D., Malone, D. A., Friehs, G. M., Rezai, A. R., et al. (2006). Three-year outcomes in deep brain stimulation for highly resistant obsessive compulsive disorder. *Neuropsychopharmacology, 31,* 2384–2393.

This article discusses the effectiveness of deep brain stimulation in the treatment of patients with OCD who have had limited or no success with conventional therapies.

Harvey, A. G., & Rapee, R. M. (1995). Cognitive-behavior therapy for generalized anxiety disorder. *Psychiatric Clinics of North America, 18*(4), 859–870.

This article offers a model for treating GAD that combines cognitive and behavioral therapeutic techniques. The authors present a summary of research findings that support the effectiveness of the model.

Kessler, R. C., Chiu, W. T., Demler, O., & Walters, E. E. (2005). Prevalence, severity and co-morbidity of twelve-month DSM-IV disorders in the National Comorbidity Survey Replication. *Archives of General Psychiatry, 62,* 617–627.

The article is a report on the face-to-face survey of 9,282 English-speaking adults, conducted between February 2001 and April 2003, reporting on the prevalence, severity, and co-morbidity of certain psychiatric disorders.

Kniele, K, & Brawman-Mintzer, O. (2006, July). Diagnosis and treatment of generalized anxiety disorder. *CNS News,* 17–23.

A clearly written, thorough review of generalized anxiety disorder, with information on etiology; treatment options, including a brief report on herbal products; and an algorithm for treatment.

Leahy, R. (1996). *Cognitive therapy: Basic principles and applications.* Northvale, NJ: Jason Aronson.

This very readable book examines the underlying assumptions and models of cognitive therapy. The specific applications, case presentations, and therapist-client dialogues are extremely instructive.

Matthews, J., Rayburn, N. R., & Otto, M. W. (2004). Cognitive-behavioral therapy. In T. A. Stern & J. B. Herman (Eds.), *Massachusetts General Hospital psychiatry update and board preparation* (2nd ed., pp. 457–465). New York: McGraw-Hill.

This chapter provides an overview of the basic principles of cognitive-behavioral therapy and their application to the treatment of specific mental disorders.

National Institute of Mental Health. (1994). *Obsessive-compulsive disorder.* Washington, DC: Author.

This excellent and hopeful summary of obsessive-compulsive disorder and treatment is directed to the client. It includes screening tests and a resource list for information and treatment.

National Institute of Mental Health. (2006). *Anxiety disorders.* Washington, DC: Author.

A detailed booklet that describes the symptoms, causes, and treatments of the major anxiety disorders, with information on getting help and coping.

Peplau, H. E. (1964). *Basic principles of patient counseling* (2nd ed.). Philadelphia: Smith Kline & French Laboratories.

This is a brief but very rich presentation of the principles of short-term counseling. It reviews basic principles of the nurse–client relationship and has an excellent nurse-teacher question-and-answer section that is very instructive. It is a classic work by one of the foremost leaders in psychiatric nursing.

Regehr, C. (2001). Crisis debriefing groups for emergency responders: Reviewing the evidence. *Brief Treatment and Crisis Intervention, 1,* 87–100.

This article discusses the conflicting data surrounding the efficacy of the Crisis Debriefing Model of intervention.

Reid, W. H. (1997). Anxiety disorders. In W. H. Reid, G. U. Balis, & B. J. Sutton (Eds.), *The treatment of psychiatric disorders* (3rd ed., pp. 239–262). Bristol, PA: Brunner/Mazel.

This comprehensive psychiatric textbook is useful to all mental health professionals. It follows the *DSM-IV* taxonomy and focuses on the treatment of each disorder.

Schnurr, P. P., Friedman, M. J., Engel, C. C., Foa, E. B., Shea, M. T., et al. (2007). Cognitive behavior therapy for posttraumatic stress disorder in women: A randomized controlled trial. *Journal of the American Medical Association, 297*(8), 820–830.

This study compared prolonged exposure therapy with supportive therapy for the treatment of PTSD in women and found a significant reduction of symptoms among the women who received prolonged exposure therapy.

Silverstone, P. H. (2004). Qualitative review of SNRIs in anxiety. *The Journal of Clinical Psychiatry, 65*(17), 19–27.

The article reviews the use of SNRIs in the treatment of anxiety disorders.

Additional Resources

Andreasen, N. C., & Black, D. W. (2006). Anxiety disorders. In N. C. Andreasen & D. W. Black (Eds.), *Introductory textbook of psychiatry* (4th ed., pp. 167–200). Washington, DC: American Psychiatric Press.

This chapter provides a succinct summary of the anxiety disorders with examples of clinical presentations.

Applegate, M. (1997). Multiphasic short-term therapy for dissociative identity disorder. *Journal of the American Psychiatric Association, 3,* 1–9.

The author presents a model for treating dissociative identity disorder in brief, time-limited phases and identifies discrete goals and interventions for each phase of treatment.

Johnson, M. R., & Lydiard, R. B. (1995). The neurobiology of anxiety disorders. *Psychiatric Clinics of North America, 18*(4), 681–725.

This heavily referenced article provides an excellent summary of research studies that contribute to understanding the neurobiologic basis for each of the anxiety disorders.

Juster, H. R., & Heimberg, R. G. (1995). Social phobia, longitudinal course and long-term outcome of cognitive-behavioral treatment. *Psychiatric Clinics of North America, 18*(4), 821–842.

This excellent article reviews the techniques of exposure, cognitive restructuring, and social skills training in the treatment of social phobia. An interesting summary of related research is included.

Kelly, V. C., & Saveanu, R. (2005). Performance anxiety: How to ease stage fright. *Current Psychiatry, 4*(6), 25–34.

A clear and concise article about performance anxiety and effective interventions currently used in treatment.

Mason, L. E. (1997, August 4). Divided she stands. *New York Magazine,* 44–49.

Written under a pseudonym, the author relates her personal experience of dissociative identity disorder. It conveys better than any text the complications of everyday functioning caused by this disorder and describes the treatment conflicts.

McDermott, S. P. (2004). Treating anxiety disorders using cognitive therapy techniques. *Psychiatric Annals, 34*(11), 858–872.

A thorough review of cognitive therapy techniques used in the treatment of anxiety, complete with many clinical examples.

U.S. Department of Health and Human Services. (1999). *Mental health: A report of the Surgeon General.* Rockville, MD: Author.

A report by the U.S. Surgeon General on mental health that specifically addresses the various anxiety disorders.

Internet Resources

http://nursing.jbpub.com/psychiatric

Visit http://nursing.jbpub.com/psychiatric for interactive exercises, NCLEX review questions, WebLinks, and more.

CHAPTER 18

Somatoform Disorders, Factitious Disorders, and Malingering

Winifred Z. Kennedy

LEARNING OBJECTIVES

After reading this chapter, you will be able to:

- Describe key characteristics of somatoform disorders.
- Differentiate among somatization disorders, hypochondriasis, factitious disorders, malingering, and pain disorders.
- Identify factors important in differentiating psychiatric disorders with physical symptoms and medical illnesses.
- Formulate nursing interventions for clients with somatoform disorders, factitious disorders, and malingering.

KEY TERMS

Body dysmorphic disorder
Briquet's syndrome
Conversion disorder
Dissociative
Factitious disorder
Hypochondriasis
La belle indifference
Malingering
Münchausen syndrome
Pain disorder
Psychosomatic
Referred pain
Reframing
Self-management training
Somatization
Somatoform disorder

http://nursing.jbpub.com/psychiatric

Visit http://nursing.jbpub.com/psychiatric for interactive exercises, NCLEX review questions, WebLinks, and more.

Introduction

Soma comes from the Greek word meaning "body." **Psychosomatic** refers to symptoms of physical illness that have a mental or emotional origin. *Mental Health: A Report of the Surgeon General* (U.S. Department of Health and Human Services, 2000) emphasizes the need to look at symptoms of medical and psychiatric illnesses as points on a continuum. It suggests that a more viable distinction than mind and body might be to discuss mental and somatic health because this is a neutral distinction acknowledging that the brain, mental functioning, and behavior are interconnected.

In somatoform disorders, physiologic changes or illness are characterized by physical symptoms originating from emotional or mental sources. Somatoform disorders may be acute or chronic, involve physical or psychologic symptoms or both, and may be exaggerated or fabricated. A client in distress seeks relief for the problem and cares little whether the symptoms arise from the mind or the body, even though this distinction may seem to be important to the healthcare provider and insurance company or may eventually influence treatment decisions. Somatoform disorders are considered psychosomatic; they affect the mind and body, and usually are not considered organic or primarily physiologic in origin. An organic disorder has an identifiable, objective, physiologic basis that can be demonstrated by examining established structural and functional changes and by diagnostic testing. In functional disorders, the signs and symptoms do not have a physiologic basis, and the diagnosis depends more upon subjective findings or connections to psychic origins.

The client may have learned that presentation of a physical complaint is a recognizable and socially sanctioned method of obtaining attention, affection, assistance, or alliances with others.

Physical disorders may appear more legitimate, tangible, and less of the client's volition than psychologic disorders. Treating a visible wound or casting a wrist fracture may seem more concrete than treating a stress-related illness perceived as imaginary or exaggerated. This psychologic manifestation of physiologic distress without a demonstrated objective causal link does not mean that there are no underlying physical findings or pathology (Nakagawa-Kogan, 1996). However, a dichotomy has been present since Descartes attempted to distinguish between the mind and the body, and this has continued through to today's distinction between traditional mainstream medicine and mental health. This is seen in both the client's willingness to seek help and society's willingness to pay for it.

Within our society, illness is often an acceptable excuse for nonperformance, and a physical illness does not have the same stigma attached to it as an admission of emotional illness. The individual's psychologic and biologic responses to the stress of a perceived illness or a diagnosed disease are similar, whether or not a clear organic or functional basis is present (see Chapters 13 and 28).

Clients with somatoform disorders experience physical symptoms without a known organic or physical cause in response to psychologic stressors or disorders. The production of symptoms is not considered to be under conscious or voluntary control. Somatoform disorders include somatization disorder, hypochondriasis, conversion disorder, body dysmorphic disorder, and pain disorder.

Factitious disorders and malingering are associated because of their link to illness symptoms and behaviors. The production of symptoms is considered to be more under conscious or voluntary control. The nature of the client's reported symptoms may be based upon problems or uncertainties in validating subjective sensory experiences (Spivak, Rodin, & Sutherland, 1994). An organic or physiologic basis is usually not found for the symptoms. Factitious disorders and malingering also may be associated with the exaggeration of an actual disorder or the intentional production of signs and symptoms of a known medical disorder. For example, a diabetic client might cover a wound with feces or self-administer an overdose of insulin.

Critical Thinking Question Does including somatoform disorders in the *Diagnostic and Statistical Manual of Mental Disorders,* Fourth Edition, Text Revision (*DSM-IV-TR*) reinforce a mind-body duality or does it emphasize how these barriers are blurred?

General Description of Disorders

The *Diagnostic and Statistical Manual of Mental Disorders,* Fourth Edition, Text Revision (*DSM-IV-TR*) divides the classification of the various somatoform disorders by the presentation of physical symptoms (American Psychiatric Association [APA], 2000). *Somatizing* is the process of expressing psychologic conflict through physical complaints or symptoms. "Butterflies in the stomach" prior to public presentations, a headache prior to tax season, or the pain of a "broken heart" are all common ways to express distress (see **Figure 18-1**). This process is universally experienced, particularly during periods of stress.

Figure 18-1 Getting a headache prior to a stressful event is common.

Somatoform Disorders

A **somatoform disorder** is a mental disorder in which physical symptoms or preoccupations that may present as a physical disorder are considered primarily psychologic in origin. Typically, clients present with multiple, vague physical complaints without a recognized or demonstrated organic cause. Somatoform disorders are diagnosed on Axis 1.

Somatization Disorder

A **somatization** disorder is a psychiatric disorder that begins before 30 years of age. Clients with this disorder have long-term, recurring, unexplained physical complaints and frequently utilize medical physicians and surgeons. Clients with **hypochondriasis** have persistent, unrealistic fears of having a medical disorder unrelated to an affective or anxiety disorder and not relieved by medical examination and explanation. A diagnosis of hypochondriasis may be further specified by adding that the client has poor insight, if this is a valid descriptor predominant in the current episode. Clients with **conversion disorder** have physical symptoms, often associated with motor or sensory deficits or seizures caused by unconscious psychologic conflicts. Conversion disorders can be further differentiated by presenting symptom as conversion disorder with motor symptom or deficit, with sensory symptom or deficit, with seizures or convulsions, or with mixed presentation if symptoms from one or more different categories are present. **Body dysmorphic disorder** is a mental disorder in which the client believes his or her body is deformed in some manner that is not readily observed by others. The diagnosis of body dysmorphic disorder is not used if symptoms can be better explained by another disorder such as anorexia or major depressive disorder. Likewise, another diagnosis can be used, such as delusion disorder, somatic type, if the symptoms of body dysmorphia disorder have a delusional quality and intensity.

Pain Disorders

Pain disorders that are influenced primarily by psychologic factors and cause significant impairment are included under somatoform disorders. Pain disorders are specified according to whether they are acute (of less than 6-month duration) or chronic (of more than 6-month duration). In

Clinical Example

Marc is a 42-year-old sales clerk who experiences painful back spasms. Neurologic and orthopedic workups indicate that his symptoms seem to be excessive compared to the physical problems shown on physical examination and repeated MRIs and x-rays. Despite physical therapy and follow-up in a pain management clinic, his pain seems to be getting worse over the past 6 months. Although he initially seemed to get better after treatment, he now is walking with a cane and asks if he can be prescribed a backbrace. He states he wishes his life would just get back to normal, but things haven't been the same since his wife was diagnosed with cancer.

addition, the *DSM-IV-TR* further differentiates between those associated primarily with psychosocial factors and those associated primarily with a general medical condition. In pain disorders associated with a general medical condition, the general medical condition or site of the pain is identified on Axis III. For example, a pain disorder is coded on Axis I, and the medical disorder, cervical radiculopathy, is specified on Axis III and identified by its proper clinical modification as coded in the *International Classification of Diseases*, 9th revision (*ICD-9-CM*; American Medical Association [AMA], 2006).

Somatic signs and symptoms found in somatoform disorders may be predominant in other disorders. If the symptoms have a known organic cause, a diagnosis of a mental disorder resulting from a general medical condition (Chapter 13), an eating disorder (Chapter 20), or a sleep disorder (Chapter 21) may be more appropriate. The clinician must differentiate between the multiple somatic symptoms found in a somatoform disorder and similar symptoms better explained by another disorder, such as the mood-congruent symptoms of a depressive disorder (Chapter 16). As noted in the *DSM-IV-TR*, what appears to be hypochondriasis in the elderly is more likely the result of an affective disorder (APA, 2000). Somatoform disorders and substance-related disorders (Chapter 14) must be differentiated from schizophrenia, other psychotic disorders, and dissociative disorders (Chapter 15).

Factitious Disorders

In a **factitious disorder**, signs and symptoms are predominantly associated with psychologic disorders, physical disorders, or combined psychologic and physical disorders. Clients appear to produce or feign symptoms intentionally by fab-

Clinical Example

Amanda is well known to the staff because of the frequent admissions of her four-year-old daughter who has had a history of multiple allergies, frequent infections, and seizures. She is a concerned parent, well informed and helpful to everyone, patiently explaining the baffling array of symptoms to new staff members and taking on many of the caretaking responsibilities herself. Amanda jokes that she is better at some things such as obtaining specimens and taking temperatures than some of the staff and has learned enough to graduate from medical school herself. However, she hasn't had the time because the child's illness has been such a strain and the family has had to move several times. During one prolonged admission, the staff observes that the patient seems to get dramatically worse at times that are associated with the mother's visits. They begin a systematic investigation and careful observation to rule out factitious disorder by proxy.

ricating symptoms, self-inflicting signs and symptoms, or exaggerating existing symptoms. Unlike the unconscious motivation of somatization disorders, factitious disorders are associated with a more conscious manipulation. However, the client is not consciously aware of the needs underlying such behavior or the impetus to continue them. Often the client has had some connection with hospitals or healthcare professions in the past and may have a pattern of switching providers when confronted. A pattern of hospitalizations or help-seeking behaviors for various unfounded disorders is seen. In addition, no obvious secondary gain or external force is observed that would explain the behavior. Factitious disorder is usually diagnosed on Axis I and is typically associated with an underlying personality disorder. Thus, the associated personality disorder (e.g., antisocial personality disorder) is specified on Axis II.

Malingering

Malingering consists of intentional or exaggerated symptoms clearly associated with external forces such as the need to avoid work or jail. It is an understandable, obvious manipulation by the client to obtain a specific result. Malingering is classified as a "v" code in the *DSM-IV-TR* because it is a condition rather than a mental disorder. It is specified on Axis I. If malingering is associated with a personality disorder, the personality disorder is specified on Axis II. For example, if malingering is coded on Axis I, the associated avoidant personality disorder is coded on Axis II (APA, 2000).

Clinical Example

Vanessa is a 27-year-old woman who was brought to the emergency department by the police. After her arrest for shoplifting, Vanessa was observed to be breathing rapidly and complained of chest pain. Vanessa had no past history of medical or psychiatric problems and her diagnostic workup in the emergency room, including EKG and cardiac enzymes, was negative.

Incidence and Prevalence

Unexplained physical symptoms are often reported in general medical practices (Feder et al., 2001) and hospital settings (Fink, Hansen, & Oxhoj, 2004). A cross-national study of somatization (Gureje, 2004) noted that there was some variability in prevalence and incidence across nations but that the most important factor appeared to be that multiple somatic complaints were more common among clients who did not have an ongoing relationship with their healthcare providers. Symptoms are found more often in older clients, women, and those who express greater functional impairment (Feder et al.). Except for factitious disorders and malingering, somatoform disorders are found more often in women. Often others in the same family have similar problems; the disorder is more prevalent in individuals with histories of family and social problems or substance, sexual, or physical abuse (Barsky, Stern, Greenberg, & Cassem, 2004).

Although the World Health Organization has limited data on the incidence of somatoform disorders, in 1995 an estimated 14 of 1,000 men and 26 of 1,000 women between 5 and 64 years of age were considered disabled by somatoform disorders. The prevalence is higher among women and occurs in approximately 1% of psychiatric disorders. The disorder is more prevalent in the least-developed areas and in economies that are in transition. The global prevalence of somatoform disorders is estimated to be 2.7% (Ustun & Sartorius, 1995). It estimated that unexplained physical symptoms are present in approximately 29% of cases presenting as part of mental health problems (Gureje, 2004).

One study reviewed 33,531 records and, based upon inconsistent or improbable symptoms, estimated that there was an aspect of malingering in approximately 29% of personal injury cases, 30% of disability cases, 19% of criminal cases, and 8% of medical cases studied. Unexplained somatic complaints were present in 39% of cases involving mild head injury, 35% of fibromyalgia/chronic fatigue cases, 31% of chronic pain cases, 27% of neurologic cases, and 22% of cases involving electrical injuries (Mittenberg, Patton, Canyock, & Condit, 2002).

Etiology

It has been suggested that "calamity, conflict, constitution ... [and] compensation ... [all] impinge on human consciousness and have a bearing on causality" (Trimble, 2004, p. 240) and can be predisposing factors for the potential development of somatoform disorders. There has often been a history of stress or trauma, underlying conflict or ambivalence, predisposition to interpreting physical or psychologic symptoms in a particular matter, and some primary or secondary gains involved in the development and maintenance of illness behaviors.

These disorders are diagnosed in adulthood but often begin in adolescence and may have roots in childhood trauma or abuse. The symptoms are associated with stress or a specific event or consequence. Cultural factors often influence how physical sensations are interpreted as well as how symptoms are described and presented. Certain culture-bound somatic syndromes, such as *koro* or *suo-yang* (a man's fear that his genitals are retracting into his abdomen) and "brain-fag" or *ode ori* (a sensation of noises or something walking around inside one's head), are usually of short duration, do not interfere with functioning, and are meaningful to others with similar cultural experience (Mezzich, Kleinman, Fabrega, & Parron, 1996). There are also cultural differences in the description of illness and treatment planning. For example, Yeung and Deguang (2002) report that in traditional Chinese medicine, there has been no model of "medically unexplained symptoms."

In today's health-conscious society where illness remedies and hygiene items are advertised and available nearly everywhere, it is almost inappropriate not to have an ache or pain that can be presented in social situations. More people may be willing to seek help because of the services and more sophisticated tests available to identify subtle changes in body structure or functioning. This may result in over-utilization of healthcare systems. Concentrating on somatic complaints without a recognizable physical cause may become a problem if it interferes with social or occupational demands or becomes the sole focus of functioning and interaction.

Social learning, family systems, and change theories may be applied to somatization disorders. Cognitive behavioral theories form the basis for behavioral interventions such as relaxation techniques and biofeedback, in which clients are taught to recognize physiologic cues and manipulate biological responses to change their response to stimuli (Nakagawa-Kogan, 1996). The client may have had a model for symptom presentation, such as another family member who had a real or imagined illness and received attention or support, or one who had a previous experience of illness where considerable secondary gain or attention was received. Symptoms may be unwittingly reinforced by cultural or social factors. Symptoms occasionally establish a balance in an unstable relationship or family system and are reinforced by this balance. The client may be the symptom bearer or someone who, through the illness, distracts others from problems in the family system or relationship. Issues of dependency and independence among members of the system may allow the client to remain in the dependent role of the sick person and reinforce illness behaviors through secondary gain.

In social learning or adaptation, a response is modified by a new experience or input. Stress may interfere with this learning process. The client may not be able to respond to a new situation in a positive way because of an overload of new input; he or she may respond by "giving up." Conversely, if there is cognitive dissonance (a situation in which the inputs are perceived as incongruous), the client may respond by not accepting or denying the new input. *Locus of control* refers to the extent to which an individual feels that he or she has control over a situation; an individual with an external locus of control feels that events are determined by outside forces such as luck or fate. Research posits an inverse relationship between the sense of personal control and somatization (the report of physical symptoms). The sense of personal control is analyzed by identifying measures of behavioral, cognitive, and decision-making control (Nakagawa-Kogan, 1996). The effects of cognitive dissonance and locus of control on learning are mitigated by other variables such as the amount of control or influence an individual has upon a situation and past experiences.

The symptoms of somatoform disorders are similar to but more specific than those for **Briquet's syndrome**, which typically occurs in women with a history of multiple somatic complaints without valid physical cause. The syndrome begins before 30 years of age and recurs frequently. Briquet's syndrome includes symptoms of overdramatization, exhibitionism, and seductiveness that previously had been associated with hysteria. The descriptors of somatoform disorder focus on the multiplicity of symptoms, their duration, and the lack of a demonstrated cause.

Pierre Briquet, an eighteenth-century physician, described numerous cases of predominantly female patients who appeared to have multiple physical symptoms attributed to hysteria. Briquet's syndrome, a psychologic disorder, formed the basis for the present diagnostic category termed *somatization disorder.*

Pain is identified according to a taxonomy proposed by the International Association for the Study of Pain. It is categorized according to anatomic region, organ system, temporal characteristics and patterns, description of intensity and time since onset, and etiology (APA, 2000). Pain may be a response to stress or can be exacerbated by it. The meanings associated with pain differ according to personality style, cultural background, environmental cues, and the presence or absence of available supports. The same physiologic pain associated with a demonstrated cause (i.e., childbirth) may be assigned different meanings by the same person in different contexts, such as in the client's experience of normal childbirth following a history of fetal demise. The physiologic pathways of pain, unless altered by disease, are similar in all people; however, the cognitive, emotional, and physical responses to pain may vary greatly in the same individual at different times and between individuals in similar circumstances.

Critical Thinking Question Emily Dickinson wrote:

Pain has an element of blank;
It cannot recollect
When it began, or if there was
A time when, it was not.

What do you think about her characterization of pain? How would you describe the effects of pain?

Physiology

Pain is associated with psychologic experiences related to early warnings and learned experiences of danger, punishment, aggression and power, loss, and sexual feelings (Engel, 1959).

Clients with somatization disorders usually present with physical symptoms that either do not have a physiologic basis or are in excess of any demonstrated or recognized cause. Diagnostic and laboratory tests usually do not show the expected pattern for the degree of symptoms described. Conversely, if a basis for the symptoms is found, the degree of impairment or discomfort exceeds normal expectations or the experiences of others in the same situation. Individuals with somatoform disorder may be more sensitive in identifying physiologic symptoms. In some cultures, more attention is paid to slight changes in body functioning, and there is more of a tendency to attribute changes or variations to a perceived norm as problematic. For example, it is not unusual for overburdened nursing students to worry that they are suffering from the exotic ailments they are studying and to experience relief from the terrible symptoms suffered during examination periods as soon as spring break arrives. Conversely, a student on a football scholarship may underestimate the pain experienced in training or deny pain to teammates and coaches. The athlete whose scholarship is dependent upon the ability to play may be able to admit to the pain only when exposed to the noncompetitive environment of home during school break.

In all cases it is important to rule out physiologic causes for the symptoms. The range of symptoms required to meet diagnostic criteria are unusual in most physical illnesses. An individual with a somatization disorder is expected to have multiple symptoms of pain, gastrointestinal problems, sexual dysfunction, and vague neurologic or **dissociative** (a distancing and disruption of usual functioning in response to psychologic conflict or trauma) complaints. The symptoms should have been problematic enough for the individual to have sought treatment or to have caused significant functional impairment. In addition, the symptoms do not follow the usual patterns for most common illnesses or syndromes and cannot be substantiated by clinical findings or diagnostic tests. Rather than focusing on one symptom or problem, the client usually presents a collection of signs and symptoms often preceded by a history of diagnostic puzzles and problematic treatments. Traditionally, this includes autonomic nervous symptoms such as rapid pulse and rapid breathing, sweating, pressure in chest, pounding heart or palpitations, muscular tension, flushing, and cold hands and feet.

In somatization disorder, multiple symptoms are identified in more than one system (APA, 2000):

- *Gastrointestinal symptoms:* Symptoms include hyperactive bowel, digestive upset, nausea, bloating, and food intolerance.
- *Pseudoneurologic symptoms:* Symptoms include weakness or tingling, loss of sensa-

tion, atypical seizures, ataxia, problems swallowing, and loss of consciousness other than fainting.

- *Sexual dysfunction:* Symptoms include painful menses, painful sexual intercourse, lack of sexual response, and ejaculatory or erectile problems.
- *Pain symptoms:* Pain is generalized or specific, unchanging, and unremitting (i.e., "nothing helps") and affects at least four areas of functioning (painful headache, backache, muscle cramping, painful sexual intercourse).

Somatization is a psychophysiologic process through which the client's response to stress is expressed. Adaptive responses such as learning, regulation of arousal, and maintenance of an organized conceptual system are regulatory coping responses. Impediments to learning, problems in regulating arousal states, and cognitive dissonance cause maladaptive coping responses and system dysregulation. Examples of this mind-body interface are found in the neural mediation of immunocompetence, cortical functioning, and sympathetic-parasympathetic imbalance; endorphins and pain responses; and autonomic nervous system arousal and anxiety. Nakagawa-Kogan (1996) postulates that **self-management training** aids in stress reduction, stating that the "completeness of cognitive content permits smooth interaction of the present encounter with successive ones, with automatic appraisal and adaptive emotional response, thus preventing the triggering of catecholamines and stimulation of the autonomic nervous system" (p. 35).

Pain is a sensory, physical, and emotional response to actual or potential tissue damage. Increased physiologic and cognitive arousal induces greater physical discomfort, muscle tension, and mental distress. Suffering is primarily an affective and cognitive response associated with the interpretation of pain. Pain may result from direct stimulation of the body or may be a response to structural or chemical changes. The number of pain receptors activated is not as important as the response to the stimulus. Pain activation involves the ratio of small-diameter and large-diameter afferent nerve fibers that trigger neurons up spinal pathways to pain centers in the thalamus or cerebral cortex and down pathways to influence the experience of pain. Small A-delta and C fibers transmit impulses to the spinal cord via the neospinothalamic tract or the paleospinothalamic tract. Ascending pathways are responsible for the sensory-discriminative component of pain. Descending pathways are responsible for inhibitory modulation or control. Interpretation of nociceptive impulses in the cerebral cortex influences the perceptual experience of pain. The endorphin, noradrenergic, and serotoninergic systems also influence the response to pain. Prolonged or excessive pain changes the nervous system and its responses. Alpha-adrenergic transmitters released during stress and negative emotional states activate C fibers termed *unmyelinated nociceptors*. Throughout the nervous system, damage results from excitation of nociceptors from cell contents such as potassium, histamine, acetylcholine, serotonin, and adenosine triphosphate; inflammatory mediators such as prostaglandins and leukotrienes; and nociceptor-releasing substances such as substance P and calcitonin gene-related peptide. Sensitization of nociceptors is known as "wind-up." When damaged cells release bradykinin, nociceptors are activated. Transmission mechanisms of acute and chronic pain differ. **Referred pain** is pain that originates in one area of the body and is referred or experienced in another part that is not receiving the noxious stimuli directly.

Clinical Presentation

The client's perception of his or her body image and the nonverbal clues given in the presentation are important in assessment and treatment but are not diagnostic of a somatoform disorder. Historically, clients have been described as having either a highly dramatic presentation or "***la belle indifference***," a calm and somewhat cheerful indifference to the catastrophes presented. Actual clients are not as predictable and may present their complaints in a hysterical or an extremely sincere and convincing manner. A matter-of-fact presentation, a limited range of affect, or even a histrionic (intense and dramatic) presentation may be more indicative of the client's characteristic style than of an underlying problem or psychologic disorder. Chronic, longstanding symptoms, such as those associated with somatization disorder, have been reinforced in the past, and the client has an interest in making his or her distress known to and recognized by others.

The client may relate a history of being more "sickly" or prone to accidents or disasters than would normally be expected, and the courses of

Somatization is a response to stress.

Factitious disorders are often associated with **Münchausen syndrome**, a disorder in which clients deliberately manipulate symptoms to obtain hospitalization, medical treatment, or surgical intervention. Baron Hieronymus Münchausen lived in the eighteenth century and was known for the wild, fantastic stories of his adventures that later became fictionalized as *The Adventures of Baron Münchausen*.

Implications for Evidence-Based Practice

As part of a nursing assessment, nursing students were asked to involve their patients with chronic illnesses to develop a symbolic representation of their experiences of illness in art, poetry, music, and the like (Michael, Candela, & Mitchell, 2002). Further research is needed to examine what kinds of information can be gleaned from these kinds of experiences and how this can be used as part of the nursing assessment. Another area of research would be in determining how such interactions affect the development of the nurse-patient relationship. It would also be interesting to find the implications for use during the assessment process and perhaps as an initiation of complementary therapies.

Research would be needed to determine if using an aesthetic representation rather than a verbal report would allow for an understanding of illness behavior across different cultures.

treatment have been more heroic or demanding than the symptoms seemed to require. The symptoms may mimic the beginning stages of physical disorders such as multiple sclerosis, but the actual course of the somatizer's illness and the symptoms themselves may vary dramatically over time. The client's description of his or her history may be overly detailed and circumstantial. The client may have had multiple caretakers and treatments, as well as reassurance from many sources that the problem is not as bad as the client thinks or does not exist at all. The client with hypochondriasis focuses on the unrealistic dread of an illness that is felt as life threatening, despite reassurance and adequate and appropriate medical follow-up. This focused anxiety persists over time and is the predominant feature of the disorder. Clients with body dysmorphia also may have a chronic history of problems and anxieties, but the focus is usually on one predominant symptom. Clients with body dysmorphic disorder feel that they are deformed by distorted physical characteristics, body or breath odor, or a dermatologic problem such as a rash or infestation that makes them unacceptable to others or the focus of unwanted attention by distinguishing them from others. Usually repeated investigations have not found the problem's source, and others do not perceive the client as deformed or unacceptable.

The acute presentation of symptoms in conversion disorder is often more clearly tied to a specific stressor or event. A conversion disorder often involves a single, isolated presentation of a dramatic symptom such as blindness or hemiplegia. Conversion disorders are changes in body functioning with a known organic cause. The presentation is often dramatic and the precipitating factors apparent and symbolic, such as the man whose hand becomes paralyzed after he raises it to strike his partner. Relief of the symptoms is often as dramatic as the symptom's onset, if the client has confidence in the healthcare provider and is open to suggestions for improvement and treatment.

Clients' descriptions of pain symptoms differ because of many variables, and symptoms are occasionally so intertwined with feelings of suffering that interpretation is difficult. Differences in personality between the client and the healthcare provider should not cause the provider to label the client's pain as imaginary or hysterical. The healthcare provider is only an observer who can help elicit the client's description and subjective experience of pain. Even when the etiology of the pain is psychologic, the clinician's role is to help alleviate the pain and associated suffering the client may be experiencing. The physiologic pathways of pain are clearly established. The descriptions and identified source of the pain may be inconsistent with

Clinical Example

Kara is a 20-year-old woman admitted to the hospital with severe abdominal pain and cramping. Medical workup has been negative. During the nursing assessment, Kara mentions that her boyfriend has been accepted into medical school and is moving to another state. He has asked her to move in with him. She says that she has been too sick to make any plans. She says she feels frustrated because she can't move out of state to be with her boyfriend. However, she acknowledges that the timing of the move is not the best because if she leaves school she would have no medical insurance or means of support. She now lives with her parents and has not told them that she has been thinking of moving in with her boyfriend.

Implications for Evidence-Based Practice

In a random telephone study of 5,584 hospitalized patients, Whelan, Jin, and Meltzer (2004) found that pain and dissatisfaction with pain management were common and that each individual patient should be considered at risk for pain. No group was identified as being at low risk for pain. Patients with higher diagnostic related group (DRG) weight tended to express greater satisfaction with pain management, suggesting that patients with more serious illnesses received more attention during hospitalizations. Further study is indicated as to the factors influencing prediction of pain and its treatment; interventional studies regarding treatment protocols also would be useful.

physical findings and known anatomic pathways. Those pain disorders associated with more than an expected degree of impairment and associated psychologic factors are classified as somatoform disorders to emphasize the need for a holistic treatment approach (Alpay, 2004).

Factitious disorders concern client behaviors associated with symptoms of psychologic or physical disorders. Intentional symptom production is not seen as lying but as an attempt to express ambiguous subjective sensory experiences, psychologic conflicts, and anxiety. Clients with factitious disorders may have a poorly differentiated sense of self and a poorly defined sense of reality. Their attempts to seek help for psychologic or physical disorders are intended to stimulate psychiatric, medical, or surgical interventions and relationships with caregivers. The "client" role and the associated relationships with others are meant to provide an externalized framework to validate their internalized experiences and sense of self (Spivak et al., 1994). The Internet may be used by the client to research information about a disease and treatment options.

Clinical Course and Complications

For many clients with somatoform disorders, presenting their complaints to healthcare providers has been a frustrating process, resulting in no adequate solution to their problems. Many healthcare providers view clients with somatization disorders as "worried but well" or "difficult." Because there is no easy cure, the client may be dissatisfied despite the best efforts of the healthcare provider. The client may be seen merely as a complainer who should be avoided because of the time and attention he or she demands. These frustrations are complicated by symptoms that present, disappear, and reappear over time. The manner in which the client normally describes symptoms may camouflage an actual physical problem that needs treatment, baffling even the most determined detective. The actual course of the disorder may be complicated by the presence or history of child or sexual abuse, substance disorders, mood disorders, and personality disorders. Clients with chronic pain need to be identified early to facilitate treatment and avoid prolonged or unnecessary treatment that could delay rehabilitation. Accurate and comprehensive assessment of pain is necessary, because both undertreating and overtreating pain can cause problems. Occasionally, treatment for pain is complicated by the healthcare provider's bias toward particular standardized protocols that are supposed to work for all clients or fears of being manipulated or fooled by an addicted client.

Clients with factitious disorders and clients with malingering may have a history of frequent help-seeking behaviors. These contacts with healthcare providers can be frustrating for both parties, because clients need to prove that their symptoms are valid and in need of attention and treatment. The primary problems affecting the clinical course include maintaining a therapeutic relationship and avoiding unnecessary and intrusive treatments that may harm the client. Confrontations by the provider or a competitive escalation of symptoms by the client to prove the illness and need for treatment are nonproductive and occasionally lead to termination of the therapeutic relationship. An angry client may feel provoked to engage in self-harm, destructive behavior, or flight (Barsky et al., 2004).

The client with somatoform disorder presents a unique challenge to the treating staff: avoid undertreating a real medical condition versus providing unnecessary treatment.

NURSING CARE PLAN Somatization Disorder

Expected Outcomes	Interventions	Evaluations
• Will minimize the potential for iatrogenic injury and self-harm. • Will identify and select a primary healthcare provider. • Will form realistic goals. • Will participate in psychotherapy.	• Evaluating, with team members, the need for diagnostic testing and medical or surgical procedures. • Demonstrating the need for clear communication and continuity of care. • Involving the client in decision making and providing feedback regarding her choices. • Encouraging the verbalization of feelings regarding the illness and hospitalization.	• Determining the extent to which the client's requests for diagnostic testing and medical or surgical intervention decrease. • Selecting and using a single primary healthcare provider to improve communication. • Observing for improvement in decision-making skills. • Determining the use of appropriate therapeutic interventions.

Visit http://nursing.jbpub.com/psychiatric for additional care plans and exercises.

CASE STUDY Ms. X.

Ms. X. is a 46-year-old woman who was brought to the emergency room with increased shortness of breath, palpitations, and chest pain. She told the emergency room staff of her history of treatment for pulmonary emboli and was started on anticoagulants. Although tests for pulmonary emboli were inconclusive, she was admitted to the hospital because she developed a hematoma at the intravenous site, weakness and tingling in her arm, and hematuria that required additional testing. Staff members on the unit requested a psychiatric consultation to evaluate the client for depression. The client had told the staff that she had had many hardships and illnesses in her life and was not certain how she could continue to manage with the terrible pain she was having due to the hematoma. The staff reported that the client was "very brave" and refused all pain medication because she had multiple allergies. Because of this, she could not participate in physical therapy and required much staff assistance with self-care.

The client told the nurse consultant that she felt overwhelmed with her situation, and "could barely feed or dress herself" because of the weakness in her arm, but was trying to emulate an aunt who had died at a young age as a result of rheumatic heart disease. The aunt had impressed the client with her courage and cheerfulness in dealing with chronic illness, and everyone loved to visit and bring flowers and keep the aunt company. The sickroom was the brightest room in her grandmother's house.

The client did not think of herself as a sickly child but had become ill in her early twenties. During the first year of her marriage, she had a miscarriage at approximately 6 weeks, "before even knowing about the pregnancy." The client said she had had "excruciating pain," "nearly bled to death," and had terrible reactions to a blood transfusion. Afterward, she always felt that she had gotten the wrong blood, although it was never proved, and had terrible pain afterward during intercourse "due to stretching during the miscarriage." She had found her husband unsympathetic and unresponsive to her medical problems, "a little rough, wanting sex all the time," but not abusive. Their relationship deteriorated in the next few years partly from the client's frequent hospitalizations for urinary tract infections and diagnostic procedures that eventually excluded endometriosis. Some of the infections caused high fevers, and she had had terrible side effects from almost every antibiotic given. The client stated that her past medical records were "all over the place" because she had moved frequently since her divorce but that she had consulted many physicians in an effort to find out just what was "draining the life out of me." She was proud of her skills as a secretary but had been unable to work full time for years because of her frequent illnesses. She now found it increasingly difficult to manage her part-time work because she found she was allergic to many office supplies. The initial clinical impression was somatization disorder (see **Table 18-1**).

NURSING CARE PLAN Conversion Disorder

Expected Outcomes	Interventions	Evaluations
• Will identify possible stressors. • Will minimize feelings of anxiety. • Will explore alternative coping mechanisms. • Will establish contact with community resources for follow-up care.	• Assessing the client and family systems. • Teaching relaxation techniques. • Assisting the client in identifying coping mechanisms that have worked in the past in similar situations. • Discussing possible community resources and support systems.	• Validating the selections and application of appropriate therapeutic techniques. • Evaluating the client's demonstration of relaxation techniques. • Observing for increased use of appropriate coping mechanisms. • Reviewing the client's participation in a parenting support group.

Visit http://nursing.jbpub.com/psychiatric for additional care plans and exercises.

Differential Diagnosis

Many clients seek medical or surgical treatment for somatoform disorders. Clearly the most important factor is to help the client avoid undertreatment for a medical condition or unnecessary treatment of an illness. Many clients complicate their care unnecessarily by seeking multiple opinions for the same complaints or enlisting multiple healthcare providers for discrete individual complaints, allowing no one to recognize the real problem. It is essential to exclude underlying medical conditions. When faced with multiple

CASE STUDY Ms. Y.

Ms. Y., a 21-year-old woman, came to her routine postpartum visit complaining of severe, constant headaches over the past week, with pain in the top and back of her head radiating to the neck. She told staff that she was worried she was going to have a stroke, because the headaches made her arms so weak she could hardly pick up the baby. When she had the headaches, she felt as if the only thing that she could do was lie down. She was concerned that she might have a headache when there was no one around to help her. She stated, "Who would take care of the baby? The older child might harm the baby or get into trouble if there were no one watching. I don't know how I would manage." She said she was eating and sleeping well and was able to enjoy her usual activities. The initial medical and neurologic findings were negative, and the client was referred to the headache clinic and eventually to mental health for evaluation. The client stated that she had not had problems during the pregnancy other than a little fatigue and that the pregnancy had been planned. She and her husband were pleased that their family now consisted of a little boy and a little girl just as they had imagined. Both sets of in-laws and other family members were happy for them and active in welcoming the new family member. This was in contrast to her first pregnancy, which was unplanned and for which she had felt unprepared, as she stated, "I was such a baby myself then." She found it very stressful and had felt sick "most of the pregnancy." She stated she had felt depressed and anxious during her first pregnancy but did not feel that way now. She said things were going well with her marriage and that the two children were "the best things that had ever happened to me." The client told the nurse that her sister had helped her initially after the baby's birth but now was returning to college after summer break. The client said she did not think she could have survived without her sister's help after the birth. She did not want to be a burden to her sister and was worried because her sister did not want to leave her when she was so sick. The client stated she did not know how she would manage without her sister because the toddler was so active and the baby was so demanding.

She had been seen by a psychiatrist on an out-patient basis during her first pregnancy and years earlier when she was 14 years of age. At 14 years of age, she had been referred to the ambulatory health center by the school nurse after she had suddenly started missing school because of the onset of severe stomach pains. She eventually confided to staff that she had been molested by a male neighbor. During both of those times, she had found behavioral health counseling helpful in dealing with her feelings of anxiety and sadness. The initial clinical impression was conversion disorder (see **Table 18-1**).

Table 18-1 Somatoform and Factitious Disorders

Disorder	Symptoms	Clinical Course	Differential
Somatoform	Pain, gastrointestinal, sexual, pseudoneurologic symptoms in more than one area	Begins when client is < 30 years of age	No physical cause or exaggeration of symptoms
Conversion disorder	Voluntary motor, sensory	Limited, reversible	Unconscious motivation, no delusional symptoms
Hypochondriasis	Fear of illness, preoccupation with illness, misinterpretation of symptoms	Transient or chronic	Not restricted to appearance, no delusional symptoms, duration > 6 months, depression
Body dysmorphia	Preoccupation with imagined defect, usually appearance	Persistent	Delusional disorders, depression
Pain disorder	Pain in more than one area; psychologic factors more likely, greater than expected disability	Acute or chronic	Not intentionally feigned, depression
Factitious	Mimics physical disorder; mimics psychological disorder	Chronic, persistent	May or may not be conscious, no recognizable benefit
Malingering	Exaggerated, prolonged	Situational, limited	Recognizable goal

and occasionally conflicting signs and symptoms, the nurse should ask what organic disorders could cause these symptoms and whether the symptoms, especially pain symptoms, follow established physiologic and pathologic patterns (Barsky et al., 2004).

Often a diagnosis of "exclusion" is made after everything else has been considered and ruled out. Many chronic illnesses begin with clients presenting a confusing or transient array of symptoms. Clients with anxiety, depressive, or psychotic disorders may exhibit somatic preoccupations or delusions. Clients with real medical problems, such as a seizure disorder, also may have an overlay of symptoms that are precipitated by psychologic stressors as well as a somatoform disorder related to nonepileptic seizures or pseudoseizures.

The index of suspicion for somatization disorder is high for clients with a long history of an unusually large number of inexplicable symptoms affecting multiple body systems. This client may be a hypochondriac, one who is often convinced that he or she has a specific illness and is going to die despite evidence to the contrary. A specific temporal or psychologic link with a specific stimulus may exist in a client with a conversion disorder; the physical symptom may be associated with a specific event or model but is not intentionally or consciously produced. Clients who repeatedly seek treatment for unrealistic concerns about their appearance or odor may have body dysmorphic disorder. These clients' symptoms seem to focus on pain more than would be expected for the type of disorder they have. Conversely, those whose lives are affected more than normally expected in similar circumstances may have a pain disorder with predominant psychologic factors.

Clients with panic or other anxiety disorders or phobias (see Chapter 17) may present with multiple somatic complaints such as paresthesias (neurologic weaknesses) and gastrointestinal symptoms, similar to clients with somatoform disorder. However, in anxiety disorders, the symptoms are usually chronic, may be generalized, and may have differing intensities. In panic disorders, physical symptoms of anxiety (e.g., rapid pulse, pounding heartbeat) are usually confined to periods of panic or situations that exacerbate anxiety.

Clients with somatization disorders, in addition to autonomic nervous system complaints similar to those of clients with anxiety, have symptoms that affect several body parts and complain of pain and sexual dysfunction not confined to specific periods. Clients with somatization disorders are more likely to seek medical intervention for their symptoms on a regular basis. Researchers believe that clients with panic or anxiety disorders are more likely to seek attention for their problematic symptoms and to accept alternative explanations for their problems as well as psychologic counseling. Some clients with underlying depression or a psychotic disorder also may appear preoccupied with pain or somatic complaints, or focused on some aspect of their physical appearance or bodily functioning. Although it may be difficult to differentiate, clients with somatoform disorder present with a multiplicity and range of symptoms and the absence of another clearly identified disorder that would explain their problems. Clients with hypochondriasis may also have underlying psychiatric disorders. If the underlying depressive or anxiety disorder is treated, hypochondriacal symptoms decrease (Barsky et al., 2004).

Clients with histories of sexual abuse or trauma may present with chronic abdominal pain or problems with sexual functioning. An underlying history of substance abuse may be causing multiple symptoms. Clients with a history of substance abuse may attribute their symptoms caused by abuse to other causes to minimize or hide their abuse or dependence or to disguise drug-seeking behaviors. Some of the symptoms of body dysmorphic disorder may lead a clinician to suspect substance abuse or withdrawal, even though the usual signs are not present and the diagnosis is not confirmed by history or toxicology screening.

In addition, specific environmental or lifestyle factors that could contribute to malingering (stimulation of a voluntary manipulation of symptoms to escape a noxious response or end) or to a factitious disorder (consciously and intentionally stimulated medical or psychiatric symptoms to obtain treatment) should be excluded. Malingering and factitious disorders are difficult to treat, because the relief of symptoms may produce an unwanted response in which the client must face negative or noxious consequences, such as the loss of disability benefits or a return to jail. Both malingering and factitious disorder are considered only after medical and psychiatric workups have identified no other possible explanations for the symptoms. Clients with malingering have an obvious associated cause for the illness behavior. For example, the client may be involved in a compensation case or be threatened with the loss of other entitlement benefits. However, no similar, readily understandable explanation for the symptoms associated with a factitious disorder exists. For example, in our society, because of the stigma attached to psychiatric disorders, most people would not believe it worthwhile to feign psychiatric symptoms.

For clients with pain disorders, it is important to establish a clear history of the onset and duration of the pain; a description of symptoms, treatments, and responses to treatment; past experiences with illness and pain; past psychiatric and substance abuse history; usual coping mechanisms; variables that increase or decrease symptoms; and past and present levels of social, psychologic, and occupational functioning.

Often, the pain is associated with periods of developmental or accidental crisis. Records of past treatment and diagnostic tests are helpful to review. Pain scales and pain logs are often helpful in pinpointing possible problems. New onset of pain or dramatic changes in presentation should be investigated to determine if there is a demonstrated basis for the pain, if it is a new medical disorder that should be treated, or if

Implications for Evidence-Based Practice

Lewandowski (2004) reviewed current literature dealing with chronic pain and identified factors associated with pain-related beliefs (sense of personal control over pain, cognitive distortion, fear avoidance), history of traumatic events (history of child or sexual abuse and PTSD), and styles of coping in an attempt to identify factors involved in the experience of chronic pain. The review found that nursing interventions depend upon accurate assessment including identification of underlying depression, history of abuse or trauma, pain beliefs, and coping styles in order to ensure appropriate treatment planning and referral for treatment of other disorders (e.g., depression, PTSD). Cognitive therapy was identified as a treatment approach to decrease excess disability and encourage alternate coping mechanisms and pain relief activities.

Treatment of symptoms, stressors, and family systems is important in dealing with somatoform disorders.

new psychosocial stressors are affecting symptom presentation.

Critical Thinking Question How do family and culture influence the development of attitudes towards pain and the expression of pain?

Management and Treatment

Teamwork and cooperation between healthcare providers and the client are important when treating any illness, but are essential when treating clients with somatoform disorders, factitious disorders, and malingering. Important points include problematic symptoms and methods of coping with them. The client needs to be assured that his or her concerns are being considered and that treatment will be helpful. Goals include relieving physiologic and psychosocial symptoms and minimizing interference with normal lifestyle requirements.

During the assessment process, the client should be encouraged to describe the symptoms as well as the context in which they appear or abate. It is helpful to identify the problems these symptoms have caused in the past and what therapies have been tried or found helpful. The identification of specific stressors or trigger factors often helps. Focusing attention on the assessment process, treatment planning, and evaluation avoids reinforcing the symptoms while providing the client with the attention necessary to maintain positive self-esteem. This focus also reassures the client of the interest and concern of the healthcare providers.

The mental health professional who treats clients with somatoform disorders must focus on engaging both the primary healthcare providers and the symptomatic client in active participation in healthcare planning and symptom management.

The clinician should help the client identify personal strengths and social supports. While recognizing that the symptoms are real, present, and problematic, the client should be assisted in managing the symptoms so that normal day-to-day activities and health are not compromised. Clients are taught problem-solving techniques and assisted in setting appropriate goals. The client and family are taught to shift their focus away from the physical symptoms to the more practical and functional management issues. Clients gain control over their symptoms and have a growing awareness of the body's responses. Exercise and physical and occupational therapies assist the client in developing a more positive and sophisticated perception of body image. These task assignments provide measurable goals, such as a gradual increase in the duration of a daily walk, doing one daily social activity with family or a group, or practicing relaxation techniques at regular intervals.

Understanding family dynamics and the client's present relationships often helps in identify-

Considerations for Client and Family Education

- Include client and family in communications and treatment planning in order to provide for use of collateral information in assessment, provide for clear communication, and maintain support systems.
- Build upon client strengths and help the client develop new coping skills.
- Assist the client to avoid unnecessary tests or procedures and recognize the need to prioritize treatment.
- Reinforce the need to recognize possible precipitants or concomitant factors associated with somatic complaints. By monitoring feelings and stressful situations and the association with somatic symptoms, the relationship between feelings, thoughts, and somatic symptoms can be identified.

Implications for Evidence-Based Practice

The Veterans Administration's (2001) consensus guidelines for treatment of medically unexplained symptoms and chronic pain focus on building a therapeutic alliance; coordinating treatment, client education, and collaboration; self-management; and follow-up to monitor treatment as well as revisit and reassess symptom severity, reinforce goals, and assess for emerging conditions. Further research is needed across varied healthcare systems to evaluate the use of consultative and interdisciplinary services and the use of adjunctive and complementary therapies.

ing causative factors and possible supports. Changes in the client's behavior or symptom presentation may affect the balance of several relationships. Knowledge of these alliances and connections is useful both in facilitating change and in anticipating problems. In addition, active family involvement in treatment helps to sustain the client's involvement. Stress-reduction and behavior-modification techniques actively involve the client in treatment. Self-management training includes assessment of the client's beliefs and behaviors, coping repertoire, problematic symptoms, and physiologic cues; instruction in physiologic control techniques such as biofeedback, relaxation, and self-monitoring techniques; and utilization of behavioral and cognitive therapies. Self-management training focuses on bodily processes that are under voluntary control. For example, cognitive-neural-physiologic responses are assessed to develop a training program that helps the client focus on breathing to control a stress-related symptom such as hyperventilation (Nakagawa-Kogan, 1996).

In somatoform disorders, medication is usually not recommended but may be indicated for the temporary treatment of problematic symptoms. Treatment of underlying psychologic disorders such as anxiety or depression may be helpful. Body dysmorphia disorders are treated with serotonin reuptake inhibitors (SRIs), clomipramine, and electroconvulsive therapy (ECT) (Barsky et al., 2004).

Analgesics, alone or in combination, are used in treatment of pain disorders, particularly those associated with a general medical condition. Various approaches are used, such as increasing the dosage strength or decreasing the dosage intervals. The drug's effect and the anticipated time to onset and duration of action should be considered. For example, a centrally acting pain medication is often combined with a peripherally acting medication, or a long-acting medication is combined with a short-acting medication to provide adequate pain relief. The presence of breakthrough pain or of different types of pain should be considered in selecting medications and dosage schedules. The client's reported history of use and experiences with the medication is helpful in determining the medication regimen and in eliciting the client's cooperation. Properly and adequately treated pain does not lead to addiction. If addiction or manipulation of drug use is suspected, other underlying, contributing factors are usually found. Undertreatment or insufficient treatment of pain is more likely to lead to chronic pain syndromes than adequately treated pain.

Peripherally acting pain medications such as acetaminophen (Tylenol), salicylates (aspirin), and nonsteroidal anti-inflammatory drugs (NSAIDs) such as ibuprofen (Advil, Motrin), ketoprofen (Orudis), and naproxen (Naprosyn) or ketoralac tromethamine (Toradol) are commonly used. Some types of pain respond to centrally acting opioid analgesics such as propoxyphene napsylate (Darvon-N), products containing codeine sulfate (Tylenol 3, Tylenol 4), hydrocodone (Vicodin), oxycodone (Roxicodone), or meperidine (Demerol). Morphine sulfate (Roxanol) and hydromorphone (Dilaudid) are relatively short acting but are available in sustained-release form (Roxanol-SR). Methadone (Dolophine), a long-acting analgesic, has a half-life that increases with prolonged use. The opioid agonists include morphine (Roxanol), codeine, hydromorphone (Dilaudid), hydrocodone (Vicodin), levorphanol (Levo-Dromoran), methadone (Dolophine), oxycodone (Roxicodone), and oxymorphone (Numorphan). Opioid agonist-antagonist and partial agonists include butorphanol (Stadol), nalbuphine (Nubain), buprenorphine (Buprenex), and pentazocine (Talwin). Medication side effects and interactions, tolerance, dependence, and withdrawal are important considerations when narcotics and opioids are used. Pregnancy, alcohol or other substance abuse history, and noncompliance or self-medication are important contraindications. Many clients prefer to use client-controlled analgesia (PCA) pumps or epidermal patch administration for more individualized pain control schedules.

Support, suggestions, self-management training, and strengthening coping and social systems are important parts of treatment.

In clients with pain disorders, a tricyclic antidepressant such as amitriptyline (Elavil), imipramine (Tofranil), or doxepin (Sinequan) is occasionally used in combination with pain medication, because tricyclic antidepressants affect the descending pain pathways, potentiate the action of most pain medications so that smaller doses can be used, and have a somewhat sedative effect along with producing skeletal muscle relaxation. Benzodiazepines and anticonvulsants are sometimes used for paroxysmal pain. These medications are thought to decrease the timing of afferent neurons and antagonize hyperexcitability. Cytokine blockers are used for arthritic pain. The goal in pain management may be to decrease the frequency or dosage of medication rather than to eliminate it entirely.

The use of placebos is never indicated, because response to a placebo does not necessarily indicate that the pain is not real.

The emphasis is not on questioning the reliability of the client's report of pain but rather on increasing the client's repertoire of coping mechanisms to manage the pain. For example, massage, guided imagery, relaxation techniques, and behavior modification techniques are helpful when used alone or with other therapies. Acupuncture, cryoanalgesia, regional block analgesics or surgical blockades, trigger point injections, transcutaneous electrical nerve stimulation (TENS), and electromagnetic stimulation therapy (TheraStim) are considered useful adjuncts for some types of chronic pain. A client with chronic pain may be referred to a pain clinic for consultation. A multidisciplinary, individualized approach is particularly helpful (Turk, 1990). Referral is suggested if there is a history of self-medication, abnormal pain behaviors, complex problems, or history of inadequate treatment (Bouckoms & Hackett, 1997).

Clinicians can put clients in charge by encouraging them to keep a log of symptom relief using simple pain scales (intensity rating scales of 0–10, from no pain to the worst pain ever). The pain's location (site or area), descriptors (dull, pressing, throbbing, burning, sharp, stabbing), and duration (constant, intermittent, periodic, with diurnal variations) are important in assessment. The pain log alerts healthcare providers to changes in symptoms, the effectiveness of the current drug regimen, and concomitant stressors or environmental changes. The pain log also demonstrates acute changes or shows changes over time that may not be readily observed.

Critical Thinking Question What are some pharmacologic and nonpharmacologic methods of pain relief, and what are their potential side effects?

Intentional symptom production to receive attention or to avoid noxious consequences should be identified. Changes in the environment to address the triggers for symptom production should be considered. Along with the client, family members should be instructed regarding somatoform disorders, factitious disorders, malingering, and the need for a holistic approach not totally dependent upon medical or surgical intervention. Similarly, a holistic approach to pain disorders is not totally dependent upon pharmacotherapy. The symptoms may serve to protect the individual client as well as the family system, and the system may need to be changed before the client can accept alternative responses. If the environment cannot be changed, the clinician should attempt to alter the client's response to the environment. **Reframing** is a process of facilitating change by developing alternative options and interpretations.

Critical Thinking Question What are some possible staff reactions to a client's behavior when staff feel they have been manipulated or purposively deceived? Discuss some ways staff can minimize these reactions when they are aware of the underlying feelings.

Summary

The five main somatoform disorders are somatization disorder, hypochondriasis, conversion disorder, body dysmorphic disorder, and pain disorders. Somatoform disorders are often frustrating both for the client who feels that her or his complaints are not receiving the proper attention and for the caretakers who feel that the client does not recognize that medical or surgical care is not needed. While unexplained physical symptoms are a common phenomenon, the client with a somatoform disorder experiences multiple symptoms affecting multiple systems and often has a history of trauma or stress, psychological symptoms, and association of illness behaviors with primary and secondary gain.

It is important that the client feels supported. The healthcare provider should suggest ways to make the client more comfortable, involve him or her in treatment, and strengthen and maintain adequate coping mechanisms. Reassuring the client, recognizing changes and strengths, and reinforcing health choices allow the professional to engage the client in managing the symptoms rather than having the symptoms control the client's life. Analgesics and various therapeutic adjuncts are used in combination to treat pain disorders. Individualized treatment strategies based upon careful client assessments are most effective.

Factitious disorders are chronic mental disorders in which the symptoms of a psychologic or physical disorder are intentionally presented to obtain medical treatment. The goal behind symptom presentation is not readily recognizable. Clients with the disorder of malingering present the symptoms of a psychologic or physical disorder for a readily recognizable goal such as avoiding school or work responsibilities. Because of the primary gain involved in a factitious disorder and the secondary gain involved in malingering, it is difficult to treat these clients. Treatment of underlying or associated personality disorders is helpful. As with somatoform disorders, treatment planning aims at preventing medical or therapeutic interventions that may be more harmful and burdensome than the physical or psychologic symptoms themselves.

Annotated References

Alpay, M. (2004). Pain. In T. A., Stern, G. Fricchione, N. H. Cassem, M. S. Jellinek, & J. F. Rosenbaum (Eds.), *Massachusetts General Hospital handbook of general hospital psychiatry* (5th ed., pp. 313–348). St. Louis, MO: Mosby-Yearbook.

Topics of pain, chronic pain, and clinical implications of treatment are discussed. Useful questions to ask the client when assessing pain are suggested.

American Medical Association. (2006). *International classification of diseases* (9th rev. ed., Vols. 1, 2). Dover, DE: Author.

This is the codebook for specifying diagnoses.

American Psychiatric Association. (2000). *Diagnostic and statistical manual of mental disorders* (4th ed., text rev.). Washington, DC: Author.

This is the fourth edition, text revision, of the American Psychiatric Association's official nomenclature of psychiatric conditions and disorders. It provides a systematic listing of the official codes and categories, a description of the multiaxial system for diagnosis, and diagnostic criteria for each of the disorders. It is used by psychiatrists, physicians, psychologists, registered nurses, social workers, therapists, and other mental health workers in all clinical settings.

Barsky, A. J., Stern, T. A., Greenberg, D. B., & Cassem, N. H. (2004). Functional somatic symptoms and somatoform disorders. In T. A. Stern, G. Fricchione, N. H. Cassem, M. S. Jellinek, & J. F. Rosenbaum (Eds.), *Massachusetts General Hospital handbook of general hospital psychiatry* (5th ed., pp. 269–291). St. Louis, MO: Mosby-Yearbook.

Typical clinical cases of somatoform disorders in hospital and general care settings are described here, including hints on diagnosis and treatment. This handbook provides practical approaches to the more common problems healthcare providers are likely to encounter.

Bouckoms, A., & Hackett, T. P. (1997). The pain patient: Evaluation and treatment. In N. H. Cassem, T. Stern, J. Rosenbaum, & M. Jellinek (Eds.), *MGH handbook of general hospital psychiatry* (4th ed., pp. 367–415). St. Louis, MO: Mosby-Yearbook.

Engel, G. L. (1959). "Psychogenic" pain and the pain-prone client. *American Journal of Medicine, 26*(6), 899–918.

This classic article provides a framework for understanding the experience of pain.

Feder, A., Olfson, M., Gameroff, M., Fuenes, M., Shea, S., et al. (2001). Medically unexplained symptoms in an urban general medical practice. *Psychosomatics, 42*(3), 261–268.

Study of patients in an urban general medical practice showed that medically unexplained symptoms were common.

Fink, P., Hansen, M. S., & Oxhoj, M-L. (2004). The prevalence of somatoform disorders among internal medical inpatients. *Journal of Psychosomatic Research, 56*(4), 412–418.

Study of hospitalized medical patients showed that 38.7% also had a psychiatric diagnosis and 17.6% had a somatoform disorder.

Gureje, O. (2004). What can we learn from a cross-national study of somatic distress? *Journal of Psychosomatic Research, 56*(4), 409–412.

Report of WHO study in 14 countries of variations in somatoform disorder using similar diagnostic standards that showed the client-doctor relationship was an important factor in client reports of multiple somatic symptoms.

Lewandowski, W. (2004). Psychological factors in chronic pain: A worthwhile undertaking for nursing? *Archives of Psychiatric Nursing, 18*(3), 97–105.

This article discusses implications of research evaluating the role of depression, personality factors, pain-related beliefs, trauma, and coping style in the experience of chronic pain.

Mezzich, J. E., Kleinman, A., Fabrega, H., & Parron, D. L. (Eds.). (1996). *Culture and psychiatric diagnosis: A DSM-IV perspective.* Washington, DC: American Psychiatric Press.

This collection of articles from the Conference on Culture and Psychiatric Diagnosis includes discussions of culture and somatoform disorders, with phenomenologic descriptions of various culture-bound syndromes and the problems of describing culturally diverse experiences in diagnostic terms.

Michael, S. R., Candela, L., & Mitchell, S. (2002). Aesthetic knowing: Understanding the experience of chronic illness. *Nurse Educator, 27*(1), 25–27.

This article discusses being involved with a client's artistic expression as part of a nursing assessment by nursing students.

Mittenberg, W., Patton, C., Canyock, E. M., & Condit, D. C. (2002). Base rates of malingering and symptom exaggeration. *Journal of Clinical and Experimental Neuropsychology, 24*(8), 1094–1102.

This is an examination of 33,531 cases to determine illness behaviors and unexplained symptoms indicating evidence of malingering and symptom exaggeration. Symptom fabrication is likely to be more evident in medicolegal and forensic than clinical contexts.

Nakagawa-Kogan, H. (1996). Using the brain to manage the body. In B. McBride & J. K. Austin (Eds.), *Psychiatric-mental health nursing: Integrating the behavioral and biological sciences* (pp. 30–52). Philadelphia: W. B. Saunders.

This text discusses psychophysiologic processes such as the stimulation of catecholamines and the autonomic nervous system, which influence system regulation and homeostasis. The text describes the use of self-management training in psychosocial nursing. Using hyperventilation as a clinical example, the psychopathophysiology of the symptom, intervention strategies, and outcome measures demonstrate a practical application of self-management training.

Spivak, H., Rodin, G., & Sutherland, A. (1994). The psychology of factitious disorders: A reconsideration. *Psychosomatics: The Journal of Consultation and Liaison Psychiatry, 35*(1), 25–34.

This article discusses the basis for the underlying motivations and psychodynamics of clients diagnosed with a factitious disorder. Defining consciousness as existing along a continuum, the text postulates that the client with factitious disorder experiences problems with reality testing and with processing sensory stimuli.

Trimble, M. (2004). *Somatization disorders: A medico-legal guide.* Cambridge, UK: Cambridge University Press.

This book discusses the factors common to the etiology and description of somatization disorders.

Turk, D. C. (1990). Customizing treatment for chronic pain clients: Who, what, and why. *Clinical Journal of Pain, 6*(4), 255–270.

This article provides a useful discussion of the many factors that complicate the treatment of pain, particularly when treatment is matched to the disease state rather than individualized to various physical, psychosocial, and behavioral measures.

U.S. Department of Health and Human Services, SAMHSA Mental Health Information Center. (2000). *Mental health: A report of the Surgeon General.* Washington, DC: Substance Abuse & Mental Health Services Administration.

This was the first Surgeon General's report on mental health issues.

Ustun, T. B., & Sartorius, N. (1995). *Mental illness in general healthcare.* London: John Wiley.

In collaboration with the World Health Organization, this book attempts to study the public health and economic impact of the major mental illnesses and project their impact across the globe. Useful for studies of statistical prevalence and impact of disability.

Veterans Administration Guidelines Committee. (2001). *VHA/DoD clinical practice guideline for the management of medically unexplained symptoms: Chronic pain and fatigue.* Washington, DC: Veterans Health Administration, Department of Defense, Office of Quality Improvement.

These are consensus guidelines from an interdisciplinary team providing a treatment algorithm for medically unexplained symptoms.

Whelan, C. T., Jin, L., & Meltzer, D. (2004). Pain and satisfaction with pain control in hospitalized medical clients. *Archives of Internal Medicine, 164,* 173–180.

This survey of general medical clients regarding their perception of pain and their satisfaction with pain control during their hospitalization supported JCAHO recommendations for a systematic approach to pain management that is individualized to the needs of each client.

Yeung, A., & Deguang, H. (2002). Case based reviews: Somatoform disorders. *Western Journal of Medicine, 176*(4), 253–256.

This article provides case examples and treatment suggestions for Asian clients experiencing somatization. It discusses traditional Chinese medicine and the concept of energy flow.

Additional Resources

Abbey, S. E. (1996). Somatization and somatoform disorders. In J. R. Rundell & M. G. Wise (Eds.), *Textbook of consultation-liaison psychiatry* (pp. 368–401). Washington, DC: American Psychiatric Press.

This chapter describes somatoform disorders using an illness behavior model that aids in dealing with the client's symptoms and responses to treatment.

Acute Pain Management Guideline Panel. (1992). *Acute pain management: Operative or medical procedures and trauma. Clinical practice guideline* (AHCR Publication No. 92-0032, pp. 1–145). Rockville, MD: Agency for Health Care Policy and Research, Public Health Service, U.S. Department of Health and Human Services.

These guidelines cover acute pain as well as conceptualizing and treating chronic pain. Clinical guidelines are available for other types of pain such as cancer pain and headaches. This series of clinical guidelines includes many other topics such as depression, incontinence, and cataracts that are essential to healthcare providers in a variety of settings. In addition, consumer guides such as the one on headaches help to educate clients.

Feldman, M. D. (2004). *Playing sick? Untangling the web of Münchausen syndrome, Münchausen by proxy, malingering, and factitious disorder.* New York: Routledge.

This text discusses factitious disorders and includes case studies, treatment options, and information on cyber-deception, use of the Internet to gather information or sympathy.

Feldman, M. D., & Ford, C. V. (1994). *Client or pretender: The strange world of factitious disorders.* New York: John Wiley.

This text emphasizes the relationship between clients and providers and teaches clinicians how to approach these disorders. A helpful guide to understanding a difficult disorder, this text explains the conflicts and ambivalence surrounding healthcare providers' relationships with these clients.

Ford, C. V. (1984). *The somatizing disorders: Illness as a way of life.* New York: Elsevier Biomedical.

This text discusses somatizing as part of the body's physiologic and psychologic defenses to variations in stress and social support. It includes case studies of common somatizing responses such as "medical student illness" in which a little knowledge, stress, and vulnerability lead to the misperception of a disease state, and "painmanship," in which psychologic responses to pain are discussed. This classic book is out of print.

Kazanowski, M., & Laccetti, M. S. (2002). *Nursing concepts: Pain.* Sudbury, MA: Jones and Bartlett.

Provides guidelines and case studies for assessment and treatment of pain at different developmental stages.

Robinette, A. (1997). Psychosocial problems of the physically ill. In J. Haber, B. Krainovich-Miller, A. H. McMahon, & P. Price-Hoskins (Eds.), *Comprehensive psychiatric nursing* (5th ed., pp. 690–714). St. Louis, MO: C.V. Mosby.

Somatoform disorders including pain and other responses to the threat of illness are covered. The entire text helps to conceptualize behavioral health problems in terms of nursing theories, interventions, and case management.

Shorter, E. (1992). *From paralysis to fatigue: A history of psychosomatic illness in the modern era.* New York: Free Press.

This text provides an interesting historical and cultural overview of psychosomatic illness. In considering how healthcare providers and clients view these symptoms, the reader is able to shift perspectives to consider the probable etiologies and conceptual frameworks of somatizations and how this process is legitimized in different cultures and time periods. Every disease has its day, but fashionable fads are fickle. For example, hysteria is no longer "politically correct." Our conceptualizations of signs, symptoms, and illness behaviors are not as objective as we believe.

Warfield, C. A., & Bajwa, Z. H. (2004). *Principles and practice in pain management.* New York: McGraw-Hill Professional.

This book is an excellent reference guide for the assessment and treatment of pain. Pharmacotherapy and other treatment methods are discussed as well as psychologic interventions and complementary treatment approaches.

Internet Resources

http://nursing.jbpub.com/psychiatric

Visit http://nursing.jbpub.com/psychiatric for interactive exercises, NCLEX review questions, WebLinks, and more.

CHAPTER 19

Sexual Disorders and Gender Identity Disorder

Blaine R. Beemer

■ LEARNING OBJECTIVES

After reading this chapter, you will be able to:

- Describe essential features of sexual dysfunctions and paraphilias.
- Describe essential features of gender identity disorder.
- Identify the nurse's role in assessing for sexual disorders.
- Identify opportunities for client education regarding sexuality.

■ KEY TERMS

Anorgasmia
Dyspareunia
Erectile dysfunction
Gender dysphoria
Gender identity
Intersex conditions
Orgasm
Paraphilias
Premature ejaculation
Sexual orientation
Sexual response cycle
Transgendered
Transsexual
Vaginismus

http://nursing.jbpub.com/psychiatric

Visit http://nursing.jbpub.com/psychiatric for interactive exercises, NCLEX review questions, WebLinks, and more.

Introduction

This chapter will present strategies for the nurse to follow when assessing clients' sexual health concerns. It will also identify the main features of sexual disorders and gender identity disorders as defined by the American Psychiatric Association (2000). Common treatment approaches for each disorder will be discussed briefly.

Sexual Health

Notions of sexuality—normal and abnormal, functional and dysfunctional—are inevitably changeable and culturally based. Changes in society's view of sexuality have influenced how these issues are addressed in the field of mental health. For instance, a common view among psychiatrists as late as the 1970s was that engaging in sexual activity actually caused or contributed to major psychiatric disorders. Now, sexual expression is broadly considered an aspect of healthy living. Another example of changing views in mental health can be found in the clinical approach to homosexuality. Homosexuality was classified as a mental disorder in the *Diagnostic and Statistical Manual of Mental Disorders* (*DSM*) until 1973 and in the *International Classification of Diseases* until 1992. Its inclusion in previous editions of diagnostic manuals was likely due to a combination of factors, including prevailing popular attitudes toward homosexuality and a dominant psychoanalytic stance that treated same-sex attraction as a failure in psychosexual development.

Early definitions of sexual health tended to concentrate on sexual functioning and the fulfillment of the sexual response cycle of excitement, plateau, orgasm, and resolution identified by Masters and Johnson (1966). Today, the World Health Organization (WHO) uses a broader definition that recognizes the varieties of healthy sexual expression, the role of emotional intimacy, the impediments caused by sexual coercion and violence, and the need for accurate information on sexuality:

> Sexual health is a state of physical, emotional, mental and social well being in relation to sexuality; it is not merely the absence of disease, dysfunction or infirmity. Sexual health requires a positive and respectful approach to sexuality and sexual relationships, as well as the possibility of having pleasurable and safe sexual experiences, free of coercion, discrimination and violence. For sexual health to be attained and maintained, the sexual rights of all persons must be respected, protected and fulfilled. (2002)

Biology of Sexual Function

The brain mechanisms of human sexual response are exceedingly complex. The pattern of brain activity associated with sexual activity appears to be extremely diverse and variable, with dominant activity at different times associated with the thalamus, the amygdala, the hippocampus, and frontal cortical structures.

Testosterone clearly acts as the central neurotransmitter for sexual libido. Testosterone reliably produces stereotypic male sexual behavior in laboratory animals, and its absence or blockade extinguishes those effects. Precipitous drops in testosterone in both males and females due to surgical intervention often cause noticeable reductions in libido and sexual functioning; however, gradual, natural reductions due to changes in the life cycle, even when testosterone levels are vastly reduced, do not inevitably lead to elimination of libido or sexual satisfaction. In fact, naturally aging men, with significantly lowered testosterone in their later years, and women, whose testosterone levels in their later years can be almost unmeasurable, generally still report high levels of sexual activity and high satisfaction with their sexual lives, even if activity levels decrease.

Types of Sexual and Gender Identity Disorders

The *DSM-IV-TR* (American Psychiatric Association [APA], 2000) recognizes four categories of sexual and gender identity disorders (**Table 19-1**):

1. *Sexual dysfunctions:* Problems with sexual response such as sexual desire, erection, ejaculation, or orgasm; also, sexual pain.
2. *Paraphilias:* Intense urges or sexual activities "that involve unusual objects, activities, or situations and cause clinically significant distress or impairment" (APA, 2000, p. 535). These include problems such as fetishes, exhibitionism, pedophilia, and sexual masochism.
3. *Gender identity disorders:* Intense cross-gender identification and "persistent discomfort with one's assigned sex" (APA, 2000, p. 535).
4. *Sexual and gender disorders not otherwise specified:* These include **intersex conditions** (congenital problems with sex-organ anatomy and sex hormones with accompanying gender identity issues) and "transient, stress related cross-dressing behavior" (APA, 2000, p. 582).

The *DSM-IV-TR* also notes that "notions of deviance, standards of sexual performance, and concepts of appropriate gender role can vary from culture to culture" (APA, 2000, p. 535).

Table 19-1 Sexual and Gender Identity Disorders

- Sexual dysfunctions
  - Sexual desire disorders
  - Sexual arousal disorders
  - Orgasmic disorders
  - Sexual pain disorders
- Paraphilias
- Gender identity disorders
- Sexual and gender disorders not otherwise specified

Axis I and III Subtypes in Diagnosis of Sexual Disorders

A variety of subtypes, reflecting differences in onset and causality, are coded on Axis I:

- *Lifelong versus acquired type:* If the condition has occurred since the beginning of sexual activity and has persisted, the condition is classified as lifelong.
- *Generalized versus situational type:* If the disorder or dysfunction occurs only in some instances (e.g., with one partner but not another), the condition is classified as situational.
- *Due to psychological factors versus due to combined factors:* If a general medical condition or substance abuse is thought to contribute to the disorder or dysfunction but is not deemed to be the main cause, a subtype of "due to combined factors" is used.

If a general medical condition is thought to primarily account for the sexual disorder, the subtype "due to a general medical condition" is used. For example, this subtype would be used for erectile dysfunction caused by diabetes. The disorder is still coded on Axis I, but the existence of the general medical condition is stated on Axis III. Substance-induced sexual dysfunction is diagnosed if the direct effects or withdrawal from an illegal drug, medication, or toxin is thought to be the primary causal agent in the condition; it is coded on Axis I.

The Nurse's Role

Nursing Assessment

The topic of sexuality often induces more anxiety for the nurse conducting the interview than for the client. This needs to be overcome in the service of holistic care. Failure to ask relevant questions about sexuality could arise for many reasons. One cause can be that these topics are seen as too private between strangers, even for therapeutic purposes. Some nurses would never even consider asking sexual questions of their clients for this reason. Another source of anxiety is that sexual questions directed at the client may bring up difficult issues for the nurse. Issues, such as sexual dysfunction, **sexual orientation**, or marital conflict, may resonate strongly with the caregiver and create a hidden "no-go zone" that reflects the clinician's sensitivities more than the client's. In other instances, nurses may sense that sexual questions are important, but feel they lack the knowledge to question intelligently or to follow up once a response is elicited.

One study among physicians uncovered impediments to the use of sexuality-related questions (Maurice, 2000):

- Unclear what to do with the answers (uncertainty about the next question; lack of familiarity with treatment approaches)
- Fear of offending clients
- Lack of obvious justification
- Generational obstacles
- Fear of sexual misconduct charge
- Sometimes perceived as irrelevant
- Lack of familiarity with some sexual practices (p. 21)

Critical Thinking Questions Do you think that any of the listed factors might inhibit you from asking a client sexually related questions? If so, what can you do to counter this?

Nurses cannot confidently assume that clinicians from other disciplines will assess for sexual concerns. It is up to nurses to raise the issue with their clients because clients are unlikely to raise the subject on their own. Most importantly, clients expect and want healthcare providers to ask about sexual concerns. The best time to begin this discussion is in the initial assessment phase; leaving sexual questions until the end may convey the impression that it is a taboo subject. It is important that sexual health be viewed as an important but unexceptional element of a holistic health assessment.

> Most patients with sexual concerns hope that healthcare professionals initiate the discussion.

> Nurses cannot rely on the patient to initiate a discussion about sexual concerns or on other healthcare professionals to assess for the presence of sexual concerns.

Nursing Interventions

Once identified, dealing with clients' sexual concerns can appear to be a daunting task. It is impractical for nurses in most general mental health settings to provide sophisticated sexual health interventions. Nurses can, however, provide holistic care by assessing and intervening to the level of their understanding. Nurses can initiate a discussion of sexual concerns at a depth consistent with their knowledge base. Nurses do not have to be able to solve sexual problems in order to identify clients' sexual concerns.

> Nurses can initiate a discussion of sexual concerns at a depth consistent with their knowledge base. Nurses do not have to be able to solve sexual problems in order to identify patients' sexual concerns.

A number of sexuality clinical care models have developed in nursing. Irwin (2002) identifies a range of potential nursing interventions, from

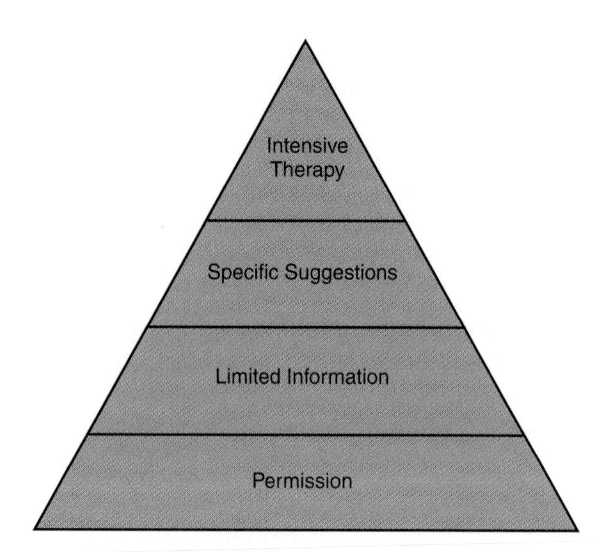

Figure 19-1 The PLISSIT model.

general information, to helping clients anticipate potential sexual consequences of a medical or surgical procedure, to detailed problem-solving around sexual difficulties. The last category is clearly the realm of highly trained nurses with specialized skills.

The PLISSIT model (Annon, 1976) (**Figure 19-1**) remains the most prominent sexual intervention model, largely due to its multidisciplinary appeal, its broad applicability to different healthcare settings, and its simplicity. It asks the clinician to identify at which of the four levels it is most appropriate for the nurse to intervene:

P = *Permission.* At this most basic level, PLISSIT involves the nurse giving permission for the client to acknowledge their existence as a sexual being, and to have a right to concern about the sexual consequences of life events, including psychiatric conditions and treatment. This level of intervention is appropriate for practically any nurse in any setting.

LI = *Limited Information.* At the level of LI, the nurse in mental health knows that there are common consequences to a person's sexuality that are associated with psychiatric conditions and their treatment. This knowledge is broadly available in psychiatric textbooks, articles, and reputable websites. Communicating this information to the client can alleviate much anxiety and may promote compliance with treatment. It is reasonable to expect nurses in mental health to be able to provide LI to all their clients, appropriate to each person's mental status.

The remaining two steps require advanced knowledge and clinical expertise that is not in the domain of the general nurse, but may be acquired by advanced practice nurses.

SS = *Specific Suggestions.* At this level, the nurse has thoroughly assessed the sexual health of the individual or couple, is aware of a range of evidence-based interventions, and can confidently offer options for the individual or couple that may improve their sexual satisfaction without compromising their overall treatment. In addition to requiring knowledge, successful SS require sensitivity to the therapeutic moment of readiness when the clients can take in these suggestions.

IT = *Intensive Therapy.* At this level, the clinician has made a thorough assessment of the individual's/couple's sexual health, can offer proven interventions personalized to the condition and the clients, and can problem-solve the outcomes of those interventions, generally through multiple visits. The nurse clinician providing IT may be collaborating with other healthcare providers in medicine, social work, occupational therapy, and rehabilitation science, among others, to optimize outcomes.

Critical Thinking Questions What are some ways that the nurse gives the client permission to speak about sexual concerns? How would you determine that a source of sexual information is reliable and valid?

A large part of the nurse's role is education for clients, sexual partners, and family, as indicated. Considerations for client and family education are addressed later in this chapter.

Essential Features of the Sexual and Gender Identity Disorders

The sexual and gender identity disorders include sexual dysfunctions, which relate to a disturbance in the sexual response pattern; paraphilias, which are intense, disturbing sexual fantasies, urges, or behaviors; and gender identity disorders or transsexualism.

Sexual Dysfunctions

The sexual dysfunctions (**Table 19-2**) correspond with the four phases of the **sexual response cycle**: desire, excitement, orgasm, and resolution.

Table 19-2 Sexual Dysfunctions

Sexual Desire Disorders	Sexual Arousal Disorders	Orgasmic Disorders	Sexual Pain Disorders
Hypoactive sexual desire disorder Sexual aversion disorder	Female sexual arousal disorder Male erectile disorder	Female orgasmic disorder Male orgasmic disorder Premature ejaculation	Dyspareunia Vaginismus

Sexual Desire Disorders

The *DSM-IV* identifies two sexual desire disorders: one related to a lack of desire, the other to an aversion to sexual activity.

- *Hypoactive sexual desire disorder (HSDD):* This is defined as a persistent or recurrent deficiency or absence of sexual fantasies and desire for sexual activity (APA, 2000). Sexual desire (and frequency of activity) varies naturally over the course of a romantic relationship, and there is no objective level at which a lack of sexual desire is normal, problematic, or pathologic. However, a lack of desire can have dramatic effects on the individual and the couple. Although couples may stabilize at a level of sexual activity in the long term, a noticeable reduction in desire by either partner may create friction and hard feelings in the relationship. Individuals who experience a drop in desire often mourn the loss. The partner often infers that they have somehow become less desirable or attractive, which has further consequences for the relationship as well as their individual self-esteem.
- *Sexual aversion disorder:* Whereas HSDD describes a lack of sexual desire, sexual aversion disorder is notable by "the aversion to and active avoidance of genital sexual contact with a partner" (APA, 2000, p. 541). This aversion may be specific to certain situations or sexual acts or may be global. The aversion must cause distress or difficulties in functioning. Diagnostically, it may be difficult to distinguish between lack of sexual desire, disinterest, discomfort with the experience of arousal, and outright aversion. However, persons with sexual aversion may experience disgust at the thought of sex, and panic when sexual activity is initiated.

Incidence and Prevalence of Desire Disorders. A loss of sexual desire is likely the most common sexual complaint of women; increasingly, however, men present to healthcare professionals with this complaint as well. Prevalence rates of female HSDD in different studies range from 10–40% (Dennerstein & Hayes, 2005). Studies of male desire problems are less common, but a prevalence of 6% has been cited (Simons & Carey, 2001). Sexual aversion disorder occurs in both men and women, but exact incidence is unknown (Shafer, 2004).

Etiology of Desire Disorders. Sexual desire problems are perhaps the most complex of sexual dysfunctions in terms of etiology. Desire is a subtle flux of love, biological drive, motivation, feelings of trust and intimacy, and self-image, especially in long-term relationships. Due to complexities in sexual response, attempts to engage in sexual activity when it is not desired through disinterest, negative emotions, or pain can turn lack of desire into outright aversion.

Some common psychosocial causes of reduced sexual desire are:

- Distractions and fatigue, especially around childrearing
- Depression and anxiety disorders
- Relational conflict and anger at partner
- Fear of sexually transmitted infections or pregnancy
- Body image issues related to age, health status, surgery, or weight
- Lack of an available partner
- Previous unsatisfying, traumatic, or physically painful sexual experiences

Biological changes such as hormonal deficiencies sometimes play a primary role in desire disorders. The sudden drop in hormones produced by genital surgery or radiation can have a profound effect. Loss of libido can be the result of a medical condition, such as hypothyroidism, diabetes mellitus, some neurological disorders, or local genital disease (Shafer, 2004). Substance abuse, depression, and prescribed medications can also contribute to a loss of sexual desire. A not-uncommon cause of sudden loss of libido in younger women is due to side effects from oral contraceptives. Some loss of libido is common in aging, but many individuals maintain libido into their eighth and ninth decades.

Treatment of Sexual Desire Disorders. Once physical and psychiatric causes have been ruled out (especially depression), individual or couples counseling with an experienced therapist can produce benefits. Few, if any, medications or compounds have been found to reliably enhance sexual desire in healthy humans. Some street drugs or medications such as alcohol and benzodiazepines may be disinhibiting, which users may perceive as prosexual. (Of course, disinhibition can interfere with sexual decision making.)

Testosterone treatment is an option for the treatment of HSDD, but its use is controversial. Although some studies suggest that testosterone replacement has some short-term effects on libido in cases where loss of testosterone has been sudden, few long-term studies exist.

Sexual Arousal Disorders

There are also two sexual arousal disorders:

- *Female sexual arousal disorder (FSAD):* Women with FSAD may attempt to engage in sexual activity but do not become physically aroused. As a consequence, sexual activity becomes unpleasant or impossible. Without physiological arousal, women may experience a lack of vaginal lubrication, leading to painful intercourse. As a consequence, they may experience frustration and anxiety, and may avoid sexual activity altogether.
- *Male erectile disorder (ED):* This disorder, referred to as **erectile dysfunction**, is experienced as a persistent or recurrent inability to attain or maintain an adequate erection until completion of the sexual activity and which causes marked distress or interpersonal difficulty (APA, 2000). Lack of erection, especially with a new partner, can be emotionally demoralizing for a man. He may doubt his ability to satisfy his partner, may doubt his own masculinity, and may fear loss of his relationship. Men may avoid intimacy altogether because of the problem. Fertility issues may arise if the problem is persistent.

Incidence and Prevalence of Sexual Arousal Disorders. Female sexual arousal disorder has a lifetime prevalence of 60% and is linked to problems with sexual desire (Shafer, 2004). Periodic erectile difficulties occur in every age group. Persistent erectile dysfunction, including the complete absence of erection, is far more common in older age groups. In a large study of men 40–70 years of age, over half experienced some form of erectile dysfunction (Feldman, Goldstein, & Hatzichristou, 1994).

Etiology of Female Sexual Arousal Disorder. Physical causes of FSAD are common when a fairly sudden loss of physical arousal is noted. Illness, surgery, radiation therapy, or medications can play a part. Fatigue, or anxiety with a new partner, can inhibit arousal, and then anticipatory anxiety can produce a chronic condition. Often, FSAD is associated with other sexual problems, such as low desire, sexual aversion, or orgasmic difficulties; FSAD may be a cause or a consequence of these other conditions.

Etiology of Male Erectile Disorder. Between 50% and 85% of all cases of ED have an organic basis (Shafer, 2004). Diabetes and cardiovascular disease are common causes of ED due to both autonomic diabetic neuropathy and penile endothelial changes. Men who smoke have a higher rate of ED, especially in younger age groups, and the effect appears to be dose-dependent. Additionally, there is a complex relationship among obesity, metabolic syndrome, hypogonadism, and reduced circulating testosterone, which has many negative general health consequences. Some categories of medications, including cardiovascular, anticonvulsant, and psychotropic agents, may also be factors.

There are also nonmedical reasons for not getting an erection, including fatigue, not being in the mood for sexual activity, alcohol or drug use, partner issues, and insufficient sexual stimulation.

Treatment of Female Sexual Arousal Disorder (FSAD). Treatment is directed at reducing anxiety and introducing behavioral exercises that focus on providing and deriving sexual pleasure, initially without the goal of intercourse or orgasm. This technique, known as "sensate focus," is intended to reduce the anxiety associated with fear of failing to achieve an orgasm. As the couple becomes better able to experience sexual pleasure through mutual touching, they progress to genital touching and eventual orgasm. Although the phosphodiesterase type 5 (PDE-5) inhibitors, such as sildenafil citrate (Viagra), may have a positive effect on a small subset of women who eperience psychological arousal but no physiological arousal, these medications have little effect on most women with FSAD.

Treatment of Erectile Dysfunction. Prior to the PDE-5 inhibitors, erection enhancement involved inhibiting venous outflow using vacuum pumps and restrictor rings; intracavernosal injection (ICI) with combinations of vasoactive agents such as phentolamine, yohimbine, papavarine, and prostaglandin E_1; and surgical options such as implantation of penile prostheses or surgery on penile outflow veins. Most of these treatments leave much to be desired, because they are often complicated, uncomfortable, and expensive. In most clinical contexts, oral agents are now the first-line treatment irrespective of the presumed organic cause of erectile difficulty, with ICI being the second-line treatment.

If the client is in a relationship, treatment of ED may involve couples therapy. Couples may benefit from coaching to optimize the use of medications and to explore sexual activities that do not involve intercourse, especially because these practices generally lead to greater sexual satisfaction for the partner.

Critical Thinking Question Imagine how a couple's sexual relationship might be affected by the need to introduce external devices, such as vacuum pumps or penile implants. What concerns might both partners have?

Orgasmic Disorders

Orgasm can be described as a sudden, subjective experience of intense pleasure usually accompanied by rhythmic contractions in the pelvic area. Orgasmic capacity varies significantly between males and females, within different individuals of the same sex, from situation to situation, and across the phase of the life cycle. Generally, males first experience orgasm at a younger age, usually through masturbation. Women who find it difficult to orgasm in their teens or 20s may find that their orgasmic capacity increases later in life, whereas men often find that orgasm becomes delayed as they age.

- *Female orgasmic disorder:* Women with orgasmic disorder (also known informally as **anorgasmia**) experience "a persistent or recurrent delay in, or absence of, orgasm following a normal sexual excitement phase" (APA, 2000, p. 547) that causes distress or interpersonal conflict. As with many other sexual dysfunctions, it can be a lifelong problem or occur at any time (acquired type); it can occur in all situations (generalized type) or only in some contexts (situational type). The dysfunction can occur in the absence of any known physical cause.

  Orgasm is a learned reflex, which is why anorgasmia (lack of orgasm) is more common in young women. Once learned, it is unusual for women to lose orgasmic capacity completely, although episodic orgasmic difficulties are not uncommon.

  Most women do not experience orgasm with intercourse alone: they require manual stimulation during intercourse. If a woman can achieve orgasm on her own but not with a partner, she in most cases does not meet the criteria for an orgasmic disorder.
- *Male orgasmic disorder.* The most frequent orgasmic disorder is the situational type wherein the man can have orgasm with masturbation and with manual or oral stimulation by a partner, but not with intercourse. Males commonly experience a longer and longer ejaculatory latency as they age, and, with increased age, they often notice that they need more intense direct stimulation to have an orgasm. Some men lose orgasmic capability at some time in their lives, or have a lifelong problem with orgasm, although either of these conditions is rarer than female orgasmic disorder.
- *Premature ejaculation:* **Premature ejaculation** (PE) is a condition wherein the male ejaculates very quickly. Although a number of formal definitions have arisen for research purposes, the key factor in PE is ejaculation prior to the wishes of the man or his partner. Premature ejaculation can be extremely severe. Some sufferers have a

Sexual problems in relationships in time often affect both partners. Seeing the patient as part of a relational system is an effective approach.

Clinical Example

Paul, a 23-year-old male, begins a new relationship after a 2-year romance with a prior partner. However, when he and his new partner attempt to become intimate, he ejaculates as soon as petting begins. The PE was a problem in the early stages of his previous relationship, but went away after a few months. Now, his embarrassment prevents him from discussing this with his new partner, so his anxiety now begins to increase as soon as the kissing starts. As a consequence, he feels forced to ignore the invitations of sexual interest from his partner. Soon, the partner starts to feel rejected and the relationship is endangered—though not directly because of the PE.

lifelong problem: they ejaculate before they remove their clothes prior to sexual activity, or with the slightest sexual touch, or while attempting to put on a condom. This can cause embarrassment, shame, enormous self-esteem issues, and relationship strain.

Incidence and Prevalence of Orgasmic Disorders. Studies vary significantly regarding the extent of female orgasmic disorder. One study found that 24% of women had experienced inability to orgasm for at least several months in the past year (Laumann, Gagnon, Michael, & Michaels, 1994). Lifetime prevalence has been estimated at 35% (Shafer, 2004).

Male orgasmic disorder is infrequent, with a lifetime prevalence of 2%, and occurs in men who are usually under the age of 35 years and who are sexually inexperienced (Shafer, 2004).

Studies place the range of prevalence of premature ejaculation at 25% to 40% of the male population (Carson & Gunn, 2006).

Etiology of Female Orgasmic Disorder. It is unclear why some women experience periodic or lifelong anorgasmia. Sociological factors such as age, education, or socioeconomic status have not been found to be consistent predictors of orgasmic disorder. Anxiety appears to play only a minor role in anorgasmia in many instances. Personality correlates of anorgasmia have yielded inconsistent results.

Female orgasmic disorder is often found with other female sexual disorders of desire or arousal; it may be difficult to determine which of these disorders might be causal or consequential to the others.

Etiology of Male Orgasmic Disorder. A variety of causes are implicated, including drugs, neurological degeneration due to disease, and surgery. Male orgasmic disorders are often associated with other sexual disorders such as ED and low libido.

Etiology of Premature Ejaculation. Premature ejaculation has a number of causes. Most young men ejaculate more quickly than they expect or want with a partner, even if they have some ejaculatory control on their own. Most notice an increase in ejaculation latency by their late 20s.

Most men will ejaculate more rapidly in adolescence and early adulthood, and early in a new relationship.

For episodic PE, situational and emotional factors explain the experience. Many men experience quicker ejaculation when with a new partner due to the excitement of the situation. Some sexual positions may increase friction and the tendency to ejaculate; some situations, such as fear of discovery, may do the same. On the other hand, lifelong PE may represent a neurobiological condition with a genetic basis.

Treatment of Female Orgasmic Disorder. No pharmacological agents have proven consistently effective in treating female orgasmic disorder. Psychoeducation and communication skills, together with physical exercises, appear to produce improvement. Various forms of directed masturbation as part of an overall cognitive behavioral therapy program have produced beneficial results.

Treatment approaches hinge on the natural history and specific circumstances of the orgasmic problem. If orgasm is possible except with a partner, clients may benefit from counseling that focuses on issues of trust and intimacy, and improving the sexual atmosphere of the relationship, plus coaching of both partners to ensure that sufficient sexual stimulation is present.

Treatment of Male Orgasmic Disorder. Treatment with medications such as amantadine or bupropion has been attempted; further research is needed. Relationship issues can play a role, although lack of sufficient stimulation is likely the most common factor.

Treatment of Premature Ejaculation. Treatment depends on the perceived causes and background to the problem. Occasional PE, especially with a new partner or in stressful circumstances, is treated with reassurance and education. Moderate PE is usually treated with the "squeeze" or "stop-start" behavioral technique, a form of systematic desensitization that teaches men and couples how to feel the physical changes prior to ejaculation. However, data on the long-term efficacy of these behavioral methods is lacking.

Lifelong PE responds poorly to reassurance or behavioral techniques alone. The use of the selective serotonin reuptake inhibitors (SSRIs) in the past decade or so has somewhat revolutionized treatment, with paroxetine being one of the most common agents used for the associated side effect of delaying ejaculation. These novel antidepressants are often used in conjunction with the PDE-5 inhibitors such as sildenafil in order to maintain erectile ability even after premature ejaculation.

For all of the orgasmic disorders, couples therapy is valuable, with a focus on communication and behavioral approaches.

Sexual Pain Disorders

There are two sexual pain disorders:

- *Dyspareunia:* **Dyspareunia** is recurrent or persistent genital pain associated with sexual intercourse in either men or women. Technically, dyspareunia is distinguished from painful intercourse caused by any other medical condition, lack of lubrication, or substance abuse, and is therefore something of a psychiatric diagnosis by exclusion. Although occasional pain may be due to lack of sufficient arousal, fatigue, or illness, more than very occasional sexual pain can become ingrained in the entire sexual experience and requires medical attention.
- *Vaginismus:* **Vaginismus** is an involuntary contraction of the muscle around the vagina that prevents penile insertion. It is often related to the existence or prior existence of a sexual pain disorder. Often, any stimulation around the introitus causes powerful contractions. Use of a tampon or performance of a specular exam may prove impossible. Vaginismus triggers a cycle of responses that then further exacerbates the disorder (**Figure 19-2**). Painful sexual episodes can lead to guarding and reflexive muscle contraction, making intercourse difficult or impossible, and sometimes interfering with fertility.

Incidence and Prevalence of Sexual Pain Disorders. Rates of dyspareunia vary significantly from study to study, as do diagnostic criteria and study methods. One large population-based study found a lifetime incidence of 16% (Harlow & Stewart, 2003). The incidence is three times greater among women than men. The frequency of vaginismus is thought to account for less than 10% of female sexual disorders (Shafer, 2004).

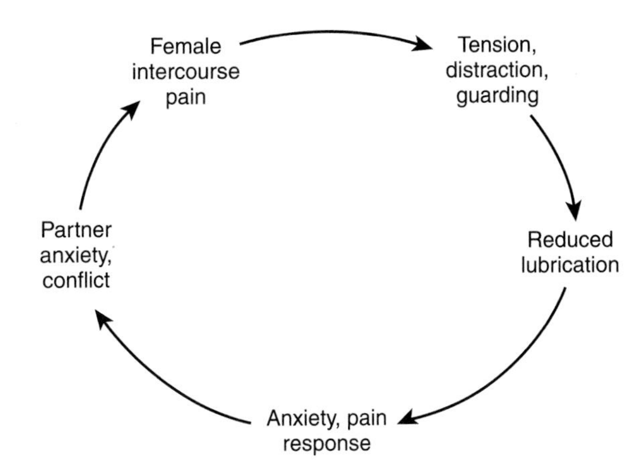

Figure 19-2 Circular pattern: Female sexual pain.

Etiology of Sexual Pain Disorders. Although psychological factors may play a role, especially in the chronicity of some of these disorders, the complex physical causes that initiate and sustain these conditions have become much better identified and understood in the past two decades. A high incidence of pelvic pathology is associated with vaginismus (Shafer, 2004). A broad consensus is emerging that efforts to distinguish between biological and psychological causes are not clinically productive.

Implications for Evidence-Based Practice

Research is needed to better understand the relationship between androgen activity and sexual function. In the future, pharmacological treatment of sexual dysfunctions may be possible using estrogen and androgen receptor modulators to enhance the sexual effects of estrogens and androgens (Basson, 2007). However, clinical experts have recommended against the generalized use of testosterone in women until issues of efficacy and long-term safety are established (Wierman et al., 2006). The necessary research to make these determinations is made difficult by the complex interactions of biology, physiology, and psychology and their effect on the role of androgens in women.

There is also interest in developing reliable assessment tools to better diagnose and evaluate treatment effects for the sexual dysfunctions. The Sexual Interest and Desire Inventory-Female (SIDI-F), a 13-item scale developed to quantify the severity of symptoms in women diagnosed with hypoactive sexual desire disorder, has shown some promise in initial studies to determine the tool's reliability and validity (Clayton et al., 2006).

Treatment of Dyspareunia. Treatment ideally involves addressing any possible physical causes such as inflammatory and infectious processes, pain medications and relaxation techniques, and counseling around the psychological issues that pre-existed the condition. Successful treatment of underlying organic conditions may not relieve the symptoms. A cascade of neurovascular, immune, and muscle tone responses can arise to sustain the initial condition, creating a complex neuropathic pain syndrome requiring multimodal management (Grazziottin & Brotto, 2004).

Treatment of Vaginismus. Treatment involves treating the underlying gynecological problems if identified, chronic pain management, hypnotherapy, and individual and couples therapy if indicated. Systematic desensitization, sometimes using successively larger vaginal dilators, is a common treatment approach.

Paraphilias

Paraphilias are recurrent, intense sexually arousing fantasies, sexual urges, or behaviors generally involving nonhuman objects, the suffering of or humiliation of oneself or one's partner, or children or other nonconsenting persons, that occur over a period of at least 6 months (APA, 2000). For some conditions, such as pedophilia and sexual sadism, acting on the urge is sufficient to merit the diagnosis; in others, "marked distress" is necessary.

A variety of paraphilias occur. In some cases, inanimate objects such as fur, leather, or female clothing become an erotic obsession; intense attraction to women's clothing (transvestitic fetishism) is a common variant. Some individuals are only aroused by experiencing pain (masochism) or providing pain (sadism). Some people find themselves attracted to persons or situations such as prepubescent children (pedophilia) or animals (bestiality). Yet others find themselves preoccupied by specific situations, such as exposing themselves to others (exhibitionism) or secretly viewing others (voyeurism).

Transvestitic fetishism (TF) is the compulsive form of cross-dressing. Identification with the opposite gender, or gender dysphoria, may manifest to varying degrees in persons with TF.

In some cases, the paraphilic object becomes the dominant or sole sexual focus. Individuals may be unable to be aroused in the absence of the paraphilic object or situation. Many individuals maintain their paraphilia as a secret activity or fantasy; in couples, the partner may find him- or herself alienated without explanation, as sexual energy is channeled into the paraphilia and not the relationship. Discovery of the paraphilia often creates intense conflict in the dyad, sometimes leading to separation and/or presentation for therapy. Acting on other paraphilias constitutes sexual offenses, and in some cases the courts mandate treatment as a condition of probation or parole.

One of the most common paraphilias is transvestitic fetishism. Cross-dressing appears to be a not-uncommon behavior in males, and was documented in the early Western sex therapy literature. Cross-dressers describe a whole range of motivations for cross-dressing, ranging from simple fun and burlesque, to "a holiday" from everyday pressures, to expression of a feminine portion of the personality.

Incidence and Prevalence of the Paraphilias

The paraphilias almost always occur in males, and have a strong association with attention deficit hyperactivity disorder in childhood and with depression, substance abuse, and phobic disorders in adults (Shafer, 2004). Varieties of definitions of what constitutes a pathological condition, and the understandable reluctance for individuals to admit to behavior that may be illegal, complicate studies of the epidemiology of the paraphilias.

Etiology of the Paraphilias

The underlying cause of the paraphilias is not well understood. Biological factors, including temporal lobe abnormalities and disturbances in the hormones that affect sexual arousal, abnormal psychosexual development, and learned experiences, have been implicated as possible causes.

Treatment of the Paraphilias

Individual therapies sometimes employ a relapse-prevention approach similar to those used in addictions treatment. In sex offender settings dealing with males, medications used include antiandrogens such as cyproterone (not approved by the Food and Drug Administration) or spironolactone, or gonadotropin hormone-releasing agonists to effect a "chemical castration." The SSRIs including fluvoxamine and paroxetine are often used for their antiobsessional properties and also for their effect of reducing libido.

Gender Identity Disorder

Gender identity is based on which gender role feels right, that of a man or a woman. Gender identity disorder (GID), commonly referred to as **transsexualism**, is a complex condition in which a person feels that their inner nature is more like that of the opposite gender. Some feel this difference between their bodies and what they see as their inner nature and experience great suffering (**gender dysphoria**).

The most intense and pervasive forms of adult gender identity disorder usually manifest in childhood. Children with gender identity disorder often assert that they are actually the opposite gender, or that they are destined to grow up to be the opposite gender. They usually show intense aversion to wearing clothes of their natal gender and may insist on using the opposite pronoun to describe themselves. They show an interest in games of the opposite sex, and prefer playmates of the opposite sex. Most cases of childhood gender identity disturbance remit in adolescence.

Strong cross-gender identification, that is, the desire to be of the other sex, and a persistent discomfort with one's assigned sex may continue into adulthood.

Elements of clinical etiquette towards **transgendered** persons include:

- Use the name and masculine or feminine pronoun preferred by the individual.
- Provide privacy for the client.
- Avoid gossip about the client's transgender condition or sexual orientation.
- Do not expect the client to educate staff on transgender issues.

Critical Thinking Questions Do you know anyone who is transsexual? What are your beliefs about this? Will these beliefs aid or impede your interactions with such clients?

Incidence and Prevalence of Gender Identity Disorder

It is difficult to obtain reliable data on the rate of GID. One study out of The Netherlands, which has an integrated reporting system and a fairly accepting social attitude to gender transition, places the incidence at 1:11,900 for persons with male to female GID (MTFs) and 1:30,400 for persons with female to male GID (FTMs) (van Kesteren, Gooren, & Megens, 1996). The 3:1 preponderance of MTFs over FTMs is consistent with the experience of most gender identity clinics. Worldwide, the age at which individuals present for treatment appears to be dropping, which might reflect increased public awareness of the condition and treatment options.

Etiology of Gender Identity Disorder

There is no clearly identified cause for GID. Neuroanatomical differences have been noted in clients with GID, specifically in the size of the central subdivision of the bed nucleus of the stria terminalis, an area of the brain responsible for sexual behavior (Zhou, Hofman, Gooren, & Swaab, 1995).

Clinical Example

A 47-year-old client presents to the emergency department (ED) for shoulder pain after a car accident. All identification lists the person as female, but old charts reveal that the client underwent sex reassignment surgery several years before. How should this be handled?

Plan: The client is legally or at least socially female, and unless the client instructs otherwise, the feminine pronoun is the only appropriate one to use. Inquiries about gender transition are relevant to ask only if strictly pertinent to other medical/surgical issues related to the condition at hand. As with other matters of personal privacy, it is intrusive and unprofessional to ask about biographical details merely out of curiosity.

Sexual orientation and gender identity are different phenomena. Sexual orientation may change after gender transition but often does not.

Treatment of Gender Identity Disorder

Treatment may involve psychotherapy, hormones, and sexual reassignment surgery. As noted earlier, most cases of childhood GID abate in adolescence. Adults with GID may choose to live nontraditional or cross-gendered lifestyles without seeking to physically change their bodies, or they may choose to receive hormone therapy and surgery.

Individuals with GID may be quite socially and sexually conservative.

Most medications used to treat psychiatric disorders can cause problems with sexual functioning.

The approval process for hormonal treatment usually takes several months of visits, then physical assessments to verify their medical safety. Approval for surgery generally takes one or more years and involves a supervised experience of the person living full-time in the desired gender, referred to as the Real Life Experience. The Real Life Experience is designed to provide the full range of experiences in the preferred gender.

After surgery, clients usually describe a sense of relief, and a wish to simply get on with their lives in their chosen gender. Most express increasing confidence in their new lives, and start ventures or relationships that they had put on hold prior to transition. However, some individuals report that they had expectations prior to surgery that remain unfulfilled in their new gender identity and need help to adjust to this major life change.

Sexual and Gender Identity Disorders Not Otherwise Specified (NOS)

The *DSM-IV* applies the term *NOS* to a disorder or disturbance that does not meet the criteria for the specific disorders already discussed. This may

NURSING CARE PLAN Male to Female Gender Identity Disorder

Expected Outcomes	Interventions	Evaluations
• Will be safe and will receive treatment for any concurrent mental disorders.	• Determine if anxiety, depression, and/or suicidal ideation are present. • Conduct mental status examination and suicide assessment. • Establish and maintain therapeutic rapport.	• Identify depression; client accepts antidepressant therapy.
• Will explore his client's attitude regarding sexual reassignment.	• Use the client's preferred name and pronoun.	• Client displays open posture, and uses nondefensive language; discusses sexual issues with nurse.
• Will be informed on GID and treatment options.	• Provide client and family education and reading materials; refer to Internet resources and community agencies; set up follow-up appointment.	• Client accepts information, contacts referral resources, returns for follow-up appointment, asks questions, and engages in discussion.
• Will increase socialization.	• Help identify client's interests; assist with social skills; connect with transgendered-friendly environments in community; educate regarding risk of experiencing violence; discuss safe and potentially unsafe environments for client while cross-dressed.	• Client reports increased comfort in social situations and increased social contacts; expresses awareness of potential societal risks.
• Will establish connections to specialized treatment services.	• Provide referral to local clinicians familiar with assessment and treatment of GID, and provide website to assist in that search.	• Client has information to secure appointment with qualified specialist.

Visit http://nursing.jbpub.com/psychiatric for additional care plans and exercises.

CASE STUDY Mr. L.

Mr. L. is an 18-year-old biological male who presents to a general out-patient mental health clinic in a large urban area with episodes of low mood and anxiety. He had made a suicide attempt 3 years before. Mr. L. was brought to the clinic by his mother.

Mr. L. says that his upbringing was very difficult: he hated the rough-and-tumble of his male classmates. In school, he was embarrassed to change into gym clothes with his male friends, and retreated to the toilet stall to change, and to sit to urinate. Mr. L. preferred to play fantasy games with the girls, often taking the role of the mother or other female figure. He was teased and roughed up frequently by his male classmates for this.

For as long as he could remember he fantasized about living life as a girl. He recalls going to bed at night as a young child hoping that he would wake up transformed into a girl. He developed a crush on a male teacher, fantasizing about marrying him one day, but did not disclose this to anyone until now.

By age 10 he began wearing female clothing when his family was out. In his teen years he began venturing outside cross-dressed, using clothes borrowed from his female friends. He found going out like this exciting, partially due to the fear of being discovered. Mr. L. is known in some circles as a female—or at least as someone who seems more female than male. Mr. L. reports that he is a virgin, and is uncomfortable touching his genitals.

Mr. L.'s mother states that Mr. L. has always seemed feminine, and despite being a fairly traditional family they have used the client's gender-neutral middle name since around age 8, when the client insisted on it. After years of consternation, the family has implicitly accepted the female gender identity of their child, though they do not understand it.

Mr. L. and his mother now present with a request for information on treatment options for Mr. L.

With Mr. L., it is important for the nurse to include an assessment for psychiatric disorders, especially given a history of depression and a past suicide attempt. A study of 31 clients with GID found that over 70% had Axis I psychiatric disorders, primarily mood and anxiety disorders (Hepp, Kraemer, Schnyder, Miller, & Delsignore, 2005).

include marked feelings of sexual inadequacy, transient cross-dressing that is experienced as stressful to the client, or persistent distress about sexual orientation.

Education for Clients and Families

Education is an important component of the nurse's role with all clients. The nurse needs to be knowledgeable regarding the basics of sexual health and needs to be comfortable providing information to clients. This is true for clients who present with a specific sexual disorder as well as for clients being treated for other psychiatric or medical disorders. The rate of sexual dysfunctions in mental health patients is extremely high, approaching 50% even in nonacute general psychiatric out-patient services (Kockott & Pfeiffer, 1996). Evidence suggests that psychiatric clients have unmet educational needs around sexuality and relationships, and they express particular interest in the effects of mental illness and medication on sexual functioning, and how to maintain long-term relationships.

Medication Side Effects

Sexual dysfunctions occur in approximately one third of clients treated with antidepressants (Norris, Cassem, Huffman, & Stern, 2004). Although clinicians are primarily concerned with the extrapyramidal side effects of conventional neuroleptics, sexual side effects may be the most distressing for the client. Sexual dysfunction is a major reason that clients discontinue their antipsychotic medications. Because medication noncompliance is a key cause of relapse in schizophrenia, addressing sexual concerns of clients would appear to be an important healthcare intervention for nurses. Clients with certain medical conditions, including hypertension and diabetes, as well as clients being treated with commonly prescribed cardiovascular, anticonvulsant, and gastrointestinal medications may also experience sexual dysfunctions. Another element is the acute and chronic adverse effects on the sexual life of the client's partner. Partners can benefit by understanding some of the common sexual and relationship consequences of mental health illness and treatment.

It is important, then, that the nurse be knowledgeable about the relationship between psychiatric and medical conditions and sexual functioning and impart this information to the client. It may take time to determine if the sexual effects experienced by the client are due to the disorder or are a side effect of medication. If the nurse is comfortable discussing this with the client, it can promote treatment compliance. The nurse can assist the client in working with the prescribing nurse practitioner or other clinician to change or adjust medications if this is indicated.

Critical Thinking Question What questions might you ask the client to determine whether sexual side effects are related to noncompliance with medications for the client's schizophrenia?

Information

Many clients with sexual dysfunctions will have knowledge deficits. By providing information, the nurse can help the client understand his or her experience, which, in turn, can decrease a sense of isolation and encourage mastery of the situation. This information should be appropriate to the skill level of the nurse, and may focus on the disorder itself, treatment alternatives, Internet and community resources, or referrals to expert clinicians. Of course, teaching about safe-sex practices is fundamental to promoting sexual health.

Behavioral Approaches

The nurse need not be an expert, but he or she should have an awareness of the behavioral approaches that are part of the treatment for sexual dysfunctions. There are many self-help books available for clients to assist in increasing sexual comfort, achieving orgasm, maintaining an erection, and reducing performance anxiety. Reduced focus on intercourse and simultaneous orgasm (which is exceedingly rare in any couple) will tend to increase sexual satisfaction, especially for the female partner. Female partners also need to know that most women do not experience orgasm most times if intercourse is engaged in exclusively. Reducing the expectations to realistic levels often has a beneficial effect on the sexual relationship. Again, clients can be referred to expert clinicians for specialized therapy.

Communication

An often underestimated aspect of client education is the teaching of communication skills. The nurse has the opportunity to model open and sensitive communication. This can be a key factor to promoting improved sexual satisfaction for clients. The communication skills learned in the relationship with the nurse can be transferred to the relationship with a sexual partner. Comfort and openness in expressing feelings and needs are important components to achieving sexual satisfaction.

Summary

Sexuality is a matter that touches every client and family. Persons with psychiatric disorders are especially vulnerable to decreases in their sexual quality of life due to elements of the disorder itself, its pharmacological treatment, and the stigma that accompanies mental illness.

A variety of sexual disorders and dysfunctions, as well as gender identity issues, can affect anyone. It is important that nurses have a basic understanding of these conditions, and feel comfortable opening up a dialogue about sexual concerns with their clients. Incorporating sexuality into nursing care is a further step towards holistic nursing practice.

Annotated References

American Psychiatric Association. (2000). *Diagnostic and statistical manual of mental disorders* (4th ed., text rev.). Washington, DC: Author.

This compendium of mental health conditions is the major diagnostic manual that guides research and clinical decision making.

Annon, J. S. (1976). *Behavioral treatment of sexual problems.* New York: Harper & Row.

This early work thoroughly outlines a multidisciplinary framework for assessment and care of sexual problems.

Basson, R. (2007). Hormones and sexuality: Current complexities and future directions. *Maturitas, 57*(1), 66–70.

This article discusses the complexities associated with studying the relationship of estrogen and androgen deficiencies to sexual dysfunction in women.

Carson, C., & Gunn, K. (2006). Premature ejaculation: Definition and prevalence. [Review]. *International Journal of Impotence Research, 18*(Suppl. 1), 5–13.

This review article documents the history of PE and the changing approaches to treatment.

Clayton, A. H., Segraves, R. T., Leiblum, S., Basson, R., Pyke, R., et al. (2006). Reliability and validity of the Sexual Interest and Desire Inventory-Female (SIDI-F), a scale designed to measure severity of female hypoactive sexual desire disorder. *Journal of Sex and Marital Therapy, 32*(2), 115–135.

The authors report findings of a study to evaluate the validity and reliability of this instrument primarily through correlation with other measures of female sexual functioning.

Dennerstein, L., & Hayes, R. (2005). Confronting the challenges: Epidemiological study of female sexual dysfunction and the menopause. *Journal of Sexual Medicine, 2*(Suppl. 3), 118–132.

This article specifically focuses on the relationship between female sexual dysfunctions and menopause.

Feldman, H. A., Goldstein, I., & Hatzichristou, D. (1994). Impotence and its medical psychosocial correlates: Results of the Massachusetts Male Aging Study. *Journal of Urology, 151*, 54–61.

The MMALES study was one of the first major population-based studies of sexual problems in men.

Grazziottin, A., & Brotto, L. (2004). Vulvar vestibulitis syndrome: A clinical approach. *Journal of Sex and Marital Therapy, 30*, 125–139.

Grazziottin and Brotto review the complexities of women's sexual pain conditions.

Harlow, B. L., & Stewart, E. G. (2003). A population-based assessment of chronic unexplained vulvar pain: Have we underestimated the prevalence of vulvodynia? *American Medical Women's Association Journal, 58*(2), 82–88.

Harlow and Stewart survey a large sample in an attempt to determine the extent of female sexual pain in the community.

Hepp, U., Kraemer, B., Schnyder, U., Miller, N., & Delsignore, A. (2005). Psychiatric comorbidity in gender identity disorder. *Journal of Psychosomatic Research, 58*(3), 259–261.

This small study shows a high rate of psychiatric disorders among clients with GID.

Irwin, R. (2002). *Psychosexual nursing.* Philadelphia: Whurr.

This book is a thorough account of assessment and nursing care of sexual problems, especially to help anticipate sexual consequences of medical care.

Kockott, G., & Pfeiffer, W. (1996). Sexual disorders in nonacute psychiatric outpatients. *Comprehensive Psychiatry, 37*(1), 56–61.

This study identifies the pervasive nature of sexual problems in psychiatric populations.

Laumann, E. O., Gagnon, J. H., Michael, R. T., & Michaels, S. (1994). *The social organization of sexuality: Sexual practices in the United States.* Chicago: University of Chicago Press.

The first of two large studies that attempted to establish the prevalence and incidence of sexual dysfunctions in the general population.

Masters, W., & Johnson, V. (1966). *Human sexual response.* New York: Little, Brown.

This classic work published the first large-scale studies of sexual response in a laboratory setting, and established the dominant physiological model of its time.

Maurice, W. L. (2000). *Sexual medicine in primary care: A selection of chapters taken from the best-selling book by the same name.* London: Mosby-Wolfe.

This short guide contains excerpts of Dr. Maurice's larger manual designed to help primary-care doctors treat sexual problems.

Norris, E. R., Cassem, N. H., Huffman, J. C., & Stern, T. A. (2004). Cardiovascular and other side effects of psychotropic medications. In T. A. Stern & J. B. Herman, (Eds.), *Massachusetts General Hospital Psychiatry and Board Update* (2nd ed., pp. 385–393). New York: McGraw-Hill.

This chapter is an excellent resource on medication side effects.

Shafer, L. (2004). Sexual disorders and sexual dysfunction. In T. A. Stern & J. B. Herman (Eds.), *Massachusetts General Hospital Psychiatry and Board Update* (2nd ed., pp. 155–164). New York: McGraw-Hill.

This chapter provides a succinct overview of the sexual disorders.

Simons, J. S., & Carey, M. P. (2001). Prevalence of sexual dysfunctions: Results from a decade of research. *Journal of Sexual Behavior, 30*(2), 177–220.

This large meta-study surveyed numerous research studies to examine the epidemiology of sexual dysfunctions.

van Kesteren, P. J., Gooren, L. J., & Megens, J. A. (1996). An epidemiological and demographic study of transsexuals in the Netherlands. *Archives of Sexual Behavior, 25*(6), 589–600.

This is a study of the incidence of GID in a small European company with national record-keeping.

Wierman, M. E., Basson, R., Davis, S. R., Khosla, S., Miller, K. K., et al. (2006). Androgen therapy in women: An Endocrine Society clinical practice guideline. *Journal of Clinical Endocrinology and Metabolism, 91*(10), 3697–3710.

A task force established by the Clinical Guidelines Subcommittee of the Endocrine Society developed recommendations for androgen therapy based on a systematic review of available evidence.

World Health Organization. (2002). Sexual health. Retrieved October 12, 2006, from http://www.who.int/reproductive-health/gender/sexual_health.html#3

This statement on the importance of sexual health is the most recent in a series of such policy statements going back over two decades.

Zhou, J. N., Hofman, M. A., Gooren, L. J., & Swaab, D. F. (1995). A sex difference in the human brain and its relation to transsexuality. *Nature,* 378(6552), 68–70.

This article identified organic differences in persons with GID.

Additional Resources

Ellison, C. R. (2003). Facilitating orgasmic responsiveness. In S. B. Levine, C. B. Risen, & S. Althof (Eds.), *Handbook of clinical sexuality* (pp. 167–186). New York: Brunner-Routledge.

Ellison takes a very nonmedical approach to clinical sexuality.

Heiman, J. R., & Palladini, D. (1987). *Becoming orgasmic: A sexual and personal growth program for women.* New York: Fireside Books.

A well-respected self-help book to overcome orgasmic difficulties.

Meston, C. M., Levin, R. J., Sipski, M. L., Hull, E. M., & Heiman, J. R. (2004). Women's orgasm. *Annual Review of Sex Research, 15,* 173–257.

An exhaustive study of orgasm in women.

Zilbergeld, B. (1999). *The new male sexuality* (Rev. ed.). New York: Bantam Books.

A classic popular work on male sexual health and sexual problems.

Internet Resources

http://nursing.jbpub.com/psychiatric

Visit http://nursing.jbpub.com/psychiatric for interactive exercises, NCLEX review questions, WebLinks, and more.

CHAPTER 20

Eating Disorders

Amy Wysoker

LEARNING OBJECTIVES

After reading this chapter, you will be able to:

- Identify factors important in the assessment of eating disorders.
- Define anorexia nervosa, bulimia nervosa, binge eating disorder, and obesity.
- Describe the diagnostic criteria for eating disorders.
- Distinguish anorexia nervosa restricting type from anorexia nervosa binge eating/purging type.
- Distinguish anorexia nervosa binge eating/purging type from bulimia nervosa.
- Delineate treatment modalities for the different types of eating disorders.
- Identify nursing interventions to assist clients experiencing eating disorders.
- Discuss the educational needs of clients and their families.

KEY TERMS

Anorexia nervosa
Anorexia nervosa (binge eating/purging type)
Anorexia nervosa (restricting type)
Bariatric surgical procedures
Binge eating
Binge eating disorder
Bulimia nervosa
Obesity
Purging

http://nursing.jbpub.com/psychiatric

Visit http://nursing.jbpub.com/psychiatric for interactive exercises, NCLEX review questions, WebLinks, and more.

Introduction

Eating disorders present a treatment challenge to healthcare practitioners. Persons with eating disorders are excessively preoccupied with food, their weight, and the shape of their body. These disorders occur most often in adolescents and young adult women ages 12 to 35 and severely affect both psychological and physiologic development (American Psychiatric Association [APA], 2000a). Nurses are often involved in both medical and psychiatric nursing interventions in the treatment of these disorders.

This chapter explains anorexia nervosa and bulimia nervosa, the most common eating disorders classified in the *Diagnostic and Statistical Manual of Mental Disorders,* Fourth Edition, Text Revision (*DSM-IV-TR*; APA, 2000a) and are coded as Axis I disorders. Both of these disorders can cause severe medical problems, even death. An additional category, eating disorder not otherwise specified (EDNOS), is used for any eating disorder that does not meet the full criteria for either anorexia nervosa or bulimia nervosa.

Binge eating disorder is one such example of EDNOS, and will also be reviewed in this chapter. All eating disorders result in severe psychological consequences. Despite the criteria set forth by the *DSM-IV-TR*, most persons entering treatment for an eating disorder do not clearly meet the criteria for anorexia nervosa or bulimia nervosa, and therefore the diagnosis of EDNOS is frequently used (Annenberg Foundation Trust, 2005).

Purging is an attempt to alleviate the perceived negative effects of binge eating on body shape and weight.

Although not classified an eating disorder, **obesity** also will be addressed in this chapter. The *DSM-IV-TR* does not consider an excess of body weight a mental disorder but rather a general medical condition. There is discussion in the psychiatric-mental health field regarding the relationship between obesity and eating disorders, especially in relationship to binge eating disorder (Annenberg Foundation Trust, 2005). This chapter will address this concern and discuss other issues related to obesity.

Anorexia Nervosa

Anorexia nervosa is the extreme pursuit of a thin body accompanied by a profoundly disturbed body image. People with anorexia nervosa have a morbid fear of gaining weight, which causes them to obsessively fear losing control of the amount of food they consume. They view themselves as fat because of their disturbed body image, even though they are actually often emaciated.

In addition to the previously mentioned characteristics, the *DSM-IV-TR* (APA, 2000a) identifies the following criterion for establishing a diagnosis of anorexia nervosa: the individual exhibits a persistent refusal to maintain his or her body weight at or above the minimum expected weight. Thus, if a person loses weight, resulting in a weight of less than 85% of the expected weight, the *DSM-IV-TR* criteria are met. Conversely, if during a period of growth the individual fails to gain the expected weight, resulting in a body weight of less than 85% of expected weight, the criteria are also met. Another criterion listed in the *DSM-IV-TR* for anorexia nervosa is the absence of at least three consecutive menstrual cycles.

There is some controversy in the field questioning the criteria as set forth by the *DSM-IV-TR*. One debate is over the word *refusal*. Refusal implies a voluntary decision to refrain from eating; however, clients with anorexia have an obsessive quality and thus have difficulty controlling the behavior that leads to low body weight. It has been suggested that *inability* is a better word to describe the criterion (Annenberg Foundation Trust, 2005). The National Institute of Mental Health (NIMH) uses the word *resistive* to describe this same criterion (NIMH, 2002).

Binge Eating/Purging Type

It is important to distinguish between the two categories of anorexia nervosa. One is termed the **binge eating/purging type**. During a period of **binge eating**, the person perceives that he or she is out of control. These individuals cannot resist the temptation to eat specific foods or cannot stop eating until someone interrupts them, the food is no longer available, or their physical condition prevents further intake. Typically, a large amount of food is consumed rapidly during a binge episode. Consensus has not been reached as to how many calories define a binge; the perception of being out of control is more important. Persons with binge eating/purging type anorexia nervosa usually consume several hundred calories during an episode. Self-induced vomiting and laxatives, diuretics, and enema abuse are purging activities (APA, 2000a).

Restricting Type

The second category of anorexia nervosa is termed the **restricting type**. During their illness, persons with this type of anorexia restrict their intake but do not regularly engage in binge eating or purging (**Figure 20-1**).

Critical Thinking Question What is the difference in the behaviors of clients with the binge eating/purging type of anorexia nervosa and the restricting type?

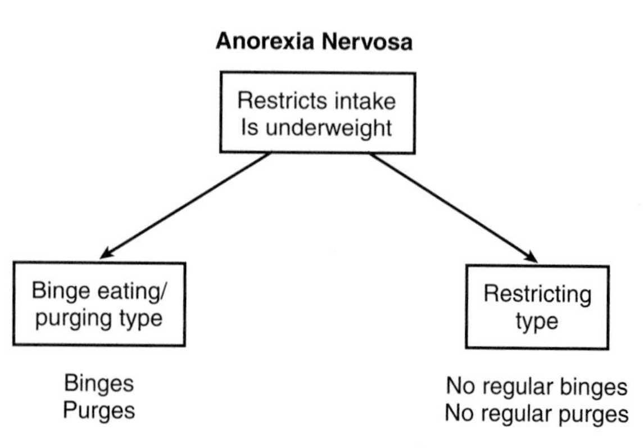

Figure 20-1 Anorexia nervosa.

Incidence and Prevalence

Statistics vary as to the prevalence of anorexia nervosa. The American Psychiatric Association's Work Group on Eating Disorders reports 0.5% to 3.7% of females experience anorexia nervosa (APA, 2000a). Research has consistently shown that females are more likely than males to develop an eating disorder (APA, 2000a; Hoek, 2002; NIMH, 2002). The mortality rate is estimated to be approximately 0.56% per year, 12 times greater than the annual death rate for females ages 15–24 years from all other causes of death (Sullivan, 1995). NIMH reports that in over 15 years of follow-up, mortality rates were found to be high as 20%.

Etiology

Many social factors may be responsible for causing anorexia nervosa. U.S. society greatly emphasizes the importance of exercise and thinness (see **Figure 20-2**). The pressures and demands placed on adolescents and young adults to be thin may significantly promote the development of this illness. Stice, Spanler, and Agras (2002) found that after exposure to the culture of thinness, for example fashion magazines where thinness is promoted, study subjects reported greater body dissatisfaction and pressure to be thin. Another study conducted in Fiji found that the influence of Western media increased rates of negative body image and body disturbances (Becker, Burwell, Gilman, Herzog, & Hamburg, 2002).

Psychological factors are also involved in the development of anorexia nervosa. Adolescents with anorexia nervosa seem to fear the normal developmental tasks of increased independence

Figure 20-2 Exercise and thinness are valued heavily in U.S. society.

Clinical Example

Casey is a 16-year-old female brought to the hospital by her parents after they found her passed out in her bedroom. Casey was extremely emaciated, and according to her parents weighed 70 pounds. The family reported that Casey consistently refused to eat, claiming she was not hungry, and when she did eat she would vigorously exercise immediately afterwards. Her parents were very concerned. However, their daughter refused to seek treatment because she did not see herself as "too thin." The only way they were able to bring her to the hospital was that she passed out and was too weak to refuse.

and increased social and sexual functioning. Their preoccupation with eating and weight gain thus allows them to avoid these normal but difficult developmental tasks. By starving themselves, these adolescents can maintain their childhood roles and avoid sexual development. Young adults with anorexia nervosa often have low self-esteem and feelings of inadequacy.

Additional psychological factors involve issues of control. The adolescent with anorexia who experiences feelings of anxiety and loss of control may counteract these feelings by using food as a source of control. Young adults with anorexia nervosa may have close but conflicting relationships with their parents. When treating these clients, therapists often find unresolved issues of individualization and separation from the mother (Bruch, 1978).

Biologic studies of anorexia nervosa have revealed a possible dysfunction of the hypothalamus as well as possible hormonal changes during adolescence. Researchers are studying the neurotransmitters that regulate appetite, fat distribution, and body size, because these are likely related to this illness (APA, 2000a). There is increased evidence that genetics contributes to the illness; however, no specific gene has been linked to either anorexia nervosa or bulimia nervosa (Annenberg Foundation Trust, 2005).

> Adolescents with anorexia nervosa are trying to maintain their childhood and avoid sexual development.

Physiology

The severely reduced intake of nutrients and calories places the client with anorexia nervosa in a state of starvation. The body literally devours itself to get the nutrients to survive. The result is a breakdown of the body's systems, often evidenced by cardiac symptoms, abnormal EKGs, and electrolyte imbalances. Anorexia can result in amenorrhea and digestive and gastrointestinal disorders; those who engage in vomiting and diuretic use can develop hypokalemic alkalosis.

Clinical Presentation

The individual with anorexia nervosa typically is a high achiever and is frequently involved in athletic activities such as ballet, gymnastics, or cheerleading. These individuals also have competitive personalities and often present with obsessive features. Frequently, the diagnosis is initially made during a medical visit prompted by the symptoms of lack of energy, physical weakness, and poor school performance. Clients with anorexic binge eating/purging type have stronger impulsive behaviors, which can present as self-mutilation, alcohol or substance abuse, and suicidal attempts (Annenberg Foundation Trust, 2005; Casper, 1990; Garfinkel, Moldofsky, & Garner, 1980).

Clients who are experiencing binge eating/purging type anorexia commonly abuse laxatives and diuretics.

Behavioral Features

Clients with anorexia present primarily with an emaciated appearance. They often wear multiple layers of loose clothing to hide their thinness and refuse to eat with their families or in public places. These clients are always thinking of food; they often collect recipes or prepare elaborate meals for others. Clients with anorexia exercise excessively and avoid being weighed. They often exhibit unusual behavior patterns, such as carrying large amounts of candy in their pockets, hiding food in their napkins or pockets when eating, rearranging food on their plates, and cutting food into small pieces. Up to 50% of these clients have eating binges (APA, 2000a). These occur secretly, often at night. Self-induced vomiting follows a binge if the client has binge eating/purging type anorexia. These clients commonly abuse laxatives and diuretics.

Clinical Features

Clients with anorexia present with many clinical features, including electrolyte disturbances and dehydration, hypothermia, and dependent edema. These clients often exhibit cardiac symptoms such as bradycardia, hypotension, cachexia (wasting), lanugo (fine downy hair on arms and torso), and metabolic changes. The most serious medical

CASE STUDY Samantha G.

Samantha G. is a 14-year-old girl who was involved in numerous athletic activities at school. She would frequently come home from practice and tell her mom that she wasn't hungry because she ate before her sporting events. Her mother would insist she sit during dinner with the family, which included her parents and two brothers. Her parents would repeatedly question why she would not eat; after all she ate many hours ago. Samantha would give various reasons, such as she doesn't get hungry after sports and was tired. When she felt pressured to eat and gave in, she would move food around her plate and play with her food, eating only small amounts. At times, Samantha would eat larger quantities and then excuse herself quickly from the table.

After many weeks of this pattern and noticeable weight loss, her parents realized that Samantha would excuse herself to go to the bathroom and would not return for some time. One evening her mother went to get something upstairs and heard her daughter retching in the bathroom. She demanded that her daughter open the door and noticed that there was vomit in the toilet and that Samantha's fingers were dirtied with vomit. There was also an open laxative bottle. Mrs. G. pleaded with her daughter to stop this behavior and would continuously tell her that she was not fat and was "too thin." Mother and daughter would get into arguments and over time nothing changed. Mrs. G. felt frustrated but did not know how to change her daughter's thinking and behaviors. She did speak to a colleague at work who encouraged seeking treatment; however, Samantha refused.

As time progressed Samantha's health became further compromised. Despite her coach telling her that her weight status was unhealthy and that she would not be allowed to continue in organized sports, she was not able to make changes. Samantha dropped out of organized sports, which upset her terribly. However, she still did not change her behaviors and would continue to excessively exercise at home. Her parents were in extreme conflict because their daughter adamantly refused help, claiming nothing was wrong with her.

One day a teacher found her on the bathroom floor too weak to stand. The nurse called 911. In the emergency department, Samantha was immediately placed on intravenous therapy and monitored for cardiac problems. She was admitted to the hospital and transferred to the eating disorder clinic for comprehensive treatment.

NURSING CARE PLAN Anorexia Nervosa

Expected Outcomes	Interventions	Evaluations
• Will have improved self-esteem/body image.	• Develop a trusting relationship. • Involve patient in decision making to allow for patient control.	• Able to talk about body image and exhibits a gradual improvement in self-esteem.
• Will demonstrate less denial.	• Provide a safe environment where the patient can express feelings and thoughts.	
• Will report feeling hungry. • Will gain sufficient weight.	• Treat malnutrition and accompanying medical problems. • Record intake and output. • Observe for vomiting. • Promote a steady weight gain of no more than 2 pounds a week.	• Gradual weight gain. • Reports being hungry and eats with others during mealtimes. • Health status stabilized. • Begins to accept illness.
• Will commit to long-term remission/rehabilitation/recovery.	• Refer for after-care treatment.	• Commits to continuation of treatment posthospitalization.

Visit http://nursing.jbpub.com/psychiatric for additional care plans and exercises.

complications result from malnutrition and cardiac arrhythmias (Annenberg Foundation Trust, 2005). Clients with anorexia restricting type have fewer medical problems compared to the subgroup with binging/purging behaviors (Annenberg Foundation Trust).

Differential Diagnosis

Because the client will persistently deny any symptoms, it is a most difficult task to diagnose anorexia nervosa. Many problems arise when attempting to obtain an accurate history and perform an adequate assessment. Other conditions must be considered; for example, extreme weight loss may be caused by many serious medical illnesses such as cancer or brain tumors. In addition, weight loss can be symptomatic of many mental health illnesses. Clients with depressive disorders may present with extreme weight loss. However, these clients report a decreased appetite, whereas anorexic clients report a normal appetite and feelings of hunger. A lack of appetite exists only in the late stages of anorexia nervosa. A preoccupation with food is not evident in depressive disorders as it is in anorexia nervosa, and depressed clients do not have an intense fear of obesity (Kaplan, Sadock, & Grebb, 1994).

Anorexia nervosa must be differentiated from bulimia nervosa, which is discussed later in this chapter. Clients with anorexia nervosa may have binge eating patterns similar to those with bulimia nervosa; however, clients with bulimia nervosa maintain their weight within the normal range.

Psychiatric co-morbidity in clients with anorexia nervosa is approximately 80% (Halmi et al., 1991). Major depressive disorder is the psychiatric illness most associated with anorexia nervosa. Fifty percent to 68% of anorexic clients also are diagnosed with major depressive disorder (Herzog, Nussbaum, & Marmor, 1996).

Clinical Course and Complications

Statistics indicate that approximately 50–70% of adolescents suffering from anorexia nervosa actually recover, whereas 20% do improve but continue to experience some symptoms and 10–20% have a chronic condition (Annenberg Foundation Trust, 2005; Herpertz-Dahlmann et al., 2001; Steinhausen, 2002; Steinhausen, Winkler, & Meier, 1997). The clinical course varies. Clients may recover, then relapse, or even die from the complications of starvation. Clients with anorexia nervosa are 12 times more likely to die than women of a similar age. Suicide is also another cause of death with a rate 57 times greater than women of similar age (Keel et al., 2003). Treatment is difficult because denial of the problem is so strong. Even clients who have regained weight remain preoccupied with food and their weight.

Unlike the client with anorexia nervosa, who is dangerously underweight, the client with bulimia nervosa maintains normal weight.

Positive outcome measures include regaining sufficient weight, reporting hunger, improved self-esteem, and less denial.

Management and Treatment

A comprehensive treatment approach is necessary for clients with anorexia nervosa. The first and most difficult task involves getting the client to accept treatment. Three phases of treatment are recommended: 1) restoring weight; 2) treating the psychological issues, such as distorted body image and low self-esteem; and 3) establishing long-term remission and rehabilitation, or full recovery (NIMH, 2001).

Medical complications and the prospect of impending medical problems from anorexia nervosa warrant hospitalization of the client.

When complications from malnutrition are evident, hospitalization should be mandatory (even if committal is necessary). In addition, if clients exhibit serious psychiatric symptoms such as severe depression, suicidal tendencies, psychosis, and self-mutilation, they should be admitted to a psychiatric hospital.

Treatment should include both family and individual therapies. Behavioral, cognitive, or interpersonal therapy can be used; all offer different approaches to treatment. Initially, the therapist must not attempt to change the client's eating behavior, because this both frustrates the practitioner and alienates the client. Clients with anorexia are invested in their symptoms; they believe the symptoms provide them with a form of control. The nurse develops a trusting relationship with the client in counseling sessions. A secure environment should be provided where clients can feel safe sharing their feelings and thoughts. It is crucial for the client to feel in control during therapy and to focus on related issues rather than eating behaviors. After progress is made in therapy, the possibility of changing eating behaviors can be addressed.

Clients with bulimia nervosa often engage in compensatory behavior (e.g., self-induced vomiting, purging with laxatives and diuretics, fasting, and excessive exercise).

During hospitalization, a more structured approach is implemented as a result of the serious nature of the malnutrition-related medical problems. These problems must be addressed before any psychotherapeutic benefits can be expected. Thus, therapy focuses to an extent on the eating behaviors but only because of the client's serious condition. Once the client's condition has stabilized, the practitioner must focus on the underlying causes based on the psychodynamics of anorexia nervosa. Throughout the client's hospitalization, the nurse and healthcare team must treat him or her accordingly. The nurse's goal is to promote in the client a steady weight gain of no more than 2 pounds per week. Rapid weight gain can cause cardiac complications. Clients must be weighed daily to monitor their progress, and malnutrition and accompanying medical problems must be treated. The nurse should record intake and output and observe for vomiting. If noted, strategies must be implemented to prevent vomiting.

Some selective serotonin reuptake inhibitors (SSRIs) have helped promote weight maintenance and do treat the related psychiatric symptoms (mood and anxiety symptoms) related to anorexia nervosa. However, these medications should be prescribed only if indicated after weight gain has occurred (NIMH, 2001).

Bulimia Nervosa

Persons with **bulimia nervosa** experience recurrent, rapid episodes of eating large amounts of food (binging) while feeling out of control. The binge eating usually terminates with abdominal pain or nausea or with an interruption during the episode. Feelings of extreme guilt, self-disgust, and depression usually follow. To compensate for their fear of weight gain, these persons may self-induce vomiting or repeatedly use laxatives or diuretics (**purging**). Fasting and excessive exercise are other compensatory behaviors (Agras, 1994).

To meet the *DSM-IV-TR* diagnostic criteria for bulimia nervosa, a person must eat large amounts of food in a discrete period of time, feel a sense of lack of control, and exhibit binge eating and compensatory behaviors at least twice a week for 3 months. In addition to a sense of lack of control, self-evaluation must be based on body shape and weight; these concerns dominate their thinking. The symptoms do not occur solely during episodes of anorexia nervosa (APA, 2000a). As previously discussed with anorexia nervosa, there is debate regarding the wording of the *DSM-IV-TR* criteria. For example, the *DSM-IV-TR* describes "amount" to mean "larger than most people would eat." Many persons with bulimia nervosa report eating large amounts that are no different than what most people eat. They also consider that the feeling of loss of control is more concerning than the amount eaten. Another concern is what constitutes "excessive exercise" (Annenberg Foundation Trust, 2005). Nurses should be aware of these issues and concerns when assess-

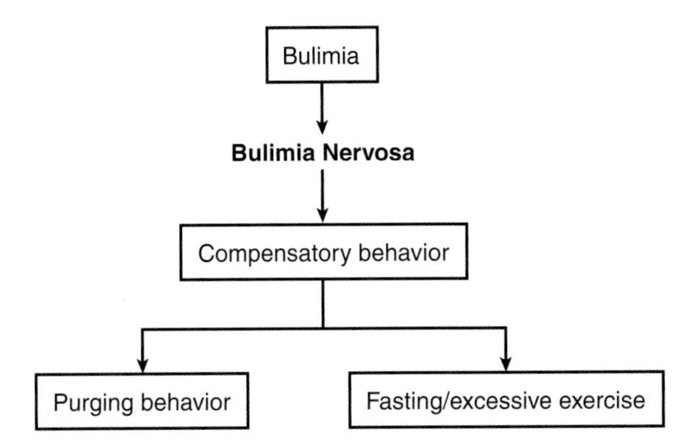

Figure 20-3 Bulimia nervosa.

ing and treating individuals for the two types of bulimia nervosa—purging and nonpurging.

Purging Type

Individuals with the purging type of bulimia regularly engage in purging activities such as self-induced vomiting or laxative or diuretic abuse after a binge episode.

Nonpurging Type

In the nonpurging type of bulimia nervosa, the individual does not purge but does exhibit other inappropriate compensatory behaviors such as fasting and excessive exercise (**Figure 20-3**).

Incidence and Prevalence

Approximately 1.1% to 4.3% of women in the Unites States have bulimia nervosa. It is seen much more often in women, 10 times more often than in males. Onset usually occurs in late adolescence. Typically, women of normal weight have this disorder; however, it has been noted in those with a history of obesity (APA, 2000a; McGilley & Pryor, 1998; NIMH, 2001).

Etiology

Many different factors have been related to the causes of bulimia nervosa. Genetic, environmental, psychological, and physiologic all have been associated with the disorder. Current research focuses on the involvement of neurotransmitters in bulimia nervosa. The success of antidepressant medications in the treatment of this disorder implicates the role of serotonin and norepinephrine.

Similar to those with anorexia, individuals with bulimia nervosa are, in part, responding to a society that emphasizes and values women who are thin. This expectation places enormous pressure on developing girls to meet unreasonable standards. The nurse must be aware of the role that family dynamics plays in this disorder. Clients with bulimia nervosa report strained family relationships and rejecting, distant, and uncaring parents (Kaplan, Sadock, & Grebb, 1994).

Physiology

The repeated vomiting in bulimia may result in gastroesophageal reflux disorder. Additionally, the use of diuretics can cause kidney problems and frequent laxative use can create irritations resulting in intestinal problems. Dehydration from loss of fluids is a serious physiological complication (APA, 2005).

Clinical Presentation

Adolescents with bulimia tend to be high achievers. These girls feel they must match society's norms. Additionally, those with bulimia nervosa have a history of obesity and dieting due to the pressures of a society that promotes thinness in women (Walsh & Devlin, 1998).

Behavioral Features

Clients with bulimia may have normal weight or fluctuate between being slightly overweight and maintaining normal weight. They appear normal and free of problems to those outside the family. These clients are occasionally impulsive or histrionic. They often act out in anger or attempt suicide. In addition to uncontrolled eating impulses, many clients lack impulse control in areas of substance dependence and self-destructive sexual relationships. They visit the bathroom regularly after meals and may eat normally or sparingly in the presence of others. Clients with bulimia may binge in private, then purge with or without fasting and excessive exercise.

Clinical Features

These clients present with several clinical features. Those who binge experience abdominal pain, malaise, and fluctuating blood sugar levels. Clients who purge by vomiting experience chronic hoarseness, hypokalemia, gastric and esophageal tears (these are rare), and cardiac symptoms such as palpitations and chest pain. Those who purge by laxatives or diuretics experience abdominal pain, diarrhea, and hypokalemia.

Critical Thinking Questions What are some of the behavioral features of bulimia nervosa that nurses need to assess? Are some more critical than others?

Differential Diagnosis

Clients with anorexia nervosa and bulimia nervosa exhibit common behaviors and symptoms. Therefore, it is important to distinguish between the binge eating and purging behaviors that occur during episodes of anorexia nervosa and those that occur during bulimia. Approximately 83% of individuals with bulimia nervosa also report a history of a psychiatric disorder (Fichter & Quadfleig, 1999). Fifty percent of clients have a lifetime history of a mood disorder; major depressive disorder is the most common mood disorder (Herzog, Keller, Sacks, Yeh, & Lavori, 1992).

Clinical Course and Complications

Bulimia nervosa is a chronic disorder with a fluctuating course. Recovery rates range from 35% to 75% after 5 years (Annenberg Foundation Trust, 2005; Fairburn, Cooper, Doll, Norman, & O'Connor, 2000). Approximately one third relapse (Keel & Mitchell, 1997). Clients may not be symptom-free after periods of improvement. Some may have a significant period of remission, while others remain disabled by their condition. The prognosis depends on the severity of the purging behavior. If the client's body has been medically compromised as a result of self-induced vomiting or abuse of laxatives and diuretics, the prognosis is less positive. Medical interventions and hospitalization become increasingly necessary. Mortality rates are very low in bulimia nervosa, approximately 0.5% (Keel, Mitchell, Miller, Davis, & Crow, 1999).

Clinical Example

Carole was very concerned about her stepdaughter Alice, who would spend extended amounts of time in the bathroom. Carole also noticed that Alice would have numerous empty "junk food bags" in her bedroom, and that upon returning home from work a significant amount of recently purchased groceries would be gone. All of Carole's three stepdaughters were very much involved in looking attractive and stylish. Their own mother was preoccupied with being thin and encouraged them to be thin. Carole intervened and asked Alice what she was doing in the bathroom for long periods of time and why there were so many empty food bags in her room. The stepdaughter denied any purging behaviors, although Carole questioned if this was true. Alice did admit to having concerns about being fat and felt pressure to be thin. She agreed to speak to a counselor and entered treatment.

Management and Treatment

The more serious the purging behaviors, the more destructive they are to the body's system, necessitating the appropriate medical interventions. Hospitalization is indicated in cases where purging results in electrolyte imbalances and metabolic disturbances.

Both types of bulimia nervosa must be treated psychologically, and cognitive-behavioral therapy is the method of choice. This type of therapy, which addresses the thoughts and feelings that occur prior to a binge episode, is helpful in recognizing the disturbed patterns that lead to destructive coping mechanisms (Agras & Apple, 1997; Agras et al., 2000; Annenberg Foundation Trust, 2005). The nurse can then help the client make the appropriate behavioral changes. Psychodynamic, interpersonal, and family therapies are also frequently used and helpful (Annenberg Foundation Trust; NIMH, 2001).

Antidepressant medication, primarily SSRIs, has successfully been used in the treatment of clients with bulimia. Antidepressants may also help prevent relapses (Annenberg Foundation Trust, 2005; NIMH, 2001).

Binge Eating Disorder

This syndrome differs from bulimia nervosa in that these individuals are usually overweight rather than normal weight, and, although both exhibit binging behaviors, clients with binge eating disorder do not involve themselves in the purging behaviors. It is estimated that approximately 2–5% of Americans have had a binge-eating disorder during a given 6-month time period (Bruce & Agras, 1992; NIMH, 2001; Spitzer et al., 1993). Because they do not self-induce vomiting or abuse laxatives and diuretics, there is far less risk of medical complications related to purging. However, physical problems from binging are still prevalent and must be addressed. Many go on to struggle with weight gain and then resort to diets. Research has shown a relationship between binge eating disorder and obesity, and in

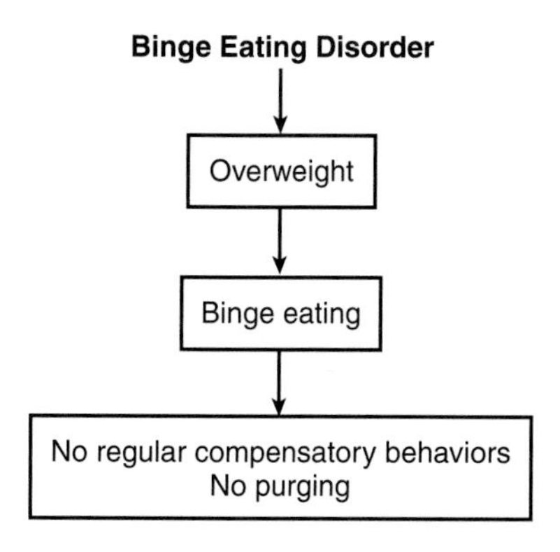

Figure 20-4 Binge eating disorder.

one study approximately 8% of the overweight population met the criteria for binge eating disorder (Bruce & Agras). In another study, approximately 29% of the subjects in the weight control programs met the criteria for binge eating disorder (Spitzer et al.). Interventions are usually required after weight gain and the medical problems resulting from episodes of weight cycling. The nurse should be concerned primarily with the cardiovascular problems associated with gaining and losing weight repeatedly (Agras, 1994; NIMH, 2001). These individuals were once referred to as compulsive overeaters or obese bingers before being classified with binge eating disorder. This classification will aid in studying and treating the disorder (**Figure 20-4**).

Critical Thinking Questions What is the difference in weight status between those persons diagnosed with bulimia nervosa and those with binge eating disorder? Why is this distinction important?

Obesity

Although not classified as an eating disorder in the *DSM-IV-TR*, obesity is considered a major health problem in the United States. Over 60 million adults (ages 20 years and older) in the United States are considered obese, 30% of the population. Over 9 million children and teens ages 6–19 are considered overweight, 16% of the population (Department of Health and Human Services [DHHS], 2006b).

The body mass index (BMI) is used to determine weight classification. Adults with a body mass index between 25 and 29.9 are considered overweight; those with a BMI of 30 or greater are considered obese (DHHS, 2006d). In children and teens BMI is age and sex specific and referred

Clinical Example

Jane is a 32-year-old fourth grade teacher who is single and lives alone. She has a body mass index (BMI) of 31 and has struggled with her weight since childhood. She has engaged in frequent dieting and has lost significant amounts of weight only to regain the weight back. After work Jane frequently goes to the gym and works out. However, when she returns home and is in for the evening watching TV, she finds herself wanting something sweet to eat. At times she will ravenously eat 2–3 quarts of ice cream and a box of cookies within a very short period of time. She explains that she won't even stop between bites. She just continues to "eat, eat, eat." Jane then experiences abdominal pain and nausea and has on certain occasions had to seek medical attention for these symptoms. Following the episodes she is disgusted with herself and feels very guilty. However, despite these feelings she will continue to partake in similar episodes and reports the inability to refrain from doing so.

to as BMI-for-age. It is calculated based on percentiles for size and growth patterns (DHHS, 2006a).

Binge eating disorder is distinguished by the presence of binge eating but an absence of purging behaviors, and clients are usually overweight.

Nutrition and physical activity determine one's weight status. An energy imbalance between how many calories are consumed and the amount of exercise performed results in obesity. There are many factors that affect how one eats and one's amount of exercise. An individual's personal characteristics, culture, finances, and environment are all contributing factors. In addition to the behavioral factors mentioned, genetics is a contributing factor as to how one's body burns calories to use for energy and how fat is stored. Considerable research is being conducted regarding the relationship between heredity and weight (DDHS, 2006c).

Obesity is related to numerous illnesses such as type 2 diabetes, hypertension, heart disease, certain cancers, stroke, osteoarthritis, and other conditions (DHHS, 2006b). Clients who are obese often have resorted to various methods of dieting to lose weight. Many experience weight cycling, losing and gaining the lost weight back repeatedly. The majority of persons who are either overweight or obese and have lost weight from dieting regain the lost weight back within 5 years (Fabricatore & Wadden, 2003; Institute of Medicine, 1995). Mood and anxiety disorders are present in one of four obese individuals (Simon et al., 2006).

The body mass index (BMI) is used to determine weight classification. Adults with a body mass index between 25 and 29.9 are considered overweight; those with a BMI of 30 or greater are considered obese and morbidly obese begins at 40.

It is the consensus among experts in the field of obesity that anyone with a BMI of greater than 30 could improve their health by losing weight. Those with BMIs between 25 and 29.9

Considerations for Client and Family Education

The public needs to be educated by nurses regarding the warning signs of eating disorders. The following is adapted from the Annenburg Foundation Trust (2005) and Anorexia Nervosa and Related Eating Disorders (ANRED) Inc. (2006):

- Withdraws socially and isolates him- or herself from activities that involve food and/or eating
- Skips meals
- Eats small portions
- Does not eat in front of others
- Has ritualistic eating patterns
- Mixes strange food combinations
- Chews food but then removes from mouth and does not swallow
- Always has an excuse to avoid eating, such as not feeling well, just ate with friends, or just not hungry
- Eats only certain foods that he or she believes are safe
- Refrains from meat; eats vegetarian but does not eat the necessary foods that provide nutrients
- Drinks diet soda excessively
- Eliminates fat from diet
- Constantly reads food labels
- Has a self-imposed rigid discipline about eating
- Tries to control what the family eats
- Engages in purging behaviors for the purpose of losing weight
- When deviating from this rigidity, will go into the bathroom to vomit
- On the other hand will gorge food, usually alone, and then vomit after the binge
- May leave evidence indicating possible desire to be discovered
- Empty food packages
- Bathroom that smells of vomit
- Overuse of mouthwash and mints
- Use of laxatives, water pills, diet pills, and natural products in health food stores that promote weight loss
- Uses alcohol and street drugs to decrease appetite, omit emotional pain
- Constant and strong concerns about his or her weight or shape
- Extreme fear of gaining weight and being obese
- Obsessive about clothing size
- Wears baggy clothes or a layer of clothes to hide what he or she thinks is fat
- Has an abnormally low weight or significant fluctuation in weight without medical reasons
- Does not like him- or herself unless he or she is thin
- Complains about being fat despite abnormally low weight
- Spends lots of time looking in the mirror
- Always finds something to criticize
- Dislikes specific body parts and constantly focuses on those parts (e.g., belly)
- Excessively and compulsively exercises
- Denies there is a problem
- Wants to be special, strives to be the best, which includes being thin
- Obsesses about food; has trouble concentrating
- Unable to talk about feelings
- Says everything is fine
- Is moody and irritable
- Throws tantrums
- Avoids people
- May engage in self-harm
- Socially tries to please everyone
- May avoid sexual activity or become involved in casual sex

Encourage patients and family members to seek treatment. The sooner the eating disorder is discovered, the better the prognosis.

and who have two of the following risk factors are also advised to lose weight: 1) family history of certain chronic illnesses (e.g., heart disease, diabetes), 2) pre-existing medical conditions (e.g., high cholesterol levels, high blood glucose), and 3) large waist circumference (for women, greater than 35 inches; for men, greater than 40 inches; National Heart, Lung, and Blood Institute [NHLBI], n.d.).

Treatment may consist of dieting, increased physical activity, behavior modification, and medication—in cases of morbid obesity (BMI greater than 40), it may include surgical interventions. Surgical interventions have been a recent choice for the severely obese person. In the year 2004, it was projected that 144,000 **bariatric surgical procedures** would be performed, a dramatic increase from earlier years (New York Health Plan

Implications for Evidence-Based Practice

Lock, LeGrange, Agras, and Dare (2001) have formulated a family-based treatment approach to manage anorexia nervosa. The treatment is called the Maudesley Approach, and further research has supported its use with bulimia nervosa as well. It is a short-term approach that promotes parent and sibling involvement in treatment. It is used with clients under the age of 18 who live with their family. Research has shown that the benefits of the treatment have been sustained for 5 years posttreatment.

Wysoker's (2002) study, entitled "A Conceptual Model of Weight Loss and Weight Regain: An Intervention for Change," provides a model for intervention in obesity. The model provides three important ways of viewing weight loss and weight regain. Additionally, Daniels's (2006) study, "Women's Descriptions of a Successful Weight-Loss Experience: A Qualitative Study," provides further information to assist nurses and nurse practitioners in helping dieters make lifestyle changes. Another study by Wysoker (2005), entitled "The Lived Experience of Choosing Bariatric Surgery to Lose Weight," elicited the four themes previously mentioned in the text that provide helpful information for nurses and other health professionals when treating the morbidly obese person.

Association, n.d.; Newman, 2004). The two most commonly performed procedures are the vertical banded gastroplasty and the Roux-en-Y gastric bypass. There have been many studies looking at the effects of the surgery on the co-morbid medical conditions accompanying the morbidly obese; however, few studies have looked at the psychological and behavioral adjustments necessary after surgery. Wysoker (2005) conducted a phenomenological study exploring the experiences of choosing bariatric surgery to lose weight. Four themes were identified: bariatric surgery was a "last resort," "surgery provides structure," "reality sets in," and "positive about the decision to have the surgery." These findings provide guidance for psychiatric nurses when treating clients who have had bariatric surgery.

Obesity treatment must be individually designed. Nurses can be instrumental in assisting clients to determine what they believe is in their best interest and help them toward meeting their goals (Wysoker, 2002). Losing and maintaining weight loss is a life-long commitment, and nurses are in a prime position to address the psychological, emotional, and behavioral components of weight loss. Nurses need to provide a holistic approach to the care of the obese person.

Clinical Example

Beth reported numerous diets were successful in helping her lose weight, but then she would gain whatever she lost back and some more. She was morbidly obese and was tired of dieting and no longer could motivate herself to go on a diet. Her experience of losing and gaining weight continuously was frustrating, and she knew her health was at extreme risk. Beth reported being desperate, and spoke to the nurse about bariatric surgery. The nurse counseled her about the risks and benefits and Beth chose to have the surgery. Following the surgery Beth lost weight rapidly, but then realized that if she wanted to keep the weight off she would need to make significant lifestyle changes.

Summary

Eating disorders are caused by numerous factors. Until nurses confront these developmental, psychological, societal, and biologic factors, the progress of treatment may be limited. Knowledge of the incidence and prevalence, etiology, behavioral, and clinical features of anorexia nervosa and bulimia nervosa prepares the nurse for confronting the life-threatening nature of these illnesses. Understanding the complexities of making a differential diagnosis, the clinical course of the diseases and their related complications, along with their management and treatment, allows the nurse to offer expert nursing care to clients with these complex diseases. Binge eating disorder and how it differs from bulimia nervosa also has been addressed. Although obesity is not classified as an eating disorder, it was also addressed in this chapter because it is considered a major health problem and involves significant medical complications. The nurse as a clinician, prevention specialist, and client advocate is instrumental in treating and preventing eating disorders and obesity.

Annotated References

Agras, W. S. (1994). Disorders of eating: Anorexia nervosa, bulimia nervosa, and binge-eating disorder. In R. Shader (Ed.), *Manual of psychiatric therapeutics* (2nd ed., pp. 59–67). Boston: Little Brown.

This text provides a review of eating disorders with an emphasis on treatment approaches.

Agras, W. S., & Apple, R. F. (1997). *Overcoming eating disorders: A cognitive-behavioral treatment for bulimia nervosa and binge eating disorder—Therapist guide.* San Antonio, TX: The Psychological Corporation.

This is a guide to using a cognitive-behavioral treatment approach in eating disorders.

Agras, W. S., Crow, S. J., Halmi, K. A., Mitchell, J. E., Wilson, G. T., & Kraemer, H. C. (2000). Outcome predictors for the cognitive-behavioral treatment of bulimia nervosa: Data from a multisite study. *American Journal of Psychiatry, 157,* 1302–1308.

The aim of this study was to discover clinically useful predictors of attrition and outcome in the treatment of bulimia nervosa with cognitive behavior therapy.

American Psychiatric Association. (2000a). *Diagnostic and statistical manual of mental disorders* (4th ed., text rev.). Washington, DC: Author.

This is the fourth edition of the APA's official nomenclature of psychiatric conditions and disorders that is used by mental health professionals in their work with clients with mental disorders and conditions.

American Psychiatric Association. (2000b). Practice guidelines for eating disorders. Revision. *American Journal of Psychiatry 157,* 1–39.

This publication provides a set of guidelines for intervening with clients who have eating disorders.

American Psychiatric Association. (2005). Let's talk facts about eating disorders. *Psychiatric News, 40*(10), 2.

This is part of the APA's popular "Let's Talk Facts" pamphlet series that educates the public about mental illnesses and mental health concerns.

Annenburg Foundation Trust (Sunnylands), Adolescent Mental Health Initiative. (2005). *Treating and preventing adolescent mental health disorder: What we know and what we don't know.* New York: Oxford University Press.

This book addresses the current state of knowledge about various mental health disorders in the teenage years and is the first to record the findings of this particular initiative.

Anorexia Nervosa and Related Eating Disorders Inc. (2006, February). Eating disorders warning signs. Retrieved October 10, 2006, from http://www.anred.com/warn.html

This fact sheet discusses the early warning signs of eating disorders.

Becker, A. E., Burwell, R. A., Gilman, S. E., Herzog, D. B., & Hamburg, P. (2002). Eating behaviours and attitudes following prolonged exposure to television among ethnic Fijian adolescent girls. *The British Journal of Psychiatry, 180,* 509–514.

This is a report on a naturalistic experiment that suggests a negative impact of television upon disordered eating attitudes and behaviors in a media-naïve population in Fiji.

Bruce, B., & Agras, W. S. (1992). Binge eating in females: A population-based investigation. *International Journal of Eating Disorders, 12*(4), 365–373.

A study of the characteristics of binge eating in an identified population of women.

Bruch, H. (1978). *The golden cage: The enigma of anorexia nervosa.* Cambridge, MA: Harvard University Press.

This is a classic text on anorexia nervosa and is still applicable today.

Casper, R. (1990). Personality features of women with good outcomes from restricting anorexia nervosa. *Psychosomatic Medicine, 52,* 156–170.

This article examines the personality characteristics of women who had physically and psychologically recovered from restricting anorexia nervosa at an 8- to 10-year follow-up.

Daniels, J. (2006). Women's descriptions of a successful weight-loss experience: A qualitative study. *The American Journal for Nurse Practitioners, 10*(10), 67–74.

Department of Health and Human Services, Centers for Disease Control and Prevention. (2006a). BMI—body mass index: About BMI for children and teens. Retrieved September 26, 2006, from http://www.cdc.gov/nccdphp/dnpa/bmi/childrens_BMI/about_childrens_BMI.htm

After BMI is calculated for children and teens, the BMI number is plotted on the CDC BMI-for-age growth charts (for either girls or boys) to obtain a percentile ranking. Percentiles are the most commonly used indicator to assess the size and growth patterns of individual children in the United States.

Department of Health and Human Services, Centers for Disease Control and Prevention. (2006b). Overweight and home. Retrieved September 26, 2006, from http://www.cdc.gov/nccdphp/dnpa/obesity/index.htm

Data from two surveys show that since the mid-1970s the prevalence of overweight and obesity has increased sharply for both adults and children.

Department of Health and Human Services, Centers for Disease Control and Prevention. (2006c). Overweight and obesity: Contributing factors. Retrieved September 26, 2006, from http://www.cdc.gov/nccdphp/dnpa/obesity/contributing_factors.htm

Obesity and overweight are chronic conditions. A variety of factors play a role in obesity. This section addresses how behavior, environment, and genetic factors may have an effect in causing people to be overweight and obese.

Department of Health and Human Services, Centers for Disease Control and Prevention. (2006d). Overweight and obesity: Defining overweight and obesity. Retrieved September 26, 2006, from http://www.cdc.gov/nccdphp/dnpa/obesity/defining.htm

Overweight and obesity are both labels for ranges of weight that are greater than what is generally considered healthy for a given height. The terms also identify ranges of weight that have been shown to increase the likelihood of certain diseases and other health problems.

Fabricatore, A. N., & Wadden, T. S. (2003). Psychological functioning of obese individuals. *Diabetes Spectrum, 16*, 245–252.

This review found that obese individuals in the general population have essentially normal psychological functioning. Obese women, however, are at greater risk than obese men of depression and related complications. Binge eating and extreme obesity further increase the likelihood of patients reporting emotional complications.

Fairburn, C. G., Cooper, Z., Doll, H. A., Norman, P., & O'Connor, M. (2000). The natural course of bulimia nervosa and binge eating disorder in young women. *Archives of General Psychiatry, 57*(7), 659–665.

This article suggests that, among young women in the study, bulimia nervosa and binge eating disorder have a different course and outcome. While the prognosis of those with bulimia nervosa was relatively poor, the great majority of those with binge eating disorder recovered.

Fichter, M., & Quadflieg, N. (1999). Six-year course of bulimia nervosa. *International Journal of Eating Disorders, 22*, 361–384.

In comparison to study samples with bulimia nervosa or binge eating disorder, the 6-year course of anorexia nervosa was less favorable.

Garfinkel, P. E., Moldofsky, H., & Garner, D. (1980). The heterogeneity of anorexia nervosa: Bulimia as a distinct group. *Archives of General Psychiatry, 9*, 1036–1140.

The bulimic group in this study displayed a variety of impulsive behaviors, including use of alcohol and street drugs, stealing, suicide attempts, and self-mutilation. With regard to family history, the high frequency of obesity in the mothers of bulimic patients was noteworthy.

Halmi, K. A., Eckert, E., Marchi, P., Sampugnaro, V., Apple, R., & Cohen, J. (1991). Comorbidity of psychiatric diagnoses in anorexia nervosa. *Archives of General Psychiatry, 48*, 712–718.

The co-morbidity of psychiatric diagnoses was examined with the Diagnostic Interview Schedule in 62 women who participated in a 10-year follow-up study of anorexia nervosa.

Herpertz-Dahlmann, B., Muller, B., Herpertz, S., Heussen, N., Hebebrand, J., & Remschmidt, H. (2001). Prospective 10-year follow-up in adolescent anorexia nervosa: Course, outcome, psychiatric comorbidity, and psychosocial adaptation. *Journal of Child Psychology and Psychiatry and Allied Disciplines, 42*, 603–612.

The study concluded that in most patients adolescent anorexia nervosa takes a prolonged course, although it seems to be more favorable than in adult-onset forms. Those who achieve complete recovery from the eating disorder have a good chance of overcoming other psychiatric disorders and adapting to social requirements.

Herzog, D. B., Keller, M. B., Sacks, N. R., Yeh, C. J., & Lavori, P. W. (1992). Psychiatric comorbidity in treatment-seeking anorexics and bulimics. *Journal of the American Academy of Child and Adolescent Psychiatry, 31*, 810–818.

High levels of co-morbidity were noted across the eating disorder samples. Mixed disorder subjects manifested the most co-morbid psychopathology and especially warrant further study.

Herzog, D. B., Nusbaum, K. M., & Marmor, A. K. (1996). Comorbidity and outcome in eating disorders. *Psychiatric Clinics of North America, 19*, 843–859.

This article reviews the data on co-morbidity, course, and outcome in anorexia nervosa and bulimia nervosa. Recovery, relapse, the process of recovery, and predictors of outcome are reviewed.

Hoek, H. W. (2002). Distribution of eating disorders. In C. G. Fairburn & K. D. Brownell (Eds.), *Eating disorders and obesity: A comprehensive handbook* (pp. 233–237). New York: Guilford Press.

This unique handbook clearly discusses both the traditional eating disorders and obesity.

Institute of Medicine. (1995). *Weighing the options: Criteria for evaluating weight-management programs.* Washington, DC: National Academy Press.

Despite widespread public concern about weight, few studies have examined the long-term results of weight-loss programs. This report presents criteria for evaluating treatment programs for obesity and explores what these criteria mean to healthcare providers, program designers, researchers, and even overweight people seeking help.

Kaplan, H., Sadock, B., & Grebb, J. (Eds.). (1994). *Kaplan and Sadock's synopsis of psychiatry* (7th ed.). Baltimore: Williams & Wilkins.

Includes the definitions and classifications of mental illness as contained in the ICD-10.

Keel, P. K., Dorer, D. J., Eddy, K. T., Franko, D., Charatan, D. L., & Herzog, D. B. (2003). Predictors of mortality in eating disorders. *Archives of General Psychiatry, 60*, 179–183.

The study concluded that clinicians treating patients with anorexia nervosa should carefully assess patterns of alcohol use during the course of care because one third of women who had alcoholism and died had no history of an alcohol use disorder at time of intake.

Keel, P. K., & Mitchell, J. E. (1997). Outcome in bulimia nervosa. *American Journal of Psychiatry, 154*, 313–321.

This study concluded that treatment interventions may speed eventual recovery but do not appear to alter outcome more than 5 years following presentation. Long-term outcome for women diagnosed with bulimia nervosa remains unclear.

Keel, P. K., Mitchell, J. E., Miller, K. B., Davis, T. L., & Crow, S. J. (1999). Long-term outcome of bulimia nervosa. *Archives of General Psychiatry, 56*, 63–69.
The findings suggest that the number of women who continue to meet full criteria for bulimia nervosa declines as the duration of follow-up increases.

Lock, J., LeGrange, D., Agras, W. S., & Dare, C. (2001). *Treatment manual for anorexia nervosa: A family-based approach*. New York: The Guilford Press.
Provides a detailed and authoritative guide to the Maudesley approach for the treatment of adolescents with anorexia nervosa and their families.

McGilley, B. M., & Pryor, T. L. (1998). Assessment and treatment of bulimia nervosa. *American Family Physician, 57*, 11.
Bulimia nervosa is characterized by binge eating and inappropriate compensatory behaviors, such as vomiting, fasting, excessive exercise, and the misuse of diuretics, laxatives, or enemas. Although the etiology of this disorder is unknown, genetic and neurochemical factors have been implicated.

National Heart, Lung, and Blood Institute. (n.d.). Clinical guidelines on the identification, evaluation, and treatment of overweight and obesity in adults—Guidelines on overweight and obesity: Electronic textbook. Retrieved October 1, 2006, from http://www.nhlbi.nih.gov/guidelines/obesity/ob_home.htm
The National Heart, Lung, and Blood Institute, in cooperation with the National Institute of Diabetes and Digestive and Kidney Diseases, released the first federal guidelines on the identification, evaluation, and treatment of overweight and obesity.

National Institute of Mental Health. (2001). *Eating disorders. Facts about eating disorders and the search for solutions*. Bethesda, MD: National Institute of Mental Health, National Institutes of Health, U.S. Department of Health and Human Services. (NIH 01-4901). Retrieved October 5, 2006, from http://www.nimh.nih.gov/publicat/eatingdisorders.cfm
A detailed booklet that describes symptoms, causes, and treatments, with information on getting help and coping.

National Institute of Mental Health. (2002). *The development of research priorities for the treatment of anorexia*. Bethesda, MD: National Institute of Mental Health, National Institutes of Health, U.S. Department of Health and Human Services. Retrieved October 5, 2006, from: http://www.nimh.nih.gov/scientificmeetings/ansummary.cfm
Given the limited progress in identifying effective treatments for anorexia nervosa, a workshop was co-sponsored by the NIH Office of Rare Diseases and the National Institute of Mental Health. This publication records the recommendations from the workshop regarding research priorities.

New York Health Plan Association. (n.d.). Bariatric surgery primer. Food for thought. *Obesity Surgery Project*. Albany, NY: Author
Bariatric surgery is a last resort for many who have struggled with being overweight and obese. This pamphlet provides information for those who are considering the surgery.

Newman, C. (2004, August). Why are we so fat? *National Geographic*, 46–61.
The obesity crisis is the result of simple math. It's a calories in, calories out calculation.

Simon, G. E., von Korff, M., Saunders, K., Miglioretti, D. L., Crane, P. K., van Belle, G., et al. (2006). Association between obesity and psychiatric disorders in the U.S. adult population. *Archives of General Psychiatry, 63*, 824–830.
An evaluation of the relationship between obesity and a range of mood, anxiety, and substance use disorders in the U.S. general population.

Spitzer, R. L., Yanovski, S., Wadden, T., Wing, R., Marcus, M. D., Stunkard, A., et al. (1993). Binge eating disorder: Its further validation in a multisite study. *International Journal of Eating Disorders, 13*(2), 137–153.
This is a study of binge eating disorder and the large number of individuals who suffer from recurrent binge eating, but who do not regularly engage in the compensatory behaviors to avoid weight gain seen in bulimia nervosa.

Steinhausen, H. C. (2002). The outcome of anorexia nervosa in the 20th century. *American Journal of Eating Disorders, 22*, 147–151.
This review addresses the outcomes of anorexia nervosa and whether they changed over the second half of the 20th century.

Steinhausen, H. C., Winkler, C., & Meier, M. (1997). Eating disorders in adolescence in a Swiss epidemiological study. *International Journal of Eating Disorders, 22*, 147–151.
This study concludes that the full clinical syndromes of anorexia nervosa and bulimia nervosa in adolescents are by far less frequent than individual symptoms of eating disorders.

Stice, E., Spangler, D. L., & Agras, W. S. (2002). Exposure to media-portrayed thin-ideal images adversely affects vulnerable girls: A longitudinal experiment. *Journal of Social and Clinical Psychology, 20*, 271–289.
A study that concluded exposure to the thin-ideal image resulted in an increase in body dissatisfaction but not negative affect or heart rate.

Sullivan, P. F. (1995). Mortality in anorexia nervosa. *American Journal of Psychiatry, 152*(7), 1073–1074.

The study indicated that the aggregate estimated mortality rate for subjects with anorexia nervosa is substantially greater than that reported for female psychiatric inpatients and for the general population.

Walsh, B. T., & Devlin, M. J. (1998). Eating disorders: Progress and problems. *Science, 280*, 1387–1390.

This article reviews current thinking on the etiology and treatment of the two major eating disorders and a related syndrome, binge eating disorder.

Wysoker, A. (2002). A conceptual model of weight loss and weight regain. An intervention for change. *Journal of the American Psychiatric Nurses Association, 8*, 168–173.

The model offers a framework for treatment and includes three different approaches: 1) one can lose weight and keep it off; 2) it may be impossible to lose weight and keep it off; and 3) women will continue to try to lose weight, despite the long history of losing weight and gaining the lost weight back.

Wysoker, A. (2005). The lived experience of choosing bariatric surgery to lose weight. *Journal of the American Psychiatric Nurses Association, 11*, 26–34.

The purpose of this research was to explore issues related to having a surgical procedure performed to lose weight.

Internet Resources

http://nursing.jbpub.com/psychiatric

Visit http://nursing.jbpub.com/psychiatric for interactive exercises, NCLEX review questions, WebLinks, and more.

CHAPTER 21

Sleep Disorders

Winifred Z. Kennedy

LEARNING OBJECTIVES

After reading this chapter, you will be able to:

- Define dyssomnias and parasomnias and give examples of each.
- Differentiate normal and abnormal sleep patterns.
- Identify factors important in the assessment of sleep disorders.
- Describe appropriate interventions for various sleep disorders.

KEY TERMS

Breathing-related sleep disorders
Cataplexy
Circadian rhythm
Dyssomnia
Hypersomnia
Insomnia
Multiple sleep latency test (MSLT)
Narcolepsy
Nightmare
Nonrapid eye movement (NREM)
Parasomnia
Periodic limb movements (PLM)
Polysomnography
Rapid eye movement (REM)
Restless leg syndrome (RLS)
Sleep architecture
Sleep terror disorder
Sleepwalking

http://nursing.jbpub.com/psychiatric

Visit http://nursing.jbpub.com/psychiatric for interactive exercises, NCLEX review questions, WebLinks, and more.

Introduction

Sleep problems are a common experience caused by variations in environment; developmental stages and psychosocial stressors; work, school, and travel schedules; use of medicines or substance abuse; and physical and mental health. Stephen King's novel *Insomnia* captures the exquisite nature of the problems encountered by an insomniac and uses them as the basis for a fantastical horror story. In the beginning of the novel, the main character begins a search for the solution to his sleeping troubles, following a rather common course of seeking advice from friends and physicians, information from popular and medical sources, treatments from folk remedies and pharmacotherapy, and trials of complementary therapies including hypnosis and acupuncture. Others with sleep problems can understand the character's discomfort, search for a cure, and accompanying physical and mental changes experienced as the sleeplessness continues. Sleep problems begin to pervade every aspect of the insomniac's life. The character in *Insomnia* eventually experiences perceptual disturbances and an altered sense of reality with continued sleep deprivation.

It is occasionally difficult to differentiate between normal, temporary variations in sleep patterns and sleep disorders. The amount of time spent sleeping normally varies and decreases with age. Most Americans report sleeping 6.8 hours on weekdays, which is below the average number of hours of sleep considered to be necessary for most people. Short sleepers, people who normally require a shortened or briefer period of sleep or less time than average when compared with others, and long sleepers, or people who normally require a greater period of sleep or more time sleeping than average, are within normal variations. Rest and activity patterns vary between people who normally function better in the morning ("larks") and those who do better at night ("owls"). Problematic symptoms such as sleepwalking or night terrors may occur during particular periods (such as in childhood). These are temporary conditions rather than sleep disorders because they are of limited duration and interference with general functioning.

General Description of Sleep Disorders

Four main divisions of sleep disorders exist: primary sleep disorder, sleep disorder related to another mental disorder, sleep disorder caused by a general medical condition, and substance-induced sleep disorder. The *Diagnostic and Statistical Manual of Mental Disorders,* Fourth Edition, Text Revision (*DSM-IV-TR*) identifies these disorders according to etiology and the disturbance in the amount, quality, and timing of sleep and associated physiologic and behavioral problems (American Psychiatric Association [APA], 2000).

Although everyone at some point may complain about the quality or quantity of their sleep, most people eventually do sleep. Clients with fatal familial insomnia, a rare prion disorder found in family clusters, are the exception. This disorder causes symptoms similar to thalamic dementia such as Creutzfeldt-Jakob disease.

Primary Sleep Disorders

Primary sleep disorders include **dyssomnias** (sleep disorders involving impaired amount, quality, and timing of sleep) and **parasomnias** (sleep disorders involving abnormal physiologic and behavioral events associated with sleep). Dyssomnias include primary **insomnia**, primary **hypersomnia**, **narcolepsy**, **breathing-related sleep disorder**, **circadian rhythm** sleep disorder, and nonspecific dyssomnias (dyssomnia not otherwise specified [NOS]). Parasomnias include **nightmare** disorder, **rapid eye movement (REM)** sleep behavior disorder, **sleep terror disorder**, **sleepwalking** disorder, and nonspecific parasomnias (parasomnia NOS). These disorders are generally coded on Axis I. Breathing-related sleep disorders also may be coded on Axis III. Some of the disorders, such as primary hypersomnia, may be further specified as recurrent if they occur repeatedly. Circadian rhythm sleep disorder also may be further specified according to type (delayed sleep phase, jet lag, shift work, or unspecified).

Sleep Disorders Related to Another Mental Disorder

Sleep disorders related to another mental disorder include insomnia related to another mental disorder and hypersomnia related to another mental disorder. These disorders are generally coded on Axis I, and the associated (Axis I or II) mental disorder is named along with the type of sleep disturbance. In addition, the associated mental disorder is appropriately coded on Axis I or II. For example, insomnia related to a major depressive disorder is coded on Axis I, and the associated mood disorder, major depressive disorder, should be coded on Axis I. Conversely, hypersomnia related to avoidant personality disorder is coded on Axis I, and the associated personality disorder, avoidant personality disorder, should be coded on Axis II.

Sleep Disorder Caused by a General Medical Condition

Sleep disorders caused by a general medical condition may be specified according to several subtypes such as insomnia, hypersomnia, parasomnia, or mixed. The diagnosis of sleep disorder caused by a general medical condition is named along with the subtype of sleep disorder and the associated general medical condition. The diagnosis is coded on Axis I. In addition, the associated general medical condition and its *International Classification of Disorders* (*ICD-9-CM*) code should be noted on Axis III. For example, sleep disorder caused by Parkinson's disease, insomnia type, is coded on Axis I and Parkinson's disease with its *ICD-9-CM* code should be coded on Axis III.

Substance-Induced Sleep Disorder

Substance-induced sleep disorder is identified according to several subtypes (insomnia, hypersomnia, parasomnia, or mixed) and further specified as either with onset during intoxication or with onset during withdrawal. The specific disorder and type is named along with the suspected causative substance. An example is amphetamine-induced sleep disorder, insomnia type, with onset during intoxication, or amphetamine-induced sleep disorder, hypersomnia type, with onset during withdrawal. If more than one substance is suspected, each should be listed separately; if the substance is unknown, unknown substance-induced sleep disorder may be used. The disorder is generally coded on Axis I. In addition, some sleep disorders may be associated with medication prescribed in therapeutic amounts for a specific general medical condition.

Incidence and Prevalence

An estimated 40% of women and 30% of men report sleep problems. More than 50% of women and men older than 65 years of age report sleep difficulties. Approximately 15% to 25% of clients seen in sleep disorder clinics for complaints of chronic insomnia are diagnosed with primary insomnia: 5–10% of those with complaints of excessive sleepiness are diagnosed with primary hypersomnia, 0.02–0.16% with narcolepsy, and 1–10% with breathing-related sleep disorders (APA, 2000). Approximately 20–60% of all shift workers report chronic sleep problems (APA). Clients with concomitant mental and medical disorders have a higher prevalence of sleep disorders. In one study, mental disorders were associated with a diagnosis of primary insomnia in approximately 77% of cases (Nowell et al., 1997).

The 2005 Omnibus Sleep in America Poll (OSAP) conducted by the National Sleep Foundation (2005) revealed that 44% of all respondents felt they had a problem with sleep and 20% reported it took them more than 30 minutes to fall asleep. Insomnia was experienced once a week by 75% of respondents, and 46% experienced excessive daytime sleepiness. Driving while drowsy was experienced by 60% of automobile drivers. In previous studies, of those who reported sleep problems, approximately 27% percent stated they used medications to sleep (10% used prescription medications, 16% used over-the-counter [OTC] medications, and 1% used both prescription and OTC medications), and approximately 11% of respondents used alcohol. The symptom of snoring loud enough to be heard through a door, which indicates a breathing-related sleep disorder, was reported by 16% of respondents. Approximately 3% of respondents reported that a physician had diagnosed them with **restless leg syndrome (RLS)**, uncomfortable pulling or crawling sensations of lower limbs that occur at times of rest or sleep, or **periodic limb movements (PLM)**, twitching or uncontrolled movements of the upper or lower limbs that occur at times of rest or sleep, or both. Among elderly clients with probable dyssomnias, PLMs were most common, affecting approximately 25–44%, followed by breathing-related sleep disorders that affected 24–42%, and RLS, affecting 29% of those over 50 years of age and 44% of those over 65 years of age (Beck-Little & Weinrich, 1998; Feinsilver & Hertz, 1993; Montplaisir, Godbout, Pelletier, & Warnes, 1994).

Etiology

Sleep disorders can be related to disturbances caused by internal or external stimuli, physiological changes and medical disorders, or pharmacokinetics and pharmacodynamics. Our ability to sleep can be affected by our habits, mood, or degree of fatigue. Sleep may vary at different developmental levels.

Environment

Many sleep disorders are caused by environmental problems and poor sleep hygiene. Ambience is important for sleep, as is establishing a basic routine. In preparing infants and young children for sleep, usually a great deal of attention is given to the surrounding comfort measures and routine. The young are fed and cleaned. The sleep space is made inviting with clean, soft bedding. Reduced environmental stimuli (dimmed lighting, decreased attractions) and perhaps soft music or a lullaby are part of the routine, as are forms of relaxation such as touch or massage, prayers or guided imagery, and reading. In contrast, in the average adult's contemporary bedroom, the bed shares space with multiple distractions such as the radio, television, telephone, and computers (see **Figure 21-1**). The person must contend with

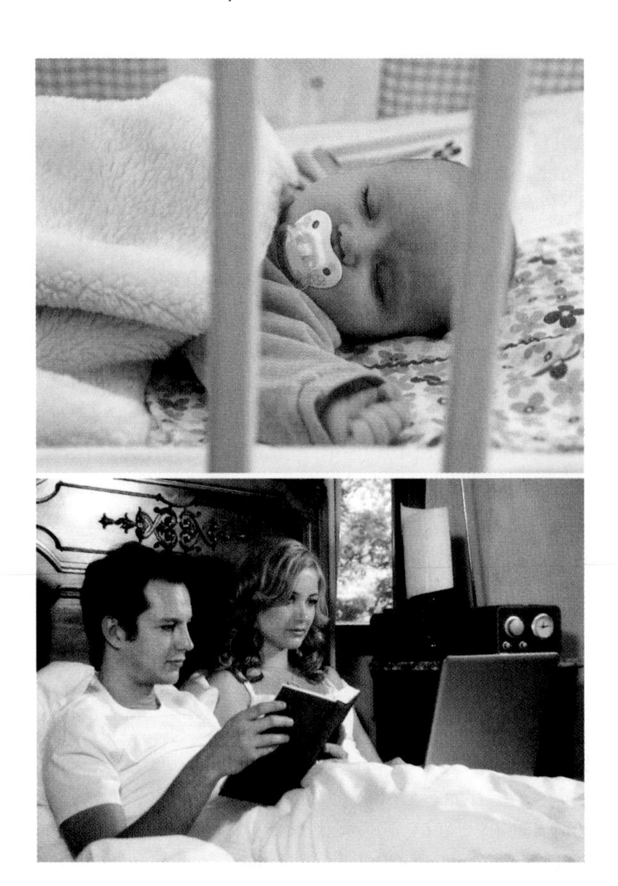

Figure 21-1 **Children and adults often sleep in rooms with very different atmospheres.**

An environment that is free from distractions and an established bedtime routine can be conducive to a good night's sleep.

the conflicting demands of multiple roles, relationships, and occupations. Overtired, under- or overfed, and overstimulated, the adult uses the bed as a battleground rather than a retreat from extrinsic stimuli.

Rhythm-Disrupting Stressors

Hospital environments may be an extrinsic source of sleep problems. This strange environment with its machines, treatments, 24-hour operating schedule, roommates, and absence of individualized control over temperature, noise, and lighting contributes to disturbances in circadian rhythms, comfort levels, and psychologic and physiologic regulatory mechanisms.

Rhythm-disrupting stressors are factors in many sleep problems. Changes in routine, such as finishing a project or studying for an examination, traveling across time zones, working overtime during the week and oversleeping on weekends, and shift work or shift rotation can temporarily or chronically disrupt sleep patterns. Women often are exposed to the common rhythm-disrupting stressors of pregnancy and childbirth, menopause, child care and other caretaking roles, and juggling multiple roles throughout their lives (Beeber, 1996). Individuals with medical, surgical, and psychiatric problems may experience rhythm-disrupting stressors related to anticipated or actual pain, treatments, pharmacotherapy, and hospitalization. Clients with mental disorders such as mood, somatoform, anxiety, and panic disorders; substance-use disorders; and posttraumatic stress disorder also may experience disruptions of sleep-wake cycles.

Critical Thinking Question How does a hospital environment contribute to sleep disturbances? Suggest some ways these factors can be mitigated.

Poorly Modulated Regulatory Function

Poorly modulated regulatory function is another cause of sleep disorders. Sleep patterns change with normal aging, and many elderly clients have a greater amount of subjective complaints concerning the amount and quality of their sleep. Some age-related changes include an increased time spent in bed, an increased proportion of stage 1 or light sleep, an increase in the number of abnormal breathing events and leg movements, a decrease in the proportion of slow-wave sleep or deep sleep, and rapid eye movement (REM) sleep latency (McCall, 1995). Many medical and psychiatric disorders are associated with sleep disturbances. Clients with cognitive disorders may experience fluctuations in states of consciousness in delirium or sleep-wake cycle variations in dementia including night-day reversal. Other neurologic disorders such as brainstem lesions, Parkinson's disease, Huntington's disease, cerebral vascular disorders, and multiple sclerosis are often associated with sleep disorders.

Physical and Mental Disorders

Clients with breathing problems such as bronchitis, chronic obstructive pulmonary disease, or restrictive lung diseases generally experience sleep disorders. Clients with chronic pain problems such as arthritis and fibromyalgia and those with medical, metabolic, and endocrine disorders such as cancer, diabetes, gastric reflux, prostatitis, and thyroid problems also experience sleep disorders. In addition, many clients with schizophrenia or manic-depressive disorder experience sleep problems related to impaired regulatory functioning. For example, a manic client may experience periods of hyperactivity, restlessness, and extreme motor agitation with continual movement and pacing that lead to complete exhaustion.

Critical Thinking Question What are some nursing interventions that could be used to reduce internal and external stimuli?

Pharmaceuticals and Other Substances

Many pharmaceuticals cause or worsen sleep disorders. Some medications and substances that may cause problems include alcohol, amphetamines, antidepressants, anesthetics, anxiolytics, antihistamines, antihypertensives, barbiturates, bromides, bronchodilators, caffeine, corticosteroids, decongestants, hallucinogens, levodopa, opioids, and tranquilizers. Even hypnotics and sedatives specifically intended to treat clients with sleep disorders occasionally worsen the problems.

Critical Thinking Question What are some of the possible etiological factors that should be assessed in a sleep disorder?

Clinical Example

Danielle is a 32-year-old woman brought to the emergency department by police after her family reported she was loud and angry as well as verbally and physically threatening them. The family reported that Danielle has been unable to sleep for the past week, and had not been eating or bathing. In the ED, Danielle was talking nonstop, singing at times, and pacing. Her family stated she had stopped wearing shoes, and her feet were swollen and covered with superficial abrasions. She told staff that she was writing a book about her life experiences as a priestess and that she had to leave immediately because she had a dinner appointment with the pope and Madonna.

Clinical Example

Saul, an 84-year-old man with a history of progressive dementia and multiple medical problems, is brought to the clinic for a routine evaluation. His daughter who is the primary caretaker reports that he is up all night and is very disruptive to the household. During the day, both she and the patient are exhausted so she lets him sleep as much as possible, and doesn't disturb him unless he awakens. She feels he needs medications to calm him down and an increase in his sleeping medications.

Physiology

Normal sleep is an essential state of consciousness that is periodic, cyclical, and reversible. Its restorative function manifests as alterations in the individual's physiologic and behavioral patterns of interaction. Metabolic and neural activity continue with some variations during sleep as they do during the waking state. During sleep, neural activity is redistributed or reorganized, changes occur in muscle tone and sensory responsiveness, and, usually, the amount and type of activity and interaction with the environment are decreased. **Sleep architecture** is the amount (total sleep time and length of sleep stages) and distribution of sleep stages (cyclical alterations in sleep states).

Sleep Stages

Sleep stages include alternating states of REM sleep and **non-REM (NREM)**, or slow wave sleep. The five sleep stages of normal sleep architecture are:

- *Stage 1:* NREM and low voltage characterize this stage. This is the transition from wakefulness to sleep characterized by drowsiness. Stage 1 normally lasts a few minutes, 2–5% of total sleep time.
- *Stage 2:* This stage is characterized by NREM and sleep complexes on the electroencephalogram (EEG). In stage 2, muscle tone and cerebral activity decrease. This stage accounts for 50% of total sleep time.
- *Stage 3:* This stage is characterized by NREM, delta waves, and slow-wave sleep. This is the transition to stage 4. Stage 3 lasts one third to one half of the night, 10–20% of total sleep time.
- *Stage 4:* This stage is characterized by NREM, deepest sleep, continued slow-wave sleep, and delta waves. The metabolic rate and temperature decrease. Stage 4 is characterized by the lowest level of body functioning. It lasts for one third to one half of the night, 10–20% of total sleep time.
- *Stage 5:* The REM dream state alternates with NREM sleep. Long periods of desynchronized activity alternate with periods of activity similar to alertness. The vital signs are irregular, atonia occurs, and the person has increased frequency of dreaming as morning approaches. Stage 5 accounts for 25% of total sleep time.

The sleep cycle usually begins in the NREM state, and NREM sleep predominates in the first one third of the cycle, while REM sleep predominates in the last one third. The cycle alternates between NREM and REM sleep, with an average NREM-REM cycle lasting approximately

Sleep architecture refers to the five stages of the normal sleep cycle. An average NREM-REM cycle lasts approximately 90 minutes.

Dreaming, the experience of emotions, images, and thoughts during sleep, occurs during REM sleep.

90 minutes with rare, brief periods of wakefulness. Variations in sleep cycles are determined by measuring the electrical potential difference between two points on the scalp with an EEG. An EEG records the frequency and amplitude of neuron activity and behavior changes during various states of consciousness and stages of sleep such as alertness, drowsiness, slow-wave NREM sleep, and paradoxical REM sleep. In the waking state, the EEG records alpha waves and mixed-frequency low-voltage activity. In the sleeping state, this alpha-wave activity decreases, and the cyclical pattern of the five sleep stages begins.

Biological rhythms can have an almost clock-like rhythm. Ultradian rhythm (e.g., periods, seconds, minutes, hours) is less than 20- to 24-hour periodicity (e.g., NREM and REM sleep stages). Circadian rhythm (about 1 day) is approximately 24-hour periodicity (e.g., sleep-wake cycles are approximately 23 to 26 hours). Infradian rhythm (e.g., periods of days, weeks, years) is more than 24-hour periodicity (e.g., menstrual cycle).

Neural System Effects

Different parts of the brain such as the cortex, hypothalamic system, and reticular system are important for wakefulness and an alert state. Neural systems affecting arousal and sleep are influenced by different parts of the brain's reticular formation. Descending, local, and ascending neural pathways converge on the reticular formation in the core of the brain stem and project from the reticular formation to the brain stem and cerebellum, spinal cord, and higher areas of the cerebellum such as the cerebral cortex, basal ganglia, and limbic system. Aside from the reticular system and noradrenergic and serotonergic nuclei, the cortex influences slow-wave NREM sleep; and stimulation of the pontine reticular formation containing cholingergic nuclei influences REM sleep. The locus coeruleus contains norepinephrine-releasing neurons active during slow-wave NREM sleep, and the raphe nuclei contain serotonergic nuclei active during slow-wave NREM sleep. Circadian rhythms are internal rhythms that affect the sleep stages. Light energy in the visual cortex and suprachiasmatic nucleus of the hypothalamus direct circadian rhythm as well as influencing neuroendocrine changes that can affect mood. REM sleep, in particular, is associated with a circadian distribution. Environmental cues and light-dark variations affect the synchronization of sleep cycles. Other rhythmic physiologic variations may affect thermoregulation; endocrine, renal, and hepatic functions; cardiovascular, immune, and respiratory systems; and pharmacokinetics. Neurotransmitters such as acetylcholine, adenosine, 5-hydroxytryptamine, dopamine, norepinephrine, and serotonin influence the initiation and maintenance of sleep-wake cycles. Neurotransmitters influence various patterns of activation, different phases of alertness and arousal, and slow-wave NREM and REM sleep.

Abnormal Sleep

Abnormal sleep is associated with disturbances in slow-wave NREM and REM sleep stages, insufficient sleep, arousals with awakenings or partial awakenings, or hypersomnia with prolonged sleep or unplanned daytime sleeping. Disruptions of normal sleep architecture, sleep efficiency (percentage of time spent asleep compared with time spent in bed), and sleep continuity (balance of sleep to wakefulness during normal sleep cycle) contribute to complaints of abnormal sleep. The National Sleep Foundation considers 8 hours of sleep to be the normal daily requirement. Many complaints regarding abnormal sleep consist of the perception of an inadequate amount of sleep (less than 7 hours). Clients with sleep deprivation (prolonged episodes of sleep loss over time) generally show disturbances of REM sleep and disruption of normal sleep cycles. Clients with sleep fragmentation (frequent interruptions of normal sleep cycles) show disturbances in daytime alertness. New parents frequently complain of this, as do hospitalized clients who are awakened for treatments and clients with RLS, PLM, and breathing-related sleep disorders. RLS and PLM are affected by circadian rhythms and are usually worse in the evening and night than in the day. Regarding excessive amounts of sleep (hypersomnia), clients generally complain of long periods (8 to 12 hours) of undisrupted sleep at night and problems awakening and staying awake in the day. In hypersomnia, the REM and NREM sleep stages are normal. Clients with narcolepsy (a less common sleep disorder) also sleep excessive amounts, and experience multiple sleep-onset REM periods, sleep attacks, sleep paralysis, and hallucinations. Circadian rhythm sleep disorders may be caused by delayed sleep phases, chronic sleep deprivation, travel-induced jet lag disturbances crossing time zones, and shift work or shift rotation. Jet lag disturbances and shift work cause a mismatch between the client's internal rhythm and need for sleep and the external rhythms of a different time zone or the environmental demands of shift work. Clients with these rhythm disruptions generally have decreased stage 2 and REM sleep. Parasomnias such as nightmare disorder, sleep terror disorder, and sleepwalking disorder are associated with REM sleep disorders and behavioral and motor manifestations of disturbed sleep and sleep-wake transitions. Studies of overtime and extended working hours show relationships with poor general health and illness, job injuries and errors, premature births, weight gain, and increased alcohol and smoking (Caruso, Hitchcock, Dick, Russo, & Schmit, 2004).

Clinical Presentation

The sleep disorder may be the primary or secondary complaint presented by the client. These clients frequently present with fatigue, the symptom of overwhelming and persistent tiredness or inertia. Common sleep disturbances reported by elderly clients include spending more time in bed but sleeping less, having problems falling asleep, waking frequently during the night, and early morning awakening (Beck-Little & Weinrich, 1998). The presentation of symptoms is often the most important factor in the differential diagnosis. Many medical and mental disorders are associated with feelings of fatigue and are often the underlying cause for the problem. Clients with a related mental disorder may report problems getting restful sleep, problems falling asleep, problems staying asleep, and early morning awakening (Nowell et al., 1997). Sleep disturbances and disorders may be associated with pain, physical illness, and hospitalization or other environmental changes. The sleep disorder may be the primary subjective complaint of clients with stress-related physiologic changes or psychiatric disorders and may be the result of an affective or behavioral disorder or of substance abuse, or a side effect of pharmacotherapy.

CASE STUDY Mr. T.

Mr. T., a 55-year-old man, came to the clinic complaining of fatigue. He stated that he found it difficult to get through a day of normal activity without feeling tired, and he just did not feel like himself at all. He stated that he felt as if he had a virus, but that he had no symptoms other than tiredness and listlessness. Mr. T.'s family medical doctor suggested that the cause might be depression after the client reported he was having problems managing at work and home. He had no history of medical problems, other than occasional sinus problems and headaches, and was taking no medications at present. He had no history of psychiatric problems or drug or alcohol abuse. Mr. T. stated that he felt he was under a great deal of stress at work and was having more problems concentrating on the tasks at hand. He stated that his job was very demanding and required long hours. Although Mr. T. reported that he felt sad and irritable at times, and was less interested in activities at home and work, he said he did not feel particularly depressed. He had an increased appetite and had gained weight. He often felt drowsy at work, found himself nodding off, and would sometimes fall asleep sitting and watching television at night. He said that, even with the daytime sleeping and napping, he just never felt rested.

Mr. T.'s wife stated she also felt that his problem was too much sleep and that he would be better off if he would just get up and do something. In contrast, Mrs. T. said she was the one who had problems sleeping, because Mr. T.'s loud snoring kept her awake. He often awakened her with what seemed to be gasping or choking noises or by sitting up in bed, but then he would quiet down again, lie down, and fall back asleep without seeming to awaken. She said he had always been a noisy and restless sleeper, but things had gotten worse as he had grown older. It had gotten to the point where she felt that separate beds or even a separate bedroom might be a good idea.

The initial clinical impression is a breathing-related sleep disorder. Asking the client's partner about sleeping habits gives valuable information. Questions regarding weight gain and collar size and other medical conditions or medication use can be included in the nursing assessment. The client should be referred for further medical evaluation or to a sleep disorder clinic. **Polysomnography**, diagnostic studies involving recordings of oximetry (oxygen saturation), breathing efforts and airflow, EEG, electromyography (EMG), electrooculogram (measurement of extraocular eye movements), and a combination of continuous positive airway pressure (CPAP) and non-CPAP trials aid in the differential diagnosis. Treatment of a possible obstructive sleep apnea syndrome involves evaluation, medical or surgical treatment of the breathing problem, CPAP, and weight loss.

NURSING CARE PLAN Breathing-Related Sleep Disorder

Expected Outcomes	Interventions	Evaluations
• Will be able to demonstrate proper use of CPAP. • Will experience decreased snoring. • Will experience decreased daytime sleepiness. • Will begin participation in weight reduction program.	• Educate the client and partner on the proper use of CPAP. • Confirm with significant others their perception of the quality of the client's sleep. • Assess exercise and activity patterns. • Reinforce client participation in the weight reduction program.	• Observing for return demonstration in CPAP use. • Validating the adaptation to and ongoing use of CPAP at continued intervals. • Taking reports of involvement in exercise program. • Monitoring involvement over time in a weight reduction program and maintenance of weight loss.

Visit http://nursing.jbpub.com/psychiatric for additional care plans and exercises.

CASE STUDY Mr. M.

Mr. M., a 55-year-old high school principal, was receiving short-term disability after knee surgery. He came to the emergency room complaining of an inability to sleep for 2 days. The problem had started approximately 2 months previously but was getting progressively worse. He was evaluated by the psychiatric clinical nurse specialist. Mr. M. stated that he had injured his knee playing tennis just before the start of the fall term and had been very nervous about the idea of surgery. At first, he thought the sleeping problems were a result of the pain he experienced and the surgery. However, the various sleep medications he used were unable to help him resume a normal sleep pattern. The client stated that he had been increasingly anxious and depressed since he had knee surgery. He said he felt as if his world were falling apart and that he was losing control of everything. Mr. M. stated that he did not know what was happening to him or how to stop it. He only knew that he felt humiliated by his inability to do anything about how he was feeling and that he was worried about everything. His worst fear, that he would never be normal again after surgery and would be permanently disabled, appeared to be coming true. He said he was particularly frightened by thoughts that his life was not worthwhile, that he had accomplished nothing, and that he would be better off dead. His wife reported that he had been increasingly dependent, had a decreased appetite with a 20-pound weight loss, and had experienced mood swings.

The client had been on various sleep medications for different periods and at different dosages over the previous 2 months, including lorazepam (Ativan), alprazolam (Xanax), buspirone (Buspar), clonazepam (Klonopin), and trifluoperazine (Stelazine). These were prescribed initially by his orthopedist, then by his family doctor, and later by a third doctor who was recommended by his managed care company. He was presently taking sertraline (Zoloft) and thioridazine (Mellaril) prescribed by a psychiatrist he had consulted as an out-patient 1 week before and oxazepam (Serax) prescribed by yet another physician to whom he was referred by his managed care company. His wife reported that for the past week, with medications, Mr. M. had continued to have problems falling asleep. He would sleep approximately 2 hours after taking the medications and then sleep restlessly, often awakening in a panic-like state in which he would be agitated and ruminating on financial problems and unrealistic fears of losing his job. She described him as an independent, high-functioning man who never had a spare moment before the accident that led to his knee surgery but who now seemed unable to do anything for himself. He had no history of psychiatric problems or drug or alcohol abuse.

The initial clinical impression is sleep disorder caused by a mental disorder (depression) that was complicated by polypharmacy. The nursing assessment can include information regarding medical and psychiatric history and validation of medication changes and actual use.

NURSING CARE PLAN **Insomnia Caused by Mental Disorder**

Expected Outcomes	Interventions	Evaluations
• Will resume normal sleep patterns. • Will decrease fears of falling asleep and staying asleep. • Will select and use appropriate sleep medications. • Will be able to fulfill normal occupational and social roles without impairment.	• Foster a safe environment conducive to sleep. • Assess and observe sleep patterns. • Monitor pharmacotherapy. • Assist client in developing short- and long-term goals.	• Subjective reports of decreased fears surrounding falling asleep and staying asleep. • Development of normal sleep patterns. • Decreased use of sleep medications/short-term use of medications. • Return to work without impaired functioning from insomnia.

Visit http://nursing.jbpub.com/psychiatric for additional care plans and exercises.

The nurse should determine if the client is getting too little or too much sleep. In addition, clients often complain of problems just before, during, or just after sleep, such as during preparation for sleep or the periods of time while just asleep or awakening. Environmental problems, situational disturbances, and recent changes in schedule or time, including travel, should be determined. Some clients' descriptions of difficulties focus on problems while sleeping (i.e., they may be aware of disturbances caused by sleep apnea, nightmares, or RLS). Family members may present additional clues by describing their observations of the client's sleeping patterns and domestic habits.

Clinical Course and Complications

Some people complain that they sleep too little and others that they sleep too much. The clinical course can vary according to the type of sleep disorder, the pattern of sleep-wakefulness, and the individual's response to normal variations in sleep. Some complications are related to things outside our control such as familial tendencies or medical disorders and others to factors more within our control such as work and travel schedules.

Insomnia

Insomnia is characterized by difficulty initiating, maintaining, or experiencing restorative sleep. It is associated with increased arousal at night, anxiety, impaired daytime performance, and negative sleep conditioning (APA, 2000). Insomnia may be temporary (associated with a rhythm-disrupting stress such as normal bereavement) or chronic. It may be related to a mental disorder, a general medical condition, or substance abuse. Chronic insomnia presents similarly to learned or psychophysiologic insomnia in that attempting to sleep becomes a struggle associated with excessive time spent in bed or trying to compensate for missed sleep (McCall, 1995). Chronic insomnia may be complicated by the negative conditioning associated with pyschophysiologic insomnia (APA, 2000). The medications used for insomnia occasionally cause or worsen insomnia.

Hypersomnia

Hypersomnia is characterized by excessive sleepiness at night or daily daytime sleep episodes. Although the quality of sleep is normal, the amount impairs daytime functioning. Hypersomnia is usually a chronic problem, but there are recurrent forms that last at least 3 days and occur several times a year for at least 2 years. Examples of recurrent forms of hypersomnia include problems of regulatory functioning such as Kleine-Levin syndrome and menstrual cycle–related symptoms of excessive sleep (APA, 2000). Complications of hypersomnia include sleep drunkenness (a state of confusion in which the client experiences a prolonged impaired state of alertness upon awakening) and automatic activity (a cognitive state in which the client engages in repetitive or stereotypic behaviors requiring little conscious thought) such as overeating.

Hypnagogic hallucinations are intense, dreamlike illusions that occur at the transition from wakefulness to sleep, just before falling asleep. Hypnopompic hallucinations are intense, dreamlike illusions that occur at the transition between sleep and awakening, just before awakening.

Narcolepsy

Narcolepsy is characterized by repeated sleep attacks (irresistible, periodic, unintended urges to sleep that are temporarily relieved by sleep periods of 10 to 20 minutes but return approximately 2 to 6 times per day), **cataplexy** (sudden periods of loss of muscle tone lasting from seconds to minutes), and recurrent episodes of REM sleep at times of sleep-wake transitions demonstrated by hypnopompic or hypnagogic hallucinations or sleep paralysis (temporary inability to move or speak). Chronic daytime sleepiness is a symptom and complication of narcolepsy. Episodes of cataplexy are triggered by strong emotions and increased by sleep deprivation. Sleep attacks and cataplexy impair social and occupational functioning and can cause traumatic injury.

The term *Pickwickian syndrome* came from a character (not Mr. Pickwick) in Charles Dickens's *The Pickwick Papers* who was forever falling asleep. The term was used to describe obesity related to hypoventilation and hypersomnia (Burwell, Robin, Whaley, & Bikelman, 1956).

Breathing-Related Sleep Disorders

Breathing-related sleep disorders are characterized by the disruption of normal sleep cycles as a result of ventilation abnormalities leading to insomnia or, more frequently, hypersomnia. Daytime sleepiness, memory problems, and irritability are frequent complications. The disorder's frequency increases with age. The development of these disorders is usually chronic, progressive, and potentially life threatening.

Obstructive sleep apnea syndrome, central sleep apnea syndrome, and central alveolar hypoventilation syndrome are breathing problems identified as sleep-related breathing conditions. Obstructive sleep apnea syndrome is associated with upper-airway structural abnormalities and obstructed respirations characterized by periods of loud snoring, gasps, silence, and body movements. It is more common among, but not limited to, heavy or overweight clients. Apneic periods resulting from airway obstruction usually last a few seconds. Central sleep apnea syndrome is characterized by periods of nonventilation or periods of Cheyne-Stokes respirations related to cardiac or neurologic problems without associated obstruction and loud snoring. Central alveolar hypoventilation is frequently seen in morbidly obese clients. It is associated with impaired ventilation with periods of decreased respirations lasting a few minutes, low arterial oxygen levels, and increased carbon dioxide levels.

Circadian Rhythm Sleep Disorders

Circadian rhythm sleep disorders include disrupted sleep patterns related to alterations of typical circadian patterns, in contrast to external and environmental demands that lead to impaired cognitive, social, or vocational functioning. The client may have problems falling asleep or staying awake at appropriate times, and the disorder may be associated with acute or chronic disruptions. Circadian rhythm sleep disorders are most commonly associated with travel across time zones (**Figure 21-2**). In addition, most people who work odd shifts or who have to rotate shifts never fully adjust to these rhythm changes. Fatigue, decreased vigilance, and poor work/school performance can be related to circadian rhythm sleep disorders.

Critical Thinking Question What are some ways in which nursing organizations, professional nurses, and employers have dealt with the ethical responsibilities of guarding against fatigue in the workplace related to shift work and voluntary or mandated extended work hours?

Clinical Example

Dylan is a 20-year-old man with no known medical problems brought to the emergency department after being involved in a motor vehicle accident, apparently after having fallen asleep while driving. Although the toxicology screen in the emergency department was negative, staff reported that the patient had acted strangely and acted as if he were unable to move or speak. Staff on the medical unit reported the patient complained of hallucinations early the next morning when he was getting up. His family reported that he always seemed to fall asleep during the day and had recently lost a job because of this, although he seemed to get enough sleep at night. They described him as very clumsy and said he had a history of falls. Because of this he was very shy and avoided activities where he might be embarrassed because this only seemed to make things worse. A recent medical exam and neurologic workup for seizures were negative.

Figure 21-2 Airline travel can cause circadian sleep rhythm disorders.

Parasomnias

Parasomnias are characterized by abnormal motor or physiologic behaviors that manifest during sleep. Nightmares and sleep terrors are usually accompanied by partial or complete awakenings. Nightmares are frequently associated with intense, frightening dreams during REM sleep that can be recalled by the client, who is easily awakened. Sleep terror disorder is associated with a high degree of autonomic arousal, unresponsiveness to others, no clear dream recall, and amnesia for the episode of sleep terror. Sleepwalking disorder is characterized by arousal, usually during NREM sleep, and complex motor activities such as walking or attempting other tasks. The event is followed by amnesia. Parasomnias are disturbing for the client and others in the same environment and interfere with sleep and daytime functioning.

Differential Diagnosis

Many variations of normal and abnormal sleep exist among individuals of different health status, developmental stage, and environmental situation. Careful physical examination and mental status evaluation are essential. Often the client's initial description of the complaint is incomplete or inaccurate, and it is helpful to obtain descriptions of the client's usual sleep habits and behaviors from others. A sleep history, a description of sleep behaviors over time, should be obtained. Sleep diaries or sleep logs also help differentiate the quality, quantity, and timing of sleep. In addition, psychophysiologic insomnia, the sleeplessness related to negative conditioning and learned sleep behaviors related to poor sleep hygiene, is common. Many clients with psychophysiologic insomnia report that their sleep improves when they are away from home (e.g., on vacation, in the sleep laboratory; McCall, 1995).

Many medical and mental disorders are associated with various sleep disorders, and identifying these factors is important in the differential diagnosis. These should be excluded before other sleep disorders are considered. Substances of abuse, therapeutic doses of pharmaceuticals, and exposure to toxins can contribute to sleep disorders. Carefully assess commonly associated problems before performing specific diagnostic tests for sleep disorders. For example, a client with a history of insomnia and travel across time zones probably has circadian rhythm disorder, whereas a client with a history of insomnia and depressive symptoms may have sleep problems resulting from a mood disorder rather than a primary sleep disorder.

Clients with medical problems such as diabetes, cardiovascular disease, gastric reflux, and prostate disease may also experience frequent nighttime arousals. Often medications, such as diuretics, or medication schedules that require nighttime awakenings or administration early in the day to avoid stimulating the client are the problem. If possible, symptoms should be controlled and medications evaluated to control for nighttime disturbances.

The diagnosis of RLS is often made based on the client's subjective experience of uncomfortable leg sensations that are particularly noted at bedtime and often relieved by movement. Clients often complain that these uncomfortable sensations prevent them from getting rest. Clients may experience problems falling asleep or experience arousals from sleep. Conversely, PLM disorder often does not wake the client; the suspected diagnosis is based on reports from others or is identified during polysomnography. The client may complain of muscle soreness or fatigue (Beck-Little & Weinrich, 1998).

Nightmares are frightening dreams that can be recalled by the client. In sleep terror disorder the client experiences amnesia, and has little or no dream recall.

The multiple, simultaneous diagnostic tests taken during the client's normal sleeping period are termed *polysomnography*. Usually done in a sleep laboratory, the tests help differentiate sleep disorders. Differences in brain activity at varying sleep stages are determined by EEG to exclude various disorders and confirm the diagnosis. The client is monitored outside of the sleep laboratory or hospital setting using wrist actigraphy, an assessment tool (Beck-Little & Weinrich, 1998). Polysomnography helps confirm whether apnea is present. Physical examination is also important in differentiating breathing-related sleep disorders. For example, identification of excessive soft tissue obstructing the upper airway is symptomatic of obstructive sleep apnea syndrome. A **multiple sleep latency test (MSLT)** confirms the duration of sleep latency periods. MSLT is a diagnostic sleep test in which the client is encouraged to take multiple daytime naps, usually at 2-hour intervals, to determine average sleep latency and REM episodes. Daytime MSLT with shortened sleep latency periods or the appearance of REM sleep during repeated MSLT indicates narcolepsy and helps differentiate narcolepsy from the excessive daytime sleepiness of hypersomnia. Wrist actigraphy allows the client to ambulate and may be used outside of a sleep laboratory. It may also be used for differential diagnosis (Beck-Little & Weinrich).

A multiple sleep latency test is used to differentiate narcolepsy from hypersomnia.

Management and Treatment

Anticipatory guidance, client education, and appropriate interventions are important to manage and treat sleep disorders. Psychophysiological or learned sleep disorders in particular are treated with behavioral therapies and changes in the sleep environment. Nonpharmacological interventions such as cognitive and behavioral therapies should be used first. Information regarding normal sleep hygiene allays the client's fears and encourages active involvement in treatment planning (McCall, 1995).

Critical Thinking Question Describe several normal variations in sleep patterns that can have their basis in situational or maturational differences. Can you think of any cultural factors that may influence sleep habits?

For most clients with sleep disorders, maintenance of a regular sleep routine and proper sleep hygiene is the first line of treatment. The evaluation and treatment of associated mental and medical disorders is secondary. All clients should avoid alcohol, drugs of abuse, and medications that can cause sleep disturbances. Pharmacologic interventions should be carefully evaluated and individualized.

Extrinsic and Intrinsic Factors

Modifying extrinsic factors, such as ventilation, lighting, and noise level in the sleep environment, or altering bedding or supports are the easiest changes to make. Changing individual routines by altering rest and activity patterns, decreasing the use of the bedroom and bed for activities other than sleep, changing the times of going to bed and awakening, and avoiding alcohol, caffeine, and other substances may be effective. Many clients find that a regular routine, perhaps including a light snack of turkey or milk (tryptophan) and a warm relaxing bath before bed, is helpful. Although strenuous exercise should be avoided because it is too stimulating, many clients, particularly those with RLS or PLM, find that some exercise or stretching routines are helpful prior to bedtime.

Considerations for Client and Family Education

- Variations in sleep patterns are normal across the lifespan and often are temporary.
- Sleep medications are not the primary means of treating sleep problems and are meant to be used as prescribed, usually on a temporary basis.
- Examination of sleep habits and sleep hygiene and change of patterns of behavior often provide long-term relief of sleep problems.
- Explain the benefits of avoiding caffeine, nicotine, alcohol, and large meals prior to going to bed.
- The administration of sleeping medications should be timed to avoid problems associated with participating in certain activities, such as use of machinery or driving.

Intrinsic factors such as perceived stress or the inability to relax occasionally are relieved using complementary therapies such as aroma therapy, deep-breathing exercises, guided meditation, or progressive relaxation exercises to aid in relaxation. Clients also may be encouraged to get out of bed rather than struggle to sleep and to engage briefly in another activity such as reading or light housekeeping until they feel tired.

Normalizing Circadian Rhythm

Circadian rhythm sleep disorder (jet lag or time zone changes, shift work) is relieved when clients attempt to normalize their routine and expectations to fit the schedule and to adapt to the new time zone or shift time. Exposure to sunlight is desirable, especially upon awakening rather than prior to bedtime, and can be helpful in adjusting to different time zones. Full-spectrum lighting and melatonin also may be helpful in circadian rhythm disorders. Most studies suggest that shift rotation should be minimized. Many people do

Implications for Evidence-Based Practice

Clients given audio tapes with educational material on sleep and relaxation reported significantly less sleep problems when compared to the control group subjects (Williams & Schreir, 2005). The tapes proved to be an effective educational tool, and the use of the diaries were helpful in self-monitoring behaviors. This study has implications for client education and nursing interventions.

Implications for Evidence-Based Practice

A study of hospital nurses indicated that suffering from sleep disorders, having night duties, and duration of natural light exposure were predictors of work stress; exposure to daylight for at least 3 hours a day was found to be a mitigating factor (Akunigkymu & Donmez, 2005). Although the authors suggest a larger and more cross-sectional sample size would be helpful, there are implications to nursing research for shift workers, prevention of burnout in nurses, and nurse retention.

not adjust to shift work, and provisions for adequate rest periods both on and off the job occasionally help. Although parents and teachers may be frustrated by adolescents who go to bed late and want to sleep later in the day, studies indicate that teens have a normal but delayed sleep cycle and may benefit from changes in scheduling.

Treating Underlying Disorders

Sleep disorders associated with medical or psychiatric disorders such as menopause, prostate problems, cancer, gastric reflux, fibrositis, breathing disorders, hypomanic states, depression, psychosis, and anxiety are helped by treating the underlying problems and disorders. For example, clients with a breathing-related sleep disorder such as obstructive sleep apnea find relief through surgery to relieve the obstructive airway or with CPAP. Laser surgery occasionally is used to cut away the soft tissue that may partially block air passages. Somnoplasty, in which an electrode is implanted in the soft palate and radio-frequency waves are used to heat tissue, causing it to shrink and tighten, is used as well. Treatment with CPAP by nose mask with low-pressure oxygen provides a pneumatic splint that prevents upper-airway collapse during inspiration and keeps the upper airway open. With CPAP, the nurse is often involved in teaching the client and monitoring home use in the early stages, in providing backup services, in fitting the mask and assessing dentition and pressure levels, and in encouraging consistent use over time. Only distilled water should be used in machines requiring water. If the client with medical problems or psychiatric disorders is hospitalized, the nurse assesses the client; provides comfort measures such as promoting hygiene, providing back rubs, turning and positioning the client, and changing bed linens; maintains a therapeutic milieu; and sets limits by ensuring client safety, reducing stimuli, and ensuring adequate rest periods.

Pharmacology

Pharmacotherapy is often used alone or in combination with other management techniques to treat sleep disorders. Underlying medical and/or psychiatric disorders should be evaluated. Often clients report subjective improvement after the first night of good sleep (McCall, 1995). Many different types of medications are available (**Table 21-1**), and selection depends on whether they are used for short or long periods. Most medications have a similar time to onset but differ in duration

Implications for Evidence-Based Practice

An algorithm developed for use with sleep disorders in long-term care settings advised initiating an evaluation of medical problems and medications and a sleep history: starting with nonpharmacologic aids and treatment of underlying problems, going on to use sleep medications in conjunction with nonpharmacologic aids if the initial methods did not work, and finally monitoring response (American Medical Directors Association, 2006). It would be useful to determine if this algorithm is effective across different settings.

Table 21-1 Common Sleep Medications

Drug Class	Medication	Selection Criteria
Melatonin receptor agonist	Ramelton (Rozerem)	Approved for long-term use
Non-benzodiazepine	Eszopiclone (Lunesta)	Approved for long-term use
Imidazopyridine	Zolpidem (Ambien)	High efficacy, low risk tolerance
Benzodiazepine	Temazepam (Restoril)	Short-term use, tolerance
	Fluzapepan (Dalmane)	
Pyrazolopyrimidines	Zaleplon (Sonata)	Non-benzo, low risk tolerance
Triazolopyridine	Trazodone	Low risk tolerance, moderate efficacy
Alprazolam	Xanax	See benzodiazepine
Salicylate	*Aspirin*	*Pain relief, possible soporiphic effect*
Alternative Medications		
5-hydroxytryptophan (5-HTP)	Tryptophan metabolite	Unpredictable, > serotonin
Melatonin	Synthetic melatonin	Unpredictable response
Valerian	Valerian root	Unpredictable response, false-positive drug test
Other Medications		
Many antidepressants, particularly SSRIs, are used for sleep.		
Antidepressant	Amitriptyline (Elavil)	Anticholinergic side effects, low risk tolerance, helpful for neuropathy, pain
	Doxepin (Sinequan)	Low risk tolerance, helpful for neuropathy, pain
	Nortriptyline (Pamelor)	
Tetracyclic	Mirtazapine (Remeron)	Strongly antihistaminic, > weight
Antihistamines are readily available and most are somewhat sedative.		
Antihistamine	Diphenhydramine (Benadryl)	Anticholinergic side effects, unpredictable, cause confusion
	Hydroxyzine (Atarax, Vistaril)	
Antianxiety medications are used for sleep.		
Anxiolytic (benzodiazepine and derivatives)	Clonazepam (Klonopin)	Short-term use, high hypnotic efficacy, high risk tolerance, increase confusion
	Diazepam (Valium)	
	Flurazepam (Dalmane)	
	Lorazepam (Ativan)	
	Oxazepam (Serax)	
	Temazepam (Restoril)	
Antipsychotic medications are used for sedation.		
Antipsychotic	Chlorpromazine (Thorazine)	Anticholinergic side effects, low risk tolerance
Barbiturates are rarely used now because of the high risk of dependency.		
Barbiturate	Pentobarbital (Nembutal)	High hypnotic efficacy, high risk tolerance
	Phenobarbital (Liminal)	
Nonbarbiturate	Chloral hydrate (Noctec)	High hypnotic efficacy, drug hangover
	Paraldehyde (Paral)	

of action. Sleep medications should only be taken before going to bed and the client should be asked about the use of other medications, alcohol, and tobacco as well as possible pregnancy. Some medications such as ramelteon (Rozerem) can be affected by grapefruit juice. One of the most commonly used medications for insomnia is zolpidem tartrate (Ambien, 5 to 10 mg), which is taken approximately 30 minutes before bedtime.

Since most benzodiazepines and benzodiazepine derivatives differ in duration and pharmacokinetics, they are prescribed cautiously for clients with liver disease; long-term use is discouraged, because it is associated with serious withdrawal effects and psychological and physical dependence. Eszopiclone zerem (Lunesta), a nonbenzodiazepine, is being studied for possible longer term use. Ramelteon, a melatonin receptor agonist that aids in sleep onset, has been approved for longer term use. Ramelteon should not be taken after a high fat meal or with other CYPaA2, CYP2C, and CYP3A4 metabolizing drugs, for example fluvoxane (Fluvox), rifonpan (Rifadin), ketoconazole (Nizoral), and fluconazole (Diflucan).

Older varieties of hypnotic medications such as chloral hydrate and barbiturates such as secobarbital and phenobarbital are rarely used because of the potential for misuse and addiction. Long-acting medications can accumulate with multiple doses and may cause confusion, particularly in elderly clients with impaired ability to metabolize medications. Using antihistamines for sleep also may be problematic because of their anticholinergic properties and unpredictable results.

Some antidepressants are prescribed for administration at night because of side effects that may make the client sleepy. Mirtazapine (Remeron), a tetracyclic antidepressant, is usually taken at night and may be helpful for clients experiencing sleep difficulties by decreasing the amount of time it takes for them to fall asleep and increasing total sleep time. Tricyclic antidepressants occasionally are used. For example, low-dose doxepin (Sinequan) is sedating and good for neuropathic pain. However, these medications also have anticholinergic properties.

Symptoms of excessive daytime sleepiness and narcolepsy have been treated with modafinil (Provigil; Mitler, Hash, Hirshkowitz, & Guilleminault, 2000; Schwartz, Feldman, Fry, & Hash, 2002). An advantage is the low potential for abuse. This medication has also been approved for use in symptoms related to shift work problems and in clients being actively treated for sleep apnea. Psychostimulants that have been used for these symptoms include dextroamphetamine (Dexedrine), dextroamphetamine and amphetamine (Adderall), and methylphenidate (Ritalin, Ritalin SR). These medications have a high potential for abuse. Cataplexy has been treated with venlafaxine (Effexor) and, less often, with atomoxetine (Strattera). Atomoxetine should not be given with albuteral or with CYP2D6 inhibitors. Another medication used for cataplexy to promote deep sleep and limit frequent awakenings is sodium oxybate (Xyrem). This medication is related to GHB (gamma hydroxybutyrate) and has a potential for abuse. Sleepwalking has also been reported by some clients who have used sodium oxybate.

Treatment for PLM may involve L-dopa (Dopar), carbidopa (Lodosyn), clonazepam (Klonopin), or trazodone (Desyrel). Opioids, benzodiazepines and derivatives, dopaminergics, and antiepileptics have been used for RLS. Ropinirole (Requip) has been approved for treatment of RLS. Ropinirole has sedative side effects and can potentiate side effects of L-dopa and exacerbate dyskinesia. Dosage of ropinirole may need to be adjusted if used with other medications that affect CYP1A2 metabolism. Treatment for RLS may also include vitamin E supplements, quinine, or clonazepam (Beck-Little & Weinrich, 1998; McCall, 1995).

Many clients try herbal supplements. There has been some research regarding the effectiveness of melatonin and tryptophan for sleep. There is limited evidence that other popular herbal remedies such as valerian root, kava kava, and St. John's wort are effective for sleep problems. With all medications, whether over the counter (OTC) and herbal remedies or controlled or noncontrolled prescription medications, there is always the possibility of side effects and/or drug interactions.

Critical Thinking Question What are some of the considerations regarding the use of prescription or OTC medications for sleep?

Summary

Sleep disorders are chronic disturbances in normal sleep patterns or behaviors that affect the amount, quality, timing, and stages or transitions of sleep and interfere with normal cognitive, physical, and psychosocial functioning. Sleep disorders include primary sleep disorders, sleep disorders related to another mental disorder, sleep disorders caused by a general medical condition, and substance-induced sleep disorder.

Primary sleep disorders include dyssomnias and parasomnias. Dyssomnias are disorders in initiating and maintaining sleep as well as problems associated with inadequate sleep (insomnia) and excessive sleep (hypersomnia). Narcolepsy is an example of dyssomnia. Parasomnias include disorders associated with sleep and sleep-wake cycles and transitions involving physical and behavioral manifestations. An example of parasomnia is sleepwalking disorder. Sleep disorders related to another mental disorder include sleep disorders attributed to a mental disorder such as anxiety (e.g., panic disorders), cognitive (e.g., dementia or delirium or both), mood (e.g., depression or mania or both), and psychotic (e.g., schizophrenia) disorders. An example is insomnia related to bipolar disorder, manic type. Sleep disorders caused by a general medical condition are those sleep disorders directly resulting from the physiologic effects of a known general medical condition (e.g., cancer, chronic obstructive pulmonary disease). An example is sleep disorder caused by Huntington's chorea, insomnia type. Substance-induced sleep disorder is related to drug use, intoxication, abuse, dependence, or withdrawal. Substances commonly associated with sleep disorders include alcohol, amphetamines, anxiolytics, caffeine, cocaine, hypnotics, opioids, and sedatives.

Management and treatment depend on a comprehensive assessment of the client's health status and sleep habits. The nurse should ask about concomitant medical and psychiatric problems and any prescribed or OTC medications or supplements. Cognitive and behavioral therapies, environmental manipulations and supportive care measures, pharmacotherapy, and other complementary therapies alone or in combination are helpful in the treatment of common sleep disorders. When selecting the appropriate pharmacologic agent for intermittent, short- or long-term use, the clinician must consider its action, onset, duration, possible drug interactions, and side effects. The potential for abuse, tolerance, and psychologic or physiological dependence also must be considered.

Annotated References

Akunigkymu, M. K., & Donmez, L. (2005). Daylight exposure and the predictors of burnout among nurses in a university hospital. *International Journal of Nursing Studies, 42*(5), 549–555.

The authors studied the effects of daylight exposure on sleep and burnout among hospital nurses.

American Medical Directors Association. (2006). *Sleep disorders*. Columbia, MD: Author.

Reviewed the evidence base for dealing with sleep disorders and developed an algorithm for dealing with sleep disorders in long-term care settings. Based upon expert consensus, the committee was composed of an interdisciplinary team including nursing input.

American Psychiatric Association. (2000). *Diagnostic and statistical manual of mental disorders* (4th ed., text rev.). Chicago: Author.

This is the American Psychiatric Association's official nomenclature of psychiatric conditions and disorders. It provides a systematic listing of the official codes and categories, a description of the multiaxial system for diagnosis, and diagnostic criteria for each of the disorders. It is used by psychiatrists, physicians, psychologists, registered nurses, social workers, therapists, and other mental health workers in all clinical settings.

Beck-Little, R., & Weinrich, S. P. (1998). Assessment and management of sleep disorders in the elderly. *Journal of Gerontological Nursing, 24*(4), 21–29.

This article discusses normal age-related sleep problems and disturbances and common sleep disorders. It provides a comprehensive overview of assessment and treatment problems as well as specific implications for nurses. The article includes an excellent summary of complaints among elderly clients, underlying pathology, suggestions for assessment, and possible interventions.

Beeber, L. S. (1996). Depression in women. In A. B. McBride & J. K. Austin (Eds.), *Psychiatric mental health nursing: Integrating the behavioral and biological sciences* (pp. 235–268). Philadelphia: W. B. Saunders.

This chapter discusses some of the regulatory functions associated with depression in women.

Burwell, C. S., Robin, E. D., Whaley, R. D., & Bikelman, A. G. (1956). Extreme obesity associated with alveolar hypoventilation—a Pickwickian syndrome. *American Journal of Medicine, 21*(11), 811–818.

This article discusses obesity as a factor in hypersomnia. Pickwickian syndrome, named for Mr. Wardle's boy, Joe, "a fat red-faced boy" who was a character in Charles Dickens's *The Pickwick Papers*, is another name for hypoventilation syndrome.

Caruso, C. C., Hitchcock, E. M, Dick, R. B., Russo, J. M., & Schmit, J. M. (2004). *Recent findings on illnesses, injuries and health behaviors.* (DHHS [NIOSH] Publication No. 204-143). Washington,

DC: U.S. Department of Health & Human Services.

This publication reviews and summarizes 52 research studies on health behaviors and work performance.

Feinsilver, S., & Hertz, G. (1993). Sleep in the elderly client. *Clinics in Chest Medicine, 13*(3), 405–411.

This article discusses problems associated with decreased sleep efficacy in the elderly.

McCall, W. V. (1995). Management of primary sleep disorders among elderly persons. *Psychiatric Services, 46*(1), 49–55.

A good review of sleep disorders in general, this article identifies common sleep problems in the elderly and various diagnostic and treatment approaches.

Mitler, M. M., Hash, J., Hirshkowitz, M., & Guilleminault, C. (2000). Long-term efficacy and safety of modafinil (Provigil) for the treatment of excessive daytime sleepiness associated with narcolepsy. *Sleep Medicine, 1*(3), 231–243.

Follow-up over 40 weeks of clients with narcolepsy who were treated with modafinil.

Montplaisir, J., Godbout, R., Pelletier, G., & Warnes, H. (1994). Restless legs syndrome and periodic limb movements during sleep. In M. H. Kryger, T. Roth, & W. C. Dement (Eds.), *Principles and practice of sleep medicine* (2nd ed., pp. 589–597). Philadelphia: W. B. Saunders.

This article discusses restless leg syndrome (RLS), which is often associated with neuropathies and periodic limb movement (PLM). Most clients with RLS will have PLM, but not all clients with PLM have RLS.

National Sleep Foundation. (2005). *2005 omnibus sleep in America poll.* Retrieved online September 30, 2006, from http://www.sleepfoundation.org/publications/2005poll.html

National poll of sleep habits and problems.

Nowell, P. D., Buysse, D. J., Reynolds, C. E., Hauri, P. J., Roth, T., Stepanski, E. J., et al. (1997). Clinical factors contributing to the differential diagnosis of primary insomnia and insomnia related to mental disorders. *American Journal of Psychiatry, 154*(10), 1412–1416.

This article identifies clinical factors to differentiate primary insomnia and insomnia related to mental disorders. The need for assessing sleep habits and providing behavioral therapies combined with pharmacotherapy is discussed.

Schwartz, J. R. L., Feldman, N. T., Fry, J. M., & Hash, J. (2002). Efficacy and safety of modafinil in improving daytime wakefulness in clients previously treated with psychostimulants. *Sleep Medicine, 4*(1), 43.

Comparison of clients treated with modafinil showed efficacy and low potential for abuse or side effects.

Williams, S. A., & Schreier, A. M. (2005). The role of education in managing fatigue, anxiety and sleep disorders in women undergoing chemotherapy for breast cancer. *Applied Nursing Research, 18*, 138–147.

Subjects in an experimental group who were given an audio tape with information on sleep and relaxation had improved self-report and logs of sleep compared to a control group.

Additional Resources

Chokroverty, S. (2008). 100 questions and answers about sleep and sleep disorders. Sudbury, MA: Jones and Bartlett.

This text provides answers to common questions about sleep and is helpful for education for clients and families.

Gottlieb, B. (Ed.). (1997). *New choices in natural healing.* Emmaus, PA: Rodale Press.

This text includes information on various complementary and homeopathic remedies for common ailments including sleep disorders and restless leg syndrome. Aromatherapy, progressive relaxation, guided imagery, and stretching exercises are some of the techniques discussed. The book includes specific instructions on how to individualize guided imagery techniques and homemade relaxation tapes.

Kryger, M. H., Roth, T., & Dement, W. C. (Eds.). (2005). *Principles and practice of sleep medicine.* Philadelphia: W. B. Saunders.

This comprehensive review of normal and abnormal sleep includes common sleep disorders and interventions. The 2005 edition includes text and an updated online edition.

Lee, K. A., & Ward T. M. (2005). Sleep assessment guide. *Issues in Mental Health Nursing, 26*(7), 739–750.

This article provides a format for nursing assessment of sleep disorders that can be used with children or adults.

McManus, C. (2003). *Progressive relaxation and autogenic training* [Audio CD]. Seattle, WA: The Wellness Series.

This commercially prepared CD is an excellent example of the types of materials available for client education and treatment. The CD includes instruction in progressive relaxation techniques and autogenic exercises. Other CDs in the series include guided imagery and mindfulness meditation and relaxation techniques accompanied by music.

Pandi-Permual, S. R., Ruoti, R., & Kramer, M. (2007). *Sleep and psychosomatic medicine.* London, England: Informa Healthcare.

This comprehensive text describes physiologic changes, medical conditions, and psychologic responses and behaviors associated with sleep and sleep disorders.

Internet Resources

http://nursing.jbpub.com/psychiatric

Visit http://nursing.jbpub.com/psychiatric for interactive exercises, NCLEX review questions, WebLinks, and more.

CHAPTER 22

Adjustment and Impulse-Control Disorders

Karen A. Ballard

LEARNING OBJECTIVES

After reading this chapter, you will be able to:

- Define adjustment and impulse-control disorders.
- Describe the specific behaviors associated with these disorders.
- Identify adaptive coping behaviors.
- Discuss various treatment modalities for these disorders.
- Identify major diagnoses and nursing interventions to assist clients with these disorders.
- Plan for the teaching needs of clients and their families including referrals to available support and resource services.

KEY TERMS

Adaptive coping behaviors
Adjustment disorder
Anxiety
Covert sensitization
Impulse-control disorders
Intermittent explosive disorder (IED)
Kleptomania
Pathologic gambling
Pyromania
Stress/stressor
Trichophagia
Trichotillomania

http://nursing.jbpub.com/psychiatric

Visit http://nursing.jbpub.com/psychiatric for interactive exercises, NCLEX review questions, WebLinks, and more.

Introduction

All people, at some time in their lives, encounter stressful events (stressors). However, not everyone develops an adjustment disorder in response to a stressor. **Adjustment disorder** is a general term referring to those situations in which the client develops particular psychological symptoms in response to stressors. The term is also used by the treating practitioner either as an interim diagnosis for adult clients or to describe psychological patterns in children or adolescents that do not lend themselves to an established mental disorder category. Many practitioners use this diagnosis especially with children and adolescents to avoid the stigma associated with other diagnoses. However, there is concern that adjustment disorder is becoming an overused diagnosis with the diagnostic criteria being poorly applied, and that the disorder is being used to "medicalize" the usual problems of daily living (Casey, 2001).

Critical Thinking Questions Why would some practitioners be concerned about the "stigma" of mental illness and choose this diagnosis instead of another one? Why are some mental health practitioners questioning the use of this diagnosis to describe usual problems of daily living?

The general classifications of adjustment disorders are identified as: with depressed mood, with **anxiety**, with mixed anxiety and depressed mood, with disturbance of conduct, and with mixed disturbance of emotions and conduct.

Classifications of adjustment disorders:
- Depressed mood
- Anxiety
- Disturbances of conduct
- Disturbances of emotions and conduct

Impulse-control disorders are categorized by the presence of uncontrollable and irresistible urges that are potentially harmful or self-destructive to the client or others. These disorders include intermittent explosive disorder, kleptomania, pyromania, pathologic gambling, and trichotillomania (hair pulling). All of these disorders are coded on Axis I in the *Diagnostic and Statistical Manual of Mental Disorders,* Fourth Edition, Text Revision (*DSM-IV-TR*; American Psychiatric Association [APA], 2000).

Adjustment Disorders

An adjustment disorder is considered to be a "superficial maladjustment to difficult situations or to newly experienced environmental factors in the absence of serious underlying personality defects" (Andreasen & Black, 2006, p. 494). According to established criteria, the symptoms must: 1) develop in response to a particular stressor within 3 months of exposure to the stress; 2) be markedly in excess of what one normally experiences when exposed to such a stressor; 3) involve significant impairment in social, occupational, or academic functioning; 4) not be an exacerbation of another, preexisting mental disorder; 5) not constitute bereavement; and 6) not generally persist for more than an additional 6 months once the stressor ceases (APA, 2000). Clients can be responding to a single stress or multiple stressors. Basically, the client feels totally overwhelmed and is unable to respond adaptively or to cope with the situation. It is important to consider the cultural, ethnic, and social background of the client when evaluating coping mechanisms to determine whether the behavior is maladaptive or acceptable and appropriate in the client's particular environment.

Stressors can be experienced by an individual, a family, or a community.

Some factors that reduce an individual's ability to cope with a stressor are lack of a trusting relationship, a misperception that change is a threat, inadequate communication skills, lack of motivation, unmet dependency needs, and low self-esteem.

Incidence and Prevalence

It has been estimated that 5% to 20% of the clients who present in the out-patient clinics of general hospitals and community mental health centers with complaints of being unable to manage their lives will fall into the category of adjustment disorder. Psychiatric consultation liaison services in general hospitals report that the frequency of this diagnosis often exceeds 20% and is over 30% in newly diagnosed cancer patients (Andreasen & Black, 2006; Spitzer, Gibbon, Skodol, Williams, & First, 2002). In other studies, approximately 13% of the adolescents receiving in-patient psychiatric care had adjustment disorders, and 13% of the adults and 42% of the adolescents seen in a psychiatric emergency room were classified as having adjustment disorders (Editor, 1992). Although some of these individuals may have major underlying mental disorders that need to be identified and treated, many will simply need assistance in responding to a specific stressor. The average age for a client with an adjustment disorder is 25 years.

Etiology

Adjustment disorder is one of the few psychiatric disorders in which there is a definite cause-and-effect relationship between an identifiable cause and the disorder as experienced by the client. The cause is the presence of a specific **stressor**. Stressors can be experienced by a single individual, an entire family, or a community. Certain individuals appear more vulnerable than others to specific stressors, experience the stress quite differently, and cope or adapt with different styles and with varying degrees of success. This is particularly noticeable when the stressor is a community-experienced event such as a natural disaster (hurricane, tornado, earthquake, flood, or tsunami; see **Figure 22-1**). Some examples of personal stressors are termination of a romantic relationship; business or financial difficulties; marital problems including fighting, infidelity, alcohol and substance abuse, separation, and divorce; being fired; being diagnosed with a serious or terminal illness; the presence of physical pain; and a variety of normal developmental events (going to school or changing schools, leaving the parental home, getting married, becoming a parent, retirement). The most common stressors for adults are marital problems, separation or divorce, moving,

Figure 22-1 Natural disasters such as hurricanes and floods can precipitate an adjustment disorder. In this photo, neighborhoods still remain flooded as a result of Hurricane Katrina in New Orleans, Louisiana, on September 3, 2005.

and financial problems. The most common stressors for young persons are school problems, parental rejection, alcohol and drug problems, and parental separation or divorce, closely followed by girlfriend or boyfriend problems (Andreasen & Black, 2006; APA, 2000).

Many factors (biological, neurological, psychological, developmental, environmental, and cultural) influence an individual's ability to respond to a particular stressor and may explain why some individuals are more vulnerable than others. Some of the contributing factors that may reduce an individual's ability to cope are lack of a trusting relationship, a misperception that change in one's life is a threat, inadequate communication skills, lack of motivation, unmet dependency needs, and low self-esteem (Krupnick & Wade, 1999).

Physiology

There are no particular physiologic parameters associated with adjustment disorders. Upon physical examination, symptoms associated with depressed mood or anxiety (insomnia, heart palpitations, and jitters) will have no physical cause. However, a thorough physical examination can help by eliminating the possibility that the symptoms are related to an underlying physical condition. If there is a physical problem, it must be treated and the client reevaluated. There are probably correlations between one's ability to handle stress and different hormonal shifts and neuroendocrine patterns (Henry, 1990; Pruessner et al., 2005).

Clinical Example

Melinda (age 45), after many months of complaints of fatigue and "just not feeling well," is diagnosed with HIV. Over 2 weeks she becomes increasingly anxious and concerned that she is going to die soon. After being afraid to travel on buses to get to work (for fear of being infected with a cold virus and further compromising her immune system), she consults a mental health practitioner.

Clinical Presentation

Clients with an adjustment disorder with depressed mood appear more disturbed, regressed, and suicidal than individuals with other types of adjustment disorder.

The client with an adjustment disorder will present with different symptoms (depressed mood, anxiety, disturbance of conduct, or disturbance of emotions and conduct), depending on how the inability to cope is being experienced. The client can have a depressed mood and have symptoms such as overall depression, tearfulness, hopelessness, lack of energy, and insomnia. Clients experiencing depressed mood often appear more disturbed, regressed, and suicidal than other clients with adjustment disorders. They express an inability to cope with anxiety and complain of nervousness, worry, jitters, palpitations, hyperventilation, or fear of separation, which is especially associated with children. Clients with disturbances of conduct usually exhibit behaviors violating the rights of others or ignoring societal norms and present with behaviors such as truancy, vandalism, reckless driving, fighting, defaulting on legal responsibilities, and difficulty fulfilling work or school obligations. In adjustment disorders with mixed disturbances of emotions and conduct, the client presents with complaints of emotions such as depression or anxiety, is increasingly socially withdrawn, and engages in some of the previously listed inappropriate conduct behaviors. Any suicidal ideation or behavior in these clients should be carefully evaluated (Andreasen & Black, 2006; Spitzer et al., 2002).

Differential Diagnosis

Clients experiencing adjustment disorders present with a variety of symptoms, so the possible differential diagnoses are many. Also, clients with other mental disorder diagnoses may develop adjustment disorders in addition to the primary diagnosis. The possible diagnoses to consider include major depression, generalized anxiety disorder, panic disorder, personality disorders, schizophrenia, posttraumatic stress disorder, and

Clinical Example

After only 12 years of marriage, James's wife died from advanced breast cancer, leaving him with 8-year-old twin girls. His mother moved in to help with the children, expecting to be there for the first few weeks. After 3 months, James begged his mother to stay, which she did. After 6 months, his father was urging his wife to return home and let James learn to cope on his own. James became tearful and depressed every time his mother tried to set a date to leave. Everyone in the family is concerned that he is "going crazy with grief."

conduct disorders in children and adolescents. Bereavement related to the loss of a loved one generally is not considered an adjustment disorder unless the course and intensity of the bereavement are excessive and do not respond to interventions or to the passage of time.

Clinical Course and Complications

Adjustment disorders can be *acute*, lasting less than 6 months, or *chronic*, lasting more than 6 months.

Depending upon the length of persistence of the symptoms, the adjustment disorder is considered either acute or chronic. An acute adjustment disorder can last a few days, weeks, or up to 6 months. Chronic duration is that persisting beyond 6 months, generally because the stressor is continuing or because the consequences of the stressful event are persisting (APA, 2000). If the symptoms continue beyond 6 months and do not meet the criteria for chronic duration, the practitioner should consider reevaluating the client for another mental disorder, such as major depression or generalized anxiety disorder, and treat accordingly.

In general, clients respond very well to treatment and, except for the potential for isolated, suicidal acts, there are usually no serious complications. In 5-year follow-up studies on clients who were treated for adjustment disorders, the results were that 71% of adults were completely well with no residual symptoms, while 21% had developed a major depressive disorder or alcoholism. For children ages 8–13, adjustment disorder did not predict future psychiatric disturbances, but for adolescents, 43% had developed a major psychiatric disorder, such as schizophrenia, schizoaffective disorder, major depression, substance use disorders, or personality disorders (Encyclopedia of Mental Disorders, 2005).

Therapies used to treat adjustment disorders include psychotherapy, relaxation techniques, guided imagery, meditation, exercise, biofeedback, occupational and physical therapy, vocational training, and specific education regarding the stressor, especially if it is a new medical condition or illness.

Management and Treatment

The goal of treatment for clients with adjustment disorders is to help the client deal with the acute symptoms, to promote a return to the previous state of mental health, and to teach effective, **adaptive coping behaviors** (cognitive, behavioral, or physiological) for dealing with a chronic stressor or its stressful consequences. Adaptive coping behaviors include, but are not limited to:

- Seeking comfort and support from a loved one
- Using self-control
- Crying, laughing, sleeping
- Eating appropriate amounts of "comfort foods"
- Participating in activities that serve as distractions
- Exercising and working out
- Talking to individuals who are familiar with the problem
- Praying or seeking spiritual advice
- Utilizing self-care activities such as massage, meditation, yoga, imagery and relaxation techniques

The psychiatric nurse should begin contact with the client through an empathetic interview to assist the client in identifying the stress, accurately assess the client's needs, and develop a plan of care. Emotional support from the psychiatric nurse and other practitioners will help the client to draw on resources such as self, family, friends, community, and religion to promote adaptive improvement and growth.

Psychotherapy is the most valuable intervention in addressing adjustment disorders. The following types of therapy, singly or in combination, have proved effective in helping these clients:

- Crisis intervention
- Brief individual psychotherapy
- Group therapy
- Family therapy
- Behavioral therapy
- Cognitive restructuring therapy
- Stress inoculation training
- Counseling

Psychotherapy provides the client with individual attention and the opportunity to be supported and guided by a therapist as the client attempts to understand the stressor and explores ways of adapting to the stress. Group therapy provides an opportunity for clients who share similar stressors, such as cancer, HIV infection, or marital problems, to support each other (Reid, Balis, & Sutton, 1997). Specific nursing interventions that can be helpful include encouraging the client to express feelings and perceptions and to discuss the present situation; encouraging the client to discuss past successes and failures with

Implications for Evidence-Based Practice

A recent study (Grassi et al., 2006) focused on 100 individuals with medical illnesses who exhibited DSM-level psychosomatic symptoms associated with various adjustment disorders. Each of the subjects was interviewed using the Diagnostic Criteria for Psychosomatic Research (DCPR). A significant overlap was demonstrated between the symptoms associated with the adjustment disorders and the DCPR criteria related to abnormal behaviors associated with medical illness, most specifically health anxiety, tanatophobia (fear of death), nosophobia (fear of having a disease), illness denial, somatization, and demoralization. Because adjustment disorder is the most common psychiatric diagnosis found in the medically ill, it is important for nurses to understand the various manifestations of the stress of a medical illness on a client and to make appropriate interventions as the symptoms present, rather than having clients become further stressed and incapacitated by the psychiatric symptoms.

handling stressful events, especially identifying adaptive coping behaviors; teaching the client to use a problem-solving approach to deal with current and future problems; focusing on supportive resources and alternative solutions; educating the client and family about the precipitating stressor; and helping the client to identify appropriate family, social, work, and community resources (Krupnick & Wade, 1999). It is also helpful to assist the client in identifying other types of therapy that might relieve symptoms. These include relaxation techniques, guided imagery, meditation, exercise, biofeedback, occupational and physical therapy, vocational training, and specific education regarding the stressor, especially if it is a new medical condition or illness.

Considerations for Client and Family Education

Teaching clients experiencing an adjustment disorder should include helping both the client and the family identify, anticipate, and understand the situations and events that are stressors and causing the reaction. When possible, the client should be helped to identify and utilize adaptive coping behaviors. The client should be encouraged to utilize a combination of therapeutic modalities to cope with the stressors and to realize the importance of medication compliance if drugs are prescribed to assist with symptom management. If there is any concern that the client may harm him- or herself or others, the family or significant others should be counseled on how to contact emergency mental health services or to access appropriate resources. The client and family should be informed of community-based support services and the availability of educational materials.

Critical Thinking Question How can complementary therapies be used in conjunction with psychotherapy to positively assist a client in dealing with an adjustment disorder?

Medication is used on a limited basis. It is particularly helpful for short-term relief of particular symptoms. For example, a client with insomnia may have symptom relief after receiving a hypnotic such as flurazepam (Dalmane) for a short period, or a client with anxiety may be better able to address ways of coping after the acute anxiety has been relieved by a brief course of diazepam (Valium). A long-term need for medication could indicate that another, underlying mental disorder has not been identified.

Impulse-Control Disorders

Five main impulse disorders:
- Intermittent explosive disorder
- Kleptomania
- Pyromania
- Pathologic gambling
- Trichotillomania

There are five types of generally accepted impulse-control disorders: intermittent explosive disorder, kleptomania, pyromania, pathologic gambling, and trichotillomania. Although these conditions appear dissimilar on the surface, they all are characterized by an experience or stimulus that is perceived by an individual as a challenge, threat, or potentially harmful.

According to the American Psychiatric Association (2000, p. 609), **intermittent explosive disorder (IED)** is characterized by "discrete episodes of failure to resist aggressive impulses resulting in serious assaults or destruction of property" that are expressed as unwarranted episodes of anger; **kleptomania** is characterized by "the recurrent failure to resist impulses to steal objects not needed for personal or monetary value"; **pyromania** is characterized by "a pattern of fire-setting for pleasure, gratification, or relief of tension"; **pathologic gambling** is characterized by "recurrent and persistent maladaptive gambling behavior"; and **trichotillomania** is characterized by "recurrent pulling out of one's hair for pleasure, gratification, or relief of tension that results in noticeable hair loss." These disorders are generally underdiagnosed, and they can cause clients considerable emotional problems while negatively impacting on family relationships, friendships, and the ability to function at work and school.

Impulse disorders are underdiagnosed; they can cause clients considerable emotional problems and negatively impact on family relationships, friendships, and the ability to function at work or school.

Critical Thinking Question Impulse-control disorders are characterized by "urges." What are the different types of urges associated with the five distinct disorders?

Incidence and Prevalence

The incidence and prevalence rates for the impulse-control disorders differ and in some conditions are not reliably known. Intermittent explosive disorder, absent of any other mental disorders or physical conditions, is generally considered to be fairly rare, occurring mostly in young males with low frustration tolerances. However, a study (2005) funded by the National Institutes of Health's (NIH) National Institute of Mental Health (NIMH) found, depending upon how broadly it is defined, IED may affect as many as 7.3% of adults (11.5–16 million Americans) in their lifetimes (Kessler et al., 2006). Kleptomania is also fairly rare, occurring in less than 5% of the individuals arrested for shoplifting, about 6 instances per 1,000 thefts,

CASE STUDY Mrs. N.

Mrs. N., a 50-year-old housewife, had been looking forward to the entrance into college of her fourth and last child. She saw this as a time in which she and her husband of 30 years would share special times again. On the trip home from their son's college, her husband announced that he had been having a 10-year affair with a colleague at work and wanted a divorce. He dropped her at their house and left to live with the other woman. Mrs. N. became tearful, anxious, and soon very sad. She kept telling herself that this could not be happening. At 2 a.m. she went into the bathroom and ingested a handful of aspirin, diphenhydramine (Benadryl), and diazepam (Valium) tablets. She called her sister immediately, who rushed her to the emergency room. She underwent gastric lavage and was seen by the emergency room's psychiatric-mental health clinical nurse specialist and the psychiatrist on call. The hospital's suicide precautions protocol was started.

Mrs. N. was admitted to the hospital's in-patient unit for 4 days. She kept stating that she was no longer suicidal. She admitted to being angry, upset, sad, and experiencing palpitations but said that she would not hurt herself again. The psychiatrist and clinical nurse specialist suggested that they speak with her and her husband together. Mrs. N. agreed somewhat reluctantly and a joint session was held. Afterward, Mrs. N. admitted that she had hoped that her husband might change his mind, but the session had shown her that this would not happen. During the session he told her that he hadn't loved her for many years and shared that he had made some bad investments, and there was limited money available. She called her sister to ask for assistance in finding a divorce lawyer. She asked the psychiatrist for help in telling her grown children about the dissolution of the marriage and her suicidal act. Mrs. N. repeatedly asked the nurses how long it takes to get over this type of "horrible disappointment." She often talked about the "good times" in the early years of the marriage and her regret that they would not have future years together. Mrs. N. was discharged and entered weekly, out-patient psychotherapy.

Four months later, Mrs. N. was still involved in the divorce process. In addition to her therapy, Mrs. N. had joined a women's support group conducted by a nurse psychotherapist and was using meditation to help control her feelings of anger and sadness. Recently, she had begun to discuss joining her oldest daughter in her small catering business. Cooking had always been a special interest for Mrs. N., and she was considering attending a renowned cooking school. Mrs. N. openly admitted that her life was different and not as happy as before, but verbalized in group and to her individual therapist her hope that once the divorce was over she could move on with her life and be her own person. She realized that financial independence was important to her.

NURSING CARE PLAN Adjustment Disorder

Expected Outcomes	Interventions	Evaluations
• Client will understand the relationship of the specific stressor (divorce) to feelings and actions.	• Listen empathetically to the client's thoughts regarding her feelings and actions and her husband's request for a divorce.	• She shares with treatment staff and in her group therapy session that she never understood before how divorce can destroy one's self-esteem and make one feel useless, almost a nonperson.
• Client will have no additional experiences of suicidal ideation or attempt to harm self.	• Assess frequently to determine if client is experiencing suicidal ideation or has a plan for self-harm. • Implement suicide precautions as needed. • Ask client to sign a no self harm/no suicide contract.	• States that she never thought that she was the type of person who would try to hurt herself because she loves her children so much and believes that only God determines when "our time on earth is over." • There are no additional attempts at self-harm and she states that "I am so glad that I did not kill myself."
• Client will experience a reduction in level of anxiety and accompanying physical symptoms.	• Explore with client other times that she has experienced anxiety as the result of a life event.	• Reports fewer symptoms such as jitteriness, insomnia, and fatigue.
• Client will utilize more appropriate, alternative coping behaviors.	• Teach relaxation techniques. • Ask the client to identify coping behaviors that have worked in the past in similar situations.	• The client is able to successfully use some of the suggested relaxation techniques. • Increasingly uses more appropriate coping behaviors.
• Client will participate in individual and group therapy while hospitalized and as an out-patient.	• Discuss the importance of participating in therapy as an in-patient and continuing therapy as an out-patient.	• Attends all scheduled sessions as an in-patient and signs a discharge treatment plan to continue them as an out-patient.
• Client will follow medication regimen.	• Review medication regimen and education with client on a daily basis.	• Can successfully repeat information about her medication schedule and the specific drug information.

Visit http://nursing.jbpub.com/psychiatric for additional care plans and exercises.

and is more common in females (Andreasen & Black, 2006). Because kleptomania results in an illegal act, it is probably underreported to practitioners by the client who is ashamed of the behavior. True pyromania is quite rare compared to single episodes of fire-setting, which is observed in some children and adolescents in different developmental stages, or deliberate fire-setting by an arsonist. Pyromania occurs more often in males with poor social skills and learning disabilities.

According to the National Gambling Impact Study Commission Final Report (1999), in any given year in the United States there are between 1.8 and 2.5 million adult pathologic gamblers. Both the incidence and prevalence rates for pathologic gambling may be as high as 1% to 3% of the adult population, and they are growing as gambling is legalized across the nation. In states where gambling has been legal for fewer than 10 years, 0.5% of the adult population has been classified as probable pathologic gamblers; in states where gambling has been legal for more than 20 years, 1.5% of the adults have been classified as pathologic gamblers, with women and minorities at greatest risk for acquiring the disorder (Volberg, 1994; APA, 2000). Approximately one third of pathologic gamblers are women, yet they are underrepresented in treatment programs. Pathologic gambling appears to start in adolescence and has many characteristics of addiction, with individuals either displaying patterns of addiction from the beginning or having a long history of progressive addiction.

According to the National Council on Problem Gambling (2007), if one answers "yes" to any of the following statements, professional help should be sought:

- You have often gambled longer than you had planned.
- You have often gambled until your last dollar was gone.
- Thoughts of gambling have caused you to lose sleep.
- You have used your income or savings to gamble while letting bills go unpaid.
- You have made repeated, unsuccessful attempts to stop gambling.
- You have broken the law or considered breaking the law to finance your gambling.
- You have borrowed money to finance your gambling.
- You have felt depressed or suicidal because of your gambling losses.
- You have been remorseful after gambling.
- You have gambled to get money to meet your financial obligations.

Clients with intermittent explosive disorder describe these episodes as spells or attacks and report a period of tension prior to the aggressive explosion followed by a sense of relief and remorse.

Trichotillomania (impulsively pulling out one's hair) was once thought to be quite rare, but recent studies indicate that 1% to 2% of college students report histories of this behavior. It is found equally in male and female children but persists into adulthood in more women than men. Most afflicted clients report a childhood onset (Andreasen & Black, 2006; APA, 2000).

Etiology

Although the specific etiology of the impulse-control disorders is unknown, they are thought to have both neurological and environmental causes and are known to be exacerbated by stress. Intermittent explosive disorder first appears somewhere between late adolescence and the third decade of life. In kleptomania, psychotherapists have suggested that the stolen items represent psychosexual fixations and gratify very primitive needs. Pyromania also appears to satisfy a primitive, unmet need. Some psychotherapists believe that pathologic gambling is derived from a childhood sense of omnipotence and a recurring need for punishment. The cause of trichotillomania is also unknown, but family histories are often positive for similar behavior in relatives and for a history of obsessive-compulsive disorder in family members (Spitzer et al., 2002).

Clients with kleptomania know that their behavior is wrong. They usually steal items that they do not need and often can afford, and then give or throw away the items.

Clients with pyromania are often fascinated with firehouses, firefighting equipment, and uniforms. They may even become firefighters.

Physiology

In intermittent explosive disorder, some individuals have changes in their electroencephalograms (EEGs), abnormal serotonin metabolism in cerebrospinal fluid, and abnormal findings in neurological and psychological screenings (reversal of letters, mirror movements, poor coordination). Some researchers believe that pathologic gambling may be associated with abnormalities of the noradrenergic system. Individuals with trichotillomania do not have any known underlying dermatologic disorders; however, skin biopsies may reveal short and broken hair shafts. Some hair follicles may appear damaged and others may contain a deeply pigmented keratinous material. Clients experience a tingling sensation in the scalp, but the skin usually shows no signs of significant inflammation or disease (Andreasen & Black, 2006; APA, 2000).

Clinical Presentation

Intermittent Explosive Disorder

Individuals with intermittent explosive disorder report having "spells" or "attacks" of explosive aggressive behavior. The explosive episode is usually preceded by a period of tension or arousal, and after the explosion the client reports a sense of relief coupled with remorse, regret, and embarrassment. The aggressive event is usually disproportionate to the precipitating cause, and the episodes recur (Lion, 1992; Spitzer et al., 2002). Some episodes of road rage, throwing and breaking objects during angry outbursts, and domestic violence may indeed be caused by this disorder.

Kleptomania

Clients who admit to kleptomania are aware that the behavior is wrong. They often steal items that they do not need or could easily afford to buy, frequently giving or throwing them away after the event. The client experiences a period of increasing tension prior to the stealing episode and feels pleasure, gratification, and relief during the episode. Kleptomania is a solitary event. Individuals with kleptomania do not purposely put themselves into a stealing episode that will likely result in arrest. Stealing as a result of kleptomania is not done in anger, for revenge, or in response to hallucinations or delusions. In some respects, kleptomania is similar to obsessive-compulsive disorder; both disorders involve irresistible, uncontrollable urges, and the stealing episode frequently appears to have a ritualistic pattern (McElroy, Pope, Hudson, Keck, & White, 1991; Spitzer et al., 2002).

Pyromania

Clients with pyromania report multiple episodes of fire-setting. This is different from the young child whose fascination with fire results in a single, albeit potentially dangerous, fire-setting episode. These individuals report tension prior to setting the fire, an almost uncontrollable attraction to remaining near the fire, perhaps participating in putting out the fire or assisting in rescue attempts. In pyromania, fire-setting is not done for money, in defense of any particular ideology, as a result of impaired judgment, or in response to hallucinations or delusions. These individuals are usually fascinated with firehouses, firefighting equipment, and uniforms and may even become firefighters. Arsonists set fires for monetary gain and do not fit into this category of impulse-control disorder (Soltys, 1992; Williams, 2002).

Pathologic Gambling

Pathologic gamblers report an ever-increasing loss of control over their behavior. The course of this disorder very closely resembles addictions such as alcoholism. Clients report preoccupation with thoughts about gambling such as what the last bet felt like and planning for the next gambling opportunity. They report that they are after the "action" more than the money, and that it takes larger and larger bets to produce the euphoria associated with the gambling event (very similar to the addict's substance-induced high; Volberg, 1994; Spitzer et al., 2002).

Trichotillomania

Clients with trichotillomania pull hair out of any part of the body (scalp, eyebrows, eyelashes, axilla, and the pubic and peri-rectal areas). The most common area is the scalp. The actual act of hair pulling can last seconds or hours. Clients report that stress can precipitate hair-pulling episodes and that they also pull out their hair when relaxed and watching television, at a movie, or involved in a pleasurable activity. Some individuals experience tension just before pulling out the hair and others as they seek to resist pulling the hair. All report feelings of relief, gratification, and pleasure during the hair-pulling episode. Clients usually are not completely bald but have discrete bald spots or patches and may be missing all or some of their eyebrows and eyelashes (Christenson, Mackenzie, & Mitchell, 1991; Woods et al., 2006).

Clinical Example

Amy has been taking objects from stores on and off for almost 10 years without being discovered. One day on a visit to Chicago, she finds herself in an exclusive women's accessory store. While there Amy becomes increasingly tense and finds herself repeatedly returning to a display of brightly colored scarves. Finally, she can no longer stand the tension and she grabs a handful of scarves and stuffs them into her handbag. Amy almost immediately experiences relief from the tension and leaves the store. Store security arrests her outside the store. She is embarrassed and unable to explain why she took the scarves. Since there is no previous criminal record, Amy is placed on probation and required to attend counseling and a 12-step program.

Clinical Example

Evan's mother has asked for an appointment with the school psychologist to discuss his "obsession with fires." She shares that after his recent 12th birthday party she found him setting fire to the party favors and throwing them up into the air. Apparently, Evan has been caught by his family playing with matches or lighters since he was about 6 years old. His mother reports that his most prized possession is a volunteer fireman's badge that his uncle gave him. When the psychologist interviews Evan, he finds that he gleefully talks about fires that he has set or times that he has played with matches in the home without being caught. He brags that he is "good at putting fires out." Not surprisingly, Evan wants to be a fireman when he is older. The psychologist recommends both individual and family therapy.

Clinical Example

David is a successful, middle-aged lawyer who was recently caught diverting funds from a client's trust fund. It turns out that he has been increasingly gambling with losses over $100,000. David borrowed $50,000 from a "loan shark" and desperately needed cash to meet this debt because he was being threatened. He is embarrassed and readily admits to his wrong-doing, stating that he cannot control himself. His mother mortgaged her house to allow him to return the lender's money. David is placed on probation by the court, given community service, told to attend Gamblers Anonymous meetings, and reported to the Bar Association for unethical behavior.

> The euphoria associated with pathologic gambling is similar to a substance-induced high.

> Individuals with trichotillomania usually pull the hair out of their scalps. Other areas for pathologic hair pulling are eyebrows, eyelashes, axilla, and the pubic and peri-rectal areas.

Differential Diagnosis

In intermittent explosive disorder, it is imperative to determine that the episodes are not related to underlying physical conditions such as brain

Some clients with impulse disorders have the potential to significantly injure others, so maintaining the safety of the client and others is a primary concern for the psychiatric nurse.

tumors or to neurological problems secondary to trauma such as an automobile accident. This disorder is excluded for individuals whose explosive, aggressive episodes are related to delirium, dementia, alcohol or substance abuse, conduct disorder, personality disorder, manic episode, or schizophrenia.

Kleptomania is not ordinary thievery or shoplifting, which are deliberate acts of taking something that belongs to someone else. Kleptomania is rare, whereas thievery and shoplifting are common and annually cost the economy millions of dollars. Kleptomania needs to be distinguished from obsessive-compulsive disorder, antisocial personality disorder, and conduct disorder.

Arson is intentional fire-setting for monetary gain or revenge; it is not pyromania.

Arson or intentional fire-setting for profit, protest, terrorism, or to attract attention is not pyromania. Fire-setting episodes that occur secondary to conduct disorder, manic episode, antisocial personality disorder, or in response to a delusion or hallucination also are not pyromania and should not be so classified.

Individuals can engage in social gambling with friends and in professional gambling as an occupation and not be pathologic gamblers. Gambling episodes occurring in relationship to manic episodes or in individuals with antisocial personality disorder are not classified in this category.

Hair pulling associated with delusions, hallucinations, obsessive-compulsive disorder, stereotypic movement disorder, and factitious disorder is not trichotillomania. Physical causes of alopecia (hair loss) should be excluded (alopecia areata, male pattern baldness, and lupus erythematosus). In childhood, some children engage in a time-limited developmental phase of twisting, tugging, and pulling at their hair. This time-limited behavior should be treated as a temporary habit, not as trichotillomania.

Clinical Course and Complications

The plan of care for clients with intermittent explosive disorder can include maintaining a journal, meditation, imagery, using time-outs, developing treatment contracts, exercise programs, teaching conflict management, and the use of medication.

For most individuals, the course of an impulse-control disorder requires a lifetime of attention to controlling the abnormal behavior. Some of these disorders, such as intermittent explosive disorder and pyromania, have the potential for significantly injuring others; therefore, maintaining the safety of others and of the client is a primary concern for the psychiatric nurse and other practitioners. When hospitalized, these individuals need to be monitored carefully to prevent aggressive outbursts or fire-setting episodes that may harm other clients or staff. Many individuals with impulse-control disorders find themselves alienated from their families, in difficulty with the legal system, even incarcerated, and not tolerated at work or in school and social situations. Individuals with intermittent explosive disorder have a high rate of hospitalization secondary to unsafe behaviors such as reckless driving and violent physical fights. Some individuals with trichotillomania eat their hair (**trichophagia**) and develop hair balls, nausea and vomiting, abdominal pain, and bowel perforation (Christenson, Mackenzie, & Mitchell, 1991; Lion, 1992; Soltys, 1992; Woods et al., 2006).

Critical Thinking Questions What types of behavior should concern a nurse that a client with an impulse-control disorder might harm him- or herself or others? What would be an appropriate nursing intervention?

Management and Treatment

Intermittent Explosive Disorder

For individuals with intermittent explosive disorder, safety for self and others is an important treatment goal. Clients should be taught to recognize when they are feeling angry and explosive and to identify the stress that produces these feelings. The next step is to help them identify ways of controlling these impulses and the concurrent angry feelings and behaviors. Individual and group therapy can assist the client in understanding these behaviors and developing personal strategies for coping and maintaining control. Since this type of behavior has probably alienated family members, family therapy sessions focused on improving the functioning of the family unit are probably essential to reintegrating the client into the family unit.

Some activities that the psychiatric nurse and other practitioners can consider are encouraging the client to keep a journal to help identify specific people, times, or events that act as triggers for the behavior; teaching relaxation techniques, such as meditation and imagery to establish control, and how to use personal time-outs as a means of escaping stress or gaining control (**Figure 22-2**); developing treatment contracts focusing on the expectations for and consequences of certain behaviors; encouraging participation in regular exercise programs; and teaching the client how to manage conflict.

Figure 22-2 Meditation is one technique for controlling intermittent explosive disorder.

Some psychotherapists believe that short-term drug therapy can help in alleviating some of the tensions or aggressive impulses associated with intermittent explosive disorder and suggest trials of lithium carbonate (Lithium), carbamazepine (Tegretol), or beta-blockers such as propranolol (Inderal).

Kerr (1990) has identified specific nursing interventions for psychiatric nurses in addressing the impulse control problems of clients on an inpatient unit. This includes informing the client on admission that harm to self, others, or property is unacceptable; telling the client that staff members are willing to assist through multiple means to help the client gain control (medication, time-outs, quiet areas); removing the client from excessive environmental stimuli; and assisting the client to identify the feeling rather than acting on it. If the client appears to be about to lose control, nurses should interrupt the behavior immediately by any appropriate means (seclusion, restraint), always explaining the need to the client. Nurses must have a standardized unified response plan for any client's impulsive behavior. Kerr suggests that nurses reinforce all efforts made by clients to exert appropriate internal controls over behavior, assist clients in understanding how maladaptive impulsive behavior is not in their best interest, and provide alternative channels for expression of physical and psychic energy such as exercise and activities. Clients in outpatient care should be monitored carefully for failure to comply with the treatment plan and for return of violent behaviors. An individual with an intermittent explosive disorder responds best to a combination of these suggested interventions. There is no single successful treatment modality for intermittent explosive disorder.

Kleptomania

There is little in the literature describing successful interventions and management of kleptomania. The client's shame and guilt associated with the behavior often keep it hidden from the practitioner. Individual psychotherapy is recommended to assist the client in dealing with the underlying guilt and need for punishment, and in maintaining control over destructive aggression and addressing behavior changes (Reid et al., 1997; Williams, 2002). Some behavior therapists recommend **covert sensitization**, a process in which the client is guided to associate images of nausea and vomiting with the desire to steal, or establishing a contract with the client in which the client agrees to be accompanied by others during all shopping activities. There has been some recent interest in using antidepressants such as fluoxetine (Prozac) to provide relief for these overwhelming urges (Andreasen & Black, 2006). Self-help recovery groups can be successful in supporting the individual to resist the urge (Shulman, 2005).

> In covert sensitization, a behavioral approach to the treatment of kleptomania, the client is guided in associating images of nausea and vomiting with the desire to steal.

Pyromania

True pyromania in adults is treated with individual psychotherapy with a focus on understanding the underlying anger, revenge, or sexual stimulus of the urges and learning alternative and adaptive behaviors to cope with the resulting stress. All fire-setting behaviors must be treated seriously because the potential for harm to others is so grave. In children and adolescents, a variety of strategies are used to interrupt the maladaptive fire-setting behavior. The practitioner usually treats this as a family problem and works with the parents to deal with any family issues that might have led to the fire-setting episode and to discuss nonpunitive methods of discipline. In addition, the child or adolescent and the family can be engaged in a mastery program that teaches cause and effect as well as how to restrain the "uncontrollable internal fire."

> Pyromania in adults is treated with individual psychotherapy focusing on the underlying anger, revenge, or sexual stimuli of the irresistible urges and learning alternative and adaptive behaviors for coping with the stress.

Local fire departments frequently have programs that teach families and children how to ignite and extinguish actual fires properly. Children are assisted in repeatedly starting and extinguishing fires, with adult supervision, in appropriate places such as barbecues and fireplaces. Some programs link fire setters with firefighters in a type of Big Brother program; others bring children and adolescents to burn units to see the effects of fire on people's bodies (Reid et al., 1997; Williams, 2002). The rate of success of treatment is higher in children than in adults.

Pathologic gambling affects the individual, similar to how alcohol and substance abuse affects an addict, with rushes, highs, withdrawal symptoms, and the need to abstain to control the disorder.

Pathologic Gambling

Treatment of pathologic gambling is usually multifaceted, including individual psychotherapy, family therapy, aversive conditioning, and a 12-step program. Individual psychotherapy appears to be more successful with this impulse-control disorder than with any of the others. Therapy focuses on helping the gambler understand the reasons for gambling and dealing with the feelings of helplessness, depression, and guilt. It is important for the client to identify the psychosocial factors or stressors that trigger gambling behaviors and learn how to either avoid them or deal with them more appropriately. Twelve-step programs help the gambler establish a new life without the addictive behavior of gambling being in control. Many clients describe the high that gambling brings them and report having the same sensation with drug and alcohol use; indeed, some clients experience withdrawal symptoms when faced with mandatory abstinence as part of the therapy (Meintz & Larson, 1994; Williams, 2002). Family therapy is particularly important because the lying, cheating, abuse, mistrust, and financial problems created by the behaviors of the pathologic gambler have alienated the family. For real recovery to take place, the family must learn to trust the client again, heal the emotional hurts, and learn to use more effective communication skills with each other and more appropriate coping behaviors.

In trichotillomania, behavior therapy that focuses on treating the hair pulling as a "bad habit" and substitutes other behaviors for the hair pulling seems to be fairly successful.

Trichotillomania

The most common type of treatment for trichotillomania is behavior therapy that focuses on hair pulling as a bad habit. Simple techniques such as positive feedback for more adaptive behavior and mild aversive conditioning (e.g., snapping a rubber band on one's wrist instead of

CASE STUDY Ms. C.

Ms. C., a 26-year-old graduate student, came to the college clinic in the middle of the spring semester. She was tearful and hesitant, unable to communicate the true nature of her problem to the nurse practitioner. She stated, "I need help with my head." In response to gentle questioning by the nurse, Ms. C. elaborated that she did not know how she was going to interview for jobs after graduation with her "head looking like this." The nurse practitioner noticed that Ms. C. had a pretty scarf wound around her head. With encouragement, Ms. C. removed it, and the nurse practitioner observed multiple circular patches of missing hair that created a polka-dot effect. In addition, Ms. C. had no eyebrows and very sparse eyelashes. She told the nurse practitioner that she had seen many physicians over the years but that no one had been able to cure her problem. After a thorough history and assessment, the nurse practitioner was satisfied that there was no underlying physical condition causing the hair loss.

With support and encouragement, Ms. C. eventually agreed to be evaluated at a local mental health clinic. During her evaluation, Ms. C. spoke glowingly of her family and how they had often urged her to seek help for her "bad habit." She recounted that her parents had taken her to dermatologists, but none of the prescribed treatments had worked. She could not remember exactly when she started pulling her hair out but said that she remembered always playing with it and that at some point in her early teens, the playful tugging became actual pulling. She said her worst time in high school was when some of the boys started to tease her and call her "Dottie"; that was when she started wearing hats and scarves that coordinated with her outfits.

Ms. C. agreed to try a course of medication and to attend twice weekly therapy sessions until the end of the semester. After 3 weeks, she reported feeling better and was not pulling at her hair as often but felt that she could not stop the behavior. Her therapy focused on improving self-esteem so that she would be successful in her job-hunting process and on encouraging her to seek ongoing therapy when she returned to her upstate hometown. Ms. C. understood that her problem was longstanding and that there was no quick fix. With her parents' assistance, a psychotherapist near her home was identified and contacted.

NURSING CARE PLAN **Impluse-Control Disorder (Trichotillomania)**

Expected Outcomes	Nursing Interventions	Evaluations
• Client will understand the relationship of specific stressors to feelings and actions.	• Assess the client and family for all types of impulse-control disorders or obsessive-compulsive disorder. • Ask client to recall situations which trigger the behavior.	• Shares with treatment staff that as a child she thought that her behavior was normal because her older brother also had bald spots as a result of hair-pulling and he "outgrew it."
• Client will experience a reduction in level of anxiety and episodes of hair-pulling.	• Listen empathetically to the client's thoughts regarding her feelings and what she experiences before, during, and after a hair-pulling episode.	• Discusses how angry she has been with her parents for forcing her to attend college and to get "steady work" when all she has ever wanted to do was to be a landscaper and to work outside making the environment beautiful.
• Client will utilize alternative coping behaviors.	• Teach relaxation techniques. • Provide positive feedback when client uses more adaptive coping behaviors. • Encourage use of mild aversive conditioning techniques (band snapping) when the urge to pull hair occurs.	• Successfully uses some of the suggested relaxation techniques. • Reports fewer symptoms such as abdominal pain. • Increasingly uses more appropriate coping behaviors. • Learns self-hypnosis to control the hair-pulling episodes.
• Client will participate in individual and group psychotherapy.	• Discuss the importance of participating in therapy sessions.	• Attends all scheduled sessions as an in-patient.
• Client follows medication regimen.	• Review medication regimen and education with client on a daily basis.	• Can successfully repeat information about medication schedule and the specific drug information.
• Client will understand the need for ongoing therapy after discharge from the in-patient unit.	• Discuss the importance of continuing therapy as an out-patient.	• Signs a discharge treatment plan to continue treatment modalities as an out-patient. • Accepts information about self-help support groups.

Visit http://nursing.jbpub.com/psychiatric for additional care plans and exercises.

Implications for Evidence-Based Practice

Recent studies into the understanding of such forces as motivation, reward, and addiction have provided new insight into the causation and pathophysiology of substance and behavioral disorders. There appears to be a strong neurobiological link between substance abuse disorders and such behavioral addictions as pathologic gambling, kleptomania, pyromania, compulsive buying, and compulsive sexual behavior. Improved understanding of the relationship of these disorders and their frequent co-occurrence can assist practitioners in improving treatment strategies for intervening with these clients (Grant, Brewer, & Potenza, 2006).

hair pulling) have good results. Individual psychotherapy addresses the client's low self-esteem, family relationships, and correction of false beliefs (e.g., no one likes the client because of the hair loss; Andreasen & Black, 2006). Hypnosis has some success in helping the client substitute behaviors, and self-hypnosis can be taught to the client for support between therapy sessions (Reid et al., 1997). The medication most successful in treating this disorder has been the tricyclic

Considerations for Client and Family Education

Nurses should encourage clients with impulse-control disorders to recognize the feelings, tensions, and stressors that produce the particular behaviors. Clients can be helped to recognize those controls within themselves, in their family relationships, and in the community that help them manage the impulse-control behavior. Nurses should discuss with the client the importance of continuing therapy (psychotherapy, family therapy, complementary therapies, 12-step programs, and medications) even when the specific symptom appears controlled. The client must recognize that control is linked directly to the therapy, and noncompliance with therapy can easily cause a relapse. Families and significant others should be advised how to intervene and whom to call if the behaviors become self-destructive or potentially harmful to others. Nurses can discuss complementary therapies such as massage, relaxation, meditation, imagery, exercise, and aversive conditioning with clients. Clients and families should be assisted in recognizing that controlling these behaviors is often a lifelong challenge.

clomipramine (Anafranil) with some clinicians suggesting success with escitalopram (Lexapro), a selective serotonin uptake inhibitor. Unfortunately, recurrence of this disorder is common, and can be precipitated by a variety of physical and emotional stressors.

Critical Thinking Question Why are 12-step programs often helpful in treating patients with impulse-control disorders?

Summary

This chapter provides an overview of adjustment disorders related to depression, anxiety, disturbances of conduct, and disturbances of emotions and conduct. The impulse-control disorders that were explored were intermittent explosive disorder, kleptomania, pyromania, pathologic gambling, and trichotillomania.

Adjustment disorders are related to a recent stress and result in significant impairment in social, occupational, or academic functioning. The feelings being expressed are in excess of what one would expect from exposure to such a stress. Any sadness associated with an adjustment disorder should not be confused with normal bereavement or major clinical depression. Symptoms usually abate within 6 months once the stress ceases.

Although impulse-control disorders appear very different, they share the presence of uncontrollable urges to perform potentially harmful or self-destructive behaviors. These disorders are generally under-diagnosed. Clients with impulse-control disorders have considerable emotional problems and behaviors that negatively impact on family relationships, friendships, and their ability to function at work or school.

Annotated References

American Psychiatric Association. (2000). *Diagnostic and statistical manual of mental disorders* (4th ed., text rev.). Washington, DC: Author.

This is the fourth edition of the American Psychiatric Association's official nomenclature of psychiatric conditions and disorders. It provides a systematic listing of the official codes and categories, a description of the multiaxial system for diagnosis, and diagnostic criteria for each of the disorders. It is used by psychiatrists, physicians, psychologists, registered nurses, social workers, therapists, and other mental health workers in all clinical settings.

Andreasen, N. C., & Black, D. W. (2006). *Introductory textbook of psychiatry* (4th ed.). Washington, DC: American Psychiatric Press.

This is a basic psychiatric medical textbook. It is simple, clear, and factual and can be used by students of medicine, nursing, psychology, social work, and other counselors and therapists.

Casey, P. (2001). Adult adjustment disorder: A review of its current diagnostic status. *Journal of Psychiatric Practice, 7*(1), 32–40.

This is a review of the information that is available on the epidemiology, clinical features, validity, measurement, and treatment of adjustment disorders.

Christenson, G., Mackenzie, T., & Mitchell, J. (1991). Characteristics of sixty adult chronic hair pullers. *American Journal of Psychiatry, 148*, 365–370.

This article carefully reviews the characteristics and histories of 60 individuals with prolonged experiences of hair pulling.

Editor. (1992). Adjustment disorders in childhood and adolescence. *The Harvard Mental Health Letter, 9*(1), 1–4.

This early article discusses adjustment disorders as they present in children and adolescents.

Encyclopedia of Mental Disorders. (2005). *Adjustment disorder.* Retrieved September 7, 2007, from http://www.minddisorders.com/A-Br/Adjustment-disorder.html

Provides information and statistics on the response rate to treatment of individuals with adjustment disorder.

Grant, J. E., Brewer, J. A., & Potenza, M. N. (2006). The neurobiology of substance and behavioral addictions. *CNS Spectrums, 11*(12), 924–930.

This article discusses the biochemical, functional neuroimaging, genetic studies, and treatment research that suggest a strong neurobiological link between behavioral addictions and substance use disorders.

Grassi, L., Mangelli, L., Fava, G. A., Grandi, S., Ottolini, F., Porcelli, P., et al. (2006). Psychosomatic characterization of adjustment disorders in the medical setting: Some suggestions for DSM-V. *Journal of Affective Disorders, 96*(3), 165–175.

This article reports on a study of 100 patients with both a medical illness and adjustment disorder. The authors concluded that utilizing criteria for psychosomatic symptoms could improve and make more specific the treatment of patients with adjustment disorders.

Henry, J. P. (1990). Stress, neuroendocrine patterns and emotional response. In J. D. Noshpitz & R. Coddington (Eds.), *Stressors and the adjustment disorders* (pp. 362–391). New York: John Wiley.

This classic psychiatric textbook examines the nature of stress, the different types of stressors, vulnerabilities, protective factors, and various methods of prevention and intervention.

Kerr, N. J. (1990). Ego competency: A framework for formulating the nursing care plan. *Perspectives in Psychiatric Care, 26*(4), 30–35.

This unique article describes how nurses can use the Ego Competency Model (ECM) in psychiatric nursing to assess ego strengths and deficits in developing nursing interventions and plans of care for different clients.

Kessler, R. C., Coccaro, E. F., Fava, M., Jaeger, S., Jin, R., et al. (2006). The prevalence and correlates of DSM-IV intermittent explosive disorder in the National Comorbidity Survey Replication. *Archives of General Psychiatry, 63*(6), 669–678.

This article reports that intermittent explosive disorder is a much more common condition than previously recognized. It also states that the early age at onset of IED behaviors, the significant associations with comorbid mental disorders, and the current low proportion of cases in treatment all make IED a promising disorder for early detection, outreach, and treatment.

Krupnick, S., & Wade, A. (1999). *Psychiatric care planning*. Springhouse, PA: Springhouse.

This excellent reference includes specific suggestions for planning the care of psychiatric patients, including psychiatric diagnostic categories, nursing diagnoses, outcome criteria, and discharge planning.

Lion, J. R. (1992). The intermittent explosive disorder. *Psychiatric Annals, 22*, 64–66.

This article extensively explores the specific characteristics and treatments associated with uncontrolled outbursts of aggressive behavior.

McElroy, S., Pope, H., Hudson, J., Keck, P., & White, K. (1991). Kleptomania: A report of twenty cases. *American Journal of Psychiatry, 148*, 652–657.

This article provides unique insight into the behaviors and characteristics of individuals with this rarely studied disorder. It focuses on demographics, phenomenology, psychopathology, and family and treatment histories.

Meintz, S., & Larson, C. (1994). Can you spot this kind of addiction? *RN, 75*(7) 42–45.

This article discusses the increase in pathologic gambling behaviors nationally and how nurses can easily monitor for the development of this problem and intervene in the early stages.

National Council on Problem Gambling. (2007). 10 questions about gambling behavior. Retrieved August 25, 2007, from http://www.ncpgambling.org/i4a/pages/Index.cfm?pageID53439

This is a listing of ten questions that can be answered by "yes" or "no" to assess if gambling may be a problem for an individual.

National Gambling Impact Study Commission Final Report. (1999). Retrieved August 25, 2007, from http://govinfo.library.unt.edu/ngisc/reports/fullrpt.html

This is a report to Congress on the status of gambling in the United States by a Presidential Commission. It reviews the expansion of gambling in the nation, types of gambling, the regulation of gambling, the problems with gambling and pathological gambling, the impact of gambling on people and places, and recommendations for future research.

Pruessner, J. C., Baldwin, M. W., Dedovic, K., Renwick, R., Mahani, N. K., et al. (2005). Self-esteem, locus of control, hippocampal volume, and cortisol regulation in young and old adulthood. *NeuroImage, 28*(4), 815–826.

This article reports on a study of two age groups who were exposed to a psychosocial stress test. Self-esteem and internal locus of control were significantly correlated with hippocampal volume in both young and elderly subjects.

Reid, W. H., Balis, G. D., & Sutton, B. J. (1997). *The treatment of psychiatric disorders* (3rd ed.). Bristol, PA: Brunner/Mazel.

This psychiatric textbook specifically addresses mental disorders as classified in the APA's manual. There is a particular emphasis on neuropsychiatric disorders, substance-related disorders, and disorders of childhood and adolescence.

Shulman, T. (2005). *Something for nothing: Shoplifting addiction and recovery.* Haverford, PA: Infinty Publishing Company.

This book presents shoplifting or kleptomania as an addiction rather than an impulse disorder and focuses on shoplifting recovery groups as the primary intervention in the behavior.

Soltys, S. (1992). Pyromania and firesetting behavior. *Psychiatric Annals, 22*, 79–83.

This article seeks to explain the motivation and behaviors of individuals who set fires.

Spitzer, R., Gibbon, M., Skodol, A. E., Williams, J. B. W., & First, M. B. (2002). *DSM-IV-TR Casebook: A learning companion to the Diagnostic and Statisti-*

cal Manual of Mental Disorders (4th ed.). Arlington, VA: American Psychiatric Publishing, Inc.

This book presents real-life case vignettes illustrating presentations of the diagnoses in *DSM-IV-TR*.

Volberg, R. (1994). The prevalence and demographics of pathological gamblers: Implications for public health. *American Journal of Public Health, 84*(2), 237–241.

This article explores the potential impact of continued legalized gambling on the overall rate of gambling problems in the general population and in specific at-risk groups.

Williams, J. (2002). *Pyromania, kleptomania, and other impulse-control disorders.* Berkeley Heights, NJ: Enslow Publishers.

This book describes the characteristics of impulse control disorders, the possible genetic, developmental, and chemical causes, and methods of treatment.

Woods, D. W., Flessner, C. A., Franklin, M. E., Keuthen, N. J., Goodwin, R. A., Stein, D. J., et al. (2006). The Trichotillomania Impact Project (TIP): Exploring phenomenology, functional impairment and treatment utilization. *Journal of Clinical Psychology, 67*(12), 1877–1888.

This is an article on the results of an Internet-based survey of self-selecting individuals who met the *DSM-IV-TR* criteria for trichotillomania.

Internet Resources

http://nursing.jbpub.com/psychiatric

Visit http://nursing.jbpub.com/psychiatric for interactive exercises, NCLEX review questions, WebLinks, and more.

CHAPTER 23

Personality Disorders

Patricia G. O'Brien

LEARNING OBJECTIVES

After reading this chapter, you will be able to:

- Differentiate between personality traits and personality disorders.
- Name the types of personality disorders.
- List the behaviors associated with each personality disorder.
- Describe the therapeutic nursing interventions to assist clients with personality disorders.

KEY TERMS

Antisocial personality disorder
Avoidant personality disorder
Borderline personality disorder
Cognitive restructuring
Dependent personality disorder
Dialectical behavior therapy (DBT)
Histrionic personality disorder
Narcissistic personality disorder
Obsessive-compulsive personality disorder
Paranoid personality disorder
Personality disorder
Personality traits
Schizoid personality disorder
Schizotypal personality disorder
Separation-individuation process
Splitting

http://nursing.jbpub.com/psychiatric

Visit http://nursing.jbpub.com/psychiatric for interactive exercises, NCLEX review questions, WebLinks, and more.

Introduction

Dominant behavioral patterns or personality traits that become pervasive and problematic may meet the diagnostic criteria for a personality disorder. In the American Psychiatric Association's *Diagnostic and Statistical Manual of Mental Disorders,* Fourth Edition, Text Revision (*DSM-IV-TR*), personality disorders are classified on Axis II and are distinguished from the major mental disorders classified on Axis I (APA, 2000).

Personality traits differ from personality disorders. Personality traits are enduring patterns of perceiving, relating to, and thinking about oneself and one's environment that are exhibited in a range of social and personal contexts. Only personality traits that are inflexible and maladaptive and cause significant functional impairment or personal distress constitute personality disorders. A **personality disorder** is an enduring pattern of inner experience and behavior that deviates markedly from the expectations of the individual's culture, is pervasive and inflexible, has an onset in adolescence or early adulthood, is stable over time, and leads to distress in important areas of functioning (APA, 2000, p. 686).

A personality change that appears suddenly, in response to a life situation, is not diagnosed as a personality disorder. This holds true even though the change may be problematic, such as increased dependency after the death of a spouse. A personality disorder can coexist with an Axis I diagnosis, but the major features of some mental disorders, such as schizophrenia and anxiety disorders, are more properly associated with the primary diagnosis rather than a personality disorder.

Everyone at one time or another exhibits behaviors that characterize the various personality disorders. A person must have functional impairment as a result of the behaviors to actually be diagnosed with a personality disorder.

Nurses are likely to encounter clients with personality disorders in all healthcare settings and clinical specialties.

Types of Personality Disorders

The *DSM-IV-TR* identifies 10 specific personality disorders and 1 additional category for a personality disorder not otherwise specified. The personality disorders are organized into three clusters that define the predominant characteristics of the disorders. A pattern of behaviors is associated with each of the personality disorders (APA, 2000).

Cluster A

Cluster A includes odd or eccentric behavior. A person with **paranoid personality disorder** is distrustful and suspicious and tends to interpret others' motives as malevolent. Those with **schizoid personality disorder** are detached from social relationships and have a restricted range of emotions. Persons with **schizotypal personality disorder** experience acute discomfort in close relationships, have cognitive or perceptual distortions, and demonstrate eccentric behavior.

Cluster B

Cluster B includes dramatic, emotional behavior. People with **antisocial personality disorder** disregard and violate the rights of others. A person with **borderline personality disorder** has unstable interpersonal relationships, self-image, and affect, as well as marked impulsivity. Those with **histrionic personality disorder** have excessive emotions and are attention seekers. Clients with **narcissistic personality disorder** are grandiose, need admiration, and lack empathy.

Cluster C

Cluster C consists of anxious, fearful behavior. People with **avoidant personality disorder** have social inhibition, feelings of inadequacy, and hypersensitivity to negative evaluation. Clients with **dependent personality disorder** are submissive, and their clinging behavior is related to an excessive need to be cared for. Those diagnosed with **obsessive-compulsive personality disorder** are preoccupied with orderliness, perfectionism, and control.

Not Otherwise Specified

Personality disorder not otherwise specified does not meet the full criteria for any one personality disorder. Rather, it has the features of more than one personality disorder that causes significant impairment in functioning.

Incidence and Prevalence

The prevalence of personality disorders is difficult to determine because the diagnosis of personality disorder varies with cultural norms, because people may display symptoms of more than one personality disorder, and because not all people who meet the diagnostic criteria for a personality disorder enter the treatment system. It is estimated that 10–20% of the general population meets the criteria for one or more personality disorders (Andreasen & Black, 2006). The percentage is significantly higher among psychiatric populations, especially those in in-patient settings. Persons with obsessive compulsive disorder have a very high incidence of personality disorders, especially the cluster C anxious type disorders. The incidence of antisocial personality disorder among psychiatric in-patients ranges from 3–30%; the highest frequency is seen among clients diagnosed with substance abuse disorder.

Borderline personality disorder accounts for 30–50% of all people diagnosed with personality disorder (Smallwood, 2004). Paranoid personality disorder is found in 1–30% of psychiatric in-patients, and dependent personality disorder is most prevalent among clients followed in mental health clinics.

Because gender bias may be a factor in diagnosing personality disorders, actual differences between men and women are uncertain. Information available on the frequency of diagnosis indicates that 75% of persons diagnosed with borderline personality disorder are women. Men are more likely to be diagnosed with narcissistic, paranoid, schizotypal, and antisocial personality disorders.

Personality disorders are usually diagnosed in adolescents and young adults. Although traits suggestive of some personality disorders, including paranoid, schizoid, and schizotypal types, may be seen in children, these traits may change as the child progresses to adulthood. Therefore, children are rarely diagnosed with personality disorders. The diagnosis of antisocial personality disorder is made only if the client is at least 18 years of age.

Etiology

Developmental Factors

An interruption in the normal course of psychologic and emotional development or a failure to achieve the defined tasks associated with individuation contribute to the development of personality disorders. Mahler, Pine, and Bergman (1975) described the individuation process as a series of phases through which the individual progresses during the first 3 years of life. Each phase is associated with a primary task (**Table 23-1**).

The child must successfully complete the **separation-individuation process** to develop effective relationships with significant others, including the ability to integrate the person's positive and negative components. A disruption in any of the tasks may predispose one to the development of a personality disorder. Kernberg's object-relations theory (1976) attributes borderline personality disorder to a failure to master the rapprochement phase, leading to a fear of abandonment evidenced by clinging, dependent behavior and an inability to achieve object constancy. This manifests as a tendency to view others as all good or all bad. This phenomenon, referred to as **splitting**, is considered a hallmark of borderline personality disorder.

Freud theorized that specific personality disorders can be matched with a fixation at a particular stage of ego development. Fixation at the oral stage was thought to result in dependent personality disorder. Fixation at the anal stage was associated with OCD, and fixation at the phallic stage was matched with histrionic personality disorder. However, there is little evidence that fixation at a particular stage of development leads to a specific personality disorder.

Although developmental stages are usually presented in a stepwise, orderly fashion, the phases actually overlap because individuals mature at different rates.

Splitting is a hallmark of borderline personality disorder.

The events and sequences that result in personality pathologies are complex and difficult to unravel.

Personalities develop in response to another person.

Table 23-1 Phases of Individuation

Age	Phase	Task
Birth–1 month	Autistic phase	Waking–sleeping
1–5 months	Symbiotic phase	Fusion with mother
5–10 months	Differentiation phase	Awareness of separateness between self and mother
10–16 months	Practicing phase	Increased independence and exploration of the environment
16–24 months	Rapprochement phase	Becomes fearful of separation from mother and seeks closeness
24–36 months	Object constancy phase	Completes the individuation process

Source: Adapted from Mahler, Pine, & Bergman, 1975.

Environmental Factors

The inadequate achievement of early developmental tasks has been attributed to environmental factors such as emotional deprivation or inconsistent parenting. The relationship between the environment and the development of personality disorders is not clearly understood, nor do researchers fully understand the neurobiology of personality disorders. Thus, it is essential to avoid harshly judging or blaming the parents of clients with personality disorders. Many consumer and mental health advocacy groups, including families of clients with personality disorders, are working with professionals to understand better what influences the development of these disorders.

The relationship between early prolonged, severe trauma and the development of borderline personality disorder remains unclear and is an area of continuing research (Goodman, New, & Siever, 2004). Humiliation and emotional trauma also have been related to paranoid personality disorder. Exposure to trauma may interfere with the development of trust and intimacy and result in an inability to modulate emotions.

Biogenetic Factors

Although the nature of personality development depends on a variety of environmental factors, an increased awareness of the underlying biology of personality disorders provides an alternative or complementary perspective for understanding them. The impulsive aggression associated with borderline personality disorder has been attributed to deficits in the neurotransmitter serotonin and to alterations in the functioning of the prefrontal cortex (Goodman, New, & Siever, 2004).

Researchers have discovered familial links between some of the personality disorders and the Axis I mental disorders that suggest a genetic basis. An increased incidence of schizotypal personality disorder is seen among the relatives of schizophrenics, and a familial link exists between paranoid personality disorder and paranoid schizophrenia. Persons with borderline personality disorder are at risk for developing major depression. Symptoms of personality disorder in elderly clients may be associated with disability and impaired social and interpersonal functioning after an acute depressive episode (Abrams, Spielman, Alexopoulos, & Klausner, 1998).

Impulsiveness, avoidance, and aggression have been associated with reduced monoamine oxidase (MAO) activity (Stalenheim, von Knorring, & Oreland, 1997). Electroencephalographic (EEG) abnormalities in persons with borderline and antisocial personality disorders suggest that a subtle brain injury or defect may cause the behavioral manifestations. A disturbance in fetal or childhood development of the brain and nervous system may be at least partially responsible for borderline personality disorder (Hampton, 1997). A recent review of the neurobiological models of personality concludes that current understanding is not sufficient to explain the structure of personality traits and disorders (Paris, 2005). However, the neurobiologic study of personality disorders is in its infancy and has the potential to influence both diagnosis and treatment.

Clinical Presentation

Few people with personality disorders display the traits of only the one disorder with which they have been diagnosed. Typically, people exhibit traits belonging to several of the defined personality disorders.

The APA (2000) offers broad criteria to identify personality disorders as well as criteria specific to the individual personality disorders.

Diagnostic Criteria

The general diagnostic criteria for personality disorder aid in distinguishing a personality disorder from personality traits, an Axis I mental disorder, or an organically based personality change (**Table 23-2**).

Paranoid personality disorder begins in early adulthood.

Table 23-2 Diagnostic Criteria for a Personality Disorder

1. A pattern of behavior that includes at least two of the following:
   - Thought disturbances, including how one perceives and interprets him- or herself, others, and events
   - Mood disturbances, including the range, intensity, lability, and appropriateness of one's emotions
   - Troublesome interpersonal relationships
   - Impulsive behavior
2. These behaviors
   - Have their onset in adolescence or early adulthood
   - Deviate from expected cultural behavior
   - Are enduring, inflexible, and extend across a range of personal, social, and occupational situations
   - Cause significant distress
   - Are not a manifestation of another mental disorder
   - Are not due to a medical condition, a medication, or other substance

Source: Adapted from American Psychiatric Association, 2000.

Additional Criteria

The *DSM-IV-TR* provides additional criteria that establish the diagnosis of each of the recognized personality disorders (APA, 2000). These criteria focus on behaviors that characterize the disorder and help inform the nurse's assessment. Behaviors associated with each personality disorder are identified in the following sections, as are the likely functional areas in which the client may be experiencing distress.

Paranoid Personality Disorder

These clients are often difficult to get along with because of their argumentative, sarcastic, and often hostile manner of relating to others. Not surprisingly, their behavior elicits a negative response in others that only serves to justify their actions to themselves. Clients with paranoid personality disorder have a fundamentally suspicious view of the world that makes them view the simple mistakes of others as deliberate intentions to cause personal harm. These people usually have problems establishing and maintaining close relationships and often are guarded during interviews, making it difficult for the nurse to obtain a personal history.

Schizoid Personality Disorder

Clients with schizoid personality disorder have a profound inability to form personal relationships, even with members of their immediate family. Even as children or teenagers these clients were viewed as different by their peers, perhaps teased by others, and often described as underachievers. As adults they seem indifferent to others, lack close friends, and show little interest in sexual relationships or marriage. However, not all "loners" have schizoid personality disorder. According to the general criteria, the diagnosis requires that the traits be inflexible and maladaptive, causing significant impairment or subjective distress. These clients may be referred for treatment resulting from difficulties in an occupational setting.

Schizotypal Personality Disorder

Clients with schizotypal personality disorder also have paranoid features and are socially isolated, but can be distinguished from clients with paranoid and schizoid personality disorder by the presence of cognitive and perceptual distortions. These distortions may take the form of magical rituals, excessive superstitions, and their belief that they can influence events through their thoughts. They are frequently described by others as odd or eccentric and may have inappropriate emotional responses in social situations. Clients with this disorder exhibit no desire for relationships and typically describe a severe social anxiety that worsens rather than abates over time. The assessment must exclude a concurrent major depressive disorder that is commonly seen with this personality disorder.

Antisocial Personality Disorder

Clients with antisocial personality disorder must be at least 18 years of age and have displayed some evidence of a conduct disorder before 15 years of age. Early symptoms include a display of aggression toward people or animals, destruction of property, deceitfulness or theft, and a violation of rules. This pattern of behavior continues into adulthood and is characterized as guiltless, exploitative, and irresponsible. These clients show little regard for others and make use of a superficial charm to deceive and manipulate others for personal gain (i.e., power, money, sex). The assessment may reveal clues to this disorder, such as a dishonorable military discharge, a criminal record, serial or multiple sexual relationships, frequent physical altercations, and an inability to support themselves. A family history is not uncommon as well as the coexistence of major depression or substance abuse.

Table 23-3 Diagnostic Criteria for Borderline Personality Disorder

A pervasive, enduring pattern of behavior beginning by early adulthood and present in a variety of contexts, as indicated by five (or more) of the following:

1. Frantic efforts to avoid abandonment
2. Unstable and intense interpersonal relationships characterized by alternating between extremes of idealization and devaluation
3. Unstable self-image or sense of self
4. Impulsiveness in at least two areas that are potentially self-damaging (e.g., spending, sex, substance abuse, reckless driving, binge eating)
5. Recurrent suicidal acts, gestures, or threats, or self-mutilating behavior
6. Marked mood swings (e.g., intense episodic dysphoria, irritability, or anxiety)
7. Chronic feelings of emptiness
8. Inappropriate, intense anger
9. Transient paranoid ideation or dissociative symptoms

Source: Adapted from American Psychiatric Association, 2000.

Borderline Personality Disorder

Clients with borderline personality disorder (see **Table 23-3**) have a fear of abandonment that results in unstable and intense interpersonal relationships. These clients often sabotage close relationships or even pending successes, fearing their inability to meet the demands of the situation. Sudden anger is a way of avoiding another person's rejection. Mood instability and intense anger characterize this disorder. The history often reveals that these clients have seen multiple therapists because they cannot tolerate risking the rejection that accompanies a close interpersonal relationship. These clients describe feeling empty and have a history of self-mutilating and suicidal behavior. Borderline personality disorder also has a familial pattern and is associated with an increased incidence of substance abuse and antisocial personality disorder.

People with antisocial personality disorder may enter treatment through the forensic system.

Borderline personality disorder behavior is unstable, and hospitalization is often precipitated by self-inflicted injury or a suicide attempt.

Histrionic Personality Disorder

Clients with histrionic personality disorder express their emotions very theatrically and dramatically. Their need for attention often interferes with establishing significant relationships. A superficial quality characterizes their approach to both people and projects. Initial enthusiasm is rapidly replaced with boredom, making a commitment to long-term goals difficult. They have an inordinate need to impress others with their appearance, and attention-seeking behaviors, including seductiveness and somatization.

Narcissistic Personality Disorder

Clients with narcissistic personality disorder convey a grandiose sense of self-importance and feel entitled to preferential treatment. They talk about themselves at length, neglecting the feelings of others. Interpersonal relationships and work performance may be impaired by an extreme need for admiration and an intolerance for criticism. These clients often overreact to criticism or defeat with deep humiliation. The clinical assessment should consider the concurrent existence of substance abuse or anorexia nervosa.

Avoidant Personality Disorder

Clients with avoidant personality disorder are sensitive to rejection in social situations because they are inhibited, anxious, and have low self-esteem. They may describe themselves as shy or timid. The absence of social skills, extreme self-consciousness, and fear of embarrassment can interfere with the development of interpersonal relationships and with job performance or advancement.

> The person with dependent personality disorder may act in a way that is anticipated to earn the nurse's approval.

Dependent Personality Disorder

Dependent personality disorder is characterized by an excessive reliance on others, typically a parent or spouse, for emotional support. The client lacks confidence in the ability to be self-reliant, is generally uncomfortable being alone, is incapable of making independent decisions, and is fearful of separation. These clients are particularly vulnerable when the dependent relationship is threatened by events such as death or divorce. The client often immediately seeks a replacement relationship. Avoidance of responsibility as a result of intrinsic self-doubt may impair interpersonal and occupational performance. Dependent personality disorder does not apply to cultural and situation-appropriate circumstances, such as a person with a disability.

Obsessive-Compulsive Personality Disorder

Persons with obsessive-compulsive personality disorder are preoccupied with orderliness and perfection. Paying strict attention to rules, details, procedures, lists, and schedules is their way of achieving control. They tend to save everything in case it may have future importance. These clients are workaholics who almost never take vacations. Even leisure activities are structured in the form of a game or sport to be "conquered." Work and structured activities allow the client to avoid situations with family or friends that may call for the expression of emotions, something that makes them uncomfortable. The perfectionism may result in missed deadlines, difficulty in delegating responsibility, and trouble adjusting to change. Depending on the nature of the client's occupation, these behaviors may be detrimental to their performance. The ambition, competitiveness, and hostility associated with this personality disorder also are risk factors for cardiac disease. Unlike obsessive-compulsive disorder, the Axis I anxiety disorder with a similar name, there is an absence of true obsessions and compulsions in clients with obsessive-compulsive personality disorder.

Assessment

When taking the history, the nurse should be alert for patterns of behavior that cause the client distress. In establishing the client's motivation for treatment, the nurse must consider the reason the client presents for help at that particular time. The clinician who elicits a history consistent with one or more personality disorders must consider the duration of the symptoms, including the age at onset, and determine that the symptoms are pervasive across a range of situations and are related to impaired functioning.

The client may not be aware of how a behavioral pattern has affected interpersonal, social, or work relationships. A person with antisocial personality disorder may not readily provide information about arrests or other aberrant behaviors. When establishing a diagnosis, it is helpful to obtain the client's consent to corroborate information with relatives, former therapists, friends, and significant others. The nurse may learn much from the client's interactions during the assessment process, but persons who have known the client for a long time can provide information from extended observation.

Organic causes, including dementia, head injury, or brain tumor, must be considered if the personality changes had a sudden onset. Substances of abuse as well as prescribed medications can alter behavior; taking a thorough drug history is essential. Other mental disorders must be excluded before establishing the diagnosis of personality disorder. A mental status examination and family medical and psychiatric histories are helpful in determining the diagnosis.

Treatment

Some form of psychotherapy, in combination with medication, and the skillful management of challenging behaviors are common approaches to the treatment of personality disorders.

Psychotherapy

Psychotherapeutic approaches to the treatment of personality disorders vary depending on the nature of the disorder and the therapist's preference and training. Regression therapy attempts to change current behavior through the exploration and understanding of early life experiences. Conversely, supportive psychotherapy avoids the past and focuses on strengthening current defenses. Cognitive and behavioral therapies have been adapted to the treatment of personality disorders and include the following techniques:

- *Cognitive restructuring:* **Cognitive restructuring** is a process in which the client identifies common negative or catastrophic thoughts that interfere with functioning. Negative thoughts are replaced with constructive thoughts that assist the client in changing feelings and behaviors.
- *Systematic desensitization:* Systematic desensitization gradually reduces the client's anxiety and fear related to situations through real or imagined exposure.
- *Dialectical behavior therapy:* **Dialectical behavior therapy (DBT)** is a cognitive-behavioral treatment for clients with borderline personality disorder (Linehan, 1993). Individual therapy utilizes validation and problem-solving strategies, emphasizes the client's strengths, and applies the principles of positive reinforcement to motivate behavioral changes. Coping skills are taught in group sessions and focus on identifying and correcting skill deficits in all aspects of the client's life. Treatment goals include reducing suicidal gestures, preventing attrition from therapy, regulating emotions, and tolerating distress (Hampton, 1997).

Psychotherapy is conducted either individually or in groups. Groups may be particularly effective for clients who have little insight into their behavior and relationships with others. The group members are helpful in pointing these out to the client. Whereas group therapy may be appropriate to counter a client's social anxiety, some clients with schizoid personality disorder may find a group too threatening, at least in the beginning of treatment. The therapist's skills are essential in controlling attention-seeking behaviors without communicating rejection. Paranoid personality disorder can result in distortions of what is said or done in a group and requires monitoring by the therapist.

Regardless of the psychotherapeutic approach, the therapist's attitude is the critical factor. The therapist must be alert to countertransference, that is, the feelings experienced by the therapist in relationship to the client. It is important for the therapist to acknowledge the client's feelings, thus validating his or her experiences and worth, and to relate to clients in a direct, open, and honest style that communicates respect and support.

Clinical Example: Cognitive Restructuring

A person with avoidant personality disorder who is tempted to cancel a job interview may be thinking, "If I go on this interview, I will be very nervous and will not know what to say. I will make a fool of myself. I have no chance of getting this job anyway." The cognitive therapist helps the client challenge the validity of these statements and gradually replace them with realistic thoughts that the client can accept. These may consist of "I am nervous, but most people are nervous on interviews. I can prepare some things to say about myself and my experience. I may not get the job, but it is good experience. I may be less nervous the next time. At least I will have a chance at the job."

Clinical Example: Systematic Desensitization

The therapist guides the client to relax while imaging the job interview situation. The client is instructed to image the events leading up to the interview, such as calling to schedule an appointment, then reviewing a resume, then calling to confirm the appointment, then dressing for the interview, traveling to the interview, and finally, imaging the actual interview. At each step, the client uses relaxation techniques and views his or her performance as going well. This gradual imagined exposure to increasingly challenging tasks when combined with social skills and assertiveness training helps to decrease isolation and improve performance in the real situation.

The angry client who interprets neutral events as intentionally directed at him or her can benefit from cognitive restructuring.

Pharmacotherapy

Medication has a limited role in the treatment of most personality disorders, except as a temporary measure to reduce anxiety. The symptoms of schizotypal and borderline personality disorders, however, respond to pharmacotherapy. Low doses of high-potency neuroleptics such as thiothixene (Navane) or haloperidol (Haldol) may be effective for both disorders, even in the absence of frank psychosis (Reid, Balis, & Sutton, 1997). The atypical antipsychotics, including clozapine (Clozaril), show promise in the treatment of both positive and negative symptoms in clients with borderline personality disorder. Olanzapine (Zyprexa), an atypical antipsychotic, has been shown to be effective in treating symptoms in women with borderline personality disorder, with the exception of depressive symptoms (Zanarini & Frankenburg, 2001). The MAO inhibitors occasionally are used for atypical depressive and suicidal symptoms and impulse control problems associated with borderline personality disorder.

Pharmacotherapy has limited applications to other personality disorders. Lithium carbonate (Eskalith), carbamazepine (Tegretol), and propranolol (Inderal) have been used to decrease physical aggression in clients with antisocial personality disorder, borderline personality disorder, and other disorders. The selective serotonin-reuptake inhibitors, including fluoxetine (Prozac), can effectively treat phobic symptoms in clients with avoidant personality disorder.

Client Behaviors and Nursing Interventions

Nursing interventions for clients diagnosed with personality disorders are directed at validating the client's experience, ensuring client safety, and teaching effective coping strategies. The interventions target the client's behavior. The schizotypal and borderline personality disorders are the personality disorders encountered most frequently on in-patient psychiatric units. The psychiatric clinical nurse specialist on the consultation-liaison service for a general hospital is called upon frequently to assist the nursing staff with persons whose personality disorders interfere with efforts to deliver care. Even in the absence of a personality disorder, behavioral traits can interfere with the client's recovery or disrupt the clinical setting. Applying specific principles and approaches to behaviors that these clients commonly display (**Table 23-4**) can increase the nurse's sense of competence and decrease frustration. As noted earlier, countertransference impairs the ability to provide effective treatment.

Control is the central issue for manipulative clients. They are always aware of who has power in personal interactions and seldom see themselves as that person.

Table 23-4 Client Behaviors Associated with Personality Disorders

Behavior	Description
Manipulation	Client attempts to communicate important need; staff may feel exploited or taken advantage of
Suicidal and self-mutilating behavior	Often precipitated by threats of rejection or separation, or increased responsibility
Splitting	Client is unable to integrate positive and negative feelings; related to fear of abandonment

Manipulative Behavior

A behavior is labeled *manipulative* if the other person feels he or she has been taken advantage of, used, or exploited. The client's behavior is likely to be termed *manipulative* if it challenges the nurse's control of a situation or if the client achieves some outcome the nurse did not intend. To provide effective therapy, the nurse needs to recognize the behavior as a symptom of the client's illness. The appropriate nursing interventions should be based on what the client is trying to accomplish.

To apply behavioral interventions, it is reasonable to start from the premise that all behavior has meaning. The client with borderline personality disorder who throws a tantrum or self-mutilates is indirectly communicating an unmet need. The client is not always able to identify what the underlying need is, and thus the nurse may have to assess the unstated goal of the client's behavior. The nurse accomplishes this by carefully observing the client's behavior, paying attention to the antecedents and consequences of the behavior.

> Manipulative behavior can be viewed as a patient's unique attempt to communicate an important need. If the staff does not respond to that need, either because of a lack of understanding, or because of negative feelings towards the patient, it may be analogous to staff withdrawal. . . . The patient, unsuccessful in meeting some need, can be expected to become more manipulative. (O'Brien, 1988, p. 239)

The therapeutic intervention the nurse chooses to use with a client is based on the individual client's need at that time. In this section's Clinical Example, for instance, the initial intervention may involve imposing a brief time-out in an effort to limit the temper tantrum behavior. The therapist then spends time with the client and discusses the avoided therapy or visitor. If the nurse feels manipulated, the accompanying frustration and anger may lead to an extended period of isolation for the client, withdrawal of privileges, or other punitive and nontherapeutic actions. If the client's need for attention is unmet, the client may see a need to "up the ante." If the client is trying to avoid therapy or a visitor and is successful, and the tantrum behavior is reinforced. The nurse must determine what purpose the behavior serves for the client, and then help the client meet that need in an acceptable way.

Clinical Example

A tantrum that occurs after a delay in responding to a client's question or in the presence of another client interacting with staff may be the client's way of communicating a need for attention. A tantrum thrown at the beginning of a therapy session or immediately prior to visiting hours may be a way of avoiding therapy or spending time with an expected visitor.

Suicidal and Self-Mutilating Behavior

The suicide rate among persons with borderline personality disorder is well over 5% (Andreasen & Black, 2006). No suicide attempt or threat should be treated casually. A half-hearted first attempt does not mean that the risk of suicide is low. People who use suicidal gestures to gain attention may, in desperation or through miscalculation, actually kill themselves. In one study of 50 teenagers who attempted suicide, 17 said they had wanted to die, although mental health professionals working with them thought only 7 did (Grinspoon, 1996).

The nurse should ask the client directly about the presence of suicidal thoughts. The risk of suicide is greater in clients who have a plausible plan and the means to carry it out. For example, a client who describes a plan to take a drug overdose and has a supply of potentially lethal medication poses a serious suicide risk. Contrary to popular opinion, inquiring about suicidal thoughts does not plant the suggestion in the mind of a client who was not already suicidal.

Client safety may dictate the search for and removal of potentially harmful objects. This search should be conducted whenever possible in the client's presence and always with the client's knowledge. The purpose should be clearly stated as an effort to protect the client from dangerous impulses and in a context of concern. The client may agree to speak to the nurse when suicidal feelings occur. This type of contract begins to identify an alternative approach to acting on suicidal feelings. An appropriate level of observation and client contact needs to be maintained. With help from the nurse, the client may begin to identify the feelings or events that trigger suicidal thoughts. Limiting the time spent discussing suicidal thoughts and extending the time spent discussing other issues or in recreational activities may reinforce nonsuicidal thoughts.

Splitting

Splitting, a phenomenon that characterizes borderline personality disorder, can be particularly disruptive on in-patient units. As a result of early developmental failure to achieve separation-individuation, the client lacks object constancy and is, therefore, unable to integrate positive and negative feelings. These clients tend to view people and situations as all good or all bad. The behavior is a primitive defense against an overwhelming fear of abandonment. The client typically idealizes some staff members and rejects others, and countertransference splits the staff's approach to the nursing care plan. The resulting inconsistencies in the staff's treatment of the client's behavior contribute to an escalation of maladaptive behavior. The staff members occasionally resort to assigning the same people to care for the client to minimize the splitting. If the staff members recognize what is happening and maintain excellent communication among themselves, they can employ an alternative approach of assigning a variety of people to care for the client. This avoids the development of dependency on particular staff members and helps diminish the underlying fear of abandonment.

Asking about suicide does *not* cause the client to consider suicide.

Critical Thinking Questions Imagine arriving to work on an in-patient psychiatric unit, and one patient greets you, saying in a loud voice, "Oh, don't tell me you're in charge today. Everything is so much better when you're not here." How might you feel? How might you react?

Setting Limits

Depending on the particular personality disorder, part of the treatment plan may include limiting certain behaviors, such as angry outbursts, excessive clinging, dependent behavior, or drug-seeking activities. Effective limit setting

Clinical Example

David, who is 8 years old, follows the nurse everywhere she goes on the unit and his constant presence is making it difficult for the nurse to do her work. The nurse assesses this behavior to represent David's need for attention. Rather than send David away or tell him that he cannot follow her, the nurse explains why this behavior is problematic. The nurse suggests some other interim activity for David to do (write her a letter, draw a picture) and agrees that, if David does this, the nurse will spend time with him at a later agreed upon time.

In this example, the nurse's explanation educates David about appropriate behavior, helps him identify alternative behaviors, and, at the same time, meets David's need for attention. The attention becomes a reward that David earns.

When setting limits, the expected behaviors must be stated clearly in a firm, nonpunitive manner.

must be clear, firm, and consistent, and it must be accompanied by the reinforcement of appropriate behavior. Rewarding appropriate behavior is likely to be more effective than imposing punishment when striving for behavioral changes.

Confirming communication validates the client's importance and promotes a trusting relationship.

In setting limits, the nurse must be careful to avoid creating a power struggle. Clients, especially those with personality disorders, are often sensitive to reminders that the nurse is "in charge." Acknowledging the client's feelings and concerns communicates respect and can be effective in disarming the client who anticipates that the nurse will be punitive and controlling. The nurse needs to have realistic goals and to be alert to the danger of using limit-setting activities as a way to act out anger toward the client.

Clinical Example

The concerns for patient safety on in-patient psychiatric units require particular vigilance regarding the presence of contraband, such as drugs or other restricted items. Some clients will challenge the staff by attempting to sneak items on the unit or taunting the staff with verbal reminders that they can do this. The implication is that the staff is not so smart, and the client is smarter.

Staff can respond by imposing further restrictions on the client, including limiting or prohibiting visitors. An alternative approach would be to acknowledge that, despite the staff's efforts, the client could probably find a way to outsmart the staff. Admitting this to the client avoids a power struggle and allows the nurse to focus on the client's need to challenge authority and his or her difficulty committing to the treatment goals.

Of course, the staff continue to conduct searches and visitor inspections, and carry out whatever procedures are in place to secure the unit. However, by choosing to not engage in the power struggle, the nurse opens the door for more meaningful dialogue with this client.

In the first response, the staff get caught up in establishing their authority and the relationship becomes defined in those terms. The alternative approach indicates an understanding that this power struggle has meaning for the client. In this case, the behavior may have served the purpose of helping this client avoid a therapeutic relationship.

Critical Thinking Questions What types of people and what behaviors are likely to make you angry? Why is that?

The Nurse-Client Relationship

Nursing interventions often involve personal interactions in which nurses use their skills and training, as well as their unique personalities, to effect growth and change (Bonnivier, 1996). The nurse models appropriate communication styles and is a safe person on whom the client can try out new skills and behaviors. The nurse must communicate acceptance and respect to help this process. Clients with low self-esteem are particularly sensitive to rejection, a symptom of several personality disorders.

The nurse's manner of relating to the client is either confirming or nonconfirming. *Confirming communication* includes listening to the client, validating the client's feelings, maintaining appropriate eye contact, asking the client's opinion, and engaging the client in problem-solving activities. Examples of nonconfirming communication include talking over the client, interrupting, not looking at the client, engaging in another activity while talking to the client, and offering solutions without considering the client's opinion.

Confirming communication validates the client's importance and promotes a trusting relationship. In a study of effective treatment for clients with borderline personality disorder, trust was the concept identified by both clients and clinicians as crucial for the establishment of the therapeutic alliance and the foundation of treatment (Langley & Klopper, 2005).

Critical Thinking Questions Can you think of a time when you were speaking with someone and you realized that the person was not really interested in what you were saying? What behaviors on the part of the other person made you think that?

Summary

Clients with personality disorders present a broad spectrum of behavioral symptoms and often require lifelong therapeutic intervention. The advanced practice nurse may be either the primary psychotherapist for these clients or the consultant to other caregivers who need direction in

Considerations for Client and Family Education

Behavioral theory states that maladaptive behaviors are to a large extent acquired through learning and represent an attempt to cope with an immediate need (O'Brien, 1997). The nursing goals are to help the client identify how the current behavior interferes with achieving satisfactory interpersonal relationships and to teach the client ways to communicate his or her needs more effectively.

An important aspect of nursing care for clients with personality disorders involves engaging the client in the process of learning new skills and adaptive behaviors. The nurse often has the advantage of observing a client's behavior over time. This provides the nurse with an understanding of the client's ineffective behaviors and the situations in which clients have the most difficulty. Certain skills and their applications have been discussed previously. The nurse can employ social skills training and role playing. This provides clients with tools to lessen their social isolation. Assertiveness training, especially learning to ask for help, aids clients who resort to self-inflicted injury or other extreme behaviors when in need of support. Problem-solving skills reduce helplessness and dependency. Clients with dependent personality disorder can utilize this approach to build confidence and experience in decision making. Groups that focus on problem solving efficiently meet the needs of a variety of clients and concurrently provide an opportunity to practice communication skills. Relaxation training teaches clients methods to reduce anger, anxiety, and impulsivity.

Family members can benefit from learning the principles of limit setting, including the importance of rewarding desired behaviors and strategies for avoiding power struggles. It is critical that family members know to take threats of suicide seriously and to seek immediate assistance in a crisis.

Compliance with medication is enhanced if the client and family understand the purpose of the medication and if the client is actively involved in evaluating the medication's effectiveness on targeted symptoms. Low initial doses of medication help to achieve an effective level with minimum side effects. The nurse is significantly involved in monitoring the effects of medication and in educating the client and family.

establishing a therapeutic relationship. The nurse who is not at the advanced level of practice is likely to encounter these clients in all clinical (medical-surgical and psychiatric) settings. These clients are most challenging, but nurses who recognize the clients' behaviors as symptoms of an illness and an expression of limited coping skills can convey an accepting and hopeful attitude to the client. The nurse's belief that the client is capable of change may be the most important part of working with those who have personality disorders.

CASE STUDY Ms. C.

Ms. C., a 23-year-old, is admitted to a psychiatric in-patient unit after cutting herself superficially on both wrists in a self-described suicide attempt. She was brought to the emergency room (ER) by her boyfriend, Mr. M., who had found Ms. C. at her apartment passed out on her couch, with a small amount of bleeding from her wrists and an empty quart-size bottle of vodka nearby. He had come to the apartment after finding a message on his voice mail from Ms. C., stating that she was going to kill herself. In the ER Ms. C. explained the precipitant for her suicide attempt was Mr. M.'s decision 2 weeks earlier to delay their plans to become engaged.

Ms. C. had one prior psychiatric admission 3 years ago when she was in college. The admission was related to an overdose of over-the-counter sleeping medications and alcohol, and was also precipitated by a breakup with her then boyfriend.

Ms. C.'s family, her mother and two younger sisters, lived in another city, approximately a 3-hour drive away. Her closest support was her roommate, Ms. G., but she has not spoken to Ms. G. in a reasonable way for the past 2 weeks because she is convinced that Ms. G. is responsible for Mr M.'s decision to delay their engagement.

On mental status examination, Ms. C. describes feeling empty, with periods of tearfulness, insomnia, and irritability over the past 2 weeks. She relates having had angry outbursts in recent weeks with Mr. M., Ms. G., her mother, and co-workers. Her diagnosis is borderline personality disorder with suicide attempt and alcohol intoxication.

To assist in developing a nursing care plan for the client with a personality disorder, refer to **Table 23-5** for a list of nursing interventions.

Table 23-5 Nursing Interventions for Clients with Personality Disorders

- Establish nurse-client relationship
  - Identify client's strengths.
  - Use confirming communication.
  - Start from the premise that all behavior has meaning.
  - Attempt to meet the client's needs in an acceptable way.
  - Reward positive behavior.
  - Focus on the process as well as the content of the client's behavior.
- Conduct a suicide assessment
  - Ask direct questions.
  - Assess the nature and frequency of the thoughts.
  - Inquire if the client has a plan.
  - Determine if the client has the means to carry out the plan.
  - Establish if there is a past history of suicide attempts, gestures, or self-mutilation.
  - Identify supports.
  - Evaluate the client's ability to resist urges and get help.
- Maintain safety from suicidal, self-mutilating, impulsive behavior (in in-patient setting)
  - Place on special observation status.
  - Provide for direct supervision.
  - Protect from sexual encounters.
  - Remove dangerous objects.
  - Encourage verbalization of feelings.
- Set limits
  - Identify the self-defeating behaviors (angry outbursts, clinging/dependent behavior) in need of limit setting.
  - Engage client in the process of reducing these behaviors.
  - Identify the client's motivation to change through observation and verbal commitment.
  - Teach the client alternative behaviors.
  - Be clear, firm, and consistent.
  - Reward positive changes.
- Provide skills training specific to client needs
  - Social skills
  - Assertive communication
  - Relaxation training
  - Anger management
  - Problem-solving skills

NURSING CARE PLAN Borderline Personality Disorder

Expected Outcomes	Interventions	Evaluations
• Client will not hurt self or engage in self-destructive behaviors.	• Assess for suicidal ideation. • Place on special observation status. • Encourage verbalization of feelings. • Remove dangerous objects. • Limit and supervise contact with male co-patients.	• Client reports absence of suicidal ideation. • Engages in therapeutic activities with staff. • Client avoids impulsive sexual encounters.
• Client will express an understanding of her behavior.	• Establish therapeutic relationship. • Identify strengths: friends/family/work. • Use confirming communication—this conveys respect and interest. The client is sensitive to rejection, so be sure to keep agreements. • Set limits with angry, clingy, or splitting behaviors: All staff must be firm, clear, and consistent. • Reward efforts to behave appropriately. • Talk about the source of feelings of anger/rejection.	• Client expresses beginning understanding of her behavior and effect on self/others. • Client demonstrates decreased angry outbursts. • Client engages in verbal therapy.

• Client will learn alternative coping skills.	• Provide skills training:
	  • Assertiveness training: ask for help; express disappointment and anger.
	  • Stress management: exercise and relaxation as substitute for alcohol; may help with anger control.
		• Client practices new skills.
		• Client reports skills helpful in meeting needs.

Visit http://nursing.jbpub.com/psychiatric for additional care plans and exercises.

Implications for Evidence-Based Practice

Most of the research and published reviews on personality disorders is related to etiology, diagnosis, co-morbidity, and treatment approaches. While these finding have some implications for nursing practice, the research finding most relevant for nursing practice is the qualitative study by Langley & Klopper (2005) referenced earlier. This study offers evidence for the importance of the nurse-client relationship in influencing client outcomes. The authors conducted individual and group interviews with clients diagnosed with borderline personality disorder and mental health clinicians experienced in treating the disorder. Themes were then identified from the interviews and trust was the concept that both the clients and the clinicians identified as the foundation for therapeutic intervention. This research supports the use of confirming communication techniques and other interventions that contribute to a trusting collaboration between the nurse and client.

Results of a study in Japan suggest that the severity of childhood separation anxiety disorder increases the risk of severe anxious-fearful personality disorders (Cluster C) in adulthood, and those with severe separation anxiety, especially women, may progress to co-morbid adult anxiety disorders (Osone & Takhashi, 2006).

There is recognition of the difficulties associated with diagnosing personality disorders and interest in the development of semi-structured interviews and self-report inventories to improve the reliability and validity of personality disorder assessment (Widiger & Chaynes, 2003). Accurate assessment and recognition of personality disorders is especially significant given the frequent co-morbidity with other mental disorders and the implications that the personality disorder may have for treatment.

There is evidence that the impaired decision making that is present in both alcohol dependence and Cluster B personality disorder may be compounded in alcoholic patients with a co-morbid Cluster B personality disorder, and this may account for more severe problems for this subset of patients (Dom, DeWilde, Hulstijn, van den Brink, & Sabbe, 2006). Another study of persons with substance use disorders found that those who had co-morbid antisocial personality disorder had more severe family and legal problems, and utilized more treatment resources than those without the personality disorder (Westermeyer & Thuras, 2005).

There also is evidence of an association between bipolar disorder and personality disorders (Swartz, Pilkonis, Frank, Proietti, & Scott, 2005). Similarly, associations have been found between personality disorders and obsessive-compulsive disorder (Torres et al., 2006) and eating disorders (Bruce & Steiger, 2005; Levitt, 2005; Sansone, Levitt, & Sansone, 2005).

The prevalence of personality disorders in the presence of these other mental disorders supports the need to routinely assess for personality disorders and design treatment with a consideration for how the personality disorder may affect the client's ability to accept and respond to treatment.

The other area of research with implications for practice has to do with treatment approaches. A recent study out of the Netherlands supports the effectiveness of cognitive-behavioral therapy in the treatment of personality disorders, specifically avoidant personality disorder (Emmelkamp et al., 2006). Clients who received cognitive-behavioral therapy showed significant improvements on a number of measures in comparison with those who had brief dynamic psychotherapy.

Two reports argue for specialized treatment centers for personality disorders. One, out of the United Kingdom, describes an in-patient setting (Nyamande & Sikabbubba, 2006); the other is an out-patient personality disorder program in Brazil (Morana & Camara, 2006). Both reports note the advantage of experienced and skilled staff in making the correct diagnosis and in implementing effective pharmacotherapy and psychosocial treatment. Prior to the economic constraints of managed health care, there were in-patient units in the United States that specialized in the treatment of borderline personality disorder. In recent times, the treatment of persons with personality disorders, with the exception of persons who are acutely suicidal, takes place in ambulatory settings. The importance of dedicated personality disorder programs has relevance regardless of the setting.

Annotated References

Abrams, R. C., Spielman, L. A., Alexopoulos, G. S., & Klausner, E. (1998). Personality disorder symptoms and functioning in elderly depressed patients. *American Journal of Geriatric Psychiatry, 6*(1), 24–30.

This article evaluates the relationship between personality disorder symptoms and disability, and social and interpersonal functioning in geriatric depression and treatment implications.

American Psychiatric Association. (2000). *Diagnostic and statistical manual of mental disorders* (4th ed., text rev.). Washington, DC: Author.

This is the American Psychiatric Association's official nomenclature of psychiatric conditions and disorders. It provides a systematic listing of the official codes and categories, a description of the multiaxial system for diagnosis, and diagnostic criteria for each of the disorders. It is used by psychiatrists, physicians, psychologists, registered nurses, social workers, therapists, and other mental health workers in all settings.

Andreasen, N. C., & Black, D. W. (2006). *Introductory textbook of psychiatry* (3rd ed.). Washington, DC: American Psychiatric Press.

This text provides a succinct summary of the personality disorders with some clinical vignettes.

Bonnivier, J. F. (1996). Management of self-destructive behaviors in an open inpatient setting. *Journal of Psychosocial Nursing, 34*(2), 38–42.

This article presents an in-patient approach that promotes client responsibility and relies on the strength of the relationship the nursing staff establishes with the clients.

Bruce, K. R., & Steiger, H. (2005). Treatment implications of Axis II comorbidity in eating disorders. *Eating Disorders, 13*(1), 93–108.

A review of the clinical research on the implications of co-morbid personality disorders, pathological personality traits, and responses to treatment of persons with eating disorders.

Dom, G., DeWilde, B., Hulstijn, W., van den Brink, W., & Sabbe, B. (2006). Decision-making deficits in alcohol-dependent patients with and without comorbid personality disorder. *Alcohol Clinical and Experimental Research, 30*(10), 1670–1677.

This research suggests that alcoholic patients with a comorbid Cluster B personality disorder are particularly impaired in their decision-making ability.

Emmelkamp, P. M., Benner, A., Kuipers, A., Feiertag, G. A., Koster, H. C., & van Apeldoorn, F. J. (2006). Comparison of brief dynamic and cognitive-behavioral therapies in avoidant personality disorder. *British Journal of Psychiatry, 189*, 60–64.

In a controlled trial, patients with avoidant personality disorder who received cognitive-behavioral therapy showed significantly more improvements on a number of measures compared with those who were treated with brief dynamic psychotherapy.

Goodman, M., New, A., & Siever, L. (2004). Trauma, genes, and the neurobiology of personality disorders. *Annals of the New York Academy of Science*, December, *1032*, 104–116.

This review article examines the current state and limitations of neurobiologic theories of personality disorders.

Grinspoon, L. (Ed.). (1996). Suicide: Part II. *The Harvard Mental Health Letter, 13*(6), 1–5.

This newsletter discusses suicide attempts, suicide prevention, the treatment of suicidal patients, and the question of physician-assisted suicide.

Hampton, N. D. (1997). Dialectical behavior therapy in the treatment of persons with borderline personality disorder. *Archives of Psychiatric Nursing, XI*(2), 96–101.

This article describes dialectical behavior therapy, a form of cognitive-behavioral therapy that has been effective in reducing hospital stays, suicide attempts, and therapy attrition.

Kernberg, O. E. (1976). *Object-relations theory and clinical psychoanalysis.* New York: Aronson.

This is the classic presentation of Kernberg's psychoanalytic ego psychology and object-relations theory. The underlying ego structure is viewed as the essence of the pathology of borderline personality disorder and is the target of expressive therapy.

Langley, G. C., & Klopper, H. (2005). Trust as a foundation for the therapeutic intervention for patients with borderline personality disorder. *Journal of Psychiatric Mental Health Nursing, 12*(1): 23–32.

A qualitative research study that supports the importance of establishing trust between client and clinician for the effective treatment of borderline personality disorder.

Levitt, J. L. (2005). A therapeutic approach to treating the eating disorder/borderline personality disorder patient. *Eating Disorders, 13*(1), 109–121.

This article discusses the treatment complications that must be considered in a subset of eating disorder patients with concomitant personality disorders.

Linehan, M. M. (1993). *Cognitive-behavioral treatment of borderline personality disorder.* New York: Guilford Press.

This text presents a comprehensive therapeutic strategy for the treatment of borderline personality disorder that focuses on coping, not curing. The core of the treatment is the balance of acceptance and change strategies, and specific strategies are provided for contingency management, exposure, cognitive modification, and skills training.

Mahler, M. S., Pine, E., & Bergman, A. (1975). *The psychological birth of the human infant: Symbiosis and individuation.* New York: Basic Books.

This book describes the separation-individuation process that occurs between birth and 3 years of age in which the child develops a sense of self, a permanent sense of significant others, and an integration of both good and bad as a component of self-concept.

Morana, H. C., & Camara, F. P. (2006). International guidelines for the management of personality disorders. *Current Opinions in Psychiatry*, *19*(5), 539–543.

This article reviews new evidence in the management of personality disorders and makes global recommendations for treatment.

Nyamande, M. M., & Sikabbubba, J. M. (2006). Managing inpatients who have personality disorders. *Nursing Times*, *102*(38), 30–32.

This article describes the increasing number of personality disorder services being developed in the United Kingdom.

O'Brien, P. G. (1988). Manipulation: A behavioral conceptualization. In M. J. Krebs & K. H. Larson (Eds.), *Applied psychiatric-mental health nursing standards in clinical practice* (pp. 225–247). New York: John Wiley & Sons.

Comprehensive presentation of therapeutic nursing interventions for clients who exhibit manipulative behavior. Offers clinical examples and guidelines for analyzing staff's feelings in relation to patients' behaviors.

O'Brien, P. G. (1997). The manipulative patient: A behavioral conceptualization. *The American Journal for Nurse Practitioners, 1*(1), 13–15, 29.

This article focuses on the need to understand the meaning behind client behavior and identifies nursing approaches for setting limits and teaching new behaviors.

Osone, A., & Takahasi, S. (2006). Possible link between childhood separation anxiety and adulthood personality disorder in patients with anxiety disorders in Japan. *Journal of Clinical Psychiatry*, *67*(9), 1451–1457.

This research study supports the relationship between childhood separation anxiety and fearful-anxious personality disorder in adults.

Paris, J. (2005). Neurobiological dimensional models of personality: A review of the models of Cloninger, Depue, and Siever. *Journal of Personality Disorders*, 19(2), 156–170.

A review of three neurobiological models of personality.

Reid, W. H., Balis, G. D., & Sutton, B. J. (1997). *The treatment of psychiatric disorders* (3rd ed.). Bristol, PA: Brunner/Mazel.

This concise volume, directed at clinicians, focuses on treatment guidelines and biopsychosocial interventions for psychiatric disorders.

Sansone, R. A., Levitt, J. L., & Sansone, L. A. (2005). The prevalence of personality disorders among those with eating disorders. *Eating Disorders*, *13*(1), 7–21.

A summary of existing data shows an association between obsessive-compulsive and borderline personality disorders and types of eating disorders.

Smallwood, P. (2004). Personality disorders. In T. A. Stern & J. B. Herman (Eds.), *Massachusetts General Hospital psychiatry update and board preparation* (2nd ed., pp. 187–194.) New York: McGraw-Hill.

A succinct presentation of the personality disorders.

Stalenheim, E. G., von Knorring, L., & Oreland, L. (1997). Platelet monoamine oxidase activity as a biological marker in a Swedish forensic psychiatric population. *Psychiatry Research*, March 24, *69*(2–3), 79–87.

This study confirmed the role of platelet MAO activity as a biological marker for personality traits, but not for personality disorders.

Swartz, H. A., Pilkonis, P. A., Frank, E., Proietti, J. M., & Scott, J. (2005). Acute treatment outcomes in patients with bipolar I disorder and co-morbid borderline personality disorder receiving medication and psychotherapy. *Bipolar Disorders*, *7*(2), 192–197.

A quasi-experimental study suggesting that treatment may be longer in patients suffering with both bipolar I disorder and borderline personality disorder.

Torres, A. R., Moran, P., Bebbington, P., Brugha, T., Bhugra, D., Coid, J. W., et al. (2006). Obsessive-compulsive disorder and personality disorder: Evidence from the British National Survey of Psychiatric Morbidity 2000. *Social Psychiatry and Psychiatric Epidemiology*, November, *41*(11), 862–867.

A study analyzing the prevalence of personality disorders in a sample of adults in the United Kingdom with obsessive-compulsive disorder.

Westermeyer, J., & Thuras, P. (2005). Association of antisocial personality disorder and substance disorder morbidity in a clinical sample. *American Journal of Drug and Alcohol Abuse, 31*(1), 93–110.

A study designed to evaluate the relationship between co-morbid substance use disorder and antisocial personality disorder.

Widiger, T. A., & Chaynes, K. (2003). Current issues in the assessment of personality disorders. *Current Psychiatry Reports, 5*(1), 28–35.

A review that discusses the major issues and developments in the assessment of personality disorders.

Zanarini, M. C., & Frankenburg, F. R. (2001). Olanzepine treatment of female borderline personality disorder patients: A double blind, placebo controlled pilot study. *Journal of Clinical Psychiatry, 62*(11), 849–854.

Early research study on the effectiveness of a particular atypical antipsychotic medication as a treatment for the symptoms of borderline personality disorder in female patients.

Additional Resources

Greene, H., & Ugarriza, D. N. (1995). Borderline personality disorder: History, theory, and nursing intervention. *Journal of Psychosocial Nursing, 33*(12), 26–30.

This article defines borderline personality disorder, presents research findings concerning the impact of childhood stress on the development of the disorder, and summarizes psychoanalytic, behavioral, and cognitive therapies for treatment of the disorder.

Krebs, M. J., & Larson, K. H. (1988). *Applied psychiatric-mental health nursing standards in clinical practice.* New York: John Wiley & Sons.

This text applies the nursing process and the American Nurses Association's standards of practice to frequently encountered client behaviors. The chapters on splitting, manipulation, control, and noncompliance are particularly relevant to personality disorders. Each chapter includes an excellent management guideline in outline form that encompasses nursing assessment, diagnosis, planning, interventions, and evaluations.

Linehan, M. M. (2006). *Treating borderline personality disorder: The dialectical approach.* A Dawkins Production. [DVD or VHS with manual (43 min., color)]. Available from Guilford Press, 72 Spring Street, New York, NY 10012; 800-365-7006; 212-966-6708 (fax).

In this video Dr. Linehan teaches clients the skills that are basic to dialectical behavior therapy (DBT) and answers questions about how DBT works. Suitable for therapists and for client and family education.

Linehan, M. M. (2006). *Understanding borderline personality disorder: The dialectical approach.* A Dawkins Production. [DVD or VHS manual (37 min., color)]. Available from Guilford Press, 72 Spring Street, New York, NY 10012; 800-365-7006; 212-966-6708 (fax).

This video presents fundamental information about borderline personality disorder and how it can be effectively treated with DBT.

Sperry, L. (2003). *Handbook of diagnosis and treatment of DSM-IV-TR personality disorders* (2nd ed.). New York: Brunner-Routledge.

A comprehensive overview of the the personality disorders, including clinical examples.

Internet Resources

http://nursing.jbpub.com/psychiatric

Visit http://nursing.jbpub.com/psychiatric for interactive exercises, NCLEX review questions, WebLinks, and more.

PART III

Nursing Management of Special Populations

CHAPTER 24

Children and Adolescents

Karen A. Ballard

LEARNING OBJECTIVES

After reading this chapter, you will be able to:

- Identify four factors that can contribute to a child developing emotional problems or mental disorders.
- Name two types of aberrant behavior in a child.
- List five components of a child's mental status examination.
- Contrast four theoretical models of childhood behaviors.
- Identify nursing interventions in assisting children and their families to cope with emotional problems or mental disorders.
- Describe four important components in teaching children about hospitalization, medications, diagnostic tests, and treatments.

KEY TERMS

Attachment
Attachment model
Behavior modification model
Bonding
Child abuse
Child psychiatry
Child's Bill of Rights
Cognitive model
Developmental history
Discipline
Extended family
Family of orientation
Family of procreation
Intrusive procedures
Maternal deprivation
Mental status examination
Nuclear family
Parenting education
Play stages
Play therapy
Play types
Psychosocial developmental model
Self-concept
Sense of self model
Sibling rivalry
System of care
Temper tantrums
Therapeutic milieu
TRIADS
VIPP teaching

http://nursing.jbpub.com/psychiatric

Visit http://nursing.jbpub.com/psychiatric for interactive exercises, NCLEX review questions, WebLinks, and more.

The Child's Bill of Rights states that children have the right to:
- Be wanted
- Be born healthy
- Live in a healthy environment
- Have basic needs met
- Experience continuous loving care
- Acquire the cognitive skills needed for life

Introduction

Childhood is viewed by society in fairly idyllic terms. What worries, what problems can occur at such a carefree time? Just the problems and cares of "growing up"! Children have been viewed by previous generations as chattel, necessary evils, progeny, and insurance against want in parental old age. Interest in a child's developmental and psychological growth is fairly recent in comparison to centuries of childrearing. Even the first theorists who expressed interest in children as individuals often described the child in terms of the parent. The child was seen as a "blank tablet" upon which the parent wrote, a form molded and shaped by the parent into the parent's own image. Children were to be seen but most definitely not heard. An early nineteenth-century writer described the world of young children as a state of "buzzing, blooming confusion." In today's society, there is a sincere interest in putting some order to this confusion.

Child's Bill of Rights

In 1978, the President's Commission on Mental Health issued special recommendations for infants, children, and adolescents and sponsored the **Child's Bill of Rights**, which is applicable today. The bill includes the child's right to be wanted, to be born healthy, to live in a healthy environment, to have basic needs met, to experience continuous loving care, and to acquire the cognitive skills needed for life (President's Commission on Mental Health, 1978). At the Surgeon General's Conference on Children's Mental Health in 2000, it was reported that "growing numbers of children are suffering needlessly because their emotional, behavioral, and developmental needs are not being met by those very institutions which were explicitly created to take care of them . . . It is time that we as a Nation took seriously the task of preventing mental health problems and treating mental illnesses in youth" (U.S. Department of Health and Human Services, 2000, para. 1.). In 2002, the Subcommittee on Children and Families of the President's New Freedom Commission on Mental Health noted that the "federal government should develop and implement a comprehensive approach for enhancing the well being of children and adolescents, based on a bio-psychosocial model, through preventive interventions prior to the onset of mental and behavioral disorders" (President's New Freedom Commission, 2002, para. 24.). The implementation options that were cited included screening all children from 0 to 5 years for social and emotional development as part of primary care visits, providing mental health screening for children and their families in community health centers, and addressing the barriers to coverage of preventative mental health services in health insurance.

Why some children appear resilient to life's critical events and stresses and other children are particularly vulnerable is unclear to many researchers. Some risk factors that can impact a child's or adolescent's mental health are poor nutrition, violence, environmental pollutants, and social and economic stresses.

Critical Thinking Question Is there evidence in today's society that children are undervalued and, if so, what can be done to remedy the situation?

Mental Health and Emotional Problems of Childhood

Children and adolescents are not miniature adults. They are developing individuals, whose focus is on coping with life as they reach maturity. It is not an easy journey. It is impossible to predict which children are vulnerable; however, nurses and other clinicians can learn to identify risk factors, contributing stresses, and the signs and symptoms of mental disorders in children and seek to intervene aggressively. Positive intervention with children and adolescents and their families and significant caretakers is critical; children with untreated emotional problems will become adults with mental health problems. Nurses should be particularly vigilant in assessing children for existing or potential emotional problems and be prepared to make the appropriate referrals to mental health agencies.

Nurses encounter children and adolescents as clients at many different points in the healthcare system—clinics, emergency rooms, schools, private physicians' offices, in-patient general pediatric or child psychiatric services, and special mental health agencies for children and adolescents. Some children are unfazed by their physical and mental experiences. These children are particularly resilient and appear protected from and invulnerable to the most extreme stresses, such as the death of a parent, divorce, abuse, and illness. Other children become stressed either as a direct result of a healthcare experience, because they have existing mental health problems that are exacerbated by current or past life events, or because they are living with mentally ill parents. During childhood, the rate of physical and mental development and the cognitive and emotional challenges faced by children make them uniquely vulnerable to multiple social, environmental, and developmental risks. Consequently, the health status of children is more at risk for negative consequences from poor nutrition, violence, environmental pollutants, and social and economic stresses (Children's Defense Fund, 2005; Stein, 1997).

Family Structure

A family is a basic cultural group, a subsystem of society. It usually shares a common residence, economic cooperation, and reproduction. It may include one or more adults of different generations and sexes and may or may not exist within the framework of marriage. A **nuclear family** is a subsystem consisting of one or more adults who undertake a parenting role for one or more children. A **family of orientation** is the nuclear family in which an individual has the status of a child. The **family of procreation** is a nuclear family in which the individual has or had the status of a parent; it can be a patriarchy or a matriarchy. An **extended family** is any family grouping that is related by descent, marriage, or adoption that is broader than the nuclear family and can include multiple generations (vertical extension) or aunts, uncles, and cousins (lateral extension).

When assessing the functioning of a family unit, the clinician examines the family's ability to do the following:

- To provide for the members' physical, emotional, and spiritual needs
- To be sensitive to the needs of family members
- To communicate with each other
- To provide support and security, and to encourage growth and positive relationships and experiences within and outside the family
- To function in a responsible manner in the community
- To help themselves and to accept appropriate help from outside resources when needed
- To perform and complete family roles
- To respond to crises as a means of individual and family unit growth
- To create a sense of family unity and loyalty
- To demonstrate the presence of mutual respect for each individual in the family

The Task Force on the Family (Schor, 2003) identified that the power and importance of families arises out of the extended duration for which children are dependent on adults to meet their basic needs. It is important for nurses and other healthcare practitioners to understand that children's self-esteem grows from being cared for, loved, and valued and being part of a social unit that shares values, communicates openly, and provides companionship. Through nursing interventions that support the family unit and parents' functioning, nurses can directly improve children's health by identifying stressors such as financial difficulties, health problems, lack of social supports, work dissatisfaction, and unfortunate life events that cause parents emotional stress interfering with their relationships with each other and their children and negatively disrupt their parenting and ability to emotionally support their children.

A family is a basic cultural group and a subsystem of society. Types of families include the nuclear family, family of orientation, family of procreation, and extended family. A family can be a patriarchy or matriarchy.

Critical Thinking Question How does the type of family in which a child is a member help or hinder that child in learning to cope with the challenges and stressors in childhood?

Incidence and Prevalence

According to the U.S. Census Bureau, in 2005 approximately 8.3 million or 11.3% of the nation's children had no health insurance (Benjamin & Young, 2006). Of this number, 17.6% of children lived below the federal poverty level, with African American and Hispanic children and children living in female-headed households being increasingly represented (U.S. Census Bureau, 2006). Hispanic children are three times more likely and African American children are 50% more likely than White children to be uninsured. African American children are 60% more likely than White children to have an unmet medical need (Children's Defense Fund, 2006). It is estimated that 6 to 8 million children either are currently dealing with mental health problems or will develop such difficulties.

One in every five children lives below the federal poverty level, and African American and Hispanic children and children living in female-headed households are disproportionately represented in those numbers.

Differential Diagnosis

The mental health conditions usually diagnosed in childhood and adolescence are mental retardation, learning disorders, motor skills disorders, communication disorders, pervasive developmental disorders, attention deficit hyperactivity disorder (ADHD), feeding and eating disorders, tics, elimination disorders, and separation anxiety

A combination of factors contributes to the development of mental health problems in children and adolescents. These factors are genetic predisposition, neurobiologic factors, prenatal influences, maternal health during pregnancy, developmental stresses, concurrent physical problems or illnesses, family factors, siblings, environmental factors, and societal stressors.

A complete mental health assessment includes the identified presenting problem, general health history, developmental milestones, family problems, school performance and intellectual functioning, level of independence, peer relationships, and ability to play at an age-appropriate level.

Children can be referred for single or multiple presenting problems. Depending on the circumstances and the developmental age of the child, some symptoms are not inappropriate nor are they a sign of a mental health problem (e.g., temper tantrums); other symptoms should always be of concern to the nurse (e.g., hurting oneself, others, or animals; fire setting; inappropriate risk taking).

disorder. The most commonly identified disorders in adolescence are conduct disorders, mood disorders, schizophrenia, eating disorders, and substance abuse. (See Chapters 11, 14, 15, 16, 19, and 24 for discussion of these disorders.)

Etiology

It is unusual for there to be a single etiology for childhood emotional problems or actual mental disorders. A combination of factors, including genetic predisposition (heredity), neurobiological factors, prenatal influences, maternal health during pregnancy, developmental stresses, concurrent physical problems or illnesses, family factors, siblings, environmental factors, and societal stresses, is most likely. Some of the factors that put children and adolescents at risk include poverty, homelessness, illness or disability, child neglect or abuse, domestic violence, parents who are either younger or older than usual, parents with histories of mental illness, substance abuse, alcoholism, criminal behaviors, and being a member of a minority community (Burgess & Hartman, 1992). Other contributing factors that can be identified include acute or chronic illness in a family member, parental separation, poor parenting techniques (especially in the area of discipline), multiple substitute caretakers, and economic changes in the family (e.g., unemployment).

Clinical Presentation

When children are identified as having mental health or emotional problems, they can be referred for treatment of single or multiple presenting problems. These problems are usually described as a more than normal inability to get along with parents, siblings, and peers; poor school performance and inability to concentrate; **temper tantrums**, impulsivity, and need for supervision; poor self-confidence; disobedience; lying; hurting oneself, animals, or others; developing somatic symptoms; unpredictable mood swings; regressive behaviors; and generally being described as sad, unhappy, or nervous (Mash & Barkley, 2003). Other problems can include inappropriate risk taking, acting-out behaviors and violence, participation in gangs or cults, running away, school delinquency, and sexual activity. It is important for the nurse to understand that, depending on the circumstances and developmental age of the child, some of these behaviors are not always inappropriate (e.g., temper tantrums), whereas others should always be of concern (e.g., hurting oneself, animals, or others).

Critical Thinking Question When working with children and adolescents, what behaviors might not always be inappropriate and what types of behaviors would be of concern and require additional evaluation?

Assessing and Interviewing a Child or Adolescent

In assessing children and adolescents, nurses can observe the child interact with others, when alone, or in play situations as well as receive reports from the family members, school teachers, other therapists, and social workers (see **Figure 24-1**). In addition to the identified presenting problem, there should be a clear understanding of the child's general health history, developmental milestones, family problems, school performance and intellectual functioning, level of independence, peer relationships, and ability to play at an age-appropriate level (House, 2002). Play and school are the work of childhood; the ability of the child or adolescent to function reasonably

Figure 24-1 Observing a child playing can help the nurse assess his or her mental health.

well in these areas is a good indicator of future mental health. When interviewing and assessing children, the nurse or clinician should explain briefly what behavior has resulted in referral and who you are (i.e., a person who helps children talk about their problems and helps them feel better). The nurse should be kind and nurturing and willing to let the child become comfortable. The interview should be conducted in a quiet, comfortable area that permits the child to move around and play with pencils, crayons, magic markers, paper, play dough, blocks, dolls (e.g., family figurines, action figures), trains, trucks, puppets, balls, jacks, and pickup sticks for younger children and more sophisticated and involved games and toys, including electronics, for older children. It may take a couple of visits before the child is comfortable sharing inner thoughts and concerns.

Child's Mental Status Examination

It was only with the development of **child psychiatry** as a subspecialty that clinicians began to appreciate that it was possible not only to test a child's intelligence, but also to consider the child's mental status, incorporating behavioral, neurological, and developmental aspects. A **mental status examination** is a descriptive document that portrays a client's appearance, perception, affect, cognition, and general intellectual development. The components of a mental status examination (Goodman & Sours, 1994; House, 2002) for a child can be found in **Table 24-1**.

A mental status examination is a descriptive document that portrays a client's appearance, perception, affect, cognition, and general intellectual development. A child's mental status examination includes size and general appearance, mobility, coordination, speech, intellectual functioning, thinking and perception, emotional reactions, manner of relating, fantasies and dreams, and character of play.

Table 24-1 A Child's Mental Status Examination

Category	Description
Size and general appearance	Large or small for age Facial features Movements of hands, feet, and face General appearance (ill health, bruising, nail biting, thumb sucking, teeth grinding, hair pulling, tics, giggles) Clean clothes Dressing (age and sex appropriate)
Mobility	Hyperactive (episodic, patterned, random) Slowness, somnolence
Coordination: motor skills and abilities	Posture, gait, and balance Ability to manipulate play objects such as puzzle pieces, pick-up sticks, tossing and catching a ball
Speech	Receptive capacity (Can the child follow directions and hear the nurse?) Expressive ability and output (baby talk, mutism, stuttering, rhyming, echolalia)
Intellectual functioning	Knowledge of general information that is age appropriate Ability to name body parts and their functions Overall and specific school performance
Thinking and perception	Use of defense mechanisms Self-concept and body image Presence of hallucinations or paranoid ideation
Emotional reactions	Fearfulness, sadness, shame Anxiety, anger Apathy Oppositional behavior
Manner of relating	Ability to separate Level of friendliness Independence of behavior Adaptability
Fantasies and dreams	Type of dreams Stories Wishes and ambitions
Character of play	Type Family and gender constellations Content

Bonding is an affectional feeling between mother or primary caretaker and child and is unidirectional. Attachment is a reciprocal affectional relationship between the mother or primary caretaker and child; it is bidirectional and develops throughout infancy.

There are three categories of attachment behaviors: signaling, approach, and following behaviors.

Maternal deprivation occurs when there is any significant separation of the infant between 3 and 15 months of age and the infant's mother figure, leading to serious emotional problems in the infant such as depression, eating disorders, and failure to thrive.

The establishment of trust is basic and critical to all future life interactions and achievements.

Tests used to evaluate a child's mental status are the Children's Apperceptive Test (CAT), Thematic Apperception Test (TAT), Rorschach Psychodiagnostic Battery, Mackover Sentence Completion, and Howells-Lickorish Family Relations Indicator. Standardized tests for evaluating expected developmental behaviors are the Denver Developmental Tests (versions DDST, DDST-R, and Denver II). Some of the abilities evaluated in the tests include the following:

- Responds to a bell (0 to 1 month)
- Follows objects to midline, coos, and gurgles (1 month)
- Displays social smile (2 months)
- Reaches for objects (4 months)
- Rolls over (5 months)
- Sits and crawls (6 to 8 months)
- Uses crude purposeful grasp (9 months)
- Uses pincer grasp (10 months)
- Walks and uses three to four words (10 to 14 months)
- Scribbles with a crayon (12 to 18 months)
- Builds a six-cube tower (24 months)
- Uses three-word sentences and pronouns (2 1/2 years)
- Rides a tricycle, draws a circle (3 years)
- Throws overhand (4 years)
- Ties knots (5 years)
- Prints name and rides a two-wheeler (6 years)

A complete evaluation of any child or adolescent should include an assessment of the child's family, school performance, **developmental history**, neurological evaluation, psychological testing results, and a complete history of the presenting problem.

Theoretical Models

Many theorists have contributed to our understanding of how children, adolescents, and adults develop and learn to cope with multiple stresses and function in society. Previous chapters discussed psychoanalytic, interpersonal, behavioral, and neurobiological theories. This chapter focuses on the **attachment**, **psychosocial**, **cognitive**, **sense of self**, and **behavior modification models**.

Attachment Model

According to John Bowlby (1994), the establishment of trust is essential to the survival of the human species. Within hours or days of a child's birth, Bowlby notes that bonding occurs between the mother and infant. **Bonding** is an affectional feeling that develops between the mother or primary caretaker and child; it is usually unidirectional, caretaker to child; occurs rapidly; and can be facilitated by physical contact. **Attachment** is a reciprocal affectional relationship between the mother or primary caretaker and child and develops throughout infancy. Once attachment occurs, one can note attachment behaviors between the caretaker and child; the child and primary caretaker produce behaviors that identify them to each other. This type of attachment and bonding sets the pattern for lifelong behaviors. There are three categories of behaviors: signaling behaviors (crying, smiling, babbling), approach behaviors (seeking, clinging, sucking), and following behaviors (crawling, walking with parent). There are identifiable phases in the mother-child relationship: first, the infant signals without discrimination at any figure; next, the infant directs signals toward a discriminated figure, usually the mother or main caretaker; third, the infant maintains proximity to the favored discriminated figure by crawling, crying, and motioning; and finally, the infant develops a goal-oriented partnership in which the child, usually around 2 years of age, predicts the caretaker's behavior and modifies his or her own behavior. This attachment to mother is the model for the child and adolescent in forming all future attachments (Bowlby). Although considerable attention is paid to encouraging early contact between mother and infant to develop attachment, mothers who cannot experience early contact should not be made to feel that they are damaging their infants. Once attachment is formed, it is believed that any significant separation of the infant and mother figure between 3 and 15 months of age can lead to serious emotional responses, depression, and failure to thrive. This is known as **maternal deprivation**.

Psychosocial Developmental Model

Erik Erikson's theory of psychosocial development (1964), although built on Freudian theory, is a developmental approach to human growth that stresses the importance of trust as a basic building block for normal psychological development. He examines critical behaviors and challenges that are central to eight stages of development, which build upon each other. Each stage has a positive and negative component. Erikson postulates that the first stage, trust versus mistrust, is the initial critical challenge to the developing person. One can have problems with subsequent stages and still be fairly well integrated, but one cannot skip or incompletely finish the establishment of trust. It is basic to all future life interactions and achievements; it is critical to learn to trust (Hockenberry, 2005; Hockenberry & Wilson, 2006). Erikson's eight stages, also known as the Eight Stages of Man, are described in **Table 24-2**.

Cognitive Model

Watching infants or children learn about themselves, their significant others, and their environment is exciting. The development of cognition is individual to each child but generally follows a pattern. Children often misinterpret adults, other children, or their environment because they simply do not have the cognitive skills or the knowledge to do otherwise. Watch an infant learn what the hand is and how to use it. The infant starts with a period of observing and moving, followed by learning to use the hand successfully to retrieve objects, which is usually accomplished by 4 to 5 months. Infants are interactive individuals who seek out stimuli and possess identifiable rhythms such as sucking, crying, sleeping, and wakefulness. They have a repertoire of behaviors such as looking, grasping, pushing, pulling, and moving. Cognitive development is cumulative; that is, the child's understanding of each new experience

Learning and the development of cognition are individual to each child but generally follow a pattern. Cognitive development is cumulative, and the understanding of a new experience develops out of what was previously learned.

Table 24-2 Erickson's Eight Stages of Development

Stage	Description
Trust versus mistrust (infancy, 0 to 1 year)	Basic trust is the critical and most important building block. It develops from a consistent and caring relationship with a nurturing figure, usually the child's mother. Mistrust develops when basic needs are either not met or met inconsistently. The outcomes of successful mastery of this stage are faith and optimism.
Autonomy versus shame and doubt (early childhood, 1 to 3 years)	This is the stage of holding on and letting go. Successful autonomy depends upon being able to experience positively activities such as walking, climbing, and toilet training. Shame and doubt develop from forced dependence, in which adults belittle the child's activities or the child is repeatedly unsuccessful in attempting new ones. The outcomes of successful mastery of this stage are self-control and willpower.
Initiative versus guilt (preschool, 3 to 6 years)	This is the stage of exploring the environment for all possible physical learning experiences. It is a period of heightened physical activity and imagination and the early development of conscience (right and wrong). Guilt develops when children are given the impression by others that their activities are wrong or unacceptable. The outcomes of successful mastery are direction and purpose.
Industry versus inferiority (school age, 6 to 12 years)	This is the stage when children apply themselves to engaging in and completing purposeful activities and tasks and to cooperating and competing with peers. Inferiority develops when expectations are too high or when children perceive that they cannot measure up to the standards of others. The outcome of successful mastery of this stage is competence.
Identity versus role confusion (adolescence, 12 to 18 years)	This stage is marked by rapid physical, emotional, and social changes in the child soon to be an adolescent and by a preoccupation with others', especially peers', perceptions of the self. Role confusion occurs when there are conflicts in the adolescent's ability to integrate these changes. The outcomes of successful mastery of this stage are devotion and fidelity.
Intimacy versus isolation (young adulthood, 18 to 25 years)	This is the stage in which one learns to form significant, loving, and intimate relationships with peers, colleagues, and, ultimately, lovers. Isolation occurs when one is unable to trust that it is safe to share oneself in a mutually giving relationship. The outcomes of successful mastery of this stage are affiliation and love.
Generativity versus stagnation (adulthood, 25 to 45 years)	This is the nourishing and nurturing stage. It focuses on caring for one's own or others' children or involvement in other creative productions. Stagnation occurs when one is so self-absorbed that focusing on creativity becomes impossible. The outcomes of successful mastery of this stage are production and caring.
Ego integrity versus despair (older adulthood, 45 years to death)	This stage occurs as one perceives that one is moving toward the final years of life, and the individual is comfortable with the previous life stages, accepting what has been or has not occurred, and is able to feel a sense of satisfaction. Despair occurs when one focuses on what might have been. The outcome of successful mastery of this stage is wisdom.

Three processes associated with cognitive development are adaptation, assimilation, and accommodation.

Self-concept is an individual's awareness of self, beliefs, thoughts, and relationships. Body image and self-esteem are inherent in self-concept.

Jean Piaget's stages of cognitive development are sensorimotor; preoperational, including preconceptual and intuitive; concrete operational; and formal operational.

Four different senses of self are described by Stern (2000):
- Emergent self
- Core self
- Subjective self
- Verbal self

grows out of what was learned previously. *Adaptation* is the continuous process of using the environment to learn and learning to adjust to changes in the environment. *Assimilation* is the process of taking new information and fitting it into a preconceived notion about objects, words, or other concepts. *Accommodation* is the process of adjusting to new experiences or objects by revising the previous plan to fit the new information. It is through the development of mental functioning that children learn about the world and all its objects, how these objects function, and the relationship between themselves and these objects. Through this cognitive or mental development children learn to reason abstractly, think logically, acquire language, develop morals and ethics, and acquire a sense of meaning, purpose, hope, and spirituality in their lives (Hockenberry & Wilson, 2006).

During childhood and culminating somewhere in adolescence, individuals develop a **self-concept**, an individual's awareness of self, beliefs, thoughts, and relationships. Inherent in self-concept are body image and self-esteem. Body image is how individuals perceive their own bodies while self-esteem reflects one's sense of worthiness and value, often influenced by others in the child's life.

Jean Piaget developed a framework for understanding how children learn and adapt (Ginsberg & Opper, 1987). Although his studies have been challenged by some current theorists, his framework for understanding cognitive development is still valuable. Piaget's stages of cognitive development are identified in **Table 24-3**.

To become fully functioning emotionally, one needs to develop the abilities to think, communicate, and understand. According to Piaget, the four factors that influence one's cognitive development are the following:

1. Emotions create the feelings that motivate learning.
2. The maturation of the nervous system promotes the development of the mental structures that permit a child to become capable of understanding.
3. The child needs to be exposed to a variety of experiences.
4. The child needs a variety of social interactions with others, such as parents, peers, and teachers.

Sense of Self Model

It is interesting to compare Bowlby's, Erikson's, and Piaget's theories with those of Daniel Stern, a child psychiatrist who has spent the last few decades describing the infant's changing concepts of self. Stern has a particular interest in the infant's preverbal understanding of self and subjective experience of life. Stern observes that all development occurs in leaps and bounds, and there are strategic leaps between 2 and 3 months, 9 and 12 months, and 15 and 18 months. These are periods of great change for the developing infant. Between 2 and 3 months, the infant smiles responsively, makes deliberate eye contact, and coos, and the parents experience a different relationship with the child. By 6 months of age, the infant has established a sense of core self—a separate, cohesive, physical being. Between the ages of 9 and 18 months, the infant is not only experiencing individuation, but also seeking and creating an intersubjective union with another being. Stern describes four different senses of self: the *emergent self* (0 to 2 months), the *core self* (2 to 6 months),

Table 24-3 Piaget's Stages of Cognition

Stage	Description
Sensorimotor (0 to 2 years)	This is preverbal intellectual development. The infant is in a world of self, learning first by repeating simple acts (*primary circular*) and then by repeating the acts and committing them to memory (*secondary circular*).
Preoperational (2 to 7 years)	This stage has two phases, preconceptual and intuitive. The world is seen from the child's point of view (egocentric thinking), including magical causation. The child is able to learn that actions have effects. Everything is literal and concrete to the child; that is, the world is either good or bad, right or wrong.
Concrete operational (7 to 12 years)	Thinking can still appear somewhat egocentric. The child knows past and present and is gaining understanding of future. The child is more flexible and is aware of the reversibility of acts.
Formal operational (12 to 16 years)	The child's conceptual organization becomes stable and coherent. The adolescent can think in abstract terms and make and test hypotheses. The child understands that death is final.

the *subjective self* (7 to 15 months), and the *verbal self* (after 15 months) (Stern, 1985, 2000).

Behavior Modification Model

Behavior modification teaches children how to establish controls from within themselves. It consists of teaching the consequences of behavior and involves such techniques as "star charts" and "token systems," time-outs, and relaxation. Three types of consequences follow one's behavior:

- *Natural consequences:* Those behaviors that occur without any interventions, such as being late and missing dinner
- *Logical consequences:* Those behaviors that are directly related to a rule, such as not being allowed to play with another toy until the used ones are put away
- *Unrelated consequences:* Those that are imposed deliberately, such as no playing until homework is completed (Hockenberry, 2005)

Time-out is when the child is sent to be alone for a short period, and nothing progresses until the time-out is taken. For some children one minute is a long time-out. Time-outs work only if they are planned, consistently used, and enforced.

It is believed that behavior that is rewarded will be repeated, and behavior that does not get a response or reward will be abandoned. One method that can be used is "star charts." The child receives a "star" for each acceptable behavior or activity and, once a number of stars are earned, the child receives a reward. A similar system can be used with older children by substituting "tokens." Contracts establishing certain behaviors and expectations can also be written simply and agreed to by the adult and the child. However, the verbal recognition given to the child by the adult is of primary importance. This positive reinforcement is ultimately sufficient reinforcement for the child as the star chart or token system is phased out.

Critical Thinking Question Which theoretical model do you believe will be most helpful to you in caring for children, and how will you incorporate it into your practice?

Parents and caregivers can learn to ignore certain unacceptable behavior as long as no one is in harm's way. Children are desperate for attention, and they will get it any way that they can, even if it means being physically disciplined or scolded by an adult. To the child, any attention means love. Studiously ignoring a child's unacceptable behavior is difficult to implement. When the adult does lose control and does not follow the behavior guidelines, it is helpful to verbalize an apology to the child for losing one's temper and leave the situation to regain control. Removing oneself from the child decreases the negative reinforcement of the behavior, gives the adult time to cool off, and teaches the child that adults can make mistakes and can be redeemed.

No adult will ever win a power struggle with a child; the adult has to demonstrate control and appropriate behavior. Verbalizing what we do, how we feel, and why we do things is good as long as we keep it simple. Children often have magical thoughts about adults, and the more they can learn to understand adult behaviors, the closer children are to learning adaptive behaviors for the rest of their lives.

Regardless of whether one focuses on a specific theorist—Freud (Sigmund and Anna), Mahler, Bowlby, Sullivan, Erikson, Fraiberg, Bowen, Yalom, or Stern—or adapts single or multiple theories—psychoanalytic, interpersonal, attachment, psychosocial, developmental, behavior, cognitive, or family systems—it is clear when working with children that as developing individuals they have critical needs to feel safe, to be able to trust others and the environment, to love, to play, and to learn. The establishment of trust in a child is absolutely essential for healthy development and the growth of a normal child into an adult. Trust is the cornerstone of a healthy personality. The child needs to feel that there is a guiding force (i.e., adult) to help the child distinguish between real and imagined dangers and fears. An example of how a child reacts negatively to a disorganized family life and the absence of a protective, caring parent is the story of Jamie.

Critical Thinking Question What are some potential emotional outcomes in adolescence and adulthood for any child who has experienced significant emotional and physical abuse in early childhood?

Management and Treatment

In developing a method of treatment for children and adolescents, it is imperative that the nurse and other clinicians be skillful in a variety of treatment methods based on the different theories and models. Children and adolescents are too

Behavior modification teaches children how to establish controls from within. There are three consequences to behavior: natural, logical, and unrelated consequences.

It appears clear that establishment of trust early in a child's life is absolutely essential for normal development and emotional and mental health.

CASE STUDY Jamie

Jamie was a 7-year-old victim of child abuse who was admitted to a general pediatric unit with lethargy, mutism, bizarre screaming episodes, and extensive abrasions, welts, and festering sores over his lower extremities and buttocks. According to his social history, Jamie was born to a 15-year-old single mother who was addicted to heroin. She left him with his godparents when he was 7 months old so she could return to her boyfriend, who did not want the baby. Jamie lived with his godparents until he was 4 years old. He then went to live with his maternal grandmother, who kept him for a year until a neighbor's report of neglect resulted in foster care placement for a year. Jamie then returned to his grandmother for 6 months, when, in an alcoholic rage, she cut him across the arm with a butcher's knife. He spent 6 more months in foster care, and then he was placed again with his godparents. After 6 months, the godparents, without informing the childcare agency, gave him to his mother, who was now married to a man who was not Jamie's father. This move occurred 4 months prior to the hospitalization.

When the mother and stepfather were asked how Jamie was hurt, they said that he was a "bad boy who needed to learn respect for adults and to stop teasing his younger sisters." A school report described a very quiet, nonverbal child who had almost no interactions with peers. He often was observed picking at his skin where he had healing sores. He had no real academic skills. He sought out the teacher for physical contact and frequently apologized for being "stupid." In the hospital, Jamie was essentially nonverbal except for isolated words, sat on the floor or his bed rocking, continually picked and ate his skin, avoided eye contact, urinated anywhere, and screamed with no observable stimulus.

It was obvious to the nursing staff that Jamie would be a challenge. The key to Jamie's care was to establish a sense of trust between him and his environment. If this could be communicated, his own internal sense of basic trust might be stimulated. Jamie remained on the general pediatric unit for 6 weeks. During this time, his behavior dramatically improved but did not become entirely appropriate. At the time of discharge, he was transferred to an in-patient child psychiatric unit because of the continued bizarre screaming episodes and his inability to stop hurting himself by continuously picking at his skin and eating it. However, he had become more verbal, made eye contact, and related tentatively to peers.

Because of his screaming, Jamie initially had been given a private room. The nursing staff created a safe, predictable environment for Jamie. A radio was placed in his room, and pictures of his family were put on a tack board. The nursing staff tried to keep the same nurses involved in his care. Even with this effort, Jamie sometimes had six different nurses caring for him every 3 days, depending on the schedule. Communication regarding nursing care goals became essential, and one nurse assumed primary responsibility for the coordination of Jamie's daily care.

The sores on Jamie's buttocks had festered and become grossly infected; they looked like severe decubiti or burns. The resultant pain and need for treatment of the sores became an overwhelming problem. Jamie's pain was accompanied by significant anxiety. While his screaming during dressing changes reflected an appropriate affective response, Jamie soon began to anticipate the pain, and his anxiety clouded his perception of reality. His screaming assumed a constant, one-tone quality and began as soon as the nurses approached him. The nurses attempted to distract Jamie from his pain fantasy and help him perceive reality. This was very difficult; every time the nurses succeeded in preventing an autistic-like state was a small victory. Jamie slowly learned what was real and not real. By the time he was discharged, Jamie was demonstrating mastery over his anxiety by helping with the dressing changes; he prided himself on being able to open the dressing sets just like a nurse. He was not expected to like the procedure, but being able to master his anxiety was critical.

Children learn about reality from caring adults. Jamie's nurses helped fill this void in his life and helped to orient him. He was often confused as to the day or time and his whereabouts. As they went through the day, the nurses would comment on the external world in a normal conversational tone—"Good morning, Jamie. I am Marie, your nurse. It is breakfast time, and you have cereal and toast in front of you. Here is your schedule for the day. Let's put it on your tack board. What clothes do you want to wear today? Look, here are your choices." A normal conversational tone is appropriate during such activities. Unfortunately, it is not unusual to observe caregivers shouting at disoriented children, as if shouting will break through the barrier. If the barrier is fear, the key is mutual trust, not shouting.

When Jamie was placed on psychotropic medication by the child psychiatrist to help control his extreme anxiety states, the nurses and staff were concerned. How could such a young child be given such strong medications? In a staff meeting, the pediatric-mental health clinical nurse specialist reviewed Jamie's chaotic life and periods of abuse and asked the nurses to imagine how Jamie was feeling. This helped the nurses to understand how serious Jamie's problems were and how the medication might actually provide him with some necessary relief.

During one visit with Jamie, the clinical nurse specialist observed an interesting event. These visits usually focused around reading a story. During the reading, Jamie reached over, picked up the nurse's finger, and slowly pulled her ring off. He rolled over onto his side, cupped the ring in his hand, and fell asleep. This was a perplexing dilemma for the clinical nurse specialist, who was frustrated with Jamie and angry at herself for having allowed him to take her ring. If she removed her ring from Jamie's hand and left, would he ever learn to trust her visits? If she left her ring with Jamie, what would he do with it when he awakened? What did Jamie's action mean, and how long would he sleep? Finally deciding that staying with Jamie was the better action, the clinical nurse specialist sat next to him and stroked his other hand. After 45 minutes, he abruptly awoke and dropped her ring on the bed. She thanked him for the ring and promised to return the same time the next day. When the clinical nurse specialist returned the next day, he looked directly at her, made deliberate eye contact and pointing to her ring, he reached out, turned it, and smiled. Obviously, the day before had been a significant breakthrough and Jamie's interaction with everyone became increasingly more deliberate and meaningful.

The next hurdle was to reintroduce Jamie to his peers. The nurses began a planned schedule of trips to the playroom where, at first, Jamie was an observer. Slowly, he was encouraged to be a participant. After 3 weeks, the decision was made to move Jamie from his single room into a room with two boys of a similar age. Initially, he seemed more withdrawn, but he soon became tentatively interactive. Within a month, Jamie was ambulating, more willing to interact with peers, and noticeably warm and responsive to his caregivers. However, there was never a period in which he was completely free of bizarre behavior; the incidence rate just decreased. He was able to play, attend the hospital school for 1 to 2 hours a day, watch and comprehend TV, and visit with his godparents and mother.

After Jamie's sores healed, the decision about where to send him had to be made. It was decided that he would be treated in an in-patient setting where he could receive intensive therapy and continue with special schooling and play therapy. His mother, stepfather, and godparents were scheduled for family therapy before he was returned to any of them. He was still too fragile. On the day of discharge, Jamie was accompanied to the other hospital by the clinical nurse specialist, his mother, and godparents. Although the other hospital had been discussed with Jamie, he became confused and thought that both he and the nurse were being transferred to the new hospital. When shown his new room, he wanted to know where the nurse would sleep. Jamie became appropriately tearful when it was time to separate. Both hospital staffs agreed that Jamie would be allowed to call the nurses in the first hospital twice a day for as long as he requested. His first call came before the clinical nurse specialist had returned to the hospital. He was pleased when she returned his telephone call, and he continued to call for almost two weeks with decreasing frequency as he became more integrated into the second hospital's routine.

Jamie remained hospitalized for an additional 3 months. During this time the godparents admitted to having physically abused him when he lived with them from the ages of 7 months to 4 years. Jamie's mother disappeared with her husband and two other children. During his continued hospitalization, Jamie's screaming episodes stopped, and he was eventually weaned from all medication. He became more overtly angry and would have more appropriate temper tantrums and angrily shout at staff. In group therapy, it was reported that he would often ask "How can moms hurt kids?" and would ask staff "What is wrong with me that mom and nanny hate me?" Jamie became a ward of the court and was placed in a small foster home with a court order forbidding any family members or previous caretakers from visiting him without a foster parent or childcare agency representative present. (For another Case Study describing child abuse, see Chapter 10.)

NURSING CARE PLAN **Abusive/Dysfunctional/Impaired Parenting**

Expected Outcomes	Interventions	Evaluations
• Child will remain safe. • Episodes of physical, verbal, and emotional abuse and neglect will be eliminated.	• Supervise the child and family interactions. • Ensure that policies and procedures are followed to maintain the child's safety. • Notify hospital security that a "child protection" protocol is in effect. • All staff adopt a nonthreatening and nonjudgmental relationship with the child's caregivers. • Connect child's feelings of ambivalence to realization that children love their parents and caregivers even when there are abusive episodes.	• Parental or caregiver visits are positive experiences. • There are no additional episodes of physical, verbal, or emotional abuse. • Child appears more comfortable when visited by parents or caregivers. • There is a decrease in the child's negative reactions to intrusive and painful procedures.
• Child will establish mastery over anxiety associated with dressing changes. • The child will develop trust and a more positive self-concept.	• Use play, family and action figures, art, and story-telling techniques with child to foster awareness of anxiety and understanding of intrusive and painful procedures. • Help the child to establish a comfort level in interacting with the nursing staff. • Help the child to engage with peers in play activities.	• Child is able to demonstrate through play mastery over anxiety and use of more appropriate coping behaviors. • Child begins to relate one to one with nurses, physicians, social workers, and therapists. • Child engages in parallel and shared play with peers in group and playroom activities.
• Contact will be established with other institutions or agencies for follow-up care.	• Have interdisciplinary team conferences to plan the child's return to the home or appropriate placement in another hospital or residential treatment center.	• Child is discharged to parental or foster home or an aftercare setting with appropriate oversight and protection.

Visit http://nursing.jbpub.com/psychiatric for additional care plans and exercises.

Mental health services for children include out-patient treatment, in-home services, special education programs, respite care, foster care, day and partial hospitalization, group homes, residential treatment centers, and in-patient psychiatric hospitalization. Different types of therapy can be provided, such as individual counseling, group therapy, family therapy, special education, play therapy, and medication therapy.

different in their individual emotional makeup, family, and cultural and societal constellations for any single method of intervention to be successful in all cases. Because adolescence is a particularly chaotic and unstable time for most individuals, some clinicians have raised the question as to whether adolescents who are hospitalized for mental health problems are truly mentally ill or just reacting differently to the many tumultuous biologic, hormonal, social, and environmental changes that they are experiencing (Smoyak, Pressler, Oppenheim, & Chapman, 1997).

A continuum of mental health services are available in the treatment of children and adolescents. These include out-patient treatment, in-home therapeutic services, special education programs, respite care, foster care, day and partial hospitalization, group homes, residential treatment centers, and in-patient psychiatric hospitalization. These treatment options, types of therapy, length of treatment, cost, and special characteristics are contrasted in **Table 24-4**.

Group homes, residential centers, and some in-patient settings seek to establish a **therapeutic milieu** that provides "adaptive experiences that a child or adolescent presumably missed in the course of growing up. . . . [It] also provides corrective experiences to offset some of the more damaging experiences; it is a safe place [that emphasizes] external structure and control"

(Lyman & Campbell, 1996, p. 45). Such a community is a flexible environment that is able to meet the individual needs of the children while maintaining predictable standards of behavior (Lyman & Campbell).

It is generally accepted that children and adolescents should be treated in the least restrictive environment and removed from the family only when there are no other options. All alternatives should be explored first, including the provision of combined services, to keep the child in the family unit. Hospitalization allows for direct observation by clinicians of a child's problems and behaviors and the initiation and adjustment of medication regimens as appropriate (Lyman & Campbell, 1996).

In-patient psychiatric hospitalization should be reserved for those children who are a danger to themselves or others, have significant bizarre behavior or a known psychiatric diagnosis, need to be on an established medication treatment regimen that must be closely monitored, or cannot be evaluated or kept safe without 24-hour skilled care and observation. Other criteria that can be used to determine the need for psychiatric hospitalization include significant emotional distress, the inability to function in school, and complete alienation from family and peers (Regan, 2006).

In group homes, residential treatment centers, and in-patient settings, programs usually use positive reinforcements with a privilege system (e.g., time-outs, debriefing, room restriction, loss of privileges). Negative responses to behavior, especially any aversion techniques, are used only when absolutely necessary (e.g., physically restraining a child). Staff members need to be trained in appropriate responses to acting out behaviors, self-injurious behaviors, suicidal thoughts or actions, intimidation, and sexual acting out. Other issues in treatment settings include the development of a coordinated multidisciplinary approach (i.e., psychiatry, psychology, nursing, social work, education, recreational and play therapy), the establishment of safety factors, the provision for **parenting education**, and planned **discipline** and limit setting.

The decision to remove a child from the family and familiar environment should never be made without due consideration. Removal is a drastic change for both the child and the family and can negatively impact on the child and family and result in stigmatization. It can lead to imitative institutionalized behaviors, and families can become disengaged from the child, while the child can become overly dependent on staff and the institution. On the positive side, removal provides the family and child with a respite from each other and the inherent conflict. It can provide everyone involved, including the clinicians on the team, the opportunity to view the problems from another perspective and provide an opportunity to maximize the therapeutic interventions. If legal assistance is requested in response to treatment suggestions, clinicians can refer children, adolescents, and their families and significant others to resources such as the American Bar Association's Center on Children and the Law (ABACCL), located in Washington, D.C., and the National Center on Women and Family Law (NCOWFL) in New York City.

> The decision to place a child or adolescent in a treatment facility outside of the family structure should never be considered without due consideration, because such placement significantly changes the family dynamic.

Finally, there are not enough mental health services available for children. Most children cannot and should not be isolated from their families forever. Treatment services must focus on improving the functioning of the child or adolescent and providing supportive therapy and services for the family unit, which in most cases will be asked to continue raising the child or adolescent. It is imperative that there be a comprehensive and coordinated network of mental health and other services available to meet the changing needs of children and their families and caregivers, a **system of care** as advanced by the Child and Adolescent Service System Program in the National Institute of Health. Such a system provides services that are community-based, child-centered, family-focused, and culturally appropriate (Arbuckle & Herrick, 2006).

Special Issues

In providing age-appropriate care for children, nurses may find themselves helping children deal with a variety of challenging life events. These include being hospitalized with medical conditions that often can be life-threatening; facing intrusive and/or complicated procedures; coping with new, and often frightening, feelings; coping with pain and death; and surviving episodes of child abuse.

Children with Medical Conditions

Multiple factors affect a child's and family's abilities to adjust to a chronic illness or hospitalization, including the actual physical condition and

Table 24-4 Treatment Options for Children and Adolescents

Treatment Option	Description	Types of Therapy	Usual Length of Treatment	Cost	Characteristics
Out-patient treatment	The goal is to maintain the child or adolescent in the family unit, school, and community. Child and family are seen once or twice a week for different types of therapy.	Individual counseling, group therapy, family therapy, play therapy, medication therapy	Can be short-term (4–6 weeks) or long-term (1–3 years)	One of the least expensive options	Least disruptive to family unit Allows mental health practitioner to address ongoing problems related to family and school Keeps child or adolescent in contact with peer group
In-home treatment	The goal is to provide brief, intensive mental health services by one or more members of a multidisciplinary team to intervene in a specific crisis.	Family therapy (on-site in the home), behavior modification therapy, parent education and training, medication therapy	Short-term (4–6 weeks); used mainly for specific periods of crisis or stress	One of the least expensive options	May be slightly disruptive to family life because all members will be asked to attend therapy at specific times Allows mental health practitioner to observe how all family members are responding to the crisis More intensive than simple out-patient treatment Disrupts normal school environment and possibly peer relationships
Special education program	The goal is to provide the child or adolescent with a positive learning experience with specially trained teachers and to provide on-site mental health practitioners.	Special education, individual counseling, family therapy, play therapy, medication therapy	Long-term (2–5 years)	One of the least expensive options	More intensive than simple out-patient treatment
Day treatment or partial hospitalization	The goal is to provide the child or adolescent with the opportunity to receive treatment in a structured environment for a portion of the day.	Individual counseling, group therapy, family therapy, play therapy, medication therapy	Short-term (a few months) or long-term (a couple of years)	Moderately expensive; may be offset by insurance	Allows child or adolescent to maintain family and peer group contact Can be an after school program or combined with a special education program May be associated with some stigmatization
Respite care	The goal is to provide the parents or caretakers with time off from providing care.	Individual counseling, family therapy, parent education or training, medication therapy	Short-term (2 weeks to 2 months)	Moderately expensive	Provides a break for child or adolescent and parents or caretakers Provides mental health practitioner with an opportunity to use intensive individual therapy with the child or adolescent

Foster care	The goal is to remove the child or adolescent from a dysfunctional home and to place the child or adolescent with foster parents who have been specially trained to work with children who have multiple emotional needs.	Individual counseling; group therapy; family therapy with foster parents, biologic parents, or both; medication therapy	Short-term (a few months during crisis times) or long-term (years)	Moderately expensive	Removal from even the most dysfunctional home can result in a major disruption in the child's life. Child or adolescent can continue to attend regular or similar school, or if necessary, a special education program can be incorporated into care. Provides the child or adolescent with a more normal, predictable family atmosphere. Mental health practitioners are available to support the foster parents and reduce burnout.
Group home care	The goal is to place the child or adolescent with 10–12 other children or adolescents who live in a structured, supervised residence, usually with specially trained house parents of both sexes.	Individual counseling, group therapy, family therapy, medication therapy	Long-term (several years)	Moderately expensive	Can result in a major disruption in the child's or adolescent's life from family and peers Less home-like than foster care Child or adolescent must adapt to group home norms and follow rules established in the home Most group homes have a treatment philosophy, such as behavior modification Usually operated by a childcare agency that is responsible for training the house parents, providing supervision, and providing a full range of mental health services as needed by the children or adolescents
Residential treatment center	The goal is to place the child or adolescent in a center that functions like a therapeutic community in which a hundred or more children may be housed in a campus-like, multiple-residence setting.	Individual counseling, group therapy, family therapy, play therapy, medication therapy	Long-term (several years)	Moderately to very expensive	Separation from family and peers can result in a major disruption in the child's or adolescent's life. Less home-like than other options House parents and multidisciplinary teams are available 24 hours. Most centers use therapeutic milieu and behavior modification techniques to influence changes in behavior.

continues

Table 24-4 Treatment Options for Children and Adolescents (continued)

Treatment Option	Description	Types of Therapy	Usual Length of Treatment	Cost	Characteristics
In-patient hospitalization	The goal is to provide safe mental health care under direct medical and nursing supervision in a secure setting.	Individual counseling and intensive psycho-therapy, group therapy, family therapy, play therapy, medication therapy	Short-term (a few weeks to a couple of months for in-patient crisis treatment or evaluation); Long-term (years for children or adolescents who are placed)	Most expensive; may be offset by insurance	Children or adolescents who are placed in these centers usually have failed at other levels of treatment intervention and have chronic and multiple mental health problems. They are usually known to social services, mental health agencies, or juvenile justice agencies. Results in the most direct disruption of the child's or adolescent's life Many units are locked or geographically very distant from the family. Schooling is on-site and is usually a special education program. Regimented schedule of daily activities assists in providing a structured environment. Usual treatment philosophy is a traditional medical model with behavior modification and therapeutic milieu techniques incorporated. Children or adolescents are placed in these settings when they are considered a potential harm to themselves or others or their behavior is chaotic. Contact with family members is structured and monitored. Passes may be provided for short visits to home.

Source: Adapted from Hendren & Berlin, 1991, p. 62; Lyman & Campbell, 1996, pp. 1–24.

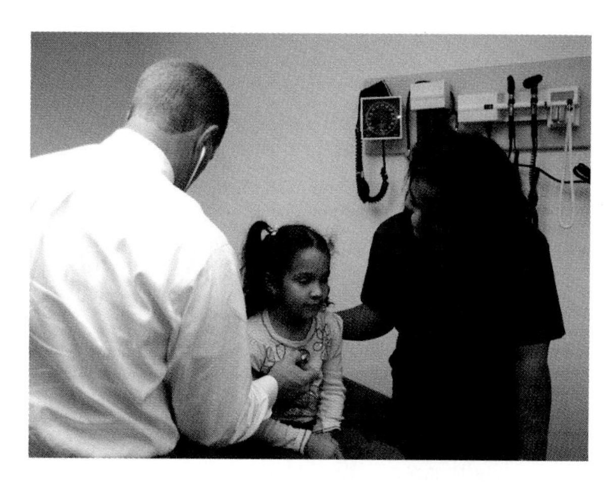

Figure 24-2 Being in a hospital can be traumatic for children.

its severity, whether the condition can be corrected, the ages of the child and the parents, sociocultural factors, financial status and availability of health insurance, accessibility of medical care, prior losses associated with illness in the family, and the parent-child and child-sibling relationships (Hayman, Mahon, & Turner, 2002).

Hospitalization is a potential trauma for all children (Figure 24-2). It includes elements of separation, strangeness of environment, pain, punishment, and threat to self, especially possible mutilation. Children react more to the fantasy aroused by medical procedures than to the procedure itself. Nurses are in a unique position on the healthcare team because they often both prepare the child for an **intrusive procedure** and carry it out, either directly or by assisting the physician, and then comfort the child after the procedure. This is no simple task. There are three types of intrusive or invasive procedures: oral procedures, such as the administration of medication, suctioning, and tracheotomy care; anal procedures, such as suppositories and enemas; and cutaneous procedures, such as injections, blood tests, intravenous (IV) therapy, and dressing changes.

Critical Thinking Question In addition to intrusive or invasive procedures, what other types of experiences during hospitalization can frighten a child, and how can nurses assist the child in feeling safe?

Children under 4 years of age tend to become more disturbed while in the hospital and to have more emotional sequelae afterward. Anxiety (e.g., crying, anorexia, bedwetting, nightmares) and regressive behaviors (e.g., loss of vocabulary, thumb sucking, masturbation, and demands to be fed) are common in hospitalized children. In younger children, imaginary companions may arise. However, these are not reasons to lie to children about what to expect. The hospitalized child is particularly at risk for problems that may not become apparent until later, even after discharge. Deception and overprotectiveness by the nurse can lead to a loss of trust and may influence the child's ability to form relationships. Adult personality patterns develop during childhood, and an early traumatic event can have lasting effects.

> Hospitalization is a potential trauma for children because it contains elements of separation, a strange environment, pain, punishment, threat to self, and possible mutilation.

Hospitalized children need play outlets, established areas of control, and consistent caretaking from the same staff. There are five **types of play** (social, explorative, imitative, group or gang, and competitive games) and four **stages of play** (solitary, parallel, associative, and cooperative). Some examples of **play therapy** that are used with hospitalized children include structured play, mutual story telling, nondirective play, behavioral play, visualization, and guided imagery.

> Play is the work of children. Some types of play therapy are structured play, mutual story telling, nondirective play, behavioral play, visualization, and guided imagery.

Children have the basic right to know. This right is mediated by the child's cognitive ability, developmental stage, ethnic and cultural experiences, and the time frame for the medical or hospital experience. Children can refuse to listen, cry in protest, or cooperate. None of these reactions alters their right to know.

Children, adolescents, and their parents should be prepared for all procedures, medical treatments, and surgeries to diminish or prevent psychological trauma. The parent or primary caretaker should always be involved in such

Clinical Examples

Some examples of children's confusion about their bodies follow:

- A 4-year-old girl with a cyanotic heart condition was asked to draw her heart on a body outline. She put little hearts in her fingers and toes and a medium heart in the middle of her belly. The child had severe clubbing and cyanosis of her fingers and toes, and, of course, she associated her heart with these extremities.
- A 9-year-old boy confined to a wheelchair to allow healing of a graft on his burned leg correctly identified neutral, nonthreatening functions of his internal organs but claimed that muscles were important because "if you could not move, you would probably have a heart attack."
- A 12-year-old mentally retarded child repeatedly referred to his bone marrow tests as "bow and arrow" tests, which is how he probably heard and perceived the test.

Considerations for Client and Family Education

Both children and families benefit from appropriate education regarding the general hospital experience, tests and procedures, medical diseases, and specific surgical interventions. If at all possible, the nurse should first meet with the parents or caregivers to determine their understanding of the hospitalization and what, if anything, the child has been told. Parents sometimes want to avoid telling the child anything, based on a belief that the child cannot possibly understand and would be better off not knowing anything. Parents will respond positively to reassurances that any teaching will be done sensitively and based on the child's stage of development and age. The teaching should be reviewed with the parents, and parents should be included in the child's teaching sessions.

When teaching, nurses should try to use less emotional words such as fix, help, open, drain, and head instead of cut, bleed, or brain. Teaching children with orthopedic problems is uniquely difficult because many individuals, even adults, have faulty knowledge of the skeletal system. Special areas on which to focus when discussing orthopedic procedures are bone pain, bone healing, cast application or removal, maintenance of bodily integrity, and implications for future life activities. To help a child understand how something can be broken but look all right, put a tongue blade inside a gauze pad and break it, use x-rays of broken limbs, build a play traction apparatus, have model casts, or have the child apply casts to a doll.

Remember that children need to know the order of events, so teach all the different elements of procedures and treatments in the order in which they occur.

Four general principles for teaching children about medical procedures are:

1. Children learn best when taught on a one-on-one basis. Although a group experience can reinforce learning, it is not a substitute for one-on-one teaching.
2. Children learn out of interest and curiosity.
3. Children learn only when ready.
4. Children learn at their own pace.

When teaching younger children, remember they often miss internal cues and rely on concrete external cues. If children displace their illnesses on a specific location, even if it is inaccurate, it should be incorporated into the child's perception to explain tests, procedures, and healing. Remember, children are visual and very literal. Therefore, it is important to teach the procedure in the order in which the child will experience it. For example, if the child is having surgery, describe the limitations on intake, preoperative medications, transportation, the attire of operating room personnel, the operating room, anesthesia, the recovery room and intensive care unit (ICU), tubes, machinery, bandages, postoperative pain, medications, and postoperative limitations on activity. The child does not need to know the details of the surgery, only what will be experienced or seen. The elements of the nursing process can be used in teaching children about healthcare experiences and hospitalization.

Teaching of children is "VIPP":

- Visual aids are used.
- Information is age appropriate.
- Preparation is done by play.

As an integral part of the teaching process, the nurse must assess:

- The child's chronological age, developmental level, and cognitive skills
- The reasons for the hospitalization or other healthcare experience (planned versus emergency)
- Previous life experiences (prior hospitalizations, recent family or peer crises, and any handicaps)
- The effect the hospitalization or healthcare experience will have on future life goals (chronicity, prognosis, body changes)
- The availability of family and peer support systems (parents, siblings, and peer relationships; transcultural and economic factors)

The nurse needs to plan a teaching program that addresses the child's individual needs, including:

- Identification of the child's and family's current knowledge base and misconceptions
- Identification of content to be taught
- Choice of appropriate methods of teaching (one-to-one, group, demonstration, video)
- Establishment of a time frame (the younger the child, the closer to the event)
- Selection of teaching materials (hospital and play equipment, books, dolls, puppets, and body diagrams) before beginning the session

The nurse implements the teaching program by:

1. Demonstrating the procedure to the child and family
2. Having the child and family participate in the experience
3. Encouraging the child and family to demonstrate the learned content

The nurse evaluates the success of the teaching program either by using a formal evaluation tool or by observing the child's and family's reactions and responses to the teaching experience and the actual event. Remember, teaching is **VIPP**:

- Visual aids are best.
- Information is age appropriate.
- The child is Prepared for the event by Play. (Ballard, 1985)

preparation, facilitating communication between the multidisciplinary team and the parents, clearing up any misconceptions the parents may have, and giving the parents and child or adolescent a common point of reference regarding the event. Parents can be particularly helpful in assisting the nursing staff in understanding any idiosyncratic language of a young child for the presenting problem (e.g., boo-boo, pimple, nasty thing), body parts (e.g., noggin, bum, peenie), and body functions (e.g., poo, pee, BM).

Feelings

Children have unique ways of conveying their feelings to caregivers. The following two poems illustrate this:

Sick Patient (by 12-year-old Chuck, with leukemia)

Part One

Come on doctor don't be slow
if I die you'll never know.
Come on doctor don't take so long
in a few minutes I may be gone.
Come on doctor don't stop to talk
at the rate I'm going I'll never walk.

Part Two

Come on social worker get off the elevator
'cause I know for a fact I won't see you later.
Come on social worker don't go to any meeting
in just a few minutes I may be leaving.
Come on social worker you're almost here
the longer you take the more I fear.

Part Three

Come on nurse don't delay
eat your Wheaties along the way.
Come on nurse don't waste time
'cause the life you save just might be mine.
Come on nurse just don't pass by
'cause in a few minutes I just may die.

The Victor (by 18-year-old Margaret, with an endocrine disorder)

When the doctors and nurses and others call me a
Stroke Victim, I say, "Wait a minute, I am
not a Stroke Victim. I am a Stroke Victor."
I can speak and walk and even write.
In life there are many things which can
claim us as their victim.
We make the decision what we will do about them.
Whether we let them victimize us or we fight
to be victorious over them. And I, for one,
with God's help will be victorious.

Pain

How do children react to pain? Children experience pain as fear, abandonment, and not being able to get help. They think that the hurt will never end, and they fear losing control. They worry that pain can kill them. Children who cannot describe pain with words can use devices such as the Wong-Baker Faces Pain Rating Scale, a series of simple round faces progressing from happy to very sad and distressed (Hockenberry, 2005). Helping children cope with pain is a challenge. Children need to be encouraged to acknowledge, describe, and rate their pain and not to refuse medication because they fear getting an injection (the little hurt from the needle takes away the bigger pain).

Death

Children also have to learn to cope with death. Erikson noted that helping children to understand death is essential to support their ability to lead productive lives (Ginsberg & Opper, 1987). Children's perceptions of death are related to their developmental stages.

- For children 1 to 3 years old, death is seen as separation.
- For children 3 to 7 years old, death is both separation and punishment.
- For children 7 to 12 years old, death is something to be feared.
- For children over 13 years of age, death is seen as the end of life.

> Helping children to understand death is essential to their ability to lead productive lives. Children respond to death based on their developmental levels. It is not until adolescence that one comprehends fully the reality of death.

Children's ability to comprehend death is quite limited until they reach adolescence. Children of different ages explain death differently. Death for younger children has no finality, because it is experienced as abandonment and separation. Children first learn that pets die, older people die, other people die, and then as adolescence approaches that they also will die. When children ask questions about death, nurses and other clinicians should listen carefully to the question and overcome the tendency to project

Clinical Examples

A pediatric-mental health clinical nurse specialist has helped many children understand death. Each child's experience has been very different:

- A 3-year-old child talks about dog and cat heaven.
- A 5-year-old child wants to write letters to God and her grandparents in heaven.
- A 7-year-old child asks to always have flowers nearby if she dies.
- A 9-year-old asks for help in getting to the next year, which he knows will be better.
- A 12-year-old child seeks reassurance that there is no pain after death and that it will not hurt to die.
- An adolescent with cancer expresses a desire to die as whole as possible—no more hair loss, no more disfiguring surgery.

their own fears and feelings. Seek clarification as to what is concerning or worrying the child.

The following poem was written by a 9-year-old girl for the nursing staff after her 14-year-old brother died from osteogenic sarcoma.

Paul

Paul was a very wonderful boy
But he isn't here for us to enjoy
The Nurses even cared for Paul
They really would give their all and all
They took care of Paul not because they were getting their pay
Just so they could see him live another day
The hospital was crying all that night
And they really gave up a terrible fight
They would care for Paul every day
And not turn their heads another way
They would cry all night or lose their pay
If Paul could see another day
But here we try to be very strong
Even though Paul has gone
If we could pray for him to come back
Even though we know he's on the right track
We know that Paul is in good hands with God.

Child Abuse and Trauma

The phenomenon of **child abuse** occurs at all levels of society. Children are physically, psychologically, and sexually abused every day. Although society attempts to identify and help the abusing dysfunctional adult, the ills that lead to abuse and sustain it—poverty, substandard housing, substance abuse, poor education, and an inadequate child welfare system—are not addressed adequately. Victims of physical child abuse, maltreatment, and neglect change ambulatory care providers with greater frequency than nonabused children. Recognition of this characteristic may allow for earlier identification of children who are at risk for additional or future neglect or abuse (Friedlaender et al., 2005).

In most states, nurses are one of many mandatory reporters of child abuse and neglect. All nurses should be knowledgeable of their state's requirements. Usually, if anyone reports a suspicion of child abuse or neglect to the authorities and it is done in good faith and without malice, the reporting individual is protected from any legal action by the family. Violence in the family is covered in Chapter 10.

In most states, nurses and other health-care practitioners are mandatory reporters of child abuse and neglect. One need only suspect that abuse or neglect has occurred.

If not successfully treated, children who have been victims of trauma will begin to identify with the offender.

Signs and symptoms of child abuse or neglect include:

- Bruises, welts, lacerations, abrasions, burns, fractures, and head injuries
- Drug withdrawal
- Poor hygiene, unattended physical or medical needs
- Torn, stained, or bloody clothing
- Genital, vaginal, or anal injuries
- Sexually transmitted diseases and pregnancy in a minor
- Lack of supervision or abandonment
- Parentally induced or fabricated illnesses
- Extreme fear of parents or adults
- Frequent behavioral or mood changes
- Sucking, biting, rocking, and head banging
- Antisocial, destructive behavior
- Hysteria and phobias
- Sleep disorders and inhibited play
- Self-destructive or suicidal acts
- Delinquency, running away, and truancy
- No explanation for injuries by parents or caretakers
- Overreaction or underreaction to the injuries by parents or caretakers
- History of "hospital shopping" for the child's care

Trauma learning occurs when "the child's attempts to modify the sensory, perceptual, and cognitive alterations that occur during abuse (physical or sexual) emerge in overt behavioral patterns that specifically reflect the abuse itself" (Burgess & Hartman, 1992, p. 362). If this behavior is not interrupted, the child will begin to identify with the offender. Burgess recommends using the **TRIADS** abuse history for assessing trauma in children (Burgess & Hartman, p. 363):

- Type of abuse (physical, psychological, sexual)
- Role relationship (family member, stranger, friend, teacher)
- Intensity (frequently, single event)
- Autonomic response (hyperarousal, numbing)
- Duration (days, weeks, years)
- Style of abuse (repetitive, patterned, ritualistic)

Children are increasingly facing traumatic events in their lives, families, schools, communities, and world. These include child abuse; domestic violence; loss of loved ones; school violence (bullying, harassment, gangs, fatal shootings); catastrophic weather events (hurricanes, tornadoes, tsunamis); epidemics of contagious diseases; terrorism; bombings; drive-by shootings, and wars (Goldman, 2005). Traumatized children must be helped to feel safe with the mental health practitioners and others involved in their treatment and to learn to trust again in their caregivers, families, and communities.

Self-Destructive Behavior

At various developmental stages when confronted with specific stressors (family, peers, school, attachment losses, illness), children and adolescents may seek to relieve themselves of overwhelming psychological pain by engaging in self-injury or suicide.

Self-Injury

Self-injury or self-mutilation has been identified as a "form of self-directed violence that is increasingly common among adolescents and adults, especially females" (Dallam, 1997, p. 152). Children and adolescents with mental retardation, autistic disorder, psychoses, posttraumatic syndrome, or attachment disorders are particularly vulnerable. Adolescents typically attempt to keep a specific stress or trauma from consciousness by engaging in non-suicidal self-injury such as biting self, cutting or carving skin, hitting self on purpose, or burning skin. When interviewed, the reasons adolescents report for engaging in such behavior include: getting a reaction from someone, getting control of a situation, or stopping bad feelings (Lloyd-Richardson, Perrine, Dierker, & Kelley, 2007). Frequently, the adolescent feels the need to be punished, needs to express anger, and attempts to use the physical pain of self-injury to distract his or her consciousness from overwhelming psychological pain. The nurse can focus on establishing a trusting and caring relationship that will encourage the adolescent to talk about the psychological pain rather than diverting it into self-mutilation.

Suicide

Children should always be assessed for behaviors that could result in accidental or planned suicide. It is generally believed that young children are incapable of suicide, but they can hurt themselves. Rates for suicide attempts and successes differ by age, gender, race, and socioeconomic status. More females attempt suicide, but more males are successful.

Because one is an adolescent before one really understands the finality of death, most children are incapable of planned suicide. However, adolescents with depression and/or impulsive behaviors are particularly vulnerable. Nurses should never underestimate ideation by any child or anyone of behaviors that could result in injury or death. Adolescents who appear particularly depressed or manic or have had an especially stressful life event should be evaluated carefully. Nurses need to rate the degree of intent, the availability of firearms, and the exposure to other suicidal events. There is a contagion factor associated with adolescent suicide that needs to be carefully monitored and responded to by mental health professionals.

> Adolescents are particularly vulnerable to self-mutilating acts, suicidal behaviors, and suicide.

Parenting Behaviors and Child Discipline

Children grow and develop based on the strength of the parenting behaviors of the main caregivers. Parenting, a critical and very serious task for adults, is often casually accepted by many members of society as something one automatically knows how to do upon the birth of a child. One need only look at the statistics for child abuse (almost 2 million children are abused annually) to know that this is not true. No parenting is perfect. We all tend to parent as we ourselves were parented. Becoming a parent, whether in a relationship and stable family unit, as a single parent, as a young parent with minimal support systems, or as an older, first time parent, results in changes in the parent's lifestyle and relationships with others. Whether or not the parent views the birth of the child as stressful or fairly routine, the parent's self-image, family economics, and levels of responsibility will all change. One's life is not the same once a child has been born into it.

> People tend to parent the way they were parented. Parents need support through all stages of normal growth and development to understand their children and their own reactions to the child's various behaviors.

There is a general lack of appreciation of the role of the father figure in a child's development. Care of infants and children must be acknowledged as natural and appropriate male behavior. Many infants form primary attachments with the father, even when the father is not the primary caretaker, and almost all infants by 3 months of age can discriminate between maternal and paternal figures. A father's play and verbalizations have positive impact on developing infants. The mother figure's interactions with the child tend to involve caretaking activities, whereas the father figure's interactions are mostly play oriented.

The role of discipline in parental activities needs to be evaluated by pediatric and mental healthcare practitioners. All families use some form of discipline. Discipline that helps children learn to control their behaviors and keep themselves safe is appropriate; discipline that is harsh, unfocused, or physically, verbally, or psychologically abusive is never appropriate.

Caregiver Stress

Caregiver burden is "the presence of problems, difficulties, or adverse events that affect the lives of the psychiatric patient's significant others" (Angold et al., 1998, p. 75). Caring for children who are emotionally healthy is not easy, and caring for children with emotional problems is significantly difficult. Such care affects the caregiver's personal well-being, puts tremendous restrictions on personal activities, and can be a social stigma. Caregiver stress can be helped through counseling focused on the specific needs of the parents or caregivers and through respite care provided on a regular and scheduled basis.

Sibling Rivalry

Children who are separated by more than 5 years in birth order seem to experience minimal **sibling rivalry**. Sibling rivalry can be constructive and is not necessarily harmful or destructive. It actually allows children to act out within the safe confines of the family many of the future challenges and competitions of adult life. Siblings' expectations of the new brother or sister must be realistic. They are not acquiring a new toy or playmate. They must be taught limitations of their interactions with the infant. They should be introduced to the reproductive process at an age-appropriate level (e.g., brothers and sisters are not delivered by storks but grow inside mommy). They must learn how everyone in the new family will fit together (e.g., sleeping arrangements, meals, family vacations). The older brother or sister can be encouraged to assist with specific, infant-directed activities; to play out feelings toward the new infant with dolls and other toys; to appreciate the specialness of older brother or older sister status; and to have their own private times with mother and father.

Sibling rivalry permits children to act out in the confines of a safe home environment many of the future challenges and competitions that will be faced in adulthood.

Summary

American society sees childhood as an idyllic stage of development; however, it is a time of tremendous growth and challenge for the child and adolescent. A child's development is affected by numerous risk factors and contributing stresses. Children experience life in a family structure. The establishment of trust early in life is critical to the child's and adolescent's ability to function in the family, with peers, in school, and in adulthood.

Nurses can gain an understanding of the functioning of a child with mental health problems by interviewing and assessing the child and by conducting a mental status examination. Five theoretical models that assist in understanding

Implications for Evidence-Based Practice

When parents are not available to a child through death or mental illness, nurses need to be sensitive to how such life situations can affect a child. The death of a parent is a major stressful event for children and their families. Children who are not supported in the early phases of grieving can develop serious emotional and behavioral problems that can lead to the development of some major psychiatric disorders (Kirwin & Hamrin, 2005). Research also reports the uncertain outcome of variables affecting the life of a child of a mentally ill parent (Atkins, 1992). Nurses should focus on assessing the child's self-care skills, deficits and adaptive and maladaptive coping behaviors to plan individual interventions for assisting the child in coping with the loss of a parent or with the behaviors of a mentally ill parent(s).

Children with acute and chronic illnesses experience multiple major stressors. One in-depth exploratory study of children diagnosed with cancer revealed that the major stressors for these children were treatment procedures such as chemotherapy, loss of control, the hospital environment, relapses, and fear of dying. The children also identified body image issues, ongoing lack of self-esteem, and issues related to returning home and back to school as stressful (McCaffrey, 2006). These types of studies reinforce the important role of nurses in teaching both children and families about any hospital experience (in-patient or out-patient), tests and procedures, medical diseases, and specific surgical interventions.

how children develop and what influences their behavior are the attachment model, the psychosocial developmental model, the cognitive model, the behavioral modification model, and the sense of self model. In the case study of a young child, the effects of a long history of poor attachment behaviors and multiple instances of loss of trust through child abuse were examined.

Various methods of management and treatment, including out-patient treatment, in-home treatment, special education programs, respite care, foster care, day and partial hospitalization, group homes, residential treatment centers, and in-patient hospitalization were explored.

Special issues such as children with medical problems, child abuse and trauma, pain, death, self-injury and suicide, and nursing interventions such as play therapy, teaching children about medical procedures, and teaching about and administering medication therapy were discussed. Caregiver stress experienced by the parents and significant others of children with emotional problems can be significant. Caregivers can be helped by counseling and with the provision of respite services.

Annotated References

Angold, A., Messer, S., Stangl, D., Farmer, E., Costello, E., & Burns, B. (1998). Perceived parental burden and service use for child and adolescent psychiatric disorders. *American Journal of Public Health, 88*(1), 75–80.

This article reports on a study of the little-known area of caregiver and parental stress as experienced by those caring for emotionally disturbed children.

Arbuckle, M., & Herrick, C. (2006). *Child & adolescent mental health—Interdisciplinary systems of care.* Sudbury, MA: Jones and Bartlett.

This text discusses the integration of the Systems of Care philosophy and approach into providing mental health care to children and adolescents. It discusses the implications and impact of such a system on the patients, families, mental health professionals, and the behavioral healthcare community.

Atkins, F. A. (1992). An uncertain future: Children of mentally ill parents. *Journal of Psychosocial Nursing, 30*(8), 13–16.

Discusses research that reports the uncertain outcome of variables affecting the life of a child of a mentally ill parent.

Ballard, K. (1985). *Preparing children for the hospital experience* [videotape]. New York: American Journal of Nursing Company and Hospital Satellite Network.

This filmed presentation of teaching methods is a classic and can be used still in preparing children of all ages for hospitalization and medical and surgical procedures. It was chosen in 1986 by the American Association for the Advancement of Science as an exceptional film.

Benjamin, M., & Young, K. (2006, August 30). 46 million in U.S. without health insurance. *Bloomberg News.* Retrieved August 21, 2006, from www.bloomberg.com/apps/news?pid5newsarchive&sid=aBo_bO.jxbvg

This article reviews the findings from the U.S. Census Bureau of the incidence and impact of no access to health insurance on individuals, families, and children in the United States.

Bowlby, J. (1994). *Attachment.* New York: Basic Books.

This is a later version of Bowlby's classic work on the formation of attachment behaviors between infants and mothers.

Burgess, A., & Hartman, C. (1992). Nursing interventions with children and adolescents experiencing sexually aggressive responses. In P. West (Ed.), *Psychiatric and mental health nursing with children and adolescents* (pp. 360–365). Gaithersburg, MD: Aspen.

This is an excellent review of trauma and its effects on children. It offers suggestions for assessment and interventions.

Children's Defense Fund. (2005). *The state of America's children—2004.* Washington, DC: Author.

This report discusses the impact of living in poverty in the United States upon children and their families and the implications of such status on their health, education, family structure, and criminal behavior.

Children's Defense Fund. (2006). *Improving children's health—Understanding children's health disparities and promising approaches to address them.* Washington, DC: Author.

This report addresses the factors contributing to health disparities, the impact of such disparities on children's health, and the access to community programs addressing infant mortality, immunizations, lead poisoning, dental care, asthma, and obesity.

Dallam, S. (1997). The identification and management of self-mutilating patients in primary care. *The Nurse Practitioner, 22*(5), 151–164.

This article presents an interesting exploration of self-mutilating behaviors, the at-risk populations, and causes and interventions.

Erikson, E. H. (1964). *Childhood and society* (2nd ed.). New York: W. W. Norton and Company.

This book is appropriately identified by the publisher as the landmark book on the social significance of childhood.

Friedlaender, E. Y., Rubin, D. M., Alpern, E. R., Mandell, D. S., Christian, C. W., & Alessandrini, E. A. (2005). Patterns of health care that might identify young children who are at risk for maltreatment. *Pediatrics, 116*(6), 1303–1308.

This paper discusses how victims of physical child abuse, maltreatment, and neglect change ambulatory care providers with greater frequency than nonabused children, and how recognizing this characteristic can lead to earlier identification of children who are at risk.

Ginsberg, H., & Opper, S. (1987). *Piaget's theory of intellectual development* (3rd ed.). Upper Saddle River, NJ: Prentice-Hall.

This book provides an excellent introduction to Piaget's life, work, and cognitive theories. It is a great introductory primer.

Goldman, L. (2005). *Raising our children to be resilient: A guide to helping children cope with trauma in today's world.* New York: Brunner-Routledge.

This book offers sound practical advice for parents, teachers, and mental health practitioners on how to support children in adapting to a frightening world.

Goodman, J. D., & Sours, J. A. (1994). *The child mental status examination.* Northvale, NJ: Jason Aronson.

This is an excellent guide for understanding the processes involved in the developmental, emotional, mental, and neurological examinations of children.

Hayman, L. L., Mahon, M. M., & Turner, J. R. (2002). *Chronic illness in children: An evidence-based approach.* New York, NY: Springer Publishing Company.

Provides a research based discussion of common childhood chronic illnesses and their etiology, diagnosis, treatment, and management. Special emphasis is placed on psychosocial management, family coping, and stress in the child.

Hendren, R., & Berlin, I. (1991). *Psychiatric inpatient care of children and adolescents: A multicultural approach.* New York: Simon & Schuster.

Hockenberry, M. (2005). *Wong's essentials of pediatric nursing* (7th ed.). St. Louis, MO: Mosby.

This is one of the premier pediatric textbooks. It provides an excellent presentation of child development, health promotion, and specific health problems organized by body systems.

Hockenberry, M., & Wilson, D. (2006). *Wong's nursing care of infants and children* (7th ed.). St. Louis, MO: Mosby.

This is an excellent pediatric nursing textbook for both nursing students and practicing nurses. It can serve as pediatric nursing guidelines, because it incorporates the latest information from many authoritative organizations.

House, A. E. (2002). *The first session with children and adolescents: Conducting a comprehensive mental health evaluation.* New York: Guilford Press.

This book provides a comprehensive approach to evaluating the mental health status of children and adolescents. It includes instructional segments, case studies, and current applicable research.

Kirwin, K. M., & Hamrin, V. (2005). Decreasing the risk of complicated bereavement and future psychiatric disorders in children. *Journal of Child and Adolescent Psychiatric Nursing, 18*(2), 62–78.

This is a discussion of the death of a parent as a major stressful event for children and their families and how to decrease its impact upon children's future mental health.

Lloyd-Richardson, E. E., Perrine, N., Dierker, L., & Kelley, M. L. (2007). *Psychological Medicine, 37*(8), 1183–1192.

This study of over 600 adolescents examines the prevalence and motivation for engaging in nonsuicidal self-injury behavior in this vulnerable population.

Lyman, R. D., & Campbell, N. R. (1996). *Treating children and adolescents in residential and inpatient settings.* Thousand Oaks, CA: Sage.

This reference provides useful guidelines for how and when to use in-patient and residential treatment in the care of children and adolescents.

Mash, E., & Barkley, R. (Eds.). (2003). *Child psychopathology* (2nd ed.). New York: Guilford Press.

This book addresses a broad range of childhood and adolescent disorders. There is particular emphasis on developmental processes, current theories of etiology, research, and adaptive and maladaptive functioning.

McCaffrey, C. N. (2006). Major stressors and their effects on the well-being of children with cancer. *Pediatric Nursing, 21*(1), 59–66.

This is an in-depth exploratory study of major stressors experienced by children diagnosed with cancer.

President's Commission on Mental Health. (1978). *Report to the president from the president's commission on mental health* (Vols. 1–4). Washington, DC: U.S. Government Printing Office.

Volume 1 contains the commission's report and recommendations; volumes 2, 3, and 4 contain the reports of the specialty panels.

President's New Freedom Commission on Mental Health. (2002). *Achieving the promise: Transforming mental health care in America.* Washington, DC: U.S. Government Printing Office.

This is a report on the commission's study of the U.S. mental health service delivery system, including both private and public sector providers. The commission provides advice to the president on methods to improve the system so that adults with serious mental illness and children with serious emotional disturbances can live, work, learn, and participate fully in their communities. This commission's report was the first comprehensive study of the nation's public and private mental health service delivery systems in nearly 25 years.

Regan, K. (2006). Paradigm shifts in inpatient psychiatric care of children: Approaching child- and family-centered care. *Journal of Child and Adolescent Psychiatric Nursing, 19*(1), 29–40.

This article describes the components of child- and family-centered care, focusing on an in-patient child psychiatric unit that has implemented an approach to care that embraces these principles.

Schor, E. L. (2003). Family pediatrics: Report of the Task Force on the Family. *Pediatrics, 111*(6 Pt 2), 1541–1571.

The task force found that stressors such as financial difficulties, health problems, lack of social supports, work dissatisfaction, and unfortunate life events can cause parents emotional stress interfering with their own relationship and disrupting their parenting.

Smoyak, S., Pressler, C., Oppenheim, J., & Chapman, V. (1997). Evaluating the decision to hospitalize SED youth using qualitative data. *Journal of Psychosocial Nursing, 35*(10), 244–249.

This article is an interesting exploration of whether seriously emotionally disturbed children are really mentally ill or simply troubled youth reacting to overwhelming factors. It is a study of a very small and limited sample group.

Stein, R. E. K. (1997). *Health care for children: What's right, what's wrong, what's next.* New York: United Hospital Fund.

This practical resource describes innovative approaches and model programs for children's health care. It raises practical, ethical, and moral questions regarding the nation's commitment to the health of its children.

Stern, D. (1985). *The interpersonal world of the infant.* New York: Basic Books.

This book is an interesting combination of psychoanalysis and developmental psychology. It discusses the importance of the first year and a half of life and the child's development of a sense of self.

Stern, D. (2000). *The interpersonal world of the infant: A view from psychoanalysis and developmental psychology.* New York: Basic Books.

This book is an interesting exploration of the early experiences of an infant and how they do or do not impact upon later development.

U.S. Census Bureau. (2006, August). *Income, poverty, and health insurance coverage in the U.S.: 2005.* Retrieved August 28, 2006, from www.census.gov/prod/2006pubs/p60-231.pdf

This reports data on income, poverty, and health insurance coverage in the United States based on information collected in the 2005 and earlier American Social and Economic Supplements to the Current Population Survey conducted by the U.S. Census Bureau.

U.S. Department of Health and Human Services. (2000). *Report of the Surgeon General's conference on children's mental health: A national action agenda.* Washington, DC: Author.

This report was a collaboration among the U.S. Departments of Health and Human Services, Education, and Justice. It contains a summary of the conference and presents sections on its vision, goals, and recommendations.

Additional Resources

Brazelton, T. B. (1992). *Touchpoints: The essential reference.* New York: Addison-Wesley.

This is an excellent child care reference by an eminent pediatrician who addresses child development from a practical approach that incorporates physical, cognitive, emotional, and behavioral information.

Clark, C. D. (2003). *In sickness and in play: Children coping with chronic illness.* Piscataway, NJ: Rutgers University Press.

This book focuses on how children and their families cope with two common childhood illnesses, diabetes and asthma.

Fraiberg, S. (1996). *The magic years.* New York: Simon & Schuster.

This later version of a classic is truly a wonderful book. If one wants to understand the mind of a child and how children confront and cope with the world, this magical book accomplishes the goal.

Johnson, B. (1995). *Child, adolescent and family psychiatric nursing.* Philadelphia: J. B. Lippincott.

This comprehensive textbook addresses the knowledge and skill needs of nurses who provide care for children and adolescents with mental health problems and for their families.

Petrillo, M., & Sanger, S. (1980). *Emotional care of hospitalized children* (2nd ed.). Philadelphia: J. B. Lippincott.

This multidisciplinary book is a classic in the specialty of pediatric health. It provides basic and practical knowledge in preparing children and their families for hospital experiences from a combined developmental and environmental approach.

Internet Resources

http://nursing.jbpub.com/psychiatric

Visit http://nursing.jbpub.com/psychiatric for interactive exercises, NCLEX review questions, WebLinks, and more.

CHAPTER 25

The Aging Client

Beverley E. Holland

LEARNING OBJECTIVES

After reading this chapter, you will be able to:

- Describe the aging population in the United States.
- Discuss the most commonly used screening tools for older people exhibiting mental disorders.
- Discuss how nutrition, elimination, sleep problems, and pain can affect an elder's mental status.
- Determine the impact polypharmacy can have on an older individual's mental status.
- Examine the effect unrecognized and untreated depression and anxiety can have on the older adult.
- Differentiate the differences in suicide in the older population versus younger adults.
- Identify the differences in late-onset and early-onset substance abuse in the older adult.

KEY TERMS

Activities of daily living (ADLs)
Competency
Dysphagia
Instrumental activities of daily living (IADLs)
Presbycusis
Presbyopia
Xerostomia

http://nursing.jbpub.com/psychiatric

Visit http://nursing.jbpub.com/psychiatric for interactive exercises, NCLEX review questions, WebLinks, and more.

Introduction

America is a youth-oriented society. No one wants to be old. In some cultures, the elderly are revered and hold a special place of honor within the society; but in highly industrialized countries such as the United States, status declines with age and a decrease in productivity and participation in the mainstream of society.

Individuals experience many changes as they age. Physical changes occur in virtually every body system, but in the absence of pathology older adults continue to function in their environment either independently or with assistance. Psychologically, there may be age-related change that could impact memory, particularly short-term memory, but again, in the absence of pathology the individual is able to function.

Older adults can experience the same spectrum of mental disorders as younger adults. However, certain conditions are particularly notable in later life, because of either increased prevalence or high

Psychiatric symptoms that develop later in life are often dismissed as normal manifestations of aging. Even psychotic symptoms may be dismissed as eccentricity or misdiagnosed as senility. Treatment can be planned only if the problem is acknowledged and identified.

Depression diagnosed after age 65 is considered late onset and is usually associated with medical illnesses.

Unsuccessful resolution of Erikson's postulated final stage of personality development, integrity vs. despair, may be related to the depression observed in the elderly. Erikson's stages of development are discussed in Chapter 3.

There is an increasing number of elderly U.S. immigrants. They follow their children to the United States and assist in child care and home maintenance. Depression may be related to acculturation problems.

morbidity. Older people often do not receive the same amount or quality of services offered to younger adults (Spar & LaRue, 2002). This may be due to limited reimbursement, limited access, and staffing patterns (Koenig, George, & Schneider, 1994). Attitudes about aging, age-related conditions, and the limited training in geriatrics of mental health professionals may also play roles in restricting the availability and quality of mental health care.

Older people themselves often fail to report mental disorders such as depression or anxiety, thinking it is normal to feel "sad" and to "worry." They often report physiological complaints to the healthcare provider as opposed to psychological problems. For many there continues to be a stigma attached to having a mental disorder. It is important to be aware of the occurrence of mental disorders in the older adult, how they may present, and various age-appropriate assessment strategies.

General Description

Life expectancy from birth has increased dramatically in the United States. Even those who are currently "old" can expect to live for many years. At age 65, men can expect to live more than 17 additional years and for women it is an additional 19.8 years (Administration on Aging [AoA], 2006). The elderly population is the only segment of the general population that is expected to grow substantially in the next 50 years. Currently individuals 65 and over make up 12.4% of the U.S. population (AoA). The baby boomers (those born between 1946 and 1964) begin turning 65 in 2011, and we will see a shift in the population age by 2030. At that time, 20% of the population will be 65 or older (AoA). "Old-old" people (those 85 years or older) constitute one of the fastest-growing subgroups.

Most people age 65 or older have at least one chronic medical illness and many have multiple conditions. Among the most frequently occurring chronic conditions are arthritis and orthopedic conditions, hypertension and heart conditions, and hearing or visual impairments (AoA, 2006). Each of these conditions can limit independent function and detract from quality of life.

Those with ongoing needs that cannot be met at home generally receive care in long-term care facilities. Although only about 5% of the elderly population is residing in nursing homes at a given time, the proportion of older persons requiring such care increases quite sharply with age (AoA, 2006).

Older people with mental disorders constitute a significant subgroup of the elderly population. Estimates indicate that about 12% of older community-dwelling adults have diagnosable mental disorders. Approximately 30% to 50% of elderly clients seen in primary care or hospitalized for medical conditions have some type of mental disorder (Spar & LaRue, 2002). In long-term care, 70% or more of residents have been found to have mental disorders; overall, it is estimated that 15% to 25% of Americans over age 65 have significant mental health problems (Spar & LaRue).

Cognitive deficits in older clients have many different possible causes, and for as many as one client in five, treatment of underlying problems can reverse or substantially alleviate cognitive symptoms (Spar & LaRue, 2002). Even individuals with dementia of the Alzheimer type can gain in functional ability by treating coexisting medical or psychiatric illnesses.

Many older people without major mental disorders experience adjustment reactions to personal stresses, bereavement, pain syndromes, and sleep disturbance. Education and interventions directed at these problems may prevent more serious psychiatric or medical problems from developing.

The Normal Aging Process

The normal aging process is generally characterized by changes in physical appearance and functional decline. As a person ages they may also have more chronic disease, which is due to pathological changes. As we age, change occurring in a physiological system can directly or indirectly influence other changes. Each individual ages differently, and aging is affected by the person's genetic makeup, health behaviors, environment, and availability of resources.

This section cannot provide a comprehensive overview of the normal aging process. **Table 25-1** gives a brief overview of normal biological changes that occur with aging. If more information is needed, please refer to a health assessment text or a gerontological nursing text.

The ability to recognize the normal and the pathological changes of aging and deal with the

Table 25-1 Normal Physiological and Functional Changes with Aging

Body System	Physiologic Change	Functional Change
Cardiovascular Heart, arteries	Enlargement, thickening, and stiffening of chambers. Arterial walls atrophy; thicken, twist, and stiffen; and show calcification and decreased elasticity.	Increased blood pressure
Respiratory Lungs, musculoskeletal	Decreased alveolar surface; decrease of lung elasticity; stiffening of chest wall due to loss of rib elasticity	Reduced vital capacity; poor gas exchange; increased residual volume
Gastrointestinal	Decreased saliva; impaired esophageal motility; atrophy of gastric mucosa; increase in gastric pH; decreased colon motility	Reduced elimination efficiency; reduced metabolism of drugs
Genitourinary	Loss of renal mass, loss of glomeruli; reduced bladder elasticity, especially in women; prostate enlargement in men	Reduced glomerular filtration rate; loss of bladder emptying capacity; decrease in clearance of some drugs
Endocrine	Atrophy and fibrosis; loss of vascularity	General decline in secretory rate
Nervous	Loss of brain weight and volume; loss of neurons; slowing of nerve conduction; decrease of secretion of most neurotransmitters	Thought processes, reasoning, and memory essentially unchanged; slower reaction time, decision making, and startle response
Musculoskeletal	Reduced muscle and bone mass; demineralization of bone; decreased number and size of muscle fibers; increased fat in muscles and calcium in cartilage; degeneration of cartilage; loss of elasticity in joints	Loss of muscular strength, endurance, and stamina; loss of bone strength; increased bone brittleness; loss of joint movement
Special senses Vision, hearing	Decreased visual acuity; decreased accommodation and focus; decreased ability to hear high-pitched sounds	**Presbycusis** (loss of auditory acuity) and decreased visual acuity, especially night vision; **presbyopia** (loss of visual accommodation)
Integumentary	Loss of subcutaneous fat and water; loss of elasticity; development of brown pigmented spots	Wrinkles, dry skin

Source: Adapted from Plahuta & Hamrick-King, 2006.

chronic conditions that may indicate impending illness or impair function is important in promoting quality of life. Many factors may contribute to the onset of illness or result in a decline in function. Some of these factors include delirium and confusion, anxiety, depression, sleep disorders, and polypharmacy, any of which can be a key cause and contributory factor for many common health problems.

Differentiating disease from normal changes of aging and the early recognition of health problems allow the early start of treatment while recovery is still possible (Amella, 2004).

Mental Health of the Older Adult

Almost 20% of adults older than age 55 experience specific mental disorders that are not part of "normal aging" (U.S. Department of Health and Human Services [DHHS], 1999). Elders with mental health problems fall into one of two groups. One group consists of those with long-term mental illnesses who have aged with their mental illness. These individuals usually understand their disorders and treatments. Unfortunately, the changes associated with aging can affect a client's control of his or her chronic mental illness. Symptoms may reappear and medications may need to be adjusted. The other group comprises individuals who are relatively free of mental health problems until their elder years. These individuals may already have other health problems and develop late-onset mental disorders, such as depression, schizophrenia, or dementia. For these individuals and their family members the development of a mental disorder can be very traumatic.

Mental health problems in the elderly can be especially complex because of co-existing medical problems and treatments. Many symptoms of somatic disorders mimic or mask psychiatric disorders. For example, fatigue may be related to anemia, but it also may be symptomatic of depression. In addition, older individuals are more likely to report somatic symptoms, rather than psychological ones, making identification of a mental disorder even more difficult.

Geriatric Mental Health Assessment

A thorough geriatric mental health nursing assessment serves as a basis for care when psychiatric or mental health issues are identified or when clients with mental illnesses reach their later years (usually about age 65 years). The overall healthcare issues for the elderly can be very complex, so it follows that certain components of the mental health nursing assessment are unique. Thus the geriatric mental health assessment emphasizes some areas that are less critical to standard adult assessment.

Nursing Assessment

The nurse assesses the client using an interview format. The nurse may also rely on self-report standardized tests, such as depression and cognitive functioning tools. A wide variety of psychologic disorders may cause changes in the mental status of older adults; therefore, the results of laboratory tests often are significant. For example, urinalysis can detect a urinary tract infection that is affecting a client's cognitive status. Other changes that can affect mental status include acid-base imbalance, dehydration, drugs (prescribed and over-the-counter), electrolyte changes, hypothyroidism, hypo- and hyperthermia, hypoxia, infection, and sepsis. In addition, medical records from other healthcare practitioners are useful in developing a complete picture of the client's health status.

Activities of daily living (ADLs) include self-care activities that people must accomplish to survive, such as eating, dressing, bathing, and toileting. **Instrumental activities of daily living (IADLs)** include performing housework, going on errands, managing finances, and making telephone calls.

An important source of client data is family members. They often notice changes that the client overlooks, fails to recognize, or will not report. A client with memory impairment may be unable to give an accurate history. By interviewing family members, the nurse expands the scope of the client assessment. Moreover, the nurse has an opportunity to evaluate the caregivers themselves to determine whether they can care for the client adequately and how they are coping with the situation. For example, a husband whose wife has Alzheimer's disease may be the sole caregiver. He may be exhausted and unable to provide safe adequate care for her but is unwilling to admit it. If the nurse can establish rapport with the husband, he or she may use the assessment interview as an opportunity to help the husband realistically examine his wife's care requirements and his capabilities (**Figure 25-1**).

Figure 25-1 Caregivers can become exhausted from caring for a loved one, and require care themselves.

Testing and evaluating the older adult can be a challenge because of a number of factors such as visual and hearing impairments, memory problems, fatigability, and distrust of psychiatric personnel. Older adults often need special attention during the interview. Hearing impaired or visually impaired individuals may need to sit closer to and directly in front of the interviewer. It is important to speak clearly and at a volume the client does not find distorted. Using distinct enunciation will help lip-reading clients understand what is being said. Sometimes, deafness is mistaken for cognitive dysfunction. The elderly client may need more physical assistance than a younger client, and the pace of the interview may need to be slower than with younger populations.

Thought Processes

Evaluating the client's thought processes and content are critical in the assessment of elderly clients. Can the client express ideas and thoughts logically? Can the client understand questions and follow the conversation of others? If the client shows any indication of hallucinations or delusions, the nurse should explore the content of the hallucination or delusion. If the client has a history of mental illness, such as schizophrenia, these symptoms may be familiar to family members, who can validate whether they are old or new problems. If this is the first time the client has experienced these abnormal thought processes, the nurse should further evaluate the content. Suspicious and delusional thoughts that characterize dementia often include: my spouse is cheating on me; people are stealing my things; this house is not my home; my relative is an impostor. If a client shares any such thoughts, further assessment should be done.

Cognition and Intellectual Performance

Cognitive functioning includes such parameters as orientation, attention, short- and long-term memory, consciousness, and executive functioning. Intellectual functioning, also considered a cognitive measure, is rarely formally assessed with a standardized intelligence test in elderly people. Considerable variability among individuals depends on lifestyle and psychosocial factors. Some changes in cognitive capacity accompany aging, but important functions are spared. Normal cognitive changes during aging include a slowing of information processing and memory retrieval. Abnormalities of consciousness, orientation, judgment, speech, or language are not related to age but to underlying neuropathologic changes. Cognitive changes in elderly people are also associated with delirium, dementia, or schizophrenia. When assessing cognitive functioning, the Mini-Mental State Examination (MMSE) is a tool that can be used for baseline information and to evaluate treatment effectiveness over time.

Behavioral Changes

Behavior changes in elderly people can indicate neuropathologic processes. If such changes occur, it is likely that family members will notice them before the client does. Behavior problems including irritability, agitation, apathy, euphoria, wandering, and aggression are often noted in individuals with dementia and other neurologic and psychologic disorders. Underlying acute infectious processes can also cause behavior changes. It is important to do a physical work-up on individuals who present with sudden onset behavior changes.

Critical Thinking Questions The most common chronic health conditions in the elderly are arthritis, hypertension, heart disease, orthopedic problems, and cataracts. What are some of the symptoms of chronic conditions that may contribute to mental status problems? How do chronic conditions complicate mental status problems?

Mental Health Screening Tools

There are many mental health screening tools available. Not all are adaptable to the older population. Screening tests should be chosen with the specific population group in mind and the ability of the tool to provide valid results.

The number-one risk factor for Alzheimer's disease is age. The older you are, the greater the risk for developing Alzheimer's disease.

Memory is the ability of the mind to recall earlier events. The two types of memory are short-term, for events that happened within the past day or so, and long-term, for events that occurred from the first recollections of childhood and up to the current week.

Cognitive assessment often requires a formal focused assessment. Individuals with advanced education or highly developed social skills may easily cover the signs of early impairment. A superficial social conversation will usually not reveal underlying disorientation to time and place or deficit in short-term memory. The most extensively used tool for assessment of mental status in geriatrics is the Mini-Mental State Examination (MMSE; Folstein, Folstein, & McHugh, 1975). The MMSE takes approximately 10 to 15 minutes to administer, and each section of the tool assesses a different aspect of cognitive function: orientation, registration, attention and calculation, recall, and language. Various studies suggest that an MMSE score below 24 of 30 has a reasonable sensitivity and specificity for discriminating between those with dementia and those without (Mulgrew, Morgenstern, Shetterly, Baxter, & Baron, 1999).

Another tool for cognitive assessment is the "clock-drawing test." The clock test has a client draw a clock face, put the numbers on it, and indicate a specific time. This evaluates cognitive and executive function and is a sensitive but nonspecific cognitive screening test (Sunderland et al., 1989). The MMSE and clock test are screening

The four A's of Alzheimer's disease:

- *Amnesia:* Loss of short- and/or long-term memory
- *Aphasia:* Loss of the ability to send or receive messages using language
- *Agnosia:* Inability to recognize objects, people, or things
- *Apraxia:* Inability to carry out purposeful tasks

tools that can indicate impairment and dementia. If they indicate a problem, further testing must be done before a diagnosis is given. Dementia evaluation should include a complete history and examination, laboratory testing, and brain imaging.

Depression is a frequently overlooked problem in the geriatric population. Often the nonspecific somatic complaints may represent physical illnesses but often are symptoms of depression. Use of the short form of the Geriatric Depression Screen (GDS; Yesavage et al., 1983) has been found to have a high sensitivity for detecting depression in elderly adults (Kurlowicz & Greenberg, 1999). Depression and dementia can coexist; the Cornell Scale for Depression in Dementia (CSDD; Alexopoulos, Abrams, Young, & Shamoian, 1998) is a reliable and valid instrument for assessing depression in older adults who also have dementia (Watson & Pignon, 2003).

The consumption of alcohol can affect different aspects of health, both physical and mental; it is important to accurately ascertain a client's alcohol intake. The CAGE (Mayfield, McLeod, & Hall, 1974) is a quick, effective screening tool for recognizing problematic drinking. "CAGE" is an acronym for the questions regarding "cutting" down on drinking, being "annoyed" when others criticize use, "guilt" regarding use, and use of an "eyeopener." It is a self-report instrument given in oral or written form and is easy and quick to administer.

A diagnostic workup for reversible causes of dementia and delirium consists of a complete physical and neurologic exam; medical history; laboratory testing (CBC, TSH, B_{12}, folate, chemistry panel, urinalysis [BUN, creatinine, bilirubin, albumin/globulin if you suspect liver disease]); VDRL/HIV, depending on history; blood glucose (fasting); EKG; and MMSE. An EEG and a head CT scan are also useful.

Factors that Impact Mental Status

A variety of factors can impact the older adult's mental status. Simple things like nutritional status, elimination problems, sleep disruption, pain issues, and polypharmacy can cause cognition changes and mental status disturbances.

Nutrition

Eating is frequently difficult for elderly individuals because they often experience a lack of appetite. Assessment of the type, amount, and frequency of food and fluids taken should be standard in any geriatric assessment. Unintentional weight loss of more than 10 pounds should be noted. Changes in eating habits and patterns and weight loss should be considered in light of mental health problems. For example, is a client's weight loss related to an underlying physical problem or is the lack of eating due to the client's belief that she is being poisoned?

A common problem of elderly people is **dysphagia**, or difficulty swallowing. Dysphagia can lead to dehydration, malnutrition, pneumonia, or asphyxiation, all of which may be an underlying cause of delirium. People who have taken conventional antipsychotics (e.g., haloperidol, chlorpromazine) may have symptoms of tardive dyskinesia, which can also make swallowing difficult. **Xerostomia**, or dry mouth, which is common in elderly people, may also impair eating. Dry mouth is also a side effect of many other anticholinergic medications and drugs that have anticholinergic activities, such as cimetidine, digoxin, and furosemide. Many of the antipsychotic medications have anticholinergic properties also. Many psychiatric medications can affect digestion and may impair an already compromised gastrointestinal tract.

Elimination

Assessment of urinary and bowel function may show problems with constipation, urinary frequency, and incontinence. This can be a cause of embarrassment, isolation, and poor self-esteem leading to depression. Elderly clients are more likely to experience constipation because the peristaltic movement of the bowel slows as people get older, but poor diet, poor fluid intake, lack of activity, and medications with anticholinergic properties can also cause constipation. Many older adults think that they must have a bowel movement daily; this can lead to abuse of laxatives and cause electrolyte imbalance and dehydration.

Urinary incontinence occurs because the strength of the sphincter muscles decreases with aging. Because of the fear of "having an accident," many older adults drink less fluids, refuse to leave their home, and become depressed. Bowel and bladder function is an important area to evaluate.

Sleep

The need for sleep is well established as affecting mental and physical health (Cole & Richards, 2006). Sleep changes become more prevalent with age. Age-related sleep disturbances are usually mild alterations in sleep that do not result in daytime sleepiness, but sleep disorders are distinctive, severe abnormalities of sleep associated with deterioration of daytime function (Cole & Richards). According to the National Sleep Foundation (NSF; 2003) Sleep in America Poll 2003, 26% of adults ages 44–65 and 21% of adults over the age of 65 rated their sleep as fair to poor.

Those with chronic illnesses, such as cardiovascular disease, stroke, endocrine disorders, depression, and Alzheimer's and Parkinson's diseases, tend to have a greater number of sleep disturbances. They sleep fewer hours, awaken more frequently, report difficulty falling asleep, awaken earlier, and report significant daytime sleepiness (NSF, 2003). Disruption in sleep can worsen chronic illness and exacerbate depression and lead to delirium in the older adult. Individuals with dementia show increasing sleep disruptions as the dementia progresses (Cole & Richards, 2006).

When working with an older person who complains of sleep disturbance and presents with daytime somnolence, disorientation, and decreased daytime functioning, it is important to obtain a good sleep assessment. Sleep assessment would include a sleep history, a sleep diary including the usual sleep pattern, and sleep hygiene or activities that enhance or deter sleep. A complete history including physical, medication, and alcohol history should also be obtained. Frequently the use of caffeinated medication, alcohol, and OTC medications contribute to sleep problems. A psychiatric history is necessary to assess for underlying stress or depression or affective disorder that may be impacting on sleep. This may need to be followed with a physiologic measure of sleep done in a sleep center or laboratory-controlled setting with polysomnography.

Interventions for sleep problems consist of re-evaluating treatment plans for medical problems, environmental alterations, behavior modifications, and short-term use of sleep medications. If a physiologic problem is contributing to the sleep disturbance, treatment of the problem can make a difference. If chronic medical conditions are causing the nighttime wakening, evaluation of treatment regimes (e.g., if the person has cardiovascular problems, evaluating medications so that diuretics are given early in the day to decrease nighttime enuresis, positioning upright, and using oxygen at night can help enhance sleep; individuals who become hypoglycemic at night related to diabetes may need a bedtime snack or adjustment of hypoglycemic medications; gastrointestinal reflux may need treatment with a nightly medication or use of warm milk and positioning) can often reduce the sleep problems.

Environmental alterations and behavioral modifications, such as a cool, darkened bedroom; quiet time or soothing music before bed; a small snack with warm milk or herbal tea; and consistent bedtime routines and supportive reassurance can reduce sleep problems. Often planning daytime activities that keep the individual active and engaged will reduce daytime napping that can cause nighttime sleep problems. Medications such as benzodiazepines, hypnotics, or antidepressants are often used on a short-term trial (2 weeks or less) to help re-establish a sleep pattern. Long-term use of sleep medications has not been shown to maintain effectiveness (Spar & LaRue, 2002).

Confusion may be evident first at night, with associated insomnia, wandering, irritability, and combativeness, known as *sundown syndrome*. Confusion in the early morning due to the prolonged half-life of medications or substances of abuse is known as *sunrise syndrome*.

Pain

Elders are more likely to experience chronic pain than younger adults (Herr, 2002). Multiple chronic medical conditions are sources of chronic pain. Most older persons report one chronic condition, and many report multiple conditions (AoA, 2006). Osteoarthritis may be a source of chronic pain in as much as 80% of the population older than age 65 (Herr). Studies of pain prevalence in older adults suggest that chronic pain occurs in 25% to 86% of community-dwelling older adults and in 45% to 80% of long-term care facility residents (Herr). Chronic pain often

Implications for Evidence-Based Practice

Poor sleep is a common problem of the elderly who make up a large proportion of hospitalized elders. Careful assessment including use of the Richards-Campbell Sleep Questionnaire is suggested. Nonpharmacological nursing interventions such as providing a warm drink, back rub, progressive relaxation exercises, and relaxation audiotapes or music have proven effective in reducing sedative-hypnotic administration. Environmental interventions include noise reduction, light adjustment, minimizing client interruptions, and increasing meaningful daytime activity (Nagel, Markie, Richards, & Taylor, 2003).

contributes to unexplained behavior and personality changes. Persistent pain has been associated with depression in community-dwelling older adults and in nursing home residents (Herr).

Evidence indicates that pain is under-reported, under-assessed, and under-treated in older clients (Herr, 2002). Assessment of pain is especially critical for those elders who are cognitively impaired and living in long-term care institutions. Kaasalainen et al. (1998) did a retrospective medication review of elderly people and pain medication orders and administration. The results indicated that residents with cognitive impairment were prescribed significantly fewer scheduled medications by their physicians and received significantly fewer pain medications (either PRN or scheduled) from their nurse than did those without cognitive impairment. The researchers theorized that nurses based their medication administration on verbal reports of pain. Because residents with cognitive impairment could not verbalize their pain, they subsequently did not receive pain medication.

Pain management in older adults can be a challenge. A major misconception is that pain is a consequence of older age and cannot be avoided. This misconception leads to a lack of effective pain assessment and intervention. Another challenge is older persons themselves. Many will not complain, thinking they want to be "good" clients or they are fearful of the meaning of their pain. Finally, the healthcare provider, whether in an institution or a family member, may not be attuned to the older person's nonverbal pain expressions, and may not be knowledgeable of appropriate pain assessment or pain treatment.

Individuals with cognitive impairment, language impairment, and dementia can give pain assessment information. Individuals with mild to moderate impairment can respond to pain scales with some adaptation (Herr, 2002). For others, observation of nonverbal pain behaviors (e.g., bracing, grimacing, guarding, restlessness, agitation), vocalizations (e.g., moaning, crying, verbal outbursts), and changes in behavior patterns (e.g., decreased activity level and interactions with others, new onset confusion, refusal to eat, resistance to care, difficulty sleeping) provide hints and information about the presence of pain from those unable to report it. Management of pain requires thorough assessment and a combination of pharmacologic and nonpharmacologic pain therapies.

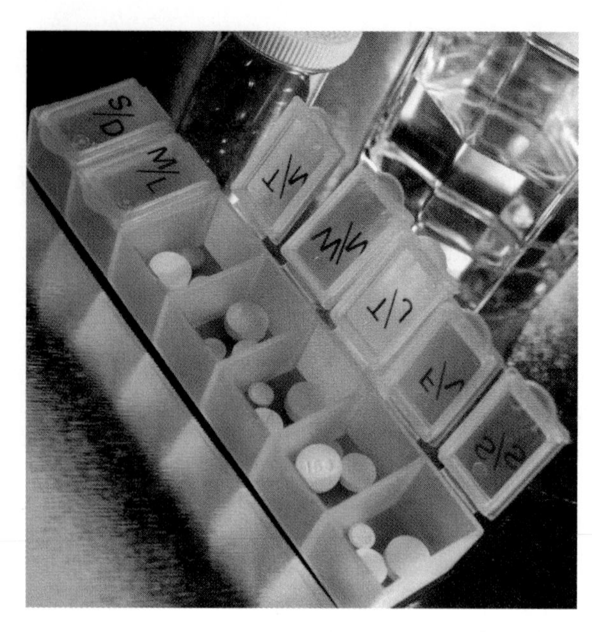

Figure 25-2 Older adults commonly take multiple prescription medications.

Polypharmacy

Older adults take considerably more medications that younger people (**Figure 25-2**). They consume 34% of all prescription medications and 40% of all nonprescription medications (American Society of Consultant Pharmacists [ASCP], 2000). Normal age-related changes result in altered pharmacokinetics (i.e., absorption, distribution, metabolism, and excretion of a drug or "what the body does to the drug") and pharmacodynamics (i.e., biochemical or physiological interactions of drugs or "what the drug does to the body"). See **Table 25-2**.

The use of multiple medications at the same time or the overprescribing of medications is called polypharmacy (Mauk, 2006). As many as 10% to 30% of hospital admissions of older adults are due to adverse drug reactions, which are often caused by taking multiple medications (ASCP, 2000). Factors contributing to polypharmacy are numerous: multiple chronic illnesses, prescribing to treat side effects, multiple specialists treating complex problems, client stockpiling of medications, use of over-the-counter (OTC) medications, use of herbal medications, and failure of healthcare providers to periodically review all medications from all sources for appropriateness and continued need.

Herbals and OTC medications can interact with prescription drugs. Usually the individual does not think to consult with or tell their physi-

Table 25-2 Drug Response in the Older Adult

Pharmacokinetics	The body's absorption, distribution, metabolism, and excretion of drugs due to changes in normal aging. • Absorption is slightly decreased. • Distribution is affected by the shift to more body fat. • Metabolism is decreased. • Excretion is slowed. Some drugs (especially lipid-soluble) may exhibit a longer half-life in older individuals, as well as slower breakdown and elimination, thus becoming drug toxic. Example: Diazepam (Valium) will have a longer half-life in an older person than a younger person.
Pharmacodynamics	The physiologic response of the drug at its site of action. • Drug concentrations may result in greater or less effects at the site of action than expected. • The older person may show increased sensitivity to certain medications. Example: Older persons show increased sensitivity to the central nervous system depressant effects of benzodiazepines, anxiolytics, and hypnotics.

cian about nonprescription drugs they are taking. OTC medications are often perceived by individuals as harmless or not considered to be a drug. Difficulty reading the product inserts can lead to inappropriate drug combinations and inaccurate dosing. Often older adults will swap drugs with others when they discuss their symptoms and treatments.

Some consequences of polypharmacy include adverse drug reactions, nonadherence to medical regimens, hospitalization resulting from confusion, delirium, electrolyte imbalance, gastrointestinal bleeding, exacerbation of chronic conditions, and falls. Recognizing that some drugs should be avoided in the elderly because their potential risk outweighs their potential benefit, the Beers criteria were developed in 1991 (Beers, 1997). It is updated annually and covers the elderly in all settings (Fick et al., 2003). There are many drugs on the list used in the treatment of mental health problems. Research has shown that following the Beers criteria, frequent medication monitoring, and decreasing and discontinuing inappropriate medications can make a difference in mental status for many elderly (Schmader et al., 2004).

Stress and Coping

Identifying stressors and coping patterns is just as important for elderly clients as it is for younger adults. Unique stresses for elderly clients include living on a fixed income, handling declining health, losing partners and friends, and ultimately confronting death. Coping ability varies depending on each client's unique circumstances. Some people respond to stressful events with amazing adaptability, whereas others become depressed and suicidal.

Loss of a spouse is common in late life. Bereavement is a normal response. Bereavement symptoms include crying and sorrow, anxiety and agitation, insomnia, and loss of appetite. These symptoms, while overlapping with those of

Implications for Evidence-Based Practice

A review of hospital records of clients ages 65 years or older admitted to the emergency department with falls indicated that nearly half were 80 years old or older. After age, polypharmacy was the greatest risk factor followed by a history of cognitive impairment and presence of more than one contributing medical factor. Elders older than 80 years old were more likely to have multiple risk factors such as polypharmacy, alcohol use, impairment of ADL, one or more medical conditions, cognitive impairment, use of an assistive device, or a gait/balance deficit. Careful assessment is needed to prevent undertreatment of potentially modifiable problems (Paniagua, Malphurs, & Phelan, 2006).

major depression, do not constitute a mental disorder. Only when these symptoms persist for 3 months or longer can a diagnosis of either adjustment disorder or major depressive disorder be made if it meets the *Diagnostic and Statistical Manual of Mental Disorders,* Fourth Edition (*DSM-IV-TR*) criteria (American Psychiatric Association, 2000). The nurse must identify normal bereavement and those at risk for prolonged grief reactions and develop interventions to help the individual successfully resolve the loss. At least 10% to 20% of widows and widowers experience symptoms of depression during the first year of bereavement (Spar & LaRue, 2002). Without interventions, depression can persist, becoming chronic and leading to further disability and other serious health problems.

Mnemonic for reversible causes for dementia:

- *D*rugs or delirium
- *E*thanol (alcohol) or eyes and ears (visual or hearing deficits)
- *M*etabolic changes
- *E*ndocrine disorders
- *N*utritional causes and normal pressure hydrocephalus
- *T*rauma, tumor, toxins
- *I*nfections
- *A*ffective disorder, arteriosclerosis

Mental Disorders of Late Life

Some elders may have had a history of mental disorders with symptoms that are in remission or stabilized by treatment. Many elders with new symptoms may not recognize these as related to psychiatric and mental health disorders that can be treated and under-report them to healthcare providers. They may fear that the symptoms may be indicative of an irreversible decline in functioning and loss of independence. Some nonspecific symptoms such as problems with memory may be related to a variety of factors and may be reversible if the underlying reason for the symptoms is treated. Other symptoms may have a slow, insidious onset that is not noticed until there is marked impairment of functioning. Careful assessment may be needed to determine if problems are related to changes in health status or response to pharmaceuticals or substances of abuse.

Definitive diagnosis of Alzheimer's disease is done by autopsy of brain tissue or brain tissue biopsy to identify the hallmark brain atrophy with neurofibrillary tangles and neuritic plaques on microscopic examination.

Dementia

Dementing disorders are the most common causes of psychopathology in the elderly. Dementia affects almost half of elderly Americans 85 years and older (Mauk, 2006). Alzheimer's disease (AD) accounts for 60% to 70% of all cases of dementia (Mauk). Dementia is a chronic and progressive illness characterized by behavioral and cognitive changes that affect memory, problem solving, judgment, and speech and can cause deficits in functional abilities. Other types of dementia include multi-infarct dementia, Parkinson's dementia, and Huntington's dementia. No curative treatment is currently available for dementia. Symptomatic treatment, including pharmacological interventions, attention to environment, and family support, can help to maximize the client's level of functioning.

Dementia is common in the elderly. The level of disability is determined by the progressive, static, or remitting course of the illness. Dementia often is confused with and coexists with depression and delirium. The five main domains involved in the clinical presentation of dementia are praxis (ability to function), memory (short- and long-term), calculation, concentration, and language.

Nurses must educate caregivers and family members to be alert to the varied presentations of dementia, because symptoms may have a slow progression to a sudden onset. Dementia often has a chronic, insidious, progressive course. Although long-lasting, some types of dementia may be slowed or reversed. Clients with potentially reversible causes of dementia (e.g., myxedema, depression, pernicious anemia, adverse drug reaction) can improve remarkably in their cognitive function with the appropriate assessment and treatment. The history, especially information provided by family members or the identified caregiver, and medical workups are key to the evaluation and appropriate diagnosis.

In the elderly, the diagnosis of dementia requires a careful, accurate assessment of altered cognitive functioning that affects the client's daily functioning. Cognitive dysfunction may present during a hospitalization or treatment for another illness. It is important for nurses to understand that several causes of dementia are potentially reversible and may partially or totally respond to treatment (e.g., antipsychotic medications for agitation causes confusion).

The Mini-Mental State Examination (MMSE) augments the physical examination and laboratory data as part of the diagnostic workup for dementia (Luggen, Meiner, & National Gerontological Nursing Association, 2002). A careful history of the memory disturbance is vital and should include any medical and psychiatric illnesses (e.g., hypertension, stroke, alcohol abuse, depression), medications (e.g., benzodiazepines, narcotics, psychotropics), and changes in the environment (e.g., a move-in with adult children, assisted living). Some general clinical features of dementia include an insidious onset, confabulation when attempting to answer questions, strug-

Implications for Evidence-Based Practice

Rigney (2006) discusses the importance of nursing assessment for delirium in hospitalized elders due to the high mortality rate when the causes of delirium are unrecognized. Risk factors include underlying dementia, lethargy, age greater than 80 years, disruption of sleep, polypharmacy, common medical conditions, and extreme stress. Careful assessment for early recognition and treatment of the underlying causes of delirium are needed.

gling with tasks, getting lost in new surroundings, personality changes, and complaints of cognitive loss with concealment of problems.

Delirium

Delirium, also referred to as acute confusional state, is a serious neuropsychiatric syndrome. It occurs in 22% to 38% of older clients in the hospital and as much as 40% of long-term care residents (Mauk, 2006). Although it occurs frequently it often goes unrecognized. It is a temporary, reversible condition. The majority of individuals presenting with delirium show cognitive-perceptual difficulties and altered level of consciousness.

Causes of delirium in older adults may include medical problems, acute illness or infections, electrolyte imbalances, abuse of alcohol or drugs, and cognitive or memory disorders. Trauma, surgery, or sudden environmental changes can also cause delirium. Medications, especially cholinergic drugs, are the most common medication cause of delirium in elderly people.

Mnemonic for delirium:
- *D*ementia
- *E*lectrolyte imbalance
- *L*ungs, liver, heart, kidney, brain dysfunction
- *I*nfection (especially pneumonia)
- *R*x (medications, polypharmacy)
- *I*njury, pain, stress
- *U*nfamiliar environment (nursing home, hospital)
- *M*etabolic changes (endocrine)

CASE STUDY Mrs. A.

Mrs. A. is a 77-year-old widow who moved into her unmarried daughter's apartment 3 months ago following a near fall at home. Shaken and slightly bruised, she did not sustain an injury but became increasingly fearful that a fall could "place me in a wheelchair for good." Her medical history includes long-standing mild hypertension and coronary artery disease, noninsulin diabetes for 15 years, and osteoarthritis for 10 years. Her medications include metoprolol (Lopressor, 100 mg orally daily), ibuprofen (Nuprin, 200 mg orally three times a day), glipizide (Glucotrol, 2.5 mg before breakfast), psyllium hydrophilic colloid (Metamucil, 1 packet in 8 oz of liquid twice a day), and calcium carbonate (Turns, 500 mg [2 tablets] daily with meals). Mrs. A. refuses to have a home health aide and states, "I can care for myself!"

Returning home after being away for the weekend, the daughter finds Mrs. A. sitting on the floor next to her bed, diaphoretic, sedated, and unable to answer the daughter's questions clearly as to what happened. Mrs. A. was easily distracted and had a decreased attention span. Fearing that her mother was having a hypoglycemic episode, she gave her some orange juice and telephoned for an ambulance. While in the emergency room, Mrs. A. complained of having pleuritic chest pain, malaise, and weakness. A chest x-ray revealed left lower lobe consolidation. She scored 15 on the MMSE. A sputum sample was yellow and mucoid. Blood glucose (fingerstick) was 40 mg/dL. Her sodium level was 117.

Mrs. A. was diagnosed with pneumonia. She was transferred to a subacute unit and later to a rehabilitation nursing home for medical treatment and rehabilitation evaluation. Arrangements were made for a visiting nurse to arrive the following day to make an evaluation and recommendations concerning ADLs and management. Mrs. A. was maintained at home with the assistance of a home healthcare aide 5 days a week, 6 hours a day. Mrs. A. has since been attending a senior citizen center three times a week at the assisted living complex, where she has made new friends. Mrs. A.'s delirium was the result of developing upper respiratory infection pneumonia. Her age, coexistent medical conditions, and lack of mobility facilitated the onset of illness. Mrs. A. had a change in living arrangements, a close-call injury that left her afraid to mobilize herself, and the onset of potential depression within a short period of time. Considering her medication regimen, noncompliance or misuse could lead to confusion and complications.

NURSING CARE PLAN Delirium

Expected Outcomes	Interventions	Evaluations
• Will experience decreased symptoms of delirium.	• Monitor for client behavior for disorientation, increased restlessness and agitation, communication problems, disturbed sensory perception, and problems interacting with environment.	• Appropriate nursing assessment and early intervention for delirium. Evaluation for possible underlying dementia. Client returns to baseline functioning.
• Will experience decreased risk of injury.	• Reduce environmental stimuli, provide regular contact with staff and family, reorientation and fall prevention.	• Minimization of use of physical and chemical restraints. Increase in client ability to interact appropriately with environment. Client is oriented and able to communicate with others. Discharge planning assessment and appropriate case management.
• Will review medication and medication administration.	• Administer medications as prescribed and monitor response to medications and possible side effects. Assess client ability to self-administer medications. Provide education for client and family regarding medications and safe administration.	• Client and family understand medications and possible interactions. Use of pre-poured medications, medication box or supervision of medication if indicated. Review of medication schedule to simplify administration and prevent errors. Client takes medications as prescribed.

Visit http://nursing.jbpub.com/psychiatric for additional care plans and exercises.

Schizophrenia

Schizophrenia and delusional disorders may accompany the individual as they age or may manifest themselves for the first time during old age (Mauk, 2006). In most instances individuals who manifest psychotic disorders early in life show a decline in psychopathology as they age. Late-onset schizophrenia (after age 60) is not common, but when it does occur, it is often characterized by delusions or hallucinations of a persecutory nature. The disease is chronic and treatment is with neuroleptics and supportive psychotherapy.

Depression

Depression is the most common and most treatable of all mental disorders in older adults. It is not a consequence of normal aging. It is a major health concern that can be life threatening if unrecognized and untreated. In the community,

Implications for Evidence-Based Practice

Risk factors for depression in elders include being single or widowed and living alone, loss and grief reactions, pain, chronic illness and functional disabilities including incontinence, death anxiety, substance abuse, medication side effects, and a history of depression or suicide attempts. Butcher and McGonigal-Kennedy (2005) examined the concept of "dispiritedness" or "being in low spirits" as a functional aspect of depression in interviews with elders. Most clients expressed this as a sense that life had lost its meaning with themes around life transitions, disengagement, loss of vigor, bewilderment, fluctuations between engagement and disengagement, and ambivalence in continuing their day to day lives. Nursing interventions to deal with these feelings centered around helping the elder to facilitate hope and spirituality, encourage activity, and maintain connectedness with their support systems.

the percentages of older people meeting strict diagnostic criteria for major depression or dysthymic disorder is quite low (Spar & LaRue, 2002). What has been found is that traditional diagnostic criteria may not be appropriate to the prevalence of depressive symptoms among older people. At least 8% of elderly community residents have serious depressive symptoms and nearly 19% have severe dysphoric symptoms (Piven, 2001). In medical hospitals at least 35% of older clients have diagnosable mood disorders and nearly 50% of admissions of older adults to psychiatric hospitals are for depressive conditions (Piven). The presence of co-morbid depression and anxiety greatly increases healthcare costs for clients in primary care.

Depression can often be difficult to recognize. Depression, dementia, and delirium can also occur simultaneously, further complicating diagnosis and treatment (Martin & Haynes, 2000). Presenting symptoms of change in feeling or mood (i.e., feeling sad, hopeless, pessimistic, or "blue"; loss of interest in pleasurable activities) may be all that is shown or the individual may also exhibit fatigue, decreased concentration and short-term memory, change in appetite, fluctuations in weight and sleep habits, irritability, and anxiety. Many older adults may avoid complaining of sadness or depression; this along with societal expectations that older adults are more fatigued and less interested in activities can disguise symptoms of depression and deprive individuals of treatment (Amella, 2004).

After assessing cognition using the MMSE, the healthcare provider should then use the Geriatric Depression Scale if the MMSE score is 23 or higher or the Cornell Scale for Depression in Dementia if the MMSE score is less than 23. This allows the healthcare provider to determine if further testing and evaluation are needed. If the individual's scores indicate depression, use of antidepressants and counseling would be indicated. Older individuals often respond to lower doses of medications and take longer to show response to antidepressants, so careful monitoring is essential. Some of the newer antidepressants such as the SSRIs show a better response for the older individual with fewer side effects. Antidepressants such as citalopram hydrobromide (Celexa), escitalopram oxalate (Lexapro), and sertraline HCL (Zoloft) are often considered for use with the elderly. Medication selection is usually based upon symptoms and possible side effects with an attempt made to minimize the use of medications that can cause orthostatic hypotension, an anticholinergic response, or interact with other medications.

Clinical Example

Lewis, a 72-year-old man, was a successful businessman for 40 years. He had enjoyed good health, took medication for hypertension that kept it under control, watched his diet, and exercised regularly. His wife died 5 years ago and he has a close relationship with his son and family. Lewis stopped visiting the family business and had decreased contact with his son. The son visited the family home and found his father sitting in the dark, unshaven and irritable. Lewis stated, "Leave me alone! I don't want to be bothered! Go away!" Lewis had lost weight, declared he had "no appetite," and stated he was taking his medication "when I remember." He had ceased his social activities and stated he "just wanted to sleep." Lewis told his longtime housekeeper to find other employment, stating, "I don't need to be a bother to anyone!"

Alarmed, his son supportively confronted his father and was able to get him to agree to see a psychiatrist the following day. The doctor diagnosed Lewis with a major depressive episode and started him on an antidepressant. He saw a psychiatric nurse practitioner for medication management and weekly group psychotherapy. The nurse practitioner's interventions and medication compliance enabled Lewis to attend and participate in weekly group psychotherapy sessions and resume his premorbid state of socialization, involving both family and business interests.

Critical Thinking Questions What are some signs of depression? What are some factors that may contribute to depression? What are some signs of passive suicidality? What are some factors that may be different in evaluating suicidality in an older person than in a younger client?

Anxiety

Anxiety is often conceptualized along a continuum from normal reactions to stress to maladaptive reactions to stress. Anxiety in later life may be reactive (i.e., a response to age-related losses and changes) or endogenous (i.e., a correlate of medical morbidity). Recurring and chronic anxiety can complicate many illnesses that are common to the elderly and can interfere with activities of daily living. The presence of anxiety in the older adult correlates with and predicts cognitive decline and impairment (Sinoff & Werner, 2003). Anxiety has also been found to significantly elevate acute pain perception (Feeney, 2004).

Anxiety disorders include generalized anxiety disorder (GAD). GAD is characterized by persistent, excessive worry with fluctuating severity

Psychiatric disorder is defined as having readily observable external symptoms that influence the mental state of the individual. Psychosocial integrity is related to both psychological and social factors, such as family relationships, living environments, and enjoyment of life.

> Use of medication is reserved for clients with psychotic behaviors such as agitation, anxiety, depression, and psychosis. Medication orders should always be questioned, especially when the dosage appears higher than standard. For the elderly, doses are typically one half the usual dosage. Neuroleptic, anticonvulsant, and antidepressant medications may cause delirium.

> It must be empl sized that suicide is ventable and depres is treatable. Electro vulsive therapy is of used for acutely sui depressed elderly cl who cannot be treat with medication.

> The initial treat step in alcohol or s stance abuse is to s drinking, stop takir drugs, or both.

> Alcohol is the n common substance abused by the elder because it is readil available and not u perceived as a drug

Specific short and long term goals should be based upon the client assessment including recognition of the client's situation and self-concept, physical status and stamina, support systems and stressors. Treatment of the elder community takes place in the community setting in out-patient clinics, mental health and community centers, medical offices as well as in the home and institutional setting. Treatment planning should involve everyone involved in care of the client.

Summary

Mental health problems in older adults are under-recognized and under-treated. The older client is less likely to receive treatment for mental health problems in either in-patient settings or by community-based healthcare practitioners (Mauk, 2006).

As individuals age they experience physical changes and there may also be age-related psychological changes. Because of these changes the impact of sleep problems, pain issues, and polypharmacy may not be correlated with mental health problems. The frequency of chronic conditions makes older adults vulnerable to depression and anxiety. Dementia disorders are the most frequent cause of psychopathology in the elderly. The growing population of individuals age 65 and older suggests that the challenge of providing care will progress well into the 21st century. Nurses who work in the field of mental health need to be able to identify and work with the older person presenting with mental health problems.

Annotated References

Administration on Aging. (2006). *A profile of older Americans: 2006*. Washington, DC: U.S. Department of Health and Human Services.

Provides demographic information about the population age 65+.

Alexopoulos, G. S., Abrams, R. C., Young, R. C., & Shamoian, C. A. (1998). Cornell scale for depression in dementia. *Biological Psychiatry, 23*, 271–284.

Information on the Cornell scale for depression for individuals with dementia.

Amella, E. J. (2004). Presentation of illness in older adults. *American Journal of Nursing, 104*(10), 40–51.

Overview of assessment, critical indicators of underlying conditions, and common diseases of the older adult.

American Psychiatric Association. (2000). *Diagnostic and statistical manual of mental disorders* (4th ed., text rev.). Washington, DC: Author.

This is the fourth edition, text revision, of the American Psychiatric Association's official nomenclature of psychiatric conditions and disorders. It provides a systematic listing of the official codes and categories, a description of the multiaxial system for diagnosis, and diagnostic criteria for each of the disorders. It is used by psychiatrists, physicians, psychologists, registered nurses, social workers, therapists, and other mental health workers in all clinical settings.

American Society of Consultant Pharmacists. (2000). Senior care pharmacy: The statistics. *Consultant Pharmacist, 15*, 310.

Discusses the senior care pharmacy concept and provides information on the medication use of the senior population.

Appelbaum, P. S., & Grisso, T. (1988). Assessing clients' capacities to consent to treatment. *New England Journal of Medicine, 319*, 1635–1638.

Information on the assessment of capacity and competency in the older adult.

Barry, K. L., Oslin, D. W., & Bow, F. C. (2001). *Alcohol problems in older adults: Prevention and management*. New York: Springer.

This book presents information on the prevention and management of alcohol abuse in older adults.

Beers, M. (1997). Explicit criteria for determining potentially inappropriate medication use by the elderly: An update. *Archives of Internal Medicine, 157*, 1531–1536.

This article presents criteria for determining the appropriateness of medications for use in the elderly. It also provides an update of inappropriate medications.

Butcher, H. K., & McGonigal-Kennedy, M. (2005). Depression and dispiritedness in later life. *American Journal of Nursing, 105*(12), 52–61.

This article discussed the difficulties in identifying depression in elders who might be less likely to describe typical depressive symptoms or report suicidal thoughts. Data obtained in interviews with clients was used to identify themes of dispiritedness in elders and three major coping mechanisms the elders utilized to deal with these feelings. Nursing interventions to inspire hope and encourage elders to keep active and maintain connections are based on this research.

Cole, C. S., & Richards, K. C. (2006). Sleep in persons with dementia: Increasing quality of life by managing sleep disorders. *Journal of Gerontological Nursing, 32*(3), 48–53.

Discusses sleep disorders and management of disorders in the older adult with dementia.

Feeney, S. L. (2004). The relationship between pain and negative affect in older adults: Anxiety as a predictor of pain. *Journal of Anxiety Disorder, 18*, 733–744.

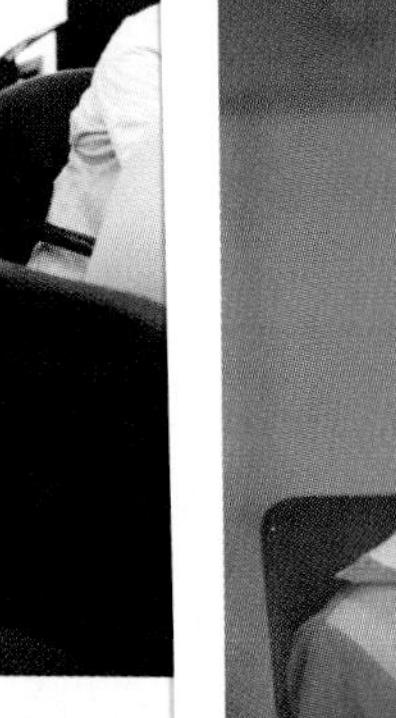

This article looks at the relationship between pain and anxiety in the older adult and discusses some of the negative aspects resulting from it.

Fick, D. M., Cooper, J. W., Wade, W. E., Waller, J. L., Maclean, R. J., & Beers, M. H. (2003). Updating the Beers criteria for potentially inappropriate medication use in older adults: Results of a U.S. consensus panel of experts. *Archives of Internal Medicine, 163*(22), 2716–2724.

Update of the Beers criteria for inappropriate medication use in the older adult.

Finfgeld-Connett, D. L. (2005). Self-management of alcohol problems among aging adults. *Journal of Gerontological Nursing, 31*(5), 51–58.

Discusses alcohol treatment using a stepped-care approach for older alcohol abusers.

Folstein, M. F., Folstein, S. E., & McHugh, P. R. (1975). "Mini-mental state." A practical method for grading the cognitive state of clients for the clinician. *Journal of Psychiatric Research, 12*, 189–198.

Discusses the Mini-Mental State Examination.

Herr, K. (2002). Chronic pain: Challenges and assessment strategies. *Journal of Gerontological Nursing, 28*(1), 20–27.

Presents assessment and management strategies for working with older adults with chronic pain.

Holkup, P. A. (2003). Evidence-based protocol: Elderly suicide—secondary prevention. *Journal of Gerontological Nursing, 29*(6), 6–17.

Discusses suicide in the older population and presents strategies for prevention and intervention.

Kaasalainen, S., Middleton, J., Knezacek, S., Hartley, T., Stewart, V., et al. (1998). Pain and cognitive status in the institutionalized elderly: Perceptions and interventions. *Journal of Gerontological Nursing, 24*(8), 24–31, 50–51.

Study of cognitively impaired institutionalized elders' pain and treatment of pain.

Koenig, H. G., George, L. K., & Schneider, R. (1994). Mental health care for older adults in the year 2020: A dangerous and avoided topic. *The Gerontologist, 34*(5), 674–679.

This article discusses the projected gap between care needs and funding for services in an aging population with psychiatric problems.

Kurlowicz, L., & Greenberg, S. A. (1999). The Geriatric Depression Scale. *Hartford Institute for Geriatric Nursing*. Retrieved November 1, 2006, from http://www.hartfordign.org/publications/trythis/issue04.pdf

Provides a copy of the Geriatric Depression Scale and a brief discussion of the strengths and limitations of the tool.

Luggen, A. S., Meiner, S. E., & National Gerontological Nursing Association. (2002). *NGNA: Core curriculum for gerontological nursing*. St. Louis, MO: Mosby.

A comprehensive text for gerontological nursing that includes information on patient assessment.

Martin, J. H., & Haynes, L. C. H. (2000). Depression, delirium and dementia in the elderly client. *Journal of the Association of Perioperative Registered Nurses, 72*(2), 209–217.

Discusses the differences in diagnosis and treatment of depression, delirium, and dementia in the elderly.

Mauk, K. L. (2006). *Gerontological nursing, competencies for care*. Boston: Jones and Bartlett.

This gerontological nursing text facilitates development of the communication and assessment skills needed to give culturally sensitive care to the older adult. It covers risk factors and health problems for this population and discusses the roles of the med-surg nurse, gerontological nurse, and case manager.

Mayfield, D., McLeod, G., & Hall, P. (1974). The CAGE questionnaire: Validation of a new alcoholism screening instrument. *American Journal of Psychiatry, 131*, 1121–1123.

This article discusses the process the CAGE questionnaire underwent for validation.

Mehta, K. M., Simonsick, E. M., Penninx, B. W., Schultz, R., Rubin, S. M., Satterfield, S., et al. (2003). Prevalence and correlates of anxiety symptoms in well-functioning older adults: Findings from the health aging and body composition study. *Journal of the American Geriatrics Society, 51*(4), 499–504.

Looks at anxiety symptoms in depressed and nondepressed older people.

Mulgrew, C., Morgenstern, N., Shetterly, S., Baxter, J., & Baron, A. E. (1999). Cognitive functioning and impairment among rural elderly Hispanics and non-Hispanic whites as assessed by the Mini-Mental State Examination. *Journal of Gerontology, 54B*(4), 223–230.

Research study looking at differences in cognitive function between rural Hispanics and non-Hispanics.

Murray, R. H. & Zentner, J. P. (2001). *Health promotion strategies through the life span* (7th ed.). Upper Saddle River, NJ: Prentice Hall.

Covers nursing assessment through the various developmental stages including persons in later adulthood.

Nagel, C. L., Markie, M. B., Richards, K. C., & Taylor, J. (2003). Sleep promotion in hospitalized elders. *MedSurg Nursing, 12*(5), 279–290.

Reviews sleep disturbances in hospitalized elders. Discusses the problems of pharmacological interventions in elders which may increase risk for falls, delirium, and functional decline as well as nonpharmacolgical nursing interventions.

National Sleep Foundation. (2003). Sleep in America poll 2003. *American Academy of Sleep Medicine*. Retrieved November 1, 2006, from http://www.sleepfoundation.org/site/c.huIXKjM0IxF/

Implications for Evidence-Based Practice

When researchers (Ailey, Miller, Heller, & Smith, 2006) utilized the Interpersonal Model of Depression (IMD) tool to evaluate the level of depression among 100 adults with Down syndrome, 32% had elevated depression scores and 40% reported feeling lonely. The relationship among depression, perceived social support, loneliness, and life satisfaction was statistically significant. Utilization of such a framework in monitoring depression in individuals with Down syndrome across their life spans could be an asset in early intervention and treatment.

In 2004, Strand, Benzein, and Saveman reported on the results of a questionnaire that was sent to 164 staff members in 17 different care settings for adults with intellectual and developmental disabilities in Sweden. Because many individuals with intellectual and psychiatric developmental disabilities are being cared for by others in either their own homes or residential settings (assisted-living or group homes), there is concern for the level of violence, abuse, and neglect that might be occurring. Seventy-four percent of respondents reported being involved in or witnessing violent incidents towards clients and 14% admitted to being the perpetrator of the violent act. Most of the violence occurred on a daily basis; it was both physical and psychological, and tended to occur in close caretaking situations. This study indicates the importance of both supportive supervision, education, and outlets for staff and increasing the training in communication skills for clients with intellectual and psychiatric developmental disabilities.

predisposition may also exhibit a learning disorder. However, many individuals with learning disorders have no specific identifiable condition to which the learning disorder can be attributed.

Physiology

There are no known physiologic processes associated with learning disorders.

Clinical Presentation

Learning disorders are classified as either verbal or nonverbal. Verbal learning disorder typically refers to deficits in reading and spelling, whereas nonverbal learning disorders refer to mathematics. Learning disorders in children are usually identified in the school. In adults, learning disorders are often observed by nurses and other healthcare practitioners when the adult fails to understand written instructions, complete health forms, take medications on schedule, or remember appointments.

Differential Diagnosis

Diagnosis of a learning disorder is usually made through administration of standardized tests by a clinician trained to administer and interpret standardized tests (e.g., a psychologist or nurse practitioner). An undiagnosed learning disorder may also be identified in adulthood. Other factors

CASE STUDY Mr. J.

Mr. J., a 28-year-old man with moderate mental retardation, has recently moved from his parents' home to a group home in the community. His parents have been overly protective, and consequently Mr. J. has had little opportunity to develop relationship skills or to explore his own sexuality. Since moving to the group home Mr. J. has appeared enthusiastic about interacting with other group members socially. Mr. J. has participated in community meetings, usually remembers to take care of his personal hygiene, is part of the housekeeping team and, most recently, volunteered to help with gardening. Mr. J. has had the most difficulty with his two roommates as he is not used to sharing a room. He has been very interested in interacting with females, and has, on occasion, frightened several young women visiting the home by grabbing them and touching them inappropriately. Mr. J. has had two fights with other male clients over female clients that he calls "his girlfriends."

NURSING CARE PLAN **Mental Retardation (Socially Immature)**

Expected Outcomes	Interventions	Evaluations
• Client will develop a positive self-concept and an understanding of own sexuality without feeling embarrassed or fearful.	• Assess client's comprehension of own sexuality. • Provide opportunities for client to discuss sexual feelings and to ask questions. • Structure opportunities to explain bodily changes, sexual functions, and issues of intimacy to client.	• Client asks questions about bodily functions as need arises. • Client talks freely with staff and family about sexual concerns. • Client refrains from inappropriate sexual behaviors and demonstrates ability to avoid inappropriate contact.
• Client will behave in socially appropriate ways. • Client will develop socially appropriate relationships.	• Provide client with information about boundaries and opportunities to distinguish between appropriate and inappropriate social behaviors. • Provide opportunities for client to engage in role-playing activities to learn to distinguish between acceptable and unacceptable social behaviors in a variety of simulated social settings.	• Client is more comfortable in social situations (one-on-one and group) and develops an appropriate social network. • Client gets along better with roommates spending more time interacting with them. • Client appears more comfortable around female clients and visitors.

Visit http://nursing.jbpub.com/psychiatric for additional care plans and exercises.

such as inadequate educational opportunities (e.g., deficient teaching, high rate of absenteeism) or sensory impairment (e.g., impaired vision or hearing) may also affect a person's ability to learn or to gain specific skills, so a diagnosis of a specific learning disorder should not be made until these other factors are eliminated as being present or causing the problem.

Management and Treatment

Treatment of learning disorders consists of special educational programs to assist children and adults to learn alternative ways of processing information as well as providing special accommodations that enable the individual to adapt to deficits they are experiencing. The underpinning of effective treatment is tailoring interventions to best meet each individual's specific needs (Dudley-Marling, 2004).

Pervasive Developmental Disorders

Pervasive developmental disorders is the official diagnostic term used in the *DSM-IV-TR* (APA, 2000) to describe a broad range of developmental disorders that are characterized by impairments in multiple areas of development and that vary in subtype and severity. The major conditions included in this diagnostic category are autistic disorder, Asperger's disorder, Rett's disorder, childhood disintegrative disorder, and other pervasive developmental disorders not otherwise specified including atypical autism. Childhood disintegrative disorder has also been called Hedler's syndrome or dementia infantilis and is a category used to describe conditions in which there is severe impairment in social and communication development in addition to stereotyped behavioral features generally observed in autistic disorder. However, criteria for the other pervasive developmental disorders, such as

Clinical Example

Chuck is a cheerful and engaging second grader who has been having temper tantrums, refusing to do homework, and is increasingly sitting alone in the classroom. During a parent-teacher conference, these behaviors are discussed and his increasing school problems with recognizing letters and simple words, spelling, and now writing is of concern. The teacher notes and his parents have observed that Chuck's speaking vocabulary is more sophisticated than his written vocabulary and he can easily follow oral directions, but becomes frustrated and struggles with written assignments. It is agreed that he will receive a physical to rule out any medical condition, and a referral to the local Developmental and Learning Center.

is often frequently misidentified as attention deficit hyperactivity disorder (ADHD; APA, 2000).

Clinical Presentation

Children with Asperger's disorder demonstrate impairments in social interactions and may show repetitive behavior patterns as well as resistance to change, similar to those with autistic disorder. Intellectual and communication function are not usually impaired. Often impairments in social interaction, communication, and imagination are subtle, and therefore difficult to diagnose (Portway & Johnson, 2005). Diagnosis of Asperger's disorder may not be made until individuals are school age and difficulties with social interaction become apparent. Individuals with Asperger's disorder are unable to recognize social cues such as body language or other forms of nonverbal behavior, or may be unable to recognize cues that indicate that their behavior is inappropriate (Safran, 2002). They do not adhere to social conventions such as respecting others' personal space, or they may talk loudly, relentlessly pursuing a subject of interest to them, even though other children or adults show no interest or are unresponsive. These children may demonstrate an abnormal need to adhere to strict routines, becoming upset and agitated if change is necessary. They also demonstrate poor gross motor function, appear clumsy, or use repetitive behaviors such as ritualistic walking patterns and obsessive-compulsive routines.

> Individuals with Asperger's disorder have significant difficulty interpreting social cues and, as a result, they may appear to be tactless or rude.

Differential Diagnosis

Distinguishing Asperger's disorder from high-functioning autism remains an unresolved issue in the mind of many practitioners (Rourke & Tsatsanis, 2000). The *DSM-IV-TR* (APA, 2000) lists diagnostic criteria as impairment in social interaction, restricted repetitive and stereotyped patterns of behavior, and significant impairment in social, occupational, or other areas of function, with no delay in language acquisition or in cognitive development as well as not meeting criteria for any other pervasive developmental disorder, ADHD, or schizophrenia.

Clinical Course and Complications

This is a lifelong disorder, with the child's social abilities waxing and waning or significantly improving into adulthood. Adolescents often learn to use areas of strength such as rote verbal skills or savant-like mathematical skills to compensate for other areas of weakness. As they age, these individuals may experience victimization from peers, social isolation, anxiety, and depression. The overall prognosis is better than for children with autistic disorder (APA, 2000).

Management and Treatment

Even though the *DSM-IV-TR* specifies diagnostic criteria for Asperger's disorder, there are many subtleties of the disorder and diagnostic boundaries that are not always clear (Wing, 2000); the disorder often is misdiagnosed or overlooked, so interventions appropriate to the diagnosis may not be forthcoming. When assessing individuals, symptoms may not be immediately apparent in a one-on-one setting. Obtaining a full history and determining how the individual interacts with other people can be an important diagnostic tool. Because Asperger's disorder is a condition in which there is social disability, the nurse can help these children and their families cope by providing referrals and resources for socially based communication and language intervention and social skills development, including helping individuals to recognize social cues (Landa, 2000). Because coping with change is difficult, the nurse should also attempt to maintain comfortable routines; when change is necessary, it should be introduced gradually.

Considerations for Client and Family Education

Teaching individuals with Asperger's disorder and their families about the symptoms of the condition can prevent misunderstanding regarding behavior that others may consider socially inappropriate. Families should also be cautioned not to focus on any savant-like behaviors to the detriment of encouraging age-appropriate skills and behaviors. Because the condition involves social skill deficits the nurse can provide encouragement and feedback, helping the child or adolescent to recognize social cues and ways in which socially appropriate behavior can be integrated into social interactions (Cole Marshall, 2002). Individuals with Asperger's disorder may experience significant stress and anxiety, so teaching individuals about outlets for stress and anxiety are also important. If individuals have had medication prescribed for their symptoms, the nurse should teach clients about the specific medication, what to expect, and what types of side effects should be reported. (See Chapter 5.)

A discussion of how individuals with Asperger's syndrome and high-functioning autism utilize and develop language skills in the social environment.

Little, L., & Clark, R. R. (2006). Wonders and worries of parenting a child with Asperger syndrome and nonverbal learning disorder. *American Journal of Maternal Child Nursing, 31*(1), 39–44.
This study describes the joys and pressing concerns of the parents of children with Asperger's syndrome and nonverbal learning disorder.

Luckasson, R., Borthwick-Duffy, S., Buntinx, W. H. E., Coulter, D. L., Craig, E. M., Reeve, A., et al. (2002). *Mental retardation: Definition, classification, and system of support.* Washington DC: American Association of Mental Retardation.
Report and recommendations regarding mental retardation.

Martin, A., Patzer, D. K., & Volkmar, F. R. (2000). Psychopharmacological treatment of higher functioning pervasive developmental disorders. In A. Klin, F. R. Volkmar, & S. S. Sparrow (Eds.), *Asperger syndrome* (pp. 210–228). New York: Guilford Press.
Discusses the aspects of medication therapy in individuals with pervasive developmental disorders.

Matson, J. L., & Minshawi, N. F. (2006). *Early intervention for autism spectrum disorders* (Vol. I). Oxford: Elsevier Science.
This book presents an overview on the assessment, management, and treatment of children with mental health disorders and developmental disabilities.

McLaughlin, P. J., & Wehman, P. (Eds.). (1996). *Mental retardation and developmental disabilities* (2nd ed.). Austin, TX: Pro-ed.
This edition expands information on a variety of developmental disabilities. The book reflects a life-span perspective, and includes information on service delivery, school issues, and transition from secondary school to adulthood. Also included is information on case management, community-based vocational training, supported employment, supported living, and social security.

Mouridsen, S. E. (2003). Childhood disintegrative disorder. *Brain and Development, 25*(4), 225–228.
Describes reviews of recent case studies of childhood disintegrative disorder. Reports use of common diagnostic systems and how they relate to treatment and outcome.

National Institute of Child Health and Human Development. (2001). *Closing the gap: A national blueprint for improving the health of persons with mental retardation.* Report of the Surgeon General's Conference on Health Disparities and Mental Retardation. Washington, DC: National Institutes of Health.
Report outlining health disparities in people with mental retardation and suggestions for remedying the problem.

Noble, J. (2001). *Textbook of primary care medicine* (3rd ed.). St. Louis: Mosby.
A comprehensive medical text discussing a wide variety of medical conditions and their diagnosis, treatment, and prognosis.

Those with Asperger's disorder may experience stress due to social deficit and may also experience depression, so medications such as antidepressants may be prescribed for associated symptoms (Martin, Patzer, & Volkmar, 2000).

Critical Thinking Question How would you expect a child's behavior to be different and/or similar if diagnosed with autistic disorder, Asperger's disorder, or a normal developmental delay?

Examples of Other Pervasive Developmental Disorders

Rett's disorder is another condition included under the category of pervasive developmental disorders, but it occurs more rarely than autism or Asperger's disorder. It occurs mainly in females at a rate of 1 in 10,000 to 1 in 23,000 females worldwide (Armstrong, 2005). Rett's disorder is often associated with severe or profound mental retardation. In most cases, Rett's disorder is thought to be due to a genetic mutation on the X chromosome (Armstrong; Glaze, 2005).

Developmental regression in Rett's disorder typically appears prior to the age of 4. After a period of normal psychomotor development, children with Rett's disorder experience progressive loss of acquired motor, cognitive, and language skills and also experience lack of coordination of movement and decrease in purposeful hand movement (Nomura & Segawa, 2005). There is impairment in expressive and receptive language function, a decreased interest in social engagement, and mental retardation and seizures may also be present.

There are no specific diagnostic tools or laboratory tests used for diagnosing Rett's disorder. Diagnosis is based on the disintegration of psychomotor skills after a previous period of normal development, including lack of coordination in trunk and gait movement, and impaired expressive and receptive language function. Deceleration of head growth has also been observed.

There is no specific treatment of Rett's disorder other than supportive care. Individuals may need assistance with feeding and other activities of daily living. Physical therapy may help prevent contractures. If a seizure disorder is present, precautions to prevent injury during seizures should be taken and medication to treat the seizure disorder may be instituted. Helping parents adjust

Clinical Example

The Walker family was overjoyed at the birth last year of a baby girl, Sally, and her three older brothers love their baby sister. In the past 2 months, her mother noticed that Sally seems to have trouble breathing and sometimes has shaking movements of her limbs that she is "afraid are seizures." At 11 months old, Sally is barely crawling and shows no interest in pulling herself up. She no longer makes cooing sounds and has stopped smiling. Both parents are tearful and not surprised when the staff at the Pediatric Development Clinic, after a battery of medical tests to rule out underlying medical conditions, suggests that Sally has a rare, chromosomal-linked, pervasive developmental disorder known as Rett's disorder.

to their child's debilitation after a period in which they were unaware that a disability existed is a major task in working with families who have a child with Rett's disorder. The nurse should inform parents of resources such as support groups and teach them the necessary skills to care for their child's physical needs as well as helping them learn how to communicate with their child. Most parents experience a grieving that is associated with the loss of the child they knew prior to onset of symptoms.

Rett's disorder is a rare pervasive developmental disorder that is thought to be caused by a genetic mutation on the X-chromosome characterized by profound developmental regression in behaviors.

Another pervasive developmental disorder is **childhood disintegrative disorder**, a condition characterized by deterioration of previously attained social, language, and play skills after the age of 2 and prior to the age of 10. It is also a rare condition, which appears to be more prevalent in males than females. The rate of childhood disintegrative disorder has been estimated as 0.11 to 0.64 per 10,000 (Mouridsen, 2003). Children with the disorder show signs of deterioration of expressive or receptive language, social skills, bowel or bladder control, and play skills after an apparent period of normal development. Deterioration of motor skills may or may not be present. Loss of previously acquired skills usually occurs between 3 and 4 years of age, but must occur prior to the age of 10.

Childhood disintegrative disorder is a condition characterized by severe deterioration of previously attained social, language, and play skills.

Because there are no specific tools currently available for the definitive diagnosis of childhood disintegrative disorder, diagnosis is based on clinical presentation. There are no specific guidelines for treatment of the disorder. In most instances management of the condition requires a multidisciplinary approach. Supportive care and support groups are important interventions. Special education, which helps the child learn adaptive skills, is also useful. As with other intellectual and developmental disabilities, the nurse should help

Communicat problems are co children and ad intellectual and mental disabilit making it difficu them to cover c in their physical emotional well-

Family violen abuse is also ass with individuals intellectual and mental disabilitie should not be dis as a potential ca changes in behav

Federal Drug Administration. (2007). Thimerosol in vaccines. Retrieved September 3, 2007, from http://www.fda.org/cber/vaccine/thimfaq.htm#q2

This is a link to a FAQ on thimerosal in vaccines covering such topics as why is exposure to mercury a concern; what is thimerosal; why is it used in vaccines; what is the difference between "thimerosal-free" and "thimerosal-reduced," and what is the government doing to make vaccines safer.

Filipek, P. A., Accardo, P. J., Ashwal, S., Barbanek, G. T., Cook, E. H. Jr., et al. (2000). Practice parameter: Screening and diagnosis of autism. *Neurology, 55*(4), 468–479.

This review of available empirical evidence proposes that appropriate tools for routine developmental screening, especially for autism, have not been developed. It advocates for earlier intervention that leads to earlier diagnosis and consequently better prognosis for autistic children.

Fisher, K. (2004). Nursing care of special populations: Issues in caring for elderly people with mental retardation. *Nursing Forum, 39*(1), 28–31.

Outlines issues associated with health care of an aging population of individuals with mental retardation. Specifies the need for nurses to be educated and have increased exposure to the clinical challenges of caring for individuals with mental retardation.

Giarelli, E., Souders, M., Pinto-Martin, J., Bloch, J., & Levy, S. E. (2005). Intervention pilot for parents of children with autistic spectrum disorder. *Pediatric Nursing, 31*(5), 389–399.

This paper describes a randomized trial to refine a nursing intervention in working with parents of children with Asperger's disorder.

Gillberg, C., & Soderstrom, H. (2003). Learning disability. *The Lancet, 362*(9386), 811–821.

A comprehensive review of learning disability (which is defined in the article as mental retardation); includes causes and pathogenesis, associated conditions, psychosocial issues, treatment, and intervention.

Glaze, D. G. (2005). Neurophysiology of Rett's syndrome. *Journal of Child Neurology, 20*(9), 740–746.

Reviews Rett's syndrome as a neurodevelopmental disorder based on a specific mutation and its effects on the central nervous system. Provides specifics on the neurophysiological, electrocardiographical, and electroencephalogical aspects of Rett's syndrome.

Goolsby, M. J., & Blackwell, J. (2001). Clinical practice guideline: Screening and diagnosing autism. *Clinical Practice Guidelines, 13*(12), 534–536.

Reviews the clinical practice guideline concerning screening and diagnosis of autism, which is developed to help primary care providers of children, including pediatric nurse practitioners and family nurse practitioners, facilitate early identification of children with autism.

Handen, B. L., Johnson, C. R., & Lubetsky, M. (2000). Efficacy of methylphenidate among children with autism and symptoms of attention-deficit hyperactivity disorder. *Journal of Autism and Developmental Disorders, 30*, 245–255.

Figure 27-1 Nicotine can interact with some pharmacologic therapies for mental disorders.

including panic attacks, phobias, and posttraumatic stress disorder; an eating disorder; a conduct disorder; an attention deficit disorder; or a personality disorder, most commonly antisocial or borderline personality disorders. According to the *Diagnostic and Statistical Manual of Mental Disorders,* 4th Edition, Text Revision *(DSM-IV-TR)* classification (American Psychiatric Association [APA], 2000), substance use disorders and the clinical mental disorders are identified on Axis I, personality disorders on Axis II.

Although dependence on nicotine and caffeine also qualify for consideration in establishing a dual diagnosis, these substances have not been a primary focus of treatment. However, nicotine addiction is receiving more attention lately. The Joint Commission on Accreditation of Healthcare Organizations (JCAHO) has made the treatment of nicotine addiction one of its core measures for the treatment of several pulmonary and cardiac diseases, thus increasing interest in the area of nicotine dependence. Nicotine dependence is particularly relevant in the treatment of psychiatric illnesses, because of nicotine's effect on some of the pharmacologic therapies prescribed for these disorders (**Figure 27-1**).

Smoking is one of the most difficult addictions to overcome.

Incidence and Prevalence

The Center for Substance Abuse Treatment (2005) estimates that 50–75% of patients in substance abuse programs have co-occurring mental illness, and 20–50% of those treated in mental health settings have co-occurring substance abuse. Most people with dual diagnoses do not receive treatment for both mental disorders and substance abuse. Many receive no treatment at all.

Some clinicians consider the co-occurrence of mental and substance use disorders so common as to be the expectation, rather than the exception (Buckley, 2006). The rate of lifetime substance use disorder among persons with schizophrenia is 70–80% (Westermeyer, 2006). This is not counting the use of nicotine, which has a prevalence rate of 80–90% among those diagnosed with schizophrenia (Ziedonis & Williams, 2002). The nurse can expect to encounter dual-diagnosed clients in all areas of practice. According to a study recently published by the Agency for Healthcare Research and Quality (AHRQ; 2007), in 2004, over 1 million adult hospital stays, or 3% of admissions to acute care hospitals, were related to a dual diagnosis—both a substance-related and a mental health disorder.

Adolescents have a high prevalence of substance use disorders associated with psychiatric disorders (Deas, 2006). The geriatric population also is vulnerable, due to a high incidence of depression compounded by significant life changes and loss. Substance abuse can be a way of dealing with feelings of anger, grief, and abandonment, common in this age group.

Etiology

The etiology of the mental and substance-related disorders have been discussed in the chapters specific to the disorders. In addition to environmental and lifestyle influences, such as availability of substances and peer pressure, the etiology of dual diagnosis is commonly explained in terms of self-medication or neurobiology.

Self-Medication

Research showing the onset of substance use after the development of a psychiatric disorder, as well as the preference for certain drugs, is often cited to support the belief that individuals with mental disorders use substances to self-medicate or treat the unpleasant symptoms of the psychiatric disorder. In most bipolar clients, substance abuse develops after multiple bipolar episodes, suggesting that the substance use may be an attempt to self-medicate. Most bipolar clients with a substance use disorder abuse cocaine, and most depressed persons abuse alcohol. It is common for persons to abuse more than one substance, such as using cocaine to get high and alternating with alcohol to come down. Cocaine may help sustain euphoria for clients with a cycling mood disorder, and the disinhibiting effects of alcohol may free the depressed client from fears of dependency and intimacy and allow some relief from painful loneliness and isolation (Kaufman & McNaul, 1992; Vornik & Brown, 2006). Persons with schizophrenia report using alcohol, cocaine, and marijuana to relieve feelings of depression and anxiety, and to feel more sociable. The psychostimulant properties of cocaine appear to diminish these negative symptoms of schizophrenia temporarily (Copersino & Serper, 1998; Green & Brown, 2006; Westermeyer, 2006).

The client who self-medicates can benefit from education regarding the relationship between mental illness and substance abuse. Although there may be a short-term relief from the symptoms of mental illness, over time, the use of substances may actually exacerbate a mental disorder. For example, substance abuse may worsen the impulsive behaviors characteristic of borderline and antisocial personality disorders, or increase the symptoms of schizophrenia or depression. The nurse may find that clients also use substances to help them cope with the side effects associated with prescribed medications. Client education on the relationship between mental illness and substance abuse is essential to the prevention and treatment of dual diagnosis.

Neurobiology

As already noted, just as a mental disorder can lead to substance use, those substances may exacerbate the mental disorder. Although this may be due in part to the disinhibiting effect of many substances, there are also neurobiological explanations.

The use of substances can lead to changes in the brain chemistry resulting in an imbalance or depletion of neurotransmitters. The frequent existence of co-occurring schizophrenia and substance abuse may have a neurobiological basis having to do with alterations in the reward system in the cortical and limbic areas of the brain (Green, 2006). Researchers hypothesize that serotonin deficits from alcohol abuse, endorphin deficits from opioid dependence, and dopamine depletion that occurs with cocaine dependence predispose one to the development of depression, and can actually increase the positive symptoms of schizophrenia, such as hallucinations and paranoia (Addington & Addington, 2001; Zauszniewski, 1995).

Hereditary and genetic factors may create predispositions for both mental and substance use disorders. There is evidence that marijuana use increases the risk of developing schizophrenia among vulnerable or psychosis-prone adolescents, with the vulnerability partially attributed to a gene that regulates the effects of cannabis (Rey, 2007). Genetic influences may also be at the root of methamphetamine psychosis (Nakamura et al., 2006).

Clinical Presentation

The co-morbidity of substance use disorder is most frequently diagnosed in persons considered to have severe mental illness, but often goes unrecognized and untreated in those with less debilitating mental disorders. As noted earlier, numerous mental disorders are commonly associated with dual diagnosis, including schizophrenia, bipolar disorder, major depressive disorder, anxiety disorders, antisocial personality disorder, and borderline personality disorder. Mood disorder was the most common mental disorder among clients diagnosed with dual diagnosis in community hospitals (AHRQ, 2007). Common substances of abuse among those with dual diagnoses are the same as those among the general population: alcohol; cocaine; heroin; morphine; marijuana; phencyclidine (PCP); methamphetamine, including the club drug ecstasy (methylenedioxymethamphetamine or MDMA); hallucinogens, such as LSD (lysergic acid diethylamide); and amphetamines. Nicotine is the most commonly used substance of abuse by clients with schizophrenia.

Depression and anxiety disorders are often masked by somatic symptoms or medical illness.

Differential Diagnosis

Assessment for dual diagnosis is complicated, because alcohol and drug abuse may contribute to the development of mental disorders as well as exacerbate, mimic, or mask symptoms of mental disorders. In the past, establishing the dual diagnosis was made more difficult by the traditionally separate diagnostic and treatment approaches to substance abuse and mental illness that had developed. The traditional chemical dependency treatment model often minimized psychiatric symptoms, attributing them to the prolonged substance use. The mental illness professional, if untrained in substance abuse treatment, was likely to focus on the mental illness as the primary disorder and view the substance use disorder as the result of the client's efforts to relieve the symptoms of the psychiatric disorder (self-medication).

The *DSM-IV-TR* offers some guidelines to aid in distinguishing between a **substance-induced mental disorder** and a **primary mental disorder**. *Primary* refers only to the fact that the symptoms of mental illness are not a temporary result of some other phenomenon such as alcohol or another drug. It is not meant to imply a greater importance or chronologic relationship to another mental or substance use disorder. According to the *DSM-IV-TR*, if the symptoms precede the onset of substance use or persist more than 4 weeks after the cessation of acute intoxication or withdrawal, the client may have a nonsubstance-induced mental disorder, in other words, a primary mental disorder (APA, 2000).

Many clients with drug or alcohol addiction may develop secondary affective or psychotic symptoms during persistent intoxication or withdrawal (**Table 27-1**). These persons are diagnosed with a primary addiction and a secondary organic psychosis. Once the client abstains, a secondary psychosis or affective syndrome usually resolves quickly, although psychotic symptoms sometimes last for weeks, or even months (Ziedonis & Williams, 2002).

Cocaine use can produce acute agitation, paranoid delusions, and even auditory hallucinations. This is referred to as a substance-induced psychosis. In this case, the client does not have a primary mental disorder and therefore is not given a dual diagnosis, even if further evaluation supports a diagnosis of substance use disorder or substance abuse. Conversely, if someone has a mental disorder, such as major depressive disorder or adjustment disorder with depressed mood, and begins to use alcohol or drugs as a way to escape the sadness, loneliness, and emptiness, a pattern consistent with a diagnosis of substance

Clinical Example

A male client, Roger, experiencing acute alcohol withdrawal presents in a way that appears guarded and suspicious. He accuses his hospital roommate of stealing his robe, and tells the nurses that he thinks they may be poisoning his food. His family states there is no history of this type of behavior. Roger's paranoia may be a temporary phenomenon related to the alcohol use. However, if the symptom persists, further evaluation for a primary mental disorder, such as schizophrenia or schizoaffective disorder, would be indicated. Only then could a diagnosis of dual disorders be established.

Table 27-1 Substance-Induced Psychotic Symptoms Associated with Intoxication and Withdrawal

Substance	Psychotic Symptoms	Onset and Duration
Cocaine	Paranoid delusions, auditory and/or visual hallucinations	During intoxication phase, with almost immediate onset and lasting up to an hour, or during a binge, effects may last 48 hours after last dose.
Alcohol	Auditory and visual hallucinations with clear sensorium, agitation, paranoia	Onset typically within 48 hours of abstinence; can last hours to weeks. Onset can occur as late as 1–3 weeks after abstinence and duration can extend for several months.
Cannabis (marijuana)	Euphoria, paranoia, auditory and visual hallucinations	Acute onset; hallucinations tend to clear after 30 days.
PCP	Dissociative state, bizarre hallucinations, agitation, aggressive behavior, suicidal and homicidal ideation	Onset during intoxication phase and usually lasting 4–6 hours; however, PCP-induced psychosis can be prolonged.
Amphetamines	Paranoia, hypersexuality, persecutory delusions, severe anxiety, agitation, panic state	Altered mental state typically lasts through intoxication, but may last days, weeks, or months.
Hallucinogens (LSD)	Delusions, visual hallucinations, panic state, anxiety, suicidal ideation	Onset within 30–90 minutes of use; effects wear off in 6–12 hours.
Anabolic steroids	Mania, depression, aggression, violence, paranoia	Symptoms occur during use; withdrawal depression sets in when drug is stopped.

Source: Adapted from Ziedonis & Williams, 2002.

abuse may be established. This example would qualify as a dual diagnosis.

The assessment to determine the presence of a primary mental disorder must include a history of medical, including psychiatric, illnesses and prescribed medications for physical and mental illnesses. Both factors can produce symptoms of a mental disorder. In the case of drug toxicity or an atypical response, a period consistent with the half-life of the medication must pass before a diagnosis can be made.

Clinical Course and Complications

Clients with a dual diagnosis can recover and lead productive lives. However, living with two chronic disorders can present formidable challenges, including relapse and hospitalizations. It is essential to recovery that both the mental and the substance use disorders be treated. Clients with a dual diagnosis may have difficulty finding a treatment setting with a multidisciplinary staff that can treat both mental illness and substance abuse. Failure to diagnose and treat a co-occurring psychiatric disorder is the most common cause for the failure of alcoholism treatment (Renner, 2004).

The impact of dual diagnosis is demonstrated in decreased productivity, dysfunctional families, emotionally deprived children, increased violence, suicide, a high incidence of physical illness, frequent hospitalization and medical treatment, homelessness, and criminal behavior. Substance abuse in the absence of a mental disorder is a recognized suicide risk, and this is true as well when the substance abuse occurs in the presence of another mental disorder, including schizophrenia, psychoses, and depression. Additional complications can occur during detoxification, withdrawal, and on-going treatment and recovery phases, related to substances of abuse as well as the effects of prescribed medications. These will be discussed in a later section on nursing care of these clients.

Integrated Treatment

SAMHSA's Co-Occurring Center for Excellence (COCE), a leading national resource for the field of co-occurring mental health and substance use disorders, advocates for an **integrated treatment approach**. According to COCE, a truly integrated system promotes the seamless delivery of mental health and substance abuse treatment services through a variety of agencies across all behavioral health settings (Center for Substance Abuse Treatment, 2006). The need for separate services for mental health and substance abuse treatment will still exist for those who do not have both diagnoses. However, those who do carry a dual diagnosis would benefit from therapists who are cross-trained in both specialties, and would be able to provide integrated screening, assessment, and treatment. An array of physical, psychological, and social service interventions would be part of an integrated treatment plan matched to the client's needs and preferences. The client would learn to manage both disorders, as well as to understand the relationship between the disorders. Integrated team treatment programs may result in an improved prognosis. Programs that employ an integrated treatment approach report decreased use of drugs and alcohol, decreased psychiatric hospitalizations, and fewer relapses of schizophrenic symptoms (Frances, 1997; Center for Substance Abuse Treatment, 2005). This approach provides treatment to address the goals of abstinence and recovery while respecting the interactive nature of the disorders.

Critical Thinking Question If a client is in treatment for schizophrenia and continues to smoke marijuana and abuse alcohol, what therapeutic approaches might the treatment team consider?

The Nurse's Role in the Treatment of the Client with a Dual Diagnosis

The nurse must be familiar with the treatment approaches utilized with clients who have a dual diagnosis and, in particular, must be knowledgeable about the unique needs and complications that these clients present.

Detoxification

When a client with a mental disorder requires detoxification for substance dependence, complications can occur related to interactions or effects of the substances of abuse and medications the client may be taking to treat the mental disorder. The nurse must monitor the client carefully and be aware of the following facts:

- Alcohol and sedative-hypnotic medications may decrease the efficacy of neuroleptic medications, making them less

Clients who are being treated with antipsychotic medications and are attempting withdrawal from alcohol or cocaine are at a high risk of developing seizures.

effective in controlling the psychotic symptoms, depression, or seizures for which they were prescribed. Clients with schizophrenia are vulnerable to hallucinations during withdrawal.

- Because neuroleptic medications lower the seizure threshold, clients taking them are at increased risk for withdrawal seizures.
- Alcohol, sedatives, and cocaine may also cause serious respiratory depression when combined with phenothiazines, a category of neuroleptic medications.
- A special classification of antidepressant medications known as monoamine oxidase inhibitors (MAOIs) can produce a life-threatening hypertensive crisis when combined with certain foods and medications, including alcohol and amphetamines. Symptoms of hypertensive crisis include chest pain, severe headache, nausea, vomiting, dilated pupils, and photosensitivity. Treatment requires the administration of intravenous phentolamine (Regitine).
- The mood-stabilizing drug lithium (Eskalith), usually prescribed for bipolar disorder, is particularly sensitive to changes in fluid and electrolyte balance. Vomiting and diarrhea associated with withdrawal can result in dehydration and elevated serum lithium levels beyond the therapeutic range (0.5 to 1.5 mEq/L). Lithium levels must be evaluated if the client is in withdrawal, and the medication should be withheld and the prescribing physician or nurse practitioner notified if the client shows signs of lithium toxicity. Signs of lithium toxicity include vomiting, diarrhea, slurred speech, drowsiness, muscle weakness or twitching, and decreased coordination.

Medication for the psychiatric disorder is essential for the client to benefit from or even participate in the process of recovery from a substance use disorder.

Benzodiazepines are avoided except for the management of withdrawal symptoms during the detoxification phase of treatment.

Disulfiram (Antabuse) increases the risk for hypotension, myocardial infarction, and stroke in elderly clients.

Clients with a dual diagnosis require special preparation to facilitate their participation in AA or other 12-step programs.

Pharmacological Treatment

Integrated treatment programs can be supportive to the client who requires pharmacologic intervention to control the symptoms of a psychiatric disorder. Therapists and counselors who have knowledge of both disorders will understand and support the need for these medications. It is helpful if the nurse partners with the prescribing nurse practitioner or other clinician to ensure that medications are appropriate for the client with a dual diagnosis. Some guiding principles are:

- When treating mental illness in the presence of a substance use disorder, the clinician avoids prescribing medications with a high potential for abuse.
- The potential for overdose with the prescription medication, either alone or in combination with substances of abuse, must also be considered. Because relapse is possible, the clinician should consider the interactions that may occur between the prescribed medication and the substance of abuse.
- To adhere to the prescribed dose, the side effects must be tolerable; the client should not need to use alcohol or other drugs to counter unpleasant side effects.
- The benzodiazepines, such as lorazepam (Ativan), alprazolam (Xanax), and diazepam (Valium), are highly addictive, mood-altering medications that are contraindicated for the dual-diagnosed client after the completion of detoxification. Buspirone (BuSpar) selectively diminishes multiple symptoms of anxiety without the acute mood alteration, sedation, and addictive potential of the benzodiazepines.

Several treatments are available to reduce drug craving or to deter the use of addictive substances. Disulfiram (Antabuse) is an alcohol abuse deterrent that can exacerbate psychotic symptoms and produce a hypertensive crisis in those who use alcohol. This drug's potential risk is too high to be an effective treatment option for dual-diagnosed clients. Naltrexone (ReVia) shows promise in blocking the craving for alcohol and opioids. It has few side effects as maintenance therapy when prescribed for alcohol dependence.

12-Step Programs

Alcoholics Anonymous (AA), Narcotics Anonymous (NA), and other 12-step programs have a demonstrated success record in helping persons achieve abstinence and improve the quality of their lives in recovery. However, the client who also has a mental disorder may need assistance in learning the social skills necessary to participate at meetings and to establish a support network. This preparation may require searching, through trial and error, for a group the client feels comfortable with. Some communities have self-help groups known as **double trouble groups** that address both addiction and mental disorders. Because many of the 12-step meetings are open to persons not in recovery, the nurse can accompany the client to meetings. Closed meetings are designated in the meeting schedule books available from each sponsoring organiza-

Considerations for Client and Family Education

The nurse can play a pivotal role in motivating and engaging the client in treatment for a dual disorder through client and family education. The neurobiology of the mental disorder and the addiction provides the foundation to help the client and family or significant other understand the relationship between the two disorders. Education reinforces the illness model of substance abuse and avoids moral blame and shame. Both mental and addictive disorders are presented as brain dysfunctions that are displayed as behavioral dysfunctions. Whereas drug use may initially be a voluntary act, addiction is not. Education about substance abuse combined with knowledge of the client's medical, social, and behavioral history can break down the denial that often prevents the client from recognizing his or her own addiction.

Compliance with the prescribed schedule and dosage of medications is a predictor of recovery, and failure to comply is a predictor of relapse. Therefore, the nurse should reinforce the differences between the prescribed medication and the drugs the client depended on prior to treatment. This issue is complicated and deserving of much time, especially because some clients have abused and become dependent on prescription medications. The client needs to appreciate that the medications, psychiatric symptoms, and drug abuse are interrelated. The role of prescribed medication must be carefully explained, as well as the importance of not stopping the medication or adjusting the dosage.

Major side effects of traditional antipsychotic medications include sedation and blurred vision (both of which usually abate within a few weeks), dry mouth, sedation, constipation, decreased libido, orthostatic hypotension, and extrapyramidal symptoms (EPS) of tremors, muscle rigidity and spasms, and involuntary movements. The nurse needs to instruct the client and family in practical ways to manage these symptoms. The client should be informed of possible side effects and be equipped with simple strategies to lessen their discomfort. Clients have been known to resort to alcohol or other drugs in an attempt to find relief from the side effects of prescribed medication.

The nurse can prepare the client to anticipate and handle criticism from other persons in recovery who do not understand the client's need for psychotropic medications. The special self-help meetings that address dual diagnosis can be helpful in these situations, and the nurse can assist the client to locate such groups.

The nurse needs to inform the client about the interaction between prescribed medications and possible substances of abuse so that the client understands the increased risks these substances present. Benztropine mesylate (Cogentin) and other anticholinergic medications are frequently prescribed to control occasional Parkinsonian symptoms for clients who take neuroleptic medications. Tricyclic antidepressants also have anticholinergic properties. The anticholinergic effects (dry mouth, dry eyes, blurred vision, constipation, difficulty urinating) are enhanced by marijuana.

Neuroleptics are not mood-altering medications and are not associated with abuse or overdose. However, some neuroleptics attenuate a cocaine high. The medication's effectiveness is decreased if the client uses alcohol, sedatives, or nicotine. MAOIs may cause a hypertensive crisis if combined with certain forms of alcohol or stimulant drugs and are therefore not the drugs of choice to treat depression in the client with a dual diagnosis.

Nicotine can decrease the blood levels of antipsychotic medications, so the dosage of these medications may need adjustment to accommodate the client's smoking habit. There is still some controversy in the field as to whether a client attempting abstinence from alcohol or other substances should simultaneously withdraw from nicotine. However, smoking is common among persons with both mental illness and substance abuse, and given the negative effects of smoking on health, this issue should be considered as part of the treatment plan. Various types of nicotine replacement therapies are available, including nicotine gum and a slow-acting transdermal patch, both available without a prescription.

Families and clients need to be informed of the warning signs of relapse, and families need to recognize early signs of noncompliance with medications or substance use. Families and significant others can be a wonderful source of support and encouragement. Of course, the client needs to consent to have family members involved in treatment. Family members and significant others can also benefit from 12-step programs specifically for them.

tion and may be attended only by persons who have the addiction being addressed by the group. Beginners' groups are usually a good way to introduce the client to the 12-step program.

Clients with dual diagnoses should be encouraged to connect with a sponsor early in the recovery process. The sponsor is an important support person and should be educated with the client about the relationship between the psychiatric illness and the addiction, as well as about the specific signs that may indicate the client has stopped medication or needs psychiatric intervention. Clients with certain mental disorders have difficulty trusting others, and thus the nurse may need to work closely with the client and sponsor to form and maintain a relationship.

Implications for Evidence-Based Practice

There are studies that support the effectiveness of integrated treatment for co-occurring disorders (Grella & Stein, 2006). However, there is a need for replicated studies, especially randomized controlled trials, to better evaluate the efficacy of this approach. A recent review of 59 studies, including 36 randomized controlled trials, examined psychosocial and medication treatments for those with a substance-related disorder and depression, anxiety disorder, schizophrenia, bipolar disorder, severe mental illness, or nonspecific mental illness. The study found that current treatments that were effective for mental or substance use disorders alone were also effective for those same disorders in clients with a dual diagnosis, but the findings on integrated treatment were still unclear (Tiet & Mausbach, 2007).

There has been an effort to match the level of treatment needs to the intensity of services, both for treatment outcome and cost-effectiveness. Not surprisingly, high-severity clients treated in high-intensity programs had better alcohol, drug, and psychiatric outcomes, as well as higher costs, than those treated in low-intensity programs. The matching of client needs to level of services provided was not significant for moderate-severity clients (Chen, Barnett, Sempel, & Timko, 2006).

Separate studies found that psychological interventions, such as talking to clients about their symptoms and medications, were effective, but underutilized with African Americans and clients with schizophrenia (Grella & Stein, 2006; Wilk et al., 2006). This is important evidence for the value of supplementing medication treatment with individual and group counseling and client education—interventions that are well-suited to nursing practice.

If an individual assessment determines that the client will not be able to participate effectively in a community-based 12-step program, or if the client is unwilling to do so, an outpatient setting provides a reasonable alternative. Integrated psychiatric and substance abuse outpatient programs incorporate 12-step programs and provide a controlled setting that may be more comfortable and supportive for some clients with a dual diagnosis.

Nonabstinence Approach

For a subset of clients, abstinence is not the best recovery model. Motivational therapy that accepts clients at their particular level of readiness to change may be much more effective. Also, for clients with a combination of opiate dependence and chronic Axis I disorders, especially psychosis, methadone maintenance may be the preferred treatment.

CASE STUDY Ms. S.

Ms. S. is a 55-year-old woman who was widowed 1 year ago. She has no children and lives alone in a suburb of a large city. Her only family is a younger first cousin who lives in the next town with her husband and two teenage children. Prior to her husband's death, Ms. S. worked as an assistant in his insurance business. She sold the business after his death and found full-time employment at a local department store. Recently, she has been disciplined at work for lateness and excessive absences.

Once a month, on a Sunday, Ms. S. and a longtime friend each drives approximately 1 hour to meet for lunch at a restaurant midway between their homes. When Ms. S. failed to show up one Sunday and did not answer her phone, her friend drove to Ms. S.'s house. She found Ms. S. intoxicated, alcohol on her breath, and an empty bottle of bourbon on the table. Ms. S.'s clothing was disheveled, her speech was slurred, and she was unsteady on her feet. When her friend arrived, Ms. S. began frantically trying to get ready to go out, but she would become distracted. She vacillated between insisting she was all right and becoming tearful. Unable to reach Ms. S.'s cousin, the friend phoned Ms. S.'s doctor, and at her direction she drove Ms. S. to the local hospital's emergency room.

Ms. S. was admitted to the hospital's in-patient alcoholism treatment unit for detoxification and treatment. During Ms. S.'s hospitalization, her cousin met with Ms. S. and her counselor and attended educational programs for family members. Ms. S. attended groups and lectures

NURSING CARE PLAN **Major Depressive Disorder and Alcohol Dependence**

Expected Outcomes	Interventions	Evaluations
• Will achieve abstinence. • Will develop strategies to reduce risk of drinking. • Will develop a healthy lifestyle. • Will feel less depressed. • Will experience improved mood and self-esteem.	• Administer medications as prescribed for detoxification and monitor response. The nurse educates Ms. S. regarding AA, including a double trouble groups. • The nurse encourages Ms. S. to attend supportive individual and group therapy to help identify antecedents to drinking. • Nurse counsels Ms. S. on sleep habits and dietary practices. • Antidepressant therapy; nurse educates Ms. S. regarding side effects and action of medication and relationship between her depression and her drinking.	• Attends AA meetings and gets sponsor from a double trouble group. • Does not drink; identifies strategies to decrease loneliness (related to antecedents to drinking): joins gym; reestablishes two friendships. • Reports regular bedtime routine and sleeps 7 hours/night; eats three meals a day. • Compliant with antidepressant medication; discusses side effects with nurse. • Absence of depressive symptoms; engages in pleasurable activities.

Visit http://nursing.jbpub.com/psychiatric for additional care plans and exercises.

Psychotherapy

Although some clients with a dual diagnosis may benefit from psychodynamic psychotherapy after 1 to 2 years of sobriety, the initial focus of therapy with these clients should be more structured. Support therapy, psychoeducation, and cognitive-behavioral interventions are effective modalities during the initial phase of treatment.

Critical Thinking Question Mr. J. is admitted to the general hospital and is scheduled for elective surgery for a hernia repair the next morning. The nurse brings Mr. J. his prescribed medications at 10 p.m., including the sleep medication, Ambien. Mr. J. asks the nurse if he must take the pill, since he is in recovery from addictions and has been "clean and sober" for 2 years. He explains to the nurse that he avoids all mood-altering medications. How might the nurse advise this patient?

The cognitive deficits associated with both mental disorders and substance use disorders need to be considered when providing client education.

where she learned about the depressant effects of alcohol. The symptoms Ms. S. reported experiencing for the past year included tearfulness, insomnia, difficulty getting up in the morning, feeling worse as the day wore on, and loss of interest in friends and activities. These were attributed to her alcohol abuse, and she was reassured by her counselor that in time these problems would disappear. Ms. S. was introduced to AA and discharged with out-patient follow-up twice a week with a substance abuse counselor. After a couple of weeks Ms. S. stopped attending AA meetings, and after 4 weeks she dropped out of treatment.

Six weeks after discharge from the alcoholism treatment unit and 10 weeks after her last drink, Ms. S. returned to work. That evening she stopped at a liquor store on the way home, and at 9 p.m. she called her cousin to tell her she had just taken over-the-counter sleeping pills and half a bottle of bourbon and was afraid she would die.

Ms. S. was treated in the emergency room and received a psychiatric consultation. She was diagnosed with major depression and alcohol dependence, started on the antidepressant venlafaxine (Effexor), and referred to a psychiatric clinical nurse specialist with certification in addictions counseling (see Nursing Care Plan). Ms. S. reconnected with AA and this time got a sponsor who met with her and the clinical specialist for educational sessions on depression and the role of antidepressant medication in recovery.

Critical Thinking Question Are there questions or information that would have helped uncover Ms. S.'s major depressive disorder during her initial hospitalization?

Summary

Dual diagnosis is a complex, multifaceted illness requiring an individualized treatment approach that integrates traditional drug dependence treatment with psychiatric treatment. A multidisciplinary staff, knowledgeable in both specialties, can accurately diagnose the co-morbid disorders and engage the client in the treatment and recovery process. It is important that the nurse be informed about the relationship between the two types of disorders in order to provide safe and effective care to the client and family.

The goals for clients in treatment for dual diagnoses are to stop using mood-altering drugs and alcohol, to understand the importance of antipsychotic or antidepressant medications in their treatment, and to learn to recognize the warning signs of relapse for each disorder. Because of the chronic nature of the illnesses, it is unrealistic to expect a complete cure, but clients can achieve sustained periods of sobriety and decreased hospitalizations.

Annotated References

Addington, J., & Addington, D. (2001). Impact of an early psychosis program on substance use. *Psychiatric Rehabilitation Journal, 25*(1), 60–67.

This article highlights the relationship between psychoses and substance-related disorders and the treatment implications.

Agency for Healthcare Research and Quality. (2007). *Care of adults with mental health and substance abuse disorders in U.S. community hospitals.* Washington, DC: Healthcare Utilization Project.

A fact book with demographic and diagnostic data related to clients with mental health and substance use disorders hospitalized in short-term, nonfederal, public and private hospitals across the United States. The survey did not include facilities specializing in the treatment of these disorders.

American Psychiatric Association. (2000). *Diagnostic and statistical manual of mental disorders* (4th ed., text rev.). Washington, DC: Author.

This is the fourth edition of the American Psychiatric Association's official nomenclature of psychiatric conditions and disorders. It provides a systematic listing of the official codes and categories, a description of the multiaxial system for diagnosis, and diagnostic criteria for each of the disorders. It is used by psychiatrists, physicians, psychologists, registered nurses, social workers, therapists, and other mental health workers in all clinical settings.

Buckley, P. F. (2006). Prevalence and consequences of the dual diagnosis of substance abuse and severe mental illness. *Journal of Clinical Psychiatry, 67*(Suppl. 7), 5–9.

This journal article provides a concise overview of dual disorders, including causes, consequences, assessment, and treatment.

Center for Substance Abuse Treatment. (2005). *Substance abuse treatment for persons with co-occurring disorders. Treatment improvement protocol (TIP) Series 42.* DHHS Publication No. (SMA) 05-3992. Rockville, MD: Substance Abuse and Mental Health Services Administration.

This protocol, created by a panel of experts, provides guidelines for the integrated treatment of clients with dual diagnoses.

Center for Substance Abuse Treatment. (2006). *Overarching principles to address the needs of persons with co-occurring disorders.* COCE Overview Paper 3, DHHS Publication No. (SMA) 06-4165. Rockville, MD: Substance Abuse and Mental Health Services Administration.

A concise introduction to the topic of co-occurring disorders, intended for administrators, policymakers, and providers.

Chen, S., Barnett, P. G., Sempel, J. M., & Timko, C. (2006). Outcomes and costs of matching the intensity of dual-diagnosis treatment to patients' symptom severity. *Journal of Substance Abuse Treatment, 31*(1), 95–105.

This study evaluated a patient treatment matching strategy intended to improve the effectiveness and cost-effectiveness of acute treatment for dual-diagnosis clients.

Copersino, M. L., & Serper, M. R. (1998). Comorbidity of schizophrenia and cocaine abuse: Phenomenology and treatment. *Medscape Mental Health, 3*(2). Retrieved March 5, 2007, from http://www.medscape.com/viewarticle/430756

This article relates dopamine depletion to both chronic cocaine administration and schizophrenia. The authors speculate on the relationship between cocaine use and decreased negative symptoms present in clients who are diagnosed with schizophrenia and discuss the role of atypical antipsychotic medications in treatment.

Deas, D. (2006). Adolescent substance abuse and psychiatric comorbidities. *Journal of Clinical Psychiatry, 67*(Suppl. 7), 18–23.

This article presents information on adolescents at risk for developing dual diagnoses.

Frances, R. J. (1997). Integrating addiction and psychiatric services in patients with dual diagnoses.

Current Approaches to Psychoses Diagnosis and Management, 6, 12–14.

This article describes the integrated team treatment approach and its advantages over the alternative fragmented approach to care for clients with a dual diagnosis. The text offers an excellent discussion concerning issues of drug therapy.

Green, A. I. (2006). Treatment of schizophrenia and comorbid substance abuse: Pharmacologic approaches. *Journal of Clinical Psychiatry, 67*(Suppl. 7), 31–35.

The author examines the pharmacologic treatment of comorbid schizophrenia and substance abuse based on a neurobiological etiology, and advocates for an integrated treatment approach.

Green, A. I. & Brown, E. S. (2006). Comorbid schizophrenia and substance abuse. *Journal of Clinical Psychiatry, 67*(9), e08.

The authors describe the prevalence, outcomes, and basis for the comorbidity of schizophrenia and substance abuse and theorize that schizophrenia may create a biologic predisposition to substance abuse by altering the brain reward system.

Grella, C. E., & Stein, J. A. (2006). Impact of program services on treatment outcomes of patients with comorbid mental and substance use disorders. *Psychiatric Services, 57*(7), 1007–1015.

This study examined the outcomes of individuals with co-occurring disorders who received drug treatment in programs that varied their integration of mental health services.

Kaufman, E., & McNaul, J. P. (1992). Recent developments in understanding and treating drug abuse and dependence. *Hospital and Community Psychiatry, 43*(3), 223–235.

This article describes developments in the areas of epidemiology, heredity, environmental influences, neuroreceptors and neurotransmitters, AIDS, diagnostic classification, psychopathology, psychodynamics, psychotherapeutic approaches, and pharmacologic treatment.

Nakamura, K., Chen, C. K., Sekine, Y., Iwata, Y., Anitha, A., et al. (2006). An association analysis of SOD2 variants with methamphetamine psychosis in Japanese and Taiwanese populations. *Human Genetics, 120*(2), 243–252.

This study examines risk factors for methamphetamine psychosis.

Renner, J. A. (2004). Alcoholism and alcohol abuse. In T. A. Stern & J. B. Herman (Eds.). *Massachusetts General Hospital Psychiatry and Board Update* (2nd ed.). New York: McGraw-Hill.

This is a comprehensive overview of alcohol abuse.

Rey, J. M. (2007). Can marijuana lead to psychotic illness? *Current Psychiatry, 6*(2), 36–41, 46.

This article reviews evidence that marijuana use can cause acute psychosis, precipitate schizophrenia, and worsen the prognosis of persons with psychotic disorders.

Tiet, Q. Q., & Mausbach, B. (2007). Treatments for patients with dual diagnosis: A review. *Alcohol Clinical and Experimental Research, 31*(4), 513–536.

This paper reviews the psychosocial and medication treatments for clients with dual diagnosis.

Vornik, L. A., & Brown, E. S. (2006). Management of comorbid bipolar disorder and substance abuse. *Journal of Clinical Psychiatry, 67*(Suppl. 7), 24–30.

The article provides an overview of substance abuse and bipolar disorder with a focus on why co-morbidity is high and treatment options.

Westermeyer, J. (2006). Comorbid schizophrenia and substance abuse: A review of epidemiology and course. *American Journal of Addictions, 15*(5), 345–355.

The author examines the increased knowledge of the relationship between schizophrenia and substance abuse, with a plea for primary prevention and early treatment.

Wilk, J., Marcus, S. C., West, J., Countis, L., Hall, R., Reiger, D. A., et al. (2006). Substance abuse and the management of medication nonadherence in schizophrenia. *Journal of Nervous and Mental Disorders, 194*(6), 454–457.

This survey studied the clinical characteristics and psychiatric management of medication noncompliance among out-patients with schizophrenia.

Zauszniewski, J. A. (1995). Severity of depression, cognitions, and functioning among depressed inpatients with and without coexisting substance abuse. *Journal of the American Psychiatric Nurses Association, 1*(2), 55–60.

This article reports on a study that found that depressed cognitions in persons with depression and substance abuse contributed to the severity of the depression and level of functioning. Based on Beck's cognitive model of depression, the study supports the use of cognitive restructuring with these clients.

Ziedonis, D., & Williams, J. (2002, Summer). Management options when psychosis and substance abuse coincide in the emergency service. *Psychiatric Issues in Emergency Care Settings*, 3–12.

This article provides guidelines for the rapid triage and treatment of patients with symptoms of both psychosis and substance abuse.

Additional Resources

Fisher, M. S., & Bentley, K. J. (1996). Two group therapy models for clients with a dual diagnosis of substance abuse and personality disorder. *Psychiatric Services, 47*(11), 1244–1250.

The disease-and-recovery model and cognitive-behavioral model are compared for effectiveness in the treatment of clients with a dual diagnosis of substance use disorder and personality disorder. The cognitive-behavioral model was more effective with out-patients, but the models were equally effective with in-patients.

Minkoff, K. (1989). An integrated treatment model for dual diagnosis of psychosis and addiction. *Hospital and Community Psychiatry, 40*(10), 1031–1036.

This author was one of the first to address the need for simultaneous treatment of the dual disorders of addiction and psychosis. This classic article describes an analogous recovery process for chronic mental illness and addiction and includes a helpful discussion of the use of Alcoholics Anonymous by clients with mental disorders.

Riley, J. A. (1994). Dual diagnosis, comorbid substance abuse or dependency and mental illness. *Nursing Clinics of North America, 29*(1), 29–34.

This article provides a nursing perspective on the progression from the traditional approach of separate treatment for the mental disorder and the addiction, to an integrated model of treatment.

Internet Resources

http://nursing.jbpub.com/psychiatric

Visit http://nursing.jbpub.com/psychiatric for interactive exercises, NCLEX review questions, WebLinks, and more.

CHAPTER 28

Clients with Chronic Mental Illness

Karen A. Ballard

LEARNING OBJECTIVES

After reading this chapter, you will be able to:

- Discuss the different theoretical frameworks for understanding chronic illness.
- Describe the parameters of chronic mental illness in a client.
- Identify the challenges to clients and families coping with chronic mental illness.
- Identify the various therapies that assist clients in coping with chronic mental illness.
- Identify nursing interventions in assisting clients and their families to cope with chronic mental illness.
- Describe the components in teaching clients and their families about chronic mental illness.

KEY TERMS

Chronic illness
Chronic mental illness
Grief
Homelessness
Loss
Persistent mental illness
Psychiatric rehabilitation
Psychoeducation
Psychosocial typology
Severe mental illness
Trajectory model

http://nursing.jbpub.com/psychiatric

Visit http://nursing.jbpub.com/psychiatric for interactive exercises, NCLEX review questions, WebLinks, and more.

Introduction

Chronic mental illness presents a considerable challenge to clients and their families or significant others because it occurs over a long period, with accompanying and varying stages of **grief** and **loss**. Nurses who practice in this specialty area of psychiatric-mental health nursing utilize their interpersonal skills to form and maintain a therapeutic relationship with clients and their families, who often have been coping with mental illness for prolonged periods. Clients with chronic mental illness (severe and persistent mental illness), like individuals with chronic physical illness, deal with the condition indefinitely, often for their entire lives.

Chronic illness, mental and physical, includes all diseases or disorders that remain with the individual for the rest of the client's lifetime once the condition has been diagnosed. Chronic illness encompasses

> all impairments or deviations from the normal which have one or more of the following characteristics: are permanent; leave residual disability; are caused by nonreversible pathologic alteration; require special training of the patient for rehabilitation, or may be expected to require a long period of supervision, observation, or care. (National Commission on Chronic Illness, 1957, p. 4)

Chronic illness, mental and physical, includes all diseases or disorders that remain with the individual for the rest of the client's lifetime once the condition has been diagnosed.

Chronic mental illness is synonymous with both persistent mental illness and severe mental illness.

Chronic mental illness is synonymous with both **persistent mental illness** and **severe mental illness**. The terms *chronic*, *persistent*, and *severe* identify the gravity of the diagnosis. Chronic mental illness tends to last for a long time, if not a lifetime, and may be characterized by periods of relapse or reoccurrence. All psychiatric disorders have the potential to persist and become chronic. However, schizophrenia, major depressive disorder, and bipolar disorder are the most prevalent major psychiatric disorders shown to develop a chronic course.

Critical Thinking Question What are some common, shared behaviors that a nurse can expect to identify in clients with chronic illness, be it a physical or mental condition?

Theoretical Frameworks

Some prominent theorists and mental health practitioners have developed theories to understand chronic illness. The conceptual frameworks of John Rolland, Juliette Corbin, Anselm Strauss, Irene Morof Lubkin, and Pamala Larsen are presented in this section.

John Rolland

Rolland's theoretical model has three dimensions: the psychosocial typology of the illness, the time phase of the illness, and the illness-specific components of family.

Rolland's theoretical model postulates that there are three time phases of chronic illness: crisis phase, chronic phase, and terminal phase.

There are two styles within the individual's and family's life cycle: centripetal (closeness) and centrifugal (disengagement).

John Rolland (1984, 1987, 1988a, 1988b, 1990) postulated that chronic illness is an impediment to health with the potential to completely consume the individual's life and the lives of those close to the person. Rolland's model has three dimensions: the **psychosocial typology** of the illness, the time phase of the illness, and the illness-specific components of family. According to Rolland's model, chronic illness affects every dimension of a person, and to understand chronic disease it is crucial to consider the psychosocial typology. Analysis of the psychosocial typology reveals the concepts of onset, course, outcome, and degree of incapacitation. The onset of the illness is classified as either acute or gradual. The course of the illness is progressive, constant, or relapsing/episodic. The outcome of the illness is its ability to cause death or limit the life span. The degree of incapacitation is the proportion of disability or impairment caused by the chronic illness (Rolland, 1984).

Rolland's model postulates three time phases of chronic illness. The initial phase is the *crisis phase*. This involves the time period prior to the diagnosis of the disease through the initial adaptation to the disease. The second phase is the *chronic phase*, involving the period after initial adaptation to the illness until issues of death and terminal illness predominate. The third phase is the *terminal phase*, which surrounds death, and includes a pretrial phase where the thought of death becomes prominent (1990).

Rolland's model also addresses family attributes that impact on chronic illness, including the family's illness belief system; the transgenerational history of illness, loss, and crisis; and the interface of the illness, the individual, and family life cycles (Rolland, 1990). He further hypothesizes that the individual's and family's values, culture, religion, belief system, world view, and family paradigm are integral components of the illness belief system (1988a). Rolland believes that how people have dealt with past stressors and the evolution of that adaptation over time are important aspects when examining the client's history of coping with illness, loss, and crisis.

Critical Thinking Question How do different family attributes impact upon how an individual with a chronic illness will be able to cope with the lifelong challenge of the disease?

For individual and family development, Rolland (1987) emphasizes the need to examine the life cycle or course of development of the individual, family, and illness and the structure of the underlying pattern of one's own or the family's life at any point in the cycle. There are two styles within the individual's and family's life cycle, centripetal (closeness) and centrifugal (disengagement). In the *centripetal style*, a person is involved with family life and works on its development rather than on the external world. In the *centrifugal style*, the person's and family's focus shifts outside themselves to the environment.

Juliette Corbin and Anselm Strauss

Corbin and Strauss (1992) developed a conceptual model to help nurses address chronic illness. Strauss and colleagues (1984) state that to treat a chronically ill individual adequately, the person must be given ample medical, psychological, and social knowledge including, but not limited to, how to deal with and manage the illness and how the illness, its management, and its symptoms affect the life of the client and the client's family and significant others.

Strauss and co-authors (1984) characterize chronic diseases differently from other pathologies. Chronic illnesses are multiple and long-term diseases, have an uncertain nature, are disproportionately intrusive, and are expensive. They require much greater efforts at palliation and a wide variety of ancillary services.

Corbin and Strauss's **trajectory model** identifies the course of the chronic illness as having an uncertain trajectory that requires those with the illness, their family members, and their healthcare practitioners to work together to shape the illness. The model comprises the following seven key concepts (Corbin & Strauss, 1991):

1. *Trajectory phasing* encompasses the various stages or modifications of chronic illness.
2. *Trajectory projection* covers the individual's feelings about and perception of the course of the illness.
3. The *trajectory scheme* is the overall plan that shapes the course of the illness, controls symptomatology, and deals with disability.
4. Conditions influence management, affecting the method by and degree to which the trajectory scheme is carried out.
5. *Trajectory management* shapes the course of the illness.
6. The *biographic and everyday living impact* is how the illness and its management modify the individual's aspects of self and the way activities of daily living are affected by the many aspects of the person.
7. The *reciprocal impact* is the consequence component that results from the interaction among biography, everyday activities, and illness.

In their conceptual model, Corbin and Strauss describe the person's need to establish a new "biography" that is a reshaping of identity, away from who the person was before the diagnosis and toward who the person becomes. This biography of self includes all experiences with the disease itself and with the healthcare system, and the person's new ways of relating to friends, colleagues, family, and even strangers (Corbin & Strauss, 1992).

They also postulate that illness is experienced in eight stages or phases (Corbin & Strauss, 1992):

- *Onset:* The diagnosis has been made and the disease begins.
- *Stable:* The person maintains everyday activities—work, school, family, and fun.
- *Unstable:* The person is unable to keep symptoms under control and life is disrupted while the person works to regain stability.
- *Acute:* Severe and unrelieved symptoms, and/or the development of complications necessitate hospitalization or bed rest to bring the illness under control.
- *Crisis:* A life-threatening episode occurs and emergency services are necessary.
- *Comeback:* The person, by working hard, gradually returns from periods of instability, acute episodes, and crisis to an acceptable way of life.
- *Downward:* Gradual physical decline is accompanied by increasing disability and continuous alterations in everyday life activities.
- *Dying:* The person relinquishes everyday life interests and activities, brings closure to his or her biography, lets go, and dies peacefully.

The client with a chronic illness moves back and forth among these stages until there are no longer any resources that can mitigate the condition's increasingly downward spiral and death occurs.

Corbin and Strauss's trajectory model identifies the course of the chronic illness as having an uncertain trajectory that requires those with the illness, their family members, and their healthcare practitioners to work together to shape the illness.

Corbin and Strauss in their conceptual model recognize that illness is experienced in eight stages or phases: onset, stable, unstable, acute, crisis, comeback, downward, and dying.

Critical Thinking Question How might a client with a chronic mental illness experience coping with the condition in a trajectory model and move among at least three stages or phases?

Rolland and Corbin and Strauss recognize how varied chronic illnesses are. Both models address the unpredictability of chronic disease as well. This unpredictability adds to the stress of managing the illness. According to these models, chronic illness is very different from acute illness. Chronic physical and mental illness cause a great deal of continual stress and loss; mental illness also involves significant loss, grieving, and diminished self-worth and self-esteem.

Chronic physical and mental illness cause a great deal of continual stress and loss; mental illness also involves significant loss, grieving, and diminished self-worth and self-esteem.

Irene Morof Lubkin and Pamala Larsen

Nurse theorists have utilized the models of Rolland and Corbin and Strauss to address various health concerns. Lubkin and Larsen (2006) challenge the nursing community to recognize that the current acute care system is grossly inadequate and that the needs of a growing elderly population (the aging "baby boomers") and others with chronic illness do not fit within the current paradigm of health care. Curtin and Lubkin offer as a definition of chronic illness, "the irreversible presence, accumulation, or latency of disease states or impairments that involve the total human environment for supportive care and self-care, maintenance of function, and prevention of further disability" (1995, pp. 6–7). When the client experiences either a physical or a mental chronic illness, such factors as the trajectory of the illness, stigma, chronic pain, social isolation, altered mobility, fatigue, body image, quality of life, family impact, caregiver stress, and powerlessness can impact on the client.

> Lubkin and Larsen define chronic illness as the irreversible presence, accumulation, or latency of disease states or impairments that involve the total human environment for supportive care and self-care, maintenance of function, and prevention of further disability.

> Chronic illness is the most important health problem in the United States, with an estimated 133 million persons currently living with one chronic illness. Approximately 157 million individuals are expected to have a chronic illness by 2020.

> The mental disorders mostly likely to result in chronic disease are schizophrenia, bipolar disorder, and major depression.

Incidence and Prevalence

Chronic disease, whether physical or mental in origin, is occurring throughout the United States with increasing prevalence every year. It is the most important health problem in America. The Partnership for Solutions (2004) estimated that 133 million persons are living with one chronic illness and that approximately 157 million individuals will have a chronic illness by 2020.

Chronic mental illness affects people of all ages, races, socioeconomic levels, and walks of life and can occur at any stage of the life cycle. The National Institute of Mental Health (NIMH)-funded study known as the National Comorbidity Survey Replication (2005) used modern psychiatric standards to estimate the prevalence of mental disorders in a nationally representative sample. Although the survey reports that 26% of the general population reported symptoms consistent with a diagnosis of a mental disorder, the prevalence rates probably were underestimated because the survey did not include the homeless or institutionalized populations in its data collection.

The study spotlighted its finding that mental disorders are the chronic disorders of young people in the United States (National Institute of Mental Health, 2005). The study also noted that:

- Mental illness begins very early in life; half of all lifetime mental disorders begin by age 14 and three quarters by age 24.
- Unlike physical conditions, young people with mental illness suffer disability when they are in the prime of their lives and when they should be most productive.
- Prevalence rates increase from the 18–29 age group to the next oldest age group of 30–44, and then decline.
- Females have a higher rate of mood and anxiety disorders; men have a higher rate of substance use disorders and impulse-control disorders.

Clinical Example

Ron (33 years old) has been diagnosed since adolescence with schizophrenia, evolving into undifferentiated chronic schizophrenia with acute exacerbations. Ron has had many losses. He lost his father at a young age, and he lost his childhood by assuming his father's responsibilities. College became impossible due to exacerbations of his illness, and he lost his dream of becoming an architect by dropping out of school. Ron lost his dyadic relationship with his wife when his daughter was born, and he lost his job and income as a result of both a physical illness and untoward side effects from his medication. Ron's successful treatment ended when his clozapine (Clozaril) had to be discontinued. His level of functioning deteriorated with each exacerbation and his poor response to other drug therapy. Ron lost his family life when he was moved into a group home, and his wife decided to leave him, taking their daughter. He refused to take medications or participate in treatment groups when he heard about losing his job and family, resulting in a rehospitalization.

Ron's recent life has changed with the exacerbation of his schizophrenic symptoms, and he is not functioning adequately in his roles of husband, father, and employee. The illness's overwhelming impact on his past, current, and future life is evident.

Etiology and Physiology

The mental disorders most likely to result in chronic disease are schizophrenia, major depressive disorder, and bipolar disorder. These are the most prevalent chronic psychiatric disorders.

Schizophrenia is a heterogeneous brain disease. The course of the disorder varies, and symptoms include hallucinations, delusions, and disordered thought. Clients with schizophrenia are unable to experience pleasure, have a diminished emotional range, experience difficulty making choices, and have an ego breakdown with boundary disruption. For a complete discussion of schizophrenia see Chapter 15.

The serious mood disorders of major depressive disorder and bipolar disorder alter affect, mood, behavior, and thought. Major depressive disorder is accompanied by restricted mood, negative affect, and diminished level of functioning that is often seen with fatigue; feelings of worthlessness, hopelessness, and helplessness; weight change (usually a loss); sleep change (usually insomnia); suicidal ideas, gestures, or both; loss of interest or pleasure; psychomotor slowing; and bodily aches and concerns. Bipolar disorder is another mood disorder in which the individual experiences cyclical changes between extreme highs (mania) and extreme lows (depression). The same individual exhibits symptoms of both mania and depression, depending on where the illness is on its cycle. For a complete discussion of mood disorders see Chapter 16.

Clinical Course and Complications

One specific clinical course for all chronic mental illnesses does not exist; however, these disorders are best understood collectively within a chronicity frame of reference.

All chronic mental illnesses impact both the client and those closest to them. The illness affects others around the client, such as family members, classmates, co-workers, peers, and neighbors. Chronic mental illness is long-term, with relapses consisting of periods of relative stability and adequate functioning to periods of more acute symptomatology. Chronic mental illnesses have additional consequences, including complications of the primary illness; pharmacotherapy reactions, including mediocre effectiveness of medication or positive effectiveness of medication with intolerable or life-threatening side or toxic effects; changes in life circumstances, such as altered income, lifestyle, and roles; and even unforeseen events, such as encounters with police, the judicial system, and incarceration.

Critical Thinking Question What types of challenges do you think that a 20-year-old, who has been coping with a mental illness since late childhood, might experience in a workplace or in college?

Clients with mental illness and their families go through stages of adjustment to the illness, often at widely varying times or levels of understanding. Families experience different losses; for example, the client is absent from family activities when hospitalized, incarcerated, or unable to participate because of disease symptomatology.

Clinical Example

Matthew (58 years old) is a recently remarried businessman who is brought into the psychiatric emergency room by the local police. He is dirty, unkempt, unshaven, and profoundly sad looking. When the staff calls his home, Matthew's wife reports that he has not been home or at work for 3 days, but he did call to say that he was alright. He refused to talk about what was bothering him, but would cry for prolonged periods on the call. In the ER, he turns away from the psychiatrist, refuses to make eye contact, crouches in a corner, and rocks back and forth crying and wringing his hands. According to his healthcare record, Matthew was previously hospitalized for depression in both his 20s and 30s.

Matthew is admitted to the in-patient unit for observation, individual therapy, and medication management. For the first 2 days, he continues to cry, refuses to care for himself, is sleeping erratically, and only picks at his food. He tries to both cut himself with a plastic knife and hang himself with a string of paper clips and tells staff that he is such a failure, "I can't even kill myself." Matthew shares with his nurse that he had been demoted at work because "the bosses don't like me, they think that I am a jerk"; according to Matthew's wife, it was because of cutbacks in the company and that he was retained because of his skills. While he accepts his medication, he frequently tells staff that he is afraid of becoming a "druggie" and that the medication will make him "less of a man to his bride." Matthew is diagnosed as having a major depressive disorder.

In another type of loss, the client cannot participate appropriately in family interactions. Permanent family disruption can occur by the client either abandoning the family or committing suicide. The individual also often experiences family-related losses, lowered economic status because of job loss, loss of a place to live because of eviction, diminished mental functioning when the illness is exacerbated, an inability or difficulty returning to premorbid functioning after the psychosis has stabilized, loss of involvement with significant others when relationships are strained consistently, an increased probability of additional psychopathology resulting from the use of substances or alcohol to cope, and impairment in physiologic functioning as a result of adverse reactions to psychopharmacologic agents.

> Chronic mental illness is long-term, with relapses consisting of periods of relative stability and adequate functioning to periods of more acute symptomatology.

Classic grief reactions are exhibited both by the individual with the mental illness and by family members—they grieve for what might have been or what has been lost. These persons experience the stages of denial, anger, bargaining, depression, acceptance, modification, and resolution. Some individuals, including the client with the mental illness as well as significant others, may not progress beyond the depression stage of grieving. These individuals are unable to reach acceptance and resolution until they receive

> Classic grief reactions are exhibited both by the individual with the mental illness and by family members as they experience the stages of denial, anger, bargaining, depression, acceptance, modification, and resolution.

Clinical Example

Bonnie (42 years old) was initially diagnosed with bipolar disorder in her senior year in high school. During college, she had frequent and major fluctuations in her mood, resulting in her changing roommates three times in her freshman year, twice in her sophomore year, and finally choosing to live alone off-campus in her last 2 years. In her senior year, she painted the apartment in combinations of dark red and black resulting in angry altercations with her landlord.

Bonnie is artistically talented, but her ability to focus on her painting and sculpture is related to how controlled her bipolar symptoms are. In her mid-30s, she destroyed a dozen paintings the night before a gallery-sponsored exhibit because of a depressive episode. The exhibit was cancelled and never rescheduled. During the same time period, she was married and divorced twice. After the second divorce, she entered individual psychotherapy, was placed on medication, and joined a support group. After a year, Bonnie reported feeling much better and opened an arts and crafts store with a member of her support group.

In the last few months she has been experiencing significant and ever increasing mood fluctuations—periods of euphoria, increased energy, hypersexuality, greatly reduced sleep patterns, and even sometimes depression. Two weeks ago in a 48-hour period, Bonnie baked 200 cupcakes for a church bake sale. She became angry, throwing cupcakes against the wall when the bake sale organizers questioned why she did so much baking. Her store partner called Bonnie's therapist who suggested that she be brought into the clinic. After a lengthy session, in which she admitted to stopping her medication because she felt really "much better and in control," Bonnie agreed with her therapist to a voluntary in-patient admission. Afterwards, Bonnie's store partner expressed her frustration that Bonnie had precipitated her relapse and worried that such behavior was jeopardizing both their business and personal relationships.

extensive support and **psychoeducation** based on the psychiatric rehabilitative model.

Management and Treatment

Ongoing integrated nursing case management can reduce the client's psychiatric symptoms, the impairments associated with the illness, and the disruptions in living caused by the chronic mental illness.

Advanced practice registered nurses functioning as psychotherapists can effectively provide individual, group, and family psychotherapy.

Clients with chronic mental and physical disorders improve more rapidly with specific, well-planned nursing interventions. Nurses should adopt caring, nonthreatening, nonjudgmental, accepting, and long-term approaches to care for all individuals with chronic mental illness.

Ongoing nursing case management is necessary to reduce psychiatric symptoms, the impairments associated with the illness, and the disruptions in living caused by the chronic mental illness. In psychiatric-mental health nursing, case management involves "population-specific nursing knowledge coupled with research, knowledge of the social and legal systems related to mental health, and expertise to engage a wide range of services for the patient, regardless of setting . . . [these] activities may be with a single client or with a designated population such as the seriously and persistent mentally ill" (ANA, 2007). Nursing management should be comprehensive and integrated with the entire multidisciplinary treatment team, social system, and community. Integrated care benefits clients by following them through the healthcare system and anticipating or eliminating problems.

Nursing management for those with chronic mental illness, whether they are in the hospital, a long-term care facility, or the community, must incorporate several elements to prevent the individual from becoming totally disabled. The nurse needs to employ an individualized and integrated approach. The nurse works with the client and family to make sure their needs are met. The nursing plan needs to be individualized, integrated with the care provided by other members of the psychiatric team, and realistic. When family members and the client are actively involved in planning, it helps in the development of realistic goals that meet and satisfy the client's and family's needs.

Counseling for grief and loss is critical because the family and the individual incur multiple losses as a result of the mental illness. If both the client and family can work through their losses, this assists them in accepting and managing the disease. Individual, group, and family psychotherapy can benefit the client and significant others. Advanced practice registered nurses (APRNs) functioning as psychotherapists can effectively provide these therapies as well as psychopharmacological management.

Stress management helps clients and their families to cope with the stressors associated with chronic mental illness. Many stressors exist for clients with major psychiatric conditions and chronic mental illness, and the clients' coping mechanisms are usually impaired. Happy life events such as weddings, holiday dinners, birthday parties, and vacations that are pleasurable to most people may be overly stressful to someone who has schizophrenia, bipolar disorder, or major depressive disorder (**Figure 28-1**). The nurse needs to utilize stress management techniques in every interaction with individuals who have chronic mental illnesses.

Critical Thinking Question Why would a happy life event become a negative stressor for a client with chronic mental illness?

Figure 28-1 **Happy life events, such as weddings, may be overly stressful to someone who has schizophrenia, bipolar disorder, or major depressive disorder.**

Empowering individuals allows them to be "pilots" of their own mental health care. The nurse's role is that of an advocate, not a "rescuer." The nurse needs to work with the client and the family on realistic expectations. Using empowering techniques allows the person and the family to control their decision making and assists in maintaining their hopefulness. Empowerment helps clients gain control over their lives, which leads to increased self-esteem, greater feelings of self-worth, improved self-concept, and a better self-image.

Community education is essential to assist the public in understanding, accepting, reducing the stigma of, and curbing resistance and discrimination against those who live with a chronic mental illness. Psychiatric rehabilitative techniques, when utilized within the community, benefit this population. For clients accessing services through a managed care system, **psychiatric rehabilitation** is a necessity (Anthony, 1997).

Comprehensive and integrated health care also is required for this population. Nurses must listen to their clients to promote their active involvement in treatment. Although difficult problems to address for clients with chronic mental illness, housing is necessary for those who are homeless, and adequate mental health care must be provided for those who are incarcerated. Nurses can orchestrate links between services so that the individual does not slip through any part of the system, especially when the client needs ongoing care to prevent reoccurrence.

Crisis intervention is necessary to address critical issues such as **homelessness**, incarceration, and recurring psychiatric symptomatology. Providing crisis intervention to assist clients during exacerbations of their illness is essential, because it reassures them that the nurse or other members of the multidisciplinary team are available. The nurse should address both personal and environmental safety to assist the client and family in addressing their anxiety and anger. This is paramount in the hospital and community settings so that the client, their families and significant others, and society are free from harm.

> Crisis intervention assists clients during exacerbations of their illness and reassures them that the nurse and other members of the multidisciplinary team are available.

The psychopharmacologic medications used in the treatment of chronic mental illness are primarily the conventional antipsychotics, antidepressants, and mood stabilizers. Nurses need to know the clinical indications for these medications, adverse and toxic reactions, and therapeutic dose information, as well as related nursing implications. (See Chapter 5 for detailed information about psychopharmacology.) The nurse must share medication information with the client and the family and stress the importance of compliance with the prescribed regimen.

The nurse also endeavors to provide to clients, as appropriate, psychiatric rehabilitation, including psychoeducation, basic cognitive and academic skills training, group work, social skills training, vocational training, interpersonal skill building, behavior modification (making small life and behavioral changes at a time), and medication management. A psychiatric rehabilitation approach allows for the active involvement by the client in his or her own mental health care. The client is taught assertiveness and appropriate decision making skills to function adequately in the least restrictive environment.

Psychiatric rehabilitation encompasses relearning skills and competencies needed for successful interpersonal, social, and vocational functioning. Psychiatric rehabilitation is critical in both hospital and community mental healthcare settings to prevent those with chronic mental illness from becoming further debilitated. According to the U.S. Psychiatric Rehabilitation Association (USPRA), psychiatric rehabilitation services promote "recovery, full community integration and improved quality of life for persons who have been diagnosed with any mental health condition that seriously impairs functioning" and these services "focus on helping individuals rediscover skills and access resources needed to increase their capacity to be successful and satisfied in the living, working, learning and social environments of their choice" (2007). This association promulgates

> Clients with chronic mental illness who are homeless must have their housing needs met, and those who are incarcerated must receive adequate mental health services within the correctional facility.

Psychiatric rehabilitation encompasses relearning skills and competencies needed for successful interpersonal, social, and vocational functioning.

Support groups for clients with chronic mental illness promote self-confidence, exposure to other adequate coping behaviors, increased problem-solving ability, and a sense of identity and belonging.

The Assertive Community Treatment (ACT) model is an interdisciplinary team approach to the care of people with severe mental illness providing services in the individual's own natural setting, regardless of place.

15 Core Principles of Psychiatric Rehabilitation (USPRA, 2007):

1. Recovery is the ultimate goal of psychiatric rehabilitation. Interventions must facilitate the process of recovery.
2. Psychiatric rehabilitation practices help people re-establish normal roles in the community and their reintegration into community life.
3. Psychiatric rehabilitation practices facilitate the development of personal support networks.
4. Psychiatric rehabilitation practices facilitate an enhanced quality of life for each person receiving services.
5. All people have the capacity to learn and grow.
6. People receiving services have the right to direct their own affairs, including those that are related to their psychiatric disability.
7. All people are to be treated with respect and dignity.
8. Psychiatric rehabilitation practitioners make conscious and consistent efforts to eliminate labeling and discrimination, particularly discrimination based upon a disabling condition.
9. Culture and/or ethnicity play an important role in recovery. They are sources of strength and enrichment for the person and the services.
10. Psychiatric rehabilitation interventions build on the strengths of each person.
11. Psychiatric rehabilitation services are to be coordinated, accessible, and available as long as needed.
12. All services are to be designed to address the unique needs of each individual, consistent with the individual's cultural values and norms.
13. Psychiatric rehabilitation practices actively encourage and support the involvement of persons in normal community activities, such as school and work, throughout the rehabilitation process.
14. The involvement and partnership of persons receiving services and family members is an essential ingredient of the process of rehabilitation and recovery.
15. Psychiatric rehabilitation practitioners should constantly strive to improve the services they provide.

Social support groups also benefit those with chronic mental illness and their family members by helping them cope with their symptoms. Participation in support groups often promotes self-confidence, exposure to other adequate coping behaviors, increased problem-solving ability, and a sense of identity and belonging. Nurses need to encourage clients to participate in appropriate psychotherapeutic and social support groups. When appropriate, clients can be encouraged to include assertiveness programs in the treatment plan to help them make decisions regarding their health care, work, and living arrangements.

Outreach is a necessary part of treatment, because it provides a support network for the client. Outreach support helps individuals with chronic mental illness and their families negotiate the system, and the nurse should be available throughout the process. Case management and monitoring are crucial in the community setting, where clients often do not have the same amount of support provided in the hospital. As a case manager, the nurse can assist in coordinating services and making them accessible to the client and family.

In community-based care, the psychiatric-mental health nurse delivers care "in partnership with patients in their homes, work sites, mental health clinics and programs, health maintenance organizations, shelters and clinics for the homeless, crisis centers, senior centers, group homes, and other community settings" (ANA, 2007, p. 25). One method is the Assertive Community Treatment (ACT) model which is "an interdisciplinary team approach to the care of people with severe mental illness. It provides services in the individual's natural setting, including homeless shelters" (ANA, 2007, p. 25). The ACT's goals are "to help patients meet the requirements of community living after discharge from another more restrictive form of care, and to reduce recurrences of hospitalization" (ANA, 2007, p. 25).

The ACT model of care evolved out of the work of Arnold Marx, MD, Leonard Stein, and Mary Ann Test, PhD, in the late 1960s. In addition to psychiatric services and case management, ACT teams (psychiatry, nursing, social work, rehabilitation, counseling) provide employment and housing assistance, family support and education, substance abuse services, and other services as needed to maintain the client in the community. ACT programs exist in the United States, Canada, and England, and the Department of Veterans Affairs has implemented the ACT model across the United States for its veterans. ACT services are available 24 hours a day, 365 days a year (Assertive Community Treatment Association, 2007).

Self-esteem, self-efficacy, life skills, and social support need to be fortified, and stressors need to be reduced for the client to benefit from treatment. The key to successful mental health treatment for the chronically mentally ill is that it should be done slowly and patiently. This allows the client and significant others to carefully institute realistic behavioral and other life changes. The various agencies must collaborate in treatment and include the client with a chronic mental illness in the care planning. The client, family, school, social services department, drug abuse treatment program, health department, housing agencies, criminal justice system, and multidisciplinary team of mental health practitioners (psychiatrists; psychiatric nurses; social workers; psychologists; medical physicians; occupational, recreational, and other activity therapists; dieticians; spiritual leaders; employment counselors; and other specialists as necessary) need to be involved collectively, providing integrated, holistic mental health care.

Considerations for Client and Family Education

Psychoeducation involves teaching clients, their families, and significant others about the disease or condition (i.e., the specific chronic mental illness), types of psychotherapy, medication management, complementary therapies, compliance with different treatment modalities, rehabilitation, signs of relapse, and community resources. By improving the client's and family's knowledge base and understanding, there is a greater potential for ongoing control of the client's condition. Clients should also be taught skills to successfully modify their lifestyles, enhance their therapies, and live productive lives.

Psychoeducation also involves teaching coping strategies to the clients' families, significant others, and caregivers in order to help them deal more effectively with the client. It can help reduce stress and anxiety within the family and community. The family is assisted in understanding the prolonged course of the chronic mental illness and its impact on family dynamics and functioning.

Summary

Individuals with chronic mental illnesses and their families need care from motivated, realistic, and caring nurses. Nurses need to employ effective approaches to properly assist individuals in living and coping with chronic illness on a daily basis. Such approaches include:

- Using concrete and simple goals to allow individuals the opportunity for successful attainment
- Teaching stress management and coping strategies
- Accepting the trajectory nature of chronic illness
- Being realistic

Nurses must continually evaluate themselves to ensure that they provide attentive care for those

Implications for Evidence-Based Practice

Over the past 40 years, practitioners caring for those with chronic mental illness have sought to reduce the re-hospitalization experiences of their clients. Husted and Jorgens (2000) proposed that therapies or procedures that work in one geographic locale might have very different results in another. They determined that mental health practitioners need to take into account where the client lives. The usual practice of placing rural clients with chronic mental illness in areas of greater population density may actually lead to more cognitive and perceptual disruptions in the clients. Therefore, decisions regarding placement of clients, who might be more comfortable and functional in a rural setting, should be considered in working toward developing a milieu that minimizes the risk of re-hospitalization for these clients.

Hayes and co-authors (2006) studied the effectiveness of using cognitive therapy in the treatment of clients with chronic mental illness. In a study that examined the added benefits of cognitive versus supportive therapy to the treatment milieu, the authors determined that the clients who participated in the cognitive groups were more motivated and active than those in the supportive group.

with chronic mental illness. Nurses need to be vigilant and active advocates in the healthcare, social service, and political arenas to ensure that the necessary services for clients with chronic mental illness are accessible, coordinated, and provided.

Annotated References

American Nurses Association. (2007). *Psychiatric-mental health nursing: Scope and standards of practice.* Silver Spring, MD: Author.

Anthony, W. (1997, September). *Psychiatric rehabilitation of schizophrenia patients in managed care: Why it is a preferred approach.* Paper presented at the conference, Psychiatric Rehabilitation of Schizophrenia: Current Trends and Future Directions, Rochester, NY.

This presentation answered the six key questions of what, where, why, how, when, and who for designing psychiatric rehabilitation within managed care systems.

Assertive Community Treatment Association. (2007). *ACT model.* Retrieved September 4, 2007, from http://www.actassociation.org/actModel

This site provides information on the history of the ACT model, persons served by ACT, and a set of guiding principles.

Corbin, J. M., & Strauss, A. (1991). A nursing model for chronic illness management based on the trajectory framework. *Scholarly Inquiry for Nursing Practice, 5*, 155–174.

This article presents Corbin and Strauss's conceptual model for nursing practice.

Corbin, J. M., & Strauss, A. (1992). A nursing model for chronic illness management based on the trajectory framework. In P. Woog (Ed.), *The chronic illness trajectory framework: The Corbin and Strauss nursing model* (pp. 9–28). New York: Springer.

In this chapter, the authors present their conceptual model, a chronic illness trajectory. They further discuss implications for nursing practice, teaching, research, and policy making.

Curtin, M., & Lubkin, I. (1995). What is chronicity? In I. Lubkin (Ed.), *Chronic illness: Impact and interventions* (3rd ed.). Sudbury, MA: Jones & Bartlett.

This textbook illustrates how healthcare professionals can effectively assist the chronically ill in better managing the course of their illness and their lives.

Hayes, S. A., Hope, D. A., Terryberry-Spohr, L. S., Spaulding, W. D., Vandyke, M., Elting, D. T., et al. (2006). Discriminating between cognitive and supportive group therapies for chronic mental illness. *Journal of Nervous and Mental Disorders, 194*(8), 603–609.

This study examined the growing evidence that cognitive therapy is effective in the treatment of clients with chronic mental illness.

Husted, J., & Jorgens, A. (2000). Best practice: Population density as a factor in the rehospitalization of persons with serious and persistent mental illness. *Psychiatric Services, 51*(5), 603–605.

This article considers the implications of placing clients with chronic mental illness in areas of greater population density and the impact on re-hospitalization.

Lubkin, I. M., & Larsen, P. D. (Eds.). (2006). *Chronic illness: Impact and interventions* (6th ed.). Sudbury, MA: Jones & Bartlett.

This textbook presents the various aspects of chronic illness that influence both patients and their families.

National Commission on Chronic Illness. (1957). *Chronic illness in the United States* (Vol. I). Cambridge, MA: Harvard University Press.

This publication gives an overview of chronic illness in the United States, including an operational definition, prevalence, incidence, prevention, and summary of information on chronic disorders.

National Institute of Mental Health. (2005). *NIMH-funded national comorbidity survey replication study (NCS-R).* Retrieved September 2, 2007, from www.nimh.nih.gov/healthinformation/ncs-r.cfm

The landmark study is described in four papers that document the prevalence and severity of specific mental disorders. The papers provide significant new data on the impairment—such as days lost from work—caused by specific disorders, including mood, anxiety, and substance abuse disorders.

Partnership for Solutions. (2004). *Chronic conditions: Making the case for ongoing care.* Retrieved April 12, 2007, from http://www.partnershipforsolutions.org/statistics/prevalence.html

The partnership, led by Johns Hopkins University and The Robert Wood Johnson Foundation, is an initiative to improve the care and quality of life for the more than 125 million Americans with chronic health conditions.

Rolland, J. S. (1984). Toward a psychosocial typology of chronic and life-threatening illness. *Family Systems Medicine, 2*, 245–263.

This article addresses Rolland's conceptual model for chronic and life-threatening illnesses.

Rolland, J. S. (1987). Family illness paradigms: Evolution and significance. *Family Systems Medicine, 5*, 482–503.

In this article Rolland clarifies important variables of family-illness paradigms and describes how beliefs shape the manner in which families adapt to chronic and life-threatening illnesses.

Rolland, J. S. (1988a). A conceptual model of chronic and life-threatening illness and its impact on families. In C. S. Chilman, E. W. Nunnally, & F. N. Cox (Eds.), *Chronic illness and disability* (pp. 17–68). Beverly Hills, CA: Sage.

In this chapter, Rolland discusses his conceptual model in relation to chronic illnesses within families.

Rolland, J. S. (1988b). Chronic illness and the family life cycle. In B. Carter & M. McGoldrick (Eds.), *The changing family life cycle: A framework for family therapy* (2nd ed., pp. 433–456). New York: Gardner Press.

In this chapter, Rolland explains chronic illness as an evolutionary thread that intertwines with the individual's and family's life cycles.

Rolland, J. S. (1990). The impact of illness on the family. In R. E. Rakel (Ed.), *Textbook of family practice* (4th ed., pp. 80–100). Philadelphia: W. B. Saunders.

In this chapter, Rolland presents his three-dimensional conceptual model and how chronic disease affects the life cycles of the person and his or her family.

Strauss, A. L., Corbin, J., Fagerhaugh, S., Glaser, B. G., Maines, D., Suczek, B., et al. (1984). *Chronic illness and the quality of life* (2nd ed.). St. Louis, MO: C. V. Mosby.

These authors give a comprehensive picture of the problems of living with chronic illness, patient hospital experiences, and the healthcare system and chronic illness.

U.S. Psychiatric Rehabilitation Association. (2007). *Psychiatric rehabilitation principles.* Retrieved September 4, 2007, from www.uspra.org

This association is a membership organization supporting mental health recovery through psychiatric rehabilitation. It brings together mental health practitioners, clients, and families.

Internet Resources

http://nursing.jbpub.com/psychiatric

Visit http://nursing.jbpub.com/psychiatric for interactive exercises, NCLEX review questions, WebLinks, and more.

Psychiatric-Mental Health Standards of Nursing Practice[1]

Psychiatric-mental health nurses, like those in other nursing specialties, follow standards and guidelines in their practice. According to the American Nurses Association (ANA), standards of nursing practice, including the standards of practice and professional performance, are "authoritative statements by which the nursing profession describes the responsibilities for which its practitioners are accountable…standards reflect the values and priorities of the profession…provide direction for professional nursing practice and a framework for the evaluation of this practice… standards also define the nursing profession's accountability to the public and the outcomes for which registered nurses are responsible" (ANA, 2003, p. 1). Meanwhile, guidelines are based on "available scientific evidence and expert opinion" and describe "a process of patient care management, which has the potential for improving the quality of clinical and patient decision-making… practice guidelines address the care of specific patient populations or phenomena, whereas standards provide a broad framework for practice" (ANA, 2003, p. 5).

The ANA has been actively engaged in the development of nursing standards since the 1960s. The first generic standards of practice were developed in 1973, and the *Standards of Clinical Nursing Practice* were first published in 1991, with a revision in 1998. In 2003, ANA published *Nursing: Scope and Standards of Practice*. These generic standards are composed of standards of practice (assessment, diagnosis, outcomes identification, planning, implementation, evaluation) and standards of professional performance (quality of practice, education, professional practice evaluation, collegiality, collaboration, ethics, research, resource utilization, leadership). Specific measurement criteria are provided by ANA in their published documents for each of the standards. Most specialty nursing organizations have agreed to use these generic practice standards as the model for the development of specialty standards of practice.

Included in this appendix are ANA's *Psychiatric-Mental Health Nursing: Scope and Standards of Practice* (2007). Also available from American Nurses Publishing are standards for many different specialty areas including *Standards for Addictions Nursing Practice with Selected Diagnoses and Criteria* (1988) and *Intellectual and Developmental Disabilities Nursing: Scope and Standards of Practice* (2004).

Standards of Psychiatric–Mental Health Nursing Practice[1]

***Standards of Practice**—These six standards "describe a competent level of nursing care as demonstrated by the critical thinking model known as the nursing process" (ANA, 2003, p. 4).*

Standard 1. Assessment

The psychiatric-mental health registered nurse collects comprehensive health data that is pertinent to the patient's health or situation.

Standard 2. Diagnosis

The psychiatric-mental health registered nurse analyzes the assessment data to determine diagnoses or problems, including level of risk.

Standard 3. Outcomes Identification

The psychiatric-mental health registered nurse identifies expected outcomes for a plan individualized to the patient or to the situation.

[1] Reprinted with permission from American Nurses Association. (2007). *Psychiatric-mental health nursing: Scope and standards of practice.* Silver Spring, MD: Author.

Standard 4. Planning

The psychiatric-mental health registered nurse develops a plan that prescribes strategies and alternatives to attain expected outcomes.

Standard 5. Implementation

The psychiatric-mental health registered nurse implements the identified plan.

Standard 5a. Coordination of Care

The psychiatric-mental health registered nurse coordinates care delivery.

Standard 5b. Health Teaching and Health Promotion

The psychiatric-mental health registered nurse employs strategies to promote health and a safe environment.

Standard 5c. Milieu Therapy

The psychiatric-mental health registered nurse provides, structures, and maintains a safe and therapeutic environment in collaboration with patients, families, and other healthcare clinicians.

Standard 5d. Pharmaceutical, Biological, Integrative Therapies

The psychiatric-mental health registered nurse incorporates knowledge of pharmacological, biological, and complementary interventions with applied clinical skills to restore the patient's health and prevent further disability.

Standard 5e. Prescriptive Authority and Treatment

The psychiatric-mental health advanced practice registered nurse uses prescriptive authority, procedures, referrals, treatments, and therapies in accordance with state and federal laws and regulations

Standard 5f. Psychotherapy

The psychiatric-mental health advanced practice registered nurse conducts individual, couples, group, and family psychotherapy using evidence-based psychotherapeutic frameworks and nurse-patient therapeutic relationships.

Standard 5g. Consultation

The psychiatric-mental health advanced practice registered nurse provides consultation to influence the identified plan, enhance the abilities of other clinicians to provide services for patients, and effect change.

Standard 6. Evaluation

The psychiatric-mental health registered nurse evaluates progress toward attainment of expected outcomes.

Standards of Professional Performance— *These nine standards "describe a competent level of behavior in the professional role" and all professional registered nurses are "expected to engage in professional role activities...appropriate to their education and position" (ANA, 2003, p. 4).*

Standard 7. Quality of Practice

The psychiatric-mental health registered nurse systematically enhances the quality and effectiveness of nursing practice.

Standard 8. Education

The psychiatric-mental health registered nurse attains knowledge and competency that reflect current nursing practice.

Standard 9. Professional Practice Evaluation

The psychiatric-mental health registered nurse evaluates one's own practice in relation to the professional practice standards and guidelines, relevant statutes, rules, and regulations.

Standard 10. Collegiality

The psychiatric-mental health registered nurse interacts with and contributes to the professional development of peers and colleagues.

Standard 11. Collaboration

The psychiatric-mental health registered nurse collaborates with patients, family, and others in the conduct of nursing practice.

Standard 12. Ethics

The psychiatric-mental health registered nurse integrates ethical provisions in all areas of practice.

Standard 13. Research

The psychiatric-mental health registered nurse integrates research findings into practice.

Standard 14. Resource Utilization

The psychiatric-mental health registered nurse considers factors related to safety, effectiveness, cost, and impact on practice in the planning and delivery of nursing services.

Standard 15. Leadership

The psychiatric-mental health registered nurse provides leadership in the professional practice setting and the profession.

References

American Nurses Association. (2003). *Nursing: Scope and standards of practice.* Washington, DC: Author.

American Nurses Association. (2007). *Psychiatric-mental health nursing: Scope and standards of practice.* Silver Spring, MD: Author.

APPENDIX II

Common NANDA-I Diagnoses Used in Psychiatric Disorders

In psychiatric-mental health nursing, the nurse should be familiar with two acceptable classification systems: NANDA-International (NANDA-I) Taxonomy II of nursing diagnoses, and the American Psychiatric Association's *Diagnostic and Statistical Manual of Mental Disorders,* 4th ed., Text Revision *(DSM-IV-TR).* The *DSM-IV-TR* classification system is the one most widely used by the four core mental health professions of psychiatry, psychology, nursing, and social work.

According to NANDA-I, a nursing diagnosis is "a clinical judgment about an individual, family, or community response to actual or potential health problems/life processes which provides the basis for definitive therapy toward achievement of outcomes for which a nurse is accountable" (NANDA-I, p. 332). It provides the basis for selection of nursing interventions to achieve outcomes for which the nurse can be held accountable. The NANDA-I Taxonomy II has three levels: domains (13), classes (47), and nursing diagnoses (188). The nursing diagnoses are organized into 13 domains with its subdivision classes. The domains are: health promotion, nutrition, elimination and exchange, activity/rest, perception/cognition, self-perception, role relationships, sexuality, coping/stress tolerance, life principles, safety/protection, comfort, and growth/development.

The psychiatric-mental health nurse should understand how the classifications are used in formulating diagnoses and developing the nursing plan of care. The **Table II-1** compares the *DSM-IV-TR* diagnostic categories with select potential corresponding NANDA-I nursing diagnoses. A complete list of the NANDA-I *Nursing Diagnoses: Definitions and Classification, 2007–2008* is found in **Table II-2.**

Table II-1 *DSM-IV-TR* **Disorders and NANDA-I Nursing Diagnoses Compared**

***DSM-IV-TR* Disorders**	**NANDA-I Nursing Diagnoses**	
Disorders First Diagnosed in Infancy, Childhood, or Adolescence	*00111*	*Delayed growth & development*
	00058	*Risk for impaired parent/infant/child/attachment*
	00060	*Interrupted family processes*
	00016	*Disorganized infant behavior*
	00056	*Impaired parenting*
	00064	*Parental role conflict*
	00130	*Disturbed thought processes*
	00051	*Impaired verbal communication*
	00121	*Disturbed personal identity*
	00140	*Risk for self-directed violence*
Dementia, Delirium, Amnesia, and Cognitive Disorders	*00127*	*Impaired environmental interpretation syndrome*
	00128	*Acute confusion*
	00128	*Chronic confusion*
	00061	*Caregiver strain*
	00155	*Risk for falls*
	00154	*Wandering*
	00101	*Adult failure to thrive*
	00122	*Disturbed sensory perception*

continues

Table II-1 ***DSM-IV-TR*** **Disorders and NANDA-I Nursing Diagnoses Compared (continued)**

Disorder	Code	Nursing Diagnosis
Substance-Related Disorders	*00079*	*Noncompliance*
	00188	*Risk-prone health behavior*
	00174	*Risk for compromised human dignity*
	00122	*Disturbed sensory perception*
	00063	*Dysfunctional family processes: Alcoholism*
	00122	*Disturbed sensory perception*
	00185	*Readiness for enhanced hope*
	00150	*Risk for suicide*
	00131	*Impaired memory*
	00138	*Risk for other-directed violence*
	00069	*Ineffective coping*
	00083	*Decisional conflict re. sobriety*
	00035	*Risk for injury*
Schizophrenia and Other Psychotic Disorders	*00130*	*Disturbed thought process*
	00051	*Impaired verbal communication*
	00109	*Dressing/grooming self-care deficit*
	00074	*Compromised family coping*
	00053	*Social isolation*
	00150	*Risk for suicide*
	00097	*Deficient diversional activity*
	00121	*Disturbed personal identity*
	00122	*Disturbed sensory perception*
	00025	*Risk for imbalanced fluid volume*
Mood Disorders	*00095*	*Insomnia*
	00119	*Chronic low self esteem*
	00137	*Chronic sorrow*
	00140	*Risk for self-directed violence*
	00150	*Risk for suicide*
	00053	*Social isolation*
	00051	*Impaired verbal communication*
	00066	*Spiritual distress*
	00002	*Imbalanced nutrition: Less than body requirements*
	00003	*Risk for imbalanced nutrition: More than body requirements*
Anxiety Disorders	*00148*	*Fear*
	00146	*Anxiety*
	00053	*Social isolation*
	00052	*Impaired social interaction*
	00124	*Hopelessness*
	00119	*Chronic low self-esteem*
	00173	*Risk for acute confusion*
	00078	*Ineffective therapeutic regimen management*
Dissociative Disorders	*00141*	*Post-trauma syndrome*
	00131	*Impaired memory*
	00138	*Risk for other-directed violence*
	00121	*Disturbed personal identity*
	00119	*Chronic low self-esteem*
	00055	*Ineffective role performance*
	00069	*Ineffective coping*
Somatoform Disorders	*00118*	*Disturbed body image*
	00059	*Ineffective sexuality pattern*
	00146	*Anxiety*
	00147	*Death anxiety*
	00132	*Acute pain*
	00133	*Chronic pain*
	00069	*Ineffective coping*
	00075	*Readiness for enhanced coping*
	00099	*Ineffective health maintenance*

Table II-1 ***DSM-IV-TR* Disorders and NANDA-I Nursing Diagnoses Compared (continued)**

Disorder	Code	Nursing Diagnosis
Factitious Disorders	00188	*Risk-prone health behavior*
	00146	*Anxiety*
	00148	*Fear*
	00125	*Powerlessness*
	00177	*Stress overload*
	00138	*Risk for other directed violence*
	00072	*Ineffective denial*
	00071	*Defensive coping*
Sexual and Gender Identity Disorders	00059	*Sexual dysfunction*
	00065	*Ineffective sexuality pattern*
	00126	*Deficient knowledge about ______*
	00153	*Risk for situational low self-esteem*
	00146	*Anxiety*
	00069	*Ineffective coping*
	00060	*Interrupted family processes*
	00142	*Post-trauma syndrome*
	00066	*Spiritual distress*
Eating Disorders	00118	*Disturbed body image*
	00002	*Imbalanced nutrition: Less than body requirements*
	00001	*Imbalanced nutrition: More than body requirements*
	00093	*Fatigue*
	00125	*Powerlessness*
	00054	*Risk for loneliness*
	00069	*Ineffective coping*
	00060	*Interrupted family processes*
	00167	*Readiness for enhanced self-concept*
Sleep Disorders	00173	*Risk for acute confusion*
	00038	*Risk for falls*
	00093	*Fatigue*
	00032	*Ineffective breathing pattern*
	00095	*Insomnia*
	00165	*Readiness for enhanced sleep*
	00078	*Ineffective therapeutic regimen management*
Adjustment and Impulse Disorders	00167	*Readiness for enhanced self-concept*
	00153	*Risk for situational low self-esteem*
	00069	*Ineffective coping*
	00067	*Risk for spiritual distress*
	00083	*Decisional conflict*
	00175	*Moral distress*
	00146	*Anxiety*
	00135	*Complicated grieving*
Personality Disorders	00119	*Chronic low self-esteem*
	00069	*Ineffective coping*
	00071	*Defensive coping*
	00139	*Risk for self-mutilation*
	00121	*Disturbed personal identity*
	00052	*Impaired social interaction*
	00167	*Readiness for enhanced self-concept*

Source: NANDA-I nursing diagnoses are reprinted with permission from: NANDA International. (2007). *Nursing diagnoses: Definitions and classification, 2007–2008*. Philadelphia: Author.

Table II-2 NANDA-I Taxonomy II Domains, Classes, and Diagnoses

Domain 1 Health Promotion

The awareness of well-being or normality of function and the strategies used to maintain control of and enhance that well-being or normality of function

Class 1 Health Awareness Recognition of normal function and well-being

Class 2 Health Management Identifying, controlling, performing, and integrating activities to maintain health and well-being

Approved Diagnoses

00082 Effective therapeutic regimen management
00078 Ineffective therapeutic regimen management
00080 Ineffective family therapeutic regimen management
00081 Ineffective community therapeutic regimen management
00084 Health-seeking behaviors (specify)
00099 Ineffective health maintenance
00098 Impaired home maintenance
00162 Readiness for enhanced therapeutic regimen management
00163 Readiness for enhanced nutrition
00186 Readiness for enhanced immunization status

Domain 2 Nutrition

The activities of taking in, assimilating, and using nutrients for the purposes of tissue maintenance, tissue repair, and the production of energy

Class 1 Ingestion Taking food or nutrients into the body

Approved Diagnoses

00107 Ineffective infant feeding pattern
00103 Impaired swallowing
00002 Imbalanced nutrition: Less than body requirements
00001 Imbalanced nutrition: More than body requirements
00003 Risk for imbalanced nutrition: More than body requirements

Class 2 Digestion The physical and chemical activities that convert foodstuffs into substances suitable for absorption and assimilation

Class 3 Absorption The act of taking up nutrients through body tissues

Class 4 Metabolism The chemical and physical processes occurring in living organisms and cells for the development and use of protoplasm, production of waste and energy, with the release of energy for all vital processes

Approved Diagnoses

00178 Risk for impaired liver function
00179 Risk for unstable glucose level

Class 5 Hydration The taking in and absorption of fluids and electrolytes

Approved Diagnoses

00027 Deficient fluid volume
00028 Risk for deficient fluid volume
00026 Excess fluid volume
00025 Risk for imbalanced fluid volume
00160 Readiness for enhanced fluid balance

Domain 3 Elimination and Exchange

Secretion and excretion of waste products from the body

Class 1 Urinary Function The process of secretion, reabsorption, and excretion of urine

Approved Diagnoses

00016 Impaired urinary elimination
00023 Urinary retention
00021 Total urinary incontinence
00020 Functional urinary incontinence
00017 Stress urinary incontinence
00019 Urge urinary incontinence
00018 Reflex urinary incontinence
00022 Risk for urge urinary incontinence
00166 Readiness for enhanced urinary elimination
00176 Overflow urinary incontinence

Class 2 Gastrointestinal Function The process of absorption and excretion of the end products of digestion

Approved Diagnoses

00014 Bowel incontinence
00013 Diarrhea
00011 Constipation
00015 Risk for constipation
00012 Perceived constipation

Class 3 Integumentary Function The process of secretion and excretion through the skin

Class 4 Respiratory Function The process of exchange of gases and removal of the end products of metabolism

Approved Diagnoses

00030 Impaired gas exchange

Domain 4 Activity/Rest

The production, conservation, expenditure, or balance of energy resources

Class 1 Sleep/Rest Slumber, repose, ease, relaxation, or inactivity

Approved Diagnoses

00096 Sleep deprivation
00165 Readiness for enhanced sleep
00095 Insomnia

Class 2 Activity/Exercise Moving parts of the body (mobility), doing work, or performing actions often (but not always) against resistance

Table II-2 NANDA-I Taxonomy II Domains, Classes, and Diagnoses (continued)

Approved Diagnoses

00040 Risk for disuse syndrome
00085 Impaired physical mobility
00091 Impaired bed mobility
00089 Impaired wheelchair mobility
00090 Impaired transfer ability
00088 Impaired walking
00097 Deficient diversional activity
00100 Delayed surgical recovery
00168 Sedentary lifestyle

Class 3 Energy Balance A dynamic state of harmony between intake and expenditure of resources

Approved Diagnoses

00050 Energy field disturbance
00093 Fatigue

Class 4 Cardiovascular/Pulmonary Responses Cardiopulmonary mechanisms that support activity/rest

Approved Diagnoses

00029 Decreased cardiac output
00033 Impaired spontaneous ventilation
00032 Ineffective breathing pattern
00092 Activity intolerance
00094 Risk for activity intolerance
00034 Dysfunctional ventilatory weaning response
00024 Ineffective tissue perfusion (specify type: renal, cerebral, cardiopulmonary, gastrointestinal, peripheral)

Class 5 Self-Care Ability to perform activities to care for one's body and bodily functions

Approved Diagnoses

00109 Dressing/grooming self-care deficit
00108 Bathing/hygiene self-care deficit
00102 Feeding self-care deficit
00110 Toileting self-care deficit
00182 Readiness for enhanced self-care

Domain 5 Perception/Cognition

The human information processing system including attention, orientation, sensation, perception, cognition, and communication

Class 1 Attention Mental readiness to notice or observe

Approved Diagnoses

00123 Unilateral neglect

Class 2 Orientation Awareness of time, place, and person

Approved Diagnoses

00127 Impaired environmental interpretation syndrome
00154 Wandering

Class 3 Sensation/Perception Receiving information through the senses of touch, taste, smell, vision, hearing, and kinesthesia and the comprehension of sense data resulting in naming, associating, and/or pattern recognition

Approved Diagnoses

00122 Disturbed sensory perception (specify: visual, auditory, kinesthetic, gustatory, tactile)

Class 4 Cognition Use of memory, learning, thinking, problem solving, abstraction, judgment, insight, intellectual capacity, calculation, and language

Approved Diagnoses

00126 Deficient knowledge (specify)
00161 Readiness for enhanced knowledge (specify)
00128 Acute confusion
00129 Chronic confusion
00131 Impaired memory
00130 Disturbed thought processes
00184 Readiness for enhanced decision making
00173 Risk for acute confusion

Class 5 Communication Sending and receiving verbal and nonverbal information

Approved Diagnoses

00051 Impaired verbal communication
00157 Readiness for enhanced communication

Domain 6 Self-Perception

Awareness about the self

Class 1 Self-Concept The perception(s) about the total self

Approved Diagnoses

00121 Disturbed personal identity
00125 Powerlessness
00152 Risk for powerlessness
00124 Hopelessness
00054 Risk for loneliness
00167 Readiness for enhanced self-concept
00187 Readiness for enhanced power
00174 Risk for compromised human dignity
00185 Readiness for enhanced hope

Class 2 Self-Esteem Assessment of one's own worth, capability, significance, and success

Approved Diagnoses

00119 Chronic low self-esteem
00120 Situational low self-esteem
00153 Risk for situational low self-esteem

Class 3 Body Image A mental image of one's own body

Approved Diagnoses

00118 Disturbed body image

Domain 7 Role Relationships

The positive and negative connections or associations between people or groups of people and the means by which those connections are demonstrated

Class 1 Caregiving Roles Socially expected behavior patterns by people providing care who are not healthcare professionals

continues

Table II-2 NANDA-I Taxonomy II Domains, Classes, and Diagnoses (continued)

Approved Diagnoses

00061 Caregiver role strain
00062 Risk for caregiver role strain
00056 Impaired parenting
00057 Risk for impaired parenting
00164 Readiness for enhanced parenting

Class 2 Family Relationships Associations of people who are biologically related or related by choice

Approved Diagnoses

00060 Interrupted family processes
00159 Readiness for enhanced family processes
00063 Dysfunctional family processes: Alcoholism
00058 Risk for impaired parent/infant/child attachment

Class 3 Role Performance Quality of functioning in socially expected behavior patterns

Approved Diagnoses

00106 Effective breastfeeding
00104 Ineffective breastfeeding
00105 Interrupted breastfeeding
00055 Ineffective role performance
00064 Parental role conflict
00052 Impaired social interaction

Domain 8 Sexuality

Sexual identity, sexual function, and reproduction

Class 1 Sexual Identity The state of being a specific person in regard to sexuality and/or gender

Class 2 Sexual Function The capacity or ability to participate in sexual activities

Approved Diagnoses

00059 Sexual dysfunction
00065 Ineffective sexuality pattern

Class 3 Reproduction Any process by which human beings are produced

Domain 9 Coping/Stress Tolerance

Contending with life events/life processes

Class 1 Post-Trauma Responses Reactions occurring after physical or psychological trauma

Approved Diagnoses

00114 Relocation stress syndrome
00149 Risk for relocation stress syndrome
00142 Rape-trauma syndrome
00144 Rape-trauma syndrome: Silent reaction
00143 Rape-trauma syndrome: Compound reaction
00141 Post-trauma syndrome
00145 Risk for post-trauma syndrome

Class 2 Coping Responses The process of managing environmental stress

Approved Diagnoses

00148 Fear
00146 Anxiety
00147 Death anxiety
00137 Chronic sorrow
00072 Ineffective denial
00136 Grieving
00135 Complicated grieving
00069 Ineffective coping
00073 Disabled family coping
00074 Compromised family coping
00071 Defensive coping
00077 Ineffective community coping
00158 Readiness for enhanced coping (individual)
00075 Readiness for enhanced family coping
00076 Readiness for enhanced community coping
00172 Risk for complicated grieving
00177 Stress overload
00188 Risk-prone health behavior

Class 3 Neurobehavioral Stress Behavioral responses reflecting nerve and brain function

Approved Diagnoses

00009 Autonomic dysreflexia
00010 Risk for autonomic dysreflexia
00116 Disorganized infant behavior
00115 Risk for disorganized infant behavior
00117 Readiness for enhanced organized infant behavior
00049 Decreased intracranial adaptive capacity

Domain 10 Life Principles

Principles underlying conduct, thought, and behavior about acts, customs, or institutions viewed as being true or having intrinsic worth

Class 1 Values The identification and ranking of preferred modes of conduct or end states

Approved Diagnoses

00185 Readiness for enhanced hope

Class 2 Beliefs Opinions, expectations, or judgments about acts, customs, or institutions viewed as being true or having intrinsic worth

Approved Diagnoses

00068 Readiness for enhanced spiritual well-being
00185 Readiness for enhanced hope

Class 3 Value/Belief/Action Congruence The correspondence or balance achieved between values, beliefs, and actions

Table II-2 NANDA-I Taxonomy II Domains, Classes, and Diagnoses (continued)

Approved Diagnoses

00066 *Spiritual distress*
00067 *Risk for spiritual distress*
00083 *Decisional conflict (specify)*
00079 *Noncompliance (specify)*
00170 *Risk for impaired religiosity*
00169 *Impaired religiosity*
00171 *Readiness for enhanced religiosity*
00175 *Moral distress*
00184 *Readiness for enhanced decision making*

Domain 11 Safety/Protection

Freedom from danger, physical injury, or immune system damage; preservation from loss; and protection of safety and security

Class 1 Infection Host responses following pathogenic invasion

Approved Diagnoses

00004 *Risk for infection*
00186 *Readiness for enhanced immunization status*

Class 2 Physical Injury Bodily harm or hurt

Approved Diagnoses

00045 *Impaired oral mucous membrane*
00035 *Risk for injury*
00087 *Risk for perioperative positioning injury*
00155 *Risk for falls*
00038 *Risk for trauma*
00046 *Impaired skin integrity*
00047 *Risk for impaired skin integrity*
00044 *Impaired tissue integrity*
00048 *Impaired dentition*
00036 *Risk for suffocation*
00039 *Risk for aspiration*
00031 *Ineffective airway clearance*
00086 *Risk for peripheral neurovascular dysfunction*
00043 *Ineffective protection*
00156 *Risk for sudden infant death syndrome*

Class 3 Violence The exertion of excessive force or power so as to cause injury or abuse

Approved Diagnoses

00139 *Risk for self-mutilation*
00151 *Self-mutilation*
00138 *Risk for other-directed violence*
00140 *Risk for self-directed violence*
00150 *Risk for suicide*

Class 4 Environmental Hazards Sources of danger in the surroundings

Approved Diagnoses

00037 *Risk for poisoning*
00180 *Risk for contamination*
00181 *Contamination*

Class 5 Defensive Processes The processes by which the self protects itself from the nonself

Approved Diagnoses

00041 *Latex allergy response*
00042 *Risk for latex allergy response*
00186 *Readiness for enhanced immunization status*

Class 6 Thermoregulation The physiologic process of regulating heat and energy within the body for purposes of protecting the organism

Approved Diagnoses

00005 *Risk for imbalanced body temperature*
00008 *Ineffective thermoregulation*
00006 *Hypothermia*
00007 *Hyperthermia*

Domain 12 Comfort

Sense of mental, physical, or social well-being or ease

Class 1 Physical Comfort Sense of well-being or ease and/or freedom from pain

Approved Diagnoses

00132 *Acute pain*
00133 *Chronic pain*
00134 *Nausea*
00183 *Readiness for enhanced comfort*

Class 2 Environmental Comfort Sense of well-being or ease in/with one's environment

Approved Diagnoses

00183 *Readiness for enhanced comfort*

Class 3 Social Comfort Sense of well-being or ease with one's social situations

Approved Diagnoses

00053 *Social isolation*

Domain 13 Growth/Development

Age-appropriate increases in physical dimensions, maturation of organ systems, and/or progression through the developmental milestone

Class 1 Growth Increases in physical dimensions or maturity of organ systems

Approved Diagnoses

00111 *Delayed growth and development*
00113 *Risk for disproportionate growth*
00101 *Adult failure to thrive*

Class 2 Development Progression or regression through a sequence of recognized milestones in life

Approved Diagnoses

00111 *Delayed growth and development*
00112 *Risk for delayed development*

Glossary

12-step program: A self-help model that aids in recovery from various addictions, compulsions, and traumatic experiences and in preventing relapse. It provides structure and relies on the support of fellow persons in recovery. Alcoholics Anonymous and Narcotics Anonymous are examples of such programs.

Acetylcholine: A brain chemical or neurotransmitter affected by many psychotropic medications.

Active neglect: Intentional failure to fulfill the caregiving obligations, inflicting physical or emotional distress.

Activities of daily living (ADLs): Self-care activities that people must accomplish to survive, such as eating, dressing, bathing, and toileting.

Acupuncture: One of the ancient arts of traditional Chinese medicine, in which specific body areas are punctured with fine needles for the purposes of relieving pain, enhancing the immune system, and treating various conditions such as asthma, addictions, or stress-related illnesses.

Acute stress disorder: A psychiatric disorder occurring 2 days to 4 weeks after a threatened or actual event that involves a combination of affective, behavioral, cognitive, and physiologic symptoms significant enough to impair normal functioning.

Adaptive coping behaviors: Positive techniques used by an individual to reduce stress, anxiety, tension, or negative feelings.

Adaptive functioning: An individual's ability to meet standards of predetermined skills related to daily living in the context of the individual's community.

Adjustment disorder: A condition in which the essential feature is the development of excessive psychological or behavioral symptoms in response to a recent stressor. These symptoms cause significant impairment in social, occupational, or academic functioning and usually subside within 6 months after the stressor is no longer present.

Advanced practice registered nurse (APRN): An umbrella classification used to describe the four major nurse specialist categories: certified registered nurse anesthetist (CRNA), certified nurse midwife (CNM), nurse practitioner (NP), and clinical nurse specialist (CNS). These individuals are educationally prepared to at least the master's degree level in the nursing specialty, have a significant depth of knowledge of theory and practice with validated clinical practice experience, and are competent in advanced clinical nursing skills

Advocacy: Those efforts aimed at educational, political, or social change in the community or society.

Affect: The external, visible expression of emotion or mood state.

Affective flattening: A blunted or constricted facial expression making the individual appear immobile, mask-like, and unresponsive, often seen in persons with schizophrenia.

Agnosia: The inability to recognize objects that cannot be explained by a reduced level of alertness.

Agonist: A medication that increases the activity of a neurotransmitter.

Agoraphobia: Anxiety about being in places or situations from which escape may be difficult or in which help may not be available should a panic attack occur.

Akathisia: A potential side effect of the antipsychotics consisting of physical restlessness and extreme difficulty remaining still.

Akinesia: A potential side effect of the antipsychotics consisting of slowing of movements.

Alogia: Decreased thought content and use of language, often seen in persons with schizophrenia.

Allostatic load: The wear and tear produced by the repeated activation of allostatic (adaptive) mechanisms.

Alzheimer's disease: A degenerative cognitive disorder that involves the development of neurofibrils, neurofibrillary tangles, and beta-plated amyloid plaques, first in the cortex and hippocampus and later in the frontal, parietal, and temporal lobes. It is characterized by cortical atrophy, ventricular dilation, and decreased acetylcholine, norepinephrine, and other neurotransmitters.

Amine neurotransmitters: These are acetylcholine, serotonin, dopamine, and norepinephrine.

Amnesia: A cognitive disorder associated with loss of memory.

Amygdala: An almond-shaped front portion of the brain's temporal lobe that plays a role in memory processing.

Anhedonia: The inability to feel pleasure.

Anorexia nervosa: The extreme pursuit of a thin body accompanied by a profoundly disturbed body image.

Anorexia nervosa, binge eating/purging type: In pursuit of a thin body, a person engages in binge eating and perceives that he or she is out of control.

Anorexia nervosa, restricting type: Persons with this type of anorexia restrict their intake but do not regularly engage in binge eating or purging.

Anorgasmia: The inability to achieve orgasm.

Antagonist: A medication that blocks the activity of a neurotransmitter.

Anterograde amnesia: Problems learning and retaining new material due to a brain injury or intoxication; past learning or memory of past events may remain unimpaired but immediate and recent recall is impaired.

Antianxiety medication: A family of psychotropic medications used primarily to treat anxiety.

Anticholinergic side effects: A group of side effects of many psychotropic medications consisting of co-existing problems with blurred vision, dry mouth, constipation, dilated pupils, and delayed urination.

Anticipatory guidance: An educative process in which individuals and families are prepared for the normal life changes at each stage of development and are told about successful coping strategies.

Anticipatory molding: The movement of a child towards the mothering figure when being held.

Antidepressants: A family of medications used primarily to treat depression.

Antidyskinetics: A family of medications used primarily to treat muscular side effects of the antipsychotics.

Antipsychotic: One of the psychotropic medications that treat psychotic symptoms.

Antisocial personality disorder: A pattern of disregard for, and violation of, the rights of others.

Anxiety: Apprehension or uneasiness in anticipation of danger; pathological when it interferes with effectiveness in living.

Apathy: A defense against anxiety wherein the person appears indifferent in a situation expected to elicit a great deal of anxiety in most persons.

Aphasia: A speech or language disorder affecting expressive and/or receptive functioning.

Apoptosis: A phase of programmed demise of cells in an organism's life cycle that characterizes aging.

Applied behavior analysis (ABA): The use of behavioral analytic methods and research findings to change socially important behaviors in meaningful ways.

Apraxia: The loss of the ability to perform motor skills or purposeful acts.

Asperger's disorder: A pervasive developmental disorder similar to autistic disorder characterized by impairment of social interactions and restricted interests and behaviors.

Asterixis: Motor tremors in which the client is unable to maintain a posture or position without moving the involved body part. Usually refers to the inability of a client with a toxic-metabolic syndrome to maintain his or her hands in a flexed position without "flapping."

Ataxia: Uncoordinated and inaccurate voluntary muscle movements as a result of cerebellar damage.

Attachment: A reciprocal affectional relationship between a mother or primary caretaker and a child.

Attachment model: A conceptual framework based upon the work of John Bowlby in which the establishment of trust, bonding, and attachment are essential to the survival of the human species.

Attention deficit hyperactivity disorder (ADHD): A persistent pattern of inattention and/or hyperactivity-impulsivity that is more frequent and more severe than typically observed in children of the same age and developmental level.

Atypical antipsychotic: A newer group of antipsychotic medications that may cause fewer side effects, including fewer muscular side effects, than previous generation of antipsychotic medications.

Autistic disorder: A pervasive developmental disorder with onset in infancy or early childhood characterized by a markedly abnormal or impaired development in social interaction and communication, typically with a restricted range of interests and activities and wide variability in one's intelligence and in the expression of the disorder.

Autogenic training: A popular relaxation technique that focuses on using self-statements suggesting heaviness and warmth.

Autonomic nervous system: The part of the nervous system that regulates involuntary body functions.

Autonomy: Self-determination, making decisions for oneself.

Avoidant personality disorder: A lifelong pattern characterized by experiences of extreme shyness, social inhibition, feelings of inadequacy, and hypersensitivity to rejection.

Avolition: The inability to initiate activity.

Axons: An extension of a neuron capable of self-propagating nervous impulses.

Bariatric surgery procedures: Different forms of surgical interventions designed to help a person lose weight.

Basal ganglia: The areas of gray matter composed of cell bodies in each cerebral hemisphere of the brain.

Battered child syndrome: When a child experiences multiple traumas and has been beaten repeatedly by a caregiver.

Battered partner syndrome: Describes a victim who is exposed to multiple physical and/or emotional traumas; characterized by passive and socially isolated behavior, and difficulty leaving the batterer.

Batterers: Abusive men or women who share certain characteristics. They deny responsibility for their actions, and they are unable to trust people; this is projected in all relationships.

Behavior modification model: An intervention based on teaching how to establish controls from within one's self and that there are consequences (natural, logical, and unrelated) to one's behavior.

Behavior therapy: A mode of treatment that focuses on modifying behavior.

Behavioral health: A term that encompasses treatment for mental health disorders and substance abuse as well as employee assistance programs.

Behavioral model: A model concerned with the here and now of behavior, not with how or why behavior developed.

Beneficence: To act in the client's welfare by preventing harm and doing no harm.

Benzodiazepine: A family of psychotropic medications used primarily to treat anxiety, agitation, and insomnia.

Binge eating: Eating large amounts of food while feeling out of control.

Binge eating disorder: A disorder where people experience recurrent, rapid episodes of eating large amounts of food (binging) while feeling out of control. These individuals do not engage in purging behaviors and are usually overweight.

Biofeedback training: A process that uses technology to measure physiologic functions to feed back information to clients so that they can use the information to regulate or change an imbalance in their systems.

Biopsychosocial history: A comprehensive assessment of the client's lifetime biologic, psychological, and social functioning.

Bipolar: A mood disorder in which both manic and depressive episodes occur.

Bipolar disorder of childhood: A pattern of severe mood instability in childhood or early adolescence that is characterized by typical or atypical mania, overactivity, a decreased need for sleep, affective storms, and in some cases hypersexuality and grandiosity.

Blackouts: Periods of amnesia during which the person appears to function normally but later does not recall the events that transpired.

Body dysmorphic disorder: A mental disorder in which the client believes his or her body is deformed in some manner that is not readily observed by others. This excessive preoccupation may lead to behaviors such as seeking constant reassurance or surgery and exercise or dieting to change the imagined defect.

Bodymindspirit: A word developed by some holistic practitioners to emphasize the interrelatedness of these three human components.

Bonding: An affectional feeling between a mother or primary caretaker and a child.

Borderline personality disorder: A serious mental disorder characterized by pervasive instability in mood and affect, interpersonal relationships, and self-image, with marked impulsivity.

Boundaries: Limits that permit the client and mental health practitioner to have a therapeutic relationship based on the needs of the client.

Brain stem: The portion of the brain that contains the medulla oblongata, pons and mesencephalon.

Breathing: In the context of complementary therapies, a simple practice for self-care for nurses and a therapeutic practice for clients offering, increased calm, relaxation awareness, and reduction of stress and discomfort.

Breathing-related sleep disorders: Dyssomnias involving disruption of sleep as a result of ventilation abnormalities and neurologic or cardiac problems that can involve upper-airway structural abnormalities, periods of nonventilation, and obstructed respirations.

Briquet's syndrome: A disorder involving symptoms of overdramatization, exhibitionism, and seductiveness associated with multiple physical complaints attributed to hysteria.

Broca's area: An area of the brain involved in speech production.

Bulimia nervosa: An disorder where people experience recurrent, rapid episodes of eating large amounts of food (binging) while feeling out of control; these individuals also engage in purging, fasting, excessive exercise, orother compensatory behaviors.

Burnout: An individual's unproductive response to an overwhelming and chronically stressful work situation that limits their productivity on and off the job.

Case management: A method of assigning the coordination of a client's care; it may be a role, a technology, a process, a service, and a system. Its goal is to decrease fragmentation and ensure access to appropriate and cost-effective care.

Catalepsy: The ability to remain in postures associated with catatonia.

Cataplexy: A temporary sudden loss of muscle tone often associated with narcolepsy.

Catatonia: A decreased reactivity to the environment that can be expressed as mutism, waxy flexibility, extreme negativism, echolalia, or echopraxia in an agitated or almost coma-like state.

Centering: A holistic nursing practice of calming, being in the present moment, and connecting with the intention to help and to heal.

Central nervous system: A major division of the brain consisting of the brain and spinal cord.

Cerebellum: The part of the brain located behind the brain stem consisting of two lobes and the vermis; controls muscle coordination and body equilibrium.

Cerebrum: The largest and uppermost section of the brain consisting of a right and left hemisphere; location of higher level mental processes.

Chief complaint: The reason for current contact with the mental health system, in the client's own words.

Child abuse: Causing physical, mental, or emotional injury to a child by action or neglect.

Childhood disintegrative disorder: A pervasive developmental disorder characterized by a marked regression in language, social skills and adaptive behaviors.

Child psychiatry: The study of medicine, psychiatry, and human development preparing one to address the mental health needs of infants, children, and adolescents

Child's Bill of Rights: A document that establishes a child's right to be wanted, to be born healthy, to live in a healthy environment, to have basic needs met, to experience continuous loving care, and to acquire the cognitive skills needed for life.

Chronic illness: All impairments or deviations from the norm that have one or more of the following characteristics: are permanent, leave residual disability, are caused by nonreversible pathologic alteration, require special training of the patient for rehabilitation, or may be expected to require a long period of supervision, observation, or care.

Chronic mental illness: Synonymous with both persistent mental illness and severe mental illness; it tends to last for a long time, if not a lifetime, and may be characterized by periods of relapse or reoccurrence.

Circadian rhythm: The underlying biologic rhythms involved in sleep/wake cycles.

Classical conditioning: A behavioral model developed by Ivan Pavlov that focuses on a person's involuntary reaction to a neutral event because the reaction and the event have become associated.

Classification of mental retardation: The four categories are intermittent, limited, extensive and pervasive.

Closed-ended questions: Focused questions that elicit specific and concise information.

CODE-C (CODE-C Disaster Mental Health Service Model): A mental health service model that includes consultation, outreach, debriefing and defusing, education, and crisis counseling to deal with psychological reactions to traumatic stress over time.

Codependence: A dynamic common among significant others of persons with substance dependence or abuse; characterized by behaviors that support or enable the substance use.

Cognitive behavioral therapy: A type of therapy that teaches the control of thought distortions and emphasizes the important role of thinking in how we feel and what we do.

Cognitive model: Model of development that examines the perceptual and intellectual growth of the individual.

Cognitive restructuring: A process of replacing negative, catastrophic thoughts that interfere with functioning with constructive thoughts.

Cognitive therapy: A treatment therapy that emphasizes the rearrangement of a person's maladaptive processes of thinking.

Collateral history: Information about the client obtained from the client's family, friends, colleagues, or mental health professionals.

Communication disorder: A disorder most often diagnosed in childhood that is characterized by severe difficulties in expressing oneself verbally or nonverbally and that is more frequent and severe than typically observed in individuals of the same age and developmental level.

Compassion fatigue: Secondary traumatic stress experienced by workers or volunteers dealing with stressful and traumatic situations related to the nature of the event, occupational and organizational support, and postevent recovery.

Competency: The capacity of an individual to manage his or her affairs and make appropriate self-care decisions on a consistent basis.

Compliance: Adherance to prescribed medications and other treatment protocols.

Compulsion: Repetitive behaviors done in response to obsessions.

Conceptual model: A framework of related concepts that address the bases for behavior in order to direct interventions; the most important conceptual models are the psychoanalytic, interpersonal, behavioral, cognitive, developmental and neurobiologic models.

Concrete thought process: A thought process in which one is able to understand only the literal meaning of words, as opposed to abstract thought process.

Conduct disorder: Behavior that constitutes a repetitive and persistent pattern in which the basic rights of others, social norms, or rules are seriously violated.

Confidentiality: Ensuring that information shared is kept private.

Conversion disorder: A psychiatric disorder in which physical symptoms, usually associated with sensory or motor deficits or seizures, are related to unconscious psychologic conflicts.

Coping mechanisms: Conscious mental strategies or behaviors used to lower anxiety and adjust to demands in a purposeful manner.

Coping skills: Mechanisms people use to manage internal and external stressors; may be adaptive or maladaptive.

Countertransference: Realistic and unrealistic feelings that the mental health professional has toward the client.

Creutzfeldt-Jakob disease: A transmissible, rapidly degenerative cognitive disorder involving sponge-like vacuoles and damage to neurons by prions, and characterized by changes in personality and functioning.

Crisis: A self-limited transitional period of disequilibrium and functional impairment experienced by an individual or family when confronted with a dangerous or threatening situation.

Crisis intervention: The use of cognitive and short-term psychotherapeutic techniques to help the client gain a realistic perception of events, become aware of feelings, develop active coping skills, and experience social support.

Critical incident stress management (CISM): A method of crisis intervention involving individual and group intervention that allows those involved in emergent and urgent disturbances to share thoughts and experiences, review events, give mutual support, normalize the experience, and provide meaning to their experiences.

Cyclothymia: A fluctuating mood disturbance ranging from hypomania to depressive symptoms.

Delirium: A temporary, potentially reversible cognitive disorder usually associated with acute changes in medical and surgical conditions or toxic metabolic syndromes.

Delusion: False beliefs not held by others in the same culture that can be non-bizarre and potentially possible, such as some jealous or persecutory false beliefs, or bizarre and not reality based, such as thought broadcasting or thought insertion. They may be paranoid, grandiose, somatic, erotic, nihilistic, guilty, bizarre, or referential in nature.

Dementia: Chronic, usually progressive, cognitive disorders associated with changes in brain structure and functioning.

Dendrites: A slender portion of a neuron's cell body that is capable of being stimulated by a neurotransmitter.

Denial: A defense mechanism that prevents an individual from recognizing reality; commonly used by individuals who are unable to recognize the destructive effects of substance use.

Dependent personality disorder: A condition characterized by submissive and clingy behaviors, an over-reliance on others, an excessive need to be taken care of, and fears of separation.

Depersonalization: Feelings of unreality or strangeness concerning either the environment, the self, or both.

Depolarization: The process that triggers the release of neurotransmitter into the synaptic cleft.

Derealization: A feeling of detachment from one's environment.

Detoxification: The process of gradual withdrawal from a substance on which the person is physiologically dependent. This process usually involves the administration of decreasing doses of a substitute medication.

Developmental crises: Crises that are predictable and occur in conjunction with normal developmental transitions.

Developmental disability: Severe chronic mental or physical disabilities that manifest before a person reaches 22 years of age, are likely to continue indefinitely, and result in substantial functional limitations in three or more of the following areas: self-care, receptive and expressive language, learning, mobility, self-direction, capacity for independent living, or economic self-sufficiency.

Developmental history: An assessment of a child's progress in attaining certain behaviors (e.g., sitting, walking, talking, playing) associated with a specific age.

***Diagnostic and Statistical Manual of Mental Disorders,* Fourth Edition, Text Revision *(DSM-IV-TR)*:** A manual published in 2000 by the American Psychiatric Association that covers all mental health disorders for children and adults. It uses a multiaxial approach (Axis I to Axis V) and can be used by psychiatrists, psychologists, nurses, social workers, and other mental health therapists.

Dialectical behavior therapy: A broad-based cognitive-behavioral treatment developed specifically for the treatment of borderline personality disorder.

Differential diagnosis: The process of differentiating one disorder from another that presents similarly.

Disaster: An unpredicted, overpowering, and traumatic event that disrupts life circumstances and threatens survival and assumptions.

Discipline: An intervention focused on helping children to learn appropriate ways to control their behaviors and to keep themselves safe.

Dissociation: An unconscious defense mechanism in which the person sustains an alteration in the integrative functions of consciousness or identity. Dissociative symptoms involve temporary changes in consciousness, identity and motor function to protect and distance the individual from painful emotions or thoughts associated with anxiety, conflict, or trauma.

Domestic violence: When an abuser acts violently toward an intimate partner.

Dopamine: A brain chemical or neurotransmitter affected by the antipsychotic medications.

Double-trouble groups: Self-help groups that address the recovery process for individuals with both addiction and other mental disorders.

Down syndrome: A congenital condition characterized by mental retardation and multiple physical defects.

Dual diagnosis: The simultaneous existence of one or more substance use disorders and at least one other primary mental disorder.

Duty to protect and duty to warn: The legal requirement to inform authorities or others if there is evidence that a client may inflict danger on a specific person.

Dynamisms: A Sullivanian concept describing the methods used by persons to reduce the tension experienced by their perception of the needs for satisfaction and security.

Dyslexia: The inability to interpret written language.

Dyspareunia: Recurrent or persistent genital pain associated with sexual intercourse.

Dysphagia: Difficulty swallowing.

Dyssomnia: Disorders of initiating or maintaining sleep involving impaired amount, quality, and timing of sleep.

Dysthymic disorder: A chronically depressed mood disorder.

Dystonia: A muscular side effect of the antipsychotics consisting of muscle spasms in any part of the body.

Echolalia: The automatic and meaningless mimicking or repetition of the words and phrases of another.

Ego defense mechanisms: As formulated by Sigmund Freud, unconscious mental mechanisms derived from the ego that are designed to alleviate anxiety by effecting a compromise between the demands of the id and the superego.

Electroconvulsive therapy (ECT): The induction of a brief convulsion by passing an electric current through the brain, primarily for the treatment of affective disorders.

Empathy: The ability to mentally put oneself in someone else's place, viewing a person's world from his or her internal frame of reference, with the goal of gaining understanding of how he or she feels in a certain situation. This involves the nurse's sensitivity to the client's current feelings and the ability to communicate this to the client in a language that can be understood. This technique is most useful in establishing trust and expresses understanding and concern.

Empowerment: The process by which an individual gains the self-esteem and self-confidence to actively engage in and control the environment.

Encopresis: Repeated passage of feces into inappropriate places, such as clothing, closets, or floors, either involuntarily or intentionally, at least once a month for at least 3 months in a child who is mentally at least 4 years of age.

Enuresis: Repeated voiding or urinating during day or night into bed or clothing, either involuntarily or intentionally, for at least 3 months in a child who is mentally at least 5 years of age.

Epraxia: The mimicking or repetition of the actions of another.

Erectile dysfunction: A persistent inability to achieve or maintain an erection.

Euphoria: An overexaggerated sense of physical and mental well-being.

Euthymia: A normal mood experience.

Evidence-based practice: A process founded on the collection, interpretation, and integration of valid, important, and applicable patient-reported, clinician-observed, and research-derived evidence.

Exposure: Used in therapy, it is the repeated experience or contact with a particular stress-provoking situation or stimulus.

Expressive language disorder: An impairment in expressive language development as demonstrated by scores on standardized measures of expressive language that are substantially below measures of both intellectual capacity and receptive language development.

Extended family: Any family grouping that is related by descent, marriage, or adoption that is broader than the nuclear family and can include multiple generations and aunts, uncles, and cousins.

Extinction: A behavioral model developed by B.F. Skinner that eliminates behavior by ignoring or not rewarding it.

Extrapyramidal: A group of muscular side effects of the antipsychotics as a result of blocking the dopamine receptor sites in the brain.

Extrapyramidal pathways: Various relays of motor neurons between the cerebral cortex, basal nuclei, thalamus, cerebellum and the brain stem.

Factitious disorder: A mental disorder in which signs and symptoms of physical and/or psychiatric disorders are intentionally and consciously produced or feigned.

Family of orientation: The nuclear family in which an individual has the status of a child.

Family of procreation: The nuclear family in which the individual has or had the status of a parent.

Family systems therapy: A treatment approach based on the belief that families are systems in which change in one aspect of the system affects the entire system. Family therapy proposes that a client's symptoms emanate from problems within the family system.

Family violence: The use or threat of physical, emotional, sexual, or economic abuse to control a family member.

Flight of ideas: As seen in mania, involves pressured speech with rapid topic changes.

Flooding: Exposure to a stress-provoking stimulus for an extended period of time for the purpose of extinguishing the negative emotional response.

Frontal lobe: The largest of the five lobes constituting the two cerebral hemispheres of the brain.

Functional imaging: A category of brain imaging that gathers information about the functioning of the brain. Functional imaging tests include positron emission tomography (PET), and functional magnetic resonance (fMRI).

Gender dysphoria: Excessive unhappiness or discomfort with one's natal gender. This discomfort may be focused on gender roles and expectations, physiognomic features, or a range of other issues.

Gender identity: The internal sense of oneself as male, female, or existing somewhere on a continuum.

General adaptation syndrome (GAS): The defense response of the body to stress as described by Hans Selye.

Generalized anxiety disorder (GAD): A pattern of persistent and excessive anxiety and worry about a wide range of subjects lasting at least 6 months.

Genes: The biologic units of inheritance.

Genogram: A diagram or map of multiple generations of a family indicating family relationships, life events, family functioning, and significant developmental events.

Glia cells: Neural cells that have a connective tissue supporting function in the CNS.

Global assessment of functioning scale: The fifth axis in a *DSM-IV-TR* diagnosis; a rating scale used by the mental health practitioner to gauge the client's total psychological, social, and occupational or academic well-being on a scale of 1 to 100.

Grief: Subjective feelings and affect that are experienced as a result of a loss or disappointment.

Group therapy: An intervention in which 3 or more persons interact for the purpose of altering their behavior patterns and developing new and more effective ways of dealing with the stressors of daily living.

Habilitation: The process of developing new skills and abilities.

Hallucination: False sensory perceptions in the absence of an external stimulus. They may be auditory, visual, tactile, olfactory, or gustatory in nature.

Hippocampus: A portion of the floor of the lateral ventricle of the brain involved in memory development.

History of present illness: A chronologic account of the events leading up to the current contact with the mental health professional, including a description of the precipitants, onset, duration, exacerbating and ameliorating factors, and change of symptoms over time.

Histrionic personality disorder: A condition characterized by pervasive and excessive emotionality and attention-seeking behaviors that become persistent and very disabling and distressing to the client.

Holistic nursing: A model of nursing practice that has the goal of healing the whole person.

Holistic psychiatric assessment: A comprehensive assessment of the client's physical, psychological, cognitive, social, and spiritual dimensions.

Homelessness: A lack of a home or residence.

Homicidal thoughts: Thoughts to kill or harm others.

HPA (hypothalamic-pituitary-adrenal) axis: Regulates the secretion of cortisol from the adrenal gland.

Huntington's disease: A genetic degenerative cognitive disorder involving destruction of neurons and causing movement disorder, personality changes, and emotional instability.

Hypersomnia: A dyssomnia characterized by prolonged or excessive sleep at night or during the day; can be related to depression or central nervous system dysfunction.

Hypnosis: The practice of working with an altered state of consciousness or trance for therapeutic benefit.

Hypnotic: A medication that induces sedation or sleep.

Hypochondriasis: An exaggerated, unrealistic preoccupation, based upon misinterpretations of physical sensations, of having a serious disease that persists despite medical evaluation and reassurance.

Hypomania: A mild form of mania.

Hypothalamus: A portion of the brain that controls and integrates the peripheral autonomic nervous system.

Imagery: The practice of assisting clients to self-heal and self-regulate by bringing them into a state of relaxation through visualization, using any or all of their senses.

Impulse control: The ability to delay, modulate, or inhibit the expression of behaviors and feelings.

Impulse control disorders: These include intermittent explosive disorder, kleptomania, pyromania, pathologic gambling, and trichotillomania.

Incest: Sexual intercourse or intimate sexual behavior with members of the same family.

Inclusion: Refers to the integration of all persons, regardless of special needs and disabilities or the environment (e.g., school, community), with typical peers in the least restrictive setting.

Individual therapy: Focuses on the person and includes other aspects of the person's life only as they relate to the individual.

Individualized Education Program (IEP): Developed for a child based on standardized testing scores; it provides for modifications in work load, assignments, and testing, or provides for specific behavioral techniques to be used in the classroom to aid in educating the child. It can also be referred to as an Individualized Education Plan.

Informed consent: The process of sharing information with the client regarding a proposed treatment; the client must be competent to understand the information provided and the consent must be voluntary.

Inner reflection: A meditative process that explores our inner awareness, thoughts, images, beliefs, attitudes, expectations, and experiences in a quiet, centered state to cultivate a deeper understanding and awareness.

Insight: The extent of the client's awareness of illness and maladaptive behaviors.

Insomnia: A dyssomnia characterized by abnormal wakefulness such as an inability to fall or remain asleep and impaired daytime performance.

Instrumental activities of daily living (IADL): These include performing housework, going on errands, managing finances, and making telephone calls.

Integrated treatment approach: A seamless treatment approach for clients with dual diagnosis that addresses both the addictive disorder and other psychiatric disorders.

Intelligence quotient (IQ): A measure of relative intelligence determined through testing.

Intention: The conscious awareness of being in the present moment in order to help facilitate the healing process.

Interdependence: Known also as mutual dependence is a method to accomplish inclusion.

Intermittent explosive disorder: Discrete episodes of failure to resist aggressive impulses resulting in serious assaults or destruction of property.

Intersex: The condition in which a person has both male and female biological characteristics.

Intimate partner violence: The use or threat of physical, emotional, sexual, or economic abuse between dating couples and current or former spouses in heterosexual or homosexual relationships.

Intoxication: A substance-specific syndrome that results from recent ingestion or exposure to a substance.

Intrusive procedures: There are three types that can be encountered during a hospitalization—oral, anal, and cutaneous procedures.

Journaling: A self-care practice that involves writing one's inner reflections, dreams, thoughts, and feelings for the purpose of reflection on one's own personal and professional processes.

Judgment: The capacity to identify possible courses of action, anticipate their consequences, and choose the appropriate behavior.

Justice: The concept that people should be treated equally and fairly.

Kleptomania: The recurrent failure to resist impulses to steal objects not needed for personal or monetary value.

Kindling: Describes the lowest threshold for setting off neuronal activity in seizure disorders.

Korsakoff's syndrome: A cognitive disorder of decreased memory associated with a deficiency of B_1, thiamine, and usually found in chronic alcoholism. It is often associated with Wernike's syndrome, a problem with gait, which appears first, and is then referred to as Wernike-Korsakoff's syndrome.

La belle indifference: A characteristic of a response in which the client is calm and somewhat indifferent to problems or catastrophes.

Lag period: The period of time between taking the first dose of a medication and experiencing the therapeutic effect.

Learning disorders: Disorders identified when an individual's achievement on standardized tests in reading, mathematics, or written expression is substantially below that expected for age, intelligence, and educational background.

Least restrictive environment: Treatment provided in a setting that meets the client's needs with the least restrictions imposed.

Levels of consciousness: Formulated by Sigmund Freud, they consist of the conscious, preconscious, and unconscious mind.

Lewy body disease: A progressive cortical dementia that affects mainly memory and motor control functioning and involves symptoms of visual hallucinations, fluctuating levels of alertness, and motor symptoms similar to Parkinson's disease.

Limbic system: A group of interconnected brain structures that function together to regulate emotion, learning, and memory.

Loss: The disappearance of something cherished; it can be a relationship, job, health, mental faculties, or control over nature or various life events.

Maintenance dose: The medication dose taken after the acute symptoms have subsided in order to prevent relapse.

Major depressive disorder: One or more episodes of depressed mood or irritability accompanied by a significant loss of interest in activities that is a change from baseline, and that persists for at least 2 weeks or is accompanied by suicidal thoughts.

Malingering: Intentional or exaggerated symptoms clearly associated with external factors such as the need to avoid work or school.

Managed care: Both a delivery and reimbursement system that aims to combine cost-effectiveness with quality care.

Mandatory outpatient treatment (MOT): Treatment mandated by the courts requiring clients to receive and attend outpatient psychiatric treatment.

MAOIs (monoamine oxidase inhibitors): A small group of antidepressants that require dietary restrictions and avoidance of certain other medications.

Material exploitation: An example of economic abuse using resources inappropriate for one's own needs.

Maternal deprivation: Occurs when there is any significant separation from the mothering figure of an infant between 3 and 15 months of age, often leading to serious emotional problems in the infant such as depression, eating disorders, and failure to thrive.

Maturational disturbance: The adaptation and transition of normal developmental phases.

Medulla: The area of the brain stem where the corticospinal tracts cross resulting in the right motor cortex controlling the muscles on the left side of the body and the left motor cortex controlling the right side.

Melancholia: A loss of interest in activities and inability to find pleasure in activities or events that are usually pleasurable.

Membrane potential: The difference in the electrical charge between two sides of a cell wall.

Mental disorder or illness: A disturbance in thoughts or mood that causes maladaptive behavior, inability to cope with normal stresses, and impaired functioning; meets diagnostic criteria established in *DSM-IV-TR*.

Mental health consumers: People who are receiving or have received mental health services.

Mental retardation: A disability that originates before 18 years of age and is characterized by significant limitation in both intellectual function and adaptive behavior as expressed in conceptual, social, and practical adaptive skills.

Mental status examination: An evaluation of a client's present state, including the client's behavior and general appearance, mood and affect, speech, thought process and content, perceptual disturbances, impulse control, cognition, knowledge, judgment, and insight.

Midbrain: The mesencephalon portion of the brain.

Milieu therapy: The use of the environment as a therapeutic tool.

Mindfulness meditation: An ancient spiritual practice of learning to be in the present moment, practicing awareness, focusing on breathing, and focusing on moment-to-moment attention.

Minor tranquilizers: A name used to refer to certain antianxiety medications or sedative/hypnotics, including barbiturates and benzodiazepines.

Mood: The internal feeling of emotion; a person's pervasive, subjective emotional state.

Mood stabilizer: A family of psychotropic medications used to prevent extreme ups and downs of mood.

Moral therapy: Introduced by Phillipe Pinel in 1792; attendants were required to treat patients kindly and keep them busy with various activities.

Multiaxial *DSM-IV-TR diagnosis:* A comprehensive diagnostic system used widely in the United States; includes major psychiatric disorders, personality disorders/mental retardation, physical/medical conditions, psychosocial and environmental stressors, and a global assessment of functioning for each client.

Multidisciplinary treatment team: Consists of the client and the family, psychiatric nurse, psychiatrist, clinical psychologist, psychiatric social worker, occupational, rehabilitation, and activities therapists, and ancillary staff.

Multiple sleep latency test (MSLT): A test of a client's daytime sleepiness; it measures sleep latency (the time it takes to fall asleep) and the amount of REM sleep.

Münchausen syndrome: Refers to factitious disorders in which there is a manipulation or invention of symptoms; named after Baron Münchausen, who was known for telling wild, fantastic tales.

Myelin: A lipoprotein that constitutes the sheath of nerve fibers throughout the body and envelops the axis of myelinated nerves.

Narcissistic personality disorder: A pervasive pattern of grandiosity, an extremely exaggerated sense of self-importance, need for admiration and lack of empathy for others.

Narcolepsy: A dyssomnia that involves uncontrollable, recurrent, brief episodes of sleep.

National Alliance on Mental Illness (NAMI): An advocacy group of families of persons with mental illness. It was instrumental in shifting the focus of the National Institute of Mental Health from education and service delivery to research.

Need for satisfaction: A Sullivanian concept stemming from a person's biological needs for food, air, water, shelter, sex, and so forth.

Need for security: A Sullivanian concept stemming from a person's emotional needs for feeling states such as interpersonal intimacy, status, and self-esteem.

Negative reinforcement: A behavioral model developed by B.F. Skinner that increases the frequency of a behavior by removing an unpleasant stimulus when a desired response occurs.

Negative symptoms: Psychotic symptoms that represent a loss or restriction of normal functioning and expression, and includes affective flattening, alogia, anhedonia, attention problems, and avolition.

Neglect: A condition in which one fails to provide essential physical and/or emotional care to a dependant person.

Neurobiologic model: A model that postulates the relationship of the brain and the nervous system as basic to the understanding of the symptoms, processes, and treatment of mental illnesses and disorders.

Neurogenesis: The process of new cells being born across one's lifetime.

Neuroimaging: Various methods of brain imaging to expand the knowledge base of the structure, function and neurochemistry of the CNS.

Neuroleptic: Refers to a class of medications, also known as major tranquilizers, that are used to treat psychotic conditions and are expected to produce a calming effect.

Neuroleptic malignant syndrome: A rare but potentially life-threatening side effect of the antipsychotic medications that causes elevated creatinine phosphokinase levels, fever, diaphoresis, muscle rigidity, and autonomic instability.

Neuron: A highly specialized cell in the nervous system that can generate and transmit bioelectric signals. The neuron is characterized by three distinct parts: the cell body (soma), the dendrites, and the axon.

Neuroplasticity: The ability of the brain to respond to the environment. This includes the development of new synapses (synaptogenesis), the myelination of axons, the development of dendritic and axonal branches (arborization), the destruction or pruning of neurons, and even the birth of new neurons (neurogenesis).

Neurotransmitters: Chemicals that are released by presynaptic cells upon stimulation and activate postsynaptic receptors of other cells.

Nightmare: Parasomnias involving intense, frightening dreams that can be recalled by the sleeper and may involve partial arousals from sleep.

Nonrapid eye movement (NREM): Slow-wave sleep that involves the three deepest and least active stages of sleep involving light sleep, sleep, and deep slow wave or delta sleep. It is measured by the relative absence of rapid eye movement and neuron activity.

Norepinephrine: A brain chemical or neurotransmitter affected by antidepressants and other psychotropic medications; a vasopressor and precursor of epinephrine.

Nuclear family: A grouping consisting of one or two adults that undertakes a parenting role for one or more children.

Nurse-patient relationship: A conceptual model developed by Hildegard Peplau that has four distinct yet overlapping phases: orientation, identification, exploitation, and resolution. As a type of therapeutic relationship, the nurse-patient or -client relationship also is described as having three phases: orientation phase, working phase, and termination phase.

Nursing roles: As developed by Hildegard Peplau, six different roles that emerge in the various phases of the nurse-client relationship: stranger, resource person, teacher, leader, surrogate, and counselor.

Obesity: The state of being significantly above one's normal weight with a body mass index of 30 or above.

Obsession: Unwanted, recurrent thoughts, ideas or impulses.

Obsessive-compulsive disorder (OCD): A pattern of recurrent obsessions or compulsions, recognized by the person as excessive or unreasonable, that are severe enough to be time-consuming or cause significant impairment in relationships with others, education, or other important areas of functioning.

Obsessive-compulsive personality disorder: A condition characterized by an inordinate preoccupation with rules, orderliness, perfectionism, and mental and interpersonal control. The condition can become persistent and disabling resulting in a loss of flexibility, openness, and efficiency.

Oculogyric crisis: An acute dystonic reaction involving the eyes resulting in an involuntary upward, lateral gaze.

Open-ended questions: A style of questioning that encourages descriptive or narrative responses, as opposed to a yes or no answer (e.g., "Tell me about your problem.").

Operant conditioning: A behavioral technique for shaping behavior; based on demonstration by B. F. Skinner that behaviors are influenced by their consequences; behaviors that have a positive consequence increase in strength and are likely to be repeated, and behaviors with negative consequences are weakened and decrease in frequency.

Opisthotonus: An extrapyramidal posturing manifested by severe spastic hyperextension of the neck that can be a side effect of antipsychotic medication.

Oppositional defiant disorder (ODD): A recurrent pattern of negative, defiant, disobedient, and hostile behavior in children toward adults that persists for at least 6 months.

Orgasm: A sudden, subjective experience of intense pleasure usually accompanied by rhythmic contractions in the pelvic area.

Pain disorder: Mental disorders in response to pain that are influenced primarily by psychologic factors, cause significant impairment, and are considered to be out of proportion to physical symptoms.

Panic attack: Sudden overwhelming anxiety of such intensity that it produces terror and physiological changes.

Paranoid personality disorder: A condition characterized by a pattern of pervasive and excessive distrust and suspiciousness of others, often interpretating others motives as malevolent.

Paraphilias: Sexual attraction to objects, materials, or situations not commonly considered erotic.

Parasomnia: Sleep disorders involving abnormal physiologic and behavioral events related to sleep characterized by dysfunctions with sleep, sleep stages, or partial arousals and associated with disturbing physiologic and behavioral events.

Parasympathetic nervous system: Regulates heart rate, increases intestinal peristalsis and gland activity and relaxes sphincters.

Parenting education: Education for adults structured to support them through all stages of child development and to understand their children and their own reactions to the various behaviors of childhood and adolescence.

Parkinson's disease: A chronic progressive cognitive disorder involving bradykinesia, tremor, and gait and posture problems.

Passive neglect: An omission or unintentional failure to deliver caregiving obligations; inflicting distress without willful intent.

Pathologic gambling: Recurrent and persistent maladaptive gambling behavior.

Pediatric autoimmune neuropsychiatric disorder associated with Group A Streptococcus (PANDAS): The rapid onset of either obsessive-compulsive symptoms or tic symptoms, directly following an infection with the Group A Streptococcus bacterium in a child who had previously not demonstrated these symptoms.

Periodic limb movements (PLM): A disorder that involves twitching and/or uncontrolled movements of the limbs that occur at times of rest or sleep, or both.

Peripheral nervous system: The motor and sensory nerves and ganglia outside of the brain and spinal cord.

Persistent mental illness: Synonymous with chronic mental illness and severe mental illness.

Personality disorder: An enduring pattern of inner experience and behavior that deviates markedly from cultural expectations, is pervasive and inflexible, begins in adolescence or young adulthood, and leads to distress and impairment.

Personality, structure of: Formulated by Sigmund Freud; comprises the id, ego, and superego.

Personality traits: Patterns enduring over a lifetime that correlate to how one perceives, relates to and thinks of oneself and one's environment as revealed in both social and personal contexts.

Pervasive developmental disorder: Conditions characterized by severe and persistent impairment in several areas of development including social interaction skills, communication skills, restricted areas of interest or activities, intelligence, or other learning disorders in the presence of stereotypical behaviors.

Phobia: Irrational, involuntary, and inappropriate fear associated with certain objects or situations.

Physical assessment: A medical work-up (including physical examination, clinical laboratory tests, and specialized diagnostic procedures) used in psychiatry to determine if medical illness is contributing to psychiatric symptoms.

Pick's disease: A progressive cognitive disorder of the frontal and temporal lobes involving deterioration in social skills and behavior, emotional blunting, and language problems.

Play stages: Solitary, parallel, associative, and cooperative.

Play therapy: Methods such as structured play, mutual story telling, nondirective play, behavioral play, visualization, and guided imagery used in treating emotional distress in children.

Play types: These are social, explorative, imitative, group, and competitive.

Polydipsia: Excessive water and fluid intake causing hyponatremia.

Polysomnography: A series of tests, often including an EEG, to measure sleep stages, usually done in a sleep lab.

Pons: A prominence on the ventral surface of the brain stem.

Positive reinforcement: A behavioral model developed by B.F. Skinner that rewards the desired behavior.

Positive symptoms: Psychotic symptoms that reflect an exaggeration or distortion of normal functions, and include hallucinations, delusions, disorganized speech.

Postpartum depression: A mood episode that occurs within 4 weeks after delivery.

Posttraumatic stress disorder (PTSD): A psychiatric disorder occurring at any point following a threatened or actual traumatic event that involves combinations of affective, behavioral, cognitive, physiologic, and relational symptoms as well as dissociative symptoms and traumatic flashbacks that impair normal functioning.

Premature ejaculation: Rapid ejaculation that occurs very early in sexual activity.

Preoccupation: A security operation that excludes the anxiety-producing reality by a consuming interest in a person, thought, or event.

Presbycusis: The hearing loss of aging.

Presbyopia: The loss of visual accommodation usually associated with aging.

Primary mental disorder: A disorder in which the symptoms of mental illness are not a temporary result of some other phenomenon.

Prion: Proteinaceous infectious particles, or infectious agents made up of protein.

Privileged communication: Confidential information provided by a client that is shared with a person in a position of trust, who has a legal duty not to disclose the shared information even in a court of law.

Progressive muscle relaxation: A sequential tensing and relaxing of each muscle group to help clients distinguish between tension and relaxation and to induce a state of relaxation.

Psychiatric advance directive (PAD): A document constructed by a client that provides information regarding the client's preferences for mental health treatment.

Psychiatric emergency: An unforeseen, acute, potentially serious and life-threatening event or situation in which a client is threatened or which may represent a danger to him- or herself or others.

Psychiatric nursing interview: A discussion between the nurse and client that is guided by the nurse with the intent of gathering the information necessary to understand and treat the client.

Psychiatric rehabilitation: The development of the necessary skills for a client with chronic mental illness to live independently.

Psychoanalytic model: A conceptual model developed by Sigmund Freud based primarily on his work with persons suffering from disabling anxiety; the treatment approach derived from this model is psychoanalysis.

Psychodynamic nursing: A theory developed by Hildegard Peplau that requires the nurse to understand his or her own behavior in order to help others to identify felt difficulties and to apply principles of human relations to the problems that arise at all levels of experience.

Psychoeducation: The teaching of clients and their families about mental diseases and disorders, treatment modalities, coping behaviors, and accessing community resources.

Psychological tests: Evaluation tools that objectively measure personality, intelligence, and symptoms of mental illness.

Psychoneuroimmunology: The field of study examining bidirectional interactions between the central nervous system and the immune system.

Psychopharmacologist: A psychiatrist who specializes in prescribing psychotropic medications.

Psychopharmacology: The study of the medications used in psychiatry.

Psychosexual theory of personality development: Formulated by Sigmund Freud, a theory of personality development that evolves from birth through young adulthood.

Psychosis: The gross impairment of reality testing usually associated with delusions, disorganized behavior and cognition, incoherent or disorganized speech, and hallucinations.

Psychosocial developmental model: An intervention based on the theories of Erik Erikson that stresses the importance of trust as a basic building block for normal psychological development; it include eight stages (trust vs. mistrust; autonomy vs. shame and doubt; initiative vs. guilt; industry vs. inferiority; identity vs. role confusion; intimacy vs. isolation; generativity vs. stagnation, and ego integrity vs. despair).

Psychosocial typology: The concepts of onset, course, outcome, and degree of incapacitation.

Psychosomatic: The relationship between the mind and the body, usually in reference to physiologic changes or physical symptoms that have mental or emotional origins.

Psychotropic medications: The drugs used to treat psychiatric illness.

Punishment: A behavioral model developed by B.F. Skinner that provides an aversive stimulus after the behavior and serves to decrease its future occurrence.

Purging: A destructive pattern of ridding one's body of excess calories (to control weight) by vomiting, abusing laxatives or diuretics, taking enemas, and/or exercising obsessively.

Pyromania: A pattern of fire-setting for pleasure, gratification, or relief of tension.

Rapid cycling: The occurrence of four or more mood disorders in a one year period.

Rapid eye movement (REM): The lightest and most active stage of sleep measured by neuron activity and rapid eye movements and characterized by dreaming.

Reactive attachment disorder (RAD): Markedly disturbed and inappropriate social relatedness that is associated with grossly pathological care; a person with RAD can be overly inhibited or overly uninhibited in interactions with others.

Referred pain: Pain that originates in one area of the body and is experienced in another that is not receiving the noxious stimuli directly.

Reframing: The process of facilitating change by developing or suggesting alternate options and interpretations.

Relaxation: A state of peaceful tranquility.

Resistance: Client behavior that impedes the progress of the interview or treatment.

Response cost: A behavioral model developed by B.F. Skinner that exacts a loss or penalty as a consequence of a certain behavior.

Restless leg syndrome: A movement disorder that involves uncomfortable pulling or crawling sensations of the lower limbs that occur at times of rest or sleep.

Restraints: Pertains to both physical restraints and drugs that are used as a means to restrain a person.

Reticular activating system (RAS): A functional system in the brain essential for wakefulness, attention, concentration and introspection.

Retrograde amnesia: The inability to recall previously retained material.

Rett's disorder: A pervasive developmental disorder that is progressive and characterized by autistic behavior, ataxia, dementia and seizures.

Right to refuse medication: The client's right to decline to take prescribed medications as long as they do not represent a danger to themselves or others.

Right to refuse treatment: The right to decline inpatient hospitalization or other mental health care unless a danger to self or others.

Right to treatment: The right to be cared for in facilities that are psychologically and physically humane, provide adequate number of staff, and use individualized treatment plans within a therapeutic setting.

Ritualistic behavior: A repetitive activity, usually a distorted or stereotyped elaboration of some routine of daily life.

Schizoid personality disorder: A condition characterized by a pervasive pattern of detachment from social relationships and a restricted range of expression of emotions in interpersonal settings that begins by early adulthood and occurs in a variety of contexts.

Schizotypal personality disorder: A condition, often disabling and extremely distressing, characterized by a pervasive pattern of social and interpersonal deficits resulting in acute discomfort and reduced capacity for close personal relationships; accompanied by cognitive or perceptual distortions and eccentric behavior; begins by early adulthood and occurs in a variety of contexts.

Seclusion: When a person is involuntarily confined in a room or an area and is physically not permitted to leave.

Security operations: A Sullivanian concept for defenses against anxiety; common security operations include apathy, somnolent detachment, selective inattention, and preoccupation.

Sedative: A medication that produces generalized CNS depression and reduces anxiety and agitation.

Selective inattention: A common security operation in which anxiety-producing aspects of a situation are not allowed into awareness.

Selective mutism: A persistent failure to speak in social situations where speaking is expected that interferes with educational achievement or social communication and that lasts at least one month

Self-care deficit nursing theory: Developed by Dorothea Orem; postulates that the actions of nurse and patient are determined by the patient's self-care agency, and nursing is seen as an interactive process based on the amount and kind of nursing agency needed.

Self-concept: A Sullivanian concept; a relatively enduring assessment of self that results from reflected appraisals of significant others.It is also an individual's awareness of self, beliefs, thoughts, relationships, body image and self-esteem.

Self-disclosure: Revealing personal information about oneself, with the goal of benefiting the client and the therapeutic process.

Self-help clearinghouses: Nonprofit services that help people to find and form self-help groups within their service areas.

Self-help groups: Nonprofit, voluntary, community-based support groups, run by and for people who join together on the basis of their common experience, to help one another as peers. They are not professionally run, although professionals frequently serve them in supportive ancillary roles. They might best be described as mutual help groups, but their description as "self-help" has become the primary phrase used in the literature to distinguish them as member-run support groups.

Self-help networks: Mutual aid networks operating primarily on the Internet, wherein peers provide mutual help to one another via message boards, electronic mailing lists, chat rooms, and other interactive means. Networks can also operate through interactive newsletters, telephone, and correspondence networks.

Self-management training: Complementary therapies in which the individual learns to control thoughts and feelings by utilizing techniques such as breathing, meditation, or self-talk to manage symptoms.

Senses of self: A theory advanced by child psychiatrist Daniel Stern in which four different senses of self are described (emergent self, core self, subjective self, and verbal self).

Sensitization: The tendency for initial mood episodes to be linked to identified stressors, but later episodes require less of a stressor or none at all.

Separation-individuation process: A developmental process, occurring in the first 3 years of life, consisting of a series of tasks critical to the development of effective interpersonal relationships and personal integration of positive and negative components in self and others.

Serotonin: A brain chemical or neurotransmitter affected by the atypical antipsychotic and antidepressant medications. It has been implicated in a number of disorders such as anxiety, depression, and migraine.

Severe mental illness: Synonymous with chronic mental illness and persistent mental illness.

Sexual misconduct: Includes the expression of any thoughts, feelings, or gestures that could be construed by the client as romantic or erotic in nature.

Sexual orientation: The gender to which one is erotically attracted. One can be androphilic (attracted to males), gynephilic (attracted to females), bisexual (attracted to both), asexual (attracted to neither), or undifferentiated.

Sexual response cycle: The physiological, cognitive, and emotional effects of sexual stimuli that occur in four phases, namely, desire, excitement, orgasm, and resolution.

Sibling rivalry: Children's interactions and experiences with brothers and sisters, often foreshadowing the many future challenges and competitions that they will encounter in adulthood.

Side effect: An unintended effect of a medication.

Situational crises: Crises that are precipitated by unpredictable events for which people cannot prepare.

Situational disturbance: Adaptation and transitions that can be accidental, planned, or imposed.

Sleep architecture: The patterns or five stages of REM (rapid eye movement) and NREM (nonrapid eye movement) representing the structure, continuity, and underlying physiologic mechanisms of sleep.

Sleep terror disorder: Parasomnias involving incomplete arousal from deep sleep and characterized by screaming and physical activity, unresponsiveness to others, and amnesia for the event.

Sleepwalking: Also known as somnambulism; the repeated action after the onset of sleep of rising from bed and ambulating.

Somatic motor system: Is responsible for voluntary control of skeletal muscle.

Somatic therapies: Physiologically based interventions designed to produce behavioral change.

Somatization: The process of expressing psychologic conflict through physical complaints or symptoms.

Somatoform disorder: A mental disorder in which physical symptoms or preoccupations present as a medical illness but are considered to be primarily psychiatric in origin.

Somnolent detachment: A primitive security operation wherein the individual falls asleep when confronted by a highly threatening, anxiety-producing experience.

Splitting: The inability to integrate positive and negative feelings, resulting in a tendency to view people and situations as all good or all bad; a primitive defense against a fear of abandonment.

SSRIs (selective serotonin reuptake inhibitors): A group of antidepressant medications that work primarily on the serotonin system in the brain.

Stimulants: A family of psychotropic medications used primarily to treat attention deficit disorder.

Stress/stressor: Any experience or stimulus that is experienced by an individual as a challenge, threat, or potentially harmful.

Stress-diathesis model: This theory explains the development of psychiatric disorders as a combination of genetic predisposition (diathesis) and environmental stress.

Structural imaging: A category of brain imaging that gathers information regarding the physical constitution of the brain at any point in time. Structural imaging tests include computed tomography (CT) and magnetic resonance imaging (MRI).

Structural family therapy: Developed by Salvador Minuchin; stresses the importance of understanding the person within a social context, specifically the family's organization and the interactional patterns between members.

Stuttering: A disturbance in the normal fluency and time patterning of speech that is inappropriate for one's age or developmental stage.

Substance abuse: Brief or chronic episodes of substance use that result in failure to meet major role obligations, legal problems, or recurrent social or interpersonal problems. There is no evidence of physiological or psychological dependence.

Substance dependence: The excessive and continued use of a substance despite significant impairment to at least one aspect of life: physiologic, psychologic, behavioral, or social. Dependence includes additional symptoms that may include tolerance, withdrawal, preoccupation with the substance, compulsive behavior, or inability to stop or reduce the use of the substance.

Substance-induced mental disorders: Refers to intoxication and withdrawal as well as to other disorders induced by substances, including delirium, dementia, amnesia, paranoia, depression, anxiety, sexual dysfunction, and sleep disorders.

Suicidal thoughts: The thought, threat, plan, or intent for self-destruction

Suicide: Intentional termination of one's own life.

Sundowning: The increased confusion experienced in dementia that occurs in the early evening.

Sympathetic nervous system: Part of the autonomic nervous system that responds to stress; prepares one to fight or flee in an emergency.

Synapse: The contact space between neurons where a neuron transfers information to another cell.

System of care: A comprehensive and coordinated system of mental health care and other services to meet the multiple and changing needs of those with mental health problems.

Systematic desensitization: Gradual exposure to an increasing hierarchy of stress-provoking stimuli for the purpose of extinguishing the negative emotional response.

Tardive dyskinesia: A late occurring, irreversible side effect of antipsychotics that involves involuntary, unwanted, repetitious movements of the muscles of the face, limbs and trunk. The risk of this problem is greatly reduced with the newer atypical antipsychotics.

Temper tantrums: The way a young child lets out strong emotions and communicates feelings; these episodes of rage, stomping, screaming, and throwing themselves to the floor are a normal part of childhood development.

Temporal lobe: The lateral region of the cerebrum.

Thalamus: Part of the diencephalon of the brain it conveys sensory information excluding smell to the cerebral cortex.

Therapeutic community: A type of participative, group-based milieu therapy that creates a microcosm of society in which persons with chronic mental illness or substance use disorders can learn and practice skills for daily living.

Therapeutic contract: The agreement between the nurse and client to work on mutually identified problems; may be written or oral in nature.

Therapeutic effect: The intended effect of a medication.

Therapeutic milieu: A nurturing environment that provides both adaptive and corrective experiences in a safe place with predictable standards for behavior.

Therapeutic touch: A form of energy healing derived from laying on of hands.

Thought disorder: Disorganized cognition displayed by disorganized speech and use of language.

Tolerance: A person's need for increasing amounts of a substance to achieve the desired effects.

Tourette's disorder (TD): Multiple motor tics and one or more vocal tics occurring many times a day over a period of at least one year and during which there is never a period of more than three consecutive months tic-free.

Trajectory model: The course of the chronic illness as an uncertain path that requires that those with the illness, their family members, and their healthcare providers work together to shape the illness; it is composed of seven key concepts.

Transdisciplinary team: A care model based on free-flowing communication, and the transfer of knowledge and skills across discipline boundaries in the service of a common, client-centered goal.

Transference: Realistic and unrealistic feelings that the client has toward the mental health professional.

Transgendered: A social umbrella term commonly used to describe individuals whose gender identity, to different degrees, varies significantly from their chromosomal sex.

Transsexual: A popular term describing an individual whose cross-gender identification is so pervasive that they seek to live in the gender role of the opposite sex.

Traumatic flashbacks: A transient, intense, intrusive, repeated re-experience in the present of thoughts, emotions, and physical sensations surrounding a past disturbance.

TRIADS: A method for assessing trauma in children; it includes types of abuse, role relationship, intensity, autonomic response, duration, and style of abuse.

Triage: Derived from the French *trier,* "to choose," triage is a classification process developed from battlefield techniques to rapidly assess acuity and attempt to balance needs and available resources, making certain that the "right" client, place, time, and care provider are identified.

Trichophagia: The act of eating one's hair, usually resulting in the development of hair balls and abdominal discomfort.

Trichotillomania: Recurrent pulling out of one's hair for pleasure, gratification, or relief of tension, resulting in noticeable hair loss.

Unipolar: A mood disorder of only depressive episodes.

Vaginismus: An involuntary contraction of the muscle around the vagina that prevents penile insertion.

Vascular dementia: A cognitive disorder, usually progressive, that is associated with cerebral vascular changes, sometimes causing speech problems and paresis.

Vicarious traumatization: A process in which traumatic damage is transferred to helpers or rescuers involved in crisis work by exposure to traumatic experiences through their work or through their intense involvement in the experiences of others.

Violence: Any activity that demonstrates that one can be physically, emotionally or sexually harmful to self or others.

Victim: Any person of any age who is violated by acts of disorderly conduct, harassment, reckless endangerment, entrapment, or assault, including attempted assault.

VIPP teaching: When providing children with information, this method stresses the use of visual aids, information appropriate for age, and preparation done using play.

Wernicke's aphasia: A form of disordered language function affecting the comprehension of written and spoken words.

Wernicke-Korsakoff syndrome: A serious neurotoxic effect of alcohol abuse; also known as alcohol-induced persisting amnestic disorder, and characterized by severe memory impairment.

Withdrawal: The process that occurs when a person who is physically addicted to a substance stops using, or reduces the intake, of that substance after heavy, prolonged consumption. The symptoms of withdrawal vary across substances.

Withdrawal delirium: Also known as delirium tremens (DTs), a life-threatening complication of alcohol withdrawal characterized by agitation, disorientation, visual hallucinations, elevated temperature, and cardiac arrhythmias.

Xerostomia: Dry mouth.

Index

B

C

E

Photo Credits

Unless otherwise indicated, photographs and art are under copyright of Jones and Bartlett Publishers.

Part and chapter openers © Handy Widiyanto/ShutterStock, Inc.

Chapter 1

Figure 1-1 William Hogarth, *The Rake's Progress: 8. The Rake in Bedlam,* 1734. Oil on canvas, 625 x 752 mm. Sir John Soane's Museum, London.

Figure 1-2 © David Buffington/Photodisc/Getty Images

Figure 1-3 © Markus Gann/ShutterStock, Inc.

Figure 1-4 © photobank.ch/ShutterStock, Inc.

Figure 1-5 Reprinted with permission from: Davis, C. (2006). Family history. In: Davis, C., (Ed.), *Patient practitioner interaction: An experiential manual for developing the art of health care* (4th ed., p. 30). Thorofare, NJ: SLACK Incorporated.

Chapter 3

Figure 3-1 © AbleStock

Chapter 4

Figure 4-11 Courtesy of Lynn E. DeLisi, MD.

Figure 4-12 Courtesy of Marcus Raichle, MD.

Chapter 5

Figure 5-1 Guy, W. (1976). *ECDEU assessment manual for psychopharmacology.* Washington, DC: U.S. Department of Health, Education and Welfare.

Chapter 6

Figure 6-1 Courtesy of Journalist 1st Class Mark D. Faram/U.S. Navy.

Figure 6-2 © Leah-Anne Thompson/ShutterStock, Inc.

Chapter 7

Figure 7-1 © Photos.com

Figure 7-2 © Renata Osinska/ShutterStock, Inc.

Chapter 9

Figure 9-2 © AbleStock

Figure 9-4 © iofoto/ShutterStock, Inc.

Figure 9-5 © Cora Reed/ShutterStock, Inc.

Chapter 11

Figure 11-1 © Terrie L. Zeller/ShutterStock, Inc.

Figure 11-2 © Lorraine Swanson/ShutterStock, Inc.

Chapter 14

Figure 14-1 © Doug Menuez/Photodisc/Getty Images

Chapter 15

Figure 15-1 © Modesty Girl/ShutterStock, Inc.

Figure 15-2 © iofoto/ShutterStock, Inc.

Chapter 16

Figure 16-1 (top left) © Raymond Kasprzak/ShutterStock, Inc.

Figure 16-1 (top right) © Photos.com

Figure 16-1 (bottom) © Tim Pleasant/ShutterStock, Inc.

Figure 16-2 © Karen Winton/ShutterStock, Inc.

Chapter 17

Figure 17-1 © Cameron Cross/ShutterStock, Inc.

Chapter 18

Figure 18-1 © Keith Brofsky/Photodisc/Getty Images

Chapter 20
Figure 20-2 © Ryan McVay/Photodisc/Getty Images

Chapter 21
Figure 21-1 (top) © Magdalena Szachowska/ShutterStock, Inc.
Figure 21-1 (bottom) © Doreen Salcher/ShutterStock, Inc.
Figure 21-2 © Kirk Peart Professional Imaging/ShutterStock, Inc.

Chapter 22
Figure 22-1
Courtesy of Jocelyn Augustino/FEMA.
Figure 22-2 © Photos.com

Chapter 24
Figure 24-1 © PhotoCreate/ShutterStock, Inc.
Figure 24-2 © NorthGeorgiaMedia/ShutterStock, Inc.

Chapter 25
Figure 25-1 © Photos.com
Figure 25-2 © AbleStock

Chapter 26
Figure 26-1 © PhotoCreate/ShutterStock, Inc.
Figure 26-2 © Photos.com

Chapter 27
Figure 27-1 © Patrick Sheandell O'Carroll/PhotoAlto/PictureQuest

Chapter 28
Figure 28-1 © Ingram Publishing/Alamy Images